Sabine Baring-Gould, Complete Collection

In this book:
Curious Myths of the Middle Ages

The Book of Were-Wolves

Historic Oddities and Strange Events, 1st Series

Historic Oddities and Strange Events, 2nd Series

A Book of Ghosts

The Rev. **Sabine Baring-Gould** (1834--1924) of Lew Trenchard in Devon, England, was an Anglican priest, hagiographer, antiquarian, novelist, folk song collector and eclectic scholar. His bibliography consists of more than 1240 publications, though this list continues to grow. His family home, the manor house of Lew Trenchard, near Okehampton, Devon, has been preserved as he had it rebuilt and is now a hotel. He is remembered particularly as a writer of hymns, the best-known being "Onward, Christian Soldiers" and "Now the Day Is Over". He also translated the carol "Gabriel's Message" from the Basque language to English.

In this book:

Curious Myths of the Middle Ages

I. — THE WANDERING JEW

WHO, that has looked on Gustave Doré's marvellous illustrations to this wild legend, can forget the impression they made upon his imagination?

I do not refer to the first illustration as striking, where the Jewish shoemaker is refusing to suffer the cross-laden Savior to rest a moment on his door-step, and is receiving with scornful lip the judgment to wander restless till the Second Coming of that same Redeemer. But I refer rather to the second, which represents the Jew, after the lapse of ages, bowed beneath the burden of the curse, worn with unrelieved toil, wearied with ceaseless travelling, trudging onward at the last lights of evening, when a rayless night of unabating rain is creeping on, along a sloppy path between dripping bushes; and suddenly he comes over against a wayside crucifix, on which the white glare of departing daylight falls, to throw it into ghastly relief against the pitch-black rain-clouds. For a moment we see the working of the miserable shoemaker's mind. We feel that he is recalling the tragedy of the first Good Friday, and his head hangs heavier on his breast, as he recalls the part he had taken in that awful catastrophe.

Or, is that other illustration more remarkable, where the wanderer is amongst the Alps, at the brink of a hideous chasm; and seeing in the contorted pine-branches the ever-haunting scene of the Via Dolorosa, he is lured to cast himself into that black gulf in quest of rest,—when an angel flashes out of the gloom with the sword of flame turning every way, keeping him back from what would be to him a Paradise indeed, the repose of Death?

Or, that last scene, when the trumpet sounds and earth is shivering to its foundations, the fire is bubbling forth through the rents in its surface, and the dead are coming together flesh to flesh, and bone to bone, and muscle to muscle—then the weary man sits down and casts off his shoes! Strange sights are around him, he sees them not; strange sounds assail his ears, he hears but one—the trumpet-note which gives the signal for him to stay his wanderings and rest his weary feet.

I can linger over those noble woodcuts, and learn from them something new each time that I study them; they are picture-poems full of latent depths of thought. And now let us to the history of this most thrilling of all mediæval myths, if a myth.

If a myth, I say, for who can say for certain that it is not true? "Verily I say unto you, There be some standing here, which shall not taste of death till they see the Son of Man coming in His kingdom,"[1] are our Lord's words, which I can hardly think apply to the destruction of Jerusalem, as commentators explain it to escape the difficulty. That some should live to see Jerusalem destroyed was not very surprising, and hardly needed the emphatic Verily which Christ only used when speaking something of peculiarly solemn or mysterious import.

[1] Matt. xvi. 28. Mark ix. 1.

Besides, St. Luke's account manifestly refers the coming in the kingdom to the Judgment, for the saying stands as follows: "Whosoever shall be ashamed of Me, and of My words, of him shall the Son of Man be ashamed, when He shall come in His own glory, and in His Father's, and of the holy angels. But I tell you of a truth, there be some standing here, which shall not taste of death till they see the kingdom of God."[2]

[2] Luke ix.

There can, I think, be no doubt in the mind of an unprejudiced person that the words of our Lord do imply that some one or more of those then living should not die till He came again. I do not mean to insist on the literal signification, but I plead that there is no improbability in our Lord's words being fulfilled to the letter. That the circumstance is unrecorded in the Gospels is no evidence that it did not take place, for we are expressly told, "Many other signs truly did Jesus in the presence of His disciples, which are not written in this book;"[3] and again, "There are also many other things which Jesus did, the which, if they should be written every one, I suppose that even the world itself could not contain the books that should be written."[4]

[3] John xx. 30.
[4] John xxi. 25.

We may remember also the mysterious witnesses who are to appear in the last eventful days of the world's history and bear testimony to the Gospel truth before the antichristian world. One of these has been often conjectured to be St. John the Evangelist, of whom Christ said to Peter, "If I will that he tarry till I come, what is that to thee?"

The historical evidence on which the tale rests is, however, too slender for us to admit for it more than the barest claim to be more than myth. The names and the circumstances connected with the Jew and his doom vary in every account, and the only point upon which all coincide is, that such an individual exists in an undying condition, wandering over the face of the earth, seeking rest and finding none.

The earliest extant mention of the Wandering Jew is to be found in the book of the chronicles of the Abbey of St. Albans, which was copied and continued by Matthew Paris. He records that in the year 1228,

"A certain Archbishop of Armenia the Greater came on a pilgrimage to England to see the relics of the saints, and visit the sacred places in the kingdom, as he had done in others; he also produced letters of recommendation from his Holiness the Pope, to the religious and the prelates of the churches, in which they were enjoined to receive and entertain him with due reverence and honor. On his arrival, he came to St. Albans, where he was received with all respect by the abbot and the monks; and at this place, being fatigued with his journey, he remained some days to rest himself and his followers, and a conversation took place between him and the inhabitants of the convent, by means of their interpreters, during which he made many inquiries relating to the religion and religious observances of this country, and told many strange things concerning the countries of the East. In the course of conversation he was asked whether he had ever seen or heard any thing of Joseph, a man of whom there was much talk in the world, who, when our Lord suffered, was present and spoke to Him, and who is still alive, in evidence of the Christian faith; in reply to which, a knight in his retinue, who was his interpreter, replied, speaking in French, 'My lord well knows that man, and a little before he took his way to the western countries, the said Joseph ate at the table of my lord the Archbishop of Armenia, and he has often seen and conversed with him.'

"He was then asked about what had passed between Christ and the said Joseph; to which he replied, 'At the time of the passion of Jesus Christ, He was seized by the Jews, and led into the hall of judgment before Pilate, the governor, that He might be judged by him on the accusation of the Jews; and Pilate, finding no fault for which he might sentence Him to death, said unto them, "Take Him and judge Him according to your law;" the shouts of the Jews, however, increasing, he, at their request, released unto them Barabbas, and delivered Jesus to them to be crucified. When, therefore, the Jews were dragging Jesus forth, and had reached the door, Cartaphilus, a porter of the hall in Pilate's service, as Jesus was going out of the door, impiously struck Him on the back with his hand, and said in mockery, "Go quicker, Jesus, go quicker; why do you loiter?" and Jesus, looking back on him with a severe countenance, said to him, "I am going, and you shall wait till I return." And according as our Lord said, this Cartaphilus is still awaiting His return. At the time of our Lord's suffering he was thirty years old, and when he attains the age of a hundred years, he always returns to the same age as he was when our Lord suffered. After Christ's death, when the Catholic faith gained ground, this Cartaphilus was baptized by Ananias (who also baptized the Apostle Paul), and was called Joseph. He dwells in one or other divisions of Armenia, and in divers Eastern countries, passing his time amongst the bishops and other prelates of the Church; he is a man of holy conversation, and religious; a man of few words, and very circumspect in his behavior; for he does not speak at all unless when questioned by the bishops and religious; and then he relates the events of olden times, and speaks of things which occurred at the suffering and resurrection of our Lord, and of the witnesses of the resurrection, namely, of those who rose with Christ, and went into the holy city, and appeared unto men. He also tells of the creed of the Apostles, and of their separation and preaching. And all this he relates without smiling, or levity of conversation, as one who is well practised in sorrow and the fear of God, always looking forward with dread to the coming of Jesus Christ, lest at the Last Judgment he should find him in anger whom, when on his way to death, he had provoked to just vengeance. Numbers came to him from different parts of the world, enjoying his society and conversation; and to them, if they are men of authority, he explains all doubts on the matters on which he is questioned. He refuses all gifts that are offered him, being content with slight food and clothing.'"

Much about the same date, Philip Mouskes, afterwards Bishop of Tournay, wrote his rhymed chronicle (1242), which contains a similar account of the Jew, derived from the same Armenian prelate:—

"Adonques vint un arceveskes
De çà mer, plains de bonnes tèques
Par samblant, et fut d'Armenie,"

and this man, having visited the shrine of "St. Tumas de Kantorbire," and then hav
devotions at "Monsigour St. Jake," he went on to Cologne to see the heads of the three kings
told in the Netherlands much resembled that related at St. Albans, only that the Jew, see
dragging Christ to his death, exclaims,—

"Atendés moi! g'i vois,
S'iert mis le faus profète en crois."

Then

"Le vrais Dieux se regarda,
Et li a dit qu'e n'i tarda,
Icist ne t'atenderont pas,
Mais saces, tu m'atenderas."

We hear no more of the wandering Jew till the sixteenth century, when we he
manner, as assisting a weaver, Kokot, at the royal palace in Bohemia (1505), to
been secreted by the great-grandfather of Kokot, sixty years before, at which tim
then had the appearance of being a man of seventy years.[5]

[5] Gubitz, Gesellsch. 1845, No. 18.

Curiously enough, we next hear of him in the East, where he is confour
Early in the century he appeared to Fadhilah, under peculiar circumstances.

After the Arabs had captured the city of Elvan, Fadhilah, at the hea
pitched his tents, late in the evening, between two mountains. Fadhilah, h
with a loud voice, heard the words "Allah akbar" (God is great) repeated
prayer was followed in a similar manner. Fadhilah, not believing this
much astonished, and cried out, "O thou! whether thou art of the angel
other order of spirits, it is well; the power of God be with thee; but if
light upon thee, that I may rejoice in thy presence and society." Sca
before an aged man, with bald head, stood before him, holding a staff
dervish in appearance. After having courteously saluted him, Fadhil
Thereupon the stranger answered, "Bassi Hadhret Issa, I am here by c
left me in this world, that I may live therein until he comes a secon
who is the Fountain of Happiness, and in obedience to his command
Fadhilah heard these words, he asked when the Lord Jesus would ap
appearing would be at the end of the world, at the Last Judgm
curiosity, so that he inquired the signs of the approach of the en
gave him an account of general, social, and moral dissolution
history.[6]

[6] Herbelot, Bibl. Orient, iii. p. 607.

In 1547 he was seen in Europe, if we are to be

"Paul von Eitzen, doctor of the Holy Scr
years past, that when he was young, havin
Hamburg in the winter of the year 1547, an
man, with his hair hanging over his shou
pulpit, listening with deepest attention to th
bowing himself profoundly and humbly, w

person who was seen in Hamburg in MDLXIV. Credat Judæus Apella! *I* did not see him, or hear anything authentic concerning him, at that time when I was in Paris."[10]

[10] J. C. Bulenger, Historia sui Temporis, p. 357.

A curious little book,[11] written against the quackery of Paracelsus, by Leonard Doldius, a Nürnberg physician, and translated into Latin and augmented, by Andreas Libavius, doctor and physician of Rotenburg, alludes to the same story, and gives the Jew a new name nowhere else met with. After having referred to a report that Paracelsus was not dead, but was seated alive, asleep or napping, in his sepulchre at Strasburg, preserved from death by some of his specifics, Libavius declares that he would sooner believe in the old man, the Jew, Ahasverus, wandering over the world, called by some Buttadæus, and otherwise, again, by others.

[11] Praxis Alchymiæ. Francfurti, MDCIV. 8vo.

He is said to have appeared in Naumburg, but the date is not given; he was noticed in church, listening to the sermon. After the service he was questioned, and he related his story. On this occasion he received presents from the burgers.[12] In 1633 he was again in Hamburg.[13] In the year 1640, two citizens, living in the Gerberstrasse, in Brussels, were walking in the Sonian wood, when they encountered an aged man, whose clothes were in tatters and of an antiquated appearance. They invited him to go with them to a house of refreshment, and he went with them, but would not seat himself, remaining on foot to drink. When he came before the doors with the two burgers, he told them a great deal; but they were mostly stories of events which had happened many hundred years before. Hence the burgers gathered that their companion was Isaac Laquedem, the Jew who had refused to permit our Blessed Lord to rest for a moment at his door-step, and they left him full of terror. In 1642 he is reported to have visited Leipzig. On the 22d July, 1721, he appeared at the gates of the city of Munich.[14] About the end of the seventeenth century or the beginning of the eighteenth, an impostor, calling himself the Wandering Jew, attracted attention in England, and was listened to by the ignorant, and despised by the educated. He, however, managed to thrust himself into the notice of the nobility, who, half in jest, half in curiosity, questioned him, and paid him as they might a juggler. He declared that he had been an officer of the Sanhedrim, and that he had struck Christ as he left the judgment hall of Pilate. He remembered all the Apostles, and described their personal appearance, their clothes, and their peculiarities. He spoke many languages, claimed the power of healing the sick, and asserted that he had travelled nearly all over the world. Those who heard him were perplexed by his familiarity with foreign tongues and places. Oxford and Cambridge sent professors to question him, and to discover the imposition, if any. An English nobleman conversed with him in Arabic. The mysterious stranger told his questioner in that language that historical works were not to be relied upon. And on being asked his opinion of Mahomet, he replied that he had been acquainted with the father of the prophet, and that he dwelt at Ormuz. As for Mahomet, he believed him to have been a man of intelligence; once when he heard the prophet deny that Christ was crucified, he answered abruptly by telling him he was a witness to the truth of that event. He related also that he was in Rome when Nero set it on fire; he had known Saladin, Tamerlane, Bajazeth, Eterlane, and could give minute details of the history of the Crusades.[15]

[12] Mitternacht, Diss. in Johann. xxi. 19.
[13] Mitternacht, ut supra.
[14] Hormayr, Taschenbuch, 1834, p. 216.
[15] Calmet, Dictionn. de la Bible, t. ii. p. 472.

Whether this wandering Jew was found out in London or not, we cannot tell, but he shortly after appeared in Denmark, thence travelled into Sweden, and vanished.

Such are the principal notices of the Wandering Jew which have appeared. It will be seen at once how wanting they are in all substantial evidence which could make us regard the story in any other light than myth.

But no myth is wholly without foundation, and there must be some substantial verity upon which this vast superstructure of legend has been raised. What that is I am unable to discover.

ever reverenced with sighs the pronunciation of the name of God, or of Jesus Christ, and could not endure to hear curses; but whenever he heard any one swear by God's death or pains, he waxed indignant, and exclaimed, with vehemence and with sighs, 'Wretched man and miserable creature, thus to misuse the name of thy Lord and God, and His bitter sufferings and passion. Hadst thou seen, as I have, how heavy and bitter were the pangs and wounds of thy Lord, endured for thee and for me, thou wouldst rather undergo great pain thyself than thus take His sacred name in vain!'

"Such is the account given to me by Doctor Paul von Eitzen, with many circumstantial proofs, and corroborated by certain of my own old acquaintances who saw this same individual with their own eyes in Hamburg.

"In the year 1575 the Secretary Christopher Krause, and Master Jacob von Holstein, legates to the Court of Spain, and afterwards sent into the Netherlands to pay the soldiers serving his Majesty in that country, related on their return home to Schleswig, and confirmed with solemn oaths, that they had come across the same mysterious individual at Madrid in Spain, in appearance, manner of life, habits, clothing, just the same as he had appeared in Hamburg. They said that they had spoken with him, and that many people of all classes had conversed with him, and found him to speak good Spanish. In the year 1599, in December, a reliable person wrote from Brunswick to Strasburg that the same mentioned strange person had been seen alive at Vienna in Austria, and that he had started for Poland and Dantzig; and that he purposed going on to Moscow. This Ahasverus was at Lubeck in 1601, also about the same date in Revel in Livonia, and in Cracow in Poland. In Moscow he was seen of many and spoken to by many.

"What thoughtful, God-fearing persons are to think of the said person, is at their option. God's works are wondrous and past finding out, and are manifested day by day, only to be revealed in full at the last great day of account.

"Dated, Revel, August 1st, 1613.

"D. W.

"D.

"Chrysostomus Dudulœus,

"Westphalus."

The statement that the Wandering Jew appeared in Lubeck in 1601, does not tally with the more precise chronicle of Henricus Bangert, which gives: "Die 14 Januarii Anno MDCIII., adnotatum reliquit Lubecæ fuisse Judæum illum immortalem, qui se Christi crucifixioni interfuisse affirmavit."[8]

[8] Henr. Bangert, Comment. de Ortu, Vita, et Excessu Coleri, I. Cti. Lubec.

In 1604 he seems to have appeared in Paris. Rudolph Botoreus says, under this date, "I fear lest I be accused of giving ear to old wives' fables, if I insert in these pages what is reported all over Europe of the Jew, coeval with the Savior Christ; however, nothing is more common, and our popular histories have not scrupled to assert it. Following the lead of those who wrote our annals, I may say that he who appeared not in one century only, in Spain, Italy, and Germany, was also in this year seen and recognized as the same individual who had appeared in Hamburg, anno MDLXVI. The common people, bold in spreading reports, relate many things of him; and this I allude to, lest anything should be left unsaid."[9]

[9] R. Botoreus, Comm. Histor. lii. p. 305.

J. C. Bulenger puts the date of the Hamburg visit earlier. "It was reported at this time that a Jew of the time of Christ was wandering without food and drink, having for a thousand and odd years been a vagabond and outcast, condemned by God to rove, because he, of that generation of vipers, was the first to cry out for the crucifixion of Christ and the release of Barabbas; and also because soon after, when Christ, panting under the burden of the rood, sought to rest before his workshop (he was a cobbler), the fellow ordered Him off with acerbity. Thereupon Christ replied, 'Because thou grudgest Me such a moment of rest, I shall enter into My rest, but thou shalt wander restless.' At once, frantic and agitated, he fled through the whole earth, and on the same account to this day he journeys through the world. It was this person who was seen in Hamburg in MDLXIV. Credat Judæus Apella! *I* did not see him, or hear anything authentic concerning him, at that time when I was in Paris."[10]

[10] J. C. Bulenger, Historia sui Temporis, p. 357.

A curious little book,[11] written against the quackery of Paracelsus, by Leonard Doldius, a Nürnberg physician, and translated into Latin and augmented, by Andreas Libavius, doctor and physician of Rotenburg, alludes to the same story, and gives the Jew a new name nowhere else met with. After having referred to a report that Paracelsus was not dead, but was seated alive, asleep or napping, in his sepulchre at Strasburg, preserved from death by some of his specifics, Libavius declares that he would sooner believe in the old man, the Jew, Ahasverus, wandering over the world, called by some Buttadæus, and otherwise, again, by others.

[11] Praxis Alchymiæ. Francfurti, MDCIV. 8vo.

He is said to have appeared in Naumburg, but the date is not given; he was noticed in church, listening to the sermon. After the service he was questioned, and he related his story. On this occasion he received presents from the burgers.[12] In 1633 he was again in Hamburg.[13] In the year 1640, two citizens, living in the Gerberstrasse, in Brussels, were walking in the Sonian wood, when they encountered an aged man, whose clothes were in tatters and of an antiquated appearance. They invited him to go with them to a house of refreshment, and he went with them, but would not seat himself, remaining on foot to drink. When he came before the doors with the two burgers, he told them a great deal; but they were mostly stories of events which had happened many hundred years before. Hence the burgers gathered that their companion was Isaac Laquedem, the Jew who had refused to permit our Blessed Lord to rest for a moment at his door-step, and they left him full of terror. In 1642 he is reported to have visited Leipzig. On the 22d July, 1721, he appeared at the gates of the city of Munich.[14] About the end of the seventeenth century or the beginning of the eighteenth, an impostor, calling himself the Wandering Jew, attracted attention in England, and was listened to by the ignorant, and despised by the educated. He, however, managed to thrust himself into the notice of the nobility, who, half in jest, half in curiosity, questioned him, and paid him as they might a juggler. He declared that he had been an officer of the Sanhedrim, and that he had struck Christ as he left the judgment hall of Pilate. He remembered all the Apostles, and described their personal appearance, their clothes, and their peculiarities. He spoke many languages, claimed the power of healing the sick, and asserted that he had travelled nearly all over the world. Those who heard him were perplexed by his familiarity with foreign tongues and places. Oxford and Cambridge sent professors to question him, and to discover the imposition, if any. An English nobleman conversed with him in Arabic. The mysterious stranger told his questioner in that language that historical works were not to be relied upon. And on being asked his opinion of Mahomet, he replied that he had been acquainted with the father of the prophet, and that he dwelt at Ormuz. As for Mahomet, he believed him to have been a man of intelligence; once when he heard the prophet deny that Christ was crucified, he answered abruptly by telling him he was a witness to the truth of that event. He related also that he was in Rome when Nero set it on fire; he had known Saladin, Tamerlane, Bajazeth, Eterlane, and could give minute details of the history of the Crusades.[15]

[12] Mitternacht, Diss. in Johann. xxi. 19.
[13] Mitternacht, ut supra.
[14] Hormayr, Taschenbuch, 1834, p. 216.
[15] Calmet, Dictionn. de la Bible, t. ii. p. 472.

Whether this wandering Jew was found out in London or not, we cannot tell, but he shortly after appeared in Denmark, thence travelled into Sweden, and vanished.

Such are the principal notices of the Wandering Jew which have appeared. It will be seen at once how wanting they are in all substantial evidence which could make us regard the story in any other light than myth.

But no myth is wholly without foundation, and there must be some substantial verity upon which this vast superstructure of legend has been raised. What that is I am unable to discover.

It has been suggested by some that the Jew Ahasverus is an impersonation of that race which wanders, Cain-like, over the earth with the brand of a brother's blood upon it, and one which is not to pass away till all be fulfilled, not to be reconciled to its angered God till the times of the Gentiles are accomplished. And yet, probable as this supposition may seem at first sight, it is not to be harmonized with some of the leading features of the story. The shoemaker becomes a penitent, and earnest Christian, whilst the Jewish nation has still the veil upon its heart; the wretched wanderer eschews money, and the avarice of the Israelite is proverbial.

According to local legend, he is identified with the Gypsies, or rather that strange people are supposed to be living under a curse somewhat similar to that inflicted on Ahasverus, because they refused shelter to the Virgin and Child on their flight into Egypt.[16] Another tradition connects the Jew with the wild huntsman, and there is a forest at Bretten, in Swabia, which he is said to haunt. Popular superstition attributes to him there a purse containing a groschen, which, as often as it is expended, returns to the spender.[17]

[16] Aventinus, Bayr. Chronik, viii.
[17] Meier, Schwäbische Sagen, i. 116.

In the Harz one form of the Wild Huntsman myth is to this effect: that he was a Jew who had refused to suffer our Blessed Lord to drink out of a river, or out of a horse-trough, but had contemptuously pointed out to Him the hoof-print of a horse, in which a little water had collected, and had bid Him quench His thirst thence.[18]

[18] Kuhn u. Schwarz Nordd. Sagen, p. 499.

As the Wild Huntsman is the personification of the storm, it is curious to find in parts of France that the sudden roar of a gale at night is attributed by the vulgar to the passing of the Everlasting Jew.

A Swiss story is, that he was seen one day standing upon the Matterberg, which is below the Matterhorn, contemplating the scene with mingled sorrow and wonder. Once before he stood on that spot, and then it was the site of a flourishing city; now it is covered with gentian and wild pinks. Once again will he revisit the hill, and that will be on the eve of Judgment.

Perhaps, of all the myths which originated in the middle ages, none is more striking than that we have been considering; indeed, there is something so calculated to arrest the attention and to excite the imagination in the outline of the story, that it is remarkable that we should find an interval of three centuries elapse between its first introduction into Europe by Matthew Paris and Philip Mouskes, and its general acceptance in the sixteenth century. As a myth, its roots lie in that great mystery of human life which is an enigma never solved, and ever originating speculation.

What was life? Was it of necessity limited to fourscore years, or could it be extended indefinitely? were questions curious minds never wearied of asking. And so the mythology of the past teemed with legends of favored or accursed mortals, who had reached beyond the term of days set to most men. Some had discovered the water of life, the fountain of perpetual youth, and were ever renewing their strength. Others had dared the power of God, and were therefore sentenced to feel the weight of His displeasure, without tasting the repose of death.

John the Divine slept at Ephesus, untouched by corruption, with the ground heaving over his breast as he breathed, waiting the summons to come forth and witness against Antichrist. The seven sleepers reposed in a cave, and centuries glided by like a watch in the night. The monk of Hildesheim, doubting how with God a thousand years could be as yesterday, listened to the melody of a bird in the green wood during three minutes, and found that in three minutes three hundred years had flown. Joseph of Arimathæa, in the blessed city of Sarras, draws perpetual life from the Saint Graal; Merlin sleeps and sighs in an old tree, spell-bound of Vivien. Charlemagne and Barbarossa wait, crowned and armed, in the heart of the mountain, till the time comes for the release of Fatherland from despotism. And, on the other hand, the curse of a deathless life has passed on the Wild Huntsman, because he desired to chase the red-deer for evermore; on the Captain of the Phantom Ship, because he vowed he would double the Cape whether God willed it or not; on the Man in the Moon, because he gathered sticks during the Sabbath rest; on the dancers of Kolbeck, because they desired to spend eternity in their mad gambols.

I began this article intending to conclude it with a bibliographical account of the tracts, letters, essays, and books, written upon the Wandering Jew; but I relinquish my intention at the sight of the multitude of works which have issued from the press upon the subject; and this I do with less compunction as the bibliographer may at little trouble and expense satisfy himself, by perusing the lists given by Grässe in his essay on the myth, and those to be found in "Notice historique et bibliographique sur les Juifs-errants: par O. B." (Gustave Brunet), Paris, Téchener, 1845; also in the article by M. Mangin, in "Causeries et Méditations historiques et littéraires," Paris, Duprat, 1843; and, lastly, in the essay by Jacob le Bibliophile (M. Lacroix) in his "Curiosités de l'Histoire des Croyances populaires," Paris, Delahays, 1859.

Of the romances of Eugène Sue and Dr. Croly, founded upon the legend, the less said the better. The original legend is so noble in its severe simplicity, that none but a master mind could develop it with any chance of success. Nor have the poetical attempts upon the story fared better. It was reserved for the pencil of Gustave Doré to treat it with the originality it merited, and in a series of woodcuts to produce at once a poem, a romance, and a chef-d'œuvre of art.

II. — PRESTER JOHN

Arms of the See of Chichester.

ABOUT the middle of the twelfth century, a rumor circulated through Europe that there reigned in Asia a powerful Christian Emperor, Presbyter Johannes. In a bloody fight he had broken the power of the Mussulmans, and was ready to come to the assistance of the Crusaders. Great was the exultation in Europe, for of late the news from the East had been gloomy and depressing, the power of the infidel had increased, overwhelming masses of men had been brought into the field against the chivalry of Christendom, and it was felt that the cross must yield before the odious crescent.

The news of the success of the Priest-King opened a door of hope to the desponding Christian world. Pope Alexander III. determined at once to effect a union with this mysterious personage, and on the 27th of September, 1177, wrote him a letter, which he intrusted to his physician, Philip, to deliver in person.

Philip started on his embassy, but never returned. The conquests of Tschengis-Khan again attracted the eyes of Christian Europe to the East. The Mongol hordes were rushing in upon the west with devastating ferocity; Russia, Poland, Hungary, and the eastern provinces of Germany, had succumbed, or suffered grievously; and the fears of other nations were roused lest they too should taste the misery of a Mongolian invasion. It was Gog and Magog come to slaughter, and the times of Antichrist were dawning. But the battle of Liegnitz stayed them in their onward career, and Europe was saved.

Pope Innocent IV. determined to convert these wild hordes of barbarians, and subject them to the cross of Christ; he therefore sent among them a number of Dominican and Franciscan missioners, and embassies of peace passed between the Pope, the King of France, and the Mogul Khan.

The result of these communications with the East was, that the travellers learned how false were the prevalent notions of a mighty Christian empire existing in Central Asia. Vulgar superstition or conviction is not, however, to be upset by evidence, and the locality of the monarchy was merely transferred by the people to Africa, and they fixed upon Abyssinia, with a show of truth, as the seat of the famous Priest-King. However, still some doubted. John de Plano Carpini and Marco Polo, though they acknowledged the existence of a Christian monarch in Abyssinia, yet stoutly maintained as well that the Prester John of popular belief reigned in splendor somewhere in the dim Orient.

But before proceeding with the history of this strange fable, it will be well to extract the different accounts given of the Priest-King and his realm by early writers; and we shall then be better able to judge of the influence the myth obtained in Europe.

Otto of Freisingen is the first author to mention the monarchy of Prester John with whom we are acquainted. Otto wrote a chronicle up to the date 1156, and he relates that in 1145 the Catholic Bishop of Cabala visited Europe to lay certain complaints before the Pope. He mentioned the fall of Edessa, and also:—

"...he stated that a few years ago a certain King and Priest called John, who lives on the farther side of Persia and Armenia, in the remote East, and who, with all his people, were Christians, though belonging to the Nestorian Church, had overcome the royal brothers Samiardi, kings of the Medes and Persians, and had captured Ecbatana, their capital and residence. The said kings had met with their Persian, Median, and Assyrian troops, and had fought for three consecutive days, each side having determined to die rather than take to flight. Prester John, for so they are wont to call him, at length routed the Persians, and after a bloody battle, remained victorious. After which victory the said John was hastening to the assistance of the Church at Jerusalem, but his host, on reaching the Tigris, was hindered from passing, through a deficiency in boats, and he directed his march North, since he had heard that the river was there covered with ice. In that place he had waited many years, expecting severe cold; but the winters having proved unpropitious, and the severity of the climate having carried off many soldiers, he had been forced to retreat to his own land. This king belongs to the family of the Magi, mentioned in the Gospel, and he rules over the very people formerly governed by the Magi; moreover, his fame and his wealth are so great, that he uses an emerald sceptre only.

"Excited by the example of his ancestors, who came to worship Christ in his cradle, he had proposed to go to Jerusalem, but had been impeded by the above-mentioned causes."[19]

[19] Otto, Ep. Frising., lib. vii. c. 33.

At the same time the story crops up in other quarters; so that we cannot look upon Otto as the inventor of the myth. The celebrated Maimonides alludes to it in a passage quoted by Joshua Lorki, a Jewish physician to Benedict XIII. Maimonides lived from 1135 to 1204. The passage is as follows: "It is evident both from the letters of Rambam (Maimonides), whose memory be blessed, and from the narration of merchants who have visited the ends of the earth, that at this time the root of our faith is to be found in the lands of Babel and Teman, where long ago Jerusalem was an exile; not reckoning those who live in the land of Paras[20] and Madai,[21] of the exiles of Schomrom, the number of which people is as the sand: of these some are still under the yoke of Paras, who is called the Great-Chief Sultan by the Arabs; others live in a place under the yoke of a strange people ... governed by a Christian chief, Preste-Cuan by name. With him they have made a compact, and he with them; and this is a matter concerning which there can be no manner of doubt."

[20] Persia.
[21] Media.

Benjamin of Tudela, another Jew, travelled in the East between the years 1159 and 1173, the last being the date of his death. He wrote an account of his travels, and gives in it some information with regard to a mythical Jew king, who reigned in the utmost splendor over a realm inhabited by Jews alone, situate somewhere in the midst of a desert of vast extent. About this period there appeared a document which produced intense excitement throughout Europe—a letter, yes! a letter from the mysterious personage himself to Manuel Comnenus, Emperor of Constantinople (1143-1180). The exact date of this extraordinary epistle cannot be fixed with any certainty, but it certainly appeared before 1241, the date of the conclusion of the chronicle of Albericus Trium Fontium. This Albericus relates that in the year 1165 "Presbyter Joannes, the Indian king, sent his wonderful letter to various Christian princes, and especially to Manuel of Constantinople, and Frederic the Roman Emperor." Similar letters were sent to Alexander III., to Louis VII. of France, and to the King of Portugal, which are alluded to in chronicles and romances, and which were indeed turned into rhyme, and sung all over Europe by minstrels and trouvères. The letter is as follows:—

"John, Priest by the Almighty power of God and the Might of our Lord Jesus Christ, King of Kings, and Lord of Lords, to his friend Emanuel, Prince of Constantinople, greeting, wishing him health, prosperity, and the continuance of Divine favor.

"Our Majesty has been informed that you hold our Excellency in love, and that the report of our greatness has reached you. Moreover, we have heard through our treasurer that you have been pleased to send to us some objects of art and interest, that our Exaltedness might be gratified thereby.

"Being human, I receive it in good part, and we have ordered our treasurer to send you some of our articles in return.

"Now we desire to be made certain that you hold the right faith, and in all things cleave to Jesus Christ, our Lord, for we have heard that your court regard you as a god, though we know that you are mortal, and subject to human infirmities.... Should you desire to learn the greatness and excellency of our Exaltedness and of the land subject to our sceptre, then hear and believe:—I, Presbyter Johannes, the Lord of Lords, surpass all under heaven in virtue, in riches, and in power; seventy-two kings pay us tribute.... In the three Indies our Magnificence rules, and our land extends beyond India, where rests the body of the holy Apostle Thomas; it reaches towards the sunrise over the wastes, and it trends towards deserted Babylon near the tower of Babel. Seventy-two provinces, of which only a few are Christian, serve us. Each has its own king, but all are tributary to us.

"Our land is the home of elephants, dromedaries, camels, crocodiles, meta-collinarum, cametennus, tensevetes, wild asses, white and red lions, white bears, white merules, crickets, griffins, tigers, lamias, hyenas, wild horses, wild oxen and wild men, men with horns, one-eyed, men with eyes before and behind, centaurs, fauns, satyrs, pygmies, forty-ell-high giants, Cyclopses, and similar women; it is the home, too, of the phœnix, and of nearly all living animals. We have some people subject to us who feed on the flesh of men and of prematurely born animals, and who never fear death. When any of these people die, their friends and relations eat him ravenously, for they regard it as a main duty to munch human flesh. Their names are Gog and Magog, Anie, Agit, Azenach, Fommeperi, Befari, Conei-Samante, Agrimandri, Vintefolei, Casbei, Alanei. These and similar nations were shut in behind lofty mountains by Alexander the Great, towards the North. We lead them at our pleasure against our foes, and neither man nor beast is left undevoured, if our Majesty gives the requisite permission. And when all our foes are eaten, then we return with our hosts home again. These accursed fifteen nations will burst forth from the four quarters of the earth at the end of the world, in the times of Antichrist, and overrun all the abodes of the Saints as well as the great city Rome, which, by the way, we are prepared to give to our son who will be born, along with all Italy, Germany, the two Gauls, Britain and Scotland. We shall also give him Spain and all the land as far as the icy sea. The nations to which I have alluded, according to the words of the prophet, shall not stand in the judgment, on account of their offensive practices, but will be consumed to ashes by a fire which will fall on them from heaven.

"Our land streams with honey, and is overflowing with milk. In one region grows no poisonous herb, nor does a querulous frog ever quack in it; no scorpion exists, nor does the serpent glide amongst the grass, nor can any poisonous animals exist in it, or injure any one.

"Among the heathen, flows through a certain province the River Indus; encircling Paradise, it spreads its arms in manifold windings through the entire province. Here are found the emeralds, sapphires, carbuncles, topazes, chrysolites, onyxes, beryls, sardius, and other costly stones. Here grows the plant Assidos, which, when worn by any one, protects him from the evil spirit, forcing it to state its business and name; consequently the foul spirits keep out of the way there. In a certain land subject to us, all kinds of pepper is gathered, and is exchanged for corn and bread, leather and cloth.... At the foot of Mount Olympus bubbles up a spring which changes its flavor hour by hour, night and day, and the spring is scarcely three days' journey from Paradise, out of which Adam was driven. If any one has tasted thrice of the fountain, from that day he will feel no fatigue, but will, as long as he lives, be as a man of thirty years. Here are found the small stones called Nudiosi, which, if borne about the body, prevent the sight from waxing feeble, and restore it where it is lost. The more the stone is looked at, the keener becomes the sight. In our territory is a certain waterless sea, consisting of tumbling billows of sand never at rest. None have crossed this sea; it lacks water altogether, yet fish are cast up upon the beach of various kinds, very tasty, and the like are nowhere else to be seen. Three days' journey from this sea are mountains from which rolls down a stony, waterless river, which opens into the sandy sea. As soon as the stream reaches the sea, its stones vanish in it, and are never seen again. As long as the river is in motion, it cannot be crossed; only four days a week is it possible to traverse it. Between the sandy sea and the said mountains, in a certain plain is a fountain of singular virtue, which purges Christians and would-be Christians from all transgressions. The water stands four inches high in a hollow stone shaped like a mussel-shell. Two saintly old men watch by it, and ask the comers whether they are Christians, or are about to become Christians, then whether they desire healing with all their hearts. If they have answered well, they are bidden to lay aside their clothes, and to step into the mussel. If what they said be true, then the water begins to rise and gush over their heads; thrice does the water thus lift itself, and every one who has entered the mussel leaves it cured of every complaint.

"Near the wilderness trickles between barren mountains a subterranean rill, which can only by chance be reached, for only occasionally the earth gapes, and he who would descend must do it with precipitation, ere the earth closes again. All that is gathered under the ground there is gem and precious stone. The brook pours into another river, and the inhabitants of the neighborhood obtain thence abundance of precious stones. Yet they never venture to sell them without having first offered them to us for our private use: should we decline them, they are at liberty to dispose of them to strangers. Boys there are trained to remain three or four days under water, diving after the stones.

"Beyond the stone river are the ten tribes of the Jews, which, though subject to their own kings, are, for all that, our slaves and tributary to our Majesty. In one of our lands, hight Zone, are worms called in our tongue Salamanders. These worms can only live in fire, and they build cocoons like silk-worms, which are unwound by the ladies of our palace, and spun into cloth and dresses, which are worn by our Exaltedness. These dresses, in order to be cleaned and washed, are cast into flames.... When we go to war, we have fourteen golden and bejewelled crosses borne before us instead of banners; each of these crosses is followed by 10,000 horsemen, and 100,000 foot soldiers fully armed, without reckoning those in charge of the luggage and provision.

"When we ride abroad plainly, we have a wooden, unadorned cross, without gold or gem about it, borne before us, in order that we may meditate on the sufferings of Our Lord Jesus Christ; also a golden bowl filled with earth, to remind us of that whence we sprung, and that to which we must return; but besides these there is borne a silver bowl full of gold, as a token to all that we are the Lord of Lords.

"All riches, such as are upon the world, our Magnificence possesses in superabundance. With us no one lies, for he who speaks a lie is thenceforth regarded as dead; he is no more thought of, or honored by us. No vice is tolerated by us. Every year we undertake a pilgrimage, with retinue of war, to the body of the holy prophet Daniel, which is near the desolated site of Babylon. In our realm fishes are caught, the blood of which dyes purple. The Amazons and the Brahmins are subject to us. The palace in which our Supereminency resides, is built after the pattern of the castle built by the Apostle Thomas for the Indian king Gundoforus. Ceilings, joists, and architrave are of Sethym wood, the roof of ebony, which can never catch fire. Over the gable of the palace are, at the extremities, two golden apples, in each of which are two carbuncles, so that the gold may shine by day, and the carbuncles by night. The greater gates of the palace are of sardius, with the horn of the horned snake inwrought, so that no one can bring poison within.

"The other portals are of ebony. The windows are of crystal; the tables are partly of gold, partly of amethyst, and the columns supporting the tables are partly of ivory, partly of amethyst. The court in which we watch the jousting is floored with onyx in order to increase the courage of the combatants. In the palace, at night, nothing is burned for light but wicks supplied with balsam.... Before our palace stands a mirror, the ascent to which consists of five and twenty steps of porphyry and serpentine."

After a description of the gems adorning this mirror, which is guarded night and day by three thousand armed men, he explains its use: "We look therein and behold all that is taking place in every province and region subject to our sceptre.

"Seven kings wait upon us monthly, in turn, with sixty-two dukes, two hundred and fifty-six counts and marquises: and twelve archbishops sit at table with us on our right, and twenty bishops on the left, besides the patriarch of St. Thomas, the Sarmatian Protopope, and the Archpope of Susa.... Our lord high steward is a primate and king, our cup-bearer is an archbishop and king, our chamberlain a bishop and king, our marshal a king and abbot."

I may be spared further extracts from this extraordinary letter, which proceeds to describe the church in which Prester John worships, by enumerating the precious stones of which it is constructed, and their special virtues.

Whether this letter was in circulation before Pope Alexander wrote his, it is not easy to decide. Alexander does not allude to it, but speaks of the reports which have reached him of the piety and the magnificence of the Priest-King. At the same time, there runs a tone of bitterness through the letter, as though the Pope had been galled at the pretensions of this mysterious personage, and perhaps winced under the prospect of the man-eaters overrunning Italy, as suggested by John the Priest. The papal epistle is an assertion of the claims of the See of Rome to universal dominion, and it assures the Eastern Prince-Pope that his Christian professions are worthless, unless he submits to the successor of Peter. "Not every one that saith unto me, Lord, Lord," &c., quotes the Pope, and then explains that the will of God is that every monarch and prelate should eat humble pie to the Sovereign Pontiff.

Sir John Maundevil gives the origin of the priestly title of the Eastern despot, in his curious book of travels.

"So it befelle, that this emperour cam, with a Cristene knyght with him, into a chirche in Egypt: and it was Saterday in Wyttson woke. And the bishop made orders. And he beheld and listened the servyse fulle tentyfly: and he asked the Cristene knyght, what men of degree thei scholden ben, that the prelate had before him. And the knyght answerede and seyde, that thei scholde ben prestes. And then the emperour seyde, that he wolde no longer ben clept kyng ne emperour, but preest: and that he wolde have the name of the first preest, that wente out of the chirche; and his name was John. And so evere more sittiens, he is clept Prestre John."

It is probable that the foundation of the whole Prester-John myth lay in the report which reached Europe of the wonderful successes of Nestorianism in the East, and there seems reason to believe that the famous letter given above was a Nestorian fabrication. It certainly looks un-European; the gorgeous imagery is thoroughly Eastern, and the disparaging tone in which Rome is spoken of could hardly have been the expression of Western feelings. The letter has the object in view of exalting the East in religion and arts to an undue eminence at the expense of the West, and it manifests some ignorance of European geography, when it speaks of the land extending from Spain to the Polar Sea. Moreover, the sites of the patriarchates, and the dignity conferred on that of St. Thomas, are indications of a Nestorian bias.

A brief glance at the history of this heretical Church may be of value here, as showing that there really was a foundation for the wild legends concerning a Christian empire in the East, so prevalent in Europe. Nestorius, a priest of Antioch and a disciple of St. Chrysostom, was elevated by the emperor to the patriarchate of Constantinople, and in the year 428 began to propagate his heresy, denying the hypostatic union. The Council of Ephesus denounced him, and, in spite of the emperor and court, Nestorius was anathematized and driven into exile. His sect spread through the East, and became a flourishing church. It reached to China, where the emperor was all but converted; its missionaries traversed the frozen tundras of Siberia, preaching their maimed Gospel to the wild hordes which haunted those dreary wastes; it faced Buddhism, and wrestled with it for the religious supremacy in Thibet; it established churches in Persia and in Bokhara; it penetrated India; it formed colonies in Ceylon, in Siam, and in Sumatra; so that the Catholicos or Pope of Bagdad exercised sway more extensive than that ever obtained by the successor of St. Peter. The number of Christians belonging to that communion probably exceeded that of the members of the true Catholic Church in East and West. But the Nestorian Church was not founded on the Rock; it rested on Nestorius; and when the rain descended, and the winds blew, and the floods came, and beat upon that house, it fell, leaving scarce a fragment behind.

Rubruquis the Franciscan, who in 1253 was sent on a mission into Tartary, was the first to let in a little light on the fable. He writes, "The Catai dwelt beyond certain mountains across which I wandered, and in a plain in the midst of the mountains lived once an important Nestorian shepherd, who ruled over the Nestorian people, called Nayman. When Coir-Khan died, the Nestorian people raised this man to be king, and called him King Johannes, and related of him ten times as much as the truth. The Nestorians thereabouts have this way with them, that about nothing they make a great fuss, and thus they have got it noised abroad that Sartach, Mangu-Khan, and Ken-Khan were Christians, simply because they treated Christians well, and showed them more honor than other people. Yet, in fact, they were not Christians at all. And in like manner the story got about that there was a great King John. However, I traversed his pastures, and no one knew anything about him, except a few Nestorians. In his pastures lives Ken-Khan, at whose court was Brother Andrew, whom I met on my way back. This Johannes had a brother, a famous shepherd, named Unc, who lived three weeks' journey beyond the mountains of Caracatais."

This Unk-Khan was a real individual; he lost his life in the year 1203. Kuschhik, prince of the Nayman, and follower of Kor-Khan, fell in 1218.

Marco Polo, the Venetian traveller (1254-1324), identifies Unk-Khan with Prester John; he says, "I will now tell you of the deeds of the Tartars, how they gained the mastery, and spread over the whole earth. The Tartars dwelt between Georgia and Bargu, where there is a vast plain and level country, on which are neither cities nor forts, but capital pasturage and water. They had no chief of their own, but paid to Prester Johannes tribute. Of the greatness of this Prester Johannes, who was properly called Un-Khan, the whole world spake; the Tartars gave him one of every ten head of cattle. When Prester John noticed that they were increasing, he feared them, and planned how he could injure them. He determined therefore to scatter them, and he sent barons to do this. But the Tartars guessed what Prester John purposed ... and they went away into the wide wastes of the North, where they might be beyond his reach." He then goes on to relate how Tschengis-(Jenghiz-)Khan became the head of the Tartars, and how he fought against Prester John, and, after a desperate fight, overcame and slew him.

The Syriac Chronicle of the Jacobite Primate, Gregory Bar-Hebræus (born 1226, died 1286), also identifies Unk-Khan with Prester John.

"In the year of the Greeks 1514, of the Arabs 599 (A. D. 1202), when Unk-Khan, who is the Christian King John, ruled over a stock of the barbarian Hunns, called Kergt, Tschingys-Khan served him with great zeal. When John observed the superiority and serviceableness of the other, he envied him, and plotted to seize and murder him. But two sons of Unk-Khan, having heard this, told it to Tschingys; whereupon he and his comrades fled by night, and secreted themselves. Next morning Unk-Khan took possession of the Tartar tents, but found them empty. Then the party of Tschingys fell upon him, and they met by the spring called Balschunah, and the side of Tschingys won the day; and the followers of Unk-Khan were compelled to yield. They met again several times, till Unk-Khan was utterly discomfited, and was slain himself, and his wives, sons, and daughters carried into captivity. Yet we must consider that King John the Kergtajer was not cast down for nought; nay, rather, because he had turned his heart from the fear of Christ his Lord, who had exalted him, and had taken a wife of the Zinish nation, called Quarakhata. Because he forsook the religion of his ancestors and followed strange gods, therefore God took the government from him, and gave it to one better than he, and whose heart was right before God."

Some of the early travellers, such as John de Plano Carpini and Marco Polo, in disabusing the popular mind of the belief in Prester John as a mighty Asiatic Christian monarch, unintentionally turned the popular faith in that individual into a new direction. They spoke of the black people of Abascia in Ethiopia, which, by the way, they called Middle India, as a great people subject to a Christian monarch.

Marco Polo says that the true monarch of Abyssinia is Christ; but that it is governed by six kings, three of whom are Christians and three Saracens, and that they are in league with the Soudan of Aden.

Bishop Jordanus, in his description of the world, accordingly sets down Abyssinia as the kingdom of Prester John; and such was the popular impression, which was confirmed by the appearance at intervals of ambassadors at European courts from the King of Abyssinia. The discovery of the Cape of Good Hope was due partly to a desire manifested in Portugal to open communications with this monarch,[22] and King John II. sent two men learned in Oriental languages through Egypt to the court of Abyssinia. The might and dominion of this prince, who had replaced the Tartar chief in the popular creed as Prester John, was of course greatly exaggerated, and was supposed to extend across Arabia and Asia to the wall of China. The spread of geographical knowledge has contracted the area of his dominions, and a critical acquaintance with history has exploded the myth which invested Unk-Khan, the nomad chief, with all the attributes of a demigod, uniting in one the utmost pretensions of a Pope and the proudest claims of a monarch.

[22] Ludolfi Hist. Æthiopica, lib. ii. cap. 1, 2. Petrus, Petri filius Lusitaniæ princeps, M. Pauli Veneti librum (qui de Indorum rebus multa: speciatim vero de Presbytero Johanne aliqua magnifice scripsit) Venetiis secum in patriam detulerat, qui (Chronologicis Lusitanorum testantibus) præcipuam Johanni Regi ansam dedit Indicæ navigationis, quam Henricus Johannis I. filius, patruus ejus, tentaverat, prosequendæ, &c.

III. — THE DIVINING ROD

FROM the remotest period a rod has been regarded as the symbol of power and authority, and Holy Scripture employs it in the popular sense. Thus David speaks of "Thy rod and Thy staff comforting me;" and Moses works his miracles before Pharaoh with the rod as emblem of Divine commission. It was his rod which became a serpent, which turned the water of Egypt into blood, which opened the waves of the Red Sea and restored them to their former level, which "smote the rock of stone so that the water gushed out abundantly." The rod of Aaron acted an oracular part in the contest with the princes; laid up before the ark, it budded and brought forth almonds. In this instance we have it no longer as a symbol of authority, but as a means of divining the will of God. And as such it became liable to abuse; thus Hosea rebukes the chosen people for practising similar divinations. "My people ask counsel at their stocks, and their staff declareth unto them."[23]

[23] Hos. iv. 12.

Long before this, Jacob had made a different use of rods, employing them as a charm to make his father-in-law's sheep bear pied and spotted lambs.

We find rhabdomancy a popular form of divination among the Greeks, and also among the Romans. Cicero in his "De Officiis" alludes to it. "If all that is needful for our nourishment and support arrives to us by means of some divine rod, as people say, then each of us, free from all care and trouble, may give himself up to the exclusive pursuit of study and science."

Probably it is to this rod that the allusion of Ennius, as the agent in discovering hidden treasures, quoted in the first book of his "De Divinatione," refers.

According to Vetranius Maurus, Varro left a satire on the "Virgula divina," which has not been preserved. Tacitus tells us that the Germans practised some sort of divination by means of rods. "For the purpose their method is simple. They cut a rod off some fruit-tree into bits, and after having distinguished them by various marks, they cast them into a white cloth.... Then the priest thrice draws each piece, and explains the oracle according to the marks." Ammianus Marcellinus says that the Alains employed an osier rod.

The fourteenth law of the Frisons ordered that the discovery of murders should be made by means of divining rods used in Church. These rods should be laid before the altar, and on the sacred relics, after which God was to be supplicated to indicate the culprit. This was called the Lot of Rods, or Tan-teen, the Rod of Rods.

But the middle ages was the date of the full development of the superstition, and the divining rod was believed to have efficacy in discovering hidden treasures, veins of precious metal, springs of water, thefts, and murders. The first notice of its general use among late writers is in the "Testamentum Novum," lib. i. cap. 25, of Basil Valentine, a Benedictine monk of the fifteenth century. Basil speaks of the general faith in and adoption of this valuable instrument for the discovery of metals, which is carried by workmen in mines, either in their belts or in their caps. He says that there are seven names by which this rod is known, and to its excellences under each title he devotes a chapter of his book. The names are: Divine Rod, Shining Rod, Leaping Rod, Transcendent Rod, Trembling Rod, Dipping Rod, Superior Rod. In his admirable treatise on metals, Agricola speaks of the rod in terms of disparagement; he considers its use as a relic of ancient magical forms, and he says that it is only irreligious workmen who employ it in their search after metals. Goclenius, however, in his treatise on the virtue of plants, stoutly does battle for the properties of the hazel rod. Whereupon Roberti, a Flemish Jesuit, falls upon him tooth and nail, disputes his facts, overwhelms him with abuse, and gibbets him for popular ridicule. Andreas Libavius, a writer I have already quoted in my article on the Wandering Jew, undertook a series of experiments upon the hazel divining rod, and concluded that there was truth in the popular belief. The Jesuit Kircher also "experimentalized several times on wooden rods which were declared to be sympathetic with regard to certain metals, by placing them on delicate pivots in equilibrium; but they never turned on the approach of metal." (De Arte Magnetica.) However, a similar course of experiments over water led him to attribute to the rod the power of indicating subterranean springs and water-courses; "I would not affirm it," he says, "unless I had established the fact by my own experience."

Dechales, another Jesuit, author of a treatise on natural springs, and of a huge tome entitled "Mundus Mathematicus," declared in the latter work, that no means of discovering sources is equal to the divining rod; and he quotes a friend of his who, with a hazel rod in his hand, could discover springs with the utmost precision and facility, and could trace on the surface of the ground the course of a subterranean conduit. Another writer, Saint-Romain, in his "Science dégagée des Chimères de l'École," exclaims, "Is it not astonishing to see a rod, which is held firmly in the hands, bow itself and turn visibly in the direction of water or metal, with more or less promptitude, according as the metal or the water are near or remote from the surface!"

In 1659 the Jesuit Gaspard Schott writes that the rod is used in every town of Germany, and that he had frequent opportunity of seeing it used in the discovery of hidden treasures. "I searched with the greatest care," he adds, "into the question whether the hazel rod had any sympathy with gold and silver, and whether any natural property set it in motion. In like manner I tried whether a ring of metal, held suspended by a thread in the midst of a tumbler, and which strikes the hours, is moved by any similar force. I ascertained that these effects could only have rise from the deception of those holding the rod or the pendulum, or, may be, from some diabolic impulsion, or, more likely still, because imagination sets the hand in motion."

The Sieur le Royer, a lawyer of Rouen, in 1674, published his "Traité du Bâton universel," in which he gives an account of a trial made with the rod in the presence of Father Jean François, who had ridiculed the operation in his treatise on the science of waters, published at Rennes in 1655, and which succeeded in convincing the blasphemer of the divine Rod. Le Royer denies to it the power of picking out criminals, which had been popularly attributed to it, and as had been unhesitatingly claimed for it by Debrio in his "Disquisitio Magica."

And now I am brought to the extraordinary story of Jacques Aymar, which attracted the attention of Europe to the marvellous properties of the divining rod. I shall give the history of this man in full, as such an account is rendered necessary by the mutilated versions I have seen current in English magazine articles, which follow the lead of Mrs. Crowe, who narrates the earlier portion of this impostor's career, but says nothing of his *exposé* and downfall.

On the 5th July, 1692, at about ten o'clock in the evening, a wine-seller of Lyons and his wife were assassinated in their cellar, and their money carried off. On the morrow, the officers of justice arrived, and examined the premises. Beside the corpses, lay a large bottle wrapped in straw, and a bloody hedging bill, which undoubtedly had been the instrument used to accomplish the murder. Not a trace of those who had committed the horrible deed was to be found, and the magistrates were quite at fault as to the direction in which they should turn for a clew to the murderer or murderers.

At this juncture a neighbor reminded the magistrates of an incident which had taken place four years previous. It was this. In 1688 a theft of clothes had been made in Grenoble. In the parish of Crôle lived a man named Jacques Aymar, supposed to be endowed with the faculty of using the divining rod. This man was sent for. On reaching the spot where the theft had been committed, his rod moved in his hand. He followed the track indicated by the rod, and it continued to rotate between his fingers as long as he followed a certain direction, but ceased to turn if he diverged from it in the smallest degree. Guided by his rod, Aymar went from street to street, till he was brought to a standstill before the prison gates. These could not be opened without leave of the magistrate, who hastened to witness the experiment. The gates were unlocked, and Aymar, under the same guidance, directed his steps towards four prisoners lately incarcerated. He ordered the four to be stood in a line, and then he placed his foot on that of the first. The rod remained immovable. He passed to the second, and the rod turned at once. Before the third prisoner there were no signs; the fourth trembled, and begged to be heard. He owned himself the thief, along with the second, who also acknowledged the theft, and mentioned the name of the receiver of the stolen goods. This was a farmer in the neighborhood of Grenoble. The magistrate and officers visited him and demanded the articles he had obtained. The farmer denied all knowledge of the theft and all participation in the booty. Aymar, however, by means of his rod, discovered the secreted property, and restored it to the persons from whom it had been stolen.

On another occasion Aymar had been in quest of a spring of water, when he felt his rod turn sharply in his hand. On digging at the spot, expecting to discover an abundant source, the body of a murdered woman was found in a barrel, with a rope twisted round her neck. The poor creature was recognized as a woman of the neighborhood who had vanished four months before. Aymar went to the house which the victim had inhabited, and presented his rod to each member of the household. It turned upon the husband of the deceased, who at once took to flight.

The magistrates of Lyons, at their wits' ends how to discover the perpetrators of the double murder in the wine shop, urged the Procureur du Roi to make experiment of the powers of Jacques Aymar. The fellow was sent for, and he boldly asserted his capacity for detecting criminals, if he were first brought to the spot of the murder, so as to be put *en rapport* with the murderers.

He was at once conducted to the scene of the outrage, with the rod in his hand. This remained stationary as he traversed the cellar, till he reached the spot where the body of the wine seller had lain; then the stick became violently agitated, and the man's pulse rose as though he were in an access of fever. The same motions and symptoms manifested themselves when he reached the place where the second victim had lain.

Having thus received his *impression*, Aymar left the cellar, and, guided by his rod, or rather by an internal instinct, he ascended into the shop, and then stepping into the street, he followed from one to another, like a hound upon the scent, the track of the murderers. It conducted him into the court of the archiepiscopal palace, across it, and down to the gate of the Rhone. It was now evening, and the city gates being all closed, the quest of blood was relinquished for the night.

Next morning Aymar returned to the scent. Accompanied by three officers, he left the gate, and descended the right bank of the Rhone. The rod gave indications of there having been three involved in the murder, and he pursued the traces till two of them led to a gardener's cottage. Into this he entered, and there he asserted with warmth, against the asseverations of the proprietor to the contrary, that the fugitives had entered his room, had seated themselves at his table, and had drunk wine out of one of the bottles which he indicated. Aymar tested each of the household with his rod, to see if they had been in contact with the murderers. The rod moved over the two children only, aged respectively ten and nine years. These little things, on being questioned, answered, with reluctance, that during their father's absence on Sunday morning, against his express commands, they had left the door open, and that two men, whom they described, had come in suddenly upon them, and had seated themselves and made free with the wine in the bottle pointed out by the man with the rod. This first verification of the talents of Jacques Aymar convinced some of the sceptical, but the Procurateur Général forbade the prosecution of the experiment till the man had been further tested.

As already stated, a hedging bill had been discovered, on the scene of the murder, smeared with blood, and unquestionably the weapon with which the crime had been committed. Three bills from the same maker, and of precisely the same description, were obtained, and the four were taken into a garden, and secretly buried at intervals. Aymar was then brought, staff in hand, into the garden, and conducted over the spots where lay the bills. The rod began to vibrate as his feet stood upon the place where was concealed the bill which had been used by the assassins, but was motionless elsewhere. Still unsatisfied, the four bills were exhumed and concealed anew. The comptroller of the province himself bandaged the sorcerer's eyes, and led him by the hand from place to place. The divining rod showed no signs of movement till it approached the blood-stained weapon, when it began to oscillate.

The magistrates were now so far satisfied as to agree that Jacques Aymar should be authorized to follow the trail of the murderers, and have a company of archers to follow him.

Guided by his rod, Aymar now recommenced his pursuit. He continued tracing down the right bank of the Rhone till he came to half a league from the bridge of Lyons. Here the footprints of three men were observed in the sand, as though engaged in entering a boat. A rowing boat was obtained, and Aymar, with his escort, descended the river; he found some difficulty in following the trail upon water; still he was able, with a little care, to detect it. It brought him under an arch of the bridge of Vienne, which boats rarely passed beneath. This proved that the fugitives were without a guide. The way in which this curious journey was made was singular. At intervals Aymar was put ashore to test the banks with his rod, and ascertain whether the murderers had landed. He discovered the places where they had slept, and indicated the chairs or benches on which they had sat. In this manner, by slow degrees, he arrived at the military camp of Sablon, between Vienne and Saint-Valier. There Aymar felt violent agitation, his cheeks flushed, and his pulse beat with rapidity. He penetrated the crowds of soldiers, but did not venture to use his rod, lest the men should take it ill, and fall upon him. He could not do more without special authority, and was constrained to return to Lyons. The magistrates then provided him with the requisite powers, and he went back to the camp. Now he declared that the murderers were not there. He recommenced his pursuit, and descended the Rhone again as far as Beaucaire.

On entering the town he ascertained by means of his rod that those whom he was pursuing had parted company. He traversed several streets, then crowded on account of the annual fair, and was brought to a standstill before the prison doors. One of the murderers was within, he declared; he would track the others afterwards. Having obtained permission to enter, he was brought into the presence of fourteen or fifteen prisoners. Amongst these was a hunchback, who had only an hour previously been incarcerated on account of a theft he had committed at the fair. Aymar applied his rod to each of the prisoners in succession: it turned upon the hunchback. The sorcerer ascertained that the other two had left the town by a little path leading into the Nismes road. Instead of following this track, he returned to Lyons with the hunchback and the guard. At Lyons a triumph awaited him. The hunchback had hitherto protested his innocence, and declared that he had never set foot in Lyons. But as he was brought to that town by the way along which Aymar had ascertained that he had left it, the fellow was recognized at the different houses where he had lodged the night, or stopped for food. At the little town of Bagnols, he was confronted with the host and hostess of a tavern where he and his comrades had slept, and they swore to his identity, and accurately described his companions: their description tallied with that given by the children of the gardener. The wretched man was so confounded by this recognition, that he avowed having staid there, a few days before, along with two Provençals. These men, he said, were the criminals; he had been their servant, and had only kept guard in the upper room whilst they committed the murders in the cellar.

On his arrival in Lyons he was committed to prison, and his trial was decided on. At his first interrogation he told his tale precisely as he had related it before, with these additions: the murderers spoke patois, and had purchased two bills. At ten o'clock in the evening all three had entered the wine shop. The Provençals had a large bottle wrapped in straw, and they persuaded the publican and his wife to descend with them into the cellar to fill it, whilst he, the hunchback, acted as watch in the shop. The two men murdered the wine-seller and his wife with their bills, and then mounted to the shop, where they opened the coffer, and stole from it one hundred and thirty crowns, eight louis-d'ors, and a silver belt. The crime accomplished, they took refuge in the court of a large house,—this was the archbishop's palace, indicated by Aymar,—and passed the night in it. Next day, early, they left Lyons, and only stopped for a moment at a gardener's cottage. Some way down the river, they found a boat moored to the bank. This they loosed from its mooring and entered. They came ashore at the spot pointed out by the man with the stick. They staid some days in the camp at Sablon, and then went on to Beaucaire.

Aymar was now sent in quest of the other murderers. He resumed their trail at the gate of Beaucaire, and that of one of them, after considerable *détours*, led him to the prison doors of Beaucaire, and he asked to be allowed to search among the prisoners for his man. This time he was mistaken. The second fugitive was not within; but the jailer affirmed that a man whom he described—and his description tallied with the known appearance of one of the Provençals—had called at the gate shortly after the removal of the hunchback to inquire after him, and on learning of his removal to Lyons, had hurried off precipitately. Aymar now followed his track from the prison, and this brought him to that of the third criminal. He pursued the double scent for some days. But it became evident that the two culprits had been alarmed at what had transpired in Beaucaire, and were flying from France. Aymar traced them to the frontier, and then returned to Lyons.

On the 30th of August, 1692, the poor hunchback was, according to sentence, broken on the wheel, in the Place des Terreaux. On his way to execution he had to pass the wine shop. There the recorder publicly read his sentence, which had been delivered by thirty judges. The criminal knelt and asked pardon of the poor wretches in whose murder he was involved, after which he continued his course to the place fixed for his execution.

It may be well here to give an account of the authorities for this extraordinary story. There are three circumstantial accounts, and numerous letters written by the magistrate who sat during the trial, and by an eye-witness of the whole transaction, men honorable and disinterested, upon whose veracity not a shadow of doubt was supposed to rest by their contemporaries.

M. Chauvin, Doctor of Medicine, published a "*Lettre à Mme. la Marquise de Senozan, sur les moyens dont on s'est servi pour découvrir les complices d'un assassinat commis à Lyon, le 5 Juillet, 1692.*" Lyons, 1692. The *procès-verbal* of the Procureur du Roi, M. de Vanini, is also extant, and published in the *Physique occulte* of the Abbé de Vallemont.

Pierre Gamier, Doctor of Medicine of the University of Montpellier, wrote a *Dissertation physique en forme de lettre, à M. de Sève, seigneur de Fléchères*, on Jacques Aymar, printed the same year at Lyons, and republished in the *Histoire critique des pratiques superstitieuses du Père Lebrun*.

Doctor Chauvin was witness of nearly all the circumstances related, as was also the Abbé Lagarde, who has written a careful account of the whole transaction as far as to the execution of the hunchback.

Another eye-witness writes to the Abbé Bignon a letter printed by Lebrun in his *Histoire critique* cited above. "The following circumstance happened to me yesterday evening," he says: "M. le Procureur du Roi here, who, by the way, is one of the wisest and cleverest men in the country, sent for me at six o'clock, and had me conducted to the scene of the murder. We found there M. Grimaut, director of the customs, whom I knew to be a very upright man, and a young attorney named Besson, with whom I am not acquainted, but who M. le Procureur du Roi told me had the power of using the rod as well as M. Grimaut. We descended into the cellar where the murder had been committed, and where there were still traces of blood. Each time that M. Grimaut and the attorney passed the spot where the murder had been perpetrated, the rods they held in their hands began to turn, but ceased when they stepped beyond the spot. We tried experiments for more than an hour, as also with the bill, which M. le Procureur had brought along with him, and they were satisfactory. I observed several curious facts in the attorney. The rod in his hands was more violently moved than in those of M. Grimaut, and when I placed one of my fingers in each of his hands, whilst the rod turned, I felt the most extraordinary throbbings of the arteries in his palms. His pulse was at fever heat. He sweated profusely, and at intervals he was compelled to go into the court to obtain fresh air."

The Sieur Pauthot, Dean of the College of Medicine at Lyons, gave his observations to the public as well. Some of them are as follows: "We began at the cellar in which the murder had been committed; into this the man with the rod (Aymar) shrank from entering, because he felt violent agitations which overcame him when he used the stick over the place where the corpses of those who had been assassinated had lain. On entering the cellar, the rod was put in my hands, and arranged by the master as most suitable for operation; I passed and repassed over the spot where the bodies had been found, but it remained immovable, and I felt no agitation. A lady of rank and merit, who was with us, took the rod after me; she felt it begin to move, and was internally agitated. Then the owner of the rod resumed it, and, passing over the same places, the stick rotated with such violence that it seemed easier to break than to stop it. The peasant then quitted our company to faint away, as was his wont after similar experiments. I followed him. He turned very pale and broke into a profuse perspiration, whilst for a quarter of an hour his pulse was violently troubled; indeed, the faintness was so considerable, that they were obliged to dash water in his face and give him water to drink in order to bring him round." He then describes experiments made over the bloody bill and others similar, which succeeded in the hands of Aymar and the lady, but failed when he attempted them himself. Pierre Garnier, physician of the medical college of Montpellier, appointed to that of Lyons, has also written an account of what he saw, as mentioned above. He gives a curious proof of Aymar's powers.

"M. le Lieutenant-Général having been robbed by one of his lackeys, seven or eight months ago, and having lost by him twenty-five crowns which had been taken out of one of the cabinets behind his library, sent for Aymar, and asked him to discover the circumstances. Aymar went several times round the chamber, rod in hand, placing one foot on the chairs, on the various articles of furniture, and on two bureaux which are in the apartment, each of which contains several drawers. He fixed on the very bureau and the identical drawer out of which the money had been stolen. M. le Lieutenant-Général bade him follow the track of the robber. He did so. With his rod he went out on a new terrace, upon which the cabinet opens, thence back into the cabinet and up to the fire, then into the library, and from thence he went direct up stairs to the lackeys' sleeping apartment, when the rod guided him to one of the beds, and turned over one side of the bed, remaining motionless over the other. The lackeys then present cried out that the thief had slept on the side indicated by the rod, the bed having been shared with another footman, who occupied the further side." Garnier gives a lengthy account of various experiments he made along with the Lieutenant-Général, the uncle of the same, the Abbé de St. Remain, and M. de Puget, to detect whether there was imposture in the man. But all their attempts failed to discover a trace of deception. He gives a report of a verbal examination of Aymar which is interesting. The man always replied with candor.

The report of the extraordinary discovery of murder made by the divining rod at Lyons attracted the attention of Paris, and Aymar was ordered up to the capital. There, however, his powers left him. The Prince de Condé submitted him to various tests, and he broke down under every one. Five holes were dug in the garden. In one was secreted gold, in another silver, in a third silver and gold, in the fourth copper, and in the fifth stones. The rod made no signs in presence of the metals, and at last actually began to move over the buried pebbles. He was sent to Chantilly to discover the perpetrators of a theft of trout made in the ponds of the park. He went round the water, rod in hand, and it turned at spots where he said the fish had been drawn out. Then, following the track of the thief, it led him to the cottage of one of the keepers, but did not move over any of the individuals then in the house. The keeper himself was absent, but arrived late at night, and, on hearing what was said, he roused Aymar from his bed, insisting on having his innocence vindicated. The divining rod, however, pronounced him guilty, and the poor fellow took to his heels, much upon the principle recommended by Montesquieu a while after. Said he, "If you are accused of having stolen the towers of Notre-Dame, bolt at once."

A peasant, taken at haphazard from the street, was brought to the sorcerer as one suspected. The rod turned slightly, and Aymar declared that the man did not steal the fish, but ate of them. A boy was then introduced, who was said to be the keeper's son. The rod rotated violently at once. This was the finishing stroke, and Aymar was sent away by the Prince in disgrace. It now transpired that the theft of fish had taken place seven years before, and the lad was no relation of the keeper, but a country boy who had only been in Chantilly eight or ten months. M. Goyonnot, Recorder of the King's Council, broke a window in his house, and sent for the diviner, to whom he related a story of his having been robbed of valuables during the night. Aymar indicated the broken window as the means whereby the thief had entered the house, and pointed out the window by which he had left it with the booty. As no such robbery had been committed, Aymar was turned out of the house as an impostor. A few similar cases brought him into such disrepute that he was obliged to leave Paris, and return to Grenoble.

Some years after, he was made use of by the Maréchal Montrevel, in his cruel pursuit of the Camisards.

Was Aymar an impostor from first to last, or did his powers fail him in Paris? and was it only then that he had recourse to fraud?

Much may be said in favor of either supposition. His *exposé* at Paris tells heavily against him, but need not be regarded as conclusive evidence of imposture throughout his career. If he really did possess the powers he claimed, it is not to be supposed that these existed in full vigor under all conditions; and Paris is a place most unsuitable for testing them, built on artificial soil, and full of disturbing influences of every description. It has been remarked with others who used the rod, that their powers languished under excitement, and that the faculties had to be in repose, the attention to be concentrated on the subject of inquiry, or the action—nervous, magnetic, or electrical, or what you will—was impeded.

Now, Paris, visited for the first time by a poor peasant, its *salons* open to him, dazzling him with their splendor, and the novelty of finding himself in the midst of princes, dukes, marquises, and their families, not only may have agitated the countryman to such an extent as to deprive him of his peculiar faculty, but may have led him into simulating what he felt had departed from him, at the moment when he was under the eyes of the grandees of the Court. We have analogous cases in Bleton and Angelique Cottin. The former was a hydroscope, who fell into convulsions whenever he passed over running water. This peculiarity was noticed in him when a child of seven years old. When brought to Paris, he failed signally to detect the presence of water conveyed underground by pipes and conduits, but he pretended to feel the influence of water where there certainly was none. Angelique Cottin was a poor girl, highly charged with electricity. Any one touching her received a violent shock; one medical gentleman, having seated her on his knee, was knocked clean out of his chair by the electric fluid, which thus exhibited its sense of propriety. But the electric condition of Angelique became feebler as she approached Paris, and failed her altogether in the capital.

I believe that the imagination is the principal motive force in those who use the divining rod; but whether it is so solely, I am unable to decide. The powers of nature are so mysterious and inscrutable that we must be cautious in limiting them, under abnormal conditions, to the ordinary laws of experience.

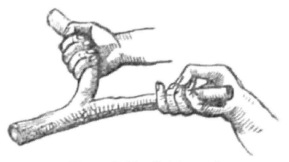

How to hold a divining rod.

The manner in which the rod was used by certain persons renders self-deception possible. The rod is generally of hazel, and is forked like a Y; the forefingers are placed against the diverging arms of the rod, and the elbows are brought back against the side; thus the implement is held in front of the operator, delicately balanced before the pit of the stomach at a distance of about eight inches. Now, if the pressure of the balls of the digits be in the least relaxed, the stalk of the rod will naturally fall. It has been assumed by some, that a restoration of the pressure will bring the stem up again, pointing towards the operator, and a little further pressure will elevate it into a perpendicular position. A relaxation of force will again lower it, and thus the rotation observed in the rod be maintained. I confess myself unable to accomplish this. The lowering of the leg of the rod is easy enough, but no efforts of mine to produce a revolution on its axis have as yet succeeded. The muscles which would contract the fingers upon the arms of the stick, pass the shoulder; and it is worthy of remark that one of the medical men who witnessed the experiments made on Bleton the hydroscope, expressly alludes to a slight rising of the shoulders during the rotation of the divining rod.

But the manner of using the rod was by no means identical in all cases. If, in all cases, it had simply been balanced between the fingers, some probability might be given to the suggestion above made, that the rotation was always effected by the involuntary action of the muscles.

The usual manner of holding the rod, however, precluded such a possibility. The most ordinary use consisted in taking a forked stick in such a manner that the palms were turned upwards, and the fingers closed upon the branching arms of the rod. Some required the normal position of the rod to be horizontal, others elevated the point, others again depressed it.

If the implement were straight, it was held in a similar manner, but the hands were brought somewhat together, so as to produce a slight arc in the rod. Some who practised rhabdomancy sustained this species of rod between their thumbs and forefingers; or else the thumb and forefingers were closed, and the rod rested on their points; or again it reposed on the flat of the hand, or on the back, the hand being held vertically and the rod held in equilibrium.

A third species of divining rod consisted in a straight staff cut in two: one extremity of the one half was hollowed out, the other half was sharpened at the end, and this end was inserted in the hollow, and the pointed stick rotated in the cavity.

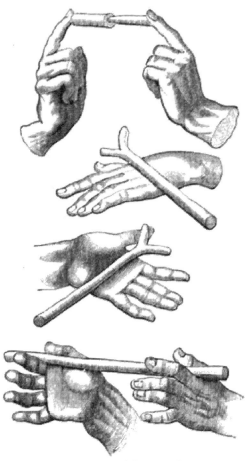

Positions of the Hands.
From "Lettres qui découvrent l'Illusion des Philosophes sur la Baguette." Paris, 1693.

The way in which Bleton used his rod is thus minutely described: "He does not grasp it, nor warm it in his hands, and he does not regard with preference a hazel branch lately cut and full of sap. He places horizontally between his forefingers a rod of any kind given to him, or picked up in the road, of any sort of wood except elder, fresh or dry, not always forked, but sometimes merely bent. If it is straight, it rises slightly at the extremities by little jerks, but does not turn. If bent, it revolves on its axis with more or less rapidity, in more or less time, according to the quantity and current of the water. I counted from thirty to thirty-five revolutions in a minute, and afterwards as many as eighty. A curious phenomenon is, that Bleton is able to make the rod turn between another person's fingers, even without seeing it or touching it, by approaching his body towards it when his feet stand over a subterranean watercourse. It is true, however, that the motion is much less strong and less durable in other fingers than his own. If Bleton stood on his head, and placed the rod between his feet, though he felt strongly the peculiar sensations produced in him by flowing water, yet the rod remained stationary. If he were insulated on glass, silk, or wax, the sensations were less vivid, and the rotation of the stick ceased."

But this experiment failed in Paris, under circumstances which either proved that Bleton's imagination produced the movement, or that his integrity was questionable. It is quite possible that in many instances the action of the muscles is purely involuntary, and is attributable to the imagination, so that the operator deceives himself as well as others.

This is probably the explanation of the story of Mdlle. Olivet, a young lady of tender conscience, who was a skilful performer with the divining rod, but shrank from putting her powers in operation, lest she should be indulging in unlawful acts. She consulted the Père Lebrun, author of a work already referred to in this paper, and he advised her to ask God to withdraw the power from her, if the exercise of it was harmful to her spiritual condition. She entered into retreat for two days, and prayed with fervor. Then she made her communion, asking God what had been recommended to her at the moment when she received the Host. In the afternoon of the same day she made experiment with her rod, and found that it would no longer operate. The girl had strong faith in it before—a faith coupled with fear; and as long as that faith was strong in her, the rod moved; now she believed that the faculty was taken from her; and the power ceased with the loss of her faith.

If the divining rod is put in motion by any other force except the involuntary action of the muscles, we must confine its powers to the property of indicating the presence of flowing water. There are numerous instances of hydroscopes thus detecting the existence of a spring, or of a subterranean watercourse; the most remarkably endowed individuals of this description are Jean-Jacques Parangue, born near Marseilles, in 1760, who experienced a horror when near water which no one else perceived. He was endowed with the faculty of seeing water through the ground, says l'Abbé Sauri, who gives his history. Jenny Leslie, a Scotch girl, about the same date claimed similar powers. In 1790, Pennet, a native of Dauphiné, attracted attention in Italy, but when carefully tested by scientific men in Padua, his attempts to discover buried metals failed; at Florence he was detected in an endeavor to find out by night what had been secreted to test his powers on the morrow. Vincent Amoretti was an Italian, who underwent peculiar sensations when brought in proximity to water, coal, and salt; he was skilful in the use of the rod, but made no public exhibition of his powers.

The rod is still employed, I have heard it asserted, by Cornish miners; but I have never been able to ascertain that such is really the case. The mining captains whom I have questioned invariably repudiated all knowledge of its use.

In Wiltshire, however, it is still employed for the purpose of detecting water; and the following extract from a letter I have just received will show that it is still in vogue on the Continent:—

"I believe the use of the divining rod for discovering springs of water has by no means been confined to mediæval times; for I was personally acquainted with a lady, now deceased, who has successfully practised with it in this way. She was a very clever and accomplished woman; Scotch by birth and education; by no means credulous; possibly a little imaginative, for she wrote not unsuccessfully; and of a remarkably open and straightforward disposition. Captain C——, her husband, had a large estate in Holstein, near Lubeck, supporting a considerable population; and whether for the wants of the people or for the improvement of the land, it now and then happened that an additional well was needed.

"On one of these occasions a man was sent for who made a regular profession of finding water by the divining rod; there happened to be a large party staying at the house, and the whole company turned out to see the fun. The rod gave indications in the usual way, and water was ultimately found at the spot. Mrs. C——, utterly sceptical, took the rod into her own hands to make experiment, believing that she would prove the man an impostor; and she said afterwards she was never more frightened in her life than when it began to move, on her walking over the spring. Several other gentlemen and ladies tried it, but it was quite inactive in their hands. 'Well,' said the host to his wife, 'we shall have no occasion to send for the man again, as you are such an adept.'

"Some months after this, water was wanted in another part of the estate, and it occurred to Mrs. C—— that she would use the rod again. After some trials, it again gave decided indications, and a well was begun and carried down a very considerable depth. At last she began to shrink from incurring more expense, but the laborers had implicit faith; and begged to be allowed to persevere. Very soon the water burst up with such force that the men escaped with difficulty; and this proved afterwards the most unfailing spring for miles round.

"You will take the above for what it is worth; the facts I have given are undoubtedly true, whatever conclusions may be drawn from them. I do not propose that you should print my narrative, but I think in these cases personal testimony, even indirect, is more useful in forming one's opinion than a hundred old volumes. I did not hear it from Mrs. C——'s own lips, but I was sufficiently acquainted with her to form a very tolerable estimate of her character; and my wife, who has known her intimately from her own childhood, was in her younger days often staying with her for months together."

I remember having been much perplexed by reading a series of experiments made with a pendulous ring over metals, by a Mr. Mayo: he ascertained that it oscillated in various directions under peculiar circumstances, when suspended by a thread over the ball of the thumb. I instituted a series of experiments, and was surprised to find the ring vibrate in an unaccountable manner in opposite directions over different metals. On consideration, I closed my eyes whilst the ring was oscillating over gold, and on opening them I found that it had become stationary. I got a friend to change the metals whilst I was blindfolded—the ring no longer vibrated. I was thus enabled to judge of the involuntary action of muscles, quite sufficient to have deceived an eminent medical man like Mr. Mayo, and to have perplexed me till I succeeded in solving the mystery.[24]

[24] A similar series of experiments was undertaken, as I learned afterwards, by M. Chevreuil in Paris, with similar results.

IV. — THE SEVEN SLEEPERS OF EPHESUS

ONE of the most picturesque myths of ancient days is that which forms the subject of this article. It is thus told by Jacques de Voragine, in his "Legenda Aurea:"—

"The seven sleepers were natives of Ephesus. The Emperor Decius, who persecuted the Christians, having come to Ephesus, ordered the erection of temples in the city, that all might come and sacrifice before him; and he commanded that the Christians should be sought out and given their choice, either to worship the idols, or to die. So great was the consternation in the city, that the friend denounced his friend, the father his son, and the son his father.

"Now there were in Ephesus seven Christians, Maximian, Malchus, Marcian, Dionysius, John, Serapion, and Constantine by name. These refused to sacrifice to the idols, and remained in their houses praying and fasting. They were accused before Decius, and they confessed themselves to be Christians. However, the emperor gave them a little time to consider what line they would adopt. They took advantage of this reprieve to dispense their goods among the poor, and then they retired, all seven, to Mount Celion, where they determined to conceal themselves.

"One of their number, Malchus, in the disguise of a physician, went to the town to obtain victuals. Decius, who had been absent from Ephesus for a little while, returned, and gave orders for the seven to be sought. Malchus, having escaped from the town, fled, full of fear, to his comrades, and told them of the emperor's fury. They were much alarmed; and Malchus handed them the loaves he had bought, bidding them eat, that, fortified by the food, they might have courage in the time of trial. They ate, and then, as they sat weeping and speaking to one another, by the will of God they fell asleep.

"The pagans sought everywhere, but could not find them, and Decius was greatly irritated at their escape. He had their parents brought before him, and threatened them with death if they did not reveal the place of concealment; but they could only answer that the seven young men had distributed their goods to the poor, and that they were quite ignorant as to their whereabouts.

"Decius, thinking it possible that they might be hiding in a cavern, blocked up the mouth with stones, that they might perish of hunger.

"Three hundred and sixty years passed, and in the thirtieth year of the reign of Theodosius, there broke forth a heresy denying the resurrection of the dead....

"Now, it happened that an Ephesian was building a stable on the side of Mount Celion, and finding a pile of stones handy, he took them for his edifice, and thus opened the mouth of the cave. Then the seven sleepers awoke, and it was to them as if they had slept but a single night. They began to ask Malchus what decision Decius had given concerning them.

"'He is going to hunt us down, so as to force us to sacrifice to the idols,' was his reply. 'God knows,' replied Maximian, 'we shall never do that.' Then exhorting his companions, he urged Malchus to go back to the town to buy some more bread, and at the same time to obtain fresh information. Malchus took five coins and left the cavern. On seeing the stones he was filled with astonishment; however, he went on towards the city; but what was his bewilderment, on approaching the gate, to see over it a cross! He went to another gate, and there he beheld the same sacred sign; and so he observed it over each gate of the city. He believed that he was suffering from the effects of a dream. Then he entered Ephesus, rubbing his eyes, and he walked to a baker's shop. He heard people using our Lord's name, and he was the more perplexed. 'Yesterday, no one dared pronounce the name of Jesus, and now it is on every one's lips. Wonderful! I can hardly believe myself to be in Ephesus.' He asked a passer-by the name of the city, and on being told it was Ephesus, he was thunderstruck. Now he entered a baker's shop, and laid down his money. The baker, examining the coin, inquired whether he had found a treasure, and began to whisper to some others in the shop. The youth, thinking that he was discovered, and that they were about to conduct him to the emperor, implored them to let him alone, offering to leave loaves and money if he might only be suffered to escape. But the shop-men, seizing him, said, 'Whoever you are, you have found a treasure; show us where it is, that we may share it with you, and then we will hide you.' Malchus was too frightened to answer. So they put a rope round his neck, and drew him through the streets into the market-place. The news soon spread that the young man had discovered a great treasure, and there was presently a vast crowd about him. He stoutly protested his innocence. No one recognized him, and his eyes, ranging over the faces which surrounded him, could not see one which he had known, or which was in the slightest degree familiar to him.

"St. Martin, the bishop, and Antipater, the governor, having heard of the excitement, ordered the young man to be brought before them, along with the bakers.

"The bishop and the governor asked him where he had found the treasure, and he replied that he had found none, but that the few coins were from his own purse. He was next asked whence he came. He replied that he was a native of Ephesus, 'if this be Ephesus.'

"'Send for your relations—your parents, if they live here,' ordered the governor.

"'They live here, certainly,' replied the youth; and he mentioned their names. No such names were known in the town. Then the governor exclaimed, 'How dare you say that this money belonged to your parents when it dates back three hundred and seventy-seven years,[25] and is as old as the beginning of the reign of Decius, and it is utterly unlike our modern coinage? Do you think to impose on the old men and sages of Ephesus? Believe me, I shall make you suffer the severities of the law till you show where you made the discovery.'

[25] This calculation is sadly inaccurate.

"'I implore you,' cried Malchus, 'in the name of God, answer me a few questions, and then I will answer yours. Where is the Emperor Decius gone to?'

"The bishop answered, 'My son, there is no emperor of that name; he who was thus called died long ago.'

"Malchus replied, 'All I hear perplexes me more and more. Follow me, and I will show you my comrades, who fled with me into a cave of Mount Celion, only yesterday, to escape the cruelty of Decius. I will lead you to them.'

"The bishop turned to the governor. 'The hand of God is here,' he said. Then they followed, and a great crowd after them. And Malchus entered first into the cavern to his companions, and the bishop after him.... And there they saw the martyrs seated in the cave, with their faces fresh and blooming as roses; so all fell down and glorified God. The bishop and the governor sent notice to Theodosius, and he hurried to Ephesus. All the inhabitants met him and conducted him to the cavern. As soon as the saints beheld the emperor, their faces shone like the sun, and the emperor gave thanks unto God, and embraced them, and said, 'I see you, as though I saw the Savior restoring Lazarus.' Maximian replied, 'Believe us! for the faith's sake, God has resuscitated us before the great resurrection day, in order that you may believe firmly in the resurrection of the dead. For as the child is in its mother's womb living and not suffering, so have we lived without suffering, fast asleep.' And having thus spoken, they bowed their heads, and their souls returned to their Maker. The emperor, rising, bent over them and embraced them weeping. He gave them orders for golden reliquaries to be made, but that night they appeared to him in a dream, and said that hitherto they had slept in the earth, and that in the earth they desired to sleep on till God should raise them again."

Such is the beautiful story. It seems to have travelled to us from the East. Jacobus Sarugiensis, a Mesopotamian bishop, in the fifth or sixth century, is said to have been the first to commit it to writing. Gregory of Tours (De Glor. Mart. i. 9) was perhaps the first to introduce it to Europe. Dionysius of Antioch (ninth century) told the story in Syrian, and Photius of Constantinople reproduced it, with the remark that Mahomet had adopted it into the Koran. Metaphrastus alludes to it as well; in the tenth century Eutychius inserted it in his annals of Arabia; it is found in the Coptic and the Maronite books, and several early historians, as Paulus Diaconus, Nicephorus, &c., have inserted it in their works.

A poem on the Seven Sleepers was composed by a trouvère named Chardri, and is mentioned by M. Fr. Michel in his "Rapports Ministre de l'Instruction Public;" a German poem on the same subject, of the thirteenth century, in 935 verses, has been published by M. Karajan; and the Spanish poet, Augustin Morreto, composed a drama on it, entitled "Los Siete Durmientes," which is inserted in the 19th volume of the rare work, "Comedias Nuevas Escogidas de los Mejores Ingenios."

Mahomet has somewhat improved on the story. He has made the Sleepers prophesy his coming, and he has given them a dog named Kratim, or Kratimir, which sleeps with them, and which is endowed with the gift of prophecy.

As a special favor this dog is to be one of the ten animals to be admitted into his paradise, the others being Jonah's whale, Solomon's ant, Ishmael's ram, Abraham's calf, the Queen of Sheba's ass, the prophet Salech's camel, Moses' ox, Belkis' cuckoo, and Mahomet's ass.

It was perhaps too much for the Seven Sleepers to ask, that their bodies should be left to rest in earth. In ages when saintly relics were valued above gold and precious stones, their request was sure to be shelved; and so we find that their remains were conveyed to Marseilles in a large stone sarcophagus, which is still exhibited in St. Victor's Church. In the Musæum Victorium at Rome is a curious and ancient representation of them in a cement of sulphur and plaster. Their names are engraved beside them, together with certain attributes. Near Constantine and John are two clubs, near Maximian a knotty club, near Malchus and Martinian two axes, near Serapion a burning torch, and near Danesius or Dionysius a great nail, such as those spoken of by Horace (Lib. 1, Od. 3) and St. Paulinus (Nat. 9, or Carm. 24) as having been used for torture.

In this group of figures, the seven are represented as young, without beards, and indeed in ancient martyrologies they are frequently called boys.

It has been inferred from this curious plaster representation, that the seven may have suffered under Decius, A. D. 250, and have been buried in the afore-mentioned cave; whilst the discovery and translation of their relics under Theodosius, in 479, may have given rise to the fable. And this I think probable enough. The story of long sleepers and the number seven connected with it is ancient enough, and dates from heathen mythology.

Like many another ancient myth, it was laid hold of by Christian hands and baptized.

Pliny relates the story of Epimenides the epic poet, who, when tending his sheep one hot day, wearied and oppressed with slumber, retreated into a cave, where he fell asleep. After fifty-seven years he awoke, and found every thing changed. His brother, whom he had left a stripling, was now a hoary man.

Epimenides was reckoned one of the seven sages by those who exclude Periander. He flourished in the time of Solon. After his death, at the age of two hundred and eighty-nine, he was revered as a god, and honored especially by the Athenians.

This story is a version of the older legend of the perpetual sleep of the shepherd Endymion, who was thus preserved in unfading youth and beauty by Jupiter.

According to an Arabic legend, St. George thrice rose from his grave, and was thrice slain.

In Scandinavian mythology we have Siegfrid or Sigurd thus resting, and awaiting his call to come forth and fight. Charlemagne sleeps in the Odenberg in Hess, or in the Untersberg near Salzburg, seated on his throne, with his crown on his head and his sword at his side, waiting till the times of Antichrist are fulfilled, when he will wake and burst forth to avenge the blood of the saints. Ogier the Dane, or Olger Dansk, will in like manner shake off his slumber and come forth from the dream-land of Avallon to avenge the right—O that he had shown himself in the Schleswig-Holstein war!

Well do I remember, as a child, contemplating with wondering awe the great Kyffhäuserberg in Thuringia, for therein, I was told, slept Frederic Barbarossa and his six knights. A shepherd once penetrated into the heart of the mountain by a cave, and discovered therein a hall where sat the emperor at a stone table, and his red beard had grown through the slab. At the tread of the shepherd Frederic awoke from his slumber, and asked, "Do the ravens still fly over the mountains?"

"Sire, they do."

"Then we must sleep another hundred years."

But when his beard has wound itself thrice round the table, then will the emperor awake with his knights, and rush forth to release Germany from its bondage, and exalt it to the first place among the kingdoms of Europe.

In Switzerland slumber three Tells at Rutli, near the Vierwaldstätter-see, waiting for the hour of their country's direst need. A shepherd crept into the cave where they rest. The third Tell rose and asked the time. "Noon," replied the shepherd lad. "The time is not yet come," said Tell, and lay down again.

In Scotland, beneath the Eilden hills, sleeps Thomas of Erceldoune; the murdered French who fell in the Sicilian Vespers at Palermo are also slumbering till the time is come when they may wake to avenge themselves. When Constantinople fell into the hands of the Turks, a priest was celebrating the sacred mysteries at the great silver altar of St. Sophia. The celebrant cried to God to protect the sacred host from profanation. Then the wall opened, and he entered, bearing the Blessed Sacrament. It closed on him, and there he is sleeping with his head bowed before the Body of Our Lord, waiting till the Turk is cast out of Constantinople, and St. Sophia is released from its profanation. God speed the time!

In Bohemia sleep three miners deep in the heart of the Kuttenberg. In North America Rip Van Winkle passed twenty years slumbering in the Katskill mountains. In Portugal it is believed that Sebastian, the chivalrous young monarch who did his best to ruin his country by his rash invasion of Morocco, is sleeping somewhere; but he will wake again to be his country's deliverer in the hour of need. Olaf Tryggvason is waiting a similar occasion in Norway. Even Napoleon Bonaparte is believed among some of the French peasantry to be sleeping on in a like manner.

St. Hippolytus relates that St. John the Divine is slumbering at Ephesus, and Sir John Mandeville relates the circumstances as follows:

"From Pathmos men gone unto Ephesim a fair citee and nyghe to the see. And there dyede Seynte Johne, and was buryed behynde the highe Awtiere, in a toumbe. And there is a faire chirche. For Christene mene weren wont to holden that place alweyes. And in the tombe of Seynt John is noughte but manna, that is clept Aungeles mete. For his body was translated into Paradys. And Turkes holden now alle that place and the citee and the Chirche. And all Asie the lesse is yclept Turkye. And ye shalle undrestond, that Seynt Johne bid make his grave there in his Lyf, and leyd himself there-inne all quyk. And therefore somme men seyn, that he dyed noughte, but that he resteth there till the Day of Doom. And forsoothe there is a gret marveule: For men may see there the erthe of the tombe apertly many tymes steren and moven, as there weren quykke thinges undre."

The connection of this legend of St. John with Ephesus may have had something to do with turning the seven martyrs of that city into seven sleepers.

The annals of Iceland relate that, in 1403, a Finn of the name of Fethmingr, living in Halogaland, in the North of Norway, happening to enter a cave, fell asleep, and woke not for three whole years, lying with his bow and arrows at his side, untouched by bird or beast.

There certainly are authentic accounts of persons having slept for an extraordinary length of time, but I shall not mention any, as I believe the legend we are considering, not to have been an exaggeration of facts, but a Christianized myth of paganism. The fact of the number seven being so prominent in many of the tales, seems to lead to this conclusion. Barbarossa changes his position every seven years. Charlemagne starts in his chair at similar intervals. Olger Dansk stamps his iron mace on the floor once every seven years. Olaf Redbeard in Sweden uncloses his eyes at precisely the same distances of time.

I believe that the mythological core of this picturesque legend is the repose of the earth through the seven winter months. In the North, Frederic and Charlemagne certainly replace Odin.

The German and Scandinavian still heathen legends represent the heroes as about to issue forth for the defence of Fatherland in the hour of direst need. The converted and Christianized tale brings the martyr youths forth in the hour when a heresy is afflicting the Church, that they may destroy the heresy by their witness to the truth of the Resurrection.

If there is something majestic in the heathen myth, there are singular grace and beauty in the Christian tale, teaching, as it does, such a glorious doctrine; but it is surpassed in delicacy by the modern form which the same myth has assumed—a form which is a real transformation, leaving the doctrine taught the same. It has been made into a romance by Hoffman, and is versified by Trinius. I may perhaps be allowed to translate with some freedom the poem of the latter:—

In an ancient shaft of Falun
Year by year a body lay,
God-preserved, as though a treasure,
Kept unto the waking day.
Not the turmoil, nor the passions,
Of the busy world o'erhead,
Sounds of war, or peace rejoicings,
Could disturb the placid dead.
Once a youthful miner, whistling,
Hewed the chamber, now his tomb:
Crash! the rocky fragments tumbled,
Closed him in abysmal gloom.
Sixty years passed by, ere miners
Toiling, hundred fathoms deep,
Broke upon the shaft where rested
That poor miner in his sleep.
As the gold-grains lie untarnished
In the dingy soil and sand,
Till they gleam and flicker, stainless,
In the digger's sifting hand;—
As the gem in virgin brilliance
Rests, till ushered into day;—
So uninjured, uncorrupted,
Fresh and fair the body lay.
And the miners bore it upward,
Laid it in the yellow sun;
Up, from out the neighboring houses,
Fast the curious peasants run.
"Who is he?" with eyes they question;
"Who is he?" they ask aloud;
Hush! a wizened hag comes hobbling,
Panting, through the wondering crowd.
O! the cry,—half joy, half sorrow,—
As she flings her at his side:
"John! the sweetheart of my girlhood,
Here am I, am I, thy bride.
"Time on thee has left no traces,
Death from wear has shielded thee;
I am agéd, worn, and wasted,
O! what life has done to me!"
Then his smooth, unfurrowed forehead
Kissed that ancient withered crone;
And the Death which had divided
Now united them in one.

V. — WILLIAM TELL

I SUPPOSE that most people regard William Tell, the hero of Switzerland, as an historical character, and visit the scenes made memorable by his exploits, with corresponding interest, when they undertake the regular Swiss round.

It is one of the painful duties of the antiquarian to dispel many a popular belief, and to probe the groundlessness of many an historical statement. The antiquarian is sometimes disposed to ask with Pilate, "What is truth?" when he finds historical facts crumbling beneath his touch into mythological fables; and he soon learns to doubt and question the most emphatic declarations of, and claims to, reliability.

Sir Walter Raleigh, in his prison, was composing the second volume of his History of the World. Leaning on the sill of his window, he meditated on the duties of the historian to mankind, when suddenly his attention was attracted by a disturbance in the court-yard before his cell. He saw one man strike another whom he supposed by his dress to be an officer; the latter at once drew his sword, and ran the former through the body. The wounded man felled his adversary with a stick, and then sank upon the pavement. At this juncture the guard came up, and carried off the officer insensible, and then the corpse of the man who had been run through.

Next day Raleigh was visited by an intimate friend, to whom he related the circumstances of the quarrel and its issue. To his astonishment, his friend unhesitatingly declared that the prisoner had mistaken the whole series of incidents which had passed before his eyes.

The supposed officer was not an officer at all, but the servant of a foreign ambassador; it was he who had dealt the first blow; he had not drawn his sword, but the other had snatched it from his side, and had run *him* through the body before any one could interfere; whereupon a stranger from among the crowd knocked the murderer down with his stick, and some of the foreigners belonging to the ambassador's retinue carried off the corpse. The friend of Raleigh added that government had ordered the arrest and immediate trial of the murderer, as the man assassinated was one of the principal servants of the Spanish ambassador.

"Excuse me," said Raleigh, "but I cannot have been deceived as you suppose, for I was eye-witness to the events which took place under my own window, and the man fell there on that spot where you see a paving-stone standing up above the rest."

"My dear Raleigh," replied his friend, "I was sitting on that stone when the fray took place, and I received this slight scratch on my cheek in snatching the sword from the murderer; and upon my word of honor, you have been deceived upon every particular."

Sir Walter, when alone, took up the second volume of his History, which was in MS., and contemplating it, thought—"If I cannot believe my own eyes, how can I be assured of the truth of a tithe of the events which happened ages before I was born?" and he flung the manuscript into the fire.[26]

[26] This anecdote is taken from the *Journal de Paris*, May, 1787; but whence did the *Journal* obtain it?

Now, I think that I can show that the story of William Tell is as fabulous as—what shall I say? any other historical event.

It is almost too well known to need repetition.

In the year 1307, Gessler, Vogt of the Emperor Albert of Hapsburg, set a hat on a pole, as symbol of imperial power, and ordered every one who passed by to do obeisance towards it. A mountaineer of the name of Tell boldly traversed the space before it without saluting the abhorred symbol. By Gessler's command he was at once seized and brought before him. As Tell was known to be an expert archer, he was ordered, by way of punishment, to shoot an apple off the head of his own son. Finding remonstrance vain, he submitted. The apple was placed on the child's head, Tell bent his bow, the arrow sped, and apple and arrow fell together to the ground. But the Vogt noticed that Tell, before shooting, had stuck another arrow into his belt, and he inquired the reason.

"It was for you," replied the sturdy archer. "Had I shot my child, know that it would not have missed your heart."

This event, observe, took place in the beginning of the fourteenth century. But Saxo Grammaticus, a Danish writer of the twelfth century, tells the story of a hero of his own country, who lived in the tenth century. He relates the incident in horrible style as follows:—

"Nor ought what follows to be enveloped in silence. Toki, who had for some time been in the king's service, had, by his deeds, surpassing those of his comrades, made enemies of his virtues. One day, when he had drunk too much, he boasted to those who sat at table with him, that his skill in archery was such, that with the first shot of an arrow he could hit the smallest apple set on the top of a stick at a considerable distance. His detractors, hearing this, lost no time in conveying what he had said to the king (Harald Bluetooth). But the wickedness of this monarch soon transformed the confidence of the father to the jeopardy of the son, for he ordered the dearest pledge of his life to stand in place of the stick, from whom, if the utterer of the boast did not at his first shot strike down the apple, he should with his head pay the penalty of having made an idle boast. The command of the king urged the soldier to do this, which was so much more than he had undertaken, the detracting artifices of the others having taken advantage of words spoken when he was hardly sober. As soon as the boy was led forth, Toki carefully admonished him to receive the whir of the arrow as calmly as possible, with attentive ears, and without moving his head, lest by a slight motion of the body he should frustrate the experience of his well-tried skill. He also made him stand with his back towards him, lest he should be frightened at the sight of the arrow. Then he drew three arrows from his quiver, and the very first he shot struck the proposed mark. Toki being asked by the king why he had taken so many more arrows out of his quiver, when he was to make but one trial with his bow, 'That I might avenge on thee,' he replied, 'the error of the first, by the points of the others, lest my innocence might happen to be afflicted, and thy injustice go unpunished.'"

The same incident is told of Egil, brother of the mythical Velundr, in the Saga of Thidrik.

In Norwegian history also it appears with variations again and again. It is told of King Olaf the Saint (d. 1030), that, desiring the conversion of a brave heathen named Eindridi, he competed with him in various athletic sports; he swam with him, wrestled, and then shot with him. The king dared Eindridi to strike a writing-tablet from off his son's head with an arrow. Eindridi prepared to attempt the difficult shot. The king bade two men bind the eyes of the child and hold the napkin, so that he might not move when he heard the whistle of the arrow. The king aimed first, and the arrow grazed the lad's head. Eindridi then prepared to shoot; but the mother of the boy interfered, and persuaded the king to abandon this dangerous test of skill. In this version, also, Eindridi is prepared to revenge himself on the king, should the child be injured.

But a closer approximation still to the Tell myth is found in the life of Hemingr, another Norse archer, who was challenged by King Harald, Sigurd's son (d. 1066). The story is thus told:—

"The island was densely overgrown with wood, and the people went into the forest. The king took a spear and set it with its point in the soil, then he laid an arrow on the string and shot up into the air. The arrow turned in the air and came down upon the spear-shaft and stood up in it. Hemingr took another arrow and shot up; his was lost to sight for some while, but it came back and pierced the nick of the king's arrow.... Then the king took a knife and stuck it into an oak; he next drew his bow and planted an arrow in the haft of the knife. Thereupon Hemingr took his arrows. The king stood by him and said, 'They are all inlaid with gold; you are a capital workman.' Hemingr answered, 'They are not my manufacture, but are presents.' He shot, and his arrow cleft the haft, and the point entered the socket of the blade.

"'We must have a keener contest,' said the king, taking an arrow and flushing with anger; then he laid the arrow on the string and drew his bow to the farthest, so that the horns were nearly brought to meet. Away flashed the arrow, and pierced a tender twig. All said that this was a most astonishing feat of dexterity. But Hemingr shot from a greater distance, and split a hazel nut. All were astonished to see this. Then said the king, 'Take a nut and set it on the head of your brother Bjorn, and aim at it from precisely the same distance. If you miss the mark, then your life goes.'

"Hemingr answered, 'Sire, my life is at your disposal, but I will not adventure that shot.' Then out spake Bjorn—'Shoot, brother, rather than die yourself.' Hemingr said, 'Have you the pluck to stand quite still without shrinking?' 'I will do my best,' said Bjorn. 'Then let the king stand by,' said Hemingr, 'and let him see whether I touch the nut.'

"The king agreed, and bade Oddr Ufeigs' son stand by Bjorn, and see that the shot was fair. Hemingr then went to the spot fixed for him by the king, and signed himself with the cross, saying, 'God be my witness that I had rather die myself than injure my brother Bjorn; let all the blame rest on King Harald.'

"Then Hemingr flung his spear. The spear went straight to the mark, and passed between the nut and the crown of the lad, who was not in the least injured. It flew farther, and stopped not till it fell.

"Then the king came up and asked Oddr what he thought about the shot."

Years after, this risk was revenged upon the hard-hearted monarch. In the battle of Stamfordbridge an arrow from a skilled archer penetrated the windpipe of the king, and it is supposed to have sped, observes the Saga writer, from the bow of Hemingr, then in the service of the English monarch.

The story is related somewhat differently in the Faroe Isles, and is told of Geyti, Aslak's son. The same Harald asks his men if they know who is his match in strength. "Yes," they reply; "there is a peasant's son in the uplands, Geyti, son of Aslak, who is the strongest of men." Forth goes the king, and at last rides up to the house of Aslak. "And where is your youngest son?"

"Alas! alas! he lies under the green sod of Kolrin kirkgarth."

"Come, then, and show me his corpse, old man, that I may judge whether he was as stout of limb as men say."

The father puts the king off with the excuse that among so many dead it would be hard to find his boy. So the king rides away over the heath. He meets a stately man returning from the chase, with a bow over his shoulder. "And who art thou, friend?" "Geyti, Aslak's son." The dead man, in short, alive and well. The king tells him he has heard of his prowess, and is come to match his strength with him. So Geyti and the king try a swimming-match.

The king swims well; but Geyti swims better, and in the end gives the monarch such a ducking, that he is borne to his house devoid of sense and motion. Harald swallows his anger, as he had swallowed the water, and bids Geyti shoot a hazel nut from off his brother's head. Aslak's son consents, and invites the king into the forest to witness his dexterity.

> *"On the string the shaft he laid,*
> *And God hath heard his prayer;*
> *He shot the little nut away,*
> *Nor hurt the lad a hair."*

Next day the king sends for the skilful bowman:—

> *"List thee, Geyti, Aslak's son,*
> *And truly tell to me,*
> *Wherefore hadst thou arrows twain*
> *In the wood yestreen with thee?"*

The bowman replies,—

> *"Therefore had I arrows twain*
> *Yestreen in the wood with me,*
> *Had I but hurt my brother dear,*
> *The other had piercéd thee."*

A very similar tale is told also in the celebrated Malleus Maleficarum of a man named Puncher, with this difference, that a coin is placed on the lad's head instead of an apple or a nut. The person who had dared Puncher to the test of skill, inquires the use of the second arrow in his belt, and receives the usual answer, that if the first arrow had missed the coin, the second would have transfixed a certain heart which was destitute of natural feeling.

We have, moreover, our English version of the same story in the venerable ballad of William of Cloudsley.

The Finn ethnologist Castrén obtained the following tale in the Finnish village of Uhtuwa:—

A fight took place between some freebooters and the inhabitants of the village of Alajäwi. The robbers plundered every house, and carried off amongst their captives an old man. As they proceeded with their spoils along the strand of the lake, a lad of twelve years old appeared from among the reeds on the opposite bank, armed with a bow, and amply provided with arrows; he threatened to shoot down the captors unless the old man, his father, were restored to him. The robbers mockingly replied that the aged man would be given to him if he could shoot an apple off his head. The boy accepted the challenge, and on successfully accomplishing it, the surrender of the venerable captive was made.

Farid-Uddin Âttar was a Persian dealer in perfumes, born in the year 1119. He one day was so impressed with the sight of a dervish, that he sold his possessions, and followed righteousness. He composed the poem Mantic Uttaïr, or the language of birds. Observe, the Persian Âttar lived at the same time as the Danish Saxo, and long before the birth of Tell. Curiously enough, we find a trace of the Tell myth in the pages of his poem. According to him, however, the king shoots the apple from the head of a beloved page, and the lad dies from sheer fright, though the arrow does not even graze his skin.

The coincidence of finding so many versions of the same story scattered through countries as remote as Persia and Iceland, Switzerland and Denmark, proves, I think, that it can in no way be regarded as history, but is rather one of the numerous household myths common to the whole stock of Aryan nations. Probably, some one more acquainted with Sanskrit literature than myself, and with better access to its unpublished stores of fable and legend, will some day light on an early Indian tale corresponding to that so prevalent among other branches of the same family. The coincidence of the Tell myth being discovered among the Finns is attributable to Russian or Swedish influence. I do not regard it as a primeval Turanian, but as an Aryan story, which, like an erratic block, is found deposited on foreign soil far from the mountain whence it was torn.

German mythologists, I suppose, consider the myth to represent the manifestation of some natural phenomena, and the individuals of the story to be impersonifications of natural forces. Most primeval stories were thus constructed, and their origin is traceable enough. In Thorn-rose, for instance, who can fail to see the earth goddess represented by the sleeping beauty in her long winter slumber, only returning to life when kissed by the golden-haired sun-god Phœbus or Baldur? But the Tell myth has not its signification thus painted on the surface; and those who suppose Gessler or Harald to be the power of evil and darkness,—the bold archer to be the storm-cloud with his arrow of lightning and his iris bow, bent against the sun, which is resting like a coin or a golden apple on the edge of the horizon, are over-straining their theories, and exacting too much from our credulity.

In these pages and elsewhere I have shown how some of the ancient myths related by the whole Aryan family of nations are reducible to allegorical explanations of certain well-known natural phenomena; but I must protest against the manner in which our German friends fasten rapaciously upon every atom of history, sacred and profane, and demonstrate all heroes to represent the sun; all villains to be the demons of night or winter; all sticks and spears and arrows to be the lightning; all cows and sheep and dragons and swans to be clouds.

In a work on the superstition of Werewolves, I have entered into this subject with some fulness, and am quite prepared to admit the premises upon which mythologists construct their theories; at the same time I am not disposed to run to the extravagant lengths reached by some of the most enthusiastic German scholars. A wholesome warning to these gentlemen was given some years ago by an ingenious French ecclesiastic, who wrote the following argument to prove that Napoleon Bonaparte was a mythological character. Archbishop Whately's "Historic Doubts" was grounded on a totally different line of argument; I subjoin the other, as a curiosity and as a caution.

Napoleon is, says the writer, an impersonification of the sun.

1. Between the name Napoleon and Apollo, or Apoleon, the god of the sun, there is but a trifling difference; indeed, the seeming difference is lessened, if we take the spelling of his name from the column of the Place Vendôme, where it stands Néapoleó. But this syllable *Ne* prefixed to the name of the sun-god is of importance; like the rest of the name it is of Greek origin, and is "νη" or "ναι", a particle of affirmation, as though indicating Napoleon as the very true Apollo, or sun.

His other name, Bonaparte, makes this apparent connection between the French hero and the luminary of the firmament conclusively certain. The day has its two parts, the good and luminous portion, and that which is bad and dark. To the sun belongs the good part, to the moon and stars belongs the bad portion. It is therefore natural that Apollo or Né-Apoleón should receive the surname of *Bonaparte*.

2. Apollo was born in Delos, a Mediterranean island; Napoleon in Corsica, an island in the same sea. According to Pausanias, Apollo was an Egyptian deity; and in the mythological history of the fabulous Napoleon we find the hero in Egypt, regarded by the inhabitants with veneration, and receiving their homage.

3. The mother of Napoleon was said to be Letitia, which signifies joy, and is an impersonification of the dawn of light dispensing joy and gladness to all creation. Letitia is no other than the break of day, which in a manner brings the sun into the world, and "with rosy fingers opes the gates of Day." It is significant that the Greek name for the mother of Apollo was Leto. From this the Romans made the name Latona, which they gave to his mother. But *Læto* is the unused form of the verb *lætor*, and signified to inspire joy; it is from this unused form that the substantive *Letitia* is derived. The identity, then, of the mother of Napoleon with the Greek Leto and the Latin Latona, is established conclusively.

4. According to the popular story, this son of Letitia had three sisters; and was it not the same with the Greek deity, who had the three Graces?

5. The modern Gallic Apollo had four brothers. It is impossible not to discern here the anthropomorphosis of the four seasons. But, it will be objected, the seasons should be females. Here the

French language interposes; for in French the seasons are masculine, with the exception of autumn, upon the gender of which grammarians are undecided, whilst Autumnus in Latin is not more feminine than the other seasons. This difficulty is therefore trifling, and what follows removes all shadow of doubt.

Of the four brothers of Napoleon, three are said to have been kings, and these of course are, Spring reigning over the flowers, Summer reigning over the harvest, Autumn holding sway over the fruits. And as these three seasons owe all to the powerful influence of the Sun, we are told in the popular myth that the three brothers of Napoleon drew their authority from him, and received from him their kingdoms. But if it be added that, of the four brothers of Napoleon, one was not a king, that was because he is the impersonification of Winter, which has no reign over anything. If, however, it be asserted, in contradiction, that the winter has an empire, he will be given the principality over snows and frosts, which, in the dreary season of the year, whiten the face of the earth. Well, the fourth brother of Napoleon is thus invested by popular tradition, commonly called history, with a vain principality accorded to him *in the decline of the power of Napoleon*. The principality was that of Canino, a name derived from *cani*, or the whitened hairs of a frozen old age,—true emblem of winter. To the eyes of poets, the forests covering the hills are their hair, and when winter frosts them, they represent the snowy locks of a decrepit nature in the old age of the year:—

"Cum gelidus crescit *canis* in montibus humor."

Consequently the Prince of Canino is an impersonification of winter;—winter whose reign begins when the kingdoms of the three fine seasons are passed from them, and when the sun is driven from his power by the children of the North, as the poets call the boreal winds. This is the origin of the fabulous invasion of France by the allied armies of the North. The story relates that these invaders—the northern gales—banished the many-colored flag, and replaced it by a white standard. This too is a graceful, but, at the same time, purely fabulous account of the Northern winds driving all the brilliant colors from the face of the soil, to replace them by the snowy sheet.

6. Napoleon is said to have had two wives. It is well known that the classic fable gave two also to Apollo. These two were the moon and the earth. Plutarch asserts that the Greeks gave the moon to Apollo for wife, whilst the Egyptians attributed to him the earth. By the moon he had no posterity, but by the other he had one son only, the little Horus. This is an Egyptian allegory, representing the fruits of agriculture produced by the earth fertilized by the Sun. The pretended son of the fabulous Napoleon is said to have been born on the 20th of March, the season of the spring equinox, when agriculture is assuming its greatest period of activity.

7. Napoleon is said to have released France from the devastating scourge which terrorized over the country, the hydra of the revolution, as it was popularly called. Who cannot see in this a Gallic version of the Greek legend of Apollo releasing Hellas from the terrible Python? The very name *revolution*, derived from the Latin verb *revolvo*, is indicative of the coils of a serpent like the Python.

8. The famous hero of the 19th century had, it is asserted, twelve Marshals at the head of his armies, and four who were stationary and inactive. The twelve first, as may be seen at once, are the signs of the zodiac, marching under the orders of the sun Napoleon, and each commanding a division of the innumerable host of stars, which are parted into twelve portions, corresponding to the twelve signs. As for the four stationary officers, immovable in the midst of general motion, they are the cardinal points.

9. It is currently reported that the chief of these brilliant armies, after having gloriously traversed the Southern kingdoms, penetrated North, and was there unable to maintain his sway. This too represents the course of the Sun, which assumes its greatest power in the South, but after the spring equinox seeks to reach the North; and after a *three months'* march towards the boreal regions, is driven back upon his traces following the sign of Cancer, a sign given to represent the retrogression of the sun in that portion of the sphere. It is on this that the story of the march of Napoleon towards Moscow, and his humbling retreat, is founded.

10. Finally, the sun rises in the East and sets in the Western sea. The poets picture him rising out of the waters in the East, and setting in the ocean after his twelve hours' reign in the sky. Such is the history of Napoleon, coming from his Mediterranean isle, holding the reins of government for twelve years, and finally disappearing in the mysterious regions of the great Atlantic.

To those who see in Samson, the image of the sun, the correlative of the classic Hercules, this clever skit of the accomplished French Abbé may prove of value as a caution.

VI. THE DOG GELLERT

HAVING demolished William Tell, I proceed to the destruction of another article of popular belief.

Who that has visited Snowdon has not seen the grave of Llewellyn's faithful hound Gellert, and been told by the guide the touching story of the death of the noble animal? How can we doubt the facts, seeing that the place, Beth-Gellert, is named after the dog, and that the grave is still visible? But unfortunately for the truth of the legend, its pedigree can be traced with the utmost precision.

The story is as follows:—

The Welsh Prince Llewellyn had a noble deerhound, Gellert, whom he trusted to watch the cradle of his baby son whilst he himself was absent.

One day, on his return, to his intense horror, he beheld the cradle empty and upset, the clothes dabbled with blood, and Gellert's mouth dripping with gore. Concluding hastily that the hound had proved unfaithful, had fallen on the child and devoured it,—in a paroxysm of rage the prince drew his sword and slew the dog. Next instant the cry of the babe from behind the cradle showed him that the child was uninjured; and, on looking farther, Llewellyn discovered the body of a huge wolf, which had entered the house to seize and devour the child, but which had been kept off and killed by the brave dog Gellert.

In his self-reproach and grief, the prince erected a stately monument to Gellert, and called the place where he was buried after the poor hound's name.

Now, I find in Russia precisely the same story told, with just the same appearance of truth, of a Czar Piras. In Germany it appears with considerable variations. A man determines on slaying his old dog Sultan, and consults with his wife how this is to be effected. Sultan overhears the conversation, and complains bitterly to the wolf, who suggests an ingenious plan by which the master may be induced to spare his dog. Next day, when the man is going to his work, the wolf undertakes to carry off the child from its cradle. Sultan is to attack him and rescue the infant. The plan succeeds admirably, and the dog spends his remaining years in comfort. (Grimm, K. M. 48.)

But there is a story in closer conformity to that of Gellert among the French collections of fabliaux made by Le Grand d'Aussy and Edéléstand du Méril. It became popular through the "Gesta Romanorum," a collection of tales made by the monks for harmless reading, in the fourteenth century.

In the "Gesta" the tale is told as follows:—

"Folliculus, a knight, was fond of hunting and tournaments. He had an only son, for whom three nurses were provided. Next to this child, he loved his falcon and his greyhound. It happened one day that he was called to a tournament, whither his wife and domestics went also, leaving the child in the cradle, the greyhound lying by him, and the falcon on his perch. A serpent that inhabited a hole near the castle, taking advantage of the profound silence that reigned, crept from his habitation, and advanced towards the cradle to devour the child. The falcon, perceiving the danger, fluttered with his wings till he awoke the dog, who instantly attacked the invader, and after a fierce conflict, in which he was sorely wounded, killed him. He then lay down on the ground to lick and heal his wounds. When the nurses returned, they found the cradle overturned, the child thrown out, and the ground covered with blood, as was also the dog, who they immediately concluded had killed the child.

"Terrified at the idea of meeting the anger of the parents, they determined to escape; but in their flight fell in with their mistress, to whom they were compelled to relate the supposed murder of the child by the greyhound. The knight soon arrived to hear the sad story, and, maddened with fury, rushed forward to the spot. The poor wounded and faithful animal made an effort to rise and welcome his master with his accustomed fondness; but the enraged knight received him on the point of his sword, and he fell lifeless to the ground. On examination of the cradle, the infant was found alive and unhurt, with the dead serpent lying by him. The knight now perceived what had happened, lamented bitterly over his faithful dog, and blamed himself for having too hastily depended on the words of his wife. Abandoning the profession of arms, he broke his lance in pieces, and vowed a pilgrimage to the Holy Land, where he spent the rest of his days in peace."

The monkish hit at the wife is amusing, and might have been supposed to have originated with those determined misogynists, as the gallant Welshmen lay all the blame on the man. But the good compilers of the "Gesta" wrote little of their own, except moral applications of the tales they relate, and the story of Folliculus and his dog, like many others in their collection, is drawn from a foreign source.

It occurs in the Seven Wise Masters, and in the "Calumnia Novercalis" as well, so that it must have been popular throughout mediæval Europe. Now, the tales of the Seven Wise Masters are translations from a Hebrew work, the Kalilah and Dimnah of Rabbi Joel, composed about A. D. 1250, or from Simeon Seth's Greek Kylile and Dimne, written in 1080. These Greek and Hebrew works were derived from kindred sources. That of Rabbi Joel was a translation from an Arabic version made by Nasr-Allah in the twelfth century, whilst Simeon Seth's was a translation of the Persian Kalilah and Dimnah. But the Persian Kalilah and Dimnah was not either an original work; it was in turn a translation from the Sanskrit Pantschatantra, made about A. D. 540.

In this ancient Indian book the story runs as follows:—

A Brahmin named Devasaman had a wife, who gave birth to a son, and also to an ichneumon. She loved both her children dearly, giving them alike the breast, and anointing them alike with salves. But she feared the ichneumon might not love his brother.

One day, having laid her boy in bed, she took up the water jar, and said to her husband, "Hear me, master! I am going to the tank to fetch water. Whilst I am absent, watch the boy, lest he gets injured by the ichneumon." After she had left the house, the Brahmin went forth begging, leaving the house empty. In crept a black snake, and attempted to bite the child; but the ichneumon rushed at it, and tore it in pieces. Then, proud of its achievement, it sallied forth, all bloody, to meet its mother. She, seeing the creature stained with blood, concluded, with feminine precipitance, that it had fallen on the baby and killed it, and she flung her water jar at it and slew it. Only on her return home did she ascertain her mistake.

The same story is also told in the Hitopadesa (iv. 13), but the animal is an otter, not an ichneumon. In the Arabic version a weasel takes the place of the ichneumon.

The Buddhist missionaries carried the story into Mongolia, and in the Mongolian Uligerun, which is a translation of the Tibetian Dsanghen, the story reappears with the pole-cat as the brave and suffering defender of the child.

Stanislaus Julien, the great Chinese scholar, has discovered the same tale in the Chinese work entitled "The Forest of Pearls from the Garden of the Law." This work dates from 668; and in it the creature is an ichneumon.

In the Persian Sindibad-nâmeh is the same tale, but the faithful animal is a cat. In Sandabar and Syntipas it has become a dog. Through the influence of Sandabar on the Hebrew translation of the Kalilah and Dimnah, the ichneumon is also replaced by a dog.

Such is the history of the Gellert legend; it is an introduction into Europe from India, every step of its transmission being clearly demonstrable. From the Gesta Romanorum it passed into a popular tale throughout Europe, and in different countries it was, like the Tell myth, localized and individualized. Many a Welsh story, such as those contained in the Mabinogion, are as easily traced to an Eastern origin.

But every story has its root. The root of the Gellert tale is this: A man forms an alliance of friendship with a beast or bird. The dumb animal renders him a signal service. He misunderstands the act, and kills his preserver.

We have tracked this myth under the Gellert form from India to Wales; but under another form it is the property of the whole Aryan family, and forms a portion of the traditional lore of all nations sprung from that stock.

Thence arose the classic fable of the peasant, who, as he slept, was bitten by a fly. He awoke, and in a rage killed the insect. When too late, he observed that the little creature had aroused him that he might avoid a snake which lay coiled up near his pillow.

In the Anvar-i-Suhaili is the following kindred tale. A king had a falcon. One day, whilst hunting, he filled a goblet with water dropping from a rock. As he put the vessel to his lips, his falcon dashed upon it, and upset it with its wings. The king, in a fury, slew the bird, and then discovered that the water dripped from the jaws of a serpent of the most poisonous description.

This story, with some variations, occurs in Æsop, Ælian, and Apthonius. In the Greek fable, a peasant liberates an eagle from the clutches of a dragon. The dragon spirts poison into the water which the peasant is about to drink, without observing what the monster had done. The grateful eagle upsets the goblet with his wings.

The story appears in Egypt under a whimsical form. A Wali once smashed a pot full of herbs which a cook had prepared. The exasperated cook thrashed the well-intentioned but unfortunate Wali within an inch of his life, and when he returned, exhausted with his efforts at belaboring the man, to examine the broken pot, he discovered amongst the herbs a poisonous snake.

How many brothers, sisters, uncles, aunts, and cousins of all degrees a little story has! And how few of the tales we listen to can lay any claim to originality! There is scarcely a story which I hear which I cannot connect with some family of myths, and whose pedigree I cannot ascertain with more or less precision. Shakespeare drew the plots of his plays from Boccaccio or Straparola; but these Italians did not invent the tales they lent to the English dramatist. King Lear does not originate with Geofry of Monmouth, but comes from early Indian stores of fable, whence also are derived the Merchant of Venice and the pound of flesh, ay, and the very incident of the three caskets.

But who would credit it, were it not proved by conclusive facts, that Johnny Sands is the inheritance of the whole Aryan family of nations, and that Peeping Tom of Coventry peeped in India and on the Tartar steppes ages before Lady Godiva was born?

If you listen to Traviata at the opera, you have set before you a tale which has lasted for centuries, and which was perhaps born in India.

If you read in classic fable of Orpheus charming woods and meadows, beasts and birds, with his magic lyre, you remember to have seen the same fable related in the Kalewala of the Finnish Wainomainen, and in the Kaleopoeg of the Esthonian Kalewa.

If you take up English history, and read of William the Conqueror slipping as he landed on British soil, and kissing the earth, saying he had come to greet and claim his own, you remember that the same story is told of Napoleon in Egypt, of King Olaf Harold's son in Norway, and in classic history of Junius Brutus on his return from the oracle.

A little while ago I cut out of a Sussex newspaper a story purporting to be the relation of a fact which had taken place at a fixed date in Lewes. This was the story. A tyrannical husband locked the door against his wife, who was out having tea with a neighbor, gossiping and scandal-mongering; when she applied for admittance, he pretended not to know her. She threatened to jump into the well unless he opened the door.

The man, not supposing that she would carry her threat into execution, declined, alleging that he was in bed, and the night was chilly; besides which he entirely disclaimed all acquaintance with the lady who claimed admittance.

The wife then flung a log into a well, and secreted herself behind the door. The man, hearing the splash, fancied that his good lady was really in the deeps, and forth he darted in his nocturnal costume, which was of the lightest, to ascertain whether his deliverance was complete. At once the lady darted into the house, locked the door, and, on the husband pleading for admittance, she declared most solemnly from the window that she did not know *him*.

Now, this story, I can positively assert, unless the events of this world move in a circle, did not happen in Lewes, or any other Sussex town.

It was told in the Gesta Romanorum six hundred years ago, and it was told, may be, as many hundred years before in India, for it is still to be found in Sanskrit collections of tales.

VII. — TAILED MEN

I WELL remember having it impressed upon me by a Devonshire nurse, as a little child, that all Cornishmen were born with tails; and it was long before I could overcome the prejudice thus early implanted in my breast against my Cornubian neighbors. I looked upon those who dwelt across the Tamar as "uncanny," as being scarcely to be classed with Christian people, and certainly not to be freely associated with by tailless Devonians. I think my eyes were first opened to the fact that I had been deceived by a worthy bookseller of L——, with whom I had contracted a warm friendship, he having at sundry times contributed pictures to my scrapbook. I remember one day resolving to broach the delicate subject with my tailed friend, whom I liked, notwithstanding his caudal appendage.

"Mr. X——, is it true that you are a Cornishman?"
"Yes, my little man; born and bred in the West country."
"I like you very much; but—have you really got a tail?"
When the bookseller had recovered from the astonishment which I had produced by my question, he stoutly repudiated the charge.
"But you are a Cornishman?"

"To be sure I am."

"And all Cornishmen have tails."

I believe I satisfied my own mind that the good man had sat his off, and my nurse assured me that such was the case with those of sedentary habits.

It is curious that Devonshire superstition should attribute the tail to Cornishmen, for it was asserted of certain men of Kent in olden times, and was referred to Divine vengeance upon them for having insulted St. Thomas à Becket, if we may believe Polydore Vergil. "There were some," he says, "to whom it seemed that the king's secret wish was, that Thomas should be got rid of. He, indeed, as one accounted to be an enemy of the king's person, was already regarded with so little respect, nay, was treated with so much contempt, that when he came to Strood, which village is situated on the Medway, the river that washes Rochester, the inhabitants of the place, being eager to show some mark of contumely to the prelate in his disgrace, did not scruple to cut off the tail of the horse on which he was riding; but by this profane and inhospitable act they covered themselves with eternal reproach; for it so happened after this, by the will of God, that all the offspring born from the men who had done this thing, were born with tails, like brute animals. But this mark of infamy, which formerly was everywhere notorious, has disappeared with the extinction of the race whose fathers perpetrated this deed."

John Bale, the zealous reformer, and Bishop of Ossory in Edward VI.'s time, refers to this story, and also mentions a variation of the scene and cause of this ignoble punishment. He writes, quoting his authorities, "John Capgrave and Alexander of Esseby sayth, that for castynge of fyshe tayles at thys Augustyne, Dorsettshyre men had tayles ever after. But Polydorus applieth it unto Kentish men at Stroud, by Rochester, for cuttinge off Thomas Becket's horse's tail. Thus hath England in all other land a perpetual infamy of tayles by theye wrytten legendes of lyes, yet can they not well tell where to bestowe them truely." Bale, a fierce and unsparing reformer, and one who stinted not hard words, applying to the inventors of these legends an epithet more strong than elegant, says, "In the legends of their sanctified sorcerers they have diffamed the English posterity with tails, as has been showed afore. That an Englyshman now cannot travayle in another land by way of marchandyse or any other honest occupyinge, but it is most contumeliously thrown in his tethe that all Englyshmen have tails. That uncomely note and report have the nation gotten, without recover, by these laisy and idle lubbers, the monkes and the priestes, which could find no matters to advance their canonized gains by, or their saintes, as they call them, but manifest lies and knaveries."[27]

[27] "Actes of English Votaries."

Andrew Marvel also makes mention of this strange judgment in his *Loyal Scot*:—

> "But who considers right will find, indeed,
> 'Tis Holy Island parts us, not the Tweed.
> Nothing but clergy could us two seclude,
> No Scotch was ever like a bishop's feud.
> All Litanys in this have wanted faith,
> There's no—Deliver us from a Bishop's wrath.
> Never shall Calvin pardoned be for sales,
> Never, for Burnet's sake, the Lauderdales;
> For Becket's sake, Kent always shall have tails."

It may be remembered that Lord Monboddo, a Scotch judge of last century, and a philosopher of some repute, though of great eccentricity, stoutly maintained the theory that man ought to have a tail, that the tail is a *desideratum*, and that the abrupt termination of the spine without caudal elongation is a sad blemish in the origination of man. The tail, the point in which man is inferior to the brute, what a delicate index of the mind it is! how it expresses the passions of love and hate! how nicely it gives token of the feelings of joy or fear which animate the soul! But Lord Monboddo did not consider that what the tail is to the brute, that the eye is to man; the lack of one member is supplied by the other. I can tell a proud man by his eye just as truly as if he stalked past one with erect tail; and anger is as plainly depicted in the human eye as in the bottle-brush tail of a cat. I know a sneak by his cowering glance, though he has not a tail between his legs; and pleasure is evident in the laughing eye, without there being any necessity for a wagging brush to express it.

Dr. Johnson paid a visit to the judge, and knocked on the head his theory that men ought to have tails, and actually were born with them occasionally; for said he, "Of a standing fact, sir, there ought to be no controversy; if there are men with tails, catch a *homo caudatus*." And, "It is a pity to see Lord Monboddo publish such notions as he has done—a man of sense, and of so much elegant learning. There would be little in a fool doing it; we should only laugh; but, when a wise man does it, we are sorry. Other people have strange notions, but they conceal them. If they have tails they hide them; but Monboddo is as jealous of his tail as a squirrel." And yet Johnson seems to have been tickled with the idea, and to have been amused with the notion of an appendage like a tail being regarded as the complement of human perfection. It may be remembered how Johnson made the acquaintance of the young Laird of Col, during his Highland tour, and how pleased he was with him. "Col," says he, "is a noble animal. He is as complete an islander as the mind can figure. He is a farmer, a sailor, a hunter, a fisher: he will run you down a dog; *if any man has a tail*, it is Col." And notwithstanding all his aversion to puns, the great Doctor was fain to yield to human weakness on one occasion, under the influence of the mirth which Monboddo's name seems to have excited. Johnson writes to Mrs. Thrale of a party he had met one night, which he thus enumerates: "There were Smelt, and the Bishop of St. Asaph, who comes to every place; and Sir Joshua, and Lord Monboddo, and ladies *out of tale*."

There is a Polish story of a witch who made a girdle of human skin and laid it across the threshold of a door where a marriage-feast was being held. On the bridal pair stepping across the girdle they were transformed into wolves. Three years after the witch sought them out, and cast over them dresses of fur with the hair turned outward, whereupon they recovered their human forms, but, unfortunately, the dress cast over the bridegroom was too scanty, and did not extend over his tail, so that, when he was restored to his former condition, he retained his lupine caudal appendage, and this became hereditary in his family; so that all Poles with tails are lineal descendants of the ancestor to whom this little misfortune happened. John Struys, a Dutch traveller, who visited the Isle of Formosa in 1677, gives a curious story, which is worth transcribing.

"Before I visited this island," he writes, "I had often heard tell that there were men who had long tails, like brute beasts; but I had never been able to believe it, and I regarded it as a thing so alien to our nature, that I should now have difficulty in accepting it, if my own senses had not removed from me every pretence for doubting the fact, by the following strange adventure: The inhabitants of Formosa, being used to see us, were in the habit of receiving us on terms which left nothing to apprehend on either side; so that, although mere foreigners, we always believed ourselves in safety, and had grown familiar enough to ramble at large without an escort, when grave experience taught us that, in so doing, we were hazarding too much. As some of our party were one day taking a stroll, one of them had occasion to withdraw about a stone's throw from the rest, who, being at the moment engaged in an eager conversation, proceeded without heeding the disappearance of their companion. After a while, however, his absence was observed, and the party paused, thinking he would rejoin them. They waited some time; but at last, tired of the delay, they returned in the direction of the spot where they remembered to have seen him last. Arriving there, they were horrified to find his mangled body lying on the ground, though the nature of the lacerations showed that he had not had to suffer long ere death released him. Whilst some remained to watch the dead body, others went off in search of the murderer; and these had not gone far, when they came upon a man of peculiar appearance, who, finding himself enclosed by the exploring party, so as to make escape from them impossible, began to foam with rage, and by cries and wild gesticulations to intimate that he would make any one repent the attempt who should venture to meddle with him. The fierceness of his desperation for a time kept our people at bay; but as his fury gradually subsided, they gathered more closely round him, and at length seized him. He then soon made them understand that it was he who had killed their comrade, but they could not learn from him any cause for this conduct. As the crime was so atrocious, and, if allowed to pass with impunity, might entail even more serious consequences, it was determined to burn the man. He was tied up to a stake, where he was kept for some hours before the time of execution arrived. It was then that I beheld what I had never thought to see. He had a tail more than a foot long, covered with red hair, and very like that of a cow. When he saw the surprise that this discovery created among the European spectators, he informed us that his tail was the effect of climate, for that all the inhabitants of the southern side of the island, where they then were, were provided with like appendages."[28]

[28] "Voyages de Jean Struys," An. 1650.

After Struys, Hornemann reported that, between the Gulf of Benin and Abyssinia, were tailed anthropophagi, named by the natives *Niam-niams*; and in 1849, M. Descouret, on his return from Mecca, affirmed that such was a common report, and added that they had long arms, low and narrow foreheads, long and erect ears, and slim legs.

Mr. Harrison, in his "Highlands of Ethiopia," alludes to the common belief among the Abyssinians, in a pygmy race of this nature.

MM. Arnault and Vayssière, travellers in the same country, in 1850, brought the subject before the Academy of Sciences.

In 1851, M. de Castelnau gave additional details relative to an expedition against these tailed men. "The Niam-niams," he says, "were sleeping in the sun: the Haoussas approached, and, falling on them, massacred them to the last man. They had all of them tails forty centimetres long, and from two to three in diameter. This organ is smooth. Among the corpses were those of several women, who were deformed in the same manner. In all other particulars, the men were precisely like all other negroes. They are of a deep black, their teeth are polished, their bodies not tattooed. They are armed with clubs and javelins; in war they utter piercing cries. They cultivate rice, maize, and other grain. They are fine looking men, and their hair is not frizzled."

M. d'Abbadie, another Abyssinian traveller, writing in 1852, gives the following account from the lips of an Abyssinian priest: "At the distance of fifteen days' journey south of Herrar is a place where all the men have tails, the length of a palm, covered with hair, and situated at the extremity of the spine. The females of that country are very beautiful and are tailless. I have seen some fifteen of these people at Besberah, and I am positive that the tail is natural."

It will be observed that there is a discrepancy between the accounts of M. de Castelnau and M. d'Abbadie. The former accords tails to the ladies, whilst the latter denies it. According to the former, the tail is smooth; according to the latter, it is covered with hair.

Dr. Wolf has improved on this in his "Travels and Adventures," vol. ii. 1861. "There are men and women in Abyssinia with tails like dogs and horses." Wolf heard also from a great many Abyssinians and Armenians (and Wolf is convinced of the truth of it), that "there are near Narea, in Abyssinia, people— men and women—with large tails, with which they are able to knock down a horse; and there are also such people near China." And in a note, "In the College of Surgeons at Dublin may still be seen a human skeleton, with a tail seven inches long! There are many known instances of this elongation of the caudal vertebra, as in the Poonangs in Borneo."

But the most interesting and circumstantial account of the Niam-niams is that given by Dr. Hubsch, physician to the hospitals of Constantinople. "It was in 1852," says he, "that I saw for the first time a tailed negress. I was struck with this phenomenon, and I questioned her master, a slave dealer. I learned from him that there exists a tribe called Niam-niam, occupying the interior of Africa. All the members of this tribe bear the caudal appendage, and, as Oriental imagination is given to exaggeration, I was assured that the tails sometimes attained the length of two feet. That which I observed was smooth and hairless. It was about two inches long, and terminated in a point. This woman was as black as ebony, her hair was frizzled, her teeth white, large, and planted in sockets which inclined considerably outward; her four canine teeth were filed, her eyes bloodshot. She ate meat raw, her clothes fidgeted her, her intellect was on a par with that of others of her condition.

"Her master had been unable, during six months, to sell her, notwithstanding the low figure at which he would have disposed of her; the abhorrence with which she was regarded was not attributed to her tail, but to the partiality, which she was unable to conceal, for human flesh. Her tribe fed on the flesh of the prisoners taken from the neighboring tribes, with whom they were constantly at war.

"As soon as one of the tribe dies, his relations, instead of burying him, cut him up and regale themselves upon his remains; consequently there are no cemeteries in this land. They do not all of them lead a wandering life, but many of them construct hovels of the branches of trees. They make for themselves weapons of war and of agriculture; they cultivate maize and wheat, and keep cattle. The Niam-niams have a language of their own, of an entirely primitive character, though containing an infusion of Arabic words.

"They live in a state of complete nudity, and seek only to satisfy their brute appetites. There is among them an utter disregard for morality, incest and adultery being common. The strongest among them becomes the chief of the tribe; and it is he who apportions the shares of the booty obtained in war. It is hard to say whether they have any religion; but in all probability they have none, as they readily adopt any one which they are taught.

"It is difficult to tame them altogether; their instinct impelling them constantly to seek for human flesh; and instances are related of slaves who have massacred and eaten the children confided to their charge.

"I have seen a man of the same race, who had a tail an inch and a half long, covered with a few hairs. He appeared to be thirty-five years old; he was robust, well built, of an ebon blackness, and had the same peculiar formation of jaw noticed above; that is to say, the tooth sockets were inclined outwards. Their four canine teeth are filed down, to diminish their power of mastication.

"I know also, at Constantinople, the son of a physician, aged two years, who was born with a tail an inch long; he belonged to the white Caucasian race. One of his grandfathers possessed the same appendage. This phenomenon is regarded generally in the East as a sign of great brute force."

About ten years ago, a newspaper paragraph recorded the birth of a boy at Newcastle-on-Tyne, provided with a tail about an inch and a quarter long. It was asserted that the child when sucking wagged this stump as token of pleasure.

Yet, notwithstanding all this testimony in favor of tailed men and women, it is simply a matter of impossibility for a human being to have a tail, for the spinal vertebræ in man do not admit of elongation, as in many animals; for the spine terminates in the os sacrum, a large and expanded bone of peculiar character, entirely precluding all possibility of production to the spine as in caudate animals.

VIII. — ANTICHRIST AND POPE JOAN

FROM the earliest ages of the Church, the advent of the Man of Sin has been looked forward to with terror, and the passages of Scripture relating to him have been studied with solemn awe, lest that day of wrath should come upon the Church unawares. As events in the world's history took place which seemed to be indications of the approach of Antichrist, a great horror fell upon men's minds, and their imaginations conjured up myths which flew from mouth to mouth, and which were implicitly believed.

Before speaking of these strange tales which produced such an effect on the minds of men in the middle ages, it will be well briefly to examine the opinions of divines of the early ages on the passages of Scripture connected with the coming of the last great persecutor of the Church. Antichrist was believed by most ancient writers to be destined to arise out of the tribe of Dan, a belief founded on the prediction of Jacob, "Dan shall be a serpent by the way, an adder in the path" (conf. Jeremiah viii. 16), and on the exclamation of the dying patriarch, when looking on his son Dan, "I have waited for Thy Salvation, O Lord," as though the long-suffering of God had borne long with that tribe, but in vain, and it was to be extinguished without hope. This, indeed, is implied in the sealing of the servants of God in their foreheads (Revelation vii.), when twelve thousand out of every tribe, except Dan, were seen by St. John to receive the seal of adoption, whilst of the tribe of Dan *not one* was sealed, as though it, to a man, had apostatized.

Opinions as to the nature of Antichrist were divided. Some held that he was to be a devil in phantom body, and of this number was Hippolytus. Others, again, believed that he would be an incarnate demon, true man and true devil; in fearful and diabolical parody of the Incarnation of our Lord. A third view was, that he would be merely a desperately wicked man, acting upon diabolical inspirations, just as the saints act upon divine inspirations. St. John Damascene expressly asserts that he will not be an incarnate demon, but a devilish man; for he says, "Not as Christ assumed humanity, so will the devil become human, but the Man will receive all the inspiration of Satan, and will suffer the devil to take up his abode within him." In this manner Antichrist could have many forerunners; and so St. Jerome and St. Augustine saw an Antichrist in Nero, not *the* Antichrist, but one of those of whom the Apostle speaks—"Even now are there many Antichrists." Thus also every enemy of the faith, such as Diocletian, Julian, and Mahomet, has been regarded as a precursor of the Arch-persecutor, who was expected to sum up in himself the cruelty of a Nero or Diocletian, the show of virtue of a Julian, and the spiritual pride of a Mahomet.

From infancy the evil one is to take possession of Antichrist, and to train him for his office, instilling into him cunning, cruelty, and pride. His doctrine will be—not downright infidelity, but a "show of godliness," whilst "denying the power thereof;" i. e., the miraculous origin and divine authority of Christianity. He will sow doubts of our Lord's manifestation "in the flesh," he will allow Christ to be an excellent Man, capable of teaching the most exalted truths, and inculcating the purest morality, yet Himself fallible and carried away by fanaticism.

In the end, however, Antichrist will "exalt himself to sit as God in the temple of God," and become "the abomination of desolation standing in the holy place." At the same time there is to be an awful alliance struck between himself, the impersonification of the world-power and the Church of God; some high pontiff of which, or the episcopacy in general, will enter into league with the unbelieving state to oppress the very elect. It is a strange instance of religionary virulence which makes some detect the Pope of Rome in the Man of Sin, the Harlot, the Beast, and the Priest going before it. The Man of Sin and the Beast are unmistakably identical, and refer to an Antichristian world-power; whilst the Harlot and the Priest are symbols of an apostasy in the Church. There is nothing Roman in this, but something very much the opposite.

How the Abomination of Desolation can be considered as set up in a Church where every sanctuary is adorned with all that can draw the heart to the Crucified, and raise the thoughts to the imposing ritual of Heaven, is a puzzle to me. To the man uninitiated in the law that Revelation is to be interpreted by contraries, it would seem more like the Abomination of Desolation in the Holy Place if he entered a Scotch Presbyterian, or a Dutch Calvinist, place of worship. Rome does not fight against the Daily Sacrifice, and endeavor to abolish it; that has been rather the labor of so-called Church Reformers, who with the suppression of the doctrine of Eucharistic Sacrifice and Sacramental Adoration have well nigh obliterated all notion of worship to be addressed to the God-Man. Rome does not deny the power of the godliness of which she makes show, but insists on that power with no broken accents. It is rather in other communities, where authority is flung aside, and any man is permitted to believe or reject what he likes, that we must look for the leaven of the Antichristian spirit at work.

It is evident that this spirit will infect the Church, and especially those in place of authority therein; so that the elect will have to wrestle against both "principalities and powers" in the state, and also "spiritual wickedness in the high places" of the Church. Perhaps it will be this feeling of antagonism between the inferior orders and the highest which will throw the Bishops into the arms of the state, and establish that unholy alliance which will be cemented for the purpose of oppressing all who hold the truth in sincerity, who are definite in their dogmatic statements of Christ's having been manifested in the flesh, who labor to establish the Daily Sacrifice, and offer in every place the pure offering spoken of by Malachi. Perhaps it was in anticipation of this, that ancient mystical interpreters explained the scene at the well in Midian as having reference to the last times.

The Church, like the daughters of Reuel, comes to the Well of living waters to water her parched flock; whereupon the shepherds—her chief pastors—arise and strive with her. "Fear not, O flock, fear not, O daughter!" exclaims the commentator; "thy true Moses is seated on the well, and He will arise out of His resting-place, and will with His own hand smite the shepherds, and water the flock." Let the sheep be in barren and dry pastures,—so long the shepherds strive not; let the sheep pant and die,—so long the shepherds show no signs of irritation; but let the Church approach the limpid well of life, and at once her prelates will, in the latter days, combine "to strive" with her, and keep back the flock from the reviving streams.

In the time of Antichrist the Church will be divided: one portion will hold to the world-power, the other will seek out the old paths, and cling to the only true Guide. The high places will be filled with unbelievers in the Incarnation, and the Church will be in a condition of the utmost spiritual degradation, but enjoying the highest State patronage. The religion in favor will be one of morality, but not of dogma; and the Man of Sin will be able to promulgate his doctrine, according to St. Anselm, through his great eloquence and wisdom, his vast learning and mightiness in the Holy Scriptures, which he will wrest to the overthrowing of dogma. He will be liberal in bribes, for he will be of unbounded wealth; he will be capable of performing great "signs and wonders," so as "to deceive—the very elect;" and at the last, he will tear the moral veil from his countenance, and a monster of impiety and cruelty, he will inaugurate that awful persecution, which is to last for three years and a half, and to excel in horror all the persecutions that have gone before.

In that terrible season of confusion faith will be all but extinguished. "When the Son of Man cometh, shall He find faith on the earth?" asks our Blessed Lord, as though expecting the answer, No; and then, says Marchantius, the vessel of the Church will disappear in the foam of that boiling deep of infidelity, and be hidden in the blackness of that storm of destruction which sweeps over the earth. The sun shall "be darkened, and the moon shall not give her light, and the stars shall fall from heaven;" the sun of faith shall have gone out; the moon, the Church, shall not give her light, being turned into blood, through stress of persecution; and the stars, the great ecclesiastical dignitaries, shall fall into apostasy. But still the Church will remain unwrecked, she will weather the storm; still will she come forth "beautiful as the moon,

41

terrible as an army with banners;" for after the lapse of those three and a half years, Christ will descend to avenge the blood of the saints, by destroying Antichrist and the world-power.

Such is a brief sketch of the scriptural doctrine of Antichrist as held by the early and mediæval Church. Let us now see to what myths it gave rise among the vulgar and the imaginative. Rabanus Maurus, in his work on the life of Antichrist, gives a full account of the miracles he will perform; he tells us that the Man-fiend will heal the sick, raise the dead, restore sight to the blind, hearing to the deaf, speech to the dumb; he will raise storms and calm them, will remove mountains, make trees flourish or wither at a word. He will rebuild the temple at Jerusalem, and making the Holy City the great capital of the world. Popular opinion added that his vast wealth would be obtained from hidden treasures, which are now being concealed by the demons for his use. Various possessed persons, when interrogated, announced that such was the case, and that the amount of buried gold was vast.

"In the year 1599," says Canon Moreau, a contemporary historian, "a rumor circulated with prodigious rapidity through Europe, that Antichrist had been born at Babylon, and that already the Jews of that part were hurrying to receive and recognize him as their Messiah. The news came from Italy and Germany, and extended to Spain, England, and other Western kingdoms, troubling many people, even the most discreet; however, the learned gave it no credence, saying that the signs predicted in Scripture to precede that event were not yet accomplished, and among other that the Roman empire was not yet abolished.... Others said that, as for the signs, the majority had already appeared to the best of their knowledge, and with regard to the rest, they might have taken place in distant regions without their having been made known to them; that the Roman empire existed but in name, and that the interpretation of the passage on which its destruction was predicted, might be incorrect; that for many centuries, the most learned and pious had believed in the near approach of Antichrist, some believing that he had already come, on account of the persecutions which had fallen on the Christians; others, on account of fires, or eclipses, or earthquakes.... Every one was in excitement; some declared that the news must be correct, others believed nothing about it, and the agitation became so excessive, that Henry IV., who was then on the throne, was compelled by edict to forbid any mention of the subject."

The report spoken of by Moreau gained additional confirmation from the announcement made by an exorcised demoniac, that in 1600, the Man of Sin had been born in the neighborhood of Paris, of a Jewess, named Blanchefleure, who had conceived by Satan. The child had been baptized at the Sabbath of Sorcerers; and a witch, under torture, acknowledged that she had rocked the infant Antichrist on her knees, and she averred that he had claws on his feet, wore no shoes, and spoke all languages.

In 1623 appeared the following startling announcement, which obtained an immense circulation among the lower orders:

"We, brothers of the Order of St. John of Jerusalem, in the Isle of Malta, have received letters from our spies, who are engaged in our service in the country of Babylon, now possessed by the Grand Turk; by the which letters we are advertised, that, on the 1st of May, in the year of our Lord 1623, a child was born in the town of Bourydot, otherwise called Calka, near Babylon, of the which child the mother is a very aged woman, of race unknown, called Fort-Juda: of the father nothing is known. The child is dusky, has pleasant mouth and eyes, teeth pointed like those of a cat, ears large, stature by no means exceeding that of other children; the said child, incontinent on his birth, walked and talked perfectly well. His speech is comprehended by every one, admonishing the people that he is the true Messiah, and the son of God, and that in him all must believe. Our spies also swear and protest that they have seen the said child with their own eyes; and they add, that, on the occasion of his nativity, there appeared marvellous signs in heaven, for at full noon the sun lost its brightness, and was for some time obscured."

This is followed by a list of other signs appearing, the most remarkable being a swarm of flying serpents, and a shower of precious stones.

According to Sebastian Michaeliz, in his history of the possessed of Flanders, on the authority of the exorcised demons, we learn that Antichrist is to be a son of Beelzebub, who will accompany his offspring under the form of a bird, with four feet and a bull's head; that he will torture Christians with the same tortures with which the lost souls are racked; that he will be able to fly, speak all languages, and will have any number of names.

We find that Antichrist is known to the Mussulmans as well as to Christians. Lane, in his edition of the "Arabian Nights," gives some curious details on Moslem ideas regarding him. According to these, Antichrist will overrun the earth, mounted on an ass, and followed by 40,000 Jews; his empire will last forty days, whereof the first day will be a year long, the duration of the second will be a month, that of the third a week, the others being of their usual length. He will devastate the whole world, leaving Mecca and Medina alone in security, as these holy cities will be guarded by angelic legions. Christ at last will descend to earth, and in a great battle will destroy the Man-devil.

Several writers, of different denominations, no less superstitious than the common people, connected the apparition of Antichrist with the fable of Pope Joan, which obtained such general credence at one time, but which modern criticism has at length succeeded in excluding from history.

Perhaps the earliest writer to mention Pope Joan is Marianus Scotus, who in his chronicle inserts the following passage: "A. D. 854, Lotharii 14, Joanna, a woman, succeeded Leo, and reigned two years, five months, and four days." Marianus Scotus died A. D. 1086. Sigebert de Gemblours (d. 5th Oct., 1112) inserts the same story in his valuable chronicle, copying from an interpolated passage in the work of Anastasius the librarian. His words are, "It is reported that this John was a female, and that she conceived by one of her servants. The Pope, becoming pregnant, gave birth to a child; wherefore some do not number her among the Pontiffs." Hence the story spread among the mediæval chroniclers, who were great plagiarists. Otto of Frisingen and Gotfrid of Viterbo mention the Lady-Pope in their histories, and Martin Polonus gives details as follows:

"After Leo IV., John Anglus, a native of Metz, reigned two years, five months, and four days. And the pontificate was vacant for a month. He died in Rome. He is related to have been a female, and, when a girl, to have accompanied her sweetheart in male costume to Athens; there she advanced in various sciences, and none could be found to equal her. So, after having studied for three years in Rome, she had great masters for her pupils and hearers. And when there arose a high opinion in the city of her virtue and knowledge, she was unanimously elected Pope. But during her papacy she became in the family way by a familiar. Not knowing the time of birth, as she was on her way from St. Peter's to the Lateran she had a painful delivery, between the Coliseum and St. Clement's Church, in the street. Having died after, it is said that she was buried on the spot; and therefore the Lord Pope always turns aside from that way, and it is supposed by some out of detestation for what happened there. Nor on that account is she placed in the catalogue of the Holy Pontiffs, not only on account of her sex, but also because of the horribleness of the circumstance."

Certainly a story at all scandalous *crescit eundo.*

William Ocham alludes to the story, and John Huss, only too happy to believe it, provides the lady with a name, and asserts that she was baptized Agnes, or, as he will have it with a strong aspirate, Hagnes. Others, however, insist upon her name having been Gilberta; and some stout Germans, not relishing the notion of her being a daughter of Fatherland, palm her off on England. As soon as we arrive at Reformation times, the German and French Protestants fasten on the story with the utmost avidity, and add sweet little touches of their own, and draw conclusions galling enough to the Roman See, illustrating their accounts with wood engravings vigorous and graphic, but hardly decent. One of these represents the event in a peculiarly startling manner. The procession of bishops, with the Host and tapers, is sweeping along, when suddenly the cross-bearer before the triple-crowned and vested Pope starts aside to witness the unexpected arrival. This engraving, which it is quite impossible for me to reproduce, is in a curious little book, entitled "Puerperium Johannis Papæ 8, 1530."

The following jingling record of the event is from the Rhythmical Vitæ Pontificum of Gulielmus Jacobus of Egmonden, a work never printed. This fragment is preserved in "Wolfii Lectionum Memorabilium centenarii, XVI.:"—

"Priusquàm reconditur Sergius, vocatur
Ad summam, qui dicitur Johannes, huic addatur
Anglicus, Moguntia iste procreatur.
Qui, ut dat sententia, fœminis aptatur
Sexu: quod sequentia monstrant, breviatur,
Hæc vox: nam prolixius chronica procedunt.

Ista, de qua brevius dicta minus lædunt.
Huic erat amasius, ut scriptores credunt.
Patria relinquitur Moguntia, Græcorum
Studiosè petitur schola. Pòst doctorum
Hæc doctrix efficitur Romæ legens: horum
Hæc auditu fungitur loquens. Hinc prostrato
Summo hæc eligitur: sexu exaltato
Quandoque negligitur. Fatur quòd hæc nato
Per servum conficitur. Tempore gignendi
Ad processum equus scanditur, vice flendi,
Papa cadit, panditur improbis ridendi
Norma, puer nascitur in vico Clementis,
Colossæum jungitur. Corpus parentis
In eodem traditur sepulturæ gentis,
Faturque scriptoribus, quòd Papa præfato,
Vico senioribus transiens amato
Congruo ductoribus sequitur negato
Loco, quo Ecclesia partu denigratur,
Quamvis inter spacia Pontificum ponatur,
Propter sexum."

Stephen Blanch, in his "Urbis Romæ Mirabilia," says that an angel of heaven appeared to Joan before the event, and asked her to choose whether she would prefer burning eternally in hell, or having her confinement in public; with sense which does her credit, she chose the latter. The Protestant writers were not satisfied that the father of the unhappy baby should have been a servant: some made him a Cardinal, and others the devil himself. According to an eminent Dutch minister, it is immaterial whether the child be fathered on Satan or a monk; at all events, the former took a lively interest in the youthful Antichrist, and, on the occasion of his birth, was seen and heard fluttering overhead, crowing and chanting in an unmusical voice the Sibylline verses announcing the birth of the Arch-persecutor:—

"Papa pater patrum, Papissæ pandito partum
Et tibi tunc eadem de corpore quando recedam!"

which lines, as being perhaps the only ones known to be of diabolic composition, are deserving of preservation.

The Reformers, in order to reconcile dates, were put to the somewhat perplexing necessity of moving Pope Joan to their own times, or else of giving to the youthful Antichrist an age of seven hundred years.

It must be allowed that the *accouchement* of a Pope in full pontificals, during a solemn procession, was a prodigy not likely to occur more than once in the world's history, and was certain to be of momentous import.

It will be seen by the curious woodcut reproduced as frontispiece from Baptista Mantuanus, that he consigned Pope Joan to the jaws of hell, notwithstanding her choice. The verses accompanying this picture are:—

"Hic pendebat adhuc sexum mentita virile
Fœmina, cui triplici Phrygiam diademate mitram
Extollebat apex: et pontificalis adulter."

It need hardly be stated that the whole story of Pope Joan is fabulous, and rests on not the slightest historical foundation. It was probably a Greek invention to throw discredit on the papal hierarchy, first circulated more than two hundred years after the date of the supposed Pope. Even Martin Polonus (A. D. 1282), who is the first to give the details, does so merely on popular report.

The great champions of the myth were the Protestants of the sixteenth century, who were thoroughly unscrupulous in distorting history and suppressing facts, so long as they could make a point. A paper war was waged upon the subject, and finally the whole story was proved conclusively to be utterly destitute of historical truth. A melancholy example of the blindness of party feeling and prejudice is seen in Mosheim, who assumes the truth of the ridiculous story, and gravely inserts it in his "Ecclesiastical History." "Between Leo IV., who died 855, and Benedict III., a woman, who concealed her sex and assumed the name of John, it is said, opened her way to the Pontifical throne by her learning and genius, and governed the Church for a time. She is commonly called the Papess Joan. During the five subsequent centuries the witnesses to this extraordinary event are without number; nor did any one, prior to the Reformation by Luther, regard the thing as either incredible or disgraceful to the Church." Such are Mosheim's words, and I give them as a specimen of the credit which is due to his opinion. The "Ecclesiastical History" he wrote is full of perversions of the plainest facts, and that under our notice is but one out of many. "During the five centuries after her reign," he says, "the witnesses to the story are innumerable." Now, for two centuries there is not an allusion to be found to the events. The only passage which can be found is a universally acknowledged interpolation of the "Lives of the Popes," by Anastasius Bibliothecarius; and this interpolation is stated in the first printed edition by Busæus, Mogunt. 1602, to be only found in two MS. copies.

From Marianus Scotus or Sigebert de Gemblours the story passed into other chronicles *totidem verbis*, and generally with hesitation and an expression of doubt in its accuracy. Martin Polonus is the first to give the particulars, some four hundred and twenty years after the reign of the fabulous Pope.

Mosheim is false again in asserting that no one prior to the Reformation regarded the thing as either incredible or disgraceful. This is but of a piece with his malignity and disregard for truth, whenever he can hit the Catholic Church hard. Bart. Platina, in his "Lives of the Popes," written before Luther was born, after relating the story, says, "These things which I relate are popular reports, but derived from uncertain and obscure authors, which I have therefore inserted briefly and baldly, lest I should seem to omit obstinately and pertinaciously what most people assert." Thus the facts were justly doubted by Platina on the legitimate grounds that they rested on popular gossip, and not on reliable history. Marianus Scotus, the first to relate the story, died in 1086. He was a monk of St. Martin of Cologne, then of Fulda, and lastly of St. Alban's, at Metz. How could he have obtained reliable information, or seen documents upon which to ground the assertion? Again, his chronicle has suffered severely from interpolations in numerous places, and there is reason to believe that the Pope-Joan passage is itself a late interpolation.

If so, we are reduced to Sigebert de Gemblours (d. 1112), placing two centuries and a half between him and the event he records, and his chronicle may have been tampered with.

The historical discrepancies are sufficiently glaring to make the story more than questionable.

Leo IV. died on the 17th July, 855; and Benedict III. was consecrated on the 1st September in the same year; so that it is impossible to insert between their pontificates a reign of two years, five months, and four days. It is, however, true that there was an antipope elected upon the death of Leo, at the instance of the Emperor Louis; but his name was Anastasius. This man possessed himself of the palace of the Popes, and obtained the incarceration of Benedict. However, his supporters almost immediately deserted him, and Benedict assumed the pontificate. The reign of Benedict was only for two years and a half, so that Anastasius cannot be the supposed Joan; nor do we hear of any charge brought against him to the effect of his being a woman. But the stout partisans of the Pope-Joan tale assert, on the authority of the "Annales Augustani,"[29] and some other, but late authorities, that the female Pope was John VIII., who consecrated Louis II. of France, and Ethelwolf of England. Here again is confusion. Ethelwolf sent Alfred to Rome in 853, and the youth received regal unction from the hands of Leo IV. In 855 Ethelwolf visited Rome, it is true, but was not consecrated by the existing Pope, whilst Charles the Bald was anointed by John VIII. in 875. John VIII. was a Roman, son of Gundus, and an archdeacon of the Eternal City. He assumed the triple crown in 872, and reigned till December 18, 882. John took an active part in the troubles of the Church under the incursions of the Sarasins, and 325 letters of his are extant, addressed to the princes and prelates of his day.

[29] These Annals were written in 1135.

Any one desirous of pursuing this examination into the untenable nature of the story may find an excellent summary of the arguments used on both sides in Gieseler, "Lehrbuch," &c., Cunningham's trans., vol. ii. pp. 20, 21, or in Bayle, "Dictionnaire," tom. iii. art. Papesse.

The arguments in favor of the myth may be seen in Spanheim, "Exercit. de Papa Fœmina," Opp. tom. ii. p. 577, or in Lenfant, "Histoire de la Papesse Jeanne," La Haye, 1736, 2 vols. 12mo.

The arguments on the other side may be had in "Allatii Confutatio Fabulæ de Johanna Papissa," Colon. 1645; in Le Quien, "Oriens Christianus," tom. iii. p. 777; and in the pages of the Lutheran Huemann, "Sylloge Diss. Sacras.," tom. i. par. ii. p. 352.

The final development of this extraordinary story, under the delicate fingers of the German and French Protestant controversialists, may not prove uninteresting.

Joan was the daughter of an English missionary, who left England to preach the Gospel to the recently converted Saxons. She was born at Engelheim, and according to different authors she was christened Agnes, Gerberta, Joanna, Margaret, Isabel, Dorothy, or Jutt—the last must have been a nickname surely! She early distinguished herself for genius and love of letters. A young monk of Fulda having conceived for her a violent passion, which she returned with ardor, she deserted her parents, dressed herself in male attire, and in the sacred precincts of Fulda divided her affections between the youthful monk and the musty books of the monastic library. Not satisfied with the restraints of conventual life, nor finding the library sufficiently well provided with books of abstruse science, she eloped with her young man, and after visiting England, France, and Italy, she brought him to Athens, where she addicted herself with unflagging devotion to her literary pursuits. Wearied out by his journey, the monk expired in the arms of the blue-stocking who had influenced his life for evil, and the young lady of so many aliases was for a while inconsolable. She left Athens and repaired to Rome. There she opened a school and acquired such a reputation for learning and feigned sanctity, that, on the death of Leo IV., she was unanimously elected Pope. For two years and five months, under the name of John VIII., she filled the papal chair with reputation, no one suspecting her sex. But having taken a fancy to one of the cardinals, by him she became pregnant. At length arrived the time of Rogation processions. Whilst passing the street between the amphitheatre and St. Clement's, she was seized with violent pains, fell to the ground amidst the crowd, and, whilst her attendants ministered to her, was delivered of a son. Some say the child and mother died on the spot, some that she survived but was incarcerated, some that the child was spirited away to be the Antichrist of the last days. A marble monument representing the papess with her baby was erected on the spot, which was declared to be accursed to all ages.

I have little doubt myself that Pope Joan is an impersonification of the great whore of Revelation, seated on the seven hills, and is the popular expression of the idea prevalent from the twelfth to the sixteenth centuries, that the mystery of iniquity was somehow working in the papal court. The scandal of the Antipopes, the utter worldliness and pride of others, the spiritual fornication with the kings of the earth, along with the words of Revelation prophesying the advent of an adulterous woman who should rule over the imperial city, and her connection with Antichrist, crystallized into this curious myth, much as the floating uncertainty as to the signification of our Lord's words, "There be some standing here which shall not taste of death till they see the kingdom of God," condensed into the myth of the Wandering Jew.

The literature connected with Antichrist is voluminous. I need only specify some of the most curious works which have appeared on the subject. St. Hippolytus and Rabanus Maurus have been already alluded to. Commodianus wrote "Carmen Apologeticum adversus Gentes," which has been published by Dom Pitra in his "Spicilegium Solesmense," with an introduction containing Jewish and Christian traditions relating to Antichrist. "De Turpissima Conceptione, Nativitate, et aliis Præsagiis Diaboliciis illius Turpissimi Hominis Antichristi," is the title of a strange little volume published by Lenoir in A. D. 1500, containing rude yet characteristic woodcuts, representing the birth, life, and death of the Man of Sin, each picture accompanied by French verses in explanation. An equally remarkable illustrated work on Antichrist is the famous "Liber de Antichristo," a blockbook of an early date. It is in twenty-seven folios, and is excessively rare. Dibdin has reproduced three of the plates in his "Bibliotheca Spenseriana," and Falckenstein has given full details of the work in his "Geschichte der Buchdruckerkunst."

There is an Easter miracle-play of the twelfth century, still extant, the subject of which is the "Life and Death of Antichrist." More curious still is the "Farce de l'Antéchrist et de Trois Femmes"—a composition of the sixteenth century, when that mysterious personage occupied all brains. The farce consists in a scene at a fish-stall, with three good ladies quarrelling over some fish. Antichrist steps in,—for no particular reason that one can see,—upsets fish and fish-women, sets them fighting, and skips off the stage. The best book on Antichrist, and that most full of learning and judgment, is Malvenda's great work in two folio volumes, "De Antichristo, libri xii." Lyons, 1647.

For the fable of the Pope Joan, see J. Lenfant, "Histoire de la Papesse Jeanne." La Haye, 1736, 2 vols. 12mo. "Allatii Confutatio Fabulæ de Johanna Papissa." Colon. 1645.

IX. — THE MAN IN THE MOON

From L. Richter.

EVERY one knows that the moon is inhabited by a man with a bundle of sticks on his back, who has been exiled thither for many centuries, and who is so far off that he is beyond the reach of death.

He has once visited this earth, if the nursery rhyme is to be credited, when it asserts that—

> *"The Man in the Moon*
> *Came down too soon,*
> *And asked his way to Norwich;"*

but whether he ever reached that city, the same authority does not state.

The story as told by nurses is, that this man was found by Moses gathering sticks on a Sabbath, and that, for this crime, he was doomed to reside in the moon till the end of all things; and they refer to Numbers xv. 32-36:—

"And while the children of Israel were in the wilderness, they found a man that gathered sticks upon the Sabbath day. And they that found him gathering sticks brought him unto Moses and Aaron, and unto all the congregation. And they put him in ward, because it was not declared what should be done to him. And the Lord said unto Moses, The man shall be surely put to death: all the congregation shall stone him with stones without the camp. And all the congregation brought him without the camp, and stoned him with stones till he died."

Of course, in the sacred writings there is no allusion to the moon.
The German tale is as follows:—

Ages ago there went one Sunday morning an old man into the wood to hew sticks. He cut a fagot and slung it on a stout staff, cast it over his shoulder, and began to trudge home with his burden. On his way he met a handsome man in Sunday suit, walking towards the Church; this man stopped and asked the fagot-bearer, "Do you know that this is Sunday on earth, when all must rest from their labors?"
"Sunday on earth, or Monday in heaven, it is all one to me!" laughed the wood-cutter.
"Then bear your bundle forever," answered the stranger; "and as you value not Sunday on earth, yours shall be a perpetual Moon-day in heaven; and you shall stand for eternity in the moon, a warning to all Sabbath-breakers." Thereupon the stranger vanished, and the man was caught up with his stock and his fagot into the moon, where he stands yet.

The superstition seems to be old in Germany, for the full moon is spoken of as *wadel*, or *wedel*, a fagot. Tobler relates the story thus: "An arma ma ket alawel am Sonnti holz ufglesa. Do hedem der liebe

Gott dwahl gloh, öb er lieber wott ider sonn verbrenna oder im mo verfrura, do willer lieber inn mo ihi. Dromm siedma no jetz an ma im mo inna, wenns wedel ist. Er hed a püscheli uffem rogga."[30] That is to say, he was given the choice of burning in the sun, or of freezing in the moon; he chose the latter; and now at full moon he is to be seen seated with his bundle of fagots on his back.

[30] Tobler, Appenz. Sprachsbuch, 20.

In Schaumburg-Lippe,[31] the story goes, that a man and a woman stand in the moon, the man because he strewed brambles and thorns on the church path, so as to hinder people from attending Mass on Sunday morning; the woman because she made butter on that day. The man carries his bundle of thorns, the woman her butter-tub. A similar tale is told in Swabia and in Marken. Fischart[32] says, that there "is to be seen in the moon a manikin who stole wood;" and Prætorius, in his description of the world,[33] that "superstitious people assert that the black flecks in the moon are a man who gathered wood on a Sabbath, and is therefore turned into stone."

[31] Wolf, Zeitschrift für Deut. Myth. i. 168.
[32] Fischart, Garg. 130.
[33] Prætorius, i. 447.

The Dutch household myth is, that the unhappy man was caught stealing vegetables. Dante calls him Cain:—

"... Now doth Cain with fork of thorns confine,
On either hemisphere, touching the wave
Beneath the towers of Seville. Yesternight
The moon was round."
Hell, cant. xx.

And again,—

"... Tell, I pray thee, whence the gloomy spots
Upon this body, which below on earth
Give rise to talk of Cain in fabling quaint?"
Paradise, cant. ii.

Chaucer, in the "Testament of Cresside," adverts to the man in the moon, and attributes to him the same idea of theft. Of Lady Cynthia, or the moon, he says,—

"Her gite was gray and full of spottis blake,
And on her brest a chorle painted ful even,
Bering a bush of thornis on his backe,
Whiche for his theft might clime so ner the heaven."

Ritson, among his "Ancient Songs," gives one extracted from a manuscript of the time of Edward II., on the Man in the Moon, but in very obscure language. The first verse, altered into more modern orthography, runs as follows:—

"Man in the Moon stand and stit,
On his bot-fork his burden he beareth,
It is much wonder that he do na doun slit,
For doubt lest he fall he shudd'reth and shivereth.

....

"When the frost freezes must chill he bide,
The thorns be keen his attire so teareth,
Nis no wight in the world there wot when he syt,
Ne bote it by the hedge what weeds he weareth."

48

Alexander Necham, or Nequam, a writer of the twelfth century, in commenting on the dispersed shadows in the moon, thus alludes to the vulgar belief: "Nonne novisti quid vulgus vocet rusticum in luna portantem spinas? Unde quidam vulgariter loquens ait:—

"Rusticus in Luna,
Quem sarcina deprimit una
Monstrat per opinas
Nulli prodesse rapinas,"

which may be translated thus: "Do you know what they call the rustic in the moon, who carries the fagot of sticks?" So that one vulgarly speaking says,—

"See the rustic in the Moon,
How his bundle weighs him down;
Thus his sticks the truth reveal,
It never profits man to steal."

Shakspeare refers to the same individual in his "Midsummer Night's Dream." Quince the carpenter, giving directions for the performance of the play of "Pyramus and Thisbe," orders: "One must come in with a bush of thorns and a lantern, and say he comes in to disfigure, or to present, the person of Moonshine." And the enacter of this part says, "All I have to say is, to tell you that the lantern is the moon; I the man in the moon; this thorn-bush my thorn-bush; and this dog my dog."

Also "Tempest," Act 2, Scene 2:—

"*Cal.* Hast thou not dropt from heaven?

"*Steph.* Out o' th' moon, I do assure thee. I was the man in th' moon when time was.

"*Cal.* I have seen thee in her; and I do adore thee. My mistress showed me thee, and thy dog, and thy bush."

The dog I have myself had pointed out to me by an old Devonshire crone. If popular superstition places a dog in the moon, it puts a lamb in the sun; for in the same county it is said that those who see the sun rise on Easter-day, may behold in the orb the lamb and flag.

I believe this idea of locating animals in the two great luminaries of heaven to be very ancient, and to be a relic of a primeval superstition of the Aryan race.

There is an ancient pictorial representation of our friend the Sabbath-breaker in Gyffyn Church, near Conway. The roof of the chancel is divided into compartments, in four of which are the Evangelistic symbols, rudely, yet effectively painted. Besides these symbols is delineated in each compartment an orb of heaven. The sun, the moon, and two stars, are placed at the feet of the Angel, the Bull, the Lion, and the Eagle. The representation of the moon is as below; in the disk is the conventional man with his bundle of sticks, but without the dog. There is also a curious seal appended to a deed preserved in the Record Office, dated the 9th year of Edward the Third (1335), bearing the man in the moon as its device. The deed is one of conveyance of a messuage, barn, and four acres of ground, in the parish of Kingston-on-Thames, from Walter de Grendesse, clerk, to Margaret his mother. On the seal we see the man carrying his sticks, and the moon surrounds him. There are also a couple of stars added, perhaps to show that he is in the sky. The legend on the seal reads:—

"Te Waltere docebo
cur spinas phebo
gero,"

which may be translated, "I will teach thee, Walter, why I carry thorns in the moon."

Representation of the moon in Gyffyn Church.

The seal with the legend visible.

The general superstition with regard to the spots in the moon may briefly be summed up thus: A man is located in the moon; he is a thief or Sabbath-breaker;[34] he has a pole over his shoulder, from which is suspended a bundle of sticks or thorns. In some places a woman is believed to accompany him, and she has a butter-tub with her; in other localities she is replaced by a dog.

[34] Hebel, in his charming poem on the Man in the Moon, in "Allemanische Gedichte," makes him both thief and Sabbath-breaker.

The belief in the Moon-man seems to exist among the natives of British Columbia; for I read in one of Mr. Duncan's letters to the Church Missionary Society, "One very dark night I was told that there was a moon to see on the beach. On going to see, there was an illuminated disk, with the figure of a man upon it. The water was then very low, and one of the conjuring parties had lit up this disk at the water's edge. They had made it of wax, with great exactness, and presently it was at full. It was an imposing sight. Nothing could be seen around it; but the Indians suppose that the medicine party are then holding converse with the man in the moon.... After a short time the moon waned away, and the conjuring party returned whooping to their house."

Now let us turn to Scandinavian mythology, and see what we learn from that source.

Mâni, the moon, stole two children from their parents, and carried them up to heaven. Their names were Hjuki and Bil. They had been drawing water from the well Byrgir, in the bucket Sœgr, suspended from the pole Simul, which they bore upon their shoulders. These children, pole, and bucket were placed in heaven, "where they could be seen from earth." This refers undoubtedly to the spots in the moon; and so the Swedish peasantry explain these spots to this day, as representing a boy and a girl bearing a pail of water between them. Are we not reminded at once of our nursery rhyme—

"Jack and Jill went up a hill
To fetch a pail of water;
Jack fell down, and broke his crown,
And Jill came tumbling after"?

This verse, which to us seems at first sight nonsense, I have no hesitation in saying has a high antiquity, and refers to the Eddaic Hjuki and Bil. The names indicate as much. Hjuki, in Norse, would be pronounced Juki, which would readily become Jack; and Bil, for the sake of euphony, and in order to give a female name to one of the children, would become Jill.

The fall of Jack, and the subsequent fall of Jill, simply represent the vanishing of one moon-spot after another, as the moon wanes.

But the old Norse myth had a deeper signification than merely an explanation of the moon-spots.

Hjuki is derived from the verb jakka, to heap or pile together, to assemble and increase; and Bil from bila, to break up or dissolve. Hjuki and Bil, therefore, signify nothing more than the waxing and waning of the moon, and the water they are represented as bearing signifies the fact that the rainfall depends on the phases of the moon. Waxing and waning were individualized, and the meteorological fact of the connection of the rain with the moon was represented by the children as water-bearers.

But though Jack and Jill became by degrees dissevered in the popular mind from the moon, the original myth went through a fresh phase, and exists still under a new form. The Norse superstition attributed *theft* to the moon, and the vulgar soon began to believe that the figure they saw in the moon was the thief. The lunar specks certainly may be made to resemble one figure, and only a lively imagination can discern two. The girl soon dropped out of popular mythology, the boy oldened into a venerable man, he retained his pole, and the bucket was transformed into the thing he had stolen—sticks or vegetables. The theft was in some places exchanged for Sabbath-breaking, especially among those in Protestant countries who were acquainted with the Bible story of the stick-gatherer.

The Indian superstition is worth examining, because of the connection existing between Indian and European mythology, on account of our belonging to the same Aryan stock.

According to a Buddhist legend, Sâkyamunni himself, in one of his earlier stages of existence, was a hare, and lived in friendship with a fox and an ape. In order to test the virtue of the Bodhisattwa, Indra came to the friends, in the form of an old man, asking for food. Hare, ape, and fox went forth in quest of victuals for their guest. The two latter returned from their foraging expedition successful, but the hare had found nothing. Then, rather than that he should treat the old man with inhospitality, the hare had a fire kindled, and cast himself into the flames, that he might himself become food for his guest. In reward for this act of self-sacrifice, Indra carried the hare to heaven, and placed him in the moon.[35]

[35] "Mémoires ... par Hjouen Thsang, traduits du Chinois par Stanislas Julien," i. 375. Upham, "Sacred Books of Ceylon," iii. 309.

Here we have an old man and a hare in connection with the lunar planet, just as in Shakspeare we have a fagot-bearer and a dog.

The fable rests upon the name of the moon in Sanskrit, çaçin, or "that marked with the hare;" but whether the belief in the spots taking the shape of a hare gave the name çaçin to the moon, or the lunar name çaçin originated the belief, it is impossible for us to say.

Grounded upon this myth is the curious story of "The Hare and the Elephant," in the "Pantschatantra," an ancient collection of Sanskrit fables. It will be found as the first tale in the third book. I have room only for an outline of the story.

THE CRAFTY HARE

In a certain forest lived a mighty elephant, king of a herd, Toothy by name. On a certain occasion there was a long drought, so that pools, tanks, swamps, and lakes were dried up. Then the elephants sent out exploring parties in search of water. A young one discovered an extensive lake surrounded with trees, and teeming with water-fowl. It went by the name of the Moon-lake. The elephants, delighted at the prospect of having an inexhaustible supply of water, marched off to the spot, and found their most sanguine hopes realized. Round about the lake, in the sandy soil, were innumerable hare warrens; and as the herd of elephants trampled on the ground, the hares were severely injured, their homes broken down, their heads, legs, and backs crushed beneath the ponderous feet of the monsters of the forest. As soon as the herd had withdrawn, the hares assembled, some halting, some dripping with blood, some bearing the corpses of their cherished infants, some with piteous tales of ruination in their houses, all with tears streaming from their eyes, and wailing forth, "Alas, we are lost! The elephant-herd will return, for there is no water elsewhere, and that will be the death of all of us."

But the wise and prudent Longear volunteered to drive the herd away; and he succeeded in this manner: Longear went to the elephants, and having singled out their king, he addressed him as follows:—

"Ha, ha! bad elephant! what brings you with such thoughtless frivolity to this strange lake? Back with you at once!"

When the king of the elephants heard this, he asked in astonishment, "Pray, who are you?"

"I," replied Longear,—"I am Vidschajadatta by name; the hare who resides in the Moon. Now am I sent by his Excellency the Moon as an ambassador to you. I speak to you in the name of the Moon."

"Ahem! Hare," said the elephant, somewhat staggered; "and what message have you brought me from his Excellency the Moon?"

"You have this day injured several hares. Are you not aware that they are the subjects of me? If you value your life, venture not near the lake again. Break my command, and I shall withdraw my beams from you at night, and your bodies will be consumed with perpetual sun."

The elephant, after a short meditation, said, "Friend! it is true that I have acted against the rights of the excellent Majesty of the Moon. I should wish to make an apology; how can I do so?"

The hare replied, "Come along with me, and I will show you."

The elephant asked, "Where is his Excellency at present?"

The other replied, "He is now in the lake, hearing the complaints of the maimed hares."

"If that be the case," said the elephant, humbly, "bring me to my lord, that I may tender him my submission."

So the hare conducted the king of the elephants to the edge of the lake, and showed him the reflection of the moon in the water, saying, "There stands our lord in the midst of the water, plunged in meditation; reverence him with devotion, and then depart with speed."

Thereupon the elephant poked his proboscis into the water, and muttered a fervent prayer. By so doing he set the water in agitation, so that the reflection of the moon was all of a quiver.

"Look!" exclaimed the hare; "his Majesty is trembling with rage at you!"

"Why is his supreme Excellency enraged with me?" asked the elephant.

"Because you have set the water in motion. Worship him, and then be off!"

The elephant let his ears droop, bowed his great head to the earth, and after having expressed in suitable terms his regret for having annoyed the Moon, and the hare dwelling in it, he vowed never to trouble the Moon-lake again. Then he departed, and the hares have ever since lived there unmolested.

X. THE MOUNTAIN OF VENUS

RAGGED, bald, and desolate, as though a curse rested upon it, rises the Hörselberg out of the rich and populous land between Eisenach and Gotha, looking, from a distance, like a huge stone sarcophagus—a sarcophagus in which rests in magical slumber, till the end of all things, a mysterious world of wonders.

High up on the north-west flank of the mountain, in a precipitous wall of rock, opens a cavern, called the Hörselloch, from the depths of which issues a muffled roar of water, as though a subterraneous stream were rushing over rapidly-whirling millwheels. "When I have stood alone on the ridge of the mountain," says Bechstein, "after having sought the chasm in vain, I have heard a mighty rush, like that of falling water, beneath my feet, and after scrambling down the scarp, have found myself—how, I never knew—in front of the cave." ("Sagenschatz des Thüringes-landes," 1835.)

In ancient days, according to the Thüringian Chronicles, bitter cries and long-drawn moans were heard issuing from this cavern; and at night, wild shrieks and the burst of diabolical laughter would ring from it over the vale, and fill the inhabitants with terror. It was supposed that this hole gave admittance to Purgatory; and the popular but faulty derivation of Hörsel was *Höre, die Seele*—Hark, the Souls!

But another popular belief respecting this mountain was, that in it Venus, the pagan Goddess of Love, held her court, in all the pomp and revelry of heathendom; and there were not a few who declared that they had seen fair forms of female beauty beckoning them from the mouth of the chasm, and that they had heard dulcet strains of music well up from the abyss above the thunder of the falling, unseen torrent. Charmed by the music, and allured by the spectral forms, various individuals had entered the cave, and none had returned, except the Tannhäuser, of whom more anon. Still does the Hörselberg go by the name of the Venusberg, a name frequently used in the middle ages, but without its locality being defined.

"In 1398, at midday, there appeared suddenly three great fires in the air, which presently ran together into one globe of flame, parted again, and finally sank into the Hörselberg," says the Thüringian Chronicle.

And now for the story of Tannhäuser.

A French knight was riding over the beauteous meadows in the Hörsel vale on his way to Wartburg, where the Landgrave Hermann was holding a gathering of minstrels, who were to contend in song for a prize.

Tannhäuser was a famous minnesinger, and all his lays were of love and of women, for his heart was full of passion, and that not of the purest and noblest description.

It was towards dusk that he passed the cliff in which is the Hörselloch, and as he rode by, he saw a white glimmering figure of matchless beauty standing before him, and beckoning him to her. He knew her at once, by her attributes and by her superhuman perfection, to be none other than Venus. As she spake to him, the sweetest strains of music floated in the air, a soft roseate light glowed around her, and nymphs of exquisite loveliness scattered roses at her feet. A thrill of passion ran through the veins of the minnesinger; and, leaving his horse, he followed the apparition. It led him up the mountain to the cave, and as it went flowers bloomed upon the soil, and a radiant track was left for Tannhäuser to follow. He entered the cavern, and descended to the palace of Venus in the heart of the mountain.

Seven years of revelry and debauch were passed, and the minstrel's heart began to feel a strange void. The beauty, the magnificence, the variety of the scenes in the pagan goddess's home, and all its heathenish pleasures, palled upon him, and he yearned for the pure fresh breezes of earth, one look up at the dark night sky spangled with stars, one glimpse of simple mountain-flowers, one tinkle of sheep-bells. At the same time his conscience began to reproach him, and he longed to make his peace with God. In vain did he entreat Venus to permit him to depart, and it was only when, in the bitterness of his grief, he called upon the Virgin-Mother, that a rift in the mountain-side appeared to him, and he stood again above ground.

How sweet was the morning air, balmy with the scent of hay, as it rolled up the mountain to him, and fanned his haggard cheek! How delightful to him was the cushion of moss and scanty grass after the downy couches of the palace of revelry below! He plucked the little heather-bells, and held them before him; the tears rolled from his eyes, and moistened his thin and wasted hands. He looked up at the soft blue sky and the newly-risen sun, and his heart overflowed. What were the golden, jewel-incrusted, lamp-lit vaults beneath to that pure dome of God's building!

The chime of a village church struck sweetly on his ear, satiated with Bacchanalian songs; and he hurried down the mountain to the church which called him. There he made his confession; but the priest, horror-struck at his recital, dared not give him absolution, but passed him on to another. And so he went from one to another, till at last he was referred to the Pope himself. To the Pope he went. Urban IV. then occupied the chair of St. Peter. To him Tannhäuser related the sickening story of his guilt, and prayed for absolution. Urban was a hard and stern man, and shocked at the immensity of the sin, he thrust the penitent indignantly from him, exclaiming, "Guilt such as thine can never, never be remitted. Sooner shall this staff in my hand grow green and blossom, than that God should pardon thee!"

Then Tannhäuser, full of despair, and with his soul darkened, went away, and returned to the only asylum open to him, the Venusberg. But lo! three days after he had gone, Urban discovered that his pastoral staff had put forth buds, and had burst into flower. Then he sent messengers after Tannhäuser, and they reached the Hörsel vale to hear that a wayworn man, with haggard brow and bowed head, had just entered the Hörselloch. Since then Tannhäuser has not been seen.

Such is the sad yet beautiful story of Tannhäuser. It is a very ancient myth Christianized, a wide-spread tradition localized. Originally heathen, it has been transformed, and has acquired new beauty by an infusion of Christianity. Scattered over Europe, it exists in various forms, but in none so graceful as that attached to the Hörselberg. There are, however, other Venusbergs in Germany; as, for instance, in Swabia, near Waldsee; another near Ufhausen, at no great distance from Freiburg (the same story is told of this Venusberg as of the Hörselberg); in Saxony there is a Venusberg not far from Wolkenstein. Paracelsus speaks of a Venusberg in Italy, referring to that in which Æneas Sylvius (Ep. 16) says Venus or a Sibyl resides, occupying a cavern, and assuming once a week the form of a serpent. Geiler v. Keysersperg, a quaint old preacher of the fifteenth century, speaks of the witches assembling on the Venusberg.

The story, either in prose or verse, has often been printed. Some of the earliest editions are the following:—

"Das Lied von dem Danhewser." Nürnberg, without date; the same, Nürnberg, 1515.—"Das Lyedt v. d. Thanheuser." Leyptzk, 1520.—"Das Lied v. d. Danheüser," reprinted by Bechstein, 1835.—"Das Lied vom edlen Tanheuser, Mons Veneris." Frankfort, 1614; Leipzig, 1668.—"Twe lede volgen Dat erste vain Danhüsser." Without date.—"Van heer Danielken." Tantwerpen, 1544.—A Danish version in "Nyerup, Danske Viser," No. VIII.

Let us now see some of the forms which this remarkable myth assumed in other countries. Every popular tale has its root, a root which may be traced among different countries, and though the accidents of the story may vary, yet the substance remains unaltered. It has been said that the common people never invent new story-radicals any more than we invent new word-roots; and this is perfectly true. The same story-root remains, but it is varied according to the temperament of the narrator or the exigencies of localization. The story-root of the Venusberg is this:—

The underground folk seek union with human beings.

a. A man is enticed into their abode, where he unites with a woman of the underground race.

b. He desires to revisit the earth, and escapes.

c. He returns again to the region below.

Now, there is scarcely a collection of folk-lore which does not contain a story founded on this root. It appears in every branch of the Aryan family, and examples might be quoted from Modern Greek, Albanian, Neapolitan, French, German, Danish, Norwegian and Swedish, Icelandic, Scotch, Welsh, and other collections of popular tales. I have only space to mention some.

There is a Norse Tháttr of a certain Helgi Thorir's son, which is, in its present form, a production of the fourteenth century. Helgi and his brother Thorstein went on a cruise to Finnmark, or Lapland. They reached a ness, and found the land covered with forest. Helgi explored this forest, and lighted suddenly on a party of red-dressed women riding upon red horses. These ladies were beautiful and of troll race. One surpassed the others in beauty, and she was their mistress. They erected a tent and prepared a feast. Helgi observed that all their vessels were of silver and gold. The lady, who named herself Ingibjorg, advanced towards the Norseman, and invited him to live with her. He feasted and lived with the trolls for three days, and then returned to his ship, bringing with him two chests of silver and gold, which Ingibjorg had given him. He had been forbidden to mention where he had been and with whom; so he told no one whence he had obtained the chests. The ships sailed, and he returned home.

One winter's night Helgi was fetched away from home, in the midst of a furious storm, by two mysterious horsemen, and no one was able to ascertain for many years what had become of him, till the prayers of the king, Olaf, obtained his release, and then he was restored to his father and brother, but he was thenceforth blind. All the time of his absence he had been with the red-vested lady in her mysterious abode of Glœsisvellir.

The Scotch story of Thomas of Ercildoune is the same story. Thomas met with a strange lady, of elfin race, beneath Eildon Tree, who led him into the underground land, where he remained with her for seven years. He then returned to earth, still, however, remaining bound to come to his royal mistress whenever she should summon him. Accordingly, while Thomas was making merry with his friends in the Tower of Ercildoune, a person came running in, and told, with marks of fear and astonishment, that a hart and a hind had left the neighboring forest, and were parading the street of the village. Thomas instantly arose, left his house, and followed the animals into the forest, from which he never returned. According to popular belief, he still "drees his weird" in Fairy Land, and is one day expected to revisit earth. (Scott, "Minstrelsy of the Scottish Border.") Compare with this the ancient ballad of Tamlane.

Debes relates that "it happened a good while since, when the burghers of Bergen had the commerce of the Faroe Isles, that there was a man in Serraade, called Jonas Soideman, who was kept by the spirits in a mountain during the space of seven years, and at length came out, but lived afterwards in great distress and fear, lest they should again take him away; wherefore people were obliged to watch him in the night." The same author mentions another young man who had been carried away, and after his return was removed a second time, upon the eve of his marriage.

Gervase of Tilbury says that "in Catalonia there is a lofty mountain, named Cavagum, at the foot of which runs a river with golden sands, in the vicinity of which there are likewise silver mines. This mountain is steep, and almost inaccessible. On its top, which is always covered with ice and snow, is a black and bottomless lake, into which if a stone be cast, a tempest suddenly arises; and near this lake is the portal of the palace of demons." He then tells how a young damsel was spirited in there, and spent seven years with the mountain spirits. On her return to earth she was thin and withered, with wandering eyes, and almost bereft of understanding.

A Swedish story is to this effect. A young man was on his way to his bride, when he was allured into a mountain by a beautiful elfin woman. With her he lived forty years, which passed as an hour; on his return to earth all his old friends and relations were dead, or had forgotten him, and finding no rest there, he returned to his mountain elf-land.

In Pomerania, a laborer's son, Jacob Dietrich of Rambin, was enticed away in the same manner.

There is a curious story told by Fordun in his "Scotichronicon," which has some interest in connection with the legend of the Tannhäuser. He relates that in the year 1050, a youth of noble birth had been married in Rome, and during the nuptial feast, being engaged in a game of ball, he took off his wedding-ring, and placed it on the finger of a statue of Venus. When he wished to resume it, he found that the stony hand had become clinched, so that it was impossible to remove the ring. Thenceforth he was haunted by the Goddess Venus, who constantly whispered in his ear, "Embrace me; I am Venus, whom you have wedded; I will never restore your ring." However, by the assistance of a priest, she was at length forced to give it up to its rightful owner.

The classic legend of Ulysses, held captive for eight years by the nymph Calypso in the Island of Ogygia, and again for one year by the enchantress Circe, contains the root of the same story of the Tannhäuser.

What may have been the significance of the primeval story-radical it is impossible for us now to ascertain; but the legend, as it shaped itself in the middle ages, is certainly indicative of the struggle between the new and the old faith.

We see thinly veiled in Tannhäuser the story of a man, Christian in name, but heathen at heart, allured by the attractions of paganism, which seems to satisfy his poetic instincts, and which gives full rein to his passions. But these excesses pall on him after a while, and the religion of sensuality leaves a great void in his breast.

He turns to Christianity, and at first it seems to promise all that he requires. But alas! he is repelled by its ministers. On all sides he is met by practice widely at variance with profession. Pride, worldliness, want of sympathy exist among those who should be the foremost to guide, sustain, and receive him. All the warm springs which gushed up in his broken heart are choked, his softened spirit is hardened again, and he returns in despair to bury his sorrows and drown his anxieties in the debauchery of his former creed.

A sad picture, but doubtless one very true.

XI. — FATALITY OF NUMBERS

The laws governing numbers are so perplexing to the uncultivated mind, and the results arrived at by calculation are so astonishing, that it cannot be matter of surprise if superstition has attached itself to numbers.

But even to those who are instructed in numeration, there is much that is mysterious and unaccountable, much that only an advanced mathematician can explain to his own satisfaction. The neophyte sees the numbers obedient to certain laws; but *why* they obey these laws he cannot understand; and the fact of his not being able so to do, tends to give to numbers an atmosphere of mystery which impresses him with awe.

For instance, the property of the number 9, discovered, I believe, by W. Green, who died in 1794, is inexplicable to any one but a mathematician. The property to which I allude is this, that when 9 is multiplied by 2, by 3, by 4, by 5, by 6, &c., it will be found that the digits composing the product, when added together, give 9. Thus:—

$$2 \times 9 = 18, \text{ and } 1 + 8 = 9$$
$$3 \times 9 = 27, \text{ " } 2 + 7 = 9$$
$$4 \times 9 = 36, \text{ " } 3 + 6 = 9$$
$$5 \times 9 = 45, \text{ " } 4 + 5 = 9$$
$$6 \times 9 = 54, \text{ " } 5 + 4 = 9$$
$$7 \times 9 = 63, \text{ " } 6 + 3 = 9$$
$$8 \times 9 = 72, \text{ " } 7 + 2 = 9$$
$$9 \times 9 = 81, \text{ " } 8 + 1 = 9$$

$10 \times 9 = 90, \; " \; 9 + 0 = 9$

It will be noticed that 9×11 makes 99, the sum of the digits of which is 18 and not 9, but the sum of the digits $1 + 8$ equals 9.

$9 \times 12 = 108$, and $1 + 0 + 8 = 9$
$9 \times 13 = 117, \; " \; 1 + 1 + 7 = 9$
$9 \times 14 = 126, \; " \; 1 + 2 + 6 = 9$

And so on to any extent.

M. de Maivan discovered another singular property of the same number. If the order of the digits expressing a number be changed, and this number be subtracted from the former, the remainder will be 9 or a multiple of 9, and, being a multiple, the sum of its digits will be 9.

For instance, take the number 21, reverse the digits, and you have 12; subtract 12 from 21, and the remainder is 9. Take 63, reverse the digits, and subtract 36 from 63; you have 27, a multiple of 9, and $2 + 7 = 9$. Once more, the number 13 is the reverse of 31; the difference between these numbers is 18, or twice 9.

Again, the same property found in two numbers thus changed, is discovered in the same numbers raised to any power.

Take 21 and 12 again. The square of 21 is 441, and the square of 12 is 144; subtract 144 from 441, and the remainder is 297, a multiple of 9; besides, the digits expressing these powers added together give 9. The cube of 21 is 9261, and that of 12 is 1728; their difference is 7533, also a multiple of 9.

The number 37 has also somewhat remarkable properties; when multiplied by 3 or a multiple of 3 up to 27, it gives in the product three digits exactly similar. From the knowledge of this the multiplication of 37 is greatly facilitated, the method to be adopted being to multiply merely the first cipher of the multiplicand by the first multiplier; it is then unnecessary to proceed with the multiplication, it being sufficient to write twice to the right hand the cipher obtained, so that the same digit will stand in the unit, tens, and hundreds places.

For instance, take the results of the following table:—

37 multiplied by 3 gives 111, and 3 times $1 = 3$
37   "   6   "   222, " 3   " $2 = 6$
37   "   9   "   333, " 3   " $3 = 9$
37   "   12   "   444, " 3   " $4 = 12$
37   "   15   "   555, " 3   " $5 = 15$
37   "   18   "   666, " 3   " $6 = 18$
37   "   21   "   777, " 3   " $7 = 21$
37   "   24   "   888, " 3   " $8 = 24$
37   "   27   "   999, " 3   " $9 = 27$

The singular property of numbers the most different, when added, to produce the same sum, originated the use of magical squares for talismans. Although the reason may be accounted for mathematically, yet numerous authors have written concerning them, as though there were something "uncanny" about them. But the most remarkable and exhaustive treatise on the subject is that by a mathematician of Dijon, which is entitled "Traité complet des Carrés magiques, pairs et impairs, simple et composés, à Bordures, Compartiments, Croix, Chassis, Équerres, Bandes détachées, &c.; suivi d'un Traité des Cubes magiques et d'un Essai sur les Cercles magiques; par M. Violle, Géomètre, Chevalier de St. Louis, avec Atlas de 54 grandes Feuilles, comprenant 400 figures." Paris, 1837. 2 vols. 8vo., the first of 593 pages, the second of 616. Price 36 fr.

I give three examples of magical squares:—

2 7 6
9 5 1
4 3 8

These nine ciphers are disposed in three horizontal lines; add the three ciphers of each line, and the sum is 15; add the three ciphers in each column, the sum is 15; add the three ciphers forming diagonals, and the sum is 15.

```
1  2  3  4
2  3  2  3
4  1  4  1
3  4  1  2
```

The sum is 10.

```
 1   7  13  19  25
18  24   5   6  12
10  11  17  23   4
22   3   9  15  16
14  20  21   2   8
```

The sum is 65.

But the connection of certain numbers with the dogmas of religion was sufficient, besides their marvellous properties, to make superstition attach itself to them. Because there were thirteen at the table when the Last Supper was celebrated, and one of the number betrayed his Master, and then hung himself, it is looked upon through Christendom as unlucky to sit down thirteen at table, the consequence being that one of the number will die before the year is out. "When I see," said Vouvenargues, "men of genius not daring to sit down thirteen at table, there is no error, ancient or modern, which astonishes me."

Nine, having been consecrated by Buddhism, is regarded with great veneration by the Moguls and Chinese: the latter bow nine times on entering the presence of their Emperor.

Three is sacred among Brahminical and Christian people, because of the Trinity of the Godhead.

Pythagoras taught that each number had its own peculiar character, virtue, and properties.

"The unit, or the monad," he says, "is the principle and the end of all; it is this sublime knot which binds together the chain of causes; it is the symbol of identity, of equality, of existence, of conservation, and of general harmony. Having no parts, the monad represents Divinity; it announces also order, peace, and tranquillity, which are founded on unity of sentiments; consequently ONE is a good principle.

"The number TWO, or the dyad, the origin of contrasts, is the symbol of diversity, or inequality, of division and of separation. TWO is accordingly an evil principle, a number of bad augury, characterizing disorder, confusion, and change.

"THREE, or the triad, is the first of unequals; it is the number containing the most sublime mysteries, for everything is composed of three substances; it represents God, the soul of the world, the spirit of man." This number, which plays so great a part in the traditions of Asia, and in the Platonic philosophy, is the image of the attributes of God.

"FOUR, or the tetrad, as the first mathematical power, is also one of the chief elements; it represents the generating virtue, whence come all combinations; it is the most perfect of numbers; it is the root of all things. It is holy by nature, since it constitutes the Divine essence, by recalling His unity, His power, His goodness, and His wisdom, the four perfections which especially characterize God. Consequently, Pythagoricians swear by the quaternary number, which gives the human soul its eternal nature.

"The number FIVE, or the pentad, has a peculiar force in sacred expiations; it is everything; it stops the power of poisons, and is redoubted by evil spirits.

"The number SIX, or the hexad, is a fortunate number, and it derives its merit from the first sculptors having divided the face into six portions; but, according to the Chaldeans, the reason is, because God created the world in six days.

"SEVEN, or the heptad, is a number very powerful for good or for evil. It belongs especially to sacred things.

"The number EIGHT, or the octad, is the first cube, that is to say, squared in all senses, as a die, proceeding from its base two, an even number; so is man four-square, or perfect.

"The number NINE, or the ennead, being the multiple of three, should be regarded as sacred.

"Finally, TEN, or the decad, is the measure of all, since it contains all the numeric relations and harmonies. As the reunion of the four first numbers, it plays an eminent part, since all the branches of science, all nomenclatures, emanate from, and retire into it."

It is hardly necessary for me here to do more than mention the peculiar character given to different numbers by Christianity. One is the numeral indicating the Unity of the Godhead; Two points to the hypostatic union; Three to the Blessed Trinity; Four to the Evangelists; Five to the Sacred Wounds; Six is the number of sin; Seven that of the gifts of the Spirit; Eight, that of the Beatitudes; Ten is the number of the commandments; Eleven speaks of the Apostles after the loss of Judas; Twelve, of the complete apostolic college.

I shall now point out certain numbers which have been regarded with superstition, and certain events connected with numbers which are of curious interest.

The number 14 has often been observed as having singularly influenced the life of Henry IV. and other French princes. Let us take the history of Henry.

On the 14th May, 1029, the first king of France named Henry was consecrated, and on the 14th May, 1610, the last Henry was assassinated.

Fourteen letters enter into the composition of the name of Henri de Bourbon, who was the 14th king bearing the titles of France and Navarre.

The 14th December, 1553, that is, 14 centuries, 14 decades, and 14 years after the birth of Christ, Henry IV. was born; the ciphers of the date 1553, when added together, giving the number 14.

The 14th May, 1554, Henry II. ordered the enlargement of the Rue de la Ferronnerie. The circumstance of this order not having been carried out, occasioned the murder of Henry IV. in that street, four times 14 years after.

The 14th May, 1552, was the date of the birth of Marguérite de Valois, first wife of Henry IV.

On the 14th May, 1588, the Parisians revolted against Henry III., at the instigation of the Duke of Guise.

On the 14th March, 1590, Henry IV. gained the battle of Ivry.

On the 14th May, 1590, Henry was repulsed from the Fauxbourgs of Paris.

On the 14th November, 1590, the Sixteen took oath to die rather than serve Henry.

On the 14th November, 1592, the Parliament registered the Papal Bull giving power to the legate to nominate a king to the exclusion of Henry.

On the 14th December, 1599, the Duke of Savoy was reconciled to Henry IV.

On the 14th September, 1606, the Dauphin, afterwards Louis XIII., was baptized.

On the 14th May, 1610, the king was stopped in the Rue de la Ferronnerie, by his carriage becoming locked with a cart, on account of the narrowness of the street. Ravaillac took advantage of the occasion for stabbing him.

Henry IV. lived four times 14 years, 14 weeks, and four times 14 days; that is to say, 56 years and 5 months.

On the 14th May, 1643, died Louis XIII., son of Henry IV.; not only on the same day of the same month as his father, but the date, 1643, when its ciphers are added together, gives the number 14, just as the ciphers of the date of the birth of his father gave 14.

Louis XIV. mounted the throne in 1643: $1 + 6 + 4 + 3 = 14$.

He died in the year 1715: $1 + 7 + 1 + 5 = 14$.

He lived 77 years, and $7 + 7 = 14$.

Louis XV. mounted the throne in the same year; he died in 1774, which also bears the stamp of 14, the extremes being 14, and the sum of the means $7 + 7$ making 14.

Louis XVI. had reigned 14 years when he convoked the States General, which was to bring about the Revolution.

The number of years between the assassination of Henry IV. and the dethronement of Louis XVI. is divisible by 14.

Louis XVII. died in 1794; the extreme digits of the date are 14, and the first two give his number.

The restoration of the Bourbons took place in 1814, also marked by the extremes being 14; also by the sum of the ciphers making 14.

The following are other curious calculations made respecting certain French kings.

Add the ciphers composing the year of the birth or of the death of some of the kings of the third race, and the result of each sum is the titular number of each prince. Thus:—

Louis IX. was born in 1215; add the four ciphers of this date, and you have IX.

Charles VII. was born in 1402; the sum of $1 + 4 + 2$ gives VII.

Louis XII. was born in 1461; and $1 + 4 + 6 + 1 = $ XII.

Henry IV. died in 1610; and $1 + 6 + 1 = $ twice IV.

Louis XIV. was crowned in 1643; and these four ciphers give XIV. The same king died in 1715; and this date gives also XIV. He was aged 77 years, and again $7 + 7 = 14$.

Louis XVIII. was born in 1755; add the digits, and you have XVIII.

What is remarkable is, that this number 18 is double the number of the king to whom the law first applies, and is triple the number of the kings to whom it has applied.

Here is another curious calculation:—

Robespierre fell in 1794;

Napoleon in 1815, and Charles X. in 1830.

Now, the remarkable fact in connection with these dates is, that the sum of the digits composing them, added to the dates, gives the date of the fall of the successor. Robespierre fell in 1794; $1 + 7 + 9 + 4 = 21$, $1794 + 21 = 1815$, the date of the fall of Napoleon; $1 + 8 + 1 + 5 = 15$, and $1815 + 15 = 1830$, the date of the fall of Charles X.

There is a singular rule which has been supposed to determine the length of the reigning Pope's life, in the earlier half of a century. Add his number to that of his predecessor, to that add ten, and the result gives the year of his death.

Pius VII. succeeded Pius VI.; $6 + 7 = 13$; add 10, and the sum is 23. Pius VII. died in 1823.

Leo XII. succeeded Pius VII.; $12 + 7 + 10 = 29$; and Leo XII. died in 1829.

Pius VIII. succeeded Leo XII.; $8 + 12 + 10 = 30$; and Pius VIII. died in 1830.

However, this calculation does not always apply.

Gregory XVI. ought to have died in 1834, but he did not actually vacate his see till 1846.

It is also well known that an ancient tradition forbids the hope of any of St. Peter's successors, *pervenire ad annos Petri*; i. e., to reign 25 years.

Those who sat longest are

	Years.	Months.	Days.
Pius VI., who reigned	24	6	14
Hadrian I. "	23	10	17
Pius VII. "	23	5	6
Alexander III. "	21	11	23
St. Silvester I. "	21	0	4

There is one numerical curiosity of a very remarkable character, which I must not omit.

The ancient Chamber of Deputies, such as it existed in 1830, was composed of 402 members, and was divided into two parties. The one, numbering 221 members, declared itself strongly for the revolution of July; the other party, numbering 181, did not favor a change. The result was the constitutional monarchy, which re-established order after the three memorable days of July. The parties were known by the following nicknames. The larger was commonly called *La queue de Robespierre*, and the smaller, *Les honnêtes gens*. Now, the remarkable fact is, that if we give to the letters of the alphabet their numerical values as they stand in their order, as 1 for A, 2 for B, 3 for C, and so on to Z, which is valued at 25, and then write vertically on the left hand the words, *La queue de Robespierre*, with the number equivalent to each letter opposite to it, and on the right hand, in like manner, *Les honnêtes gens*, if each column of numbers be summed up, the result is the number of members who formed each party.

```
1  2  3  4  5  6  7  8  9  10  11  12  13
A  B  C  D  E  F  G  H  I   J   K   L   M
14 15 16 17 18 19 20 21 22  23  24  25
N  O  P  Q  R  S  T  U  V   X   Y   Z
L—12   L—12
A— 1   E— 5
       S—19
Q—17
```

U—21 H—8
E—5 O—15
U—5 N—14
E—5 N—14
 E—5
D—4 T—20
E—5 E—5
 S—19
R—18
O—15 G—7
B—2 E—5
E—5 N—14
S—19 S—19
P—16 181
I—9
E—5
R—18
R—18
E—5
221

Majority 221
Minority 181
Total 402

Some coincidences of dates are very remarkable.

On the 25th August, 1569, the Calvinists massacred the Catholic nobles and priests at Béarn and Navarre.

On the same day of the same month, in 1572, the Calvinists were massacred in Paris and elsewhere.

On the 25th October, 1615, Louis XIII. married Anne of Austria, infanta of Spain, whereupon we may remark the following coincidences:—

The name Loys[36] de Bourbon contains 13 letters; so does the name Anne d'Austriche.

[36] Up to Louis XIII. all the kings of this name spelled Louis as Loys.

Louis was 13 years old when this marriage was decided on; Anne was the same age.

He was the thirteenth king of France bearing the name of Louis, and she was the thirteenth infanta of the name of Anne of Austria.

On the 23d April, 1616, died Shakspeare: on the same day of the same month, in the same year, died the great poet Cervantes.

On the 29th May, 1630, King Charles II. was born.

On the 29th May, 1660, he was restored.

On the 29th May, 1672, the fleet was beaten by the Dutch.

On the 29th May, 1679, the rebellion of the Covenanters broke out in Scotland.

The Emperor Charles V. was born on February 24, 1500; on that day he won the battle of Pavia, in 1525, and on the same day was crowned in 1530.

On the 29th January, 1697, M. de Broquemar, president of the Parliament of Paris, died suddenly in that city; next day his brother, an officer, died suddenly at Bergue, where he was governor. The lives of these brothers present remarkable coincidences. One day the officer, being engaged in battle, was wounded in his leg by a sword-blow. On the same day, at the same moment, the president was afflicted with acute pain, which attacked him suddenly in the same leg as that of his brother which had been injured.

John Aubrey mentions the case of a friend of his who was born on the 15th November; his eldest son was born on the 15th November; and his second son's first son on the same day of the same month.

At the hour of prime, April 6, 1327, Petrarch first saw his mistress Laura, in the Church of St. Clara in Avignon. In the same city, same month, same hour, 1348, she died.

The deputation charged with offering the crown of Greece to Prince Otho, arrived in Munich on the 13th October, 1832; and it was on the 13th October, 1862, that King Otho left Athens, to return to it no more.

On the 21st April, 1770, Louis XVI. was married at Vienna, by the sending of the ring.

On the 21st June, in the same year, took place the fatal festivities of his marriage.

On the 21st January, 1781, was the *fête* at the Hôtel de Ville, for the birth of the Dauphin.

On the 21st June, 1791, took place the flight to Varennes.

On the 21st January, 1793, he died on the scaffold.

There is said to be a tradition of Norman-monkish origin, that the number 3 is stamped on the Royal line of England, so that there shall not be more than three princes in succession without a revolution.

William I., William II., Henry I.; then followed the revolution of Stephen.

Henry II., Richard I., John; invasion of Louis, Dauphin of France, who claimed the throne.

Henry III., Edward I., Edward II., who was dethroned and put to death.

Edward III., Richard II., who was dethroned.

Henry IV., Henry V., Henry VI.; the crown passed to the house of York.

Edward IV., Edward V., Richard III.; the crown claimed and won by Henry Tudor.

Henry VII., Henry VIII., Edward VI.; usurpation of Lady Jane Grey.

Mary I., Elizabeth; the crown passed to the house of Stuart.

James I., Charles I.; Revolution.

Charles II., James II.; invasion of William of Orange.

William of Orange and Mary II., Anne; arrival of the house of Brunswick.

George I., George II., George III., George IV., William IV., Victoria. The law has proved faulty in the last case; but certainly there was a crisis in the reign of George IV.

As I am on the subject of the English princes, I will add another singular coincidence, though it has nothing to do with the fatality of numbers.

It is that Saturday has been a day of ill omen to the later kings.

William of Orange died Saturday, 18th March, 1702.

Anne died Saturday, 1st August, 1704.

George I. died Saturday, 10th June, 1727.

George II. died Saturday, 25th October, 1760.

George III. died Saturday, 30th January, 1820.

George IV. died Saturday, 26th June, 1830.

XII. — THE TERRESTRIAL PARADISE

THE exact position of Eden, and its present condition, do not seem to have occupied the minds of our Anglo-Saxon ancestors, nor to have given rise among them to wild speculations.

The map of the tenth century in the British Museum, accompanying the Periegesis of Priscian, is far more correct than the generality of maps which we find in MSS. at a later period; and Paradise does not occupy the place of Cochin China, or the isles of Japan, as it did later, after that the fabulous voyage of St. Brandan had become popular in the eleventh century.[37] The site, however, had been already indicated by Cosmas, who wrote in the seventh century, and had been specified by him as occupying a continent east of China, beyond the ocean, and still watered by the four great rivers Pison, Gihon, Hiddekel, and Euphrates, which sprang from subterranean canals. In a map of the ninth century, preserved in the Strasbourg library, the terrestrial Paradise is, however, on the Continent, placed at the extreme east of Asia; in fact, is situated in the Celestial Empire. It occupies the same position in a Turin MS., and also in a map accompanying a commentary on the Apocalypse in the British Museum.

[37] St. Brandan was an Irish monk, living at the close of the sixth century; he founded the Monastery of Clonfert, and is commemorated on May 16. His voyage seems to be founded on that of Sinbad, and is full of absurdities. It has been republished by M. Jubinal from MSS. in the Bibliothèque du Roi, Paris, 8vo. 1836; the earliest printed English edition is that of Wynkyn de Worde, London, 1516.

According to the fictitious letter of Prester John to the Emperor Emanuel Comnenus, Paradise was situated close to—within three days' journey of—his own territories, but where those territories were, is not distinctly specified.

"The River Indus, which issues out of Paradise," writes the mythical king, "flows among the plains, through a certain province, and it expands, embracing the whole province with its various windings: there are found emeralds, sapphires, carbuncles, topazes, chrysolites, onyx, beryl, sardius, and many other precious stones. There too grows the plant called Asbetos." A wonderful fountain, moreover, breaks out at the roots of Olympus, a mountain in Prester John's domain, and "from hour to hour, and day by day, the taste of this fountain varies; and its source is hardly three days' journey from Paradise, from which Adam was expelled. If any man drinks thrice of this spring, he will from that day feel no infirmity, and he will, as long as he lives, appear of the age of thirty." This Olympus is a corruption of Alumbo, which is no other than Columbo in Ceylon, as is abundantly evident from Sir John Mandeville's Travels; though this important fountain has escaped the observation of Sir Emmerson Tennant.

"Toward the heed of that forest (he writes) is the cytee of Polombe, and above the cytee is a great mountayne, also clept Polombe. And of that mount, the Cytee hathe his name. And at the foot of that Mount is a fayr welle and a gret, that hathe odour and savour of all spices; and at every hour of the day, he chaungethe his odour and his savour dyversely. And whoso drynkethe 3 times fasting of that watre of that welle, he is hool of alle maner sykenesse, that he hathe. And thei that duellen there and drynken often of that welle, thei nevere han sykenesse, and thei semen alle weys yonge. I have dronken there of 3 of 4 sithes; and zit, methinkethe, I fare the better. Some men clepen it the Welle of Youthe: for thei that often drynken thereat, semen alle weys yongly, and lyven withouten sykenesse. And men seyn, that that welle comethe out of Paradys: and therefore it is so vertuous."

Gautier de Metz, in his poem on the "Image du Monde," written in the thirteenth century, places the terrestrial Paradise in an unapproachable region of Asia, surrounded by flames, and having an armed angel to guard the only gate.

Lambertus Floridus, in a MS. of the twelfth century, preserved in the Imperial Library in Paris, describes it as "Paradisus insula in oceano in oriente:" and in the map accompanying it, Paradise is represented as an island, a little south-east of Asia, surrounded by rays, and at some distance from the main land; and in another MS. of the same library,—a mediæval encyclopædia,—under the word Paradisus is a passage which states that in the centre of Paradise is a fountain which waters the garden—that in fact described by Prester John, and that of which story-telling Sir John Mandeville declared he had "dronken 3 or 4 sithes." Close to this fountain is the Tree of Life. The temperature of the country is equable; neither frosts nor burning heats destroy the vegetation. The four rivers already mentioned rise in it. Paradise is, however, inaccessible to the traveller on account of the wall of fire which surrounds it.

Paludanus relates in his "Thesaurus Novus," of course on incontrovertible authority, that Alexander the Great was full of desire to see the terrestrial Paradise, and that he undertook his wars in the East for the express purpose of reaching it, and obtaining admission into it. He states that on his nearing Eden an old man was captured in a ravine by some of Alexander's soldiers, and they were about to conduct him to their monarch, when the venerable man said, "Go and announce to Alexander that it is in vain he seeks Paradise; his efforts will be perfectly fruitless; for the way of Paradise is the way of humility, a way of which he knows nothing. Take this stone and give it to Alexander, and say to him, 'From this stone learn what you must think of yourself.'" Now, this stone was of great value and excessively heavy, outweighing and excelling in value all other gems; but when reduced to powder, it was as light as a tuft of hay, and as worthless. By which token the mysterious old man meant, that Alexander alive was the greatest of monarchs, but Alexander dead would be a thing of nought.

That strangest of mediæval preachers, Meffreth, who got into trouble by denying the Immaculate Conception of the Blessed Virgin, in his second sermon for the Third Sunday in Advent, discusses the locality of the terrestrial Paradise, and claims St. Basil and St. Ambrose as his authorities for stating that it is situated on the top of a very lofty mountain in Eastern Asia; so lofty indeed is the mountain, that the waters of the four rivers fall in cascade down to a lake at its foot, with such a roar that the natives who live on the shores of the lake are stone-deaf. Meffreth also explains the escape of Paradise from submergence at the Deluge, on the same grounds as does the Master of Sentences (lib. 2, dist. 17, c. 5), by the mountain being so very high that the waters which rose over Ararat were only able to wash the base of the mountain of Paradise.

The Hereford map of the thirteenth century represents the terrestrial Paradise as a circular island near India, cut off from the continent not only by the sea, but also by a battlemented wall, with a gateway to the west.

Rupert of Duytz regards it as having been situated in Armenia. Radulphus Highden, in the thirteenth century, relying on the authority of St. Basil and St. Isidore of Seville, places Eden in an inaccessible region of Oriental Asia; and this was also the opinion of Philostorgus. Hugo de St. Victor, in his book "De Situ Terrarum," expresses himself thus: "Paradise is a spot in the Orient productive of all kind of woods and pomiferous trees. It contains the Tree of Life: there is neither cold nor heat there, but perpetual equable temperature. It contains a fountain which flows forth in four rivers."

Rabanus Maurus, with more discretion, says, "Many folk want to make out that the site of Paradise is in the east of the earth, though cut off by the longest intervening space of ocean or earth from all regions which man now inhabits. Consequently, the waters of the Deluge, which covered the highest points of the surface of our orb, were unable to reach it. However, whether it be there, or whether it be anywhere else, God knows; but that there *was* such a spot once, and that it was on earth, that is certain."

Jacques de Vitry ("Historia Orientalis"), Gervais of Tilbury, in his "Otia Imperialia," and many others, hold the same views, as to the site of Paradise, that were entertained by Hugo de St. Victor.

Jourdain de Sèverac, monk and traveller in the beginning of the fourteenth century, places the terrestrial Paradise in the "Third India;" that is to say, in trans-Gangic India.

Leonardo Dati, a Florentine poet of the fifteenth century, composed a geographical treatise in verse, entitled "Della Sfera;" and it is in Asia that he locates the garden:—

"Asia e le prima parte dove l'huomo
Sendo innocente stava in Paradiso."

But perhaps the most remarkable account of the terrestrial Paradise ever furnished, is that of the "Eireks Saga Vídförla," an Icelandic narrative of the fourteenth century, giving the adventures of a certain Norwegian, named Eirek, who had vowed, whilst a heathen, that he would explore the fabulous Deathless Land of pagan Scandinavian mythology. The romance is possibly a Christian recension of an ancient heathen myth; and Paradise has taken the place in it of Glœsisvellir.

According to the majority of the MSS. the story purports to be nothing more than a religious novel; but one audacious copyist has ventured to assert that it is all fact, and that the details are taken down from the lips of those who heard them from Eirek himself. The account is briefly this:—

Eirek was a son of Thrand, king of Drontheim, and having taken upon him a vow to explore the Deathless Land, he went to Denmark, where he picked up a friend of the same name as himself. They then went to Constantinople, and called upon the Emperor, who held a long conversation with them, which is duly reported, relative to the truths of Christianity and the site of the Deathless Land, which, he assures them, is nothing more nor less than Paradise.

"The world," said the monarch, who had not forgotten his geography since he left school, "is precisely 180,000 stages round (about 1,000,000 English miles), and it is not propped up on posts—not a bit!—it is supported by the power of God; and the distance between earth and heaven is 100,045 miles (another MS. reads 9382 miles—the difference is immaterial); and round about the earth is a big sea called Ocean." "And what's to the south of the earth?" asked Eirek. "O! there is the end of the world, and that is India." "And pray where am I to find the Deathless Land?" "That lies—Paradise, I suppose, you mean—well, it lies slightly east of India."

Having obtained this information, the two Eireks started, furnished with letters from the Greek Emperor.

They traversed Syria, and took ship—probably at Balsora; then, reaching India, they proceeded on their journey on horseback, till they came to a dense forest, the gloom of which was so great, through the interlacing of the boughs, that even by day the stars could be observed twinkling, as though they were seen from the bottom of a well.

On emerging from the forest, the two Eireks came upon a strait, separating them from a beautiful land, which was unmistakably Paradise; and the Danish Eirek, intent on displaying his scriptural knowledge, pronounced the strait to be the River Pison. This was crossed by a stone bridge, guarded by a dragon.

The Danish Eirek, deterred by the prospect of an encounter with this monster, refused to advance, and even endeavored to persuade his friend to give up the attempt to enter Paradise as hopeless, after that they had come within sight of the favored land. But the Norseman deliberately walked, sword in hand, into the maw of the dragon, and next moment, to his infinite surprise and delight, found himself liberated from the gloom of the monster's interior, and safely placed in Paradise.

"The land was most beautiful, and the grass as gorgeous as purple; it was studded with flowers, and was traversed by honey rills. The land was extensive and level, so that there was not to be seen mountain or hill, and the sun shone cloudless, without night and darkness; the calm of the air was great, and there was but a feeble murmur of wind, and that which there was, breathed redolent with the odor of blossoms." After a short walk, Eirek observed what certainly must have been a remarkable object, namely, a tower or steeple self-suspended in the air, without any support whatever, though access might be had to it by means of a slender ladder. By this Eirek ascended into a loft of the tower, and found there an excellent cold collation prepared for him. After having partaken of this he went to sleep, and in vision beheld and conversed with his guardian angel, who promised to conduct him back to his fatherland, but to come for him again and fetch him away from it forever at the expiration of the tenth year after his return to Dronheim.

Eirek then retraced his steps to India, unmolested by the dragon, which did not affect any surprise at having to disgorge him, and, indeed, which seems to have been, notwithstanding his looks, but a harmless and passive dragon.

After a tedious journey of seven years, Eirek reached his native land, where he related his adventures, to the confusion of the heathen, and to the delight and edification of the faithful. "And in the tenth year, and at break of day, as Eirek went to prayer, God's Spirit caught him away, and he was never seen again in this world: so here ends all we have to say of him."[38]

[38] Compare with this the death of Sir Galahad in the "Morte d'Arthur" of Sir Thomas Malory.

The saga, of which I have given the merest outline, is certainly striking, and contains some beautiful passages. It follows the commonly-received opinion which identified Paradise with Ceylon; and, indeed, an earlier Icelandic work, the "Rymbegla," indicates the locality of the terrestrial Paradise as being near India, for it speaks of the Ganges as taking its rise in the mountains of Eden. It is not unlikely that the curious history of Eirek, if not a Christianized version of a heathen myth, may contain the tradition of a real expedition to India, by one of the hardy adventurers who overran Europe, explored the north of Russia, harrowed the shores of Africa, and discovered America.

Later than the fifteenth century, we find no theories propounded concerning the terrestrial Paradise, though there are many treatises on the presumed situation of the ancient Eden. At Madrid was published a poem on the subject, entitled "Patriana decas," in 1629. In 1662 G. C. Kirchmayer, a Wittemberg professor, composed a thoughtful dissertation, "De Paradiso," which he inserted in his "Deliciæ Æstivæ." Fr. Arnoulx wrote a work on Paradise in 1665, full of the grossest absurdities. In 1666 appeared Carver's "Discourse on the Terrestrian Paradise." Bochart composed a tract on the subject; Huet wrote on it also, and his work passed through seven editions, the last dated from Amsterdam, 1701. The Père Hardouin composed a "Nouveau Traité de la Situation du Paradis Terrestre," La Haye, 1730. An Armenian work on the rivers of Paradise was translated by M. Saint Marten in 1819; and in 1842 Sir W. Ouseley read a paper on the situation of Eden, before the Literary Society in London.

THE END

The Book of Were-Wolves

I. — INTRODUCTORY

I SHALL never forget the walk I took one night in Vienne, after having accomplished the examination of an unknown Druidical relic, the Pierre labie, at La Rondelle, near Champigni. I had learned of the existence of this cromlech only on my arrival at Champigni in the afternoon, and I had started to visit the curiosity without calculating the time it would take me to reach it and to return. Suffice it to say that I discovered the venerable pile of grey stones as the sun set, and that I expended the last lights of evening in planning and sketching. I then turned my face homeward. My walk of about ten miles had wearied me, coming at the end of a long day's posting, and I had lamed myself in scrambling over some stones to the Gaulish relic.

A small hamlet was at no great distance, and I betook myself thither, in the hopes of hiring a trap to convey me to the posthouse, but I was disappointed. Few in the place could speak French, and the priest, when I applied to him, assured me that he believed there was no better conveyance in the place than a common charrue with its solid wooden wheels; nor was a riding horse to be procured. The good man offered to house me for the night; but I was obliged to decline, as my family intended starting early on the following morning.

Out spake then the mayor—"Monsieur can never go back to-night across the flats, because of the— the—" and his voice dropped; "the loups-garoux."

"He says that he must return!" replied the priest in patois. "But who will go with him?"

"Ah, ha, M. le Curé. It is all very well for one of us to accompany him, but think of the coming back alone!"

"Then two must go with him," said the priest, and you can take care of each other as you return."

"Picou tells me that he saw the were-wolf only this day se'nnight," said a peasant; "he was down by the hedge of his buckwheat field, and the sun had set, and he was thinking of coming home, when he heard a rustle on the far side of the hedge. He looked over, and there stood the wolf as big as a calf against the horizon, its tongue out, and its eyes glaring like marsh-fires. Mon Dieu! catch me going over the marais to-night. Why, what could two men do if they were attacked by that wolf-fiend?"

"It is tempting Providence," said one of the elders of the village;" no man must expect the help of God if he throws himself wilfully in the way of danger. Is it not so, M. le Curé? I heard you say as much from the pulpit on the first Sunday in Lent, preaching from the Gospel."

"That is true," observed several, shaking their heads.

"His tongue hanging out, and his eyes glaring like marsh-fires!" said the confidant of Picou.

"Mon Dieu! if I met the monster, I should run," quoth another.

"I quite believe you, Cortrez; I can answer for it that you would," said the mayor.

"As big as a calf," threw in Picou's friend.

"If the loup-garou were *only* a natural wolf, why then, you see"—the mayor cleared his throat—"you see we should think nothing of it; but, M. le Curé, it is a fiend, a worse than fiend, a man-fiend,—a worse than man-fiend, a man-wolf-fiend."

"But what is the young monsieur to do?" asked the priest, looking from one to another.

"Never mind," said I, who had been quietly listening to their patois, which I understood. "Never mind; I will walk back by myself, and if I meet the loup-garou I will crop his ears and tail, and send them to M. le Maire with my compliments."

A sigh of relief from the assembly, as they found themselves clear of the difficulty.

"Il est Anglais," said the mayor, shaking his head, as though he meant that an Englishman might face the devil with impunity.

A melancholy flat was the marais, looking desolate enough by day, but now, in the gloaming, tenfold as desolate. The sky was perfectly clear, and of a soft, blue-grey tinge; illumined by the new moon, a curve of light approaching its western bed. To the horizon reached a fen, blacked with pools of stagnant water, from which the frogs kept up an incessant trill through the summer night. Heath and fern covered the ground, but near the water grew dense masses of flag and bulrush, amongst which the light wind sighed wearily. Here and there stood a sandy knoll, capped with firs, looking like black splashes against the grey sky; not a sign of habitation anywhere; the only trace of men being the white, straight road extending for miles across the fen.

That this district harboured wolves is not improbable, and I confess that I armed myself with a strong stick at the first clump of trees through which the road dived.

This was my first introduction to were-wolves, and the circumstance of finding the superstition still so prevalent, first gave me the idea of investigating the history and the habits of these mythical creatures.

I must acknowledge that I have been quite unsuccessful in obtaining a specimen of the animal, but I have found its traces in all directions. And just as the palæontologist has constructed the labyrinthodon out of its foot-prints in marl, and one splinter of bone, so may this monograph be complete and accurate, although I have no chained were-wolf before me which I may sketch and describe from the life.

The traces left are indeed numerous enough, and though perhaps like the dodo or the dinormis, the werewolf may have become extinct in our age, yet he has left his stamp on classic antiquity, he has trodden deep in Northern snows. has ridden rough-shod over the mediævals, and has howled amongst Oriental sepulchres. He belonged to a bad breed, and we are quite content to be freed from him and his kindred, the vampire and the ghoul. Yet who knows! We may be a little too hasty in concluding that he is extinct. He may still prowl in Abyssinian forests, range still over Asiatic steppes, and be found howling dismally in some padded room of a Hanwell or a Bedlam.

In the following pages I design to investigate the notices of were-wolves to be found in the ancient writers of classic antiquity, those contained in the Northern Sagas, and, lastly, the numerous details afforded by the mediæval authors. In connection with this I shall give a sketch of modern folklore relating to Lycanthropy.

It will then be seen that under the veil of mythology lies a solid reality, that a floating superstition holds in solution a positive truth.

This I shall show to be an innate craving for blood implanted in certain natures, restrained under ordinary circumstances, but breaking forth occasionally, accompanied with hallucination, leading in most cases to cannibalism. I shall then give instances of persons thus afflicted, who were believed by others, and who believed themselves, to be transformed into beasts, and who, in the paroxysms of their madness, committed numerous murders, and devoured their victims.

I shall next give instances of persons suffering from the same passion for blood, who murdered for the mere gratification of their natural cruelty, but who were not subject to hallucinations, nor were addicted to cannibalism.

I shall also give instances of persons filled with the same propensities who murdered and ate their victims, but who were perfectly free from hallucination.

II. — LYCANTHROPY AMONG THE ANCIENTS

Definition of Lycanthropy—Marcellus Sidetes—Virgil—Herodotus—Ovid—
Pliny—Agriopas—Story from Petronius—Arcadian Legends—Explanation offered

WHAT is Lycanthropy? The change of man or woman into the form of a wolf, either through magical means, so as to enable him or her to gratify the taste for human flesh, or through judgment of the gods in punishment for some great offence.

This is the popular definition. Truly it consists in a form of madness, such as may be found in most asylums.

Among the ancients this kind of insanity went by the names of Lycanthropy, Kuanthropy, or Boanthropy, because those afflicted with it believed themselves to be turned into wolves, dogs, or cows. But in the North of Europe, as we shall see, the shape of a bear, and in

Africa that of a hyæna, were often selected in preference. A mere matter of taste! According to Marcellus Sidetes, of whose poem {Greek *perì lukanðrw'pou*} a fragment exists, men are attacked with this madness chiefly in the beginning of the year, and become most furious in February; retiring for the night to lone cemeteries, and living precisely in the manner of dogs and wolves.

Virgil writes in his eighth Eclogue:—

Has herbas, atque hæc Ponto mihi lecta venena
Ipse dedit Mris; nascuntur plurima Ponto.
His ego sæpe lupum fieri et se conducere sylvis
Mrim, sæpe animas imis excire sepulchris,
Atque satas alio, vidi traducere messes.

And Herodotus:—"It seems that the Neuri are sorcerers, if one is to believe the Scythians and the Greeks established in Scythia; for each Neurian changes himself, once in the year, into the form of a wolf, and he continues in that form for several days, after which he resumes his former shape."—(Lib. iv. c. 105.)

See also Pomponius Mela (lib. ii. c. 1) "There is a fixed time for each Neurian, at which they change, if they like, into wolves, and back again into their former condition."

But the most remarkable story among the ancients is that related by Ovid in his "Metamorphoses," of Lycaon, king of Arcadia, who, entertaining Jupiter one day, set before him a hash of human flesh, to prove his omniscience, whereupon the god transferred him into a wolf:— [*]

[*. OVID. Met. i. 237; PAUSANIAS, viii. 2, § 1; TZETZE *ad Lycoph.* 481; ERATOSTH. *Catas.* i. 8.]

In vain he attempted to speak; from that very instant
His jaws were bespluttered with foam, and only he thirsted
For blood, as he raged amongst flocks and panted for slaughter.
His vesture was changed into hair, his limbs became crooked;
A wolf,—he retains yet large trace of his ancient expression,
Hoary he is as afore, his countenance rabid,
His eyes glitter savagely still, the picture of fury.

Pliny relates from Evanthes, that on the festival of Jupiter Lycæus, one of the family of Antæus was selected by lot, and conducted to the brink of the Arcadian lake. He then hung his clothes on a tree and plunged into the water, whereupon he was transformed into a wolf. Nine years after, if he had not tasted human flesh, he was at liberty to swim back and resume his former shape, which had in the meantime become aged, as though he had worn it for nine years.

Agriopas relates, that Demænetus, having assisted at an Arcadian human sacrifice to Jupiter Lycæus, ate of the flesh, and was at once transformed into a wolf, in which shape he prowled about for ten years, after which he recovered his human form, and took part in the Olympic games.

The following story is from Petronius:—

"My master had gone to Capua to sell some old clothes. I seized the opportunity, and persuaded our guest to bear me company about five miles out of town; for he was a soldier, and as bold as death. We set out about cockcrow, and the moon shone bright as day, when, coming among some monuments. my man began to converse with the stars, whilst I jogged along singing and counting them. Presently I looked back after him, and saw him strip and lay his clothes by the side of the road. My heart was in my mouth in an instant, I stood like a corpse; when, in a crack, he was turned into a wolf. Don't think I'm joking: I would not tell you a lie for the finest fortune in the world.

"But to continue: after he was turned into a wolf, he set up a howl and made straight for the woods. At first I did not know whether I was on my head or my heels; but at last going to take up his clothes, I found them turned into stone. The sweat streamed from me, and I never expected to get over it. Melissa began to wonder why I walked so late. 'Had you come a little sooner,' she said, 'you might at least have lent us a hand; for a wolf broke into the farm and has butchered all our cattle; but though be got off, it was no laughing matter for him, for a servant of ours ran him through with a pike. Hearing this I could not close an eye; but as soon as it was daylight, I ran home like a pedlar that has been eased of his pack. Coming to the place where the clothes had been turned into stone, I saw nothing but a pool of blood; and when I got home, I found my soldier lying in bed, like an ox in a stall, and a surgeon dressing his neck. I saw at once that he was a fellow who could change his skin (*versipellis*), and never after could I eat bread with him, no, not if you would have killed me. Those who would have taken a different view of the case are welcome to their opinion; if I tell you a lie, may your genii confound me!"

As every one knows, Jupiter changed himself into a bull; Hecuba became a bitch; Actæon a stag; the comrades of Ulysses were transformed into swine; and the daughters of Prtus fled through the fields believing themselves to be cows, and would not allow any one to come near them, lest they should be caught and yoked.

S. Augustine declared, in his *De Civitate Dei*, that he knew an old woman who was said to turn men into asses by her enchantments.

Apuleius has left us his charming romance of the *Golden Ass*, in which the hero, through injudicious use of a magical salve, is transformed into that long-eared animal.

It is to be observed that the chief seat of Lycanthropy was Arcadia, and it has been very plausibly suggested that the cause might he traced to the following circumstance:—The natives were a pastoral people, and would consequently suffer very severely from the attacks and depredations of wolves. They would naturally institute a sacrifice to obtain deliverance from this pest, and security for their flocks. This sacrifice consisted in the offering of a child, and it was instituted by Lycaon. From the circumstance of the sacrifice being human, and from the peculiarity of the name of its originator, rose the myth.

But, on the other hand, the story is far too widely spread for us to attribute it to an accidental origin, or to trace it to a local source.

Half the world believes, or believed in, were-wolves, and they were supposed to haunt the Norwegian forests by those who had never remotely been connected with Arcadia: and the superstition had probably struck deep its roots into the Scandinavian and Teutonic minds, ages before Lycaon existed; and we have only to glance at Oriental literature, to see it as firmly engrafted in the imagination of the Easterns.

III. — THE WERE-WOLF IN THE NORTH

Norse Traditions—Manner in which the Change was effected—Vlundar Kvda—
Instances from the Völsung Saga—Hrolf's Saga—Kraka—Faroëse Poem—
Helga Kvida—Vatnsdæla Saga—Eyrbyggja Saga

IN Norway and Iceland certain men were said to be *eigi einhamir*, not of one skin, an idea which had its roots in paganism. The full form of this strange superstition was, that men could take upon them other bodies, and the natures of those beings whose bodies they assumed. The second adopted shape was called by the same name as the original shape,*hamr*, and the expression made use of to designate the transition from one body to another, was at *skipta hömum*, or *at hamaz*; whilst the expedition made in the second form, was the hamför. By this transfiguration extraordinary powers were acquired; the natural strength of the individual was doubled, or quadrupled; he acquired the strength of the beast in whose body he travelled, in addition to his own, and a man thus invigorated was called *hamrammr*.

The manner in which the change was effected, varied. At times, a dress of skin was cast over the body, and at once the transformation was complete; at others, the human body was deserted, and the soul entered the second form, leaving the first body in a cataleptic state, to all appearance dead. The second hamr was either borrowed or created for the purpose. There was yet a third manner of producing this effect-it was by incantation; but then the form of the individual remained unaltered, though the eyes of all beholders were charmed so that they could only perceive him under the selected form.

Having assumed some bestial shape, the man who is *eigi einhammr* is only to be recognized by his eyes, which by no power can be changed. He then pursues his course, follows the instincts of the beast whose body he has taken, yet without quenching his own intelligence. He is able to do what the body of the animal can do, and do what he, as man, can do as well. He may fly or swim, if be is in the shape of bird or fish; if he has taken the form of a wolf, or if he goes on a *gandreið*, or wolf's-ride, he is fall of the rage and malignity of the creatures whose powers and passions he has assumed.

I will give a few instances of each of the three methods of changing bodies mentioned above. Freyja and Frigg had their falcon dresses in which they visited different regions of the earth, and Loki is said to have borrowed these, and to have then appeared so precisely like a falcon, that he would have escaped detection, but for the malicious twinkle of his eyes. In the Vælundar kviða is the following passage:—

I. I.
Meyjar flugu sunnan
Myrkvið igögnum

Alvitr unga
Orlög drýgja;
þær á savarströnd
Settusk at hvilask,
Dró sir suðrnar
Dýrt lín spunnu.   From the south flew the maidens
Athwart the gloom,
Alvit the young,
To fix destinies;
They on the sea-strand
Sat them to rest,
These damsels of the south
Fair linen spun.
II. II.
Ein nam þeirra
Egil at verja
Fögr mær fíra
Faðmi ljósum;
Önnur var Svanhvít,
Svanfjaðrar dró;
En in þriðja
þeirra systir
Var i hvítan
Háls Völundar.   One of them took
Egil to press,
Fair maid, in her
Dazzling arms.
Another was Svanhwit,
Who wore swan feathers;
And the third,
Their sister,
Pressed the white
Neck of Vlund.

The introduction of Smund tells us that these charming young ladies were caught when they had laid their swan-skins beside them on the shore, and were consequently not in a condition to fly.

In like manner were wolves' dresses used. The following curious passage is from the wild Saga of the Völsungs:—

"It is now to be told that Sigmund thought Sinfjötli too young to help him in his revenge, and he wished first to test his powers; so during the summer they plunged deep into the wood and slew men for their goods, and Sigmund saw that he was quite of the Völsung stock. . . . Now it fell out that as they went through the forest, collecting monies, that they lighted on a house in which were two men sleeping, with great gold rings an them; they had dealings with witchcraft, for wolf-skins hung up in the house above them; it was the tenth day on which they might come out of their second state. They were kings' sons. Sigmund and Sinfjötli got into the habits, and could not get out of them again, and the nature of the original beasts came over them, and they howled as wolves—they learned "both of them to howl. Now they went into the forest, and each took his own course; they made the agreement together that they should try their strength against as many as seven men, but not more, and. that he who was ware of strife should utter his wolf's howl.

"'Do not fail in this,' said Sigmund, 'for you are young and daring, and men would be glad to chase you.' Now each went his own course; and after that they had parted Sigmund found men, so he howled; and when Sinfjötli heard that, he ran up and slew them all-then they separated. And Sinfjötli had not been long in the wood before he met with. eleven men; he fell upon them and slew them every one. Then he was tired, so he flung himself under an oak to rest. Up came Sigmund and said, 'Why did you not call out?' Sinfjötli replied, 'What was the need of asking your help to kill eleven men?'

"Sigmund flew at him and rent him so that he fell, for he had bitten through his throat. That day they could not leave their wolf-forms. Sigmund laid him on his back and bare him home to the hall, and sat beside him, and said, 'Deuce take the wolf-forms!'"—Völsung Saga, c. 8.

There is another curious story of a were-wolf in the same Saga, which I must relate.

"Now he did as she requested, and hewed down a great piece of timber, and cast it across the feet of those ten brothers seated in a row, in the forest; and there they sat all that day and on till night. And at midnight there came an old she-wolf out of the forest to them, as they sat in the stocks, and she was both huge and grimly. Now she fell upon one of them, and bit him to death, and after she had eaten him all up, she went away. And next morning Signy sent a trusty man to her brothers, to know how it had fared with them. When he returned he told her of the death of one, and that grieved her much, for she feared it might fare thus with them all, and she would be unable to assist them.

"In short, nine nights following came the same she-wolf at midnight, and devoured them one after another till all were dead, except Sigmund, and he was left alone. So when the tenth night came, Signy sent her trusty man to Sigmund, her brother, with honey in his hand, and said that he was to smear it over the face of Sigmund, and to fill his mouth with it. Now he went to Sigmund, and did as he was bid, after which he returned home. And during the night came the same she-wolf, as was her wont, and reckoned to devour him, like his brothers.

"Now she snuffed at him, where the honey was smeared, and began to lick his face with her tongue, and presently thrust her tongue into his mouth. He bore it ill, and bit into the tongue of the she-wolf; she sprang up and tried to break loose, setting her feet against the stock, so as to snap it asunder: but he held firm, and ripped the tongue out by the roots, so that it was the death of the wolf. It is the opinion of some men that this beast was the mother of King Siggeir, and that she had taken this form upon her through devilry and witchcraft."—(c. 5.)

There is another story bearing on the subject in the Hrolfs Saga Kraka, which is pretty; it is as follows:—

"In the north of Norway, in upland-dales, reigned a king called Hring; and he had a son named Björn. Now it fell out that the queen died, much lamented by the king, and by all. The people advised him to marry again, and so be sent men south to get him a wife. A gale and fierce storm fell upon them, so that they had to turn the helm, and run before the wind, and so they came north to Finnmark, where they spent the winter. One day they went inland, and came to a house in which sat two beautiful women, who greeted them well, and inquired whence they had come. They replied by giving an account of their journey and their errand, and then asked the women who they were, and why they were alone, and far from the haunts of men, although they were so comely and engaging. The elder replied—that her name was Ingibjorg, and that her daughter was called Hvit, and that she was the Finn king's sweetheart. The messengers decided that they would return home, if Hvit would come with them and marry King Hring. She agreed, and they took her with them and met the king who was pleased with her, and had his wedding feast made, and said that he cared not though she was not rich. But the king was very old, and that the queen soon found out.

"There was a Carle who had a farm not far from the king's dwelling; he had a wife, and a daughter, who was but a child, and her name was Bera; she was very young and lovely. Björn the king's son, and Bera the Carle's daughter, were wont, as children, to play together, and they loved each other well. The Carle was well to do, he had been out harrying in his young days, and he was a doughty champion. Björn and Bera loved each other more and more, and they were often together.

"Time passed, and nothing worth relating occurred; but Björn, the king's son, waxed strong and tall; and he was well skilled in all manly exercises.

"King Hring was often absent for long, harrying foreign shores, and Hvit remained at home and governed the land. She was not liked of the people. She was always very pleasant with Björn, but he cared little for her. It fell out once that the King Hring went abroad, and he spake with his queen that Björn should remain at home with her, to assist in the government, for he thought it advisable, the queen being haughty and inflated with pride.

"The king told his son Björn that he was to remain at home, and rule the land with the queen; Björn replied that he disliked the plan, and that he had no love for the queen; but the king was inflexible, and left the land with a great following. Björn walked home after his conversation with the king, and went up to his place, ill-pleased and red as blood. The queen came to speak with him, and to cheer him; and spake friendly with him, but he bade her be of. She obeyed him that time. She often came to talk with him, and said how much pleasanter it was for them to be together, than to have an old fellow like Hring in the house.

"Björn resented this speech, and struck her a box in the ear, and bade her depart, and he spurned her from him. She replied that this was ill-done to drive and thrust her away: and 'You think it better, Björn, to sweetheart a Carle's daughter, than to have my love and favour, a fine piece of condescension and a disgrace it is to you! But, before long, something will stand in the way of your fancy, and your folly.' Then she struck at him with a wolf-skin glove, and said, that he should become a rabid and grim wild bear; and 'You shall eat nothing but your father's sheep, which you shall slay for your food, and never shall you leave this state.'

After that, Björn disappeared, and none knew what had become of him; and men sought but found him not, as was to be expected. We must now relate how that the king's sheep were slaughtered, half a score at a time, and it was all the work of a grey bear, both huge and grimly.

"One evening it chanced that the Carle's daughter saw this savage bear coming towards her, looking tenderly at her, and she fancied that she recognized the eyes of Björn, the king's son, so she made a slight attempt to escape; then the beast retreated, but she followed it, till she came to a cave. Now when she entered the cave there stood before her a man, who greeted Bera, the Carle's daughter; and she recognized him, for he was Björn, Hring's son. Overjoyed were they to meet. So they were together in the cave awhile, for she would not part from him when she had the chance of being with him; but he said that this was not proper that she should be there by him, for by day he was a beast, and by night a man.

"Hring returned from his harrying, and he was told the news, of what had taken place during his absence; how that Björn, his son, had vanished, and also, how that a monstrous beast was up the country, and was destroying his flocks. The queen urged the king to have the beast slain, but he delayed awhile.

"One night, as Bera and Björn were together, he said to her:—'Methinks to-morrow will be the day of my death, for they will come out to hunt me down. But for myself I care not, for it is little pleasure to live with this charm upon me, and my only comfort is that we are together; but now our union must be broken. I will give you the ring which is under my left hand. You will see the troop of hunters to-morrow coming to seek me; and when I am dead go to the king, and ask him to give you what is under the beast's left front leg. He will consent.'

"He spoke to her of many other things, till the bear's form stole over him, and he went forth a bear. She followed him, and saw that a great body of hunters had come over the mountain ridges, and had a number of dogs with them. The bear rushed away from the cavern, but the dogs and the king's men came upon him, and there was a desperate struggle. He wearied many men before he was brought to bay, and had slain all the dogs. But now they made a ring about him, and he ranged around it., but could see no means of escape, so he turned to where the king stood, and he seized a man who stood next him, and rent him asunder; then was the bear so exhausted that he cast himself down flat, and, at once, the men rushed in upon him and slew him. The Carle's daughter saw this, and she went up to the king, and said,—'Sire! wilt thou grant me that which is under the bear's left fore-shoulder?' The king consented. By this time his men had nearly flayed the bear; Bera went up and plucked away the ring, and kept it, but none saw what she took, nor had they looked for anything. The king asked her who she was, and she gave a name, but not her true name.

"The king now went home, and Bera was in his company. The queen was very joyous, and treated her well, and asked who she was; but Bera answered as before.

"The queen now made a great feast, and had the bear's flesh cooked for the banquet. The Carle's daughter was in the bower of the queen, and could not escape, for the queen had a suspicion who she was. Then she came to Bera with a dish, quite unexpectedly, and on it was bear's flesh, and she bade Bera eat it. She would not do so. 'Here is a marvel!' said the queen; 'you reject the offer which a queen herself deigns to make to you. Take it at once, or something worse will befall you.' She bit before her, and she ate of that bite; the queen cut another piece, and looked into her mouth; she saw that one little grain of the bite had gone down, but Bera spat out all the rest from her mouth, and said she would take no more, though she were tortured or killed.

"'Maybe you have had sufficient,' said the queen, and she laughed."—(Hrolfs Saga Kraka, c. 24-27, condensed.)

In the Faroëse song of Finnur hin friði, we have the following verse:—

Hegar íð Finnur hetta sær,	When this peril Finn saw,
Mannspell var at meini,	That witchcraft did him harm,
Skapti hann seg í varglíki:	ᴉen he changed himself into a wer
.....	wolf:
Hann feldi allvæl fleiri.	.....
	He slew many thus.

The following is from the second Kviða of Helga Hundingsbana (stroph. 31):—

May the blade bite,
Which thou brandishest
Only on thyself,
when it Chimes on thy head.
Then avenged will be
The death of Helgi,
When thou, as a wolf,
Wanderest in the woods,
Knowing nor fortune
Nor any pleasure,
Haying no meat,
Save rivings of corpses.

In all these cases the change is of the form: we shall now come to instances in which the person who is changed has a double shape, and the soul animates one after the other.

The Ynglinga Saga (c. 7) says of Odin, that "he changed form; the bodies lay as though sleeping or dead, but he was a bird or a beast, a fish, or a woman, and went in a twinkling to far distant lands, doing his own or other people's business." In like manner the Danish king Harold sent a warlock to Iceland in the form of a whale, whilst his body lay stiff and stark at home. The already quoted Saga of Hrolf Krake gives us another example, where Bödvar Bjarki, in the shape of a huge bear, fights desperately with the enemy, which has surrounded the hall of his king, whilst his human body lies drunkenly beside the embers within.

In the Vatnsdæla Saga, there is a curious account of three Finns, who were shut up in a hut for three nights, and ordered by Ingimund, a Norwegian chief, to visit Iceland and inform him of the lie of the country, where he was to settle. Their bodies became rigid, and they sent their souls the errand, and, on their awaking at the end of three days, gave an accurate description of the Vatnsdal, in which Ingimund was eventually to establish himself. But the Saga does not relate whether these Finns projected their souls into the bodies of birds or beasts.

The third manner of transformation mentioned, was that in which the individual was not changed himself, but the eyes of others were bewitched, so that they could not detect him, but saw him only under a certain form. Of this there are several examples in the Sagas; as, for instance, in the Hromundar Saga Greypsonar, and in the Fostbræðra Saga. But I will translate the most curious, which is that of Odd, Katla's son, in the Eyrbyggja Saga.—(c. 20.)

"Geirrid, housewife in Mafvahlið, sent word into Bolstad, that she was ware of the fact that Odd, Katla's son, had hewn off Aud's hand.

"Now when Thorarinn and Arnkell heard that, they rode from home with twelve men. They spent the night in Mafvahlið, and rode on next morning to Holt: and Odd was the only man in the house.

"Katla sat on the high seat spinning yarn, and she bade Odd sit beside her; also, she bade her women sit each in her place, and hold their tongues. 'For,' said she, 'I shall do all the talking.' Now when Arnkell and his company arrived, they walked straight in, and when they came into the chamber, Katla greeted Arnkell, and asked the news. He replied that there was none, and he inquired after Odd. Katla said that he had gone to Breidavik. 'We shall ransack the house though,' quoth Arnkell. 'Be it so,' replied Katla, and she ordered a girl to carry a light before them, and unlock the different parts of the house. All they saw was Katla spinning yarn off her distaff. Now they search the house, but find no Odd, so they depart. But when they had gone a little way from the garth, Arnkell stood still and said: 'How know we but that Katla has hoodwinked us, and that the distaff in her hand was nothing more than Odd.' 'Not impossible!' said Thorarinn; 'let us turn back.' They did so; and when those at Holt raw that they were returning, Katla said to her maids, 'Sit still in your places, Odd and I shall go out.'

"Now as they approached the door, she went into the porch, and began to comb and clip the hair of her son Odd. Arnkell came to the door and saw where Katla was, and she seemed to be stroking her goat, and disentangling its mane and beard and smoothing its wool. So he and his men went into the house, but found not Odd. Katla's distaff lay against the bench, so they thought that it could not have been Odd, and they went away. However, when they had come near the spot where they had turned before, Arnkell said, 'Think you not that Odd may have been in the goat's form?' 'There is no saying,' replied Thorarinn; 'but if we turn back we will lay hands on Katla.' 'We can try our luck again,' quoth Arnkell; 'and see what comes of it.' So they returned.

"Now when they were seen on their way back, Katla bade Odd follow her; and she lea him to the ash-heap, and told him to lie there and not to stir on any account. But when Arnkell, and his men came to the farm, they rushed into the chamber, and saw Katla seated in her place, spinning. She greeted them and said that their visits followed with rapidity. Arnkell replied that what she said was true. His comrades took the distaff and cut it in twain. 'Come now!' said Katla, 'you cannot say, when you get home, that you have done nothing, for you have chopped up my distaff.' Then Arnkell and the rest hunted high and low for Odd, but could not find him; indeed they saw nothing living about the place, beside a boar-pig which lay under the ash-heap, so they went away once more.

"Well, when they got half-way to Mafvahlið, came Geirrid to meet them, with her workmen. 'They had not gone the right way to work in seeking Odd,' she said, 'but she would help them.' So they turned back again. Geirrid had a blue cloak on her. Now when the party was seen and reported to Katla, and it was said that they were thirteen in number, and one had on a coloured dress, Katla exclaimed, 'That troll Geirrid is come! I shall not be able to throw a glamour over their eyes any more.' She started up from her place and lifted the cushion of the seat, and there was a hole and a cavity beneath: into this she thrust Odd, clapped the cushion over him, and sat down, saying she felt sick at heart.

"Now when they came into the room, there were small greetings. Geirrid cast of her the cloak and went up to Katla, and took the seal-skin bag which she had in her hand, and drew it over the head of Katla. [*] Then Geirrid bade them break up the seat. They did so, and found Odd. Him they took and carried to Buland's head, where they hanged him. . . . But Katla they stoned to death under the headland."

[* A precaution against the "evil eye." Compare *Gisla Saga Surssonnar*, p. 34. *Laxdœla Saga*, cc. 37, 38.]

IV. — THE ORIGIN OF THE SCANDINAVIAN WERE-WOLF

Advantage of the Study of Norse Literature—Bear and Wolf-skin Dresses—
The Berserkir—Their Rage—The Story of Thorir—Passages from the Aigla—
The Evening Wolf—Skallagrim and his Son-Derivation of the Word "Hamr:" of
"Vargr"—Laws affecting Outlaws—"To become a Boar"—Recapitulation

ONE of the great advantages of the study of old Norse or Icelandic literature is the insight given by it into the origin of world-wide superstitions. Norse tradition is transparent as glacier ice, and its origin is as unmistakable.

Mediæval mythology, rich and gorgeous, is a compound like Corinthian brass, into which many pure ores have been fused, or it is a full turbid river drawn from numerous feeders, which had their sources in remote climes. It is a blending of primæval Keltic, Teutonic, Scandinavian, Italic, and Arab traditions, each adding a beauty, each yielding a charm, bat each accretion rendering the analysis more difficult.

Pacciuchelli says:—"The Anio flows into the Tiber; pure as crystal it meets the tawny stream, and is lost in it, so that there is no more Anio, but the united stream is all Tiber." So is it with each tributary to the tide of mediæval mythology. The moment it has blended its waters with the great and onward rolling flood, it is impossible to detect it with certainty; it has swollen the stream, but has lost its own identity. If we would analyse a particular myth, we must not go at once to the body of mediæval superstition, but strike at one of the tributaries before its absorption. This we shall proceed to do, and in selecting Norse mythology, we come upon abundant material, pointing naturally to the spot whence it has been derived, as glacial moraines indicate the direction which they have taken, and point to the mountains whence they have fallen. It will not be difficult for us to arrive at the origin of the Northern belief in were-wolves, and the data thus obtained will be useful in assisting us to elucidate much that would otherwise prove obscure in mediæval tradition.

Among the old Norse, it was the custom for certain warriors to dress in the skins of the beasts they had slain, and thus to give themselves an air of ferocity, calculated to strike terror into the hearts of their foes.

Such dresses are mentioned in some Sagas, without there being any supernatural qualities attached to them. For instance, in the Njála there is mention of a man *i geitheðni*, in goatskin dress. Much in the same way do we hear of Harold Harfagr having in his company a band of berserkir, who were all dressed in wolf-skins, *ulfheðnir*, and this expression, wolf-skin coated, is met with as a man's name. Thus in the Holmverja Saga, there is mention of a Björn, "son of *Ulfheðin*, wolfskin coat, son of *Ulfhamr*, wolf-shaped, son of *Ulf*, wolf, son of *Ulfhamr*, wolf-shaped, who could change forms."

But the most conclusive passage is in the Vatnsdæla Saga, and is as follows:—"Those berserkir who were called *ulfheðnir*, had got wolf-skins over their mail coats" (c. xvi.) In like manner the word *berserkr*, used of a man possessed of superhuman powers, and subject. to accesses of diabolical fury, was originally applied to one of those doughty champions who went about in bear-sarks, or habits made of bear-skin over their armour. I am well aware that Björn Halldorson's derivation of berserkr, bare of sark, or destitute of clothing, has been hitherto generally received, but Sveibjörn Egilsson, an indisputable authority, rejects this derivation as untenable, and substitutes for it that which I have adopted.

It may be well imagined that a wolf or a bear-skin would make a warm and comfortable great-coat to a man, whose manner of living required him to defy all weathers, and that the dress would not only give him an appearance of grimness and ferocity, likely to produce an unpleasant emotion in the breast of a foe, but also that the thick fur might prove effectual in deadening the blows rained on him in conflict.

The berserkr was an object of aversion and terror to the peaceful inhabitants of the land, his avocation being to challenge quiet country farmers to single combat. As the law of the land stood in Norway, a man who declined to accept a challenge, forfeited all his possessions, even to the wife of his bosom, as a poltroon unworthy of the protection of the law, and every item of his property passed into the hands of his challenger. The berserkr accordingly had the unhappy man at his mercy. If he slew him, the farmer's possessions became his, and if the poor fellow declined to fight, he lost all legal right to his inheritance. A berserkr would invite himself to any feast, and contribute his quota to the hilarity of the entertainment, by snapping the backbone, or cleaving the skull, of some merrymaker who incurred his displeasure, or whom he might single out to murder, for no other reason than a desire to keep his hand in practice.

It may well be imagined that popular superstition went along with the popular dread of these wolf-and-bear-skinned rovers, and that they were believed to be endued with the force, as they certainly were with the ferocity, of the beasts whose skins they wore.

Nor would superstition stop there, but the imagination of the trembling peasants would speedily invest these unscrupulous disturbers of the public peace with the attributes hitherto appropriated to trolls and jötuns.

The incident mentioned in the Völsung Saga, of the sleeping men being found with their wolf-skins hanging to the wall above their heads, is divested of its improbability, if we regard these skins as worn over their armour, and the marvellous in the whole story is reduced to a minimum, when we suppose that Sigmund and Sinfjötli stole these for the purpose of disguising themselves, whilst they lived a life of violence and robbery.

In a similar manner the story of the northern "Beauty and Beast," in Hrolf's Saga Kraka, is rendered less improbable, on the supposition that Björn was living as an outlaw among the mountain fastnesses in a bearskin dress, which would effectually disguise him—*all but his eyes*—which would gleam out of the sockets in his hideous visor, unmistakably human. His very name, Björn, signifies a bear; and these two circumstances may well have invested a kernel of historic fact with all the romance of fable; and if divested of these supernatural embellishments, the story would resolve itself into the very simple fact of there having been a King Hring of the Updales, who was at variance with his son, and whose son took to the woods, and lived a berserkr life, in company with his mistress, till he was captured and slain by his father.

I think that the circumstance insisted on by the Saga-writers, of the eyes of the person remaining unchanged, is very significant, and points to the fact that the skin was merely drawn over the body as a disguise.

But there was other ground for superstition to fasten on the berserkir, and invest them with supernatural attributes.

No fact in connection with the history of the Northmen is more firmly established, on reliable evidence, than that of the berserkr rage being a species of diabolical possession. The berserkir were said to work themselves up into a state of frenzy, in which a demoniacal power came over them, impelling them to acts from which in their sober senses they would have recoiled. They acquired superhuman force, and were as invulnerable and as insensible to pain as the Jansenist convulsionists of S. Medard. No sword would wound them, no fire would barn them, a club alone could destroy them, by breaking their bones, or crushing in their skulls. Their eyes glared as though a flame burned in the sockets, they ground their teeth, and frothed at the mouth; they gnawed at their shield rims, and are said to have sometimes bitten them through, and as they rushed into conflict they yelped as dogs or howled as wolves. [*]

[* Hic (Syraldus) septem filios habebat, tanto veneficiorum usu callentes, ut sæpe subitis furoris viribus instincti solerent ore torvum infremere, scuta morsibus attrectare, torridas fauce prunas absumere, extructa quævis incendia penetrare, nec posset conceptis dementiæ motus alio remedii genere quam aut vinculorum injuriis aut cædis humanæ piaculo temperari. Tantam illis rabiem site sævitia ingenii sive furiaram ferocitas inspirabat.—*Saxo Gramm*. VII.]

According to the unanimous testimony of the old Norse historians, the berserkr rage was extinguished by baptism, and as Christianity advanced, the number of these berserkir decreased.

But it must not be supposed that this madness or possession came only on those persons who predisposed themselves to be attacked by it; others were afflicted with it, who vainly struggled against its influence, and who deeply lamented their own liability to be seized with these terrible accesses of frenzy. Such was Thorir Ingimund's son, of whom it is said, in the *Vatnsdæla Saga*, that "at times there came over Thorir berserkr fits, and it was considered a sad misfortune to such a man, as they were quite beyond control."

The manner in which he was cured is remarkable; pointing as it does to the craving in the heathen mind for a better and more merciful creed:—

"Thorgrim of Kornsá had a child by his concubine Vereydr, and, by order of his wife, the child was carried out to perish.

"The brothers (Thorsteinn and Thorir) often met, and it was now the turn of Thorsteinn to visit Thorir, and Thorir accompanied him homeward. On their way Thorsteinn asked Thorir which he thought was the first among the brethren; Thorir answered that the reply was easy, for 'you are above us all in discretion and talent; Jökull is the best in all perilous adventures, but I,' he added, 'I am the least worth of us brothers, because the berserkr fits come over me, quite against my will, and I wish that you, my brother, with your shrewdness, would devise some help for me.'

"Thorsteinn said,—'I have heard that our kinsman, Thorgrim, has just suffered his little babe to be carried out, at the instigation of his wife. That is ill done. I think also that it is a grievous matter for you to be different in nature from other men.'

"Thorir asked how he could obtain release from his affliction . . . . Then said Thorsteinn, 'Now will I make a vow to Him who created the sun, for I ween that he is most able to take the ban of you, and I will undertake for His sake, in return, to rescue the babe and to bring it up for him, till He who created man shall take it to Himself-for this I reckon He will do!' After this they left their horses and sought the child, and a thrall of Thorir had found it near the Marram river. They saw that a kerchief had been spread over its face, but it had rumpled it up over its nose; the little thing was all but dead, but they took it up and flitted it home to Thorir's house, and he brought the lad up, and called him Thorkell Rumple; as for the berserkr fits, they came on him no more." (c. 37)

But the most remarkable passages bearing on our subject will be found in the *Aigla*.

There was a man, Ulf (the wolf) by name, son of Bjálfi and Hallbera. Ulf was a man so tall and strong that the like of him was not to be seen in the land at that time. And when he was young he was out viking expeditions and harrying . . . He was a great landed proprietor. It was his wont to rise early, and to go about the men's work, or to the smithies, and inspect all his goods and his acres; and sometimes he talked with those men who wanted his advice; for he was a good adviser, he was so clear-headed; however, every day, when it drew towards dusk, he became so savage that few dared exchange a word with him, for he was given to dozing in the afternoon.

"People said that he was much given to changing form (*hamrammr*), so he was called the evening-wolf, *kveldúlfr*."—(c. 1.) In this and the following passages, I do not consider *hamrammr* to have its primary signification of actual transformation, but simply to mean subject to fits of diabolical possession, under the influence of which the bodily powers were greatly exaggerated. I shall translate pretty freely from this most interesting Saga, as I consider that the description given in it of Kveldulf in his fits greatly elucidates our subject.

"Kveldulf and Skallagrim got news during summer of an expedition. Skallagrim. was the keenest-sighted of men, and he caught sight of the vessel of Hallvard and his brother, and recognized it at once. He followed their course and marked the haven into which they entered at even. Then he returned to his company, and told Kveldulf of what he had seen . . . . Then they busked them and got ready both their boats; in each they put twenty men, Kveldulf steering one and Skallagrim the other, and they rowed in quest of the ship. Now when they came to the place where it was, they lay to. Hallvard and his men had spread an awning over the deck, and were asleep. Now when Kveldulf and his party came upon them, the watchers who were seated at the end of the bridge sprang up and called to the people on board to wake up, for there was danger in the wind. So Hallvard and his men sprang to arms. Then came Kveldulf over the bridge and Skallagrim with him into the ship. Kveldulf had in his hand a cleaver, and he bade his men go through the vessel and hack away the awning. But he pressed on to the quarter-deck. It is said the were-wolf fit came over him and many of his companions. They slow all the men who were before them. Skallagrim did the same as he went round the vessel. He and his father paused not till they had cleared it. Now when Kveldulf came upon the quarter-deck he raised his cleaver, and smote Hallvard through helm and head, so that the haft was buried in the flesh; but he dragged it to him so violently that he whisked Hallvard into the air., and flung him overboard. Skallagrim cleared the forecastle and slew Sigtrygg. Many men flung themselves overboard, but Skallagrim's men took to the boat and rowed about, killing all they found. Thus perished Hallvard with fifty men. Skallagrim and his party took the ship and all the goods which had belonged to Hallvard . . . and flitted it and the wares to their own vessel, and then exchanged ships, lading their capture, but quitting their own. After which they filled their old ship with stones, brake it up and sank it. A good breeze sprang up, and they stood out to sea.

It is said of these men in the engagement who were were-wolves, or those on whom came the berserkr rage, that as long as the fit was on them no one could oppose them, they were so strong; but when it had passed off they were feebler than usual. It was the same with Kveldulf when the were-wolf fit went off him—he then felt the exhaustion consequent on the fight, and he was so completely 'done up,' that he was obliged to take to his bed."

In like manner Skallagrim had his fits of frenzy, taking after his amiable father.

"Thord and his companion were opposed to Skallagrim in the game, and they were too much for him, he wearied, and the game went better with them. But at dusk, after sunset, it went worse with Egill and Thord, for Skallagrim became so strong that he caught up Thord and cast him down, so that he broke his bones, and that was the death of him. Then he caught at Egill. Thorgerd Brák was the name of a servant of Skallagrim, who had been foster-mother to Egill. She was a woman of great stature, strong as a man and a bit of a witch. Brák exclaimed,—'Skallagrim! are you now falling upon your son?' (hamaz þú at syni þínum). Then Skallagrim let go his hold of Egill and clutched at her. She started aside and fled. Skallagrim. followed. They ran out upon Digraness, and she sprang off the headland into the water. Skallagrim cast after her a huge stone which struck her between the shoulders, and she never rose after it. The place is now called Brak's Sound."—(c. 40.)

Let it be observed that in these passages from the *Aigla*, the words að hamaz, hamrammr, &c. are used without any intention of conveying the idea of a change of bodily shape, though the words taken literally assert it. For they are derived from *hamr*, a skin or habit; a word which has its representatives in other Aryan languages, and is therefore a primitive word expressive of the skin of a beast.

The Sanskrit — *carmma*; the Hindustanee — *cam*, hide or skin; and — *camra*, leather; the Persian — *game*, clothing, disguise; the Gothic *ham* or *hams*, skin; and even the Italian *camicia*, and the French *chemise*, are cognate words. [*]

[* I shall have more to say on this subject in the chapter on the Mythology of Lycanthropy.]

It seems probable accordingly that the verb *að hamaz* was first applied to those who wore the skins of savage animals, and went about the country as freebooters; but that popular superstition soon invested them with supernatural powers, and they were supposed to assume the forms of the beasts in whose skins they were disguised. The verb then acquired the significance "to become a were-wolf, to change shape." It did not stop there, but went through another change of meaning, and was finally applied to those who were afflicted with paroxysms of madness or demoniacal possession.

This was not the only word connected with were-wolves which helped on the superstition. The word *vargr*, a wolf, had a double significance, which would be the means of originating many a were-wolf story. *Vargr* is the same as *u-argr*, restless; *argr* being the same as the Anglo-Saxon *earg*. *Vargr* had its double signification in Norse. It signified a wolf, and also a godless man. This *vargr* is the English *were*, in the word were- wolf, and the *garou* or *varou* in French. The Danish word for were-wolf is *var-ulf*, the Gothic *vaira-ulf*. In the *Romans de Garin*, it is "Leu warou, sanglante beste." In the *Vie de S. Hildefons* by Gauthier de Coinsi,—

> *Cil lon desve, cil lou garol,*
> *Ce sunt deable, que saul*
> *Ne puent estre de nos mordre.*

Here the loup-garou is a devil. The Anglo-Saxons regarded him as an evil man: *wearg*, a scoundrel; Gothic *varys*, a fiend. But very often the word meant no more than an outlaw. Pluquet in his *Contes Populaires* tells us that the ancient Norman laws said of the criminals condemned to outlawry for certain offences, *Wargus esto*: be an outlaw!

In like manner the Lex Ripuaria, tit. 87, "Wargus sit, hoe est expulsus." In the laws of Canute, he is called verevulf. (*Leges Canuti*, Schmid, i. 148.) And the Salic Law (tit. 57) orders: "Si quis corpus jam sepultum effoderit, aut expoliaverit, *wargus* sit." "If any one shall have dug up or despoiled an already buried corpse, let him be a varg."

Sidonius Apollinaris.[*] says, "Unam feminam quam forte *vargorum*, hoc enim nomine indigenas latrunculos nuncupant," as though the common name by which those who lived a freebooter life were designated, was varg.

[* SIDONIUS APOLLINARIS: Opera, lib. vi. ep. 4.]

In like manner Palgrave assures us in his *Rise and Progress of the English Commonwealth*, that among the Anglo, Saxons an *utlagh*, or out-law, was said to have the head of a wolf. If then the term *vargr* was applied at one time to a wolf, at another to an outlaw who lived the life of a wild beast, away from the haunts of men "he shall be driven away as a wolf, and chased so far as men chase wolves farthest," was the legal form of sentence—it is certainly no matter of wonder that stories of out-laws should have become surrounded with mythical accounts of their transformation into wolves.

But the very idiom of the Norse was calculated to foster this superstition. The Icelanders had curious expressions which are sufficiently likely to have produced misconceptions.

Snorri not only relates that Odin changed himself into another form, but he adds that by his spells he turned his enemies into boars. In precisely the same manner does a hag, Ljot, in the Vatnsdæla Saga, say that she could have turned Thorsteinn and Jökull into boars to run about with the wild beasts (c. xxvi.); and the expression *verða at gjalti*, or at *gjöltum*, to become a boar, is frequently met with in the Sagas.

"Thereupon came Thorarinn and his men upon them, and Nagli led the way; but when he saw weapons drawn he was frightened, and ran away up the mountain, and became a boar. . . . And Thorarinn and his men took to run, so as to help Nagli, lest he should tumble off the cliffs into the sea" (Eyrbyggja Saga, c. xviii.) A similar expression occurs in the Gisla Saga Surssonar, p. 50. In the Hrolfs Saga Kraka, we meet with a troll in boar's shape, to whom divine honours are paid; and in the Kjalnessinga Saga, c. xv., men are likened to boars—"Then it began to fare with them as it fares with boars when they fight each other, for in the same manner dropped their foam." The true signification of *verða at gjalti* is to be in such a state of fear as to lose the senses; but it is sufficiently peculiar to have given rise to superstitious stories.

I have dwelt at some length on the Northern myths relative to were-wolves and animal transformations, because I have considered the investigation of these all-important towards the elucidation of the truth which lies at the bottom of mediæval superstition, and which is nowhere so obtainable as through the Norse literature. As may be seen from the passages quoted above at length, and from an examination of those merely referred to, the result arrived at is pretty conclusive, and may be summed up in very few words.

The whole superstructure of fable and romance relative to transformation into wild beasts, reposes simply on this basis of truth—that among the Scandinavian nations there existed a form of madness or possession, under the influence of which men acted as though they were changed into wild and savage brutes, howling, foaming at the mouth, ravening for blood and slaughter, ready to commit any act of atrocity, and as irresponsible for their actions as the wolves and bears, in whose skins they often equipped themselves.

The manner in which this fact became invested with supernatural adjuncts I have also pointed out, to wit, the change in the significance of the word designating the madness, the double meaning of the word *vargr*, and above all, the habits and appearance of the maniacs. We shall see instances of berserkr rage reappearing in the middle ages, and late down into our own times, not exclusively in the North, but throughout France, Germany, and England, and instead of rejecting the accounts given by chroniclers as fabulous, because there is much connected with them which seems to be fabulous, we shall be able to refer them to their true origin.

It may be accepted as an axiom, that no superstition of general acceptance is destitute of a foundation of truth; and if we discover the myth of the were-wolf to be widely spread, not only throughout Europe, but through the whole world, we may rest assured that there is a solid core of fact, round which popular superstition has crystallized; and that fact is the existence of a species of madness, during the accesses of which the person afflicted believes himself to be a wild beast, and acts like a wild beast.

In some cases this madness amounts apparently to positive possession, and the diabolical acts into which the possessed is impelled are so horrible, that the blood curdles in reading them, and it is impossible to recall them without a shudder.

V. — THE WERE-WOLF IN THE MIDDLE-AGES.

Stories from Olaus Magnus of Livonian Were-wolves—Story from Bishop Majolus—
Story of Albertus Pericofcius—Similar occurrence at Prague—Saint Patrick—
Strange incident related by John of Nüremberg—Bisclaveret—Courland Were-wolves
—Pierre Vidal—Pavian Lycanthropist—Bodin's Stories—Forestus' Account of a
Lycanthropist—Neapolitan Were-wolf

OLAUS MAGNUS relates that—"In Prussia, Livonia, and Lithuania, although the inhabitants suffer considerably from the rapacity of wolves throughout the year, in that these animals rend their cattle, which are scattered in great numbers through the woods, whenever they stray in the very least, yet this is not regarded by them as such a serious matter as what they endure from men turned into wolves.

"On the feast of the Nativity of Christ, at night, such a multitude of wolves transformed from men gather together in a certain spot, arranged among themselves, and then spread to rage with wondrous ferocity against human beings, and those animals which are not wild, that the natives of these regions suffer more detriment from these, than they do from true and natural wolves; for when a human habitation has been detected by them isolated in the woods, they besiege it with atrocity, striving to break in the doors, and in the event of their doing so, they devour all the human beings, and every animal which is found within. They burst into the beer-cellars, and there they empty the tuns of beer or mead, and pile up the empty casks one above another in the middle of the cellar, thus showing their difference from natural and genuine wolves. . . . Between Lithuania, Livonia, and Courland are the walls of a certain old ruined castle. At this spot congregate thousands, on a fixed occasion, and try their agility in jumping. Those who are unable to bound over the wall, as; is often the case with the fattest, are fallen upon with scourges by the captains and slain." [*] Olaus relates also in c. xlvii. the story of a certain nobleman who was travelling through a large forest with some peasants in his retinue who dabbled in the black art. They found no house where they could lodge for the night, and were well-nigh famished. Then one of the peasants offered, if all the rest would hold their tongues as to what he should do, that he would bring them a lamb from a distant flock.

[* OLAUS MAGNUS: *Historia de Vent. Septent.* Basil. 15, lib. xviii. cap. 45.]

He thereupon retired into the depths of the forest and changed his form into that of a wolf, fell upon the flock, and brought a lamb to his companions in his mouth. They received it with gratitude. Then he retired once more into the thicket, and transformed himself back again into his human shape.

The wife of a nobleman in Livonia expressed her doubts to one of her slaves whether it were possible for man or woman thus to change shape. The servant at once volunteered to give her evidence of the possibility. He left the room, and in another moment a wolf was observed running over the country. The dogs followed him, and notwithstanding his resistance, tore out one of his eyes. Next day the slave appeared before his mistress blind of an eye.

Bp. Majolus [*] and Caspar Peucer [†] relate the following circumstances of the Livonians:—

[* MAJOLI *Episc. Vulturoniensis Dier. Canicul.* Helenopolis, 1612, tom. ii. colloq. 3.]
[† CASPAR PEUCER: *Comment. de Præcipuis Divin. Generibus*, 1591, p. 169.]

At Christmas a boy lame of a leg goes round the country summoning the devil's followers, who are countless, to a general conclave. Whoever remains behind, or goes reluctantly, is scourged by another with an iron whip till the blood flows, and his traces are left in blood. The human form vanishes, and the whole multitude become wolves. Many thousands assemble. Foremost goes the leader armed with an iron whip, and the troop follow, "firmly convinced in their imaginations that they are transformed into wolves." They fall upon herds of cattle and flocks of sheep, but they have no power to slay men. When they come to a river, the leader smites the water with his scourge, and it divides, leaving a dry path through the midst, by which the pack may go. The transformation lasts during twelve days, at the expiration of which period the wolf-skin vanishes, and the human form reappears. This superstition was expressly forbidden by the church. "Credidisti, quod quidam credere solent, ut illæ quæ a vulgo Parcæ vocantur, ipsæ, vel sint vel possint hoc facere quod creduntur, id est, dum aliquis homo nascitur, et tunc valeant illum designare ad hoc quod velint, ut quandocunque homo ille voluerit, in lupum transformari possit, quod vulgaris stultitia, *werwolf* vocat, aut in aliam aliquam figuram?"—Ap. Burchard. (d. 1024). In like manner did S. Boniface preach against those who believed superstitiously in it strigas et fictos lupos." (*Serm.* apud Mart. et Durand. ix. 217.)

In a dissertation by Müller [*] we learn, on the authority of Cluverius and Dannhaverus (*Acad. Homilet.* p. ii.), that a certain Albertus Pericofcius in Muscovy was wont to tyrannize over and harass his subjects in the most unscrupulous manner. One night when he was absent from home, his whole herd of cattle, acquired by extortion, perished. On his return he was informed of his loss, and the wicked man broke out into the most horrible blasphemies, exclaiming, "Let him who has slain, eat; if God chooses, let him devour me as well."

[* De {Greek *Lukanðrwpía*}. Lipsiæ, 1736.]

As he spoke, drops of blood fell to earth, and the nobleman, transformed into a wild dog, rushed upon his dead cattle, tore and mangled the carcasses and began to devour them; possibly he may be devouring them still (*ac forsan hodie que pascitur*). His wife, then near her confinement, died of fear. Of these circumstances there were not only ear but also eye witnesses. (*Non ab auritis tantum, sed et ocidatis accepi, quod narro*). Similarly it is related of a nobleman in the neighbourhood of Prague, that he robbed his subjects of their goods and reduced them to penury through his exactions. He took the last cow from a poor widow with five children, but as a judgment, all his own cattle died. He then broke into fearful oaths, and God transformed him into a dog: his human head, however, remained.

S. Patrick is said to have changed Vereticus, king of Wales, into a wolf, and S. Natalis, the abbot, to have pronounced anathema upon an illustrious family in Ireland; in consequence of which, every male and female take the form of wolves for seven years and live in the forests and career over the bogs, howling mournfully, and appeasing their hunger upon the sheep of the peasants. [*] A duke of Prussia, according to Majolus, had a countryman brought for sentence before him, because he had devoured his neighbour's cattle. The fellow was an ill-favoured, deformed man, with great wounds in his face, which he had received from dogs' bites whilst he had been in his wolf's form. It was believed that he changed shape twice in the year, at Christmas and at Midsummer. He was said to exhibit much uneasiness and discomfort when the wolf-hair began to break out and his bodily shape to change.

[* PHIL. HARTUNG: *Conciones Tergeminæ*, pars ii. p. 367.]

He was kept long in prison and closely watched, lest he should become a were-wolf during his confinement and attempt to escape, but nothing remarkable took place. If this is the same individual as that mentioned by Olaus Magnus, as there seems to be a probability, the poor fellow was burned alive.

John of Nüremberg relates the following curious story. [*] A priest was once travelling in a strange country, and lost his way in a forest. Seeing a fire, he made towards it, and beheld a wolf seated over it. The wolf addressed him in human-voice, and bade him not fear, as "he was of the Ossyrian race, of which a man and a woman were doomed to spend a certain number of years in wolf's form. Only after seven years might they return home and resume their former shapes, if they were still alive." He begged the priest to visit and console his sick wife, and to give her the last sacraments. This the priest consented to do, after some hesitation, and only when convinced of the beasts being human beings, by observing that the wolf used his front paws as hands, and when he saw the she-wolf peel off her wolf-skin from her head to her navel, exhibiting the features of an aged woman.

[* JOHN EUS. NIERENBERG *de Miracul. in Europa*, lib. ii. cap. 42.]

Marie de France says in the Lais du Bisclaveret:— [*]

> *Bisclaveret ad nun en Bretan*
> *Garwall Papelent li Norman.*
>
> ....
>
> *Jadis le poet-hum oir*
> *Et souvent suleit avenir,*
> *Humes pluseirs Garwall deviendrent*
> *E es boscages meisun tindrent*

[* An epitome of this curious were-wolf tale will be found in Ellis's *Early English Metrical Romances*.]

There is an interesting paper by Rhanæus, on the Courland were-wolves, in the Breslauer Sammlung. [*] The author says,—"There are too many examples derived not merely from hearsay, but received on indisputable evidence, for us to dispute the fact, that Satan—if we do not deny that such a being exists, and that he has his work in the children of darkness—holds the Lycanthropists in his net in three ways:—

[* Supplement III. *Curieuser* und nutzbarer Anmerkungen von Natur und Kunstgeschichten, gesammelt von Kanold. 1728.]

"1. They execute as wolves certain acts, such as seizing a sheep, or destroying cattle, &c., not changed into wolves, which no scientific man in Courland believes, but in their human frames, and with their human limbs, yet in such a state of phantasy and hallucination, that they believe themselves transformed into wolves, and are regarded as such by others suffering under similar hallucination, and in this manner run these people in packs as wolves, though not true wolves.

"2. They imagine, in deep sleep or dream, that they injure the cattle, and this without leaving their conch; but it is their master who does, in their stead, what their fancy points out, or suggests to him.

"3. The evil one drives natural wolves to do some act, and then pictures it so well to the sleeper, immovable in his place, both in dreams and at awaking, that he believes the act to have been committed by himself."

Rhanæus, under these heads, relates three stories, which he believes be has on good authority. The first is of a gentleman starting on a journey, who came upon a wolf engaged in the act of seizing a sheep in his own flock; he fired at it, and wounded it, so that it fled howling to the thicket. When the gentleman returned from his expedition he found the whole neighbourhood impressed with the belief that he had, on a given day and hour, shot at one of his tenants, a publican, Mickel. On inquiry, the man's Wife, called Lebba, related the following circumstances, which were fully corroborated by numerous witnesses:— When her husband had sown his rye he had consulted with his wife how he was to get some meat, so as to have a good feast. The woman urged him on no account to steal from his landlord's flock, because it was guarded by fierce dogs. He, however, rejected her advice, and Mickel fell upon his landlord's sheep, but he had suffered and had come limping home, and in his rage at the ill success of his attempt, had fallen upon his own horse and had bitten its throat completely through. This took place in the year 1684.

In 1684, a man was about to fire upon a pack of wolves, when he heard from among the troop a voice exclaiming—"Gossip! Gossip! don't fire. No good will come of it."

The third story is as follows:—A lycanthropist was brought before a judge and accused of witchcraft, but as nothing could be proved against him, the judge ordered one of his peasants to visit the man in his prison, and to worm the truth out of him, and to persuade the prisoner to assist him in revenging himself upon another peasant who had injured him; and this was to be effected by destroying one of the man's cows; but the peasant was to urge the prisoner to do it secretly, and, if possible, in the disguise of a wolf. The fellow undertook the task, but he had great difficulty in persuading the prisoner to fall in with his wishes: eventually, however, he succeeded. Next morning the cow was found in its stall frightfully mangled, but the prisoner had not left his cell: for the watch, who had been placed to observe him, declared that he had spent the night in profound sleep, and that he had only at one time made a slight motion with his head and hands and feet.

Wierius and Forestus quote Gulielmus Brabantinus as an authority for the fact, that a man of high position had been so possessed by the evil one, that often during the year he fell into a condition in which he believed himself to be turned into a wolf, and at that time he roved in the woods and tried to seize and devour little children, but that at last, by God's mercy, he recovered his senses.

Certainly the famous Pierre Vidal, the Don Quixote of Provençal troubadours, must have had a touch of this madness, when, after having fallen in love with a lady of Carcassone, named Loba, or the Wolfess, the excess of his passion drove him over the country, howling like a wolf, and demeaning himself more like an irrational beast than a rational man.

He commemorates his lupine madness in the poem *A tal Donna*:—[*]

[* BRUCE WHYTE: *Histoire des Langues Romaines*, tom. ii. p. 248.]

> *Crowned with immortal joys I mount*
> *The proudest emperors above,*
> *For I am honoured with the love*
> *Of the fair daughter of a count.*
> *A lace from Na Raymbauda's hand*
> *I value more than all the land*
> *Of Richard, with his Poïctou,*
> *His rich Touraine and famed Anjou.*
> *When loup-garou the rabble call me,*
> *When vagrant shepherds hoot,*
> *Pursue, and buffet me to boot,*
> *It doth not for a moment gall me;*
> *I seek not palaces or halls,*
> *Or refuge when the winter falls;*
> *Exposed to winds and frosts at night,*
> *My soul is ravished with delight.*
> *Me claims my she-wolf (Loba) so divine:*
> *And justly she that claim prefers,*
> *For, by my troth, my life is hers*
> *More than another's, more than mine.*

Job Fincelius [*] relates the sad story of a farmer of Pavia, who, as a wolf, fell upon many men in the open country and tore them to pieces. After much trouble the maniac was caught, and he then assured his captors that the only difference which existed between himself and a natural wolf, was that in a true wolf the hair grew outward, whilst in him it struck inward. In order to put this assertion to the proof, the magistrates, themselves most certainly cruel and bloodthirsty wolves, cut off his arms and legs; the poor wretch died of the mutilation. This took place in 1541. The idea of the skin being reversed is a very ancient one: *versipellis* occurs as a name of reproach in Petronius, Lucilius, and Plautus, and resembles the Norse *hamrammr*.

[* FINCELIUS *de Mirabilibus*, lib. xi.]

Fincelius relates also that, in 1542, there was such a multitude of were-wolves about Constantinople that the Emperor, accompanied by his guard, left the city to give them a severe correction, and slew one hundred and fifty of them.

Spranger speaks of three young ladies who attacked a labourer, under the form of cats, and were wounded by him. They were found bleeding in their beds next morning.

Majolus relates that a man afflicted with lycanthropy was brought to Pomponatius. The poor fellow had been found buried in hay, and when people approached, he called to them to flee, as he was a were wolf, and would rend them. The country-folk wanted to flay him, to discover whether the hair grew inwards, but Pomponatius rescued the man and cured him.

Bodin tells some were-wolf stories on good authority; it is a pity that the good authorities of Bodin were such liars, but that, by the way. He says that the Royal Procurator-General Bourdin had assured him that he had shot a wolf, and that the arrow had stuck in the beast's thigh. A few hours after, the arrow was found in the thigh of a man in bed. In Vernon, about the year 1566, the witches and warlocks gathered in great multitudes, under the shape of cats. Four or five men were attacked in a lone place by a number of these beasts. The men stood their ground with the utmost heroism, succeeded in slaying one puss, and in wounding many others. Next day a number of wounded women were found in the town, and they gave the judge an accurate account of all the circumstances connected with their wounding.

Bodin quotes Pierre Marner, the author of a treatise on sorcerers, as having witnessed in Savoy the transformation of men into wolves. Nynauld [*] relates that in a village of Switzerland, near Lucerne, a peasant was attacked by a wolf, whilst he was hewing timber; he defended himself, and smote off a fore-leg of the beast. The moment that the blood began to flow the wolf's form changed, and he recognized a woman without her arm. She was burnt alive.

[* NYNAULD, *De la Lycanthropie*. Paris, 1615, p. 52.]

An evidence that beasts are transformed witches is to be found in their having no tails. When the devil takes human form, however, he keeps his club-foot of the Satyr, as a token by which he may be recognized. So animals deficient in caudal appendages are to be avoided, as they are witches in disguise. The Thingwald should consider the case of the Manx cats in its next session.

Forestus, in his chapter on maladies of the brain, relates a circumstance which came under his own observation, in the middle of the sixteenth century, at Alcmaar in the Netherlands. A peasant there was attacked every spring with a fit of insanity; under the influence of this he rushed about the churchyard, ran into the church, jumped over the benches, danced, was filled with fury, climbed up, descended, and never remained quiet. He carried a long staff in his hand, with which he drove away the dogs, which flew at him and wounded him, so that his thighs were covered with scars. His face was pale, his eyes deep sunk in their sockets. Forestus pronounces the man to be a lycanthropist, but he does not say that the poor fellow believed himself to be transformed into a wolf. In reference to this case, however, he mentions that of a Spanish nobleman who believed himself to be changed into a bear, and who wandered filled with fury among the woods.

Donatus of Altomare [*] affirms that he saw a man in the streets of Naples, surrounded by a ring of people, who in his were-wolf frenzy had dug up a corpse and was carrying off the leg upon his shoulders. This was in the middle of the sixteenth century.

[* *De Medend. Human. Corp.* lib. i. cap. 9.]

VI. — A CHAMBER OF HORRORS.

Pierre Bourgot and Michel Verdung—The Hermit of S. Bonnot—
The Gandillon Family—Thievenne Paget—The Tailor of Châlons—Roulet

IN December, 1521, the Inquisitor-General for the diocese of Besançon, Boin by name, heard a case of a sufficiently terrible nature to produce a profound sensation of alarm in the neighbourhood. Two men were under accusation of witchcraft and cannibalism. Their names were Pierre Bourgot, or Peter the Great, as the people had nicknamed him from his stature, and Michel Verdung. Peter had not been long under trial, before he volunteered a full confession of his crimes. It amounted to this:—

About nineteen years before, on the occasion of a New Year's market at Poligny, a terrible storm had broken over the country, and among other mischiefs done by it, was the scattering of Pierre's flock. "In vain," said the prisoner, "did I labour, in company with other peasants, to find the sheep and bring them together. I went everywhere in search of them.

"Then there rode up three black horsemen, and the last said to me: 'Whither away? you seem to be in trouble?'

"I related to him my misfortune with my flock. He bade me pluck up my spirits, and promised that his master would henceforth take charge of and protect my flock., if I would only rely upon him. He told me, as well, that I should find my strayed sheep very shortly, and he promised to provide me with money. We agreed to meet again in four or five days. My flock I soon found collected together. At my second meeting I learned of the stranger that he was a servant of the devil. I forswore God and our Lady and all saints and dwellers in Paradise. I renounced Christianity, kissed his left hand, which was black and ice-cold as that of a corpse. Then I fell on my knees and gave in my allegiance to Satan. I remained in the service of the devil for two years, and never entered a church before the end of mass, or at all events till the holy water had been sprinkled, according to the desire of my master, whose name I afterwards learned was Moyset.

"All anxiety about my flock was removed, for the devil had undertaken to protect it and to keep off the wolves.

"This freedom from care, however, made me begin to tire of the devil's service, and I recommenced my attendance at church, till I was brought back into obedience to the evil one by Michel Verdung, when I renewed my compact on the understanding that I should be supplied with money.

"In a wood near Chastel Charnon we met with many others whom I did not recognize; we danced, and each had in his or her hand a green taper with a blue flame. Still under the delusion that I should obtain money, Michel persuaded me to move with the greatest celerity, and in order to do this, after I had stripped myself, he smeared me with a salve, and I believed myself then to be transformed into a wolf. I was at first somewhat horrified at my four wolf's feet, and the fur with which I was covered all at once, but I found that I could now travel with the speed of the wind. This could not have taken place without the help of our powerful master, who was present during our excursion, though I did not perceive him till I had recovered my human form. Michel did the same as myself.

"When we had been one or two hours in this condition of metamorphosis, Michel smeared us again, and quick as thought we resumed our human forms. The salve was given us by our masters; to me it was given by Moyset, to Michel by his own master, Guillemin."

Pierre declared that he felt no exhaustion after his excursions, though the judge inquired particularly whether he felt that prostration after his unusual exertion, of which witches usually complained. Indeed the exhaustion consequent on a were-wolf raid was so great that the lycanthropist was often confined to his bed for days, and could hardly move hand or foot, much in the same way as the berserkir and *ham rammir* in the North were utterly prostrated after their fit had left them.

In one of his were-wolf runs, Pierre fell upon a boy of six or seven years old, with his teeth, intending to rend and devour him, but the lad screamed so loud that he was obliged to beat a retreat to his clothes, and smear himself again, in order to recover his form and escape detection. He and Michel, however, one day tore to pieces a woman as she was gathering peas; and a M. de Chusnée, who came to her rescue, was attacked by them and killed.

On another occasion they fell upon a little girl of four years old, and ate her up, with the exception of one arm. Michel thought the flesh most delicious.

Another girl was strangled by them, and her blood lapped up. Of a third they ate merely a portion of the stomach. One evening at dusk, Pierre leaped over a garden wall, and came upon a little maiden of nine years old, engaged upon the weeding of the garden beds. She fell on her knees and entreated Pierre to spare her; but he snapped the neck, and left her a corpse, lying among her flowers. On this occasion he does not seem to have been in his wolf's shape. He fell upon a goat which he found in the field of Pierre Lerugen, and bit it in the throat, but he killed it with a knife.

Michel was transformed in his clothes into a wolf, but Pierre was obliged to strip, and the metamorphosis could not take place with him unless he were stark naked.

He was unable to account for the manner in which the hair vanished when he recovered his natural condition.

The statements of Pierre Bourgot were fully corroborated by Michel Verdung.

Towards the close of the autumn of 1573, the peasants of the neighbourhood of Dôle, in Franche Comté, were authorized by the Court of Parliament at Dôle, to hunt down the were-wolves which infested the country. The authorization was as follows:— "According to the advertisement made to the sovereign Court of Parliament at Dole, that, in the territories of Espagny, Salvange, Courchapon, and the neighbouring villages, has often been seen and met, for some time past, a were-wolf, who, it is said, has already seized and carried off several little children, so that they have not been seen since, and since he has attacked and done injury in the country to some horsemen, who kept him of only with great difficulty and danger to their persons: the said Court, desiring to prevent any greater danger, has permitted, and does permit, those who are abiding or dwelling in the said places and others, notwithstanding all edicts concerning the chase, to assemble with pikes, halberts, arquebuses, and sticks, to chase and to pursue the said were-wolf in every place where they may find or seize him; to tie and to kill, without incurring any pains or penalties. . . . Given at the meeting of the said Court, on the thirteenth day of the month September, 1573." It was some time, however, before the loup-garou was caught.

In a retired spot near Amanges, half shrouded in trees, stood a small hovel of the rudest construction; its roof was of turf, and its walls were blotched with lichen. The garden to this cot was run to waste, and the fence round it broken through. As the hovel was far from any road, and was only reached by a path over moorland and through forest, it was seldom visited, and the couple who lived in it were not such as would make many friends. The man, Gilles Garnier, was a sombre, ill-looking fellow, who walked in a stooping attitude, and whose pale face, livid complexion, and deep-set eyes under a pair of coarse and bushy brows, which met across the forehead, were sufficient to repel any one from seeking his acquaintance. Gilles seldom spoke, and when he did it was in the broadest patois of his country. His long grey beard and retiring habits procured for him the name of the Hermit of St. Bonnot, though no one for a moment attributed to him any extraordinary amount of sanctity.

The hermit does not seem to have been suspected for some time, but one day, as some of the peasants of Chastenoy were returning home from their work, through the forest, the screams of a child and the deep baying of a wolf, attracted their notice, and on running in the direction whence the cries sounded, they found a little girl defending herself against a monstrous creature, which was attacking her tooth and nail, and had already wounded her severely in five places. As the peasants came up, the creature fled on all fours into the gloom of the thicket; it was so dark that it could not be identified with certainty, and whilst some affirmed that it was a wolf, others thought they had recognized the features of the hermit. This took place on the 8th November.

On the 14th a little boy of ten years old was missing, who had been last seen at a short distance from the gates of Dole.

The hermit of S. Bonnot was now seized and brought to trial at Dole, when the following evidence was extracted from him and his wife, and substantiated in many particulars by witnesses.

On the last day of Michaelmas, under the form of a wolf, at a mile from Dole, in the farm of Gorge, a vineyard belonging to Chastenoy, near the wood of La Serre, Gilles Gamier had attacked a little maiden of ten or twelve years old, and had slain her with his teeth and claws; he had then drawn her into the wood, stripped her, gnawed the flesh from her legs and arms, and had enjoyed his meal so much, that, inspired with conjugal affection, he had brought some of the flesh home for his wife Apolline.

Eight days after the feast of All Saints, again in the form of a were-wolf, he had seized another girl, near the meadow land of La Pouppe, on the territory of Athume and Chastenoy, and was on the point of slaying and devouring her, when three persons came up, and he was compelled to escape. On the fourteenth day after All Saints, also as a wolf, he had attacked a boy of ten years old, a mile from Dôle, between Gredisans and Menoté, and had strangled him. On that occasion he had eaten all the flesh off his legs and arms, and had also devoured a great part of the belly; one of the legs he had rent completely from the trunk with his fangs.

On the Friday before the last feast of S. Bartholomew, he had seized a boy of twelve or thirteen, under a large pear-trees near the wood of the village Perrouze, and had drawn him into the thicket and killed him, intending to eat him as he had eaten the other children, but the approach of men hindered him from fulfilling his intention. The boy was, however, quite dead, and the men who came up declared that Gilles appeared as a man and not as a wolf. The hermit of S. Bonnot was sentenced to be dragged to the place of public execution, and there to be burned alive, a sentence which was rigorously carried out.

In this instance the poor maniac fully believed that actual transformation into a wolf took place; he was apparently perfectly reasonable on other points, and quite conscious of the acts he had committed.

We come now to a more remarkable circumstance, the affliction of a whole family with the same form of insanity. Our information is derived from Boguet's *Discours de Sorciers*, 1603-1610.

Pernette Gandillon was a poor girl in the Jura, who in 1598 ran about the country on all fours, in the belief that she was a wolf. One day as she was ranging the country in a fit of lycanthropic madness, she came upon two children who were plucking wild strawberries. Filled with a sudden passion for blood, she flew at the little girl and would have brought her down, had not her brother, a lad of four years old, defended her lustily with a knife. Pernette, however, wrenched the weapon from his tiny hand, flung him down and gashed his throat, so that he died of the wound. Pernette was torn to pieces by the people in their rage and horror.

Directly after, Pierre, the brother of Pernette Gandillon, was accused of witchcraft. He was charged with having led children to the sabbath, having made hail, and having run about the country in the form of a wolf. The transformation was effected by means of a salve which he had received from the devil. He had on one occasion assumed the form of a hare, but usually he appeared as a wolf, and his skin became covered with shaggy grey hair. He readily acknowledged that the charges brought against him were well founded, and he allowed that he had, during the period of his transformation, fallen on, and devoured, both beasts and human beings. When he desired to recover his true form, he rolled himself in the dewy grass. His son Georges asserted that he had also been anointed with the salve, and had gone to the sabbath in the shape of a wolf. According to his own testimony, he had fallen upon two goats in one of his expeditions.

One Maundy-Thursday night he had lain for three hours in his bed in a cataleptic state, and at the end of that time had sprung out of bed. During this period he had been in the form of a wolf to the witches' sabbath.

His sister Antoinnette confessed that she had made hail, and that she had sold herself to the devil, who had appeared to her in the shape of a black he-goat. She had been to the sabbath on several occasions.

Pierre and Georges in prison behaved as maniacs, running on all fours about their cells and howling dismally. Their faces, arms, and legs were frightfully scarred with the wounds they had received from dogs when they had been on their raids. Boguet accounts for the transformation not taking place, by the fact of their not having the necessary salves by them.

All three, Pierre, Georges, and Antoinnette, were hung and burned.

Thievenne Paget, who was a witch of the most unmistakable character, was also frequently changed into a she-wolf, according to her own confession, in which state she had often accompanied the devil over hill and dale, slaying cattle, and falling on and devouring children. The same thing may be said of Clauda Isan Prost, a lame woman, Clauda Isan Guillaume, and Isan Roquet, who owned to the murder of five children.

On the 14th of December, in the same year as the execution of the Gandillon family (1598), a tailor of Châlons was sentenced to the flames by the Parliament of Paris for lycanthropy. This wretched man had decoyed children into his shop, or attacked them in the gloaming when they strayed in the woods, had torn them with his teeth, and killed them, after which he seems calmly to have dressed their flesh as ordinary meat, and to have eaten it with great relish. The number of little innocents whom he destroyed is unknown. A whole cask full of bones was discovered in his house. The man was perfectly hardened, and the details of his trial were so full of horrors and abominations of all kinds, that the judges ordered the documents to be burned.

Again in 1598, a year memorable in the annals of lycanthropy, a trial took place in Angers, the details of which are very terrible.

In a wild and unfrequented spot near Caude, some countrymen came one day upon the corpse of a boy of fifteen, horribly mutilated and bespattered with blood. As the men approached, two wolves, which had been rending the body, bounded away into the thicket. The men gave chase immediately, following their bloody tracks till they lost them; when suddenly crouching among the bushes, his teeth chattering with fear, they found a man half naked, with long hair and beard, and with his hands dyed in blood. His nails were long as claws, and were clotted with fresh gore, and shreds of human flesh.

This is one of the most puzzling and peculiar cases which come under our notice.

The wretched man, whose name was Roulet, of his own accord stated that he had fallen upon the lad and had killed him by smothering him, and that he had been prevented from devouring the body completely by the arrival of men on the spot.

Roulet proved on investigation to be a beggar from house to house, in the most abject state of poverty. His companions in mendicity were his brother John and his cousin Julien. He had been given lodging out of charity in a neighbouring village, but before his apprehension he had been absent for eight days.

Before the judges, Roulet acknowledged that he was able to transform himself into a wolf by means of a salve which his parents had given him. When questioned about the two wolves which had been seen leaving the corpse, he said that he knew perfectly well who they were, for they were his companions, Jean and Julian, who possessed the same secret as himself. He was shown the clothes he had worn on the day of his seizure, and he recognized them immediately; he described the boy whom he had murdered, gave the date correctly, indicated the precise spot where the deed had been done, and recognized the father of the boy as the man who had first run up when the screams of the lad had been heard. In prison, Roulet behaved like an idiot. When seized, his belly was distended and hard; in prison he drank one evening a whole pailful of water, and from that moment refused to eat or drink.

His parents, on inquiry, proved to be respectable and pious people, and they proved that his brother John and his cousin Julien had been engaged at a distance on the day of Roulet's apprehension.

"What is your name, and what your estate?" asked the judge, Pierre Hérault.

"My name is Jacques Roulet, my age thirty-five; I am poor, and a mendicant."

"What are you accused of having done?"

"Of being a thief—of having offended God. My parents gave me an ointment; I do not know its composition."

"When rubbed with this ointment do you become a wolf?"

"No; but for all that, I killed and ate the child Cornier: I was a wolf."

"Were you dressed as a wolf?"

"I was dressed as I am now. I had my hands and my face bloody, because I had been eating the flesh of the said child."

"Do your hands and feet become paws of a wolf?"

"Yes, they do."

"Does your head become like that of a wolf-your mouth become larger?"

"I do not know how my head was at the time; I used my teeth; my head was as it is to-day. I have wounded and eaten many other little children; I have also been to the sabbath."

The *lieutenant criminel* sentenced Roulet to death. He, however, appealed to the Parliament at Paris; and this decided that as there was more folly in the poor idiot than malice and witchcraft, his sentence of death should be commuted to two years' imprisonment in a madhouse, that he might be instructed in the knowledge of God, whom he had forgotten in his utter poverty. [*]

[* "La cour du Parliament, par arrêt, mist l'appellation et la sentence dont il avoit esté appel au néant, et, néanmoins, ordonna que le dit Roulet serait mis à l'hospital Saint Germain des Prés, où on a accoustumé de mettre les folz, pour y demeurer l'espace de deux ans, afin d'y estre instruit et redressé tant de son esprit, que ramené à la cognoissance de Dieu, que l'extrême pauvreté lui avoit fait mescognoistre."]

VII. — JEAN GRENIER

On the Sand-dunes—A Wolf attacks Marguerite Poirier—Jean Grenier brought to Trial—His Confessions—Charges of Cannibalism proved—His Sentence— Behaviour in the Monastery—Visit of Del'ancre

ONE fine afternoon in the spring, some village girls were tending their sheep on the sand-dunes which intervene between the vast forests of pine covering the greater portion of the present department of *Landes* in the south of France, and the sea.

The brightness of the sky, the freshness of the air puffing up off the blue twinkling Bay of Biscay, the hum or song of the wind as it made rich music among the pines which stood like a green uplifted wave on the East, the beauty of the sand-hills speckled with golden cistus, or patched with gentian-blue, by the low growing *Gremille couchée*, the charm of the forest-skirts, tinted variously with the foliage of cork-trees, pines, and acacia, the latter in full bloom, a pile of rose-coloured or snowy flowers,—all conspired to fill the peasant maidens with joy, and to make their voices rise in song and laughter, which rung merrily over the hills, and through the dark avenues of evergreen trees.

Now a gorgeous butterfly attracted their attention, then a flight of quails skimming the surface.

"Ah!" exclaimed Jacquiline Auzun," ah, if I had my stilts and bats, I would strike the little birds down, and we should have a fine supper."

"Now, if they would fly ready cooked into one's mouth, as they do in foreign parts!" said another girl.

"Have you got any new clothes for the S. Jean?" asked a third; "my mother has laid by to purchase me a smart cap with gold lace."

"You will turn the head of Etienne altogether, Annette!" said Jeanne Gaboriant. "But what is the matter with the sheep?"

She asked because the sheep which had been quietly browsing before her, on reaching a small depression in the dune, had started away as though frightened at something. At the same time one of the dogs began to growl and show his fangs.

The girls ran to the spot, and saw a little fall in the ground, in which, seated on a log of fir, was a boy of thirteen. The appearance of the lad was peculiar. His hair was of a tawny red and thickly matted, falling over his shoulders and completely covering his narrow brow. His small pale-grey eyes twinkled with an expression of horrible ferocity and cunning, from deep sunken hollows. The complexion was of a dark olive colour; the teeth were strong and white, and the canine teeth protruded over the lower lip when the mouth was closed. The boy's hands were large and powerful, the nails black and pointed like bird's talons. He was ill clothed, and seemed to be in the most abject poverty. The few garments he had on him were in tatters, and through the rents the emaciation of his limbs was plainly visible.

The girls stood round him, half frightened and much surprised, but the boy showed no symptoms of astonishment. His face relaxed into a ghastly leer, which showed the whole range of his glittering white fangs.

"Well, my maidens," said he in a harsh voice, "which of you is the prettiest, I should like to know; can you decide among you?"

"What do you want to know for?" asked Jeanne Gaboriant, the eldest of the girls, aged eighteen, who took upon herself to be spokesman for the rest.

"Because I shall marry the prettiest," was the answer.

"Ah!" said Jeanne jokingly; "that is if she will have you, which is not very likely, as we none of us know you, or anything about you."

"I am the son of a priest," replied the boy curtly.

"Is that why you look so dingy and black?"

"No, I am dark-coloured, because I wear a wolf-skin sometimes."

"A wolf-skin!" echoed the girl; "and pray who gave it you?"

"One called Pierre Labourant."

"There is no man of that name hereabouts. Where does he live?"

A scream of laughter mingled with howls, and breaking into strange gulping bursts of fiendlike merriment from the strange boy.

The little girls recoiled, and the youngest took refuge behind Jeanne.

"Do you want to know Pierre Labourant, lass? Hey, he is a man with an iron chain about his neck, which he is ever engaged in gnawing. Do you want to know where he lives, lass? Ha., in a place of gloom and fire, where there are many companions, some seated on iron chairs, burning, burning; others stretched on glowing beds, burning too. Some cast men upon blazing coals, others roast men before fierce flames, others again plunge them into caldrons of liquid fire."

The girls trembled and looked at each other with scared faces, and then again at the hideous being which crouched before them.

"You want to know about the wolf-skin cape?" continued he. "Pierre Labourant gave me that; he wraps it round me, and every Monday, Friday, and Sunday, and for about an hour at dusk every other day, I am a wolf, a were-wolf. I have killed dogs and drunk their blood; but little girls taste better, their flesh is tender and sweet, their blood rich and warm. I have eaten many a maiden, as I have been on my raids together with my nine companions. I am a were-wolf! Ah, ha! if the sun were to set I would soon fall on one of you and make a meal of you!" Again he burst into one of his frightful paroxysms of laughter, and the girls unable to endure it any longer, fled with precipitation.

Near the village of S. Antoine de Pizon, a little girl of the name of Marguerite Poirier, thirteen years old, was in the habit of tending her sheep, in company with a lad of the same age, whose name was Jean Grenier. The same lad whom Jeanne Gaboriant had questioned.

The little girl often complained to her parents of the conduct of the boy: she said that he frightened her with his horrible stories; but her father and mother thought little of her complaints, till one day she returned home before her usual time so thoroughly alarmed that she had deserted her flock. Her parents now took the matter up and investigated it. Her story was as follows:—

Jean had often told her that he had sold himself to the devil, and that he had acquired the power of ranging the country after dusk, and sometimes in broad day, in the form of a wolf. He had assured her that he had killed and devoured many dogs, but that he found their flesh less palatable than the flesh of little girls, which he regarded as a supreme delicacy. He had told her that this had been tasted by him not unfrequently, but he had specified only two instances: in one he had eaten as much as he could, and had thrown the rest to a wolf, which had come up during the repast. In the other instance he had bitten to death another little girl, had lapped her blood, and, being in a famished condition at the time, had devoured every portion of her, with the exception of the arms and shoulders.

The child told her parents, on the occasion of her return home in a fit of terror, that she had been guiding her sheep as usual, but Grenier had not been present. Hearing a rustle in the bushes she had looked round, and a wild beast bad leaped upon her, and torn her clothes on her left side with its sharp fangs. She added that she had defended herself lustily with her shepherd's staff, and had beaten the creature off. It had then retreated a few paces, had seated itself on its hind legs like a dog when it is begging, and had regarded her with such a look of rage, that she had fled in terror. She described the animal as resembling a wolf, but as being shorter and stouter; its hair was red, its tail stumpy, and the head smaller than that of a genuine wolf.

The statement of the child produced general consternation in the parish. It was well known that several little girls had vanished in a most mysterious way of late, and the parents of these little ones were thrown into an agony of terror lest their children had become the prey of the wretched boy accused by Marguerite Poirier. The case was now taken up by the authorities and brought before the parliament of Bordeaux.

The investigation which followed was as complete as could be desired.

Jean Grenier was the son of a poor labourer in the village of S. Antoine do Pizon, and not the son of a priest, as he had asserted. Three months before his seizure he had left home, and had been with several masters doing odd work, or wandering about the country begging. He had been engaged several times to take charge of the flocks belonging to farmers, and had as often been discharged for neglect of his duties. The lad exhibited no reluctance to communicate all he knew about himself, and his statements were tested one by one, and were often proved to be correct.

The story he related of himself before the court was as follows:—

"When I was ten or eleven years old, my neighbour, Duthillaire, introduced me, in the depths of the forest, to a M. de la Forest, a black man, who signed me with his nail, and then gave to me and Duthillaire a salve and a wolf-skin. From that time have I run about the country as a wolf.

"The charge of Marguerite Poirier is correct. My intention was to have killed and devoured her, but she kept me off with a stick. I have only killed one dog, a white one, and I did not drink its blood."

When questioned touching the children, whom he said he had killed and eaten as a wolf, he allowed that he had once entered an empty house on the way between S. Coutras and S. Anlaye, in a small village, the name of which he did not remember, and had found a child asleep in its cradle; and as no one was within to hinder him, he dragged the baby out of its cradle, carried it into the garden, leaped the hedge, and devoured as much of it as satisfied his hunger. What remained he had given to a wolf. In the parish of S. Antoine do Pizon he had attacked a little girl, as she was keeping sheep. She was dressed in a black frock; he did not know her name. He tore her with his nails and teeth, and ate her. Six weeks before his capture he had fallen upon another child, near the stone-bridge, in the same parish. In Eparon he had assaulted the hound of a certain M. Millon, and would have killed the beast, had not the owner come out with his rapier in his hand.

Jean said that he had the wolf-skin in his possession, and that he went out hunting for children, at the command of his master, the Lord of the Forest. Before transformation he smeared himself with the salve, which be preserved in a small pot, and hid his clothes in the thicket.

He usually ran his courses from one to two hours in the day, when the moon was at the wane, but very often he made his expeditions at night. On one occasion he had accompanied Duthillaire, but they had killed no one.

He accused his father of having assisted him, and of possessing a wolf-skin; he charged him also with having accompanied him on one occasion, when he attacked and ate a girl in the village of Grilland, whom he had found tending a flock of geese. He said that his stepmother was separated from his father. He believed the reason to be, because she had seen him once vomit the paws of a dog and the fingers of a child. He added that the Lord of the Forest had strictly forbidden him to bite the thumb-nail of his left hand, which nail was thicker and longer than the others, and had warned him never to lose sight of it, as long as he was in his were-wolf disguise.

Duthillaire was apprehended, and the father of Jean Grenier himself claimed to be heard by examination.

The account given by the father and stepmother of Jean coincided in many particulars with the statements made by their son.

The localities where Grenier declared he had fallen on children were identified, the times when he said the deeds had been done accorded with the dates given by the parents of the missing little ones, when their losses had occurred.

The wounds which Jean affirmed that he had made, and the manner in which he had dealt them, coincided with the descriptions given by the children he had assaulted.

He was confronted with Marguerite Poirier, and he singled her out from among five other girls, pointed to the still open gashes in her body, and stated that he had made them with his teeth, when he attacked her in wolf-form, and she had beaten him off with a stick. He described an attack he had made on a little boy whom he would have slain, had not a man come to the rescue, and exclaimed, "I'll have you presently."

The man who saved the child was found, and proved to be the uncle of the rescued lad, and he corroborated the statement of Grenier, that he had used the words mentioned above.

Jean was then confronted with his father. He now began to falter in his story, and to change his statements. The examination had lasted long, and it was seen that the feeble intellect of the boy was wearied out, so the case was adjourned. When next confronted with the elder Grenier, Jean told his story as at first, without changing it in any important particular.

The fact of Jean Grenier having killed and eaten several children, and of his having attacked and wounded others, with intent to take their life, were fully established; but there was no proof whatever of the father having had the least hand in any of the murders, so that he was dismissed the court without a shadow of guilt upon him.

The only witness who corroborated the assertion of Jean that he changed his shape into that of a wolf was Marguerite Poirier.

Before the court gave judgment, the first president of assize, in an eloquent speech, put on one side all questions of witchcraft and diabolical compact, and bestial transformation, and boldly stated that the court had only to consider the age and the imbecility of the child, who was so dull and idiotic—that children of seven or eight years old have usually a larger amount of reason than he. The president went on to say that Lycanthropy and Kuanthropy were mere hallucinations, and that the change of shape existed only in the disorganized brain of the insane, consequently it was not a crime which could be punished. The tender age of the boy must be taken into consideration, and the utter neglect of his education and moral development. The court sentenced Grenier to perpetual imprisonment within the walls of a monastery at Bordeaux, where he might be instructed in his Christian and moral obligations; but any attempt to escape would be punished with death.

A pleasant companion for the monks! a promising pupil for them to instruct! No sooner was he admitted into the precincts of the religious house, than he ran frantically about the cloister and gardens upon all fours, and finding a heap of bloody and raw offal, fell upon it and devoured it in an incredibly short space of time.

Delancre visited him seven years after, and found him diminutive in stature, very shy, and unwilling to look any one in the face. His eyes were deep set and restless; his teeth long and protruding; his nails black, and in places worn away; his mind was completely barren; he seemed unable to comprehend the smallest things. He related his story to Delancre, and told him how he had run about formerly in the woods as a wolf, and he said that he still felt a craving for raw flesh, especially for that of little girls, which he said was delicious, and he added that but for his confinement it would not be long before he tasted it again. He said that the Lord of the Forest had visited him twice in the prison, but that he had driven him off with the sign of the cross. The account be then gave of his murders coincided exactly with what had come out in his trial; and beside this, his story of the compact he had made with the Black One, and the manner in which his transformation was effected, also coincided with his former statements.

He died at the age of twenty, after an imprisonment of seven years, shortly after Delancre's visit. [*]

[* DELANCRE: *Tableau de l'Iinconstance*, p 305.]

In the two cases of Roulet and Grenier the courts referred the whole matter of Lycanthropy, or animal transformation, to its true and legitimate cause, an aberration of the brain. From this time medical men seem to have regarded it as a form of mental malady to be brought under their treatment, rather than as a crime to be punished by law. But it is very fearful to contemplate that there may still exist persons in the world filled with a morbid craving for human blood, which is ready to impel them to commit the most horrible atrocities, should they escape the vigilante of their guards, or break the bars of the madhouse which restrains them.

VIII. — FOLK-LORE RELATING TO WERE-WOLVES

Barrenness of English Folk-lore—Devonshire Traditions—Derivation of Were-wolf
—Cannibalism in Scotland—The Angus Robber—The Carle of Perth—
French Superstitions—Norwegian Traditions—Danish Tales of Were- wolves—
Holstein Stories—The Werewolf in the Netherlands—Among the Greeks;
the Serbs; the White Russians; the Poles; the Russians—A Russian Receipt
for becoming a Were-wolf—The Bohemian Vlkodlak—Armenian Story—Indian Tales
—Abyssinian Budas—American Transformation Tales—A Slovakian Household Tale—
Similar Greek, Béarnais, and Icelandic Tales

ENGLISH folk-lore is singularly barren of were-wolf stories, the reason being that wolves had been extirpated from England under the Anglo-Saxon kings, and therefore ceased to be objects of dread to the people. The traditional belief in were-wolfism must, however, have remained long in the popular mind, though at present it has disappeared, for the word occurs in old ballads and romances. Thus in Kempion—

O was it war-wolf in the wood?
Or was it mermaid in the sea?
Or was it man, or vile woman,
My ain true love, that mis-shaped thee?

There is also the romance of *William and the Were-wolf* in Hartshorn;[*] but this professes to be a translation from the French:—

[* HARTSHORN: *Ancient Metrical Tales*, p. 256. See also "The Witch Cake," in CRUMEK'S *Remains of Nithsdale Song.*]

For he of Frenche this fayre tale ferst dede translate,
In ese of Englysch men in Englysch speche.

In the popular mind the cat or the hare have taken the place of the wolf for witches' transformation, and we hear often of the hags attending the devil's Sabbath in these forms.

In Devonshire they range the moors in the shape of black dogs, and I know a story of two such creatures appearing in an inn and nightly drinking the cider, till the publican shot a silver button over their heads, when they were instantly transformed into two ill-favoured old ladies of his acquaintance. On Heathfield, near Tavistock, the wild huntsman rides by full moon with his "wush hounds;" and a white hare which they pursued was once rescued by a goody returning from market, and discovered to be a transformed young lady.

Gervaise of Tilbury says in his *Otia Imperalia*—

"Vidimus frequenter in Anglia, per lunationes, homines in lupos mutari, quod hominum genus *gerulfos* Galli vocant, Angli vero *wer-wlf,*dicunt: *wer* enim Anglice virum sonat, *wlf,* lupum." Gervaise may be right in his derivation of the name, and were-wolf may mean man-wolf, though I have elsewhere given a different derivation, and one which I suspect is truer. But Gervaise has grounds for his assertion that *wér* signifies man; it is so in Anglo-Saxon, *vair* in Gothic, *vir* in Latin, *verr*, in Icelandic, *vîra,* Zend, *wirs*, old Prussian, *wirs*, Lettish, *vîra,* Sanskrit, *bîr,* Bengalee.

There have been cases of cannibalism in Scotland, but no bestial transformation is hinted at in connection with them.

Thus Bthius, in his history of Scotland, tells us of a robber and his daughter who devoured children, and Lindsay of Pitscottie gives a full account.

"About this time (1460) there was ane brigand ta'en with his haill family, who haunted a place in Angus. This mischievous man had ane execrable fashion to take all young men and children he could steal away quietly, or tak' away without knowledge, and eat them, and the younger they were, esteemed them the mair tender and delicious. For the whilk cause and damnable abuse, he with his wife and bairns were all burnt, except ane young wench of a year old who was saved and brought to Dandee, where she was brought up and fostered; and when she came to a woman's years, she was condemned and burnt quick for that crime. It is said that when she was coming to the place of execution, there gathered ane huge multitude of people, and specially of women, cursing her that she was so unhappy to commit so damnable deeds. To whom she turned about with an ireful countenance, saying:—'Wherefore chide ye with me, as if I had committed ane unworthy act? Give me credence and trow me, if ye had experience of eating men and women's flesh, ye wold think it so delicious that ye wold never forbear it again.' So, but any sign of repentance, this unhappy traitor died in the sight of the people." [*]

[* LINDSAY'S *Chronicles of Scotland*, 1814, p. 163.]

Wyntoun also has a passage in his metrical chronicle regarding a cannibal who lived shortly before his own time, and he may easily have heard about him from surviving contemporaries. It was about the year 1340, when a large portion of Scotland had been devastated by the arms of Edward III.

> *About Perth thare was the countrie*
> *Sae waste, that wonder wes to see;*
>
> ....
>
> *For intill well-great space thereby,*
> *Wes nother house left nor herb'ry.*
> *Of deer thare wes then sic foison (profusion),*
> *That they wold near come to the town,*
> *Sae great default was near that stead,*
> *That mony were in hunger dead.*
> *A carle they said was near thereby,*
> *That wold act settis (traps) commonly,*
> *Children and women for to slay,*
> *And swains that he might over-ta;*
> *And ate them all that he get might;*
> *Chwsten Cleek till name behight.*
> *That sa'ry life continued he,*
> *While waste but folk was the countrie.[*]*

[* WYNTOUN'S *Chronicle*, ii. 236.]

We have only to compare these two cases with those recorded in the last two chapters, and we see at once how the popular mind in Great Britain had lost the idea of connecting change of form with cannibalism. A man guilty of the crimes committed by the Angus brigand, or the carle of Perth, would have been regarded as a were-wolf in France or Germany, and would have been tried for Lycanthropy.

S. Jerome, by the way, brought a sweeping charge against the Scots. He visited Gaul in his youth, about 880, and he writes:—"When I was a young man in Gaul, I may have seen the Attacotti, a British people who live upon human flesh; and when they find herds of pigs, droves of cattle, or flocks of sheep in the woods, they cut off the haunches of the men and the breasts of the women, and these they regard as great dainties;" in other words they prefer the shepherd to his flock. Gibbon who quotes this passage says on it: "If in the neighbourhood of the commercial and literary town of Glasgow, a race of cannibals has really existed, we may contemplate, in the period of the Scottish history, the opposite extremes of savage and civilized life. Such reflections tend to enlarge the circle of our ideas, and to encourage the pleasing hope that New Zealand may produce in a future age, the Hume of the Southern hemisphere."

If traditions of were-wolves are scanty in England, it is quite the reverse if we cross the water.

In the south of France, it is still believed that fate has destined certain men to be lycanthropists—that they are transformed into wolves at full moon. The desire to run comes upon them at night. They leave their beds, jump out of a window, and plunge into a fountain. After the bath, they come out covered with dense fur, walking on all fours, and commence a raid over fields and meadows, through woods and villages, biting all beasts and human beings that come in their way. At the approach of dawn, they return to the spring, plunge into it, lose their furry skins, and regain their deserted beds. Sometimes the loup-garou is said to appear under the form of a white dog, or to be loaded with chains; but there is probably a confusion of ideas between the were-wolf and the church-dog, bar-ghest, pad-foit, wush-hound, or by whatever name the animal supposed to haunt a churchyard is designated.

In the Périgord, the were-wolf is called louléerou. Certain men, especially bastards, are obliged at each full moon to transform themselves into these diabolic beasts.

It is always at night that the fit comes on. The lycanthropist dashes out of a window, springs into a well, and, after having struggled in the water for a few moments, rises from it, dripping, and invested with a goatskin which the devil has given him. In this condition, the louléerous run upon four legs, pass the night in ranging over the country, and in biting and devouring all the dogs they meet. At break of day they lay aside their goatskins and return home. Often they are ill in consequence of having eaten tough old hounds, and they vomit up their undigested paws. One great nuisance to them is the fact that they may be wounded or killed in their louléerou state. With the first effusion of blood their diabolic covering vanishes, and they are recognized, to the disgrace of their families.

A were-wolf may easily be detected, even when devoid of his skin; for his hands are broad, and his fingers short, and there are always some hairs in the hollow of his hand.

In Normandy, those who are doomed to be loups-garoux, clothe themselves every evening with a skin called their *hère* or *hure*, which is a loan from the devil. When they run in their transformed state, the evil one accompanies them and scourges them at the foot of every cross they pass. The only way in which a werewolf can be liberated from this cruel bondage, is by stabbing him three times in the forehead with a knife. However, some people less addicted to allopathic treatment, consider that three drops of blood drawn by a needle, will be sufficient to procure release.

According to an opinion of the vulgar in the same province, the loup-garou is sometimes a metamorphosis forced upon the body of a damned person, who, after having been tormented in his grave, has torn his way out of it. The first stage in the process consists in his devouring the cerecloth which enveloped his face; then his moans and muffled howls ring from the tomb, through the gloom of night, the earth of the grave begins to heave, and at last, with a scream, surrounded by a phosphorescent glare, and exhaling a ftid odour, he bursts away as a wolf.

In Le Bessin, they attribute to sorcerers the power of metamorphosing certain men into beasts, but the form of a dog is that principally affected by them.

In Norway it is believed that there are persons who can assume the form of a wolf or a bear (Huse-björn), and again resume their own; this property is either imparted to them by the Trollmen, or those possessing it are themselves Trolls.

In a hamlet in the midst of a forest, there dwelt a cottager named Lasse, and his wife. One day he went out in the forest to fell a tree, but had forgot to cross himself and say his paternoster, so that some troll or wolf-witch (varga mor) obtained power over him and transformed him into a wolf. His wife mourned him for many years, but, one Christmas-eve, there came a beggar-woman, very poor and ragged, to the door, and the good woman of the house took her in, fed her well, and entreated her kindly. At her departure the beggar-woman said that the wife would probably see her husband again, as he was not dead, but was wandering in the forest as a wolf. Towards night-fall the wife went to her pantry to place in it a piece of meat for the morrow, when, on turning to go out, she perceived a wolf standing before her, raising itself with its paws on the pantry steps, regarding her with sorrowful and hungry looks. Seeing this she exclaimed, "If I were sure that thou wert my own Lasse, I would give thee a bit of meat." At that instant the wolf-skin fell off, and her husband stood before her in the clothes he wore on the unlucky morning when she had last beheld him.

Finns, Lapps, and Russians are held in particular aversion, because the Swedes believe that they have power to change people into wild beasts. During the last year of the war with Russia, when Calmar was overrun with an unusual number of wolves, it was generally said that the Russians had transformed their Swedish prisoners into wolves, and sent them home to invest the country.

In Denmark the following stories are told:—

A man, who from his childhood had been a were-wolf, when returning one night with his wife from a merrymaking, observed that the hour was at hand when the evil usually came upon him; giving therefore the reins to his wife, he descended from the vehicle, saying to her, "If anything comes to thee, only strike at it with thine apron." He then withdrew, but immediately after, the woman, as she was sitting in the vehicle, was attached by a were-wolf. She did as the man had enjoined her, and struck it with her apron, from which it rived a portion, and then ran away. After some time the man returned, holding in his mouth the rent portion of his wife's apron, on seeing which, she cried out in terror,—"Good Lord, man, why, thou art a were-wolf!" "Thank thee, wife," said he, "now I am free." And from that time he was no more afflicted.

If a female at midnight stretches between four sticks the membrane which envelopes the foal when it is brought forth, and creeps through it, naked, she will bear children without pain; but all the boys will be were-wolves, and all the girls maras. By day the were-wolf has the human form, though he may be known by the meeting of his eyebrows above the nose. At a certain time of the night he has the form of a dog on three legs. It is only when another person tells him that he is a were-wolf, or reproaches him with being such, that a man can be freed from the ban.

According to a Danish popular song, a hero transformed by his step-mother into a bear, fights with a knight:—

For 'tis she who bath bewitched me,
A woman false and fell,
Bound an iron girdle round me,
If thou can'st not break this belt,
Knight, I'll thee destroy!
. . . .
The noble made the Christian sign,
The girdle snapped, the bear was changed,
And see! he was a lusty knight,
His father's realm regained.
—Kjæmpeviser, p. 147.

When an old bear in Ofodens Priestegjeld was killed, after it had caused the death of six men und sixty horses, it was found to be girded with a similar girdle.

In Schleswig and Holstein they say that if the were-wolf be thrice addressed by his baptismal name, he resumes his human form.

On a hot harvest day some reapers lay down in the field to take their noontide sleep, when one who could not sleep observed that the fellow next to him rose softly, and having girded himself with a strap, became a were-wolf.

A young man belonging to Jägerup returning late one night from Billund, was attacked, when near Jägerup, by three were-wolves, and would probably have been torn to pieces, had he not saved himself by leaping into a rye-field, for there they had no more power over him.

At Caseburg, on the isle of Usedom, a man and his wife were busy in the field making hay, when after some time the woman said to the man that she had no more peace, she could stay no longer, and went away. But she had previously desired her husband to promise, that if perchance a wild beast should come that way, he would cast his hat at it and then run away, and it would do him no injury. She had been gone but a short while, when a wolf came swimming across the Swine, and ran directly towards the haymakers.

The man threw his hat at it, which the animal instantly tore to rags. But in the meantime a boy had run up with a pitchfork, and he dabbed the wolf from behind: in the same moment it became changed, and all saw that the boy had killed the man's wife.

Formerly there were individuals in the neighbourhood of Steina, who, by putting on a certain girdle, could transform themselves into were-wolves. A man of the neighbourhood, who had such a girdle, forgot one day when going out to lock it up, as was his wont. During his absence, his little son chanced to find it; he buckled it round him., and was instantaneously turned into an animal, to all outward appearance like a bundle of peat-straw, and he rolled about like an unwieldy bear. When those who were in the room perceived this, they hastened in search of the father, who was found in time to come and unbuckle the belt, before the child had done any mischief. The boy afterwards said, that when he had put on the girdle, he was seized with such a raging hunger, that he was ready to tear in pieces and devour all that came in his way.

The girdle is supposed to be made of human skin, and to be three finger-breadths wide.

In East Friesland, it is believed, when seven girls succeed each other in one family, that among them one is of necessity a were-wolf, so that youths are slow in seeking one of seven sisters in marriage.

According to a curious Lithuanian story related by Schleicher in his *Litauische Märchen*, a person who is a were-wolf or bear has to remain kneeling in one spot for one hundred years before he can hope to obtain release from his bestial form.

In the Netherlands they relate the following tale:—A man had once gone out with his bow to attend a shooting match at Rousse, but when about half way to the place, he saw on a sudden, a large wolf spring from a thicket, and rush towards a young girl, who was sitting in a meadow by the roadside watching cows. The man did not long hesitate, but quickly drawing forth an arrow, took aim, and luckily hit the wolf in the right side, so that the arrow remained sticking in the wound, and the animal fled howling to the wood.

On the following day he heard that a serving-man of the burgomaster's household lay at the point of death, in consequence of having been shot in the right side, on the preceding day. This so excited the archer's curiosity, that he went to the wounded man, and requested to see the arrow. He recognized it immediately as one of his own. Then, having desired all present to leave the room, he persuaded the man to confess that he was a were-wolf and that he had devoured little children. On the following day he died.

Among the Bulgarians and Sloyakians the were-wolf is called *vrkolak*, a name resembling that given it by the modern Greeks {Greek *brúkolakas*}. The Greek were-wolf is closely related to the vampire. The lycanthropist falls into a cataleptic trance, during which his soul leaves his body, enters that of a wolf and ravens for blood. On the return of the soul, the body is exhausted and aches as though it had been put through violent exercise. After death lycanthropists become vampires. They are believed to frequent battlefields in wolf or hyæna shapes, and to suck the breath from dying soldiers, or to enter houses and steal the infants from their cradles. Modern Greeks call any savage-looking man, with dark complexion, and with distorted, misshapen limbs, a {Greek *brúkolakas*}, and suppose him to be invested with power of running in wolf-form.

The Serbs connect the vampire and the were-wolf together, and call them by one name *vlkoslak*. These rage chiefly in the depths of winter: they hold their annual gatherings, and at them divest themselves of their wolf-skins, which they hang on the trees around them. If any one succeeds in obtaining the skin and burning it, the vlkoslak is thenceforth disenchanted.

The power to become a were-wolf is obtained by drinking the water which settles in a foot-print left in clay by a wolf.

Among the White Russians the *wawkalak* is a man who has incurred the wrath of the devil, and the evil one punishes him by transforming him into a wolf and sending him among his relations, who recognize him and feed him well. He is a most amiably disposed were-wolf, for he does no mischief, and testifies his affection for his kindred by licking their hands. He cannot, however, remain long in any place, but is driven from house to house, and from hamlet to hamlet, by an irresistible passion for change of scene. This is an ugly superstition, for it sets a premium on standing well with the evil one.

The Sloyakians merrily term a drunkard a vlkodlak, because, forsooth, he makes a beast of himself. A Slovakian household were-wolf tale closes this chapter.

The Poles have their were-wolves, which rage twice in the year—at Christmas and at midsummer.

According to a Polish story, if a witch lays a girdle of human skin on the threshold of a house in which a marriage is being celebrated, the bride and bridegroom, and bridesmaids and groomsmen, should they step across it, are transformed into wolves. After three years, however, the witch will cover them with skins with the hair. turned outward; immediately they will recover their natural form. On one occasion, a witch cast a skin of too scanty dimensions over the bridegroom, so that his tail was left uncovered: he resumed his human form, but retained his lupine caudal appendage {*i.e. tail—jbh*}.

The Russians call the were-wolf *oborot*, which signifies "one transformed." The following receipt is given by them for becoming one.

"He who desires to become an oborot, let him seek in the forest a hewn-down tree; let him stab it with a small copper knife, and walk round the tree, repeating the following incantation:—

> *On the sea, on the ocean, on the island, on Bujan,*
> *On the empty pasture gleams the moon, on an ashstock lying*
> *In a green wood, in a gloomy vale.*
> *Toward the stock wandereth a shaggy wolf.*
> *Horned cattle seeking for his sharp white fangs;*
> *But the wolf enters not the forest,*
> *But the wolf dives not into the shadowy vale,*
> *Moon, moon, gold-horned moon,*
> *Cheek the flight of bullets, blunt the hunters' knives,*
> *Break the shepherds' cudgels,*
> *Cast wild fear upon all cattle,*
> *On men, on all creeping things,*
> *That they may not catch the grey wolf,*
> *That they may not rend his warm skin*
> *My word is binding, more binding than sleep,*
> *More binding than the promise of a hero!*

"Then he springs thrice over the tree and runs into the forest, transformed into a wolf." [*]

[* SACHAROW: *Inland*, 1838, No. 17.]

In the ancient Bohemian Lexicon of Vacerad (A. D. 1202) the were-wolf is called vilkodlak, and is explained as faunus. Safarik says under that head,-

"Incubi sepe improbi existunt mulieribus, et earum peragunt concubitum, quos demones Galli *dusios* nuncupant." And in another place: "Vilkodlaci, incubi, sive invidi, ab inviando passim cum animalibus, unde et incubi dicuntur ab incubando homines, i. e. stuprando, quos Romani faunos ficarios dicunt."

That the same belief in lycanthropy exists in Armenia is evident from the following story told by Haxthausen, in his *Trans-Caucasia* (Leipzig, i. 322):—"A man once saw a wolf, which had carried off a child, dash past him. He pursued it hastily, but was unable to overtake it. At last he came upon the hands and feet of a child, and a little further on he found a cave, in which lay a wolf-skin. This he cast into a fire, and immediately a woman appeared, who howled and tried to rescue the skin from the flames. The man, however, resisted, and, as soon as the hide was consumed, the woman had vanished in the smoke."

In India, on account of the prevalence of the doctrine of metempsychosis, the belief in transformation is widely diffused. Traces of genuine lycanthropy are abundant in all regions whither Buddism has reached. In Ceylon, in Thibet, and in China, we find it still forming a portion of the national creed.

In the Pantschatantra is a story of an enchanted Brahmin's son, who by day was a serpent, by night a man.

Vikramâditya's father, the son of Indra, was condemned to be an ass by day and a man by night.

A modern Indian tale is to this effect:—A prince marries a female ape, but his brothers wed handsome princesses. At a feast given by the queen to her stepdaughters, there appears an exquisitely beautiful lady in gorgeous robes. This is none other than the she-ape, who has laid aside her skin for the occasion: the prince slips out of the room and burns the skin, so that his wife is prevented from resuming her favourite appearance.

Nathaniel Pierce [*] gives an account of an Abyssinian superstition very similar to that prevalent in Europe.

[* *Life and Adventures of Nathaniel Pierce*, written by himself during a residence in Abyssinia from 1810-19. London, 1831.]

He says that in Abyssinia the gold. and silversmiths are highly regarded, but that the ironworkers are looked upon with contempt, as an inferior grade of beings. Their kinsmen even ascribe to them the power of transforming themselves into hyænas, or other savage beasts. All convulsions and hysterical disorders are attributed to the effect of their evil eye. The Amhara call them *Buda*, the Tigré, *Tebbib*. There are also Mahomedan and Jewish Budas. It is difficult to explain the origin of this strange superstition. These Budas are distinguished from other people by wearing gold ear-rings, and Coffin declares that he has often found hyænas with these rings in their ears, even among the beasts which he has shot or speared himself. But how the rings got into their ears is more than Coffin was able to ascertain.

Beside their power to transform themselves into hyænas or other wild beasts, all sorts of other strange things are ascribed to them; and the Abyssinians are firmly persuaded that they rob the graves by midnight, and no one would venture to touch what is called *quanter*, or dried meat in their houses, though they would not object to partake of fresh meat, if they had seen the animal, from which it came, killed before them. Coffin relates, as eye-witness of the fact, the following story:—

Among his servants was a Buda, who, one evening, whilst it was still light, came to his master and asked leave of absence till the following morning. He obtained the required leave and departed; but scarcely had Coffin turned his head, when one of his men exclaimed,—"Look! there he is, changing himself into hyæna," pointing in the direction taken by the Buda. Coffin turned to look, and although he did not witness the process of transformation, the young man had vanished from the spot on which he had been standing, not a hundred paces distant, and in his place was a hyæna running away. The place was a plain without either bush or tree to impede the view. Next morning the young man returned, and was charged by his companions with the transformation: this he rather acknowledged than denied, for he excused himself on the plea that it was the habit of his class. This statement of Pierce is corroborated by a note contributed by Sir Gardner Wilkinson to Rawlinson's *Herodotus*(book iv. chap. 105). "A class of people in Abyssinia are believed to change themselves into hyænas when they like. On my appearing to discredit it, I was told by one who lived for years there, that no well-informed person doubted it, and that he was once walking with one of them, when he happened to look away for a moment, and on turning again towards his companion, he saw him trotting off in the shape of a hyæna. He met him afterwards in his old form. These worthies are blacksmiths.—G. W."

A precisely similar superstition seems to have existed in America, for Joseph Acosta (*Hist. Nat. des Indes*) relates that the ruler of a city in Mexico, who was sent for by the predecessor of Montezuma, transformed himself, before the eyes of those who were sent to seize him, into an eagle, a tiger, and an enormous serpent. He yielded at last, and was condemned to death. No longer in his own house, he was unable to work miracles so as to save his life. The Bishop of Chiapa, a province of Guatemala, in a writing published in 1702, ascribes the same power to the Naguals, or national priests, who laboured to bring back to the religion of their ancestors, the children brought up as Christians by the government. After various ceremonies, when the child instructed advanced to embrace him, the Nagual suddenly assumed a frightful aspect, and under the form of a lion or tiger, appeared chained to the young Christian convert.—(*Recueil de Voyages*, tom. ii. 187.)

Among the North American Indians, the belief in transformation is very prevalent. The following story closely resembles one very prevalent all over the world.

"One Indian fixed his residence on the borders of the Great Bear lake, taking with him only a dog big with young. In due time, this dog brought forth eight pups. Whenever the Indian went out to fish, he tied up the pups, to prevent the straying of the litter. Several times, as he approached his tent, he heard noises proceeding from it, which sounded like the talking, the laughing, the crying, the wail, and the merriment of children; but, on entering it, he only perceived the pups tied up as usual. His curiosity being excited by the noises he had heard, he determined to watch and learn whence these sounds proceeded, and what they were. One day he pretended to go out to fish, but, instead of doing so, he concealed himself in a convenient place. In a short time he again heard -voices, and, rushing suddenly into the tent, beheld some beautiful children sporting and laughing, with the dog-skins lying by their side. He threw the dog-skins into the fire, and the children, retaining their proper forms, grew up, and were the ancestors of the dog-rib nation."—(*Traditions of the North American Indians*, by T. A. Jones, 1830, Vol. ii. p. 18.)

In the same work is a curious story entitled *The Mother of the World*, which bears a close analogy to another world-wide myth: a woman marries a dog, by night the dog lays aside its skin, and appears as a man. This may be compared with the tale of Björn and Bera already given.

I shall close this chapter with a Slovakian household tale given by T. T. Hanush in the third volume of *Zeitschrift für Deutsche Mythologie*.

"THERE was once a father, who had nine daughters, and they were all marriageable, but the youngest was the most beautiful. The father was a were-wolf. One day it came into his head: 'What is the good of having to support so many girls?' so he determined to put them all out of the way.

"He went accordingly into the forest to hew wood, and he ordered his daughters to let one of them bring him his dinner. It was the eldest who brought it.

"'Why, how come you so early with the food?' asked the woodcutter.

"'Truly, father, I wished to strengthen you, lest you should fall upon us, if famished!'

"'A good lass! Sit down whilst I eat.' He ate, and whilst he ate he thought of a scheme. He rose and said: I My girl, come, and I will show you a pit I have been digging.'

"'And what is the pit for?'

"'That we may be buried in it when we die, for poor folk will not be cared for much after they are dead and gone.'

"So the girl went with him to the side of the deep pit. 'Now hear,' said the were-wolf, 'you must die and be cast in there.'

"She begged for her life, but all in vain, so he laid hold of her and cast her into the grave. Then he took a great stone and flung it in upon her and crushed her head, so the poor thing breathed out her soul. When the were-wolf had done this he went back to his work, and as dusk came on, the second daughter arrived, bringing him food. He told her of the pit, and brought her to it, and cast her in, and killed her as the first. And so he dealt with all his girls up to the last. The youngest knew well that her father was a were-wolf, and she was grieved that her sisters did not return; she thought, 'Now where can they be? Has my father kept them for companionship; or to help him in his work?' So she made the food which she was to take him, and crept cautiously through the wood. When she came near the place where her father worked, she heard his strokes felling timber, and smelt smoke. She saw presently a large fire and two human heads roasting at it. Turning from the fire, she went in the direction of the axe-strokes, and found her father.

"See,' said she, 'father, I have brought you food.'

"That is a good lass,' said he. 'Now stack the wood for me whilst I eat.'

"'But where are my sisters?' she asked.

"'Down in yon valley drawing wood,' he replied 'follow me, and I will bring you to them.'

"They came to the pit; then he told her that he had dug it for a grave. 'Now,' said he, 'you must die, and be cast into the pit with your sisters. '

"'Turn aside, father,' she asked, 'whilst I strip of my clothes, and then slay me if you will.'

"He turned aside as she requested, and then—tchich! she gave him a push, and he tumbled headlong into the hole he had dug for her.

"She fled for her life, for the were-wolf was not injured, and he soon would scramble out of the pit.

"Now she hears his howls resounding through the gloomy alleys of the forest, and swift as the wind she runs. She hears the tramp of his approaching feet, and the snuffle of his breath. Then she casts behind her her handkerchief. The were-wolf seizes this with teeth and nails, and rends it till it is reduced to tiny ribands. In another moment he is again in pursuit foaming at the mouth, and howling dismally, whilst his red eyes gleam like burning coals. As he gains on her, she casts behind her her gown, and bids him tear that. He seizes the gown and rives it to shreds, then again he pursues. This time she casts behind her her apron, next her petticoat, then her shift, and at last rums much in the condition in which she was born. Again the were-wolf approaches; she bounds out of the forest into a hay-field, and hides herself in the smallest heap of hay. Her father enters the field, runs howling about it in search of her, cannot find her, and begins to upset the different haycocks, all the while growling and gnashing his gleaming white fangs in his rage at her having escaped him. The foam flakes drop at every step from his mouth, and his skin is reeking with sweat. Before he has reached the smallest bundle of hay his strength leaves him, he feels exhaustion begin to creep over him, and he retires to the forest.

"The king goes out hunting every clay; one of his dogs carries food to the hay-field, which has most unaccountably been neglected by the hay-makers for three days. The king, following the dog, discovers the fair damsel, not exactly 'in the straw,' but up to her neck in hay. She is carried, hay and all, to the palace, where she becomes his wife, making only one stipulation before becoming his bride, and that is, that no beggar shall be permitted to enter the palace.

"After some years a beggar does get in, the beggar being, of course, none other than her were-wolf father. He steals upstairs, enters the nursery, cuts the throats of the two children borne by the queen to her lord, and lays the knife under her pillow.

"In the morning, the king, supposing his wife to be the murderess, drives her from home, with the dead princes hung about her neck. A hermit comes to the rescue, and restores the babies to life. The king finds out his mistake, is reunited to the lady out of the hay, and the were-wolf is cast off a high cliff into the sea, and that is the end of him. The king, the queen, and the princes live happily, and may be living yet, for no notice of their death has appeared in the newspaper."

This story bears some resemblance to one told by Von Hahn in his *Griechische und Albanesische Märchen*; I remember having heard a very similar one in the Pyrenees; but the man who flies from the were-wolf is one who, after having stripped off all his clothes, rushes into a cottage and jumps into a bed. The were-wolf dares not, or cannot, follow. The cause of his flight was also different. He was a freemason who had divulged the secret, and the were-wolf was the master of his lodge in pursuit of him. In the Bearnais story, there is nothing similar to the last part of the Slovakian tale, and in the Greek one the transformation and the pursuit are omitted, though the woman-eater is called "dog's-head," much as an outlaw in the north of Europe was said to be wolf-headed.

It is worthy of notice in the tale of *The Daughter of the Ulkolak*, that the were-wolf fit is followed by great exhaustion, [*] and that the wolf is given clothes to tear, much as in the Danish stories already related. There does not seem to be any indication of his Laving changed his shape, at least no change is mentioned, his hands are spoken of, and he swears and curses his daughter in broad Slovakian. The fit very closely resembles that to which Skallagrim, the Icelander, was subject. It is a pity that the maid Bràk in the Icelandic tale did not fall upon her legs like the young lady in the hay.

[* Compare this with the exhaustion following a Berserkir fit, and that which succeeded the attacks to which M. Bertrand was subject.]

CHAPTER IX. — NATURAL CAUSES OF LYCANTHROPY

Innate Cruelty—Its Three Forms—Dumollard—Andreas Bichel—A Dutch Priest—
Other instances of Inherent Cruelty—Cruelty united to Refinement—A Hungarian
Bather in Blood—Suddenness with which the Passion is developed—Cannibalism;
in pregnant Women; in Maniacs—Hallucination; how Produced—Salves—The Story
of Lucius—Self-deception

WHAT I have related from the chronicles of antiquity, or from the traditional lore of the people, is veiled under the form of myth or legend; and it is only from Scandinavian descriptions of those afflicted with the wolf-madness, and from the trials of those charged with the crime of lycanthropy in the later Middle Ages, that we can arrive at the truth respecting that form of madness which was invested by the superstitious with so much mystery.

It was not till the close of the Middle Ages that lycanthropy was recognized as a disease; but it is one which has so much that is ghastly and revolting in its form, and it is so remote from all our ordinary experience, that it is not surprising that the casual observer should leave the consideration of it, as a subject isolated and perplexing, and be disposed to regard as a myth that which the feared investigation might prove a reality.

In this chapter I purpose briefly examining the conditions under which men have been regarded as werewolves.

Startling though the assertion may be, it is a matter of fact, that man, naturally, in common with other carnivora, is actuated by an impulse to kill, and by a love of destroying life.

It is positively true that there are many to whom the sight of suffering causes genuine pleasure, and in whom the passion to kill or torture is as strong as any other passion. Witness the number of boys who assemble around a sheep or pig when it is about to be killed, and who watch the struggle of the dying brute with hearts beating fast with pleasure, and eyes sparkling with delight. Often have I seen an eager crowd of children assembled around the slaughterhouses of French towns, absorbed in the expiring agonies of the sheep and cattle, and hushed into silence as they watched the flow of blood.

The propensity, however, exists in different degrees. In some it is manifest simply as indifference to suffering, in others it appears as simple pleasure in seeing killed, and in others again it is dominant as an irresistible desire to torture and destroy.

This propensity is widely diffused; it exists in children and adults, in the gross-minded and the refined., in the well-educated and the ignorant, in those who have never had the opportunity of gratifying it, and those who gratify it habitually, in spite of morality, religion, laws, so that it can only depend on constitutional causes.

The sportsman and the fisherman follow a natural instinct to destroy, when they make wax on bird, beast, and fish: the pretence that the spoil is sought for the table cannot be made with justice, as the sportsman cares little for the game he has obtained, when once it is consigned to his pouch. The motive for his eager pursuit of bird or beast must be sought elsewhere; it will be found in the natural craving to extinguish life, which exists in his soul. Why does a child impulsively strike at a butterfly as it flits past him? He cares nothing for the insect when once it is beaten down at his feet, unless it be quivering in its agony, when he will watch it with interest. The child strikes at the fluttering creature because it has *life* in it, and he has an instinct within him impelling him to destroy life wherever he finds it.

Parents and nurses know well that children by nature are cruel, and that humanity has to be acquired by education. A child will gloat over the sufferings of a wounded animal till his mother bids him "put it out of its misery." An unsophisticated child would not dream of terminating the poor creature's agonies abruptly, any more than he would swallow whole a bon-bon till he had well sucked it. Inherent cruelty may be obscured by after impressions, or may be kept under moral restraint; the person who is constitutionally a Nero, may scarcely know his own nature, till by some accident the master passion becomes dominant, and sweeps all before it. A relaxation of the moral check, a shock to the controlling intellect, an abnormal condition of body, are sufficient to allow the passion to assert itself.

As I have already observed, this passion exists in different persons in different degrees.

In some it is exhibited in simple want of feeling for other people's sufferings. This temperament may lead to crime, for the individual who is regardless of pain in another, will be ready to destroy that other, if it suit his own purposes. Such an one was the pauper Dumollard, who was the murderer of at least six poor girls, and who attempted to kill several others. He seems not to have felt much gratification in murdering them, but to have been so utterly indifferent to their sufferings, that he killed them solely for the sake of their clothes, which were of the poorest description. He was sentenced to the guillotine, and executed in 1862. [*]

[* A full account of this man's trial is given by one who was present, in *All the Year Round*, No. 162.]

In others, the passion for blood is developed alongside with indifference to suffering.

Thus Andreas Bichel enticed young women into his house, under the pretence that he was possessed of a magic mirror, in which he would show them their future husbands; when he had them in his power he bound their hands behind their backs, and stunned them with a blow. He then stabbed them and despoiled them of their clothes, for the sake of which he committed the murders; but as he killed the young women the passion of cruelty took possession of him, and he hacked the poor girls to pieces whilst they were still alive, in his anxiety to examine their insides. Catherine Seidel he opened with a hammer and a wedge, from her breast downwards, whilst still breathing. "I may say," he remarked at his trial, "that during the operation I was so eager, that I trembled all over, and I longed to rive off a piece and eat it."

Andreas Bichel was executed in 1809. [*]

[* The case of Andreas Bichel is given in Lady Duff Gordon's *Remarkable Criminal Trials*.]

Again, a third class of persons are cruel and bloodthirsty, because in them bloodthirstiness is a raging insatiable passion. In a civilized country those possessed by this passion are forced to control it through fear of the consequences, or to gratify it upon the brute creation. But in earlier days, when feudal lords were supreme in their domains, there have been frightful instances of their excesses, and the extent to which some of the Roman emperors indulged their passion for blood is matter of history.

Gall gives several authentic instances of bloodthirstiness. [*] A Dutch priest had such a desire to kill and to see killed, that he became chaplain to a regiment that he might have the satisfaction of seeing deaths occurring wholesale in engagements. The same man kept a large collection of various kinds of domestic animals, that he might be able to torture their young. He killed the animals for his kitchen, and was acquainted with all the hangmen in the country, who sent him notice of executions, and he would walk for days that he might have the gratification of seeing a man executed.

[* GALL: *Sur les Fonctions du Cerveau*, tom. iv.]

In the field of battle the passion is variously developed; some feel positive delight in slaying, others are indifferent. An old soldier, who had been in Waterloo, informed me that to his mind there was no pleasure equal to running a man through the body, and that he could lie awake at night musing on the pleasurable sensations afforded him by that act.

Highwaymen are frequently not content with robbery, but manifest a bloody inclination to torment and kill. John Rosbeck, for instance, is well known to have invented and exercised the most atrocious cruelties, merely that he might witness the sufferings of his victims, who were especially women and children. Neither fear nor torture could break him of the dreadful passion till he was executed.

Gall tells of a violin-player, who, being arrested, confessed to thirty-four murders, all of which he had committed, not from enmity or intent to rob, but solely because it afforded him an intense pleasure to kill.

Spurzheim [*] tells of a priest at Strasbourg, who, though rich, and uninfluenced by envy or revenge, from exactly the same motive, killed three persons.

[* *Doctrine of the Mind*, p. 158.]

Gall relates the case of a brother of the Duke of Bourbon, Condé, Count of Charlois, who, from infancy, had an inveterate pleasure in torturing animals: growing older, he lived to shed the blood of human beings, and to exercise various kinds of cruelty. He also murdered many from no other motive, and shot at slaters for the pleasure of seeing them fall from the roofs of houses.

Louis XI. of France caused the death of 4,000 people during his reign; he used to watch their executions from a neighbouring lattice. He had gibbets placed outside his own palace, and himself conducted the executions.

It must not be supposed that cruelty exists merely in the coarse and rude; it is quite as frequently observed in the refined and educated. Among the former it is manifest chiefly in insensibility to the sufferings of others; in the latter it appears as a passion, the indulgence of which causes intense pleasure.

Those bloody tyrants, Nero and Caligula, Alexander Borgia, and Robespierre, whose highest enjoyment consisted in witnessing the agonies of their fellow-men, were full of delicate sensibilities and great refinement of taste and manner.

I have seen an accomplished young woman of considerable refinement and of a highly strung nervous temperament, string flies with her needle on a piece of thread, and watch complacently their flutterings. Cruelty may remain latent till, by some accident. it is aroused, and then it will break forth in a devouring flame. It is the same with the passion for blood as with the passions of love and hate; we have no conception of the violence with which they can rage till circumstances occur which call them into action. Love or hate will be dominant in a breast which has been in serenity, till suddenly the spark falls, passion blazes forth, and the serenity of the quiet breast is shattered for ever. A word, a glance, a touch, are sufficient to fire the magazine of passion in the heart, and to desolate for ever an existence. It is the same with bloodthirstiness. It may lurk in the deeps of some heart very dear to us. It may smoulder in the bosom which is most cherished by us, and we may be perfectly unconscious of its existence there. Perhaps circumstances will not cause its development; perhaps moral principle may have bound it down with fetters it can never break.

Michael Wagener [*] relates a horrible story which occurred in Hungary, suppressing the name of the person, as it was that of a still powerful family in the country. It illustrates what I have been saying, and shows how trifling a matter may develope the passion in its most hideous proportions.

[* *Beiträge zur philosophischen Anthropologie*, Wien, 1796.]

"Elizabeth ———— was wont to dress well in order to please her husband, and she spent half the day over her toilet. On one occasion, a lady's-maid saw something wrong in her head-dress, and as a recompence for observing it, received such a severe box on the ears that the blood gushed from her nose, and spirted on to her mistress's face. When the blood drops were washed off her face, her skin appeared much more beautiful—whiter and more transparent on the spots where the blood had been.

"Elizabeth formed the resolution to bathe her face and her whole body in human blood so as to enhance her beauty. Two old women and a certain Fitzko assisted her in her undertaking. This monster used to kill the luckless victim, and the old women caught the blood, in which Elizabeth was wont to bathe at the hour of four in the morning. After the bath she appeared more beautiful than before.

"She continued this habit after the death of her husband (1604) in the hopes of gaining new suitors. The unhappy girls who were allured to the castle, under the plea that they were to be taken into service there, were locked up in a cellar. Here they were beaten till their bodies were swollen. Elizabeth not unfrequently tortured the victims herself; often she changed their clothes which dripped with blood, and then renewed her cruelties. The swollen bodies were then cut up with razors.

"Occasionally she had the girls burned, and then cut up, but the great majority were beaten to death.

"At last her cruelty became so great, that she would stick needles into those who sat with her in a carriage, especially if they were of her own sex. One of her servant-girls she stripped naked, smeared her with honey, and so drove her out of the house.

"When she was ill, and could not indulge her cruelty, she bit a person who came near her sick bed as though she were a wild beast.

"She caused, in all, the death of 650 girls, some in Tscheita, on the neutral ground, where she had a cellar constructed for the purpose; others in different localities; for murder and bloodshed became with her a necessity.

"When at last the parents of the lost children could no longer be cajoled, the castle was seized, and the traces of the murders were discovered. Her accomplices were executed, and she was imprisoned for life."

An equally remarkable example will be found in the account of the Mareschal de Retz given at some length in the sequel. He vas an accomplished man, a scholar, an able general, and a courtier; but suddenly the impulse to murder and destroy came upon him whilst sitting in the library reading Suetonius; he yielded to the impulse, and became one of the greatest monsters of cruelty the world has produced.

The case of Sviatek, the Gallician cannibal, is also to the purpose. This man was a harmless pauper, till one day accident brought him to the scene of a conflagration. Hunger impelled him to taste of the roast fragments of a human being who had perished in the fire, and from that moment he ravened for man's flesh.

M. Bertrand was a French gentleman of taste and education. He one day lounged over the churchyard wall in a quiet country village and watched a funeral. Instantly an overwhelming desire to dig up and rend the corpse which he had seen committed to the ground came upon him, and for years he lived as a human hyæna, preying upon the dead. His story is given in detail in the fifteenth chapter.

An abnormal condition of body sometimes produces this desire for blood. It is manifest in certain cases of pregnancy, when the constitution loses its balance, and the appetite becomes diseased. Schenk [*] gives instances.

[* *Observationes Medic.* lib. iv. De Gravidis.]

A pregnant woman saw a baker carrying loaves on his bare shoulder. She was at once filled with such a craving for his flesh that she refused to taste any food till her husband persuaded the baker, by the offer of a large sum, to allow his wife to bite him. The man yielded, and the woman fleshed her teeth in his shoulder twice; but he held out no longer. The wife bore twins on three occasions, twice living, the third time dead.

A woman in an interesting condition, near Andernach on the Rhine, murdered her husband, to whom she was warmly attached, ate half his body, and salted the rest. When the passion left her she became conscious of the horrible nature of her act, and she gave herself up to justice.

In 1553, a wife cut her husband's throat, and gnawed the nose and the left arm, whilst the body was yet warm. She then gutted the corpse, and salted it for future consumption. Shortly after, she gave birth to three children, and she only became conscious of what she had done when her neighbours asked after the father, that they might announce to him the arrival of the little ones.

In the summer of 1845, the Greek papers contained an account of a pregnant woman murdering her husband for the purpose of roasting and eating his liver.

That the passion to destroy is prevalent in certain maniacs is well known; this is sometimes accompanied by cannibalism.

Gruner [*] gives an account of a shepherd who was evidently deranged, who killed and ate two men. Marc [†] relates that a woman of Unterelsas, during the absence of her husband, a poor labourer, murdered her son, a lad fifteen months old. She chopped of his legs and stewed them with cabbage. She ate a portion, and offered the rest to her husband. It is true that the family were very poor, but there was food in the house at the time. In prison the woman gave evident signs of derangement.

[* *De Anthropophago Bucano*. Jen. 1792.]
[† *Die Geistes-Krankheiten*. Berlin, 1844.]

The cases in which bloodthirstiness and cannibalism are united with insanity are those which properly fall under the head of Lycanthropy. The instances recorded in the preceding chapter point unmistakably to hallucination accompanying the lust for blood. Jean Grenier, Roulet, and others, were firmly convinced that they had undergone transformation. A disordered condition of mind or body may produce hallucination in a form depending on the character and instincts of the individual. Thus, an ambitious man labouring under monomania will imagine himself to be a king; a covetous man will be plunged in despair, believing himself to be penniless, or exult at the vastness of the treasure which he imagines that he has discovered.

The old man suffering from rheumatism or gout conceives himself to be formed of china or glass, and the foxhunter tallyhos! at each new moon, as though he were following a pack. In like manner, the naturally cruel man, if the least affected in his brain, will suppose himself to be transformed into the most cruel and bloodthirsty animal with which he is acquainted.

The hallucinations under which lycanthropists suffered may have arisen from various causes. The older writers, as Forestus and Burton, regard the were-wolf mania as a species of melancholy madness, and some do not deem it necessary for the patient to believe in his transformation for them to regard him as a lycanthropist.

In the present state of medical knowledge, we know that very different conditions may give rise to hallucinations.

In fever cases the sensibility is so disturbed that the patient is often deceived as to the space occupied by his limbs, and he supposes them to be preternaturally distended or contracted. In the case of typhus, it is not uncommon for the sick person, with deranged nervous system, to believe himself to be double in the bed, or to be severed in half, or to have lost his limbs. He may regard his members as composed of foreign and often fragile materials, as glass, or he may so lose his personality as to suppose himself to have become a woman.

A monomaniac who believes himself to be some one else, seeks to enter into the feelings, thoughts, and habits of the assumed personality, and from the facility with which this is effected, he draws an argument, conclusive to himself, of the reality of the change. He thenceforth speaks of himself under the assumed character, and experiences all its needs, wishes, passions, and the like. The closer the identification becomes, the more confirmed is the monomaniac in his madness, the character of which varies with the temperament of the individual. If the person's mind be weak, or rude and uncultivated, the tenacity with which he clings to his metamorphosis is feebler, and it becomes more difficult to draw the line between his lucid and insane utterances. Thus Jean Grenier, who laboured under this form of mania, said in his trial much that was true, but it was mixed with the ramblings of insanity.

Hallucination may also be produced by artificial means, and there are evidences afforded by the confessions of those tried for lycanthropy, that these artificial means were employed by them. I refer to the salve so frequently mentioned in witch and were-wolf trials. The following passage is from the charming *Golden Ass of Apuleius*; it proves that salves were extensively used by witches for the purpose of transformation, even in his day:—

"Fotis showed me a crack in the door, and bade me look through it, upon which I looked and saw Pamphile first divest herself of all her garments, and then, having unlocked a chest, take from it several little boxes, and open one of the latter, which contained a certain ointment. Rubbing this ointment a good while previously between the palms of her hands, she anointed her whole body, from the very nails of her toes to the hair on the crown of her head, and when she was anointed all over, she whispered many magic words to a lamp, as if she were talking to it. Then she began to move her arms, first with tremulous jerks, and afterwards by a gentle undulating motion, till a glittering, downy surface by degrees overspread her body, feathers and strong quills burst forth suddenly, her nose became a hard crooked beak, her toes changed to curved talons, and Pamphile was no longer Pamphile, but it was an owl I saw before me. And now, uttering a harsh, querulous scream, leaping from the ground by little and little, in order to try her powers, and presently poising herself aloft on her pinions, she stretched forth her wings on either Side to their full extent, and flew straight away.

"Having now been actually a witness of the performance of the magical art, and of the metamorphosis of Pamphile, I remained for some time in a stupefied state of astonishment. . . . At last, after I had rubbed my eyes some time, had recovered a little from the amazement and abstraction of mind, and begun to feel a consciousness of the reality of things about me, I took hold of the hand of Fotis and said,—'Sweet damsel, bring me, I beseech thee, a portion of the ointment with which thy mistress hath just now anointed, and when thou hast made me a bird, I will be thy slave, and even wait upon thee like a winged Cupid.' Accordingly she crept gently into the apartment, quickly returned with the box of ointment, hastily placed it in my hands, and then immediately departed.

"Elated to an extraordinary degree at the sight of the precious treasure, I kissed the box several times successively; and uttering repeated aspirations in hopes of a prosperous flight, I stripped off my clothes as quick as possible, dipped my fingers greedily into the box, and having thence extracted a good large lump of ointment, rubbed it all over my body and limbs. When I was thoroughly anointed, I swung my arms up and down, in imitation of the movement of a bird's pinions, and continued to do so a little while, when instead of any perceptible token of feathers or wings making their appearance, my own thin skin, alas! grew into a hard leathern hide, covered with bristly hair, my fingers and toes disappeared, the palms of my hands and the soles of my feet became four solid hoofs, and from the end of my spine a long tail projected. My face was enormous, my mouth wide, my nostrils gaping, my lips pendulous, and I had a pair of immoderately long, rough, hairy ears. In short, when I came to contemplate my transformation to its full extent, I found that, instead of a bird, I had become—an ASS." [*]

[* APULEIUS, Sir George Head's translation, bk. iii.]

Of what these magical salves were composed we know. They were composed of narcotics, to wit, *Solanum somniferum*, aconite, hyoscyamus, belladonna, opium, *acorus vulgaris*, *sium*. These were boiled down with oil, or the fat of little children who were murdered for the purpose. The blood of a bat was added, but its effects could have been *nil*. To these may have been added other foreign narcotics, the names of which have not transpired.

Whatever may have been the cause of the hallucination, it is not surprising that the lycanthropist should have imagined himself transformed into a beast. The cases I have instanced are those of shepherds, who were by nature of their employment, brought into collision with wolves; and it is not surprising that these persons, in a condition liable to hallucinations, should imagine themselves to be transformed into wild beasts, and that their minds reverting to the injuries sustained from these animals, they should, in their state of temporary insanity, accuse themselves of the acts of rapacity committed by the beasts into which they believed themselves to be transformed. It is a well-known fact that men, whose minds are unhinged, will deliver themselves up to justice, accusing themselves of having committed crimes which have actually taken place, and it is only on investigation that their self-accusation proves to be false; and yet they will describe the circumstances with the greatest minuteness, and be thoroughly convinced of their own criminality. I need give but a single instance.

In the war of the French Revolution, the *Hermione* frigate was commanded by Capt. Pigot, a harsh man and a severe commander. His crew mutinied, and carried the ship into an enemy's port, having murdered the captain and several of the officers, under circumstances of extreme barbarity. One midshipman escaped, by whom many of the criminals, who were afterwards taken and delivered over to justice, one by one, were identified. Mr. Finlayson, the Government actuary, who at that time held an official situation in the Admiralty, states:—"In my own experience I have known, on separate occasions, *more than six sailors* who voluntarily confessed to having struck the first blow at Capt. Pigot. These men detailed all the horrid circumstances of the mutiny with extreme minuteness and perfect accuracy; nevertheless, not one of them had ever been in the ship, nor had so much as seen Capt. Pigot in their lives. They had obtained by tradition, from their messmates, the particulars of the story. When long on a foreign station, hungering and thirsting for home, their minds became enfeebled; at length they actually believed themselves guilty of the crime over which they had so long brooded, and submitted with a gloomy pleasure to being sent to England in irons, for judgment. At the Admiralty we were always able to detect and establish their innocence, in defiance of their own solemn asseverations."—(*London Judicial Gazette*, January, 1803.)

X. — MYTHOLOGICAL ORIGIN OF THE WERE-WOLF MYTH

Metempsychosis—Sympathy between Men and Beasts—Finnbog and the Bear—
Osage and the Beaver—The Connexion of Soul and Body—Buddism—
Case of Mr. Holloway—Popular ideas concerning the Body—The derivation
of the German Leichnam—Feather Dresses—Transmigration of Souls—A Basque Story
—Story from the Pantschatantra—Savage ideas regarding Natural Phenomena—
Thunder, Lightning, and Cloud—The origin of the Dragon—John of Bromton's Dragon
a Waterspout—The Legend of Typhoeus—Allegorizing of the Effects of a Hurricane—
Anthropomorphosis—The Cirrus Cloud, a Heavenly Swan—Urvaci—The Storm-cloud a
Daemon—Vritra and Rakschasas—Story of a Brahmin and a Rakschasas

TRANSFORMATION into beasts forms an integral portion of all mythological systems. The gods of Greece were wont to change themselves into animals in order to carry out their designs with greater speed, security, and secrecy, than in human forms. In Scandinavian mythology, Odin changed himself into the shape of an eagle, Loki into that of a salmon. Eastern religions abound in stories of transformation.

The line of demarcation between this and the translation of a beast's soul into man, or a man's soul into a beast's (metempsychosis) is very narrow.

The doctrine of metempsychosis is founded on the consciousness of gradation between beasts and men. The belief in a soul-endowed animal world was present among the ancients, and the laws of intelligence and instinct were misconstrued, or were regarded as a puzzle, which no man might solve.

The human soul with its consciousness seemed to be something already perfected in a pre-existing state, and, in the myth of metempsychosis, we trace the yearnings and gropings of the soul after the source whence its own consciousness was derived, counting its dreams and hallucinations as gleams of memory, recording acts which had taken place in a former state of existence.

Modern philosophy has resumed the same thread of conjecture, and thinks to see in man the perfected development of lower organisms.

After death the translation of the soul was supposed to continue. It became either absorbed into the *nous*, into Brahma, into the deity, or it sank in the scale of creation, and was degraded to animate a brute. Thus the doctrine of metempsychosis was emphatically one of rewards and punishments, for the condition of the soul after death depended on its training during life. A savage and bloodthirsty man was exiled, as in the case of Lycaon, into the body of a wild beast: the soul of a timorous man entered a hare, and drunkards or gluttons became swine.

The intelligence which was manifest in the beasts bore such a close resemblance to that of man, in the childhood and youth of the world, that it is not to be wondered at, if our forefathers failed to detect the line of demarcation drawn between instinct and reason. And failing to distinguish this, they naturally fell into the belief in metempsychosis.

It was not merely a fancied external resemblance between the beast and man, but it was the perception of skill, pursuits, desires, sufferings, and griefs like his own, in the animal creation, which led man to detect within the beast something analogous to the soul within himself; and this, notwithstanding the points of contrast existing between them, elicited in his mind so strong a sympathy that, without a great stretch of imagination, he invested the beast with his own attributes, and with the full powers of his own understanding. He regarded it as actuated by the same motives, as subject to the same laws of honour, as moved by the same prejudices, and the higher the beast was in the scale, the more he regarded it as an equal. A singular illustration of this will be found in the Finnboga Saga, c. xi.

"Now we must relate about Finnbog. Afterward in the evening, when men slept, he rose, took his weapons, and went forth, following the tracks which led to the dairy farm. As was his wont, he stepped out briskly along the spoor till he came to the dairy. There he found the bear lying down, and he had slain the sheep, and he was lying on them lapping their blood. Then said Finnbog: 'Stand up, Brain! make ready against me; that becomes you more than crouching over those sheep's carcases.'

"The bear sat up, looked at him, and lay down again. Finnbog said, 'If you think that I am too fully armed to match with you, I will do this,' and he took of his helmet and laid aside his shield. Then he said, Stand up now, if you dare! '

"The bear sat up, shook his head, and then cast himself down again. "Finnbog exclaimed, 'I see, you want us both to be *boune* alike!' so he flung aside his sword and said, 'Be it as you will; now stand up if you have the heart that I believe you have, rather than one such as was possessed by these rent sheep.'

"Then Bruin stood up and prepared to fight."

The following story taken from the mouth of an Osage Indian by J. A. Jones, and published in his *Traditions of the North American Indians*, shows how thoroughly the savage mind misses the line of demarcation between instinct and reason, and how the man of the woods looks upon beasts as standing on an equality with himself.

An Osage warrior is in search of a wife: he admires the tidy and shrewd habits of the beaver. He accordingly goes to a beaver-hut to obtain one of that race for a bride. "In one corner of the room sat a beaver-woman combing the heads of some little beavers, whose ears she boxed very soundly when they would not lie still. The warrior, *i. e.* the beaver-chief, whispered the Osage that she was his second wife, and was very apt to be cross when there was work to be done, which prevented her from going to see her neighbours. Those whose heads she was combing were her children, he said, and she who had made them rub their noses against each other and be friends, was his eldest daughter. Then calling aloud, 'Wife,' said he, 'what have you to eat? The stranger is undoubtedly hungry; see, he is pale, his eye has no fire, and his step is like that of a moose.'

"Without replying to him, for it was a sulky day with her, she called aloud, and a dirty-looking beaver entered. 'Go,' said she, 'and fetch the stranger something to eat.' With that the beaver girl passed through a small door into another room, from which she soon returned, bringing some large pieces of willow-bark, which she laid at the feet of the warrior and his guest. While the warrior-beaver was chewing the willow, and the Osage was pretending to do so, they fell to talking over many matters, particularly the wars of the beavers with the otters, and their frequent victories over them. He told our father by what means the beavers felled large trees, and moved them to the places where they wished to make dams; how they raised to an erect position the poles for their lodges, and how they plastered them so as to keep out rain. Then he spoke of their employments when they had buried the hatchet; of the peace and happiness and tranquillity they enjoyed when gathered into companies, they rested from their labours, and passed their time in talking and feasting, and bathing, and playing the game of bones, and making love. All the while the young beaver-maiden sat with her eyes fixed upon the Osage, at every pause moving a little nearer, till at length she was at his side with her forepaw upon his arm; a minute more and she had placed it around his neck, and was rubbing her soft furry cheek against his. Our ancestor, on his part, betrayed no disinclination to receive her caresses, but returned them with equal ardour. The old beaver seeing what was going on, turned his back upon them, and suffered them to be as kind to each other as they pleased. At last, turning quickly round, while the maiden, suspecting what was coming, and pretending to be abashed, ran behind her mother, he said, 'To end this foolery, what say you to marrying my daughter? She is well brought up, and is the most industrious girl in the village. She will flap more wall with her tail in a day than any maiden in the nation; she will gnaw down a larger tree betwixt the rising of the sun and the coming of the shadows than many a smart beaver of the other sex. As for her wit, try her at the game of the dish, and see who gets up master; and for cleanliness, look at her petticoat?' Our father answered that he did not doubt that she was industrious and cleanly, able to gnaw down a very large tree, and to use her tail to very good purpose; that he loved her much, and wished to make her the mother of his children. And thereupon the bargain was concluded."

These two stories, the one taken from Icelandic saga, the other from American Indian tradition, shew clearly the oneness which the uncultivated mind believes to exist between the soul of man and the soul of beast. The same sentiments actuate both man and brute, and if their actions are unlike, it is because of the difference in their formation. The soul within is identical, but the external accidents of body are unlike.

Among many rude as well as cultivated people, the body is regarded as a mere garment wrapped around the soul. The Buddist looks upon identity as existing in the soul alone, and the body as no more constituting identity, than the clothes he puts on or takes off. He exists as a spirit; for convenience he vests himself in a body; sometimes that body is human, sometimes it is bestial. As his soul rises in the spiritual scale, the nobler is the animal form which it tenants. Budda himself passed through various stages of existence; in one he was a hare, and his soul being noble, led him to immolate himself, in order that he might offer hospitality to Indra, who, in the form of an old man, craved of him food and shelter. The Buddist regards animals with reverence; an ancestor may be tenanting the body of the ox he is driving, or a descendant may be running at his side barking, and wagging his tail. When he falls into an ecstasy, his soul is leaving his body for a little while, it is laying aside its raiment of flesh and blood and bone, to return to it once more when the trance is over. But this idea is not confined to Buddists, it is common everywhere. The spirit or soul is supposed to be imprisoned in the body, the body is but the lantern through which the spirit shines, "the corruptible body" is believed to "press down the soul," and the soul is unable to attain to perfect happiness till it has shuffled off this earthy coil. Butler regards the members of the body as so many instruments used by the soul for the purpose of seeing, hearing, feeling, &c., just as we use telescopes or crutches, and which may be rejected without injury to our individuality.

The late Mr. J. Holloway, of the Bank of England, brother to the engraver of that name, related of himself that, being one night in bed, and unable to sleep, he had fixed his eyes and thoughts with uncommon intensity on a beautiful star that was shining in at the window, when he suddenly found his spirit released from his body and soaring into space. But instantly seized with anxiety for the anguish of his wife, if she discovered his body apparently dead beside her, he returned, and re-entered it with difficulty. He described that returning as a returning from light into darkness, and that whilst the spirit was free, he was alternately in the light or the dark, accordingly as his thoughts were with his wife or with the star. Popular mythology in most lands regards the soul as oppressed by the body, and its liberation is considered a deliverance from the "burden" of the flesh. Whether the soul is at all able to act or express itself without a body, any more than a fire is able to make cloth without the apparatus of boiler and machinery, is a question which has not commended itself to the popular mind. But it may be remarked that the Christian religion alone is that which raises the body to a dignity equal to that of the soul, and gives it a hope of ennoblement and resurrection never dreamed of in any mythological system.

But the popular creed, in spite of the most emphatic testimony of Scripture, is that the soul is in bondage so long as it is united to a body, a creed entirely in accordance with that of Buddism.

If the body be but the cage, as a poet [*] of our own has been pleased to call it, in which dwells the imprisoned soul, it is quite possible for the soul to change its cage. If the body be but a vesture clothing the soul, as the Buddist asserts, it is not improbable that it may occasionally change its vesture.

[* VAUGHN, *Sitex Scintillans*.]

This is self-evident, and thus have arisen the countless tales of transformation and transmigration which are found all over the world. That the same view of the body as a mere clothing of the soul was taken by our Teutonic and Scandinavian ancestors, is evident even from the etymology of the words *leichnam*, *lîkhama*, used to express the soulless body.

I have already spoken of the Norse word *hamr*, I wish now to make some further remarks upon it. *Hamr* is represented in Anglo-Saxon by *hama*, *homa*, in Saxon by *hamo*, in old High German by *hamo*, in old French by *homa*, *hama*, to which are related the Gothic *gahamon*, *ufar-hamon*, *ana-hamon*, {Greek *e?ndúesðai*}, {Greek *e?pendúesðai*}; *and-hamon*, *af-hamon*, {Greek *a?pekdúein*} {Greek *e?kdúesðai?*} thence also the old High German *hemidi*, and the modern *Hemde*, garment. In composition we find this word, as *lîk-hagnr*, in old Norse; in old High German *lîk- hamo*, Anglo-Saxon *lîk-hama*, and *flæsc-hama*, Old Saxon, *lîk-hamo*, modern German *Leich-nam*, a body, *i. e.* a garment of flesh, precisely as the bodies of birds are called in old Norse *fjaðr-hamr*, in Anglo-Saxon *feðerhoma*, in Old Saxon *fetherhamo*, or feather-dresses and the bodies of wolves are called in old Norse *úlfshamr*, and seals' bodies in Faroëse *kôpahamr*. The significance of the old verb *að hamaz* is now evident; it is to migrate from one body to another, and *hama-skipti* is a transmigration of the soul. The method of this transmigration consisted in simply investing the body with the skin of the animal into which the soul was to migrate. When Loki, the Northern god of evil, went in quest of the stolen Idunn, he borrowed of Freyja her falcon dress, and at once became, to all intents and purposes, a falcon. Thiassi pursued him as he left Thrymheimr, having first taken upon him an eagle's dress, and thereby become an eagle.

In order to seek Thor's lost hammer, Loki borrowed again of Freyja her feather dress, and as be flew away in it, the feathers sounded as they winnowed the breeze (*fjaðrhamr dunði*).

In like manner Cædmon speaks of an evil spirit flying away in feather-dress: "þät he mid feðerhomon fleôgan meahte, windan on wolkne" (Gen. ed. Gr. 417), and of an angel, "þuo þar suogan quam engil þes alowaldon obhana fun radure faran an feðerhamon" (Hêlj. 171, 23), the very expression made use of when speaking of a bird: "farad an feðarhamun" (Hêlj. 50,11).

The soul, in certain cases, is able to free itself from the body and to enter that of beast or man—in this form stood the myth in various theological systems.

106

Among the Finns and Lapps it is not uncommon for a magician to fall into a cataleptic condition, and during the period his soul is believed to travel very frequently in bodily form, having assumed that of any animal most suitable for its purpose. I have given instances in a former chapter. The same doctrine is evident in most cases of lycanthropy. The patient is in a state of trance, his body is watched, and it remains motionless, but his soul has migrated into the carcase of a wolf, which it vivifies, and in which it runs its course. A curious Basque story shows that among this strange Turanian people, cut off by such a flood of Aryan nations from any other members of its family, the same superstition remains. A huntsman was once engaged in the chase of it bear among the Pyreneean peaks, when Bruin turned suddenly on him and hugged him to death, but not before he had dealt the brute its mortal wound. As the huntsman expired, he breathed his soul into the body of the bear, and thenceforward ranged the mountains as a beast.

One of the tales of the Sanskrit book of fables, the *Pantschatantra*, affords such a remarkable testimony to the Indian belief in metempsychosis, that I am tempted to give it in abstract.

A king was one day passing through the marketplace of his city, when he observed a hunchbacked merryandrew, whose contortions and jokes kept the bystanders in a roar of laughter. Amused with the fellow, the king brought him to his palace. Shortly after, in the hearing of the clown, a necromancer taught the monarch the art of sending his soul into a body not his own.

Some little while after this, the monarch, anxious to put in practice his newly acquired knowledge, rode into the forest accompanied by his fool, who, he believed, had not heard, or, at all events comprehended, the lesson. They came upon the corpse of a Brahmin lying in the depth of the jungle, where he had died of thirst. The king, leaving his horse, performed the requisite ceremony, and instantly his soul had migrated into the body of the, Brahmin, and his own lay as dead upon the ground. At the same moment, however, the hunchback deserted his body, and possessed himself of that which had been the king's, and shouting farewell to the dismayed monarch, he rode back to the palace, where he was received with royal honours. But it was not long before the queen and one of the ministers discovered that a screw was somewhere loose, and when the quondam king, but now Brahmin, arrived and told his tale, a plot was laid for the recovery of his body. The queen asked her false husband whether it were possible to make her parrot talk, and he in a moment of uxorious weakness promised to make it speak. He laid his body aside, and sent his soul into the parrot. Immediately the true king jumped out of his Brahmin body and resumed that which was legitimately his own, and then proceeded, with the queen, to wring the neck of the parrot.

But besides the doctrine of metempsychosis, which proved such a fertile mother of fable, there was another article of popular mythology which gave rise to stories of transformation. Among the abundant superstitions existing relative to transformation, three shapes seem to have been pre-eminently affected— that of the swan, that of the wolf, and that of the serpent. In many of the stories of those transformed, it is evident that the individual who changes shape is regarded with superstitious reverence, as a being of a higher order—of a divine nature. In Christian countries, everything relating to heathen mythology was regarded with a suspicious eye by the clergy, and any miraculous powers not sanctioned by the church were attributed to the evil one. The heathen gods became devils, and the marvels related of them were supposed to be effected by diabolic agency. A case of transformation which had shown the power of an ancient god, was in Christian times considered as an instance of witchcraft. Thus stories of transformation fell into bad odour, and those who changed shapes were no longer regarded as heavenly beings, commanding reverence, but as miserable witches deserving the stake.

In the infancy of the world, when natural phenomena were ill-understood, expressions which to us are poetical were of a real significance. When we speak of thunder rolling, we use an expression which conveys no further idea than a certain likeness observed between the detonations and the roll of a vehicle; but to the uninstructed mind it was more. The primæval savage knew not what caused thunder, and tracing the resemblance between it and the sound of wheels, he at once concluded that the chariot of the gods was going abroad, or that the celestial spirits were enjoying a game of bowls.

We speak of fleecy clouds, because they appear to us soft and light as wool, but the first men tracing the same resemblance, believed the light vapours to be flocks of heavenly sheep. Or we say that the clouds are flying: the savage used the same expression, as he looked up at the mackerel sky, and saw in it flights of swans coursing over the heavenly lake. Once more, we creep nearer to the winter fire, shivering at the wind, which we remark is howling around the house, and yet we do not suppose that the wind has a voice. The wild primæval men thought that it had, and because dogs and wolves howl, and the wind howled, and because they had seen dogs and wolves, they concluded that the storm-wind was a night-hound, or a monstrous wolf, racing over the country in the darkness of the winter night, ravening for prey.

Along with the rise of this system of explaining the operations of nature by analogies in the bestial world, another conclusion forced itself on the untaught mind. The flocks which strayed in heaven were no earthly sheep, but were the property of spiritual beings, and were themselves perhaps spiritual; the swans which flew aloft, far above the topmost peak of the Himalaya, were no ordinary swans, but were divine and heavenly. The wolf which howled so wildly in the long winter night, the hounds, whose bay sounded so. dismally through the shaking black forest, were no mundane wolves and hounds, but issued from the home of a divine hunter, and were themselves wondrous, supernatural beings of godlike race.

And so, the clouds having become swans, the swan-clouds were next believed to be divine beings, valkyries, apsaras, and the like, seen by mortals in their feather-dresses, but appearing among the gods as damsels. The storm-wind having been supposed to be a wolf, next was taken to be a tempestuous god, who delighted to hunt on earth in lupine form.

I have mentioned also the serpent shape, as being one very favourite in mythology. The ancient people saw the forked and writhing lightning, and supposed it to be a heavenly fiery serpent, a serpent which had godlike powers, which was in fact a divine being, manifesting himself to mortals under that form. Among the North American Indians, the lightning is still regarded as the great serpent, and the thunder is supposed to be his hissing.

"Ah!" exclaimed a Magdeburg peasant to a German professor, during a thunder-storm, as a vivid forked gleam shot to earth, "what a glorious snake was that!" And this resemblance did not escape the Greeks.

{Greek *é!likes d? e?klámpousi steroph~s ksápuroi*}.
Æsch. Prom. 1064.
{Greek *drákonta pursónwton, ó!s á?platon a?mfeliktòs é!lik? e?froúrei, ktanw'n*}.
Eurip. Herc. F. 395.
And according to Aristotle, {Greek *e!likíai*} are the lightnings, {Greek *grammoeidw~s ferómenoi*}.

It is so difficult for us to unlearn all we know of the nature of meteorological phenomena, so hard for us to look upon atmospheric changes as though we knew nothing of the laws that govern them, that we are disposed to treat such explanations of popular myths as I have given above, as fantastic and improbable.

But among the ancients all solutions of natural problems were tentative, and it is only after the failure of every attempt made to explain these phenomena on supernatural grounds that we have been driven to the discovery of the true interpretation. Yet among the vulgar a vast amount of mythology remains, and is used still to explain atmospheric mysteries. The other day a Yorkshire girl, when asked why she was not afraid of thunder, replied because it was only her Father's voice; what knew she of the rushing together of air to fill the vacuum caused by the transit of the electric fluid? to her the thunder-clap was the utterance of the Almighty. Still in North Germany does the peasant say of thunder, that the angels are playing skittles aloft, and of the snow, that they are shaking up the feather-beds in heaven.

The myth of the dragon is one which admits, perhaps more than any other, of identification with a meteorological phenomenon, and presents to us as well the phase of transition from theriomorphosis to anthropomorphosis.

The dragon of popular mythology is nothing else than the thunderstorm, rising at the horizon, rushing with expanded, winnowing, black pennons across the sky, darting out its forked fiery tongue, and belching fire. In a Slovakian legend, the dragon sleeps in a mountain cave through the winter months, but, at the equinox, bursts forth—"In a moment the heaven was darkened and became black as pitch, only illumined by the fire which flashed from dragon's jaws and eyes. The earth shuddered, the stones rattled down the mountain sides into the glens. Right and left, left and right, did the dragon lash his tail, overthrowing pines and beeches, snapping them as rods. He evacuated such floods of water that the mountain torrents were full. But after a while his power was exhausted, he lashed no more with his tail, ejected no more water, and spat no more fire."

I think it is impossible not to see in this description, a spring-tide thunderstorm. But to make it more evident that the untaught mind did regard such a storm as a dragon, I think the following quotation from *John of Brompton's Chronicle* will convince the most sceptical: "Another remarkable thing is this, that took place during a certain month in the Gulf of Satalia (on the coast of Pamphylia). There appeared a great and black dragon which came in clouds, and let down his head into the water, whilst his tail seemed turned to the sky; and the dragon drew the water to him by drinking, with such avidity, that, if any ship, even though laden with men or any other heavy articles, had been near him when drinking, it would nevertheless have been sucked up and carried on high. In order however to avoid this danger, it is necessary, when people see it, at once to make a great uproar, and to shout and hammer tables, so that the dragon, hearing the noise, and the voices of those shouting, may withdraw himself far off. Some people, however, assert that this is not a dragon, but the sun drawing up the waters of the sea; which seems more probable." [*] Such is John of Brompton's account of a waterspout. In Greek mythology the dragon of the storm has begun to undergo anthropomorphosis. Typhus is the son of Tartarus and Terra; the storm rising from the horizon may well be supposed to issue from the earth's womb, and its characteristics are sufficient to decide its paternity. Typhus, the whirlwind or typhoon, has a hundred dragon or serpent heads, the long writhing strive of vapour which run before the hurricane cloud. He belches fire, that is, lightnings issue from the clouds, and his roaring is like the howling of wild dogs. Typhus ascends to heaven to make war on the gods, who fly from him in various fantastic shapes; who cannot see in this ascent the hurricane climbing up the vault of sky, and in the flying gods, the many fleeting fragments of white cloud which are seen drifting across the heavens before the gale!

[* Apud TWYSDEN, Hist. Anglicæ Script. x. 1652. p. 1216.]

Typhus, according to Hesiod, is the father of all bad winds, which destroy with rain and tempest, all in fact which went among the Greeks by the name of {Greek *laílaps*}, bringing injury to the agriculturist and peril to the voyager.

> {Greek
> ?Ek dè Tufwéos é?st? a?némwn ménos u!gròn á?eptwn,
> nósfi Nótou Boréw te, kaì a?rgéstew Zefúrou te.
> oí! ge mèn e?n ðeófin geneh`, ðnhtoïs még? ó?neiar.
> ai! d? á?llai mapsau~rai e?pipneíousi ðalassan.
> ai! d? h?'toi píptousai e?s heroeideá pónton,
> ph~ma méga ðnhtoi~si, kakh~j ðúousin a?éllhj.
> á?llote d? á?llai a?eísi, diaskidna~si te nh~as,
> naútas te fðeírousi. kakou~ d? ou? gígnetai a?lkh`
> a?ndrásin, oí! keínhjsi sinántwntai katà pónton.
> ai! d? aû? kaì katà gai~an a?peíriton, a?nðemóessan
> é?rg? e?ratà fðeírousi xamaigenéwn a?nðrw'pwn,
> pimpleu~sai kóniós te kaì a?rgaléou kolosurtou~}
> —Hesiod. Theog. 870, seq.

In both modern Greek and Lithuanian household mythology the dragon or drake has become an ogre, a gigantic man with few of the dracontine attributes remaining. Von Hahn, in his *Griechische und Albanesische Märchen*, tells many tales of drakes, and in all, the old characteristics have been lost, and the drake is simply a gigantic man with magical and superhuman powers.

It is the same among the Lithuanian peasantry. A dragon walks on two legs, talks, flirts with a lady, and marries her. He retains his evil disposition, but has sloughed off his scales and wings.

Such is the change which has taken place in the popular conception of the dragon, which is an impersonification of the thunderstorm. A similar change has taken place in the swan-maiden and were-wolf myths.

In ancient Indian Vedaic mythology the apsaras were heavenly damsels who dwelt in the tether, between earth and sun. Their name, which signifies "the shapeless," or "those who go in the water "—it is uncertain which. is the correct derivation—is expressive of the white cirrus, constantly changing form, and apparently floating swan-like on the blue heaven-sea. These apsaras, according to the Vedaic creed, were fond of changing their shapes, appearing generally as ducks or swans, occasionally as human beings. The souls of heroes were given to them for lovers and husbands. One of the most graceful of the early Indian myths is the story of the apsaras, Urvaçî. Urvaçî loved Puravaras and became his 'wife, on the condition that she was n-ever to behold him in a state of nudity. They remained together for years, till the heavenly companions of Urvaçî determined to secure her return to them. They accordingly beguiled Puravaras into leaving his bed in the darkness of night, and then with a lightning flash they disclosed him, in his nudity, to his wife, who was thereupon constrained to leave him. He pursued her, full of sorrow at his loss, and found her at length swimming in a large lotus pond, in swan's shape.

That this story is not a mere invention, but rests on some mythological explanation of natural phenomena, I think more than probable, as it is found all over the world with few variations. As every Aryan branch retains the story, or traces of it, there can be no doubt that the belief in swan-maidens, who swam in the heavenly sea, and who sometimes became the wives of those fortunate men who managed to steal from them their feather dresses, formed an integral portion of the old mythological system of the Aryan family, before it was broken up into Indian, Persian, Greek, Latin, Russian, Scandinavian, Teutonic, and other races. But more, as the same myth is found. in tribes not Aryan, and far removed from contact with European or Indian superstition,—as, for instance, among Samoyeds and American Indians,—it is even possible that this story may be a tradition of the first primæval stock of men.

But it is time for me to leave the summer cirrus and turn to the tempest-born rain-cloud. It is represented in ancient Indian mythology by the Vritra or Râkshasas. At first the form of these dæmons was uncertain and obscure. Vritra is often used as an appellative for a cloud, and kabhanda, an old name for a rain-cloud, in later times became the name of a devil. Of Vritra, who envelopes the mountains with vapour, it is said, "The darkness stood retaining the water, the mountains lay in the belly of Vritra." By degrees Vritra stood out more prominently as a dæmon, and he is described as a "devourer" of gigantic proportions. In the same way Râkshasas obtained corporeal form and individuality. He is a misshapen giant "like to a cloud," with a red beard and red hair, with pointed protruding teeth, ready to lacerate and devour human flesh. His body is covered with coarse bristling hair, his huge mouth is open, he looks from side to side as he walks, lusting after the flesh and blood of men, to satisfy his raging hunger, and quench his consuming thirst. Towards nightfall his strength increases manifold. He can change his shape at will. He haunts the woods, and roams howling through the jungle; in short, he is to the Hindoo what the were-wolf is to the European.

A certain wood was haunted by a Râkschasa; he one day came across a Brahmin, and with a bound reached his shoulders, and clung to them, exclaiming, "Heh! go on with you!" And the Brahmin, quaking with fear, advanced with him. But when he observed that the feet of the Râkschasa were as delicate as the stamens of the lotus, he asked him, How is it that you have such weak and slender feet? The Râkschasa replied, "I never walk nor touch the earth with my feet. I have made a vow not to do so." Presently they came to a large pond. Then the Râkschasa bade the Brahmin wait at the edge whilst he bathed and prayed to the gods. But the Brahmin thought: "As soon as these prayers and ablutions are over, he will tear me to pieces with his fangs and eat me. He has vowed not to walk; I will be off post haste!" so he ran away, and the Râkschasa dared not follow him for fear of breaking his VOW. (*Pantschatantra*, v. 13.) There is a similar story in the Mahâbhârata, xiii., and in the Kathâ Sarit Sâgara, v. 49-53.

I have said sufficient to show that natural phenomena gave rise to mythological stories, and that these stories have gradually deteriorated, and have been degraded into vulgar superstitions. And I have shown that both the doctrine of metempsychosis and the mythological explanations of meteorological changes have given rise to abundant fable, and among others to the popular and wide-spread superstition of lycanthropy. I shall now pass from myth to history, and shall give instances of bloodthirstiness, cruelty, and cannibalism.

XI. THE MARÉCHAL DE RETZ. I. — THE INVESTIGATION OF CHARGES

Introduction—History of Gilles de Laval—The Castle of Machecoul—
Surrender of the Marshal—Examination of Witnesses—Letter of De Retz—
The Duke of Brittany reluctant to move—The Bishop of Nantes

THE history of the man whose name heads this chapter I purpose giving in detail, as the circumstances I shall narrate have, I believe, never before been given with accuracy to the English public. The name of Gilles de Laval may be well known, as sketches of his bloody career have appeared in many biographies, but these sketches have been very incomplete, as the material from which they were composed was meagre. M. Michelet alone ventured to give the public an idea of the crimes which brought a marshal of France to the gallows, and his revelations were such that, in the words of M. Henri

Martin, "this iron age, which seemed unable to feel surprise at any amount of evil, was struck with dismay."

M. Michelet derived his information from the abstract of the papers relating, to the case, made by order of Ann of Brittany, in the Imperial Library. The original documents were in the library at Nantcs, and a great portion of them were destroyed in the Revolution of 1789. But a careful analysis had been made of them, and this valuable abridgment, which was inaccessible to M. Michelet, came into the hands of M. Lacroix, the eminent French antiquarian, who published a memoir of the marshal from the information he had thus obtained, and it is his work, by far the most complete and circumstantial which has appeared, that I condense into the following chapters.

"The most monstrously depraved imagination," says M. Henri Martin, "never could have conceived what the trial reveals." M. Lacroix has been obliged to draw a veil over much that transpired, and I must draw it closer still. I have, however, said enough to show that this memorable trial presents horrors probably unsurpassed in the whole volume of the world's history.

During the year 1440, a terrible rumour spread through Brittany, and especially through the ancient *pays de Retz*, which extends along the south of the Loire from Nantes to Paimbuf, to the effect that one of the most famous and powerful noblemen in Brittany, Gilles de Laval, Maréchal de Retz, was guilty of crimes of the most diabolical nature.

Gilles de Laval, eldest son of Gay de Laval, second of his name, Sire de Retz, had raised the junior branch of the illustrious house of Laval above the elder branch, which was related to the reigning family of Brittany. He lost his father when he was aged twenty, and remained master of a vast territorial inheritance, which was increased by his marriage with Catharine de Thouars in 1420. He employed a portion of their fortune in the cause of Charles VII., and in strengthening the French crown. During seven consecutive years, from 1426 to 1433, he was engaged in military enterprises against the English; his name is always cited along with those of Dunois, Xaintrailles, Florent d'Illiers, Gaucourt, Richemont, and the most faithful servants of the king. His services were speedily acknowledged by the king creating him Marshal of France. In 1427, he assaulted the Castle of Lude, and carried it by storm; he killed with his own hand the commander of the place; next year he captured from the English the fortress of Rennefort, and the Castle of Malicorne; in 1429, he took an active part in the expedition of Joan of Arc for the deliverance of Orleans, and the occupation of Jargeau, and he was with her in the moat, when she was wounded by an arrow under the walls of Paris.

The marshal, councillor, and chamberlain of the king participated in the direction of public affairs, and soon obtained the entire confidence of his master. He accompanied Charles to Rheims on the occasion of his coronation, and had the honour of bearing the oriflamme, brought for the occasion from the abbey of S. Remi. His intrepidity on the field of battle was as remarkable as his sagacity in council, and he proved himself to be both an excellent warrior and a shrewd politician.

Suddenly, to the surprise of every one, he quitted the service of Charles VII., and sheathed for ever his sword, in the retirement of the country. The death of his maternal grandfather, Jean de Craon, in 1432, made him so enormously wealthy, that his revenues were estimated at 800,000 livres; nevertheless, in two years, by his excessive prodigality, he managed to lose a considerable portion of his inheritance. Mauléon, S. Etienne de Malemort, Loroux-Botereau, Pornic, and Chantolé, he sold to John V., Duke of Brittany, his kinsman, and other lands and seigneurial rights he ceded to the Bishop of Nantes, and to the chapter of the cathedral in that city.

The rumour soon spread that these extensive cessions of territory were sops thrown to the duke and to the bishop, to restrain the one from confiscating his goods, and the other from pronouncing excommunication, for the crimes of which the people whisperingly accused him; but these rumours were probably without foundation, for eventually it was found hard to persuade the duke of the guilt of his kinsman, and the bishop was the most determined instigator of the trial.

The marshal seldom visited the ducal court, but he often appeared in the city of Nantes, where he inhabited the Hôtel de la Suze, with a princely retinue. He had, always accompanying him, a guard of two hundred men at arms, and a numerous suit of pages, esquires, chaplains, singers, astrologers, &c., all of whom he paid handsomely.

Whenever he left the town, or moved to one of his other seats, the cries of the poor, which had been restrained during the time of his presence, broke forth. Tears flowed, curses were uttered, a long-continued wail rose to heaven, the moment that the last of the marshal's party had left the neighbourhood. Mothers had lost their children, babes had been snatched from the cradle, infants had been spirited away almost from the maternal arms, and it was known by sad experience that the vanished little ones would never be seen again.

But on no part of the country did the shadow of this great fear fall so deeply as on the villages in the neighbourhood of the Castle of Machecoul, a gloomy château, composed of huge towers, and surrounded by deep moats, a residence much frequented by Do Retz, notwithstanding its sombre and repulsive appearance. This fortress was always in a condition to resist a siege: the drawbridge was raised, the portcullis down, the gates closed, the men under arms, the culverins on the bastion always loaded. No one, except the servants, had penetrated into this mysterious asylum and had come forth alive. In the surrounding country strange tales of horror and devilry circulated in whispers, and yet it was observed that the chapel of the castle was gorgeously decked with tapestries of silk and cloth of gold, that the sacred vessels were encrusted with gems, and that the vestments of the priests were of the most sumptuous character. The excessive devotion of the marshal was also noticed; he was said to hear mass thrice daily, and to be passionately fond of ecclesiastical music. He was said to have asked permission of the pope, that a crucifer should precede him in processions. But when dusk settled down over the forest, and one by one the windows of the castle became illumined, peasants would point to one casement high up in an isolated tower, from which a clear light streamed through the gloom of night; they spoke of a fierce red glare which irradiated the chamber at times, and of sharp cries ringing out of it, through the hushed woods, to be answered only by the howl of the wolf as it rose from its lair to begin its nocturnal rambles.

On certain days, at fixed hours, the drawbridge sank, and the servants of De Retz stood in the gateway distributing clothes, money, and food to the mendicants who crowded round them soliciting alms. It often happened that children were among the beggars: as often one of the servants would promise them some dainty if they would go to the kitchen for it. Those children who accepted the offer were never seen again.

In 1440 the long-pent-up exasperation of the people broke all bounds, and with one voice they charged the marshal with the murder of their children, whom they said he had sacrificed to the devil.

This charge came to the ears of the Duke of Brittany, but he pooh-poohed it, and would have taken no steps to investigate the truth, had not one of his nobles insisted on his doing so. At the same time Jean do Châteaugiron, bishop of Nantes, and the noble and sage Pierre de l'Hospital, grand-seneschal of Brittany, wrote to the duke, expressing very decidedly their views, that the charge demanded thorough investigation.

John V., reluctant to move against a relation, a man who had served his country so well, and was in such a high position, at last yielded to their request, and authorized them to seize the persons of the Sire de Retz and his accomplices. A *serjent d'armes*, Jean Labbé, was charged with this difficult commission. He picked a band of resolute fellows, twenty in all, and in the middle of September they presented themselves at the gate of the castle, and summoned the Sire do Retz to surrender. As soon as Gilles heard that a troop in the livery of Brittany was at the gate, he inquired who was their leader? On receiving the answer "Labbé," he started, turned pale, crossed himself, and prepared to surrender, observing that it was impossible to resist fate.

Years before, one of his astrologers had assured him that he would one day pass into the hands of an Abbé, and, till this moment, De Retz had supposed that the prophecy signified that he should eventually become a monk.

Gilles de Sillé, Roger de Briqueville, and other of the accomplices of the marshal, took to flight, but Henriet and Pontou remained with him.

The drawbridge was lowered and the marshal offered his sword to Jean Labbé. The gallant serjeant approached, knelt to the marshal, and unrolled before him a parchment sealed with the seal of Brittany.

"Tell me the tenor of this parchment?" said Gilles de Retz with dignity.

"Our good Sire of Brittany enjoins you, my lord, by these presents, to follow me to the good town of Nantes, there to clear yourself of certain criminal charges brought against you."

"I will follow immediately, my friend, glad to obey the will of my lord of Brittany: but, that it may not be said that the Seigneur de Retz has received a message without largess, I order my treasurer, Henriet, to hand over to you and your followers twenty gold crowns."

"Grand-merci, monseigneur! I pray God that he may give you good and long life."

"Pray God only to have mercy upon me, and to pardon my sins."

The marshal had his horses saddled, and left Machecoul with Pontou and Henriet, who had thrown in their lot with him.

It was with lively emotion that the people in the villages traversed by the little troop, saw the redoubted Gilles de Laval ride through their streets, surrounded by soldiers in the livery of the Duke of Brittany, and unaccompanied by a single soldier of his own. The roads and streets were thronged, peasants left the fields, women their kitchens, labourers deserted their cattle at the plough, to throng the road to Nantes. The cavalcade proceeded in silence. The very crowd which had gathered to see it, was hushed. Presently a shrill woman's voice was raised:—

"My child! restore my child!"

Then a wild, wrathful howl broke from the lips of the throng, rang along the Nantes road, and only died away, as the great gates of the Chateau de Bouffay closed on the prisoner.

The whole population of Nantes was in commotion, and it was said that the investigation would be fictitious, that the duke would screen his kinsman, and that the object of general execration would escape with the surrender of some of his lands.

And such would probably have been the event of the trial, had not the Bishop of Nantes and the grand-seneschal taken a very decided course in the matter. They gave the duke no peace till he had yielded to their demand for a thorough investigation and a public trial.

John V. nominated Jean de Toucheronde to collect information, and to take down the charges brought against the marshal. At the same time he was given to understand that the matter was not to be pressed, and that the charges upon which the marshal was to be tried were to be softened down as much as possible.

The commissioner, Jean de Toucheronde, opened the investigation on the 18th September, assisted only by his clerk, Jean Thomas. The witnesses were introduced either singly, or in groups, if they were relations. On entering, the witness knelt before the commissioner, kissed the crucifix, and swore with his hand on the Gospels that he would speak the truth, and nothing but the truth: after this he related all the facts referring to the charge, which came under his cognizance, without being interrupted or interrogated.

The first to present herself was Perrine Loessard, living at la Roche-Bernard.

She related, with tears in her eyes, that two years ago, in the month of September, the Sire de Retz had passed with all his retinue through la Roche-Bernard, on his way from Vannes, and had lodged with Jean Collin. She lived opposite the house in which the nobleman was staying.

Her child, the finest in the village, a lad aged ten, had attracted the notice of Pontou, and perhaps of the marshal himself, who stood at a window, leaning on his squire's shoulder.

Pontou spoke to the child, and asked him whether he would like to be a chorister; the boy replied that his ambition was to be a soldier.

"Well, then," said the squire, "I will equip you."

The lad then laid hold of Pontou's dagger, and expressed his desire to have such a weapon in his belt. Thereupon the mother had ran up and had made him leave hold of the dagger, saying that the boy was doing very well at school, and was getting on with his letters, for he was one day to be a monk. Pontou had dissuaded her from this project, and had proposed to take the child with him to Machecoul, and to educate him to be a soldier. Thereupon he had paid her clown a hundred sols to buy the lad a dress, and had obtained permission to carry him off.

Next day her son had been mounted on a horse purchased for him from Jean Collin, and had left the village in the retinue of the Sire de Retz. The poor mother at parting had gone in tears to the marshal, and had entreated him to be kind to her child. From that time she had been able to obtain no information regarding her son. She had watched the Sire de Retz whenever he had passed through La Roche Bernard, but had never observed her child among his pages. She had questioned several of the marshal's people, but they had laughed at her; the only answer she had obtained was: "Be not afraid. He is either at Machecoul, or else at Tiffauges, or else at Pornic, or somewhere." Perrine's story was corroborated by Jean Collin, his wife, and his mother-in-law.

Jean Lemegren and his wife, Alain Dulix, Perrot Duponest, Guillaume Guillon, Guillaume Portayer, Etienne de Monclades, and Jean Lefebure, all inhabitants of S. Etienne de Montluc, deposed that a little child, son of Guillaume Brice of the said parish, having lost his father at the age of nine, lived on alms, and went round the country begging.

This child, named Jamet, had vanished suddenly at midsummer, and nothing was known of what had become of him; but strong suspicions were entertained of his having been carried off by an aged hag who had appeared shortly before in the neighbourhood, and who had vanished along with the child.

On the 27th September, Jean de Toucheronde, assisted by Nicolas Chateau, notary of the court at Nantes, received the depositions of several inhabitants of Pont-de-Launay, near Bouvron: to wit, Guillaume Fourage and wife; Jeanne, wife of Jean Leflou; and Richarde, wife of Jean Gandeau.

These depositions, though very vague, afforded sufficient cause for suspicion to rest on the marshal. Two years before, a child of twelve, son of Jean Bernard, and another child of the same age, son of Ménégué, had gone to Machecoul. The son of Ménégué had returned alone in the evening, relating that his companion had asked him to wait for him on the road whilst he begged at the gates of the Sire de Retz. The son of Ménégué said that he had waited three hours, but his companion had not returned. The wife of Guillaume Fourage deposed that she had seen the lad at this time with an old hag, who was leading him by the hand towards Machecoul. That same evening this hag passed over the bridge of Launay, and the wife of Fourage asked her what had become of little Bernard. The old woman neither stopped nor answered further than by saying he was well provided for. The boy had not been seen since. On the 28th September, the Duke of Brittany joined another commissioner, Jean Couppegorge, and a second notary, Michel Estallure, to Toucheronde and Chateau.

The inhabitants of Machecoul, a little town over which the Sire de Retz exercised supreme power, appeared now to depose against their lord. André Barbier, shoemaker, declared that last Easter, a child, son of his neighbour Georges Lebarbier, had disappeared. He was last seen gathering plums behind the hotel Rondeau. This disappearance surprised none in Machecoul, and no one ventured to comment on it. André and his wife were in daily terror of losing their own child. They had been a pilgrimage to S. Jean d'Angely, and had been asked there whether it was the custom at Machecoul to eat children. On their return they had heard of two children having vanished—the son of Jean Gendron, and that of Alexandre Châtellier. André Barbier had made some inquiries about the circumstances of their disappearance, and had been advised to hold his tongue, and to shut his ears and eyes, unless he were prepared to be thrown into a dungeon by the lord of Machecoul.

"But, bless me!" he had said, "am I to believe that a fairy spirits off and eats our little ones?"

"Believe what you like," was the advice given to him; "but ask no questions." As this conversation had taken place, one of the marshal's men at arms had passed, when all those who had been speaking took to their heels. André, who had run with the rest, without knowing exactly why he fled, came upon a man near the church of the Holy Trinity, who was weeping bitterly, and crying out,—"O my God, wilt Thou not restore to me my little one?" This man had also been robbed of his child.

Licette, wife of Guillaume Sergent, living at La Boneardière, in the parish of S. Croix de Machecoul, had lost her son two years before, and had not seen him since; she besought the commissioners, with tears in her eyes, to restore him to her.

"I left him," said she, "at home whilst I went into the field with my husband to sow flax. He was a bonny little lad, and he was as good as he was bonny. He had to look after his tiny sister, who was a year and a half old. On my return home, the little girl was found, but she could not tell me what had become of him. Afterwards we found in the marsh a small red woollen cap which had belonged to my poor darling; but it was in vain that we dragged the marsh, nothing was found more, except good evidence that he had not been drowned. A hawker who sold needles and thread passed through Machecoul at the time, and told me that an old woman in grey, with a black hood on her head, had bought of him some children's toys, and had a few moments after passed him, leading a little boy by the hand."

Georges Lebarbier, living near the gate of the châtelet de Machecoul, gave an account of the manner in which his son had evanesced. The boy was apprenticed to Jean Pelletier, tailor to Mme. de Retz and to the household of the castle. He seemed to be getting on in his profession, when last year, about S. Barnabas' day, he went to play at ball on the castle green. He never returned from the game.

This youth and his master, Jean Pelletier, had been in the habit of eating and drinking at the castle, and bad always laughed at the ominous stories told by the people.

Guillaume Hilaire and his wife confirmed the statements of Lebarbier. They also said that they knew of the loss of the sons of Jean Gendron, Jeanne Rouen, and Alexandre Châtellier. The son of Jean Gendron, aged twelve, lived with the said Hilaire and learned of him the trade of skinner. He had been working in the shop for seven or eight years, and was a steady, hardworking lad. One day Messieurs Gilles de Sillé and Roger de Briqueville entered the shop to purchase a pair of hunting gloves. They asked if little Gendron might take a message for them to the castle. Hilaire readily consented, and the boy received beforehand the payment for going—a gold angelus, and he started, promising to be back directly. But he had never returned. That evening Hiliare and his wife, observing Gilles de Sillé and Roger de Briqueville returning to the castle, ran to them and asked what had become of the apprentice. They replied that they had no notion of where he was, as they had been absent hunting, but that it was possible he might have been sent to Tiffauges, another castle of De Retz.

Guillaume Hilaire, whose depositions were more grave and explicit than the others, positively asserted that Jean Dujardin, valet to Roger de Briqueville had told him he knew of a cask secreted in the castle, full of children's corpses. He said that he had often heard people say that children were enticed to the château and then murdered, but had treated it as an idle tale. He said, moreover, that the marshal was not accused of having any hand in the murders, but that his servants were supposed to be guilty.

Jean Gendron himself deposed to the loss of his son, and he added that his was not the only child which had vanished mysteriously at Machecoul. He knew of thirty that had disappeared.

Jean Chipholon, elder and junior, Jean Aubin, and Clement Doré, all inhabitants of the parish of Thomage, deposed that they had known a poor man of the same parish, named Mathelin Thomas, who had lost his son, aged twelve, and that he had died of grief in consequence.

Jeanne Rouen, of Machecoul, who for nine years had been in a state of uncertainty whether her son were alive or dead, deposed that the child had been carried off whilst keeping sheep. She had thought that he had been devoured of wolves, but two women of Machecoul, now deceased, had seen Gilles de Sillé approach the little shepherd, speak to him, and point to the castle. Shortly after the lad had walked off in that direction. The husband of Jeanne Rouen went to the château to inquire after his son, but could obtain no information. When next Gilles de Sillé appeared in the town, the disconsolate mother entreated him to restore her child to her. Gilles replied that he knew nothing about him, as he had been to the king at Amboise.

Jeanne, widow of Aymery Hedelin, living at Machecoul, had also lost, eight years before, a little child as he had pursued some butterflies into the wood. At the same time four other children had been carried off, those of Gendron, Rouen, and Macé Sorin. She said that the story circulated through the country was, that Gilles de Sillé stole children to make them over to the English, in order to obtain the ransom of his brother who was a captive. But she added that this report was traced to the servants of Sillé, and that it was propagated by them.

One of the last children to disappear was that of Noël Aise, living in the parish of S. Croix.

A man from Tiffauges had said to her (Jeanne Hedelin) that for one child stolen at Machecoul, there were seven carried away at Tiffauges.

Macé Sorin confirmed the deposition of the widow Hedelin., and repeated the circumstances connected with the loss of the children of Châtellier, Rouen, Gendron, and Lebarbier.

Perrine Rondeau had entered the castle with the company of Jean Labbé. She had entered a stable, and had found a heap of ashes and powder, which had a sickly and peculiar smell. At the bottom of a trough she had found a child's shirt covered with blood.

Several inhabitants of the bourg of Fresnay, to wit, Perrot, Parqueteau, Jean Soreau, Catherine Degrépie, Gilles Garnier, Perrine Viellard, Marguerite Rediern, Marie Carfin, Jeanne Laudais, said that they had heard Guillaume Hamelin, last Easter, lamenting the loss of two children.

Isabeau, wife of Guillaume Hamelin, confirmed these depositions, saving that she had lost them seven years before. She had at that time four children; the eldest aged fifteen, the youngest aged seven, went together to Machecoul to buy some bread, but they did not return. She sat up for them all night and next morning. She heard that another child had been lost, the son of Michaut Bonnel of S. Ciré de Retz.

Guillemette, wife of Michaut Bonnel, said that her son had been carried off whilst guarding cows.

Guillaume Rodigo and his wife, living at Bourg-neuf-en-Retz, deposed that on the eve of last S. Bartholomew's day, the Sire do Retz lodged with Guillaume Plumet in his village.

Pontou, who accompanied the marshal, saw a lad of fifteen, named Bernard Lecanino, servant to Rodigo, standing at the door of his house. The lad could not speak much French, but only bas-Breton. Pontou beckoned to him and spoke to him in a low tone. That evening, at ten o'clock, Bernard left his master's house, Rodigo and his wife being absent. The servant maid, who saw him go out, called to him that the supper table was not yet cleared, but he paid no attention to what she said. Rodigo, annoyed at the loss of his servant, asked some of the marshal's men what had become of him. They replied mockingly that they knew nothing of the little Breton, but that he had probably been sent to Tiffauges to be trained as page to their lord.

Marguerite Sorain, the chambermaid alluded to above, confirmed the statement of Rodigo, adding that Pontou had entered the house and spoken with Bernard. Guillaume Plumet and wife confirmed what Rodigo and Sorain had said.

Thomas Aysée and wife deposed to the loss of their son, aged ten, who had gone to beg at the gate of the castle of Machecoul; and a little girl had seen him drawn by an offer of meat into the château.

Jamette, wife of Eustache Drouet of S. Léger, had sent two sons, one aged ten, the other seven, to the castle to obtain alms. They had not been seen since.

On the 2nd October the commissioners sat again, and the charges became graver, and the servants of the marshal became more and more implicated.

The disappearance of thirteen other children was substantiated under circumstances throwing strong suspicion on the inmates of the castle. I will not give the details, for they much resemble those of the former depositions. Suffice it to say that before the commissioners closed the inquiry, a herald of the Duke of Brittany in tabard blew three calls on the trumpet, from the steps of the tower of Bouffay, summoning all who had additional charges to bring against the Sire de Retz, to present themselves without delay. As no fresh witnesses arrived, the case was considered to be made out, and the commissioners visited the duke, with the information they had collected, in their hands.

The duke hesitated long as to the steps he should take. Should he judge and sentence a kinsman, the most powerful of his vassals, the bravest of his captains, a councillor of the king, a marshal of France?

Whilst still unsettled in his mind as to the course he should pursue, he received a letter from Gilles de Retz, which produced quite a different effect from that which it had been intended to produce.

"Monsieur My Cousin and Honoured Sire,—

"It is quite true that I am perhaps the most detestable of all sinners, having sinned horribly again and again, yet have I never failed in my religious duties. I have heard many masses, vespers, &c., have fasted in Lent and on vigils, have confessed my sins, deploring them heartily, and have received the blood of our Lord at least once in the year.

Since I have been languishing in prison, awaiting your honoured justice, I have been overwhelmed with incomparable repentance for my crimes, which I am ready to acknowledge and to expiate as is suitable.

"Wherefore I supplicate you, M. my cousin, to give me licence to retire into a monastery, and there to lead a good and exemplary life. I care not into what monastery I am sent, but I intend that all my goods, &c., should be distributed among the poor, who are the members of Jesus Christ on earth . . . . Awaiting your glorious clemency, on which I rely, I pray God our Lord to protect you and your kingdom.

He who addresses you is in all earthly humility,"

"FRIAR   GILLES,

Carmelite in intention."

The duke read this letter to Pierre de l'Hospital, president of Brittany, and to the Bishop of Nantes, who were those most resolute in pressing on the trial. They were horrified at the tone of this dreadful communication, and assured the duke that the case was so clear, and the steps taken had been so decided, that it was impossible for him to allow De Retz to escape trial by such an impious device as he suggested. In the meantime, the bishop and the grand-seneschal had set on foot an investigation at the castle of Machecoul, and had found numerous traces of human remains. But a complete examination could not be made, as the duke was anxious to screen his kinsman as much as possible, and refused to authorize one.

The duke now summoned his principal officers and held a council with them. They unanimously sided with the bishop and de l'Hospital, and when John still hesitated, the Bishop of Nantes rose and said: "Monseigneur, this case is one for the church as much as for your court to take up. Consequently, if your President of Brittany does not bring the case into secular court, by the Judge of heaven and earth! I will cite the author of these execrable crimes to appear before our ecclesiastical tribunal."

The resolution of the bishop compelled the duke to yield, and it was decided that the trial should take its course without let or hindrance.

In the meantime, the unhappy wife of Gilles de Retz, who had been separated from him for some while, and who loathed his crimes, though she still felt for him as her husband, hurried to the duke with her daughter to entreat pardon for the wretched man. But the duke refused to hear her. Thereupon she went to Amboise to intercede with the king for him who bad once been his close friend and adviser.

XII. — THE MARÉCHAL DE RETZ II. — THE TRIAL

The Appearance of the Marshal—Pierre de l'Hospital—The Requisition—
The Trial adjourned—Meeting of the Marshal and his Servants—The Confession of
Henriet—Pontou persuaded to confess all—The adjourned Trial not hurried on—
The hesitation of the Duke of Brittany

ON the 10th October, Nicolas Chateau, notary of the duke, went to the Château of Bouffay, to read to the prisoner the summons to appear in person on the morrow before Messire de l'Hospital, President of Brittany, Seneschal of Rennes, and Chief Justice of the Duchy of Brittany.

The Sire de Retz, who believed himself already a novice in the Carmelite order, had dressed in white, and was engaged in singing litanies. When the summons had been read, he ordered a page to give the notary wine and cake, and then he returned to his prayers with every appearance of compunction and piety.

On the morrow Jean Labbé and four soldiers conducted him to the hall of justice. He asked for Pontou and Henriet to accompany him, but this was not permitted.

He was adorned with all his military insignia, as though to impose on his judges; he had around his neck massive chains of gold, and several collars of knightly orders. His costume, with the exception of his purpoint, was white, in token of his repentance. His purpoint was of pearl-grey silk, studded with gold stars, and girded around his waist by a scarlet belt, from which dangled a poignard in scarlet velvet sheath. His collar, cufs, and the edging of his purpoint were of white ermine, his little round cap or *chapel* was white, surrounded with a belt of ermine—a fur which only the great feudal lords of Brittany had a right to wear. All the rest of his dress, to the shoes which were long and pointed, was white.

No one at a first glance would have thought the Sire do Retz to be by nature so cruel and vicious as he was supposed to be. On the contrary, his physiognomy was calm and phlegmatic, somewhat pale, and expressive of melancholy. His hair and moustache were light brown, and his beard was clipped to a point. This beard, which resembled no other beard, was black, but under certain lights it assumed a blue hue, and it was this peculiarity which obtained for the Sire do Retz the surname of Blue-beard, a name which has attached to him in popular romance, at the same time that his story has undergone strange metamorphoses.

But on closer examination of the countenance of Gilles de Retz, contraction in the muscles of the face, nervous quivering of the mouth, spasmodic twitchings of the brows, and above all, the sinister expression of the eyes, showed that there was something strange and frightful in the man. At intervals he ground his teeth like a wild beast preparing to dash upon his prey, and then his lips became so contracted, as they were drawn in and glued, as it were, to his teeth, that their very colour was indiscernible.

At times also his eyes became fixed, and the pupils dilated to such an extent, with a sombre fire quivering in them, that the iris seemed to fill the whole orbit, which became circular, and sank back into the head. At these moments his complexion became livid and cadaverous; his brow, especially just over the nose, was covered with deep wrinkles, and his beard appeared to bristle, and to assume its bluish hues. But, after a few moments, his features became again serene, with a sweet smile reposing upon them, and his expression relaxed into a vague and tender melancholy.

"Messires," said he, saluting his judges, "I pray you to expedite my matter, and despatch as speedily as possible my unfortunate case; for I am peculiarly anxious to consecrate myself to the service of God, who has pardoned my great sins. I shall not fail, I assure you, to endow several of the churches in Nantes, and I shall distribute the greater portion of my goods among the poor, to secure the salvation of my soul."

"Monseigneur," replied gravely Pierre de l'Hospital: "It is always well to think of the salvation of one's soul; but, if you please, think now that we are concerned with the salvation of your body."

"I have confessed to the father superior of the Carmelites," replied the marshal, with tranquillity; "and through his absolution I have been able to communicate: I am, therefore, guiltless and purified."

"Men's justice is not in common with that of God, monseigneur, and I cannot tell you what will be your sentence. Be ready to make your defence, and listen to the charges brought against you, which M. le lieutenant du Procureur de Nantes will read."

The officer rose, and read the following paper of charges, which I shall condense:—

"Having heard the bitter complaints of several of the inhabitants of the diocese of Nantes, whose names follow hereinafter (here follow the names of the parents of the lost children), we, Philippe do Livron, lieutenant assesseur of Messire le Procureur de Nantes, have invited, and do invite, the very noble and very wise Messire Pierre de l'Hospital, President of Brittany, &c., to bring to trial the very high and very powerful lord, Gilles de Laval, Sire de Retz, Machecoul, Ingrande and other places, Councillor of his Majesty the King, and Marshal of France:

"Forasmuch as the said Sire de Retz has seized and caused to be seized several little children, not only ten or twenty, but thirty, forty, fifty, sixty, one hundred, two hundred, and more, and has murdered and slain them inhumanly, and then burned their bodies to convert them to ashes:

"Forasmuch as persevering in evil, the said Sire, notwithstanding that the powers that be are ordained of God, and that every one should be an obedient subject to his prince, . . . has assaulted Jean Leferon, subject of the Duke of Brittany, the said Jean Leferon being guardian of the fortress of Malemort, in the name of Geoffrey Leferon, his brother, to whom the said lord had made over the possession of the said place:

"Forasmuch as the said Sire forced Jean Leferon to give up to him the said place, and moreover retook the lordship of Malemort in despite of the order of the duke and of justice:

117

"Forasmuch as the said Sire arrested Master Jean Rousseau, sergeant of the duke, who was sent to him with injunctions from the said duke, and beat his men with their own staves, although their persons were under the protection of his grace:

"We conclude that the said Sire de Retz, homicide in fact and in intent according to the first count, rebel and felon according to the second, should be condemned to suffer corporal punishment, and to pay a fine of his possessions in lands and goods held in fief to the said nobleman, and that these should be confiscated and remitted to the crown of Brittany."

This requisition was evidently drawn up with the view of saving the life of the Sire de Retz; for the crime of homicide was presented without aggravating circumstances, in such a manner that it could be denied or shelved, whilst the crimes of felony and rebellion against the Duke of Brittany were brought into exaggerated prominence.

Gilles de Retz had undoubtedly been forewarned of the course which was to be pursued, and he was prepared to deny totally the charges made in the first count.

"Monseigneur," said Pierre de l'Hospital, whom the form of the requisition had visibly astonished: "What justification have you to make? Take an oath on the Gospels to declare the truth."

"No, messire!" answered the marshal. "The witnesses are bound to declare what they know upon oath, but the accused is never put on his oath."

"Quite so," replied the judge. "Because the accused may be put on the rack and constrained to speak the truth, an' please you."

Gilles de Retz turned pale, bit his lips, and cast a glance of malignant hate at Pierre de l'Hospital; then, composing his countenance, he spoke with an appearance of calm:—

"Messires, I shall not deny that I behaved wrongfully in the case of Jean Rousseau; but, in excuse, let me say that the said Rousseau was full of wine, and he behaved with such indecorum towards me in the presence of my servants, that it was quite intolerable. Nor will I deny my revenge on the brothers Leferon: Jean had declared that the said Grace of Brittany had confiscated my fortress of Malemort, which I had sold to him, and for which I have not yet received payment; and Geoffrey Leferon had announced far and wide that I was about to be expelled Brittany as a traitor and a rebel. To punish them I re-entered my fortress of Malemort.—As for the other charges, I shall say nothing about them, they are simply false and calumnious."

"Indeed exclaimed Pierre de l'Hospital, whose blood boiled with indignation against the wretch who stood before him with such effrontery. "All these witnesses who complain of having lost their children, lied under oath!"

"Undoubtedly, if they accuse me of having anything to do with their loss. What am I to know about them, am I their keeper?"

"The answer of Cain!" exclaimed Pierre de l'Hospital, rising from his seat in the vehemence of his emotion. "However, as you solemnly deny these charges, we must question Henriet and Pontou."

"Henriet, Pontou!" cried the marshal, trembling; "they accuse me of nothing, surely!"

"Not as yet, they have not been questioned, but they are about to be brought into court, and I do not expect that they will lie in the face of justice."

"I demand that my servants be not brought forward as witnesses against their master," said the marshal, his eyes dilating, his brow wrinkling, and his beard bristling blue upon his chin: "a master is above the gossiping tales and charges of his servants."

"Do you think then, messire, that your servants will accuse you?"

"I demand that I, a marshal of France, a baron of the duchy, should be sheltered from the slanders of small folk, whom I disown as my servants if they are untrue to their master."

"Messire, I see we must put you on the rack, or nothing will be got from you."

"Hola! I appeal to his grace the Duke of Brittany, and ask an adjournment, that I may take advice on the charges brought against me, which I have denied, and which I deny still."

"Well, I shall adjourn the case till the 25th of this month, that you may be well prepared to meet the accusations."

On his way back to prison, the marshal passed Henriet and Pontou as they were being conducted to the court. Henriet pretended not to see his master, but Pontou burst into tears on meeting him. The marshal held out his hand, and Pontou kissed it affectionately.

"Remember what I have done for you, and be faithful servants," said Gilles de Retz. Henriet recoiled from him with a shudder, and the marshal passed on.

"I shall speak," whispered Henriet; "for we have another master beside our poor master of Retz, and we shall soon be with the heavenly one."

The president ordered the clerk to read again the requisition of the lieutenant, that the two presumed accomplices of Gilles de Retz might be informed of the charges brought against their master. Henriet burst into tears, trembled violently, and cried out that he would tell all. Pontou, alarmed, tried to hinder his companion, and said that Henriet was touched in his head, and that what he was about to say would be the ravings of insanity.

Silence was imposed upon him.

"I will speak out," continued Henriet and yet I dare not speak of the horrors which I know have taken place, before that image of my Lord Christ; "and he pointed tremblingly to a large crucifix above the seat of the judge.

"Henriet." moaned Pontou, squeezing his hand, "you will destroy yourself as well as your master."

Pierre de l'Hospital rose, and the figure of our Redeemer was solemnly veiled.

Henriet, who had great difficulty in overcoming his agitation, than began his revelations.

The following is the substance of them:—

On leaving the university of Angers, he had taken the situation of reader in the house of Gilles de Retz. The marshal took a liking to him, and made him his chamberlain and confidant.

On the occasion of the Sire de la Suze, brother of the Sire de Retz, taking possession of the castle of Chantoncé, Charles de Soenne, who had arrived at Chantoncé, assured Henriet that he had found in the oubliettes of a tower a number of dead children, some headless, others frightfully mutilated. Henriet then thought that this was but a calumny invented by the Sire de la Suze.

But when, some while after, the Sire de Retz retook the castle of Chantoncé and had ceded it to the Duke of Brittany, he one evening summoned Henriet, Pontou, and a certain Petit Robin to his room; the two latter were already deep in the secrets of their master. But before confiding anything to Henriet, De Retz made him take a solemn oath never to reveal what he was about to tell him. The oath taken, the Sire de Retz, addressing the three, said that on the morrow an officer of the duke would take possession of the castle in the name of the duke, and that it was necessary, before this took place, that a certain well should be emptied of children's corpses, and that their bodies should be put into boxes and transported to Machecoul.

Henriet, Pontou, and Petit Robin went together, furnished with ropes and hooks, to the tower where were the corpses. They toiled all night in removing the half-decayed bodies, and with them they filled three large cases, which they sent by a boat down the Loire to Machecoul, where they were reduced to ashes.

Henriet counted thirty-six children's heads, but there were more bodies than heads. This night's work, he said, bad produced a profound impression on his imagination, and he was constantly haunted with a vision of these heads rolling as in a game of skittles, and clashing with a mournful wail. Henriet soon began to collect children for his master, and was present whilst he massacred them. They were murdered invariably in one room at Machecoul. The marshal used to bathe in their blood; he was fond of making Gilles do Sillé, Pontou, or Henriet torture them, and he experienced intense pleasure in seeing them in their agonies. But his great passion was to welter in their blood. His servants would stab a child in the jugular vein, and let the blood squirt over him. The room was often steeped in blood. When the horrible deed was done, and the child was dead, the marshal would be filled with grief for what he had done, and would toss weeping and praying on a bed, or recite fervent prayers and litanies on his knees, whilst his servants washed the floor, and burned in the huge fireplace the bodies of the murdered children. With the bodies were burned the clothes and everything that had belonged to the little victims.

An insupportable odour filled the room, but the Maréchal do Retz inhaled it with delight.

Henriet acknowledged that he had seen forty children put to death in this manner, and he was able to give an account of several, so that it was possible to identify them with the children reported to be lost.

"It is quite impossible," said the lieutenant, who had been given the cue to do all that was possible to save the marshal—"It is impossible that bodies could be burned in a chamber fireplace."

"It was done, for all that, messire," replied Henriet. "The fireplace was very large, both at the hotel Suze, and also at Machecoul; we piled up great faggots and logs, and laid the dead children among them. In a few hours the operation was complete, and we flung the ashes out of the window into the moat."

Henriet remembered the case of the two sons of Hamelin; he said that, whilst the one child was being tortured, the other was on its knees sobbing and praying to God, till its own turn came.

"What you have said concerning the excesses of Messire de Retz," exclaimed the lieutenant du procureur, "seems to be pure invention, and destitute of all probability. The greatest monsters of iniquity never committed such crimes, except perhaps some Cæsars of old Rome."

"Messire, it was the acts of these Cæsars that my Lord of Retz desired to imitate. I used to read to him the chronicles of Suetonius, and Tacitus, in which their cruelties are recorded. He used to delight in hearing of them, and he said that it gave him greater pleasure to hack off a child's head than to assist at a banquet. Sometimes he would seat himself on the breast of a little one, and with a knife sever the head from the body at a single blow; sometimes he cut the throat half through very gently, that the child might languish, and he would wash his hands and his beard in its blood. Sometimes he had all the limbs chopped off at once from the trunk; at other times he ordered us to hang the infants till they were nearly dead, and then take them down and cut their throats. I remember having brought to him three little girls who were asking charity at the castle gates. He bade me cut their throats whilst he looked on. André Bricket found another little girl crying on the steps of the house at Vannes because she had lost her mother. He brought the little thing—it was but a babe—in his arms to my lord, and it was killed before him. Pontou and I had to make away with the body. We threw it down a privy in one of the towers, but the corpse caught on a nail in the outer wall, so that it would be visible to all who passed. Pontou was let down by a rope, and he disengaged it with great difficulty."

"How many children do you estimate that the Sire de Retz and his servants have killed?"

"The reckoning is long. I, for my part, confess to having killed twelve with my own hand, by my master's orders, and I have brought him about sixty. I knew that things of the kind went on before I was admitted to the secret; for the castle of Machecoul had been occupied a short while by the Sire do la Sage. My lord recovered it speedily, for he knew that there were many children's corpses hidden in a hayloft. There were forty there quite dry and black as coal, because they had been charred. One of the women of Madame de Retz came by chance into the loft and saw the corpses. Roger de Briqueville wanted to kill her, but the maréchal would not let him."

"Have you nothing more to declare?

"Nothing. I ask Pontou, my friend, to corroborate what I have said."

This deposition, so circumstantial and detailed, produced on the judges a profound impression of horror. Human imagination at this time had not penetrated such mysteries of refined cruelty. Several times, as Henriet spake, the president had shown his astonishment and indignation by signing himself with the cross. Several times his face had become scarlet, and his eyes had fallen; he had pressed his hand to his brow, to assure himself that he was not labouring under a hideous dream, and a quiver of horror had run through his whole frame.

Pontou had taken no part in the revelation of Henriet; but when the latter appealed to him he raised his head, looked sadly round the court, and sighed.

"Etienne Cornillant, alias Pontou, I command you in the name of God and of justice, to declare what you know."

This injunction of Pierre do l'Hospital remained unresponded to, and Pontou seemed to strengthen himself in his resolution not to accuse his master.

But Henriet, flinging himself into the arms of his accomplice, implored him, as he valued his soul, no longer to harden his heart to the calls of God; but to bring to light the crimes he had committed along with the Sire do Retz.

The lieutenant du procureur, who hitherto had endeavoured to extenuate or discredit the charges brought against Gilles do Retz, tried a last expedient to counterbalance the damaging confessions of Henriet, and to withhold Pontou from giving way.

"You have heard, monseigneur," said he to the president, "the atrocities which have been acknowledged by Henriet, and you, as I do, consider them to be pure inventions of the aforesaid, made out of bitter hatred and envy with the purpose of ruining his master. I therefore demand that Henriet should be put on the rack, that he may be brought to give the lie to his former statements."

"You forget," replied de l'Hospital, "that the rack is for those who do *not* confess, and not for those who freely acknowledge their crimes. Therefore I order the second accused, Etienne Cornillant, alias Pontou, to be placed on the rack if he continues silent. Pontou! will you speak or will you not?"

"Monseigneur, he will speak!" exclaimed Henriet. Oh, Pontou, dear friend, resist not God any more."

"Well then, messeigneurs," said Pontou, with emotion; "I will satisfy you; I cannot defend my poor lord against the allegations of Henriet, who has confessed all through dread of eternal damnation."

He then fully substantiated all the statements of the other, adding other facts of the same character, known only to himself.

Notwithstanding the avowal of Pontou and Henriet, the adjourned trial was not hurried on. It would have been easy to have captured some of the accomplices of the wretched man; but the duke, who was informed of the whole of the proceedings, did not wish to augment the scandal by increasing the number of the accused. He even forbade researches to be made in the castles and mansions of the Sire de Retz, fearing lest proofs of fresh crimes, more mysterious and more horrible than those already divulged, should come to light.

The dismay spread through the country by the revelations already made, demanded that religion and morality, which had been so grossly outraged, should be speedily avenged. People wondered at the delay in pronouncing sentence, and it was loudly proclaimed in Nantes that the Sire de Retz was rich enough to purchase his life. It is true that Madame de Retz solicited the king and the duke again to give pardon to her husband; but the duke, counselled by the bishop, refused to extend his authority to interfere with the course of justice; and the king, after having sent one of his councillors to Nantes to investigate the case, determined not to stir in it.

XIII. — MARÉCHAL DE RETZ III. — THE SENTENCE AND EXECUTION.

The adjourned Trial—The Marshal Confesses—The Case handed over to the
Ecclesiastical Tribunal—Prompt steps taken by the Bishop—The Sentence—
Ratified by the Secular Court—The Execution

ON the 24th October the trial of the Maréchal de Retz was resumed. The prisoner entered in a Carmelite habit, knelt and prayed in silence before the examination began. Then he ran his eye over the court, and the sight of the rack, windlass, and cords made a slight shudder run through him.

"Messire Gilles de Laval," began the president; "you appear before me now for the second time to answer to a certain requisition read by M. le Lieutenant du Procureur de Nantes."

"I shall answer frankly, monseigneur," said the prisoner calmly; "but I reserve the right of appeal to the benign intervention of the very venerated majesty of the King of France, of whom I am, or have been, chamberlain and marshal, as may be proved by my letters patent duly enregistered in the parliament at Paris—"

"This is no affair of the King of France," interrupted Pierre de l'Hospital; "if you were chamberlain and marshal of his Majesty, you are also vassal of his grace the Duke of Brittany."

"I do not deny it; but, on the contrary, I trust to his Grace of Brittany to allow me to retire to a convent of Carmelites, there to repent me of my sins."

"That is as may be; will you confess, or must I send you to the rack?"

"Torture me not!" exclaimed Gilles de Retz "I will confess all. Tell me first, what have Henriet and Pontou said?"

"They have confessed. M. le Lieutenant du Procureur shall read you their allegations."

"Not so," said the lieutenant, who continued to show favour to the accused; "I pronounce them false, unless Messire de Retz confirms them by oath, which God forbid!"

Pierre de l'Hospital made a motion of anger to check this scandalous pleading in favour of the accused, and then nodded to the clerk to read the evidence.

The Sire do Retz, on hearing that his servants had made such explicit avowals of their acts, remained motionless, as though thunderstruck. He saw that it was in vain for him to equivocate, and that he would have to confess all.

"What have you to say?" asked the president, when the confessions of Henriet and Pontou had been read.

"Say what befits you, my lord," interrupted the lieutenant du procureur, as though to indicate to the accused the line he was to take: "are not these abominable lies and calumnies trumped up to ruin you?"

"Alas, no!" replied the Sire do Retz; and his face was pale as death: "Henriet and Pontou have spoken the truth. God has loosened their tongues."

"My lord! relieve yourself of the burden of your crimes by acknowledging them at once," said M. do l'Hospital earnestly.

"Messires!" said the prisoner, after a moment's silence: "it is quite true that I have robbed mothers of their little ones; and that I have killed their children, or caused them to be killed, either by cutting their throats with daggers or knives, or by chopping off their heads with cleavers; or else I have had their skulls broken by hammers or sticks; sometimes I had their limbs hewn off one after another; at other times I have ripped them open, that I might examine their entrails and hearts; I have occasionally strangled them or put them to a slow death; and when the children were dead I had their bodies burned and reduced to ashes."

"When did you begin your execrable practices?" asked Pierre de l'Hospital, staggered by the frankness of these horrible avowals: "the evil one must have possessed you."

"It came to me from myself,—no doubt at the instigation of the devil: but still these acts of cruelty afforded me incomparable delight. The desire to commit these atrocities came upon me eight years ago. I left court to go to Chantoncé, that I might claim the property of my grandfather, deceased. In the library of the castle I found a Latin book—*Suetonius*, I believe—full of accounts of the cruelties of the Roman Emperors. I read the charming history of Tiberius, Caracalla, and other Cæsars, and the pleasure they took in watching the agonies of tortured children. Thereupon I resolved to imitate and surpass these same Cæsars, and that very night I began to do so. For some while I confided my secret to no one, but afterwards I communicated it to my cousin, Gilles de Sillé, then to Master Roger de Briqueville, next in succession to Henriet, Pontou, Rossignol, and Robin." He then confirmed all the accounts given by his two servants. He confessed to about one hundred and twenty murders in a single year.

"An average of eight hundred in less than seven years!" exclaimed Pierre de l'Hospital, with a cry of pain: "Ah! messire, you were possessed! "

His confession was too explicit and circumstantial for the Lieutenant du Procureur to say another word in his defence; but he pleaded that the case should be made over to the ecclesiastical court, as there were confessions of invocations of the devil and of witchcraft mixed up with those of murder. Pierre de l'Hospital saw that the object of the lieutenant was to gain time for Mme. de Retz to make a fresh attempt to obtain a pardon; however he was unable to resist, so he consented that the case should be transferred to the bishop's court.

But the bishop was not a man to let the matter slip, and there and then a sergeant of the bishop summoned Gilles de Laval, Sire do Retz, to appear forthwith before the ecclesiastical tribunal. The marshal was staggered by this unexpected citation, and he did not think of appealing against it to the president; he merely signed his readiness to follow, and he was at once conducted into the ecclesiastical court assembled hurriedly to try him.

This new trial lasted only a few hours.

The marshal, now thoroughly cowed, made no attempt to defend himself, but he endeavoured to bribe the bishop into leniency, by promises of the surrender of all his lands and goods to the Church, and begged to be allowed to retire into the Carmelite monastery at Nantes.

His request was peremptorily refused, and sentence of death was pronounced against him.

On the 25th October, the ecclesiastical court having pronounced judgment, the sentence was transmitted to the secular court, which had now no pretext upon which to withhold ratification.

There was some hesitation as to the kind of death the marshal was to suffer. The members of the secular tribunal were not unanimous on this point. The president put it to the vote, and collected the votes himself; then he reseated himself, covered his head, and said in a solemn voice:—

"The court, notwithstanding the quality, dignity, and nobility of the accused, condemns him to be hung and burned. Wherefore I admonish you who are condemned, to ask pardon of God, and grace to die well, in great contrition for having committed the said crimes. And the said sentence shall be carried into execution to-morrow morning between eleven and twelve o'clock." A similar sentence was pronounced upon Henriet and Pontou.

On the morrow, October 26th, at nine o'clock in the morning, a general procession composed of half the people of Nantes, the clergy and the bishop bearing the blessed Sacrament, left the cathedral and went round the city visiting each of the principal churches, where masses were said for the three under sentence.

At eleven the prisoners were conducted to the place of execution, which was in the meadow of Biesse, on the further side of the Loire.

Three gibbets had been erected, one higher than the others, and beneath each was a pile of faggots, tar, and brushwood.

It was a glorious, breezy day, not a cloud was to be seen in the blue heavens; the Loire rolled silently towards the sea its mighty volumes of turbid water, seeming bright and blue as it reflected the brilliancy and colour of the sky. The poplars shivered and whitened in the fresh air with a pleasant rustle, and the willows flickered and wavered above the stream.

A vast crowd had assembled round the gallows; it was with difficulty that a way was made for the condemned, who came on chanting the *De profundis*. The spectators of all ages took up the psalm and chanted it with them, so that the surge of the old Gregorian tone might have been heard by the duke and the bishop, who had shut themselves up in the château of Nantes during the hour of execution.

After the close of the psalm, which was terminated by the *Requiem æternam* instead of the *Gloria*, the Sire de Retz thanked those who had conducted him, and then embraced Pontou and Henriet, before delivering himself of the following address, or rather sermon:—

"My very dear friends and servants, be strong and courageous against the assaults of the devil, and feel great displeasure and contrition for your ill deeds, without despairing of God's mercy. Believe with me, that there is no sin, however great, in the world, which God, in his grace and loving kindness, will not pardon, when one asks it of Him with contrition of heart. Remember that the Lord God is always more ready to receive the sinner than is the sinner to ask of Him pardon. Moreover, let us very humbly thank Him for his great love to us in letting us die in full possession of our faculties, and not cutting us off suddenly in the midst of our misdeeds. Let us conceive such a love of God, and such repentance, that we shall not fear death, which is only a little pang, without which we could not see God in his glory. Besides we must desire to be freed from this world, in which is only misery, that we may go to everlasting glory. Let us rejoice rather, for although we have sinned grievously here below, yet we shall be united in Paradise, our souls being parted from our bodies, and we shall be together for ever and ever, if only we endure in our pious and honourable contrition to our last sigh." [*] Then the marshal, who was to be executed first, left his companions and placed himself in the hands of his executioners. He took off his cap, knelt, kissed a crucifix, and made a pious oration to the crowd much in the style of his address to his friends Pontou and Henriet.

[* The case of the Sire de Retz is one to make us see the great danger there is in trusting to feelings in matters of religion. "If thou wilt enter into life, keep the commandments," said our Lord. How many hope to go to heaven because they have pious emotions!]

Then he commenced reciting the prayers of the dying; the executioner passed the cord round his neck, and adjusted the knot. He mounted a tall stool, erected at the foot of the gallows as a last honour paid to the nobility of the criminal. The pile of firewood was lighted before the executioners had left him.

Pontou and Henriet, who were still on their knees, raised their eyes to their master and cried to him, extending their arms,—

"At this last hour, monseigneur, be a good and valiant soldier of God, and remember the passion of Jesus Christ which wrought our redemption. Farewell, we hope soon to meet in Paradise!

The stool was cast down, and the Sire de Retz dropped. The fire roared up, the flames leaped about him, and enveloped him as be swung.

Suddenly, mingling with the deep booming of the cathedral bell, swelled up the wild unearthly wail of the *Dies iræ*.

No sound among the crowd, only the growl of the fire, and the solemn strain of the hymn

Lo, the Book, exactly worded,
Wherein all hath been recorded;
Thence shall judgment be awarded.

When the Judge his seat attaineth,
And each hidden deed arraigneth,
Nothing unavenged remaineth.

What shall I, frail man, be pleading?
Who for me be interceding?
When the just are mercy needing.

King of Majesty tremendous,
Who dost free salvation send us,

Fount of pity! then befriend us.
. . . .
Low I kneel, with heart-submission;
See, like ashes, my contrition—
Help me in my last condition!

Ah I that day of tears and mourning!
From the dust of earth returning,
Man for judgment must prepare him!

Spare, O, God, in mercy spare him!
Lord, who didst our souls redeem,
Grant a blessed requiem!
AMEN.

Six women, veiled, and robed in white, and six Carmelites advanced. bearing a coffin.

It was whispered that one of the veiled women was Madame de Retz, and that the others were members of the most illustrious houses of Brittany.

The cord by which the marshal was hung was cut, and he fell into a cradle of iron prepared to receive the corpse. The body was removed before the fire had gained any mastery over it. It was placed in the coffin., and the monks and the women transported it to the Carmelite monastery of Nantes, according to the wishes of the deceased.

In the meantime, the sentence had been executed upon Pontou and Henriet; they were hung and burned to dust. Their ashes were cast to the winds; whilst in the Carmelite church of Our Lady were celebrated with pomp the obsequies of the very high, very powerful, very illustrious Seigneur Gilles de Laval, Sire de Retz, late Chamberlain of King Charles VII., and Marshal of France!

XIV. — A GALICIAN WERE-WOLF

The Inhabitants of Austrian Galicia—The Hamlet of Polomyja—Summer Evening in
the Forest—The Beggar Swiatek—A Girl disappears—A School-boy vanishes—
A Servant-girl lost—Another Boy carried of—The Discovery made by the Publican
of Polomyja—Swiatek locked up—Brought to Dabkow—Commits suicide

THE inhabitants of Austrian Galicia are quiet, inoffensive people, take them as a whole. The Jews, who number a twelfth of the population, are the most intelligent, energetic, and certainly the most money-making individuals in the province, though the Poles proper, or Mazurs, are not devoid of natural parts.

Perhaps as remarkable a phenomenon as any other in that kingdom—for kingdom of Waldimir it was—is the enormous numerical preponderance of the nobility over the untitled. In 1837 the proportions stood thus: 32,190 nobles to 2,076 tradesmen.

The average of execution for crime is nine a year, out of a population of four and a half millions,—by no means a high figure, considering the peremptory way in which justice is dealt forth in that province. Yet, in the most quiet and well-disposed neighbourhoods, occasionally the most startling atrocities are committed, occurring when least expected, and sometimes perpetrated by the very person who is least suspected.

Just sixteen years ago there happened in the circle of Tornow, in Western Galicia-the province is divided into nine circles-a circumstance which will probably furnish the grandames with a story for their firesides, during their bitter Galician winters, for many a long year.

In the circle of Tornow, in the lordship of Parkost, is a little hamlet called Polomyja, consisting of eight hovels and a Jewish tavern. The inhabitants are mostly woodcutters, hewing down the firs of the dense forest in which their village is situated, and conveying them to the nearest water, down which they are floated to the Vistula. Each tenant pays no rent for his cottage and pitch of field, but is bound to work a fixed number of days for his landlord: a practice universal in Galicia, and often productive of much discontent and injustice, as the proprietor exacts labour from his tenant on those days when the harvest has to be got in, or the land is m best condition for tillage, and just when the peasant would gladly be engaged upon his own small plot. Money is scarce in the province, and this is accordingly the only way in which the landlord can be sure of his dues.

Most of the villagers of Polomyja are miserably poor; but by cultivating a little maize, and keeping a few fowls or a pig, they scrape together sufficient to sustain life. During the summer the men collect resin from the pines, from each of which, once in twelve Years, they strip a slip of bark, leaving the resin to exude and trickle into a small earthenware jar at its roots; and, during the winter, as already stated, they fell the trees and roll them down to the river.

Polomyja is not a cheerful spot—nested among dense masses of pine, which shed a gloom over the little hamlet; yet, on a fine day, it is pleasant enough for the old women to sit at their cottage doors, scenting that matchless pine fragrance, sweeter than the balm of the Spice Islands, for there is nothing cloying in that exquisite and exhilarating odour; listening to the harp-like thrill of the breeze in the old grey tree-tops, and knitting quietly at long stockings, whilst their little grandchildren romp in the heather and tufted fern.

Towards evening, too, there is something indescribably beautiful in the firwood. The sun dives among the trees, and paints their boles with patches of luminous saffron, or falling over a level clearing, glorifies it with its orange dye, so visibly contrasting with the blue-purple shadow on the western rim of unreclaimed forest, deep and luscious as the bloom on a plum. The birds then are hastening to their nests, a ger-falcon, high overhead, is kindled with sunlight; capering and gambolling among the branches, the merry squirrel skips home for the night.

The sun goes down, but the sky is still shining with twilight. The wild cat begins to hiss and squall in the forest, the heron to flap hastily by, the stork on the top of the tavern chimney to poise itself on one leg for sleep. To-whoo! an owl begins to wake up. Hark! the woodcutters are coming home with a song.

Such is Polomyja in summer time, and much resembling it are the hamlets scattered about the forest, at intervals of a few miles; in each, the public-house being the most commodious and best-built edifice, the church, whenever there is one, not remarkable for anything but its bulbous steeple.

You would hardly believe that amidst all this poverty a beggar could have picked up any subsistence, and yet, a few years ago, Sunday after Sunday, there sat a white-bearded venerable man at the church door, asking alms.

Poor people are proverbially compassionate and liberal, so that the old man generally got a few coppers, and often some good woman bade him come into her cottage, and let him have some food.

Occasionally Swiatek—that was the beggar's name, went his rounds selling small pinchbeck ornaments and beads; generally, however, only appealing to charity.

One Sunday, after church, a Mazur and his wife invited the old man into their hut and gave him a crust of pie and some meat. There were several children about, but a little girl, of nine or ten, attracted the old man's attention by her artless tricks.

Swiatek felt in his pocket and produced a ring, enclosing a piece of coloured glass set over foil. This he presented to the child, who ran off delighted to show her acquisition to her companions.

"Is that little maid your daughter?" asked the beggar.

"No," answered the house-wife, "she is an orphan; there was a widow in this place who died, leaving the child, and I have taken charge of her; one mouth more will not matter much, and the good God will bless us."

"Ay, ay! to be sure He will; the orphans and fatherless are under His own peculiar care."

"She's a good little thing, and gives no trouble," observed the woman. "You go back to Polomyja tonight, I reckon."

"I do—ah!" exclaimed Swiatek, as the little girl ran up to him. You like the ring, is it not beautiful? I found it under a big fir to the left of the churchyard,there may be dozens there. You must turn round three times, bow to the moon, and say, 'Zaboï!' then look among the tree-roots till you find one."

"Come along!" screamed the child to its comrades; "we will go and look for rings."

"You must seek separately," said Swiatek.

The children scampered off into the wood.

"I have done one good thing for you," laughed the beggar, "in ridding you, for a time, of the noise of those children."

"I am glad of a little quiet now and then," said the woman; "the children will not let the baby sleep at times with their clatter. Are you going?"

"Yes; I must reach Polomyja to-night. I am old and very feeble, and poor"—he began to fall into his customary whine— very poor, but I thank and pray to God for you."

Swiatek left the cottage.

That little orphan was never seen again.

The Austrian Government has, of late years, been vigorously advancing education among the lower orders, and establishing schools throughout the province.

The children were returning from class one day, and were scattered among the trees, some pursuing a field-mouse, others collecting juniper-berries, and some sauntering with their hands in their pockets, whistling.

"Where's Peter?" asked one little boy of another who was beside him. "We three go home the same way, let us go together."

"Peter!" shouted the lad.

"Here I am!" was the answer from among the trees; "I'll be with you directly."

"Oh, I see him!" said the elder boy. "There is some one talking to him."

"Where?"

"Yonder, among the pines. Ah! they have gone further into the shadow, and I cannot see them any more. I wonder who was with him; a man, I think."

The boys waited till they were tired, and then they sauntered home, determined to thrash Peter for having kept them waiting. *But Peter was never seen again.*

Some time after this a servant-girl, belonging to a small store kept by a Russian, disappeared from a village five miles from Polomyja. She had been sent with a parcel of grocery to a cottage at no very great distance, but lying apart from the main cluster of hovels, and surrounded by trees.

The day closed in, and her master waited her return anxiously, but as several hours elapsed without any sign of her, he—assisted by the neighbours—went in search of her.

A slight powdering of snow covered the ground, and her footsteps could be traced at intervals where she had diverged from the beaten track. In that part of the road where the trees were thickest, there were marks of two pair of feet leaving the path; but owing to the density of the trees at that spot and to the slightness of the fall of snow, which did not reach the soil, where shaded by the pines, the footprints were immediately lost. By the following morning a heavy fall had obliterated any further traces which day-light might have discovered.

The servant-girl also was never seen again.

During the winter of 1849 the wolves were supposed to have been particularly ravenous, for thus alone did people account for the mysterious disappearances of children.

A little boy had been sent to a fountain to fetch water; the pitcher was found standing by the well, but *the boy had vanished*. The villagers turned out, and those wolves which could be found were despatched.

We have already introduced our readers to Polomyja, although the occurrences above related did not take place among those eight hovels, but in neighbouring villages. The reason for our having given a more detailed account of this cluster of houses—rude cabins they were—will now become apparent.

In May, 1849, the innkeeper of Polomyja missed a couple of ducks, and his suspicions fell upon the beggar who lived there, and whom he held in no esteem, as he himself was a hard-working industrious man, whilst Swiatek maintained himself, his wife, and children by mendicity, although possessed of sufficient arable land to yield an excellent crop of maize, and produce vegetables, if tilled with ordinary care.

As the publican approached the cottage a fragrant whiff of roast greeted his nostrils.

"I'll catch the fellow in the act," said the innkeeper to himself, stealing up to the door, and taking good care not to be observed.

As he threw open the door, he saw the mendicant hurriedly shuffle something under his feet, and conceal it beneath his long clothes. The publican was on him in an instant, had him by the throat, charged him with theft, and dragged him from his seat. Judge of his sickening horror when from beneath the pauper's clothes rolled forth the head of a girl about the age of fourteen or fifteen years, carefully separated from the trunk.

In a short while the neighbours came up. The venerable Swiatek was locked up, along with his wife, his daughter—a girl of sixteen—and a son, aged five.

The hut was thoroughly examined, and the mutilated remains of the poor girl discovered. In a vat were found the legs and thighs, partly raw, partly stewed or roasted. In a chest were the heart, liver, and entrails, all prepared and cleaned, as neatly as though done by a skilful butcher; and, finally, under the oven was a bowl full of fresh blood. On his way to the magistrate of the district. the wretched man flung himself repeatedly on the ground, struggled with his guards, and endeavoured to suffocate himself by gulping clown clods of earth and stones, but was prevented by his conductors.

When taken before the Protokoll at Dabkow, he stated that he had already killed and—assisted by his family—eaten six persons: his children, however, asserted most positively that the number was much greater than he had represented, and their testimony is borne out by the fact, that the remains of *fourteen* different caps and suits of clothes, male as well as female, were found in his house.

The origin of this horrible and depraved taste was as follows, according to Swiatek's own confession:—

In 1846, three years previous, a Jewish tavern in the neighbourhood had been burned down, and the host had himself perished in the flames. Swiatek, whilst examining the ruins, had found the half-roasted corpse of the publican among the charred rafters of the house. At that time the old man was craving with hunger, having been destitute of food for some time. The scent and the sight of the roasted flesh inspired him with an uncontrollable desire to taste of it. He tore off a portion of the carcase and satiated his hunger upon it, and at the same time he conceived such a liking for it, that he could feel no rest till he had tasted again. His second victim was the orphan above alluded to; since then—that is, during the period of no less than three years—he had frequently subsisted in the same manner, and had actually grown sleek and fat upon his frightful meals.

The excitement roused by the discovery of these atrocities was intense; several poor mothers who had bewailed the loss of their little ones, felt their wounds reopened agonisingly. Popular indignation rose to the highest pitch: there was some fear lest the criminal should be torn in pieces himself by the enraged people, as soon as he was brought to trial: but he saved the necessity of precautions being taken to ensure his safety, for, on the first night of his confinement, he hanged himself from the bars of the prison-window.

XV. — ANOMALOUS CASE: THE HUMAN HYÆNA

Ghouls—Story from Fornari—Quotation from Apuleius—Incident mentioned
by Marcassus—Cemeteries of Paris violated—Discovery of Violator—
Confession of M. Bertrand

IT is well known that Oriental romance is full of stories of violators of graves. Eastern superstition attributes to certain individuals a passion for unearthing corpses and mangling them. Of a moonlight night weird forms are seen stealing among the tombs, and burrowing into them with their long nails, desiring to reach the bodies of the dead ere the first streak of dawn compels them to retire. These ghouls, as they are called, are supposed generally to require the flesh of the dead for incantations or magical compositions, but very often they are actuated by the sole desire of rending the sleeping corpse, and disturbing its repose. There is every probability that these ghouls were no mere creations of the imagination, but were actual resurrectionists. Human fat and the hair of a corpse which has grown in the grave, form ingredients in many a necromantic receipt, and the witches who compounded these diabolical mixtures, would unearth corpses in order to obtain the requisite ingredients. It was the same in the middle ages, and to such an extent did the fear of ghouls extend, that it was common in Brittany for churchyards to be provided with lamps, kept burning during the night, that witches might be deterred from venturing under cover of darkness to open the graves.

Fornari gives the following story of a ghoul in his *History of Sorcerers*:—

In the beginning of the 15th century, there lived at Bagdad an aged merchant who had grown wealthy in his business, and who had an only son to whom he was tenderly attached. He resolved to marry him to the daughter of another merchant, a girl of considerable fortune, but without any personal attractions. Abul-Hassan, the merchant's son, on being shown the portrait of the lady, requested his father to delay the marriage till he could reconcile his mind to it. Instead, however, of doing this, he fell in love with another girl, the daughter of a sage, and he gave his father no peace till he consented to the marriage with the object of his affections. The old man stood out as long as he could, but finding that his son was bent on acquiring the hand of the fair Nadilla, and was equally resolute not to accept the rich and ugly lady, he did what most fathers, under such circumstances, are constrained to do, he acquiesced.

The wedding took place with great pomp and ceremony, and a happy honeymoon ensued, which might have been happier but for one little circumstance which led to very serious consequences.

Abul-Hassan noticed that his bride quitted the nuptial couch as soon as she thought her husband was asleep, and did not return to it, till an boar before dawn.

Filled with curiosity, Hassan one night feigned sleep, and saw his wife rise and leave the room as usual. He followed cautiously, and saw her enter a cemetery. By the straggling moonbeams he beheld her go into a tomb; he stepped in after her.

The scene within was horrible. A party of ghouls were assembled with the spoils of the graves they had violated., and were feasting on the flesh of the long-buried corpses. His own wife, who, by the way, never touched supper at home, played no inconsiderable part in the hideous banquet.

As soon as he could safely escape, Abul-Hassan stole back to his bed.

He said nothing to his bride till next evening when supper was laid, and she declined to eat; then he insisted on her partaking, and when she positively refused, he exclaimed wrathfully,—"Yes, you keep your appetite for your feast with the ghouls!" Nadilla was silent; she turned pale and trembled, and without a word sought her bed. At midnight she rose, fell on her husband with her nails and teeth, tore his throat, and having opened a vein, attempted to suck his blood; but Abul-Hassan springing to his feet threw her down, and with a blow killed her. She was buried next day.

Three days after, at midnight, she re-appeared, attacked her husband again, and again attempted to suck his blood. He fled from her, and on the morrow opened her tomb, burned her to ashes, and cast them into the Tigris.

This story connects the ghoul with the vampire. As will be seen by a former chapter, the were-wolf and the vampire are closely related.

That the ancients held the same belief that the witches violate corpses, is evident from the third episode in the *Golden Ass* of Apuleius. I will only quote the words of the crier:—

"I pray thee, tell me," replied I, "of what kind are the duties attached to this funeral guardianship?" "Duties!" quoth the crier; "why, keep wide awake all night, with thine eyes fixed steadily upon the corpse, neither winking nor blinking, nor looking to the right nor looking to the left, either to one side or the other, be it even little; for the witches, infamous wretches that they are! can slip out of their skins in an instant and change themselves into the form of any animal they have a mind; and then they crawl along so slyly, that the eyes of justice, nay, the eyes of the sun himself, are not keen enough to perceive them. At all events, their wicked devices are infinite in number and variety; and whether it be in the shape of a bird, or a dog, or a mouse, or even of a common house-fly, that they exercise their dire incantations, if thou art not vigilant in the extreme, they will deceive thee one way or other, and overwhelm thee with sleep; nevertheless, as regards the reward, 'twill be from four to six aurei; nor, although 'tis a perilous service, wilt thou receive more. Nay, hold! I had almost forgotten to give thee a necessary caution. Clearly understand, that it the corpse be not restored to the relatives entire, the deficient pieces of flesh torn off by the teeth of the witches must be replaced from the face of the sleepy guardian."

Here we have the rending of corpses connected with change of form.

Marcassus relates that after a long war in Syria, during the night, troops of lamias, female evil spirits, appeared upon the field of battle, unearthing the hastily buried bodies of the soldiers, and devouring the flesh off their bones. They were pursued and fired upon, and some young men succeeded in killing a considerable number; but during the day they had all of them the forms of wolves or hyænas. That there is a foundation of truth in these horrible stories, and that it is quite possible for a human being to be possessed of a depraved appetite for rending corpses, is proved by an extraordinary case brought before a court-martial in Paris, so late as July 10th, 1849.

The details are given with fulness in the *Annales Medico- psychologiques* for that month and year. They are too revolting for reproduction. I will, however, give an outline of this remarkable case.

In the autumn of 1848, several of the cemeteries in the neighbourhood of Paris were found to have been entered during the night, and graves to have been rifled. The deeds were not those of medical students, for the bodies had not been carried of, but were found lying about the tombs in fragments. It was at first supposed that the perpetration of these outrages must have been a wild beast, but footprints in the soft earth left no doubt that it was a man. Close watch was kept at Père la Chaise; but after a few corpses had been mangled there, the outrages ceased.

In the winter, another cemetery was ravaged, and it was not till March in 1849, that a spring gun which had been set in the cemetery of S. Parnasse, went off during the night, and warned the guardians of the place that the mysterious visitor had fallen into their trap. They rushed to the spot, only to see a dark figure in a military mantle leap the wall, and disappear in the gloom. Marks of blood, however, gave evidence that he had been hit by the gun when it had discharged. At the same time, a fragment of blue cloth, torn from the mantle, was obtained, and afforded a clue towards the identification of the ravisher of the tombs.

On the following day, the police went from barrack to barrack, inquiring whether officer or man were suffering from a gun-shot wound. By this means they discovered the person. He was a junior officer in the 1st Infantry regiment, of the name of Bertrand.

He was taken to the hospital to be cured of his wound, and on his recovery, he was tried by court-martial.

His history was this.

He had been educated in the theological seminary of Langres, till, at the age of twenty, he entered the army. He was a young man of retiring habits, frank and cheerful to his comrades, so as to be greatly beloved by them, of feminine delicacy and refinement, and subject to fits of depression and melancholy. In February, 1847, as he was walking with a friend in the country, he came to a churchyard, the gate of which stood open. The day before a woman had been buried, but the sexton had not completed filling in the grave, and he had been engaged upon it on the present occasion, when a storm of rain had driven him to shelter. Bertrand noticed the spade and pick lying beside the grave, and—to use his own words:—"A cette vue des idées noires me vinrent, j'eus comme un violent mal de tête, mon cur battait avec force, je no me possédais plus." He managed by some excuse to get rid of his companion, and then returning to the churchyard, he caught up a spade and began to dig into the grave. "Soon I dragged the corpse out of the earth, and I began to hash it with the spade, without well knowing what I was about. A labourer saw me, and I laid myself flat on the ground till he was out of sight, and then I cast the body back into the grave. I then went away, bathed in a cold sweat, to a little grove, where I reposed for several hours, notwithstanding the cold rain which fell, in a condition of complete exhaustion. When I rose, my limbs were as if broken, and my head weak. The same prostration and sensation followed each attack.

Two days after, I returned to the cemetery, and opened the grave with my hands. My hands bled, but I did not feel the pain; I tore the corpse to shreds, and flung it back into the pit."

He had no further attack for four months, till his regiment came to Paris. As he was one day walking in the gloomy, shadowy, alleys of Père la Chaise, the same feeling came over him like a flood. In the night he climbed the wall, and dug up a little girl of seven years old. He tore her in half. A few days later, he opened the grave of a woman who had died in childbirth, and had lain in the grave for thirteen days. On the 16th November, he dug up an old woman of fifty, and, ripping her to pieces, rolled among the fragments. He did the same to another corpse on the 12th December. These are only a few of the numerous cases of violation of tombs to which he owned. It was on the night of the 15th March that the spring-gun shot him.

Bertrand declared at his trial, that whilst he was in the hospital he had not felt any desire to renew his attempts, and that he considered himself cured of his horrible propensities, for he had seen men dying in the beds around him, and now: "Je suis guéri, car aujourd'hui j'ai peur d'un mort."

The fits of exhaustion which followed his accesses are very remarkable, as they precisely resemble those which followed the berserkir rages of the Northmen, and the expeditions of the Lycanthropists.

The case of M. Bertrand is indubitably most singular and anomalous; it scarcely bears the character of insanity, but seems to point rather to a species of diabolical possession. At first the accesses chiefly followed upon his drinking wine, but after a while they came upon him without exciting cause. The manner in which he mutilated the dead was different. Some he chopped with the spade, others he tore and ripped with his teeth and nails. Sometimes he tore the mouth open and rent the face back to the ears, he opened the stomachs, and pulled off the limbs. Although he dug up the bodies of several men he felt no inclination to mutilate them, whereas he delighted in rending female corpses. He was sentenced to a year's imprisonment.

XVI. — A SERMON ON WERE-WOLVES

The Discourses of Dr. Johann—The Sermon—Remarks

THE following curious specimen of a late mediæval sermon is taken from the old German edition of the discourses of Dr. Johann Geiler von Keysersperg, a famous preacher in Strasbourg. The volume is entitled: "*Die Emeis*. Dis ist das Büch von der Omeissen, und durch Herr der Künnig ich diente gern. Und sagt von Eigenschafft der Omeissen, und gibt underweisung von der Unholden oder Hexen, und von Gespenst, der Geist, und von dem Wütenden Heer Wunderbarlich."

This strange series of sermons was preached at Strasbourg in the year 1508, and was taken down and written out by a barefooted friar, Johann Pauli, and by him published in 1517. The doctor died on Mid-Lent Sunday, 1510. There is a Latin edition of his sermons, but whether of the same series or not I cannot tell, as I have been unable to obtain a sight of the volume. The German edition is illustrated with bold and clever woodcuts. Among other, there are representations of the Witches' Sabbath, the Wild Huntsman, and a Werewolf attacking a Man.

The sermon was preached on the third Sunday in Lent. No text is given, but there is a general reference to the gospel for the day. This is the discourse:— [*]

[* Headed thus:—"Am drittë sontag à fastê, occuli, predigt dé doctor vô dê Werwölffenn."]

"What shall we say about were-wolves? for there are were-wolves which run about the villages devouring men and children. As men say about them, they run about full gallop, injuring men, and are called ber-wölff, or wer-wölff. Do you ask me if I know aught about them? I answer, Yes. They are apparently wolves which cat men and children, and that happens on seven accounts:—

1. Esuriem — Hunger.
2. Rabiem — Savageness.
3. Senectutem — Old age.
4. Experientiam — Experience.
5. Insaniem — Madness.
6. Diabolum —The Devil.
7. Deum — God.

The first happens through hunger; when the wolves find nothing to eat in the woods, they must come to people and eat men when hunger drives them to it. You see well, when it is very cold, that the stags come in search of food up to the villages, and the birds actually into the dining-room in search of victuals.

"Under the second head, wolves eat children through their innate savageness, because they are savage, and that is (propter locum coitum ferum). Their savageness arises first from their condition. Wolves which live in cold places are smaller on that account, and more savage than other wolves. Secondly, their savageness depends on the season; they are more savage about Candlemas than at any other time of the year, and men must be more on their guard against them then than at other times. It is a proverb, 'He who seeks a wolf at Candlemas, a peasant on Shrove Tuesday, and a parson in Lent, is a man of pluck.' . . . Thirdly, their savageness depends on their having young. When the wolves have young, they are more savage than when they have not. You see it so in all beasts. A wild duck, when it has young poults, you see what an uproar it makes. A cat fights for its young kittens; the wolves do ditto.

"Under the third head, the wolves do injury on account of their age. When a wolf is old, it is weak and feeble in its leas, so it can't ran fast enough to catch stags, and therefore it rends a man, whom it can catch easier than a wild animal. It also tears children and men easier than wild animals, because of its teeth, for its teeth break off when it is very old; you see it well in old women: how the last teeth wobble, and they have scarcely a tooth left in their heads, and they open their mouths for men to feed them with mash and stewed substances.

"Under the fourth head, the injury the were-wolves do arises from experience. It is said that human flesh is far sweeter than other flesh; so when a wolf has once tasted human flesh, he desires to taste it again. So he acts like old topers, who, when they know the best wine, will not be put off with inferior quality.

"Under the fifth head, the injury arises from ignorance. A dog when it is mad is also inconsiderate, and it bites any man; it does not recognize its own lord: and what is a wolf but a wild dog which is mad and inconsiderate, so that it regards no man.

"Under the sixth head, the injury comes of the Devil, who transforms himself, and takes on him the form of a wolf So writes Vincentius in his *Speculum Historiale*. And he has taken it from Valerius Maximus in the Punic war. When the Romans fought against the men of Africa, when the captain lay asleep, there came a wolf and drew his sword, and carried it off. That was the Devil in a, wolf's form. The like writes William of Paris,—that a wolf will kill and devour children, and do the greatest mischief. There was a man who had the phantasy that he himself was a wolf. And afterwards he was found lying in the wood, and he was dead out of sheer hunger.

"Under the seventh head, the injury comes of God's ordinance. For God will sometimes punish certain lands and villages with wolves. So we read of Elisha,—that when Elisha wanted to go up a mountain out of Jericho, some naughty boys made a mock of him and said, 'O bald head, step up! O glossy pate, step up!' What happened? He cursed them. Then came two bears out of the desert and tore about forty-two of the children. That was God's ordinance. The like we read of a prophet who would set at naught the commands he had received of God, for he was persuaded to eat bread at the house of another. As he went home he rode upon his ass. Then came a lion which slew him and left the ass alone. That was God's ordinance. Therefore must man turn to God when He brings wild beasts to do him a mischief: which same brutes may He not bring now or evermore. Amen."

It will be seen from this extraordinary sermon that Dr. Johann Geiler von Keysersperg did not regard werewolves in any other light than natural wolves filled with a lust for human flesh; and he puts aside altogether the view that they are men in a state of metamorphosis. However, he alludes to this superstition in his sermon on wild-men of the woods, but translates his lycanthropists to Spain.

Historic Oddities and Strange Events, 1st Series

I. — THE DISAPPEARANCE OF BATHURST

THE mystery of the disappearance of Benjamin Bathurst on November 25, 1809, is one which can never with certainty be cleared up. At the time public opinion in England was convinced that he had been secretly murdered by order of Napoleon, and the *Times* in a leader on January 23, 1810, so decisively asserted this, that the *Moniteur* of January 29 ensuing, in sharp and indignant terms repudiated the charge. Nevertheless, not in England only, but in Germany, was the impression so strong that Napoleon had ordered the murder, if murder had been committed, that the Emperor saw fit, in the spring of the same year, solemnly to assure the wife of the vanished man, on his word of honour, that he knew nothing about the disappearance of her husband. Thirty years later Varnhagen von Ense, a well-known German author, reproduced the story and reiterated the accusation against Napoleon, or at all events against the French. Later still, the *Spectator*, in an article in 1862, gave a brief sketch of the disappearance of Bathurst, and again repeated the charge against French police agents or soldiers of having made away with the Englishman. At that time a skeleton was said to have been discovered in the citadel of Magdeburg with the hands bound, in an upright position, and the writer of the article sought to identify the skeleton with the lost man.[1]

[1] The discovery of a skeleton as described was denied afterwards by the Magdeburg papers. It was a newspaper sensational paragraph, and unfounded.

We shall see whether other discoveries do not upset this identification, and afford us another solution of the problem—What became of Benjamin Bathurst?

Benjamin Bathurst was the third son of Dr. Henry Bathurst, Bishop of Norwich, Canon of Christchurch, and the Prebendary of Durham, by Grace, daughter of Charles Coote, Dean of Kilfenora, and sister of Lord Castlecoote. His eldest brother, Henry, was Archdeacon of Norwich; his next, Sir James, K.C.B., was in the army and was aide-de-camp to Lord Wellington in the Peninsula.

Benjamin, the third son of the bishop, was born March 14, 1784,[2] and had been secretary of the Legation at Leghorn. In May, 1805, he married Phillida, daughter of Sir John Call, Bart., of Whiteford, in Cornwall, and sister of Sir William Pratt Call, the second baronet. Benjamin is a Christian name that occurs repeatedly in the Bathurst family after the founder of it, Sir Benjamin, Governor of the East India Company and of the Royal African Company. He died in 1703. The grandfather of the subject of our memoir was a Benjamin, brother of Allen, who was created Baron in 1711, and Earl in 1772.

[2] Register of Baptisms, Christchurch, Oxford, 1784, March 14, Benjamin, s. of Henry Bathurst, Canon, and Grace his wife, born, and bap. April 19.

Benjamin had three children: a son who died, some years after his father's disappearance, in consequence of a fall from a horse at a race in Rome; a daughter, who was drowned in the Tiber; and another who married the Earl of Castlestuart in 1830, and after his death married Signor Pistocchi.

In 1809, early in the year, Benjamin was sent to Vienna by his kinsman, Earl Bathurst, who was in the ministry of Lord Castlereagh, and, in October, Secretary of State for the Foreign Department. He was sent on a secret embassy from the English Government to the Court of the Emperor Francis. The time was one of great and critical importance to Austria. Since the Peace of Pressburg she had been quiet; the Cabinet of Vienna had adhered with cautious prudence to a system of neutrality, but she only waited her time, and in 1808 the government issued a decree by which a militia, raised by a conscription, under the name of the "*Landwehr*," was instituted, and this speedily reached the number of 300,000 men. Napoleon, who was harassed by the insurrection in the Peninsula, demanded angrily an explanation, which was evaded. To overawe Austria, he met the Emperor Alexander of Russia at Erfurth, and the latter when sounded by Austria refused to have any part in the confederation against Napoleon. England, in the meantime, was urging Austria to cast down the gauntlet. In pledge of amity, the port of Trieste was thrown open to the English and Spanish flags. In December, a declaration of the King of England openly alluded to the hostile preparations of Austria, but the Cabinet at Vienna were as yet undecided as to the course they would finally adopt. The extreme peril which the monarchy had undergone already in the wars with Napoleon made them hesitate. England was about to send fifty thousand men to the Peninsula, and desired the diversion of a war in the heart of Germany. Prussia resolved to remain neutral. Napoleon rapidly returned from Spain, and orders were despatched to Davoust to concentrate his immense corps at Bamberg; Massena was to repair to Strasburg, and press on to Ulm; Oudenot to move on Augsburg, and Bernadotte, at the head of the Saxons, was to menace Bohemia. It was at this juncture that Benjamin Bathurst hurried as Ambassador Extraordinary to Vienna, to assure the Cabinet there of the intentions of England to send a powerful contingent into Spain, and to do all in his power to urge Austria to declare war. Encouraged by England, the Cabinet of Vienna took the initiative, and on April 8 the Austrian troops crossed the frontier at once on the Inn, in Bohemia, in Tyrol, and in Italy.

The irritation and exasperation of Napoleon were great; and Bathurst, who remained with the Court, laboured under the impression that the Emperor of the French bore him especial enmity, on account of his exertions to provoke the Austrian Ministry to declaration of war. Whether this opinion of his were well founded, or whether he had been warned that Napoleon would take the opportunity, if given him, of revenging himself, we do not know; but what is certain is, that Bathurst was prepossessed with the conviction that Napoleon regarded him with implacable hostility and would leave no stone unturned to compass his destruction.

On July 6 came the battle of Wagram, then the humiliating armistice of Znaim, which was agreed to by the Emperor Francis at Komorn in spite of the urgency of Metternich and Lord Walpole, who sought to persuade him to reject the proposals. This armistice was the preliminary to a peace which was concluded at Schönbrun in October. With this, Bathurst's office at Vienna came to an end, and he set out on his way home. Now it was that he repeatedly spoke of the danger that menaced him, and of his fears lest Napoleon should arrest him on his journey to England. He hesitated for some time which road to take, and concluding that if he went by Trieste and Malta he might run the worst risks, he resolved to make his way to London by Berlin and the north of Germany. He took with him his private secretary and a valet; and, to evade observation, assumed the name of Koch, and pretended that he was a travelling merchant. His secretary was instructed to act as courier, and he passed under the name of Fisher. Benjamin Bathurst carried pistols about his person, and there were firearms in the back of the carriage.

On November 25, 1809, about midday, he arrived at Perleberg, with post-horses, on the route from Berlin to Hamburg, halted at the post-house for refreshments, and ordered fresh horses to be harnessed to the carriage for the journey to Lenzen, which was the next station.

Bathurst had come along the highway from Berlin to Schwerin, in Brandenburg, as far as the little town of Perleberg, which lies on the Stepnitz, that flows after a few miles into the Elbe at Wittenberge. He might have gone on to Ludwigslust, and thence to Hamburg, but this was a considerable détour, and he was anxious to be home. He had now before him a road that led along the Elbe close to the frontier of Saxony. The Elbe was about four miles distant. At Magdeburg were French troops. If he were in danger anywhere, it would be during the next few hours—that is, till he reached Dömitz. About a hundred paces from the post-house was an inn, the White Swan, the host of which was named Leger. By the side of the inn was the Parchimer gate of the town, furnished with a tower, and the road to Hamburg led through this gate, outside of which was a sort of suburb consisting of poor cottagers' and artisans' houses.

Benjamin Bathurst went to the Swan and ordered an early dinner; the horses were not to be put in till he had dined. He wore a pair of grey trousers, a grey frogged short coat, and over it a handsome sable greatcoat lined with violet velvet. On his head was a fur cap to match. In his scarf was a diamond pin of some value.

As soon as he had finished his meal, Bathurst inquired who was in command of the soldiers quartered in the town, and where he lodged. He was told that a squadron of the Brandenburg cuirassiers was there under Captain Klitzing, who was residing in a house behind the Town Hall. Mr. Bathurst then crossed the market place and called on the officer, who was at the time indisposed with a swollen neck. To Captain Klitzing he said that he was a traveller on his way to Hamburg, that he had strong and well-grounded suspicions that his person was endangered, and he requested that he might be given a guard in the inn, where he was staying. A lady who was present noticed that he seemed profoundly agitated, that he trembled as though ague-stricken, and was unable to raise a cup of tea that was offered him to his lips without spilling it.

The captain laughed at his fears, but consented to let him have a couple of soldiers, and gave the requisite orders for their despatch; then Mr. Bathurst rose, resumed his sable overcoat, and, to account for his nervous difficulty in getting into his furs again, explained that he was much shaken by something that had alarmed him.

Not long after the arrival of Mr. Bathurst at the Swan, two Jewish merchants arrived from Lenzen with post-horses, and left before nightfall.

On Mr. Bathurst's return to the inn, he countermanded the horses; he said he would not start till night. He considered that it would be safer for him to spin along the dangerous portion of the route by night when Napoleon's spies would be less likely to be on the alert. He remained in the inn writing and burning papers. At seven o'clock he dismissed the soldiers on guard, and ordered the horses to be ready by nine. He stood outside the inn watching his portmanteau, which had been taken within, being replaced on the carriage, stepped round to the heads of the horses—*and was never seen again.*

It must be remembered that this was at the end of November. Darkness had closed in before 5 P.M., as the sun set at four. An oil lantern hung across the street, emitting a feeble light; the ostler had a horn lantern, wherewith he and the postillion adjusted the harness of the horses. The landlord was in the doorway talking to the secretary, who, as courier, was paying the account. No one particularly observed the movements of Mr. Bathurst at the moment. He had gone to the horses' heads, where the ostler's lantern had fallen on him. The horses were in, the postillion ready, the valet stood by the carriage door, the landlord had his cap in hand ready to wish the gentleman a "lucky journey;" the secretary was impatient, as the wind was cold. They waited; they sent up to the room which Mr. Bathurst had engaged; they called. All in vain. Suddenly, inexplicably, without a word, a cry, an alarm of any sort, he was gone—spirited away, and what really became of him will never be known with certainty.

Whilst the whole house was in amazement and perplexity the Jewish merchants ordered their carriage to be got ready, and departed.

Some little time elapsed before it was realised that the case was serious. Then it occurred to the secretary that Mr. Bathurst might have gone again to the captain in command to solicit guards to attend his carriage. He at once sent to the captain, but Mr. Bathurst was not with him. The moment, however, that Klitzing heard that the traveller had disappeared, he remembered the alarm expressed by the gentleman, and acted with great promptitude. He sent soldiers to seize the carriage and all the effects of the missing man. He went, in spite of his swollen neck, immediately to the Swan, ordered a chaise, and required the secretary to enter it; he placed a cuirassier and the valet on the box, and, stepping into the carriage, ordered it to be driven to the Golden Crown, an inn at the further end of the town, where he installed the companions of Bathurst, and placed a soldier in guard over them. A guard was also placed over the Swan, and next morning every possible search was made for the lost man. The river was dragged, outhouses, woods, marshes, ditches were examined, but not a trace of him could be found. That day was Sunday. Klitzing remained at Perleberg only till noon, to wait some discovery, and then, without delay, hurried to Kyritz, where was his commandant, Colonel Bismark, to lay the case before him, and solicit leave to hasten direct to Berlin, there to receive further instructions what was to be done.

He was back on Monday with full authority to investigate the matter.

Before he left he had gone over the effects of Mr. Bathurst, and had learned that the fur coat belonging to him was missing; he communicated this fact to the civil magistrate of the district, and whilst he was away search was instituted for this. It was the sable coat lined with violet velvet already mentioned, and this, along with another belonging to the secretary, Fisher was under the impression had been left in the post-house.

The amazing part of the matter is that the city authorities—and, indeed, on his return, Captain Klitzing—for a while confined themselves to a search for the fur coat, and valuable time was lost by this means. Moreover, the city authorities, the police, and the military were all independent, and all jealous of each other. The military commander, Klitzing, and the burgomaster were in open quarrel, and sent up to headquarters charges against each other for interference in the matter beyond their rights. The head of the police was inert, a man afterwards dismissed for allowing defalcation in the monies entrusted to him. There was no system in the investigation, and the proper clues were not followed.

On December 16th, two poor women went out of Perleberg to a little fir wood in the direction of Quitzow, to pick up broken sticks for fuel. There they found, a few paces from a path leading through the wood, spread out on the grass, a pair of trousers turned inside out. On turning them back they observed that they were stained on the outside, as if the man who had worn them had lain on the earth. In the pocket was a paper with writing on it; this, as well as the trousers, was sodden with water. Two bullet holes were in the trousers, but no traces of blood about them, which could hardly have been the case had the bullets struck a man wearing the trousers. The women took what they had found to the burgomaster. The trousers were certainly those of the missing man. The paper in the pocket was a half-finished letter from Mr. Bathurst to his wife, scratched in pencil, stating that he was afraid he would never reach England, and that his ruin would be the work of Count d'Entraigues, and he requested her not to marry again in the event of his not returning.

The English Government offered £1,000 reward, and his family another £1,000; Prince Frederick of Prussia, who took a lively interest in the matter, offered in addition 100 Friedrichs d'or for the discovery of the body, or for information which might lead to the solution of the mystery, but no information to be depended upon ever transpired. Various rumours circulated; and Mrs. Thistlethwaite, the sister of Benjamin Bathurst, in her Memoirs of Dr. Henry Bathurst, Bishop of Norwich, published by Bentley in 1853, gives them. He was said to have been lost at sea. Another report was that he was murdered by his valet, who took an open boat on the Elbe, and escaped. Another report again was that he had been lost in a vessel which was crossing to Sweden and which foundered about this time. These reports are all totally void of truth. Mrs. Thistlethwaite declares that Count d'Entraigues, who was afterwards so cruelly murdered along with his wife by their Italian servant, was heard to say that he could prove that Mr. Bathurst was murdered in the fortress of Magdeburg. In a letter to his wife, dated October 14, 1809, Benjamin Bathurst said that he trusted to reach home by way of Colberg and Sweden. D'Entraigues had been a French spy in London; and Mrs. Thistlethwaite says that he himself told Mrs. Bathurst that her husband had been carried off by *douaniers-montés* from Perleberg to Magdeburg, and murdered there. This it is hard to believe.

Thomas Richard Underwood, in a letter from Paris, November 24, 1816, says he was a prisoner of war in Paris in 1809, and that both the English and French there believed that the crime of his abduction and murder had been committed by the French Government.

The *European Magazine* for January, 1810, says that he was apparently carried off by a party of French troops stationed at Lenzen, but this was not the case. No French troops were on that side of the Elbe. It further says, "The French Executive, with a view to ascertain by his papers the nature of the relations subsisting between this country and the Austrian Government, has added to the catalogue of its crimes by the seizure, or probably the murder, of this gentleman."

If there had been French troops seen we should have known of it; but none were. Every effort was made by the civil and military authorities to trace Bathurst. Bloodhounds were employed to track the lost man, in vain. Every well was explored, the bed of the Stepnitz thoroughly searched. Every suspicious house in Perleberg was examined from attic to cellar, the gardens were turned up, the swamps sounded, but every effort to trace and discover him was in vain.

On January 23, 1810, in a Hamburg paper, appeared a paragraph, which for the first time informed the people of Perleberg who the merchant Koch really was who had so mysteriously vanished. The paragraph was in the form of a letter, dated from London, January 6, 1810—that is, six weeks after the disappearance. It ran thus: "Sir Bathurst, Ambassador Extraordinary of England to the Court of Austria, concerning whom a German newspaper, under date of December 10, stated that he had committed suicide in a fit of insanity, is well in mind and body. His friends have received a letter from him dated December 13, which, therefore, must have been written after the date of his supposed death."

Who inserted this, and for what purpose? It was absolutely untrue. Was it designed to cause the authorities to relax their efforts to probe the mystery, and perhaps to abandon them altogether?

The Jewish merchants were examined, but were at once discharged; they were persons well-to-do, and generally respected.

Was it possible that Mr. Bathurst had committed suicide? This was the view taken of his disappearance in France, where, in the *Moniteur* of December 12, 1809, a letter from the correspondent in Berlin stated: "Sir Bathurst on his way from Berlin showed signs of insanity, and destroyed himself in the neighbourhood of Perleberg." On January 23, 1810, as already said, the *Times* took the matter up, and not obscurely charged the Emperor Napoleon with having made away with Mr. Bathurst, who was peculiarly obnoxious to him.

In the mean time, the fur coat had been found, hidden in the cellar of a family named Schmidt, behind some firewood. Frau Schmidt declared that it had been left at the post house, where she had found it; and had conveyed it away, and given it to her son Augustus, a fellow of notoriously bad character. Now, it is remarkable that one witness declared that she had seen the stranger who had disappeared go out of the square down the narrow lane in which the Schmidts lived, and where eventually the fur coat was found. When questioned, Augustus Schmidt said that "his mother had told him the stranger had two pistols, and had sent her to buy him some powder. He supposed therefore that the gentleman had shot himself." Unfortunately the conflict of authorities acted prejudicially at this point, and the questions how the Schmidts came to know anything about the pistols, whether Frau Schmidt really was sent for powder, and whether Bathurst was really seen entering the alley in which they lived, and at what hour, were never properly entered into. Whatever information Klitzing obtained, was forwarded to Berlin, and there his reports remain in the archives. They have not been examined.

Fresh quarrels broke out between Klitzing and the Burgomaster, and Klitzing instead of pursuing the main investigations, set to work to investigate the proceedings of the Burgomaster. So more time was lost.

On Thursday, November 30th, that is to say, five days after the disappearance of Bathurst, Captain Klitzing ordered the town magistrates; 1. To have all ditches and canals round the place examined; 2. To have the neighbourhood of the town explored by foresters with hounds; 3. To let off the river Stepnitz and examine the bed. Then he added, "as I have ascertained that Augustus Schmidt, who is now under arrest for the theft of the fur coat, was *not at home at the time that the stranger disappeared*, I require that this fact be taken into consideration, and investigated"—and this, as far as we can ascertain, was not done; it was just one of those valuable clues which were left untraced.

The whole neighbourhood was searched, ditches, ponds, the river bed, drains, every cellar, and garden, and nothing found. The search went on to December 6, and proved wholly resultless. It was not till December 16 that the trousers were found. It is almost certain that they were laid in the Quitzow wood after the search had been given over, on December 6th.

As nothing could be proved against the Schmidt family, except that they had taken the fur coat, Frau Schmidt and her son were sentenced to eight weeks' imprisonment.

The matter of the pistols was not properly cleared up. That, again, was a point, and an important point that remained uninvestigated.

The military authorities who examined the goods of Mr. Bathurst declared that nothing was missing except the fur cloak, which was afterwards recovered, and we suppose these pistols were included. If not, one may be sure that some notice would have been taken of the fact that he had gone off with his pistols, and had not returned. This would have lent colour to the opinion that he destroyed himself. Besides no shot was heard. A little way outside the gateway of the town beyond the Swan inn is a bridge over the small and sluggish stream of the Stepnitz. It was possible he might have shot himself there, and fallen into the water; but this theory will not bear looking closely into. A shot fired there would certainly have been heard at night in the cottages beside the road; the river was searched shortly after without a trace of him having been found, and his trousers with bullet holes made in them after they had been taken off him had been discovered in another direction.

The *Moniteur* of January 29 said: "Among the civilised races, England is the only one that sets an example of having bandits[3] in pay, and inciting to crime. From information we have received from Berlin, we believe that Mr. Bathurst had gone off his head. It is the manner of the British Cabinet to commit diplomatic commissions to persons whom the whole nation knows are half fools. It is only the English diplomatic service which contains crazy people."

[3] When, in 1815, Napoleon was at St. Helena, on his first introduction to Sir Hudson Lowe, he addressed the governor with the insulting words, "Monsieur, vous avez commandé des brigands." He alluded to the Corsican rangers in the British service, which Lowe had commanded.

This violent language was at the time attributed to Napoleon's dictation, stung with the charge made by the *Times*, a charge ranking him with "vulgar murderers," and which attributed to him two other and somewhat similar cases, that of Wagstaff, and that of Sir George Rumbold. It is very certain that the *Moniteur* would not have ventured on such insulting language without his permission.

In April Mrs. Bathurst, along with some relatives, arrived in Perleberg. The poor lady was in great distress and anxiety to have the intolerable suspense alleviated by a discovery of some sort, and the most liberal offers were made and published to induce a disclosure of the secret. At this time a woman named Hacker, the wife of a peasant who lived in the shoe-market, was lying in the town gaol—the tower already mentioned, adjoining the White Swan. She was imprisoned for various fraudulent acts. She now offered to make a confession, and this was her statement:

"A few weeks before Christmas I was on my way to Perleberg from a place in Holstein, where my husband had found work. In the little town of Seeberg, twelve miles from Hamburg, I met the shoemaker's assistant Goldberger, of Perleberg, whom I knew from having danced with him. He was well-dressed, and had from his fob hanging a hair-chain with gold seals. His knitted silk purse was stuffed with louis d'ors. When I asked him how he came by so much money, he said, 'Oh, I got 500 dollars and the watch as hush-money when the Englishman was murdered.' He told me no more particulars, except that one of the seals was engraved with a name, and he had had that altered in Hamburg."

No credit was given to this story, and no inquiry was instituted into the whereabouts of Goldberger. It was suspected that the woman had concocted it in the hopes of getting Mrs. Bathurst to interest herself in obtaining her release, and of getting some of the money offered to informers.

Mrs. Bathurst did not return immediately to England; she appealed to Napoleon to grant her information, and he assured her through Cambacières, and on his word of honour, that he knew nothing of the matter beyond what he had seen in the papers.

So the matter rested, an unsolved mystery.

In Prussia, among the great bulk of the educated, in the higher and official classes, the prevailing conviction was that Napoleon had caused the disappearance of Bathurst, not out of personal feeling, but in political interests, for the purpose of getting hold of the dispatches which he was believed to be conveying to England from the Austrian Government. The murder was held to be an accident, or an unavoidable consequence. And in Perleberg itself this was the view taken of the matter as soon as it was known who the stranger was. But then, another opinion prevailed there, that Klitzing had secretly conveyed him over the frontier, so as to save him from the spies, and the pursuit which, as he and Bathurst knew, endangered the safety of the returning envoy.

In Perleberg two opinions were formed, by such as conceived that he had been murdered, as to the manner in which he had been made away with.

Not far from the post-house was at the time a low tavern kept by Hacker, who has been mentioned above; the man combined shoemaking with the sale of brandy. Augustus Schmidt spent a good deal of his time in this house. Now shortly after this affair, Hacker left Perleberg, and set up at Altona, where he showed himself possessed of a great deal of money. He was also said to have disposed of a gold repeater watch to a jeweller in Hamburg. This was never gone into; and how far it was true, or idle rumour, cannot be said. One view was that Bathurst had been robbed and murdered by Hacker and Schmidt.

The other opinion was this. Opposite the post-house was a house occupied at the time by a fellow who was a paid French spy; a man who was tried for holding secret communication with the enemy of his Fatherland. He was a petty lawyer, who stirred up quarrels among the peasants, and lived by the result. He was a man of the worst possible character, capable of anything. The opinion of one section of the people of Perleberg was, that Bathurst, before entering the carriage, had gone across the square, and had entered into conversation with this man, who had persuaded him to enter his door, where he had strangled him, and buried him in his cellar. The widow of this man on her death-bed appeared anxious to confess something, but died before she could speak.

In 1852 a discovery was made at Perleberg which may or may not give the requisite solution.

We may state before mentioning this that Captain Klitzing never believed that Bathurst had been spirited away by French agents. He maintained that he had been murdered for his money.

On April 15, 1852, a house on the Hamburg road that belonged to the mason Kiesewetter was being pulled down, when a human skeleton was discovered under the stone threshold of the stable. The skeleton lay stretched out, face upwards, on the black peat earth, covered with mortar and stone chips, the head embedded in walling-stones and mortar. In the back of the skull was a fracture, as if a blow of a heavy instrument had fallen on it. All the upper teeth were perfect, but one of the molars in the lower jaw was absent, and there were indications of its having been removed by a dentist. The house where these human remains were found had been purchased in 1834 by the mason Kiesewetter from Christian Mertens, who had inherited it from his father, which latter had bought it in 1803 of a shoemaker. *Mertens, the father, had been a serving man in the White Swan at the time of the disappearance of Mr. Bathurst.*

Inquiry was made into what was known of old Mertens. Everyone spoke highly of him as a saving, steady man, God-fearing; who had scraped together during his service in the Swan sufficient money to dower his two daughters with respectively £150 and £120. After a long illness he had died, generally respected.

Information of the discovery was forwarded to the Bathurst family, and on August 23, Mrs. Thistlethwaite, sister of Benjamin, came to Perleberg, bringing with her a portrait of her brother, but she was quite unable to say that the skull that was shown her belonged to the missing man, whom she had not seen for forty-three years. And—no wonder! When Goethe was shown the skull of his intimate friend Schiller he could hardly trace any likeness to the head he remembered so well. Mrs. Thistlethwaite left, believing that the discovery had no connection with the mystery of her brother's disappearance, so ineradicably fixed in the convictions of the family was the belief that he had been carried away by French agents.

However, let us consider this discovery a little closer, and perhaps we shall be led to another conclusion.

In the first place, the skeleton was that of a man who had been murdered by a blow on the back of his head, which had fractured the skull. It had been stripped before being buried, for not a trace of clothing could be found.

Secondly, the house of the Mertens family lay on the Hamburg road, on the way to Lenzen, outside the Parchimer Gate, only three hundred paces from the White Swan. In fact, it was separated from the White Swan only by the old town-gate and prison tower, and a small patch of garden ground.

At the time of the disappearance of Mr. Bathurst it was inhabited by Christian Mertens, who was servant at the White Swan. No examination was made at the time of the loss of Bathurst into the whereabouts of Mertens, nor was his cottage searched. It was assumed that he was at the inn waiting for his "vale," like the ostler and the *Kellner*. It is quite possible that he may have been standing near the horses' heads, and that he may have gone on with Mr. Bathurst a few steps to show him the direction he was to go; or, with the pretence that he had important information to give him, he may have allured him into his cottage, and there murdered him, or, again, he may have drawn him on to where by pre-arrangement Goldberger was lying in wait with a hammer or hatchet to strike him down from behind. Considering how uneasy Mr. Bathurst was about the road, and how preoccupied with the idea that French spies and secret agents were on the look-out for him, he might easily have been induced by a servant of the inn where he was staying to go a few steps through the gate, beyond earshot of the post-boy and landlord and ostler, to hear something which the boots pretended was of importance to him. Goldberger or another may have lain in wait in the blackness of the shadow of the gateway but a short distance from the lights about the carriage, and by one stroke have silenced him. It is possible that Augustus Schmidt may have been mixed up in the matter, and that the sable coat was taken off Mr. Bathurst when dead.

Again, Mertens was able on the marriage of his two daughters to give one 150*l.* and the other 120*l.* This would mean that Mertens had saved as boots of the Swan at the least 300*l.*, for he would not give every penny to his children. Surely this was a considerable sum for a boots in a little inn to amass from his wage and from "vales."

Mrs. Thistlethwaite asserts in her Memoirs of Bishop Bathurst that shortly after the disappearance of her brother the ostler—can she mean Mertens?—also disappeared, ran away. But we do not know of any corroborating evidence.

Lastly, the discovery of the trousers in the wood near Quitzow points to the traveller having been murdered in Perleberg; the murderers, whoever they were, finding that an investigation of houses, barns, gardens and stables was being made, took the garments of the unfortunate man, discharged a couple of shots through them to make believe he had been fired at by several persons lying in wait for him, and then exposed them in a place away from the road along which Mr. Bathurst was going. The man who carried these garments was afraid of being observed, and he probably did not go through the town with them, but made a circuit to the wood, and for the same reason did not take them very far. The road to Lenzen ran S.W. and that to Quitzow N.W. He placed the trousers near the latter, but did not venture to cross the highway. He could get to the wood over the fields unperceived.

Supposing that this is the solution of the mystery, one thing remains to be accounted for—the paragraph in the Hamburg paper dated from London, announcing that Mr. Bathurst was alive and had been heard of since the disappearance.

This, certainly, seems to have been inserted with a design to divert or allay suspicion, and it was generally held to have been sent from London by a French agent, on instruction from Paris. But it is possible that the London correspondent may have heard a coffee-house rumour that Bathurst was still alive, and at once reported it to the paper. Its falsehood was palpable, and would be demonstrated at once by the family of the lost man to the authorities at Perleberg. It could not answer the purpose of arresting inquiry and staying investigation.

It remains only to inquire whether it was probable that Napoleon had any hand in the matter.

What could induce him to lay hands on an envoy? He could not expect to find on the person of Mr. Bathurst any important dispatches, for the war was over, peace with Austria was concluded. He was doubtless angry at Austria having declared war, and angry at England having instigated her to do so, but Mr. Bathurst was very small game indeed on which to wreak his anger; moreover, the peace that had been concluded with Austria gave great advantages to France. He can have had no personal dislike to Bathurst, for he never saw him. When Napoleon entered Vienna, Bathurst was with the Emperor Francis in Hungary, at Komorn.

And yet, he may have suspected that Austria was insincere, and was anxious to renew the conflict, if she could obtain assurance of assistance from England. He may have thought that by securing the papers carried to England by Bathurst, he would get at the real intentions of Austria, and so might be prepared for consequences. We cannot say. The discovery of the body in Mertens' house, under the threshold—supposing it to be that of Bathurst, does not by any means prove that the murder was a mere murder for the purpose of robbery.

If Napoleon had given instructions for the capture of Bathurst, and the taking from him of his papers, it does not follow that he ordered his murder, on the contrary, he would have given instructions that he should be robbed—as if by highwaymen—and let go with his life. The murder was against his wishes, if he did give orders for him to be robbed.

The Bathurst family never doubted that Benjamin had been murdered by the agents of Napoleon. It is certain that he was well aware that his safety was menaced, and menaced at Perleberg. That was why he at once on reaching the place asked for the protection of a guard. He had received warning from some one, and such warning shows that an attempt to rob him of his papers was in contemplation.

That caution to be on his guard must have been given him, before he left Vienna. He probably received another before he reached Perleberg, for he appeared before the Commandant in a state of great alarm and agitation. That this was mere spiritual presage of evil is hardly credible. We cannot doubt—and his letter to his wife leads to this conviction—that he had been warned that spies in the pay of the French Government were on the look-out for him. Who the agents were that were employed to get hold of his papers, supposing that the French Government did attempt to waylay him, can never be determined, whether Mertens or Augustus Schmidt.

In 1815 Earl Bathurst was Secretary of State for War and the Colonial Department. May we not suspect that there was some mingling of personal exultation along with political satisfaction, in being able to send to St. Helena the man who had not only been the scourge of Europe, and the terror of kings, but who, as he supposed—quite erroneously we believe—had inflicted on his own family an agony of suspense and doubt that was never to be wholly removed?

II. — THE DUCHESS OF KINGSTON

ELIZABETH CHUDLEIGH, Countess of Bristol and Duchess of Kingston, who was tried for bigamy in Westminster Hall by the Peers in 1776, was, it can hardly be doubted, the original from whom Thackeray drew his detailed portrait of Beatrix Esmond, both as young Trix and as the old Baroness Bernstein; nor can one doubt that what he knew of his prototype was taken from that scandalous little book, "An Authentic Detail of Particulars relative to the late Duchess of Kingston," published by G. Kearsley in 1788. Thackeray not only reproduced some of the incidents of her life, but more especially caught the features of her character.

Poor Trix! Who does not remember her coming down the great staircase at Walcote, candle in hand, in her red stockings and with a new cherry ribbon round her neck, her eyes like blue stars, her brown hair curling about her head, and not feel a lingering liking for the little coquette, trying to catch my Lord Mohun, and the Duke of Hamilton, and many another, and missing all? and for the naughty old baroness, with her scandalous stories, her tainted past, her love of cards, her complete unscrupulousness, and yet with one soft corner in the withered heart for the young Virginians?

The famous, or infamous, Duchess has had hard measure dealt out to her, which she in part deserved; but some of the stories told of her are certainly not true, and one circumstance in her life, if true, goes far to palliate her naughtiness. Unfortunately, almost all we know of her is taken from unfriendly sources. The only really impartial source of information is the "Trial," published by order of the Peers, but that covers only one portion of her life, and one set of incidents.

Elizabeth Chudleigh was the daughter of Colonel Thomas Chudleigh, of Chelsea, and his wife Henrietta, who was his first cousin, the fourth daughter of Hugh Chudleigh, of Chalmington, in Dorset. Thomas was the only brother of Sir George Chudleigh, fourth baronet of Asheton, in Devon. As Sir George left only daughters, Thomas, the brother of Elizabeth, whose baptism in 1718 is recorded in the Chelsea registers, succeeded as fifth baronet in 1738. Unfortunately the Chelsea registers do not give the baptism of Elizabeth, and we are not able to state her precise age, about which there is some difference. Her father had a post in Chelsea College, but apparently she was not born there. There can, however, be little doubt that she saw the light for the first time in 1726, and not in 1720, as is generally asserted.

Her family was one of great antiquity in the county of Devon, and was connected by marriage with the first families of the west of England. The old seat, Asheton, lies in a pleasant coombe under the ridge of

Haldon; some remains of the old mansion, and venerable trees of the park, linger on; and in the picturesque parish church, perched on a rock in the valley, are many family monuments and heraldic blazonings of the Chudleigh lions, gules on an ermine field. Elizabeth lost her father very early, and the widow was left on a poor pension to support and advance the prospects of her two children. Though narrowed in fortune, Mrs. Chudleigh had good connections, and she availed herself of these to push her way in the world. At the age of sixteen—that is, in 1743—Elizabeth was given the appointment of maid of honour to the Princess of Wales, through the favour of Mr. Pulteney, afterwards Earl of Bath, who had met her one day while out shooting. The old beau was taken with the vivacity, intelligence and beauty of the girl. She was then not only remarkable for her beauty, delicacy of complexion, and sparkling eyes, but also for the brilliancy of her wit and the liveliness of her humour. Even her rival, the Marquise de la Touche, of whom more hereafter, bears testimony to her charms. Pulteney, himself a witty, pungent, and convivial man, was delighted with the cleverness of the lovely girl, and amused himself with drawing it out. In after years, when she was asked the secret of her sparkling repartee, she replied, "I always aim to be short, clear, and surprising."

The Princess of Wales, Augusta, daughter of Frederick of Saxe-Gotha, who with the Prince, Frederick Lewis, had their court at Leicester House, became greatly attached to her young maid of honour. The beautiful Miss Chudleigh was speedily surrounded by admirers, among whom was James, sixth Duke of Hamilton, born in 1724, and therefore two years her senior.

According to the "Authentic Detail," the Duke obtained from her a solemn engagement that, on his return from a tour on the Continent which he was about to take, she would become his wife. Then he departed, having arranged for a mutual correspondence.

In the summer of 1744 she went on a visit to Lainston, near Winchester, to her maternal aunt, Anne Hanmer, who was then living at the house of Mr. Merrill, the son of another aunt, Susanna, who was dead.

To understand the relationship of the parties, a look will suffice at the following pedigree.[4]

[4] In Col. Vivian's "Visitations of the County of Devon," the pedigree is not so complete. He was unaware who the wife of Thos. Chudleigh was, and he had not seen the will of the duchess.

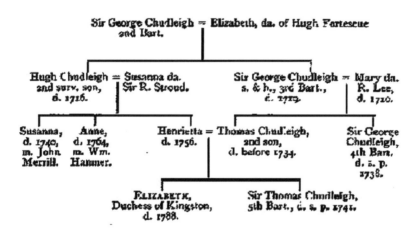

Mrs. Hanmer, a widow, kept house for her nephew, who was squire. At the Winchester races, to which she went with a party, Elizabeth met Lieutenant Hervey, second son of the late John, Lord Hervey, and grandson of the Earl of Bristol. Lieutenant Hervey, who was in the *Cornwall*, then lying at Portsmouth, a vessel in Sir John Danver's squadron, was born in 1724, and was therefore two years the senior of Elizabeth; indeed, at the time he was only just twenty. He was fascinated by the beautiful girl, and was invited by Mrs. Hanmer to Lainston. "To this gentleman," says the "Authentic Detail," "Mrs. Hanmer became so exceedingly partial that she favoured his views on her niece, and engaged her efforts to effect, if possible, a matrimonial connexion. There were two difficulties which would have been insurmountable if not opposed by the fertile genius of a female: Miss Chudleigh disliked Captain Hervey, and she was betrothed to the Duke of Hamilton. To render this last nugatory, the letters of his Grace were intercepted by Mrs. Hanmer, and his supposed silence giving offence to her niece, she worked so successfully on her pride as to induce her to abandon all thoughts of the lover, whose passion she had cherished with delight."

Is this story true? It seems incredible that Mrs. Hanmer should have urged her niece to throw over such a splendid prospect of family advancement as that offered by marriage with the Duke of Hamilton, for the sake of an impecunious young sailor who was without the means of supporting his wife, and who, at that time, had not the faintest expectation of succeeding to the Earldom of Bristol.

It is allowable to hope that the story of the engagement to the Duke of Hamilton, broken through the intrigues of the aunt, is true, as it forms some excuse for the after conduct of Elizabeth Chudleigh.

It is more probable that the Duke of Hamilton had not said anything to Elizabeth, and did not write to her, at all events not till later. She may have entertained a liking for him, but not receiving any token that the liking was reciprocated, she allowed her aunt to engage and marry her to young Hervey. That the poor girl had no fancy for the young man is abundantly clear. The Attorney General, in the trial, said that Mrs. Hanmer urged on the match "as advantageous to her niece;" but advantageous it certainly was not, and gave no prospect of being.

In August, Augustus John Hervey got leave from his ship and came to Lainston. The house, which had belonged to the Dawleys, had passed into the possession of the Merrills. In the grounds stands the parish church, but as the only house in the parish is the mansion, it came to be regarded very much as the private chapel of the manor house. The living went with Sparsholt. There was no parsonage attached, and though the Dawleys had their children baptized in Lainston, they were registered in the book of Sparsholt. The church is now an ivy-covered ruin, and the mansion is much reduced in size from what it was in the time when it belonged to the Merrills.

"Lainston is a small parish, the value of the living being £15 a year; Mr. Merrill's the only house in it, and the parish church at the end of his garden. On the 4th August, 1744, Mr. Amis, the then rector, was appointed to be at the church, alone, late at night. At eleven o'clock Mr. Hervey and Miss Chudleigh went out, as if to walk in the garden, followed by Mrs. Hanmer, her servant—Anne Craddock, Mr. Merrill, and Mr. Mountenay, which last carried a taper to read the service by. They found Mr. Amis in the church, according to his appointment, and there the service was celebrated, Mr. Mountenay holding the taper in his hat. The ceremony being performed, Mrs. Hanmer's maid was despatched to see that the coast was clear, and they returned into the house without being observed by any of the servants."

This is the account of the wedding given at the trial by the Attorney General, from the evidence of Anne Craddock, then the sole surviving witness.

There was no signing of registers, Mr. Amis was left to make the proper entry in the Sparsholt book—and he forgot to do this. The happiness of the newly-married couple lasted but a few days—two, or at the outside, three; and then Lieutenant Hervey left to rejoin his vessel, and in November sailed for the West Indies. The "Authentic Detail" declares that a violent quarrel broke out immediately on marriage between the young people, and that Elizabeth declared her aversion, and vowed never to associate with him again.

So little was the marriage to her present advantage that Elizabeth was unable to proclaim it, and thereby forfeit her situation as maid of honour to the Princess, with its pay and perquisites. Consequently, by her aunt's advice, she kept it concealed.

"Miss Chudleigh, now Mrs. Hervey,—a maid in appearance, a wife in disguise,—seemed from those who judge from externals only, to be in an enviable situation. Of the higher circles she was the attractive centre, of gayer life the invigorating spirit. Her royal mistress not only smiled on, but actually approved her. A few friendships she cemented, and conquests she made in such abundance that, like Cæsar in a triumph, she had a train of captives at her heels. Her husband, quieted for a time, grew obstreperous as she became more the object of admiration. He felt his right, and was determined to assert it. She endeavoured by letter to negotiate him into peace, but her efforts succeeded not. He demanded a private interview, and, enforcing his demands by threats of exposure in case of refusal, she complied through compulsion."

The Duke of Hamilton returned from the grand tour, and he at once sought Elizabeth to know why his letters had not been answered. Then the fraud that had been practised on her was discovered, and the Duke laid his coronet at her feet. She was unable to accept the offer, and unable also to explain the reasons of her refusal. Rage at having been duped, disappointment at having lost the strawberry leaves, embittered Elizabeth, and stifled the germs of good principle in her.

This is the generally received story. It is that given by the author, or authoress, of the "Authentic Detail," usually well informed. But, as we have seen, it is hardly possible to suppose that Mrs. Hanmer can have suppressed the Duke's letters. No doubt she was a fool, and a woman, when a fool, is of abnormal folly, yet she never loses sight of her own interest; and it was not Mrs. Hanmer's interest to spoil the chances of her niece with the Duke.

After the Duke of Hamilton had been refused, and his visits to her house in Conduit Street prohibited, the Duke of Ancaster, Lord Howe, and other nobles made offers, and experienced a fate similar to that of his Grace of Hamilton. This astonished the fashionable world, and Mrs. Chudleigh, her mother, who was a stranger to the private marriage of her daughter, reprehended her folly with warmth.[5] To be freed from her embarrassments, Elizabeth resolved to travel. She embarked for the Continent, and visited Dresden, where she became an attached friend of the Electress of Saxony.

[5] Mrs. Chudleigh died in 1756, and her will mentions her daughter by her maiden name.

On her return to England she was subjected to annoyance from her husband. She could not forgive him the deception practised on her, though he was probably innocent of connivance in it.

"Captain Hervey, like a perturbed spirit, was eternally crossing the path trodden by his wife. Was she in the rooms at Bath? he was sure to be there. At a rout, ridotto, or ball, there was this fell destroyer of peace, embittering every pleasure and blighting the fruit of happiness by the pestilential malignity of his presence. As a proof of his disposition to annoy, he menaced his wife with an intimation that he would disclose the marriage to the Princess of Wales. In this Miss Chudleigh anticipated him by being the first relater of the circumstance. Her royal mistress heard and pitied her. She continued her patronage to the hour of her death."

In 1749, Elizabeth attended a masquerade ball in the dress, or rather undress, of the character of Iphigenia. In a letter of Mrs. Montague to her sister, she says, "Miss Chudleigh's dress, or rather undress, was remarkable, she was Iphigenia for the sacrifice, but so naked, the high priest might easily inspect the entrails of the victim. The Maids of Honour (not of maids the strictest) were so offended they would not speak to her." Horace Walpole says, "Miss Chudleigh was Iphigenia, but so naked that you would have taken her for Andromeda." It was of her that the witty remark was then first made that she resembled Eve in that she was "naked and not ashamed." On May 17th Walpole writes: "I told you we were to have another masquerade; there was one by the King's command for Miss Chudleigh, the Maid of Honour, with whom our gracious monarch has a mind to believe himself in love, so much in love, that at one of the booths he gave her a fairing for her watch, which cost him five-and-thirty guineas, actually disbursed out of his privy purse, and not charged on the civil list. I hope some future Holinshed or Speed will acquaint posterity that five-and-thirty guineas were an immense sum in those days."

In December 1750, George II. gave the situation of Housekeeper at Windsor to Mrs. Chudleigh, Elizabeth's mother. Walpole says, "Two days ago, the gallant Orondates (the King) strode up to Miss Chudleigh, and told her he was glad to have the opportunity of obeying her commands, that he appointed her mother Housekeeper at Windsor, and hoped she would not think a kiss too great a reward—against all precedent he kissed her in the circle. He has had a hankering these two years. Her life, which is now of thirty years' standing, has been a little historic. Why should not experience and a charming face on her side, and near seventy years on his, produce a title?"

In 1760 she gave a soirée on the Prince's birthday, which Horace Walpole describes: "Poor thing," he writes, "I fear she has thrown away above a quarter's salary!"

The Duke of Kingston saw and was captivated by Elizabeth. Evelyn Pierrepoint, Duke of Kingston, Marquis of Dorchester, Earl of Kingston, and Viscount Newark, was born in 1711. Horace Walpole says of him that he was "a very weak man, of the greatest beauty and finest person in England."

He had been to Paris along with Lord Scarborough, taking with him an entire horse as a present to the Duke of Bourbon, and was unable to do this without a special Act of Parliament to authorise him. The Duke of Bourbon, in return for the compliment, placed his palace at Paris, and his château of Chantilly at the disposal of the visitor.

The Duke was handsome, young, wealthy and unmarried. A strong set was made at him by the young ladies of the French court; but of all the women he there met, none attracted his attentions and engaged his heart but the Marquise de la Touche, a lady who had been married for ten years and was the mother of three children. He finally persuaded her to elope with him to England, where, however, he grew cold towards her, and when he fell under the fascinations of Elizabeth Chudleigh he dismissed her. The Marquise returned to France, and was reconciled to her husband; there in 1786 she published her version of the story, and gave a history of her rival, whom naturally she paints in the blackest colours.

Now follows an incident which is stated in the English accounts of the life of Elizabeth Chudleigh; but of which there is no mention in the trial, and which is of more than doubtful truth.

She had become desperate, resolved at all hazard to break the miserable tie that bound her to Captain Hervey. She made a sudden descent on Lainston—so runs the tale—visited the parsonage, and whilst Mr. Amis was kept in conversation with one of her attendants, she tore out the leaf of the register book that contained the entry of her marriage.

This story cannot possibly be true. As already said, Lainston has no parsonage, and never had. Lainston goes with Sparsholt, half-a-mile off. But Mr. Amis never held Sparsholt, but acted as curate there for a while in 1756 and 1757. Lainston had no original register. What Elizabeth did was probably to convince herself that through inadvertence, her marriage had not been registered in the parish book of Sparsholt.

In 1751 died John, Earl of Bristol, and was succeeded by his grandson, George William, who was unmarried. He was in delicate health; at one time seriously ill, and it was thought he would die. In that case Augustus John, Elizabeth's husband, would succeed to the Earldom of Bristol. She saw now that it was to her interest to establish her marriage. She accordingly took means to do so.

She went at once to Winchester and sent for the wife of Mr. Amis, who had married her. She told Mrs. Amis that she wanted the register of her marriage to be made out. Mr. Amis then lay on his death-bed, but, nevertheless, she went to the rectory to obtain of him what she desired. What ensued shall be told in the words of Mrs. Amis at the trial.

"I went up to Mr. Amis and told him her request. Then Mr. Merrill and the lady consulted together whom to send for, and they desired me to send for Mr. Spearing, the attorney. I did send for him, and during the time the messenger was gone the lady concealed herself in a closet; she said she did not care that Mr. Spearing should know that she was there. When Mr. Spearing came, Mr. Merrill produced a sheet of stamped paper that he brought to make the register upon. Mr. Spearing said it would not do; it must be a book, and that the lady must be at the making of it. Then I went to the closet and told the lady. Then the lady came to Mr. Spearing, and Mr. Spearing told the lady a sheet of stamped paper would not do, it must be a book. Then the lady desired Mr. Spearing to go and buy one. Mr. Spearing went and bought one, and when brought, the register was made. Then Mr. Amis delivered it to the lady; the lady thanked him, and said it might be an hundred thousand pounds in her way. Before Mr. Merrill and the lady left my house the lady sealed up the register and gave it to me, and desired I would take care of it until Mr. Amis's death, and then deliver it to Mr. Merrill."

The entries made thus were those:

"2 August, Mrs. Susanna Merrill, relict of John Merrill, Esq. buried.
"4 August, 1744, married the Honourable Augustus Hervey, Esq., in the parish Church of Lainston, to Miss Elizabeth Chudleigh, daughter of Col. Thomas Chudleigh, late of Chelsea College, by me, Thos. Amis."

Unfortunately this register book was taken up to Westminster at the trial of the Duchess and was never returned. Application was made to Elbrow Woodcock, solicitor in the trial, for the return of the book, by the then rector and patron of the living, but in vain; and in December, 1777, a new register book was purchased for the parish.

The Earl recovered, and did not die till some years later, in 1775, when Augustus John did succeed to the earldom.

In 1751, the Prince of Wales died, and this necessitated a rearrangement of the household of the Princess. Elizabeth was reappointed maid of honour to her, still in her maiden name. Soon after—that is, in 1752—the Duke of Hamilton married the beautiful Miss Gunning.

In 1760 the king was dead. "Charles Townshend, receiving an account of the impression the king's death had made," writes Walpole, "was told Miss Chudleigh cried. 'What,' said he, 'oysters?'" "There is no keeping off age," he writes in 1767, "as Miss Chudleigh does, by sticking roses and sweet peas in one's hair."

Before this, in 1765, the Duke of Kingston's affection for her seeming to wane, Elizabeth, who was getting fat as well as old, started for Carlsbad to drink the waters. "She has no more wanted the Carlsbad waters than you did," wrote Lord Chesterfield. "Is it to show the Duke of Kingston he can not live without her? A dangerous experiment, which may possibly convince him that he can. There is a trick, no doubt, in it, but what, I neither know nor care." "Is the fair, or, at least, the fat Miss Chudleigh with you still? It must be confessed she knows the arts of courts to be so received at Dresden and so connived at in Leicester Fields."

At last the bonds of a marriage in which he was never allowed even to speak with his wife became intolerable to Captain Hervey; and some negotiations were entered into between them, whereby it was agreed that she should institute a suit in the Consistory Court of the Bishop of London for the jactitation of the marriage, and that he should not produce evidence to establish it. The case came on in the Michaelmas term, 1768, and was in form, proceedings to restrain the Hon. Augustus John Hervey from asserting that Elizabeth Chudleigh was his wife, "to the great danger of his soul's health, no small prejudice to the said Hon. Elizabeth Chudleigh, and pernicious example of others."

There was a counter-suit of Captain Hervey against her, in which he asserted that in 1743 or 1744, being then a minor of the age of seventeen or eighteen, he had contracted himself in marriage to Elizabeth Chudleigh, and she to him; and that they had been married in the house of Mr. Merrill, on August 9, 1744, at eleven o'clock at night, by the Rev. Thomas Amis, since deceased, and in the presence of Mrs. Hanmer and Mr. Mountenay, both also deceased.

As will be seen, the counter-libel was incorrectly drawn. The marriage had not taken place in the house, but in the church; Mr. Hervey was aged twenty, not seventeen or eighteen; and Anne Craddock, the sole surviving witness of the ceremony, was not mentioned. The register of the marriage was not produced,[6] and no serious attempt was made to establish it. Accordingly, on February 10, 1769, sentence was given, declaring the marriage form gone through in 1744 to have been null and void, and to restrain Mr. Hervey from asserting his claim to be husband to Miss Elizabeth Chudleigh, and condemning him in costs to the sum of one hundred pounds.

[6] Mr. John Merrill died February 1767, and his burial was entered in it. Mr. Bathurst, who had married his daughter, found the register book in the hall, and handed it over to the rector, Mr. Kinchin. Nevertheless it was not produced at the hearing of the case for jactitation in the Consistory Court.

As the Attorney-General said at her subsequent trial, "a grosser artifice, I believe, than this suit was never fabricated."

On March 8, 1769, the Duke of Kingston married Elizabeth Chudleigh by special licence from the Archbishop, the minister who performed it being the Rev. Samuel Harper, of the British Museum, and the Church, St. Margaret's, Westminster. The Prince and Princess of Wales wore favours on the occasion.

No attempt was made during the lifetime of the Duke to dispute the legality of the marriage. Neither he nor Elizabeth had the least doubt that the former marriage had been legally dissolved. It was, no doubt, the case that Captain Hervey made no real attempt to prove his marriage, he was as impatient of the bond as was she. It can hardly be doubted that the sentence of the Ecclesiastical Court was just. Captain Hervey was a minor at the time, and the poor girl had been deluded into marrying him by her wretched aunt. Advantage had been taken of her—a mere girl—by the woman who was her natural guardian in the absence of her mother. Such a marriage would at once be annulled in the Court of the Church of Rome; it would be annulled in a modern English divorce court.

The fortune of the Duke was not entailed; his Grace had, therefore, the option to bequeath it as seemed best to his inclination. His nearest of kin were his nephews, Evelyn and Charles Meadows, sons of Lady Francis Pierrepont; Charles was in 1806 created Earl Manners; he had previously changed his name to Pierrepont, and been created Baron Pierrepont and Viscount Newark in 1796.

The Duke was and remained warmly attached to the Duchess. She made him happy. She had plenty of conversation, had her mind stored with gossip, and though old, oldened gracefully and pleasantly. Her bitter enemy—an old servant and confidant, who furnished the materials for the "Authentic Detail," says, "Contrarily gifted and disposed, they were frequently on discordant terms, but she had a strong hold on his mind."

On September 23, 1773, the Duke died. The Duchess had anticipated his death. He had already made his will, bequeathing to her the entire income of his estates during her life, subject to the proviso that she remained in a state of widowhood. This did not at all please the Duchess, and directly she saw that her husband was dying she sent for a solicitor, a Mr. Field, to draw up a new will, omitting the obnoxious proviso; she was only by two years on the right side of fifty, and might marry again. When Mr. Field was introduced to the Duke, he saw that the dying man was not in a mental condition capable of executing a will, and he refused to have anything to do with an attempt to extort his signature from him. The Duchess was very angry; but the refusal of Mr. Field was most fortunate for her, as, had the will proposed been executed, it would most indubitably have been set aside.

As soon as the Duke was dead the dowager Duchess determined to enjoy life. She had a pleasure yacht built, placed in command of it an officer who had served in the navy, fitted it up with every luxury, sailed for Italy, and visited Rome, where the Pope and the cardinals received her with great courtesy. Indeed, she was given up one of the palaces of the cardinals for her residence. Whilst she was amusing herself in Italy something happened in England that was destined to materially spoil her happiness. Anne Craddock was still alive, the sole witness of her marriage that survived. She was in bad circumstances, and applied to Mr. Field for pecuniary relief. He refused it, but the Duchess sent to offer her twenty guineas per annum. This Anne Craddock refused, and gave intimation to Mr. Evelyn Meadows that she had information of importance which she could divulge.

When Mr. Meadows heard what Anne Craddock had to say, he set the machinery of the law in motion to obtain the prosecution of the Duchess, in the hopes of convicting her of bigamy, and then of upsetting the will of the late Duke in her favour. A bill of indictment for bigamy was preferred against her; the bill was found, Mr. Field had notice of the procedure, and the Duchess was advised to return instantly to England and appear to the indictment, to prevent an outlawry.

At this time—that is, in 1775—the Earl of Bristol died without issue, and Augustus John, her first husband, succeeded to the title.

The anxieties of the Duchess were not confined to the probable issue of the trial. Samuel Foote, the comedian, took a despicable advantage of her situation to attempt to extort money from her. He wrote a farce, entitled "A Trip to Calais," in which he introduced her Grace under the sobriquet of Lady Kitty Crocodile, and stuffed the piece with particulars relative to the private history of the Duchess, which he had obtained from Miss Penrose, a young lady who had been about her person for many years. When the piece was finished, he contrived to have it communicated to her Grace that the Haymarket Theatre would open with the entertainment in which she was held up to ridicule and scorn. She was alarmed, and sent for Foote. He attended with the piece in his pocket. She desired him to read a part of it. He obeyed; and had not read far before she could no longer control herself, but, starting up in a rage, exclaimed, "This is scandalous, Mr. Foote! Why, what a wretch you have made me!" After a few turns round the room, she composed herself to inquire on what terms he would suppress the play. Foote had the effrontery to demand two thousand pounds. She offered him fourteen, then sixteen hundred pounds; but he, grasping at too much, lost all. She consulted the Duke of Newcastle, and the Lord Chamberlain was apprised of the circumstances, and his interference solicited. He sent for the manuscript copy of the "Trip to Calais," perused, and censured it. In the event of its publication she threatened to prosecute Foote for libel. Public opinion ranged itself on the side of the Duchess, and Dr. Schomberg only expressed its opinion when he said that "Foote deserved to be run through the body for such an attempt. It was more ignoble than the conduct of a highwayman."

On April 17, 1776, the trial of the Duchess came on in Westminster Hall, and lasted five days. The principal object argued was the admission, or not, of a sentence of the Spiritual Court, in a suit for jactitation of marriage, in an indictment for polygamy. As the judges decided against the admission of such a sentence in bar to evidence, the fact of the two marriages was most clearly proved, and a conviction of course followed. The Duchess was tried by the Peers, a hundred and nineteen of whom sat and passed judgment upon her, all declaring "Guilty, upon mine honour," except the Duke of Newcastle, who pronounced "Guilty, erroneously; but not intentionally, upon mine honour."

No sooner did the Duchess see that her cause was lost than she determined to escape out of England. The penalty for bigamy was death, but she could escape this sentence by claiming the benefits of the statute 3 and 4 William and Mary, which left her in a condition to be burnt in the hand, or imprisoned; but she claimed the benefit of the peerage, and the Lord Chief Baron, having conferred with the rest of the judges, delivered their unanimous opinion that she ought "to be immediately discharged." However, her prosecutors prepared a writ "ne exeat regno," to obtain her arrest and the deprivation of her personal property. To escape this she fled to Dover, where her yacht was in waiting, and crossed to Calais, whilst amusing the public and her prosecutors by issuing invitations to a dinner at Kingston House, and causing her carriage to appear in the most fashionable quarters of the town. Mr. Meadows had carried his first point; she could no longer call herself Dowager Duchess of Kingston in England, but she was reinstated in her position of wife to Augustus John Hervey, and was therefore now Countess of Bristol. Mr. Meadows next proceeded to attack the will of the late Duke, but in this attempt he utterly failed. The will was confirmed, and Elizabeth, Countess of Bristol, was acknowledged as lawfully possessed of life interest in the property of the Duke so long as she remained unmarried. Mr. Meadows was completely ruined, and his sole gain was to keep the unhappy woman an exile from England.

Abroad the Countess was still received as Duchess of Kingston. She lived in considerable state, and visited Italy, Russia, and France. Her visit to St. Petersburg was splendid, and to ensure a favourable reception by the Empress Catharine she sent her a present of some of the valuable paintings by old masters from Kingston House. When in Russia she purchased an estate near the capital, to which she gave the name of Chudleigh, and which cost her 25,000*l*.[7] The Empress also gave her a property on the Neva. She had a corvette built of mahogany which was to be a present to the Empress, but the vessel stranded on the coast of Ingermanland. Eight of the cannons out of her are now at Chudleigh, almost the only things there that recall the Duchess. She gave magnificent entertainments; at one of these, to which the Empress was invited, a hundred and forty of her own servants attended in the Kingston livery of black turned up with red and silver.

[7] This place still bears the name. It is on the main road through Livland and Esthonia to St. Petersburg; about twenty miles from Narwa. It also goes by the name of Fockenhof. The present mansion is more modern, and belongs to the family of Von Wilcken.

On her return from Russia she bought an estate at Montmartre, which cost her 9,000*l*., and another that belonged to one of the French royal princes at Saint Assise, which cost her 55,000*l*. The château was so large that three hundred beds could be made up in it.

She was getting on in years, but did not lose her energy, her vivacity, and her selfishness. Once in Rome, the story goes, she had been invited to visit some tombs that were famous. She replied with a touch of real feeling: "Ce n'est pas la peine de chercher des tombeaux, on en porte assez dans son coeur."

The account of her death shall be given in the words of the author of "Authentic Detail."

"She was at dinner, when her servants received intelligence of a sentence respecting the house near Paris having been awarded against her. She flew into a violent passion, and, in the agitation of her mind and body, burst an internal blood-vessel. Even this she appeared to have surmounted, until a few days afterwards, on the morning of the 26th August (1788), when about to rise from her bed, a servant who had long been with her endeavoured at dissuasion. The Duchess addressed her thus: 'I am not very well, but I *will* rise. At your peril disobey me; I will get up and walk about the room. Ring for the secretary to assist me.' She was obeyed, dressed, and the secretary entered the chamber. The Duchess then walked about, complained of thirst, and said, 'I could drink a glass of my fine Madeira and eat a slice of toasted bread; I shall be quite well afterwards; but let it be a large glass of wine.' The attendant reluctantly brought and the Duchess drank the wine. She then said, 'I knew the Madeira would do me good. My heart feels oddly; I will have another glass.' She then walked a little about the room, and afterwards said, 'I will lie on the couch.' She sat on the couch, a female having hold of each hand. In this situation she soon appeared to have fallen into a profound sleep, until the women found her hands colder than ordinary; other domestics were rung for, and the Duchess was found to have expired, as the wearied labourer sinks into the arms of rest."

Was it a touch of final malice or of real regret that caused the old lady, by codicil to her will dated May 10, 1787, to leave pearl earrings and necklace to the Marquise de la Touche? Was it a token that she forgave her the cruel book, "Les aventures trop amoureuses; ou, Elizabeth Chudleigh," which she wrote, or caused to be written, for the blackening of her rival, and the whitewashing of herself? Let us hope it was so. The proviso in the Duke's will saved her from herself; but for that she would have married an adventurer who called himself the Chevalier de Wortha, a man who obtained great influence over her, and finally died by his own hand.

Elizabeth Chudleigh's character and career have never been sketched by friends; her enemies, those jealous of her fascinations, angry at her success, discontented with not having been sufficiently considered in her will, have given us their impressions of her, have poured out all the evil they knew and imagined of her. She has been hardly used. The only perfectly reliable authority for her history is the report of her trial, and that covers only one portion of her story. The "Authentic Detail" published by G. Kearsley, London, in 1788, is anonymous. It is fairly reliable, but tinctured by animosity. The book "Les Aventures trop Amoureuses, ou, Elizabeth Chudleigh, ex-duchesse douairière de Kingston, aujourd'hui Comtesse de Bristol, et la Marquise de la Touche. Londres, aux depens des Interessez, 1776," was composed for the justification of Madame de la Touche, and with all the venom of a discomfited and supplanted rival.

An utterly worthless book, "Histoire de la vie et des Aventures de la Duchesse de Kingston, a Londres, et se trouve à Paris, Chez Quillot, 1789," is fiction. It pretends to be based on family papers. At the commencement it gives a portion of the diary of Col. Thomas Chudleigh, in which, among other impossibilities, he records his having reduced the rents of his tenants on his estates twenty per cent. because the year was bad. As it happened, Col. Thomas Chudleigh neither possessed an acre of land, nor a tenant.

In 1813 appeared "La Duchesse de Kingston, memoires rédigés par M. de Favolle," in two volumes; this is based solely on the preceding with rich additions from the imagination of the author. Not a statement in it can be trusted.

Some little reliable information may be found in the "Memoires de la Baronne d'Oberkirch," Paris 1853.

III. — GENERAL MALLET

ON the return of Napoleon to Paris from Moscow, he was depressed with news that troubled him more than the loss of his legions. The news that had reached him related to perhaps the most extraordinary conspiracy that was ever devised, and which was within an ace of complete success. It was the news of this conspiracy that induced him to desert the army in the snows of Russia and hasten to Paris. The thoughts of this conspiracy frustrated by an accident, as Alison says, "incessantly occupied his mind during his long and solitary journey."

"Gentlemen," said Napoleon, when the report of the conspiracy was read over to him, "we must no longer disbelieve in miracles."

Claude François Mallet belonged to a noble family in the Franche Comté. He was born on June 28th, 1754, at Dole, and passed his early life in the army, where he commanded one of the first battalions of the Jura at the commencement of the Revolution. In May 1793, he was elevated to the rank of adjutant-General, and in August 1799, made General of Brigade, and commanded a division under Championnet. He was a man of enthusiastically Republican views, and viewed the progress of Napoleon with dissatisfaction mingled with envy. There can be no question as to what his opinions were at first; whether he changed them afterwards is not so certain. He was a reserved, hard, and bitter man, ambitious and restless. Envy of Napoleon, jealousy of his success seems to have been the ruling motive in his heart that made of him a conspirator, and not genuine disgust at Cæsarism.

Bonaparte knew his political opinions; and though he did not fear the man, he did not trust him. He became implicated in some illegal exactions at Civita Vecchia, in the Roman States, and was in consequence deprived of his command, and sent before a commission of enquiry at Paris, in July 1807; and, in virtue of their sentence, he was confined for a short while, and then again set at liberty and reinstated. In 1808, when the war in the Peninsula broke out, Mallet entered at Dijon into a plot, along with some old anarchists, for the overthrow of the Emperor, among them the ex-General Guillaume, who betrayed the plot, and Mallet was arrested and imprisoned in La Force. Napoleon did not care that conspiracies against himself and his throne should be made public, and consequently he contented himself with the detention of Mallet alone.

In prison, the General did not abandon his schemes, and he had the lack of prudence to commit them to paper. This fell into the hands of the Government. The minister regarded the scheme as chimerical and unimportant. The papers were shown to Napoleon, who apparently regarded the scheme or the man as really dangerous, and ordered him to perpetual detention in prison.

Time passed, and Mallet and his schemes were forgotten. Who could suppose that a solitary prisoner, without means, without the opportunity of making confederates, could menace the safety of the Empire?

Then came the Russian campaign, in 1812. Mallet saw what Napoleon did not; the inevitable failure that must attend it; and he immediately renewed his attempts to form a plot against the Emperor.

But the prison of La Force was bad headquarters from which to work. He pretended to be ill, and he was removed to a hospital, that of the Doctor Belhomme near the Barrière du Trône. In this house were the two brothers Polignac, a M. de Puyvert, and the Abbé Lafon, who in 1814 wrote and published an account of this conspiracy of Mallet. These men were Royalists, and Mallet was a Republican. It did not matter so long as Napoleon could be overthrown, how divergent their views might be as to what form of Government was to take the place of the Empire.

They came to discussion, and the Royalists supposed that they had succeeded in convincing Mallet. He, on his side, was content to dissemble his real views, and to make use of these men as his agents.

The Polignac brothers were uneasy, they were afraid of the consequences, and they mistrusted the man who tried to draw them into his plot. Perhaps, also, they considered his scheme too daring to succeed. Accordingly they withdrew from the hospital, to be out of his reach. It was not so with the others. The Polignacs had been mixed up in the enterprise of Georges, and had no wish to be again involved. Whether there were many others in the plot we do not know, Lafon names only four, and it does not seem that M. de Puyvert took a very active part in it.

Mallet's new scheme was identical with the old one that had been taken from him and shown to Napoleon. Napoleon had recognized its daring and ability, and had not despised it. That no further fear of Mallet was entertained is clear, or he would never have been transferred from the prison to a private hospital, where he would be under very little supervision.

In his hospital, Mallet drew up the following report of a Session of the Senate, imagined by himself:

"SÉNAT CONSERVATEUR
"Session of 22 October, 1812.
"The Session was opened at 8 P.M., under the presidency of Senator Sieyes.

"The occasion of this extraordinary Session was the receipt of the news of the death of the Emperor Napoleon, under the walls of Moscow, on the 8th of the month.

"The Senate, after mature consideration of the condition of affairs caused by this event, named a Commission to consider the danger of the situation, and to arrange for the maintenance of Government and order. After having received the report of this Commission, the following orders were passed by the Senate.

"That as the Imperial Government has failed to satisfy the aspirations of the French people, and secure peace, it be decreed annulled forthwith.

"That all such officers military and civil as shall use their authority prejudicially to the re-establishment of the Republic, shall be declared outlawed.

"That a Provisional Government be established, to consist of 13 members:—Moreau, President; Carnot, Vice-President; General Augereau, Bigonet, Destutt-Tracy, Florent Guyot, Frochot; Mathieu Montmorency, General Mallet, Noailles, Truguet; Volney, Garat.

"That this Provisional Government be required to watch over the internal and external safety of the State, and to enter into negociations with the military powers for the re-establishment of peace.

"That a constitution shall be drawn up and submitted to the General Assembly of the French realm.

"That the National Guard be reconstituted as formerly.

"That a general Amnesty be proclaimed for all political offences; that all emigrants, exiles, be permitted to return.

"That the freedom of the Press be restored.

"That the command of the army of the Centre, and which consists of 50,000 men, and is stationed near Paris, be given to General Lecombe.

"That General Mallet replaces General Hulin as commandant of Paris, and in the first division. He will have the right to nominate the officers in the general staff that will surround him."

There were many other orders, 19 in all, but these will suffice to indicate the tendency of the document. It was signed by the President and his Secretaries.

President, SIEYES.
Secretaries, LANJUINAIS, et GREGOIRE.
"Approved, and compared with a similar paper in my own hands,
Signed, MALLET, General of Division, Commandant of the main army of Paris, and of the forces of the First Division."

This document, which was designed to be shown to the troops, to the officers and officials, was drawn up in a form so close to the genuine form, and the signatures and seals were so accurately imitated, that the document was not likely at the first glance to excite mistrust.

Moreover, Mallet had drawn up an order for the day, and a proclamation, which was printed in many thousand copies.

On the 22nd October, 1812, at 10 o'clock at night, after he had been playing cards with great composure in the hospital, Mallet made his escape, along with four others, one was the Abbé Lafon, another a corporal named Rateau, whom he had named as his aide-de-camp. Mallet had just twelve francs in his pocket, and so furnished he embarked on his undertaking to upset the throne of the Emperor. He at once went to a Spanish monk, whose acquaintance he had made in prison; and in his rooms found his general's uniform which had been brought there by a woman the evening before. Uniforms and swords for his confederates were also ready. But it rained that night—it rained in torrents, and the streets of Paris ran with water. It has been remarked that rain in Paris has a very sobering effect on political agitations, and acts even better than bayonets in preventing a disturbance of the public peace.

Mallet and his confederates could not leave their shelter till after midnight, and some of them did not appear at the place of rendezvous till 6 o'clock in the morning. Indisputably this had much to do with the defeat of the plot.

The success of the undertaking depended on darkness, on the sudden bewilderment of minds, and the paralysis of the government through the assassination of some of the ministers. About 2 A.M. Mallet appeared in his general's uniform, attended by some of his confederates also in uniform, at the Popincour barracks, and demanded to see the Commandant Soulier at once, giving his name as Lamothe. Soulier was in bed asleep. He was also unwell. He was roused from his slumbers, hastily dressed himself, and received a sealed letter, which he broke open, and read:

"To the General of Division, Commandant-in-Chief of the troops under arms in Paris, and the troops of the First Division, Soulier, Commandant of the 10th Cohort."

"General Headquarters, "Place Vendôme. "23rd Oct., 1812, 10 o'clock a.m.

"M. LE COMMANDANT,—I have given orders to the General Lamothe with a police commissioner to attend at your barracks, and to read before you and your Cohort the decree of the senate consequent on the receipt of the news of the death of the Emperor, and the cessation of the Imperial Government. The said general will communicate to you the Order for the Day, which you will be pleased to further to the General of Brigade. You are required to get the troops under arms with all possible despatch and quietness. By daybreak, the officers who are in barracks will be sent to the Place de Grève, there to await their companies, which will there assemble, after the instructions which General Lamothe will furnish have been carried out."

Then ensued a series of dispositions for the troops, and the whole was signed by Mallet.

When Soulier had read this letter, Mallet, who pretended to be General Lamothe, handed him the document already given, relating to the assembly of the Senate, and its decisions. Then he gave him the Order for the Day, for the 23rd and 24th October.

Colonel Soulier, raised from sleep, out of health, bewildered, did not for a moment mistrust the messenger, or the documents handed to him. He hastened at once to put in execution the orders he had received.

The same proceedings were gone through in the barracks of Les Minimes, and of Picpus; the decree of the Senate, the Order of the Day, and a Proclamation, were read by torchlight.

Everywhere the same success. The officers had not the smallest doubt as to the authenticity of the papers presented to them. Everywhere also the Proclamation announcing the death of the Emperor, the cessation of the Empire, and the establishment of the Provisional Government was being placarded about.

At 6 A.M., at the head of a troop, Mallet, still acting as General Lamothe, marched before the prison of La Force, and the Governor was ordered to open the gates. The Decree of the Senate and the Order of the Day were read to him, and he was required at once to discharge three state prisoners he held, General Guidal, Lahorie, and a Corsican, Bocchejampe, together with certain officers there confined. He did as required, and Mallet separated his troops into four detachments, keeping one under his own command, and placing the others under the orders of Guidal, Lahorie and Bocchejampe.

Guidal and Lahorie, by his orders, now marched to the Ministry of Police, where they arrested Savary, Duke of Rovigo, Minister of Police. At the same time Boutreux, another confederate, had gone to the prefecture of the Paris police, had arrested the prefect, Pasquier, and sent him to be confined in La Force.

Mallet, now at the head of 150 men, went to the État-Major de-la-place, to go through the same farce with the Commandant-de-place, and get him to subscribe the Order for the Day. Count Hullin refused. Mallet presented a pistol at his head, fired, and Hullin fell covered with blood to the ground. Mallet left him for dead, but fortunately only his jaw was broken. By means of a forged order addressed to the commandant of one of the regiments of the paid guard of Paris, he occupied the National Bank, in which, at the time, there was a considerable treasure in specie.

The État-Major of Paris was a post of the highest importance, as it was the headquarters of the whole military authority in Paris. Before Mallet approached it, he sent a packet to the Adjutant-General Doucet, of a similar tenor to that given to Soulier and the other colonels, and containing his nomination as general of brigade, and a treasury order for a hundred thousand francs.

Soulier, Colonel of the 10th Cohort, obeying the orders he had received, the authenticity of which he did not for a moment dispute, had in the meantime made himself master of the Hôtel-de-Ville, and had stationed a strong force in the square before the building. Frochot, Prefect of the Seine, was riding into Paris from his country house at half-past eight in the morning, when he was met by his servants, in great excitement, with a note from Mallet, on the outside of which were written the ominous words "Fuit Imperator." Now it so happened that no tidings of the Emperor had been received for twenty-five days, and much uneasiness was felt concerning him. When Frochot therefore received this notice, he believed it, and hurried to the Hôtel-de-Ville. There he received a despatch from Mallet, under the title of Governor of Paris, ordering him to make ready the principal apartment in the building for the use of the Provisional Government. Not for a moment did Frochot remember that—even if the Emperor were dead, there was the young Napoleon, to whom his allegiance was due; he at once obeyed the orders he had received, and began to make the Hôtel ready for the meeting of the Provisional Government. Afterwards when he was reminded that there was a son to Napoleon, and that his duty was to support him, Frochot answered, "Ah! I forgot that. I was distracted with the news."

By means of the forged orders despatched everywhere, all the barriers of Paris had been seized and were closed, and positive orders were issued that no one was to be allowed to enter or leave Paris.

Mallet now drew up before the État-Major-Général, still accompanied and obeyed by the officer and detachment. Nothing was wanting now but the command of the adjutant-general's office to give to Mallet the entire direction of the military force of Paris, with command of the telegraph, and with it of all France. With that, and with the treasury already seized, he would be master of the situation. In another ten minutes Paris would be in his hand, and with Paris the whole of France.

An accident—an accident only—at that moment saved the throne of Napoleon. Doucet was a little suspicious about the orders—or allowed it afterwards to be supposed that he was. He read them, and stood in perplexity. He would have put what doubts presented themselves aside, had it not been for his aide-de-camp, Laborde. It happened that Laborde had had charge of Mallet in La Force, and had seen him there quite recently. He came down to enter the room where was Doucet, standing in doubt before Mallet. Mallet's guard was before the door, and would have prevented him from entering; however, he peremptorily called to them to suffer him to pass, and the men, accustomed to obey his voice, allowed him to enter. The moment he saw Mallet in his general's uniform, he recognised him and said, "But—how the devil!— That is my prisoner. How came he to escape?" Doucet still hesitated, and attempted to explain, when Laborde cut his superior officer short with, "There is something wrong here. Arrest the fellow, and I will go at once to the minister of police."

Mallet put his hand in his pocket to draw out the pistol with which he had shot Hullin, when the gesture was observed in a mirror opposite, and before he had time to draw and cock the pistol, Doucet and Laborde were on him, and had disarmed him.

Laborde, with great promptitude, threw open the door, and announced to the soldiers the deceit that had been practised on them, and assured them that the tidings of the death of the Emperor were false.

The arrest of Mallet disconcerted the whole conspiracy. Had Generals Lahorie and Guidal been men of decision and resolution they might still have saved it, but this they were not; though at the head of considerable bodies of men, the moment they saw that their chief had met with a hitch in carrying out his plan, they concluded that all was lost, and made the best of their way from their posts to places of concealment.

It was not till 8 o'clock that Saulnier, General Secretary of Police, heard of the arrest and imprisonment of his chief, Savary, Duke of Rovigo. He at once hastened to Cambacérès, the President of the Ministry in the absence of the Emperor, and astonished and alarmed him with the tidings. Then Saulnier hastened to Hullin, whom he found weltering in his blood, and unable to speak.

Baron Pasquier, released from La Force, attempted to return to his prefecture. The soldiers posted before it refused to admit him, and threatened to shoot him, believing that he had escaped from prison, and he was obliged to take refuge in an adjoining house. Laborde, who about noon came there, was arrested by the soldiers, and conducted by them as a prisoner to the État-Major-Gênéral, to deliver him over to General Mallet; and it was with difficulty that they could be persuaded that they had been deceived, and that Mallet was himself, at that moment, in irons.

Savary, released from La Force, had Mallet and the rest of the conspirators brought before him. Soulier also, for having given too ready a credence to the forged orders, was also placed under arrest, to be tried along with the organisers and carriers out of the plot.

Mallet confessed with great composure that he had planned the whole, but he peremptorily refused to say whether he had aiders or sympathisers elsewhere.

Lahorie could not deny that he had taken an active part, but declared that it was against his will, his whole intention being to make a run for the United States, there to spend the rest of his days in tranquillity. He asserted that he had really believed that the Emperor was dead.

Guidal tried to pass the whole off as a joke; but when he saw that he was being tried for his life, he became greatly and abjectly alarmed.

Next day the generals and those in the army who were under charge were brought before a military commission. Saulnier had an interesting interview with Mallet that day. He passed through the hall where Mallet was dining, when the prisoner complained that he was not allowed the use of a knife. Saulnier at once ordered that he might be permitted one; and this consideration seems to have touched Mallet, for he spoke with more frankness to Saulnier than he did before his judges. When the General Secretary of Police asked him how he could dream of success attending such a mad enterprise, Mallet replied, "I had already three regiments of infantry on my side. Very shortly I would have been surrounded by the thousands who are weary of the Napoleonic yoke, and are longing for a change of order. Now, I was convinced that the moment the news of my success in Paris reached him, Napoleon would leave his army and fly home, I would have been prepared for him at Mayence, and have had him shot there. If it had not been for the cowardice of Guidal and Lahorie, my plot would have succeeded. I had resolved to collect 50,000 men at Chalons sur Marne to cover Paris. The promise I would have made to send all the conscripts to their homes, the moment the crisis was over, would have rallied all the soldiers to my side."

On October 23, the prisoners to the number of twenty-four were tried, and fourteen were condemned to be shot, among these, Mallet, Guidai, Lahorie, and the unfortunate Soulier. Mallet at the trial behaved with great intrepidity. "Who are your accomplices?" asked the President. "The whole of France," answered Mallet, "and if I had succeeded, you yourself at their head. One who openly attacks a government by force, if he fails, expects to die." When he was asked to make his defence, "Monsieur," he said, "a man who has constituted himself defender of the rights of his Fatherland, needs no defence."

Soulier put in as an apology, that the news of the death of the Emperor had produced such a sudorific effect on him, that he had been obliged to change his shirt four times in a quarter of an hour. This was not considered sufficient to establish his attachment to the Imperial government.

In the afternoon of the same day the fourteen were conveyed to the plain of Grenelle to be shot, when pardon was accorded by the Empress Regent to two of the condemned, the Corporal Rateau, and Colonel Rabbe. When the procession passed through the Rue Grenelle, Mallet saw a group of students looking on; "Young men," he called to them, "remember the 23rd October." Arrived on the place of execution, some of the condemned cried out, "Vive l'empereur!" only a few "Vive la République."

Mallet requested that his eyes might not be bandaged, and maintained the utmost coolness. He received permission, at his own desire, to give the requisite orders to the soldiers drawn up to shoot him and his party. "Peloton! Present!" The soldiers, moved by the tragic catastrophe, obeyed, but not promptly. "That is bad!" called Mallet, "imagine you are before the foe. Once again—Attention!—Present!" This time it was better. "Not so bad this time, but still not well," said the General; "now pay attention, and mind, when I say Fire, that all your guns are discharged as one. It is a good lesson for you to see how brave men die. Now then, again, Attention!" For a quarter of an hour he put the men through their drill, till he observed that his comrades were in the most deplorable condition. Some had fainted, some were in convulsions. Then he gave the command: Fire! the guns rattled and the ten fell to the ground, never to rise again. Mallet alone reeled, for a moment or two maintaining his feet, and then he also fell over, without a sound, and was dead.

"But for the singular accident," says Savary, "which caused the arrest of the Minister of War to fail, Mallet, in a few moments, would have been master of almost everything; and in a country so much influenced by the contagion of example, there is no saying where his success would have stopped. He would have had possession of the treasury, then extremely rich; the post office, the telegraph, and the command of the hundred cohorts of the National Guard. He would soon have learned the alarming situation in Russia; and nothing could have prevented him from making prisoner of the Emperor himself if he returned alone, or from marching to meet him, if he had come at the head of his shattered forces."

As Alison says, "When the news reached Napoleon, one only idea took possession of his imagination—that in this crisis the succession of his son was, by common consent, set aside; one only truth was ever present to his mind—that the Imperial Crown rested on himself alone. The fatal truth was brought home to him that the Revolution had destroyed the foundations of hereditary succession; and that the greatest achievements by him who wore the diadem afforded no security that it would descend to his progeny. These reflections, which seem to have burst on Napoleon all at once, when the news of this extraordinary affair reached him in Russia, weighed him down more than all the disasters of the Moscow retreat."

IV. — SCHWEINICHEN'S MEMOIRS

MEMOIRS, says Addison, in the *Tatler*, are so untrustworthy, so stuffed with lies, that, "I do hereby give notice to all booksellers and translators whatsoever, that the word *memoir* is French for a novel; and to require of them, that they sell and translate it accordingly."

There are, however, some memoirs that are trustworthy and dull, and others, again, that are conspicuously trustworthy, and yet are as entertaining as a novel, and to this latter category belong the memoirs of Hans von Schweinichen, the Silesian Knight, Marshal and Chamberlain to the Dukes of Liegnitz and Brieg at the close of the 16th century. Scherr, a well known writer on German Culture, and a scrupulous observer and annotator of all that is ugly and unseemly in the past, says of the diary of Schweinichen: "It carries us into a noble family at the end of the 16th century and reveals boorish meanness, coarseness and lack of culture." That is, in a measure, true, but, as is invariably the case with Scherr, he leaves out of sight all the redeeming elements, and there are many, that this transparently sincere diarist discloses.

The MS. was first discovered and published in 1823, by Büsching; it was republished in 1878 at Breslau by Oesterley. The diary extends to the year 1602, and Schweinichen begins with an account of his birth in 1552, and his childish years. But we are wrong in saying that he begins with his birth—characteristic of the protestant theological spirit of his times, he begins with a confession of his faith.

As a picture of the manners and customs of the highest classes in the age just after the Reformation it is unrivalled for its minuteness, and for its interest. The writer, who had not an idea that his diary would be printed, wrote for his own amusement, and, without intending it, drew a perfect portraiture of himself, without exaggeration of his virtues and observation of his faults; indeed the virtues we admire in him, he hardly recognised as virtues, and scarcely considered as serious the faults we deplore. In reading his truthful record we are angry with him, and yet, he makes us love and respect him, and acknowledge what sterling goodness, integrity, fidelity and honour were in the man.

Hans was son of George, Knight of Schweinichen and Mertschütz, and was born in the Castle of Gröditzberg belonging to the Dukes of Silesia, of which his father was castellan, and warden of the Ducal Estates thereabouts. The Schweinichens were a very ancient noble Silesian family, and Hans could prove his purity of blood through the sixteen descents, eight paternal and eight maternal.

In 1559, Duke Frederick III. was summoned before the Emperor Ferdinand I. at Breslau, to answer the accusations of extravagance and oppression brought against him by the Silesian Estates, and was deposed, imprisoned, and his son Henry XI. given the Ducal crown instead. The deposition of the Duke obliged the father of our hero to leave Gröditzberg and retire to his own estates, where Hans was given the village notary as teacher in reading and writing for a couple of years, and was then sent, young noble though he was, to keep the geese for the family. However, as he played tricks with the geese, put spills into their beaks, pegging them open, the flock was then withdrawn from his charge. This reminds us of Grettir the Strong, the Icelandic hero, who also as a boy was sent to drive the family geese to pasture, and who maltreated his charge.

His father sent Hans to be page to the imprisoned Duke Frederick at Liegnitz, where also he was to study with the Duke's younger son, afterwards Frederick IV. Hans tells us he did not get as many whippings as his companion, because he slipped his money-allowance into the tutor's palm, and so his delinquencies were passed over. As page, he had to serve the Duke at table. A certain measure of wine was allowed the imprisoned Duke daily by his son, the reigning Duke; what he did not drink every day, Hans was required to empty into a cask, and when the cask was full, the Duke invited some good topers to him, and they sat and drank the cask out, then rolled over on the floor. All night Hans had to sit or lie on the floor and watch the drunken Duke.

Duke Frederick took a dislike to the chaplain, and scribbled a lampoon on him, which may be thus rendered, without injustice to the original:—

"All the mischief ever done Twixt the old Duke and his son, Comes from that curs't snuffy one Franconian Parson Cut-and-run."

The Duke ordered Hans to pin this to the pulpit cushion, and he did so. When the pastor ascended the pulpit he saw the paper, and instead of a text read it out. The reigning Duke Henry was very angry, and Hans was made the scape-goat, and sent home in disgrace to his father.

In 1564, Hans attended his father, himself as page, his father as Marshal, when Duke Henry and his Duchess visited Stuttgard and Dresden. Pages were not then allowed to sit astride a horse, they stood in a sort of stirrup slung to the pommel, to which they held. At Dresden old Schweinichen ran a tilt in a tournament with the elector Augustus and unhorsed him, but had sufficient courtesy to at once throw himself off his own horse, as though he also had been cast by the elector. This so gratified the latter, that he sent old Schweinichen a gold chain, and a double florin worth about 4 shillings to the young one.

When Hans was fifteen, he went to the marriage of Duke Wenceslas of Teschen with the daughter of Duke Franz of Saxony, and received from his father a present of a sword, which, he tells us, cost his father a little under a pound. One of the interesting features of this diary is that Hans enters the value of everything. For instance, we are given the price of wheat, barley, rye, oats, meat, &c., in 1562, and we learn from this that all kinds of grain cost one fifth or one sixth of what it costs now, and that meat— mutton, was one eighteenth or one twentieth the present cost. For a thaler, 3 shillings, in 1562 as much food could be purchased as would now cost from 25 to 30 shillings. Hans tells us what pocket money he received from his parents; he put a value on every present he was given, and tells what everything cost him which he give away.

In the early spring of 1569 Duke Henry XI. went to Lublin in Poland to a diet. King Sigismund was old, and the Duke hoped to get elected to the kingdom of Poland on his death. This was a costly expedition, as the Duke had to make many presents, and to go in great state. Hans went with him, and gives an infinitely droll account of their reception, the miserable housing, his own dress, one leg black, the other yellow, and how many ells of ribbon went to make the bows on his jacket. His father and he, and a nobleman called Zedlitz and his son were put in a garret under the tiles in bitter frost—and "faith," says Hans, "our pigs at home are warmer in their styes."

This expedition which led to no such result as the Duke hoped, exhausted his treasury, and exasperated the Silesian Estates. All the nobles had to stand surety for their Duke, Schweinichen and the rest to the amount of—in modern money £100,000.

When Hans was aged eighteen he was drunk for the first time in his life, so drunk that he lay like a dead man for two days and two nights, and his life was in danger.

Portia characterised the German as a drunkard, she liked him "very vilely in the morning, when he is sober; and most vilely in the afternoon, when he is drunk. Set a deep glass of Rhenish wine on the contrary casket: for, if the devil be within, and that temptation without, I know he will choose it. I will do anything, Nerissa, ere I will be married to a sponge."

How true this characterisation was of the old German noble, Schweinichen's memoirs show; it is a record of drunken bouts at small intervals. There was no escape, he who would live at court must drink and get drunken.

At the age of nineteen old Schweinichen made his son keep the accounts at home, and look after the mill; he had the charge of the fish-ponds, and attended to the thrashing of the corn, and the feeding of the horses and cattle.

Once Hans was invited to a wedding, and met at it four sisters from Glogau, two were widows and two unmarried. Their maiden name was Von Schaben. Hans, aged twenty, danced with the youngest a good deal, and before leaving invited the four sisters to pay his father and him a visit. A friend of his called Eicholz galloped ahead to forewarn old Schweinichen. Some hours later up drove Hans in a waggon with the four sisters; but he did not dare to bring them in till he had seen his father, so he went into the house, and was at once saluted with a burst of laughter, and the shout, "Here comes the bridegroom," and Eicholz sang at the top of his voice an improvised verse:

"Rosie von Schaben Hans er will haben."

"Where are the ladies?" asked the old knight.

"In the waggon outside," answered Hans.

"Send for the fiddlers, bring them in. We will eat, drink, dance and be merry," said the old man.

But Hans was offended at being boisterously saluted as bridegroom, and he now kept Rosie at a distance. Somewhat later, the Duke tried to get him to marry a charming young heiress called Hese von Promnitz, and very amusing is Hans' account of how he kept himself clear of engagement. When he first met her at court she was aged fourteen, and was passionately fond of sugar. Hans says he spent as much as £3 in our modern money on sweets for her, but he would make no proposal, because, as he concluded, she was too young to be able "to cook a bowl of soup." Two years passed, and then an old fellow called Geisler, "looking more like a Jew than a gentleman," who offered Hese a box of sweets every day, proposed for her. Hese would not answer till she knew the intentions of Hans, and she frankly asked him whether he meant to propose for her hand or not. "My heart's best love, Hese," answered Schweinichen, "at the right time, and when God wills I shall marry, but I do not think I can do that for three years. So follow your own desires, take the old Jew, or wait, as you like."

Hese said she would wait any number of years for Hans. This made Hans the colder. The Duke determined that the matter should be settled one way or other at once, so he sent a crown of gold roses to Hans, and said it was to be Hese's bridal wreath, if he desired that she should wear it for him, he was to lay hold of it; Hans thereupon put his hands behind his back. Then he went to his Schweinichen coat-of-arms and painted under it the motto, "I bide my time, when the old man dies, I'll get the prize." This Geisler read, and—says Hans, didn't like.

Hans was now installed as gentleman-in-waiting to the Duke, and was henceforth always about his person. He got for his service free bed and board, a gala coat that cost in our modern money about £36, and an every day livery costing £18. His father made him a small allowance, but pay in addition to liveries and keep he got none. The Duke's great amusement consisted in mumming. For a whole year he rambled about every evening in masquerade, dropping in on the burghers unexpectedly. Some were, we are told, pleased to see and entertain him, others objected to these impromptu visits. The special costume in which the Duke delighted to run about the town making these visits was that of a Nun. Hans admits that this was very distasteful to him, but he could not help himself, he was obliged to accommodate himself to the whims of his master. He made an effort to free himself from the service of the Duke, so as to go out of the country to some other court—he felt intuitively that this association would be fatal to his best interests, but the Duke at once took him by his better side, pleaded with him to remain and be faithful to him, his proper master and sovereign, and Hans with misgivings at heart consented.

There was at Court an old lady, Frau von Kittlitz, who acted as stewardess, and exercised great influence over the Duke, whom she had known from a boy. The Duchess resented her managing ways, and interference, and was jealous of her influence. One day in 1575 she refused to come down from her room and dine with the Duke unless the old Kittlitz were sent to sit at the table below the dais. This led to words and hot blood on both sides. The Duchess used a gross expression in reference to the stewardess, and the Duke who had already some wine under his belt, struck the Duchess in the face, saying, "I'll teach you not to call people names they do not deserve." Hans, who was present, threw himself between the angry couple; the Duke stormed and struck about. Hans entreated the Duchess to retire, and then he stood in her door and prevented the Duke following, though he shouted, "She is my wife, I can serve her as I like. Who are you to poke yourself in between married folk?"

As soon as the Duchess had locked herself in, Hans escaped and fled; but an hour after the Duke sent for him, and stormed at him again for his meddlesomeness. Hans entreated the Duke to be quiet and get reconciled to the Duchess, but he would not hear of it, and dismissed Schweinichen. A quarter of an hour later another messenger came from his master, and Hans returned to him, to find him in a better mood. "Hans," said his Highness, "try if you can't get my wife to come round and come down to table—all fun is at an end with this."

Hans went up and was admitted. The Duchess, in a towering rage, had already written a letter to her brother the Margrave of Anspach, telling him how her husband had struck her in the face and given her a black eye, and she had already dispatched a messenger with the letter. After much arguing, Hans wrung from her her consent to come down, on two conditions, one that the Duke should visit her at once and beg her pardon, the other that the old Kittlitz should sit at the table with the pages. The Duke was now in a yielding mood and ate his leek humbly. The Duchess consented to tell the Court that she had got her black eye from striking her face against a lamp, and the Duke ordered ten trumpeters and a kettledrum to make all the noise they could to celebrate the reconciliation.

The Duchess in an aside to Schweinichen admitted that she had been rash and unjust, and regretted having sent off that letter. An unlucky letter—says our author—for it cost the duchy untold gold and years of trouble.

The Duke had made several visits to Poland, chasing that Jack o' lantern—the Polish crown, and it had cost him so much money that he had quarrelled with his Estates, bullied and oppressed his subjects to extort money, and at last the Estates appealed to the Emperor against him, as they had against his father; and the Emperor summoned him to Prague. The Duke had great difficulty in scraping together money enough to convey him so far; and on reaching Prague, he begged permission of the Kaiser to be allowed to visit the Electors and the Free Cities, and see whether he could not obtain from them some relief from his embarrassments, and money wherewith to pacify the angry Estates of the Silesian Duchy. The consent required was given, and then the Duke with his faithful Schweinichen, and several other retainers, started on a grand begging and borrowing round of the Empire. Hans was constituted treasurer, and he had in his purse about £400. The Duke took with him five squires, two pages, three serving men, a cook, and several kitchen boys, one carriage drawn by six horses, another by four. And not only was this train to make the round of the Empire, but also to visit Italy—and all on £400.

The first visit was paid, three days' journey from Prague, at Theusing to a half-sister of the Duchess. She received him coolly, and lectured him on his conduct to his wife. When the Duke asked her to lend him money, she answered that she would pay his expenses home, if he chose to go back to Liegnitz, but not one penny otherwise should he have. Not content with this refusal, the Duke went on to Nurnberg, where he sent Hans to the town council to invite them to lend him money; he asked for 4,000 florins. The council declined the honour. The two daughters of the Duke were in the charge of the Margrave of Anspach, their mother's brother. The Duke sent Hans to Anspach to urge the Margrave to send the little girls to him, or invite him to visit Anspach to see them. He was shy of visiting his brother-in-law uninvited, because of the box in the ear and the black eye. He confided to Hans that if he got his children at Nurnberg, he would not return them to their uncle, without a loan or a honorarium.

This shabby transaction was not to Schweinichen's taste, but he was obliged to undertake it. It proved unsuccessful, the Margrave refused to give up the children till the Duke returned to his wife and duchy and set a better example.

Whilst Hans was away, the Duke won a large sum of money at play, enough to pay his own bill, but instead of doing this with it, he had it melted up and made into silver cups. When he came to leave Nurnberg he was unable to pay his inn bill, and obliged to leave in pawn with the taverner a valuable jewel. Then he and his suite went to Augsburg and settled into an inn till the town council could agree to lend him money.

One day, whilst there, Hans was invited to a wedding. The Duke wanted to go also, but, as he was not invited, he went as Hans' servant, but got so drunk that Hans was obliged to carry him home to the tavern, after which he returned to the wedding. In the evening, when dancing began, the Duke reappeared, he had slept off his drunkenness and was fresh for more entertainment. He was now recognized, and according to etiquette, two town councillors, in robes of office and gold chains, danced solemnly before his Highness. Hans tells us that it was customary for all dances to be led by two persons habited in scarlet with white sleeves, and these called the dance and set the figures, no one might execute any figure or do anything which had not been done by the leaders. Now as Hans vows he never saw so many pretty girls anywhere as on that evening, he tipped the leaders with half a thaler to kiss each other, whereupon the two solemn dancing councillors had also to kiss each other, and the Duke, nothing loth, his partner, and Hans, with zest, his. That evening he gave plenty of kisses, and what with the many lights, and the music and the dancing and the pretty girls he thought himself in Paradise. Shortly after this, the Duke was invited to dine with Fugger, the merchant prince, who showed him his treasury, gold to the worth of a million, and one tower lined within from top half way down with nothing but silver thalers. The Duke's mouth watered, and he graciously invited Fugger to lend him £5,000; this the merchant declined, but made him a present of 200 crowns and a good horse. The town council consented to lend the Duke £1,200 on his I.O.U. for a year; and then to pay his host he melted up his silver mugs again, pawned his plate and gave him a promissory note for two months.

From Augsburg the Duke went about the abbeys, trying to squeeze loans out of the abbots, but found that they had always the excuse ready, that they would not lend to Lutheran princes. Then he stuck on in the abbeys, eating up all their provisions and rioting in their guest-apartments, till the abbots were fain to make him a present to be rid of him.

All at once an opening offered for the Duke to gain both renown and money. Henry I. of Condé was at the court of the Elector Palatine at Heidelsberg, soliciting assistance in behalf of the Huguenots against the King of France. The Elector agreed to send a force under his son John Casimir, and the Duke of Liegnitz offered his services, which were readily accepted. He was to lead the rearguard, and to receive a liberal pay for his services. Whilst he was collecting this force and getting underway, John Casimir and the Prince of Condé marched through Lorraine to Metz, and Hans went with John Casimir. He trusted he was now on his way to fortune. But it was not so to be. The Duke, his master, insisted that he should return to him, and Hans, on doing so, found him rioting and gambling away, at Frankfort and Nassau, the money paid him in advance for his useless services. Almost the first duty imposed on Hans, on his return, was to negociate a loan for £5,000 with the magistrates of Frankfort, which was peremptorily refused; whereupon the Duke went to Cologne and stayed there seven months, endeavouring to cajole the town council there into advancing him money.

But we can not follow any further the miserable story of the degradation of the Silesian Duke, till at the beginning of the new year, 1577, the Duke ran away from the town of Emmerich, leaving his servants to pay his debts as best they could. Hans sold the horses and whatever was left, and then, not sorry to be quit of such a master, returned on foot to his Silesian home.

It is, perhaps, worth while quoting Duke Henry's letter, which Hans found in the morning announcing his master's evasion.

"Dear Hans,—Here is a chain, do what you can with it. Weigh it and sell it, also the horses for ready money; I will not pillow my head in feathers till, by God's help, I have got some money, to enable me to clear out of this vile land, and away from these people. Good morning, best-loved Hans.
"With mine own hand, HENRY, DUKE."

As he neared home, sad news reached Hans. The Ducal creditors had come down on his father, who had made himself responsible, and had seized the family estates; whereat the old man's heart broke, and he had died in January. When Hans heard this, he sat for two hours on a stone beside the road, utterly unmanned, before he could recover himself sufficiently to pursue his journey.

In the meantime an Imperial commission had sat on the Duke, deposed him, and appointed his brother Frederick duke in his room. Schweinichen's fidelity to Duke Henry ensured his disfavour with Duke Frederick, and he was not summoned to court, but was left quietly at Mertschütz to do his best along with his brother to bring the family affairs into some sort of order. His old master did not, however, allow him much rest. By the Imperial decision, he was to be provided with a daily allowance of money, food and wine. This drew Duke Henry home, and no sooner was he back in Silesia than he insisted on Hans returning to his service, and for some years more he led the faithful soul a troubled life, and involved him in miserable pecuniary perplexities. This was the more trying to Hans as he had now fallen in love with Margaret von Schellendorff, whom he married eventually. The tenderness and goodness of Schweinichen's heart break out whenever he speaks of his dear Margaretta, and of the children which came and were taken from him. His sorrows as he lingered over the sick-beds of his little ones, and the closeness with which he was drawn by domestic bereavements and pecuniary distresses, to his Margaretta, come out clearly in his narrative. The whole story is far too long to tell in its entirety. Hans was a voluminous diarist. His memoirs cease at the year 1602, when he was suffering from gout, but he lived on some years longer.

In the church of S. John at Liegnitz was at one time his monument, with life-sized figure of Hans von Schweinichen, and above it his banner and an inscription stating that he died on the 23rd Aug., 1616. Alas! the hand of the destroyer has been there. The church and monument are destroyed, and we can no longer see what manner of face Hans wore; but of the inner man, of a good, faithful, God fearing, and loving soul, strong and true, he has himself left us the most accurate portrait in his precious memoirs.

V. — THE LOCKSMITH GAMAIN

AMONG the many episodes of the French Revolution there is one which deserves to be somewhat closely examined, because of the gravity of the accusation which it involves against the King and Queen, and because a good deal of controversy has raged round it. The episode is that of the locksmith Gamain, whom the King and Queen are charged with having attempted to poison.

That the accusation was believed during "the Terror" goes without saying; the heated heads and angry hearts at that time were in no condition to sift evidence with impartiality. Afterwards, the charge was regarded as preposterous, till the late M. Paul Lacroix—better known as le Bibliophile Jacob—a student of history, very careful and diligent as a collector, gave it a new spell of life in 1836, when he reformulated the accusation in a *feuilleton* of the *Siècle*. Not content to let it sleep or die in the ephemeral pages of a newspaper, he republished the whole story in 1838, in his "Dissertations sur quelques points curieux de l'histoire de France." This he again reproduced in his "Curiosités de l'histoire de France," in 1858. M. Louis Blanc, convinced that the case was made out, has reasserted the charge in his work on the French Revolution, and it has since been accepted by popular writers—as Décembre-Alonnier—who seek to justify the execution of the King and Queen, and to glorify the Revolution.

M. Thiers rejected the accusation; M. Eckard pointed out the improbabilities in the story in the "Biographie Universelle," and M. Mortimer-Ternaux has also shown its falsity in his "Histoire de la Terreur;" and finally, M. Le Roy, librarian of Versailles, in 1867, devoted his special attention to it, and completely disproved the poisoning of Gamain. But in spite of disproval the slanderous accusation does not die, and no doubt is still largely believed in Paris.

So tenacious of life is a lie—like the bacteria that can be steeped in sulphuric acid without destroying their vitality—that the story has been again recently raked up, and given to the public, from Lacroix, in a number of the Cornhill Magazine (December, 1887); the writer of course knew only Lacroix' myth, and had never seen how it had been disproved. It is well now to review the whole story.

François Gamain was born at Versailles on August 29, 1751. He belonged to an hereditary locksmith family. His father Nicolas had been in the same trade, and had charge of the locks in the royal palaces in Versailles and elsewhere.

The love of Louis XVI. for mechanical works is well known. He had a little workshop at Versailles, where he amused himself making locks, assisted by François Gamain, to whom he was much attached, and with whom he spent many hours in projecting and executing mechanical contrivances. The story is told of the Intendant Thierry, that when one day the King showed him a lock he had made, he replied, "Sire, when kings occupy themselves with the works of the common people, the common people will assume the functions of kings," but the *mot* was probably made after the fact.

After the terrible days of the 5th and 6th of October, 1789, the King was brought to Paris. Gamain remained at Versailles, which was his home, and retained the King's full confidence.

When, later, the King was surrounded by enemies, and he felt the necessity for having some secret place where he could conceal papers of importance which might yet fall into the hands of the rabble if the palace was again invaded, as it had been at Versailles, he sent for Gamain to make for him an iron chest in a place of concealment, that could only be opened by one knowing the secret of the lock.

Unfortunately, the man was not as trustworthy as Louis XVI. supposed. Surrounded by those who had adopted the principles of the Revolution, and being a man without strong mind, he followed the current, and in 1792 he was nominated member of the Council General of the Commune of Versailles, and on September 24 he was one of the commissioners appointed "to cause to disappear all such paintings, sculptures, and inscriptions from the monuments of the Commune as might serve to recall royalty and despotism."

The records of the debates of the Communal Council show that Gamain attended regularly and took part in the discussions, which were often tumultuous.

The Queen heard of Gamain's Jacobinism, and warned the King, who, however, could not believe that Gamain would betray him. Marie Antoinette insisted on the most important papers being removed from the iron chest, and they were confided to Mme. de Campan.

When the trial of the King was begun, on November 20, Gamain went to Roland, Minister of the Interior, and told him the secret of the iron chest. Roland, alarmed at the consequences of such a discovery, hastened to consult his wife, who was in reality more minister than himself.

From August 10, a commission had been appointed to collect all the papers found in the Tuileries; this commission, therefore, ought to be made acquainted with the discovery; but here lay the danger. Mme.

Roland, as an instrument of the Girondins, feared that among the papers in the chest might be discovered some which would show in what close relations the Girondins stood to the Court. She decided that her husband should go to the Tuileries, accompanied by Gamain, an architect, and a servant. The chest was opened by the locksmith, Roland removed all the papers, tied them up in a napkin, and took them home. They were taken the same day to the Convention; and the commission charged the minister with having abstracted such papers as would have been inconvenient to him to deliver up.

When Roland surrendered the papers he declared, without naming Gamain, that they had been discovered in a hole in the wall closed by an iron door, behind a wainscot panel, in so secret a place "that they could not have been found had not the secret been disclosed by the workman who had himself made the place of concealment."

On December 24 following, Gamain was summoned to Paris by the Convention to give his evidence to prove that a key discovered in the desk of Thierry de Ville-d'Avray fitted the iron chest.

After the execution of the King, on January 21, 1793, the Convention sent deputies into all the departments "to stimulate the authorities to act with the energy requisite under the circumstances." Crassous was sent into the department of Seine-et-Oise; and not finding the municipality of Versailles, of which Gamain was a member, "up to the requisite pitch," he discharged them from office; and by a law of September 17, all such discharged functionaries were declared to be "suspected persons," who were liable to be brought before the revolutionary tribunal on that charge alone.

Thus, in spite of all the proofs he had given of his fidelity to the principles of the Revolution, Gamain was at any moment liable to arrest, and to being brought before that terrible tribunal from which the only exit was to the guillotine. Moreover, Gamain had lost his place and emoluments as Court locksmith; he had fallen into great poverty, was without work, and without health.

On April 27, 1794, he presented a petition to the Convention which was supported by Musset, the deputy and constitutional curé. "It was not enough," said Musset from the tribune, "that the last of our tyrants should have delivered over thousands of citizens to be slain by the sword of the enemy. You will see by the petition I am about to read that he was familiarised with the most refined cruelty, and that he himself administered poison to the father of a family, in the hopes thereby of destroying evidence of his perfidy. You will see that his ferocious mind had adopted the maxim that to a king everything is permissible."

After this preamble Musset read the petition of Gamain, which is as follows:

"François Gamain, locksmith to the cabinets and to the laboratory of the late King, and for three years member of the Council General of the Commune of Versailles, declares that at the beginning of May 1792 he was ordered to go to Paris. On reaching it, Capet required him to make a cupboard in the thickness of one of the walls of his room, and to fasten it with an iron door; and he further states that he was thus engaged up to the 22nd of the said month, and that he worked in the King's presence. When the chest was completed, Capet himself offered citizen Gamain a large tumbler of wine, and asked him to drink it, as he, the said Gamain, was very hot.

"*A few hours later* he was attacked by a violent colic, which did not abate till he had taken two spoonfuls of elixir, which made him vomit all he had eaten and drunk that day. This was the prelude to a terrible illness, which lasted fourteen months, during which he lost the use of his limbs, and which has left him at present without hope of recovering his full health, and of working so as to provide for the necessities of his family."

After reading the petition Musset added: "I hold in my hands the certificate of the doctors, that testifies to the bad state of the health of the citizen petitioner.

"Citizens! If wickedness is common to kings, generosity is the prerogative of the free people. I demand that this petition be referred to the Committee of Public Assistance to be promptly dealt with. I demand that after the request all the papers relating to it be deposed in the national archives, as a monument of the atrocity of tyrants, and be inserted in the bulletin, that all those who have supposed that Capet did evil only at the instigation of others may know that crime was rooted in his very heart."

This proposition was decreed. On May 17, 1794, the representative Peyssard mounted the tribune, and read the report of the Committee, which we must condense.

"Citizens! At the tribunal of liberty the crimes of the oppressors of the human race stand to be judged. To paint a king in all his hideousness I need name only Louis XVI. This name sums in itself all crimes; it recalls a prodigy of iniquity and of perfidy. Hardly escaped from infancy, the germs of the ferocious perversity which characterise a despot appeared in him. His earliest sports were with blood, and his brutality grew with his years, and he delighted in wreaking his ferocity on all the animals he met. He was known to be cruel, treacherous, and murderous. The object of this report is to exhibit him to France cold-bloodedly offering a cup of poison to the unhappy artist whom he had just employed to construct a cupboard in which to conceal the plots of tyranny. It was no stranger he marked as his victim, but a workman whom he had employed for five-and-twenty years, and the father of a family, his own instructor in the locksmith's art. Monsters who thus treat their chosen servants, how will they deal with the rest of men?"

The National Convention thereupon ordered that "François Gamain, poisoned by Louis Capet on May 22, 1792, should enjoy an annual pension of the sum of 1,200 livres, dating from the day on which he was poisoned."

It will be noticed by the most careless reader that the evidence is *nil*. Gamain does not feel the colic till some hours after he has drunk the wine; he had eaten or drunk other things besides during the day; and finally the testimony of the doctors is, not that he was poisoned, but that, at the time of his presenting the petition, he was in a bad state of health. Accordingly, all reasonable historians, unblinded by party passion, have scouted the idea of an attempt on Gamain's life by the King. Thus the matter would have remained had not M. Paul Lacroix taken it up and propped the old slander on new legs. We will take his account, which he pretends to have received from several persons to whom Gamain related it repeatedly. This is his *mise en scène*.

"The old inhabitants of Versailles will remember with pity the man whom they often encountered alone, bowed on his stick like one bent with years. Gamain was aged only fifty-eight when he died, but he bore all the marks of decrepitude."

Here is a blunder, to begin with; he died, as the Versailles registers testify, on May 8, 1795, and was accordingly only forty-four years old,—that is, he died *one* year after the grant of the annuity. M. Parrott, in his article on Gamain in the "Dictionnaire de la Révolution Française," says that he died in 1799, five years after having received his pension; but the Versailles registers are explicit.

M. Lacroix goes on: "His hair had fallen off, and the little that remained had turned white over a brow furrowed deeply; the loss of his teeth made his cheeks hollow; his dull eyes only glared with sombre fire when the name of Louis XVI was pronounced. Sometimes even tears then filled them. Gamain lived very quietly with his family on his humble pension, which, notwithstanding the many changes of government, was always accorded him. It was not suppressed, lest the reason of its being granted should again be raked up before the public."

As we have seen, Gamain died under the Government which granted the pension. M. Lacroix goes on to say "that the old locksmith bore to his dying day an implacable hatred of Louis XVI., whom he accused of having been guilty of an abominable act of treachery."

"This act of treachery was the fixed and sole idea in Gamain's head, he recurred to it incessantly, and poured forth a flood of bitter and savage recriminations against the King. It was Gamain who disclosed the secret of the iron chest in the Tuileries, and the papers it contained, which furnished the chief accusation against Louis XVI.; it was he, therefore, who had, so to speak, prepared the guillotine for the royal head; it was he, finally, who provoked the decree of the Convention which blackened the memory of the King as that of a vulgar murderer. But this did not suffice the hate of Gamain, who went about everywhere pursuing the dead beyond the tomb, with his charge of having attempted murder as payment of life-long and devoted service. Gamain ordinarily passed his evenings in a cafe at Versailles, the name of which I have been told, but which I do not divulge lest I should make a mistake. He was generally in the society of two old notaries, who are still alive (in 1836), and of the doctor Lameyran, who attended him when he was poisoned. These three persons were prepared to attest all the particulars of the poisoning which had been proved at the *procès verbal*. Gamain, indeed, lacked witnesses to establish the incidents of the 22nd May, 1792, at the Tuileries; but his air of veracity and expression of pain, his accent of conviction, his face full of suffering, his burning eyes, his pathetic pantomime, were the guarantees of good faith."

These three men, the notaries and the doctor, which latter M. Lacroix hints was living when he wrote, were his authorities for what follows. The notaries he does not name, nor the café where they met. His account published in the *Siècle* at once attracted attention, and M. Lacroix was challenged to produce his witnesses. As for M. Lameyran, the doctor, he had died in 1811; consequently his testimony was not to be had in 1836. The other doctor who had attended Gamain was M. Voisin, who died in 1823, but M. Le Roy asserts positively that in 1813 M. Voisin told him, "Never was Gamain poisoned. Lameyran and I had long attended him for chronic malady of the stomach. This is all we testified to in our certificate, when he applied for a pension. In our certificate we stated that he was in weak health—not a word was in it about poisoning, which existed only in his fancy."

These certificates are no longer in existence. They were not preserved in the archives of the Convention. Even this fact is taken as evidence in favour of the attempt. M. Emile Bonnet, in an article on Gamain in the "Intermédiaire des Chercheurs," declares that they have been substracted since the Restoration of Charles;[8] but there is no trace in the archives of them ever having been there. Moreover, we have M. Le Roy's word that M. Voisin assured him he had not testified to poisoning, and, what is more important, we have Musset's declaration before the Convention that the certificate of the doctors "asserted the ill-health of the claimant." If there had been a word about poison in it, he would assuredly have said so.

[8] Le Bibliophile Jacob says the same: "Les pièces détournées maladroitement par la Restauration."

M. Lacroix was asked to name his authorities—the two advocates who, as M. Lameyran was dead, were alive and would testify to the fact that they had heard the story from the lips of Gamain. He remained silent. He would not even name the café where they met, and which might lead to the identification. M. Eckard, who wrote the notice on Gamain in the "Biographie Universelle," consulted the family of the locksmith on the case, and was assured by them that the bad health of Gamain was due to no other cause than disappointment at the loss of his fortune, the privations he underwent, and, above all, his terror for his life after his dismissal from the Communal Council.

We will now continue M. Lacroix's account, which he proceeds, not a little disingenuously, to put into the mouth of Gamain himself, so that the accusation may not be charged on the author.

"On May 21, 1792," says Gamain, according to the "Bibliophile Jacob," "whilst I was working in my shop, a horseman drew up at my door and called me out. His disguise as a carter did not prevent me from recognising Durey, the King's forge assistant. I refused. I congratulated myself that evening at having done so, as the rumour spread in Versailles that the Tuileries had been attacked by the mob, but this did not really take place till a month later. Next morning Durey returned and showed me a note in the King's own hand, entreating me to lend my assistance in a difficult job past his unaided powers. My pride was flattered. I embraced my wife and children, without telling them whither I was going, but I promised to return that night. It was not without anxiety that they saw me depart with a stranger for Paris."

We need merely point out that Durey was no stranger to the family: he had been for years associated daily with Gamain.

"Durey conducted me to the Tuileries, where the King was guarded as in a prison. We went at once to the royal workshop, where Durey left me, whilst he went to announce my arrival. Whilst I was alone, I observed an iron door, recently forged, a mortise lock, well executed, and a little iron box with a secret spring which I did not at once discover. Then in came Durey with the King. 'The times are bad,' said Louis XVI., 'and I do not know how matters will end.' Then he showed me the works I had noticed, and said, 'What do you say to my skill? It took me ten days to execute these things. I am your apprentice, Gamain.' I protested my entire devotion. Then the King assured me that he always had confidence in me, and that he did not scruple to trust the fate of himself and his family in my hands. Thereupon he conducted me into the dark passage that led from his room to the chamber of the Dauphin. Durey lit a taper, and removed a panel in the passage, behind which I perceived a round hole, about two feet in diameter, bored in the wall. The King told me he intended to secrete his money in it, and that Durey, who had helped to make it, threw the dust and chips into the river during the night. Then the King told me that he was unable to fit the iron door to the hole unassisted. I went to work immediately. I went over all the parts of the lock, and got them into working order; then I fashioned a key to the lock, then made hinges and fastened them into the wall as firmly as I could, without letting the hammering be heard. The King helped as well as he was able, entreating me every moment to strike with less noise, and to be quicker over my work. The key was put in the little iron casket, and this casket was concealed under a slab of pavement in the corridor."

It will be seen that this story does not agree with the account in the petition made by Gamain to the Convention. In that he said he was summoned to Paris at the beginning of the month of May, and that "Capet ordered him to make a cupboard in the thickness of the wall of his apartment, and to close it with an iron door, the whole of which was not accomplished till the 22nd of the same month." He was three weeks over the job, not a few hours. "I had been working," continues Gamain, or M. Lacroix for him, "for eight consecutive hours. The sweat poured from my brow; I was impatient to repose, and faint with hunger, as I had eaten nothing since I got up."

But, according to his account before the Convention, the elixir made him throw up "all he had eaten and drunk during the day."

"I seated myself a moment in the King's chamber, and he asked me to count for him two thousand double louis and tie them up in four leather bags. Whilst so doing I observed that Durey was carrying some bundles of papers which I conjectured were destined for the secret closet; and, indeed, the money-counting was designed to distract my attention from what Durey was about."

What a clumsy story! Why were not the papers hidden after Gamain was gone? Was it necessary that this should be done in his presence, and he set to count money, so as not to observe what was going on?

"As I was about to leave, the Queen suddenly entered by a masked door at the foot of the King's bed, holding in her hands a plate, in which was a cake (brioche) and a glass of wine. She came up to me, and I saluted her with surprise, because the King had assured me that she knew nothing about the fabrication of the chest. 'My dear Gamain,' said she in a caressing tone, 'how hot you are! Drink this tumbler of wine and eat this cake, and they will sustain you on your journey home.' I thanked her, confounded by this consideration for a poor workman, and I emptied the tumbler to her health. I put the cake in my pocket, intending to take it home to my children."

Here again is a discrepancy. In his petition Gamain says that the King gave him a glass of wine, and makes no mention of the Queen.

On leaving the Tuileries, Gamain set out on foot for Versailles, but was attacked by a violent colic in the Champs Elysées. His agonies increased; he was no longer able to walk; he fell, and rolled on the ground, uttering cries and moans. A carriage that was passing stopped, and an English gentleman got out—wonderful to relate!—extraordinary coincidence!—a physician, and an acquaintance.

"The Englishman took me to his carriage, and ordered the coachman to drive at full gallop to an apothecary's shop. The conveyance halted at last before one in the Rue de Bac; the Englishman left me alone, whilst he prepared an elixir which might counteract the withering power of the poison. When I had swallowed this draught I ejected the venomous substances. An hour later nothing could have saved me. I recovered in part my sight and hearing; the cold that circulated in my veins was dissipated by degrees, and the Englishman judged that I might be safely removed to Versailles, which we reached at two o'clock in the morning. A physician, M. de Lameyran, and a surgeon, M. Voisin, were called in; they recognised the unequivocal tokens of poison.

"After three days of fever, delirium, and inconceivable suffering, I triumphed over the poison, but suffered ever after from a paralysis almost complete, and a general inflammation of the digestive organs.

"A few days after this catastrophe the servant maid, whilst cleaning my coat, which I had worn on the occasion of my accident, found my handkerchief, stained black, and the cake. She took a bite of the latter, and threw the rest into the yard, where a dog ate it and died. The girl, who had consumed only a morsel of the cake, fell dangerously ill. The dog was opened by M. Voisin, and a chemical analysis disclosed the presence of poison, both on my kerchief stained by my vomit, and in the cake. The cake alone contained enough corrosive sublimate to kill ten persons."

So—the poison was found. But how is it that in Gamain's petition none of this occurs? According to that document, Gamain was offered a goblet of wine by the King himself. "A few hours later he was attacked by a violent colic. This was the prelude to a terrible illness." Only a vague hint as to poison, no specific statement that he had been poisoned, and that the kind of poison had been determined.

Now, corrosive sublimate, when put in red wine, forms a violet precipitate, and alters the taste of the wine, giving it a characteristic metallic, harsh flavour, so disagreeable that it insures its immediate rejection. Gamain tasted nothing. Again, the action of corrosive sublimate is immediate or very nearly so; but Gamain was not affected till several hours after having drunk the wine.

According to the petition, Gamain asserted that he was paralysed in all his limbs for fourteen months, from May 22, 1792; but the Communal registers of Versailles show that he attended a session of the Council and took part in the discussion on June 4 following, that is, less than a fortnight after; that he was present at the sessions of June 8, 17, 20, and on August 22, and that he was sufficiently hearty and active to be elected on the commission which was to obliterate the insignia of monarchy on September 24 following, which certainly would not have been the case had he been a sick man paralysed in all his members.

Why, we may further inquire, did not Louis the XVI. or Queen Marie Antoinette attempt to poison Durey also, if they desired to make away with all those who knew the secret of the iron locker?

Now, Durey was alive in 1800, and Eckard, who wrote the article on Gamain in the "Biographie Universelle," knew him and saw him at that date, and Durey told him that Gamain's story was a lie; the iron safe was made, not in 1792, but in May, 1791; and this is probable, as it would have been easier for the King to have the locker made before his escape to Varennes, than in 1792, when he was under the closest supervision.

According to the version attributed to Gamain by M. Paul Lacroix, Gamain was paralysed for five months only. Why this change? Because either M. Lacroix or the locksmith had discovered that it was an anachronism for him to appear in November before Roland, and assist him in opening the case which he had made in May—five months before, and afterwards to declare that he was paralysed in all his members from May till the year following. We think this correction is due to the Bibliophile. But he was not acquainted with the Versailles archives proving him to have been at a session a few days after the pretended poisoning.

There is not much difficulty in discovering Gamain's motive for formulating the accusation against the King. He betrayed his king, who trusted him, and then, to excuse his meanness, invented an odious calumny against him.

But what was M. Lacroix's object in revivifying the base charge? We are not sure that he comes cleaner out of the slough than the despicable locksmith. He gave the story a new spell of life; he based his "facts" on testimonies, who, he said, were ready at any moment to vouch for the truth. When challenged to produce them he would not do so. His "facts" were proved again and again to be fables, and yet he dared to republish his slanderous story again and again, without a word of apology, explanation, or retractation. M. Lacroix died only a year or two ago, and it may seem ungenerous to attack a dead man, but one is forced to do this in defence of the honour of a dead Queen whom he grossly calumniated. The calumny was ingeniously put. M. Lacroix set it in the mouth of Gamain, thinking thereby to free himself from responsibility, but the responsibility sticks when he refuses to withdraw what has been demonstrated to be false.

There is something offensive to the last degree in the pose of M. Lacroix as he opens his charge.

"For some years I have kept by me, with a sort of terror, the materials for an historic revelation, without venturing to use them, and yet the fact, now almost unknown, on which I purpose casting a sinister light, is one that has been the object of my most active preoccupations. For long I condemned myself to silence and to fresh research, hitherto fruitless, hoping that the truth would come to light.... Well! now, at the moment of lifting the veil which covers a half-effaced page of history, with the documents I have consulted and the evidence I have gleaned lying before me, surrounded by a crowd of witnesses, one sustaining the testimony of the other, relying on my conscience and on my sentiments as a man of honour—still I hesitate to open my mouth and call up the remembrance of an event monstrous in itself, that has not found an echo even in the writings of the blindest partisans of a hideous epoch. Yes, I feel a certain repugnance in seeming to associate in thought, though not in act, with the enemies of Louis XVI. I have just re-read the sublime death of this unhappy political martyr; I have felt my eyes moisten with tears at the contemplation of the picture of the death inflicted by an inexorable state necessity, and I felt I must break my pen lest I should mix my ink with the yet warm blood of the innocent victim. Let my hand wither rather than rob Louis XVI. of the mantle of probity and goodness, which the outrages of '93 succeeded neither in staining nor in rending to rags."

And so on—M. Lacroix is only acting under a high sense of the sacred duty of seeking the truth, "of forcing the disclosure of facts, before it be too late," which may establish the innocence of Louis XVI. Now, be it noted that M. Lacroix is the first to accuse the Queen of attempting the murder; his assault is on her as much as, more than, on the poor King—in the sacred interests of historic truth!

What are his evidences, his crowd of witnesses, his documents that he has collected? What proof is there of his active preoccupations and fresh researches? He produced nothing that can be called proof, and refused the names of his witnesses when asked for them. We can quite understand that the Bibliophile Jacob may have heard some gossiping story such as he narrates, and may have believed it when he wrote the story; but then, where are the high sense of honour, the tender conscience, the enthusiasm for truth, when his story is proved to be a tissue of improbabilities and impossibilities, that permit him to republish, and again republish at intervals of years, this cruel and calumnious fabrication?

VI. ABRAM THE USURER.[9]

[9] This account is taken from a sermon preached in the Church of St. Sophia at Constantinople on Orthodoxy Sunday, printed by Combefisius (Auctuarium novum, pars post. col. 644), from a MS. in the National Library at Paris. Another copy of the sermon is in the Library at Turin. The probable date of the composition is the tenth century. Orthodoxy Sunday was not instituted till 842.

IN the reign of Heraclius, when Sergius was patriarch of Constantinople, there lived in Byzantium a merchant named Theodore, a good man and just, fearing God, and serving him with all his heart. He went on a voyage to the ports of Syria and Palestine with his wares, in a large well-laden vessel, sold his goods to profit, and turned his ship's head homewards with a good lading of silks and spices, the former some of the produce of the looms of distant China, brought in caravans through Persia and Syria to the emporiums on the Mediterranean.

It was late in the year when Theodore began his voyage home, the equinoctial gales had begun to blow, and prudence would have suggested that he should winter in Cyprus; but he was eager to return to Byzantium to his beloved wife, and to prepare for another adventure in the ensuing spring.

But he was overtaken by a storm as he was sailing up the Propontis, and to save the vessel he was obliged to throw all the lading overboard. He reached Constantinople in safety, but with the loss of his goods. His grief and despair were excessive. His wife was unable to console him. He declared that he was weary of the world, his loss was sent him as a warning from heaven not to set his heart on Mammon, and that he was resolved to enter a monastery, and spend the rest of his days in devotion.

"Hasten, husband mine," said the wife, "put this scheme into execution at once; for if you delay you may change your mind."

The manifest impatience of his wife to get rid of him somewhat cooled the ardour of Theodore for the monastic profession, and before taking the irrevocable step, he consulted a friend. "I think, dearest brother, nay, I am certain, that this misfortune came on me as the indication of the finger of Providence that I should give up merchandise and care only for the saving of my soul."

"My friend," answered the other, "I do not see this in the same light as you. Every merchant must expect loss. It is one of the ordinary risks of sailors. It is absurd to despair. Go to your friends and borrow of them sufficient to load your vessel again, and try your luck once more. You are known as a merchant, and trusted as an honest man, and will have no difficulty in raising the sum requisite."

Theodore rushed home, and announced to his wife that he had already changed his mind, and that he was going to borrow money.

"Whatever pleases you is right in my eyes," said the lady.

Theodore then went the round of his acquaintances, told them of his misfortune, and then asked them to lend him enough to restock his vessel, promising to pay them a good percentage on the money lent. But the autumn had been fatal to more vessels than that of Theodore, and he found that no one was disposed to advance him the large sum he required. He went from door to door, but a cold refusal met him everywhere. Disappointed, and sick at heart, distressed at finding friends so unfriendly, he returned home, and said to his wife, "Woman! the world is hard and heartless, I will have nothing more to do with it. I will become a monk."

"Dearest husband, do so by all means, and I shall be well pleased," answered the wife.

Theodore tossed on his bed all night, unable to sleep; before dawn an idea struck him. There was a Jew named Abram who had often importuned him to trade with his money, but whom he had invariably refused. He would try this man as a last resource.

So when morning came, Theodore rose and went to the shop of Abram. The Hebrew listened attentively to his story, and then said, smiling, "Master Theodore, when thou wast rich, I often asked thee to take my money and trade with it in foreign parts, so that I might turn it over with advantage. But I always met with refusal. And now that thou art poor, with only an empty ship, thou comest to me to ask for a loan. What if again tempest should fall on thee, and wreck and ruin be thy lot, where should I look for my money? Thou art poor. If I were to sell thy house it would not fetch much. Nay, if I am to lend thee money thou must provide a surety, to whom I may apply, and who will repay me, should accident befall thee. Go, find security, and I will find the money."

So Theodore went to his best friend, and told him the circumstances, and asked him to stand surety for him to the Jew.

"Dear friend," answered he, "I should be most happy to oblige you; but I am a poor man, I have not as much money in the world as would suffice. The Hebrew would not accept me as surety, he knows the state of my affairs too well. But I will do for you what little I can. We will go together to some merchants, and together beseech them to stand security for you to the Jew."

So the two friends went to a rich merchant with whom they were acquainted, and told him what they wanted; but he blustered and turned red, and said, "Away with you, fellows; who ever heard of such insolence as that two needy beggars should ask a man of substance like me to go with them to the den of a cursed infidel Jew. God be thanked! I have no dealings with Jews. I never have spoken to one in my life, and never give them a greeting when I pass any in street or market-place. A man who goes to the Jews to-day, goes to the dogs to-morrow, and to the devil the day after."

The friends visited other merchants, but with like ill-success. Theodore had spent the day fasting, and he went supperless to bed, very hopeless, and with the prospect growing more distinct of being obliged to put on the cowl of the monk, a prospect which somehow or other he did not relish.

Next morning he started from home to tell Abram his failure. His way was through the great square called the Copper-Market before the Imperial palace. Now there stood there a porch consisting of four pillars, which supported a dome covered with brazen tiles, the whole surmounted by a cross, on the east side of which, looking down on the square, and across over the sparkling Bosphorus to the hills of Asia, was a large, solemn figure of the Crucified. This porch and cross had been set up by Constantine the Great,[10] and had been restored by Anastasius.

[10] This famous figure was cast down and broken by Leo the Isaurian in 730, a riot ensued, the market-women interfering with the soldiers, who were engaged on pulling down the figure, they shook the ladders and threw down one who was engaged in hacking the face of the figure. This led to the execution of ten persons, among them Gregory, head of the bodyguard, and Mary, a lady of the Imperial family. The Empress Irene set up a mosaic figure in its place. This was again destroyed by Leo the Armenian, and again restored after his death by Theophilus in 829.

As Theodore sped through the Copper-Market in the morning, he looked up; the sky was of the deepest gentian blue. Against it, glittering like gold in the early sun, above the blazing, brazen tiles, stood the great cross with the holy form thereon. Theodore halted, in his desolation, doubt and despair, and looked up at the figure. It was in the old, grave Byzantine style, very solemn, without the pain expressed in Mediæval crucifixes, and like so many early figures of the sort was probably vested and crowned.

A sudden inspiration took hold of the ruined man. He fell on his knees, stretched his hands towards the shining form, and cried, "Lord Jesus Christ! the hope of the whole earth, the only succour of all who are cast down, the sure confidence of those that look to Thee! All on whom I could lean have failed me. I have none on earth on whom I can call. Do Thou, Lord, be surety for me, though I am unworthy to ask it." Then filled with confidence he rose from his knees, and ran to the house of Abram, and bursting in on him said, "Be of good cheer, I have found a Surety very great and noble and mighty. Trust thy money, He will keep it safe."

Abram answered, "Let the man come, and sign the deed and see the money paid over."

"Nay, my brother," said Theodore; "come thou with me. I have hurried in thus to bring thee to him."

Then Abram went with Theodore, who led him to the Copper-Market, and bade him be seated, and then raising his finger, he pointed to the sacred form hanging on the cross, and, full of confidence, said to the Hebrew, "There, friend, thou could'st not have a better security than the Lord of heaven and earth. I have besought Him to stand for me, and I know He is so good that He will not deny me."

The Jew was perplexed. He said nothing for a moment or two, and then, wondering at the man's faith, answered, "Friend, dost thou not know the difference between the faith of a Christian and of a Hebrew? How can'st thou ask me to accept as thy surety, One whom thou believest my people to have rejected and crucified? However, I will trust thee, for thou art a God-fearing and an honest man, and I will risk my money."

So they twain returned to the Jew's quarters, and Abram counted out fifty pounds of gold, in our money about £2,400. He tied the money up in bags, and bade his servants bear it after Theodore. And Abram and the glad merchant came to the Copper-Market, and then the Jew ordered that the money bags should be set down under the Tetrastyle where was the great crucifix. Then said the Hebrew usurer, "See, Theodore, I make over to thee the loan here before thy God." And there, in the face of the great image of his Saviour, Theodore received the loan, and swore to deal faithfully by the Jew, and to restore the money to him with usury.

After this, the merchant bought a cargo for his vessel, and hired sailors, and set sail for Syria. He put into port at Tyre and Sidon, and traded with his goods, and bought in place of them many rich Oriental stuffs, with spices and gums, and when his ship was well laden, he sailed for Constantinople.

But again misfortune befell him. A storm arose, and the sailors were constrained to throw the bales of silk, and bags of costly gums, and vessels of Oriental chasing into the greedy waves. But as the ship began to fill, they were obliged to get into the boat and escape to land. The ship keeled over and drifted into shallow water. When the storm abated they got to her, succeeded in floating her, and made the best of their way in the battered ship to Constantinople, thankful that they had preserved their lives. But Theodore was in sad distress, chiefly because he had lost Abram's money. "How shall I dare to face the man who dealt so generously by me?" he said to himself. "What shall I say, when he reproaches me? What answer can I make to my Surety for having lost the money entrusted to me?"

Now when Abram heard that Theodore had arrived in Constantinople in his wrecked vessel with the loss of all his cargo, he went to him at once, and found the man prostrate in his chamber, the pavement wet with his tears of shame and disappointment. Abram laid his hand gently on his shoulder, and said, in a kind voice, "Rise, my brother, do not be downcast; give glory to God who rules all things as He wills, and follow me home. God will order all for the best."

Then the merchant rose, and followed the Jew, but he would not lift his eyes from the ground, for he was ashamed to look him in the face. Abram was troubled at the distress of his friend, and he said to him, as he shut the door of his house, "Let not thy heart be broken with overmuch grief, dearest friend, for it is the mark of a wise man to bear all things with firm mind. See! I am ready again to lend thee fifty pounds of gold, and may better fortune attend thee this time. I trust that our God will bless the money and multiply it, so that in the end we shall lose nothing by our former misadventure."

"Then," said Theodore, "Christ shall again stand security for me. Bring the money to the Tetrastyle."

Therefore again the bags of gold were brought before the cross, and when they had then been made over to the merchant, Abram said, "Accept, Master Theodore, this sum of fifty pounds of gold, paid over to thee before thy Surety, and go in peace. And may the Lord God prosper thee on thy journey, and make plain the way before thee. And remember, that before this thy Surety thou art bound to me for a hundred pounds of gold."

Having thus spoken, Abram returned home. Theodore repaired and reloaded his ship, engaged mariners and made ready to sail. But on the day that he was about to depart, he went into the Copper-Market, and kneeling down, with his face towards the cross, he prayed the Lord to be his companion and captain, and to guide him on his journey, and bring him safe through all perils with his goods back to Byzantium once more.

Then he went on to the house of Abram to bid him farewell. And the Jew said to him, "Keep thyself safe, brother, and beware now of trusting thy ship to the sea at the time of equinoctial gales. Thou hast twice experienced the risk, run not into it again. Winter at the place whither thou goest, and that I may know how thou farest, if thou hast the opportunity, send me some of the money by a sure hand. Then there is less chance of total ruin, for if one portion fails, the other is likely to be secure."

Theodore approved of this advice, and promised to follow it; so then the Jew and the Christian parted with much affection and mutual respect, for each knew the other to be a good and true man, fearing God, and seeking to do that which is right. This time Theodore turned his ship's head towards the West, intending to carry his wares to the markets of Spain. He passed safely through the Straits of Hercules, and sailed North. Then a succession of steady strong breezes blew from the South and swept him on so that he could not get into harbour till he reached Britain. He anchored in a bay on the rugged Cornish coast, in the very emporium of tin and lead, in the Cassiterides famed of old for supplying ore precious in the manufacture of bronze. He readily disposed of all his merchandise, and bought as much tin and lead as his ship would hold. His goods had sold so well, and tin and lead were so cheap that he found he had fifty pounds in gold in addition to the cargo.

The voyage back from Britain to Byzantium was long and dangerous, and Theodore was uneasy. He found no other ships from Constantinople where he was, and no means presented themselves for sending back the money in part, as he had promised. He was a conscientious man, and he wished to keep his word.

He set sail from Cornwall before the summer was over, passed safely through the straits into the Mediterranean, but saw no chance of reaching Constantinople before winter. He would not again risk his vessel in the gales of the equinox, and he resolved to winter in Sicily. He arrived too late in the year to be able to send a message and the money to Abram. His promise troubled him, and he cast about in his mind how to keep his word.

At last, in the simple faith which coloured the whole life of the man, he made a very solid wooden box and tarred it well internally and externally. Then he inclosed in it the fifty pounds of gold he had made by his goods in Britain over and above his lading of lead and tin, and with the money he put a letter, couched in these terms:

"In the name of my heir and God, my Lord and Saviour Jesus Christ who is also my Surety for a large sum of money, I, Theodore, humbly address my master Abram, who, with God, is my benefactor and creditor.

"I would have thee know, Master Abram, that we all, by the mercy of God, are in good health. God has verily prospered us well and brought our merchandise to a good market. And now, see! I send thee fifty pounds of gold, which I commit to the care of my Surety, and He will convey the money safely to thy hands. Receive it from me and do not forget us. Farewell."

Then he fastened up the box, and raised his eyes to heaven, and prayed to God, saying: "O Lord Jesus Christ, Mediator between God and Man, Who dwellest in Heaven, but hast respect unto the lowly; hear the voice of thy servant this day; because Thou hast proved Thyself to me a good and kind Surety, I trust to Thee to return to my benefactor and creditor, Abram, the money I promised to send him. Trusting in Thee, Lord, I commit this little box to the sea!"

So saying he flung the case containing the gold and the letter into the waves; and standing on a cliff watched it floating on the waters, rising and falling on the glittering wavelets, gradually drifting further and further out to sea, till it was lost to his sight, and then, nothing doubting but that the Lord Christ would look after the little box and guide it over the waste of waters to its proper destination, he went back to his lodging, and told the ship pilot what he had done. The sailor remained silent wondering in his mind at the great faith of his master. Then his rough heart softened, and he knelt down and blessed and praised God.

That night Theodore had a dream, and in the morning he told it to the pilot.

"I thought," said he, "that I was back in Byzantium, and standing in the Copper-Market before the great cross with Christ on it. And I fancied in my dream that Abram was at my side. And I looked, and saw him hold up his hands, and receive the box in them, and the great figure of Christ said, 'See, Abram, I give thee what Theodore committed to my trust.' And, thereupon, I awoke trembling. So now I am quite satisfied that the gold is in safe keeping, and will infallibly reach its destination."

The summer passed, the storms of autumn had swept over the grey sea, and torn away from the trees the last russet leaves; winter had set in; yet Abram had received no news of Theodore.

He did not doubt the good faith of his friend, but he began to fear that ill-luck attended him. He had risked a large sum, and would feel the loss severely should this cargo be lost like the former one. He talked the matter over with his steward, and considered it from every imaginable point of view. His anxiety took him constantly to the shore to watch the ships that arrived, hoping to hear news by some of them, and to recover part of his money. He hardly expected the return of Theodore after the injunctions he had given him not to risk his vessel in a stormy season.

One day he was walking with his steward by the sea-side, when the waves were more boisterous than usual. Not a ship was visible. All were in winter quarters. Abram drew off his sandals, and began to wash his feet in the sea water. Whilst so doing he observed something floating at a little distance. With the assistance of his steward he fished out a box black with tar, firmly fastened up, like a solid cube of wood. Moved by curiosity he carried the box home, and succeeded with a little difficulty in forcing it open. Inside he found a letter, not directed, but marked with three crosses, and a bag of gold. It need hardly be said that this was the box Theodore had entrusted to Christ, and his Surety had fulfilled His trust and conveyed it to the hands of the creditor.

Next spring Theodore returned to Constantinople in safety. As soon as he had disembarked, he hastened to the house of Abram to tell him the results of his voyage.

The Jewish usurer, wishing to prove him, feigned not to understand, when Theodore related how he had sent him fifty pounds of gold, and made as though he had not received the money. But the merchant was full of confidence, and he said, "I cannot understand this, brother, for I enclosed the money in a box along with a letter, and committed it to the custody of my Saviour Christ, Who has acted as Surety for me unworthy. But as thou sayest that thou hast not received it, come with me, and let us go together before the crucifix, and say before it that thou hast not had the money conveyed to thee, and then I will believe thy word."

Abram promised to accompany his friend, and rising from their seats, they went together to the Copper-Market. And when they came to the Tetrastyle, Theodore raised his hands to the Crucified, and said, "My Saviour and Surety, didst Thou not restore the gold to Abram that I entrusted to Thee for that purpose?"

There was something so wonderful, so beautiful, in the man's faith, that Abram was overpowered; and withal there was the evidence that it was not misplaced so clear to the Jew, that the light of conviction like a dazzling sunbeam darted into his soul, and Theodore saw the Hebrew usurer fall prostrate on the pavement, half fainting with the emotion which oppressed him.

Theodore ran and fetched water in his hands and sprinkled his face, and brought the usurer round. And Abram said, "As God liveth, my friend, I will not enter into my house till I have taken thy Lord and Surety for my Master." A crowd began to gather, and it was bruited abroad that the Jewish usurer sought baptism. And when the story reached the ears of the Emperor Heraclius, he glorified God. So Abram was put under instruction, and was baptised by the patriarch Sergius.[11]

[11] Sergius was patriarch of Constantinople between 610 and 638. He embraced the Monothelite heresy.

And after seven days a solemn procession was instituted through the streets of Constantinople to the Copper-Market, in which walked the emperor and the patriarch, and all the clergy of the city; and the box which had contained the money was conveyed by them to the Tetrastyle and laid up, along with the gold and the letter before the image, to be a memorial of what had taken place to all generations. And thenceforth the crucifix received the common appellation of Antiphonetos, or the Surety.

As for the tin and lead with which the vessel of Theodore was freighted, it sold for a great price, so that both he and Abram realised a large sum by the transaction. But neither would keep to himself any portion of it, but gave it all to the Church of S. Sophia, and therewith a part of the sanctuary was overlaid with silver. Then Theodore and his wife, with mutual consent, gave up the world and retired into monastic institutions.

Abram afterwards built and endowed an oratory near the Tetrastyle, and Sergius ordained him priest and his two sons deacons.

Thus ends this strange and very beautiful story, which I have merely condensed from the somewhat prolix narrative of the Byzantine preacher. The reader will probably agree with me that if sermons in the 19th century were as entertaining as this of the 10th, fewer people would be found to go to sleep during their delivery.

I have told the tale as related by the preacher. But there are reasons which awaken suspicion that he somewhat erred as to his dates; but that, nevertheless the story is really not without a foundation of fact. Towards the close of the oration the preacher points to the ambone, and the thusiasterion, and bids his hearers remark how they are overlaid with silver, and this he says was the silver that Abram, the wealthy Jewish usurer, and Theodore, the merchant, gave to the Church of S. Sophia.

Now it happens that we have got a contemporary record of this overlaying of the sanctuary with silver; we know from the pen of Procopius of Gaza that it took place in the reign of Justinian in A.D. 537.[12]

[12] Fabricius, Bibl. Græca, Ed. Harles, T.X. p. 124, 125.

This was preparatory to the dedication of the great Church, when the Emperor and the wealthy citizens of Byzantium were lavishly contributing to the adornment of the glorious building.

We can quite understand how that the new convert and the grateful merchant were carried away by the current of the general enthusiasm, and gave all their silver to the plating of the sanctuary of the new Church. Procopius tells us that forty thousand pounds of silver were spent in this work. Not all of this, however, could have been given by Abram and Theodore.

If this then were the date of the conversion of Abram, for Heraclius we must read Justinian, and for Sergius we must substitute Mennas. As the sermon was not preached till four hundred years after, the error can be accounted for, one imperial benefactor of the Church was mistaken for another.

Now about the time of Justinian, we know from other sources that there was a converted Jew named Abram who founded and built a church and monastery in Constantinople, and which in after times was known as the Abramite Monastery. We are told this by John Moschus. We can not fix the exact date of the foundation, Moschus heard about A.D. 600 from the abbot John Rutilus, who had heard it from Stephen the Moabite, that the Monastery of the Abramites had been constructed by Abram who afterwards was raised to the metropolitan See of Ephesus. We may put then the foundation of the monastery at about A.D. 540.

Now Abram of Ephesus succeeded Procopius who was bishop in 560; and his successor was Rufinus in 597. The date of the elevation of Abram to the metropolitan throne of Ephesus is not known exactly, but it was probably about 565.

There is, of course, much conjecture in thus identifying the usurer Abram with Abram, Bishop of Ephesus; but there is certainly a probability that they were identical; and if so, then one more pretty story of the good man survives. After having built the monastery in Constantinople, Moschus tells us that Abram went to Jerusalem, the home to which a Jewish heart naturally turns, and there he set to work to erect another monastery. Now there was among the workmen engaged on the building a mason who ate but sparingly, conversed with none, but worked diligently, and prayed much in his hours of relaxation from labour.

Abram became interested in the man, and called him to him, and learned from him his story. It was this. The mason had been a monk in the Theodorian Monastery along with his brother. The brother weary of the life, had left and fallen into grave moral disorders. Then this one now acting as mason had gone after him, laid aside his cowl and undertaken the same daily toil as the erring brother, that he might be with him, waiting his time when by means of advice or example he might draw the young man from his life of sin. But though he had laid aside the outward emblems of his monastic profession, he kept the rule of life as closely as he was able, cultivating prayer and silence and fasting. Then Abram deeply moved, said to the monk-mason: "God will look on thy fraternal charity; be of good courage, He will give thee thy brother at thy petition."

VII. — SOPHIE APITZSCH

"SOME are born great," said Malvolio, strutting in yellow stockings, cross-gartered, before Olivia, "some achieve greatness," and with a smile, "some have greatness thrust upon them."

Of the latter was Sophie Sabine Apitzsch. She was not born great, she was the daughter of an armourer. She hardly can be said to have achieved greatness, though she did attain to notoriety; what greatness she had was thrust on her, not altogether reluctant to receive it. But the greatness was not much, and was of an ambiguous description. She was treated for a while as a prince in disguise, and then became the theme of an opera, of a drama, and of a novel. For a hundred years her top-boots were preserved as historical relics in the archives of the House of Saxony, till in 1813 a Cossack of the Russian army passing through Augustenburg, saw, desired, tried on, and marched off with them; and her boots entered Paris with the Allies.

About five-and-twenty miles from Dresden lived in 1714 a couple of landed proprietors, the one called Volkmar, and the other von Günther, who fumed with fiery hostility against each other, and the cause of disagreement was, that the latter wrote himself von Günther. Now, to get a *von* before the name makes a great deal of difference: it purifies, nay, it alters the colour of the blood, turning it from red to blue. No one in Germany can prefix *von* to his name as any one in England can append Esq. to his. He must receive authorisation by diploma of nobility from his sovereign.

George von Günther had been, not long before, plain George Günther, but in 1712 he had obtained from the Emperor Charles VI. a patent of nobility, or gentility, they are the same abroad, and the motive that moved his sacred apostolic majesty to grant the patent was—as set forth therein—that an ancestor of George Günther of the same name "had sat down to table with the elector John George II. of Saxony;" and it was inconceivable that a mere citizen could have been suffered to do this, unless there were some nobility in him. George von Günther possessed an estate which was a manor, a knight's fee, at Jägerhof, and he was moreover upper Forester and Master of the Fisheries to the King-elector of Saxony, and Sheriff of Chemnitz and Frankenberg. He managed to marry his daughters to men blessed with *von* before their names, one to von Bretschneider, Privy- Councillor of War, the other to a Major von Wöllner.

Now, all this was gall and wormwood to Councillor-of-Agriculture, Daniel Volkmar, who lived on his paternal acres at Hetzdorf, of which he was hereditary chief magistrate by virtue of his lordship of the acres. This man had made vain efforts to be ennobled. He could not find that any ancestor of his had sat at table with an elector; and, perhaps, he could not scrape together sufficient money to induce his sacred apostolic majesty to overlook this defect. As he could not get his diploma, he sought how he might injure his more fortunate neighbour, and this he did by spying out his acts, watching for neglect of his duties to the fishes or the game, and reporting him anonymously to head-quarters. Günther knew well enough who it was that sought to injure him, and, as Volkmar believed, had invited some of the gamekeepers to shoot him; accordingly, Volkmar never rode or walked in the neighbourhood of the royal forests and fish-ponds unarmed, and without servants carrying loaded muskets.

One day a brother magistrate, Pöckel by name, came over to see him about a matter that puzzled him. There had appeared in the district under his jurisdiction a young man, tall, well-built, handsome, but slightly small-pox-pitted, who had been arrested by the police for blowing a hunting-horn. Now ignoble lips might not touch a hunting-horn, and for any other than breath that issued out of noble lungs to sound a note on such a horn was against the laws.

"Oh," said Volkmar, "if he has done this, and is not a gentleman—lock him up. What is his name?"

"He calls himself Karl Marbitz."

"But I, even I, may not blow a blast on a horn—that scoundrel Günther may. Deal with the fellow Marbitz with the utmost severity."

"But—suppose he may have the necessary qualification?"

"How can he without a von before his name?"

"Suppose he be a nobleman, or something even higher, in disguise?"

"What, in disguise? Travelling incognito? Our Crown Prince is not at Dresden."[13]

[13] Augustus the Strong was King of Poland and Elector of Saxony.

"Exactly. All kinds of rumours are afloat concerning this young man, who is, indeed, about the Crown Prince's age; he has been lodging with a baker at Aue, and there blowing the horn."

"I'll go with you and see him. I will stand bail for him. Let him come to me. Hah-hah! George von Günther, hah-hah!"

So Volkmar, already more than half disposed to believe that the horn-blower was a prince in disguise, rode over to the place where he was in confinement, saw him, and lost what little doubt he had. The upright carriage, the aristocratic cast of features, the stand-off manners, all betokened the purest of blue blood—all were glimmerings of that halo which surrounds sovereignty.

The Crown Prince of Saxony was away—it was alleged, in France—making the grand tour, but, was it not more likely that he was going the round of the duchy of Saxony, inquiring into the wants and wrongs of the people? If so, who could better assist him to the knowledge of these things, than he, Volkmar, and who could better open his eyes to the delinquencies of high-placed, high-salaried officials—notably of the fisheries and forests?

"There is one thing shakes my faith," said Pöckel: "our Crown Prince is not small-pox marked."

"That is nothing," answered Volkmar eagerly. "His Serenity has caught the infection in making his studies among the people."

"And then—he is so shabbily dressed."

"That is nothing—it is the perfection of disguise."

Volkmar carried off the young man to his house, and showed him the greatest respect, insisted on his sitting in the carriage facing the horses, and would on no account take a place at his side, but seated himself deferentially opposite him.

On reaching Hetzdorf, Volkmar introduced his wife and his daughter Joanna to the distinguished prince, who behaved to them very graciously, and with the most courtly air expressed himself charmed with the room prepared for him.

Dinner was served, and politics were discussed; the reserve with which the guest treated such subjects, the caution with which he expressed an opinion, served to deepen in Volkmar's mind the conviction that he had caught the Crown Prince travelling incog. After the servants had withdrawn, and when a good deal of wine—the best in the cellar—had been drunk, the host said confidentially in a whisper, "I see clearly enough what you are."

"Indeed," answered the guest, "I can tell you what I am—by trade an armourer."

"Ah, ha! but by birth—what?" said Volkmar, slyly, holding up his glass and winking over it.

"Well," answered the guest, "I will admit this—I am not what I appear."

"And may I further ask your—I mean you—where you are at home?"

"I am a child of Saxony," was the answer.

Afterwards, at the trial, the defendant insisted that this was exactly the reply made, whereas Volkmar asserted that the words were, "I am a child of the House of Saxony." But there can be no doubt that his imagination supplemented the actual words used with those he wished to hear.

"The small-pox has altered you since you left home," said Volkmar.

"Very likely. I have had the small-pox since I left my home."

Volkmar at once placed his house, his servants, his purse, at the disposal of his guest, and his offer was readily accepted.

It is now advisable to turn back and explain the situation, by relating the early history of this person, who passed under the name of Karl Marbitz, an armourer; but whom a good number of people suspected of being something other than what he gave himself out to be, though only Volkmar and Pöckel and one or two others supposed him to be the Crown Prince of Saxony.

Sophie Sabine Apitzsch was born at Lunzenau in Saxony in 1692, was well brought up, kept to school, and learned to write orthographically, and to have a fair general knowledge of history and geography. When she left school she was employed by her father in his trade, which was that of an armourer. She was tall and handsome, somewhat masculine—in after years a Cossack got into her boots—had the small-pox, which, however, only slightly disfigured her. In 1710 she had a suitor, a gamekeeper, Melchior Leonhart. But Sophie entertained a rooted dislike to marriage, and she kept her lover off for three years, till her father peremptorily ordered her to marry Melchior, and fixed the day for the wedding. Then Sophie one night got out of her own clothing, stepped into her father's best suit, and walked away in the garments of a man, and shortly afterwards appeared in Anspach under a feigned name, as a barber's assistant. Here she got into difficulties with the police, as she had no papers of legitimation, and to escape them, enlisted. She carried a musket for a month only, deserted, and resumed her vagabond life in civil attire, as a barber's assistant, and came to Leipzig, where she lodged at the Golden Cock. How she acquired the art, and how those liked it on whose faces she made her experiments with the razor, we are not told.

At the Golden Cock lodged an athletic lady of the name of Anna Franke, stout, muscular, and able to lift great weights with her teeth, and with a jerk throw them over her shoulders. Anna Franke gave daily exhibitions of her powers, and on the proceeds maintained herself and her daughter, a girl of seventeen. The stout and muscular lady also danced on a tight rope, which with her bounces acted like a taut bowstring, projecting the athlete high into the air.

The Fräulein Franke very speedily fell in love with the fine young barber, and proposed to her mother that Herr Karl should be taken into the concern, as he would be useful to stretch the ropes, and go round for coppers. Sophie was nothing loth to have her inn bill paid on these terms, but when finally the bouncing mother announced that her daughter's hand was at the disposal of Karl, then the situation became even more embarrassing than that at home from which Sophie had run away. The barber maintained her place as long as she could, but at last, when the endearments of the daughter became oppressive, and the urgency of the mother for speedy nuptials became vexatious, she pretended that the father, who was represented as a well-to-do citizen of Hamburg, must first be consulted. On this plea Sophie borrowed of Mother Franke the requisite money for her journey and departed, promising to return in a few weeks. Instead of fulfilling her promise, Sophie wrote to ask for a further advance of money, and when this was refused, disappeared altogether from the knowledge of the athlete and her daughter.

On this second flight from marriage, Sophie Apitzsch met with an armourer named Karl Marbitz, and by some means or other contrived to get possession of his pass, leaving him instead a paper of legitimation made out under the name of Karl Gottfried, which old Mother Franke had induced the police to grant to the young barber who was engaged to marry her daughter.

In June 1714, under the name of Marbitz, Sophie appeared among the Erz-Gebirge, the chain of mountains that separate Saxony from Bohemia, and begged her way from place to place, pretending to be a schoolmaster out of employ. After rambling about for some time, she took up her quarters with a baker at Elterlein. Here it was that for the first time a suspicion was aroused that she was a person of greater consequence than she gave out. The rumour reached the nearest magistrate that there was a mysterious stranger there who wore a ribbon and star of some order, and he at once went to the place to make inquiries, but found that Sophie had neither ribbon nor order, and that her papers declared in proper form who and what she was. At this time she fell ill at the baker's house, and the man, perhaps moved by the reports abroad concerning her, was ready to advance her money to the amount of £6 or £7. When recovered, she left the village where she had been ill, and went to another one, where she took up her abode with another baker, named Fischer, whom she helped in his trade, or went about practising upon the huntsman's horn.

This amusement it was which brought her into trouble. Possibly she may not have known that the horn was a reserved instrument that might not be played by the ignoble.

At the time that Volkmar took her out of the lockup, and carried her off to his mansion in his carriage, she was absolutely without money, in threadbare black coat, stockings ill darned, and her hair very much in want of powder.

Hitherto her associates had been of the lowest classes; she had been superior to them in education, in morals, and in character, and had to some extent imposed on them. They acknowledged in her an undefined dignity and quiet reserve, with unquestioned superiority in attainments and general tone of mind, and this they attributed to her belonging to a vastly higher class in society.

Now, all at once she was translated into another condition of life, one in which she had never moved before; but she did not lose her head; she maintained the same caution and reserve in it, and never once exposed her ignorance so as to arouse suspicion that she was not what people insisted on believing her to be. She was sufficiently shrewd never by word to compromise herself, and afterwards, when brought to trial, she insisted that she had not once asserted that she was other than Karl Marbitz the armourer. Others had imagined she was a prince, but she had not encouraged them in their delusion by as much as a word. That, no doubt, was true, but she accepted the honours offered and presents made her under this erroneous impression, without an attempt to open the eyes of the deluded to their own folly.

Perhaps this was more than could be expected of her. "Foolery," said the clown in "Twelfth Night," "does walk about the orb, like the sun; it shines everywhere"—and what are fools but the natural prey of the clever?

Sophie had been ill, reduced to abject poverty, was in need of good food, new clothes, and shelter; all were offered, even forced upon her. Was she called upon to reject them? She thought not.

Now that Volkmar had a supposed prince under his roof he threw open his house to the neighbourhood, and invited every gentleman he knew—except the von Günthers. He provided the prince with a coat of scarlet cloth frogged and laced with gold, with a new hat, gave him a horse, filled his purse, and provided him with those identical boots in which a century later a Cossack marched into Paris.

She was addressed by her host and hostess as "Your Highness," and "Your Serenity," and they sought to kiss her hand, but she waived away these exhibitions of servility, saying, "Let be—we will regard each other as on a common level." Once Volkmar said slyly to her, "What would your august father say if he knew you were here?"

"He would be surprised," was all the answer that could be drawn from her. One day the newspaper contained information of the Crown Prince's doings in Paris with his tutor and attendants. Volkmar pointed it out to her with a twinkle of the eye, saying, "Do not suppose I am to be hoodwinked by such attempts to deceive the public as that."

In the mornings when the pseudo prince left the bedroom, outside the door stood Herr Volkmar, cap in hand, bowing. As he offered her a pinch of snuff from a gold *tabatière* one day, he saw her eyes rest on it; he at once said, "This belonged formerly to the Königsmark."

"Then," she replied, "it will have the double initials on it. 'A' for Aurora."

Now, argued Volkmar, how was it likely that his guest should know the scandalous story of Augustus I. and the fair Aurora of Königsmark, mother of the famous French marshal, unless he had belonged to the royal family of Saxony?[14] He left out of account that Court scandal is talked about everywhere, and is in the mouths of all. Then he presented her with the snuff-box. Next he purchased for her a set of silver plate for her cover, and ordered a ribbon and a star of diamonds, because it became one of such distinguished rank not to appear without a decoration! As the girl said afterwards at her trial, she had but to hint a desire for anything, and it was granted her at once. Her host somewhat bored her with political disquisitions; he was desirous of impressing on his illustrious guest what a political genius he was, and in his own mind had resolved to become prime minister of Saxony in the place of the fallen Beichlingen, who was said to have made so much money out of the State that he could buy a principality, and who, indeed, struck a medal with his arms on it surmounted by a princely crown.

[14] Aurora v. Königsmark went out of favour in 1698—probably then sold the gold snuff-box. She died in 1728.

But Volkmar's ambition went further. As already stated he had a daughter—the modest Joanna; what a splendid opportunity was in the hands of the scheming parents! If the young prince formed an attachment for Joanna, surely he might get the emperor to elevate her by diploma to the rank of a princess, and thus Volkmar would see his Joanna Queen of Poland and Electress of Saxony. He and Frau Volkmar were far too good people to scheme to get their daughter such a place as the old Königsmark had occupied with the reigning sovereign. Besides, Königsmark had been merely created a countess, and who would crave to be a countess when she might be Queen? and a favourite, when, by playing her cards well, she might become a legitimate wife?

So the old couple threw Joanna at the head of their guest, and did their utmost to entangle him. In the meantime the von Günthers were flaming with envy and rage. They no more doubted that the Volkmars had got the Crown Prince living with them, than did the Volkmars themselves. The whole neighbourhood flowed to the entertainments given in his honour at Hetzdorf; only the von Günthers were shut out. But von Günther met the mysterious stranger at one or two of the return festivities given by the gentry who had been entertained at Hetzdorf, and he seized on one of these occasions boldly to invite his Highness to pay him also a visit at his "little place;" and what was more than he expected, the offer was accepted.

In fact, the Apitzsch who had twice run away from matrimony, was becoming embarrassed again by the tenderness of Joanna and the ambition of the parents.

The dismay of the Volkmars passes description when their guest informed them he was going to pay a visit to the hated rivals.

Sophie was fetched away in the von Günther carriage, and by servants put into new liveries for the occasion, and was received and entertained with the best at Jägerhof. Here, also, presents were made; among others a silver cover for table was given her by the daughter of her host, who had married a major, and who hoped, in return, to see her husband advanced to be a general.

She was taken to see the royal castle of Augustusburg, and here a little difference of testimony occurs as to the observation she made in the chapel, which was found to be without an organ. At her trial it was asserted that she had said, "I must order an organ," but she positively swore she had said, "An organ ought to be provided." She was taken also to the mansion of the Duke of Holstein at Weisenburg, where she purchased one of his horses—that is to say, agreed to take it, and let her hosts find the money.

The visit to the von Günthers did not last ten days, and then she was back again with the Volkmars, to their exuberant delight. Why she remained so short a time at Jägerhof does not appear. Possibly she may have been there more in fear of detection than at Hetzdorf. Now that the Volkmars had her back they would not let her out of their sight. They gave her two servants in livery to attend her; they assured her that her absence had so affected Joanna that the girl had done nothing but weep, and had refused to eat. They began to press in their daughter's interest for a declaration of intentions, and that negotiations with the Emperor should be opened that a title of princess of the Holy Roman Empire might be obtained for her as preliminary to the nuptials.

Sophie Apitzsch saw that she must again make a bolt to escape the marriage ring, and she looked about for an opportunity. But there was no evading the watch of the Volkmars, who were alarmed lest their guest should again go to the hated von Günthers.

Well would it have been for the Volkmars had they kept the "prince" under less close surveillance, and allowed him to succeed in his attempts to get away. It would have been to their advantage in many ways.

A fortnight or three weeks passed, and the horse bought of the Duke of Holstein had not been sent In fact the Duke, when the matter was communicated to him, was puzzled. He knew that the Crown Prince was in Paris, and could not have visited his stables, and promised to purchase his horse. So he instituted inquiries before he consented to part with the horse, and at once the bubble burst. Police arrived at Hetzdorf to arrest the pretender, and convey her to Augustusburg, where she was imprisoned, till her trial. This was in February, 1715. In her prison she had an apoplectic stroke, but recovered. Sentence was pronounced against her by the court at Leipzig in 1716, that she should be publicly whipped out of the country. That is to say, sent from town to town, and whipped in the market-place of each, till she was sent over the frontier. In consideration of her having had a stroke, the king commuted the sentence to whipping in private, and imprisonment at his majesty's pleasure.

She does not seem to have been harshly treated by the gaoler of Waldheim, the prison to which she was sent. She was given her own room, she dined at the table of the gaoler, continued to wear male clothes, and was cheerful, obedient, and contented. In 1717 both she and her father appealed to the king for further relaxation of her sentence, but this was refused. The prison authorities gave her the best testimony for good conduct whilst in their hands.

In the same year, 1717, the unfortunate Volkmar made a claim for the scarlet coat—which he said the moths were likely to eat unless placed on some one's back—the gold snuff-box, the silver spoons, dishes, forks, the horse, the watch, and various other things he had given Sophie, being induced to do so by false representations. The horse as well as the plate, the star, the snuff-box, the coat and the boots had all been requisitioned as evidence before her trial. The question was a hard one to solve, whether Herr Volkmar could recover presents, and it had to be transmitted from one court to another. An order of court dated January, 1722, required further evidence to be produced before purse, coat, boots, &c., could be returned to Volkmar—that is, *seven* years after they had been taken into the custody of the Court. The horse must have eaten more than his cost by this time, and the coat must have lost all value through moth-eating. The cost of proceedings was heavy, and Volkmar then withdrew from his attempt to recover the objects given to the false prince.

But already—long before, by decree of October 1717—Sophie Apitzsch had been liberated. She left prison in half male, half female costume, and in this dress took service with a baker at Waldheim; and we hear no more of her, whether she married, and when she died.

VIII. — PETER NIELSEN

ON the 29th day of April in the year 1465, died Henry Strangebjerg, bishop of Ribe in Denmark, after having occupied the See for just ten years. For some days before his decease public, official prayer had been made for his recovery by the Cathedral Chapter, but in their hearts the Canons were impatient for his departure. Not, be it understood, that the Bishop was an unworthy occupant of the See of Liafdag the Martyr—on the contrary, he had been a man of exemplary conduct; nor because he was harsh in his rule—on the contrary, he had been a lenient prelate. The reason why, when official prayer was made for his recovery, it was neutralised by private intercession for his removal, was solely this—his removal opened a prospect of advancement.

The Cathedral Chapter of Ribe consisted of fifteen Canons, and a Dean or Provost, all men of family, learning and morals. Before the doctors had shaken their heads over the sick bed of Henry Strangebjerg, it was known throughout Ribe that there would be four candidates for the vacant throne. It was, of course, impossible for more than one man to be elected; but as the election lay entirely and uncontrolledly in the hands of the Chapter, it was quite possible for a Canon to make a good thing out of an election without being himself elected. The bishops nominated to many benefices, and there existed then no law against pluralities. The newly chosen prelate, if he had a spark of gratitude, must reward those faithful men who had made him bishop.

At 4 p.m. on April 29th the breath left the body of Henry Strangebjerg. At 4.15 p.m. the Chapter were rubbing their hands and drawing sighs of relief. But Thomas Lange, the Dean, rubbed his hands and drew his sigh of relief ten minutes earlier, viz., at 4.5 p.m., for he stood by the bed of the dying bishop. At 3.25 p.m. Thomas Lange's nerves had received a great shock, for a flicker as of returning life had manifested itself in the sick man, and for a few minutes he really feared he might recover. At 4.10 p.m. Hartwig Juel, the Archdeacon, who had been standing outside the bishop's door, was seen running down the corridor with a flush in his cheeks. Through the keyhole he had heard the Dean exclaim: "Thank God!" and when he heard that pious ejaculation, he knew that all dread of the Bishop's restoration was over. It was not till so late as 4.20 p.m. that Olaf Petersen knew it. Olaf was kneeling in the Cathedral, in the Chapel of St. Lambert, the yellow chapel as it was called, absorbed in devotion, consequently the news did not reach him till five minutes after the Chapter, twenty minutes after the vacation of the See. Olaf Petersen was a very holy man; he was earnest and sincere. He was, above everything, desirous of the welfare of the Church and the advancement of religion. He was ascetic, denying himself in food, sleep and clothing, and was profuse in his alms and in his devotions. He saw the worldliness, the self-seeking, the greed of gain and honours that possessed his fellows, and he was convinced that one thing was necessary for the salvation of Christianity in Ribe, and that one thing was his own election to the See.

The other candidates were moved by selfish interests. He cared only for true religion. Providence would do a manifest injustice if it did not take cognizance of his integrity and interfere to give him the mitre. He was resolved to use no unworthy means to secure it. He would make no promises, offer no bribes—that is, to his fellow Canons, but he promised a silver candlestick to St. Lambert, and bribed St. Gertrude to intervene with the assurance of a pilgrimage to her shrine.

We have mentioned only three of the candidates. The fourth was Jep Mundelstrup, an old and amiable man, who had not thrust himself forward, but had been put forward by his friends, who considered him sufficiently malleable to be moulded to their purposes.

Jep was, as has been said, old; he was so old that it was thought (and hoped), if chosen, his tenure of office would be but brief. Four or five years—under favourable circumstances, such as a changeable winter, a raw spring with east winds—he might drop off even sooner, and leave the mitre free for another scramble.

The Kings of Denmark no longer nominated to the Sees, sent no *congé d'élire* to the Chapter. They did not even appoint to the Canonries. Consequently the Canons had everything pretty much their own way, and had only two things to consider, to guide their determination—the good of the Church and their own petty interests. The expression "good of the Church" demands comment. "The good of the Church" was the motive, the only recognised motive, on which the Chapter were supposed to act. Practically, however, it was non-existent as a motive. It was a mere figure of speech used to cloak selfish ambition.

From this sweeping characterisation we must, however, exclude Olaf Petersen, who did indeed regard pre-eminently the good of the Church, but then that good was, in his mind, inextricably involved with his own fortunes. He was the man to make religion a living reality. He was the man to bring the Church back to primitive purity. He could not blind his eyes to the fact that not one of the Canons beside himself cared a farthing for spiritual matters; therefore he desired the mitre for his own brows.

The conclave at which the election was to be made was fixed for the afternoon of the day on which Henry Strangebjerg was to be buried, and the burial was appointed to take place as soon as was consistent with decency.

The whole of the time between the death and the funeral was taken up by the Canons with hurrying to and from each other's residences, canvassing for votes.

Olaf Petersen alone refrained from canvassing, he spent his whole time in fasting and prayer, so anxious was he for the welfare of the Church and the advancement of true religion.

At length—Boom! Boom! Boom! The great bell of the minster tower summoned the Chapter to the hall of conclave. Every Canon was in his place, fifteen Canons and the provost, sixteen in all. It was certain that the provost, although chairman, would claim his right to vote, and exercise it, voting for himself. It was ruled that all voting should be open, for two reasons—that the successful candidate might know who had given him their shoulders on which to mount, and so reward these shoulders by laying many benefices upon them, and secondly, that he might know who had been his adversaries, and so might exclude them from preferments. Every one believed he would be on the winning side, no one supposed the other alternative possible.

The candidates, as already intimated, were four. Thomas Lange, the Dean, who belonged to a good, though not wealthy family. He had been in business before taking orders, and brought with him into the

Church practical shrewdness and business habits. He had husbanded well the resources of the Chapter, and had even enlarged its revenue by the purchase of three farms and a manor.

The second candidate, Hartwig Juel, was a member of a powerful noble family. His brother was at Court and highly regarded by King Christian. His election would gratify the king. Hartwig Juel was Archdeacon.

The third candidate was the good old Jep Mundelstrup; and the fourth was the representative of the ascetic, religious party, which was also the party of reform, Olaf Petersen.

The Dean was, naturally, chairman. Before taking the chair he announced his intention of voting. The four candidates were proposed, and the votes taken.

The Dean numbered 4.

Hartwig Juel numbered 4.

Jep Mundelstrup numbered 4.

Olaf Petersen numbered 4.

Moreover, each candidate had voted for himself.

What was to be done? The Chapter sat silent, looking about them in each others' faces.

Then the venerable Jep Mundelstrup, assisted by those who sat by him, staggered to his feet, and leaning on his staff, he mumbled forth this address: "My reverend brothers, it was wholly without my desire and not in furtherance of any ambition of mine, that my name was put up as that of a candidate for the vacant mitre of the Holy See of Ribe. I am old and infirm. With the patriarch Jacob I may say, 'Few and evil have been the days of the years of my life.' and I am not worthy to receive so great an honour. Evil my days have been, because I have had only my Canonry and one sorry living to support me; and there are comforts I should desire in my old age which I cannot afford. My health is not sound. I shrink from the responsibilities and labours of a bishopric. If I withdraw my candidature, I feel confident that the successful candidate will not forget my infirmities, and the facility I have afforded for his election. I decline to stand, and at the same time, lest I should seem to pose in opposition to three of my excellent brethren, I decline also to vote." Then he sat down, amidst general applause.

Here was an unexpected simplification of matters. The Dean and Hartwig Juel cast kindly, even affectionate glances at those who had previously voted for Jep, Olaf Petersen looked up to heaven and prayed.

Again, the votes were taken, and again the chairman claimed his right to vote.

When taken they stood thus:

The Dean, 5.

Hartwig Juel, 5.

Olaf Petersen, 5.

What was to be done? Again the Chapter sat silent, rubbing their chins, and casting furtive glances at each other. The Chapter was adjourned to the same hour on the morrow. The intervening hours were spent in negociations between the several parties, and attempts made by the two first in combination to force Olaf Petersen to resign his candidature. But Olaf was too conscientious a man to do this. He felt that the salvation of souls depended on his staying the plague like Phinehas with his censer.

Boom! Boom! Boom! The Cathedral bell again summoned the conclave to the Chapter House.

Before proceeding to business the Dean, as chairman, addressed the electors. He was an eloquent man, and he set in moving words before them the solemnity of the duty imposed on them, the importance of considering only the welfare of the Church, and the responsibility that would weigh on them should they choose an unworthy prelate. He conjured them in tones vibrating with pathos, to put far from them all self-seeking thoughts, and to be guided only by conscience. Then he sat down. The votes were again taken. Jep Mundelstrup again shaking his head, and refusing to vote. When counted, they stood thus.

Thomas Lange, 5.

Hartwig Juel, 5.

Olaf Petersen, 5.

Then up started the Dean, very red in the face, and said, "Really this is preposterous! Are we to continue this farce? Some of the brethren must yield for the general good. I would cheerfully withdraw my candidature, but for one consideration. You all know that the temporal affairs of the See have fallen into confusion. Our late excellent prelate was not a man of business, and there has been alienation, and underletting, and racking out of church lands, which I have marked with anxiety, and which I am desirous to remedy. You all know that I have this one good quality, I am a business man, understand account keeping, and look sharp after the pecuniary interests of the Chapter lands. It is essential that the lands of the See should be attended to by some practical man like myself, therefore I do not withdraw from my candidature, but therefore only—"

Then up sprang Hartwig Juel, and said, "The very Reverend the Dean has well said, this farce must not continue. Some must yield if a bishop is to be elected. I would cheerfully withdraw from candidature but for one little matter. I hold in my hand a letter received this morning from my brother, who tells me that his most gracious majesty, King Christian, expressed himself to my brother in terms of hope that I should be elected. You, my reverend brothers, all know that we are living in a critical time when it is most necessary that a close relation, a cordial relation, should be maintained between the Church and the State. Therefore, in the political interests of the See, but only in these interests, I cannot withdraw my candidature."

Then all eyes turned on Olaf Petersen. His face was pale, his lips set. He stood up, and leaning forward said firmly, "The pecuniary and the political interests of the See are as nothing to me, its spiritual interests are supreme. Heaven is my witness, I have no personal ambition to wear the mitre. I know it will cause exhausting labour and terrible responsibilities, from which I shrink. Nevertheless, seeing as I do that this is a period in the history of the Church when self-seeking and corruption have penetrated her veins and are poisoning her life-blood, seeing as I do that unless there be a revival of religion, and an attempt at reform be made within the Church, there will ensue such a convulsion as will overthrow her, therefore, and only therefore do I feel that I can not withdraw from my candidature."

"Very well," said the Dean in a crusty tone. "There is nothing for it but for us to vote again. Now at least we have clear issues before us, the temporal, the political, and the spiritual interests of the Church." The votes were again taken, and stood thus.

The temporal interests, 5.

The political interests, 5.

The spiritual interests, 5.

Here was a dead lock. It was clear that parties were exactly divided, and that none would yield.

After a pause of ten minutes, Jep Mundelstrup was again helped to his feet. He looked round the Chapter with blinking eyes, and opened and shut his mouth several times before he came to speak. At last he said, in faltering tones, "My reverend brethren, it is clear to me that my resignation has complicated, rather than helped matters forward. Do not think I am about to renew my candidature, *that* I am not, but I am going to make a proposition to which I hope you will give attentive hearing. If we go on in this manner, we shall elect no one, and then his Majesty, whom God bless, will step in and nominate."

"Hear, hear!" from the adherents of Hartwig Juel.

"I do not for a moment pretend that the nominee of his Majesty would not prove an excellent bishop, but I do fear that a nomination by the crown would be the establishment of a dangerous precedent."

"Hear! hear!" from the adherents of Olaf Petersen.

"At the same time it must be borne in mind that the temporal welfare of the See ought to be put in the hands of some one conversant with the condition into which they have been allowed to lapse."

"Hear! hear!" from the adherents of Thomas Lange.

"I would suggest, as we none of us can agree, that we refer the decision to an umpire."

General commotion, and whispers, and looks of alarm.

"How are we to obtain one at once conversant with the condition of the diocese, and not a partizan?" asked the Dean.

"There is a wretched little village in the midst of the Roager Heath, cut off from communication with the world, in which lives a priest named Peter Nielsen on his cure, a man who is related to no one here, belongs, I believe, to no gentle family, and, therefore, would have no family interests one way or the other to bias him. He has the character of being a shrewd man of business, some of the estates of the Church are on the Roager Heath, and he knows how they have been treated, and I have always heard that he is a good preacher and an indefatigable parish priest. Let him be umpire. I can think of none other who would not be a partizan."

The proposition was so extraordinary and unexpected that the Chapter, at first, did not know what to think of it. Who was this Peter Nielsen? No one knew of him anything more than what Jep Mundelstrup had said, and he, it was believed, had drawn largely on his imagination for his facts. Indeed, he was the least known man among the diocesan clergy. It was disputed whether he was a good preacher. Who had heard him? no one. Was it true that he was not a gentleman by birth? No one knew to what family he belonged. In default of any other solution to the dead lock in which the Chapter stood, it was agreed by all that the selection of a bishop for Ribe should be left to Peter Nielsen of Roager.

That same day, indeed as soon after the dissolution of the meeting as was possible, one of the Canons mounted his horse, and rode away to the Roager Heath.

The village of Ro or Raa-ager, literally the rough or barren field, lay in the dead flat of sandy heath that occupies so large a portion of the centre and west coast of Jutland, and which goes by various names, as Randböll Heath and Varde Moor. In many places it is mere fen, where the water lies and stagnates. In others it is a dry waste of sand strewn with coarse grass and a few scant bushes. The village itself consisted of one street of cottages thatched with turf, and with walls built of the same, heather and grass sprouting from the interstices of the blocks. The church was little more dignified than the hovels. It was without tower and bell. Near the church was the parsonage.

The Canon descended from his cob; he had ridden faster than was his wont, and was hot. He drew his sleeve across his face and bald head, and then threw the bridle over the gate-post.

In the door of the parsonage stood a short, stout, rosy-faced, dark-eyed woman, with two little children pulling at her skirts. This was Maren Grubbe, the housekeeper of the pastor, at least that was her official designation. She had been many years at Roager with Peter Nielsen, and was believed to manage him as well as the cattle and pigs and poultry of the glebe. From behind her peered a shock-headed boy of about eight years with a very dirty face and cunning eyes.

The Canon stood and looked at the woman, then at the children, and the woman and children stood and looked at him.

"Is this the house of the priest, Peter Nielsen?" he asked.

"Certainly, do you want him?" inquired the housekeeper.

"I have come from Ribe to see him on diocesan business."

"Step inside," said the housekeeper curtly. "His reverence is not in the house at this moment, he is in the church saying his offices."

"That's lies!" shouted the dirty boy from behind. "Dada is in the pigstye setting a trap for the rats."

"Hold your tongue, Jens!" exclaimed the woman, giving the boy a cuff which knocked him over. Then to the Canon she said, "Take a seat and I will go to the church after him."

She went out with the two smaller children staggering at her skirts, tumbling, picking themselves up, going head over heels, crowing and squealing.

When she was outside the house, the dirty boy sat upright on the floor, winked at the Canon, crooked his fingers, and said, "Follow me, and I will show you Dada."

The bald-headed ecclesiastic rose, and guided by the boy went into a back room, through a small window in which he saw into the pig-styes, and there, without his coat, in a pair of stained and patched breeches, and a blue worsted night-cap, over ankles in filth, was the parish priest engaged in setting a rat-trap. Outside, in the yard, the pigs were enjoying their freedom. Leisurely round the corner came the housekeeper with the satellites. "There, Peers!" said she, "There is a reverend gentleman from the cathedral come after thee."

"Then," said the pastor, slowly rising, "do thou, Maren, keep out of sight, and especially be careful not to produce the brats. Their presence opens the door to misconstruction."

The Canon stole back to his seat, mopped his brow and head, and thought to himself that the Chapter had put the selection of a chief pastor into very queer hands. The nasty little boy began to giggle and snuffle simultaneously. "Have you seen Dada? Dada saying his prayers in there."

"Who are you?" asked the ecclesiastic stiffly of the child.

"I'm Jens," answered the boy.

"I know you are Jens, I heard your mother call you so. I presume that person is your mother."

"That is my mother, but Dada is not my dada."

"O, Jens, boy, Jens! Truth above all things. Magna est veritas et prævalebit." The Reverend Peter Nielsen entered, clean, in a cassock, and with a shovel hat on his head.

"The children whom you have seen," said Peter Nielsen, "are the nephews and nieces of my worthy housekeeper, Maria Grubbe. She is a charitable woman, and as her sister is very poor, and has a large family, my Maren, I mean my housekeeper, takes charge of some of the overflow."[15]

[15] In Norway, Denmark, Sweden, and Iceland, clerical celibacy was never enforced before the Reformation. Now and then a formal prohibition was issued by the bishops, but it was generally ignored. The clergy were married, openly and undisguisedly.

"It is a great burden to you," said the Canon.

Peter Nielsen shrugged his shoulders. "To clothe the naked and give food to the hungry are deeds of mercy."

"I quite understand, quite," said the Canon.

"I only mentioned it," continued the parish priest, "lest you should suppose—"

"I quite understand," said the Canon, interrupting him, with a bow and a benignant smile.

"And now," said Peter Nielsen, "I am at your service."

Thereupon the Canon unfolded to his astonished hearer the nature of his mission. The pastor sat listening attentively with his head bowed, and his hands planted on his knees. Then, when his visitor had done speaking, he thrust his left hand into his trouser pocket and produced a palmful of carraway seed. He put some into his mouth, and began to chew it; whereupon the whole room became scented with carraway.

"I am fond of this seed," said the priest composedly, whilst he turned over the grains in his hand with the five fingers of his right. "It is good for the stomach, and it clears the brain. So I understand that there are three parties?"

"Exactly, there is that of Olaf Petersen, a narrow, uncompromising man, very sharp on the morals of the clergy; there is also that of the Dean, Thomas Lange, an ambitious and scheming ecclesiastic; and there is lastly that of the Archdeacon Hartwig Juel, one of the most amiable men in the world."

"And you incline strongly to the latter?"

"I do—how could you discover that? Juel is not a man to forget a friend who has done him a favour."

"Now, see!" exclaimed Peter Nielsen, "See the advantage of chewing carraway seed. Three minutes ago I knew or recollected nothing about Hartwig Juel, but I do now remember that five years ago he passed through Roager, and did me the honour of partaking of such poor hospitality as I was able to give. I supplied him and his four attendants, and six horses, with refreshment. Bless my soul! the efficacy of carraway is prodigious! I can now recall all that took place. I recollect that I had only hogs' puddings to offer the Archdeacon, his chaplain, and servants, and they ate up all I had. I remember also that I had a little barrel of ale which I broached for them, and they drank the whole dry. To be sure!—I had a bin of oats, and the horses consumed every grain! I know that the Archdeacon regretted that I had no bell to my church, and that he promised to send me one. He also assured me he would not leave a stone unturned till he had secured for me a better and more lucrative cure. I even sent a side of bacon away with him as a present—but nothing came of the promises. I ought to have given him a bushel of carraway. You really have no notion of the poverty of this living. I cannot now offer you any other food than buck-wheat brose, as I have no meat in the house. I can only give you water to drink as I am without beer. I cannot even furnish you with butter and milk, as I have not a cow."

"Not even a cow!" exclaimed the Canon. "I really am thankful for your having spoken so plainly to me. I had no conception that your cure was so poor. That the Archdeacon should not have fulfilled the promises he made you is due to forgetfulness. Indeed, I assure you, for the last five years I have repeatedly seen Hartwig Juel strike his brow and exclaim, 'Something troubles me. I have made a promise, and cannot recall it. This lies on my conscience, and I shall have no peace till I recollect and discharge it.' This is plain fact."

"Take him a handful of carraway," urged the parish priest.

"No—he will remember all when I speak to him, unaided by carraway."

"There is one thing I can offer you," said Peter Nielsen, "a mug of dill-water."

"Dill-water! what is that?"

"It is made from carraway. It is given to infants to enable them to retain their milk. It is good for adults to make them recollect their promises."

"My dear good friend," said the Canon rising, "your requirements shall be complied with to-morrow. I see you have excellent pasture here for sheep. Have you any?"

The parish priest shook his head.

"That is a pity. That however can be rectified. Good-bye, rely on me. *Qui pacem habet, se primum pacat.*"

When the Canon was gone, Peter Nielsen, who had attended him to the door, turned, and found Maren Grubbe behind him.

"I say, Peers!" spoke the housekeeper, nudging him, "What is the meaning of all this? What was that Latin he said as he went away?"

"My dear, good Maren," answered the priest, "he quoted a saying familiar to us clergy. At the altar is a little metal plate with a cross on it, and this is called the Pax, or Peace. During the mass the priest kisses it, and then hands it to his assistant, who kisses it in turn and passes it on so throughout the attendance. The

Latin means this, 'Let him who has the Pax bless himself with it before giving it out of his hands,' and means nothing more than this: 'Charity begins at Home,' or—put more boldly still, 'Look out for Number I.'"

"Now, see here," said the housekeeper, "you have been too moderate, Peers, you have not looked out sufficiently for Number I. Leave the next comer to me. No doubt that the Dean will send to you, in like manner as the Archdeacon sent to-day."

"As you like, Maren, but keep the children in the background. Charity that thinketh no ill, is an uncommon virtue."

Next morning early there arrived at the parsonage a waggon laden with sides of bacon, smoked beef, a hogshead of prime ale, a barrel of claret, and several sacks of wheat. It had scarcely been unloaded when a couple of milch cows arrived; half an hour later came a drove of sheep. Peter Nielsen disposed of everything satisfactorily about the house and glebe. His eye twinkled, he rubbed his hands, and said to himself with a chuckle, "He who blesses, blesses first himself."

In the course of the morning a rider drew up at the house door. Maren flattened her nose at the little window of the guest-room, and scrutinized the arrival before admitting him. Then she nodded her head, and whispered to the priest to disappear. A moment later she opened the door, and ushered a stout red-faced ecclesiastic into the room.

"Is the Reverend Pastor at home?" he asked, bowing to Maren Grubbe; "I have come to see him on important business."

"He is at the present moment engaged with a sick parishioner. He will be here in a quarter of an hour. He left word before going out, that should your reverence arrive before his return—"

"What! I was expected!"

"The venerable the Archdeacon sent a deputation to see my master yesterday, and he thought it probable that a deputation from the very Reverend the Dean would arrive to-day."

"Indeed! So Hartwig Juel has stolen a march on us."

"Hartwig Juel had on a visit some little while ago made promises to my master of a couple of cows, a herd of sheep, some ale, wine, wheat, and so on, and he took advantage of the occasion to send all these things to us."

"Indeed! Hartwig Juel's practice is sharp."

"Thomas Lange will make up no doubt for dilatoriness."

"Humph! and Olaf Petersen, has he sent?"

"His deputation will, doubtless, come to-morrow, or even this afternoon."

The Canon folded his hands over his ample paunch, and looked hard at Maren Grubbe. She was attired in her best. Her cheeks shone like quarendon apples, as red and glossy; full of health—with a threat of temper, just as a hot sky has in it indications of a tempest. Her eyes were dark as sloes, and looked as sharp. She was past middle age, but ripe and strong; for all that.

The fat Canon sat looking at her, twirling his thumbs like a little windmill, over his paunch, without speaking. She also sat demurely with her hands flat on her knees, and looked him full and firm in the face.

"I have been thinking," said the Canon, "how well a set of silver chains would look about that neck, and pendant over that ample bosom."

"Gold would look better," said Maren, and shut her mouth again.

"And a crimson silk kerchief—"

"Would do," interrupted the housekeeper, "for one who has not expectations of a crimson silk skirt."

"Quite so." A pause, and the windmills recommenced working. Presently squeals were heard in the back premises. One of the children had fallen and hurt itself.

"Cats?" asked the Canon.

"Cats," answered Maren.

"Quite so," said the Canon. "I am fond of cats.'

"So am I," said Maren.

Then ensued an uproar. The door burst open, and in tumbled little Jens with one child in his arms, the other clinging to the seat of his pantaloons. These same articles of clothing had belonged to the Reverend Peter Nielsen, till worn out, when at the request of Maren, they had been given to her and cut down in length for Jens. In length they answered. The waistband was under the arms, indeed, but the legs were not too long. In breadth and capacity they were uncurtailed.

"I cannot manage them, mother," said the boy. "It is of no use making me nurse. Besides, I want to see the stranger."

"These children," said Maren, looking firmly in the face of the Canon, "call me mother, but they are the offspring of my sister, whose husband was lost last winter at sea. Poor thing, she was left with fourteen, and I—"

She put her apron to her eyes and wept.

"O, noble charity!" said the fat priest enthusiastically. "You—I see it all—you took charge of the little orphans. You sacrifice your savings for them, your time is given to them. Emotion overcomes me. What is their name?"

"Katts."

"Cats?"

"John Katts, and little Kristine and Sissely Katts."

"And the worthy pastor assists in supporting these poor orphans?"

"Yes, in spite of his poverty. And now we are on this point, let me ask you if you have not been struck with the meanness of this parsonage house. I can assure you, there is not a decent room in it, upstairs the chambers are open to the rafters, unceiled."

"My worthy woman," said the Canon, "I will see to this myself. Rely upon it, if the Dean becomes Bishop, he will see that the manses of his best clergy are put into thorough repair."

"I should prefer to see the repairs begun at once," said Maren. "When the Dean becomes Bishop he will have so much to think about, that he might forget our parsonage house."

"Madam," said the visitor, as he rose, "they shall be executed at once. When I see the charity shown in this humble dwelling, by pastor and housekeeper alike, I feel that it demands instantaneous acknowledgment."

Then in came Peter Nielsen, and said, "I have not sufficient cattle-sheds. Sheep yards are also needed."

"They shall be erected."

Then the Canon caught up little Kirsten and little Sissel, and kissed their dirty faces. Maren's radiant countenance assured the Canon that the cause of Thomas Lange was won with Maren Grubbe.

He took the parish priest by the hand, pressed it, and said in a low tone, "*Qui pacem habet, se primum pacat.* You understand me?"

"Perfectly," answered Peter Nielsen, with a smile.

Next morning early there arrived at Roager a party of masons from Ribe, ready to pull down the old parsonage and build one more commodious and extensive. The pastor went over the plans with the master mason, suggested alterations and enlargements, and then, with a chuckle, he muttered to himself, "That is an excellent saying, *Qui pacem habet, se primum pacat.*" Then looking up, he saw before him an ascetic, hollow-eyed, pale-faced priest.

"I am Olaf Petersen," said the new comer. "I thought best to come over and see you myself; I think the true condition of the Church ought to be set before you, and that you should consider the spiritual welfare of the poor sheep in the Ribe fold, and give them a chief pastor who will care for the sheep and not for the wool."

"I have got a flock of sheep already," said Peter Nielsen, coldly. "Hartwig Juel sent it me."

"I think," continued Olaf, "that you should consider the edification of the spiritual building."

"I am going to have a new parsonage erected," said Peter Nielsen, stiffly; "Thomas Lange has seen to that."

"The Bishop needed for this diocese," Olaf Petersen went on, "should combine the harmlessness of the dove with the wisdom of the serpent."

"If he does that," said Nielsen, roughly, "he will be half knave and half fool. Let us have the wisdom, that is what we want now; and one of the first maxims of wisdom in Church and State is, *Qui pacem habet, se primum pacat.* You take me?"

Olaf sighed, and shook his head.

"Do you see this plan," said Peter Nielsen. "I am going to have a byre fashioned on that, with room for a dozen oxen. I have but two cows; stables for two horses, I have not one; a waggon shed, I am without a wheeled conveyance. I shall have new rooms, and have no furniture to put in them. Now, to stock and furnish farm and parsonage will cost much money. I have not a hundred shillings in the world. What am I to do? The man who would be Bishop of Ribe should consider the welfare of one of the most influential, learned, and moral of the priests in the diocese, and do what he can to make him comfortable. Before we choose a cow we go over her, feel her, examine her parts; before we purchase a horse we look at the teeth and explore the hoofs, and try the wind. When we select a bishop we naturally try the stuff of which he is made, if liberal, generous, open-handed, amiable. You understand me?"

180

Olaf sighed, and drops of cold perspiration stood on his brow. A contest was going on within. Simony was a mortal sin. Was there a savour of simony in offering a present to the man in whose hands the choice of a chief pastor lay? He feared so. But then—did not the end sometimes justify the means? As these questions rose in his mind and refused to be answered, something heavy fell at his feet. His hand had been plucking at his purse, and in his nervousness he had detached it from his girdle, and had let it slip through his fingers. He did not look down. He seemed not to notice his loss, but he moved away without another word, with bent head and troubled conscience. When he was gone, Peter Nielsen bowed himself, picked up the pouch, counted the gold coins in it, laughed, rubbed his hands, and said, "He who blesses, blesses first himself."

Next day a litter stayed at the parsonage gate, and out of it, with great difficulty, supported on the arms of two servants, came the aged Jep Mundelstrup. He entered the guest-room and was accommodated with a seat. When he got his breath, he said, extending a roll of parchment to the incumbent of Roager, "You will not fail to remember that it was at *my* suggestion that the choice of a bishop was left with you. You are deeply indebted to me. But for me you would not have been visited and canvassed by the Dean, the Arch-deacon, and the Ascetic, either in person or by their representatives. You will please to remember that I was nominated, but seeing so many others proposed, I withdrew my name. I think you will allow that this exhibited great humility and shrinking from honour. In these worldly, self-seeking days such an example deserves notice and reward. I am old, and perhaps unequal to the labours of office, but I think I ought to be considered; although I did formally withdraw my candidature, I am not sure that I would refuse the mitre were it pressed on me. At all events it would be a compliment to offer it me and I might refuse it. *Qui pacem habet, se primum pacat.* You will not regret the return courtesy."

* * * * *

Boom! Boom! Boom! The cathedral bell was summoning all Ribe to the minster to be present at the nomination of its bishop. All Ribe answered the summons.

The cathedral stands on a hill called the Mount of Lilies, but the mount is of so slight an elevation that it does not protect the cathedral from overflow, and a spring tide with N.W. wind has been known to flood both town and minster and leave fishes on the sacred floor. The church is built of granite, brick and sandstone; originally the contrast may have been striking, but weather has smudged the colours together into an ugly brown-grey. The tower is lofty, narrow, and wanting a spire. It resembles a square ruler set up on end; it is too tall for its base. The church is stately, of early architecture with transepts, and the choir at their intersection with the nave, domed over, and a small semi-circular apse beyond, for the altar. The nave was crowded, the canons occupied the stalls in their purple tippets edged with crimson; purple, because the chapter of a cathedral; crimson edged, because the founder of the See was a martyr. Fifteen, and the Dean, sixteen in all, were in their places. On the altar steps, in the apse, in the centre, sat Peter Nielsen in his old, worn cassock, without surplice. On the left side of the altar stood the richly-sculptured Episcopal throne, and on the seat was placed the jewelled mitre, over the arm the cloth of gold cope was cast, and against the back leaned the pastoral crook of silver gilt, encrusted with precious stones.

When the last note of the bell sounded, the Dean rose from his stall, and stepping up to the apse, made oath before heaven, the whole congregation and Peter Nielsen, that he was prepared to abide by the decision of this said Peter, son of Nicolas, parish priest of Roager. Amen. He was followed by the Archdeacon, then by each of the canons to the last.

Then mass was said, during which the man in whose hands the fortunes of the See reposed, knelt with unimpassioned countenance and folded hands.

At the conclusion he resumed his seat, the crucifix was brought forth and he kissed it.

A moment of anxious silence. The moment for the decision had arrived. He remained for a short while seated, with his eyes fixed on the ground, then he turned them on the anxious face of the Dean, and after having allowed them to rest scrutinisingly there for a minute, he looked at Hartwig Juel, then at Olaf Petersen, who was deadly white, and whose frame shook like an aspen leaf. Then he looked long at Jep Mundelstrup and rose suddenly to his feet.

The fall of a pin might have been heard in the cathedral at that moment.

He said—and his voice was distinctly audible by every one present—"I have been summoned here from my barren heath, into this city, out of a poor hamlet, by these worthy and reverend fathers, to choose for them a prelate who shall be at once careful of the temporal and the spiritual welfare of the See. I have scrupulously considered the merits of all those who have been presented to me as candidates for the mitre. I find that in only one man are all the requisite qualities combined in proper proportion and degree—not in Thomas Lange," the Dean's head fell on his bosom, "nor in Hartwig Juel," the Archdeacon sank back in his stall; "nor in Olaf Petersen," the man designated uttered a faint cry and dropped on his knees, "nor in

181

Jep Mundelstrup—but in myself. I therefore nominate Peter, son of Nicolas, commonly called Nielsen, Curate of Roager, to be Bishop of Ribe, twenty-ninth in descent from Liafdag the martyr. *Qui pacem habet, se primum pacat.* Amen. He who has to bless, blesses first himself."

Then he sat down.

For a moment there was silence, and then a storm broke loose. Peter sat motionless, with his eyes fixed on the ground, motionless as a rock round which the waves toss and tear themselves to foam.

Thus it came about that the twenty-ninth bishop of Ribe was Peter Nielsen.

IX. — *THE WONDER-WORKING PRINCE HOHENLOHE*

IN the year 1821, much interest was excited in Germany and, indeed, throughout Europe by the report that miracles of healing were being wrought by Prince Leopold Alexander of Hohenlohe-Waldenburg-Schillingsfürst at Würzburg, Bamberg, and elsewhere. The wonders soon came to an end, for, after the ensuing year, no more was heard of his extraordinary powers.

At the time, as might be expected, his claims to be a miracle-worker were hotly disputed, and as hotly asserted. Evidence was produced that some of his miracles were genuine; counter evidence was brought forward reducing them to nothing.

The whole story of Prince Hohenlohe's sudden blaze into fame, and speedy extinction, is both curious and instructive. In the Baden village of Wittighausen, at the beginning of this century, lived a peasant named Martin Michel, owning a farm, and in fairly prosperous circumstances. His age, according to one authority, was fifty, according to another sixty-seven, when he became acquainted with Prince Hohenlohe. This peasant was unquestionably a devout, guileless man. He had been afflicted in youth with a rupture, but, in answer to continuous and earnest prayer, he asserted that he had been completely healed. Then, for some while he prayed over other afflicted persons, and it was rumoured that he had effected several miraculous cures. He emphatically and earnestly repudiated every claim to superior sanctity. The cures, he declared, depended on the faith of the patient, and on the power of the Almighty. The most solemn promises had been made in the gospel to those who asked in faith, and all he did was to act upon these evangelical promises.

The Government speedily interfered, and Michel was forbidden by the police to work any more miracles by prayer or faith, or any other means except the recognised pharmacopoeia.

He had received no payment for his cures in money or in kind, but he took occasion through them to impress on his patients the duty of prayer, and the efficacy of faith.

By some means he met Prince Alexander Hohenlohe, and the prince was interested and excited by what he heard, and by the apparent sincerity of the man. A few days later the prince was in Würzburg, where he called on the Princess Mathilde Schwarzenberg, a young girl of seventeen who was a cripple, and who had already spent a year and a half at Würzburg, under the hands of the orthopædic physician Heine, and the surgeon Textor. She had been to the best medical men in Vienna and Paris, and the case had been given up as hopeless. Then Prince Schwarzenberg placed her under the treatment of Heine. She was so contracted, with her knees drawn up to her body, that she could neither stand nor walk.

Prince Hohenlohe first met her at dinner, on June 18, 1821, and the sight of her distortion filled him with pity. He thought over her case, and communicated with Michel, who at his summons came to Würzburg. As Würzburg is in Bavaria, the orders of the Baden Government did not extend to it, and the peasant might freely conduct his experiments there.

Prince Alexander called on the Princess at ten o'clock in the morning of June 20, taking with him Michel, but leaving him outside the house, in the court. Then Prince Hohenlohe began to speak to the suffering girl of the power of faith, and mentioned the wonders wrought by the prayers of Michel. She became interested, and the Prince asked her if she would like to put the powers of Michel to the test, warning her that the man could do nothing unless she had full and perfect belief in the mercy of God. The Princess expressed her eagerness to try the new remedy and assured her interrogator that she had the requisite faith. Thereupon he went to the window, and signed to the peasant to come up.

What follows shall be given in the Princess's own words, from her account written a day or two later:—"The peasant knelt down and prayed in German aloud and distinctly, and, after his prayer, he said to me, 'In the Name of Jesus, stand up. You are whole, and can both stand and walk!' The peasant and the

Prince then went into an adjoining room, and I rose from my couch, without assistance, in the name of God, well and sound, and so I have continued to this moment."

A much fuller and minuter account of the proceedings was published, probably from the pen of the governess, who was present at the time; but as it is anonymous we need not concern ourselves with it.

The news of the miraculous recovery spread through the town; Dr. Heine heard of it, and ran to the house, and stood silent and amazed at what he saw. The Princess descended the stone staircase towards the garden, but hesitated, and, instead of going into the garden, returned upstairs, leaning on the arm of Prince Hohenlohe.

Next day was Corpus Christi. The excitement in the town was immense, when the poor cripple, who had been seen for more than a year carried into her carriage and carried out of it into church, walked to church, and thence strolled into the gardens of the palace.

On the following day she visited the Julius Hospital, a noble institution founded by one of the bishops of Würzburg. On the 24th she called on the Princess Lichtenstein, the Duke of Aremberg, and the Prince of Baar, and moreover, attended a sermon preached by Prince Hohenlohe in the Haugh parish church. Her recovery was complete.

Now, at first sight, nothing seems more satisfactorily established than this miracle. Let us, however, see what Dr. Heine, who had attended her for nineteen months, had to say on it. We cannot quote his account in its entirety, as it is long, but we will take the principal points in it:—"The Princess of Schwarzenberg came under my treatment at the end of October, 1819, afflicted with several abnormities of the thorax, with a twisted spine, ribs, &c. Moreover, she could not rise to her feet from a sitting posture, nor endure to be so raised; but this was not in consequence of malformation or weakness of the system, for when sitting or lying down she could freely move her limbs. She complained of acute pain when placed in any other position, and when she was made to assume an angle of 100° her agony became so intense that her extremities were in a nervous quiver, and partial paralysis ensued, which, however, ceased when she was restored to her habitual contracted position.

"The Princess lost her power of locomotion when she was three years old, and the contraction was the result of abscesses on the loins. She was taken to France and Italy, and got so far in Paris as to be able to hop about a room supported on crutches. But she suffered a relapse on her return to Vienna in 1813, and thenceforth was able neither to stand nor to move about. She was placed in my hands, and I contrived an apparatus by which the angle at which she rested was gradually extended, and her position gradually changed from horizontal to vertical. At the same time I manipulated her almost daily, and had the satisfaction by the end of last April to see her occupy an angle of 50°, without complaining of suffering. By the close of May further advance was made, and she was able to assume a vertical position, with her feet resting on the ground, but with her body supported, and to remain in this position for four or five hours. Moreover, in this situation I made her go through all the motions of walking. The extremities had, in every position, retained their natural muscular powers and movements, and the contraction was simply a nervous affection. I made no attempt to force her to walk unsupported, because I would not do this till I was well assured such a trial would not be injurious to her.

"On the 30th of May I revisited her, after having been unable, on account of a slight indisposition, to see my patients for several days. Her governess then told me that the Princess had made great progress. She lay at an angle of 80°. The governess placed herself at the foot of the couch, held out her hands to the Princess, and drew her up into an upright position, and she told me that this had been done several times of late during my enforced absence. Whilst she was thus standing I made the Princess raise and depress her feet, and go through all the motions of walking. Immediately on my return home I set to work to construct a machine which might enable her to walk without risk of a fall and of hurting herself. On the 19th of June, in the evening, I told the Princess that the apparatus was nearly finished. Next day, a little after 10 A.M., I visited her. When I opened her door she rose up from a chair in which she was seated, and came towards me with short, somewhat uncertain steps. I bowed myself, in token of joy and thanks to God.

"At that moment a gentleman I had never seen before entered the room and exclaimed, 'Mathilde! you have had faith in God!' The Princess replied, 'I have had, and I have now, entire faith.' The gentleman said, 'Your faith has saved and healed you. God has succoured you.' Then I began to suspect that some strange influence was at work, and that something had been going on of which I was not cognizant. I asked the gentleman what was the meaning of this. He raised his right hand to heaven, and replied that he had prayed and thought of the Princess that morning at mass, and that Prince Wallerstein was privy to the whole proceeding. I was puzzled and amazed. Then I asked the Princess to walk again. She did so, and shortly after I left, and only then did I learn that the stranger was the Prince of Hohenlohe.

"Next month, on July 21, her aunt, the Princess Eleanor of Schwarzenberg, came with three of the sisters of Princess Mathilde to fetch her away and to take her back to her father. Her Highness did me the honour of visiting me along with the Princesses on the second day after their arrival, to thank me for the pains I had taken to cure the Princess Mathilde. Before they left, Dr. Schäfer, who had attended her at Ratisbon, Herr Textor, and myself were allowed to examine the Princess. Dr. Schäfer found that the condition of the thorax was mightily improved since she had been in my hands. I, however, saw that her condition had retrograded since I had last seen her on June 20, and it was agreed that the Princess was to occupy her extension-couch at night, and by day wear the steel apparatus for support I had contrived for her. At the same time Dr. Schäfer distinctly assured her and the Princess, her aunt, that under my management the patient had recovered the power of walking *before* the 19th of June."

This account puts a different complexion on the cure, and shows that it was not in any way miraculous. The Prince and the peasant stepped in and snatched the credit of having cured the Princess from the doctor, to whom it rightly belonged.

Before we proceed, it will be well to say a few words about this Prince Alexander Hohenlohe. The Hohenlohe family takes its name from a bare elevated plateau in Franconia. About the beginning of the 16th century it broke into two branches; the elder is Hohenlohe-Neuenstein, the younger is Hohenlohe-Waldenburg.

The elder branch has its sub-ramifications—Hohenlohe-Langenburg, which possesses also the county of Gleichen; and the Hohenlohe-Oehringen and the Hohenlohe-Kirchberg sub-branches. The second main branch of Hohenlohe-Waldenburg has also its lateral branches, as those of Hohenlohe-Bartenstein and Hohenlohe-Schillingsfürst; the last of these being Catholic.

Prince Leopold Alexander was born in 1794 at Kupferzell, near Waldenburg, and was the eighteenth child of Prince Karl Albrecht and his wife Judith, Baroness Reviczky. His father never became reigning prince, from intellectual incapacity, and Alexander lost him when he was one year old. He was educated for the Church by the ex-Jesuit Riel, and went to school first in Vienna, then at Berne; in 1810 he entered the Episcopal seminary at Vienna, and finished his theological studies at Ellwangen in 1814. He was ordained priest in 1816, and went to Rome.

Dr. Wolff, the father of Sir Henry Drummond Wolff, in his "Travels and Adventures," which is really his autobiography, says (vol i. p. 31):—

"Wolff left the house of Count Stolberg on the 3rd April, 1815, and went to Ellwangen, and there met again an old pupil from Vienna, Prince Alexander Hohenlohe-Schillingsfürst, afterwards so celebrated for his miracles—to which so many men of the highest rank and intelligence have borne witness that Wolff dares not give a decided opinion about them. But Niebuhr relates that the Pope said to him himself, speaking about Hohenlohe in a sneering manner, '*Questo far dei miracoli!' This* fellow performing miracles!

"It may be best to offer some slight sketch of Hohenlohe's life. His person was beautiful. He was placed under the direction of Vock, the Roman Catholic parish priest at Berne. One Sunday he was invited to dinner with Vock, his tutor, at the Spanish ambassador's. The next day there was a great noise in the Spanish embassy, because the mass-robe, with the silver chalice and all its appurtenances, had been stolen. It was advertised in the paper, but nothing could be discovered, until Vock took Prince Hohenlohe aside, and said to him, 'Prince, confess to me; have you not stolen the mass-robe?' He at once confessed it, and said that he made use of it every morning in practising the celebration of the mass in his room; which was true." (This was when Hohenlohe was twenty-one years old.) "He was afterwards sent to Tyrnau, to the ecclesiastical seminary in Hungary, whence he was expelled, on account of levity. But, being a Prince, the Chapter of Olmütz, in Moravia, elected him titular canon of the cathedral; nevertheless, the Emperor Francis was too honest to confirm it. Wolff taught him Hebrew in Vienna. He had but little talent for languages, but his conversation on religion was sometimes very charming; and at other times he broke out into most indecent discourses. He was ordained priest, and Sailer[16] preached a sermon on the day of his ordination, which was published under the title of 'The Priest without Reproach.' On the same day money was collected for building a Roman Catholic Church at Zürich, and the money collected was given to Prince Hohenlohe, to be remitted to the parish priest of Zürich (Moritz Mayer); but the money never reached its destination. Wolff saw him once at the bed of the sick and dying, and his discourse, exhortations, and treatment of these sick people were wonderfully beautiful. When he mounted the pulpit to preach, one imagined one saw a saint of the Middle Ages. His devotion was penetrating, and commanded silence in a church where there were 4,000 people collected. Wolff one day called on him, when Hohenlohe said to him, 'I never read any other book than the Bible. I never look in a sermon-book by anybody else, not even at the sermons of Sailer.' But Wolff after this heard him preach, and the whole sermon was copied from one of Sailer's, which Wolff had read only the day before.

[16] Johann M. Sailer was a famous ex-Jesuit preacher, at this time Professor at the University of Landshut, afterwards Bishop of Ratisbon. He died, 1832.

"With all his faults, Hohenlohe cannot be charged with avarice, for he give away every farthing he got, perhaps even that which he obtained dishonestly. They afterwards met at Rome, where Hohenlohe lodged with the Jesuits, and there it was said he composed a Latin poem. Wolff, knowing his incapacity to do such a thing, asked him boldly, 'Who is the author of this poem?' Hohenlohe confessed at once that it was written by a Jesuit priest. At that time Madame Schlegel wrote to Wolff: 'Prince Hohenlohe is a man who struggles with heaven and hell, and heaven will gain the victory with him.' Hohenlohe was on the point of being made a bishop at Rome, but, on the strength of his previous knowledge of him, Wolff protested against his consecration. Several princes, amongst them Kaunitz, the ambassador, took Hohenlohe's part on this occasion; but the matter was investigated, and Hohenlohe walked off from Rome without being made a bishop. In his protest against the man, Wolff stated that Hohenlohe's pretensions to being a canon of Olmütz were false; that he had been expelled the seminary of Tyrnau; that he sometimes spoke like a saint, and at others like a profligate."

And now let us return to Würzburg, and see the result of the cure of Princess Schwarzenberg. The people who had seen the poor cripple one day carried into her carriage and into church, and a day or two after saw her walk to church and in the gardens, and who knew nothing of Dr. Heine's operations, concluded that this was a miracle, and gave the credit of it quite as much to Prince Hohenlohe as to the peasant Michel.

The police at once sent an official letter to the Prince, requesting to be informed authoritatively what he had done, by what right he had interfered, and how he had acted. He replied that he had done nothing, faith and the Almighty had wrought the miracle. "The instantaneous cure of the Princess is a *fact*, which cannot be disputed; it was the result of a living faith. That is the truth. It happened to the Princess according to her faith." The peasant Michel now fell into the background, and was forgotten, and the Prince stood forward as the worker of miraculous cures. Immense excitement was caused by the restoration of the Princess Schwarzenberg, and patients streamed into Würzburg from all the country round, seeking health at the hands of Prince Alexander. The local papers published marvellous details of his successful cures. The blind saw, the lame walked, the deaf heard. Among the deaf who recovered was His Royal Highness the Crown Prince of Bavaria, three years later King Ludwig I., grandfather of the late King of Bavaria. Unfortunately we have not exact details of this cure, but a letter of the Crown Prince written shortly after merely states that he heard *better* than before. Now the spring of 1821 was very raw and wet, and about June 20 there set in some dry hot weather. It is therefore quite possible that the change of weather may have had to do with this cure. However, we can say nothing for certain about it, as no data were published, merely the announcement that the Crown Prince had recovered his hearing at the prayer of Prince Hohenlohe. Here are some better-authenticated cases, as given by Herr Scharold, an eye-witness; he was city councillor and secretary.

"The Prince had dined at midday with General von D——. All the entrances to the house from two streets were blocked by hundreds of persons, and they said that he had already healed four individuals crippled with rheumatism in this house. I convinced myself on the spot that one of these cases was as said. The patient was the young wife of a fisherman, who was crippled in the right hand, so that she could not lift anything with it, or use it in any way; and all at once she was enabled to raise a heavy chair, with the hand hitherto powerless, and hold it aloft. She went home weeping tears of joy and thankfulness.

"The Prince was then entreated to go to another house, at another end of the town, and he consented. There he found many paralysed persons. He began with a poor man whose left arm was quite useless and stiff. After he had asked him if he had perfect faith, and had received a satisfactory answer, the Prince prayed with folded hands and closed eyes. Then he raised the kneeling patient; and said, 'Move your arm.' Weeping and trembling in all his limbs the man did as he was bid; but as he said that he obeyed with difficulty, the Prince prayed again, and said, 'Now move your arm again.' This time the man easily moved his arm forwards, backwards, and raised it. The cure was complete. Equally successful was he with the next two cases. One was a tailor's wife, named Lanzamer. 'What do you want?' asked the Prince, who was bathed in perspiration. Answer: 'I have had a paralytic stroke, and have lost the use of one side of my body, so that I cannot walk unsupported.' 'Kneel down!' But this could only be effected with difficulty, and it was rather a tumbling down of an inert body, painful to behold. I never saw a face more full of expression of faith in the strongly marked features. The Prince, deeply moved, prayed with great fervour, and then said, 'Stand up!' The good woman, much agitated, was unable to do so, in spite of all her efforts, without the assistance of her boy, who was by her, crying, and then her lame leg seemed to crack. When she had reached her feet, he said, 'Now walk the length of the room without pain.' She tried to do so, but succeeded with difficulty, yet with only a little suffering. Again he prayed, and the healing was complete; she walked lightly and painlessly up and down, and finally out of the room; and the boy, crying more than before, but now with joy, exclaimed, 'O my God! mother can walk, mother can walk!' Whilst this was going on, an old woman, called Siebert, wife of a bookbinder, who had been brought in a sedan-chair, was admitted to the room. She suffered from paralysis and incessant headaches that left her neither night nor day. The first attempt made to heal her failed. The second only brought on the paroxysm of headache worse than ever, so that the poor creature could hardly keep her feet or open her eyes. The Prince began to doubt her faith, but when she assured him of it, he prayed again with redoubled earnestness. And, all at once, she was cured. This woman left the room, conducted by her daughter, and all present were filled with astonishment." This account was written on June 26. On June 28 Herr Scharold wrote a further account of other cures he had witnessed; but those already given are sufficient. That this witness was convinced and sincere appears from his description, but how far valuable his evidence is we are not so well assured.

A curious little pamphlet was published the same year at Darmstadt, entitled, "Das Mährchen vom Wunder," that professed to be the result of the observations of a medical man who attended one or two of these *séances*. Unfortunately the pamphlet is anonymous, and this deprives it of most of its authority. Another writer who attacked the genuineness of the miracles was Dr. Paulus, in his "Quintessenz aus den Wundercurversuchen durch Michel und Hohenlohe," Leipzig, 1822; but this author also wrote anonymously, and did not profess to have seen any of the cures. On the other hand, Scharold and a Dr. Onymus, and two or three priests published their testimonies as witnesses to their genuineness, and gave the names and particulars of those cured.

Those who assailed the Prince and his cures dipped their pens in gall. It is only just to add that they cast on his character none of the reflections for honesty which Dr. Wolff flung on him.

The author of the Darmstadt pamphlet, mentioned above, says that when he was present the Prince was attended by two sergeants of police, as the crowd thronging on him was so great that he needed protection from its pressure. He speaks sneeringly of him as spending his time in eating, smoking, and miracle-working, when not sleeping, and says he was plump and good-looking.

"A girl of eighteen, who was paralysed in her limbs, was brought from a carriage to the feet of the prophet. After he had asked her if she believed, and he had prayed for about twelve seconds, he exclaimed in a threatening rather than gentle voice, 'You are healed!' But I observed that he had to thunder this thrice into the ear of the frightened girl, before she made an effort to move, which was painful and distressing; and, groaning and supported by others, she made her way to the rear. 'You will be better shortly—only believe!' he cried to her. I, who was looking on, observed her conveyed away as much a cripple as she came.

"The next case was a peasant of fifty-eight, a cripple on crutches. Without his crutches he was doubled up, and could only shuffle with his feet on the ground. After the Prince had asked the usual questions and had prayed, he ordered the kneeling man to stand up, his crutches having been removed. As he was unable to do so, the miracle-worker seemed irritated, and repeated his order in an angry tone. One of the policemen at the side threw in 'Up! in the name of the Trinity,' and pulled him to his feet. The man seemed bewildered. He stood, indeed, but doubled as before, and the sweat streamed from his face, and he was not a ha'porth better than previously; but as he had come with crutches, and now stood without them, there arose a shout of 'A miracle!' and all pressed round to congratulate the poor wretch. His son helped him away. 'Have faith and courage!' cried to him the Prince; and the policeman added, 'Only believe, and rub in a little spirits of camphor!' Many pressed alms into the man's hand, and he smiled; this was regarded as a token of his perfect cure. I saw, however, that his knees were as stiff as before, and that the rogue cast longing eyes at his crutches, which had been taken away, but which he insisted on having back. No one thought of asking how it fared with the poor wretch later, and, as a fact, he died shortly after.

"The next to come up was a deaf girl of eighteen. The wonder-worker was bathed in perspiration, and evidently exhausted with his continuous prayer night and day. After a few questions as to the duration of her infirmity, the Prince prayed, then signed a cross over the girl, and, stepping back from her, asked her questions, at each in succession somewhat lowering his tone; but she only heard those spoken as loudly as before the experiment was made, and she remained for the most part staring stupidly at the wonder-worker. To cut the matter short, he declared her healed. I took the mother aside soon after, and inquired what was the result. She assured me that the girl heard no better than before.

"In her place came a stone-deaf man of twenty-five. The result was very similar; but as the Prince, when bidding him depart healed, made a sign of withdrawal with his hand, the man rose and departed, and this was taken as evidence that he had heard the command addressed to him."

The author gives other cases that he witnessed, not one of which was other than a failure, though they were all declared to be cures.

On June 29 the Prince practised his miracle-working at the palace, in the presence of the Crown Prince and of Prince Esterhazy, the Austrian ambassador who was on his way to London to attend the coronation of George IV. in July. The attempts were probably as great failures as those described in the Darmstadt pamphlet. The Prince was somewhat discouraged at the invitation of the physicians attached to the Julius Hospital; he had visited that institution the day before, and had experimented on twenty cases, and was unsuccessful in every one. Full particulars of these were published in the "Bamberger Briefe," Nos. 28-33. We will give only a very few:—

"1. Barbara Uhlen, of Oberschleichach, aged 39, suffering from dropsy. The Prince said to her, 'Do you sincerely believe that you can be helped and are helped?' The sick woman replied, 'Yes. I had resolved to leave the hospital, where no good has been done to me, and to seek health from God and the Prince.' He raised his eyes to heaven and prayed; then assured the patient of her cure. Her case became worse rapidly, instead of better.

"7. Margaretta Löhlein, of Randersacher, aged 56. Suffering from dropsy owing to disorganisation of the liver. Another failure. Shortly after the Prince left, she had to be operated on to save her from suffocation.

"10. Susanna Söllnerin, servant maid of Aub, aged 22, had already been thirteen weeks in hospital, suffering from roaring noises in the head and deafness. The Prince, observing the fervour of her faith, cried out, 'You shall see now how speedily she will be cured!' Prayers, blessing, as before, and—as before, no results.

"11. George Forchheimer, butcher, suffering from rheumatism. One foot is immovable, and he can only walk with the assistance of a stick. During the prayer of the Prince the patient wept and sobbed, and was profoundly agitated. The Prince ordered him to stand up and go without his stick. His efforts to obey were unavailing; he fell several times on the ground, though the Prince repeated over him his prayers."

These are sufficient as instances; not a single case in the hospital was more successfully treated by him.

On July 5 Prince Hohenlohe went to Bamberg, where he was eagerly awaited by many sick and credulous persons. The Burgomaster Hornthal, however, interfered, and forbade the attempt at performing miracles till the authorities at Baireuth had been instructed of his arrival, and till a commission had been appointed of men of judgment, and physicians to take note of the previous condition of every patient who was submitted to him, and of the subsequent condition. Thus hampered the Prince could do nothing; he failed as signally as in the Julius Hospital at Würzburg, and the only cases of cures claimed to have been wrought were among a mixed crowd in the street to whom he gave a blessing from the balcony of his lodging.

Finding that Bamberg was uncongenial, he accepted a call to the Baths of Brückenau, and thence news reached the incredulous of Bamberg and Würzburg that extraordinary cures had been wrought at the prayers of the Prince. As, however, we have no details respecting these, we may pass them over.

Hohenlohe, who had no notion of hiding his light under a bushel, drew up a detailed account of over a hundred cures which he claimed to have worked, had them attested by witnesses, and sent this precious document to the Pope, who, with good sense, took no notice of it; at least no public notice, though it is probable that he administered a sharp private reprimand, for Hohenlohe collapsed very speedily.

From Brückenau the Prince went to Vienna, but was not favourably received there, so he departed to Hungary, where his mother's relations lived. Though he was applied to by sick people who had heard of his fame, he did not make any more direct attempts to heal them. He, however, gave them cards on which a day and hour were fixed, and a prayer written, and exhorted them to pray for recovery earnestly on the day and at the hour indicated, and promised to pray for them at the same time. But this was also discontinued, having proved inefficacious, and Hohenlohe relapsed into a quiet unostentatious life. He was appointed, through family interest, Canon of Grosswardein, and in 1829 advanced to be Provost of the Cathedral. His powers as a preacher long survived his powers of working miracles. He spent his time in good works, and in writing little manuals of devotion. In 1844 he was consecrated titular Bishop of Sardica *in partibus*, that is, without a See. He died at Vöslau, near Vienna, in 1849. That Hohenlohe was a conscious hypocrite we are far from supposing. He was clearly a man of small mental powers, very conceited, and wanting in judgment. We must not place too much reliance on the scandalous gossip of Dr. Wolff. Probably Hohenlohe's vanity received a severe check in 1821, when both the Roman See and the world united to discredit his miracles; and he had sufficient good sense to accept the verdict.

X. — THE SNAIL-TELEGRAPH

THE writer well remembers, as a child, the sense of awe not unmixed with fear, with which he observed the mysterious movements of the telegraph erected on church towers in France along all the main roads.

Many a beautiful tower was spoiled by these abominable erections. There were huge arms like those of a windmill, painted black, and jointed, so as to describe a great number of cabalistic signs in the air. Indeed, the movements were like the writhings of some monstrous spider.

Glanvil who wrote in the middle of the 17th century says, "To those that come after us, it may be as ordinary to buy a pair of wings to fly into the remotest regions, as now a pair of boots to ride a journey. *And to confer, at the distance of the Indies, by sympathetic conveyances*, may be as usual to future times as to us is literary correspondence." He further remarks, "Antiquity would not have believed the almost incredible force of our cannons, and would as coldly have entertained the wonders of the telescope. In these we all condemn antique incredulity. And it is likely posterity will have as much cause to pity ours. But those who are acquainted with the diligent and ingenious endeavours of true philosophers will despair of nothing."

In 1633 the Marquis of Worcester suggested a scheme of telegraphing by means of signs. Another, but similar scheme, was mooted in 1660 by the Frenchman Amonton. In 1763 Mr. Edgeworth erected for his private use a telegraph between London and Newmarket. But it was in 1789 that the Optical Telegraph came into practical use in France—Claude Chappe was the inventor. When he was a boy, he contrived a means of communication by signals with his brothers at a distance of two or three miles. He laid down the first line between Lille and Paris at a cost of about two thousand pounds, and the first message sent along it was the announcement of the capture of Lille by Condé. This led to the construction of many similar lines communicating with each other by means of stations. Some idea of the celerity with which messages were sent may be gained from the fact that it took only two minutes to reproduce in Paris a sign given in Lille at a distance of 140 miles. On this line there were 22 stations. The objections to this system lay in its being useless at night and in rainy weather. The French system of telegraph consisted of one main beam—the regulator, at the end of which were two shorter wings, so that it formed a letter Z. The regulator and its flags could be turned about in various ways, making in all 196 signs. Sometimes the regulator stood horizontally, sometimes perpendicularly.

Lord Murray introduced one of a different construction in England in 1795 consisting of two rows of three octangular flags revolving on their axis. This gave 64 different signs, but was defective in the same point as that of Chappe. Poor Chappe was so troubled in mind because his claim to be the inventor of his telegraph was disputed, that he drowned himself in a well, 1805.

Besides the fact that the optical telegraph was paralysed by darkness and storm, it was very difficult to manage in mountainous and well-wooded country, and required there a great number of stations.

After that Sömmering had discovered at Munich in 1808 the means of signalling through the galvanic current obtained by decomposition of water, and Schilling at Canstadt and Ampère in Paris (1820) had made further advances in the science of electrology, and Oersted had established the deflexion of the magnetic needle, it was felt that the day of the cumbrous and disfiguring optical telegraph was over. A new power had been discovered, though the extent and the applicability of this power were not known. Gauss and Weber in 1833 made the first attempt to set up an electric telegraph; in 1837 Wheatstone and Morse utilised the needle and made the telegraph print its messages. In 1833 the telegraph of Gauss and Weber supplanted the optical contrivance on the line between Trèves and Berlin. The first line in America was laid from Washington to Baltimore in 1844. The first attempt at submarine telegraphy was made at Portsmouth in 1846, and in 1850 a cable was laid between England and France.

It was precisely in this year when men's minds were excited over the wonderful powers of the galvanic current, and a wide prospect was opened of its future advantage to men, when, indeed, the general public understood very little about the principle and were in a condition of mind to accept almost any scientific marvel, that there appeared in Paris an adventurer, who undertook to open communications between all parts of the world without the expense and difficulty of laying cables of communication. The line laid across the channel in 1850 was not very successful; it broke several times, and had to be taken up again, and relaid in 1851. If it did not answer in conveying messages across so narrow a strip of water, was it likely to be utilized for Transatlantic telegraphy? The *Presse*, a respectable Paris paper, conducted by a journalist of note, M. de Girardin, answered emphatically, No. The means of communication was not to be sought in a chain. The gutta percha casing would decompose under the sea, and when the brine touched the wires, the cable would be useless. The Chappe telegraph was superseded by the electric telegraph which answered well on dry land, but fatal objections stood in the way of its answering for communication between places divided by belts of sea or oceans. Moreover, it was an intricate system. Now the tendency of science in modern times was towards simplification; and it was always found that the key to unlock difficulties which had puzzled the inventors of the past, lay at their hands. The electric telegraph was certainly more elaborate, complicated and expensive than the optical telegraph. Was it such a decided advance on it? Yes—in one way. It could be worked at all hours of night and day. But had the last word in telegraphy been spoken, when it was invented? Most assuredly not.

Along with electricity and terrestrial magnetism, another power, vaguely perceived, the full utility of which was also unknown, had been recognised—animal magnetism. Why should not this force be used as a means for the conveyance of messages?

M. Jules Allix after a long preamble in *La Presse*, in an article signed by himself, announced that a French inventor, M. Jacques Toussaint Benoît (de l'Hérault), and a fellow worker of Gallic origin, living in America, M. Biat-Chrétien, had hit on "a new system of universal intercommunication of thought, which operates instantaneously."

After a long introduction in true French rhodomontade, tracing the progress of humanity from the publication of the Gospel to the 19th century, M. Allix continued, "The discovery of MM. Benoît and Biat depends on galvanism, terrestrial and animal magnetism, also on natural sympathy, that is to say, the base of communication is a sort of special sympathetic fluid which is composed of the union or blending of the galvanic, magnetic and sympathetic currents, by a process to be described shortly. And as the various fluids vary according to the organic or inorganic bodies whence they are derived, it is necessary further to state that the forces or fluids here married are: (*a*) The terrestrial-galvanic current, (*b*) the animal-sympathetic current, in this case derived from *snails*, (*c*) the adamic or human current, or animal-magnetic current in man. Consequently, to describe concisely the basis of the new system of intercommunication, we shall have to call the force, '*The galvano-terrestrial-magnetic-animal and adamic force!*'" Is not this something like a piece of Jules Verne's delicious scientific *hocus-pocus*? Will the reader believe that it was written in good faith? It was, there can be no question, written in perfect good faith. The character of *La Presse*, of the journalist, M. Jules Allix, would not allow of a hoax wilfully perpetrated on the public. We are quoting from the number for October 27th, 1850, of the paper.

"According to the experiments made by MM. Benoît and Biat, it seems that snails which have once been put in contact, are always in sympathetic communication. When separated, there disengages itself from them a species of fluid of which the earth is the conductor, which develops and unrolls, so to speak, like the almost invisible thread of the spider, or that of the silk worm, which can be uncoiled and prolonged almost indefinitely in space without its breaking, but with this vital difference that the thread of the escargotic fluid is invisible as completely and the pulsation along it is as rapid as the electric fluid.

"But, it may be objected with some plausibility, granted the existence in the snails of this sympathetic fluid, will it radiate from them in all directions, after the analogy of electric, galvanic and magnetic fluids, unless there be some conductor established between them? At first sight, this objection has some weight, but for all that it is more specious than serious."

The solution of this difficulty is exquisitely absurd. We must summarise.

At first the discoverers of the galvanic current thought it necessary to establish a return wire, to complete the circle, till it was found to be sufficient to carry the two ends of the wire in communication with the earth, when the earth itself completed the circle. There is no visible line between the ends underground, yet the current completes the circle through it. Moreover, it is impossible to think of two points without establishing, in idea, a line between them, indeed, according to Euclid's definition, a straight line is that which lies evenly between its extreme points, and a line is length without breadth or substance. So, if we conceive of two snails, we establish a line between them, an unsubstantial line, still a line along which the sympathetic current can travel. "Now MM. Benoît and Biat, by means of balloons in the atmosphere," had established beyond doubt that a visible tangible line of communication was only necessary when raised above the earth.

"Consequently, there remains nothing more to be considered than the means, the apparatus, whereby the transmission of thought is effected.

"This apparatus consists of a square box, in which is a Voltaic pile, of which the metallic plates, instead of being superposed, as in the pile of Volta, are disposed in order, attached in holes formed in a wheel or circular disc, that revolves about a steel axis. To these metallic plates used by Volta, MM. Benoît and Biat have substituted others in the shape of cups or circular basins, composed of zinc lined with cloth steeped in a solution of sulphate of copper maintained in place by a blade of copper riveted to the cup. At the bottom of each of these bowls, is fixed, by aid of a composition that shall be given presently, a living snail, whose sympathetic influence may unite and be woven with the galvanic current, when the wheel of the pile is set in motion and with it the snails that are adhering to it.

"Each galvanic basin rests on a delicate spring, so that it may respond to every escargotic commotion. Now; it is obvious that such an apparatus requires a corresponding apparatus, disposed as has been described, and containing in it snails in sympathy with those in the other apparatus, so that the escargotic vibration may pass from one precise point in one of the piles to a precise point in the other and complementary pile. When these dispositions have been grasped the rest follows as a matter of course. MM. Benoît and Biat have fixed letters to the wheels, corresponding the one with the other, and at each sympathetic touch on one, the other is touched; consequently it is easy by this means, naturally and instantaneously, to communicate ideas at vast distances, by the indication of the letters touched by the snails. The apparatus described is in shape like a mariner's compass, and to distinguish it from that, it is termed the *pasilalinic—sympathetic compass*, as descriptive at once of its effects and the means of operation."

But, who were these inventors, Benoît and Biat-Chrétien? We will begin with the latter. As Pontoppidon in his History of Norway heads a chapter, "Of Snakes," and says, "Of these there are none," so we may say of M. Biat-Chrétien; there was no such man; at least he never rose to the surface and was seen. Apparently his existence was as much a hallucination or creation of the fancy of M. Benoît, as was Mrs. Harris a creature of the imagination of Mrs. Betsy Gamp. Certainly no Biat-Chrétien was known in America as a discoverer.

Jacques Toussaint Benoît (de l'Hérault) was a man who had been devoted since his youth to the secret sciences. His studies in magic and astrology, in mesmerism, and electricity, had turned his head. Together with real eagerness to pursue his studies, and real belief in them, was added a certain spice of rascality.

One day Benoît, who had by some means made the acquaintance of M. Triat, founder and manager of a gymnasium in Paris for athletic exercises, came to Triat, and told him that he had made a discovery which would supersede electric telegraphy. The director was a man of common sense, but not of much education, certainly of no scientific acquirements. He was, therefore, quite unable to distinguish between true and false science. Benoît spoke with conviction, and carried away his hearer with his enthusiasm.

"What is needed for the construction of the machine?" asked M. Triat.

"Only two or three bits of wood," replied Benoît.

M. Triat took him into his carpenter's shop. "There, my friend," he said, "here you have wood, and a man to help you."

M. Triat did more. The future inventor of the instantaneous communication of thought was house-less and hungry. The manager rented a lodging for him, and advanced him money for his entertainment. Benoît set to work. He used a great many bits of wood, and occupied the carpenter a good part of his time. Other things became necessary as well as wood, things that cost money, and the money was found by M. Triat. So passed a twelvemonth. At the end of that time, which had been spent at the cost of his protector, Benoît had arrived at no result. It was apparent that, in applying to M. Triat, he had sought, not so much to construct a machine already invented, as to devote himself to the pursuit of his favourite studies. The director became impatient. He declined to furnish further funds. Then Benoît declared that the machine was complete.

This machine, for the construction of which he had asked for two or three pieces of wood, was an enormous scaffold formed of beams ten feet long, supporting the Voltaic pile described by M. Allix, ensconced in the bowls of which were the wretched snails stuck to the bottom of the basins by some sort of glue, at intervals. This was the Pasilalinic-sympathetic compass. It occupied one end of the apartment. At the other end was a second, exactly similar. Each contained twenty-four alphabetic-sympathetic snails. These poor beasts, glued to the bottom of the zinc cups with little dribbles of sulphate of copper trickling down the sides of the bowls from the saturated cloth placed on them, were uncomfortable, and naturally tried to get away. They thrust themselves from their shells and poked forth their horns groping for some congenial spot on which to crawl, and came in contact with the wood on which was painted the letters. But if they came across a drop of solution of sulphate of copper, they went precipitately back into their shells.

Properly, the two machines should have been established in different rooms, but no second room was available on the flat where Benoît was lodged, so he was forced to erect both vis-à-vis. That, however, was a matter wholly immaterial, as he explained to those who visited the laboratory. Space was not considered by snails. Place one in Paris, the other at the antipodes, the transmission of thought along their sympathetic current was as complete, instantaneous and effective as in his room on the *troisième*. In proof of this, Benoît undertook to correspond with his friend and fellow-worker Biat-Chrétien in America, who had constructed a similar apparatus. He assured all who came to inspect his invention that he conversed daily by means of the snails with his absent friend. When the machine was complete, the inventor was in no hurry to show it in working order; however M. Triat urged performance on him. He said, and there was reason in what he said, that an exhibition of the pasilalinic telegraph before it was perfected, would be putting others on the track, who might, having more means at their command, forestall him, and so rob him of the fruit of his labours. At last he invited M. Triat and M. Allix, as representative of an influential journal, to witness the apparatus in working order, on October 2nd. He assured them that since September 30, he had been in constant correspondence with Biat-Chrétien, who, without crossing the sea, would assist at the experiments conducted at Paris on Wednesday, October 2nd, in the lodging of M. Benoît.

On the appointed day, M. Triat and M. Allix were at the appointed place. The former at once objected to the position of the two compasses, but was constrained to be satisfied with the reason given by the operator. If they could not be in different rooms, at least a division should be made in the apartment by means of a curtain, so that the operator at one compass could not see him at the other. But there was insuperable difficulty in doing this, so M. Triat had to waive this objection also. M. Jules Allix was asked to attend one of the compasses, whilst the inventor stood on the scaffold managing the other. M. Allix was to send the message, by touching the snails which represented the letters forming the words to be transmitted, whereupon the corresponding snail on M. Benoît's apparatus was supposed to thrust forth his horns. But, under one pretext or another, the inventor ran from one apparatus to the other, the whole time, so that it was not very difficult, with a little management, to reproduce on his animated compass the letters transmitted by M. Jules Allix.

The transmission, moreover, was not as exact as it ought to have been. M. Jules Allix had touched the snails in such order as to form the word *gymnase*; Benoît on his compass read the word *gymoate*. Then M. Triat, taking the place of the inventor, sent the words *lumiere divine* to M. Jules Allix, who read on his compass *lumhere divine*. Evidently the snails were bad in their orthography. The whole thing, moreover, was a farce, and the correspondence, such as it was, was due to the incessant voyages of the inventor from one compass to the other, under the pretext of supervising the mechanism of the two apparatuses.

Benoît was then desired to place himself in communication with his American friend, planted before his compass on the other side of the Atlantic. He transmitted to him the signal to be on the alert. Then he touched with a live snail he held in his hand the four snails that corresponded to the letters of the name

BIAT; then they awaited the reply from America. After a few moments, the poor glued snails began to poke out their horns in a desultory, irregular manner, and by putting the letters together, with some accommodation CESTBIEN was made out, which when divided, and the apostrophe added, made *C'est bien*.

M. Triat was much disconcerted. He considered himself as hoaxed. Not so M. Allix. He was so completely satisfied, that on the 27th October, appeared the article from his pen which we have quoted. M. Triat then went to the inventor and told him point blank, that he withdrew his protection from him. Benoît entreated him not to throw up the matter, before the telegraph was perfected.

"Look here!" said M. Triat; "nothing is easier than for you to make me change my intention. Let one of your compasses be set up in my gymnasium, and the other in the side apartment. If that seems too much, then let a simple screen be drawn between the two, and do you refrain from passing between them whilst the experiment is being carried on. If under these conditions you succeed in transmitting a single word from one apparatus to the other, I will give you a thousand francs a day whilst your experiments are successful."

M. Triat then visited M. de Girardin who was interested in the matter, half believed in it, and had accordingly opened the columns of *La Presse* to the article of M. Allix. M. de Girardin wished to be present at the crucial experiment, and M. Triat gladly invited him to attend. He offered another thousand francs so long as the compasses worked. "My plan is this," said M. de Girardin: "If Benoît's invention is a success, we will hire the *Jardin d'hiver* and make Benoît perform his experiments in public. That will bring us in a great deal more than two thousand francs a day."

Benoît accepted all the conditions with apparent alacrity; but, before the day arrived for the experiment, after the removal of the two great scaffolds to the gymnasiums—he had disappeared. He was, however, seen afterwards several times in Paris, very thin, with eager restless eyes, apparently partly deranged. He died in 1852!

Alas for Benoît. He died a few years too soon. A little later, and he might have become a personage of importance in the great invasion of the table-turning craze which shortly after inundated Europe, and turned many heads as well as tables.

XI. — *THE COUNTESS GOERLITZ*

ONE of the most strange and terrible tragedies of this century was the murder of the Countess Goerlitz; and it excited immense interest in Germany, both because of the high position of the unfortunate lady, the mystery attaching to her death, and because the charge of having murdered her rested on her husband, the Count Goerlitz, Chamberlain to the Grand-Duke of Hesse, Privy Councillor, a man of fortune as well as rank, and of unimpeachable character. There was another reason why the case excited general interest: the solution remained a mystery for three whole years, from 1847 to 1850.

The Count Goerlitz was a man of forty-six, a great favourite at the Court, and of fine appearance. He had married, in 1820, the daughter of the Privy Councillor, Plitt. They had no children. The Countess was aged forty-six when the terrible event occurred which we are about to relate.

The Count and Countess lived in their mansion in the Neckarstrasse in Darmstadt—a large, palatial house, handsomely furnished. Although living under the same roof, husband and wife lived apart. She occupied the first floor, and he the parterre, or ground floor. They dined together. The cause of the unfriendly terms on which they lived was the fact that the Countess was wealthy, her family was of citizen origin, and had amassed a large fortune in trade. Her father had been ennobled by the Grand-Duke, and she had been his heiress. The Count, himself, had not much of his own, and his wife cast this fact in his teeth. She loved to talk of the "beggar nobility," who were obliged to look out for rich burghers' daughters to gild their coronets. The Count may have been hot of temper, and have aggravated matters by sharpness of repartee; but, according to all accounts, it was her miserliness and bitter tongue which caused the estrangement.

There were but four servants in the house—the Count's valet, the coachman, a manservant of the Countess, and the cook.

Every Sunday the Count Goerlitz dined at the palace. On Sunday, June 13, 1847, he had dined at the Grand-Duke's table as usual. As we know from the letters of the Princess Alice, life was simple at that Court. Hours were, as usual in South Germany, early. The carriage took the Count to dinner at the palace at 3 P.M., and he returned home in it to the Neckar Street at half-past six. When he came in he asked the servant of the Countess, a man named John Stauff, whether his wife was at home, as he wanted to see her. As a matter of fact, he had brought away from the dinner-table at the palace some maccaroons and bonbons for her, as she had a sweet tooth, and he thought the attention might please her.

As John Stauff told him the Countess was in, he ascended the stone staircase. A glass door led into the anteroom. He put his hand to it and found it fastened. Thinking that his wife was asleep, or did not want to be disturbed, he went downstairs to his own room, which was under her sitting-room. There he listened for her tread, intending, on hearing it, to reascend and present her with the bonbons. As he heard nothing, he went out for a walk. The time was half-past seven. A little before nine o'clock he returned from his stroll, drew on his dressing-gown and slippers, and asked for his supper, a light meal he was wont to take by himself in his own room, though not always, for the Countess frequently joined him. Her mood was capricious. As he had the bonbons in his pocket, and had not yet been able to present them, he sent her man Stauff to tell her ladyship that supper was served, and that it would give him great satisfaction if she would honour him with her presence. Stauff came back in a few moments to say that the Countess was not at home. "Nonsense!" said the husband, "of course she is at home. She may, however, be asleep. I will go myself and find her." Thereupon he ascended the stairs, and found, as before, the glass door to the anteroom fastened. He looked in, but saw nothing. He knocked, and received no answer. Then he went to the bedroom door, knocked, without result; listened, and heard no sound. The Count had a key to the dressing-room; he opened, and went in, and through that he passed into the bed-chamber. That was empty. The bed-clothes were turned down for the night, but were otherwise undisturbed. He had no key to the anteroom and drawing-room.

Then the Count went upstairs to the laundry, which was on the highest storey, and where were also some rooms. The Countess was particular about her lace and linen, and often attended to them herself, getting up some of the collars and frills with her own hands. She was not in the laundry. Evidently she was, as Stauff had said, not at home. The Count questioned the manservant. Had his mistress intimated her intention of supping abroad? No, she had not. Nevertheless, it was possible she might have gone to intimate friends. Accordingly, he sent to the palace of Prince Wittgenstein, and to the house of Councillor von Storch, to inquire if she were at either. She had been seen at neither.

The Count was puzzled, without, however, being seriously alarmed. He bade Stauff call the valet, Schiller, and the coachman, Schämbs, who slept out of the house, and then go for a locksmith. Stauff departed. Presently the valet and coachman arrived, and, after, Stauff, without the locksmith, who, he said, was ill, and his man was at the tavern. The Count was angry and scolded. Then the coachman went forth, and soon came back with the locksmith's apprentice, who was set at once to open the locked doors in the top storey. The Countess was not in them. At the same time the young man noticed a smell of burning, but whence it came they could not decide. Thinking that this smell came from the kitchen on the first storey— that is, the floor above where the Count lived—they attacked the door of the kitchen, which was also locked. She was not there. Then the Count led the way to the private sitting-room of the Countess. As yet only the young locksmith had noticed the fire, the others were uncertain whether they smelt anything unusual or not. The key of the apprentice would not fit the lock of the Countess' ante-room, so he ran home to get another. Then the Count went back to his own apartment, and on entering it, himself perceived the smell of burning. Accordingly, he went upstairs again, to find that the coachman had opened an iron stove door in the passage, and that a thick pungent smoke was pouring out of it. We must enter here into an explanation. In many cases the porcelain stove of a German house has no opening into the room. It is lighted outside through a door into the passage. Several stoves communicate with one chimney. The Count and his servants ran out into the courtyard to look at the chimney stack to see if smoke were issuing from it. None was. Then they returned to the house. The apprentice had not yet returned. Looking through the glass door, they saw that there was smoke in the room. It had been unperceived before, for it was evening and dusk. At once the Count's valet, Schiller, smashed the plate glass, and through the broken glass smoke rolled towards them.

The hour was half-past ten. The search had occupied an hour and a half. It had not been prosecuted with great activity; but then, no suspicion of anything to cause alarm had been entertained. If the Countess were at home, she must be in the sitting-room. From this room the smoke must come which pervaded the ante-chamber. The fire must be within, and if the Countess were there, she must run the danger of suffocation. Consequently, as the keys were not at hand, the doors ought to be broken open at once. This was not done. Count Goerlitz sent the servants away. Stauff he bade run for a chimney-sweep, and Schiller for his medical man, Dr. Stegmayer. The coachman had lost his head and ran out into the street, yelling, "Fire! fire!" The wife of Schiller, who had come in, ran out to summon assistance.

The Count was left alone outside the glass door; and there he remained passive till the arrival of the locksmith's man with the keys. More time was wasted. None of the keys would open the door, and still the smoke rolled out. Then the apprentice beat the door open with a stroke of his hammer. He did it of his own accord, without orders from the Count. That was remembered afterwards. At once a dense, black, sickly-smelling smoke poured forth, and prevented the entrance of those who stood without.

In the meantime, the coachman and others had put ladders against the wall, one to the window of the ante-room, the other to that of the parlour. Seitz, the apprentice, ran up the ladder, and peered in. The room was quite dark. He broke two panes in the window, and at once a blue flame danced up, caught the curtains, flushed yellow, and shot out a fiery tongue through the broken window. Seitz, who seems to have been the only man with presence of mind, boldly put his arm through and unfastened the valves, and, catching the burning curtains, tore them down and flung them into the street. Then he cast down two chairs which were flaming from the window. He did not venture in because of the smoke.

In the meanwhile the coachman had broken the window panes of the ante-room. This produced a draught through the room, as the glass door had been broken in by Seitz. The smoke cleared sufficiently to allow of admission to the parlour door. This door was also found to be locked, and not only locked, but with the key withdrawn from it, as had been from the ante-chamber door. This door was also burst open, and then it was seen that the writing-desk of the Countess was on fire. That was all that could be distinguished at the first glance. The room was full of smoke, and the heat was so great that no one could enter.

Water was brought in jugs and pails, and thrown upon the floor. The current of air gradually dissipated the smoke, and something white was observed on the floor near the burning desk. "Good heavens!" exclaimed the Count, "there she lies!"

The Countess lay on the floor beside her writing-desk; the white object was her stockings.

Among those who entered was a smith called Wetzell; he dashed forward, flung a pail of water over the burning table, caught hold of the feet of the dead body, and dragged it into the ante-room. Then he sought to raise it, but it slipped through his hands. A second came to his assistance, with the same result. The corpse was like melted butter. When he seized it by the arm, the flesh came away from the bone.

The body was laid on a mat, and so transported into a cabinet. The upper portion was burnt to coal; one hand was charred; on the left foot was a shoe, the other was found, later, in another room. More water was brought, and the fire in the parlour was completely quenched. Then only was it possible to examine the place. The fire had, apparently, originated at the writing-desk or secretaire of the Countess; the body had lain before the table, and near it was a chair, thrown over. From the drawing-room a door, which was found open, led into the boudoir. This boudoir had a window that looked into a side street. In the ante-room were no traces of fire. In the drawing-room only the secretaire and the floor beneath it had been burnt. On a chiffonier against the wall were candlesticks, the stearine candles in them had been melted by the heat of the room and run over the chiffonier.

In this room was also a sofa, opposite the door leading from the ante-chamber, some way from the desk and the seat of the fire. In the middle of the sofa was a hole fourteen inches long by six inches broad, burnt through the cretonne cover, the canvas below, and into the horse hair beneath. A looking-glass hung against the wall above; this glass was broken and covered with a deposit as of smoke. It was apparent, therefore, that a flame had leaped up on the sofa sufficiently high and hot to snap the mirror and obscure it.

Left of the entrance-door was a bell-rope, torn down and cast on the ground.

Beyond the parlour was the boudoir. It had a little corner divan. Its cover was burnt through in two places. The cushion at the back was also marked with holes burnt through. Above this seat against the wall hung an oil painting. It was blistered with heat. Near it was an étagère, on which were candles; these also were found melted completely away. In this boudoir was found the slipper from the right foot of the Countess.

If the reader will consider what we have described, he will see that something very mysterious must have occurred. There were traces of burning in three distinct places—on the sofa, and at the secretaire in the parlour, and on the corner seat in the boudoir. It was clear also that the Countess had been in both rooms, for her one slipper was in the boudoir, the other on her foot in the drawing-room. Apparently, also, she had rung for assistance, and torn down the bell-rope.

Another very significant and mysterious feature of the case was the fact that the two doors were found locked, and that the key was not found with the body, nor anywhere in the rooms. Consequently, the Countess had not locked herself in.

Again:—the appearance of the corpse was peculiar. The head and face were burnt to cinder, especially the face, less so the back of the head. All the upper part of the body had been subjected to fire, as far as the lower ribs, and there the traces of burning ceased absolutely. Also, the floor was burnt in proximity to the corpse, but not where it lay. The body had protected the floor where it lay from fire.

The police were at once informed of what had taken place, and the magistrates examined the scene and the witnesses. This was done in a reprehensibly inefficient manner. The first opinion entertained was that the Countess had been writing at her desk, and had set fire to herself, had run from room to room, tried to obtain assistance by ringing the bell, had failed, fallen, and died. Three medical men were called in to examine the body. One decided that this was a case of spontaneous combustion. The second that it was not a case of spontaneous combustion. The third simply stated that she had been burnt, but how the fire originated he was unable to say. No minute examination of the corpse was made. It was not even stripped of the half-burnt clothes upon it. It was not dissected. The family physician signed a certificate of "accidental death," and two days after the body was buried.

Only three or, at the outside, four hypotheses could account for the death of the Countess.

1. She had caught fire accidentally, whilst writing at her desk.

2. She had died of spontaneous combustion.

3. She had been murdered.

There is, indeed, a fourth hypothesis—that she had committed suicide; but this was too improbable to be entertained. The manner of death was not one to be reconciled with the idea of suicide.

The first idea was that in the minds of the magistrates. They were prepossessed with it. They saw nothing that could militate against it. Moreover, the Count was Chamberlain at Court, a favourite of the sovereign and much liked by the princes, also a man generally respected. Unquestionably this had something to do with the hasty and superficial manner in which the examination was gone through. The magistrates desired to have the tragedy hushed up.

A little consideration shows that the theory of accident was untenable. The candles were on the chiffonier, and no traces of candlesticks were found on the spot where the fire had burned. Moreover, the appearance of the secretaire was against this theory. The writing-desk and table consisted of a falling flap, on which the Countess wrote, and which she could close and lock. Above this table were several small drawers which contained her letters, receipted bills, and her jewelry. Below it were larger drawers. The upper drawers were not completely burnt; on the other hand, the lower drawers were completely consumed, and their bottoms and contents had fallen in cinders on the floor beneath, which was also burnt through to the depth of an inch and a half to two inches. It was apparent, therefore, that the secretaire had been set on fire from below. Moreover, there was more charcoal found under it than could be accounted for, by supposing it had fallen from above. Now it will be remembered that only the upper portion of the body was consumed. The Countess had not set fire to herself whilst writing, and so set fire to the papers on the desk. That was impossible.

The supposition that she had died of spontaneous combustion was also entertained by a good many. But no well-authenticated case of spontaneous combustion is known. Professor Liebig, when afterwards examined on this case, stated that spontaneous combustion of the human body was absolutely impossible, and such an idea must be relegated to the region of myths.

There remained, therefore, no other conclusion at which it was possible for a rational person to arrive who weighed the circumstances than that the Countess had been murdered.

The Magisterial Court of the city of Darmstadt had attempted to hush-up the case. The German press took it up. It excited great interest and indignation throughout the country. It was intimated pretty pointedly that the case had been scandalously slurred over, because of the rank of the Count and the intimate relation in which he stood to the royal family. The papers did not shrink from more than insinuating that this was a case of murder, and that the murderer was the husband of the unfortunate woman. Some suspicion that this was so seems to have crossed the minds of the servants of the house. They recollected his dilatoriness in entering the rooms of the Countess; the time that was protracted in idle sending for keys, and trying key after key, when a kick of the foot or a blow of the hammer would have sufficed to give admission to the room where she lay. It was well known that the couple did not live on the best terms. To maintain appearances before the world, they dined and occasionally supped together. They rarely met alone, and when they did fell into dispute, and high words passed which the servants heard.

The Countess was mean and miserly, she grudged allowing her husband any of her money. She had, however, made her will the year before, leaving all her large fortune to her husband for life. Consequently her death released him from domestic and pecuniary annoyances. On the morning after the death he sent for the agent of the insurance company with whom the furniture and other effects were insured and made his claim. He claimed, in addition to the value of the furniture destroyed, the worth of a necklace of diamonds and pearls which had been so injured by the fire that it had lost the greater part of its value. The pearls were quite spoiled, and the diamonds reduced in worth by a half. The agent refused this claim, as he contended that the jewelry was not included in the insurance, and the Count abstained from pressing it.

To the Count the situation became at length intolerable. He perceived a decline of cordiality in his reception at Court, his friends grew cold, and acquaintances cut him. He must clear himself of the charge which now weighed on him. The death of the Countess had occurred on June 13, 1847. On October 6, that is four months later, Count Goerlitz appeared before the Grand-Ducal Criminal Court of Darmstadt, and produced a bundle of German newspapers charging him with having murdered his wife, and set fire to the room to conceal the evidence of his crime. He therefore asked to have the case re-opened, and the witnesses re-examined. Nothing followed. The Court hesitated to take up the case again, and throw discredit on the magistrates' decision in June. Again, on October 16, the Count renewed his request, and desired, if this were refused, that he and his solicitor might be allowed access to the minutes of the examination, that they might be enabled to take decided measures for the clearing of the Count's character, and the chastisement of those who charged him with an atrocious crime. On October 21, he received a reply, "that his request could not be granted, unless he produced such additional evidence as would show the Court that the former examination was defective."

On October 25, the Count laid a mass of evidence before the Court which, he contended, would materially modify, if not absolutely upset the conclusion arrived at by the previous investigation.

Then, at last, consent was given; but proceedings did not begin till November, and dragged on till the end of October in the following year, when a new law of criminal trial having been passed in the grand-duchy, the whole of what had gone before became invalid, save as preliminary investigation, and it was not till March 4, 1850—that is, not till *three years* after the death of the Countess—that the case was thoroughly sifted and settled. Before the promulgation of the law of October, 1848, all trials were private, then trial by jury, and in public, was introduced.

However, something had been done. In August 1848—that is, over a year after the burial of the Countess—the body was exhumed and submitted to examination. Two facts were then revealed. The skull of the Countess had been fractured by some blunt instrument; and she had been strangled. The condition in which the tongue had been found when the body was first discovered had pointed to strangulation, the state of the jaws when exhumed proved it.

So much, then, was made probable. A murderer had entered the room, struck the Countess on the head, and when that did not kill her, he had throttled her. Then, apparently, so it was argued, he had burnt the body, and next, before it was more than half consumed, had placed it near the secretaire, and, finally, had set fire to the secretaire.

He had set fire to the writing-desk to lead to the supposition that the Countess had set fire to herself whilst writing at it; and this was the first conclusion formed.

That a struggle had taken place appeared from several circumstances. The bell-rope was torn down. Probably no servant had been in the house that Sunday evening when the bell rang desperately for aid. The seat flung over seemed to point to her having been surprised at the desk. One shoe was in the boudoir. The struggle had been continued as she fled from the sitting-room into the inner apartment.

Now, only, were the fire-marks on the divan and sofa explicable. The Countess had taken refuge first on one, then on the other, after having been wounded, and her blood had stained them. The murderer had burnt out the marks of blood.

She had fled from the sitting-room to the boudoir, and thence had hoped to escape through the next door into a corner room, but the door of that room was locked.

The next point to be determined was, where had her body been burnt.

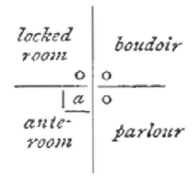

In the sitting-room, the boudoir, and a locked corner room were stoves. The walls of these rooms met, and in the angles were the stoves. They all communicated with one chimney. They were all heated from an opening in the anteroom, marked *a*, which closed with an iron door, and was covered with tapestry. The opening was large enough for a human being to be thrust through, and the fire-chamber amply large enough also for its consumption.

Much time had passed since a serious examination was begun, and it was too late to think of finding evidence of the burning of the body in this place. The stoves had been used since, each winter. However, some new and surprising evidence did come to light. At five minutes past eight on the evening that the mysterious death took place, Colonel von Stockhausen was on the opposite side of the street talking to a lady, when his attention was arrested by a dense black smoke issuing suddenly from the chimney of the Count Goerlitz' palace. He continued looking at the column of smoke whilst conversing with the lady, uncertain whether the chimney were on fire or not, and whether he ought to give the alarm. When the lady left him, after about ten minutes, or a quarter of an hour, he saw that smoke ceased to issue from the chimney. He accordingly went his way without giving notice of the smoke.

So far every piece of evidence went to show that the Countess had been murdered. The conclusion now arrived at was this: she had been struck on the head, chased from room to room bleeding, had been caught, strangled, then thrust into the fire-chamber of the stove over a fire which only half consumed her; taken out again and laid before the secretaire, and the secretaire deliberately set fire to, and all the blood-marks obliterated by fire. That something of this kind had taken place was evident. Who had done it was not so clear. The efforts of the Count to clear himself had established the fact that his wife was murdered, but did not establish his innocence.

Suddenly—the case assumed a new aspect, through an incident wholly unexpected and extraordinary.

The result of inquiry into the case of the death of the Countess Goerlitz was, that the decision that she had come to her end by accident, given by the city magistrates, was upset, and it was made abundantly clear that she had been murdered. By whom murdered was not so clear.

Inquiry carried the conclusion still further. She had been robbed as well as murdered.

We have already described the writing-desk of the Countess. There were drawers below the flap, and other smaller drawers concealed by it when closed. In the smaller drawers she kept her letters, her bills, her vouchers for investments, and her jewelry. Among the latter was the pearl and diamond necklace, which she desired by her will might be sold, and the money given to a charitable institution. The necklace was indeed discovered seriously injured; but what had become of her bracelets, brooches, rings, her other necklets, her earrings? She had also a chain of pearls, which was nowhere to be found. All these articles were gone. No trace of them had been found in the cinders under the secretaire; moreover, the drawers in which she preserved them were not among those burnt through. In the first excitement and bewilderment caused by her death, the Count had not observed the loss, and the magistrates had not thought fit to inquire whether any robbery had been committed.

A very important fact was now determined. The Countess had been robbed, and murdered, probably for the sake of her jewels. Consequently the murderer was not likely to be the Count.

When the case was re-opened, at Count Goerlitz's repeated demand, an "Inquirent" was appointed by the Count to examine the case—that is, an official investigator of all the circumstances; and on November 2, 1847, in the morning, notice was given to the Count that the "Inquirent" would visit his mansion on the morrow and examine both the scene of the murder and the servants. The Count at once convoked his domestics and bade them be in the house next day, ready for examination.

That same afternoon the cook, Margaret Eyrich by name, was engaged in the kitchen preparing dinner for the master, who dined at 4 P.M. At three o'clock the servant-man, John Stauff, came into the kitchen and told the cook that her master wanted a fire lit in one of the upper rooms. She refused to go because she was busy at the stove. Stauff remained a quarter of an hour there talking to her. Then he said it was high time for him to lay the table for dinner, a remark to which she gave an assent, wondering in her own mind why he had delayed so long. He took up a soup dish, observed that it was not quite clean, and asked her to wash it. She was then engaged on some sauce over the fire.

"I will wash it, if you will stir the sauce," she said. "If I leave the pan, the sauce will be burnt."

Stauff consented, and she went with the dish to the sink. Whilst thus engaged, she turned her head, and was surprised to see that Stauff had a small phial in his hand, and was pouring its contents into the sauce.

She asked him what he was about; he denied having done anything, and the woman, with great prudence, said nothing further, so as not to let him think that her suspicions were aroused. Directly, however, that he had left the kitchen, she examined the sauce, saw it was discoloured, and on trying it, that the taste was unpleasant. She called in the coachman and the housekeeper. On consultation they decided that this matter must be further investigated. The housekeeper took charge of the sauce, and carried it to Dr. Stegmayer, the family physician, who at once said that verdigris had been mixed with it, and desired that the police should be communicated with. This was done, the sauce was analysed, and found to contain 15½ grains of verdigris, enough to poison a man. Thereupon Stauff was arrested.

We see now that an attempt had been made on the life of the Count, on the day on which he had announced that an official inquiry into the murder was to be made in his house and among his domestics.

Stauff, then, was apparently desirous of putting the Count out of the way before that inquiry was made. At this very time a terrible tragedy had occurred in France, and was in all the papers. The Duke of Praslin had murdered his wife, and when he was about to be arrested, the duke had poisoned himself.

Did Stauff wish that the Count should be found poisoned that night, in order that the public might come to the conclusion he had committed suicide to escape arrest? It would seem so.

John Stauff's arrest took place on November 3, 1847, four months and a half after the death of the Countess. He was, however, only arrested on a charge of attempting to poison the Count, and the further charge of having murdered the Countess was not brought against him till August 28, 1848. The body of the murdered woman, it will be remembered, was not exhumed and examined till August 11, 1848—eight months after the re-opening of the investigation! It is really wonderful that the mystery should have been cleared and the Count's character satisfactorily vindicated, with such dilatoriness of proceeding. One more instance of the stupid way in which the whole thing was managed. Although John Stauff was charged with the attempt to poison on November 3, 1847, he was not questioned on the charge till January 10, 1849, that is, till he had been fourteen months in prison.

It will be remembered that the bell-rope in the Countess's parlour was torn down. It would suggest itself to the meanest capacity that here was a point of departure for inquiry. If the bell had been torn down, it must have pealed its summons for help through the house. Who was in the house at the time? If anyone was, why did he not answer the appeal? Inconceivable was the neglect of the magistrates of Darmstadt in the first examination—they did not inquire. Only several months later was this matter subjected to investigation.

In the house lived the Count and Countess, the cook, who also acted as chambermaid to the Countess, Schiller, the valet to the Count, Schämbs, the coachman, and the Countess's own servant-man, John Stauff. Of these Schiller and Schämbs did not sleep in the house.

June 13, the day of the murder, was a Sunday. The Count went as usual to the grand-ducal palace in his coach at 3 P.M. The coachman drove him; Stauff sat on the box beside the coachman. They left the Count at the palace and returned home. They were ordered to return to the palace to fetch him at 6 P.M. On Sundays, the Count usually spent his day in his own suite of apartments, and the Countess in hers. On the morning in question she had come downstairs to her husband with a bundle of coupons which she wanted him to cash for her on the morrow. He managed her fortune for her. The sum was small, only £30. At 2 P.M. she went to the kitchen to tell the cook she might go out for the afternoon, as she would not be wanted, and that she must return by 9 P.M.

At three o'clock the cook left. The cook saw and spoke to her as she left. The Countess was then partially undressed, and the cook supposed she was changing her clothes. Shortly after this, Schiller, the Count's valet, saw and spoke with her. She was then upstairs in the laundry arranging the linen for the mangle. She was then in her morning cotton dress. Consequently she had not dressed herself to go out, as the cook supposed. At the same time the carriage left the court of the house for the palace. That was the last seen of her alive, except by John Stauff, and, if he was not the murderer, by one other.

About a quarter past three the coach returned with Schämbs and Stauff on the box. The Count had been left at the palace. The coachman took out his horses, without unharnessing them, and left for his own house, at half-past three, to remain there till 5 o'clock, when he must return, put the horses in, and drive back to the palace to fetch the Count. A quarter of an hour after the coachman left, Schiller went out for a walk with his little boy.

Consequently—none were in the house but the Countess and Stauff, and Stauff knew that the house was clear till 5 o'clock, when Schämbs would return to the stables. What happened during that time?

At a quarter past four, the wife of Schiller came to the house with a little child, and a stocking she was knitting. She wanted to know if her husband had gone with the boy to Eberstadt, a place about four miles distant. She went to the back-door. It was not fastened, but on being opened rang a bell, like a shop door. Near it were two rooms, one occupied by Schiller, the other by Stauff. The wife went into her husband's room and found it empty. Then she went into that of Stauff. It also was empty. She returned into the entrance hall and listened. Everything was still in the house. She stood there some little while knitting and listening. Presently she heard steps descending the backstairs, and saw Stauff, with an apron about him, and a duster in his hand. She asked him if her husband had gone to Eberstadt, and he said that he had. Then she left the house. Stauff, however, called to her from the window to hold up the child to him, to kiss. She did so, and then departed.

Shortly after five, Schämbs returned to the stable, put in the horses, and drove to the palace without seeing Stauff. He thought nothing of this, as Stauff usually followed on foot, in time to open the coach door for the Count. On this occasion, Stauff appeared at his post in livery, at a quarter to six. At half-past six both returned with their master to the house in Neckar Street.

Accordingly, from half-past three to a quarter past four, and from half-past four to half-past five, Stauff was alone in the house with the Countess. But then, from a quarter to five to half-past five she was quite alone, and it was possible that the murder was committed at that time. The Count, it will be remembered, on his return, went upstairs and knocked at the door of the Countess' apartments, without meeting with a response. Probably, therefore, she was then dead.

At seven o'clock the coachman went away, and Stauff helped the Count to take off his court dining dress, and put on a light suit. He was with him till half-past seven, when the Count went out for a walk. The Count returned at half-past eight; during an hour, therefore, Stauff was alone in the house with the Countess, or—her corpse.

What occurred during that hour? Here two independent pieces of evidence come in to assist us in determining what took place. At five minutes past eight, Colonel von Stockhausen had seen the column of black smoke issue from the chimney of the house; it ascended, he said, some fifteen feet above the chimney, and was so dense that it riveted his attention whilst he was talking to a lady.

At about a quarter-past eight the smoke ceased.

The reader may remember that the window of the inner boudoir did not look into the Neckar Street, but into a small side street. Immediately opposite lived a widow lady named Kekule. On the evening in question, her daughter, Augusta, a girl of eighteen, came in from a walk, and went upstairs to the room the window of which was exactly opposite, though at a somewhat higher level than the window of the boudoir. Looking out of her window, Augusta Kekule saw to her astonishment a flickering light like a lambent flame in the boudoir. A blind was down, so that she could see nothing distinctly. She was, however, alarmed, and called her brother Augustus, aged twenty years, and both watched the flames flashing in the room. They called their mother also, and all three saw it flare up high, then decrease, and go out. The time was 8.15. On examination of the spot, it was seen that the window of Miss Kekule commanded the corner of the boudoir, where was the divan partly burnt through in several places.

What was the meaning of these two appearances, the smoke and the flame? Apparently, from half-past seven to half-past eight the murderer was engaged in burning the body, and in effacing with fire the blood-stains on the sofas. During this time John Stauff was in the house, and, beside the Countess, alive or dead, John Stauff only.

Stauff was now subjected to examination. He was required to account for his time on the afternoon and evening of Sunday, June 13.

He said, that after his return from the palace, that is, about ten minutes past three, he went into his room on the basement, and ate bread and cheese. When told that the wife of Schiller stated she had seen him come downstairs, he admitted that he had run upstairs to fetch a duster, to brush away the bread crumbs from the table at which he had eaten. After the woman left, according to his own account, he remained in his room below till five o'clock, when the Countess came to the head of the stairs and called him. He went up and found her on the topmost landing; she went into the laundry, and he stood in the door whilst she spoke to him, and gave him some orders for the butcher and baker. She wore, he said, a black stuff gown. Whilst he was talking to her, Schämbs drove away to fetch the Count. He gave a correct account of what followed, up to the departure of the Count on his walk. After that, he said, he had written a letter to his sweetheart, and at eight went out to get his supper at an outdoor restaurant where he remained till half-past nine. He was unable to produce evidence of anyone who had seen him and spoken to him there; but, of course, much cannot be made of this, owing to the distance of time at which the evidence was taken from the event of the murder. According to his account, therefore, no one was in the house at the time when the smoke rose from the chimney, and the flame was seen in the boudoir.

If we sum up the points determined concerning the murder of the Countess, we shall see how heavily the evidence told against Stauff.

She had been attacked in her room, and after a desperate struggle, which went on in both parlour and boudoir, she had been killed.

Her secretaire had been robbed.

Her body had been burnt.

The blood-stains had been effaced by fire.

The secretaire had been set fire to; and, apparently, the body removed from where it had been partially consumed, and placed near it.

Now all this must have taken time. It could only be done by one who knew that he had time in which to effect it undisturbed.

John Stauff was at two separate times, in the afternoon and evening, alone in the house for an hour, knowing that during that time he would be undisturbed.

If his account were true, the murder must have been committed during his brief absence with the coach, and the burning of the body, and setting fire to the room, done when he went out to get his supper. But—how could the murderer suppose he would leave the house open and unprotected at eight o'clock? Was it likely that a murderer and robber, after having killed the Countess and taken her jewels at six o'clock, would hang about till eight, waiting the chance of getting back to the scene of his crime unobserved, to attempt to disguise it? not knowing, moreover, how much time he would have for effecting his purpose?

It was possible that this had been done, but it was not probable.

Evidence was forthcoming from a new quarter that served to establish the guilt of Stauff.

On October 6, 1847, an oilman, Henry Stauff, in Oberohmen, in Hesse Cassel, was arrested, because he was found to be disposing of several articles of jewelry, without being able to give a satisfactory account of where he got them. The jewelry consisted of a lump of molten gold, and some brooches, bracelets and rings.

Henry Stauff had been a whitesmith in his youth, then he became a carrier, but in the last few years, since the death of his wife, he had sold knives, and been a knife-grinder. He was very poor, and had been unable to pay his rates. In July of 1847, however, his affairs seemed to have mended; he wore a silver watch, and took out a licence to deal in oil and seeds. When he applied for the patent, the burgomaster was surprised, and asked him how he could get stock to set up business, in his state of poverty. Thereupon, Henry Stauff opened his purse and showed that it contained a good amount of silver, and—with the coins was a gold ring with, apparently, a precious stone in it.

The cause of his arrest was his offering the lump of gold to a silversmith in Cassel. It looked so much as if it was the melting up of jewelry, that the smith communicated with the police. On his arrest, Henry Stauff said he was the father of four children, two sons and two daughters; that his sons, one of whom was in the army, had sent him money, that his daughter in America had given him the jewelry, and that the gold he had had by him for several years, it had been given him by a widow, who was dead. The silver watch he had bought in Frankfort. Henry Stauff had a daughter at home, name Anna Margaretta, who often received letters from Darmstadt. One of these letters had not been stamped, and as she declined to pay double for it, it lay in the post-office till opened to be returned. Then it was found to be dated September 29, 1847, and to be from her brother, John Stauff. It simply contained an inclosure to her father; this was opened; it contained an angry remonstrance with him for not having done what he was required, and sent the money at once to the writer.

Was it possible that this had reference to the disposal of the jewelry?

On July 7, three weeks after the death of the Countess, Henry Stauff was at Darmstadt, where one son, Jacob, was in the army; the other, John, was in service with the Goerlitz family.

This led the magistrates in Cassel to communicate with those in Darmstadt. On November 10, John Stauff was questioned with reference to his father. He said he had often sent him money. He was shown the jewelry, and asked if he recognised it. He denied having ever seen it, and having sent it to his father.

The jewelry was shown to Count Goerlitz, and he immediately identified it as having belonged to his wife. A former lady's-maid of the Countess also identified the articles. The Count, and a maid, asserted that these articles had always been kept by the deceased lady in the small upper drawers of her secretaire. The Countess was vain and miserly, and often looked over her jewelry. She would, certainly, have missed her things had they been stolen before June 13.

The articles had not been stolen since, found among the ashes, and carried off surreptitiously, for they showed no trace of fire.

Here we must again remark on the extraordinary character of the proceedings in this case. The articles were identified and shown to John Stauff on November 10, 1847, but it was not till ten months after, on August 28, 1848, that he was told that he was suspected of the murder of the Countess, and of having robbed her of these ornaments. Another of the eccentricities of the administration of justice in Darmstadt consisted in allowing the father Henry, and his son John, to have free private communication with each other, whilst the latter was in prison, and thus allowing them to concoct together a plausible account of their conduct, with which, however, we need not trouble ourselves.

On September 1, 1848, on the fourth day after Stauff knew that he was charged with the murder of the Countess, he asked to make his statement of what really took place. This was the account he gave. It will be seen that, from the moment he knew the charge of murder was brought against him, he altered his defence.

He said, "On June 20, 1847," (that is, a week after the murder), "about ten o'clock in the evening, after the Count had partaken of his supper and undressed, he brought me a box containing jewelry, and told me he would give it to me, as I was so poor, and that it would place my father and me in comfortable circumstances. I then told the Count that I did not know what to do with these jewels, whereupon he exhorted me to send them to my father, and get him to dispose of them. He told me that he required me solemnly to swear that I would not tell anyone about the jewels. I hid the box in a stocking and concealed it in some bushes on the Bessungen road. Later I told my brother Jacob where they were, and bade him give them to my father on his visit to Darmstadt."

When Stauff was asked what reason he could assign for the Count giving him the jewels, he said that the Count saw that he, John Stauff, suspected him of the murder, and he named several circumstances, such as observing blood on the Count's handkerchief on the evening of the murder, which had led him to believe that the Count was guilty, and the Count was aware of his suspicions.

On March 4, 1850, began the trial of John Stauff for the murder of the Countess, for robbery, for arson, and for attempt to poison the Count.

At the same time his father, Henry Stauff, and his brother, Jacob Stauff, were tried for concealment of stolen goods. The trial came to an end on April 11. As many as 118 witnesses were heard; among these was the Count Goerlitz, as to whose innocence no further doubts were entertained.

John Stauff was at that time aged twenty-six, he was therefore twenty-four years old at the time of the murder. He had been at school at Oberohmen, where he had shown himself an apt and intelligent scholar. In 1844 he had entered the grand-ducal army, and in May 1846 had become servant in the Goerlitz house, as footman to the Countess. In his regiment he had behaved well; he had been accounted an excellent servant, and both his master and mistress placed confidence in him. Curiously enough, in the autumn of 1846, he had expressed a wish to a chambermaid of the Countess "that both the Countess and her pack of jewels, bracelets and all, might be burnt in one heap."

When the maid heard of the death of the Countess in the following year, "Ah!" she said, "now Stauff's wish has been fulfilled to the letter."

He was fond of talking of religion, and had the character among his fellow-servants of being pious. He was, however, deep in debt, and associated with women of bad character. Throughout the trial he maintained his composure, his lips closed, his colour pale, without token of agitation. But the man who could have stood by without showing emotion at the opening of the coffin of his mistress, at the sight of the half-burnt, half-decomposed remains of his victim, must have had powers of self-control of no ordinary description. During the trial he seemed determined to show that he was a man of some culture; he exhibited ease of manner and courtesy towards judges, jury, and lawyers. He never interrupted a witness, and when he questioned them, did so with intelligence and moderation. He often looked at the public, especially the women, who attended in great numbers, watching the effect of the evidence on their minds. When, as now and then happened, some ludicrous incident occurred, he laughed over it as heartily as the most innocent looker-on.

The jury unanimously found him "guilty" on every count. They unanimously gave a verdict of "guilty" against his father and brother. Henry Stauff was sentenced to six months' imprisonment; Jacob Stauff to detention for three months, and John to imprisonment for life. At that time capital punishment could not be inflicted in Hesse.

On June 3, he was taken to the convict prison of Marienschloss. On July 1, he appealed to the Grand-Duke to give him a free pardon, as he was innocent of the crimes for which he was sentenced. The appeal was rejected. Then he professed his intention of making full confession. He asked to see the Count. He professed himself a broken-hearted penitent, desirous of undoing, by a sincere confession, as much of the evil as was possible.

We will give his confession in his own words.

"When, at five o'clock, I went to announce to the Countess that I was about to go to the palace, I found both the glass door of the ante-room, and that into the sitting-room, open, and I walked in through them. I did not find the Countess in her parlour, of which the curtains were drawn. Nor was she in her boudoir. I saw the door into the little corner room ajar, so I presumed she was in there. The flap of her desk was down, so that I saw the little drawers, in which I knew she kept her valuables, accessible to my hand. Opportunity makes the thief. I was unable to resist the temptation to enrich myself by these precious articles. I opened one of the drawers, took out a gold bracelet, one of gold filigree, two of bronze, a pair of gold ear-rings, a gold brooch, and a triple chain of beads or Roman pearls; and pocketed these articles, which my father afterwards had, and, for the most part, melted up.

"Most of these articles were in their cases. At that moment the Countess appeared on the threshold of her boudoir and rushed towards me. I do not remember what she exclaimed; fear for the consequences, and anxiety to prevent the Countess from making a noise and calling assistance, and thereby obtaining my arrest, prevailed in my mind, and I thought only how I might save myself. I grasped her by the neck, and pressed my thumbs into her throat. She struggled desperately. I was obliged to use all my strength to hold her. After a wrestle of between five and seven minutes, her eyes closed, her face became purple, and I felt her limbs relax.

"When I saw she was dead I was overcome with terror. I let the body fall, whereby the head struck the corner of the left side of the secretaire, and this made a wound which began to bleed. Then I ran and locked both the doors, hid what I had taken in my bed, and left the house. On my way to the palace, I stepped into Frey's tavern and drank three glasses of wine. I was afraid I should arrive too late at the palace, where I appeared, however, at half-past five. The Count did not return till half-past six, as dinner that day lasted rather longer than usual.

"When the Count went upstairs to see his wife and take her something good he had brought away with him from table, I was not uneasy at all, for I knew that he would knock and come away if he met with no response. So he did. He came down without being discomposed, and remarked that he fancied the Countess had gone out. At half-past seven he left the house. In the mean time I had been considering what to do, and had formed my plan. Now my opportunity had arrived, and I hastened to put it into execution. My plan was to efface every trace of my deed by fire, and to commit suicide if interrupted.

"As the weather was chilly, the Count had some fire in his stove. I fetched the still glowing charcoal, collected splinters of firwood and other combustibles, and matches, and went upstairs with them. Only the wine sustained me through what I carried out. I took up the body. I put a chair before the open desk, seated the corpse on it, placed one arm on the desk, laid the head on the arm, so that the body reposed in a position of sleep, leaning on the flap of the desk. I threw the red hot charcoal down under the head, heaped matches, paper, and wood splinters over them; took one of the blazing bits of wood and threw it on the divan in the boudoir; locked both doors, and flung away the keys.

"Then I went to my own room and lighted a fire in the stove, and put the jewel cases on the fire. The fire would not burn well, and thick smoke came into the room. Then I saw that the damper was closed. I opened that, and the smoke flew up the chimney; this is what Colonel von Stockhausen saw. There were a lot of empty match-boxes also in the stove, and these burnt with the rest."

Such was the confession of Stauff. How far true, it is impossible to say. He said nothing about the bell-pull being torn down, nothing about the holes burnt in the sofa of the sitting-room. According to the opinion of some experimentalists, the way in which he pretended to have burnt the Countess would not account for the appearance of the corpse.

His object was to represent himself as the victim of an over-mastering temptation—to show that the crime was wholly unpremeditated.

This was the sole plea on which he could appeal for sympathy, and expect a relaxation of his sentence. That sentence was relaxed.

In 1872 he obtained a free pardon from the Grand-Duke, on condition that he left the country and settled in America. Including his imprisonment before his trial, he had, therefore, undergone twenty-five years of incarceration.

When released he went to America, where he probably still is.

XII. — A WAX-AND-HONEY MOON

IN the history of Selenography, John Henry Maedler holds a distinguished place. He was the very first to publish a large map of the lunar surface; and his map was a good one, very accurate, and beautifully executed, in four sheets (1834-6). For elucidation of this map he wrote a book concerning the moon, entitled "The Universal Selenography." Not content with this, he published a second map of the moon in 1837, embodying fresh discoveries. Indeed as an astronomer, Maedler was a specialist. Lord Dufferin when in Iceland met a German naturalist who had gone to that inclement island to look for one moth. It is of the nature of Teutonic scientific men not to diffuse their interests over many branches of natural history or other pursuits, but to focus them on a single point. Maedler was comparatively indifferent to the planets, cold towards the comets, and callous to the attractions of the nebulæ. On the subject of the moon, he was a sheer lunatic.

He died at Hanover in 1874 at the age of eighty, a moon gazer to the last. Indeed, he appeared before the public as the historian of that science in a work published at Brunswick, the year previous to his death. The study of astronomy, more than any other,—even than theology—detaches a man from the world and its interests. Indeed theology as a study has a tendency to ruffle a man, and make him bark and snap at his fellow men who use other telescopes than himself; it is not so with astronomy. This science exercises a soothing influence on those who make it their study, so that an Adams and a Le Verrier can simultaneously discover a Neptune without flying at each other's noses.

Astronomy is certainly an alluring science; set an astronomer before a telescope, and an overwhelming attraction draws his soul away through the tube up into heaven, and leaves his body without mundane interests. An astronomer is necessarily a mathematician, and mathematics are the hardest and most petrifying of studies. The "humane letters," as classic studies are called, draw out the human interests, they necessarily carry men among men, but mathematics draw men away from all the interests of their fellows. The last man one expects to find in love, the last man in whose life one looks for a romantic episode, is a mathematician and astronomer. But as even Cæsar nods, so an astronomer may lapse into spooning. The life of Professor Maedler does not contain much of animated interest; but it had its poetic incident. The curious story of his courtship and marriage may be related without indiscretion, now that the old Selenographer is no more.

Even the most prosaic of men have their time of poetry. The swan is said to sing only once—just before it dies. The man of business—the stockbroker, the insurance-company manager, the solicitor, banker, the ironmonger, butcher, greengrocer, postman, have all passed through a "moment," as Hegel would call it, when the soul burst through its rind of common-place and vulgar routine, sang its nightingale song, and then was hushed for ever after. It is said that there are certain flowers which take many years coming to the point of bloom, they open, exhale a flood of incense, and in an hour wither. It is so with many. Even the astronomer has his blooming time. Then, after the honeymoon, the flower withers, the song ceases, the sunshine fades, and folds of the fog of common-place settle deeper than before.

Ivan Turgenieff, the Russian novelist, says of love, "It is not an emotion, it is a malady, attacking soul and body. It is developed without rule, it cannot be reckoned with, it cannot be overreached. It lays hold of a man, without asking leave, like a fever or the cholera. It seizes on its prey as a falcon on a dove, and carries it, where it wills. There is no equality in love. The so-termed free inclination of souls towards each other is an idle dream of German professors, who have never loved. No! of two who love, one is the slave, the other is the lord, and not inaccurately have the poets told of the chains of love."

But love when it does lay hold of a man assumes some features congruent to his natural habit. It is hardly tempestuous in a phlegmatic temperament, nor is a man of sanguine nature liable to be much influenced by calculations of material advantages. That calculations should form a constituent portion of the multiform web of a mathematician's passion is what we might anticipate.

It will be interesting to see in a German professor devoted to the severest, most abstract and super-mundane of studies, the appearance, course, and dying away of the "malady" of love. We almost believe that this case is so easy of analysis that the very *bacillus* may be discovered.

Before, however, we come to the story of Professor Maedler's love episode, we must say a word about his previous history.

Maedler was born at Berlin on May 29th, 1794, in the very month of love, though at its extreme end. He began life as a schoolmaster, but soared in his leisure hours into a purer atmosphere than that of the schoolroom; he began to study the stars, and found them brighter and more interesting than the heads of his pupils.

In 1828 William Beer, the Berlin banker, brother of the great composer, Meyerbeer, a Jew, built a small observatory in the suburbs of Berlin. He had made the acquaintance of Maedler, they had the same love of the stars, and they became close friends.

The Beers were a gifted family, running out in different directions. Michael, a third brother, was a poet, and wrote tragedies, one or two of which occasionally reappear on the boards.

The result of the nightly star gazings was an article on Mars when in opposition, with a drawing of the surface as it appeared to Beer and Maedler, through the telescope of the former.

But Mars did not admit of much further scrutiny, it presented no more problems they were capable of solving, so they devoted themselves to the moon. A gourmand exists from dinner to dinner, that meal is the climax of his vitality, that past he lapses into inertness, indifference, quiescence. Full moon was the exciting moment of the periods in Maedler's life, which was divided, not like a gourmand's day, into periods of twenty-four hours, but into lunar months. When the moon began to show, Maedler began to live; his interest, the pulses of his life quickened as full moon approached, then declined and went to sleep when there was no lunar disc in the sky. From 1834 to 1836 he issued his great map of the moon, and so made his name. But beyond that, in the summer of 1833 he was employed by the Russian Government on a chronometrical expedition in the Baltic.

When his map came out, he was at once secured by the Prussian Government as assistant astronomer to the observatory at Berlin, recently erected. In 1840 he became a professor, and was summoned to take charge of the observatory, and lecture on astronomy, in the Russian University of Dorpat. There he spent six uneventful years. He was unmarried, indifferent to female society, and as cold as his beloved moon. He was as solitary, as far removed from the ideas of love and matrimony, as the Man in the Moon.

At last, one vacation time, he paid a long deferred visit to a friend, a Selenologist, at Gröningen, the University of the Kingdom of Hanover. Whilst smoking, drinking beer, and talking over the craters and luminous streaks in the moon, with his friend, who was also a professor, that gentleman drew his pipe from his mouth, blew a long spiral from between his lips, and then said slowly, "By the way, professor, are you aware that we have here, in this kingdom, not, indeed, in Gröningen, but in the town of Hanover, a lady, the wife of the Herr Councillor Witte, who is, like yourself, devoted to the moon; a lady, who spends entire nights on the roof of her house peering at the face of the moon through one end—the smaller—of her telescope, observing all the prominences, measuring their altitudes, and sounding all the cavities. Indeed, it is asserted that she studies the face and changes of the moon much more closely than the features and moods of her husband. Also, it is asserted, that when the moon is shining, the household duties are neglected, the dinners are bad, the maids—"

"O dinners! maids! you need not consider them; there are always dinners and maids," said the Dorpat astronomer contemptuously, "but the moon is seen so comparatively rarely. The moon must be made much of when she shows. Everything must then be sacrificed to her."

Dr. Maedler did not call the moon *she*, but *he*; however, we are writing in English, not in German, so we change the gender.

The Astronomer Royal of the University of Gröningen went on, without noticing the interruption: "Frau von Witte has spent a good deal of her husband's money in getting the largest procurable telescope, and has built an observatory for it with a dome that revolves on cannon balls, on the top of her house. Whilst Herr von Witte slumbers and snores beneath, like a Philistine, his enlightened lady is aloft, studying the moon. The Frau Councilloress has done more than observe Luna, she has done more than you and Beer together, with your maps—she has modelled it."

"Modelled it!—modelled the moon!—in what?"

"In white wax."

Professor Maedler's countenance fell. He had gained great renown, not in Germany only, but throughout Europe by his maps of the moon. Here was an unknown lady, as enthusiastic a devotee to the satellite as himself, who had surpassed him. "You see," continued the Hanoverian professor, "the idea is superb, the undertaking colossal. You have a fixed strong light, you make the wax moon to revolve on its axis, and you reproduce in the most surprising and exact manner, all the phases of the moon itself."

This was indeed an idea. Maedler looked at his hands, his fingers. Would they be capable of modelling such a globe? Hardly, he had very broad coarse hands, and thick flat fingers, like paddles. He suddenly stood up.

"What is the matter? Whither are you going?" asked his friend.

"To Hanover, to Frau Witte, to see the wax moon." No persuasion would restrain him, he was in a selenological fever, he could not sleep, he could not eat, he could not read, he must see the wax moon.

And now, pray observe the craft of Cupid. The professor was aged fifty-two. In vain had the damsels of Berlin and Dorpat set their caps at him. Not a blonde beauty of Saxon race with blue eyes had caught his fancy, not a dark Russian with large hazel eyes and thick black hair, had arrested his attention. His heart had been given to the cold, chaste Diana. It was, with him, the reverse of the tale of Endymion.

He had written a treatise on the occultation of Mars, he had described the belts of Saturn, he had even measured his waist. Venus he had neglected, and now Cupid was about to avenge the slight passed on his mother. There was but one avenue by which access might be had to the professor's heart. The God of Love knew it, and resolved to storm the citadel through this avenue. Dr. Maedler packed his trunk himself in the way in which unmarried men and abstract thinkers do pack their portmanteaus. He bundled all his clothes in together, higglety-pigglety. The only bit of prudence he showed was to put the pomatum pot into a stocking. His collars he curled up in the legs of his boots. Copies of his astronomical pamphlets for presentation, lay in layers between his shirts. Then as the trunk would not close, the Professor of Astronomy sat down heavily on it, stood up, then sharply sat down on it again, and repeated this operation, till coats, trousers, linen, pamphlets, brushes and combs had been crushed together into one cohesive mass, and so the lock would fasten.

No sooner was Dr. Maedler arrived at his inn in Hanover, and had dusted the collar of his coat, and revolved before the *garçon* who went over him with a clothes brush, revolved like the moon he loved, than he sallied forth in quest of the house of the Wittes. There was no mistaking it—with the domed observatory on the roof.

Dr. Maedler stood in the square, looking up at it. The sight of an observatory touched him; and now, hard and dry as he was, moisture came into his eyes, as he thought that there, on that elevated station, an admirable woman spent her nights in the contemplation of the moon. What was Moses on Pisgah, viewing the Promised Land, what was Simeon Stylites braving storm and cold, to this spectacle?

Never before had the astronomer met with one of the weaker sex who cared a button for the moon, *qua* moon, and not as a convenience for illumining lovers' meetings, or for an allusion in a valentine. Here was an heroic soul which surged, positively surged above the frivolities of her sex, one who aspired to be the rival of man in intelligence and love of scientific research.

Professor Maedler sent in his card, and a letter of introduction from his friend at Gröningen, and was at once admitted. He had formed an ideal picture of the Selenographic lady, tall, worn with night watching, with an arched brow, large, clear eyes. He found her a fat little woman, with a face as round and as flat as that of the moon, not by any means pale, but red as the moon in a fog.

The lady was delighted to make the acquaintance of so renowned an astronomer. She made him pretty speeches about his map, at the same time letting him understand that a map was all very well, but she knew of something better. Then she launched out into a criticism of his pamphlets on Mars and Saturn, on which, as it happened, he was then sitting. He had put a crumpled copy in each of his tail-coat pockets for an offering, and was now doubly crumpling them. Then she asked his opinion about the revolution and orbit of Biela's comet, which had been seen the preceding year. Next she carried him to Hencke's recently discovered planet, Astræa; after that she dashed away, away with him to the nebulæ, and sought to resolve them with his aid. Then down they whirled together through space to the sun, and the luminous red protuberances observable at an eclipse. Another step, and they were plunging down to earth, had reached it in safety, and were discussing Lord Rosse's recently erected telescope. It was like Dante and Beatrix, with this difference, that Maedler was not a poet, and Frau Witte was a married woman.

The Professor was uneasy. Charming as is a telescope, delightful as is the sun, fascinating as Astræa may be, still, the moon, the moon was what he had come to discuss, and wax moon what he had come to see.

So he exercised all his skill, and with great dialectic ability conducted his Beatrix away on another round. They gave the fixed stars a wide berth, dived in and out among the circling planets and planetoids without encountering one, avoided the comets, kept their feet off nebulous matter, and at last he planted his companion firmly on the moon, and when there, there he held her.

To her words of commendation of his lunar map, he replied by expressing his astonishment at her knowledge of the several craters and so-called seas. Presently Frau Witte rose with a smile, and said, "Herr Professor, I may, perhaps, be allowed to exhibit a trifle on which I have been engaged for many years:—an independent work that I have compared with, but not copied from, your excellent selenic map."

The doctor's heart fluttered; his eyes brightened; a hectic flush came into his cheeks.

Frau Witte took a key and led the way to her study, where she threw open a mahogany cupboard, and exposed to view something very much like a meat cover. This also she removed, it was composed of the finest silk stretched on a frame, and exposed to view—the wax moon.

The globe was composed of the purest white beeswax, it stood upon a steel needle that passed through it, and rested on pivots, so that the globe was held up and held firm, and could be easily made to revolve. Frau Witte closed the shutters, leaving open only one orifice through which the light could penetrate and fall on the wax ball.

The doctor raised his hands in admiration. Never had he seen anything that so delighted him. The globe's surface had been most delicately manipulated. The mountains were pinched into peaks, the hollows indented to the requisite depth, the craters were rendered with extraordinary precision, the striæ being indicated by insertions of other tinted wax. A shadow hung sombre over the mysterious Sea of Storms.

Professor Maedler returned to his hotel a prey to emotion. He inquired the address of a certain Rollmann, whom he had known in former years at Berlin, and who was now professor in the Polytechnic school at Hanover. Then he rushed off in quest of Rollmann. The Polytechnic Professor was delighted to see his friend, but disturbed at the condition of mind in which he found him.

"What has brought you to Hanover, dear Professor?" he asked.

"The moon! the moon! I have come after the moon."

"The moon! How can that be? She shines over Dorpat as surely as over our roofs in Hanover."

"I've just seen her."

"Impossible. The moon is new. Besides, it is broad daylight."

"New! of course she is new. Only made lately."

Professor Rollman was puzzled.

"The moon is certainly as old as the world, and even if we give the world so limited an age as four thousand years—"

"I was not allowed to touch her, scarcely to breathe near her," interrupted Maedler.

"My dear colleague, what is the matter with you? You are—what do you say, seen, touched, breathed on the moon? The distance of the moon from the earth is two hundred and forty thousand miles."

"Not the old moon—I mean the other."

"There is no other, that is, not another satellite to this world. I am well aware that Jupiter has four moons, two of which are smaller than the planet Mars. I know also that Mars—"

"My dear Rollman, there is another—here in Hanover."

"I give it up, I cannot understand."

"Happy Hanover to possess such an unique treasure," continued the excited Maedler, "and such a woman as Frau Witte."

"Oh! her wax moon!" said Rollmann, with a sigh of relief.

"Of what else could I speak?"

"So you have seen that. The old lady is very proud of her performance."

"She has cause to be proud of it. It is simply superb."

"And the sight of it has nearly sent you off your head!"

"Rollmann! what will become of that model? Frau Councilloress Witte will not live for ever. She is old, puffy, and red, and might have apoplexy any day. Is her husband an astronomer?"

"O dear no! he regards astronomy as as unprofitable a study as astrology. It is quite as expensive a pursuit, he says."

"Merciful heavens! Suppose she were to predecease—he would have the moon, and be unable to appreciate it. He might let it get dusty, have the craters and seas choked; perhaps the mountain-tops knocked off. He must not have it."

"It cannot be helped. The moon must take its chance."

"It must not be. She *must* outlive the Councillor."

"If you can manage that—well."

"But—supposing she does outlive him, she is not immortal. Some day she must die. Who will have the moon then?"

"I suppose, her daughter."

"What will the daughter do with it?"

"Melt it up for waxing the floors."

Professor Maedler uttered a cry of dismay.

"The object is one of incalculable scientific value. Has the daughter no husband, a man of intelligence, to stay her hand?"

"The daughter is unmarried. There was some talk of a theological candidate—"

"A theological candidate! An embryo pastor! Just powers! These men are all obscurantists. He will melt up the moon thinking thereby to establish the authority of Moses."

"That came to nothing. She is disengaged."

Professor Maedler paced the room. Perspiration bedewed his brow. He wiped his forehead, more drops formed. Suddenly he stood still. "Rollmann," he said, in a hollow voice, "I must—I will have that moon, even if I have to marry the daughter to secure it."

"By all means. Minna is a pleasant young lady."

"Minna! Minna! is that her name?" asked the distracted professor; then, more coolly, "I do not care a rush what her name is. I want, not her, but the moon."

"She is no longer in the bloom of early youth."

"She is an exhausted world; a globe of volcanic cinder."

"She is of real solid worth."

"Solid—she is of solid wax—white beeswax."

"If she becomes yours—"

"I will exhibit her at my lectures to the students."

"As you are so much older, some provision will have to be made in the event of your death."

"I will leave her to the Dorpat museum, with directions to the curator to keep the dust off her."

"My dear Professor Maedler, I am speaking of the young lady, *you* of the moon."

"Ah so! I had forgotten the incumbrance. Yes, I will marry the moon. I will carry her about with me, hug her in my arms, protect her most carefully from the fingers of the Custom House officers. I will procure an ukase from the Emperor to admit her unfingered over the frontier."

"And Minna!"

"What Minna?"

"The young lady."

"Ah so! She had slipped out of my reckoning. She shall watch the box whilst I sleep, and whilst she sleeps I will keep guard."

"Be reasonable, Maedler. Do you mean, in sober earnest, to invite Minna Witte to be your wife?"

"If I cannot get the moon any other way."

"But you have not even seen her yet."

"What does that matter? I have seen the moon."

"And you are in earnest!"

"I *will* have the moon."

"Then, of course, you will have to propose."

"I propose!"

"And, of course, to make love."

"I make love!"

Professor Maedler's colour died away. He stood still before his friend, his pocket-handkerchief in hand, and stared.

"I have not the remotest idea how to do it."

"You must try."

"I've had no experience. I am going on to fifty-three. As well ask me to dance on the trapeze. It is not proper. It is downright indecent."

"Then you must do without the wax moon."

"I cannot do without the wax moon."

"Then, there is no help for it, you must make love to and propose to the fair Minna."

"Friend," said the Russian-imperial-professor-of-astronomy-of-the-University-of-Dorpat, as he clasped Rollmann's hand. "You are experienced in the ways of the world. I have lived in an observatory, and associated only with fixed stars, revolving moons, and comets. Tell me how to do it, and I will obey as a lamb."

"You will have to sigh."

"O! I can do that."

"And ogle the lady."

"Ogle!—when going fifty-three!"

"Learn a few lines of poetry."

"Yes, Milton's Paradise Lost. Go on."

"Tell the young lady that your heart is consumed with love."

"Consumed with love, yes, go on."

"Squeeze her hand."

"I cannot! That I cannot!" gasped Professor Maedler. "Look at my whiskers. They are grey. There is a point beyond which I cannot go. Rollmann, why may I not settle it all with the mother, and let you court the young lady for me by proxy."

"No, no, you must do it yourself."

"I would not be jealous. Consider, I care nothing for the young girl. It is the moon I want. That you shall not touch or breathe on."

"My dear Maedler, you and I are sure to be invited to dine with the family on Sunday. After dinner we will take a stroll in the garden. During dinner mind and be attentive to Miss Minna, and feed her with honeyed words. When we visit the garden I will tackle the mother, as Mephistopheles engages Martha, and you, you gay Faust, will have to be the gallant to Minna."

"My good Rollmann! I dislike the simile. It offends me. Consider my age, my whiskers, my position at the Dorpat University, my map of the moon in four sheets, my paper on the occultation of Mars."

"Pay attention to me, if you want your wax globe. Frau Witte, the Councillor and I will sit drinking coffee in the arbour. You ask Minna to show you the garden. When you are gone I will begin at once with the mother, praise you, and say how comfortably you are provided for at Dorpat, laud your good qualities, and bring her to understand that you are a suitor for the hand of her daughter. Meanwhile press your cause with ardour."

"With ardour! I shall not be able to get up any warmth."

"Think of the wax moon! direct your raptures to that."

"This is all very well," said Maedler fretfully, "but you have forgotten the main thing. I know you will make a mistake. You have asked for the hand of the daughter, and said nothing about the moon."

"Do not be concerned."

"But I am concerned. It would be a pretty mischief if I got the daughter's hand instead of the face of the moon."

"I will manage that you have what you want. But the moon must not rise over the matrimonial scene till the preliminaries are settled. I will represent to the old lady what credit will accrue to her if her moon be exhibited and lectured on at the Dorpat University by so distinguished an astronomer as yourself. Then, be well assured, she will give you the wax moon along with her daughter."

"Very well, I will do what I can. Only, further, explain to me the whole process, that I may learn it by heart. It seems to me as knotty to a beginner as Euler's proof of the Binomial Theorem."

"It is very easy. Pay attention. You must begin to talk about the fascination which a domestic life exerts on you; you then say that the sight of such an united household as that in which you find yourself influences you profoundly."

"I see. Causes a deflection in my perihelion. That deflection is calculable, the force excited calculable, the position of the attractive body estimable. I direct my telescope in the direction, and discover—Minna. Put astronomically, I can understand it."

"But you must *not* put it astronomically to her. Paint in glowing tints the charms of the domestic hearth—that is to say, of the stove. Touch sadly on your forlorn condition, your unloved heart—are you paying attention, or thinking of the moon?"

"On the contrary, I was thinking of myself, from a planetary point of view. I see, a wife is a satellite revolving round her man. I see it all now. Jupiter has four."

"Sigh; let the corners of your mouth droop. Throw, if you can, an emotional vibration into your tones, and say that hitherto life has been to you a school, where you have been set hard tasks; not a home. Here shake your head slowly, drop a tear if you can, and say again, in a low and thrilling voice, 'Not a home!' Now for the poetry. Till now, you add, you have looked into the starry vault—"

"It is not a vault at all."

"Never mind; say this. Till now you have looked into the starry vault for your heaven, and not dreamed that a heaven full of peaceful lights was twinkling invitingly about your feet. That is poetical, is it not? It must succeed."

"Quite so, I should never have thought of it."

"Then turn, and look into Miss Minna's eyes."

"But suppose she is looking in another direction?"

"She will not be. A lady is always ready to help a stumbling lover over the impediments in the way of a declaration. She will have her eyes at command, ready to meet yours."

"Go on."

"You will presently come to a rose tree. You must stop there and be silent. Then you must admire the roses, and beg Miss Minna to present you with one."

"But I do not want any roses. What can I do with them? I am lodging at an hotel."

"Never mind, you *must* want one. When she has picked and offered it—"

"But perhaps she will not."

"Fiddlesticks! Of course she will. Then take the rose, press your lips to it, and burst forth into raptures."

"Excuse me, how am I to do the raptures?"

"Think of the wax moon, man. Exclaim, 'Oh that I might take the fair Minna, fairer than this rose, to my heart, as I apply this flower to my buttonhole!'"

"Shall I say nothing about the wax moon?"

"Not a word. Leave me to manage that."

"Go on."

"Then she will look down, confused, at the gravel, and stammer. Press her for a Yes or No. Promise to destroy yourself if she says No. Take her hand and squeeze it."

"Must I squeeze it? About how much pressure to the square-foot should I apply?"

"Then say, 'Come, let us go to your parents, and obtain their blessing.' The thing is done."

"But suppose she were to say No?"

Rollmann stamped with impatience. "I tell you she will not say No, now that the theological candidate has dropped through."

"Well," said Professor Maedler, "I must go along with it, now I have made up my mind to it. But, on my word, as an exact reasoner, I had no idea of the difficulties men have to go through to get married. Why, the calculation of the deflections of the planets is nothing to it. And the Grand Turk, like Jupiter, has more satellites than one!"

A few months after the incident above recorded Professor Maedler returned to Dorpat, not alone; with him was the Frau Professorinn—Minna. Everything had gone off in the garden as Rollmann had planned.

The moon and Minna, or Minna and the moon, put it which way you will, were secured.

When the Professor arrived at Dorpat with his wife, the students gave him an ovation after the German style, that is to say, they organized a Fackel-zug, or torch-light procession.

Three hundred young men, some wearing white caps, some green caps, some red, and some purple, marched along the street headed by a band, bearing torches of twisted tow steeped in tar, blazing and smoking, or, to be more exact, smoking and blazing. Each corps was followed by a hired droschky, in which sat the captain and stewards of the white, red, green, or purple corps, with sashes of their respective colours. Behind the last corps followed the elephants, two and two. By elephants is not meant the greatest of quadrupeds, but the smallest esteemed of the students, those who belong to no corps.

The whole procession gathered before the house of the Professor, and brandished their torches and cheered. Then the glass door opening on the balcony was thrown back, and the Professor John Henry Maedler appeared on the balcony leading forth his wife. The astronomer looked younger than he had been known to look for the last twenty years. His whiskers in the torchlight looked not grey, but red. The eyes, no longer blear with star-gazing, watered with sentiment. His expression was no longer that of a man troubled with integral calculus, but of a man in an ecstasy. He waved his hand. Instantly the cheers subsided. "My highly-worthy-and-ever-to-be-honoured sirs," began the Professor, "this is a moment never to be forgotten. It sends a *fackel-zug* of fiery emotion through every artery and vein. Highly-worthy-and-ever-to-be-honoured sirs, I am not so proud as to suppose that this reception is accorded to me alone. It is an ovation offered to my highly-beloved-and-evermore-to-be-beloved-and-respected consort, Frau Minna Maedler, born Witte, the daughter of a distinguished lady, who, like myself, has laboured on Selenography, and loved Selenology. Highly-worthy-and-ever-to-be-respected sirs, when I announce to you that I have returned to Dorpat to endow that most-eminent-and-ever-to-become-more-eminent-University with one of the most priceless treasures of art the world has ever seen, a monument of infinite patience and exact observation; I mean a wax moon; I am sure I need only allude to the fact to elicit your unbounded enthusiasm. But, highly-worthy-and-ever-to-be-honoured sirs, allow me to assure you that my expedition to Hanover has not resulted in a gain to the highly eminent University of Dorpat only, but to me, individually as well.

"That highly-eminent-and-evermore-to-become-more-eminent University is now enriched through my agency with a moon of wax, but I—I, sirs—excuse my emotion, I have also been enriched with a moon, not of wax, but of honey. The wax moon, gentlemen, may it last undissolved as long as the very-eminent-and-evermore-to-become-more-eminent University of Dorpat lasts. The honey moon, gentlemen, with which I have been blessed, I feel assured will expand into a lifetime, at least will last also undissolved as long as Minna and I exist."

XIII. — THE ELECTRESS'S PLOT

THE Elector Frederick Christian of Saxony reigned only a few weeks, from October 5th to December 13, 1763; in his forty-first year he died of small-pox. He never had enjoyed rude health. The mother of the unfortunate prince, Marie Josepha of Austria, was an exceedingly ugly, but prolific lady, vastly proud of her Hapsburg descent. The three first children followed each other with considerable punctuality, but the two first, both sons, died early. Frederick Christian was the third. The Electress, a few months before his birth, was hunting, when a deer that had been struck, turned to her, dragging its broken legs behind it. This produced a powerful impression on her mind; and when her son was born, he was found to be a cripple in his legs. His head and arms were well formed, but his spine was twisted, and his knees, according to the English ambassador, Sir Charles Williams—were drawn up over his stomach. He could not stand, and had to be lifted about from place to place. At the age of five-and-twenty he had been married to Maria Antonia, daughter of the Elector of Bavaria, afterwards the Emperor Charles VII.

His brother, Francis Xavier, was a sturdy fellow, like his father, and the Electress mother tried very hard to get Frederick Christian to resign his pretentions in favour of his brother, and take holy orders. This he refused to do, and was then married to Maria Antonia, aged twenty-three. Her mother had also been an Austrian princess, Amalia, and also remarkable for her ugliness. The choice was not happy, it brought about a marriage between cousins, and an union of blood that was afflicted with ugliness and infirmity of body.

Maria Antonia had not only inherited her mother's ugliness, but was further disfigured with small-pox. She was small of stature, but of a resolute will, and of unbounded ambition. English tourists liked her, they said that she laid herself out to make the Court of Dresden agreeable to them. Wraxall tells a good story of her, which shows a certain frankness, not to say coarseness in her conversation—a story we will not reproduce.

She had already made her personality felt at the Bavarian Court. Shortly after the death of her father, in imitation of Louisa Dorothea, Duchess of Gotha, she had founded an "Order of Friendship, or the Society of the Incas." The founding of the Order took place one fine spring day on a gondola in the canal at Nymphenburg. Her brother, the Elector of Bavaria, was instituted a member, the Prince of Fürstenberg was made chancellor, and was given the custody of the seal of the confraternity which had as its legend "La fidelité mêne." The badge of the Order was a gold ring on the little finger of the left hand, with the inscription, "L'ordre de l'amitié—Maria Antonia." Each member went by a name descriptive of his character, or of that virtue he or she was supposed to represent. Thus the chancellor was called "Le Solide."

Sir Charles Williams says that on the very first night of her appearance in Dresden she made an attempt to force herself into a position for which she had no right; to the great annoyance of the King of Poland (Augustus, Elector of Saxony).

At Dresden, she favoured the arts, especially music and painting. She became the patroness of the family Mengs. She sang, and played on the piano, and indeed composed a couple of operas, "Thalestris" and "Il trionfo della fidelita," and the former was actually put on the stage. Sir Charles Williams in 1747 wrote that, in spite of her profession that in her eyes no woman ought to meddle in the affairs of state, he ventured to prophecy, she would rule the whole land in the name of her unfortunate husband.

Nor was he wrong. The moment that her father-in-law died, she put her hand on the reins. She was not likely to meet with resistance from her husband, he was not merely a cripple in body, but was contracted in his intellect; he was amiable, but weak and ignorant. Sir Charles Williams says that he once asked at table whether it was not possible to reach England by land—*although* it was an island.

Frederick Christian began to reign on 5th October 1763, and immediately orders were given for the increase of the army to 50,000 men. Maria Antonia was bent on becoming a queen, and for this end she must get her husband proclaimed like his father, King of Poland. She was allied to all the Courts of Europe, her agreeable manners, her energy, gained her friends in all quarters. She felt herself quite capable of wearing a royal crown, and she wrote to all the courts to urge the claims of her husband, the Elector, when—the unfortunate cripple was attacked by small-pox, had a stroke, and died December 17th. Small-pox had carried off his ancestor John George IV., and in that same century it occasioned the death of his brother-in-law, Max Joseph of Bavaria, and of the Emperor Joseph I.

He left behind him four sons, his successor, Frederick Augustus, and the three other princes, Charles, his mother's favourite, Anthony, and Maximilian Joseph, the third of whom died the same year as his father. He had also two daughters.

The death of her husband was a severe blow to the ambition of the Electress; her eldest son, Frederick Augustus, was under age, and the reins of government were snatched from her hands and put into those of the uncle of the young Elector, Xavier, who had been his mother's favourite, and in favour of whom his elder brother had been urged to resign his pretensions. Xavier was appointed administrator of Saxony, and acted as such for five years.

When, at the age of eighteen, Frederick Augustus III. assumed the power, he endeavoured to fulfil his duties with great diligence and conscientiousness, and allowed of no interference. He had, indeed, his advisers, but these were men whom he selected for himself from among those who had been well tried and who had proved themselves trusty.

The Electress-mother had, during the administration of Prince Xavier, exercised some little authority; she now suddenly found herself deprived of every shred. Her son was too firm and self-determined to admit of her interference. Moody and dissatisfied, she left Dresden and went to Potsdam to Frederick II., in 1769, apparently to feel the way towards the execution of a plan that was already forming in her restless brain. She does not seem to have met with any encouragement, and she then started for Italy, where she visited Rome in 1772, and sought Mengs out, whose artistic talents had been fostered under her care.

Under the administration of Prince Xavier, the Electress Dowager had received an income of sixty thousand dollars; after her son had mounted the throne, her appanage was doubled, more than doubled, for she was granted 130,000 dollars, and in addition her son gave her a present of 500,000 dollars. This did not satisfy her, for she had no notion of cutting her coat according to her cloth, she would everywhere maintain a splendid court. Moreover, she was bitten with the fever of speculation. The year before her son came of age and assumed the power, she had erected a great cotton factory at Grossenhain, but as it brought her in no revenue, and cost her money besides, she was glad to dispose of it in 1774. The visitor to Dresden almost certainly knows the Bavarian tavern at the end of the bridge leading into Little Dresden. It is a tavern now mediævalised, with panelled walls, bull's eye glass in the windows, old German glass and pottery—even an old German kalendar hanging from the walls, and with a couple of pretty Bavarian Kellnerins in costume, to wait on the visitor. There also in the evening Bavarian minstrels jodel, and play the zither.

This Bavarian tavern was established by the Electress Mother, who thought that the Saxons did not drink good or enough beer, and must be supplied with that brewed in her native land.

But this speculation also failed, and her capital of five hundred thousand dollars was swallowed up to the last farthing, and to meet her creditors she was obliged to pawn her diamond necklace and the rest of her jewels. This happened in Genoa. When her allowance came in again she redeemed her jewelry, but in 1775 had to pawn it again in Rome. Unable to pay her debts, and in distress for money, she appealed repeatedly, but in vain, to her son.

Frederick Augustus was, like his father, of feeble constitution, and moreover, as he himself complained later on in life, had been at once spoiled and neglected in his youth; and he was unable through weakness to ascend a height. He did not walk or ride, but went about in a carriage. The January

(1769) after he came to the Electoral crown, he married Amelia Augusta of Zweibrücken, sister of Max Joseph, afterwards first King of Bavaria. She was only seventeen at the time.

The favourite son of his mother was Charles. This prince had been hearty and in full possession of his limbs in his early age, but when he reached the years of eleven or twelve, he became crippled and doubled up like his father. Wraxal says that beside him Scarron would have passed as a beauty. He was so feeble and paralysed that he could only be moved about on a wheeled chair. He died in 1781. His elder brother, the Elector, though not a vigorous man, was not a cripple.

One of the attendant gentry on the Electress Mother, in Rome, was the Marquis Aloysius Peter d'Agdolo, son of the Saxon Consul in Venice, Colonel of the Lifeguard, and Adjutant General to Prince Xavier whilst he was Administrator.

Agdolo advised the Electress Mother to raise money to meet her difficulties by selling to her son, the Elector, her claims on the Bavarian inheritance. Her brother, Maximilian Joseph, was without children; and the nearest male claimant to the Electoral Crown of Bavaria was the Count Palatine of Sulzbach, only remotely connected. It was, therefore, quite possible that Bavaria might fall to a sister. Now on the death of her brother, the Dowager Electress of Saxony certainly intended to advance her claims against any remote kinsman hailing through a common ancestor two centuries ago. But whether she would be able to enforce her claim was another matter. She might sell it to her son, who would have the means of advancing his claim by force of arms and gold. This was in 1776. Maria Antonia was delighted with the scheme and at once hastened to Munich to put it in execution, taking with her all her diamonds which she had managed to redeem from pawn.

Whilst she was on her way to Munich, Agdolo was despatched to Dresden, to open the negociation with her son, not only for the transference of her rights on Bavaria, but also for the pawning of her diamonds, to her son.

She had urgent need of money, and in her extremity she conceived an audacious scheme to enable her at the same time to get hold of the money, and to retain her rights on Bavaria. The plan was this:—As soon as she had got the full payment from the Elector for the resignation of her claims in his favour, she had resolved suddenly to proclaim to the world that he was no son at all of the late Elector Frederick Christian—that he was a bastard, smuggled into the palace and passed off as the son of the Elector, much as, according to Whig gossip, James the Pretender was smuggled into the palace of James II. in a warming pan, and passed off as of blood royal, when he was of base origin.

Frederick Augustus thus declared to be no son of the House of Saxony, the Electoral crown would come to her favourite son Charles, who was a cripple. The Elector was not deformed—evidence against his origin; Charles was doubled up and distorted—he was certainly the true son of the late Elector, and the legitimate successor.

If Maria Antonia should succeed—she would rule Saxony in the name, and over the head of her unfortunate son Charles, and her rights on Bavaria would not have been lost or made away with.

Arrived in Munich, she confided the whole plan to her ladies-in-waiting. She told them her hopes, her confidence in Agdolo, who was gone to Dresden to negociate the sale, and who was thoroughly aware of her intentions.

Agdolo, as all the ladies knew, was a great rascal. He had been pensioned by Prince Xavier with six hundred dollars per annum, and he had what he received from the Electress Mother as her gentleman-in-waiting. He was married to the Princess Lubomirska, widow of Count Rutowska, had quarrelled with her, and they lived separate, but he had no scruple to receive of an insulted wife an annual allowance. All these sources of income were insufficient to meet his expenses; and no one who knew him doubted for a moment that he would lend himself to any intrigue which would promise him wealth and position. The plot of the Dowager Electress was a risky one—but, should it succeed, his fortune was assured.

At Dresden he was well received by the Elector; and Frederick Augustus at once accepted the proposition of his mother. He consented to purchase Maria Antonia's resignation in his favour of her claims on the allodial inheritance of the family on the extinction of the Bavarian Electoral house in the male line, and to pay all her debts, and to find a sum sufficient to redeem the diamonds, which were represented as still in pawn at Rome.

Maria Antonia and her confidant appeared to be on the eve of success, when the plan was upset, from a quarter in which they had not dreamed of danger. Among the ladies of the court of the Dowager Electress was one whose name does not transpire, who seems to have entertained an ardent passion for Agdolo. He, however, disregarded her, and paid his attentions to another of the ladies. Rage and jealousy consumed the heart of this slighted beauty, and when the Electress Mother confided to her the plan she had formed, the lady-in-waiting saw that her opportunity had arrived for the destruction of the man who had slighted her charms. She managed to get hold of her mistress' keys and to make a transcript of her papers, wherein the whole plan was detailed, also of copies of her letters to Agdolo, and of the Marquis's letters to her. When she had these, she at once despatched them—not to the Elector of Saxony, but to Frederick II. at Berlin, who stood in close relations of friendship with the Elector of Saxony. She had reckoned aright. Such tidings, received through the Court of Prussia, would produce a far deeper impression on Frederick Augustus, than if received from her unknown and insignificant self. It is possible also that she may have known of her mistress having been at Berlin and there thrown out hints of something of the sort, so that Frederick II. would at once recognise in this matured plan the outcome of the vague hints of mischief poured out at Potsdam a few years before.

All was going on well at Berlin. Adolphus von Zehmen, Electoral Treasurer, had already started for Munich, furnished with the requisite sums. He was empowered to receive the deed of relinquishment from the Dowager Electress, and also her diamond necklace, which, in the meantime, was to be brought by a special courier from Rome. Maria Antonia, on her side, had constituted Councillor Hewald her plenipotentiary; she wrote to say that he would transact all the requisite negociation with the Treasurer Zehmen, and that the diamond necklace had arrived and was in his hands.

Agdolo received orders from the Electress Mother on no account to leave Dresden till the middle of September, 1776, lest his departure should arouse suspicion.

The conduct of the Marquis was not in any way remarkable, he moved about among old friends with perfect openness, often appeared in Court, and was satisfied that he was perfectly safe. He was not in the least aware that all his proceedings were watched and reported on, not by order of the Elector, but of his own mistress, who received regular reports from this emissary as to the behaviour and proceedings of the Marquis, so that she was able to compare with this private report that sent her by Agdolo, and so satisfy herself whether he was acting in her interest, or playing a double game.

This bit of cunning on her part, was not surprising, considering what a man Agdolo was, and, as we shall see, it proved of great advantage to her, but in a way she least expected.

The Marchese d'Agdolo had paid his farewell visit to the Elector, and received leave to depart. Frederick Augustus had not the remotest suspicion that his mother was playing a crooked part, and he seemed heartily satisfied with the negociation, and made the Marquis a present.

On September 15, 1776, Agdolo was intending to start from Dresden, on his return to Munich, and the evening before leaving he spent at the house of a friend, Ferber, playing cards. Little did he suspect that whilst he was winning one stake after another at the table, the greatest stake of all was lost. That evening, whilst he was playing cards, a courier arrived from Berlin, in all haste, and demanded to see the Elector in person, instantly, as he had a communication of the utmost importance to make from Frederick II. He was admitted without delay, and the whole of his mother's plot was detailed before the astonished Elector.

"The originals of these transcripts," said the courier, "are in the hands of the Marchese d'Agdolo, let him be arrested, and a comparison of the documents made."

The Privy Council was at once assembled, and the papers received from Frederick II. were laid before it. The members voted unanimously that the Marquis should be arrested, and General Schiebell was entrusted with the execution of the decree. No surprise was occasioned by the entry of General Schiebell into the house of Ferber. It was a place of resort of the best society in Dresden; but when the General announced that he had come to make an arrest, many cheeks lost their colour.

"In the name of his Serene Highness the Elector," said the General, "I make this man my prisoner," and he laid his hand on the shoulder of Agdolo, who had served under him in the Seven Years' War. He was taken at once to his own lodgings, where his desks and boxes—already packed for departure—were opened, and all his papers removed. The same night, under a strong guard, he was transported at 10 o'clock, to Königstein. In that strong fortress and state prison, perched on an isolated limestone crag, the rest of his life was to be spent in confinement.

But the Marchese, like a crafty Italian, had made his preparations against something of the sort; for among his papers was found a communication addressed by him to the Elector, revealing the whole plot. It was undated. If the search of his rooms and the discovery of his papers had been made earlier, the Elector might have believed that the man had really intended to betray his mistress, but, he had postponed the delivery of the communication too late.[17]

[17] This is supposed to have been the contents of the packet addressed to the Elector, the contents have never been revealed.

A few days later, the Marchese received a sealed letter from the Elector; and he was treated in his prison without undue severity; his pension was not withdrawn; and the Elector seems never to have quite made up his mind whether Agdolo really intended to make him aware of the plot at the last minute, or to go on with the plan after his mistress's orders.

After some years, when Agdolo began to suffer in his chest, he was allowed to go to the baths of Pirna, under a guard. His wife never visited him in prison. She died, however, only two years later, in 1778, at the age of fifty-six. Agdolo lived on for twenty-three years and a half, and died August 27, 1800. All his papers were then sent to Frederick Augustus III., who read them, dissolved into tears, and burnt them.

We must return for a moment to Munich. No sooner had the emissary of the Electress Mother heard of the news of the arrest of Agdolo, than he hastened to Munich with post horses as hard as he could fly over the roads. Maria Antonia, when she heard the news, at once made fresh dispositions. She sent word that same night to Hewald to make off, and in another half hour he had disappeared with the diamonds.

Next day the completion of the resignation of claims was to be made. The Electress Mother requested the Treasurer Zehmen to go to the dwelling of her Councillor Hewald, who, as we can understand, was not to be found anywhere. Herr von Zehmen was much surprised and disconcerted, and the Dowager Electress affected extreme indignation and distress, charging her plenipotentiary with having robbed her of her diamonds, and bolted with them. Then she took to her bed, and pretended to be dangerously ill. Next day the news reached Zehmen of what had occurred at Dresden, and with the news came his recall. She saw the treasurer before his departure, and implored him to get both Agdolo and Hewald arrested and punished, because, as she declared, they had between them fabricated a wicked plot for her robbery and ruin.

Hewald went to Frankfort with the jewels, where he was stopped and taken by an officer of Frederick Augustus, and brought on Jan. 27, 1777, to Dresden. He was sent to the Königstein, but was released in 1778.

In 1777 died the Elector of Bavaria, but his sister was unable to obtain any recognition of her claims; and she died 23rd April, 1780, without any reconciliation with the eldest son. Next year died her favourite son, the cripple, Charles.

XIV. — SUESS OPPENHEIM

ON December 16th, 1733, Charles Alexander, Duke of Würtemberg, entered Stuttgart in state. It was a brilliant though brief winter day. The sun streamed out of a cloudless heaven on the snowy roofs of the old town, and the castle park trees frosted as though covered with jewels. The streets were hung with tapestries, crimson drapery, and wreaths of artificial flowers. Peasants in their quaint costume poured in from all the country round to salute their new prince. From the old castle towers floated the banners of the Duchy and the Empire—for Würtemberg three stag-horns quartered with the Hohenstauffen black lions. The Duke was not young: he was hard on fifty—an age when a man has got the better of youthful impetuosity and regrets early indiscretions—an age at which, if a man has stuff in him, he is at his best.

The land of Würtemberg is a favoured and smiling land. At the period of which we write, it was not so ample as the present kingdom, but fruitful, favoured, and called the Garden of the Empire. For twenty years this Duchy had been badly governed; the inhabitants had been cruelly oppressed by the incompetent Duke Eberhardt Ludwig, or rather by his favourites. The country was burdened with debt; the treasury was exhausted. It had, as it were, lain under winter frost for twenty years and more, and now though on a winter day laughed and bloomed with a promise of spring.

And every good Würtemberger had a right to be glad and proud of the new duke, who had stormed Belgrade under Prince Eugene, and was held to be one of the bravest, noblest minded, and most generous of the German princes of his time.

As he rode through the streets of Stuttgart all admired his stately form, his rich fair hair flowing over his shoulders, his bright commanding eye, and the pleasant smile on his lip; every Würtemberger waved his hat, and shouted, and leaped with enthusiasm. Now at last the Garden of Germany would blossom and be fruitful under so noble a duke.

But in the same procession walked, not rode, another man whom none regarded—a handsome man with dark brown hair and keen olive eyes, a sallow complexion, and a finely moulded Greek nose. He had a broad forehead and well arched brows. He was tall, and had something noble and commanding in his person and manner. But his most remarkable feature was the eye—bright, eager, ever restless.

This man, whom the Würtembergers did not observe, was destined to play a terrible and tragic part in their history—to be the evil genius of the duke and of the land. His name was Joseph Suess Oppenheim.

Joseph's mother, Michaela, a Jewess, had been a woman of extraordinary beauty, the only child of the Rabbi Salomon of Frankfort. She had been married when quite young to the Rabbi Isachar Suess Oppenheim, a singer. Joseph was born at Heidelberg in 1692, and was her child by the Baron George of Heydersdorf, a soldier who had distinguished himself in the Turkish war, and with whom she carried on a guilty intrigue. From his father Joseph Suess derived a dignified, almost military bearing, and his personal beauty from his mother.

The Baron's romance with the lovely Jewess came to an end in 1693, when he held the castle of Heidelberg against the French. He surrendered after a gallant defence; too soon, however, as the court-martial held on him decided; and he was sentenced to death, but was pardoned by the Emperor Leopold, with the loss of all his honours and offices, and he was banished the Empire.

Suess had a sister who married a rich Jew of Vienna, but followed her mother in laxity of morals, and, after having wasted a good fortune in extravagance, fell back on her mother and brother for a maintenance. He had a brother who became a factor at the court of Darmstadt. They lived on bad terms with each other, and were engaged in repeated lawsuits with one another. This brother abjured Judaism, was baptised, and assumed the name of Tauffenberg. Joseph Suess was connected, or nominally connected, through Isachar, his reputed though not his real father, with the great and wealthy Jewish family of Oppenheim. The branch established in Vienna had become rich on contracts for the army, and had been ennobled. One member failed because the Emperor Leopold I. owed him many millions of dollars and was unable to pay. Joseph began life in the office of the court bankers and army contractors of his family at Vienna. Here it was that he obtained his first ideas of how money could be raised through lotteries, monopolies, and imposts of all kinds. But though Joseph was put on the road that led to wealth, in the Oppenheim house at Vienna, he missed his chance there, and was dismissed for some misconduct or other, the particulars of which we do not know.

Then, in disgrace and distress, he came to Bavaria, where he served a while as barber's assistant. Probably through the influence of some of the Oppenheims, Joseph was introduced into the court of the family of Thurn and Taxis, which had acquired vast wealth through the monopoly of the post-office. Thence he made his way into an office of the palatine court at Mannheim.

This was a period in which the German princes were possessed with the passion of imitating the splendour and extravagance of Louis XIV. Everyone must have his Versailles, must crowd his court with functionaries, and maintain armies in glittering and showy uniforms.

Germany, to the present day, abounds in vast and magnificent palaces, for the most part in wretched repair, if not ruinous. The houses of our English nobility are nothing as compared in size with these palaces of petty princes, counts, and barons.

To build these mansions, and when built to fill them with officials and servants, to keep up their armies, and to satisfy the greed of their mistresses, these German princes needed a good deal of money, and were ready to show favour to any man who could help them to obtain it—show where to bore to tap fresh financial springs. All kinds of new methods of taxation were had recourse to, arousing the bitter mockery of the oppressed. The tobacco monopoly was called the nose-tax; it was felt to be oppressive only by the snuff-takers and smokers; and perhaps the stamp on paper only by those who wrote; but the boot and shoe stamp imposed by one of the little princes touched everyone but those who went barefoot.

Joseph Suess introduced the stamp on paper into the palatinate. He did not invent this duty, which had been imposed elsewhere; but he obtained the concession of the impost, and sold it to a subfactor for 12,000 florins, and with the money invested in a speculation in the coinage of Hesse-Darmstadt. All the little German princes at this time had their own coinage, down to trumpery little states of a few miles in diameter, as Waldeck, Fulda, Hechingen, and Montfort; and Germany was full to overflow of bad money, and barren of gold and silver. Suess, in his peregrinations, had obtained a thorough insight into the mysteries of this branch of business. He not only thoroughly understood the practical part of the matter— the coinage—but also where the cheapest markets were, in which to purchase the metals to be coined. Now that he had some money at his command, he undertook to farm the coinage of Hesse-Darmstadt; but almost immediately undersold it, with a profit to himself of 9,000 florins. He took other contracts for the courts, and soon realised a comfortable fortune. Even the Archbishop of Cologne called in his aid, and contributed to enrich him, in his efforts to get a little more for himself out of the subjects of his palatinate. In the summer of 1732 Joseph Suess visited the Blackforest baths of Wildbad, for the sake of the waters.

At the same time Charles Alexander of Würtemberg and his wife were also undergoing the same cure. Oppenheim's pleasant manners, his handsome face, and his cleverness caught the fancy of Charles Alexander, and he appointed him his agent and steward; and as the Prince was then in want of money, Suess lent him a trifle of 2,000 florins. Charles Alexander had not at this time any assurance that he would ascend the ducal throne of Würtemberg, though it was probable.[18] The reigning Duke, Eberhardt Louis, had, indeed, just lost his only son; but it was not impossible that a posthumous grandson might be born. Charles Alexander was first-cousin of the Duke. It is said that Suess on this occasion foretold the future greatness of the Prince, and pretended to extract his prophecy from the Cabala. It is certain that Charles Alexander was very superstitious, and believed in astrology, and it is by no means improbable that Suess practised on his credulity. He had at his disposal plenty of means of learning whether the young Princess of Würtemberg was likely soon to become a mother—her husband had died in November—and he was very well aware that the old Duke was failing. The loan made by Suess came acceptably to Prince Charles Alexander just as a Jewish banker, Isaac Simon of Landau, with whom he had hitherto dealt, had declined to make further advances.

[18] There was some idea of a younger brother being elected.

When the Prince returned to Belgrade, where he resided as stadtholder of Servia, under the Emperor, he was fully convinced that he had discovered in Suess an able, intelligent, and devoted servant. His wife was a princess of Thurn and Taxis, and it is possible that Suess, who had been for some time about that court at Ratisbon, had used her influence, and his acquaintance with her family affairs, to push his interests with the Prince, her husband.

On October 31, 1733, died the old Duke Eberhardt Louis, and Charles Alexander at once hastened from Belgrade to Vienna, where, in an interview with the Emperor, without any consultation with the Estates, or consideration for the treasury of Würtemberg, he promised Leopold a contingent of 12,000 men to aid in the war against France. Then he went on to Stuttgart.

Poor Würtemberg groaned under the burdens that had been imposed on it; the favourites had been allowed to do with it what they liked; and Charles Alexander's first public declaration on entering his capital was: "From henceforth I will reign over you immediately, and myself see to the reform of every grievance, and put away from my people every burden which has galled its shoulders. If my people cry to me, my ears shall be open to hear their call. I will not endure the disorder which has penetrated everywhere, into every department of the State; my own hand shall sweep it away."

And as a token of his sincerity he ordered every office-holder in Church and State to put on paper and present to him a schedule of every payment that had been made, by way of fee and bribe, to obtain his office. This was published on December 28, 1733. The older and wiser heads were shaken; the Duke, they said, was only heaping trouble on his shoulders; let the past be buried. He replied, "I must get to the bottom of all this iniquity. I must get inured to work."

But the hero of Belgrade had all his life been more accustomed to the saddle than the desk, and to command in battle—a much simpler matter—than to rule in peace. The amount of grievances brought before him, the innumerable scandals, peculations, bewildered him. The people were wild with enthusiasm, but the entire bureaucracy was filled with sullen and dogged opposition.

Würtemberg enjoyed a constitution more liberal than any other German principality. The old Duke Eberhardt with the Beard, who died in 1496, by his will contrived for the good government of his land by providing checks against despotic rule by the dukes his successors. On the strength of this testament the Estates deposed his successor. The provisions of this will were ratified in the Capitulation of Tübingen, in 1514, and every duke on assuming the reins of government was required to swear to observe the capitulation. Duke Charles Alexander took the oath without perhaps very closely examining it, and found out after it was taken that he was hampered in various ways, and was incapacitated from raising the body of men with which he had undertaken to furnish the Emperor, independent of the consent of the Parliament. It may here be said that there was no hereditary house of nobles in Würtemberg; the policy of the former dukes had been to drive the hereditary petty nobles out of the country, and to create in their place a clique of court officials absolutely dependent on themselves. By the constitution, no standing army was to be maintained, and no troops raised without the consent of the Estates; the tenure of property was guaranteed by the State, all serfage was abolished, and no taxes could be imposed or monopolies created without the consent of the Estates.

The Estates consisted of fourteen prelates, pastors invested with dignities which entitled them to sit in the House, and seventy deputies—some elected by the constituencies, others holders of certain offices, who sat *ex officio*. The Estates had great power; indeed the Duke could do little but ask its consent to the measures he proposed, and to swallow humble pie at refusal. It not only imposed the taxes, but the collectors were directly responsible to the Estates for what was collected, and paid into its hands the sum gathered. Moreover, any agreement entered into between the Duke and another prince was invalid unless ratified by the Estates.

When Duke Charles Alexander, who had been accustomed to the despotic command of an army as field-marshal, found how his hands were tied and how he was surrounded by impediments to free action on all sides, he was very angry, and quarrelled with the Ministers who had presented the capitulation to him for signature. He declared that the paper presented for him to sign had not been read to him in full, or had the obnoxious passages folded under that he should not see them, or that they had been added after his signature had been affixed.

He became irritable, not knowing how to keep his promise with the Emperor, and disgusted to find himself a ruler without real authority.

Now, as it was inconvenient to call the Assembly together on every occasion when something was wanted, a permanent committee sat in Stuttgart, consisting of two parts. This committee acted for the Estates and were responsible to it.

Wanting advice and help, unwilling to seek that of the reliable Ministers—and there were some honest and patriotic—the Duke asked Joseph Suess to assist him, and Suess was only too delighted to show him a way out of his difficulties. The redress of grievances was thrust aside, abuses were left uncorrected, and the Duke's attention was turned towards two main objects—the establishment of a standing army, and the upsetting of the old constitution.

Würtemberg was then a state whose limits were not very extensive, nor did they lie within a ring fence. The imperial cities of Reutlingen, Ulm, Heilsbronn, Weil, and Gmünd were free. It might not be convenient for the Emperor to pay with hard cash for the troops the Duke had promised to furnish, but he might allow of the incorporation of these independent and wealthy cities in the duchy. Moreover, it was a feature of the times for the princes to seek to conquer fresh districts and incorporate them. France had recently snatched away Mompelgard from Würtemberg, and Charles Alexander recovered it. The duchy had suffered so severely from having been overrun by French troops that the Estates acquiesced, though reluctantly, in the Duke's proposal that a standing army should be maintained. Having obtained this concession, Suess instructed him how to make it a means of acquiring money, by calling men to arms who would be thankful to purchase their discharge. The army soon numbered 18,000 soldiers. His general-in-chief was Remchingen, a man who had served with him in the Imperial army and was devoted to his interests. The Duke placed his army under officers who were none of them Würtembergers. At the head of an army officered by his own creatures, the Duke hoped to carry his next purpose—the abrogation of the capitulation, and the conversion of the State from a constitutional to a despotic monarchy. Suess now became the Duke's most confidential adviser, and, guided by him, Charles Alexander got rid of all his Ministers and courtiers who would not become the assistants in this policy, and filled their places with creatures of his own, chief of whom was a fellow named Hallwachs. In order to paralyse the Assembly the Duke did not summon it to meet, and managed to pack the committee with men in his interest; for, curiously enough, the committee was not elected by the delegates, but itself elected into the vacancies created in it. By means of the committee the Duke imposed on the country in 1736 a double tax, and the grant of a thirtieth of all the fruits; and this was to last "as long as the necessities of the case required it."

Suess himself was careful to keep in the background. He accepted no office about court, became Minister of no branch of the State; but every Minister and officer was nominated by him and devoted to him. Towards these creatures of his own he behaved with rudeness and arrogance, so that they feared him almost more than the Duke. If the least opposition was manifested, Suess threatened the gallows or the block, forfeiture of goods, and banishment; and as the Duke subscribed every order Suess brought him, it was well known that his threats were not idle.

Suess employed Weissensee, a pastor, the prelate of Hirsau, as his court spy. This worthless man brought to the favourite every whisper that passed within his hearing among the courtiers of the Duke, everything that was said in the committee, and advised whether the adhesion of this or that man was doubtful.

Suess so completely enveloped the Duke in the threads of the web he spun about him, that Charles Alexander followed his advice blindly, and did nothing without consulting him.

In 1734 Suess farmed the coinage of Würtemberg, with great profit to himself, and, having got it into his own hands, kept it there to the end. But there is this to be said for his coinage, that it was far better than that of all the other states of Germany; so that the Würtemberg silver was sought throughout Germany.

There was nothing fraudulent in this transaction, and though at his trial the matter was closely investigated, no evidence of his having exceeded what was just could be produced against him.

It was quite another matter with the "Land Commission," a well-intentioned institution with which the Duke began his reign. Charles Alexander was overwhelmed with the evidence sent in to him of bribery under the late Duke, and, unable to investigate the cases himself, he appointed commissioners to do so, and of course these commissioners were nominated by Suess. The commission not only examined into evidence of bribery in the purchase of offices, but also into peculation and neglect of duty in the discharge of offices. Those against whom evidence was strong were sentenced to pay a heavy fine, but were not necessarily deprived. Those, on the other hand, who had acquired their offices honourably and had discharged their functions conscientiously were harassed by repeated trials, terrified with threats, and were forced to purchase their discharge at a sum fixed according to an arbitrary tariff. Those who proved stubborn, or did not see at what the commissioners aimed, were subjected to false witnesses, found guilty, and fined. These fines amounted in some instances to £2,000.

After the commission had exhausted the bureaucracy, and money was still needed, private individuals became the prey of their inquisitorial and extortive action.

Any citizen who was reported to be rich was summoned before the tribunal to give an account of the manner in which he had obtained his wealth; his private affairs were investigated, his books examined, and his trial protracted till he was glad to purchase his dismissal for a sum calculated according to his income as revealed to the prying eyes of the inquisitors.

But as this did not suffice to fill the empty treasury, recurrence was had to the old abuse which the Land Commission had been instituted to inquire into and correct. Every office was sold, and to increase the revenue from this source fresh offices were created, fresh titles invented, and all were sold for ready money. Every office in Church as well as State was bought; indeed, a sort of auction was held at every vacancy, and the office was knocked down to the highest bidder.

This sort of commerce had been bad enough under the late Duke, but it became fourfold as bad now under the redresser of abuses, for what had before been inchoate was now organised by Suess into a system.

Not only were the offices sold, but after they had been entered upon, the tenant was expected to pay a second sum, entitled the gratuity, which was to go, it was announced, towards a sustentation fund for widows and orphans and the aged. It is needless to say that none of this money ever reached widows, orphans, or aged.

A special bureau of gratuities was organised by decree of the Duke, and filled with men appointed by Suess, who paid into his hands the sums received; and he, after having sifted them, and retained what he thought fit, shook the rest into the ducal treasury. This bureau was founded by ducal rescript in 1736.

Side by side with the Office of Gratuities came the Fiscal Office into being, whose function it was to revise the magisterial and judicial proceedings of the courts of justice. This also was filled by Suess with his creatures. The ground given to the world for its establishment was the correction of judicial errors and injustices committed by the courts of law. It was the final court of revision, before which every decision went before it was carried into effect. Legal proceedings, moreover, were long and costly, and the Fiscal Court undertook to interfere when any suit threatened to be unduly protracted to the prejudice of justice. But the practical working of the Fiscal Court was something very different. It interfered with the course of justice, reversing judgments, not according to equity, but according to the bribes paid into the hands of the board. In a very short time the sources of justice were completely poisoned by it, and no crime, however great and however clearly established, led to chastisement if sufficient money were paid into the hands of the court of revision. The whole country was overrun with spies, who denounced as guilty of imaginary crimes those who were rich, and such never escaped without leaving some of their gold sticking to the hands of the fiscal counsellors.

As usual with Joseph Suess, he endeavoured to keep officially clear of this court, as he had of the Office of Gratuities, and of all others. But the Duke nominated him assistant counsellor. Suess protested, and endeavoured to shirk the honour; but as the Duke refused to release him, he took care never once to attend the court, and when the proceedings and judgments were sent him for his signature he always sent them back unsigned; and he never was easy till relieved of the unacceptable title. For Suess was a clever rogue. In every transaction that was public, and of which documentary evidence was producible that he had been mixed up with it, he acted with integrity; but whenever he engaged on a proceeding which might render him liable to be tried in the event of his falling into disfavour, he kept himself in the background and acted through his agents; so that when, eventually, he was tried for his treasonable and fraudulent conduct, documentary evidence incriminating him was wholly wanting.

After the death of the Duke, it was estimated from the records of the two courts that they had in the year 1736-7 squeezed sixty-five thousand pounds out of the small and poor duchy.

Suess had constituted himself jeweller to the Duke, who had a fancy for precious stones, but knew nothing of their relative values. When Suess offered him a jewel he was unable to resist the temptation of buying it, and very little of the money of the Bureau of Gratuities ever reached him; he took the value out in stones at Suess' estimation. When some of his intimates ventured to suggest that the Jew was deceiving him as to the worth of the stones, Duke Charles Alexander shrugged his shoulders and said with a laugh, "It may be so, but I can't do without that coujon" (*cochon*).[19] At the beginning of 1736 a new edict for wards was issued by the Duke, probably on Suess' suggestion, whereby he constituted a chancery which should act as guardian to all orphans under age, managing their property for them, and was accountable to none but the Duke for the way in which it dealt with the trust. Then a commission was instituted to take charge of all charitable bequests in the duchy; and by this means Suess got the fingering of property to the amount of two hundred thousand pounds, for which the State paid to the Charities at the rate of three per cent.

[19] In three years Suess gained a profit of 20,000 florins out of the sale of jewellery alone.

Then came the imposition of duties and taxes. Salt was taxed, playing-cards, groceries, leather, tobacco, carriages, even the sweeping of chimneys. A gazette was issued containing decrees of the Duke and official appointments, and every officer and holder of any place, however insignificant, under Government was compelled to subscribe to this weekly paper, the profits of which came to the Duke and his adviser. Then came a property and income tax; then in quick succession one tormenting edict after another, irritating and disturbing the people, and all meaning one thing—money.

Lotteries were established by order of the Duke. Suess paid the Duke £300 for one, and pocketed the profits, which were considerable. At the court balls and masquerades Suess had his roulette tables in an adjoining room, and what fell to the *croupier* went into his pocket.[20]

[20] The Duke, at Suess's instigation, wrote to the Emperor to get the Jew factotum ennobled, but was refused.

At last his sun declined. The Duke became more and more engrossed in his ideas of upsetting the constitution by means of his army, and listened more to his general, Remchingen, than to Suess. He entered into a compact with the elector of Bavaria and with the Bishops of Würzburg and Bamberg to send him troops to assist him in his great project, and, as a price for this assistance, promised to introduce the Roman Catholic religion into Würtemberg.

The enemies of Suess, finding that he was losing hold of the Duke, took advantage of a precious stone which the Jew had sold him for a thousand pounds, and which proved to be worth only four hundred, to open the eyes of Charles Alexander to the character of the man who had exercised such unbounded influence over him. Suess, finding his power slipping from him, resolved to quit the country. The Duke stopped him. Suess offered five thousand pounds for permission to depart; it was refused. Charles Alexander was aware that Suess knew too many court secrets to be allowed to quit the country. Moreover, the necessities of the Duke made him feel that he might still need the ingenuity of Suess to help him to raise money. As a means of retaining him he granted him a so-called "absolutorium"—a rescript which made him responsible to no one for any of his actions in the past or in the future. Furnished with this document, the Jew consented to remain, and then the Duke required of him a loan of four thousand pounds for the expenses of a journey he meditated to Danzig to consult a physician about a foot from which he suffered. The "absolutorium" was signed in February 1737.

On March 12 following, Charles Alexander started on his journey from Stuttgart, but went no farther than his palace at Ludwigsburg.

Although the utmost secrecy had been maintained, it had nevertheless transpired that the constitution was to be upset as soon as the Duke had left the country. He had given sealed orders to his general, Remchingen, to this effect. The Bavarian and Würtemberg troops, to the number of 19,000 men, were already on the march. The Würtemberg army was entirely officered by the Duke's own men. Orders had been issued to forbid the Stuttgart Civil Guard from exercising and assembling, and ordering that a general disarmament of the Civil Guard and of the peasants and citizens should be enforced immediately the Duke had crossed the frontier. All the fortresses in the duchy had been provided with abundance of ammunition and ordnance.

219

At Ludwigsburg the Duke halted to consult an astrologer as to the prospect of his undertaking. Suess laughed contemptuously at the pretences of this man, and, pointing to a cannon, said to Charles Alexander, "This is your best telescope."

The sealed orders were to be opened on the 13th, and on that day the stroke was to be dealt. Already Ludwigsburg was full of Würzburg soldiers. A courier of the Duke with a letter had, in a drunken squabble, been deprived of the dispatch; this was opened and shown to the Assembly, which assembled in all haste and alarm. It revealed the plot. At once some of the notables hastened to Ludwigsburg to have an interview with their prince. He received them roughly, and dismissed them without disavowing his intentions. The consternation became general. The day was stormy; clouds were whirled across the sky, then came a drift of hail, then a gleam of sun. At Ludwigsburg, the wind blew in whole ranges of windows, shivering the glass. The alarm-bells rang in the church towers, for fire had broken out in the village of Eglosheim.

The Assembly sent another deputation to Ludwigsburg, consisting of their oldest and most respected members. They did not arrive till late, and unable to obtain access through the front gates, crept round by the kitchen entrance, and presented themselves unexpectedly before the Duke at ten o'clock at night, as he was retiring to rest from a ball that had been given. Dancing was still going on in one of the wings, and the strains of music entered the chamber when the old notables of Würtemberg, men of venerable age and high character, forced their way into the Duke's presence.

Charles Alexander had but just come away from the ball-room, seated himself in an arm-chair, and drunk a powerful medicine presented him by his chamberlain, Neuffer, in a silver bowl. Neuffer belonged to a family which had long been influential in Würtemberg, honourable and patriotic. Scarce had the Duke swallowed this draught when the deputation appeared. He became livid with fury, and though the interview took place with closed doors the servants without heard a violent altercation, and the Duke's voice raised as if he were vehemently excited. Presently the doors opened and the deputation came forth, greatly agitated, one of the old men in his hurry forgetting to take his cap away with him. Scarcely were they gone when Neuffer dismissed the servants, and himself went to a further wing of the palace.

The Duke, still excited, suddenly felt himself unwell, ran into the antechamber, found no one there, staggered into a third, then a fourth room, tore open a window, and shouted into the great court for help; but his voice was drowned by the band in the illumined ball-room, playing a valse. Then giddiness came over the Duke, and he fell to the ground. The first to arrive was Neuffer, and he found him insensible. He drew his knife and lanced him. Blood flowed. The Duke opened his eyes and gasped, "What is the matter with me? I am dying!" He was placed in an armchair, and died instantly.

That night not a window in Stuttgart had shown light. The town was as a city of the dead. Everyone was in alarm as to what would ensue on the morrow, but in secret arms were being distributed among the citizens and guilds. They would fight for their constitution. Suddenly, at midnight, the news spread that the Duke was dead. At once the streets were full of people, laughing, shouting, throwing themselves into each other's arms, and before another hour the windows were illuminated with countless candles.[21]

[21] On the following night a confectioner set up a transparency exhibiting the Devil carrying off the Duke.

Not a moment was lost. Duke Charles Rudolf of Würtemberg-Neuenstadt was invested with the regency, and on March 19, General Remchingen was arrested and deprived of his office.

For once Suess' cleverness failed him. Relying on his "absolutorium," he did not fly the country the moment he heard of the death of the Duke. He waited till he could place his valuables in safety. He waited just too long, for he was arrested and confined to his house. Then he did manage to escape, and got the start of his enemies by an hour, but was recognised and stopped by a Würtemberg officer, and reconducted to Stuttgart, where he was almost torn to pieces by the infuriated populace, and with difficulty rescued from their hands. On March 19, he was sent to the fortress of Hohenneuffen; but thence he almost succeeded in effecting his escape by bribing the guards with the diamonds he had secreted about his person.

At first Suess bore his imprisonment with dignity. He was confident, in the first place, that the "absolutorium" would not be impeached, and in the second, that there was no documentary evidence discoverable which could incriminate him. But as his imprisonment was protracted, and as he saw that the country demanded a victim for the wrongs it had suffered, his confidence and self-respect left him. Nevertheless, it was not till the last that he was convinced that his life as well as his ill-gotten gains would be taken from him, and then he became a despicable figure, entreating mercy, and eagerly seeking to incriminate others in the hopes of saving his own wretched life thereby.

There were plenty of others as guilty as Suess—nay, more so, for they were natives of Würtemberg, and he an alien in blood and religion. But these others had relations and friends to intercede for them, and all felt that Suess was the man to be made a scape-goat of, because he was friendless.

The mode of his execution was barbarous. His trial had been protracted for eleven months; at length, on February 4, 1738, he was led forth to execution—to be hung in an iron cage. This cage had been made in 1596, and stood eight feet high, and was four feet in diameter. It was composed of seventeen bars and fourteen cross-bars, and was circular. The gallows was thirty-five feet high. The wretched man was first strangled in the cage, hung up in it like a dead bird, and then the cage with him in it was hoisted up to the full height of the gallows-tree. His wealth was confiscated.

Hallwachs and the other rascals who had been confederated with him in plundering their country were banished, but were allowed to depart with all their plunder.

Remchingen also escaped; when arrested, he managed to get rid of all compromising papers, which were given by him to a chimney-sweep sent to him down the chimney by some of the agents of the Bishop of Würzburg.

Such is the tragic story of the life of Suess Oppenheim, a man of no ordinary abilities, remarkable shrewdness, but without a spark of principle. But the chief tragedy is to be found in the deterioration of the character of Duke Charles Alexander, who, as Austrian field-marshal and governor of Servia, had been the soul of honour, generous and beloved; who entered on his duchy not only promising good government, but heartily desiring to rule well for his people's good; and who in less than four years had forfeited the love and respect of his subjects, and died meditating an act which would have branded him as perjured—died without having executed one of his good purposes, and so hated by the people who had cheered him on his entry into the capital, that, by general consent, the mode of his death was not too curiously and closely inquired into.

XV. — IGNATIUS FESSLER

ON December 15th, 1839, in his eighty-fourth year, died Ignatius Fessler, Lutheran Bishop, at St. Petersburg, a man who had gone through several phases of religious belief and unbelief, a Hungarian by birth, a Roman Catholic by education, a Capuchin friar, then a deist, almost, if not quite, an atheist, professor of Oriental languages in the university of Lemberg, finally Lutheran Bishop in Finland.

He was principally remarkable as having been largely instrumental in producing one of the most salutary reforms of the Emperor Joseph II.

His autobiography published by him in 1824, when he was seventy years old, affords a curious picture of the way in which Joseph carried out those reforms, and enables us to see how it was that they roused so much opposition, and in so many cases failed to effect the good that was designed.

Fessler, in his autobiography, paints himself in as bright colours as he can lay on, but it is impossible not to see that he was a man of little principle, selfish and heartless.

The autobiography is so curious, and the experiences of Fessler so varied, the times in which he lived so eventful, and the book itself so little known, that a short account of his career may perhaps interest, and must be new to the generality of readers.

Ignatius Fessler was the son of parents in a humble walk of life resident in Hungary, but Germans by extraction. Ignatius was born in the year 1754, and as the first child, was dedicated by his mother to God. It was usual at that time for such children to be dressed in ecclesiastical habits. Ignatius as soon as he could walk was invested in a black cassock. His earliest reading was in the lives of the saints and martyrs, but at his first Communion his mother gave him a Bible. That book and Thomas à Kempis were her only literature. Long-continued prayer, daily reading of religious books, and no others, moulded the opening mind of her child. Exactly the same process goes on in countless peasant houses in Catholic Austria and Germany and Switzerland at the present day. No such education, no such walling off of the mind from secular influences is possible in England or France. The first enthusiasm of the child was to become a saint, his highest ambition to be a hermit or a martyr. At the age of seven he was given to be instructed by a Jesuit father, and was shortly after admitted to communion. At the age of nine Ignatius could read and speak Latin, and then he read with avidity Cardinal Bona's *Manductio ad Coelum*. His education was in the hands of the Carmelites at Raab. Dr. Fessler records his affectionate remembrance of his master, Father Raphael. Ignatius lounged, and was lazy. "Boy!" said the Father, "have done with lounging or you will live to be no good, but the laughing stock of old women. Look at me aged seventy, full of life and vigour, that comes of not being a lounger when a boy." From the Carmelite school Ignatius passed into that of the Jesuits. His advance was rapid; but his reading was still in Mystical Theology and his aim the attainment of the contemplative, ecstatic life of devotion. So he reached his seventeenth year.

Then his mother took him to Buda, to visit his uncle who was lecturer on Philosophy in the Capuchin Convent. The boy declared his desire to become a Franciscan. His mother and uncle gave their ready consent, and he entered on his noviciate, under the name of Francis Innocent. "The name Innocent became me well—really, at that time, I did not know the difference between the sexes."

In 1774, when aged twenty, he took the oaths constituting him a friar. All the fathers in the convent approved, except one old man, Peregrinus, who remonstrated gravely, declaring that he foresaw that Fessler would bring trouble on the fraternity. Father Peregrinus was right, Fessler was one to whom the life and rules and aim of the Order could never be congenial. He had an eager, hungry mind, an insatiable craving for knowledge, and a passion for books. The Capuchins were, and still are, recruited from the lowest of the people, ignorant peasants with a traditional contempt for learning, and their teachers embued with the shallowest smattering of knowledge. Fessler, being devoid of means, could not enter one of the cultured Orders, the Benedictines or the Jesuits. Moreover, the Franciscan is, by his vow, without property, he must live by begging, a rule fatal to self-respect, and fostering idleness. S. Francis, the founder, was a scion of a mercantile class, and the beggary which he imposed on his Order, was due to his revolt against the money-greed of his class. But it has been a fruitful source of mischief. It deters men with any sense of personal dignity from entering the Order, and it invites into it the idle and the ignorant. The Franciscan Order has been a fruitful nursery of heresies, schisms and scandals. Now old Father Peregrinus had sufficient insight into human nature to see and judge that a man of pride, intellectual power, and culture of mind, would be as a fish on dry land in the Capuchin fraternity. He was not listened to. Fessler was too young to know himself, and the fathers too eager to secure a man of promise and ability.

"The guardian, Coelestine, an amiable man, took a liking to me. He taught me to play chess, and he played more readily with me than with any of the rest, which, not a little, puffed up my self-esteem. The librarian, Leonidas, was an old, learned, obliging man, dearly loving his flowers. I fetched the water for him to his flower-beds, and he showed me his gratitude by letting me have the run of the library."

The library was not extensive, the books nearly all theological, and the volume which Fessler was most attracted by was Barbanson's "Ways of Divine Love."

In 1775, Fessler made the acquaintance of a Calvinist Baron, who lent him Fleury's "Ecclesiastical History." This opened the young man's eyes to the fact that the Church was not perfect, that the world outside the Church was not utterly graceless. He read his New Testament over seven times in that year. Then his Calvinist friend lent him Muratori's "Treatise on the Mystical Devotions of the Monks." His confidence was shaken. He no longer saw in the Church the ideal of purity and perfect infallibility; he saw that Mystical Theology was a geography of cloud castles. What profit was there in it? To what end did the friars live? To grow cabbages, make snuff-boxes, cardboard cases, which they painted—these were their practical labours; the rest of their time was spent in prayer and meditation.

Then the young friar got hold of Hofmann-Waldau's poems, and the sensuousness of their pictures inflamed his imagination at the very time when religious ecstasy ceased to attract him.

What the result might have been, Fessler says, he trembles to think, had he not been fortified by Seneca. It is curious to note, and characteristic of the man, that he was saved from demoralisation, not by the New Testament, which did not touch his heart, but by Seneca's moral axioms, which convinced his reason. The Franciscans are allowed great liberty. They run over the country collecting alms, they visit whom they will, and to a man without principle, such liberty offers dangerous occasions.

Fessler now resolved to leave an Order which was odious to him. "Somewhat tranquillized by Seneca, I now determined to shake myself loose from the trammels of the cloister, without causing scandal. The most easy way to do this was for me to take Orders, and get a cure of souls or a chaplaincy to a nobleman." He had no vocation for the ministry; he looked to it merely as a means of escape from uncongenial surroundings. On signifying his desire to become a priest, he was transferred to Gross Wardein, there to pass the requisite course of studies. At Wardein he gained the favour of the bishop and some of the canons, who lent him books on the ecclesiastical and political history of his native land. He also made acquaintance with some families in the town, a lady with two daughters, with the elder of whom he fell in love. He had, however, sufficient decency not to declare his passion. It was otherwise with a young Calvinist tailor's widow, Sophie; she replied to his declaration very sensibly by a letter, which, he declares, produced a lasting effect upon him.

In 1776 he was removed to Schwächat to go through a course of Moral Theology. His disgust at his enforced studies, which he regarded as the thrashing of empty husks, increased. He was angry at his removal from the friends he had made at Wardein. Vexation, irritation, doubt, threw him into a fever, and he was transferred to the convent in the suburbs of Vienna, where he could be under better medical care. The physician who attended him soon saw that his patient's malady was mental. Fessler opened his heart to him, and begged for the loan of books more feeding to the brain than the mystical rubbish in the convent library. The doctor advised him to visit him, when discharged as cured from the convent infirmary, instead of at once returning to Schwächat. This he did, and the doctor introduced him to two men of eminence and influence, Von Eybel and the prelate Rautenstrauch, a Benedictine abbot, the director of the Theological Faculties in the Austrian Monarchy. This latter promised Fessler to assist him in his studies, and urged him to study Greek and Hebrew, also to widen the circle of his reading, to make acquaintance with law, history, with natural science and geography, and undertook to provide him with the requisite books.

On his return to Schwächat, Fessler appealed to the Provincial against his Master of Studies whom he pronounced to be an incompetent pedant. At his request he was moved to Wiener-Neustadt. There he found the lecturer on Ecclesiastical Studies as superficial as the man from whom he had escaped. This man did not object to Fessler pursuing his Greek and Hebrew studies, nor to his taking from the library what books he liked.

The young candidate now borrowed and devoured deistical works, Hobbes, Tindal, Edelmann, and the Wolfenbüttel Fragments. He had to be careful not to let these books be seen, accordingly he hid them under the floor in the choir. After midnight, when matins had been sung, instead of returning to bed with the rest, he remained, on the plea of devotion, in the church, seated on the altar steps, reading deistical works by the light of the sanctuary lamp, which he pulled down to a proper level. He now completely lost his faith, not in Christianity only, but in natural religion as well. Nevertheless, he did not desist from his purpose of seeking orders. He was ordained deacon in 1778, and priest in 1779. "On the Sunday after Corpus Christi, I celebrated without faith, without unction, my first mass, in the presence of my mother, her brother, and the rest of my family. They all received the communion from my hand, bathed in tears of emotion. I, who administered to them, was frozen in unbelief."

The cure of souls he desired was not given him, no chaplaincy was offered him. His prospect of escape seemed no better than before. He became very impatient, and made himself troublesome in his convent. As might have been suspected, he became restive under the priestly obligations, as he had been under the monastic rule. It is curious that, late in life, when Fessler wrote his memoirs, he showed himself blind to the unworthiness of his conduct in taking on him the most sacred responsibilities to God and the Church, when he disbelieved in both. He is, however, careful to assure us that though without faith in his functions, he executed them punctually, hearing confessions, preaching and saying mass. But his conduct is so odious, his after callousness so conspicuous, that it is difficult to feel the smallest conviction of his conscientiousness at any time of his life.

As he made himself disagreeable to his superiors at Neustadt, he was transferred to Mödling. There he made acquaintance with a Herr Von Molinari and was much at his house, where he met a young Countess Louise. "I cannot describe her stately form, her arching brows, the expression of her large blue eyes, the delicacy of her mouth, the music of her tones, the exquisite harmony that exists in all her movements, and what affects me more than all—she speaks Latin easily, and only reads serious books." So wrote Fessler in a letter at the time. He read Ovid's Metamorphoses with her in the morning, and walked with her in the evening. When, at the end of October, the family went to Vienna, "the absence of that noble soul," he wrote, "filled me with the most poignant grief." The Molinari family were bitten with Jansenism, and hoped to bring the young Capuchin to their views. Next year, in the spring of 1781, they returned to Mödling.

"This year passed like the former; in the convent I was a model of obedience, in the school a master of scholastic theology: in Molinari's family a humble disciple of Jansen, in the morning a worshipper of the muse of Louise, in the evening an agreeable social companion,"—in heart—an unbeliever in Christianity.

A letter written to an uncle on March 12th, 1782, must be quoted verbatim, containing as it does a startling discovery, which gave him the opportunity so long desired, of breaking with the Order:—

"Since the 23rd February, I sing without intermission after David, in my inmost heart, 'Praise and Glory be to God, who has delivered my enemies into my hand!' Listen to the wonderful way in which this has happened. On the night of the 23rd to 24th of February, after eleven o'clock, I was roused from sleep by a lay-brother. 'Take your crucifix,' said he 'and follow me.'

"'Whither?' I asked, panic struck.

"'Whither I am about to lead you.'

"'What am I to do?'

"'I will tell you, when you are on the spot.'

"'Without knowing whither I go, and for what purpose, go I will not.'

"'The Guardian has given the order; by virtue of holy obedience you are bound to follow whither I lead.'

"As soon as holy obedience is involved, no resistance can be offered. Full of terror, I took my crucifix and followed the lay-brother, who went before with a dark lantern. Passing the cell of one of my fellow scholars, I slipped in, shook him out of sleep, and whispered in Latin twice in his ear, 'I am carried off, God knows whither. If I do not appear to-morrow, communicate with Rautenstrauch.'

"Our way led through the kitchen, and beyond it through a couple of chambers; on opening the last, the brother said, 'Seven steps down.' My heart contracted, I thought I was doomed to see the last of day-light. We entered a narrow passage, in which I saw, half way down it, on the right, a little altar, on the left some doors fastened with padlocks. My guide unlocked one of these, and said, 'Here is a dying man, Brother Nicomede, a Hungarian, who knows little German, give him your spiritual assistance. I will wait here. When he is dead, call me.'

"Before me lay an old man on his pallet, in a worn-out habit, on a straw palliasse, under a blanket; his hood covered his grey head, a snow-white beard reached to his girdle. Beside the bedstead was an old straw-covered chair, a dirty table, on which was a lamp burning. I spoke a few words to the dying man, who had almost lost his speech; he gave me a sign that he understood me. There was no possibility of a confession. I spoke to him about love to God, contrition for sin, and hope in the mercy of heaven; and when he squeezed my hand in token of inward emotion, I pronounced over him the General Absolution. The rest of the while I was with him, I uttered slowly, and at intervals, words of comfort and hope of eternal blessedness. About three o'clock, after a death agony of a quarter-of-an-hour, he had passed out of the reach of trouble.

"Before I called the lay-brother, I looked round the prison, and then swore over the corpse to inform the Emperor of these horrors. Then I summoned the lay-brother, and said, coldly, 'Brother Nicomede is gone.'

"'A good thing for him, too,' answered my guide, in a tone equally indifferent.

"'How long has he been here?'

"'Two and fifty years.'

"'He has been severely punished for his fault.'

"'Yes, yes. He has never been ill before. He had a stroke yesterday, when I brought him his meal.'

"'What is the altar for in the passage?'

"'One of the fathers says mass there on all festivals for the lions, and communicates them. Do you see, there is a little window in each of the doors, which is then opened, and through it the lions make their confession, hear mass, and receive communion.'

"'Have you many lions here?'

"'Four, two priests and two lay-brothers to be attended on.'

"'How long have they been here?'

"'One for fifty, another for forty-two, the third for fifteen, and the last for nine years.'

"'Why are they here?'

"'I don't know.'

"'Why are they called lions?'

"'Because I am called the lion-ward.'

"I deemed it expedient to ask no more questions. I got the lion-ward to light me to my cell, and there in calmness considered what to do.

"Next day, or rather, that same day, Feb. 24th, I wrote in full all that had occurred, in a letter addressed to the Emperor, with my signature attached. Shortly after my arrival in Vienna I had made the acquaintance of a Bohemian secular student named Bokorny, a trusty man. On the morning of Feb. 25th, I made him swear to give my letter to the Emperor, and keep silence as to my proceeding.

"At 8 o'clock he was with my letter in the Couriers' lobby of the palace, where there is usually a crowd of persons with petitions awaiting the Emperor. Joseph took my paper from my messenger, glanced hastily at it, put it apart from the rest of the petitions, and let my messenger go, after he had cautioned him most seriously to hold his tongue.

"The blow is fallen; what will be the result—whether anything will come of it, I do not yet know."

For many months no notice was taken of the letter. It was not possible for the Emperor to take action at once, for a few days later Pius VI. arrived in Vienna on a visit to Joseph.

Joseph II. was an enthusiastic reformer; he had the liveliest regard for Frederick the Great, and tried to copy him, but, as Frederick said, Joseph always began where he ought to leave off. He had no sooner become Emperor (1780) than he began a multitude of reforms, with headlong impetuosity. He supposed that every abuse was to be rooted up by an exercise of despotic power, and that his subjects would hail freedom and enlightenment with enthusiasm. Regardless of the power of hereditary association, he arbitrarily upset existing institutions, in the conviction that he was promoting the welfare of his subjects. He emancipated the Jews, and proclaimed liberty of worship to all religious bodies except the Deists, whom he condemned to receive five-and-twenty strokes of the cane. He abolished the use of torture, and reorganised the courts of justice.

The Pope, alarmed at the reforming spirit of Joseph, and the innovations he was introducing into the management of the Church, crossed the Alps with the hope that in a personal interview he might moderate the Emperor's zeal. He arrived only a few days after Joseph had received the letter of Ignatius Fessler, which was calculated to spur him to enact still more sweeping reforms, and to steel his heart against the papal blandishments. Nothing could have come to his hands more opportunely.

In Vienna, in St. Stephen's, the Pope held a pontifical mass. The Emperor did not honour it by his presence. By order of Joseph, the back door of the papal lodging was walled up, that Pius might receive no visitors unknown to the Emperor, and guards were placed at the entrance, to scrutinize those who sought the presence of the Pope. Joseph lost dignity by studied discourtesy; and Kaunitz, his minister, was allowed to be insulting. The latter received the Pope when he visited him, in his dressing-gown, and instead of kissing his hand, shook it heartily. Pius, after spending five weeks in Vienna without affecting anything, was constrained to depart.

Fessler saw him thrice, once, when the Pope said mass in the Capuchin Church, he stood only three paces from him. "Never did faith and unbelief, Jansenism and Deism, struggle for the mastery in me more furiously than then; tears flowed from my eyes, excited by my emotion, and at the end of the mass, I felt convinced that I had seen either a man as full of the burning love of God as a seraph, or the most accomplished actor in the world." Of the sincerity and piety of Pius VI. there can be no question. He was a good man, but not an able man. "At the conclusion he turned to us young priests, asked of each his name, length of time in the Order, and priesthood, about our studies, and exhorted us, in a fatherly tone, to be stout stones in the wall of the house of Israel, in times of trouble present and to come."

Before Pius departed, he gave his blessing to the people from the balcony of the Jesuit Church. "The Pope was seated on a throne under a gold-embroidered canopy. Fifty thousand persons must have been assembled below. Windows were full of heads, every roof crowded. The Pope wore his triple-crowned tiara, and was attended by three cardinals and two bishops in full pontificals. He intoned the form of absolution, in far-reaching voice, which was taken up by the court choir of four hundred voices. When this was done, Pius rose from his throne, the tiara was removed from his head, he stepped forward, raised eyes and arms to heaven, and in a pure ecstasy of devotion poured forth a fervent prayer. Only sighs and sobs broke occasionally the perfect silence which reigned among the vast throng of kneeling persons in the great square. The Pope seemed rather to be raised in ecstasy from his feet, than to stand. The prayer lasted long, and the bishops put their hands to stay up his arms; it was like Moses on the mountain top, with the rod of God in his hand, supported by Aaron and Hur, as he prayed for his people striving below with Amalek. At last this second Moses let his arms fall, he raised his right hand, and blessed the people in the name of the Triune God. At the Amen, the cannon of the Freiung boomed, and were answered by all the artillery on the fortifications of the city."

The Pope was gone, and still no notice taken of the petition. Molinari spoke to Fessler, who was very hot about reform, and had drawn up a scheme for the readjustment of the Church in the Empire, which he sent to some of the ministers of the Emperor. "My friend," said Molinari, "to pull down and to rebuild, to destroy and to re-create, are serious matters, only to be taken in hand by one who has an earnest vocation, and not to be made a means for self-seeking."

Fessler admits that there was truth in the reproach, he was desirous of pushing himself into notice, and he cared for the matter of "the lions," only because he thought they would serve his selfish purpose. Joseph now issued an order that no member of a monastic order was to be admitted to a benefice who had not passed an examination before the teachers of the Seminaries. The superiors of the Capuchins forbade their candidates going into these examinations. Fessler stirred up revolt, and he and some others, acting under his advice, demanded to be admitted to examination. His superior then informed him that he was not intended by the Order to take a cure of souls, he was about to be appointed lecturer on Philosophy in one of the convents in Hungary. In order to prevent his removal, and to force the Order to an open rupture with him, Fessler had recourse to a most unseemly and ungenerous act. Whilst in Vienna, he had made the acquaintance of an unmarried lady, the Baroness E. He had assisted her in her studies, giving her instructions usually by letter. His acquaintance, Von Eybel, had written a book or tract, which had made a great stir, entitled, "Who is the Pope?" Fessler wrote another, entitled, "Who is the Emperor?" He sent a copy to the publisher, but retained the original MS. Fessler now wrote under a feigned name, and in a disguised hand, a letter to Father Maximus, guardian of the convent, charging himself with carrying on a guilty correspondence with the Baroness E., and with the composition of an inflammatory and anti-religious pamphlet, "Who is the Emperor?" Maximus at once visited the Baroness, and showed her the letter. The lady in great indignation produced the entire correspondence, and handed the letters to him. Maximus put them in the hands of the Lector of the convent, who visited Fessler, and asked him if he acknowledged the authorship of "these scandalous letters."

"Scandalous, they are not," answered Fessler.

"*Impius, cum in profundum venerit, contemnit,*" roared the friar. "They are not only scandalous, but impious. Look at this letter on platonic love. Is that a fit letter for such as you to write to a lady?"

In consequence of these letters, and the MS. of the pamphlet being found upon him, Fessler was denounced to the Consistorial Court of the Archbishop. He was summoned before it at the beginning of August, when he was forced to admit he had been wont to kiss the lady to whom he wrote on platonic love, and the Consistory suspended him from the exercise of his priestly functions for a month.

"I and the Lector returned to the convent silent, as if strangers. When we arrived, the friars were at table. I do not know how I got to my place; but after I had drunk my goblet of wine, all was clearer about me. I seemed to hear the voice of Horace calling to me from heaven, *Perfer et obdura!* and in a moment my self-respect revived, and I looked with scorn on the seventy friars hungrily eating their dinner."

Of his own despicable conduct, that he had richly deserved his punishment, Fessler never seems to have arrived at the perception. He was, indeed, a very pitiful creature, arousing disgust and contempt in a well-ordered mind; and his Memoirs only deserve notice because of the curious insight they afford into the inner life of convents, and because he was the means of bringing great scandals to light, and in assisting Joseph II. in his work of reform.

At the beginning of September, 1782, Fessler was the means of bringing a fresh scandal before the eyes of the Emperor. During the preceding year, a saddler in Schwächat had lost his wife, and was left, not only a widower, but childless. His niece now kept house for him, and was much afraid lest her uncle should marry again, and that thus she should not become his heir. She consulted a Capuchin, Father Brictius. Fessler had been in the Schwächat convent, and knew the man. Soon after, the niece assured her uncle that the ghost of her aunt had appeared to her, and told her she was suffering in Purgatory. For her release, she must have ten masses said, and some wax candles burnt. The saddler was content to have his old woman "laid" at this price. But, after the tenth mass, the niece declared she had seen her aunt again, and that the spirit had appeared to her in the presence of Father Brictius, and told her, that what troubled her most of all was the suspicion she was under, that her husband purposed marrying again; and she assured him, that were he so to do, he would lose his soul, in token whereof, she laid her hand on the cover of the niece's prayer-book, and left the impression burnt into it.

Father Brictius carried the scorched book all round the neighbourhood, the marks of thumb and five fingers were clearly to be seen, burnt into the wooden cover. Great was the excitement, and on all sides masses for souls were in demand. Some foolish pastors even preached on the marvel.

It happened that a Viennese boy was apprenticed to a tinker at Schwächat; and the boy came home every Saturday evening, to spend the day with his parents, at Vienna. He generally brought Fessler some little presents or messages from his friends at Schwächat. One day, the boy complained to Fessler that he had been severely beaten by his master. On being asked the reason, he replied, that he had been engaged with the tinker making an iron hand, and that he had spoiled it. Shortly after this, the rumour of the miraculous hand laid on the prayer-book, reached the convent. Fessler put the circumstances together, and suspected he was on the track of a fraud. He went at once to one of the ministers of the Emperor, and told him what he knew.

An imperial commission was issued, the tinker, the saddler's niece, and Father Brictius, were arrested, cross-questioned, and finally, confessed the trick. The tinker was sent to prison for some months, the woman, for some weeks, and the Franciscan was first imprisoned, and then banished the country. An account of the fraud was issued, by Government authority, and every parish priest was ordered to read it to his parishioners from the pulpit.

The Capuchins at Vienna, after this, were more impatient than before to send Fessler to Hungary, and he was forced to appeal to the Emperor to prevent his removal.

Suddenly, quite unexpectedly, in the beginning of October—seven months after Fessler had sent the Emperor an account of the prison in the convent, and when he despaired of notice being taken of it—some imperial commissioners visited the convent, and demanded in the name of the Emperor to be shown all over it. At the head of the Commission was Hägelin, to whom Fessler had told his suspicions about the iron hand.

The commissioners visited all the cells, and the infirmary, then asked the Guardian thrice on his honour, and in the name of the Emperor, whether there was a prison in the convent. Thrice the Guardian replied that there was not. "Let us now visit the kitchen," said Hägelin, and in spite of the protests and excuses of the Guardian, he insisted on being taken there. Beyond the kitchen was the wash-house. The commissioners went further, and found a small locked door. They insisted on its being opened. Then the Guardian turned pale and nearly fainted. The door was thrown open, the cells were unlocked, and the lay brothers ordered to bring the prisoners into the refectory. There the commissioners remained alone with the unfortunates to take down their depositions. It was found that three, Fathers Florentine, and Paternus, and the lay brother, Nemesian, were out of their minds. The "lion-ward" was summoned to answer for them. From his account, it transpired that Nemesian had gone out of his mind through religious enthusiasm; he was aged seventy-one, and had been fifty years in the dungeon. Father Florentine was aged seventy-three, he had been in confinement for forty-two years for boxing the Guardian's ears in a fit of temper. Father Paternus was locked up because he used to leave his convent without permission, and when rebuked would not give up his independent conduct. He had been fifteen years in prison. His confinement had bereft him of his senses. As the remaining two were in full possession of their faculties, the "lion-ward" was now dismissed. The lay brother Barnabas said he had been a shopkeeper's servant in Vienna, he had fallen in love with his master's daughter. As his master refused to have him as his son-in-law, out of despair he had gone into the Capuchin Order. During his noviciate, the master died; the master of the novices stopped the letter informing him of this, and he took the vows, to discover, when too late, that the girl loved him, and was ready to take him. In his mad rage, he flung his rosary at the feet of the Guardian, declaring he would never confess to, or receive the communion from the hands of a father of this accursed Order. He had been nine years in prison, and was thirty-eight years old.

Father Thuribius had been caught reading Wieland, Gellert, Rabener, &c.; they had been taken from him. He got hold of other copies, they were taken away a second time. A third time he procured them, and when discovered, fought with his fists for their retention. He had been repeatedly given the cat o' nine tails, and had been locked up five months and ten days. His age was twenty-eight.

The commissioners at once suspended the Provincial and the Guardian till further notice, and the five unfortunates were handed over to the care of the Brothers of Charity.

That same day, throughout the entire monarchy, every monastery and nunnery was visited by imperial commissioners.

At the same time, the Emperor Joseph issued an order that Fessler was on no account to be allowed to leave Vienna, and that he took him under his imperial protection against all the devices of his monastic enemies.

"Now came the sentence on the Guardian and the Provincial from the Emperor. They were more severely punished than perhaps they really deserved. I felt for their sufferings more keenly, because I was well aware that I had been moved to report against them by any other motive rather than humanity; and even the consequences of my revelation, the setting at liberty of a not inconsiderable number of unfortunate monks and nuns throughout the Austrian Empire, could not set my conscience at rest. Only the orders made by the Emperor rendering it impossible to repeat such abuses, brought me any satisfaction. The monastic prisons were everywhere destroyed. Transgression of rules was henceforth to be punished only by short periods of seclusion, and cases of insanity were to be sent to the Brothers of Charity, who managed the asylums."

If Joseph II. had but possessed commonsense as well as enthusiasm, he would have left his mark deeper on his country than he did.

Fessler laid before him the schedule of studies in the Franciscan Convents. Joseph then issued an order (6th April, 1782), absolutely prohibiting the course of studies in the cloisters. When Fessler saw that the Guardian of his convent was transgressing the decree, he appealed against him to the Emperor, and had him dismissed. Next year Joseph required all the students of the Capuchin Order to enter the seminaries, and pass thence through the Universities. But, unfortunately, Joseph had taken a step to alienate from him the bishops and secular clergy, as well as the monks and friars. He arbitrarily closed all the diocesan seminaries, and created seminaries of his own for the candidates for Orders, to which he appointed the professors, thus entirely removing the education of the clergy from the hands of the Church. When the Bishop of Goritz expressed his dissatisfaction, Joseph suppressed his see and banished him. The professors he appointed to the universities, to the chairs which were attended by candidates for Orders, were in many cases free-thinkers and rationalists. The professor of Biblical Exegesis at Vienna was an ex-Jesuit, Monsperger, "His religious system," says Fessler, who attended his course, "was simply this,—a wise enjoyment of life, submission to the inevitable, and prudence of conduct. That was all. He had no other idea of Church than a reciprocal bond of rights and duties. In his lectures he whittled all the supernatural out of the Old Testament, and taught his pupils to regard the book as a collection of myths, romance, and contradictions. His lectures brought me back from my trifling with Jansenism to the point I had been at four years before under the teaching of Hobbes, Tindal, and the Wolfenbüttel Fragments. I resolved to doubt everything supernatural and divine, without actually denying such thing.—Strange! I resolved to disbelieve, when I never had believed."

On Feb. 6th, 1784, he received the Emperor's appointment to the professorships of Biblical Exegesis and Oriental languages in the University of Lemberg. On the 20th Feb., on the eve of starting for Lemberg, for ever to cast off the hated habit of S. Francis, and to shake off, as much as he dare, the trammels of the priesthood, Fessler was in his cell at midnight, counting the money he had received for his journey. "To the right of me, on the table was a dagger, given me as a parting present by the court secretary, Grossinger. I was thinking of retiring to rest, when my cell door was burst open, and in rushed Father Sergius, a great meat-knife in his hand, shouting, *Moriere hoeretice!* he struck at my breast. In an instant I seized my dagger, parried the blow, and wounded my assailant in the hand. He let the knife fall and ran away. I roused the Guardian, told him what had occurred, and advised what was to be done. Sergius, armed with two similar knives, had locked himself into his cell. At the command of the Guardian six lay-brothers burst open the door, and beat the knives from his hands with sticks, then dragged him off to the punishment-cell, where they placed him under watch. Next morning I went with the Guardian, as I had advised, to the president of the Spiritual Commission, the Baron von Kresel, to inform him that Father Sergius had gone raving mad, and to ask that he might be committed to the custody of the Brothers of Mercy. This was at once granted; and I left the Guardian to instruct the fanatic how to comport himself in the hospital as a lunatic, so as not to bring his superiors into further difficulties."

The first acquaintance Fessler made in Lemberg, was a renegade Franciscan friar, who had been appointed Professor of Physic, "He was a man of unbounded ambition and avarice, a political fanatic, and a complete atheist." Joseph afterwards appointed this man to be mitred abbot of Zazvár. He died on the scaffold in 1795, executed for high treason.

The seminarists of the Catholic and of the Uniat Churches as well as the pupils from the religious Orders were obliged to attend Fessler's lectures. These were on the lines of these of Monsperger. Some of the clergy in charge of the Seminarists were so uneasy at Fessler's teaching that they stood up at his lectures and disputed his assertions; but Fessler boasts that after a couple of months he got the young men round to his views, and they groaned, hooted and stamped down the remonstrants. He published at this time two works, *Institutiones linguarum orientalium*, and a Hebrew anthology for the use of the students. In the latter he laid down certain canons for the interpretation of the Old Testament, by means of which everything miraculous might be explained away.

It was really intolerable that the candidates for orders should be forcibly taught to disbelieve everything their Church required them to hold. In his inspection of the monasteries, in the suppression of many, Joseph acted with justice, and the conscience of the people approved, but in this matter of the education of the clergy he violated the principles of common justice, and the consequence was such wide-spread irritation, that Joseph for a moment seemed inclined to give way. That Joseph knew the rationalism of Fessler is certain. The latter gives a conversation he had with the Emperor, in which they discussed the "Ruah," the Spirit of God, which moved on the face of the waters, as said in the first chapter of Genesis. Fessler told him that he considered "the expression to be a Hebrew superlative, and to mean no more than that a violent gale was blowing. Possibly," he added, "Moses may have thought of the Schiva in the Hindoo Trimurti; for he was reared in all the wisdom of the Egyptians, who were an Ethiopic race, which was in turn an Indian colony." Dr. Fessler's Ethnology was faulty, whatever may be thought of his Theology.

After having given this explanation to the Emperor, Fessler boldly asked him for a bishopric—he who loathed his priesthood and disbelieved in revealed religion!

Joseph did not give him a mitre, but made him Professor of Doctrinal Theology and Catholic Polemics as well as of Biblical Exegesis. This did not satisfy the ambitious soul of Fessler, he was bent on a mitre. He waited with growing impatience. He sent his books to Joseph. He did his utmost to force himself into his notice. But the desired mitre did not come.

Fessler complains that scandalous stories circulated about him whilst at Lemberg, and these possibly may have reached the imperial ears. He asserts, and no doubt with perfect truth, that these were unfounded. He had made himself bitter enemies, and they would not scruple to defame him. He boasts that at Lemberg he contracted no Platonic alliances; he had no *attachements de coeur* there at all.

The Emperor seemed to have forgotten him, to have cast aside his useful tool. Filled with the bitterness of defeated ambition, in 1788 he wrote a drama, entitled James II., a covert attack on his protector, Joseph II., whom he represented as falling away in his enthusiasm for reform, and succumbing to the gathering hostility of Obscurantists and Jesuits.

This was not the case, but Joseph was in trouble with his refractory subjects in the Low Countries, who would not have his seminaries and professors, who subscribed for the support of the ousted teachers, and rioted at the introduction of the new professors to the University of Louvain.

The play was put into rehearsal, but the police interfered, and it was forbidden. Fessler either feared or was warned that he was about to be arrested, and he escaped over the frontier into Prussian Silesia. Joseph II. died in 1790, broken in spirit by his failures.

Fessler, after his escape from Austria, became a salaried reader and secretary to the Count of Carolath, whose wife was a princess of Saxe-Meiningen.

After a while he married a young woman of the middle class; he seems to have doubted whether they would be happy together, after he had proposed, accordingly he wrote her a long epistle, in the most pedantic and dictorial style, informing her of what his requirements were, and warning her to withdraw from the contemplated union, if she were not sure she would come up to the level of the perfect wife. The poor creature no doubt wondered at the marvellous love letter, but had no hesitation in saying she would do her duty up to her lights. The result was not happy. They led together a cat-and-dog life for ten years. She was a homely person without intellectual parts, and he was essentially a book-worm. He admits that he did not shine in society, and leaves it to be understood that the loss was on the side of inappreciative society, but we can not help suspecting that he was opinionated, sour, and uncouth. All these qualities were intensified in the narrow circle of home. After ten years of misery he divorced his wife on the ground of mutual incompatibility. For a livelihood he took up Freemasonry, and went about founding lodges. There were three rogues at that period who worked Freemasonry for their own ends, the Darmstadt Court Chaplain, Starck, a Baron von Hundt, and a certain Becker, who called himself Johnson, and pretended to be a delegate from the mysterious, unknown head of the Society in Aberdeen. They called themselves Masons of the Strict Observance, but were mere swindlers.

After a while, Freemasonry lost its attractions for Fessler, probably it ceased to pay, and then he left Breslau, and wandered into Prussia. He wrote a novel called "Marcus Aurelius," glorifying that emperor, for whom he entertained great veneration, and did other literary work, which brought him in a little money. Then he married again, a young, beautiful and gifted woman, with a small property. He was very happy in his choice, but less happy in the speculation in which he invested her money and that of her sisters. It failed, and they were reduced to extreme poverty. What became of the sisters we do not know. Fessler with his wife and children went into Russia, and sponged for some time on the Moravian Brothers, who treated him with great kindness, and lent him money, "Which," he says, in his autobiography, "I have not yet been able to pay back altogether."

He lost some of his children. Distress, pecuniary embarrassments, and sickness, softened his heart, and perhaps with that was combined a perception that if he could get a pastorate he would be provided for;[22] this led to a conversion, which looks very much as if it were copied from the famous conversion of St. Augustine. It possibly was, to some extent, sincere; he recovered faith in God, and joined the Lutheran community.

[22] He had, however, just received a pension from the Czar, so that he was relieved from abject poverty.

Then he had his case and attainments brought under the notice of the Czar, who was, at the time, as Fessler probably knew, engaged in a scheme for organising the Lutheran bodies in Finland into a Church under Episcopal government. He chose Fessler to be bishop of Saratow, and had him consecrated by the Swedish bishops, "Who," says Fessler, "like the Anglican bishops, have preserved the Apostolic succession." He makes much of this point, a curious instance of the revival in his mind of old ideas imbibed in his time of Catholicity. . According to his own account, he was a bishop quite on the Apostolic model, and worked very hard to bring his diocese into order. His ordination was in 1820. In 1833, the Saratow consistory was dissolved, and he retired to St. Petersburg, where he was appointed general superintendent of the Lutheran community in the capital. He married a third time, but says very little of the last wife. He concludes with this estimate of his own character, which is hardly that at which a reader of his autobiography would arrive. "Earnestness and cheerfulness, rapid decision, and unbending determination, manly firmness and childlike trueheartedness—these are the ever recurring fundamental characteristics of my nature. Add to these a gentle mysticism, to surround the others with colour and unite them in harmony. Sometimes it may be that dissonances occur, it may be true that occasionally I thunder with powerful lungs in my house, as if I were about to wreck and shatter everything, but that is called forth only by what is wrong. In my inmost being calm, peace, and untroubled cheerfulness reign supreme. Discontent, wrath, venom and gall, have not embittered one moment of my life."[23]

[23] "Of myself," he says, "I must confess that I have heard great and famous preachers, true Bourdaloues, Massillons, Zollikofers, &c, in Vienna, Carolath, Breslau, Berlin, Dresden, Leipzig, Hanover, and have been pleased with the contents, arrangement, and delivery of their sermons; but never once have I felt my heart stirred with religious emotion. On the contrary, on the 25th March, 1782, when Pius VI. said mass in the Capuchin Church, and on the 31st March, when he blessed the people, I trembled on the edge of conviction and religious faith, and was only held back by my inability to distinguish between religion and the Church system. Still more now does the Sermon on the Mount move me, and for the last 23 years the divine liturgical prayer in John xvii., does not fail to stir my very soul."

Historic Oddities and Strange Events, 2nd Series

I. — A SWISS PASSION PLAY

WE are a little surprised, and perhaps a little shocked, at the illiberality of the Swiss Government, in even such Protestant cantons as Geneva, Zürich, and Berne, in forbidding the performances on their ground of the "Salvation Army," and think that such conduct is not in accordance with Protestant liberty of judgment and democratic independence. But the experiences gone through in Switzerland as in Germany of the confusion and mischief sometimes wrought by fanaticism, we will not say justify, but in a measure explain, the objection the Government has to a recrudescence of religious mysticism in its more flagrant forms. The following story exemplifies the extravagance to which such spiritual exaltation runs occasionally—fortunately only occasionally.

About eight miles from Schaffhausen, a little way on one side of the road to Winterthür, in a valley, lies the insignificant hamlet of Wildisbuch, its meadows overshadowed by leafy walnut trees. The hamlet is in the parish of Trüllikon. Here, at the beginning of this century, in a farmhouse, standing by itself, lived John Peter, a widower, with several of his children. He had but one son, Caspar, married in 1812, and divorced from his wife; he was, however, blessed with five daughters—Barbara, married to a blacksmith in Trüllikon; Susanna, Elizabeth, Magdalena married to John Moser, a shoemaker; and Margaretta, born in 1794, his youngest, and favourite child. Not long after the birth of Margaretta, her mother died, and thenceforth the child was the object of the tenderest and most devoted solicitude to her sisters and to her father. Margaretta grew up to be a remarkable child. At school she distinguished herself by her aptitude in learning, and in church by the devotion with which she followed the tedious Zwinglian service. The pastor who prepared her for confirmation was struck by her enthusiasm and eagerness to know about religion. She was clearly an imaginative person, and to one constituted as she was, the barnlike church, destitute of every element of beauty, studiously made as hideous as a perverse fancy could scheme, and the sacred functions reduced to utter dreariness, with every element of devotion bled out of them, were incapable of satisfying the internal spiritual fire that consumed her.

There is in every human soul a divine aspiration, a tension after the invisible and spiritual, in some more developed than in others, in certain souls existing only in that rudimentary condition in which, it is said, feet are found in the eel, and eyes in the oyster, but in others it is a predominating faculty, a veritable passion. Unless this faculty be given legitimate scope, be disciplined and guided, it breaks forth in abnormal and unhealthy manifestations. We know what is the result when the regular action of the pores of the skin is prevented, or the circulation of the blood is impeded. Fever and hallucination ensue. So is it with the spiritual life in man. If that be not given free passage for healthy discharge of its activity, it will resolve itself into fanaticism, that is to say it will assume a diseased form of manifestation.

Margaretta was far ahead of her father, brother and sisters in intellectual culture, and in moral force of character. Susanna, the second daughter of John Peter, was an amiable, industrious, young woman, without independence of character. The third daughter, Elizabeth, was a quiet girl, rather dull in brain; Barbara was married when Margaretta was only nine, and Magdalena not long after; neither of them, however, escaped the influence of their youngest sister, who dominated over their wills almost as completely as she did over those of her two unmarried sisters, with whom she consorted daily.

How great her power over her sisters was may be judged from what they declared in after years in prison, and from what they endured for her sake.

Barbara, the eldest, professed to the prison chaplain in Zürich, in 1823, "I am satisfied that God worked in mighty power, and in grace through Margaret, up to the hour of her death." The father himself declared after the ruin of his family and the death of two of his daughters, "I am assured that my youngest daughter was set apart by God for some extraordinary purpose."

When Margaret was six, she was able to read her Bible, and would summon the family about her to listen to her lectures out of the sacred volume. She would also at the same time pray with great ardour, and exhort her father and sisters to lead God-fearing lives. When she read the narrative of the Passion, she was unable to refrain from tears; her emotion communicated itself to all assembled round her, and the whole family sobbed and prayed aloud. She was a veritable "ministering child" to her household in all things spiritual. As she had been born at Christmas, it was thought that this very fact indicated some special privilege and grace accorded to her. In 1811, when aged seventeen, she received her first communion and edified all the church with the unction and exaltation of soul with which she presented herself at the table. In after years the pastor of Trüllikon said of her, "Unquestionably Margaretta was the cleverest of the family. She often came to thank me for the instructions I had given her in spiritual things. Her promises to observe all I had taught her were most fervent. I had the best hopes for her, although I observed somewhat of extravagance in her. Margaretta speedily obtained an absolute supremacy in her father's house. All must do what she ordered. Her will expressed by word of mouth, or by letter when absent, was obeyed as the will of God."

In personal appearance Margaretta was engaging. She was finely moulded, had a well-proportioned body, a long neck on which her head was held very upright; large, grey-blue eyes, fair hair, a lofty, well-arched brow. The nose was well-shaped, but the chin and mouth were somewhat coarse.

In 1816, her mother's brother, a small farmer at Rudolfingen, invited her to come and manage his house for him. She went, and was of the utmost assistance. Everything prospered under her hand. Her uncle thought that she had brought the blessing of the Almighty on both his house and his land.

Whilst at Rudolfingen, the holy maiden was brought in contact with the Pietists of Schaffhausen. She attended their prayer-meetings and expositions of Scripture. This deepened her religious convictions, and produced a depression in her manner that struck her sisters when she visited them. In answer to their inquiries why she was reserved and melancholy, she replied that God was revealing Himself to her more and more every day, so that she became daily more conscious of her own sinfulness. If this had really been the case it would have saved her from what ensued, but this sense of her own sinfulness was a mere phrase, that meant actually an overweening self-consciousness. She endured only about a twelve month of the pietistic exercises at Schaffhausen, and then felt a call to preach, testify and prophesy herself, instead of sitting at the feet of others. Accordingly, she threw up her place with her uncle, and returned to Wildisbuch, in March, 1817, when she began operations as a revivalist.

The paternal household was now somewhat enlarged. The old farmer had taken on a hand to help him in field and stable, called Heinrich Ernst, and a young woman as maid called Margaret Jäggli. Ernst was a faithful, amiable young fellow whom old Peters thoroughly trusted, and he became devoted heart and soul to the family. Margaret Jäggli was a person of very indifferent character, who, for her immoralities, had been turned out of her native village. She was subject to epileptic fits, which she supposed were possession by the devil, and she came to the farm of the Peter's family in hopes of being there cured by the prayers of the saintly Margaretta.

Another inmate of the house was Ursula Kündig, who entered it at the age of nineteen, and lived there as a veritable maid-of-all-work, though paid no wages. This damsel was of the sweetest, gentlest disposition. Her parish pastor gave testimony to her, "She was always so good that even scandal-mongers were unable to find occasion for slander in her conduct." Her countenance was full of intelligence, purity, and had in it a nobility above her birth and education. Her home had been unhappy; she had been engaged to be married to a young man, but finding that he did not care for her, and sought only her small property, she broke off the engagement, to her father's great annoyance. It was owing to a quarrel at home relative to this, that she went to Wildisbuch to entreat Margaretta Peter to be "her spiritual guide through life into eternity." Ursula had at first only paid occasional visits to Wildisbuch, but gradually these visits became long, and finally she took up her residence in the house. The soul of the unhappy girl was as wax in the hands of the saint, whom she venerated with intensest admiration as the Elect of the Lord; and she professed her unshaken conviction "that Christ revealed Himself in the flesh through her, and that through her many thousands of souls were saved." The house at Wildisbuch became thenceforth a great gathering place for all the spiritually-minded in the neighbourhood, who desired instruction, guidance, enlightenment, and Margaretta, the high priestess of mysticism to all such as could find no satisfaction for the deepest hunger of their souls in the Zwinglian services of their parish church.

Man is composed of two parts; he has a spiritual nature which he shares with the angels, and an animal nature that he possesses in common with the beasts. There is in him, consequently, a double tendency, one to the indefinite, unconfined, spiritual; the other to the limited, sensible and material. The religious history of all times shows us this higher nature striving after emancipation from the law of the body, and never succeeding in accomplishing the escape, always falling back, like Dædalus, into destruction, when attempting to defy the laws of nature and soar too near to the ineffable light. The mysticism of the old heathen world, the mysticism of the Gnostic sects, the mysticism of mediæval heretics, almost invariably resolved itself into orgies of licentiousness. God has bound soul and body together, and an attempt to dissociate them in religion is fatally doomed to ruin.

The incarnation of the Son of God was the indissoluble union of Spirit with form as the basis of true religion. Thenceforth, Spirit was no more to be dissociated from matter, authority from a visible Church, grace from a sacramental sign, morality from a fixed law. All the great revolts against Catholicism in the middle-ages, were more or less revolts against this principle and were reversions to pure spiritualism. The Reformation was taken advantage of for the mystic aspirations of men to run riot. Individual emotion became the supreme and sole criticism of right and wrong, of truth and falsehood, and sole authority to which submission must be tendered.

In the autumn of 1817, Margaretta of Wildisbuch met a woman who was also remarkable in her way, and the head of another revivalist movement. This was Julianne von Krüdner; about whom a word must now be said.

Julianne was born in 1766, at Riga, the daughter of a noble and wealthy family. Her father visited Paris and took the child with him, where she made the acquaintance of the rationalistic and speculative spirits of French society, before the Revolution. In a Voltairean atmosphere, the little Julianne grew up without religious faith or moral principle. At the age of fourteen she was married to a man much older than herself, the Baron von Krüdner, Russian Ambassador at Venice. There her notorious immoralities resulted in a separation, and Julianne was obliged to return to her father's house at Riga. This did not satisfy her love of pleasure and vanity, and she went to St. Petersburg and then to Paris, where she threw herself into every sort of dissipation. She wrote a novel, "Valérie," in which she frankly admitted that woman, when young, must give herself up to pleasure, then take up with art, and finally, when nothing else was left her, devote herself to religion. At the age of forty she had already entered on this final phase. She went to Berlin, was admitted to companionship with the Queen, Louise, and endeavoured to "convert" her. The sweet, holy queen required no conversion, and the Baroness von Krüdner was obliged to leave Berlin. She wandered thenceforth from place to place, was now in Paris, then in Geneva, and then in Germany. At Karlsruhe she met Jung-Stilling; and thenceforth threw herself heart and soul into the pietistic revival. Her mission now was—so she conceived—to preach the Gospel to the poor. In 1814 she obtained access to the Russian Court, where her prophecies and exhortations produced such an effect on the spirit of the Czar, Alexander I., that he entreated her to accompany him to Paris. She did so, and held spiritual conferences and prayer meetings in the French capital. Alexander soon tired of her, and she departed to Basel, where she won to her the Genevan Pastor Empeytaz and the Basel Professor Lachenal. Her meetings for revival, which were largely attended, caused general excitement, but led to many domestic quarrels, so that the city council gave her notice to leave the town. She then made a pilgrimage along the Rhine, but her proceedings were everywhere objected to by the police and town authorities, and she was sent back under police supervision first to Leipzig, and thence into Russia.

Thence in 1824 she departed for the Crimea, where she had resolved to start a colony on the plan of the Moravian settlements, and there died before accomplishing her intention.

It was in 1817, when she was conducting her apostolic progress along the Rhine, that she and Margaretta of Wildisbuch met. Apparently the latter made a deeper impression on the excitable baroness than had the holy Julianne on Margaretta. The two aruspices did not laugh when they met, for they were both in deadly earnest, and had not the smallest suspicion that they were deluding themselves first, and then others.

The meeting with the Krüdner had a double effect. In the first place, the holy Julianne, when forced to leave the neighbourhood by the unregenerate police, commended her disciples to the blessed Margaret; and, in the second place, the latter had the shrewdness to perceive, that, if she was to play anything like the part of her fellow-apostle, she must acquire a little more education. Consequently Margaret took pains to write grammatically, and to spell correctly.

The result of the commendation by Saint Julianne of her disciples to Margaret was that thenceforth a regular pilgrimage set in to Wildisbuch of devout persons in landaus and buggies, on horse and on foot.

Some additional actors in the drama must now be introduced.

Magdalena Peter, the fourth daughter of John Peter, was married to the cobbler, John Moser. The influence of Margaret speedily made itself felt in their house. At first Moser's old mother lived with the couple, along with Conrad, John Moser's younger brother. The first token of the conversion of Moser and his wife was that they kicked the old mother out of the house, because she was worldly and void of "saving grace." Conrad was a plodding, hard-working lad, very useful, and therefore not to be dispensed with. The chosen vessels finding he did not sympathise with them, and finding him too valuable to be done without, starved him till he yielded to their fancies, saw visions, and professed himself "saved." Barbara, also, married to the blacksmith Baumann, was next converted, and brought all her spiritual artillery to bear on the blacksmith, but in vain. He let her go her own way, but he would have nothing himself to say to the great spiritual revival in the house of the Peters. Barbara, not finding a kindred soul in her husband, had taken up with a man of like soaring piety, a tailor, named Hablützel.

Another person who comes into this story is Jacob Ganz, a tailor, who had been mixed up with the movement at Basel under Julianne the Holy.

Margaret's brother Caspar was a man of infamous character; he was separated from his wife, whom he had treated with brutality; had become the father of an illegitimate child, and now loafed about the country preaching the Gospel.

Ganz, the tailor, had thrown aside his shears, and constituted himself a roving preacher. In one of his apostolic tours he had made the acquaintance of Saint Margaret, and had been deeply impressed by her. He had an elect disciple at Illnau, in the Kempthal, south of Winterthür. This was a shoemaker named Jacob Morf, a married man, aged thirty; small; with a head like a pumpkin. To this shoemaker Ganz spoke with enthusiasm of the spiritual elevation of the holy Margaret, and Morf was filled with a lively desire of seeing and hearing her.

Margaretta seems after a while to have wearied of the monotony of life in her father's house, or else the spirit within her drove her abroad to carry her light into the many dark corners of her native canton. She resolved to be like Ganz, a roving apostle. Sometimes she started on her missionary journeys alone, sometimes along with her sister Elizabeth, who submitted to her with blind and stanch obedience, or else with Ursula Kündig. These journeys began in 1820, and extended as far Zürich and along the shores of that lovely lake. In May of the same year she visited Illnau, where she was received with enthusiasm by the faithful, who assembled in the house of a certain Ruegg, and there for the first time she met with Jacob Morf. The acquaintance then begun soon quickened into friendship. When a few weeks later he went to Schaffhausen to purchase leather, he turned aside to Wildisbuch. After this his visits there became not only frequent, but were protracted.

Margaret was the greatest comfort to him in his troubled state of soul. She described to him the searchings and anxieties she had undergone, so that he cried "for very joy that he had encountered one who had gone through the same experience as himself."

In November, 1820, Margaret took up her abode for some time in the house of a disciple, Caspar Notz, near Zürich, and made it the centre whence she started on a series of missionary excursions. Here also gathered the elect out of Zürich to hear her expound Scripture, and pray. And hither also came the cobbler Morf seeking ease for his troubled soul, and on occasions stayed in the house there with her for a week at a time. At last his wife, the worthy Regula Morf, came from Illnau to find her husband, and persuaded him to return with her to his cobbling at home.

At the end of January in 1821, Margaret visited Illnau again, and drew away after her the bewitched Jacob, who followed her all the way home, to Wildisbuch, and remained at her father's house ten days further.

On Ascension Day following, he was again with her, and then she revealed to him that it was the will of heaven that they should ascend together, without tasting death, into the mansions of the blessed, and were to occupy one throne together for all eternity. Throughout this year, when the cobbler, Jacob, was not at Wildisbuch, or Saint Margaretta at Illnau, the pair were writing incessantly to each other, and their correspondence is still preserved in the archives of Zürich. Here is a specimen of the style of the holy Margaret. "My dear child! your dear letter filled me with joy. O, my dear child, how gladly would I tell you how it fares with me! When we parted, I was forced to go aside where none might see, to relieve my heart with tears. O, my heart, I cannot describe to you the distress into which I fell. I lay as one senseless for an hour. For anguish of heart I could not go home, such unspeakable pains did I suffer! My former separation from you was but a shadow of this parting. O, why are you so unutterably dear to me, &c.," and then a flow of sickly, pious twaddle that makes the gorge rise.

Regula Morf read this letter and shook her head over it. She had shaken her head over another letter received by her husband a month earlier, in which the holy damsel had written: "O, how great is my love! It is stronger than death. O, how dear are you to me. I could hug you to my heart a thousand times." And had scribbled on the margin, "These words are for your eye alone." However, Regula saw them, shook her head and told her husband that the letter seemed to her unenlightened mind to be very much like a love-letter. "Nothing of the sort," answered the cobbler, "it speaks of spiritual affection only."

We must now pass over a trait in the life of the holy maid which is to the last degree unedifying, but which is merely another exemplification of that truth which the history of mysticism enforces in every age, that spiritual exaltation runs naturally, inevitably, into licentiousness, unless held in the iron bands of discipline to the moral law. A mystic is a law to himself. He bows before no exterior authority. However much he may transgress the code laid down by religion, he feels no compunction, no scruples, for his heart condemns him not. It was so with the holy Margaret. Her lapse or lapses in no way roused her to a sense of sin, but served only to drive her further forward on the mad career of self-righteous exaltation.

She had disappeared for many months from her father's house, along with her sister Elizabeth. The police had inquired as to their whereabouts of old John Peter, but he had given them no information as to where his daughters were. He professed not to know. He was threatened unless they were produced by a certain day that he would be fined. The police were sent in search in every direction but the right one.

Suddenly in the night of January 11th, 1823, the sisters re-appeared, Margaret, white, weak, and prostrate with sickness.

A fortnight after her return, Jacob Morf was again at Wildisbuch, as he said afterwards before court, "led thither because assured by Margaret that they were to ascend together to heaven without dying."

From this time forward, Margaretta's conduct went into another phase. Instead of resuming her pilgrim's staff and travelling round the country preaching the Gospel, she remained all day in one room with her sister Elizabeth, the shutters closed, reading the Bible, meditating, and praying, and writing letters to her "dear child" Jacob. The transgressions she had committed were crosses laid on her shoulder by God. "Oh! why," she wrote in one of her epistles, "did my Heavenly Father choose *that* from all eternity in His providence for me? There were thousands upon thousands of other crosses He might have laid on me. But He elected that one which would be heaviest for me, heavier than all the persecutions to which I am subjected by the devil, and which all but overthrow me. From the foundation of the world He has never so tried any of His saints as He has us. It gives joy to all the host of heaven when we suffer to the end." Again, "the greater the humiliation and shame we undergo, and have to endure from our enemies here below"—consider, brought on herself by her own scandalous conduct—"the more unspeakable our glorification in heaven."

In the evening, Margaretta would come downstairs and receive visitors, and preach and prophesy to them. The entire house was given over to religious ecstasy that intensified as Easter approached. Every now and then the saint assembled the household and exhorted them to watch and pray, for a great trial of their faith was at hand. Once she asked them whether they were ready to lay down their lives for Christ. One day she said, in the spirit of prophecy, "Behold! I see the host of Satan drawing nearer and nearer to encompass me. He strives to overcome me. Let me alone that I may fight him." Then she flung her arms about and struck in the air with her open hands.

The idea grew in her that the world was in danger, that the devil was gaining supremacy over it, and would carry all souls into captivity once more, and that she—and almost only she—stood in his way and was protecting the world of men against his power.

For years she had exercised her authority, that grew with every year, over everyone in the house, and not a soul there had thought of resisting her, of evading the commands she laid on them, of questioning her word.

The house was closed against all but the very elect. The pastor of the parish, as "worldly," was not suffered to cross the threshold. At a tap, the door was opened, and those deemed worthy were admitted, and the door hastily barred and bolted behind them. Everything was viewed in a spiritual light. One evening Ursula Kündig and Margaretta Jäggli were sitting spinning near the stove. Suddenly there was a pop. A knot in the pine-logs in the stove had exploded. But up sprang Jäggli, threw over her spinning-wheel, and shrieked out—"Hearken! Satan is banging at the window. He wants me. He will fetch me!" She fell convulsed on the floor, foaming at the mouth. Margaret, the saint, was summoned. The writhing girl shrieked out, "Pray for me! Save me! Fight for my soul!" and Margaretta at once began her spiritual exercises to ban the evil spirit from the afflicted and possessed servant maid. She beat with her hands in the air, cried out, "Depart, thou murderer of souls, accursed one, to hell-fire. Wilt thou try to rob me of my sheep that was lost? My sheep—whom I have pledged myself to save?"

One day, the maid had a specially bad epileptic fit. Around her bed stood old John Peter, Elizabeth and Susanna, Ursula Kündig, and John Moser, as well as the saint. Margaret was fighting with the Evil One with her fists and her cries, when John Moser fell into ecstasy and saw a vision. His account shall be given in his own words: "I saw Christ and Satan, and the latter held a book open before Christ and bade Him see how many claims he had on the soul of Jäggli. The book was scored diagonally with red lines on all the pages. I saw this distinctly, and therefore concluded that the account was cancelled. Then I saw all the saints in heaven snatch the book away, and tear it into a thousand pieces that fell down in a rain."

But Satan was not to be defeated and driven away so easily. He had made himself a nest, so Margaret stated, under the roof of the house, and only a desperate effort of faith and contest with spiritual arms could expel him. For this Armageddon she bade all prepare. It is hardly necessary to add that it could not be fought without the presence of the dearly beloved Jacob. She wrote to him and invited him to come to the great and final struggle with the devil and all his host, and the obedient cobbler girded his loins and hastened to Wildisbuch, where he arrived on Saturday the 8th March, 1823.

On Monday, in answer, probably, to her summons, came also John Moser and his brother Conrad. Then also Margaret's own and only brother, Caspar.

Before proceeding to the climax of this story we may well pause to ask whether the heroine was in her senses or not; whether she set the avalanche in motion that overwhelmed herself and her house, with deliberation and consciousness as to the end to which she was aiming. The woman was no vulgar impostor; she deceived herself to her own destruction. In her senses, so far, she had set plainly before her the object to which she was about to hurry her dupes, but her reason and intelligence were smothered under her overweening self-esteem, that had grown like a great spiritual cancer, till it had sapped common-sense, and all natural affection, even the very instinct of self-preservation. Before her diseased eyes, the salvation of the whole world depended on herself. If she failed in her struggle with the evil principle, all mankind fell under the bondage of Satan; but she could not fail—she was all-powerful, exalted above every chance of failure in the battle, just as she was exalted above every lapse in virtue, do what she might, which to the ordinary sense of mankind is immoral. Every mystic does not go as far as Margaret Peter, happily, but all take some strides along that road that leads to self-deification and *anomia*. In Margaret's conduct, in preparation for the final tragedy, there was a good deal of shrewd calculation; she led up to it by a long isolation and envelopment of herself and her doings in mystery; and she called her chosen disciples to witness it. Each stage in the drama was calculated to produce a certain effect, and she measured her influence over her creatures before she advanced another step. On Monday all were assembled and in expectation; Armageddon was to be fought, but when the battle would begin, and how it would be carried through, were unknown. Tuesday arrived; some of the household went about their daily work, the rest were gathered together in the room where Margaret was, lost in silent prayer. Every now and then the hush in the darkened room was broken by a wail of the saint: "I am sore straitened! I am in anguish!—but I refresh my soul at the prospect of the coming exaltation!" or, "My struggle with Satan is severe. He strives to retain the souls which I will wrest from his hold; some have been for two hundred, even three hundred years in his power."

One can imagine the scene—the effect produced on those assembled about the pale, striving ecstatic. All who were present afterwards testified that on the Tuesday and the following days they hardly left the room, hardly allowed themselves time to snatch a hasty meal, so full of expectation were they that some great and awful event was about to take place. The holy enthusiasm was general, and if one or two, such as old Peter and his son, Caspar, were less magnetised than the rest, they were far removed from the thought of in any way contesting the will of the prophetess, or putting the smallest impediment in the way of her accomplishing what she desired.

When evening came, she ascended to an upper room, followed by the whole company, and there she declared, "Lo! I see Satan and his first-born floating in the air. They are dispersing their emissaries to all corners of the earth to summon their armies together." Elizabeth, somewhat tired of playing a passive part, added, "Yes—I see them also." Then the holy maid relapsed into her mysterious silence. After waiting another hour, all went to bed, seeing that nothing further would happen that night. Next day, Wednesday, she summoned the household into her bedroom; seated on her bed, she bade them all kneel down and pray to the Lord to strengthen her hands for the great contest. They continued striving in prayer till noon, and then, feeling hungry, all went downstairs to get some food. When they had stilled their appetites, Margaret was again seized by the spirit of prophecy, and declared, "The Lord has revealed to me what will happen in the latter days. The son of Napoleon" (that poor, feeble mortal the Duke of Reichstadt) "will appear before the world as anti-Christ, and will strive to bring the world over to his side. He will undergo a great conflict; but what will be the result is not shown me at the present moment; but I am promised a spiritual token of this revelation." And the token followed. The dearly-loved Jacob, John Moser, and Ursula Kündig cried out that they saw two evil spirits, one in the form of Napoleon, pass into Margaret Jäggli, and the other, in that of his son, enter into Elizabeth. Whereupon Elizabeth, possessed by the spirit of that poor, little, sickly Duke of Reichstadt, began to march about the room and assume a haughty, military air. Thereupon the prophetess wrestled in spirit and overcame these devils and expelled them. Thereat Elizabeth gave up her military flourishes.

From daybreak on the following day the blessed Margaret "had again a desperate struggle," but without the assistance of the household, which was summoned to take their share in the battle in the afternoon only. She bade them follow her to the upper chamber, and a procession ascended the steep stairs, consisting of Margaret, followed by Elizabeth and Susanna Peter, Ursula Kündig and Jäggli, the old father and his son, Caspar, the serving-man, Heinrich Ernst, then Jacob Morf, John Moser, and the rear was brought up by the young Conrad. As soon as the prophetess had taken her seat on the bed, she declared, "Last night it was revealed to me that you are all of you to unite with me in the battle with the devil, lest he should conquer Christ. I must strive, lest your souls and those of so many, many others should be lost. Come, then! strive with me; but first of all, kneel down, lay your faces in the dust and pray." Thereupon, all prostrated themselves on the floor and prayed in silence. Presently the prophetess exclaimed from her throne on the bed, "The hour is come in which the conflict must take place, so that Christ may gather together His Church, and contend with anti-Christ. After Christ has assembled His Church, 1260 days will elapse, and then anti-Christ will appear in human form, and with sweet and enticing words will strive to seduce the elect; but all true Christians will hold aloof." After a pause, she said solemnly, "In verity, anti-Christ is already among us."

Then with a leap she was off the bed, turning her eyes about, throwing up her hands, rushing about the room, striking the chairs and clothes-boxes with her fists, crying, "The scoundrel, the murderer of souls!" And, finding a hammer, she began to beat the wall with it.

The company looked on in breathless amaze. But the epileptic Jäggli went into convulsions, writhed on the ground, groaned, shrieked and wrung her hands. Then the holy Margaretta cried, "I see in spirit the old Napoleon gathering a mighty host, and marching against me. The contest will be terrible. You must wrestle unto blood. Go! fly! fetch me axes, clubs, whatever you can find. Bar the doors, curtain all the windows in the house, and close every shutter."

Whilst her commands were being fulfilled in all haste, and the required weapons were sought out, John Moser, who remained behind, saw the room "filled with a dazzling glory, such as no tongue could describe," and wept for joy. The excitement had already mounted to visionary ecstasy. It was five o'clock when the weapons were brought upstairs. The holy Margaretta was then seated on her bed, wringing her hands, and crying to all to pray, "Help! help! all of you, that Christ may not be overcome in me. Strike, smite, cleave—everywhere, on all sides—the floor, the walls! It is the will of God! smite on till I bid you stay. Smite and lose your lives if need be."

It was a wonder that lives were not lost in the extraordinary scene that ensued; the room was full of men and women; there were ten of them armed with hatchets, crowbars, clubs, pick-axes, raining blows on walls and floors, on chairs, tables, cupboards and chests. This lasted for three hours. Margaret remained on the bed, encouraging the party to continue; when any arm flagged she singled out the weary person, and exhorted him, as he loved his soul, to fight more valiantly and utterly defeat and destroy the devil. "Strike him! cut him down! the old adversary! the arch-fiend! whoso loseth his life shall find it. Fear nothing! smite till your blood runs down as sweat. There he is in yonder corner; now at him," and Elizabeth served as her echo, "Smite! strike on! He is a murderer, he is the young Napoleon, the coming anti-Christ, who entered into me and almost destroyed me."

This lasted, as already said, for three hours. The room was full of dust. The warriors steamed with their exertions, and the sweat rolled off them. Never had men and women fought with greater enthusiasm. The battle of Don Quixote against the wind-mills was nothing to this. What blows and wounds the devil and the young Duke of Reichstadt obtained is unrecorded, but walls and floor and furniture in the room were wrecked; indeed pitchfork and axe had broken down one wall of the house and exposed what went on inside to the eyes of a gaping crowd that had assembled without, amazed at the riot that went on in the house that was regarded as a very sanctuary of religion.

No sooner did the saint behold the faces of the crowd outside than she shrieked forth, "Behold them! the enemies of God! the host of Satan, coming on! But fear them not, we shall overcome."

At last the combatants were no longer able to raise their arms or maintain themselves on their feet. Then Margaret exclaimed, "The victory is won! follow me!" She led them downstairs into the common sitting-room, where close-drawn curtains and fastened shutters excluded the rude gaze of the profane. Here a rushlight was kindled, and by its light the battle continued with an alteration in the tactics.

In complete indifference to the mob that surrounded the house and clamoured at the door for admission, the saint ordered all to throw themselves on the ground and thank heaven for the victory they had won. Then, after a pause of more than an hour the same scene began again, and that it could recommence is evidence how much a man can do and endure, when possessed by a holy craze.

It was afterwards supposed that the whole pious community was drunk with schnaps; but with injustice. Their stomachs were empty; it was their brains that were drunk.

The holy Margaret, standing in the midst of the prostrate worshippers, now ordered them to beat themselves with their fists on their heads and breasts, and they obeyed. Elizabeth yelled, "O, Margaret! Do thou strike me! Let me die for Christ."

Thereupon the holy one struck her sister repeatedly with her fists, so that Elizabeth cried out with pain, "Bear it!" exclaimed Margaret; "It is the wrath of God!"

The prima-donna of the whole comedy in the meanwhile looked well about her to see that none of the actors spared themselves. When she saw anyone slack in his self-chastisement, she called to him to redouble his blows. As the old man did not exhibit quite sufficient enthusiasm in self-torture, she cried, "Father, you do not beat yourself sufficiently!" and then began to batter him with her own fists. The ill-treated old man groaned under her blows, but she cheered him with, "I am only driving out the old Adam, father! It does not hurt you," and redoubled her pommelling of his head and back. Then out went the light.

All this while the crowd listened and passed remarks outside. No one would interfere, as it was no one's duty to interfere. Tidings of what was going on did, however, reach the amtmann of the parish, but he was an underling, and did not care to meddle without higher authority, so sent word to the amtmann of the district. This latter called to him his secretary, his constable and a policeman, and reached the house of the Peter's family at ten o'clock. In his report to the police at Zürich he says: "On the 13th about 10 o'clock at night I reached Wildisbuch, and then heard that the noise in the house of the Peter's family had ceased, that all lights were. out, and that no one was stirring. I thought it advisable not to disturb this tranquillity, so left orders that the house should be watched," and then he went into the house of a neighbour. At midnight, the policeman who had been left on guard came to announce that there was a renewal of disturbance in the house of the Peters. The amtmann went to the spot and heard muffled cries of "Save us! have mercy on us! Strike away! he is a murderer! spare him not!" and a trampling, and a sound of blows, "as though falling on soft bodies." The amtmann knocked at the window and ordered those within to admit him. As no attention was paid to his commands, he bade the constable break open the house door. This was done, but the sitting-room door was now found to be fast barred. The constable then ascended to the upper room and saw in what a condition of wreckage it was. He descended and informed the amtmann of what he had seen. Again the window was knocked at, and orders were repeated that the door should be opened. No notice was taken of this; whereupon the worthy magistrate broke in a pane of glass, and thrust a candle through the window into the room.

"I now went to the opened window, and observed four or five men standing with their backs against the door. Another lay as dead on the floor. At a little distance was a coil of human beings, men and women, lying in a heap on the floor, beside them a woman on her knees beating the rest, and crying out at every blow, 'Lord, have mercy!' Finally, near the stove was another similar group."

The amtmann now ordered the sitting-room door to be broken open. Conrad Moser, who had offered to open to the magistrate, was rebuked by the saint, who cried out to him: "What, will you give admission to the devil?"

"The men," says the magistrate in his report, "offered resistance excited thereto by the women, who continued screaming. The holy Margaret especially distinguished herself, and was on her knees vigorously beating another woman who lay flat on the floor on her face. A second group consisted of a coil of two men and two women lying on the floor, the head of one woman on the body of a man, and the head of a man on that of a girl. The rest staggered to their feet one after another. I tried remonstrances, but they were unavailing in the hubbub. Then I ordered the old Peter to be removed from the room. Thereupon men and women flung themselves upon him, in spite of all our assurances that no harm would be done him. With difficulty we got him out of the room, with all the rest hanging on him, so that he was thrown on the floor, and the rest clinging to him tumbled over him in a heap. I repeated my remonstrance, and insisted on silence, but without avail. When old Peter prepared to answer, the holy Margaret stayed him with, 'Father, make no reply. Pray!' All then recommenced the uproar. Margaret cried out: 'Let us all die! I will die for Christ!' Others called out, 'Lord, save us!' and others, 'Have mercy on us!'"

The amtmann gave orders that the police were to divide the party and keep guard over some in the kitchen, and the rest in the sitting-room, through the night, and not to allow them to speak to each other. The latter order was, however, more than the police could execute. In spite of all their efforts, Margaretta and the others continued to exhort and comfort one another through the night.

Next morning each was brought before the magistrate and subjected to examination. All were sullen, resolute, and convinced that they were doing God's will. As the holy Margaretta was led away from examination, she said to Ursula and the servant Heinrich, "The world opposes, but can not frustrate my work."

Her words came true, the world was too slow in its movements. The amtmann did not send in his report to the authorities of Zürich till the 16th, whereupon it was taken into consideration, and orders were transmitted to him that Margaret and Elizabeth were to be sent to an asylum. It was then too late.

After the investigation, the amtmann required the cobbler, John Morf, to march home to Illnau, John and Conrad Moser to return to their home, and Ursula Kündig to be sent back to her father. This command was not properly executed. Ursula remained, and though John Moser obeyed, he was prepared to return to the holy Margaret directly he was summoned.

As soon as the high priestess had come out of the room where she had been examined by the amtmann, she went to her own bed-chamber, where boards had been laid over the gaps between the rafters broken by the axes and picks, during the night. Elizabeth, Susanna, Ursula, and the maid sat or stood round her and prayed.

At eight o'clock, the father and his son, Caspar, rejoined her, also her eldest sister, Barbara, arrived from Trüllikon. The servant, Heinrich, formed one more in the re-assembled community, and the ensuing night was passed in prayer and spiritual exercises. These were not conducted in quiet. To the exhortations of Margaret, both Elizabeth and the housemaid entreated that the devil might be beaten out of them. But now Ursula interfered, as the poor girl Elizabeth had been badly bruised in her bosom by the blows she had received on the preceding night. When the Saturday morning dawned, Margaret stood up on her bed and said, "I see the many souls seeking salvation through me. They must be assisted; would that a sword were in my hand that I might fight for them." A little later she said, with a sigh of relief, "The Lamb has conquered. Go to your work."

Tranquillity lasted for but a few hours. Magdalena, Moser's wife, had arrived, together with her husband and Conrad. The only one missing was the dearly beloved Jacob, who was far on his way homeward to Illnau and his hardly used wife, Regula.

At ten o'clock, the old father, his five daughters, his son, the two brothers, John and Conrad Moser, Ursula Kündig, the maid Jäggli, and the man Heinrich Ernst, twelve in all, were assembled in the upper room.

Margaret and Elizabeth sat side by side on the bed, the latter half stupified, looking fixedly before her, Margaret, however, in a condition of violent nervous surrexitation. Many of the weapons used in wrecking the furniture lay about; among these were the large hammer, and an iron wedge used for splitting wood. All there assembled felt that something extraordinary was about to happen. They had everyone passed the line that divides healthy common-sense from mania.

Margaretta now solemnly announced, "I have given a pledge for many souls that Satan may not have them. Among these is the soul of my brother Caspar. But I cannot conquer in the strife for him without the shedding of blood." Thereupon she bade all present recommence beating themselves with their fists, so as to expel the devil, and they executed her orders with wildest fanaticism.

The holy maid now laid hold of the iron wedge, drew her brother Caspar to her, and said, "Behold, the Evil One is striving to possess thy soul!" and thereupon she began to strike him on head and breast with the wedge. Caspar staggered back; she pursued him, striking him and cutting his head open, so that he was covered with blood. As he afterwards declared, he had not the smallest thought of resistance; the power to oppose her seemed to be taken from him. At length, half stunned, he fell to the ground, and was carried to his bed by his father and the maid Jäggli. The old man no more returned upstairs, consequently he was not present at the terrible scene that ensued. But he took no steps to prevent it. Not only so, but he warded off all interruption from without. Whilst he was below, someone knocked at the door. At that moment Susanna was in the room with him, and he bade her inquire who was without. The man gave his name as Elias Vogal, a mason, and asked leave to come in. Old Peter refused, as he said the surgeon was within. Elias endeavoured to push his way in but was resisted, and the door barred against him. Vogel went away, and meeting a policeman told him what had taken place, and added that he had noticed blood-stains on the sleeves of both old Peter and Susanna. The policeman, thinking that Peter's lie was truth, and that the surgeon was really in the house, and had been bleeding the half-crazy people there, took no further notice of what he had heard, and went his way.

Meanwhile, in the upper room the comedy had been changed into a ghastly tragedy. As soon as the wounded Caspar had been removed, the three sisters, Barbara, Magdalena, and Susanna left the room, the two latter, however, only for a short while. Then the holy Margaret said to those who remained with her, "To-day is a day of great events. The contest has been long and must now be decided. Blood must flow. I see the spirit of my mother calling to me to offer up my life." After a pause she said, "And you—all—are you ready to give your lives?" They all responded eagerly that they were. Then said Margaret, "No, no; I see you will not readily die. But I—I must die."

Thereupon Elizabeth exclaimed, "I will gladly die for the saving of the souls of my brother and father. Strike me dead, strike me dead!" Then she threw herself on the bed and began to batter her head with a wooden mallet.

"It has been revealed to me," said Margaret, "that Elizabeth will sacrifice herself." Then taking up the iron hammer, she struck her sister on the head. At once a spiritual fury seized on all the elect souls, and seizing weapons they began to beat the poor girl to death. Margaret in her mania struck at random about her, and wounded both John Moser and Ursula Kündig. Then she suddenly caught the latter by the wrist and bade her kill Elizabeth with the iron wedge. Ursula shrank back, "I cannot! I love her too dearly!" "You must," screamed the saint; "it is ordained." "I am ready to die" moaned Elizabeth. "I cannot! I cannot!" cried Ursula. "You must," shouted Margaret. "I will raise my sister again, and I also will rise again after three days. May God strengthen your arm."

As though a demoniacal influence flowed out of the holy maid, and maddened those about her, all were again seized with frenzy. John Moser snatched the hammer out of her hand, and smote the prostrate girl with it again, and yet again, on head and bosom and shoulders. Susanna brought down a crow-bar across her body, the servant-man Heinrich belaboured her with a fragment of the floor planking, and Ursula, swept away by the current, beat in her skull with the wedge. Throughout the turmoil, the holy maid yelled: "God strengthen your arms! Ursula, strike home! Die for Christ, Elizabeth!" The last words heard from the martyred girl were an exclamation of resignation to the will of God, as expressed by her sister.

One would have supposed that when the life was thus battered out of the unfortunate victim, the murderers would have come to their senses and been filled with terror and remorse. But it was not so. Margaret sat beside the body of her murdered sister, the blaze of spiritual ecstasy in her eyes, the blood-stained hammer in her right hand, terrible in her inflexible determination, and in the demoniacal energy which was to possess her to the last breath she drew. Her bosom heaved, her body quivered, but her voice was firm and her tone authoritative, as she said, "More blood must flow. I have pledged myself for the saving of many souls. I must die now. You must crucify me." John Moser and Ursula, shivering with horror, entreated, "O do not demand that of us." She replied, "It is better that I should die than that thousands of souls should perish."

So saying she struck herself with the hammer on the left temple. Then she held out the weapon to John Moser, and ordered him and Ursula to batter her with it. Both hesitated for a moment.

"What!" cried Margaret turning to her favourite disciple, "will you not do this? Strike and may God brace your arm!" Moser and Ursula now struck her with the hammer, but not so as to stun her.

"And now," said she with raised voice, "crucify me! You, Ursula, must do the deed."

"I cannot! I cannot!" sobbed the wretched girl.

"What! will you withdraw your hand from the work of God, now the hour approaches? You will be responsible for all the souls that will be lost, unless you fulfil what I have appointed you to do."

"But O! not I—!" pleaded Ursula.

"Yes—you. If the police authorities had executed me, it would not have fallen to you to do this, but now it is for you to accomplish the work. Go, Susan, and fetch nails, and the rest of you make ready the cross."

In the meantime, Heinrich, the man-servant, frightened at what had taken place, and not wishing to have anything more to do with the horrible scene in the upper chamber, had gone quietly down into the wood-house, and was making stakes for the vines. There Susanna found him, and asked him for nails, telling him for what they were designed. He composedly picked her out nails of suitable length, and then resumed his work of making vine stakes. Susanna re-ascended to the upper room, and found Margaret extended on the bed beside the body of Elizabeth, with the arms, breast, and feet resting on blocks of wood, arranged, whilst Susanna was absent, by John Moser and Ursula, under her in the fashion of a cross.

Then began the horrible act of crucifixion, which is only conceivable as an outburst of religious mania, depriving all who took part in it of every feeling of humanity, and degrading them to the level of beasts of prey. At the subsequent trial, both Ursula and John Moser described their condition as one of spiritual intoxication.

The hands and feet of the victim were nailed to the blocks of wood. Then Ursula's head swam, and she drew back. Again Margaret called her to continue her horrible work. "Go on! go on! God strengthen your arm. I will raise Elizabeth from the dead, and rise myself in three days." Nails were driven through both elbows and also through the breasts of Margaret; not for one moment did the victim express pain, nor did her courage fail her. No Indian at the stake endured the cruel ingenuity of his tormentors with more stoicism than did this young woman bear the martyrdom she had invoked for herself. She impressed her murderers with the idea that she was endowed with supernatural strength. It could not be otherwise, for what she endured was beyond the measure of human strength. That in the place of human endurance she was possessed with the Berserker strength of the *furor religiosus*, was what these ignorant peasants could not possibly know. Conrad Moser could barely support himself from fainting, sick and horror-struck at the scene. He exclaimed, "Is not this enough?" His brother, John, standing at the foot of the bed, looked into space with glassy eyes. Ursula, bathed in tears, was bowed over the victim. Magdalena Moser had taken no active part in the crucifixion; she remained the whole time, weeping, leaning against a chest.

The dying woman smiled. "I feel no pain. Be yourselves strong," she whispered. "Now, drive a nail or a knife through my heart."

Ursula endeavoured to do as bidden, but her hand shook and the knife was bent. "Beat in my skull!" this was the last word spoken by Margaret. In their madness Conrad Moser and Ursula Kündig obeyed, one with the crowbar, the other with the hammer.

It was noon when the sacrifice was accomplished—dinner-time. Accordingly, all descended to the sitting-room, where the meal that Margaret Jäggli had been in the meantime preparing was served and eaten.

They had scarce finished before a policeman entered with a paper for old Peter to sign, in which he made himself answerable to produce his daughters before the magistrates when and where required. He signed it with composure, "I declare that I will cause my daughters, if in good health, to appear before the Upper Amtsmann in Andelfingen when so required." Then the policeman departed without a suspicion that the two girls were lying dead in the room above. On Sunday the 16th, the servant Heinrich was sent on horseback to Illnau to summon Jacob Morf to come to Wildisbuch and witness a great miracle. Jacob came there with Heinrich, but was not told the circumstances of the crucifixion till he reached the house. When he heard what had happened, he was frightened almost out of his few wits, and when taken upstairs to see the bodies, he fainted away. Nothing—no representations would induce him to remain for the miraculous resurrection, and he hastened back to Illnau, where he took to his bed. In his alarm and horror he sent for the pastor, and told him what he had seen.

But the rest of the holy community remained stead-fast in their faith. On the night of Sunday before Monday morning broke, Ursula Kündig and the servant man Heinrich went upstairs with pincers and drew out the nails that transfixed Margaretta. When asked their reason for so doing, at the subsequent trial, they said that they supposed this would facilitate Margaretta's resurrection. *Sanctus furor* had made way for *sancta simplicitas*.

The night of Monday to Tuesday was spent in prayer and Scripture-reading in the upper chamber, and eager expectation of the promised miracle, which never took place. The catastrophe could no longer be concealed. Something must be done. On Tuesday, old John Peter pulled on his jacket and walked to Trüllikon to inform the pastor that his daughter Elizabeth had died on the Saturday at 10 a.m., and his daughter Margaretta at noon of the same day.

We need say little more. On Dec. 3rd, 1823, the trial of all incriminated in this frightful tragedy took place at Zürich and sentence was pronounced on the following day. Ursula Kündig was sentenced to sixteen years' imprisonment, Conrad Moser and John Peter to eight years, Susanna Peter and John Moser to six years, Heinrich Ernst to four years, Jacob Morf to three, Margaret Jäggli to two years, Barbara Baumann and Casper Peter to one year, and Magdalena Moser to six months with hard labour. The house at Wildisbuch was ordered to be levelled with the dust, the plough drawn over the foundation, and that no house should again be erected on the spot.

Before the destruction, however, a pilgrimage of Pietists and believers in Margaret Peter had visited the scene of her death, and many had been the exclamations of admiration at her conduct. "Oh, that it had been I who had died!" "Oh, how many souls must she have delivered!" and the like. *Magna est stultitia et prævalebit.*

At a time like the present, when there is a wave of warm, mystic fever sweeping over the country, and carrying away with it thousands of ignorant and impetuous souls, it is well that the story—repulsive though it be—should be brought into notice, as a warning of what this spiritual excitement may lead to—not, indeed, again, maybe, into bloodshed. It is far more likely to lead to, as it has persistently, in every similar outbreak, into moral disorders, the record of which, in the case of Margaretta Peter, we have passed over almost without a word.

AUTHORITY

Die Gekreuzigte von Wildisbuch, von J. Scherr, 2nd Edit., St. Gall. 1867. Scherr visited the spot, collected information from eye-witnesses, and made copious extracts from the records of the trial in the Zürich archives, where they are contained in Vol. 166, folio 1044, under the heading: "Akten betreffened die Gräuel—Scenen in Wildisbuch."

II. — A NORTHERN RAPHAEL

HERE and there in the galleries of North Germany and Russia may be seen paintings of delicacy and purity, delicacy of colour and purity of design, the author of which was Gerhard von Kügelgen. The majority of his paintings are in private hands; but an Apollo, holding the dying Hyacinthus in his arms, is in the possession of the German Emperor; Moses on Horeb is in the gallery of the Academy of Fine Arts at Dresden; a St. Cæcilia and an Adonis, painted in 1794 and 1795, were purchased by the Earl of Bristol; a Holy Family is in the Gallery at Cassel; and some of the sacred subjects have found their way into churches.

In 1772, the wife of Franz Kügelgen, a merchant of Bacharach on the Rhine, presented her husband with twin sons, the elder of whom by fifteen minutes is the subject of this notice. His brother was named Karl. Their resemblance was so great that even their mother found a difficulty in their early childhood in distinguishing one from the other.

Bacharach was in the Electorate of Cologne, and when the Archbishop-Elector, Maximilian Franz, learned that the twins were fond of art, in 1791 he very liberally gave them a handsome sum of money to enable them to visit Rome and there prosecute their studies.

Gerhard was at once fascinated by the statuary in the Vatican, and by the pictures of Raphael. The ambition of his life thenceforward was to combine the beauty of modelling of the human form that he saw in the Græco-Roman statues with the beauty of colour that he recognised in Raphael's canvases. Karl, on the other hand, devoted himself to landscapes.

In 1795 the brothers separated, Gerhard that he might visit Munich. Thence, in the autumn, he went to Riga with a friend, and there he remained rather over two years, and painted and disposed of some fifty-four pictures. Then he painted in St. Petersburg and Revel, and finally settled into married life and regular work at Dresden in 1806. There he became a general favourite, not only on account of his artistic genius, but also because of the fascination of his modest and genial manner. He was honoured by the Court, and respected by everyone for his virtues. Orders flowed in on him, and his paintings commanded good prices. The king of Saxony ennobled him, that is to say, raised him out of the bürger-stand, by giving him the privilege of writing a *Von* before his patronymic.

Having received an order from Riga for a large altar picture, he bought a vineyard on the banks of the Elbe, commanding a charming prospect of the river and the distant blue Bohemian mountains. Here he resolved to erect a country house for the summer, with a large studio lighted from the north. The construction of this residence was to him a great pleasure and occupation. In November, 1819, he wrote to his brother, "My house shall be to us a veritable fairy palace, in which to dwell till the time comes, when through a little, narrow and dark door we pass through into that great habitation of the Heavenly Father in which are many mansions, and where our whole family will be re-united. Should it please God to call me away, then Lily (his wife) will find this an agreeable dower-house, in which she can supervise the education of the children, as the distance from the town is only an hour's walk."

The words were written, perhaps, without much thought, but they foreshadowed a terrible catastrophe. Kügelgen would pass, before his fairy palace was ready to receive him, through that little, narrow door into the heavenly mansions.

The holy week of 1820 found him in a condition of singularly deep religious emotion. He was a Catholic, but had, nevertheless, allowed his son to be confirmed by a Protestant pastor. The ceremony had greatly affected him, and he said to a friend, who was struck at the intensity of his feeling, "I know I shall never be as happy again till I reach Heaven."

On March 27th, on the very day of the confirmation, he went in the afternoon a walk by himself to his vineyard, to look at his buildings. He invited one of his pupils to accompany him, but the young man had some engagement and declined.

At 5 p.m. he was at the new house, where he paid the workmen, gave some instructions, and pointed out where he would do some planting, so as to enchance the picturesqueness of the spot. At some time between six and seven he left, to walk back to Dresden, along the road from Bautzen.

Every one who has been at the Saxon capital knows that road. The right bank of the Elbe above Dresden rises in picturesque heights covered with gardens and vineyards, from the river, and about a mile from the bridge is the Linkes Bad, with its pleasant gardens, theatre, music and baths. That road is one of the most charming, and, therefore, the most frequented outside the capital. On the evening in question the Easter moon was shining.

Kügelgen did not return home. His wife sent his son, the just confirmed boy, aged 17 years, to the new house, to inquire for her husband. The boy learned there that he had left some hours before. He returned home, and found that still his father had not come in. The police were communicated with, and the night was spent in inquiries and search, but all in vain. On the following morning, at 9 a.m., as the boy was traversing the same road, along with a gensdarme, he deemed it well to explore a footpath beside the river, which was overflown by the Elbe, and there, finally, amongst some reeds they discovered the dead body of the artist, stripped of his clothes to his shirt and drawers, lying on his face.

Gerhard von Kügelgen had been murdered. His features were cut and bruised, his left temple and jaw were broken. Footsteps, as of two persons, were traceable through the river mud and across a field to the highway. Apparently the artist had been murdered on the road, then carried or dragged to the path, stripped there, and then cast among the rushes. About twenty-four paces from where he lay, between him and the highway, his cap was found.

The excitement, the alarm, aroused in Dresden was immense. Not only was Kügelgen universally respected, but everyone was in dismay at the thought that his own safety was jeopardised, if a murder such as this could be perpetrated on the open road, within a few paces of the gates. Indeed, the place where the crime was committed was but a hundred strides from the Linkes Bad, one of the most popular resorts of the Dresdeners.

It was now remembered that only a few months before, near the same spot, another murder had been committed, that had remained undiscovered. In that case the victim had been a poor carpenter's apprentice.

On the same day as the body of Kügelgen was found, the Government offered a sum equal to £150 for the discovery of the murderer. A little later, some children found among the rubbish, outside the Black Gate of the Dresdener Vorstadt, a blue cloth cloak, folded up and buried under some stones. It was recognised as having belonged to Kügelgen. Moreover, in the pocket was the little "Thomas-à-Kempis" he always carried about with him.

It was concluded that the murderer had not ventured to bring all the clothing of Kügelgen into the town, through the gate, and had, therefore, hidden portions in places whence he could remove them one by one, unobserved. The murderer was, undoubtedly, an inhabitant of the city.

From March 29th to April 4th the police remained without any clue, although a description of the garments worn by the murdered man, and of his watch, was posted up at every corner, and sent round to the nearest towns and villages.

The workmen who had been engaged on Kügelgen's house were brought before the police. They had left after his departure, and had received money from him; but they were discharged, as there was no evidence against them.

As no light seemed to fall on this mysterious case, the police looked up the circumstances of the previous murder. On December 29th, 1819, a carrier on the highroad had found a body on the way. It was ascertained to be that of a carpenter's apprentice, named Winter. His skull had been broken in. Not a trace of the murderer was found; not even footprints had been observed. However, it was learned that the wife of a labourer had been attacked almost at the same spot, on the 28th December, by a man wearing a military cap and cloak; and she had only escaped him by the approach of a carriage, the sound of the wheels having alarmed him, and induced him to fly. He had fled in the direction of the Black Gate and the barracks.

The anxiety of the Dresdeners seemed justified. There was some murderous ruffian inhabiting the Vorstadt, who hovered about the gates, waylaying, not wealthy men only, but poor charwomen and apprentices.

The military cloak and cap, the direction taken by the assailant in his flight, gave a sort of clue—and the police suspected that the murderer must be sought among the soldiers.

On April 4th two Jewish pawnbrokers appeared before the police, and handed over a silver watch which had been left with them at 9 a.m. on the 20th March—that is to say on the morning after the murder of Kügelgen—and which agreed with the advertised description of the artist's lost watch. It was identified at once. The man who had pawned it, the Jews said, wore the uniform of an artillery soldier.

At the request of the civil authorities, the military officers held an inquisition in the barracks. All the artillery soldiers were made to pass before the Jew brokers, but they were unable to identify the man who had deposited the watch with them. Somewhat later in the day one of these Jews, as he was going through the street, saw a man in civil dress, whom he thought he recognised as the fellow who had given him the watch. He went up to him at once and spoke about the watch. The man at first acknowledged that he had pawned one, then denied, and threatened the Jew when he persevered in clinging to him. A gendarme came up, and hearing what the controversy was about, arrested the man, who gave his name as Fischer, a gunner.

Fischer was at once examined, and he doggedly refused to allow that he had given up a watch to the Jew.

Suspicion against him was deepened by his declaring that he had heard nothing of the murder—a matter of general talk in Dresden—and that he had not seen the notices with the offer of reward for the discovery of the murderer. On the following day, April 5th, however, he admitted having pawned the watch, which he pretended to have found outside the Black Gate. A few hours later he withdrew this confession, saying that he was so bewildered with the questions put to him, and so alarmed at his arrest, that he did not well know what he said. It was observed that Fischer was a man of very low intellectual power.

The same day he was invested in his uniform, and presented before the pawnbrokers. Both unanimously declared that he was *not* the man who had entered their shop and deposited the watch with them. They both declared that though Fischer had the same height and general build as the man in question, and the same fair hair, yet that the face was different.

With this, the case against Fischer broke down; nevertheless, though he had been handed over by the military authorities to the civil power, he remained under arrest. The public was convinced of his guilt, and the police hoped by keeping him in prison to draw from him later some information which might prove serviceable.

And, in fact, after he had been a fortnight under arrest, he volunteered a statement. He was conducted at once before the magistrate, and confessed that he had murdered Von Kügelgen. He, however, stoutly denied having laid hands on the carpenter Winter. Nevertheless, on the way back to his cell he told his gaoler that he had committed this murder as well. Next day he was again brought before the magistrate, and confessed to both murders. He was taken to the spots where the two corpses had been found, and there he renewed his confession, though without entering into any details.

But on the next morning, April 21, he begged to be again heard, and he then asserted that his former confessions were false. He had confessed merely because he was weary of his imprisonment and the poor food he was given, and decided to die. When spoken to by the magistrates seriously, and remonstrated with for his contradictions, he cried out that he was innocent. Let them torture him as much as they pleased, he wished to die.

But hardly was he back in his prison than he told the gaoler that it was true that he was the murderer of both Kügelgen and Winter. Again he confessed before the magistrate, and again, on the 27th, withdrew his confession and protested his innocence.

On the 21st April a new element in the case came to light, that perplexed the question not a little.

A Jewish pawnbroker, Löbel Graff, announced that on February 3, 1820, he had received from the gunner Kaltofen, a green coat, and on the 4th April a dark-blue cloth coat, stained with spots of oil, also a pair of cloth trousers. As both coats seemed to him suspicious, and to resemble those described in the advertisements, he had questioned Kaltofen about them, but had received equivocal answers, and Kaltofen at last admitted that he had bought them from the gunner Fischer.

John Gottfried Kaltofen was a young man of 24 years, servant to one of the officers, and therefore did not live in the barracks. He was now taken up. His manner and appearance were in his favour. He was frank, and at once admitted that he had disposed of the two coats to Graff, and that he had bought them of Fischer. On confrontation with the latter he repeated what he had said. Fischer fell into confusion, denied all knowledge of Kaltofen, protested his innocence, and denied the sale of the coats, one of which had in the meantime been identified as having belonged to Winter, and the other to Kügelgen.

On April 27th a search was made in the lodgings of Kaltofen, and three keys were found there, hidden away, and these proved to have belonged to Kügelgen. At first Kaltofen declared that he knew nothing of these keys, but afterwards said that he remembered on consideration that he had found them in the pocket of the blue coat he had purchased from Fischer, and had put them away before disposing of the coat, and had given them no further thought. Not many minutes after Fischer had been sent back to prison, he begged to be brought before the magistrate again, and now admitted that it was quite true that he had sold both coats to Kaltofen.

Whilst this confession was being taken down, however, he again hesitated, broke down, and denied having sold them to Kaltofen, or any one else. "I can't say anything more," he cried out; "my head is dazed."

By this statement he remained, protesting his innocence, and he declared that he had only confessed his guilt because he was afraid of ill-treatment in the prison if he continued to assert his innocence. It must be remembered that the gaolers were as convinced of his guilt as were the public of Dresden; and it is noticeable that under pressure from them Fischer always acknowledged his guilt; whereas, when before the magistrates he was ready to proclaim that he was innocent. At this time it was part of the duty of a gaoler, or was supposed to be such, to use every possible effort to bring a prisoner to confession. And now, on April 27th, a third gunner appeared on the scene. His name was Kiessling, and he asked the magistrate to take down his statement, which was to the effect that Kaltofen, who had been discharged, had admitted to him that he had murdered Kügelgen with a cudgel, and that he had still got some of his garments hidden in his lodgings. But—so said Kiessling—Kaltofen had jauntily said he would lay it all on Fischer. Kiessling, moreover, produced a pair of boots, that he said Kaltofen had left with him to be re-soled, as he was regimental shoemaker. And these boots were at once recognised as having been those worn by Kügelgen when he was murdered.

Kaltofen was at once re-arrested, and brought into confrontation with Kiessling. He retained his composure, and said that it was quite true that he had given a pair of boots to Kiessling to re-sole, but they were a pair that he had bought in the market. But, in the meantime, another investigation of his lodgings had been made, and a number of articles found that had certainly belonged to the murdered men, Winter and Kügelgen. They were ranged on the table, together with the pair of boots confided to Kiessling, and Kaltofen was shown them. Hitherto, the young man had displayed phlegmatic composure, and an openness of manner that had impressed all who saw him in his favour. His intelligence, had, moreover, contrasted favourably with that of Fischer. But the sight of all these articles, produced before him, staggered Kaltofen, and, losing his presence of mind, he turned in a fury upon his comrade, the shoemaker, and swore at him for having betrayed his confidence. Only after he had poured forth a torrent of abuse, could the magistrate bring him to say anything about the charge, and then—still hot and panting from his onslaught on Kiessling—he admitted that he, not Fischer, was the murderer in both cases. Fischer, he said, was wholly innocent, not only of participation in, but of knowledge of the crimes. The summary of his confession, oft repeated and never withdrawn, was as follows:—Being in need of money, he had gone outside the town thrice in one week, at the end of December, 1819, with the intent of murdering and robbing the first person he could attack with security. For this purpose, he had provided himself with a cudgel under his cloak. On the 29th December he selected Winter as his first victim. He allowed him to pass, then stole after him, and suddenly dealt him a blow on the back of his head, before the young man turned to see who was following him. Winter dropped, whereupon he, Kaltofen, had struck him twice again on the head. Then he divested his victim of collar, coat, hat, kerchief, watch, and a little money—not more than four shillings in English coins, and a few tools. He was engaged on pulling off his boots and trousers, when he was alarmed by hearing the tramp of horses and the sound of wheels, and he ran off across the fields with his spoil. He got Kiessling to dispose of the hat for him, the other articles he himself sold to Jews. Whether it was he also who assaulted the poor woman we are not informed. In like manner Kaltofen proceeded with Kügelgen. He was again in want of money. He had been gambling, and had lost what little he had. On the Monday in Holy Week, 1820, he took his cudgel again and went out along the Bautzen Road. The moon shone brightly, and he met a gentleman walking slowly towards Dresden, in a blue cloak. He allowed him to pass, then followed him. As a woman was walking in the same direction, but at a quicker rate, he delayed his purpose till she had disappeared behind the first houses of the suburb. Then he hastened on, walking lightly, and springing up behind Kügelgen, struck him on the right temple with his cudgel from behind. Kügelgen fell without uttering a cry. Kaltofen at once seized him by the collar and dragged him across a field to the edge of the river. There he dealt him several additional blows, and then proceeded to strip him. Whilst thus engaged, he remembered that the dead man had dropped his walking-stick on the high road when first struck. Kaltofen at once desisted from what he was about, to return to the road and recover the walking-stick. On coming back to his victim, he thought there was still life in him; Kügelgen was moving and endeavouring to rise. Whereupon, with his cudgel, Kaltofen repeatedly struck him, till all signs of life disappeared. He now completed his work of spoliation, pulled off the boots, untied the neckerchief, and ransacked the pockets. He found in addition to the watch the sum of about half-a-guinea. He then stole away among the rushes till he reached the Linkes Bad, where he returned to the main road. He concealed the cloak at the Black Gate, but carried the rest of his plunder to his lodgings.

His confession was confirmed by several circumstances. Kiessling was again required to repeat what he had heard from Kaltofen, and the story as told by him agreed exactly with that now confessed by the murderer. Kiessling added that Kaltofen had told him he was puzzled to account for Fischer's self-examination, as he knew that the man had nothing to do with the murder. A third examination of Kaltofen's lodgings resulted in the discovery of all the rest of the murdered man's effects. Moreover, when Kaltofen was confronted with the two Jews who had taken the silver watch on the 24th, they immediately recognised him as the man who had disposed of it to them.

Finally, he confessed to having been associated with Kiessling in two robberies, one of which was a burglarious attack on his own master.

The case was made out clearly enough against Kaltofen, and it seemed equally clear that Fischer was innocent. Moreover, from the 24th April onwards, Fischer never swerved from his protestation of complete innocence. When questioned why he had confessed himself guilty, he said that he had been pressed to do so by the gaoler, who had several times fastened him for a whole night into the stocks, and had threatened him with severer measures unless he admitted his guilt. The gaoler admitted having so treated Fischer once, but Fischer insisted that he had been thus tortured on two consecutive nights.

It was ascertained that Fischer had not only known about the murder of Kügelgen, but had attended his funeral, and yet he had pretended entire, or almost entire, ignorance when first arrested. When asked to explain this, he replied that he was so frightened that he took refuge in lies. That he was a dull-minded, extremely ignorant man, was obvious to the judges and to all who had to do with him; he was aged thirty, and had spent thirteen years in the army, had conducted himself well, but had never been trusted with any important duties on account of his stupidity. He had a dull eye, and a heavy countenance. Kaltofen, on the other hand, was a good-looking, well-built young fellow, of twenty-four, with a bright, intelligent face; his education was above what was ordinary in his class. It was precisely this that had excited in him vanity, and craving for pleasures and amusements which he could not afford. His obliging manners, his trimness, and cheerfulness, had made him a favourite with the officers.

As already intimated, he was fond of play, and it was this that had induced him to commit his murders. He admitted that he had felt little or no compunction, and he said frankly that it was as well for society that he was taken, otherwise the death of Kügelgen would have been followed by others. He spoke of the crimes he had committed with openness and indifference, and maintained this condition of callousness to the end. It seems to have been customary on several occasions for the Lutheran pastors who attended the last hours of criminals to publish their opinions as to the manner in which they prepared for death, and their ideas as to the motives for the crimes committed, an eminently indecent proceeding to our notions. In this case, the chaplain who attended on Kaltofen rushed into the priest after the execution. He said, "Play may have occasioned that want of feeling which will commit the most atrocious crime, without compunction, for the gratification of a temporary requirement. Kaltofen, without being rude and rough towards his fellows, but on the contrary obliging and courteous, came to regard them with brutal indifference." Only twice did he feel any twinge of conscience, he said, once before his first murder, and again at the funeral of his second victim, which he attended. The criminal was now known, had confessed, and had confessed that he had no accomplice. Moreover, he declared that Fischer was wholly innocent. Not a single particle of evidence was forthcoming to incriminate Fischer, apart from his own retracted confessions. Nevertheless he was not liberated.

The police could not believe that Kaltofen had been without an accomplice. There were stabs in the face and body of Kügelgen, and Kaltofen had professed to have used no other weapon than a cudgel. The murderer said that he had dragged the body over the field to the rushes, and it was agreed that there must have been evidence of this dragging. Some witnesses had, indeed, said they had seen such, but others protested that there were footprints as of two men. This, however, could be explained by Kaltofen's admission that he had gone back to the road for the walking-stick.

Then, again, Fischer, when interrogated, had given particulars which agreed with the circumstances in a remarkable manner. He was asked to explain this. "Well," said he, "he had heard a good deal of talk about the murders, and he was miserable at the thought of spending long years in prison, and so had confessed." When asked how he knew the particulars of the murder of Winter, he said that he had been helped to it by the gaoler. He had said first, "I went to his left side"—whereupon the gaoler had said, "Surely you are wrong, it was on the right," thereat Fischer had corrected himself and said, "Yes, of course—on the right."

The case was now ready for final sentence, and for this purpose all the depositions were forwarded on September 12th to the Judicial Court at Leipzig. But, before judgment was pronounced, the depositions were hastily sent for back to Dresden—for, in the meantime, the case had passed into a new phase. On October 5th, the gaoler—the same man who had brought about the confession of Fischer—announced that Kaltofen had confided to him that Fischer really had been his accomplice in both the murders. Kaltofen at once was summoned before the magistrate, and he calmly, and with emphasis, declared that Fischer had assisted him on both occasions, and that he had not allowed this before, because he and Fischer had sworn that neither would betray the other. Fischer had never mentioned his name, and he had accordingly done his utmost to exculpate Fischer.

According to his account, he and Fischer had been walking together on the morning of March 26th, between 9 and 10, when they planned a murder together for the following day. However, there was rebutting evidence to the effect that on the morning in question Fischer had been on guard, at the hour named, before the powder magazine; he had not been released till noon. Other statements of Kaltofen proved to be equally untrue.

What could have induced Kaltofen to deliberately charge a comrade in arms with participation in the crime, if he were guiltless? There was no apparent motive. He could gain no reprieve by it. It did not greatly diminish his own guilt.

It was necessary to enter into as close investigation as was possible into the whereabouts of Fischer at the time of the two murders. It was not found possible to determine where he was at the time when Winter was killed, but some of his comrades swore that on March 27th he had been present at the roll-call at 6 p.m., and had come into barrack before the second roll-call at half-past eight. The murder of Kügelgen had taken place at eight o'clock, and the distance between the barrack and the spot where it had been committed was 3487 paces, which would take a man about 25 minutes to traverse. If, as his comrades asserted, Fischer had come in shortly after eight, then it was quite impossible that he could have been present when Kügelgen was murdered; but not great reliance can be placed on the testimony of soldiers as to the hour at which a comrade came into barrack just seven months before on a given day.

The case was perplexing. The counsel for Fischer—his name was Eisenstück—took a bold line of defence. He charged the gaoler with having manipulated Kaltofen, as he had Fischer. This gaoler's self-esteem was wounded by the discovery that Kaltofen and not Fischer was the murderer, and his credit was damaged by the proceedings which showed that he had goaded an unhappy man, confided to his care, into charging himself with a crime he had never committed. Eisenstück asserted that this new charge was fabricated in the prison by the gaoler in concert with Kaltofen for his own justification. But, whatever may be thought of the character and conduct of this turnkey, it is difficult to understand how he could prevail on a cool-headed man like Kaltofen thus to take on himself the additional guilt of perjury, and such perjury as risked the life of an innocent man. Kaltofen never withdrew this assertion that Fischer was an accomplice. He persisted in it to his last breath.

The depositions were again sent to the faculty at Leipzig, on Dec. 18th, to give judgment on the following points.

1. The examination of the body of Kügelgen had revealed stabs made with a sharp, two-edged instrument, as well as blows dealt by a blunt weapon. Kaltofen would admit that he had used no other instrument than a cudgel.

2. It would have been a difficult matter for one man to drag a dead body from the road to the bed of rushes, without leaving unmistakable traces on the field traversed; and such were not, for certain, found. It was therefore more probable that the dead man had been carried by two persons to the place where found.

It must be observed that crowds poured out of Dresden to see the place where the body lay as soon as it was known that Kügelgen had been discovered, and consequently no accurate and early examination of tracks across the field had been made.

3. That it would have been difficult for Kaltofen alone to strip the body. This may be doubted; it would be difficult possibly, but not impossible, whilst the body was flexible.

4. A witness had said that she had met two men outside the Black Gate on the evening of the 27th March, of whom one was wrapped in a cloak and seemed to be carrying something under it. We should much like to know when the woman gave this evidence. Unfortunately, that is what is not told us.

5. Kaltofen, in a letter to his parents, had stated that he had an accomplice, but had not named him.

These were the points that made it appear that Kaltofen had an accomplice. An accomplice in some of his crimes he had—Kiessling.

There were other points that made it appear that Fischer had assisted him in the murders.

6. Fischer's denial that he knew anything about the murder of Kügelgen when he was arrested, whereas it was established that he had attended the funeral of the murdered man.

7. His repeated confessions that he had assisted at the murders, and his acquaintance with the particulars and with the localities.

8. Kaltofen's asseverations that Fischer was his associate in the murders.

In favour of Fischer it may be said that his conduct in the army had for thirteen years been uniformly good, and there was no evidence that he had been in any way guilty of dishonesty. Nor was he a man of extravagant habits like Kaltofen, needing money for his pleasures. He was a simple, inoffensive, and very stupid man. His confessions lose all their effect when we consider how they were extorted from him by undue influence.

Against Kaltofen's later accusation must be set his repeated declaration, during six months, that Fischer was innocent. Not only this, but his assertion in confidence to Kiessling that he was puzzled what could have induced Fischer to avow himself guilty of a crime, of which he—Kaltofen—knew him to be innocent. When Kiessling gave this evidence on April 24th, Kaltofen did not deny that he had said this, but flew into a paroxysm of fury with his comrade for betraying their private conversation.

Again, not a single article appertaining to either of the murdered men was found with Fischer. All had been traced, without exception, to Kaltofen. It was the latter who had concealed Kügelgen's coat, and had given his watch to the Jews. It was he who had got Kiessling to dispose of Winter's hat for him, and had given the boots of the last victim to Kiessling to be repaired.

On January 4th, 1821, the Court at Leipzig issued its judgment; that Kaltofen, on account of two murders committed and confessed, was to be put to death on the wheel; "but that John George Fischer be discharged on account of lack of evidence of complicity in the murders." The gaoler was discharged his office.

Kaltofen appealed against the sentence, but in vain. The sentence was confirmed. The ground of his appeal was, that he was not alone guilty. The King commuted the penalty of the wheel into execution by the sword.

The sentence of the court produced the liveliest commotion in Dresden. The feeling against Fischer was strong and general; the gaoler had but represented the universal opinion. Fischer—who had confessed to the murder—Fischer, whom Kaltofen protested was as deeply stained in crime as himself, was to go scot free. The police authorities did not carry out the sentence of discharge in its integrity; they indeed released him from prison, but placed him under police supervision, and he was discharged from the Artillery on the plea that he had forsworn himself. The pastor Jaspis was entrusted with the preparation of Kaltofen for death; and we know pretty well what passed between him and the condemned man, as he had the indecency to publish it to the world. Jaspis had, indeed, visited him in prison when he was first arrested, and then Kaltofen had asserted that he had committed the murders entirely unassisted. On Jaspis remarking to him in April, 1820, that there were circumstances that rendered this eminently improbable, Kaltofen cut him short with the answer, "I was by myself." Afterwards, when he had changed his note, Jaspis reminded him of his previous declaration, but Kaltofen pretended not to remember ever having made it.

Towards the end of his days, Kaltofen was profoundly agitated, and was very restless. When Jaspis gave him a book of prayers and meditations for such as were in trouble, he put it from him, and said the book was unsuitable, and was adapted only to the innocent. He had visitors who combined piety with inquisitiveness, and came to discuss with him the state of his soul. Kaltofen's vanity was inflamed, and he was delighted to pose before these zealots. When he heard that Jaspis had preached about him in the Kreuz Kirche on the Sunday before his execution, he was greatly gratified, and said, "He would really like to hear what had been said about him."

Jaspis thereupon produced his sermon, and read it over to the wretched man—but tells us that even the most touching portions of the address failed to awake any genuine compunction in his soul. Unless he could play the saint, before company, he was cold and indifferent. His great vanity, however, was hurt at the thought that his assertion was disbelieved, that Fischer was his associate in his crimes. He was always eager and inquisitive to know what rumours circulated in the town concerning him, and was gratified to think that he was the topic of the general conversation.

On the night before his execution he slept soundly for five hours, and then lit his pipe and smoked composedly. His condition was, however, not one of bluntness of sense, for he manifested considerable readiness and consciousness up to the last. He had drawn up a dying address which he handed to pastor Jaspis, and on which he evidently placed great importance, as when his first copy had caught fire when he was drying it, he set to work to compose a second. He knew his man—Jaspis—and was sure he would publish it after the execution. The paper was a rigmarole in which he posed to the world.

On reaching the market-place where the execution was to take place, he repeated his confession, but on this occasion without mention of a confederate. His composure gave way, and he began to sob. On reaching the scaffold, however, the sight of the vast crowd assembled to see him die restored to him some of his composure, as it pleased his vanity; but he again broke down, as he made his last confession to the Lutheran pastor. His voice trembled, and the sweat broke out on his brow. Then he sprang up and shouted, so that all could hear—"Gentlemen, Fischer deserved the same punishment as myself." In another moment his head fell from his body.

The words had been audible throughout the market-place by everyone. Who could doubt that his last words were true?

Fischer happened that very day (July 12th) to be in Dresden. He had been seen, and had been recognised.

He had come to Dresden to see his counsel, and ask him to use his influence to obtain his complete discharge from police supervision, and restoration to his rights as an honest man and a soldier, with a claim to a pension.

A vast crowd of people rolled from the place of execution to the house of Eisenstück, shouting, and threatening to tear Fischer to pieces.

But Eisenstück was not the man to be terrified. He summoned a carriage, entered it along with Fischer, and drove slowly, with the utmost composure, through the angry crowd.

On August 26th, 1822, by command of the king, Fischer's name was replaced in the army list, and he received his complete discharge from all the consequences of the accusations made against him. He was guaranteed his pension for his "faithful services through 16 years, and in the campaigns of 1813, 1814, and 1815, in which he had conducted himself to the approval of all his officers."

How are we to explain the conduct of Kaltofen? The simplest way is to admit that he spoke the truth; but against this is to be opposed his denial that Fischer was guilty during the first six months that he was under arrest. And it is impossible to believe that Fischer was guilty, on the sole testimony of Kaltofen, without any confirmatory evidence.

It is rather to be supposed that the inordinate vanity of the young culprit induced him to persist in denouncing his innocent brother gunner, so as to throw off his own shoulders some of the burden of that crime, which, he felt, made him hateful in the eyes of his fellow-citizens, and perhaps to induce them to regard him as misled by an older man, more hardened and experienced in crime, thus arousing their pity and sympathy in place of their disgust.

Jaspis, the pastor, did not himself believe in the criminality of Fischer, and proposes a solution which he gives conjecturally only. He suggests that Kaltofen was misled by the confession of Fischer into the belief that he really had committed a murder or two, though not those of Winter and Kügelgen, and that when he declared on the scaffold that "Fischer deserved to die as much as himself," he spoke under this conviction. This explanation is untenable, for the miserable man had repeatedly charged Fischer with assisting him in committing these two particular crimes. The explanation must be found in his self-conceit and eagerness to present himself in the best and most affecting light before the public. And he gained his point to some extent. The mob believed him, pitied him, became sentimental over him, wept tears at his death, and cursed the unfortunate Fischer. The apparent piety, the mock heroics, the graceful attitudes, and the good looks of the murderer had won their sympathies, and the general opinion of the vulgar was that they had assisted at the sublimation of a saint to the seventh heaven, and not at the well-deserved execution of a peculiarly heartless and brutal murderer.

A month had hardly passed since Kaltofen's execution before Dresden was shocked to hear of another murder—on this occasion by a young woman. On August 12th, 1821, this person, who had been in a state of excitement ever since the edifying death of Kaltofen, invited to her house a young girl, just engaged to be married, and deliberately murdered her; then marched off to the police and confessed her crime—the nature of which she did not disguise. She desired to make the same affecting and edifying end as Kaltofen. Above all, she wanted to get herself talked about by all the mouths in Dresden. The police on visiting her house found the murdered girl lying on the bed. On the door in large letters the murderer had inscribed the date of Kaltofen's martyrdom, July 12th, and she had committed her crime on the same day one month after, desirous to share his glory.

Such was one consequence of this execution. A small farce also succeeded it. Influenced by the general excitement provoked by the murder of Kügelgen, the Jews had assembled and agreed, should any of them be able to discover the murderer, that they would decline the £150 offered by Government for information that might lead to the apprehension of the guilty. But Hirschel Mendel, the Jew who had produced the watch, put in his claim; whereupon Löbel Graff, who had produced the coat, put in a counter claim. This occasioned a lawsuit between the two Jews for the money. A compromise was finally patched up, by which each received half.

Gerhard von Kügelgen had been buried in the Catholic cemetery at Dresden on Maundy Thursday evening by moonlight. A great procession of art students attended the funeral cortège with lighted torches, and an oration was pronounced over his grave by his friend Councillor Böttiger.

His tomb may still be seen in the cemetery; on it is inscribed:—

FRANZ GERHARD VON KÜGELGEN. Born 6 Feb., 1772. Died 27 March, 1820.

On the other side is the text, St. John xiv. 27.

Kügelgen left behind him two sons and a daughter. The eldest son, Wilhelm, pursued his father's profession as an artist, and the Emperor of Russia sent an annual grant of money to assist him in his studies. There is a pleasant book, published anonymously by him, "An Old Man's Youthful Reminiscences," the first edition of which was issued in 1870, and which had reached its eighth edition in 1876.

Kügelgen's twin brother, Karl Ferdinand, after spending some years in St. Petersburg and in Livonia, settled at Reval, and died in 1832. He was the author of a "Picturesque Journey in the Crimea," published in 1823.

AUTHORITY

F. Ch. A. Hasse: Das Leben Gerhards von Kügelgen. Leipzig, 1824. He gives in the Supplement an excerpt from the records of the trial. As frontispiece is a portrait of the artist by himself, very Raphaelesque.

III. — THE POISONED PARSNIPS

AT the time when the banished Bourbons were wandering about Europe seeking temporary asylums, during the period of Napoleon's supremacy, a story circulated in 1804 relative to an attempt made in Warsaw, which then belonged to Prussia, upon the life of the Royal Family then residing there. It was said that a plot had been formed, that was well nigh successful, to kill Louis XVIII., his wife, the Duke and Duchess of Angoulême, and such of the Court as sat at the Royal table, with a dish of poisoned parsnips. It was, moreover, whispered that at the bottom of the plot was no other than Napoleon himself, who sought to remove out of his way the legitimate claimants to the Gallic throne.

The article in which the account of the attempt was made public was in the *London Courier* for August 20th, 1804, from which we will now take the leading facts.

The Royal Family was living in Warsaw. Napoleon Bonaparte employed an agent of the name of Galon Boyer at Warsaw to keep an eye on them, and this man, it was reported, had engaged assassins at the instigation of Napoleon to poison Louis XVIII. and the rest of the Royal Family. The *Courier* of August 21st, 1804, says: "Some of the daily papers, which were not over anxious to discredit the conspiracy imputed to Mr. Drake,[1] affect to throw some doubt upon the account of the attempt upon the lives of the Royal Family at Warsaw. They seem to think that had Bonaparte desired such a plan, he could have executed it with more secrecy and effect. Undoubtedly his plans of assassination have hitherto been more successful, because his hapless victims were within his power—his wounded soldiers at Jaffa, Toussaint L'Ouverture, Pichegru, and the Duke D'Enghien. He could send his bloodhounds into Germany to seize his prey; but Warsaw was too remote for him; he was under the necessity of having recourse to less open means of sending his assassins to act secretly. But it is deemed extraordinary that the diabolical attempt should have failed. Why is it extraordinary that a beneficent Providence should interpose to save the life of a just prince? Have we not had signal instances of that interposition in this country? For the accuracy of the account we published yesterday, we pledge ourselves[2] that the fullest details, authenticated by all Louis XVIII.'s Ministers—by the venerable Archbishop of Rheims—by the Abbé Edgeworth, who administered the last consolation of religion to Louis the XVI., have been received in this country. All those persons were present when the poisoned preparation was analysed by very eminent physicians, *who are the subjects of the King of Prussia.*

[1] Drake was envoy of the British Government at Munich; he and Spencer Smith, Chargé d'Affaires at Würtemberg, were accused by Napoleon of being at the bottom of a counter revolution, and an attempt to obtain his assassination. It was true that Drake and Smith were in correspondence with parties in France with the object of securing Hagenau and Strassburg and throwing discord among the troops of the

Republic, but they never for a moment thought of obtaining the assassination of the First Consul, as far as we can judge from their correspondence that fell into the hands of the French police.

[2] Unfortunately the British Museum file is imperfect, and does not contain the Number for August 20th.

"The two wretches who attempted to corrupt the poor Frenchman were openly protected by the French Consul or Commercial Agent.

"The Prussian Governor would not suffer them to be arrested in order that their guilt or innocence might be legally investigated. Is it to be believed that had there been no foundation for the charge against them, the French agent would have afforded them less open protection, and thereby strengthened the charge brought against them? If they were protected and paid by the French agent, is it probable that he paid them out of his own pocket, employed them in such a plot of his own accord, and without order and instructions from his own Government, from Bonaparte? Besides, did not the President Hoym acknowledge his fears that some attempt would be made upon the life of Louis the XVIII.?

"The accounts transmitted to this country were sent from Warsaw one hour after the king had set out for Grodno."

The *Courier* for August 24th, 1804, has the following note:—"We have another strong fact which is no slight evidence in our minds of Bonaparte's guilt. The plot against Louis the XVIII. was to be executed at the end of July—it would be known about the beginning of August. At that very period Bonaparte prohibits the importation of all foreign journals without exception—that is, of all the means by which the people could be informed of the diabolical deed. Why does he issue this prohibition at the present moment, or why does he issue it at all? Fouché says in his justification of it that it is to prevent our knowing when the expedition sails. Have we ever received any news about the expedition from the French papers? No, no! the prohibition was with a view to the bloody scene to be acted at Warsaw."

The *Courier* of August 22nd contained full particulars. We will now tell the whole story, from beginning to end, first of all as dressed out by the fancy of Legitimists, and then according to the real facts of the case as far as known.

Napoleon, it will be remembered, had been appointed First Consul for life on August 2nd, 1802, but the Republic came to an end, and the French Empire was established by the Senate on May 18th, 1804.

It was supposed—and we can excuse the excitement and intoxication of wrath in the minds of all adherents of the Bourbons which could suppose it—that Napoleon, who was thus refounding the Empire of Charlemagne, desired to secure the stability of this new throne by sweeping out of his way the legitimate claimants to that of France. The whole legend of the attempt to assassinate Louis XVIII. by means of a dish of poisoned parsnips is given us in complete form by the author of a life of that prince twenty years after the event.[3] It is to this effect:

When the King (Louis XVIII.) was preparing for his journey from Warsaw to Grodno an atrocious attempt to assassinate him was brought to light, which leaves no manner of doubt that it was the purpose of those who were the secret movers in the plot to remove by poison both the King and Queen and also the Duke of Angoulême and his wife. Two delegates of Napoleon had been in Warsaw seeking for a man who could execute the plan. A certain Coulon appeared most adapted to their purpose, a man indigent and eager for money. He had previously been in the service of one of the emigré nobles, and had access to the kitchen of the Royal Family.

[3] A. de Beauchamp, Vie de Louis XVIII. Paris, 1824.

The agents of Napoleon gave Coulon drink, and as he became friendly and lively under the influence of punch, they communicated to him their scheme, and promised him money, the payment of his debts, and to effect his escape if he would be their faithful servant in the intrigue. Coulon pretended to yield to their solicitations, and a rendezvous was appointed where the plans were to be matured. But no sooner was Coulon at liberty than he went to his former master, the Baron de Milleville, master of horse to the Queen, and told him all. The Baron sought the Duc de Pienne, first gentleman of the Royal household, and he on receiving the information communicated it to the Count d'Avaray, Minister of Louis XVIII. Coulon received orders to pretend to be ready to carry on the plot. He did this with reluctance, but he did it. He told the agents of Napoleon that he was in their hands and would blindly execute their orders. They treated him now to champagne, and revealed to him the details of the attempt. He was to get into the kitchen of the Royal household, and was to pour the contents of a packet they gave him into one of the pots in which the dinner for the Royal table was being cooked. Coulon then demanded an instalment of his pay, and asked to be given 400 louis d'or. One of the agents then turned to the other and asked if he thought Boyer would be disposed to advance so much—this was Galon Boyer, the head agent sent purposely to Warsaw as spy on the Royal Family, and the principal mover in the attempt.

The other agent replied that Boyer was not at the moment in Warsaw, but he would be back in a couple of days. Coulon stuck to his point, like a clever rascal, and refused to do anything till he felt gold in his palm, and he was bidden wait till Boyer had been communicated with. He was appointed another meeting on the moors at Novawies outside the city.

As, next evening, Coulon was on his way to the place named, he observed that he was followed by a man. Suddenly out of the corn growing beside the road started a second. They were the agents. They paid him a few dollars, promised to provide handsomely for him in France, by giving him 400 louis d'or and a situation under Government; and handed him a bottle of liquor that was to stimulate his courage at the crucial moment, and also a paper packet that contained three parsnips, that had been scooped out and filled with poison. These he was to insinuate into one of the pots cooking for dinner, and induce the cook to overlook what he had done, and serve them up to the Royal Family.

The King then lived in a chateau at Lazienki, about a mile out of Warsaw. Thither hastened Coulon as fast as his legs could carry him, and he committed the parsnips to the Baron de Milleville. The Count d'Avaray and the Archbishop of Rheims put their seals on the parcel; after that the parsnips had first been shown to the Prussian authorities, and they had been asked in all form to attest the production of the poisoned roots, and to order the arrest of the two agents of Napoleon, and to confront them with Coulon—and had declined. Louis, when informed of the attempt, showed his wonted composure. He wrote immediately to the Prussian President, Von Hoym, and requested him to visit him at Lazienki, and consult what was to be done.

Herr Von Hoym did not answer; nor did he go to the King, but communicated with his superiors. Finally there arrived a diplomatic reply declining to interfere in the matter, as it was the concern of the police to investigate it, and it should be taken up in the ordinary way.

Thereupon the King requested that Coulon and his wife should be secured, and that specialists should be appointed who, along with the Royal physician, might examine the parsnips alleged to be poisoned.

But the Prussian Courts declined again to take any steps. The policy of the Prussian Cabinet under Count Haugwitz was favourable to a French alliance, and the King of Prussia was among the first of the greater Powers which had formally recognised the French Emperor. On condition that the French troops occupying Hanover should not be augmented, and that war, if it broke out with Russia, should be so carried on as not to inconvenience and sweep over Prussian territory, Prussia had undertaken to observe a strict neutrality. In return for these concessions, which were of great moment to Napoleon, he openly proclaimed his intention to augment the strength of Prussia, and it was hoped at Berlin that the price paid would be the incorporation of Hanover with Prussia.

At this moment, consequently, the Prussian Government was most unwilling to meddle in an investigation which threatened to lead to revelations most compromising to the character of Napoleon, and most inconvenient for itself.

As the Prussian courts would not take up the matter of the parsnips, a private investigation was made by the Count d'Avaray, with the Royal physician, Dr. Lefèvre, and the Warsaw physician, Dr. Gagatkiewicz, together with the Apothecary Guidel and a certain Dr. Bergozoni. The seals were broken in their presence, and the three roots were examined. It was ascertained that they were stuffed with a mixture of white, yellow, and red arsenic. This having been ascertained, and a statement of the fact duly drawn up, and signed, the president of the police, Herr von Tilly, was communicated with. He, however, declined to interfere, as had the President von Hoym. "Thus," says M. Beauchamp, "one court shuffled the matter off on another, backwards and forwards, so as not to have to decide on the matter, a specimen of the results of the system adopted at this time by the Prussian Cabinet."

No other means of investigation remained but for Count d'Avaray to have the matter gone into by the court of the exiled King. They examined Coulon, who held firmly to his story as told to the Baron de Milleville, and all present were convinced that he spoke the truth.

As the King could obtain no justice from the hands of Prussia, he suffered the story to be made public in order that the opinion of all honourable men in Europe might be expressed on the conduct of both Napoleon and of the Prussian Ministry. "The impression made," says M. Beauchamp, "especially in England, was deep. Men recalled Bonaparte's former crimes that had been proved—the poisoning at Jaffa, the—at the time—very fresh indignation provoked by the murder of the Count de Frotté, of Pichegru, of Captain Wright, of the Duke d'Enghien, of Toussaint l'Ouverture; they recalled the lack of success he had experienced in demanding of Louis XVIII. a formal renunciation of his claims, and weighed well the determination of his character. Even the refusal of the Prussian courts to go into the charge (for if it had been investigated they must needs have pronounced judgment on it)—encouraged suspicion. Hardly an English newspaper did not condemn Napoleon as the instigator of an attempt that providentially failed."

Such is the legend as formulated by M. de Beauchamp. Fortunately there exists documentary evidence in the archives of the courts at Berlin that gives an altogether different complexion to the story, and entirely clears the name of Napoleon from stain of complicity in this matter. It throws, moreover, a light, by no means favourable, on those of the Legitimist party clustered about the fallen monarch.

Louis XVIII., obliged to fly from one land to another before the forces of Napoleon, was staying for a while at Warsaw, in the year 1804, under the incognito of the Count de l'Isle. His misfortunes had not broken his spirit or diminished his pretensions. He was surrounded by a little court in spite of his incognito; and as this little court had no affairs of State to transact, it played a niggling game at petty intrigue. This court consisted of the Count d'Avaray, the Archbishop of Rheims, the Duke de Pienne, the Marquis de Bonney, the Duke d'Avré de Croy, the Count de la Chapelle, the Counts Damas Crux and Stephen de Damas, and the Abbés Edgeworth and Frimont. Louis had assured Napoleon he would rather eat black bread than resign his pretensions. At Warsaw he maintained his pretensions to the full, but did not eat black bread; he kept a very respectable kitchen. The close alliance between Prussia and France forced him to leave Warsaw and migrate into Russia.

At this time there lived in Warsaw a certain Jean Coulon, son of a small shopkeeper at Lyons, who had led an adventurous life. At the age of nine he had run away from home and attached himself to a wandering dramatic company; then had gone into service to a wigmaker, and had lived for three years at Barcelona at his handicraft. But wigs were going out of fashion, and he threw up an unprofitable trade, and enlisted in a legion of emigrés, but in consequence of some quarrel with a Spaniard was handed over to the Spanish authorities. He purchased his pardon by enlisting in the Spanish army, but deserted and joined the French Republican troops, was in the battle of Novi, ran away, and joined the corps raised at Naples by Cardinal Ruffo. When this corps was dispersed, he went back to Spain, again enlisted, and was shipped for St. Lucia. The vessel in which he was, was captured by an English cruiser, and he was taken into Plymouth and sent up to Dartmoor as prisoner of war. After two years he was exchanged and was shipped to Cuxhaven. Thence he went to Altona, where he asked the intervention of the Duke d'Avré in his favour. The Duke recommended him to the Countess de l'Isle, and he was taken into the service of her master of horse, the Baron de Milleville, and came to Warsaw in September, 1803. There he married, left his service and set up a café and billiard room that was frequented by the retainers and servants of the emigré nobility that hovered about the King and Queen. He was then aged 32, could speak Italian and Spanish as well as French, and was a thorough soldier of fortune, impecunious, loving pleasure, and wholly without principles, political or religious.

The French Chargé d'Affaires at Warsaw was Galon Boyer; he does not appear in the documents relative to the *Affaire Coulon*, not because the Prussian Government shirked its duty, but because he was in no way mixed up with the matter of the parsnips. It is quite true that, as M. de Beauchamp asserts, the Court of Louis XVIII. did endeavour to involve the Prussian authorities in the investigation, but it was in such a manner that it was not possible for them to act. On July 23rd, when the Count de l'Isle was determined to leave Warsaw, Count d'Avaray called on the President von Hoym, and told him in mysterious language that he was aware of a conspiracy in which were involved several Frenchmen and as many as a dozen Poles that sought the life of his august master. Herr von Hoym doubted. He asked for the grounds of this assertion, and was promised full particulars that same evening at eight o'clock. At the hour appointed, the Count appeared breathless before him, and declared that now he was prepared with a complete disclosure. However, he told nothing, and postponed the revelation to 10 o'clock. Then Avaray informed him that the keeper of the Café Coulon had been hired by some strangers to meet him that same night on the road to Novawies, to plan with him the murder, by poison, of the Count de l'Isle. The whole story seemed suspicious to von Hoym. It was now too late for him to send police to watch the spot where the meeting was to take place, which he might have done had d'Avaray condescended to tell him in time, two hours earlier. He asked d'Avaray where Coulon lived that he might send for him, and the Count professed he did not know the address.

Next day Count d'Avaray read to the President von Hoym a document, which he said had been drawn up by members of the court of the Count de l'Isle, showed him a paper that contained twelve small parsnips, and requested him to subscribe the document and seal the parcel of parsnips. Naturally, the President declined to do this. He had not seen Coulon, he did not know from whom Coulon had received the parcel, and he mistrusted the whole story. However, he requested that he might be furnished with an exact description of the two mysterious strangers, and when he had received it, communicated with the police, and had inquiry made for them in and about Warsaw. No one had seen or heard of any persons answering to the description.

Presently the Marquis de Bonney arrived to request the President, in the name of the Count de l'Isle, to have the parsnips examined by specialists. He declined to do so.

On July 26th, the Count d'Avaray appeared before the head of the Police, the President von Tilly, and showed him an attestation made by several doctors that they had examined three parsnips that had been shown them, and they had found in them a paste composed of arsenic and orpiment. Von Tilly thought the whole story so questionable that he refused to meddle with it. Moreover, a notary of Warsaw, who had been requested to take down Coulon's statement, had declined to testify to the genuineness of the confession, probably because, as Coulon afterwards insinuated, he had been helped to make it consistent by those who questioned him.

Louis XVIII. left Warsaw on July 30, and as the rumour spread that Coulon's wife had bought some arsenic a week before at an apothecary's shop in the place, the police inspector ordered her arrest. She was questioned and declared that she had, indeed, bought some rat poison, without the knowledge of her husband. Coulon was now taken up and questioned, and he pretended that he had given his wife orders to buy the rat poison, because he was plagued with vermin in the house.

Then the authorities in Warsaw sent all the documents relating to this matter, including the *procès verbal* drawn up by the courtiers of Louis XVIII., to Berlin, and asked for further instructions.

According to this *procès verbal* Coulon had confessed as follows: On the 20th July two strangers had entered his billiard room, and had assured him that, if he were disposed to make his fortune, they could help him to it. They made him promise silence, and threatened him with death if he disclosed what they said. After he had sworn fidelity and secrecy, they told him that he was required to throw something into the pot in which the soup was being prepared for the King's table. For so doing they would pay him 400 louis d'or. Coulon considered a moment; then the strangers promised they would provide a situation for his wife in France. After that one of them said to his fellow in Italian, "We must be off. We have no time to lose." Next day, in the evening, a third stranger appeared at his door, called him forth into the street, walked about with him through the streets of old and new Warsaw, till he was thoroughly bewildered, and did not know where he was, and, finally, entered with him a house, where he saw the two strangers who had been with him previously. Champagne was brought on the table, and they all drank, and one of the strangers became tipsy. When Coulon promised to do what was required of him, he was told to secure some of the mutton-chops that were being prepared for the Royal table, and to manipulate them with the powder that was to be given him. That the cook might not notice what he was about, he was to treat him to large draughts of brandy. Coulon agreed, but asked first to touch the 400 louis d'or. Then the tipsy man shouted out, "That is all right, but will Boyer consent to it?" The other stranger tried to check him, and said, "What are you saying? Boyer is not here, he has gone out of town and will not be back for a couple of days." After Coulon had insisted on prepayment, he had been put off till the next evening, when he was to meet the strangers at 11 o'clock on the road to Novawies. There he was to receive money, and the powder for the King. He was then given one ducat, and led home at one o'clock in the morning. On the following night, at 11 o'clock, he went on the way to Novawies, and then followed what we have already given from the story of the man, as recorded by M. de Beauchamp. He received from the men a packet containing the parsnips, and some money—only six dollars. They put a kerchief under the earth beneath a tree, and bade him, if he had accomplished his task, come to the tree and remove the kerchief, as a token to them; if, however, he failed, the kerchief was to be left undisturbed. The tree he had marked well, it was the forty-fifth along the road to Novawies. A small end of the kerchief peeped out from under the soil. The strangers had then given him a bottle of liqueur to stimulate his courage for the undertaking.

After that Coulon was left alone, he said that he staggered homewards, but felt so faint that he would have fallen to the ground had not a Prussian officer, who came by, noticed his condition and helped him home. At the conclusion of the *procès verbal* came an exact description of the conspirators. Such was the document produced originally by the Count d'Avaray, and we can hardly wonder that, on hearing it, the Prussian civil and police authorities had hesitated about taking action. The so-called confession of Coulon seemed to them to be a rhodomontade got up for the purpose of obtaining money out of the ex-King and his Court.

From Berlin orders were sent to Warsaw to have the matter thoroughly sifted. Coulon and his wife were now again subjected to examination. He adhered at first to his story, but when he endeavoured to explain the purchase of the arsenic, and to fit it into his previous tale, he involved himself in contradictions.

The President at this point addressed him gravely, and warned him of the consequences. His story compromised the French chargé d'affaires, M. Galon Boyer, and this could not be allowed to be passed over without a very searching examination that must inevitably reveal the truth. Coulon was staggered, and hastily asked how matters would stand with him if he told the truth. Then, after a little hesitation, he admitted that "he thought before the departure of the Count de l'Isle he would obtain for himself a sum of money, with which to escape out of his difficulties. He had reckoned on making 100 ducats out of this affair." He now told quite a different tale. With the departure of the court of the emigrés, he would lose his clientelle, and he was concerned because he owed money for the café and billiard table. He had therefore invented the whole story in hopes of imposing on the court and getting from them a little subvention. But he said he had been dragged on further than he intended by the Count d'Avaray, who had swallowed his lie with avidity, and had urged him to go on with the intrigue so as to produce evidence against the conspirators.

That was why he had made up the figment of the meeting with the strangers on the road and their gift to him of the parsnips, which he admitted that he had himself scooped out and filled with the rat poison paste he had bought at the apothecary's.

So far so good. What he now said was precisely what the cool heads of the Prussian authorities had believed from the first. But Coulon did not adhere to this second confession. After a few days in prison he professed his desire to make another. He was brought before the magistrate, and now he said that the whole story was got up by the Count d'Avaray, M. de Milleville, and others of the surroundings of the exiled King, for the purpose of creating an outbreak of disgust in Europe against Napoleon, and of bringing about a revolt in France. He declared that he had been promised a pension of six ducats monthly, that when he gave his evidence M. de Milleville had paid him 35 ducats, and that he had been taken into the service, along with his wife, of the ex-Queen, as reward for what he had done.

There were several particulars which gave colour to this last version of Coulon's story. It was true that he had been given some money by Milleville; it was perhaps true that in their eagerness to prove a case of attempted assassination, some of those who conducted the inquiry had helped him to correct certain discrepancies in his narrative. Then, again, it was remarkable that, although the Count d'Avaray knew about the projected murder, he would not tell the Prussian President the facts till 10 o'clock at night, when it was too late to send the police to observe the pretended meeting on the Novawies road; and when Herr von Hoym asked for directions as to where Coulon lived that the police might be sent to arrest him on his return, and during his absence to search the house, the Count had pretended to be unable to say where Coulon lived. It was also true that de Milleville had repeatedly visited Coulon's house during the course of the intrigue, and that it was immediately after Coulon had been at Milleville's house that his wife was sent to buy the rat poison.

Coulon pretended to have heard M. de Milleville say that "This affair might cause a complete change in the situation in France, when tidings of what had been done were published." Moreover, he said that he had been despatched to the Archbishop of Rheim's with the message "Le coup est manqué."

But it is impossible to believe that the emigré court can have fabricated such a plot by which to cast on the name of Napoleon the stain of attempted assassination. The whole story reads like the clumsy invention of a vulgar adventurer. Coulon's second confession is obviously that of his true motives. He was in debt, he was losing his clientelle by the departure of the Count, and it is precisely what such a scoundrel would do, to invent a lie whereby to enlist their sympathies for himself, and obtain from them some pecuniary acknowledgment for services he pretended to have rendered. The little court was to blame in its gullibility. Its blind hatred of Napoleon led it to believe such a gross and palpable lie, and, if doubts arose in any of their minds as to the verity of the tale told them, they suppressed them.

Coulon was found guilty by the court and was sentenced to five years' imprisonment. The judgment of the court was that he had acted in concert with certain members of the retinue of the Count de l'Isle, but it refrained from naming them.

IV. — THE MURDER OF FATHER THOMAS IN DAMASCUS

THE remarkable case we are about to relate awoke great interest and excitement throughout three quarters of the world, and stirred up that hatred of the Jews which had been laid asleep after the persecutions of the Middle Ages, just at the time when in all European lands the emancipation of the Jew was being recognised as an act of justice. At the time the circumstances were imperfectly known, or were laid before the public in such a partial light that it was difficult to form a correct judgment upon them. Since then, a good deal of light has been thrown on the incident, and it is possible to arrive at a conclusion concerning the murder with more unbiased mind and with fuller information than was possible at the time.

The Latin convents of Syria stand under the immediate jurisdiction of the Pope, and are, for the most part, supplied with recruits from Italy. They are very serviceable to travellers, whom they receive with genial hospitality, and without distinction of creed. They are nurseries of culture and of industry. Every monk and friar is required to exercise a profession or trade, and the old charge against monks of being drones is in no way applicable to the busy members of the religious orders in Palestine.

In the Capuchin Convent at Damascus dwelt, in 1840, a friar named Father Thomas, a Sardinian by birth. For thirty-three years he had lived there, and had acted as physician and surgeon, attending to whoever called for his services, Mussulman or Christian, Turk, Jew or Frank alike. He set limbs, dosed with quinine for fever, and vaccinated against smallpox. Being well known and trusted, he was in constant practice, and his practice brought him, or, at all events, his order, a handsome annual income. His manners were, unfortunately, not amiable. He was curt, even rude, and somewhat dictatorial; his manners impressed as authoritative in the sickroom, but were resented in the market-place as insolent.

On February 5th, 1840, Father Thomas disappeared, together with his servant, a lay brother who always attended him. This disappearance caused great commotion in Damascus.

France has been considered in the East as the protector of Christians of the Latin confession. The French Consul, the Count Ratti-Menton, considered it his duty to investigate the matter.

Father Thomas had been seen to enter the Jews' quarter. Several Israelites admitted having seen him there. No one saw him leave it: consequently, it was concluded he had disappeared, been made away with, there. As none but Jews occupied the Ghetto, it was argued that Father Thomas had been murdered by Israelites. That was settled as a preliminary. But in the meantime the Austrian Consul had been making investigation as well as the Count Ratti-Menton, and he had obtained information that Father Thomas and his servant had been noticed engaged in a violent quarrel and contest of words with some Mohammedans of the lowest class, in the market-place. No weight was attached to this, and the French Consul pursued his investigations in the Jews' quarter, and in that quarter alone.

Sheriff Pacha was Governor of Syria, and Count Ratti-Menton required him to allow of his using every means at his disposal for the discovery of the criminal. He also requested the Austrian Consul to allow a domiciliary visitation of all the Jews' houses, the Austrian Government being regarded as the protector of the Hebrews. In both cases consent was given, and the search was begun with zeal.

Then a Turk, named Mohammed-el-Telli, who was in prison for non-payment of taxes, sent word to the French Consul that, if he would obtain his release, he would give such information as would lead to the discovery of the murderer or murderers. He received his freedom, and denounced, in return, several Jews' houses as suspicious. Count Ratti-Menton at the head of a troop of soldiers and workmen, and a rabble assembled in the street, invaded all these houses, and explored them from attic to cellar.

One of the first names given by Mohammed-el-Telli was that of a Jewish barber, Negrin. He gave a confused and contradictory account of himself, but absolutely denied having any knowledge of the murder. In vain were every means used during three days at the French Consulate to bring him to a confession; after that he was handed over to the Turkish authorities. They had him bastinadoed, then tortured. During his torture, Mohammed-el-Telli was at his side urging him to make a clean breast. Unable to endure his sufferings longer, the barbar declared his readiness to tell all. Whether what he said was based on reports circulating in the town, or was put into his mouth by his tormentors, we cannot tell. According to his story, on the evening of February the 5th a servant of David Arari summoned him into his house. He found the master of the house along with six other Israelitish rabbis and merchants, to wit, Aaron and Isaac Arari, Mussa Abul Afia, Moses Salonichi, and Joseph Laniado. In a corner of the room lay or leaned against the wall Father Thomas, gagged and bound hand and foot. The merchants urged Negrin to murder the Capuchin in their presence, but he stedfastly refused to do so. Finally finding him inflexible, they bought his silence with 600 piastres (hardly £6) and dismissed him.

Thereupon, the governor ordered the arrest of David Arari and the other Jews named, all of whom were the richest merchants in the town—at all events the richest Jewish merchants. They, with one consent, solemnly protested their innocence. They, also, were subjected to the bastinado; but as most of them were aged men, and it was feared that they might succumb under the blows, after a few lashes had been administered, they were raised from the ground and subjected to other tortures. For thirty-six hours the unhappy men were forced to stand upright, and were prevented from sleeping. They still persisted in denial, whereupon some of them were again beaten. At the twentieth blow they fainted. The French

Consul complained that the beating was inefficient—so the Austrian Consul reported, and at his instigation they were again bastinadoed, but again without bringing them to confession.

In the meantime, David Arari's servant, Murad-el-Fallat, was arrested, the man who was said to have been sent for the barber. He was dealt with more sharply than the others. He was beaten most cruelly, and to heighten his pain cold water was poured over his bruised and mangled flesh. Under the anguish he confessed that he had indeed been sent for the barber.

That was an insufficient confession. He was threatened with the bastinado again, and promised his release if he would reveal all he knew. Thereupon he repeated the story of the barber, with additions of his own. He and Negrin, said he, had by command of the seven rich merchants put the Father to death, and had then cut up the body and hidden the remains in a remote water conduit.

The barber, threatened with fresh tortures, confessed to the murder.

Count Ratti-Menton explored the conduit where the two men pretended the mutilated body was concealed, in the presence of the servant and barber, both of whom were in such a condition through the barbarous treatment to which they had been subjected, that they could not walk, and had to be carried to the spot. And actually there some bones were found, together with a cap. A surgeon pronounced that these were human bones. It was at once concluded that these were the remains of Father Thomas, and as such were solemnly buried in the cemetery of the Capuchin Convent.

David Arari's servant, Murad-el-Fallet, had related that the blood of Father Thomas had been collected in a copper vessel and drawn off and distributed among the Jews for religious purposes. It was an old and favourite belief among the ignorant that the Jews drank the blood of Christians at Easter, or mingled it with the Paschal unleavened dough. At the same time the rumour spread that the rich Hebrew Picciotto, a young man, nephew of the Austrian Consul at Aleppo, had sent his uncle a bottle of blood.

The seven merchants were led before the bones that had been discovered. They persisted in the declaration of their innocence. From this time forward, all scruple as to their treatment vanished, and they were tortured with diabolical barbarity. They received the bastinado again, they were burned where their flesh was tenderest with red hot pincers. Red hot wires were passed through their flesh. A German traveller, present at the time, declares that the first to acknowledge the truth of the charge was brought to do so by immersing him after all these torments for several hours in ice cold water; after which the other six were lashed with a scourge made of hippopotamus hide, till half unconscious, and streaming with blood, they were ready to admit whatever their tormentors strove to worry out of them.

The Protestant missionary, Wildon Pieritz, in his account enumerates the sufferings to which these unhappy men were subjected.

They were, 1st, bastinadoed.

2nd. Plunged in large vessels of cold water.

3rd. Placed under pressure till their eyes started out of their sockets.

4th. Their flesh, where most sensitive, was twisted and nipped till they went almost mad with agony.

5th. They were forced to stand upright for three whole days, and not suffered even to lean against a wall. Those who fell with exhaustion were goaded to rise again by the bayonets of the guard.

6th. They were dragged about by their ears, so that they were torn and bled.

7th. Thorns were driven up the quick of their nails on fingers and toes.

8th. Their beards were singed off, so that the skin was scorched and blistered.

9th. Flames were put under their noses so as to burn their nostrils.

The French Consul—let his name go down to posterity steeped in ignominy—Count Ratti-Menton, was not yet satisfied. He was bent on finding the vials filled with the blood. Each of the seven questioned said he had not got one, but had given his vial to another. The last, Mussa Abul Afia, unable to endure his torments any longer, gave way, and professed his willingness to turn Mussulman. Nevertheless, he was again subjected to the scourge, and whipped till he named another confederate—the Chief Rabbi Jacob Antibi, as the man to whom the blood had been committed. Mussa's confession, committed to writing, was as follows:—"I am *commanded* to say what I know relative to the murder of Father Thomas, and why I have submitted to become a Mussulman. It is, therefore, my duty to declare the truth. Jacob Antibi, Chief Rabbi, about a fortnight before the event, said to me—'You know that according to our religion we must have blood. I have already arranged with David Arari, to obtain it in the house of one of our people, and you must be present and bring me the blood.' I replied that I had not the nerve to see blood flow; whereupon, the Chief Rabbi answered that I could stand in the ante-chamber, and I would find Moses Salonichi and Joseph Laniado there. I then consented. On the 10th of the month, Achach, about an hour and a half before sun-down, as I was on my way to the synagogue, I met David Arari, who said to me: 'Come along to my house, you are wanted there.' I replied that I would come as soon as I had ended my prayers. 'No, no—come immediately!' he said. I obeyed. Then he told me that Father Thomas was in his house, and that he was to be sacrificed that evening. We went to his house. There we entered a newly-furnished apartment. Father Thomas lay bound in the midst of all there assembled. After sunset we adjourned to an unfurnished chamber, where David cut the throat of the monk. Aaron and Isaac Arari finished him. The blood was caught in a vat and then poured into a bottle, which was to be taken to the Chief Rabbi Jacob. I took the bottle and went to him. I found him in his court waiting for me. When he saw me enter, he retreated to his cabinet, and I followed him thither, saying, 'Here, I bring you what you desired.' He took the bottle and put it behind a book-case. Then I went home. I have forgotten to say that, when I left Arari's house, the body was undisturbed. I heard David and his brother say that they had made a bad choice of a victim, as Father Thomas was a priest, and a well-known individual, and would therefore be sought for, high and low. They answered that there was no fear, no one would betray what had taken place. The clothing would be now burnt, the body cut to pieces, and conveyed by the servants to the conduit, and what remained would be concealed under some secret stairs. I knew nothing about the servant of Father Thomas. The Wednesday following, I met David, Isaac, and Joseph Arari, near the shop of Bahal. Isaac asked David how all had gone on. David replied that all was done that was necessary, and that there was no cause for fear. As they began to talk together privately, I withdrew, as I was not one who associated with the wealthiest of the Jews, and the Arari were of that class. The blood is required by the Jews for the preparation of the Paschal bread. They have been often accused of the same, and been condemned on that account. They have a book called Serir Hadurut (no such a book really exists) which concerns this matter; now that the light of Islam has shone on me, I place myself under the protection of those who hold the power in their hands."

Such was his confession. The French Consul, unable to find the blood, was bent on discovering more criminals; and the servant of David Arari, after further pressure, was ready to give further particulars. He said that, after the Father had been murdered, he was sent to a rich Israelite, Marad Farhi, to invite him to slaughter the servant of the Capuchin friar in the same way as his master had been slaughtered. When he took the message, he found the young merchant, Isaac Picciotto, present, and delivered his message before him. Next day this Picciotto and four other Jews, Marad Farhi, Meir, and Assan Farhi, and Aaron Stamboli, all men of wealth, came to his master's house, and informed David Arari that they had together murdered the Capuchin's serving-man in the house of Meir Farhi. On another occasion this same witness, Murad-el-Fallat, said that the murder of the servant took place in the house of David Arari; but no importance was attached in this remarkable case to contradictions in the evidence.

Picciotto, as son of a former Austrian Consul, a nephew of the Consul at Aleppo, was able to take refuge under the protection of Merlato, the Austrian Consul at Damascus. On the demand of Count Ratti-Menton, he was placed on his trial, but proved an *alibi*; on the evening in question, he and his wife had been visiting an English gentleman, Mr. George Macson.

Arari's servant now extended his revelations. He said that he had been present at the murder of the attendant on the Capuchin. This man had been bound and put to death by seven Jews, namely, by the four already mentioned, young Picciotto, Jacob Abul Afia, and Joseph Menachem Farhi.

The French Consul was dissatisfied that Picciotto should escape. He demanded of the Austrian Consul that he should be delivered over to the Mussulman Court to be tortured like the rest into confession. The Austrian Consul was in a difficult position. He stood alone over against a fanatical Christian and an embittered Mohammedan mob, and in resistance to the Egyptian Government and the representative of France. But he did not hesitate, he absolutely refused to surrender Picciotto. The general excitement was now directed against the Consul; he was subjected to suspicion as a favourer of the murderers, as even incriminated in the murder. His house was surrounded by spies, and every one who entered or left it was an object of mistrust.

All Damascus was in agitation; everyone sought to bring some evidence forward to help on the case against the Jews. According to one account, thirty-three—according to the report of the Austrian Consul, sixty-three Jewish children, of from four to ten years old, were seized, thrown into prison and tortured, to extract information from them as to the whereabouts of their parents and relations—those charged with the murder of the servant, and who had fled and concealed themselves. Those witnesses who had appeared before the court to testify to the innocence of the accused, were arrested, and treated with Oriental barbarity. Because Farach Katasch and Isaac Javoh had declared that they had seen Father Thomas on the day of the murder in another quarter of the town than the Ghetto, they were put to the torture. Isaac Javoh said he had seen Father Thomas on the road to Salachia, two miles from the Jews' quarter, and had there spoken to him. He was racked, and died on the rack.

A boy admitted that he had noticed Father Thomas and his servant in another part of the town. For so saying, he was beaten with such barbarity that he died twenty-four hours after. A Jewish account from Beyrut says: "A Jew dedicated himself to martyrdom for the sanctity of the ever-blessed Name. He went before the Governor, and said to him, 'Is this justice you do? It is a slander that we employ blood for our Paschal bread; and that it is so is known to all civilized governments. You say that the barber, who is a Jew, confessed it. I reply that he did so only under the stress of torture. Very likely the Father was murdered by Christians or by Turks.' The Governor, and the dragoman of the French Consul, Baudin by name, retorted, 'What! you dare to charge the murder on Turks or Christians?' and he was ordered to be beaten and tortured to death. He was barbarously scourged and hideously tormented, and urged all the while to confess the truth. But he cried ever, 'Hear, O Israel! The Lord thy God is one Lord!' and so crying he died."

As the second murder, according to one account, was committed in the house of Meir Farhi, Count Ratti-Menton had the water conduits and drains torn up all round it, and in the drain near them was found a heap of bones, a bit of flesh, and a fragment of leather—according to one account a portion of a shoe, according to that of the Austrian Consul, a portion of a girdle. It had—supposing it to have belonged to the murdered man—been soaking for a month in the drain, nevertheless, the brother of the servant who had disappeared identified it as having belonged to the murdered man! Dr. Massari, Italian physician to Sheriff Pacha, and Dr. Rinaldo, a doctor practising in Damascus, declared that the bones were human remains, but they were examined by Dr. Yograssi, who proved them to be—sheep bones. One may judge from this what reliance can be placed on the assumption that the first collection of bones that were given Christian burial were those of a man, and of Father Thomas. As for the bit of flesh, it was thought to be a piece of liver, but whether of a human being or of a beast was uncertain or unascertained. The Jews' houses were now subjected to search. Count Ratti-Menton swept through the streets at the head of twenty sbirri, entering and ransacking houses at his own caprice, the Jews' houses first of all, and then such houses of Christians as were supposed to be open as a harbour of shelter to the persecuted Israelites. Thus one night he rushed not only into the house of, but even the women's bedrooms of a merchant, Aiub, who stood under Austrian protection, hunting after secreted Jews, an outrage, in popular opinion, even in the East.

The Jews charged with the murder of the servant had not been secured. The greater number of the well-to-do Hebrews had fled the town. A hue-and-cry was set up, and the country round was searched. Their families were taken up and tortured into confessing where they were. A German traveller then in Damascus says that the prisons were crowded with unfortunates, and that the pen refuses to detail the torments to which they were subjected to wring from them the information required. The wife of Meir Farhi and their child were imprisoned, and the child bastinadoed before its mother's eyes. At the three hundredth blow the mother's heart gave way, and she betrayed the hiding-place of her husband. He was seized. The hippopotamus scourge was flourished over his head, and knowing what his fellows had suffered, he confessed himself guilty. Assan Farhi, who was caught in his hiding-place, was imprisoned for a week in the French Consulate, and then delivered over to Turkish justice. Bastinado and the rack convinced him of his guilt, but he found means to despatch from his dungeon a letter to Ibrahim Pacha protesting his innocence.

It is as impossible as it is unnecessary to follow the story of the persecution in all its details. The circumstances have been given by various hands, and as names are not always recorded, it is not always possible to distinguish whether single cases are recorded by different writers with slight variations, or whether they are reporting different incidents in the long story.

The porter of the Jews' quarters, a man of sixty, died under bastinado, to which he was subjected for no other crime than not confessing that he had seen the murdered men enter the Ghetto.

In the meantime, whilst this chase after those accused of the second murder was going on, the seven merchants who had confessed to the murder of the Father had been lying in prison recovering from their wounds and bruises. As they recovered, the sense of their innocence became stronger in them than fear for the future and consideration of the past. They withdrew their confessions. Again were they beaten and tormented. Thenceforth they remained stedfast. Two of the seven, David Arari, aged eighty and Joseph Laniado, not much younger, died of their sufferings. Laniado had protested that he could bring evidence—the unimpeachable evidence of Christian merchants at Khasbin—that he had been with them at the time when it was pretended he had been engaged on the murder. But he died before these witnesses reached Damascus. Then Count Ratti-Menton pressed for the execution of the rest.

So stood matters when Herr von Hailbronner, whose report on the whole case is both fullest and most reliable, for the sequence of events, arrived in Damascus. He took pains to collect all the most authentic information he could on every particular.

Damascus was in the wildest commotion. All classes of the people were in a condition of fanatic excitement. The suffering caused by the pressure of the Egyptian government of Mohamed Ali, the threat of an Oriental war, the plague which had broken out in Syria, the quarantine, impeding all trade, were matters that were thrust into the background by the all-engrossing story of the murder and the persecution of the Jews.

The condition of the Hebrews in Damascus became daily more precarious. The old antagonism, jealousy of their riches, hatred caused by extortionate usury, were roused and armed for revenge. The barber, though he had confessed that he was guilty of the murder, was allowed to go scot-free, because he had betrayed his confederates. What an encouragement was offered to the rabble to indulge in false witness against rich Jews, whose wealth was coveted!

Mohamed Ali's government desired nothing better than the confiscation of their goods. A pack of ruffians sought occasion to extract money out of this persecution by bribes, or to purchase pardon for past offences by denouncing the innocent.

It is well at this point to look a little closer at the French Consul, the Count Ratti-Menton. On him rests the guilt of this iniquitous proceeding, rather than on the Mussulman judges. He had been twice bankrupt when French Consul in Sicily. Then he had been sent as Consul to Tiflis, where his conduct had been so disreputable, that on the representation of the Russian Government he had been recalled. He had then been appointed Consul at Damascus. In spite of all this, and the discredit with which his conduct with regard to the Jews, on account of the murder of Father Thomas, had covered him, his part was warmly taken up by the Ultramontane Press, and the French Government did its utmost to shield him. M. Thiers even warmly defended him. The credit of France was thought to be at stake, and it was deemed advisable to stand by the agent of France, and make out a case for him as best might be.

It is quite possible, it is probable, that he was thoroughly convinced that the Jews were guilty, but that does not justify his mode of procedure. It is possible also that bribes may—as was said—have been offered him by the Jews if he would desist from his persecution, but that he refused these bribes shows that he was either not an unredeemed rascal, or that he conceived he had gone too far to withdraw.

The Turkish and Egyptian authorities acted as always has been and will be their manner, after their nature, and in their own interest. We expect of them nothing else, but that the representative of one of the most enlightened nations of Europe, a man professing himself to be a Christian, and civilized, a member of a noble house, should hound on the ignorant and superstitious, and give rein to all the worst passions of an Oriental rabble, against a helpless and harmless race, that has been oppressed, and ill-treated, and slandered for centuries, is never to be looked over and forgiven. The name of Ratti-Menton must go down branded to posterity; and it is to be regretted that M. Thiers should have allowed his love of his country to so carry him away as to induce him to throw the shield over a man of whose guilt he must have been perfectly aware, having full information in his hands. This shows us to what an extent Gallic vanity will blind the Gallic eye to the plain principles of truth and right.

Ratti-Menton had his agents to assist him—Baudin, chief of his bureau at the Consulate; Francois Salins, a native of Aleppo, who acted as interpreter, spy, and guard to the Consulate; Father Tosti, a French Lazarist, who, according to the Austrian Consul, "seemed to find in this case an opportunity for avenging on the race the death of his Divine Master; also a Christian Arab, Sehibli Ayub, a man of bad character, who was well received by Ratti-Menton, because of his keenness as spy, and readiness as denunciator.

What followed now passes all belief. After that countless poor Jews had been accused, beaten, tortured, and killed, it occurred to the judges that it would be as well to ascertain the motive for the crime. It had been said by those who had confessed that the Pater and his servant had been put to death in order to obtain their blood to mingle with the dough for the Paschal wafer. The disappearance of the two men took place on February 5th. Easter fell that year on April 18th, so that the blood would have to be preserved two months and a half. That was an inconsequence which neither the French Consul nor the Egyptian authorities stooped to consider. Orders were issued that the Talmud and other sacred books of the Jews should be explored to see whether, or rather where in them, the order was given that human blood should be mingled with the Paschal dough. When no such commands could be discovered, it was concluded that the editions presented for examination were purposely falsified.

Now, there were distinct indications pointing in quite another direction, which, if followed, might have elucidated the case, and revealed the actual criminals. But these indications were in no case followed.

Wildon Pieritz, an Evangelical Missionary, then in Damascus, as well as the Austrian Consul, agree in stating that three days before the disappearance of Father Thomas he was seen in violent altercation with a Turkish mule-driver, who was heard to swear he would be the death of the priest. The altercation was so violent that the servant of Father Thomas seized the mule-driver by the throat and maltreated him so that blood flowed—probably from his nose. Father Thomas lost his temper and cursed the mussulman and his religion. The scene created great commotion, and a number of Turks were very angry, amongst them was one, a merchant, Abu Yekhyeh, who distinguished himself. Wildon Pieritz in a letter to the *Journal de Smyrne* on May 14th, 1840, declares that when the news of the disappearance of Father Thomas began to excite attention, this merchant, Abu Yekhyeh, hanged himself.

We may well inquire how it was that none of these facts came to be noticed. The answer is to hand. Every witness that gave evidence which might exculpate the accused Jews, and turn attention in another direction, was beaten and tortured, consequently, those who could have revealed the truth were afraid to do so.

Even among the Mohammedans complaints arose that the French Consul was acting in contravention to their law, and a feeling gradually grew that a great injustice was being committed—that the Jews were innocent. Few dared allow this in the first fever of popular excitement, but nevertheless it awoke and spread.

At first the Austrian Consul had been subjected not to annoyance only, but to danger of life, so violent had been the popular feeling against him because of the protection he accorded to one of the accused. Fortunately Herr Merlato was a man of pluck. He was an old soldier who had distinguished himself as a marine officer. He not only resolutely protected young Picciotto, but he did his utmost to hinder the proceedings of Ratti-Menton; he invoked the assistance of the representatives of the other European Powers, and finally every Consul, except the French, agreed to unite with him in representations to their governments of the iniquitous proceedings of Ratti-Menton, and to use their influence with the Egyptian authorities to obtain the release of the unhappy accused.

The bastinadoes and tortures now ceased. Merlato obtained the release of several of those who were in confinement; and finally the only Jews who remained in prison were the brothers Arari, Mussa Salonichi, and the renegade Abul Afia. Of the supposed murderers of the servant only the brothers Farhi were still held in chains.

Matters were in this condition when the news of what had taken place at Damascus reached Europe and set all the Jews in commotion. Every effort was made by them, in Vienna, Leipzig, Paris and London, indeed in all the great cities of Europe, to convince the public of the absurdity of the charge, and to urge the governments to interfere in behalf of the sufferers.

Finally all the representatives of the European governments at Alexandria, with the exception of the French, remonstrated with Mohamed Ali. They demanded that the investigation should be begun *de novo*; the French Consul-General, M. Cochelet, alone objected. But the action of the Jews of Europe had more influence with Mohamed Pacha than the representations of the Consuls. The house of Rothschild had taken the matter up, and Sir Moses Montefiore started from London, and M. Cremieux from Paris as a diplomatic embassy to the Viceroy at Alexandria to convince him, by such means as is most efficacious to an Oriental despot, of the innocence of the accused at Damascus.

The arguments these delegates employed were so extremely satisfactory to the mind of Mohamed Pacha, that he quashed the charges against the Jews of Damascus, in spite of the vehement protest of M. Cochelet, the representative of France. When the Viceroy issued a firman ordering the incarcerated Jews to be discharged as innocent and suffered to abide in peace, M. Cochelet strove in vain to have the firman qualified or altered into a pardon.

Thus ended one of the most scandalous cases of this century. Unfortunate, innocent men were tortured and put to death for a crime that had never been proved. That the two Europeans had been murdered was merely matter of conjecture. No bodies had been found. There was no evidence worth a rush against the accused, and no motive adduced deserving of grave consideration. "What inhumanities were committed during the eight months of this persecution," wrote Herr Von Hailbronner, "will never be wholly known. But it must call up a blush of shame in the face of an European to remember that Europeans provoked, favoured and stimulated it to the last."

AUTHORITIES

"Morgenland und Abendland," by Herr Von Hailbronner,—who, as already mentioned, was present in Damascus through part of the time. "Damascia," by C. H. Löwenstein, Rödelheim, 1840. Reports and debates in the English Parliament at the time. The recently published Diaries of Sir Moses Montefiore, 2 vols., 1890; his Centenal Biography, 1884, vol. I., p. 213-288; and the article summing up the whole case in "Der Neue Pitaval," by Dr. J. C. Hitzig and Dr. W. Häring, 1857, Vol. I.

V. — *SOME ACCUSATIONS AGAINST JEWS*

THE story just given of the atrocious treatment of the Jews of Damascus on a false accusation naturally leads to a brief sketch of their treatment in the Middle Ages on similar charges. Not, indeed, that we can deal with all of the outrages committed on the sons of Abraham, Isaac, and Jacob—that would require volumes—but only notice some of those which they have had to suffer on the same or analogous false charges.

These false accusations range under three heads:—
1. They have been charged with poisoning the wells when there has been an outbreak of plague and malignant fever.
2. They have been charged with stealing the Host and with stabbing it.
3. Lastly, with having committed murders in order to possess themselves of Christian blood, to mingle with the dough wherewith to make their Paschal cakes.

We will leave the first case on one side altogether, and as we have already considered one instance—not by any means the last case of such an accusation levied against them in Europe—we will take it before we come to the instances of their being accused of stealing the Host.

But *why* should they be supposed to require Christian blood? One theory was that by common participation in it, the Jewish community was closer bound together; another, that it had a salutary medicinal effect. That is to say, having made up their minds in the Middle Ages that Jews did sacrifice human beings and drink their blood, they beat about for the explanation, and caught at any wild theory that was proposed.[4]

[4] Antonius Bonfinius: Rer. Hungaricarum Dec., v. 1., 3, gives *four* reasons. Thomas Cantipratensis, Lib. II., c. 29, gives another and preposterous one, not to be quoted even in Latin.

John Dubravius in his Bohemian History, under the year 1305, relates: "On Good Friday the Jews committed an atrocious crime against a Christian man, for they stretched him naked to a cross in a concealed place, and then, standing round, spat on him, beat him, and did all they could to him which is recorded of their having done to Christ. This atrocious act was avenged by the people of Prague upon the Jews, with newly-invented punishments, and of their property that was confiscated, a monument was erected." But there were cases earlier than this. Perhaps the earliest is that of S. William of Norwich, in 1144; next, S. Richard of Paris, 1179; then S. Henry of Weissemburg, in Alsace, in 1220; then S. Hugh of Lincoln, in 1255, the case of which is recorded by Matthew Paris. A woman at Lincoln lost her son, a child eight years old. He was found in a well near a Jew's house. The Jew was arrested, and promised his life if he would accuse his brethren of the murder. He did so, but was hanged nevertheless. On this accusation ninety-two of the richest Jews in Lincoln were arrested, their goods seized to replenish the exhausted Royal exchequer; eighteen were hung forthwith, the rest were reserved in the Tower of London for a similar fate, but escaped through the intervention of the Franciscans, who, says Matthew Paris, were bribed by the Jews of England to obtain their release. On May 15th, 1256, thirty-five of the wretched Jews were released. We are not told what became of the remaining thirty-nine, whether they had been discharged as innocent, or died in prison. The story of little Hugh has been charmingly told in Chaucer's Canterbury Tales.

A girl of seven years was found murdered at Pforzheim, in 1271; the Jews were accused, mobbed, maltreated, and executed. In 1286, a boy, name unknown, disappeared in Munich, with the same results to the Jews. In 1292, a boy of nine, at Constance—same results. In 1303 "the perfidious Jews, accustomed to the shedding of Christian blood," says Siffrid, priest of Meisen, in 1307, "cruelly murdered a certain scholar, named Conrad, son of a knight of Weissensee, in Thuringia, after that they had tortured him, cut all his sinews, and opened his veins. This took place before Easter. The Almighty, who is glorious in His Saints, however did not suffer the murder of the innocent boy to remain concealed, but destroyed the murderers, and adorned the martyrdom of their innocent victim with miracles. For when the said Jews had taken the body of the lad to many places in Thuringia to bury it secretly, by God's disposition they were always foiled in their attempt to make away with it. Wherefore, returning to Weissensee, they hung it to a vine. Then the truth having been revealed, the soldiers rushed out of the castle, and the citizens rose together with the common people, headed by Frederick, son of Albert Landgrave of Thuringia, and killed the Jews tumultuously."

The story of St. Werner, the boy murdered by the Jews in 1287, at Wesel, on the Rhine, and buried at Bacharach, is well known. The lovely chapel erected over his body is now a ruin. But Werner was not the only boy martyred by the Jews on the Rhine. Another was St. Johanettus of Siegburg.

St. Andrew of Heiligenwasser, near Innsbrück, is another case, in 1462; St. Ludwig of Ravensburg, in 1429, again another. Six boys were said to have been murdered by Jews at Ratisborn, in 1486; and several cases come to us out of Spanish history. In Poland, in 1598, in the village of Swinarzew, near Lositz, lived a peasant, Matthias Petrenioff, with his wife, Anna. They had several children, among them a boy named Adalbert. One day in Holy Week the boy was in the fields ploughing with his father. In the evening he was sent home, but instead of going home directly, he turned aside to visit the village of Woznik, in which lived a Jew, Mark, who owned a pawnshop, and had some mills. The son of Mark, named Aaron, and the son-in-law, Isaac, overtook the boy as they were returning to Wosnik in their cart and took him up into it.

As the child did not return home, his father went in search of him, and hearing that he had been seen in the cart between the two Jews, he went to the house of Mark and inquired for him. Mark's wife said she had not seen him. The peasant now became frightened. He remembered the stories that floated about concerning the murder of Christian children by Jews, and concluded that his boy had been put to death by Mark and his co-religionists. At length the body of the child was discovered in a pond, probably gnawed by rats—but the marks on the body were at once supposed to be due to the weapons of the Jews. Immense excitement reigned in the district, and finally two servants of the Jews, both Christians, one Athanasia, belonging to the Greek Church, and another, Christina, a Latin, confessed that their masters had murdered the boy. He had been concealed in a cellar till the eve of the Passover, when the chief Jews of the district had been assembled, and the boy had been bled to death in their presence. The blood was put into small phials and each Jew provided with one at least. This led to a general arrest of the Jews, when the rack produced the requisite confession. Isaac, son-in-law of Mark, in whose house the butchery was said to have taken place, declared under torture that the Jews partook of the blood of Christians in bread, and also in wine, but he professed to be unable to account for the custom. Filled, however, with remorse for having thus falsely accused his people and his relatives, he hung himself in prison. Mark and Aaron were condemned to be torn to pieces alive; and, of course, the usual spoliation ensued. We have the account of this atrocious judicial murder from the pen of a Jesuit, Szembeck, who extracted the particulars from the acts of the court of Lublin, in which the case was tried, and from those drawn up by order of the bishop of the diocese of Luz, in which the murder occurred, and who obtained or sanctioned a canonization of the boy-martyr.

Another still more famous case is that of S. Simeon, of Trent, in 1475, very full details of which are given in the Acta Sanctorum of the Bollandists, as the victim was formally canonized by Pope Benedict XIV., and the Roman Martyrology asserts the murder by the Jews in these terms:—

"At Trent (on March 24th) the martyrdom of S. Simeon, a little child, cruelly slain by the Jews, who was glorified afterwards by several miracles."

The story as told and approved at the canonization was as follows: On Tuesday, in Holy Week, 1475, the Jews met to prepare for the approaching Passover, in the house of one of their number, named Samuel; and it was agreed between three of them, Samuel, Tobias, and Angelus, that a child should be crucified, as an act of revenge against the Christians who cruelly maltreated them. Their difficulty, however, was how to get one. Samuel sounded his servant Lazarus, and attempted to bribe him into procuring one, but the suggestion so scared the fellow that he ran away. On the Thursday, Tobias undertook to get the boy, and going out in the evening, whilst the people were in church, he prowled about till he found a child sitting on the threshold of his father's door, aged twenty-nine months, and named Simeon. The Jew began to coax the little fellow to follow him, and the boy, after being lured away, was led to the house of Samuel, whence during the night he was conveyed to the synagogue, where he was bled to death, and his body pierced with awls.

All Friday the parents sought their son, but found him not. The Jews, alarmed at the proceedings of the magistrates, who had taken the matter up, consulted together what was to be done. It was resolved to put the body back into its clothes and throw it into the stream that ran under Samuel's window, but which was there crossed by a grating. Tobias was to go to the bishop and magistrates and inform them that a child's body was entangled in the grate. This was done. Thereupon John de Salis, the bishop, and James de

Sporo, the governor, went to see the spot, had the body removed, and conveyed to the cathedral. As, according to popular superstition, blood was supposed to flow from the wound when a murderer drew near, the officers of justice were cautioned to observe the crowds as they passed.

It was declared that blood exuded as Tobias approached. On the strength of this, the house of Samuel and the synagogue were examined, and it is asserted that blood and other traces of the butchery were found. The most eminent physicians were called to investigate the condition of the corpse, and they pronounced that the child had been strangled, and that the wounds were due to stabs. The popular voice now accusing the Jews, the magistrates seized on them and threw them into prison, and on the accusation of a renegade more than five of the Jews were sentenced to death. They were broken on the wheel and then burnt. The body of the child is enshrined at Trent, and a basin of the blood preserved as a relic in the cathedral.

This must suffice for instances of accusations of murder for religious purposes brought against the Jews, in every case false. Another charge brought against them was Sacrilege. Fleury in his Ecclesiastical History gives one instance. "In the little town of Pulca, in Passau, a layman found a bloody Host before the house of a Jew, lying in the street upon some straw. The people thought that this Host was consecrated, and washed it and took it to the priest, that it might be taken to the church, where a crowd of devotees assembled, concluding that the blood had flowed miraculously from wounds dealt it by the Jews. On this supposition, and without any other examination, or any other judicial procedure, the Christians fell on the Jews, and killed several of them; but wiser heads judged that this was rather for the sake of pillage than to avenge a sacrilege. This conjecture was justified by a similar event, that took place a little while before at Neuburg, in the same diocese, where a certain clerk placed an unconsecrated Host steeped in blood in a church, but confessed afterwards before the bishop that he had dipped this Host in blood for the purpose of raising hostility against the Jews."[5]

[5] Fleury, Hist. Eccl., vi. p. 110.

In 1290, a Jew named Jonathan was accused in Paris of having thrown a Host into the Seine. It floated. Then he stabbed it with his knife, and blood flowed. The Jew was burnt alive, and the people clamored for a general persecution of the Hebrews.

In Bavaria, in 1337, at Dechendorf, some Hosts were discovered which the Jews had stabbed. The unhappy Hebrews were burnt alive.

In 1326, a Jew convert, a favourite of Count William the Good, of Flanders, was accused of having struck an image of the Madonna, which thereupon bled. The Jew was tortured, but denied the accusation. Then he was challenged to a duel by a fanatic. He, wholly unaccustomed to the use of weapons, succumbed. That sufficed to prove his guilt. He was burnt.

In 1351, a Jew convert was accused, at Brussels, of having pretended, on three occasions, to communicate, in order that he might send the Hosts to his brethren at Cologne, who stabbed them, and blood flowed.

The traveller who has been in Brussels must certainly have noticed the painted windows all down the nave of S. Gudule, in the side aisles, to left and right. They represent, in glowing colours, the story of the miraculous Hosts preserved in the chancel to the north of the choir, where seven red lamps burn perpetually before them.

The story is as follows: In 1370, a rich Jew of Enghien bribed a converted Hebrew, named John of Louvain, for 60 pieces of gold, to steal for him some Hosts from the Chapel of S. Catherine. Hardly, however, had the Jew, Jonathan, received the wafers, before he was attacked by robbers and murdered. His wife, alarmed, and thinking that his death was due to the sacrilege, resolved to get rid of the wafers. It may have been remarked in the stories of murders by Jews, that they were represented as finding great difficulty in getting rid of the dead bodies. In these stories of sacrilege, no less difficulty was encountered in causing the disappearance of the Hosts. Moreover, the Jews invariably proceeded in the most roundabout and clumsy way, inviting discovery. The widow of the murdered Jonathan conveyed the Hosts to the synagogue at Brussels. There, on Good Friday, the Jews took advantage of the Hosts to stab them with their knives, in mockery of Christ and the Christian religion. But blood squirted from the transfixed wafers. In terror, they also resolved to get rid of the miraculous Hosts, and found no better means of so doing than bribing a renegade Jewess, named Catharine, to carry them to Cologne. They promised her twenty pieces of gold for her pains. She took the Hosts, but, troubled in conscience, revealed what she had undertaken to her confessor. The ecclesiastical authorities were informed, Catherine was arrested, imprisoned, and confessed. All the Jews dwelling in Brussels were taken up and tortured; but in spite of all torture refused to acknowledge their guilt. However, a chaplain of the prince, a man named Jean Morelli, pretended to have overheard a converted Jew say, "Why do not these dogs make a clean breast? They know that they are guilty." This man was that John of Louvain who had procured the theft of the wafers. He was seized. He at once confessed his participation in the crime. That sufficed. All the accused, he himself included, were condemned to death. They were executed with hideous cruelty; after having had their flesh torn off by red-hot pinchers, they were attached to stakes and burnt alive, on the Vigil of the Ascension, 1370. Every year a solemn procession of the Saint Sacrement de Miracle commemorates this atrocity, or the miracle which led to it.

Unfortunately, there exists no doubt whatever as to the horrible execution of the Jews on the false charge of having stolen the Hosts, but there is very good reason for disbelieving altogether the story of the miracle of the bleeding Hosts.

Now, it is somewhat remarkable that not a word is said about this miracle before 1435, that is to say, for 65 years, by any writer of the period and of the country. The very first mention of it is found in a Papal bull of that date, addressed to the Dean and Chapter of S. Gudule, relative to a petition made by them that, as they wanted money for the erection of a chapel to contain these Hosts, indulgences might be granted to those who would contribute thereto. The Pope granted their request.

Now, it so happens that the official archives at Brussels contains two documents of the date, 1370, relative to this trial. The first of these is the register of the accounts of the receiver-general of the Duke of Brabant. In that are the items of expenditure for the burning of these Jews, a receipt, and the text is as follows: "Item, recepta de bonis dictorum judeorum, postquam combusti fuerant circa ascensionem Domini lxx, quæ defamata fuerant de sacramentis punicè et furtivè acceptis." That is to say, that a certain sum flowed into the Duke's exchequer from the goods of the Jews, burnt for having "guiltily and furtively obtained the Hosts." "Punice" is an odd word, but its signification is clear enough. Now, in 1581, on May 1st, the magistrates of Brussels forbade the exercise of the Catholic religion, in a proclamation in which, when mentioning certain frauds committed by the Roman Church, they speak of "The Sacrament of the Miracle, which," say they, "by documentary evidence can be proved never to have bled nor to have been stabbed." No question—they had seen this entry in which no mention is made of the stabbing—no allusion made to the bleeding. Moreover, in the same archives is the contemporary episcopal letter addressed to the Dean of S. Gudule on the subject of these Hosts. In this document there is no mention made by the bishop of the stabbing or of the miracle. It is stated that the Hosts were obtained by the Jews in order that they might insult and outrage them. It is curious that the letter should not specify their having done this, and done it effectually, with their knives and daggers. Most assuredly, also, had there been any suspicion of a miracle, the bishop would have referred to it in the letter relative to the custody of these very Hosts.

After the whole fable of the stabbing and bleeding had grown up, no doubt applied to these Hosts from a preceding case of accusation against Jews, that of 1351, less than thirty years before, it was thought advisable, if not necessary, to produce some evidence in favour of the story; but as no such evidence was obtainable, it was manufactured in a very ingenious manner. The entry in the register of accounts was published by the Père Ydens, after a notary had been required to collate the text. This notary—his name was Van Asbroek—gave his testimony that he had made an exact and literal transcript of the entry. What he and the Père Ydens gave as their exact, literal transcript was "recepta de bonis dictorum Judoeorum ... quæ defamata fuerant de sacramen*to puncto* et furtive accep*to*." Ingenious, but disingenuous. In the first place they altered "sacramentis" from plural into singular, and then, the adverb *punicè*, "guiltily," into *puncto*, stabbed.

Subsequently, Father Ydens and his notary have been quoted and requoted as authoritative witnesses. However, the document is now in the Archives at Brussels, and has been lithographed from a photograph for the examination of such as have not the means of obtaining access to the original.[6] The last jubilee of this apocryphal miracle was celebrated at Brussels in July, 1870.

[6] Le Jubilé d'un faux Miracle (extrait de la Revue de Belgique), Bruxelles 1870.

VI. — THE COBURG MAUSOLEUM

AT the east end of the garden of the Ducal residence of Coburg is a small, tastefully constructed mausoleum, adorned with allegorical subjects, in which are laid the remains of the deceased dukes. Near the mausoleum rise a stately oak, a clump of rhododendron, a cluster of acacias, and a group of yews and weeping-willows.

The mausoleum is hidden from the palace by a plantation of young pines.

The Castle of Coburg is one of the most interesting and best preserved in Germany. It stands on a height, above the little town, and contains much rich wood-carving of the 15th and 16th centuries. Below the height, but a little above the town, is the more modern residence of the Dukes Ehrenburg, erected in 1626 by the Italian architect Bonallisso, and finished in 1693. It has that character of perverse revolt against picturesqueness that marked all the edifices of the period. It has been restored, not in the best style, at the worst possible epoch, 1816. The south front remains least altered; it is adorned with a handsome gateway, over which is the inscription, "Fried ernährt, Unfried verzehrt"—not easily rendered in English:—

"Peace doth cherish— Strife makes perish."

The princes of Coburg by their worth and kindly behaviour have for a century drawn to them the hearts of their subjects, and hardly a princely house in Germany is, and has been, more respected and loved.

Duke Franz died shortly after the battle of Jena. During his reign, by his thrift, geniality, and love of justice he had won to his person the affections of his people, though they resented the despotic character of his government under his Minister Kretschmann. He was twice married, but left issue only by the second wife, Augusta, a princess of Reuss, who inherited the piety and virtues which seem to be inrooted in that worthy house.

Only a few weeks after her return from Brussels, where she had seen her son, recently crowned King of the Belgians, did the Duchess Augusta of Sachsen-Coburg die in her seventy-sixth year, November 16th, 1831. The admiration and love this admirable princess had inspired drew crowds to visit the body, as it lay in state in the residence at Coburg, prior to the funeral, which took place on the 19th, before day-break, by the light of torches. The funeral was attended by men and women of all classes eager to express their attachment to the deceased, and respect for the family. A great deal was said, and fabled, concerning this funeral. It was told and believed that the Dowager Duchess had been laid in the family vault adorned with her diamond rings and richest necklaces. She was the mother of kings, and the vulgar believed that every royal and princely house with which she was allied had contributed some jewel towards the decoration of her body.

Her eldest son, Ernst I., succeeded his father in 1806 as Duke of Sachsen-Coburg-Saalfeld, and in 1826 became Duke of Sachsen-Coburg-Gotha. The second son, Ferdinand, married in 1816 the wealthiest heiress of Hungary, the Princess Rohary, and his son, Ferdinand, became in 1836 King of Portugal, and his grandson, Ferdinand, by his second son, is the present reigning Prince of Bulgaria.

The third son, Leopold, married Charlotte, only daughter of George IV. of England, and in 1831 became King of the Belgians. Of the five daughters, the eldest was married to the Grand-Duke Constantine of Russia, the second married the Duke of Kent, in 1818, and was the mother of our Queen, Victoria. The third married Duke Alexander of Würtemberg.

Among those who were present at the funeral of the Duchess Augusta was a Bavarian, named Andreas Stubenrauch, an artisan then at Coburg. He was the son of an armourer, followed his father's profession, and had settled at Coburg as locksmith. He was a peculiarly ugly man, with low but broad brow, dark-brown bristly hair, heavy eyebrows and small cunning grey eyes. His nose was a snub, very broad with huge nostrils, his complexion was pale; he had a large mouth, and big drooping underlip. His short stature, his lack of proportion in build, and his uncomely features, gave him the appearance of a half-witted man. But though he was not clever he was by no means a fool. His character was in accordance with his appearance. He was a sullen, ill-conditioned, intemperate man.

Stubenrauch had been one of the crowd that had passed by the bed on which the Duchess lay in state, and had cast covetous eyes at the jewellery with which the body was adorned. He had also attended the funeral, and had come to the conclusion that the Duchess was buried with all the precious articles he had noticed about her, as exposed to view before the burial, and with a great deal more, which popular gossip asserted to have been laid in the coffin with her.

The thought of all this waste of wealth clung to his mind, and Stubenrauch resolved to enter the mausoleum and rob the body. The position of the vault suited his plans, far removed and concealed from the palace, and he made little account of locks and bars, which were likely to prove small hindrances to an accomplished locksmith.

To carry his plan into execution, he resolved on choosing the night of August 18-19, 1832. On this evening he sat drinking in a low tavern till 10 o'clock, when he left, returned to his lodgings, where he collected the tools he believed he would require, a candle and flint and steel, and then betook himself to the mausoleum.

In the first place, he found it necessary to climb over a wall of boards that encircled the portion of the grounds where was the mausoleum, and then, when he stood before the building, he found that to effect an entrance would take him more time and give him more work than he had anticipated.

The mausoleum was closed by an iron gate formed of strong bars eight feet high, radiating from a centre in a sort of semicircle and armed with sharp spikes. He found it impossible to open the lock, and he was therefore obliged to climb over the gate, regardless of the danger of tearing himself on the barbs. There was but a small space between the spikes and the arch of the entrance, but through this he managed to squeeze his way, and so reach the interior of the building, without doing himself any injury.

Here he found a double stout oaken door in the floor that gave access to the vault. The two valves were so closely dovetailed into one another and fitted so exactly, that he found the utmost difficulty in getting a tool between them. He tried his false keys in vain on the lock, and for a long time his efforts to prise the lock open with a lever were equally futile. At length by means of a wedge he succeeded in breaking a way through the junction of the doors, into which he could insert a bar, and then he heaved at one valve with all his might, throwing his weight on the lever. It took him fully an hour before he could break open the door. Midnight struck as the valve, grating on its hinges, was thrown back. But now a new and unexpected difficulty presented itself. There was no flight of steps descending into the vault, as he had anticipated, and he did not know the depth of the lower pavement from where he stooped, and he was afraid to light a candle and let it down to explore the distance.

But Stubenrauch was not a man to be dismayed by difficulties. He climbed back over the iron-spiked gates into the open air, and sought out a long and stout pole, with which to sound the depth, so as to know what measures he was to take to descend. Going into the Ducal orchard, he pulled up a pole to which a fruit tree was tied, and dragged it to the mausoleum, and with considerable difficulty got it through the gateway, which he again surmounted with caution and without injury to himself.

Then, leaning over the opening, holding the pole in both hands, he endeavoured to feel the depth of the vault. In so doing he lost his balance, and the weight of the pole dragged him down, and he fell between two coffins some twelve feet below the floor of the upper chamber. There he lay for some little while unconscious, stunned by his fall. When he came to himself, he sat up, felt about with his hands to ascertain where he was, and considered what next should be done.

Without a moment's thought as to how he was to escape from his position, about the possibility of which he was not in the smallest doubt, knowing as he did his own agility and readiness with expedients, he set to work to accomplish his undertaking. With composure Stubenrauch now struck a light and kindled the candle. When he had done this, he examined the interior of the vault, and the coffins he found there, so as to select the right one. Those of the Duchess Augusta and her husband the late Duke were very much alike, so much so that the ruffian had some difficulty in deciding which was the right one. He chose, however, correctly that which seemed freshest, and he tore off it the black cover. Under this he found the coffin very solid, fastened by two locks, which were so rusted that his tools would not turn in them. He had not his iron bar and other implements with him now; they were above on the floor of the upper chamber. With great difficulty he succeeded at length in breaking one of the hinges, and he was then able to snap the lower lock, whereas that at the top resisted all his efforts. However, the broken hinge and lock enabled him to lift the lid sufficiently for him to look inside. Now he hoped to be able to insert his hand, and remove all the jewellery he supposed was laid there with the dead lady. To his grievous disappointment he saw nothing save the fading remains of the Duchess, covered with a glimmering white mould, that seemed to him to be phosphorescent. The body was in black velvet, the white luminous hands crossed over the breast. Stubenrauch was not the man to feel either respect for the dead or fear of aught supernatural. With both hands he sustained the heavy lid of the coffin as he peered in, and the necessity for using both to support the weight prevented his profane hand from being laid on the remains of an august and pious princess. Stubenrauch did indeed try more than once to sustain the lid with one hand, that he might grope with the other for the treasures he fancied must be concealed there, but the moment he removed one hand the lid crashed down.

Disappointed in his expectations, Stubenrauch now replaced the cover, and began to consider how he might escape. But now—and now only—did he discover that it was not possible for him to get out of the vault into which he had fallen. The pole on which he had placed his confidence was too short to reach to the opening above. Every effort made by Stubenrauch to scramble out failed. He was caught in a trap— and what a trap! Nemesis had fallen on the ruffian at once, on the scene of his crime, and condemned him to betray himself.

Although now for the first time deadly fear came over him, as he afterward asserted, it was fear because he anticipated punishment from men, not any dread of the wrath of the spirits of those into whose domain he had entered. When he had convinced himself that escape was quite impossible, he submitted to the inevitable, lay down between the two coffins and tried to go to sleep; but, as he himself admitted, he was not able to sleep soundly.

Morning broke—it was Sunday, and a special festival at Coburg, for it was the twenty-fifth anniversary of the accession of the Duke, so that the town was in lively commotion, and park and palace were also in a stir.

Stubenrauch sat up and waited in hopes of hearing someone draw near who could release him. About 9 o'clock in the morning he heard steps on the gravel, and at once began to shout for assistance.

The person who had approached ran away in alarm, declaring that strange and unearthly noises issued from the Ducal mausoleum. The guard was apprised, but would not at first believe the report. At length one of the sentinels was despatched to the spot, and he returned speedily with the tidings that there certainly was a man in the vault. He had peered through the grating at the entrance and had seen the door broken open and a crowbar and other articles lying about.

The gate was now opened, and Stubenrauch removed in the midst of an assembled crowd of angry and dismayed spectators. He was removed to prison, tried, and condemned to eighteen months with hard labour.

That is not the end of the story. After his discharge, Stubenrauch never settled into regular work. In 1836 he was taken up for theft, and again on the same charge in 1844. In the year 1854 he was discovered dead in a little wood near his home; between the fingers of his right hand was a pinch of snuff, and in his left hand a pistol with which he had blown out his own brains. In his pockets were found a purse and a brandy bottle, both empty.

VII. — JEAN AYMON

JEAN AYMON was born in Dauphiné, in 1661, of Catholic parents. He studied in the college of Grenoble. His family, loving him, neglected nothing which might contribute to the improvement of his mind, and the professors of Grenoble laboured to perfect their intelligent pupil in mathematics, languages, and history.

From Grenoble, Aymon betook himself to Turin, where he studied theology and philosophy. But there was one thing neither parents nor professors were able to implant in the young man—a conscience. He was thoroughly well versed in all the intricacies of moral theology and the subtleties of the school-men; he regarded crime and sin as something deadly indeed, but deadly only to other persons. Theft was a mortal sin to every one but himself. Truth was a virtue to be strictly inculcated, but not to be practised in his own case.

His parents, thinking he would grow out of this obliquity of moral vision, persisted in their scheme of education for the lad—probably the very worst which, with his peculiar bent of mind, they could have chosen for him. Having finished his studies at Turin, his evil star led him to Rome, where his talents soon drew attention to him, and Hercules de Berzet, Bishop of Saint Jean de Maurienne, in Savoy, named him chaplain, and had him ordained, by brief of Innocent XI., before the age fixed by the Council of Trent, "because of the probity of his life, his virtues and other merits!"—such were the reasons.

Shortly after his installation as chaplain to the bishop, his patron entrusted him with a delicate case. De Berzet had lately been deep in an intrigue to obtain a cardinal's hat. He had been disappointed, and he was either bent on revenge, or, perhaps, hoped to frighten the Pope into giving him that which he had solicited in vain. He set to work, raking up all the scandal of the Papal household, and acting the spy upon all the movements of the familiars of the court. After a very little while, this worthy prelate had succeeded in gathering together enough material to make all the ears in Europe tingle, and this was put into the hands of the young priest to work into form for publication.

As Aymon looked through these scandalous memoirs, he made his own reflections. "The publication of this will raise a storm, undoubtedly; but the first who will perish in it will be my patron, and all who sail in his boat." Aymon noticed that M. de Camus, Bishop of Grenoble, was most compromised by the papers in his hands, and would be most interested in their suppression. Aymon, without hesitation, tied up the bundle, put it in his pocket, and presented himself before the bishop, ready to make them over to him for a consideration. He was well received, as may be supposed, and in return for the papers was given a living in the diocese. But this did not satisfy the restless spirit of Aymon; he had imbibed a taste for intrigue, and there was no place like the Eternal City for indulging this taste. He was, moreover, dissatisfied with his benefice, and expected greater rewards for the service he had done to the Church. Innocent XI. received him well, and in 1687 appointed him his protonotary. Further he did not advance. At the Papal Court he made his observations, and whether it was that he was felt to be somewhat of a spy, or through some intrigue, his star began to set, when Aymon, too well aware that a falling man may sink very low, suddenly fled from Rome, crossed the border into Switzerland, and in a few days was a convert to the straitest sect of the Calvinists. But the Swiss are poor, and their ministers are in comfortable, though not lucrative positions. Holland was the paradise of Calvinism, and to Holland Aymon repaired. Here he obtained a cure of importance, and married a lady of rank.

But even now, Aymon was not satisfied. Among the Protestants of the Low Countries there are no bishops, and no man can soar higher than the pulpit of a parish church. Aymon was convinced that he had climbed as high as he could in the Church of Calvin, and that he had a soul for something higher still. His next step was extraordinary enough. He wrote in December, 1705, to M. Clement, of the Bibliothèque du Roi, at Paris, stating that he had in his possession the "Herbal" of the celebrated Paul Hermann, in forty folio volumes, and that he offered it to the King for 3200 livres, a trifle over what it had cost him. He added that he was a renegade priest, who had sought rest in Protestantism, but had found none—nay! he had discovered it to be a hot-bed of every kind of vice, and that he yearned for the Church of his baptism. He hinted that he had made some discoveries of the utmost political importance, and that he would communicate them to the King if he could be provided with a passport.

Clement made inquiries of the superintendent of the Jardin-Royal as to the expediency of purchasing the "Herbal," and received a reply in the negative.

Aymon wrote again, saying little more of the "Herbal," and developing his schemes. He said that he had State secrets to confide to the Ministers of the Crown, besides which, he volunteered to compose a large and important work on the state of Protestantism, "full of proofs so authentic, and so numerous, that, if given to the light of day, as I purpose, it would probably not only restrain all those who meditate seceding from the Roman Church, but also would persuade all those, who are not blinded by their passions, to return to the Catholic faith."

Clement, uncertain what to answer, showed these letters to some clergy of his acquaintance, and, acting on their advice, he presented them to M. de Pontchartrain, who communicated the proposal of Aymon to the King.

A passport was immediately granted, and Aymon left Holland, assuring his congregation that he was going for a little while to Constantinople on important matters of religion.

On his arrival in Paris, he presented himself before M. Clement, to assure him of the fervour of his zeal and the earnestness of his conversion. Clement received him cordially, and took him to Versailles to see M. de Pontchartrain. In this interview Aymon made great promises of being serviceable to the Church and to the State, by the revelations he was about to make; but M. de Pontchartrain treated his protestations very lightly, and handed him over to the Cardinal de Noailles, Archbishop of Paris.

The conference with the cardinal was long. The archbishop addressed a homily to the repentant sinner, who listened with hands crossed on his breast, his eyes bent to earth, and his cheeks suffused with tears. Aymon sighed forth that he had quitted the camp of the Amalekites for ever, and that he was determined to turn against them their own weapons. Clement, who was present, now stepped forward and reminded the prelate that Aymon had abandoned a lucrative situation, at the dictates of conscience, and that though he might, of course, expect to be rewarded hereafter, still that remuneration in this life would not interfere with these future prospects. The cardinal quite approved of this sentiment, and promised to see what he could do for the convert. In the meantime, he wished Aymon to spend a retreat in some religious house, where he could meditate on the error of his past life, and expiate, as far as in him lay, his late delinquencies by rigorous penances. Aymon thanked the cardinal for thus, unasked, granting him the request which was uppermost in his thoughts, and then begged to be allowed the use of the Royal Library, in which to pursue his theological researches, and to examine the documents which were necessary for the execution of his design of writing a triumphant vindication of the Catholic faith, and a complete exposure of the abominations of Protestantism. M. Clement readily accorded this, at the request of the archbishop, and Jean Aymon was sent to the seminary of the Missions Etrangères.

Aymon now appeared as a model penitent. He spent a considerable part of the night in prayer before the altar, he was punctual in his attendance on all the public exercises of religion, and his conversation, morning, noon, and night, was on the errors and disorders of the Calvinist Church. When not engaged in devotions, he was at the library, where he was indefatigable in his research among manuscripts which could throw light on the subject upon which he was engaged. Indeed, his enthusiasm and his zeal for discoveries wearied the assistants. Clement himself was occupied upon the catalogues, and was unable to dance attendance on Aymon; and the assistants soon learned to regard him as a bookworm who would keep them on the run, supplying him with fresh materials, if they did not leave him to do pretty much what he liked.

Time passed, and Aymon heard no more of the reward promised by the cardinal. He began to murmur, and to pour his complaints into the reluctant ear of Clement, who soon became so tired of hearing them, that the appearance of Aymon's discontented face in the library was a signal for him to plead business and hurry into another apartment. Aymon declared that he should most positively publish nothing till the king or the cardinal made up to him the losses he had endured by resigning his post in Holland.

All of a sudden, to Clement's great relief, Aymon disappeared from the library. At first he was satisfied to be freed from him, and made no inquiries; but after a while, hearing that he had also left the Missions Etrangères, he made search for the missing man. He was nowhere to be found.

About this time Aymon's congregation at the Hague were gratified by the return of their pastor, not much bronzed by exposure to the sun of Constantinople, certainly, but with his trunks well-stocked with valuable MSS.

A little while after, M. Clement received the following note from a French agent resident at the Hague:—

"Information is required relative to a certain Aymon, who says that he was chaplain to M. le Cardinal de Camus, and apostolic protonotary. After having lived some while at the Hague, whither he had come from Switzerland, where he had embraced the so-called Reformed religion, he disappeared, and it was ascertained that he was at Paris, whither he had taken an Arabic Koran in MS., which he had stolen from a bookseller at the Hague. He has only lately returned, laden with spoils—thefts, one would rather say, which he must have made at Paris, where he has been spending five or six months in some publicity.... He has with him the Acts of the last Council of Jerusalem held by the Greeks on the subject of Transubstantiation, and some other documents supposed to be stolen from the Bibliothèque du Roi. The man has powerful supporters in this country.—March 10, 1707."

The "Council of Jerusalem" was one of the most valuable MSS. of the library—and it was in the hands of Aymon! Clement flew to the cabinet where this inestimable treasure was preserved under lock and key. The cabinet was safely enough locked—but alas! the MS. was no longer there.

A few days after, Clement heard that Aymon had crossed the frontier with several heavy boxes, which, on inquiry, proved to be full of books. What volumes were they? The collections in the Royal Library consisted of 12,500 MSS. The whole had to be gone through. It was soon ascertained that another missing book was the original Italian despatches and letters of Carlo Visconti, Apostolic Nuncio at the Council of Trent.

There was no time to be lost. Clement wrote to the Hague to claim the stolen volumes, and to institute legal proceedings for their recovery, before the collection could be dispersed, and he appointed, with full powers, William de Voys, bookseller at the Hague, to seize the two volumes said to be in the possession of Aymon.

A little while after some more MSS. volumes were missed; they were "The Italian Letters of Prospero S Croce, Nuncio of Pius IV," "The Embassy of the Bishop of Angoulême to Rome in 1560-4," "Le Registre des taxes de la Chancellerie Romaine," "Dialogo politico sopra i tumulti di Francia," nine Chinese MSS., a copy of the Gospels of high antiquity in uncial characters, another copy of the Gospels, no less valuable, and the Epistles of S. Paul, also very ancient.

Shortly after this, two Swiss, passing through the Hague, were shown by Aymon some MSS. which agreed with those mentioned as lost from the Royal Library; but besides these, they saw numerous loose sheets, inscribed with letters of gold, and apparently belonging to a MS. of the Bible. Clement had now to go through each MS. in the library and find what had been subtracted from them. Fourteen sheets were gone from the celebrated Bible of S. Denys. From the Pauline Epistles and Apocalypse, a MS. of the seventh century, and one of the most valuable treasures of the library, thirty-five sheets had been cut. There were other losses of less importance.

Whilst Clement was making these discoveries, De Voys brought an action against Aymon for the recovery of the "Council of Jerusalem" and the "Letters of Visconti."

Jean Aymon was not, however, a man to be despoiled of what he had once got. He knew his position perfectly, and he knew the temper of those around him. He was well aware that in order to gain his cause he had only to excite popular passion. His judges were enemies to both France and Catholicism, he had but to make them believe that a plot was formed against him by French Papists for obtaining possession of certain MSS. which he had, and which contained a harvest of scandals and revelations overwhelming to Catholics, and he knew that his cause was safe.

He accordingly published a defence, bearing the following title:—"Letter of the Sieur Aymon, Minister of the Holy Gospel, to M. N., Professor of Theology, to inform people of honour and savants of the extraordinary frauds of certain Papistical doctors and of the vast efforts they are now making, along with some perverted Protestants, who are striving together to ruin, by their impostures, the Sieur Aymon, and to deprive him of several MSS., &c."—La Haye, dated 1707. Aymon in his pamphlet took high moral ground. He was not pleading his own cause. Persecuted, hunted down by Papists, by enemies of the Republic and of the religion of Christ, he scorned their calumnies and despised their rage. He would bow under the storm, he would endure the persecution cheerfully—for "Blessed are those that are persecuted for righteousness' sake;" but higher interests were at stake than his own fair fame. For himself he cared little; for the Protestant faith he cared everything. If the Papists obtained their suit, they would wrest from his grasp documents most compromising to themselves. They would leave no stone unturned to secure them—they *dare not* leave them in the hands of a Protestant pastor. Their story of the "Acts of the Council of Jerusalem" was false. They said that it had been obtained by Olier de Nanteuil, Ambassador of France at Constantinople, in 1672, and had been transmitted to Paris, where Arnauld had seen and made use of it in preparing his great work on the "Perpetuity of the Faith." They further said that the Bibliothèque du Roi had obtained it in 1696. On the other hand, Aymon asserted that Arnauld had falsified the text in his treatise on the "Perpetuity of the Faith," and that, not daring to let his fraud appear, he had never given the MS. to the Royal Library, but had committed it to a Benedictine monk of S. Maur, who had assisted him in falsifying it and making an incorrect translation. This monk would never have surrendered the MS. but that conscience had given him no rest till he had transmitted it to one who would know how to use it aright. He, Aymon, had solemnly promised never to divulge the name of this monk, and even though he and the Protestant cause were to suffer for it, that promise should be held sacred. He challenged the library of the King to prove its claim to the "Council of Jerusalem!" All books in the Bibliothèque du Roi have the seal of the library on them. This volume had three seals—that of the Sultan, that of the Patriarch of Jerusalem, and that of Olier de Nanteuil; but he defied any one to see the library mark on its cover, or on any of its sheets. Aymon wound up his audacious pamphlet by prophesying that the Papists of France would not be satisfied with this claim, but would advance many others, for they knew that in his hands were documents of the utmost importance to them to conceal. Aymon was too clever for Clement: he had mixed up truth with fiction in such a way that the points which Clement had to admit tended to make even those who were not bigoted hesitate about condemning Aymon.

Clement replied to this letter by stating the whole story of Aymon's deception of the Cardinal de Noailles and others. With regard to the "Council of Jerusalem," it was false that it had ever been in a Benedicient monastery. "It is true," he said, "that in the Monastery of S. Germain-des-Prés there are documents relating to the controversies between the Catholics and Greek schismatics, but they are all in French." He produced an attestation, signed by the prior, to the effect that the MS. in question had never been within the walls of his monastery. Clement was obliged to allow that a Benedictine monk had been employed by Arnauld to translate the text of the Council; he even found him out, his name was Michel Foucquère; he was still alive, and the librarian made him affirm in writing that he had restored the volume, on the completion of his translation, to Dom Luc d'Achery. Clement sent a copy of the register in the library, which related how and when the volume had come into the possession of the King. It was true that it bore no library seal, but that was through an oversight.

Aymon wrote a second pamphlet, exposing Clement more completely, pointing out the concessions he was obliged to make, and finally, in indignant terms, hurling back on him the base assertion made to injure him in the eyes of an enlightened Protestant public, that he had ever treated with the government or clergy of Paris relative to a secession to the ranks of Popery. But that he had been to Paris; that he had met the Cardinal Archbishop, he admitted; but on what ground? He had met him and twenty-four prelates besides, gathered in solemn conclave, and had lifted up his voice in testimony against them; had disputed with them, and, with the Word of God in his mouth, had put them all to silence! No idea of his ever leaving the reformed faith had ever entered his head. No! he had been on a mission to the Papists of France, to open their eyes and to convert them.

The news of the robbery had, however, reached the ears of the King, Louis XIV., and he instructed M. de Torcy to demand on the part of Government the restitution of the stolen MSS. M. de Torcy first wrote to a M. Hennequin at Rotterdam, who replied that Aymon had justified himself before the Council of State from the imputations cast upon him. He had been interrogated, not upon the theft committed in

Paris, but on his journey to France. Aymon had proved that this expedition had been undertaken with excellent intentions, and had been attended with supreme success, since he had returned laden with manuscripts the publication of which would cause the greatest confusion in the Catholic camp. Hennequin added, that after having been deprived of his stipend, as suspected, on it having been ascertained that he had visited Paris instead of Constantinople, Aymon, having cleared his character, had recovered it. Such was the first result of the intervention of Louis XIV. in this affair.

"The stamp of the Royal Library is on all the MSS., except the 'Council of Jerusalem,'" said Clement. "Let the judges insist on examining the books in the possession of Aymon, and all doubt as to the theft will be removed."

But this the judges refused to do.

It was pretended that Aymon was persecuted; it was the duty of the Netherland Government to protect a subject from persecution. He had made discovries, and the Catholics dreaded the publication of his discoveries, therefore a deep plot had been laid to ruin him.

Aymon had now formed around him a powerful party, and the Calvinist preachers took his side unanimously. It was enough to read the titles of the books stolen to be certain that they contained curious details on the affairs which agitated Catholics and Protestants from the sixteenth century.

All that the Dutch authorities cared for now was to find some excuse for retaining these important papers, and the inquiry was mainly directed to the proceedings of Aymon in France. If, as it was said, he had gone thither to abjure Calvinism and betray his brethren, he deserved reprimand, but if, on the other hand, he had penetrated the camp of the enemy to defy it, and to witness a good confession in the heart of the foe, he deserved a crown. Clement, to display Aymon in his true colours, acting on the advice of the Minister, sent copies of Aymon's letters. It was not thought that the good faith of the French administration would be doubted. Aymon swore that the letters were not his own, but that they had been fabricated by the Government; and he offered to stake his head on the truth of what he said. At the same time he dared De Torcy to produce the originals.

He had guessed aright: he knew exactly how far he could go. The Dutch court actually questioned the good faith of these copies, and demanded the originals. This, as Aymon had expected, was taken by De Torcy as an insult, and all further communication on the subject was abruptly stopped. It was a clever move of Aymon. He inverted by one bold stroke the relative positions of himself and his accuser: the judges at the Hague required M. de Torcy to re-establish his own honour before proceeding with the question of Aymon's culpability. In short, they supposed that one of the Ministers of the Crown, for the sake of ruining a Protestant refugee, had deliberately committed forgery.

The matter was dropped. After a while Aymon published translations of some of the MSS. in his possession, and those who had expected great results were disappointed. In the meantime poor Clement died, heart-broken at the losses of the library committed to his care.

At last the Dutch Government, after the publication of Aymon's book, and after renewed negotiation, restored the "Council of Jerusalem" to the Bibliothèque du Roi. It still bears traces of the mutilations and additions of Aymon.

In 1710, the imposter published the letters of Prospero S. Croce, which he said he had copied in the Vatican, but which he had in fact stolen from the Royal Library. In 1716 he published other stolen papers. Clement was succeeded by the Abbé de Targny, who made vain attempts to recover the lost treasures. The Abbé Bignon succeeded De Targny, and he discovered fresh losses. Aymon had stolen Arabic books as well as Greek and Italian MSS. There was no chance of recovering the lost works through the courts of law, and Bignon contented himself with writing to Holland, England, and Germany to inquire whether any of the MSS. had been bought there.

The Baron von Stocks wrote to say that he had purchased some leaves of the Epistles of S. Paul, some pages of the S. Denis Bible, and an Arabic volume from Aymon for a hundred florins, and that he would return them to the library for that sum. They were recovered in March, 1720.

About the same time Mr. Bentley, librarian to the King of England, announced that some more of the pages from the Epistles of S. Paul were in Lord Harley's library; and that the Duke of Sunderland had purchased various MSS. at the Hague from Aymon. In giving this information to the Abbé Bignon, Mr. Bentley entreated him not to mention the source of his information. M. de Bozé thereupon resolved to visit England and endeavour to recover the MSS. But he was detained by various causes.

In 1729, Earl Middleton offered, on the part of Lord Harley, to return the thirty-four leaves of the Epistles in his possession, asking only in return an acknowledgment sealed with the grand seal. Cardinal Fleury, finding that the Royal signature could hardly be employed for such a purpose, wrote in the King's name a letter to the Earl of Oxford of a flattering nature, and the lost MSS. were restored in September, 1729.

Those in the Sunderland collection have not, I believe, been returned.

And what became of Aymon? In 1718 he inhabited the Chateau of Riswyck. Thence he sent to the brothers Wetstein, publishers at Amsterdam, the proofs of his edition of the letters of Visconti. It appeared in 1719 in two 12mo volumes, under the title "Lettres, Anecdotes, et Mémoires historiques du nonce Visconti, Cardinel Préconisé et Ministre Secret de Pie IV. et de ses créatures." The date of his death is not known.

AUTHORITY

Hauréau, J. Singularités Historiques et Litéraires. Paris, 1881.

VIII. — THE PATARINES OF MILAN
I.

IN the eleventh century, nearly all the clergy in the north of Italy were married.[7] It was the same in Sicily, and it had been the same in Rome,[8] but there the authority and presence of the Popes had sufficed to convert open marriage into secret concubinage.

[7] "Cuncti fere cum publicis uxoribus ... ducebant vitam." "Et ipsi, ut cernitur, sicut laici, palam uxores ducunt."—*Andr. Strum. "Vit. Arialdi."* "Quis clericorum non esset uxoratus vel concubinarius?"—*Andr. Strum. "Vit. S. Joan. Gualberti."*

[8] "Coeperunt ipsi presbyteri et diacones laicorum more uxores ducere suscepsosque filios hæredes relinquere. Nonnulli etiam episcoporum verecund â omni contemptâ, cum uxoribus domo simul in unâ habitare."—*Victor Papa "in Dialog."*

But concubinage did not in those times mean exactly what it means now. A *concubina* was an *uxor* in an inferior degree; the woman was married in both cases with the ring and religious rite, but the children of the concubine could not inherit legally the possessions of their father. When priests were without wives, concubines were tolerated wives without the legal status of wives, lest on the death of the priest his children should claim and alienate to their own use property belonging to the Church. In noble and royal families it was sometimes the same, lest estates should be dismembered. On the death of a wife, her place was occupied by a concubine, and the sons of the latter could not dispute inheritance with the sons of the former. Nor did the Church look sternly on the concubine. In the first Toledian Council a canon was passed with regard to communicating those who had one wife or one concubine;—such were not to be excluded from the Lord's Table,[9] so long only as each man had but one wife or concubine, and the union was perpetual.

[9] "Qui unius mulieris, aut uxoris, aut concubinæ (ut ei placuerit) sit conjunctione contentus."—1st Conc. of Toledo, can. 17. "Hæ quippe, licet nec uxoribus, nec Reginarum decore et privilegiis gaudebant, erant tamen veræ uxores," say the Bollandist Fathers, and add, that it is a vulgar error "Concubinæ appellationem solis iis tribuere, quæ corporis sui usum uni viro commodant, nullo interim legitimo nexu devinctæ."—Acta SS., Jun. T. L. p. 178.

But, though concubinage was universal among the clergy in Italy, at Milan the priests openly, boldly claimed for their wives a position as honourable as could be accorded them; and they asserted without fear of contradiction that their privilege had received the sanction of the great Ambrose himself. Married bishops had been common, and saintly married prelates not unknown. St. Severus of Ravenna had a wife and daughter, and though the late biographer asserts that he lived with his wife as with a sister after he became a bishop, this statement is probably made to get over an awkward fact.[10] When he was about to die, he went to the tomb where his wife and daughter lay, and had the stone removed. Then he addressed them thus—"My dear ones, with whom I lived so long in love, make room for me, for this is my grave, and in death we shall not be divided." Thereupon he descended into the grave, laid himself between his wife and daughter, and died. St. Heribert, Archbishop of Milan, had been a married man with a wife esteemed for her virtues.[11]

[10] It is the same with St. Gregory, Nyssen, Baronius, Alban, Butler, and other modern Hagiographers make this assertion boldly, but there is not a shadow of evidence, in any ancient authorities for his life, that this was the case.

[11] "Hic Archiepiscopus habuit uxorem nobilem mulierem; quæ donavit dotem suam monasterii S. Dionysii, quæ usque hodie Uxoria dicitur."—*Calvaneus Fiamma, sub ann. 1040.*

By all accounts, friendly and hostile, the Lombard priests were married openly, legally, with religious rite, exchange of ring, and notarial deed. There was no shame felt, no supposition entertained that such was an offence.[12]

[12] "Nec vos terreat," writes St. Peter Damiani to the wives of the clergy "quod forte, non dicam fidei, sed perfidiæ vos annulus subarrhavit; quod rata et monimenta dotalia notarius quasi matrimonii jure conscripserit: quod juramentum ad confirmandam quodammodo conjugii copulam utrinque processit. Ignorantes quia pro uniuscujusque fugaci voluptate concubitus mlle annorum negotiantur incendium."

How was this inveterate custom to be broken through? How the open, honest marriage to be perverted into clandestine union? For to abolish it wholly was beyond the power of the Popes and Councils. It was in vain to appeal to the bishops, they sympathised with their clergy. It was in vain to invoke the secular arm; the emperors, the podestas, supported the parish-priests in their contumacious adherence to immemorial privilege.

To carry through the reform on which they were bent, to utterly abolish the marriage of the clergy, the appeal must be made to the people.

In Milan this was practicable, for the laity, at least the lower rabble, were deeply tinged with Patarinism, and bore a grudge against the clergy, who had been foremost in bringing the luckless heretics to the rack and the flames; and one of the most cherished doctrines of the Patarines was the unlawfulness of marriage. What if this anti-connubial prejudice could be enlisted by the strict reformers of the Church, and turned to expend its fury on the clergy who refused to listen to the expostulations of the Holy Father?

The Patarines, whom the Popes were about to enlist in their cause against the Ambrosian clergy, already swarmed in Italy. Of their origin and tenets we must say a word.

It is a curious fact that, instead of Paganism affecting Christianity in the earliest ages of the Church, it was Christianity which affected Paganism, and that not the Greek and Roman idolatry, which was rotten through and through, but the far subtler and more mystical heathenism of Syria, Egypt, Persia, and Mesopotamia. The numerous Gnostic sects, so called from their claim to be the possessors of the true *gnosis*, or knowledge of wisdom, were not, save in the rarest cases, of Christian origin. They were Pagan philosophical schools which had adopted and incorporated various Christian ideas. They worked up Biblical names and notions into the strange new creeds they devised, and, according as they blended more or less of Christian teaching with their own, they drew to themselves disciples of various tempers. Manes, who flourished in the middle of the third century, a temporary and nominal convert to the Gospel, blended some of these elder Gnostic systems with the Persian doctrines of Zoroaster, added to a somewhat larger element of Christianity than his predecessors had chosen to adopt. His doctrines spread and gained an extensive and lasting hold on the minds of men, suppressed repeatedly, but never disappearing wholly, adopting fresh names, emerging in new countries, exhibiting an irrepressible vitality, which confounded the Popes and Churchmen from the third to the tenth centuries.

The tradition of Western Manicheism breaks off about the sixth century; but in the East, under the name of Paulicians, the adherents of Manichean doctrines endured savage persecutions during two whole centuries, and spread, as they fled from the sword and stake in the East, over Europe, entering it in two streams—one by Bulgaria, Servia, and Croatia, to break out in the wild fanaticism of the Taborites under Zisca of the Flail; the other, by way of the sea, inundating northern Italy and Provence. In Piedmont it obtained the name of Patarinism; in Provence, of Albigensianism.

With Oriental Manicheism, the Patarines and Albigenses of the West held that there were two co-equal conflicting principles of good and evil; that matter was eternal, and waged everlasting war against spirit. Their moral life was strict and severe. They fasted, dressed in coarse clothing, and hardly, reluctantly suffered marriage to the weaker, inferior disciples. It was absolutely forbidden to those who were, or esteemed themselves to be, perfect.

Already, in Milan, St Heribert, the married archbishop, had kindled fires, and cast these denouncers of wedlock into them. In 1031 the heretics held the castle of Montforte, in the diocese of Asti. They were questioned: they declared themselves ready to witness to their faith by their blood. They esteemed virginity, and lived in chastity with their wives, never touched meat, and prayed incessantly. They had their goods in common. Their castle stood a siege. It was at length captured by the Archbishop. In the market-place were raised a cross on one side, a blazing pyre on the other. The Patarines were brought forth, commanded to cast themselves before the cross, confess themselves to be heretics, or plunge into the flames. A few knelt to the cross; the greater number covered their faces, rushed into the fire, and were consumed.[13]

[13] Landulf Sen. ii. c. 27.

St. Augustine, in his book on Heresies, had already described these heretics. He, who had been involved in the fascinating wiles of Manicheism, could not be ignorant of them. He calls them Paternians, or Venustians, and says that they regarded the flesh as the work of the devil—that is, of the evil principle, because made of matter.

In the eleventh century, in Lombardy, they are called Patarines, Patrins, or Cathari. Muratori says that they derived their name from the part of the town of Milan in which they swarmed, near the Contrada di Patari; but it is more probable that the quarter was called after them.

In 1074 Gregory VII. in solemn conclave will bless them altogether, by name, as the champions of the Holy See, and of the Truth; in 1179 Alexander III. will anathematise them altogether, as heretics meet to be burned. Frederick II., when seeking reconciliation with Honorius III. and Gregory IX., will be never weary of offering hecatombs of Patarines, in token of his orthodoxy.

Ariald, a native of Cuzago, a village near Milan, of ignoble birth, in deacon's orders, was chosen for the dangerous expedient of enlisting the Patarine heretics against the orthodox but relaxed clergy of that city. Milan, said a proverb, was famous for its clergy; Ravenna for its churches. In morals, in learning, in exact observance of their religious duties, the clergy of Milan were prominent among the priests of Lombardy. But they were all married. The Popes could expect no support from the Archbishop, Guido Vavasour; none from the Emperor Henry IV., then a child. Ariald was a woman-hater from infancy, deeply tinged with Patarinism. We are told that even as a little boy the sight of his sisters was odious to him.[14] He began to preach in Milan in 1057, and the populace was at once set on fire[15] by his sermons. They applauded vociferously his declaration that the married clergy were no longer to be treated as priests, but as "the enemies of God, and the deceivers of souls."

[14] For authorities we have Andrew of Vallombrosa, d. A.D. 1170, a disciple of Ariald. He was a native of Parma. He afterwards went to Florence, where he was mixed up with the riots occasioned by St. John Gualberto in 1063. He joined the Order of Vallombrosa, and became Abbot of Strumi. At least, I judge, and so do the Bollandists, that Andrew of Vallombrosa and Andrew of Strumi are the same.

[15] "Plebs fere universa sic est accensa."

Then up rose from among the mob a clerk named Landulf, a man of loud voice and vehement gesture, and offered to join Ariald in his crusade. The crowd, or, at least, a part of it, enthusiastically cheered; another part of the audience, disapproving, deeming it an explosion of long-suppressed Manicheism, which would meet with stern repression, thought it prudent to withdraw.

A layman of fortune, named Nazarius, offered his substance to advance the cause, and his house as a harbour for its apostles.

The sermon was followed by a tumult. The whole city was in an uproar, and the married clergy were threatened or maltreated by the mob. Guido Vavasour de Velati, the Archbishop, was obliged to interfere. He summoned Ariald and Landulf before him, and remonstrated. "It is unseemly for a priest to denounce priests. It is impolitic for him to stir up tumult against his brethren. Let not brothers condemn brothers, for whose salvation Christ died." Then turning to Landulf, "Why do not you return to your own wife and children whom you have deserted, and live with them as heretofore, and set an example of peace and order? Cast the beam out of thine own eye, before thou pluckest motes out of the eyes of thy brethren. If they have done wrong, reprove them privately, but do not storm against them before all the people." He concluded by affirming the lawfulness of priests marrying, and insisted on the cessation of the contest.[16] Ariald obstinately refused to desist. "Private expostulation is in vain. As for obstinate disorders you apply fire and steel, so for this abuse we must have recourse to desperate remedies."

[16] "Hæc cum Guido placide dixisset; eo finem orationis dixerit, ut sacerdotibus fas esset dicere uxores ducere."—*Alicatus, "Vit. Arialdi."*

He left the Archbishop to renew his appeals to the people. But dreading lest Guido should use force to restrain him, Ariald invoked the support of Anselm de Badagio, Bishop of Lucca, and received promise of his countenance and advocacy at Rome.

Guido Vavasour had succeeded the married Archbishop Heribert in 1040. His election had not satisfied the people, who had chosen, and proposed for consecration, four priests, one of whom the nobles were expected to select. But the nobles rejected the popular candidates, and set up in their place Guido Vavasour, and his nomination was ratified by the Emperor and by the Pope. He was afterwards, as we shall see, charged with having bribed Henry III. to give him the See, but was acquitted of the charge, which was denounced as unfounded by Leo IX. in 1059. The people, in token of their resentment, refused to be present at the first mass he sang. "He is a country bumpkin," said they. "Faugh! he smells of the cow-house."[17] Consequently there was simmering discontent against the Archbishop for Ariald to work upon; he could unite the lower people, whose wishes had been disregarded by the nobles, with the Patarines, who had been haled before ecclesiastical courts for their heresy, in one common insurrection against the clergy and the pontiff.

[17] Arnulf., Gesta Archiepisc. Mediol. ap. Pertz, x. p. 17.

According to Landulf the elder, a strong partisan of the Archbishop, another element of discontent was united to those above enumerated. The clergy of Milan had oppressed the country people. The Church had estates outside of Milan, vine and olive yards and corn-fields. The clergy had been harsh in exacting feudal rights and legal dues.

Ariald, as a native of a country village, knew the temper of the peasants, and their readiness to resent these extortions. Ariald worked upon the country-folk; Landulf, rich and noble, and eloquent in speech, on the town rabble; and the two mobs united against the common enemy.

Anselm de Badagio, priest and popular preacher at Milan, had been mixed up with Landulf and Ariald in the controversy relative to clerical marriage; but to stop his mouth the Archbishop had given him the bishopric of Lucca, in 1057, and had supplied his place as preacher at Milan by seven deacons. Landulf the elder relates that these deacons preached with such success that Anselm, in a fit of jealousy, returned to Milan to listen to their sermons, and scornfully exclaimed, "They may become preachers, but they must first put away their wives."

According to the same authority, Ariald bore a grudge against the Archbishop for having had occasion to rebuke him on account of some irregularity of which he had been guilty. But Landulf the elder is not to be trusted implicitly; he is as bigoted on one side as is Andrew of Strumi on the other.

In the meantime the priests and their wives were exposed to every sort of violence, and "a great horror fell on the Ambrosian clergy." The poor women were torn from their husbands, and driven from the city; the priests who refused to be separated from their companions were interdicted from the altar.[18]

[18] "Sic ab eodem populo sunt persecuta et deleta (clericorum connubia) ut nullus existeret quin aut cogeretur tantum nefas dimittere, vel ad altare non accedere."—*Andr. Strum.*

Landulf was sent to Rome to report progress, and obtain confirmation of the proceedings of the party from the Pope. He reached Piacenza, but was unable to proceed farther; he was knocked down, and finding the way barred by the enemies of his party, returned to Milan. Ariald then started, and eluding his adversaries, arrived safely at Rome. He presented himself before Pope Stephen X., who was under the influence of Hildebrand, and, therefore, disposed to receive him with favour. Stephen bade him return to Milan, prosecute the holy war, and, if need be, shed his blood in the sacred cause.

The appeal to Rome was necessary, as the Archbishop and a large party of the citizens, together with all the clergy, had denounced Ariald and Landulf as Patarines. The fact was notorious that the secret and suspected Manichees in Milan were now holding up their heads and defying those who had hitherto controlled them. The Manichees suddenly found that from proscribed heretics they had been exalted into champions of orthodoxy. It was a satisfactory change for those who had been persecuted to become persecutors, and turn their former tyrants into victims. But now, to the confusion and dismay of the clergy, they found themselves betrayed by the Pope, and at the mercy of those who had old wrongs to resent. Fortified with the blessing of the Pope on his work, his orthodoxy triumphantly established by the supreme authority, Ariald rushed back to Milan, accompanied by papal legates to protect him, and proclaim his mission as divine. He was unmeasured in his denunciations. Dissension fast ripened into civil war. Ariald, at the head of a roaring mob, swept the clergy together into a church, and producing a paper which bound all of them by oath to put away their wives, endeavoured to enforce their subscription.

A priest, maddened to resentment, struck the demagogue in the mouth. This was the signal for a general tumult. The adherents of Ariald rushed through the streets, the alarm bells pealed, the populace gathered from all quarters, and a general hunting down of the married clergy ensued.

"How can the blind lead the blind?" preached Landulf Cotta. "Let these Simoniacs, these Nicolaitans be despised. You who wish to have salvation from the Lord, drive them from their functions; esteem their sacrifices as dogs' dung (*canina stercora*)! Confiscate their goods, and every one of you take what he likes![19] We can imagine the results of such license given to the lowest rabble. The nobles, over-awed, dared not interfere.

[19] Arnulf., *Gesta Ep. Mediol.* ap. Pertz, x. p. 18. It is necessary not to confound Landulf Cotta, the demagogue, with Landulf the elder, the historian, and Landulf the younger, the disciple and biographer of Ariald.

Nor were the clergy of the city alone exposed to this popular persecution. The preachers roved round the country, creating riots everywhere. This led to retaliation, but retaliation of a feeble, harmless sort. A chapel built by Ariald on his paternal estate was pulled down; and the married clergy resentfully talked of barking his chestnut trees and breaking down his vines, but thought better of it, and refrained.

A more serious attempt at revenge was the act of a private individual. Landulf Cotta was praying in a church, when a priest aimed at him with a sword, but without seriously hurting him. A cripple at the church door caught the flying would-be assassin; a crowd assembled, and Landulf with difficulty extricated the priest alive from their hands.

Ariald and Cotta now began to denounce those who had bought their cures of souls, or had paid fees on their institution to them. They stimulated the people to put down simony, as they had put down concubinage. "Cursed is he that withholdeth his hand from blood!" was the fiery peroration of a sermon on this subject by Ariald.

"Landulf Cotta," says Arnulf, "being master of the lay folk, made them swear to combat both simony and concubinage. Presently he forced this oath on the clergy. From this time forward he was constantly followed by a crowd of men and women, who watched around him night and day. He despised the churches, and rejected priests as well as their functions, under pretext that they were defiled with simony. They were called Patari, that is to say, beggars, because the greater part of them belonged to the lowest orders."[20]

[20] Ap. Pertz, l.c., pp. 19, 20.

"What shall we do?" asked a large party at Milan. "This Ariald tells us that if we receive the Holy Sacrament from married or simoniacal priests, we eat our own damnation. We cannot live without sacraments, and he has driven all the priests out of Milan."

The parties were so divided, that those who held with Ariald would not receive sacraments from the priests, the heavenly gift on their altars they esteemed as "dogs' dung;" they would not even join with them, or those who adhered to them, in prayer. "One house was all faithful," says Andrew of Strumi; "the next all unfaithful. In the third, the mother and one son were believing, but the father and the other son were unbelieving; so that the whole city was a scene of confusion and contention."

In 1058 Guido assembled a synod at Fontanetum near Novara, and summoned Ariald and Landulf Cotta to attend it. The synod awaited their arrival for three days, and as they did not come, excommunicated them as contumacious.

Landulf the younger, the biographer of Ariald, says that Pope Stephen X. reversed the sentence of the synod; but this account does not agree with what is related by Arnulf. Landulf the elder confounds the dates, and places the synod in the reign of Alexander II., and says that the Pope adopted a middle course, and sent ambassadors to Milan to investigate the matter. Bonizo of Sutri says the same. All agree that Hildebrand was one of these commissioners. Hildebrand was therefore able to judge on the spot of the results of an appeal to the passions of the people. It is the severest condemnation to his conduct in 1073, to know for certain that he had seen the working of the power he afterwards called out. He then saw how great was that power; he must have been cruelly, recklessly, wickedly indifferent to the crimes which accompanied its invocation. Landulf the elder says that the second commissary was Anselm of Lucca, whilst Bonizo speaks indifferently of the "bishops *a latere*" as constituting the deputation. Guido was not in Milan when it arrived, he did not dare to venture his person in the midst of the people. The ambassadors were received with the utmost respect; they took on themselves to brand the Archbishop as a simoniac and a schismatic, and, according to Landulf, to do many other things which they were not authorised by the Pope to do; so that the dissension, so far from being allayed by their visit, only waxed more furious.

At the end of the year 1058, or the beginning of 1059, the Pope sent Peter Damiani, the harsh Bishop of Ostia, and Anselm, Bishop of Lucca, on a new embassy to Milan.[21] They were received with respect by the Archbishop and clergy; but the pride of the Milanese of all ranks was wounded by seeing the Bishop of Ostia enthroned in the middle, with Anselm of Lucca, the suffragan of Milan, upon his right, and their Archbishop degraded to the left of the Legate, and seated on a stool at his feet. Milan assembled at the ringing of the bells in all the churches, and the summons of an enormous brazen trumpet which shrieked through the streets. The fickle people asked if the Church of St. Ambrose was to be trodden under the foot of the Roman Pontiff. "I was threatened with death," wrote Peter Damiani to Hildebrand, "and many assured me that there were persons panting for my blood. It is not necessary for me to repeat all the remarks the people made on this occasion."

[21] We have a full account of this embassy in a letter of St. Peter Damiani to the Archdeacon Hildebrand (Petri Dam. *Opp.* iii; *Opusc.* v. p. 37), besides the accounts by Bonizo, Arnulf, and Landulf the elder.

But Peter Damiani was not the man to be daunted at a popular outbreak. He placidly mounted the ambone, and asserted boldly the supreme jurisdiction of the chair of St. Peter. "The Roman Church is the mother, that of Ambrose is the daughter. St. Ambrose always recognised that mistress. Study the sacred books, and hold us as liars, if you do not find that it is as I have said."

Then the charges against the clergy were investigated by the legates, and not a single clerk in Milan was found who had not paid a fee on his ordination; "for that was the custom, and the charge was fixed," says the Bishop of Ostia. Here was a difficulty. He could not deprive every priest and deacon in Milan, and leave the great city without pastors. He was therefore obliged to content his zeal with exacting from the bishops a promise that ordination in future should be made gratuitously; and the Archbishop was constrained to deposit on the altar a paper in which he pronounced his own excommunication, in the event of his relaxing his rigour in suppressing the heresy of the Simoniacs and Nicolaitans, by which latter name those who insisted on the lawfulness of clerical marriage were described.

To make atonement for the past, the Archbishop was required to do penance for one hundred years, but to pay money into the papal treasury in acquittal of each year; which, to our simple understanding, looks almost as scandalous a traffic as imposing a fee on all clergy ordained. But then, in the one case the money went into the pocket of the bishops, and in the other into that of the Pope.

The clergy who had paid a certain sum were to be put to penance for five years; those who had paid more, for ten (also to be compensated by a payment to Rome!), and to make pilgrimages to Rome or Tours. After having accomplished this penance they were to receive again the insignia of their offices.

Then Peter Damiani re-imposed on the clergy the oaths forced on them by Ariald, and departed.

The Milanese contemporary historian, Arnulf, exclaims, "Who has bewitched you, ye foolish Milanese? Yesterday you made loud outcries for the priority of a see, and now you trouble the whole organisation of the Church. You are gnats swallowing camels. You say, perhaps, Rome must be honoured because of the Apostle. Well, but the memory of St. Ambrose should deliver Milan from such an affront as has been inflicted on her. In future it will be said that Milan is subject to Rome."[22]

[22] Pertz, x. p. 21.

Guido attended a council held in Rome (April 1059), shortly after this visitation. Ariald also was present, to accuse the Archbishop of favouring simony and concubinage. The legates had dealt too leniently with the scandal. Guido was defended by his suffragans of Asti, Novara, Turin, Vercelli, Alba, Lodi, and Brescia. "Mad bulls, they," says Bonizo; and Ariald was forced to retire, covered with confusion. The Council pronounced a decree that no mercy should be shown to the simoniacal and married clergy.[23] An encyclical was addressed by Nicholas II. to all Christendom, informing it that the Council had passed thirteen canons, one of which prevented a layman from assisting at a mass said by a priest who had a concubine or a *subintroducta mulier*. Priests, deacons, and sub-deacons who should take

278

"publicly" a concubine, or not send away those with whom they lived, were to be inhibited from exercising all ministerial acts and receiving ecclesiastical dues.

[23] "Nulla misericordia habenda est."

On the return of the bishops to their sees, one only of them, Adelmann of Brescia, ventured to publish these decrees. He was nearly torn to pieces by his clergy; an act of violence which greatly furthered the cause of the Patarines.[24]

[24] Bonizo. It is deserving of remark that Bonizo, an ardent supporter of Hildebrand and the reforming party, calls that Papal party by the name of *Patari*, thus showing that it was really made up of the Manichean heretics.

In the same year Pope Nicholas sent legates into different countries to execute, or attempt to execute, the decrees passed against simony and concubinage—as clerical marriage was called. Peter Damiani travelled through several cities of Italy to exhort the clergy to celibacy, and especially to press this matter on the bishops. Peter Damiani was not satisfied with the conduct of the Pope in assuming a stern attitude towards the priests, but overlooking the fact that the bishops were themselves guilty of the same offence. A letter from him to the Pope exists, in which he exhorts him to be a second Phinehas (Numb. xxv. 7), and deal severely with the bishops, without which no real reform could be affected.[25]

[25] *Opp.* t. iii.; *Opusc.* xiii. p. 188.

Anselm de Badagio, Bishop of Lucca, the instigator of Landulf and Ariald, or at least their staunch supporter, was summoned on the death of Nicholas to occupy the throne of St. Peter, under the title of Alexander II. But his election was contested, and Cadalus, an anti-Pope, was chosen by a Council of German and Lombard prelates assembled at Basle. The contests which ensued between the rival Pontiffs and their adherents distracted attention from the question of clerical marriage, and the clergy recalled their wives.

In 1063, in Florence, similar troubles occurred. The instigator of these was St. John Gualberto, founder of the Vallombrosian Order. The offence there was rather simony than concubinage.

The custom of giving fees to those who appointed to benefices had become inveterate, and in many cases had degenerated into the purchase of them. A Pope could not assume the tiara without a lavish largess to the Roman populace. A bishop could not grasp his pastoral staff without paying heavy sums to the Emperor and to the Pope. The former payment was denounced as simony, the latter was exacted as an obligation. But under some of the Emperors the bishoprics were sold to the highest bidder. What was customary on promotion to a bishopric became customary on acceptance of lesser benefices, and no priest could assume a spiritual charge without paying a bounty to the episcopal treasury. When a bishop had bought his throne, he was rarely indisposed to sell the benefices in his gift, and to recoup a scandalous outlay by an equally scandalous traffic. The Bishop of Florence was thought by St. John Gualberto to have bought the see. He was a Pavian, Peter Mediabardi. His father came to Florence to visit his son. The Florentines took advantage of the unguarded simplicity of the old man to extract the desired secret from him.[26]

[26] "Cui Florentini clam insidiantes tentando dicere coeperunt," &c.... "ille utpote simplicissimus homo coepit jurejurando dicere," &c.—*Andrew of Genoa*, c. 62.

"Master Teulo," said they, "had you a large sum to pay to the King for your son's elevation?"

"By the body of St. Syrus," answered the father, "you cannot get a millstone out of the King's house without paying for it."

"Then what did you pay?" asked the Florentines greedily.[27]

[27] "Alacres et avidi rem scisitari."

"By the body of St. Syrus!" replied the old man, "not less than three thousand pounds."

No sooner was the unguarded avowal made, than it was spread through the city by the enemies of the bishop.[28]

[28] For the account of what follows, in addition to the biography by Andrew of Strumi, we have the *Dialogues* of Desiderius of Monte Cassino, lib. iii.

St. John Gualberto took up the quarrel. He appeared in Florence, where he had a monastery dedicated to St. Salvius, and began vehemently to denounce the prelate as a simoniac, and therefore a heretic. His monks, fired by his zeal, spread through the city, and exhorted the people to refuse to accept the sacramental acts of their bishop and resist his authority.

The people broke out into tumult. The bishop appealed to the secular arm to arrest the disorder, and officers were sent to coerce the monks of St. Salvius. They broke into the monastery at night, sought Gualberto, but, unable to find him, maltreated the monks. One received a blow on his forehead which laid bare the bone, and another had his nose and lips gashed with a sword. The monks were stripped, and the monastery fired. The abbot rolled himself in an old cloak extracted from under a bed, where it had been cast as ragged, and awaited day, when the wounds and tears of the fraternity might be exhibited to a sympathising and excitable people. Nor were they disappointed. At daybreak all the town was gathered around the dilapidated monastery, and people were eagerly mopping up the sacred blood that had been shed, with their napkins, thinking that they secured valuable relics. Sympathy with the injured was fanned into frenzied abhorrence of the persecutor.

St. John Gualberto appeared on the scene, blazing with the desire of martyrdom,[29] and congratulated the sufferers on having become confessors of Christ. "Now are ye true monks! But why did ye suffer without me?"

[29] "Martyrii flagrans amore."—*Andr. Strum.*

The secular clergy of Florence were, it is asserted, deeply tainted with the same vice as their bishop. They had all paid fees at their institution, or had bought their benefices. They lived in private houses, and were for the most part married. Some were even suspected to be of immoral life.[30]

[30] "Quis clericorum propriis et paternis rebus solummodo non studebat? Qui potius inveniretur, proh dolor! qui non esset uxoratus vel concubinarius? De simoniâ quid dicam? Omnes pene ecclesiasticos ordines hæc mortifera bellua devoraverat, ut, qui ejus morsum evaserit, rarus inveniretur."—*Andr. Strum.*

But the preaching of the Saint, the wounds of the monks, converted some of the clergy. Those who were convinced by their appeals, and those who were wearied of their wives, threw themselves into the party of Gualberto, and clubbed together in common life.[31]

[31] "Exemplo vero ipsius et admonitionibus delicati clerici, spretis connubiis, coeperunt simul in ecclesiis stare, et communem ducere vitam."—Atto Pistor., *Vit. S. Joan. Gualb.*

The Vallombrosian monks appealed to Pope Alexander II. against the bishop,[32] their thirst for martyrdom whetted not quenched.[33] If the Pope desired it, they would try the ordeal of fire to prove their charge. Hildebrand, then only sub-deacon, but a power in the councils of the Pope, urged on their case, and demanded the deposition of the bishop. But Alexander, himself among the most resolute opponents of simony, felt that there was no case. There was no evidence, save the prattle of an old man over his wine-cups. He refused the petition of the monks, and was supported by the vast majority of the bishops—there were over a hundred present.[34]

[32] For what follows, in addition to the above-quoted authorities, we have Berthold's *Chronicle* from 1054 to 1100; Pertz, *Mon. Sacr.* v. pp. 264-326.

[33] "Securiores de corona, quam jam gustaverant, martyrii."—*Andr. Strum.*

[34] "Favebat enim maxima pars Episcoporum parti Petri, et omnes pene erant monachis adversi."—*Andr. Strum.*

Even St. Peter Damiani, generally unmeasured in his invectives against simony, wrote to moderate the frantic zeal of the Vallombrosian monks, which he denounced as unreasonable, intemperate, unjust.

But the refusal of the Pope to gratify their resentment did not quell the vehemence of the monks and the faction adverse to the bishop. The city was in a condition of chronic insubordination and occasional rioting. Godfrey Duke of Tuscany was obliged to interfere; and the monks were driven from their monastery of St. Salvi, and compelled to retire to that of St. Settimo outside of the gates.

Shortly after, Pope Alexander visited Florence. The monks piled up a couple of bonfires, and offered to pass between them in proof of the truth of their allegation. He refused to permit the ordeal, and withdrew, leaving the bishop unconvicted, and therefore unrebuked.

The clergy of Florence now determined to demand of the bishop that he should either go through the ordeal himself, or suffer the monks to do so. As they went to the palace, the people hooted them: "Go, ye heretics, to a heretic! You who have driven Christ out of the city! You who adore Simon Magus as your God!"

The bishop sullenly refused; he would neither establish his innocence in the fire, nor suffer the monks to convict him by the ordeal.

The Podesta of Florence then, with a high hand, drove from the town the clergy who had joined the monastic faction. They went forth on the first Saturday in Lent, 1067, amidst a sympathising crowd, composed mostly of women,[35] who tore off their veils, and with hair scattered wildly over their faces, threw themselves down in the road before the confessors, crying, "Alas! alas! O Christ, Thou art expelled this city, and how dost Thou leave us desolate? Thou art not tolerated here, and how can we live without Thee? Thou canst not dwell with Simon Magus. O holy Peter, didst thou once overcome Simon? and now dost thou permit him to have the mastery? We deemed him bound and writhing in infernal flames, and lo! he is loose, and risen again to thy dishonour."

[35] "Maxime feminarum."

And the men said to one another, "Let us set fire to this accursed city, which hates Christ."[36]

[36] "Et nos, viri fratres, civitatem hanc incendamus atque cum parvulis et uxoribus nostris, quocumque Christus ierit, secum camus. Si Christiani sumus, Christum sequamur."—*Andr. Strum.*

The secular clergy were in dismay; denounced, deserted, threatened by the people, they sang no psalms, offered no masses. Unable to endure their position, they again visited the bishop, and entreated him to sanction the ordeal of fire. He refused, and requested the priests not to countenance such an unauthorised venture, should it be made. But the whole town was bent on seeing this ordeal tried, and on the Wednesday following, the populace poured to the monastery of St. Settimo. Two piles of sticks were heaped near the monastery gate, measuring ten feet long by five wide, and four and a half feet high. Between them lay a path the length of an arm in width.

Litanies were chanted whilst the piles were reared, and then the monks proceeded to elect one who was to undergo the fire. The lot fell on a priest named Peter, and St. John Gualberto ordered him at once to the altar to say mass. All assisted with great devotion, the people crying with excitement. At the *Agnus Dei* four monks, one with the crucifix, another with holy water, the third with twelve lighted tapers, the fourth with a full censer, proceeded to the pyres, and set them both on fire.

This threw the people into an ecstasy of excitement, and the voice of the priest was drowned in the clamour of their tongues. The priest finished mass, and laid aside his chasuble. Holding the cross, in alb and stole and maniple, he came forth, followed by St. John Gualberto and the monks, chanting. Suddenly a silence fell on the tossing concourse, and a monk appointed by the abbot stood forth, and in a clear voice said to the people, "Men, brethren, and sisters! we do this for the salvation of your souls, that henceforth ye may learn to avoid the leprosy of simony, which has infected nearly the whole world; for the crime of simony is so great, that beside it every other crime is as nothing."

The two piles were burning vigorously. The priest Peter prayed, "Lord Christ, I beseech Thee, if Peter of Pavia, called Bishop of Florence, has obtained the episcopal throne by money, do Thou assist me in this terrible ordeal, and deliver me from being burned, as of old Thou didst deliver the three children in the midst of the burning furnace." Then, giving the brethren the kiss of peace, he stepped fearlessly between the burning pyres, and came forth on the farther side uninjured.

His linen alb, his silken stole and maniple, were unburnt. He would have again rushed through the flames in the excess of his confidence, but was prevented by the pious vehemence of the people, who surrounded him, kissed his feet, clung to his vestments, and would have crushed him to death in their eagerness to touch and see him, had he not been rescued by the strong arms of burly monks.

In after years he told, and talked himself into believing, that as he passed through the fire, his maniple fell off. Discovering his loss ere he emerged, he turned back, and deliberately picked it up. But of this nothing was said at the time.[37]

[37] It is not mentioned in the epistle of the Florentines to the Pope, narrating the ordeal and supposed miracle, which is given by Andrew of Strumi and Atto of Pistoja.

A letter was then drawn up, appealing to the Pope in the most vehement terms, to deliver the sheep of the Florentine flock from the ravening wolf who shepherded them, and urging him, not obscurely, to use force if need be, and compel by his troops the evacuation of the Florentine episcopal throne. Peter of Pavia, the bishop, a man of gentle character, yielded to the storm. He withdrew from Florence, and was succeeded by another Peter, whom the people called Peter the Catholic, to distinguish him from the Simoniac. But Muratori adduces evidence that the former continued to be recognised by the Pope some time after his supposed degradation. Thus ended the schism of Florence in the entire triumph of the Patarines. Hildebrand was not unobservant; he proved afterwards not to be forgetful of the lesson taught by this schism,—the utilization of the rude mob as a powerful engine in the hands of the fanatical or designing. It bore its fruit in the canons of 1074.

II.

ANSELMO DE BADAGIO, Bishop of Lucca, had succeeded Nicholas II. to the Papal throne in 1061. Cadalus of Parma had been chosen by the German and Lombard prelates on October 28th, and he assumed the name of Honorius II. But no Roman Cardinal was present to sanction this election. Cadalus was acknowledged by all the simoniacal and married clergy, when he entered Italy; but the Princess Beatrice and the Duke of Tuscany prevented him from advancing to Rome. From Parma Cadalus excommunicated Alexander, and from Rome, Alexander banned Honorius. The cause of Alexander was that of the Patarines, but the question of marriage and simony paled before the more glaring one, of which of the rival claimants was the actual Pope.

The voice of Landulf Cotta was silenced. A terrible cancer had consumed the tongue which had kept Milan for six years in a blaze of faction. But his room was speedily filled by a more implacable adversary of the married clergy—his brother, Herlembald, a stern, able soldier. An event in Herlembald's early life had embittered his heart against the less rigid clergy. His plighted bride had behaved lightly with a priest. He was just returned from a pilgrimage to Jerusalem, his zeal kindled to enthusiasm. He went to Rome, where he was well received by Alexander II. He came for authority to use his sword for the Patarines. The sectaries in Milan had said to him, "We desire to deliver the Church, besieged and degraded by the married priests; do thou deliver by the law of the sword, we will do so by the law of God." Alexander II., in a public consistory, created Herlembald "Defender of the Church," gave him the sacred banner of St. Peter, and bade him go back to Milan and shed blood—his, if necessary, those of the anti-Patarines certainly—in this miserable quarrel.

The result was that the Patarines were filled with new zeal, and lost all compunction at shedding blood and pillaging houses. Herlembald established himself in a large mansion, which he fortified and filled with mercenaries; over it waved the consecrated banner of St. Peter. From this stronghold he issued forth to assail the obnoxious clergy. They were dragged from their altars and consigned to shame and insult. The services of the Church, the celebration of the sacraments, were suspended, or administered only by the one or two priests who adhered to the Patari. It is said that, in order to keep his rude soldiery in pay, Herlembald made every clerk take a solemn oath that he had ever kept innocence, and would wholly abstain from marriage or concubinage. Those who could not, or would not, take this oath were expelled the city, and their whole property confiscated to support the standing corps of hireling ruffians maintained by the Crusader. The lowest rabble, poor artisans and ass-drivers, furtively placed female ornaments in the chambers of the priests, and then, attacking their houses, dragged them out and plundered their property. By 1064, when a synod was held at Mantua by the Pope, Milan was purged of "Simoniacs and Nicolaitans," and the clergy who remained were gathered together into a house to live in common, under rule.

Guido of Milan and all the Lombard prelates attended that important synod, which saw the triumph of Alexander, his reconciliation with the Emperor, and the general abandonment of the anti-Pope, Cadalus.

In the following year, Henry IV. was under the tutelage of Adalbert of Bremen; he had escaped from Anno, Archbishop of Cologne, who had favoured the strict faction and Alexander II. The situation in Lombardy changed simultaneously. Herlembald had assumed a power, an authority higher than that of the archbishop, whom he refused to recognise, and denounced as a heretic. Guido, weary of the nine years of strife he had endured, relieved from the fear of interference from Germany, resolved on an attempt to throw off the hateful yoke. The churches of Milan were for the most part without pastors. The married clergy had been expelled, and there were none to take their place. The Archbishop had been an obedient penitent for five years, compromising his one hundred years of penitence by payments into the Papal treasury; but as the cause of Alexander declined, his contrition languished, died out; and he resumed his demands for fees at ordinations and institutions, at least so clamoured Ariald and Herlembald in the ears of Rome.

A party in Milan had long resented the despotism of the "Law of God and the law of the sword" of Ariald and Herlembald, and an effort was made to break it, with the sanction, no doubt, of the Archbishop. A large body of the citizens rose, "headed," says Andrew of Strumi, "by the sons of the priests," and attacked the church and house of Ariald, but, unable to find him, contented themselves with wrecking the buildings. Thereupon Herlembald swept down at the head of his mercenaries, surrounded the crowd, and hewed them to pieces to the last man, "like the vilest cattle."[38]

[38] Hæc ut nobilis Herembaldus ceterique Fideles audiere, sumptis armis, in audacem plebem et temerariam irruere; quos protinus exterminavere omnes, quasi essent vilissimæ pecudes,"—*Andr. Strum.*

Guido, the Archbishop, now acted with resolution, and boldly took up the cause of the married clergy. Having heard that two priests of Monza, infected with Patarinism, had turned their wives out of their houses, he ordered the arrest of the priests, and punished them with imprisonment in the castle of Lecco. On hearing this, the Patarines flew to arms, and swarmed out of Milan after Ariald, who bore the banner of St. Peter, as Herlembald was absent at Rome. They met the mounted servants of the Archbishop near Monza, surprised them, and wrested from them a promise to surrender the priests. Three days after, the curates were delivered up. Ariald, at the head of the people, met them outside the gates, received them with enthusiasm, crying, "See, these are the brave martyrs of Christ!" and escorted them to a church, where they intoned a triumphant *Te Deum.*

Herlembald returned from Rome to Milan with a bull of excommunication fulminated by the Pope against the Archbishop. Guido summoned the Milanese to assemble in the cathedral church on the vigil of Pentecost.

In the meantime the Patarines were torn into factions on a subtle point mooted by Ariald. That demagogue had ventured to assail in a sermon the venerable custom of the Milanese, which required them to fast during the Rogation days. Was he greater than St. Ambrose? Did he despise the authority of the great doctor? On this awful subject the Patarines divided, and with the division lost their strength.

Neither Herlembald nor Ariald seems to have been prepared for the bold action of the Archbishop. On the appointed day the cathedral was filled with substantial citizens and nobles. Herlembald missed the wolfish eyes, ragged hair, and hollow cheeks of his sectaries, and, fearing danger, leaped over the chancel rails, and took up his position near the altar. The Archbishop mounted the ambone with the bull of excommunication in his hand. "See!" he exclaimed, "this is the result of the turbulence of these demagogues, Ariald and Herlembald. This city, out of reverence to St. Ambrose, has never obeyed the Roman Church. Shall we be crushed? Take away out of the land of the living these disturbers of the public peace who labour day and night to rob us of our ancient liberties."

He was interrupted by a shout of "Let them be killed." Guido paused, and then cried out, "All who honour and cleave to St. Ambrose, leave the church, that we may know who are our adversaries." Instantly from the doors rolled out the dense crowd, seven hundred in number, according to the estimation of Andrew, the biographer of Ariald. Only twelve men were left within who stood firm to the Patarine cause. Ariald had, in the meantime, taken refuge in the choir beside Herlembald. The clergy selected Ariald, the laity Herlembald, for their victims. Ariald was dragged from the church, severely wounded. Herlembald escaped better; using his truncheon, he beat off his assailants till he had climbed to a place of safety, whence he could not be easily dislodged.

As night fell, the Patarines gathered, stormed, and pillaged the palace of the Archbishop, and, bursting into the church, liberated Herlembald. Guido hardly escaped on horseback, sorely maltreated in the tumult. His adherents fled like smoke before the tempest. Ariald was found bleeding and faint, and was conveyed by the multitude in triumph to the church of St. Sepolcro. Then Herlembald called to the roaring mob to be still. "Let us ask Master Ariald whose house is to be first given up to sack."

But Ariald earnestly dissuaded from further violence, and entreated the vehement dictator to spare the lives and property of their enemies.

The surprise to the Archbishop's party was, however, temporary only. By morning they had rallied, and the city was again in their hands. Guido published an interdict against Milan, which was to remain in force as long as it harboured Ariald. No mass was said, no bells rang, the church doors were bolted and barred. Ariald was secretly removed by some of his friends to the village of St. Victor, where also Herlembald had been constrained to take refuge with a party of mercenaries. Thence they made their way to Pavia and to Padua, where they hoped to obtain a boat, and escape to Rome. But the whole country was up against them, and Herlembald was obliged to disband his soldiers, and attempt to escape in disguise. Ariald was left with a priest whose acquaintance Herlembald had made in Jerusalem. But a priest was the last person likely to secrete the tyrant and persecutor of the clergy. He treacherously sent word to the Archbishop, and Ariald was taken by the servants of Olivia, the niece of Guido, and conveyed to an island on the Lago Maggiore. He was handed over to the cruel mercies of two married priests, who directed his murder with cold-blooded heartlessness, if we may trust the gossips picked up later. His ears, nose and lips were cut off. He was asked if he would acknowledge Guido for archbishop. "As long as my tongue can speak," he replied, "I will not." The servants of Olivia tore out his tongue; he was beaten by the two savage priests, and when he fainted, was flung into the calm waters of the lovely lake. Andrew of Vallombrosa, or Strumi, followed in his trace, and hung about the neighbourhood till he heard from a peasant the awful story. He sought the mangled body.[39] It was found and transported to Milan on the feast of the Ascension following. For ten days it was exposed in the church of St. Ambrose, that all might venerate it, and was finally disposed in the convent of St. Celsus. In the memory of man, never had such a crowd been seen. The Archbishop deemed it prudent to retire, and Herlembald profited by his absence to recover his power, and make the people swear to avenge the martyr, and unite to the death for the "good cause." The events in Milan had their counterpart in the other cities of Lombardy, especially at Cremona, where the bishopric had been obtained by Arnulf, nephew of Guido of Milan. In that city, twelve men, headed by one Christopher, took the Patarine oath to fight the married clergy; the people joined them, and forced their oath on the bishop-elect before he was ordained. But, as in 1067, he seized a Patarine priest, a sedition broke out, in which the bishop was seriously injured. The inhabitants of Cremona, after Easter, sent ambassadors to the Pope, and received from him a reply, given by Bonizo, exhorting them not to allow a priest, deacon or sub-deacon, suspected of concubinage or simony, to hold a benefice or execute his ministry. The consequence of this letter was that all suspected clerks were excluded from their offices; and shortly after, the same course was followed at Piacenza. Asti, Lodi, and Ravenna also threw in their lot with the Patarines.

[39] Ariald was murdered on June 27, 1065. Andrew of Strumi says 1066; but he followed the Florentine computation—he had been a priest of Florence—which made the year begin on March 25.

In 1067, Alexander II. sent legates to Milan to settle the disturbances therein. Adalbert of Bremen had fallen, and again the Papal party were in the ascendant. The fortunes of Milan fluctuated with the politics of those who held the regency in the minority of Henry IV.

Guido, now advanced in years, and weary of ruling so turbulent a diocese, determined to vacate a see which he had held for twenty-seven years; the last ten of incessant civil war. He burdened it with a pension to himself, and then made it over to Godfrey, the sub-deacon, along with the pastoral staff and ring. Godfrey crossed the Alps, took the oath of allegiance to the Emperor, promised to use his utmost endeavours to exterminate the Patarines, and to deliver Herlembald alive into the hands of the Emperor, laden with chains. Friend and foe, without scruple, designate the followers of the Papal policy as Patarines; it is therefore startling, a few years later, when the Popes had carried their point, to find them insisting on the luckless Patarines being given in wholesale hecatombs to the flames, as damnable heretics. It was an ungracious return for the battle these heretics had fought under the banner of St. Peter.

But Herlembald refused to acknowledge Godfrey, he devastated the country with fire and sword wherever Godfrey was acknowledged, and created such havoc that not a day passed in the holy Lenten fast without the effusion of much Christian blood. Finally, Herlembald drove the archbishop-elect to take refuge in the strong fortress of Castiglione. Guido, not receiving his pension, annulled his resignation, and resumed his state. But he unwisely trusted to the good faith of Herlembald; he was seized,[40] and shut up in a monastery till his death, which took place August 23, 1071.

[40] "Gloriosus hac vice delusus," says Arnulf.

The year before this, 1070, Adelheid, Margravine of Turin, mother-in-law of the young Emperor, attacked the Patarines, and burnt the cities of Lodi and Asti. On March 19, 1071, as Herlembald was besieging Castiglione, a terrible conflagration broke out in Milan, and consumed a great part of the city and several of the stateliest churches. Whilst the army of Herlembald was agitated by the report of the fire, Godfrey burst out of Castiglione, and almost routed the besiegers. Before the death of Guido, Herlembald, with the sanction of the Pope, had set up a certain Otto to be Archbishop, nominated by himself and the Papal legate, without consulting the electors of Milan or the Emperor, January 6, A.D. 1072.

Otto was but a youth, just admitted into holy orders, likely to prove a pliant tool in the strong hand of the dictator. It was the Feast of the Epiphany, and the streets were thronged with people, when the news leaked out that an archbishop had been chosen, and was now holding the customary banquet after election in the archiepiscopal palace.

The people were furious, rose and attacked the house, hunted the youthful prelate out of an attic, where he had taken refuge, dragged him by his legs and arms into the church, and compelled him to swear to renounce his dignity. The Roman legate hardly escaped with his robes torn.

Herlembald, who had been surprised, recovered the upper hand in Milan on the morrow, but not in the open country, which was swept by the imperial troops. The suffragan bishops of Lombardy assembled at Novara directly they heard of what had taken place in Milan, and consecrated Godfrey as their archbishop.

Otto appealed to Rome (January, 1072), and a few weeks later the Pope assembled a synod, and absolved Otto of his oath extorted from him at Milan, acknowledged him as archbishop, and struck Godfrey with interdict. Alexander II. died April 21, 1073, and the tiara rested on the brows of the great Hildebrand.

On June 24, Hildebrand, now Gregory VII., wrote to the Margravine Beatrice to abstain from all relations with the excommunicated bishops of Lombardy; on June 28, to William, Bishop of Pavia, to oppose the usurper, the excommunicate Godfrey of Milan; on July 1, to all the faithful of Lombardy to refrain from that false bishop, who lay under the apostolic ban. From Capua, on September 27, he wrote to Herlembald, exhorting him to fight valiantly, and hold out Milan against the usurper Godfrey. Again, on October 9, to Herlembald, bidding him be of good courage; he hoped to detach the young Emperor from the party of Godfrey, and bade him receive amicably those who, with true sentiments of contrition, came over to the Patarine, that is, the Papal side.

On March 10, 1074, Gregory held one of the most important synods, not of his reign only, but ever held by any Pope. The acts of this assembly have been lost or suppressed, but its most important decisions were summed up in a letter from Gregory to the Bishop of Constance. This letter has not been printed in the Registrum; but fortunately it has been preserved by two contemporary writers, Paul of Bernried, and Bernold of Constance, the latter of whom has supplied a detailed apology for the law of celibacy promulgated in that synod. Gregory absolutely forbade all priests sullied with the *crimen fornicationis*, which embraced legitimate marriage, either to say a mass or to serve at one; and the people were strictly enjoined to shun their churches and their sacraments; and when the bishops were remiss, he exhorted them themselves to enforce the pontifical sentence.[41]

[41] "Audivimus quod quidam Episcoporum apud vos commorantium, aut sacerdotes, et diaconi, et subdiaconi, mulieribus commisceantur aut consentiant aut negligant. His præcipimus vos nullo modo obedire, vel illorum præceptis consentire, sicut ipsi apostolicæ sedis præceptis non obediunt neque auctoritati sanctorum patrum consentiunt." "Quapropter ad omnes de quorum fide et devotione confidimus nunc convertimur, rogantes vos et apostolicâ auctoritate admonentes ut quidquid Episcopi dehinc loquantur aut taceant, vos officium eorum quos aut simoniace promotos et ordinatos aut in crimine fornicationis jacentes cognoveritis, nullatenus recipiatis."—Letter to the Franconians (Baluze, *Misc.* vii. p. 125).

The results shall be described in the words of a contemporary historian, Sigebert of Gemblours. "Many," says he, "seeing in this prohibition to hear a mass said by a married priest a manifest contradiction to the doctrine of the Fathers, who believed that the efficacy of sacrament, such as baptism, chrism, and the Body and Blood of Christ, is independent of the dignity of the minister, thence resulted a grievous scandal; never, perhaps, even in the time of the great heresies, was the Church divided by a greater schism. Some did not abandon their simony, others disguised their avarice under a more acceptable name; what they boasted they had given gratuitously, they in reality sold; very few preserved continence. Some through greed of lucre, or sentiments of pride, simulated chastity, but many added false oaths and numerous adulteries to their debaucheries. The laity seized the opportunity to rise against the clerical order, and to excuse themselves for disobedience to the Church. They profaned the holy mysteries, administering baptism themselves, and using the wax out of their ears as chrism. They refused on their death-beds to receive the *viaticum* from the married priests; they would not even be buried by them. Some went so far as to trample under foot the Host, and pour out the precious Blood consecrated by married priests."[42]

[42] Pertz, viii. p. 362.

The affairs of the church of Milan continued in the same unsatisfactory condition. The contest between the Patarines and their adversaries had taken greater dimensions. The question which divided them was now less that of the marriage of the clergy than which of the rival archbishops was to be acknowledged. Godfrey was supported by the Emperor, Otto by the Pope. The parties were about even; neither Godfrey nor Otto could maintain himself in Milan; the former fortified himself in the castle of Brebbio, the latter resided at Rome. Henry IV., in spite of all the admonitions of the Pope, persisted in supporting the cause of Godfrey. Milan was thus without a pastor. The suffragan bishops wished to execute their episcopal functions in the city, and to consecrate the holy oils for the benediction of the fonts at Whitsuntide. Herlembald, when one of the bishops had sent chrism into the city for the purpose, poured it out on the ground and stamped on it, because it had been consecrated by an excommunicated prelate.

In March, 1075, another conflagration broke out in the city, and raged with even greater violence than the fire of 1071. Herlembald had again poured forth the oils, as he had the year before; and had ordered Leutprand, a priest, as Easter came, to proceed to the consecration of chrism. This innovation roused the alarm of the Milanese; the subsequent conflagration convinced them that it was abhorrent to heaven. All the adversaries of the Patarines assembled outside the city, and swore to preserve intact the privileges of St. Ambrose, and to receive only the bishop nominated or approved by the King. Then, entering the city, they fell unexpectedly on the Patarines. Leutprand was taken and mutilated, his ears and nose were cut off. The standard of St. Peter was draggled in the dust, and Herlembald fell with it, cut down by a noble, Arnold de Rauda. Every insult was heaped on the body of the "Defender of the Church," and the sacred banner was trampled under foot.

Messengers were sent to Henry IV. to announce the triumph, and to ask him to appoint a new Archbishop of Milan. Henry was so rejoiced at the victory, that he abandoned Godfrey, and promised the Milanese a worthy prelate. His choice fell on Tebald, a Milanese sub-deacon in his Court.

Pope Urban II. canonised Herlembald. Ariald seems never to have been formally enrolled among the saints, but he received honours as a saint at Milan, and has been admitted into several Italian Martyrologies, and into the collection of the Bollandists. Baronius wisely expunged Herlembald and Ariald from the Roman Martyrology; nevertheless, the disgraceful fact remains, that the ruffian Herlembald has been canonised by Papal bull.

The seeds of fresh discord remained. Leutprand, or Liprand, the priest, was curate of the Church of St. Paul;[43] having suffered mutilation in the riot, he was regarded in the light of a Patarine confessor. But no outbreak took place till the death of Anselm IV., Archbishop of Milan (September 30, 1101), at Constantinople, where he was on his way with the Crusaders to the Holy Land. His vicar, the Greek, Peter Chrysolaus, Bishop of Savonia, whom the Lombards called Grossulani, perhaps because of the coarse habit he wore (more probably as a corruption for Chrysolaus), had been left in charge of the see of Milan. On the news of the death of the Archbishop reaching that city, the Primicerius convoked the electors to choose a successor. The vote fell on Landulf, Ordinary of Milan; but he was not yet returned from Jerusalem, whither he had gone as a crusader. Grossulani declared the election informal. Thereupon the Abbot of St. Dionysius, at the head of a large party of the electors, chose Peter Grossulani. There is no evidence of his having used bribery in any form; but he may have acted unjustly in cancelling the election of Landulf. It is, however, fair to observe that Landulf, on his return, supported Grossulani; consequently, it is probable that the latter acted strictly in accordance with law and precedent.

[43] The life of Liprand was written by Landulf the younger, his sister's son, in his *Hist. Mediolan.*1095-1137.

But the election displeased Liprand and the remains of the Patarines. They appealed to Rome, but Grossulani, supported by the Countess Matilda and St. Bernard, abbot of Vallombrosa, overcame their objections. Pope Paschal II. ratified the election, and sent the pall to the Archbishop. Ardericus de Carinate had been sent to Rome on behalf of Grossulani. The people came out of the gates, on his approach, to learn the result. Ardericus, hanging the pall across his umbrella (*protensi virga*), waved it over his head, shouting, "Ecco la stola! Ecco la stola!" (Here is the pall!) and led the way into the cathedral, whither Grossulani also hastened, and ascending the pulpit in his pontifical habit, placed the coveted insignia about his neck.

Liprand was not satisfied. By means of private agitation, he disturbed the tranquillity of public feeling, and the Archbishop, to calm the minds of the populace, was obliged to convoke a provincial synod at Milan (1103), in which, in the presence of his suffragans, the clergy and the people, he said, "If anyone has a charge to make against me, let him speak openly at the present time, or he shall not be heard."

Liprand would not appear before the council and formally make charge, but he mounted the pulpit in the Church of St. Paul and preached against the Archbishop as a simoniac. He declared his readiness to prove his charge by the ordeal of fire. The bishops assembled in council refused to suffer the attempt to be made.

However, Liprand was not deterred. "Look at my amputated nose and ears!" he cried, "I am a confessor for Christ. I will try the ordeal by fire to substantiate my charge. Grossulani is a simoniac, by gift of hand, gift of tongue, and gift of homage." And he gave his wolf-skin cloak and some bottles of wine in exchange for wood, which the crowd carried off and heaped up in a great pile against the wall of the monastery of St. Ambrogio. The Archbishop sent his servants, and they overturned the stack, and scattered the wood. Then the crowd of "boys and girls, men and women," poured through the main streets, roaring, "Away with Grossulani, away with him!" and clamoured around the doors of the archiepiscopal palace, so that Grossulani, fearing for his life, said, "Be it so, let the fellow try the fire, or let him leave Milan." His servants with difficulty appeased the people, by promising that the ordeal should be undergone on the following Palm Sunday evening. "I will not leave the city," said Liprand; "but now I have no money for buying wood, and I will not sell my books, as I keep them for my nephew Landulf, now at school." So the magistrates of the city prepared a pile of billets of oak wood.

On the appointed day Liprand, barefooted, in sackcloth, bearing a cross, went to the Church of Saints Gervasius and Protasius and sung mass. Grossulani also, bearing a cross, entered the same church and mounted the pulpit, attended by Ariald de Marignano, and Berard, Judge of Asti. Silence being made, and Liprand having taken his place barefooted "on the marble stone at the entrance to the choir, containing an image of Hercules," Grossulani addressed the people; "Listen, and I will silence this man in three words." Then turning to Liprand, he asked, "You have charged me with being a simoniac. To whom have I given anything? Answer me."

Liprand, raising his eyes to the pulpit, pointed to those who occupied it and said, "Look at those three great devils, who think to confound me by their wit and wealth.[44] I appeal to the judgment of God."

[44] "Proposuisti quod ego sum simoniacus per munus a manu. Modo die: cui dedi; Tunc presbyter super populum oculos aperuit, et digitum ad eos, qui stabunt in pulpito, extendit, dicens, Videte tres grandissimos diabolos, qui per ingenium et pecuniam suam putant me confundere."

Grossulani said, "But I ask what act of simony do you lay to my charge?"
Liprand answered, "Do you answer me, What is the lightest form of simony?"
The Archbishop, after some consideration, answered, "To refrain from deposing a simoniac."
"And I say that is simony which consists in deposing an abbot from his abbacy, a bishop from his bishopric, and an archbishop from his archbishopric."[45]

[45] It is very evident from this discussion that Grossulani was innocent of true simony; the whole charge against him was due to his having quashed the election of Landulf, and thus of having deposed, after a fashion, "an archbishop from his archbishopric."

The people became impatient, and began to shout, "Come out, come out to the ordeal!" Then Liprand "jumped down from the stone, containing the image of Hercules," and went forth accompanied by the multitude to the field where the pyre was made. There arose then a difficulty about the form of oath to be administered. Liprand, seeing that there was some hesitation, said, "Let me manage it, and see if I do not satisfy you all!" Whereupon he took hold of the hood of the Archbishop and shook it, and said in a loud voice, "That Grossulani, who is under this hood, he, and no other, has obtained the archbishopric of Milan simoniacally, by gift of hand, gift of tongue, and gift of service. And I, who enter on this ordeal, swear that I have used no charm, or incantation, or witchcraft."

The Archbishop, unwilling to remain, remounted his horse and rode to the Church of St. John "ad concham," but Ariald of Marignano remained to see that the ordeal was rightly carried out. When the pile was lighted, he said to the priest, "In heaven's name, return to your duty, and do not rush on certain death." But Liprand answered, "Get thee behind me, Satan," and signing himself, and blessing the fire with consecrated water, he rushed through the flames, barefooted, in sackcloth cassock and silk chasuble. He came out on the other side uninjured; a sudden draught had parted the flames as he entered, and when he emerged his feet were not burnt, nor was his silk chasuble scorched.

The people shouted at the miracle, and Grossulani was obliged to fly from the city.

It was soon rumoured, however, that Liprand was suffering from a scorched hand and an injured foot. It was in vain for his friends to assure the people that his hand had been burnt when he was throwing the holy water on the flames before he entered them, and that his foot was injured not by the fire, but by the hoof of a horse as he emerged from the flames. One part of the mob began to clamour against Liprand that he was an impostor, the other to exalt him as a saint, and the streets became the scene of riot and bloodshed. At this juncture Landulf of Vereglate, who had been just elected to the vacant see, arrived from Jerusalem, and finding that the Archbishop had fled the city, he appealed to the people to cease from their riots, and promised to have Grossulani deposed, or at least the charges brought against him properly investigated at Rome. The tumults were with difficulty allayed, and the Archbishop, Landulf, and Liprand went to Rome (A.D. 1103). A Synod was convened and Liprand brought his vague accusations of simony against the Archbishop. Landulf refused to support him, so that it is hardly probable that he can have felt himself aggrieved by the conduct of Grossulani. Liprand, being unable to substantiate his charge of simony, was obliged to change the nature of his accusation, and charged the Archbishop with having forced him to submit to the ordeal of fire. The Pope and the Synod required the Archbishop to clear himself by oath; accordingly Grossulani did so, in the following terms: "I, Grossulani, by the grace of God Archbishop, did not force Liprand to enter the fire." Azo, Bishop of Acqui, and Arderic, Bishop of Lodi, took the oath with him; at the same time the pastoral staff slipped from the hands of the Archbishop and fell on the floor, a sign, the biographer of Liprand says, that he forswore himself.[46]

[46] It is evident from the account of Landulf the younger himself, that the Archbishop did not force the priest to enter on the ordeal.

The Archbishop withdrew his authority confirmed by the Holy See, and he returned to Milan, where he was well received.

The Archbishop took an unworthy opportunity, in 1110, of ridding the city of the presence of Liprand for that priest having taken into his house and cured a certain Herebert of Bruzano, an enemy of the Archbishop, who was ill with fever. Grossulani deprived Liprand of his benefice, and the priest retired into the Valteline. Troubles broke out in Milan between the two parties, which produced civil war, and the Archbishop was driven out of the city, whereupon Liprand returned to it. The friends of Grossulani persuaded him to visit Jerusalem, and he started, after having appointed Arderic, Bishop of Lodi, his vicar (A.D. 1111). During his absence both parties united to reject him, and they elected Jordano of Cliva in his room (Jan. 1, A.D. 1112). Mainnard, Archbishop of Turin, hastened to Rome, and received the pall from the Pope, on condition that it should not be worn for six months. But the rumours having spread that Grossulani was returning from Jerusalem, Mainnard came to Milan, and placed the pall on the altar of St. Ambrose, whence Jordano took it and laid it about his shoulders.

On the return of Grossulani, civil war broke out again between the two factions, which ended in both Archbishops being summoned to Rome in 1116; and the Pope ordered Grossulani to return to his bishopric of Savonia, and confirmed Jordano in the archbishopric of Milan. But before this Liprand had died 3rd January, 1113. His sanctity was almost immediately attested by a miracle, in spite of the disparagement of his virtues by the party of the Archbishop Grossulani; for a certain knight of Piacenza, having swallowed a fish-bone which stuck in his throat, in sleep saw the priest appear to him and touch his throat, whereupon a violent fit of coughing ensued, in which the bone was ejected; this was considered quite sufficient to establish the claim of Liprand to be regarded as a saint.

TO the year 1524 Münster, the capital of Westphalia, had remained faithful to the religion which S. Swibert, coadjutor of S. Willibrord, first Bishop of Utrecht, had brought to it in the 7th century. But then Lutheranism was introduced into it.

Frederick von Wied at that time occupied the Episcopal throne. He was brother to Hermann, Archbishop of Cologne, who was afterwards deprived for his secession to Lutheranism.

The religious revolution in the Westphalian capital at its commencement presents the same symptoms which characterised the beginning of the Reformation elsewhere. The town council were prepared to hail it as a means of overthrowing the Episcopal authority, and establishing the municipal power as supreme in the city.

Already the State of Juliers had embraced the new religion, and faith had been shaken in Osnabrück, Minden, and Paderborn, when the first symptoms appeared in Münster.

Four priests, the incumbents of the parishes of St. Lambert, St. Ludger, St. Martin, and the Lieb-Frau Church, commonly called Ueberwasser, declared for the Reform. The contemporary historian, Kerssenbroeck, an eye-witness of all he describes, says of them, "They indulged in the most violent abuse of the clergy, they cursed good works, assured their auditors that such works would not receive the smallest recompense, and permitted every one to give way to all the excesses of so-called Evangelical liberty."[47] They stirred up their hearers against the religious orders, and the people clamoured daily at the gates of the monasteries and nunneries, insisting on being given food; and the monks and nuns were too much frightened to refuse those whom impunity rendered daily more exacting.[48] On the night of the 22nd March, 1525, they attacked the rich convent of nuns at Nizink, with intentions of pillaging it. They failed in this attempt, and the ringleaders were seized and led before the magistrates, followed by an excited and tumultuous crowd of men and women, "evangelically disposed," as the chronicler says. Hoping to ally the effervescence, the magistrates asked the cause of complaint against the nuns of Nizink, and then came out the true reason, for which religious prejudice had served as a cloak. They complained that the monks and nuns exercised professions to the prejudice of the artisans; and they demanded of the magistracy that their looms should be broken, the religious forbidden to work at trades, and their superabundant goods to be distributed among the poor. The orators of the band declared in conclusion "that if the magistrates refused to grant these requests, the people would disregard their orders, displace them by force of arms, and put in their stead men trustworthy and loyal, and devoted to the interests of the citizens."[49] Alarmed at these threats, the magistrates yielded, and promised to take every measure satisfactory to the insurgents.[50] On the 25th May, accordingly, the Friars of St. Francis and the nuns of Nizink were ordered to give up their looms and accounts. The friars yielded, but the ladies stoutly refused. The magistrates, however, had all the looms carried away, whilst a mob howled at the gates, and agitators, excited by the four renegade priests, ran about the town stirring up the people against the religious. "All the worst characters," says the old chronicler, "joined the rioters; the curious came to swell the crowd, and people of means shut themselves into their houses."[51] For Johann Groeten, the orator of the band, now proclaimed that having emptied the strong boxes of the monks and nuns, they would despoil all those whose fortunes exceeded two thousand ducats.

[47] Kerssenbroeck, p. 114.
[48] *Ibid.* p. 115.
[49] Kerssenbroeck, p. 116.
[50] *Ibid.* p. 117.
[51] *Ibid.* p. 120.

The rioters next marched to the town hall, where the senators sat trembling, and they demanded the immediate confirmation of a petition in thirty-four articles that had been drawn up for them by their leaders. At the same time the mob announced that unless their petition was granted they would execute its requirements with their own hands.

It asked that the canons of the cathedral should be required to pay the debts of the bishop deceased; that criminal jurisdiction should be withdrawn from the hands of the clergy; that the monks and nuns should be forbidden to exercise any manufacture, to dry grain, make linen, and rear cattle; that the burden of taxation should be shared by the clergy; that rectors should not be allowed to appoint or dismiss their curates without consent of the parish; that lawsuits should not be allowed to be protracted beyond six weeks; that beer licences should be abolished, and tolls on the bridges done away with; that monks and nuns should be allowed free permission to leave their religious societies and return to the world; that the property of religious houses should be sold and distributed amongst the needy, and that the municipality should allow them enough for their subsistence; that the Carmelites, the Augustinians, and the Dominicans should be suppressed; that pious foundations for masses for the repose of souls should be confiscated; and that people should be allowed to marry in Lent and Advent. The magistrates yielded at once, and promised to endeavour to get the consent of the other estates of the diocese to the legalising of these articles.[52]

[52] Kerssenbroeck, p. 126.

On the morrow of the Ascension, 1525, the magistrates closed the gates of the town, and betook themselves to the clergy of the chapter to request them to accept the thirty-four articles. The canons refused at first, but, in fear of the people, they consented, but wrote to the bishop to tell him what had taken place, and to urge him to act with promptitude, and not to forget that the rights and privileges of the Church were in jeopardy.

It was one of the misfortunes in Germany, as it was in France, that the clergy were exempt from taxation. This precipitated the Revolution in France, and aroused the people against the clergy; and in Germany it served as a strong motive for the adoption of the Reformation.

The canons now fled the town, protesting that their signatures had been wrested from them by violence, and that they withdrew their consent to the articles. The inferior clergy remained at their post, and exhibited great energy and decision. They deprived Lubert Causen, minister of St. Martins, one of the most zealous fautors of Lutheranism in Münster, and the head of the reforming party. When his parishioners objected, a packet of love-letters he had written to several girls in the town, and amongst others some to a young woman of respectable position whom he had seduced, came to light, and were read in the Senate. The reformer had in his letters used scriptural texts to excuse and justify the most shameless libertinage.[53] Johann Tante, preacher at St. Lambert, and Gottfried Reining, of Ueberwasser, were also deprived. As for the Lutheran preacher at St. Ludger, Johann Fink, "his mouth was stopped by the gift of a fat prebendal stall, and from that moment he entirely lost his zeal for the gospel of Wittenberg, and never uttered another word against the Catholic religion."[54]

[53] Kerssenbroeck, p. 128.
[54] *Ibid.*

By means of the mediation of the Archbishop of Cologne, a reconciliation was effected. The articles were abolished and the signatures annulled, and the members of the chapter returned to Münster, which had felt their absence by the decrease in trade, and the inconstant people "showed at least as much joy at their return as they had shown hatred at their departure."[55]

[55] *Ibid.* p. 138.

There can be no question but that the Reformation in Germany was provoked to a large extent by abuses and corruptions in the Church. To a much larger extent it was a revolt against the Papacy which had weakened and numbed the powers of the Empire throughout the Middle Ages from the time of the Emperor Henry IV. But chiefly as a social and political movement it was the revolt of municipalities against the authority of collegiate bodies of clergy and the temporal jurisdiction of prince-bishops, or of grand dukes and margraves and electors favouring the change because it allowed them at a sweep to confiscate vast properties and melt down tons of chalices and reliquaries into coin.

In Münster lived a draper, Bernhard Knipperdolling by name, who assembled the malcontents in his house, or in a tavern, and poured forth in their ears his sarcasms against the Pope, the bishops, the clergy and the Church. He was well known for his dangerous influence, and the bishop, Frederic von Wied, arrested him as he passed near his residence at Vecht. The people of Münster, exasperated at the news of the captivity of their favourite, obliged the magistrates and the chapter to ask the bishop to release him. Frederick von Wied yielded with reluctance, using these prophetic words, "I consent, but I fear that this man will turn everything in Münster and the whole diocese upside down." Knipperdolling left prison, after having taken an oath to keep the peace; but on his return to Münster he registered a vow that he would terribly revenge his incarceration and would make the diocese pay as many ducats as his captivity had cost him hellers.[56]

[56] Kerssenbroeck, p. 143.

There was another man in Münster destined to exercise a fatal influence on the unfortunate city. This was a priest named Bernard Rottmann.[57] As a child he had been chorister at St. Maurice's Church at Münster, where his exquisite voice had attracted notice. He was educated in the choir school, then went to Mainz, where in 1524 he took his Master's degree, and returning to Münster, was ordained priest in 1529. He was then given the lectureship of the church in which, as a boy, he had sung so sweetly. He shortly exhibited a leaning towards Lutheranism, and the canons of St. Maurice, who had placed great hopes on the young preacher, thinking that he acted from inexperience and without bad intent, gave him a paternal reprimand, and provided him with funds to go to the University of Cologne, and study there dogmatic and controversial theology; at the same time undertaking to retain Rottmann in the receipt of his salary as lecturer, and to this they added a handsome pension to assist him in his studies.

[57] *Ibid.* 148; Latin edition, p. 1517-9; Dorpius, f. 391 a.

The young man received this money, and then, instead of going to Cologne, betook himself to Wittenberg, where he attached himself to Melancthon. On his return to Münster, the canons, unaware of the fraud that had been played upon them, reinstated Rottmann in the pulpit. He was too crafty to publish his new tenets in his discourses, and thus to insure the loss of his situation, but he employed his secret influence in society to spread Lutheranism. After a while, when he considered his party strong enough to support him, he threw off the mask, and preached boldly against the priests and the bishops, and certain doctrines of the Catholic Church. The more violent he became in his attacks, the more personal and caustic in his language, the greater grew the throng of people to hear him. Then he preached against Confession, which he called "the disturber of consciences," and contrasted it with Justification by Faith only, which set consciences at ease; he preached against good works, against the obligation to observe the moral law, and assured his hearers that grace was freely imputed to them, live as they liked, and that the Gospel afforded them entire freedom from all restraints. "The shameless dissolution which now began to spread through the town," says Kerssenbroeck, "proved that the mob adopted the belief in the impunity of sin; all those who were ruined in pocket, hoping to get the possessions of others, joined the party of innovators, and Rottmann was extolled by them to the skies."[58]

[58] Kerssenbroeck, p. 152.

The Senate forbade the citizens to attend Rottmann's sermons, but their orders were disregarded. The populace declared that Master Bernard was the only preacher of the true Gospel, and they covered with slander and abuse those who strove to oppose his seductive doctrine. "Some of the episcopal councillors, however," says the historian, "favoured the innovator. The private secretary of the bishop, Leonhard Mosz, encouraged him secretly, and promised him his support in the event of danger."[59]

[59] Kerssenbroeck, p. 152.

But the faithful clergy informed the bishop of the scandal, and before Mosz and others could interfere, a sentence of deprivation was pronounced against him.

Rottmann, startled by this decisive measure, wrote a series of letters to Frederick von Wied, which have been preserved by Kerssenbroeck, in which he pretended that he had been calumniated before "the best and most just of bishops," and excused himself, instead of boldly and frankly announcing his secession from the Catholic Church. In reply, the bishop ordered him to quit Münster, and charged his councillors to announce to him that his case would be submitted to the next synod. Rottmann then wrote to the councillors a letter which exhibits his duplicity in a clearer light. Frederick von Wied, hearing of this letter, ordered the recalcitrant preacher to quit the convent adjoining the church of St. Maurice, and to leave the town. Rottmann thereupon took refuge in the house of Knipperdolling and his companions. Under the protection of these turbulent men, the young preacher assumed a bolder line, and wrote to the bishop demanding a public discussion, and announcing that shortly his doctrine would be published in a pamphlet, and thus be popularised.

On the 23rd of January, 1532, Rottmann's profession of faith appeared, addressed in the form of a letter to the clergy of Münster.[60] Like all the professions of faith of the period, it consisted chiefly of a string of negations, with a few positive statements retained from the Catholic creed on God, the Incarnation, &c. He denied the special authority of the priesthood, reduced the Sacraments to signs, going thereby beyond Luther; rejected doctrines of the Eucharistic Sacrifice, Purgatory, the intercession of saints, and the use of images, pilgrimages, vows, benedictions, and the like. It would certainly have been more appropriately designated a Confession of Disbelief. This pamphlet was widely circulated amongst the people, and the party of Lutheran malcontents, headed by Knipperdolling, and Herman Bispink, a coiner and forger of title-deeds, grew in power, in numbers, and in audacity.

[60] Kerssenbroeck, p. 165 *et seq.*; Latin edition, Mencken, p. 1520-8: Sleidan, French tr., p. 406.

On the 23rd of February, 1532, Knipperdolling and his associates assembled the populace early, and carried Rottmann in triumph to the church of St. Lambert. Finding the doors shut, they mounted the preacher on a wooden pulpit before the bone-house. The Reformer then addressed the people on the necessity of proclaiming evangelical liberty and of destroying idolatry; of overthrowing images and the Host preserved in the tabernacles. His doctrine might be summed up in two words: liberty for the Evangelicals to do what they liked, and compulsion for the Catholics. The sermon produced a tremendous effect; before it was concluded the rioters rushed towards the different churches, burst open the doors, tore down the altars, reliquaries, statues; and the Sacrament was taken from the tabernacles and trampled under foot. The cathedral alone, defended by massive gates, escaped their fury.[61]

[61] Kerssenbroeck, p. 185; Bullinger, "Adversus Anabaptist." lib. ii. c. 8.

Proud of this achievement, the insurgents defied all authority, secular and ecclesiastical, and installed Bernhard Rottmann as preacher and pastor of the Evangelical religion in St. Lambert's Church. "Thenceforth," says the Münster contemporary historian, "it may well be understood that they did not limit themselves to simple tumults, but that murders, pillage, and the overthrow of all public order followed. The success of this first enterprise had rendered the leaders masters of the city."

Bishop Frederick von Wied felt that his power was at an end. He was a man with no very strong religious zeal or moral courage. He resigned his dignity in the sacristy of the church of Werne, reserving to himself a yearly income of 2,000 florins. Duke Eric of Brunswick, Prince of Grubenhagen, Bishop of Paderborn and Osnabrück, was elected in his room. The nomination of Eric irritated the Lutheran party. He was a man zealous for his religion, and with powerful relations. Rottmann at once sent him his twenty-nine articles, and the artisans of Münster, who had embraced the cause of Rottmann, handed in a petition to the magistrates (April 16th, 1532) to request that compulsion might be used to force every one to become Lutheran, "because it seems to us," said they, "that this doctrine is in all points and entirely conformable to the Gospel, whilst that which is taught by the rest of the clergy is absurd, and ought to be rejected."[62] The bishop-elect wrote to the magistrates, insisting on the dismissal of Rottmann, but in their answer they not only declined to obey, but offered an apology for his conduct.

[62] Kerssenbroeck, pp. 189-90.

The bishop wrote again, but received no answer. Wishing to use every means of conciliation, before adopting forcible measures, he sent a deputation to Münster to demand the expulsion of the preacher, but without success.

The people, becoming more insubordinate, determined to take possession of other churches. One of the most important is the church of Unsere Lieb-frau, or Ueberwasser, a church whose beautiful tower and choir attract the admiration of the traveller visiting Münster. This church and parish depended on the convent of Ueberwasser; the rector was a man of zeal and power, a Dr. Martin, who was peculiarly obnoxious to the Lutheran party. A deputation was sent to the abbess, Ida von Merfelt, to insist on the dismissal of the rector and the substitution of an Evangelical preacher.[63] The lady was a woman of courage; she recommended the deputation to return to their shops and to attend to their own business, and announced that Dr. Martin should stay at his post; and stay he did, for a time.

[63] *Ibid.* p. 203.

The bishop was resolved to try force of arms, when suddenly he died, May 9th, 1532, after having drunk a goblet of wine. Several writers of the period state that it was poisoned. A modern historian says he died of excess of drink—on what authority I do not know.[64] He had brought down upon himself the dislike of the Lutherans for having vigorously suppressed the reforming movement in Paderborn. The history of that movement in this other Westphalian diocese is too suggestive to be passed over. In 1527 the Elector John Frederick of Saxony passed through Paderborn and ordered his Lutheran preachers to address the people in the streets through the windows of the house in which he lodged, as the clergy refused them the use of the churches. Next year the agitation began by a quarrel between some of the young citizens and the servants of the chapter, and ended in the plundering and devastation of the cathedral and the residences of the canons. The leader of the Evangelical party in Paderborn was Johann Molner of Buren, a man who had been expelled from the city in 1531 for murder and adultery; he left, taking with him as his mistress the wife of the man he had murdered, and retired to Soest, "where," says a contemporary writer, Daniel von Soest, "he did not remain satisfied with this woman only." He returned to Paderborn as a burning and shining gospel light, and led the iconoclastic riot. Duke Philip of Grubenhagen supported his brother, and the town was forced to pay 2,000 gulden for the damage done, and to promise to pay damages if any further mischief took place, and this so cooled the zeal of the citizens of Paderborn for the Gospel that it died out.[65]

[64] Stürc, "Gerchichte v. Osnabrück." Osnab. 1826, pt. iii. p. 25.

[65] Vehse, "Geschichte der Deutschen Höfe." Hamburg, 1859, vol. xlvii. p. 4-6. Bessen, "Geschichte v. Paderborn"; Paderb. 1820, vol. ii. p. 33.

The chapter retired to Ludwigshausen for the purpose of electing the successor to Bishop Eric, who had only occupied the see three months; their choice fell on Francis von Waldeck, Bishop of Minden, and then of Osnabrück. The choice was not fortunate; it was dictated by the exigencies of the times, which required a man of rank and power to occupy the vacant throne, so as to reduce the disorder by force of arms. Francis of Waldeck was all this, but the canons were not at that time aware that he had himself strong leanings towards Lutheranism; and after he became Bishop of Münster he would have readily changed the religion of the place, had it not been that such a proceeding would, under the circumstances, have involved the loss of his income as prince-bishop. Later, when the disturbances were at an end, he proposed to the Estates the establishment of Lutheranism and the suppression of Catholicism, as we shall see in the sequel. He even joined the Smalkald union of the Protestant princes against the Catholics in 1544.

With sentiments so favourable to the Reform, the new bishop would have yielded everything to the agitators, had they not assumed a threatening attitude, and menaced his temporal position and revenue, which were the only things connected with the office for which he cared.

The inferior clergy of Münster wrote energetically to him on his appointment, complaining of the innovations which succeeded each other with rapidity in the town. "The Lutheran party," said they in this letter, "are growing daily more invasive and insolent," and they implored the bishop to protect their rights and liberty of conscience against the tyranny of the new party, who, not content with worshipping God in their own way, refused toleration to others, outraged their feelings by violating all they held most sacred, and disturbed their services by unseemly interruptions.

Francis of Waldeck renewed the orders of his predecessor. The senate acknowledged the receipt of his letter, and promised to answer it on a future occasion.

However, the warmest partisans of Rottmann were resolved to carry matters to a climax, and at once to overthrow both the episcopal and the civil authority. Knipperdolling persuaded the butcher Modersohn and the skinner Redekker that, as provosts of their guilds, they were entitled to convene the members of their trades without the intervention of the magistrates. These two men accordingly convoked the people for the 1st July.[66] The assembly was numerously attended, and opened tumultuously. When silence was obtained, a certain Johann Windemuller rose and proclaimed the purpose of the convention. "The affair is one of importance," said he; "we have to maintain the glory of God, our eternal welfare, the happiness of all our fellow-citizens, and the development of our franchises; all these things depend on the sacred ecclesiastical liberty announced to us by the worthy Rottmann. We must conclude an alliance against the oppressors of the Gospel, that the doctrine of Rottmann, which is incontestably the true one, may be protected." These words produced such enthusiasm, that the audience shouted with one voice that "they would defend Rottmann and his doctrine to their last farthing, and the last drop of their blood." Some of those present, by their silence, expressed their displeasure, but a draper named Johann Mennemann had the courage to raise his voice against the proposal. A furious band at once attacked him with their fists, crying out that the enemies of the pure Gospel must be destroyed; "already the bold draper was menaced with their daggers, when one of his friends succeeded in effecting his escape from the popular rage." However, he was obliged to appear before the heads of the guilds and answer for his opposition. Mennemann replied, that in weighty matters concerning the welfare of the commonwealth, tumultuous proceedings were not likely to produce good resolutions, and that he advised the separation of the corporations, that the questions might be maturely considered and properly weighed.[67]

[66] Kerssenbroeck, p. 207; Dorpius, f. 391 b. 392.
[67] *Ibid.* p. 208.

The corporations of trades now appointed twenty-six individuals, in addition to the provosts, to decide on measures adapted to carry out the resolution. This committee decided "that one religion alone should be taught in the town for the future and for ever after;" and that "if any opposition was offered by the magistrates, the whole body of the citizens should be appealed to."[68]

[68] Kerssenbroeck, p. 209.

These decisions were presented to the senate on the 11th July, which replied that they were willing not to separate themselves from evangelical truth, but that they were not yet satisfied on which side it was to be found, and that they would ask the bishop to send them learned theologians who should investigate the matter.

This reply irritated Rottmann, Knipperdolling, and their followers. On the 12th July fresh messengers were sent to the Rath (senate) to know whether it might be reckoned upon. The answer was equivocal. A third deputation insisted on an answer of "Yes" or "No," and threatened a general rising of the people unless their demands were acceded to.[69] The magistrates, in alarm, promised their adhesion to the wishes of the insurgents, who demanded at once that "sincere preachers of the pure Gospel" should be installed in every church of Münster. The councillors accordingly issued orders to all the clergy of the city to adopt the articles of Bernard Rottmann, or to refute them by scriptural arguments, or they must expect the Council to proceed against them with the extremest rigour of the law.

[69] *Ibid.* pp. 210, 211.

Then, to place the seal on their cowardly conduct, they wrote to the prince-bishop on the 25th, to excuse themselves of complicity in the institution of Rottmann, but at the same time they undertook the defence of the Reformer, and assured the bishop that his doctrine was sound and irrefutable. At the same time they opened a communication with the Landgrave Philip of Hesse, asking that bulwark of the Reformation to protect them. Philip wrote back, promising his intervention, but warning them not to make the Gospel an excuse for revolt and disorder, and not to imagine that Christian liberty allowed them to seize on all the property of the Church. At the same time he wrote to the prince-bishop to urge upon him not to deprive the good and simple people of Münster of their evangelical preachers.[70]

[70] Kerssenbroeck, pp. 213-23.

In the meantime the seditious members of the town guilds grew impatient; and on the 6th August they sent a deputation to the town council reminding it of its promise, and insisting on the immediate deprivation of all the Catholic clergy. The magistrates sought to gain time, but the deputation threatened them with the people taking the law into their own hands, rejecting the authority of the council, and electing another set of magistrates.

"The Rath, on hearing this," says Kerssenbroeck, "were filled with alarm, and they considered it expedient to yield, in part at least, to the populace, and to deprive the clergy of their rights, rather than to expose themselves rashly to the greatest dangers."[71]

[71] *Ibid.* p. 272.

They resolved therefore to forbid the Catholic clergy the use of the pulpits of the churches, and to address the people in any form. This was done at once, and all ceremonies "contrary to the pure word of God" were abolished, and the faithful in the different parishes were required to receive and maintain the new pastors commissioned by the burgomaster and corporation to minister to them in things divine.

On the 10th August, a crowd, headed by Rottmann, the preacher Brixius, and Knipperdolling, fell upon the churches and completed the work of devastation which had been begun in February. The Cathedral and the Church of Ueberwasser alone escaped their Vandalism, because the fanatics were afraid of arousing too strong an opposition. The same day the celebration of mass and communion in one kind were forbidden under the severest penalties; the priests were driven out of their churches, and Rottmann, Brixius, Glandorp, Rolle, Wertheim, and Gottfried Ninnhoven, Lutheran preachers, were intruded in their room.[72]

[72] *Ibid.* pp. 228-34.

The peace among these new apostles of the true Gospel was, however, subject to danger. Pastor Brixius had fallen in love with the sister of Pastor Rottmann, and the appearance of the girl proved to every one that the lovers had not waited for the ceremony of marriage. Rottmann insisted on this brother pastor marrying the young woman to repair the scandal. But no sooner was the bride introduced into the parsonage of St. Martin, of which Brixius was in possession, than the first wife of the evangelical minister arrived in Münster with her two children. Brixius was obliged to send away the new wife, but a coldness ensued between him and Rottmann; "however, fearing to cause dissension amongst their adherents by an open quarrel, they came to some arrangement, and Brixius retained his situation."[73]

[73] Kerssenbroeck, pp. 228, 229.

These acts of violence and scandals had inspired many of the citizens with alarm. Those who were able sent their goods out of the town; the nuns of Ueberwasser despatched their title-deeds and sacred vessels to a place of safety. Several of the wealthy citizens and senators, who would not give up their religion, deserted Münster, and settled elsewhere. The two burgomasters, Ebroin Drost and Willebrand Plonies, resigned their offices and left the city never to return.[74] The provosts of the guilds next insisted on the severe repression of all Catholic usages and the performance of sacraments by the priests; they went further, and insisted on belief in the sacrifice of the altar and adoration of the Host being made penal. The clergy wrote to the bishop imploring his aid, and assuring him that their position was daily becoming more intolerable; but Francis of Waldeck recommended patience, and promised his aid when it lay in his power to assist them.

[74] *Ibid.* p. 230.

On the 17th September, 1532, he convoked the nobles of the principality at Wollbeck, gave them an account of the condition of Münster, and conjured them to assist him in suppressing the rebellion.[75] The nobles replied, that before adopting violent measures, it would be advisable to attempt a reconciliation. Eight commissioners were chosen from amongst the barons, who wrote to the magistrates, and requested them to send their deputies to Wollbeck on Monday, September 23rd, "so as to come to some decision on what is necessary for the welfare of the republic." The envoys of the city appeared, and after the opening of the assembly, the grand marshal of the diocese described the condition of the city, and declared that if it pursued its course of disobedience, the nobility were prepared to assist their prince in re-establishing order. The delegates were given eight days to frame an answer. The agitation in Münster during these days was great. The evangelical preachers lost no time in exciting the people. The deputies returned to the conference with a vague answer that the best way to settle the differences would be to submit them to competent and enlightened judges; and so the matter dropped.

[75] *Ibid.* p. 248 *et seq.*

The bishop's officers now captured a herd of fat cattle belonging to some citizens of Münster, which were on their way to Cologne, and refused to surrender them till the preachers of disaffection were sent away.[76]

[76] Kerssenbroeck, pp. 268-9.

The party of Rottmann and Knipperdolling now required the town council to raise 500 soldiers for the defence of the town, should it be attacked by the prince-bishop—to strike 2000 ducats in copper for the payment of the mercenaries, such money to circulate in Münster alone—to order the sentinels to forbid egress to the Catholic clergy, should they attempt to fly—and to impose on the Catholic clergy a tax of 4000 florins a month for the support of the troops. As the clergy had been deprived of their benefices, forbidden to preach and minister the sacraments, this additional act of persecution was intolerable in its injustice. The senate accepted these requisitions with some abatement—the number of soldiers was reduced to 300.[77]

[77] *Ibid.* p. 279 *et seq.*

The bishop, finding that the confiscation of the oxen had not produced the required results, adopted another expedient which proved equally ineffectual. He closed all the roads by his cavalry, declared the city in a state of blockade, and forbade the peasantry taking provisions into Münster. The artizans then marched out and took the necessary food; they paid for it, but threatened the peasants with spoliation without repayment, unless they frequented the market with their goods as usual. This menace produced its effect; Münster continued to be provisioned as before.[78]

[78] *Ibid.* p. 283 *et seq.*

Proud of their success, the innovators attacked Ueberwasser Church, and ordered the abbess to dismiss the Catholic clergy who ministered there, and to replace them by Gospel preachers. She declined peremptorily, and the mob then drove the priests out of the church and presbytery, and instituted Lutherans in their place.[79]

[79] *Ibid.* pp. 284, 285.

Notwithstanding the decrees of the senate, the priests continued their exhortations and their ministrations in such churches as the Evangelicals were unable to supply with pastors, of whom there was a lack. Brixius, the bigamist minister of St. Martin's, having found in one of them a monk preaching to a crowd of women, rushed up into the pulpit, crying out that the man was telling them lies; "but," says Kerssenbroeck, "the devotees surrounded the unfortunate orator, beat him with their fists, slippers, wooden shoes and staves, so that he fled the church, his face and body black and blue." Probably these women bore him a grudge also for his treatment of Rottmann's sister, which was no secret. "Furious at this, he went next day to exhibit the traces of the combat to the senate, entreating them to revenge the outrage he had received—he a minister of the Holy Gospel; but, for the first time, the magistrates showed some sense, and declared that they would not meddle in the matter, because the guilty persons were too numerous, and that some indulgence ought to be shown to the fair sex."[80]

[80] Kerssenbroeck, p. 330.

The town council now sent deputies to the Protestant princes, Dukes Ernest and Francis of Lüneburg, the Landgrave Philip of Hesse, and Count Philip of Waldeck, brother of the prince-bishop, to promise the adhesion of the city to the Smalkald union, and to request their assistance against their bishop. The situation was singular. The city sought assistance of the Protestant union against their prince, desiring to overthrow his power, under the plea that he was a Catholic bishop. And the bishop, at heart a Lutheran, and utterly indifferent to his religious position and responsibilities, was determined to coerce his subjects into obedience, that he might retain his rank and revenue as prince, intending, when the city returned to its obedience, to shake off his episcopal office, to Lutheranize his subjects, and remain their sovereign prince, and possibly transform the ecclesiastical into a hereditary principality, the appanage of a family of which he would be the founder. He had already provided himself with a concubine, Anna Pölmann, by whom he had children.

Whilst the senate was engaged in treating with the Protestant princes, negotiations continued with the bishop, at the diets convoked successively at Dulmen and Wollbeck, but they were as fruitless as before. The deputies separated on the 9th December, agreeing to meet again on the 21st of the same month.

At this time there arrived in Münster a formal refutation of the theses of Rottmann, by John of Deventer, provincial of the Franciscans at Cologne.[81] The magistrates had repeatedly complained that "the refusal of the Catholics to reply to Bernard Rottmann was the sole cause of all the evil." At the same time they had forbidden the Catholic clergy to preach or to make use of the press in Münster. This answer came like a surprise upon them. It was carried by the foes of the clergy to the magistrates. The news of the appearance of this counterblast created the wildest excitement. "The citizens, assembled in great crowds, ran about the streets to hear what was being said. Some announced that the victory would remain with Rottmann, others declared that he would never recover the blow."

[81] Kerssenbroeck, p. 332.

The provosts of the guilds hastily drew up a petition to the senate to expel the clergy from the town, and to confiscate their goods; but the magistrates refused to comply with this requisition, which would have at once stirred up civil war.[82]

[82] *Ibid.* pp. 335-7.

Rottmann mounted the pulpit on St. Andrew's day, and declared that on the following Sunday he would refute the arguments of John of Deventer. Accordingly, on the day appointed, he preached to an immense crowd, taking for his text the words of St. Paul (Rom. xiii. 12), "The night is far spent, the day is at hand." The sermon was not an answer to the arguments of John of Deventer, but a furious attack upon the Pope and Catholicism. Knipperdolling also informed the people that he would rather have his children killed and cooked and served up for dinner than surrender his evangelical principles and return to the errors of the past.[83]

[83] *Ibid.* p. 338.

On the 21st December, 1532, Francis of Waldeck assembled the diet of the principality, and asked its advice as to the advisability of proclaiming war against Münster, should the city persist in its obstinacy.[84] The clergy and nobles replied that, according to immemorial custom, the prince must engage in war at his own cost, and that they were too heavily burdened with taxes for the Turkish war to enable them to undertake fresh charges. Francis of Waldeck reminded them that he was obliged to pay a pension of 2000 florins to his predecessor, Frederick von Wied, and he affirmed that he also was not in a condition to have recourse to arms.

[84] *Ibid.* p. 340 *et seq.*

Whilst the prince, his barons and canons were deliberating, Rottmann had assumed the ecclesiastical dictatorship in the cathedral city, and had ordered, on his sole authority, the suppression of the observance of fast-days.

The spirit of opposition and protestation that had been evoked already manifested itself in strange excesses. "Some of the Evangelicals refused to have the bread put into their mouths at Communion," says Kerssenbroeck, "but insisted on helping themselves from the table, or they stained themselves in taking long draughts at the large chalices. It is even said that some placed the bread in large soup tureens, and poured the wine upon it, and took it out with spoons and forks, so that they might communicate in both kinds at one and the same moment."[85]

[85] Kerssenbroeck, p. 347.

The Reformer of Münster began to entertain and to express doubts as to the validity of the baptism of infants, which he considered had not the warrant of Holy Scripture. Melancthon wrote urgently to him, imploring him not to create dissensions in the Evangelical Church by disturbing the arrangement many wise men had agreed upon. "We have enemies enough," added Melancthon; "they will be rejoiced to see us tearing each other and destroying one another.... I speak with good intention, and I take the liberty of giving my advice, because I am devoted to you and to the Church."[86]

[86] *Ibid.* p. 348.

Luther wrote as well, not to Rottmann, but to the magistrates of Münster, praising their love of the Gospel, and urging them to beware of being drawn away by the damnable errors of the Sacramentarians, Zwinglians, *aliorumque schwermerorum.*[87] The senators received this apostolic epistle with the utmost respect and reverence imaginable; they communicated it to Rottmann and his colleagues, and ordered them to obey it. But the senate had long lost its authority; and this injunction was disregarded.[88] "Disorder and infidelity made progress; the idle, rogues, spendthrifts, thieves, and ruined persons swelled the crowd of Evangelists."[89]

[87] *Ibid.* p. 349.
[88] Kerssenbroeck, p. 351.
[89] *Ibid.* p. 351.

However, it was not enough to have introduced the new religion, to satisfy the Evangelicals the Catholics must be completely deprived of the exercise of their religion. In spite of every hindrance, mass had been celebrated every Sunday in the cathedral. All the parish churches had been deprived of their priests, but the minster remained in the hands of the Catholics. As Christmas approached, many men and women prepared by fasting, alms, and confession, to make their communion at the cathedral on the festival of the Nativity.

The magistrates, hearing of their design, forbade them communicating, offering, as an excuse, that it would cause scandal to the partisans of the Reform. They also published a decree forbidding baptisms to be performed elsewhere than in the parish churches; so as to force the faithful to bring their children to the ministrations of men whom they regarded with aversion as heretics and apostates.[90]

[90] *Ibid.* p. 353.

No envoys from the capital attended the reunion of the chambers at Wollbeck on the 20th December. But Münster sent a letter expressing a hope that the difference between the city and the prince might be terminated by mediation.

This letter gave the diet a chance of escaping from its very difficult position of enforcing the rule of the prince without money to pay the soldiers. The diet undertook to lay the suggestion before the prince-bishop, and to transmit his reply to the envoys of Münster.

Francis of Waldeck then quitted his diocese of Minden, and betook himself to Telgte,[91] a little town about four miles from Münster, where he was to receive the oath of allegiance and homage of his subjects in the principality. The estates assembled at Wollbeck, and all the leading nobles and clergy of the diocese hastened to Telgte and assembled around their sovereign on the same day. A letter was at once addressed to the senate of Münster by the assembled estates, urging it to send deputies to Telgte, the following morning, at eight o'clock, to labour together with them at the re-establishment of peace.

[91] *Ibid.* p. 354 *et seq.* Sleidan, French tr. p. 407.

The deputies did not appear; the senate addressed to the diet, instead, a letter of excuses. The estates at once replied that in the interest of peace, they regretted the obstinacy with which the senate had refused to send deputies to Telgte; but that this had not prevented them from supplicating the bishop to yield to their wishes; and that they were glad to announce that he was ready to submit the mutual differences to the arbitration of two princes of the Empire, one to be named by himself, the other by the city of Münster. And until the arbitration took place, the prince-bishop would provisionally suspend all measures of severity, on condition that the ancient usages should be restored in the churches, the preachers should cease to innovate, and that the imprisoned vassals of the bishop should be released.

This missive was sent into the town on the 25th; the magistrates represented to the bearer "that it would be scandalous to occupy themselves with temporal affairs on Christmas-day," and on this pretext they persuaded him to remain till the morrow in Münster. Then orders were given for the gates of the town to be closed, and egress to be forbidden to every one.

Having taken these precautions, the magistrates assembled the provosts of the guilds, and held with them a conference, which terminated shortly before nine o'clock the same evening; after which the subaltern officers of the senate were sent round to rap at every door, and order the citizens to assemble at midnight, before the town-hall. A nocturnal expedition had been resolved upon; but the movement in the town had excited the alarm of the Catholics, who, thinking that a general massacre of those who adhered to the old religion was in contemplation, hid themselves in drains and cellars and chimneys.

Arms were brought out of the arsenal, cannons were mounted, waggons were laden with powder, shot, beams, planks and ladders. At the appointed hour, the crowd, armed in various fashions, assembled before the Rath-haus.[92] The magistrates and provosts then selected six hundred trusty Evangelicals, and united them to a band of three hundred mercenaries and a small troop of horse. The rest were dispersed upon the ramparts and were recommended to keep watch; then it was announced to the party in marching order that they were to hasten stealthily to Telgte and capture the prince-bishop, his councillors, the barons, and all the members of the estates then assembled in that little town.

[92] Kerssenbroeck, p. 358 *et seq.* Sleidan, French tr. p. 408. Sleidan also gives the number as 900; Dorpius, f. 392 b.

However, the diet, surprised at not seeing their messenger return, conceived a slight suspicion. Whether he feared that his person was in danger so near Münster is not known, but fortunately for himself, the prince, that same evening, left Telgte for his castle of Iburg. The members of the diet, after long waiting, sent some men along the road to the capital to ascertain whether their messenger was within sight. These men returned, saying that the gates of Münster were closed and that no one was to be seen stirring.

The fact was singular, not to say suspicious, and a troop of horse was ordered to make a reconnaissance in the direction of Münster. It was already late at night, so, having given the order, the members of the diet retired to their beds. The horse soldiers beat the country, found all quiet, withdrew some planks from a bridge over the Werse, between Telgte and Münster, to intercept the passage, and then returned to their quarters, for the night was bitterly cold. On surmounting a hill, crowned by a gibbet, they, however, turned once more and looked over the plain towards the city. A profound silence reigned; but a number of what they believed to be will-o'-the-wisps flitted here and there over the dark ground. As, according to popular superstition in Westphalia, these little lights are to be seen in great abundance at Yuletide, the horsemen paid no attention to them, but continued their return. These lights, mistaken for marsh fires, were in fact the burning matches of the arquebuses carried by those engaged in the sortie. On their return to Telgte, the horse soldiers retired to their quarters, and in half-an-hour all the inhabitants of the town were fast asleep.

Meanwhile, the men of Münster advanced, replaced the bridge over the Werse, traversed the plain, and reached Telgte at two o'clock in the morning. They at once occupied all the streets, according to a plan concerted beforehand, then invaded the houses, and captured the members of the diet, clergy, nobles and commons. Three only of the cathedral chapter escaped in their night shirts with bare feet across the frozen river Ems. The Münsterians, having laid their hands on all the money, jewels, seals, and gold chains they could find, retreated as rapidly as they had advanced, carrying off with them their captives and the booty, but disappointed in not having secured the person of the prince. They entered the cathedral city in triumph on the morning of the 26th December, highly elated at their success, and nothing doubting that with such hostages in their hands, they would be able to dictate their own terms to the sovereign.

But the expedition of Telgte had made a great sensation in the empire. Francis of Waldeck addressed himself to all the members of the Germanic body, and appealed especially to his metropolitan, the Elector of Cologne, for assistance, and also to the Dukes of Cleves and Gueldres. The elector wrote at once to Münster in terms the most pressing, because some of his own councillors were among the prisoners. He received an evasive answer. The Protestant princes of the Smalkald league even addressed letters to the senate, blaming energetically their high-handed proceeding. Philip Melancthon also wrote a letter of mingled remonstrance and entreaty.[93] The only result of their appeals was the restoration to the prisoners of their money and the jewels taken from them.

[93] Kerssenbroeck, p. 368.

John von Wyck, syndic of Bremen, was despatched by the senate of Münster to the Landgrave Philip of Hesse, to ask him to undertake the office of mediator between them and their prince. The Landgrave readily accepted the invitation, and Francis of Waldeck was equally ready to admit his mediation, as he was himself, as has been already stated, a Lutheran at heart. The people of Münster, finding that the bishop was eager for a pacific settlement, insisted on the payment of the value of the oxen he had confiscated, as a preliminary, before the subject of differences was entered upon. The prince-bishop consented, paid 450 florins, and allowed the Landgrave of Hesse to draw up sixteen articles of treaty, which met with the approval of both the senate and himself.

The terms of the agreement were as follows:[94]—

I. The prince-bishop was to offer no violence to the inhabitants of Münster in anything touching religion. "The people of Münster shall keep the pure Word of God," said the article; "it shall be preached to them, without any human additions by their preachers, in the six parish churches. These same preachers shall minister the sacraments and order their services and ceremonies as they please. The citizens shall submit in religious matters to the judgment of the magistrates alone, till the questions at issue are decided by a General Council."

[94] *Ibid.* p. 392 *et seq.*

II. The Catholics were to exercise their religion freely in the cathedral and in the capitular churches not included in the preceding article, *until Divine Providence should order otherwise.* The Lutheran ministers were forbidden to attack the Catholics, their dogmas and rights, *unless the Word of God imperiously required it*;—a clause opening a door to any amount of abuse. As the speciality of Protestantism of every sort consists in negation, it would be impossible for an Evangelical pastor to hold his position without denouncing what he disbelieved.

Article III. interdicted mutual recriminations. Article IV., in strange contradiction with Article I., declared that the town of Münster should obey the prince-bishop as legitimate sovereign in matters spiritual and temporal. The bishop in the Vth Article promised to respect the privileges of the subject.

The VIth Article forbade any one making an arbitrary use of the Word of God to justify refusal of obedience to the magistrates. Article VII. reserved to the clergy their revenues, with the exception of the six parish churches, of which the revenues were to be employed for the maintenance of the Evangelical pastors. By the VIIIth Article the senate promised not to interfere with the collation to benefices not in their hands by right. The IXth Article allowed the citizens to deprive their pastors in the Lutheran churches, without the intervention of the bishop. The rest of the Articles secured a general amnesty, permission to the refugees to return, and to the imprisoned members of the diet to obtain their freedom.

This treaty was fair enough in its general provisions. If, as was the case, a large number of the citizens were disposed to adopt Lutheranism, no power on earth had any right to constrain them, and they might justly claim the free exercise of their religion. But there were suspicious clauses inserted in the 1st and 2nd Articles which pointed to the renewal of animosity and the re-opening of the whole question.

This treaty was signed on the 14th February, 1533, by Philip of Hesse, as mediator, Francis, Count of Waldeck, Prince and Bishop of Münster, the members of chapter, the representatives of the nobles of the principality, and the burgomasters and senators of Münster, together with those of the towns of Coesfeld and Warendorf, in their own name and in behalf of the other towns of the diocese. The captive estates were liberated on the 18th February. How the magistrates and town kept the other requirements of the treaty we shall soon see.

The senate having been constituted supreme authority in spiritual things by the Lutheran party, now undertook the organisation of the Evangelical Church in the city; and a few days after the treaty had been signed, it published an "Evangelical Constitution," consisting of ten articles, for the government of the new Church.[95]

[95] Kerssenbroeck, p. 398 *et seq.*

The 8th article had a threatening aspect. "The ministers of the Divine Word shall use their utmost endeavours to gain souls to the true faith, and to direct them in the ways of perfection. *As for those who shall refuse to accept the pure doctrine*, and those who shall blaspheme and be guilty of public crimes, the senate will employ against them all the rigour of the laws, and the sword of justice."

Rottmann was appointed by the magistrates Superintendent of the Lutheran Church in Münster, a function bearing a certain resemblance to that of a bishop.[96] Then, thinking that a bishop should be the husband of one wife at least, Rottmann married the widow of Johann Vigers, late syndic of Münster. "She was a person of bad character," says Kerssenbroeck, "whom Rottmann had inspired during her husband's life with Evangelical principles and an adulterous love."[97] It is asserted, with what truth it is impossible at this distance of time to decide, that Vigers was drowned in his bath at Ems, in a fit, and that his wife allowed him to perish without attempting to save him. Anyhow, no sooner was he dead, than she returned full speed to Münster and married her lover.[98]

[96] *Ibid.* p. 402.
[97] *Ibid.* p. 403.
[98] *Ibid.* p. 404.

The reformer and his adherents had been given their own way, and the senate hoped they would rest satisfied, and that tranquillity would be re-established in the city. But their hopes were doomed to disappointment. Certain people, if given an inch, insist on taking an ell; of these people Rottmann was one. Excited by him, the Evangelicals of the town complained that the magistrates had treated the Papists with too great leniency, that the clergy had not been expelled and their goods confiscated according to the original programme. It was decided tumultuously that the elections must be anticipated; and on the 3rd March, the people deposed the magistrates and elected in their room the leaders of the extreme reforming party.[99] Knipperdolling was of their number; only four of the former magistrates were allowed to retain office, and these were men whom they could trust. Hermann Tilbeck and Kaspar Judenfeld were named burgomasters; Heinrich Modersohn and Heinrich Redekker were chosen provosts or tribunes of the people.[100]

[99] Kerssenbroeck, p. 404.
[100] *Ibid.* p. 405.

Next to the senate came the turn of the parishes. On the 17th March, under the direction of Rottmann, the people proceeded to appoint the ministers to the churches in the town. Their choice was not happy; it fell on those most unqualified to exercise a salutary influence, and restrain the excitement of a mob already become nearly ungovernable.[101]

[101] *Ibid.* p. 406.

The new senate endeavoured to strengthen the Evangelical cause by uniting the other towns of the diocese in a common bond of resistance. They invited these towns to send their deputies to meet those of the capital at a little inn between Münster and Coesfeld, on the 20th March. The assembly took place; but so far from the other cities agreeing to support Münster, their deputies read those of the capital a severe lecture, and refused to throw off their old religion and their allegiance to the bishop.[102]

[102] Kerssenbroeck, p. 407 *et seq.*

On the 24th March, 1533, the burgomaster Tilbeck, accompanied by the citizen Kerbink, went to Ueberwasser, summoned the abbess before him, and ordered her to maintain at the expense of the abbey the preachers lately appointed to the church in connection with the convent. She was forced to submit.[103]

[103] *Ibid.* p. 413.

On the 27th of the same month one of the preachers invaded the church of St. Ledger, still in the hands of the Catholics, at the head of his congregation, broke open the tabernacle, drew out the Host, broke it, and blowing the fragments into the air, screamed to the assembled multitude, "Look at your good God flying away."

The same day the treaty was violated towards the Franciscans. Some of the senators ordered them to quit their convent, their habit, and their order, unless they desired still more rigorous treatment, "because the magistrates were resolved to make the Church flourish again in her ancient purity, and because they wanted to convert the convent into a school."[104]

[104] *Ibid.* p. 413.

The superior replied that he and his brethren followed strictly the rule of their founder, and that this house belonged to them by right of succession, and that they were no charge to the town. He said that if a building was needed for an Evangelical school, he was ready to surrender to the magistrates a portion of the convent buildings; all he asked in return was that he and his brethren should be allowed to live in tranquillity. This proposal saved the Franciscans for a time. The Evangelical school was established in their convent, "but at the end of a month it had fallen into complete disorder, whereas the old Papist school had not lost one of its pupils, and was as flourishing as ever."[105]

[105] Kerssenbroeck, p. 415.

Whilst the senators menaced the monasteries, Knipperdolling and his friend Gerhardt Kibbenbroeck pillaged the church of S. Lambert. Scarcely a day now passed without some fresh act of violence done to the Catholics, or Vandalism perpetrated on the churches.

On the 5th April the prior and monks of Bispinkhoff were forbidden by the magistrates to hear confessions in their own church. The same day the Lutherans broke the altar and images in the church of Ueberwasser, and scraped the paintings off the walls.

On Palm Sunday, April 6th,[106] at Ueberwasser, some of the nuns, urged by the preachers in their church, cast off their vows, and joining the people, chanted the 7th verse of the 124th Psalm according to Luther's translation—

"Der Strich ist entzwei, Und wir sind frei."

[106] *Ibid.* p. 416.

"The snare is broken, and we are delivered;" and then they received Communion with the pastors.

On the 7th the mob pillaged the church of the Servites, and defaced it. Next day the Franciscans, who had made the wafers for the Holy Sacrament for the churches in the diocese, were forbidden to make them any more. On the 9th Knipperdolling, heading a party of the reformed, broke into the cathedral during the celebration of the Holy Eucharist, rushed up to the altar, and drove away the priest, exclaiming, "Greedy fop, haven't you enough good Gods yet?" Two days later the magistrates ordered the chapter to surrender into their hands their title deeds and sacred vessels. On the 14th, Belkot, head of the city tribunal of Münster, entered the church of S. Ledger, and carried off all its chalices, patens, and ciboriums, whilst others who accompanied him destroyed the altars, paintings, and statuary, and profaned the church in the most disgusting manner. The unhappy Catholics, unable to resist, uttered loud lamentations, and did not refrain from calling the perpetrators of the outrage "robbers and sacrilegious," for which they were summoned before the magistrates, and threatened with imprisonment unless they apologised.[107]

[107] Kerssenbroeck 417.

As the news of the conversion of the city of Münster to the Gospel spread, strangers came to it from all parts, to hear and to learn, as they gave out, pure Evangelical truth.

Amongst these adventurers was a man destined to play a terribly prominent part in the great drama that was about to be enacted at Münster. This was John Bockelson, a tailor, a native of Leyden, in Holland. He had quitted his country and his wife secretly to hear Rottmann. He entered Münster on the 25th July, and lodged with a citizen named Hermann Ramers. Having been instructed in the Gospel according to Luther, he went to preach in Osnabrück, but from thence he was driven. He then returned to his own home. There he became an Anabaptist, under the instruction of John Matthisson, who sent him with Gerrit Buchbinder as apostles of the sect to Westphalia in the month of November, 1533.

The time had now arrived when the Lutheran party, which had so tyrannically treated the Catholics in the city of Münster, was itself to be despotically put down and trampled upon by a sect which sprang from its own womb.

Rottmann had for some while been wavering in his adhesion to Lutheranism.[108] He doubted first, and then disbelieved in the Real Presence, which Luther insisted upon. He thought that the reformation of the Wittenberg doctor was not sufficiently thoroughgoing in the matter of ceremonial; then he doubted the scriptural authority for the baptism of infants. Two preachers, Heinrich Rott and Herman Strapedius, fell in with his views. The former had been a monk at Haarlem, but had become a Lutheran preacher. He regarded the baptism of infants as one of those things which are indifferent to salvation. Strapedius was more decided; he preached against infant baptism as an abomination in the sight of God. He was named by the people preacher at S. Lambert's, the head church of the city, in spite of the opposition of the authorities.[109]

[108] Kerssenbroeck, p. 429 et seq.; Sleidan, French tr. p. 409; Bullinger, "Adv. Anabapt.," 116, ii. c. 8.

[109] Kerssenbroeck, pp. 431, 432; Dorp., f. 322-3.

The Lutheran senate of Münster, which a few months previously had been elected enthusiastically by the people, now felt that before these fiery preachers, drifting into Anabaptism, their power was in as precarious a position as was that of those whom they had supplanted. Alarmed at the rapid extension of the new forms of disbelief, they twice forbade Rottmann to preach against the baptism of infants and the Real Presence, and ordered him to conform in his teaching to authorised Lutheran doctrine. He treated their orders with contempt. Then they summoned him before them: he appeared, but on leaving the Rathhaus, preached in the square to the people with redoubled violence.

The senate, at their wits' end, ordered a public discussion between Rottmann and the orthodox Lutherans, represented by Hermann Busch. The discussion took place before the city Rath, and the senate decided that Busch had gained the day, and they therefore forbade all innovation in the administration of baptism and the Lord's Supper.

Rottmann and his colleague disregarded the monition, and continued their sermons against the rags of Popery which still disfigured the Lutheran Church. Several of the ministers in the town, whether from conviction or from interest, finding that their congregations drained away to the churches where the stronger-spiced doctrine was preached, joined the movement. It was simply a carrying of negation beyond the pillars of Hercules planted by Luther. Luther had denied of the sum total of Catholic dogmas, say ten, and had retained ten. The Anabaptist denied two more, and retained only eight. On the 10th August a tumultuous scene took place in the church of S. Giles.[110] A Dutch preacher began declaiming against baptism of children. Johann Windemoller, ex-senator, a vehement opponent of Anabaptist disintegration of Lutheran doctrine, who was in the congregation, rushed up the pulpit stairs, and pulled the preacher down, exclaiming, "Scoundrel! how dare you take upon you the office of preacher—you who, a few years ago, were thrust into the iron-collar, and branded on the cheek for your crimes? Do you think I do not know your antecedents? You talk of virtue, you gibbet-bird? You who are guilty of so many crimes and impieties? Go along with you, take your doctrine and your brand elsewhere."

[110] Kerssenbroeck, p. 434.

Windemoller was about to turn the pastor out of the church, when a number of women, who had joined the Anabaptist party, fell, howling, upon Windemoller, crying that he wanted to deprive them of the saving Gospel and Word of Truth, and they would have strangled him had he not beat a precipitate retreat. The same afternoon, some citizens who brought their children to this church to be baptized were driven from the doors with shouts of derision.

The magistrates played a trump card, and ordered Rottmann to leave the town, together with the ministers who followed his teaching.[111] Bernard Rottmann replied much in the same strain as he had answered the bishop, stating that his doctrine was strictly conformable to the pure word of God, and that he demanded a public discussion, in which his doctrines might be tested by Scripture alone, without human additions. Finally he protested that he would not abstain from preaching, nor desert his flock, whether the senate persisted in its sentence or not. Five ministers signed this defiant letter—Rottmann, Johann Clopris, Heinrich Roll, Gottfried Strahl, and Denis Vinnius. These men at once hastened to collect the heads of the corporations and provosts together, and urge them to take their part against the Rath. They were quite prepared to do so, and the magistrates yielded on condition that Bernard and his following of preachers should abstain from speaking on the disputed questions of infant baptism and the Eucharist. Rottmann consented, in his own name and in that of his friends, in a paper dated October 3rd, 1533.[112] The senate was, however, well aware that its power was tottering to its fall, and that the preachers had not the remotest intention of fulfilling their engagement. They saw that these men were gradually absorbing into themselves the supreme authority in the city, and that a magistracy which opposed them could at any moment be by them dismissed their office. In alarm they wrote to the prince-bishop, and sent him messengers to lay before him the precarious condition of the affairs in the capital, imploring him to consider the imminence of the peril, and to send them learned theologians who could combat the spread of erroneous doctrine, and introduce those conformable to the pure word of God.[113]

[111] *Ibid.* p. 436.
[112] Kerssenbroeck, pp. 437-9.
[113] *Ibid.* p. 441.

It was a singular state of affairs indeed. The magistrates had appealed to the pure word of God, as understood by Luther, against Catholicism, and now the Anabaptists appealed to the same oracle, with equal confidence against Lutheranism; the two parties leaned on the same support—who was to decide which party Scripture upheld?

The answer of Francis of Waldeck was such as might have been expected from a man endowed with some common sense. He reminded the magistrates that it was their own fault if things had come to such a pass; he feared that now the evil had gained the upper hand, and that gentleness was out of place; a decided face could alone secure to the magistrates moral authority. He was ready to support them if they would maintain their allegiance for the future. He would send them a learned theologian, Dr. Heinrich Mumpert, prior of the Franciscans of Bispinkhoff, to preach against error in the cathedral.

The senate was in a dilemma. They had no wish to return to Catholicism, and they dreaded the progress of schism. They stood on an inclined plane. Above was the rock of an infallible authority; below, faith shelved into an abyss of negation they shrank from fathoming. If they looked back, they saw Catholicism; if they looked forward, they beheld the dissolution of all positive belief. Like all timorous men they shrank from either alternative, and attempted for a little longer to maintain their slippery position. They declined the offer of the Catholic doctor, and turned to the Landgrave Philip of Hesse for assistance. The Landgrave at once acceded to the request of the magistrates, and sent them Theodore Fabricius and Johann Melsinger, guaranteeing to their senate their orthodoxy.[114]

[114] Kerssenbroeck, p. 443; Sleidan, p. 410; Dorpius, f. 393 b.

While these preachers were on their way, disorder increased in Münster. The faction of Rottmann grew apace, and spread into the Convent of Ueberwasser, where the nuns were daily compelled to hear the harangues of two zealous Evangelical pastors, who exerted themselves strenuously to demolish the faith of the sisters down to the point fixed as the limit of negation by Luther. But these pastors having become infected with Rottmann's views, continued the work of destruction, and lowered the temple of faith two additional stages.

The result of these sermons on the excitable nuns was that the majority broke out into revolt, and refused to observe abstinence and practise self-mortification; and proclaimed their intention of returning to the world and marrying. The bishop wrote to them, imploring them to consider that they were all of them members of noble families, and that they must be careful in no way to dishonour their families by scandalous behaviour. The mutineers seemed disposed to yield, but we shall presently see that their submission was only temporary.[115]

[115] Kerssenbroeck, p. 443.

On the 15th October, the senate wrote to the bishop, and informed him that they would not permit the prior Mumpert to preach in the cathedral.[116] They acknowledged that according to the treaty of Telgte, the city had consented to allow the Catholics the use of the cathedral, "until such time as the Lord shall dispose otherwise," but, they said, at the time of the conclusion of the treaty, there was no preacher at the minster; which was true, for the Catholic clergy had been forbidden the use of the pulpit; and they declared that "in all good conscience, they could not permit the institution of one whose doctrine and manner of life were not conformable to the gospel."

[116] *Ibid.* p. 444.

Francis of Waldeck, without paying attention to this refusal, ordered Mumpert to preach and celebrate the Eucharist in the cathedral church, on Sunday, 26th October, 1533. The prior obeyed. The fury of the

Evangelicals was without limits; and in a second letter, more insolent than the first, the magistrates told the bishop that "they would not suffer a fanatical friar to come and teach error to the people." The bishop's sole reply was a command to the prior to continue his course.

At this moment the learned divines sent by Philip of Hesse arrived in the city, and hearing of the sermons in the minster, to which the people flocked, and which were likely to produce a counter current in a Catholic direction, they insisted, as a preliminary to their mission, that the mouth of the Catholic preacher should be stopped. "We pray you," said they to the magistrates, "to forbid this man permission to reside in the town, lest our pure doctrine be choked by his abominable sermons. An authority claiming to be Christian should not tolerate such a scandal."

The senate hastened to satisfy the Hessian theologians, by not merely ordering the Catholic preacher to leave the city, but by outlawing him, so that he was obliged in haste to fly a place where his life might be taken by any unscrupulous persons with impunity.[117]

[117] Kerssenbroeck, p. 444 *et seq.*

Francis of Waldeck, justly irritated, wrote to Philip of Hesse, remonstrating at the interference of his commissioners in the affairs of another man's principality.[118] The Landgrave replied that, so far from deserving reproach, he merited thanks for having sent to Münster two divines of the first class, who would preach there the pure Word of God, and would strangle the monster of Anabaptism. With the outlawry of the Catholic preacher, the struggle between Catholicism and Lutheranism closed; the struggle for the future was to be between Lutheranism and Anabaptism; a struggle desperate on the part of the Lutherans, for what basis had they for operation? The Catholics had an intrenched position in the authority of a Church, which they claimed to be invested with divine inerrancy, by commission from Christ; but the Lutheran and Anabaptist fought over the pages of the Bible, each claiming Scripture as on his side. It was a war within a camp, to decide which should pitch the other outside the rampart of the letter.

[118] *Ibid.* p. 457 *et seq.*

Fabricius and Melsinger fought for Infant Baptism and the Real Presence, Rottmann and Strapedius against both. "Do you call this the body and blood of Christ?" exclaimed Master Bernard one day, whilst he was distributing the Sacrament; and flinging it on the ground, he continued, "Were it so, it would get up from the ground and mount the altar of itself without my help. Know by this that neither the body nor blood of Christ are here."[119]

[119] Dorpius, f. 394.

Peter Wyrthemius, a Lutheran preacher, was interrupted, when he attempted to preach, by the shouts and jeers of the Anabaptists, and was at last driven from his pulpit.

Rottmann kept his promise not to preach Anabaptist doctrine in the pulpit, but he printed and circulated a number of tracts and pamphlets, and held meetings in private houses for the purpose of disseminating his views.[120] His reputation increased rapidly, and extended afar. Disciples came from Holland, Brabant, and Friesland, to place themselves under his direction; women even confided to him the custody of their children.

[120] Kerssenbroeck, p. 448.

The most lively anxiety inspired the senate to make another attempt to regain their supremacy in the direction of affairs.

On the 3rd or 4th November, the heads of the guilds and the provosts and patricians of the city were assembled to deliberate, and it was resolved that Rottmann and his colleagues should be expelled the town and the diocese; and to remove from them the excuse that they feared arrest when they quitted the walls of Münster, the magistrates obtained for them a safe-conduct, signed by the bishop and the upper chapter.[121]

[121] *Ibid.* p. 449.

Next day, the magistrates and chief citizens reassembled in the market square, and voted that "not only should the Anabaptist preachers be exiled, but also those of the magistrates who had supported them; and that this sentence should receive immediate execution."[122]

[122] Kerssenbroeck, p. 450 *et seq.*

This was too sweeping a measure to pass without provoking resistance. The burgomaster, Tilbeck, who felt that the blow was aimed at himself, exclaimed, angrily: "Is this the reward I receive for having prudently governed the republic? But we will not suffer the innocent to be oppressed, and we shall treat you in such a manner as will calm your insolence."

These words gave the signal for an open rupture.

Knipperdolling and Hermann Krampe, both members of the senate, drew their swords and ranged themselves beside the burgomaster, calling the people to arms. The mob at once rushed upon the senators. The servants of the chapter and the clergy in the cathedral close, hastened carrying arms to the assistance of the magistrates. Both parties sought a place of defence, each anticipating an attack. The Lutherans occupied the Rath-haus and barricaded the doors. The Anabaptists retired behind the strong walls of the cemetery of St. Lambert. The night was spent by both parties under arms, and a fight appeared imminent on the morrow. Then the syndic Johann von Wyck persuaded the frightened senate to moderate their sentence, and hurrying to the Anabaptists, he urged them to be reconciled to the magistrates. An agreement was finally concluded, whereby Rottmann was forbidden for the future to preach, and every one was to be allowed to believe what he liked, and to disbelieve what he chose.

Master Bernard, however, evaded his obligation by holding meetings in private houses at night, to which his followers were summoned by the discharge of a gun.[123] Considering that it was now necessary that his adherents should have their articles of belief, or rather of disbelief, as a bond of union and of distinction between themselves and the Lutherans, he drew up a profession of faith in nineteen articles. That which he had published nine months before was antiquated, and represented the creed of the Lutheran faction, against which he was now at variance.

[123] Kerssenbroeck, p. 453 *et seq.*

This second creed contained the following propositions:—

The baptism of children is abominable before God.

The habitual ceremonies used at baptism are the work of the devil and of the Pope, who is Antichrist.

The consecrated Host is the great Baal.

A Christian (that is, a member of Rottmann's sect) does not set foot in the religious assemblies of the impious (*i.e.*, of the Catholics and Lutherans).

He holds no communication and has no relations with them; he is not bound to obey their authorities; he has nothing in common with their tribunals; nor does he unite with them in marriage.

The Sabbath was instituted by the Lord God, and there is no scriptural warrant for transferring the obligation to the Sunday.

Papists and Lutherans are to be regarded as equally infamous, and those who give faith to the inventions of priests are veritable pagans.

During fourteen centuries there have been no true Christians. Christ was the last priest; the apostles did not enjoy the priestly office.

Jesus Christ did not derive His human nature from Mary.[124]

[124] This is corroborated by the Acta, Handlungen, &c., fol. 385. "*The Preachers*: Do you believe that Christ received His flesh off the flesh of Mary, by the operation of the Holy Ghost? *John of Leyden*: No; such is not the teaching of Scripture." And he explained that if the flesh had been taken from Mary, it must have been sinful, for she was not immaculate.

Every marriage concluded before re-baptism is invalid.

Faith in Christ must precede baptism.

Wives shall call their husbands lords.

Usury is forbidden.

The faithful shall possess all things in common.

The publication of this formulary of faith, if such it may be called, which is a string of negative propositions, increased the alarm of the more sober citizens, who, feeling the insecurity of property and life under a powerless magistracy, prepared to leave the town. Many fled and left their Lutheranism behind them. Lening, one of the preachers sent by the Landgrave of Hesse, ran away.

Fabricius had more courage. He preached energetically against Rottmann, assisted by Dr. Johann Westermann, a Lutheran theologian of Lippe.[125]

[125] Kerssenbroeck, p. 456; Sleidan, p. 411.

According to Kerssenbroeck, however, half the town followed by the Anabaptist leader, and brought their goods and money to lay them at his feet. Those who had nothing of their own, in a body joined the society which proclaimed community of goods.

The bishop again wrote to the magistrates, urging them to permit the Catholic preacher, Mumpert, the use of the cathedral pulpit, but the senate refused, and continued their vain efforts to build their theological system on a slide. At their request, Fabricius and Westermann drew up (November 28, 1533) a symbol of belief in opposition to that formulated by Rottmann, and it was read and adopted by the Lutherans in the Church of St. Lambert. A large number of the people gave in their adhesion to this last and newest creed, and the magistrates, emboldened thereby, made a descent upon the house of the ex-superintendent, and confiscated his private press, with which he had printed his tracts.[126]

[126] *Ibid.* p. 456.

It was then that the two apostles, Buchbinder and Bockelson, sent by Matthisson into Westphalia, appeared in the city. They remained there only four days, during which they re-baptised the preachers and several of their adepts, and then retired prophesying their speedy return and the advent of the reign of grace.

Rottmann, highly exasperated against Fabricius for having drawn up his counter-creed, went on the 30th November to the churchyard of St. Lambert, and standing in an elevated situation, preached to the people on his own new creed, whilst Fabricius was discoursing within to his congregation on his own profession of faith.

When service was over Fabricius came out, and was immediately attacked by Rottmann with injurious expressions, which, however, so exasperated the congregation of the Lutheran, that they fell upon the late superintendent of the Evangelical Church, and threatened him with their sticks and fists.

On the 1st December, Fabricius complained in the pulpit of the insult he had received, and appealed to the people to judge between his doctrine and that of Master Bernard by the difference there was between their respective behaviour.[127]

[127] Kerssenbroeck, p. 461.

A new Anabaptist orator now appeared on the stage; he was a blacksmith's apprentice, named Johann Schroeder. On the 8th December he occupied the position in the cemetery of St. Lambert from which Rottmann had been forced to fly, and defied the Lutherans to oppose him with the pure Word of God. He denounced them as still in darkness, as wrapped in the trappings of Popery, and as enemies to the Gospel of Christ and Evangelical liberty. Then he dared Fabricius to meet him in a public discussion, and prove his doctrine by the text of Scripture.[128]

[128] *Ibid.* p. 461.

The magistrates resolved on one more attempt to arrest the disorder. On the 11th November they informed Rottmann that, unless he immediately left the city, they would decree his outlawry. Rottmann sent a message to them in reply, "That he would not go; that he was not afraid; and that exile was to him an empty word, for, wherever he was, the heavenly Father would cover him with His wings." He took no further notice of the order, except only that he instituted a bodyguard of armed citizens to accompany him wherever he went. On the Sunday following, December 14th, he betook himself, surrounded by his guard, to the church of the Servites, where he intended to preach. But finding the doors locked, he placed himself under a lime-tree near the building and pronounced his discourse, without any one venturing to lay a hand upon him.[129]

[129] Kerssenbroeck, p. 163; Dorpius, f. 394 a.

The magistrates were equally unsuccessful in silencing the blacksmith Schroeder. This man, having preached again on the 15th December, was taken by the police and thrown into prison. Next day the members of the Blacksmiths' Guild marched to the Rath-haus, armed with their hammers and with bars of iron, to demand the release of their comrade. A violent dispute arose between the senators and the exasperated artisans. The former declared that Schroeder, whose trade was to shoe horses and not to preach, had deserved death for having incited to sedition. The reply of the blacksmiths was very similar to that made by the senate to the bishop when he ordered the expulsion of Rottmann. "Schroeder," said they, "has been urged on by love of truth, and he has preached with so much zeal that he has made himself hoarse. He has been guilty neither of murder nor of any crime worthy of death. How dare you maltreat this one who has given edifying instruction to his fellow citizens? Must nothing be done without your authorisation?" Upon the heels of the arguments came menaces. The senate yielded again, and promised to release Schroeder on the morrow.

"Not to-morrow," shouted the blacksmiths; "restore our comrade to us immediately, or we will burst open the prison doors."

The magistrates bowed to the storm, taking, however, the worse than useless precaution of making Schroeder swear, before they knocked off his chains, that he would not attempt to revenge on them his captivity.[130]

[130] Kerssenbroeck, p. 464.

On the 21st December, Rottmann resumed the use of his pulpit in the church of the Servites, treating the orders of the senate with supreme contempt. Westermann, tired of a struggle with the swelling tide, deserted Münster, leaving Fabricius alone to fight against the growing power of the Anabaptists.

The year 1534 opened under gloomy auspices at Münster. In the first few days of January, the new sect dealt the Lutherans the same measure these latter had dealt the Catholics a twelvemonth before. They invaded their churches and disturbed divine worship.

Fabricius attacked Rottmann violently in a sermon preached on the 4th January, and offered to have a public discussion with him on the moot points of doctrine. The senate accepted the proposition with transport, but Rottmann refused. "Not," said he, "that I am afraid of entering the lists against this Lutheran, but that men are so corrupt that they would certainly condemn that side which had for its support right and the word of Scripture."[131]

[131] *Ibid.* pp. 466, 467.

On the same day that Rottmann sent in his refusal, a band of women tumultuously entered the town-hall and demanded that "the miserable foreign vagabond Fabricius, who could not even speak the dialect of the country, and who, inspired by an evil spirit, preaches all kinds of absurdities in a tongue scarcely intelligible, should be driven out of the city. Set in his place the worthy Rottmann," said the women; "he is prudent, eloquent, instructed in every kind of knowledge, and he can speak our language. Grant us this favour, Herrn Burgmeistern, and we will pray God for you." The burgomasters requested the ladies not to meddle with matters that concerned them not, but to return to their families and kitchens. This invitation drove them into a paroxysm of rage, and they shouted at the top of their shrill voices: "Here are fine burgomasters! They are neglecting the interests of the town! Here are tender fathers of their country who attend to nothing! You are worse than murderers, for *they* kill the body, but *you* assassinate souls by depriving them of the Evangelical Word which is their nourishment." The women then retired, but returned next day reinforced by others, and among them were six nuns who had deserted the convent of Ueberwasser and exhibited greater violence than the rest.

The women entered the hall where the senators were sitting and demanded peremptorily that Rottmann should be instituted to the church of St. Lambert. They were turned out of the hall without much ceremony, but they waited the exit of the magistrates when their session was at an end; then they bespattered them with cow and horse dung, and cursed them as Papists. "At first you favoured our holy enterprise, but you have returned to Popery like dogs to their vomit. Since you have devoured the good Hessian God which Fabricius offers you in communion, you oppress the pure Word of God. To the gallows, to the gallows with you all!" The senators fled to their houses, pursued by the women, covered with filth, and deafened by their yells.[132]

[132] Kerssenbroeck, p. 468.

Rottmann and his colleagues exercised an extraordinary influence over the people; they persuaded the rich ladies and citizens' wives of substance to sell their goods, give up their jewels, and cast everything they had into a common fund. The prompt submission of so many proves that the number of fanatics who were sincere in their convictions was considerable. These proceedings led to estrangement in families. Kerssenbroeck relates that the wife of one of the senators, named Wardemann, having been rebaptised by Rottmann, "was so vigorously confirmed in her faith by her husband, who had been informed by a servant maid of the circumstance, that she could not walk for several weeks." Other women, who had given up their jewels and money to Rottmann, were also severely chastised by their husbands.[133]

[133] *Ibid.* p. 472.

The magistrates, afraid to touch Rottmann's person, hoped to weaken him by dismissing his assistants. They therefore, on the 15th January, 1534, ordered their officers to take the Anabaptist preachers, Clopris, Roll, and Strahl, and to turn them out of the town, with orders never to re-enter it. The mandate was executed; but the ministers returned by another gate, and were conducted in triumph to their parsonages by the whole body of the Anabaptists.[134]

[134] Kerssenbroeck, p. 473.

The fugitive nuns of Ueberwasser, to the number of eight, were re-baptised by Rottmann on the 11th January, and became some of his most devoted adherents. Their conduct in the sequel was characterised by the most shameless lubricity.

The prince-bishop at this time published a decree against the Anabaptists, outlawed Rottmann and five other preachers of that sect in Münster, and ordered his officers to check the spread of the schism through the other towns of his principality.

On the 23rd January, Rottmann having noticed some Catholics and Lutherans amongst his audience in the church of the Servites, abruptly stopped his sermon, saying that it was not meet to cast the pearls of the new revelation before swine.[135] Then he descended from the pulpit, and refused to remount it again. But probably the real cause of this sudden cessation was, that the views of the leader were undergoing a third change, and he was unwilling to announce his new doctrine to an audience of which all were not prepared to receive it. He continued to assemble the faithful in private houses, and to hold daily assemblies, in which they were initiated into the further mysteries of his revelation. In every parish a house was provided for the purpose, and none were admitted without a pass-word. In these gatherings the mystic was able to give full development to his views without the restraint of an only partially sympathising audience.

[135] *Ibid.* p. 476.

On the evening of the 28th January, at seven o'clock, the Anabaptists stretched chains across the streets, assembled in armed bands, closed the city gates, and placed sentinels in all directions. A terrible anxiety reigned in the city. The Lutherans remained up and awake all night, a prey to fear, with their doors and windows barricaded, waiting to see what these preparations signified. The night passed, broken only by the tramp of the sectarian fanatics, and lighted by the glare of their torches.

Dawn broke and nothing further had taken place, when suddenly two men, dressed like prophets, with long ragged beards, ample garments, and flowing mantles, staff in hand paced through the town solemnly, up one street and down another, raising their eyes to heaven, sighing, and then looking down with an expression of compassion on the multitude, which bowed before them and saluted them as Enoch and Elias. After having traversed the greater part of the town, the two men entered the door of Knipperdolling's house.[136]

[136] Kerssenbroeck, p. 476.

The names of these prophets were John Matthisson and John Bockelson. The first was the chief of the Anabaptist sect in Holland. The part which the second was destined to play in Münster demands that his antecedents should be more fully given. Bockelson was the bastard son of Bockel, bailiff of the Hague, and a certain Adelhaid, daughter of a serf of the Lord of Zoelcken, in the diocese of Münster. This Adelhaid purchased her liberty afterwards and married her seducer. John was brought up at Leyden, where he was apprenticed to a tailor. He visited England, Portugal, and Lubeck, and returned to Leyden in his twenty-first year. He then married the widow of a boatman, who presented him with two sons. John Bockelson was endowed by nature with a ready wit and with a retentive memory. He amused himself by learning nearly the whole of the Bible by heart, and by composing obscene verses and plays. In addition to his business of tailoring, he opened a public-house under the sign of "The Three Herrings," which became a haunt of women of bad repute. The passion for change came over Bockelson after leading this sort of life for a while, and he visited Münster in 1533, as we have already seen, and thence passed to Osnabrück, from which place he was expelled. After wandering about Westphalia for a while he returned to Leyden. Next year, in company with Matthisson, the head of the Anabaptists, he visited Münster, which the latter declared prophetically was destined to be the new Jerusalem, the capital of a regenerate world, where the millennial kingdom was to be set up.[137]

[137] Kerssenbroeck, part ii. p. 51 *et seq.*; Heresbach, p. 31; Hast, p. 324.

The two adventurers reached their destination on the 13th January, and Knipperdolling received them into his house. Some of the preachers were informed of their arrival, but were required to keep the matter secret till the time ordained of God should come for their revealing themselves to the world.

A council was being held in the house of Knipperdolling, when the prophets entered it after having finished their peregrination of the town. Rottmann, Roll, Clopris, Strapedius, Vinnius, and Strahl were engaged in a warm discussion. Some of the party were of opinion that the moment had arrived, now that all the Anabaptists were under arms, for a general purification of the city by the massacre or expulsion of Catholics and Lutherans; the others thought that the hour of vengeance had not yet struck, and that the day of the Lord must not be antedated. The quarrel was appeased by the appearance of the two prophets, who were hailed as messengers sent from heaven to announce the will of God. Then Matthisson and his companion knelt down and wept, and having meditated some moments, they uttered their decision in voices broken by sobs. "The time for cleansing the threshing-floor of the Lord is not yet come. The slaughter of the ungodly must be delayed, that souls may be gathered in, and that souls may be formed and educated in houses set apart, and not in churches which were lately filled with idols. But," said they in conclusion, "the day of the Lord is at hand."

These words reconciled the council. On the evening of the 29th, the Anabaptists laid aside their arms and returned to their homes.[138] The events of the night had utterly dispelled the last traces of courage in the magistrates; they did not venture to notice the threatening aspect of the armed fanatics, or to remonstrate with them for barricading the streets. To avert all possible danger from themselves was their only object; and to effect this they published an act of toleration, permitting every man to worship God and perform his public and private devotions as he thought proper.

[138] Kerssenbroeck, part i. p. 477 *et seq.*

The power of Rottmann had become so great, through the events just recorded, that a false prophecy did not serve to upset his authority. On the 6th February, at the head of a troop of his admirers, he invaded the Church of Ueberwasser, "to prevent the Evangelical flame kindled in the hearts of the nuns from dying out."[139] Having summoned all the sisters into the church, he mounted the pulpit and preached to them a sermon on matrimony, in which he denounced convents and monasteries, in which the most imperious laws of nature were left unfulfilled, and "he urged the nuns to labour heartily for the propagation of the human race;" and then he completely turned the heads of the young women, by announcing to them with an inspired air, that their convent would fall at midnight, and would bury beneath its ruins every one who was found within its walls. "This salutary announcement has been made to me," said he, "by one of the prophets now present in this town, and the Heavenly Father has also favoured me with a direct and special revelation to the same effect."[140]

[139] Kerssenbroeck, p. 479.
[140] Hast, p. 329 *et seq.*

This was enough to complete the conversion of the nuns, already shaken in their faith by the sermons they had been compelled to listen to for some time past. In vain did the Abbess Ida and two other sisters implore them to remain and despise the prophecy. The infatuated women, in paroxysms of fear and excitement, fled the convent and took refuge in the house of Rottmann, where they changed their clothes, and then ran about the town uttering cries of joy.

The prophecy of Rottmann had been repeated by one to another throughout Münster. No one slept that night. Crowds poured down the streets in the direction of Ueberwasser, and the square in front of the convent was densely packed with breathless spectators, awaiting the ruin of the house.

Midnight tolled from the cathedral tower. The crowd waited another hour. It struck one, and the convent had not fallen. Master Bernard was not the man to be disconcerted by so small a matter. "Prophecies," cried he, "are always conditional. Jonah foretold that Nineveh should be destroyed in forty days, but since the inhabitants repented, it remained standing. The same has taken place here. Nearly all the nuns have repented, have quitted their cloister and their habit, have renounced their vows—thus the anger of the Heavenly Father has been allayed."[141]

[141] Kerssenbroeck, p. 479.

The preacher Roll was next seized with prophetic inspiration. He ran through the town, foaming at the mouth, his eyes rolling, his hair and garments in disorder, his face haggard, uttering at one moment inarticulate howls, and at another, exhortations to the impenitent to turn and be saved, for that the day of the Lord was at hand.[142]

[142] Dorpius, p. 394.

A young girl of eighteen, the daughter of a tailor named Gregory Zumberge, was next seized. "On the 8th February she was possessed with a sort of oratorical fury, and she preached with fire and extraordinary volubility before an astonished crowd."

The same day the spirit fell on Knipperdolling and Bockelson; they ran about the streets with bare heads and uplifted eyes, repeating incessantly in shrill tones, "Repent, repent, repent, ye sinners; woe, woe!" Having reached the market-place, they fell into one another's arms before a crowd of citizens and artizans who ran up from all directions. At the same moment, the tailor, Gregory Zumberge, father of the preaching damsel, arrived with his hair flying, his arms extended, his face contorted, and a wild light playing in his eyes, and cried, "Lift up your heads, O men, O dear brothers! I see the majesty of God in the clouds, and Jesus waving the standard of victory. Woe to ye impious ones who have resisted the truth! Repent, repent! I see the Heavenly Father surrounded by thousands of angels menacing you with destruction! Be converted! the great and terrible day of the Lord is come.... God will truly purge His floor, and burn the chaff with unquenchable fire.... Renounce your evil ways and adopt the sign of the New Convenant, if you wish to escape the wrath of the Lord."

"It is impossible," says the oft-quoted writer, who was eye-witness in the town of all he describes, "impossible to imagine the gestures and antics which accompanied this discourse. Now the tailor leaped about on the stones and seemed as though about to fly; then he turned his head with extraordinary rapidity, beating his hands together, and looking up to heaven and then down to earth. Then, all at once, an expression of despair came over his face, and he fell on the pavement in the form of a cross, and rolled in the mud. A good number of us young fellows were there," continues Kerssenbroeck, "much astonished at their howling, and looking attentively at the sky to see if there really was anything extraordinary to be seen there; but not distinguishing anything we began to make fun of the illuminati, and this decided them to retire to the house of Knipperdolling."[143]

[143] Kerssenbroeck, p. 483.

There a new scene commenced. The ecstatics left doors and windows wide open, that all that passed within might be seen and heard by the dense crowd which packed the street without. Those in the street saw Knipperdolling place himself in a corner, his face to the wall, and carry on in broken accents a familiar conversation with God the Father. At one moment he was seen to be listening, then to be replying, making the strangest gestures. This went on for some time, till another actor appeared. This was a blind Scottish beggar, very tall and gaunt—a zealous Anabaptist. He was fantastically dressed in rags, and wore high-heeled boots to add to his stature. Although blind, he ran about exclaiming that he saw strange visions in the sky. This was enough to attract a crowd, which followed him to the corner of the König's Strasse, when, just as he was exclaiming, "Alas, alas! Heaven is going this instant to fall!" he tumbled over a dung-heap which was in his way. This accident woke him from his ecstasy, and he picked himself up in great confusion, and never prophesied again.[144]

[144] *Ibid.* p. 479.

But his place was speedily supplied by another man named Jodocus Culenburg, who, in order to convey himself with greater rapidity whither the Spirit called him, rode about the town on a horse, announcing in every street that he heard the peal of the Last Trumpet. Several women also were taken with the prophetic spirit, and one, named Timmermann, declared that "the King of Heaven was about to appear like a lightning-flash, and would re-establish Jerusalem." Another woman, whose cries and calls to repentance had caused her to lose her voice, ran about with a bell attached to her girdle, urging the bystanders with expressive gestures to join the number of the elect and be saved.[145]

[145] Kerssenbroeck, p. 484.

These fantastic scenes had made a profound impression on many of the citizens of Münster. A nervous affection accompanying mystic excitement is always infectious. The agitation of minds and consciences became general; men and women had trances, prayed in public, screamed, had visions, and fell into cataleptic fits. In those days people knew nothing of physical and psychological causes; the general excitement was attributed by them to supernatural agency. It was simply a question whether these signs were produced by the devil or by the Spirit of God. The Catholics attributed the signs to the agency of Satan; the Lutherans were in nervous uncertainty. Were they resisting God or the devil? Fear lest they should be found in the ranks of those fighting against the Holy Spirit drew off numbers of the timorous and most conscientious to swell the ranks of the mystical sect. Münster was exhibiting on a large scale what is reproduced in our own land in many a Wesleyan and Ranter revival meeting.

The time had now come, thought Rottmann, for the destruction of the enemies of God. Secret notice was sent to the different Anabaptist congregations to be prepared to strike the blow on the 9th of February. Accordingly, early in the morning, 500 fanatics seized on the gates of the city, the Rath-haus, and the arms it contained; cannons were planted in the chapel of St. Michael, the tower of St. Lambert's church, and in the market place; barricades of stones, barrels, and benches from the church were thrown up. The common danger united Catholics and Lutherans; they saw clearly that the intention of their adversaries was either to massacre them, or to drive them out of the town. They retreated in haste to the Ueberwasser quarter, and took up their position in the cemetery, planted cannons, placed bodies of armed men in the tower of the cathedral, and retook two of the city gates. They also arrested several of the senators who had joined the Anabaptist sect, but they had not the courage to lay their hands on the burgomaster, Tilbeck, who was also of that party. Two of the preachers, Strahl and Vinnius, were caught, and were lodged in the tower of Ueberwasser church.[146]

[146] Dorpius, f. 394.

Messages were sent to the villages and towns around announcing the state of affairs, and imploring assistance. The magistrates even wrote in the stress of their terror to the prince-bishop, asking him to come speedily to their rescue from a position of imminent peril. Francis of Waldeck at once replied by letter, promising to march with the utmost rapidity to Münster, and demanding that one of the gates might be opened to admit him. This letter was taken to Hermann Tilbeck; but the burgomaster, intent on securing the triumph of the fanatics, with whom he was in league, suppressed the letter, and did not mention either its arrival or its contents to the senate. He, however, informed the Anabaptists of their danger, and urged them to come to terms with the Lutherans as speedily as possible.

At the same time the pastor, Fabricius, unable to restrain his religious prejudices, even in the face of danger, sped among the Lutheran ranks, inciting his followers against the Catholics, and urging them to make terms with the fanatics rather than submit to the bishop. "Beware," said he, "lest, in the event of your gaining a victory, the Papists should recover their power, for it is they who are the real cause of all these evils and disorders."[147]

[147] Kerssenbroeck, p. 405 *et seq.* Montfort., "Tumult. Anabap.," p. 15 *et seq.*; Bullinger, lib. ii. c. 8.

Whilst the preacher was sowing discord in the ranks of the party of order, Rottmann and the two prophets, Matthisson and Bockelson, roused the enthusiasm of their disciples to the highest pitch, by announcing to them a glorious victory, and that the Father would render His elect invulnerable before the weapons of their adversaries.

The Anabaptist women ran about the streets making the most extraordinary contortions and prodigious leaps, crying out that they saw the Lord surrounded by a host of angels coming to exterminate the worshippers of Baal.

Thus passed the night. At daybreak Knipperdolling recommenced his course through the streets, uttering his doleful wail of "Repent, repent! woe, woe!" Approaching too near the churchyard wall of Ueberwasser, he was taken and thrown into the tower with Strahl and Vinnius.

At eight o'clock the drossar of Wollbeck arrived at the head of a troop of armed peasants to reinforce the party of order, and several ecclesiastics entered the town to inform the magistrates that the prince-bishop was approaching at the head of his cavalry.

Before the lapse of many hours the city might have been pacified and order re-established, had it not been for the efforts of Tilbeck the burgomaster, and Fabricius the divine. Mistrust of their allies had now fully gained possession of the Lutherans, and the burgomaster took advantage of the hesitation to dismiss the drossar of Wollbeck and his armed band, and to send to the prince, declining his aid. By his advice, also, the Anabaptists agreed to lay down their arms and make a covenant with the senate for the establishment of harmony. Hostages were given on either side and the prisoners were liberated. Peace was finally concluded on these conditions: 1st. That faith should be absolutely free. 2nd. That each party should support the other. 3rd. That all should obey the magistrates.

The treaty having been signed, the two armed bodies separated, the cannons were fired into the air, the drossar of Wollbeck and the ecclesiastics withdrew, with grief at their hearts, predicting the approaching ruin of Münster. The prince-bishop was near the town with his troops when the fatal news was brought him. He shed tears of mortification, turned his horse and departed.[148]

[148] Same authorities; Sleidan, p. 411.

Peace was secured for the moment by this treaty, but order was not re-established. No sooner had the armed Anabaptists quitted the market-place than it swarmed with women who had received from Rottmann the sign of the New Covenant. "The madness of the pagan bacchantes," says the eye-witness of these scenes, Kerssenbroeck,[149] "cannot have surpassed that of these women. It is impossible to imagine a more terrible, crazy, indecent, and ridiculous exhibition than they made. Their conduct was so frenzied that one might have supposed them to be the furies of the poets. Some had their hair disordered, others ran about almost naked, without the least sense of shame; others again made prodigious gambles, others flung themselves on the ground with arms extended in the shape of a cross; then rose, clapped their hands, knelt down, and cried with all their might, invoking the Father, rolling their eyes, grinding their teeth, foaming at the mouth, beating their breasts, weeping, laughing, howling, and uttering the most strange inarticulate sounds.... Their words were stranger than their gestures. Some implored grace and light for us, others besought that we might be struck with blindness and damnation. All pretended that they saw in heaven some strange sights; they saw the Father descending to judge their holy cause, myriads of angels, clouds of blood, black and blue fires falling upon the city, and above the clouds a rider mounted on a white horse, brandishing his sword against the impenitent who refused to turn from their evil ways.... But the scene was constantly varying. Kneeling on the ground, and turning their eyes in one direction, they all at once exclaimed together, with joined hands, 'O Father! Father! O most excellent King of Zion, spare the people!' Then they repeated these words for some while, raising the pitch of their voices, till they attained to such a shriek that a host of pigs could not have produced a louder noise when assembled on market-day.

[149] Kerssenbroeck, p. 495 *et seq.*

"There was on the gable of one of the houses in the market-place a weathercock of a peculiar form, lately gilt, which just then caught the sun's rays and blazed with light. This weathercock caused the error of the women. They mistook it for the most excellent King of Zion. One of the citizens discovering the cause, climbed the roof of the house and removed this new sort of majesty. A calm at once succeeded to the uproar; ashamed and full of confusion, the visionaries dispersed and returned to their homes. Unfortunately the lesson did not restore them to their senses."

Shortly after the treaty was signed, the burgomaster, Tilbeck, openly joined the Anabaptists, and was rebaptised with all his family by Rottmann.[150]

[150] Kerssenbroeck, p. 496.

The more sensible and prudent citizens, including nearly all the Catholics and a good number of Lutherans, being well aware that the treaty was, in fact, a surrender of all authority into the hands of the fanatics, deserted the town in great numbers, carrying with them all their valuables. The emigration began on 12th February. The Anabaptists ordered that neither weapons nor victuals should be carried out of the gates, and appointed a guard to examine the effects of all those who left the city. The emigration was so extensive, that in a few days several quarters of the town were entirely depopulated.[151]

[151] Kerssenbroeck; Dorpius, ff. 394-5.

Then Rottmann addressed a circular letter to the Anabaptists of all the neighbouring towns to come and fill the deserted mansions from which the apostates had fallen. "The Father has sent me several prophets," said he, "full of His Spirit and endowed with exalted sanctity; they teach the pure word of God, without human additions, and with sublime eloquence. Come then, with your wives and children, if you hope for eternal salvation; come to the holy Jerusalem, to Zion, and to the new temple of Solomon. Come and assist us to re-establish the true worship of God, and to banish idolatry. Leave your worldly goods behind, you will find here a sufficiency, and in heaven a treasure."[152]

[152] *Ibid.*, p. 502; Mencken, p. 1545.

In response to this appeal, the Anabaptists streamed into the city from all quarters, from Holland, Friesland, Brabant, Hesse, Osnabrück, and from the neighbouring towns, where the magistrates exerted themselves to suppress a sect which they saw imperilled the safety of the commonwealth.

In a short while the deserted houses were peopled by these fanatics. Bernhard Krechting, pastor of Gildehaus, arrived at the head of a large portion of his parishioners. Hermann Regewart, the ex-Lutheran preacher of Warendorf, sought a home in the new Jerusalem. Rich and well-born persons, bitten with the madness, arrived, such were Peter Schwering and his wife, the wealthiest citizens of Coesfeld; Werner von Scheiffort, a country gentleman; the Lady von Becke with her three daughters, of whom the two eldest were broken nuns, and the youngest was betrothed to the Lord of Dörlö; and the Grograff of Schoppingen, Heinrich Krechting, with his wife, his children, and a number of the inhabitants of that town, with carts laden with their effects. The Grograff took up his abode in Kerssenbroeck's house, along with his family and servants, and, as the chronicler bitterly remarks, he took care to occupy the best part of the mansion.[153]

[153] Kerssenbroeck, p. 503.

Amongst those who escaped from the town were the syndic, Von Wyck, who had led the opposition against the bishop, and the burgomaster, Caspar Judenfeld. The latter retired to Hamm and was left unmolested, but Von Wyck had played too conspicuous a part to escape so easily. By the orders of the prince-bishop he was arrested and executed at Vastenau.[154]

[154] *Ibid.* p. 505.

Münster now became the theatre of the wildest orgies ever perpetrated under the name of religion. It is apparently a law that mysticism should rapidly pass from the stage of asceticism into that of licence. At any rate, such has been the invariable succession of stages in every mystic society that is allowed unchecked to follow its own course. In the Roman Church those thus psychologically affected are locked up in convents. The religious passion verges so closely on the sexual passion that a slight additional pressure given to it bursts the partition, and both are confused in a frenzy of religious debauch. The Anabaptist fanatics were rapidly approaching this stage. The prophet Matthisson led the way by instituting a second baptism, administered only to the inner circle of the elect, which was called the baptism of fire.

The adepts were sworn to secrecy, and refused to explain the mode of administration. But public curiosity was aroused, and by learning the password, some were enabled to slip into the assembly and see what took place. Amongst these was a woman who was an acquaintance of Kerssenbroeck, and from whose lips he had an account of the rite. "Matthisson," says he, "secretly assembled the initiated of both sexes during the night, in the vast mansion of Knipperdolling. When all were assembled, the prophet placed himself under a copper chandelier, hung in the centre of the ceiling, lighted with three tapers." He then made an instruction on the new revelation of the Divine will, which he pretended had been made to him, and the assembly became a scene of frantic orgies too horrible to be described.

The assemblies in which these abominations were perpetrated, prepared the way for the utter subversion of all the laws of decency and morality, which followed in the course of a few months.

When Carnival arrived, a grand anti-Catholic procession was organised, to incite afresh the hostility of the people to the ancient Church, its rites and ceremonies. First, a company of maskers dressed like monks, nuns, and priests in their sacred vestments, led the way, capering and singing ribald songs. Then followed a great chariot, drawn by six men in the habits of the religious orders. On the box sat a fellow dressed as a bishop, with mitre and crosier, scourging on the labouring monks and friars. On the car was a man represented as dying, with a priest leaning over him, a huge pair of spectacles on his nose, administering to the sick man the last sacraments of the Church, and addressing him in the most absurd manner, loudly, that the bystanders might hear and laugh at his farcical parody of the most sacred things of the old religion. The next car was drawn by a man dressed as a priest in surplice and stole. The other cars contained groups suitable for turning into ridicule devotion to saints, belief in purgatory, the mass, &c.[155]

[155] Kerssenbroeck, p. 509.

The prophets now decided that it was necessary to be prepared in the event of a siege. They, therefore, commissioned the preacher Roll to visit Holland and raise the Anabaptists there, urge them to arm and to march to the defence of the New Jerusalem. Roll started from Münster on the 21st of February, but the Spanish Government in the Netherlands, alarmed at what was taking place in the capital of Westphalia, ordered a strict watch to be kept on the movements of the fanatics, and Roll was seized and executed at Utrecht.

The next step taken by the prophets was to discharge the members of the senate from the performance of their office, because they had been elected "according to the flesh," and to choose to fill their room another body of men "elected according to the Spirit." Bernard Knipperdolling and Gerhardt Kippenbroeck, both drapers, were appointed burgomasters.

One of the first acts of the new magistrates was to forbid the removal of furniture, articles of food, and money from the town, and to permit a general pillage of all the churches and convents in the city. The Anabaptist mob first attacked the religious houses, and carried off all the sacred vessels, the gold, the silver, and the vestments. Then they visited the chapel of St. Anthony, outside the gate of St. Maurice, and after having sacked it completely, they tore it down. They burnt the church of St. Maurice, then fell upon the church of St. Ledger, but had not the patience to complete its demolition. Thence they betook themselves to the cathedral, broke it open, and destroyed altars, with their beautiful sculptured and painted oak retables, miracles of delicate workmanship and Gothic beauty, the choir stalls, statues, paintings, frescoes, stained glass, organ, vestments, and carried off the chalices and ciboriums. The great clock, the pride of Münster, as that of Strasburg is of the Alsatian capital, was broken to pieces with hammers. A valuable collection of MSS., collected by the poet Rudolf Lange, and presented to the minister, together with the rest of the volumes in the library, were burned. Two noble paintings, one of the Blessed Virgin, the other of St. John the Baptist, on panel, by Franco, were split up and turned into seats for privies to the guard-house near the Jews' cemetery. The heads and arms were broken off the statues that could not be overthrown—statues of apostles, prophets, and sibyls, which decorated the interior of the cathedral and the neighbouring square. The tabernacle was broken open, and the Blessed Sacrament was danced and stamped on. The font was shattered with crowbars, in token of the abhorrence borne by the fanatics to infant baptism; the tombs of the bishops and canons were destroyed, and the bodies torn from their graves, and their dust was scattered to the winds.[156]

[156] Kerssenbroeck, p. 510; Sleidan, p. 411; Dorpius, f. 395.

But whilst this was taking place in Münster, Francis von Waldeck was preparing for war. On the 23rd February he held a meeting at Telgte to consolidate plans, and now from all sides assistance came. The Elector of Cologne, the Duke of Cleves, even the Landgrave of Hesse, now exasperated at the ill-success of his endeavours to establish tranquillity and to effect a compromise, the Duke of Brunswick, the Regent of Brabant, the Counts of Lippe and Berntheim, and many other nobles and cities sent soldiers, artillery, and munitions.

The bishop appointed the generals and principal officers, then he made all the soldiers take an oath of fidelity to himself, and concluded with them an agreement, consisting of the following ten articles:

1. The soldiers are to be faithful to the prince, and to obey their officers.

2. The towns, arms, and munitions taken in war shall belong to the prince.

3. If, after the capture of the city, the prince-bishop permits its pillage by the troops, he shall not be obliged to pay them any prize-money.

4. If the pillage be accorded, the town hall is not to be touched.

5. The prince shall have half the plunder.

6. The nobles, canons, and those who have escaped from the city shall be allowed the first bid for their articles when offered for sale.

7. No fixtures shall be removed by the soldiery.

8. After the capture of the town, the custody of the gates and ramparts shall be confided to those whom the prince-bishop shall appoint.

9. The city taken, and its pillage permitted, the soldiers shall be allowed eight days for distribution and sale of the plunder. The soldiers shall receive their pay with punctuality.

10. The heads of the revolt shall, as far as possible, be taken alive and delivered up to the bishop for a recompense.[157]

[157] Kerssenbroeck, p. 513 *et seq.* Sleidan, lib. x. pp. 412-3; Heresbach, p. 36.

The Anabaptists were not afraid at these preparations; they made ready vigorously for the defence of the New Zion. As a preliminary, a body of five hundred burnt the convent of St. Maurice, outside the city gates, and levelled all the houses of the suburbs, which obscured the view, and might serve as cover for the besiegers.

On the 26th February Matthisson preached in the afternoon to a congregation summoned by the discharge of a culverin. At the end of the sermon he assumed an inspired air, and announced that he had an important revelation to communicate. Having arrested the attention of his hearers, he said in a solemn tone, "The Father requires the purification of the New Jerusalem and of His temple; for our republic, which has begun so prosperously, cannot grow and endure if a prey to the confusion produced by the presence of impious sects. My advice is that we kill without further delay the Lutherans, the Papists, and all those who have not the right faith, that there may remain in Zion but one body, one society, which is truly Christian, and which can offer to the Father a pure and well-pleasing worship. There is but one way of preserving the faithful from the contagion of the impious, and that is to sweep them off the face of the earth. Nothing is easier than the execution of this scheme. We form the majority in a strong city, abundantly supplied with all necessaries; there is nothing to fear from within or from without."[158]

[158] Kerssenbroeck, p. 516.

This suggestion would have been carried into immediate execution by the frenzied sectarians, had it not been for the intervention of Knipperdolling, who, fearing that a general massacre of Lutherans and Catholics would combine the forces of the Smalkald union and of the Imperialists against the city, urgently insisted on milder measures. "Let us be content," said he, "with driving, to-morrow, out of the city those miserable creatures who refuse the sign of the New Covenant; thus shall we thoroughly purge the floor of the Lord, and nothing that is impure will remain in the New Jerusalem."[159]

[159] *Ibid.* p. 517; Sleidan, p. 412.

This advice was accepted, and it was unanimously decided that the morrow should witness the expulsion of Catholics and Lutherans. The 27th February was a bitterly cold day. A hard frost had set in, the north wind blew, cutting to the bone all exposed to the blast, the country was white with snow, and the streams were crusted over with ice. At every gate was a double guard; the squares were thronged with armed fanatics, and in and out among them passed the prophets, staff in hand, uttering maledictions on the Lord's enemies, and words of encouragement to those sealed on their brows and hands.

Matthisson sought out those who did not belong to the sect, and with menacing gestures and flaring eyes called them to repentance before the door was shut. "Turn ye, turn ye, sinners," he cried in his harsh tones. "Judgment is preparing for you. The elements are in league against you; your iniquities have made nature rise to scourge you. The sword of the Lord's anger is hung above your heads. Turn, ye sinners, and receive the sign of our alliance, that ye be not cast out from the chosen people!" Then he flung himself down in the great square, and called on the Father; and lying with arms extended on the frozen ground, and his face pinched with cold turned towards the sky, he fell into a trance. The Anabaptists knelt around him, and lifting their hands to heaven besought the Father to reveal His will by the mouth of the prophet whom He had sent.

Then Matthisson, slowly returning from his ecstasy, like one awaking out of a dream, said, "This is the will and order of the Father: the miscreants, unless they be converted and be baptised, must be expelled this place. This holy city shall be purified of all that is unclean, for the conversation of the ungodly corrupts and defiles the people of God. Away with the sons of Esau! this place, this New Zion, this habitation belongs to the sons of Jacob, to the true Israel."

The enthusiasm of Matthisson communicated itself to the assembly. The Anabaptists separated to sweep the streets, sword and pike in hand, and drove the ungodly beyond their walls, shouting, "The lot is ours; the tares must be gathered from among the wheat; the goats from the sheep; the unholy from the godly; away, away!" Doors were burst open, and the fanatics invaded every house, driving before them men, women, and children, from garret and cellar, wherever concealed, in spite of their cries and entreaties. Men of all professions, men and women of every age were banished; they were not allowed to take anything with them. The sword of the Lord was brandished against them; the hale and the infirm, the master and the servant, none were spared. Those who lagged were beaten; those who were sick and unable to fly were carried to the market-place to be rebaptised by Rottmann.

Through the gates streamed the terrified crowd, shivering, half clothed, mothers clasping their babes to their breasts, children sustaining between them their aged parents, all blue with cold, as the fierce wind thick strewn with sleet rushed upon them at the corners, and over the bare plain without the city walls, growling and cruel, as though it too were wrought up into religious frenzy, and came as an auxiliary to the savage work.

Thousands traversed the frozen plans, uncertain whither to fly for refuge, uttering piteous cries, lamentations, or low moans; whilst from the walls of the heavenly city thundered a salvo of joy, and the Anabaptists shouted, because the Lord's day of vengeance had come, and the millennium was set up on earth.

"Never," says Kerssenbroeck, "never did I see anything more afflicting. The women carried their naked nurslings in their arms, and in vain sought rags wherewith to clothe them; miserable children, hanging to their fathers' coats, ran barefooted, uttering piercing cries; old people, bent by age, tottered along calling down God's vengeance on their persecutors; lastly, some sick women driven from their beds during the pangs of maternity fell in labour in the snow, deprived of all human succour."[160]

[160] Kerssenbroeck, p. 5222.

Amongst those expelled was Fabricius, the Lutheran divine, who escaped in disguise. He was so greatly hated by the sectarians, that had he been recognised, he would not have been suffered to quit the city alive.

The Frau Werneche, a rich lady, too stout to walk, and unable to find a conveyance, was obliged to remain in Münster. Rottmann insisted on her receiving the sign of the New Covenant.

"I have been baptised already, as were my ancestors," said the good woman. Rottmann replied that if she persisted in her impiety she must be slain with the sword, lest the wrath of the Father should be kindled against the Holy City. The poor lady, who had no desire for martyrdom, cried out, impatiently, "Well, then, be it so! baptise me in the name of all the devils of hell, for I have already been baptised in the name of God." Rottmann, not very particular, administered the rite, and the stout lady remained in Münster.

The apostle now sent letters into all the country, announcing the glad tidings of the approaching reign of Christ on earth, and inviting the Anabaptists of the neighbourhood to flock into Zion. One of these epistles of Rottmann has been preserved.[161]

[161] Kerssenbroeck, p. 520; Dorpius, f. 395.

"Bernard, servant of Jesus Christ in His Church of Münster, salutes affectionately his very dear brother Henry Schlachtschap. Grace and peace from God, and the strength of the Holy Spirit, be with you and with all the faithful.

"Dear Brother in Christ,—

"The marvellous works of God are so great and so diverse that it would not be possible for me to describe them all, had I a hundred tongues. I am, therefore, unable to do so with my single pen. The Lord has splendidly assisted us. He has delivered us out of the hands of our enemies, and has driven them from the city. Seized by a panic terror, they fled in multitudes. This is the beginning of what the Lord announced by His prophets—that all the saints would assemble in this New Zion. These prophets have charged me to write to you, that you may order all the brethren to hasten to us with all the gold and silver they can collect; as for their other goods, let them be left to the sisters, who will dispose of them, and then join us here also. Beware of doing anything after the flesh; do all in the Spirit. The rest by word of mouth. Health in the Lord."

This appeal had all the more success because several executions had taken place at Wollbeck and Bevergern and other places, together with confiscation of goods, and this had struck alarm into the Anabaptists scattered throughout the principality. Numbers, therefore, answered the appeal, and went up, as the tribes of the Lord, to Jerusalem, out of Leyden, Coesfeld, Warendorf, and Gröningen. The vacated houses were re-occupied, the Münster Baptists selecting for themselves the best. Knipperdolling, Kippenbroeck, and others, took possession of the residences of the canons; servants installed themselves in the dwellings of their masters as if they were their own; and the deserted monasteries were given up as hostels to receive the influx from the country, till houses could be provided for them.[162]

[162] Kerssenbroeck, p. 523.

On the 28th February, Francis von Waldeck left Telgte at the head of his army and invested the capital. Batteries were planted, seven camps were established for the infantry, and six for the cavalry around Münster. These camps were in connection with one another, for mutual support in the event of a sortie, and were rapidly fortified.

Thus began the siege which was to last sixteen months minus four days, during which a multitude of untrained, undisciplined fanatics, commanded by a Dutch tailor-innkeeper, held out against a numerous and well-armed force. But there was an element of strength in the besieged that lacked in the besiegers. Those within the walls were members of a vast confraternity, which ramified over Germany, Switzerland, and the Low Countries, its members bound together by a common enthusiasm, in more or less direct relation with the chiefs who commanded in the Westphalian capital. In spite of the siege, news from without was constantly brought into the city, and messengers were sent out to stir up the members of the society in other countries and provinces to rise and march to the relief of the city which, they all believed, was destined to be their religious capital. The Münster brothers looked for a speedy deliverance wrought by the efficacy of the arms of their brothers in Holland, Juliers, Cleves, and Brabant. The Low Countries swarmed with Anabaptists who had organised communities in Amsterdam, Leyden, Utrecht, Haarlem, Antwerp, and Ghent; they had arms stored in cellars and garrets, and waited only the proper moment to rise in a body, massacre their opponents, and deliver the Holy City. Several attempts to rise were made, but the vigilance of the Spanish Government in the Netherlands prevented the rising; and the hopes of the besieged were never realised.

On the other hand, the army of the prince-bishop was composed of mercenaries, of soldiers from different provinces and principalities, speaking different dialects, with different interests, and differing also in faith. The Lutheran troops would not cordially unite with the Catholics, and the latter mistrusted their Protestant allies, whose sympathies they believed lay with the Anabaptist besieged. And the head of the whole army was a Catholic prelate with Lutheran proclivities, who knew nothing of war, had an empty purse, and desired to reduce his own subjects by the aid of foreign mercenaries, with little expense to himself, and damage to his subjects.

The Anabaptists organised their defence with prudence. They elected captains and standard-bearers, and divided all the citizens capable of bearing arms into regiments and companies. Every one was given his place and his functions, and it was decided that the magistrates should be required to mount guard when it came to their turn. Boys were drilled and taught the use of the arquebus; women prepared brands steeped in pitch and sulphur to fling at the enemy, and they melted lead from the roofs into bullets. Mines were dug and charged with powder, fresh bastions were thrown up, and curtains were erected before the gates, into which were built the tombs and sarcophagi of the bishops and canons.[163]

[163] Kerssenbroeck, p. 531 *et seq.*; Hast, p. 344.

The newly-elected senate, though composed of the most zealous Anabaptists, was powerless before Matthisson. A sect governed by the inspiration of the moment, professing to be guided by the Spirit speaking through the mouths of prophets, ready to spring into the maddest excesses at the dictates of visionaries, could not long submit to the government of a magistracy whose power was temporal. The way was rapidly preparing for the establishment of a spiritual despotism.

It was in vain for the senate to pass an order without the sanction of Matthisson, in vain for them to attempt resistance to the execution of his mandates. One day he announced that it was the will of the Father that all the goods of the citizens who had fled, or had been expelled, should be collected into one place, that they might be distributed amongst the saints, as every man had need. He thereupon despatched men to bring together all that was left behind in the city by the refugees, and convey the articles to houses which he designated in every parish. He was promptly obeyed. Garments, linen, beds, furniture, crockery, food, wine—everything was brought away in carts. The jewels, the gold, and the silver, were deposited in the chancery. Then the prophet ordered three days of prayer to be instituted, "that God might reveal to him the persons chosen by Him to keep guard over the accumulated treasure."[164]

[164] Kerssenbroeck; Dorpius, f. 395.

When the three days were at an end, Matthisson announced that the Father had indicated to him seven individuals who were to be the deacons to serve tables in the New Jerusalem. He therefore appointed the men to distribute out of the common store to those who needed that which would satisfy their necessities.[165]

[165] *Ibid.* p. 585.

It must not, however, be supposed that, with the expulsion of the impious from the holy city, all opposition had disappeared. A very considerable number of citizens, shopkeepers, and merchants, rather than desert their houses, abandon their goods to pillage, and lose their trade, had consented to be re-baptised. The reign of the prophets was becoming to them daily more irksome. A blacksmith, named Hubert Rüscher, or Trutling, had the courage to oppose Matthisson, to charge him with being a false prophet, and an impostor.[166] The prophet, feeling the danger of his position, saw that a measure, decided and terrible, must be adopted to suppress the murmurs, and frighten those who desired to shake off his yoke. "Judgment must begin at the house of God," said Matthisson; and he ordered the immediate execution of the smith. Tilbeck, the burgomaster, and Redecker, a magistrate, interposed, but were, by order of the prophet, cast into prison. Then Bockelson, bursting through the crowd, announced with frantic gesture that the Father had commissioned him to slay with the sword he bore all those who withstood the will of Heaven as interpreted by the prophets whom He had sent. Then brandishing his weapon, he rushed upon the blacksmith, but Matthisson forestalled him, by running his halbert through the body of the unfortunate man. Finding that he still breathed, he despatched him with a carbine, crying, "So perish all who are guilty of similar crimes." Then, at his command, the multitude chanted a hymn of praise, and dispersed, silent and trembling, to their homes.[167]

[166] Kerssenbroeck, p. 535 *et seq.*; Monfortius, p. 19; Sleidan and Dorpius call the man Truteling; Sleidan, p. 412; Dorpius, f. 395 b.
[167] Monfortius, p. 19.

Matthisson took immediate advantage of the power this bold stroke had given him to deal another blow. When the treasure of the enemies of Zion had been confided to the care of deacons, the faithful had kept their own goods. But this was to be no longer tolerated. The prophet issued a decree, requiring all, old and young, male and female, under pain of death, to bring all their possessions in gold and silver, under whatever form it might be, into the treasury; "Because," said he, "such things profit not the true Christian."

The majority of the citizens obeyed, in fear and trembling; but many buried their vessels and ornaments of precious metal, and declared that they possessed no jewels.[168] However, the amount of money, chains, rings, brooches, and cups, brought together was very considerable. It was placed in the chancery, and confided to four of Matthisson's most devoted adherents.

[168] Kerssenbroeck, p. 538.

A few days after, he summoned all the inhabitants into the Cathedral square, where, in a long discourse, he announced that the wrath of God was excited against those who had allowed themselves to be rebaptised on the 26th of February, out of human considerations, because they did not desire to leave their homes and their effects, or out of fear; and he advised them all to betake themselves to the church of St. Lambert, to entreat the Father to pardon them for having lied to the Holy Ghost, and soiled by their presence the city of the children of God; "and if the Father does not remit your offence," concluded he in a loud and terrible voice, "you must perish by the sword of the Just One."

In an agony of terror, the unfortunate citizens crowded the church, and the doors were fastened behind them. They passed several hours within, weeping, groaning, and deploring their lot, a prey to inexpressible terror.[169]

[169] Kerssenbroeck, p. 539.

At length Matthisson entered, accompanied by armed men, and the prisoners, supposing they were about to be slaughtered, fell at his feet and embraced his knees, entreating him, with tears, as the favourite of God, to mediate with Him and obtain their pardon. The prophet replied that he must consult the Father; he knelt down, and fell into an ecstasy. After a few moments he rose, leaped with joy, and declared that the Father, though greatly irritated, had granted his prayer, and suffered the penitents to live. Then the poor creatures were purified, hymns of praise were sung, and they were pronounced admitted into the household of the true Israel. The doors were thrown open, and they were allowed to disperse.

On the 15th of March, a new decree appeared, forbidding the faithful to possess, read, or look at any books except the Bible, and requiring all the books, in print or MS., and all legal documents that were found in the town, to be brought to the Cathedral square, and there to be consigned to the flames. Thus perished many a treasure of inappreciable value.

In the meantime the appeal of Rottmann to the Anabaptists of the Low Countries to come and deliver Zion had produced its effect. Thousands assembled in the neighbourhood of Amsterdam, crossed the Zuyder Zee, landed at Zwoll, and marched towards Münster, pillaging and burning churches and convents. But Baron Schenk von Teutenburg, imperial lieutenant, met them, utterly routed them, cut to pieces a large number, and made many prisoners.[170]

[170] Kerssenbroeck, pp. 541, 542; Bullinger, ii. c. 10.

The prophets of Münster, warned of their advance, but ignorant of their dispersion, reckoned on an approaching deliverance, and continued their follies. On Good Friday, April 3, 1534, they organised a general festival, with bells pealing, and a mock procession carrying candles. The treaty concluded with the prince-bishop, through the intervention of Philip of Hesse, was attached to the tail of an old horse, and the beast was driven out of the gate of St. Maurice in the direction of the enemy's camp.[171]

[171] *Ibid.* p. 542.

Easter approached, and with it great things were expected. A rumour circulated that a mighty deliverance of Israel would be wrought on the Feast of the Resurrection. Whether Matthisson started the report or was carried away by it, it is impossible to decide; but it is certain that, on the eve, he announced in an access of enthusiasm, after a trance, that he had received orders from the Father to put to flight the armies of the aliens with a handful of true believers.[172]

[172] *Ibid.*, 542; Hast, p. 348.

Accordingly, on the morrow, carrying a halbert, he headed a few zealots who shared his confidence; the gate of St. Ludgar was thrown open, and he rushed forth with his followers upon the army of the prince-bishop; whilst the ramparts were crowded by the inhabitants of Münster, shouting and praying, and expecting to see a miracle wrought in his favour. But he had not advanced very far before a troop of the enemy surrounded his little band, and, in spite of a desperate resistance, he and his companions were cut to pieces.[173]

[173] Kerssenbroeck, 542; Sleidan, p. 413; Bullinger, lib. ii. c. 9; Heresbach, p. 138; Buissierre, p. 310.

John Bockelson, seeing that the confidence of the Anabaptists was shaken by the failure of this prediction and the fall of the great prophet, lost not a moment in establishing his own supremacy. He called all the people together, and declared to them that Matthisson had died by the just judgment of God, because he had disobeyed the commandment of the Father to go forth with a very small handful, and because he had relied on his own strength instead of on Divine aid. "But," added he, "he neglected all those precautions he ought to have taken, solemn prayer and fasting, after the example of Judith; and he forgot that victory is in the hands of God; he was proud and vain, therefore was he forsaken of the Lord. His terrible end was revealed to me eight days ago by the Holy Ghost; for, as I was sleeping in the house of Knipperdolling, after having meditated on the Divine Law, Matthisson appeared to me pierced through by the lance of an armed man, with all his bowels gushing forth. Then was I frightened beyond measure at this terrible spectacle; but the armed man said to me, 'Fear not, well-beloved son of the Father, but be faithful to thy calling, for the judgment of God will fall upon Matthisson; and when he is dead, marry his widow.' These words cast me into profound amazement, for I have already a legitimate wife at Leyden. Nevertheless, that I might have a witness worthy of confidence to this extraordinary revelation, I trusted the secret to Knipperdolling; he is present, let him be brought forth."[174]

[174] Kerssenbroeck, p. 543; Montfort., p. 24.

Thereupon Knipperdolling stepped forward and declared by oath that Bockelson had spoken the truth, and he mentioned the place, the day, and the hour when the revelation was confided to him.

From that moment Bockelson passed with the people not only as a prophet, but as a favourite of Heaven, one specially chosen of the Father, and was held in far higher estimation, accordingly, than had been the fallen prophet. He was seized with inspiration. On the 9th of April, he declared that "the Father ordered, under pain of incurring his dire wrath, that every exalted thing should be laid low, and that the work was to begin at the church steeples." Consequently three architects of the town were ordered to demolish them. They succeeded in pulling down all the spires in Münster. That of Ueberwasser church was singularly beautiful. It was reduced to a stump; and the modern visitor to the ancient Westphalian capital has cause to deplore its loss. The towers were only saved to be used as positions for cannon to play upon the besiegers.[175]

[175] Bullinger, ii. c. 8; Sleidan, p. 271; Dorpius, f. 396.

Bockelson had another vision, which served to consolidate his power. "The Father," said he, "had appeared to him, and had commanded him to appoint Knipperdolling to be the executioner of the new republic."

This was not precisely satisfactory to Knipperdolling; he aimed at a higher office, but he dissembled his irritation, and accepted the sword offered him by John of Leyden with apparent transports of joy.[176] Four under-executioners were named to assist him, and to accompany him wherever he went.

[176] Kerssenbroeck, p. 545; Heresbach, p. 139; Sleidan, p. 413; Dorpius, f. 396.

The nomination of Knipperdolling was the prelude to other important changes. Bockelson aspired to exercise absolute power, without opposition or control. To arrive at his ends, a wild prophetic scene was enacted. He ran, during the night, through the streets of Münster stark naked, uttering howls and crying, "Ye men of Israel who inhabit this holy Zion! fear the Lord, and repent for your past lives. Turn ye, turn ye! The glorious King of Zion, surrounded by multitudes of angels, is about to descend and judge the world, at the peal of His terrible trumpet. Turn, ye blind ones, and be converted." [177]

[177] Kerssenbroeck, p. 596; Monfort, pp. 25, 26; Heresbach, p. 99 *et seq.*

Exhausted with his run and his shouts, and satisfied with having thoroughly alarmed the inhabitants, he returned to the house of Knipperdolling, who was also in a paroxysm of inspiration, foaming, leaping, rolling on the ground, and performing many other extravagant actions. Bockelson, on entering, cast himself down in a corner and pretended to have lost the power of speech; and as the crowd, assembled round him, asked him the meaning of what had taken place, he signed to them to bring him tablets, on which he wrote, "By the order of the Father, I remain dumb for three days."

At the expiration of this period he convoked the people, and declared to them that the Father had revealed to him that Israel must have a new constitution, with new laws and new magistrates, divinely appointed. The former magistracy had been elected by men, but the new one was to be designated by the Holy Ghost. Bockelson then dissolved the senate, and, as the mouthpiece of God, he declared the names of the new officers, to the number of twelve, who were to bear the title of The Elders of the Tribes of Israel, in whose hands all power, temporal and spiritual, was to be placed. Those appointed were, as might have been expected, the prophet's most devoted adherents.[178] Hermann Tilbeck, the old burgomaster, was brought out of prison, and it was announced to him that he was to be of the number of elders; but perhaps a little cooled in this enthusiasm by his sojourn in chains, he burst into tears, and in accents of humility prayed, "Oh, Father! I am not worthy so great an honour; give me strength and light to govern with wisdom."

[178] Dorpius, f. 396 b.

Rottmann, who, since the arrival of the prophet, had played but a subordinate part, judged the occasion favourable for thrusting himself into prominence. He therefore preached a long sermon, in which he declared that God was the author of the new constitution, and then, calling the elders before him by name, he committed to each a drawn sword, with the words, "Receive with this weapon the right of life or death, which the Father has ordered me to confer upon you, and use the sword conformably to the Lord's will." Then the proceedings closed with the multitude singing the *Gloria in excelsis* in German, on their knees.

The senate resigned its functions without apparent regret or opposition, and the twelve elders assumed the plenitude of power. They abolished the laws and formulated new ones, published edicts, resolved difficulties, judged causes, subject to no control save the will of the prophet; but that will they regarded as identical with the Divine will, as superior to all law, and every one obeyed its smallest requirements.

Immediately after the installation of the government, an edict in ten parts was published.[179] The first part, divided into thirteen articles, contained the moral law; the second part, in thirty-three articles, contained the civil law.

[179] Kerssenbroeck, pt. ii. pp. 1-9; Monfortius, pp. 26, 27; Hast, p, 352 *et seq.*

The first part forbade thirteen crimes under pain of death: blasphemy, disobedience, adultery, impurity, avarice, theft, fraud, lying and slander, idle conversation, disputes, anger, envy, and discontent against the government.

The second part required every citizen to conform his life and belief to the Word of God; to fulfil exactly his duties to others and to the State. It ordered a strict system of vigilance against night surprises by the enemy, and required one of the elders to sit in rotation every day as judge to try cases brought before him; also, that whatsoever was decided by the elders as necessary for the welfare of the New Jerusalem should be announced to the assembly-general of Israel, by the prophet John of Leyden, servant of the Most High; that Bernard Knipperdolling, the executioner, should denounce to the elders the crimes committed within the holy city; and that he might exercise his office with greater security he was never to go forth unaccompanied by his four assistants.

It ordered that henceforth repasts should be taken publicly and in common; that every one should accept what was set before him, should eat it modestly, in silence; that the brothers and the sisters should eat at separate tables; and that, during the meal, portions of the Old Testament should be read to them.

The next articles named the individuals who were to execute the offices of butcher, shoemaker, smith, tailor, brewer, and the like, to the Lord's people. Two articles forbade the introduction of new fashions, and the wearing of garments with holes in them. Article XXIX. ordered every stranger belonging to another religion, who should enter the city of Münster, to be examined by Knipperdolling. No communication of any sort with strangers was permitted to the children of Zion.

Article XXXII. forbade, under pain of death, desertion from the military service, or exchange of companies without the sanction of the elders.

Article XXXIII. required that in the event of a decease, all the goods and chattels of the defunct should be taken to Knipperdolling, who would convey them to the elders, and they would distribute them as they judged fitting.

That some of these provisions were indicative of great prudence is not to be doubted. All food having been seized upon and being served out publicly to all the citizens alike, and in moderation, the capabilities of prolonging the defence were greatly increased; and the military dictatorship and strict discipline within the city maintained by the prophet, enabled the Anabaptists to preserve an invulnerable front to an enemy torn by faction and with divided responsibilities.

To increase the disaffection and party strife in the hostile camp, the people of Münster sent arrows amongst the besiegers, to which were attached letters, one of which has been preserved by Kerssenbroeck.[180] It is an exhortation to the enemy to beware lest by attacking the people of the Lord, who held to the pure Word of God, they should be regarded by him as in league with Antichrist, and urging them to repentance.

[180] Kerssenbroeck, pt. ii. p. 9.

Besiegers and besieged heaped on each other reciprocal insults, exhibiting themselves to one another in postures more expressive of contempt than decent.[181]

[181] *Ibid.* pp. 11, 12.

A chimney-sweep, named William Bast, had about this time a vision ordering him to burn the cities of the ungodly. Bast announced his mission to the elders and to the prophet, and was bidden go forth in the Lord's name. He accordingly left Münster, eluded the vigilance of the enemy's sentinals, and reached Wollbeck, where was the powder magazine of the Episcopal army. He fired several houses, and the flames spread, but were fortunately extinguished before they reached the powder. Bast had escaped to Dreusteindorf, where also he attempted to execute his mission, but was caught, brought back to Wollbeck, and burnt alive.

In the meantime various sorties had taken place, in which the besiegers suffered, being caught off their guard. On May 22nd, the prince-bishop, finding the siege much more serious than he had anticipated, began to bombard the town; but as fast as the walls gave way, they were repaired by the women and children at night.

A general assault was resolved on for the 26th May; of this the besieged were forewarned by their spies. Unfortunately for the investing army, the soldiers of Guelders got drunk on the preceding day in anticipation of their victory, and marched reeling and shouting against the city as the dusk closed in. The Anabaptists manned the walls, and easily repulsed their tipsy assailants; but in the meantime the rest of the army, observing the march of the men of Guelders, and hearing the discharge of firearms, rushed to their assistance, without order; the Münsterians rallied, repulsed them with great carnage, and they fled in confusion to the camp. The Anabaptists had only lost two officers and eight soldiers in the fray; and their success convinced them that they were under the special providence of God, which had rendered them invincible.[182] They, therefore, repaired their walls with energy, erected several additional bastions, and continued their sorties.

[182] Kerssenbroeck, pp. 15, 16; Sleidan, p. 413.

On the 30th May, a party of the fanatics issued from a subterraneous passage upon the sentinels opposite the Judenfeld gate, spiked nineteen cannon, and laid a train of gunpowder from the store, which they reached, to the mouth of their passage. The troops stationed within sight marched hastily to repulse the sortie, when the train was fired, the store exploded, and a large number of soldiers were destroyed.[183]

[183] Kerssenbroeck, pp. 15, 16.

The prince-bishop next adopted an antiquated expedient, which proved singularly inefficacious. He raised a huge bank against the walls, by requisitioning the services of the peasants of the country round. The besieged poured a shower of bullets amongst the unfortunate labourers, who perished in great numbers, and the mole remained unfinished.[184]

[184] *Ibid.* p. 21.

Francis of Waldeck, discouraged, and at the end of his resources, sent his deputies to the Diet of Neuss on the 25th June, to announce to the Archbishop of Cologne and the Duke of Juliers his failures, and to ask for additional troops. The two princes replied that they would not abandon their ally in his difficulties, and they promised to bear a part of the cost of the siege, advanced 40,000 florins for the purchase of gunpowder, promised to despatch forces to his assistance, and sent at once prudent advisers.[185] The prince was, in fact, utterly incompetent as a general and incompetent as a bishop. The pastoral staff has a crook at the head and a spike at the bottom. Liturgiologists assure us that this signifies the mode in which a bishop should exercise discipline—the gentle he should restrain or direct with mercy, the rebellious he should treat with severity. To the former he should be lenient, with the latter prompt. Francis of Waldeck wielded gracefully and effectively neither end of his staff.

[185] Hast, p. 357; Sleidan, p. 413.

He shortly incurred a risk, and but for the fidelity of one of his subjects in Münster, he would have fallen a victim to assassination.

A young Anabaptist maiden, named Hilla Phnicon, of singular beauty, conceived the notion that she had been called by God to be the Judith of this new Bethulia, and was to take the head from off the shoulders of the great, soft, bungling Holophernes, Francis of Waldeck.[186]

[186] Kerssenbroeck, p. 26 *et seq.*

Rottmann, Bockelson, and Knipperdolling encouraged the girl in her delusion, and urged her not to resist the inspirations of the Father. Accordingly, on the 16th June, Hilla dressed herself in the most beautiful robes she could procure, adorned her hair with pearls, and her arms with bracelets, selecting from the treasury of the city whatever articles she judged most conducive to the end; the treasury being for the purpose placed at her disposal by order of the prophet. Furnished with a linen shirt steeped in deadly poison, which she had herself made, as an offering to the prince, she left Münster, and delivered herself up into the hands of the drossar of Wollbeck, who, after having dispoiled her of her jewels, questioned her as to her object in deserting the city. She replied with the utmost composure, that she was a native of Holland, and that she had lived in Münster with her husband, till the change of religion had so disgusted her that she could endure it no longer, and that she had fled on the first opportunity, and that her husband would follow her on a suitable occasion. "It is to ask pardon for him that I am come," said she; "and he will be able to indicate to his highness a means of entering the city without loss."

The perfect self-possession of the lady convinced the drossar of her sincerity, and he promised to introduce her to the prince at Iburg within two days. Everything seemed to favour the adventuress; but an unexpected event occurred on the 18th, the day appointed for the audience, which spoiled the plot.

The secret had been badly kept, and it was a matter of conversation, hope, and prayer in Münster. A citizen named Ramers, who had remained in the city, and had been rebaptised rather than lose his business and give up his house to pillage, having heard of it, escaped from the town on the 18th, and revealed the projects of Hilla to one of the generals of the besieging army. The unfortunate young woman was thereupon put to the question, and confessed. She was conducted to Bevergern and decapitated. At the moment when she was being prepared for execution, she assured the bystanders that they would not be able to take her life, for the prophet John "chosen friend of the Father, had assured her that she would return safe and sound to Zion."

The bishop sent for Ramers, provided for his necessities, and ordered that his house and goods should be spared in the event of the capture of Münster.

As soon as one danger disappeared, another rose up in its place. The letters attached to arrows fired by the Anabaptists into the hostile camp, as well as their secret agents, had wrought their effect. The Lutheran auxiliaries from Meissen complained that they were called to fight against the friends of the Gospel, and on the night of the 30th June they deserted in a body.[187] Other soldiers escaped into Münster and offered their arms to the Anabaptists. Disaffection was widely spread. Disorder, misunderstandings, and ill-concealed hatred reigned in the camp. The besieged reckoned among their assailants numerous and warm friends, and were regularly informed of all the projects of the general. Their emissaries bearing letters to the Anabaptists in other territories easily traversed the ranks of the investing army, and when they had accomplished their mission they returned with equal ease to the gates of Münster, which opened to receive them.

[187] Kerssenbroeck, p. 36.

One of the soldiers of the Episcopal army, who had taken refuge in Münster, was lodged in the house of Knipperdolling, in which also dwelt John Bockleson. The deserter observed that the Leyden prophet was wont to leave his bedroom at night, and he ventured to watch his conduct and satisfy himself that it was not what it ought to be.[188] He mentioned to others what he had observed. The scandal would soon get wind. One only way remained to cut it short. John Bockleson consulted with Rottmann and the other preachers, and urged that polygamy should be not only sanctioned but enjoined on the elect.

[188] *Ibid.* p. 38; H. Montfort., p. 28.

Some of those present having objected to this new doctrine, the prophet cast his mantle and the New Testament on the ground, and solemnly swore that this which he enjoined was the direct revelation of the Almighty. He threatened the recalcitrant ministers, and at last, half-persuaded and wholly frightened, they withdrew their objections; and he appointed the pastors three days in which to preach polygamy to the people.[189] The new doctrine having been ventilated, an assembly of the people was called, and it was formerly laid down by the prophet as the will of God, that every man was to have as many wives as he wanted.[190]

[189] Sleidan, p. 414; Dorp. f 396.
[190] Kerssenbroeck, p. 38.

The result of this new step was to bring about a reaction which for a moment threatened the prophet's domination with downfall.

On the 30th July, Heinrich Mollenhecke, a blacksmith, supported by two hundred citizens, burghers and artisans, declared openly that he was resolved to put down the new masters of Münster, and to restore everything upon the ancient footing. With the assistance of his companions, he captured Bockleson, Knipperdolling, and the preachers Rottmann, Schlachtscap, Clopris, and Vinnius, and cast them into prison. Then a council was held, and it was resolved that the gates should be opened to the bishop, the old magistracy should be restored, and the exiled burgesses should be recalled, and their property restored to them: and that all this should be done *on the morrow*. Had it been done on the spot we should have heard no more of John of Leyden. The delay saved him and ruined the reactionary party. It allowed time for his adherents to muster.[191] Mollenhecke and his party, when they met on the following morning to execute their design, were attacked and surrounded by a multitude of fanatics headed by Heinrich Redecker. The blacksmith had succeeded in collecting only a handful. "No pen can describe the rage with which their adversaries fell upon them, and the refinements of cruelty to which they became victims. After having overwhelmed them with blows and curses, they were imprisoned, but they continued inflicting upon them such horrible tortures that the majority of these unfortunates would have a thousand times preferred death."[192] Ninety-one were ordered to instant execution. Twenty-five were shot, the other sixty-six were decapitated by Knipperdolling to economize powder, and lest the sound of the discharge of firearms within the city should lead the besiegers to believe that fighting was going on in the streets. Some had their heads cut off, others were tied to a tree and shot, others again were cut asunder at the waist, and others were slowly mutilated. Knipperdolling himself executed the men, so many every day, in the presence of the prophet, till all were slain.[193]

[191] Kerssenbroeck, p. 39 *et seq.*; Heresbach, pp. 41, 42; H. Montfort., pp. 29, 30; Bullinger, lib. ii. c. 9, p. 56.
[192] Kerssenbroeck, p. 40.
[193] *Ibid.* p. 41; Dorpius, f. 536 b.

"The partisans of the emancipation of the flesh having thus obtained the mastery in Münster," says the eye-witness, "it was impossible, a few days later, to discover in the capital of Westphalia the last and feeble traces of modesty, chastity, and self-restraint."

Three men, John [OE]chinckfeld, Henry Arnheim, and Hermann Bispinck, having, however, the hardihood to assert that they still believed that Christian marriage consisted in the union of one man with one woman, were decapitated by order of John of Leyden.[194]

[194] H. Montfort., p. 29; C. Heresbach, p. 42.

With the death of these men disappeared every attempt at resistance.

The horrors which were perpetrated in Münster under the name of religious liberty almost exceed belief. The most frantic licence and savage debauchery were practised. The prophet took two wives, besides his favourite sultana, the beautiful Divara, widow of Matthisson, and his lawful wife at Leyden. These were soon discovered to be too few, and the harem swelled daily.[195]

[195] Kerssenbroeck, p. 42. Dorpius confirms the horrible account given by Kerssenbroeck from what he saw himself, f. 498.

"We must draw a veil," says Kerssenbroeck, "over what took place, for we should scandalise our readers were we to relate in detail the outrageous scenes of immorality which took place in the town, and the villanies which these maniacs committed to satisfy their abominable lusts. They were no more human beings, they were foul and furious beasts. The hideous word *Spiritus meus concupiscit carnem tuam* was in every mouth; those who resisted these magic words were shut up in the convent of Rosenthal; and if they persisted in their obstinacy after exhortation, their heads were cut off. In one day four were simultaneously executed on this account. On another occasion a woman was sentenced to be decapitated, after childbirth, for having complained of her husband having taken to himself a second wife."[196]

[196] Kerssenbroeck, p. 43 *et seq.*

Henry Schlachtscap preached that no man after the Ascension of Christ had lived in true matrimony, if he had contracted marriage on account of beauty, wealth, family, and similar causes, for that true marriage consisted solely in that which was instigated by the Spirit.

A new prophet now appeared upon the scene, named Dusentscheuer, a native of Warendorf. He rushed into the market-place uttering piercing cries, and performing such extraordinary antics that a crowd was speedily gathered around him.

Then, addressing himself to the multitude, he exclaimed, "Christian brothers, the celestial Father has revealed to me, and has commanded me to announce to you, that John Bockelson of Leyden, the saint and prophet of God, must be king of the whole earth; his authority will extend over emperors, kings, princes, and all the powers of the world; he will be the chief authority; and none shall arise above him. He will occupy the throne of his father David, and will carry the sceptre till the Lord reclaims it from him."[197]

[197] *Ibid.* p. 47; Sleidan, p. 419; Bullinger, lib. ii. p. 56; Montfort., p. 31; Heresbach, pp. 136-7, "Historia von d. Münsterischen Widerteuffer," f. 328 b; Dorpius, f. 397.

Bockelson and the twelve elders were present. A profound silence reigned in the assembly. Dusentscheuer, advancing to the elders, demanded their swords of office; they surrendered them into his hands; he placed eleven at the feet of Bockelson, and put the twelfth into his hand, saying—"Receive the sword of justice, and with it the power to subjugate all nations. Use it so that thou mayst be able to give a good account thereof to Christ, when He shall come to judge the quick and the dead."[198] Then drawing from his pocket a phial of fragrant oil, he poured it over the tailor's head, pronouncing solemnly the words, "I consecrate thee in the presence of thy people, in the name of God, and by His command, and I proclaim thee king of the new Zion." When the unction was performed, Bockelson cast himself in the dust and exclaimed, "O Father! I have neither years, nor wisdom, nor experience, necessary for such sovereignty; I appeal to Thy grace, I implore Thy assistance and Thy all-powerful protection!... Send down upon me, therefore, Thy divine wisdom. May Thy glorious throne descend on me, may it dwell with me, may it illumine my labours; then shall I be able to accomplish Thy will and Thy good pleasure, and thus shall I be able to govern Thy people with equity and justice."

[198] Kerssenbroeck, p. 43 *et seq.*

Then, turning himself towards the crowd, Bockelson declared that he had long known by revelation the glory that was to be his, but he had never mentioned it, lest he should be deemed ambitious, but had awaited in patience and humility the accomplishment of God's holy will. He concluded by saying that, destined by the Father to reign over the whole world, he would use the sword, and slay all those who should venture to oppose him.[199]

Nevertheless murmurs of disapprobation were heard. "What!" thundered the Leyden tailor, "you dare to resist the designs of God! Know then, that even were you all to oppose me, I should nevertheless become king of the whole earth, and that my royalty, which begins now in this spot, will last eternally."

The new prophet Dusentscheuer and the other preachers harangued the people during three consecutive days on the new revelation, read to the people the 23rd chapter of Jeremiah and the 27th of Ezekiel, and announced that in the King John the prophecies of the old seers were accomplished, for that he was the new David whom God had promised to raise up in the latter days. They also read aloud the 13th chapter of St. Paul's Epistle to the Romans, and accompanied the lecture with commentaries on the necessity and divine obligation of submission to authority.[199]

[199] Kerssenbroeck, p. 47; and the authors before quoted.

At the expiration of these three days, Dusentscheuer requested John of Leyden to complete the spoliation of the inhabitants, so that everything they possessed might be placed in a common fund. "It has been revealed to me," said he, "that the Father is violently irritated against the men and women because they have abused grievously their food and drink and clothing. The Father requires for the future, that no one of either sex shall retain more than two complete suits and four shirts; the rest must be collected and placed in security. It is the will of the Lord that the provisions of beef and pork found in every house shall also be seized and be consecrated to the general use."[200]

[200] Kerssenbroeck, p. 49.

The order was promptly obeyed. Eighty-three large waggons were laden with confiscated clothes, and all the provisions found in the city were brought to the king, who confided the care and apportionment of them to Dusentscheuer.

Bockelson now organised his court with splendour. He appointed his officers, chamberlain, stewards, marshals, and equerries, in imitation of the Court of the Emperor and Princes of Germany. Rottmann was named his chaplain; Andrew von Coesfeld, director of police; Hermann Tilbeck, grand-marshal; Henry Krechting, chancellor; Christopher Waldeck, the bishop's son, who had fallen into his power, was in derision made one of the pages; and a privy council of four, composed of Bernard Krechting, Henry Redecker, and two others of inferior note, was instituted under the presidency of Christian Kerkering. John had also a grand-master of the kitchen, a cup-bearer, taster, carver, gentlemen of the bedchamber, &c.[201]

[201] *Ibid.* p. 55 Montfort., pp. 31-3; Sleidan, p. 418; Bullinger, p. 57; Heresbach, pp. 137-8.

But John Bockelson not only desired to be surrounded by a court; he determined also to display all the personal splendour of royalty. Accordingly, at his order, two crowns of pure gold were made, one royal, the other imperial, encrusted with jewels. Around his neck hung a gold chain enriched with precious stones, from which depended a globe of the same metal transfixed by two swords, one of gold, the other of silver. The globe was surmounted by a cross which bore the inscription, "Ein König der Gerechtigkeit über all" (a King of Righteousness over all). His sceptre, spurs, baldrick and scabbard were also of gold, and his fingers blazed with diamonds. On one of the rings, which was exceedingly massive, was cut, "Der König in dem nyen Tempel furet dit zeichen vur sein Exempel" (the King of the new Temple bears this symbol as his token). The royal garments were magnificent, of crimson and purple, and costly stuffs of velvet, silk, and gold and silver damask, with superb lace cuffs and collars, and his mantle lined with costly furs. The elders, the prophets, and the preachers followed suit, and exchanged their sad-coloured garments for robes of honour in gay colours. The small house of Knipperdolling no longer contented the tailor-king; he therefore furnished, and moved into, a handsome mansion belonging to the noble family of Von Büren. The house next door was converted into the palace of his queens, and was adorned with royal splendour. A door of communication, broken through the partition wall, allowed King John to visit his wives at all hours.

He now took to himself thirteen additional wives, and a large train of concubines. Among his sixteen legitimate wives was a daughter of Knipperdolling. Divara of Haarlem remained the head queen, though she was the oldest. The rest were all under twenty, and were the most beautiful girls of Münster. They all bore the title of queens, but Divara alone had a court, officers, and bodyguard, habited in a livery of chestnut brown and green; the livery of the king being scarlet and blue.[202]

[202] Kerssenbroeck, p. 55 *et seq.*; and the authors above cited. Kerssenbroeck gives long details of the dress, ornaments, and manner of life of the king; also "Historia von d. Münsterischen Widerteuffer," f. 329.

The king usually had his meals with his wives, and during the repasts he examined them with great attention, feasting his eyes on their beauty. The names of the sixteen queens were inscribed on a tablet on which the king, after dinner, designated the lady who had attracted his favour.[203]

[203] Kerssenbroeck gives the names of all the wives except one, which he conceals charitably, as the poor child—she was very young—fell ill, but recovered, and was living respectably after the siege with her relatives in the city.

The King of Zion had abolished the names of the days of the weeks, and had replaced them by the seven first letters of the alphabet. He ordered that whenever a child was born in the town, it should be announced to him, and then he gave it a name, whose initial letter corresponded with the letter of the day on which it entered the world. But, as Kerssenbroeck observes, the debauchery which reigned in Münster had the result of diminishing the births, so that the number of children born during the latter part of the siege was extraordinarily small.

Bockelson had only two children by all his wives, and both were daughters. Divara was the first to give birth; the event took place on a Sunday, designated by the letter A; it was given the name of Averall (for Ueberall—Above all); the second child, born on Monday, was called Blydam (the Blythe).[204]

[204] Kerssenbroeck, p. 59.

Thrice in the week Bockelson sat in judgment in the market-place on a throne decked in purple silk, and richly adorned with gold. He betook himself to this place of audience with great pomp. A band of musical instruments headed the pageant, then followed the councillors in purple, and the grand-marshal with the white wand in his hand. John, wearing the royal insignia, mounted on a white horse, splendidly caparisoned, followed between two pages fantastically dressed, one bearing a Bible, the other a naked sword, symbols of the spiritual and temporal jurisdiction exercised by his majesty. The bodyguard surrounded his royal person, to keep off the crowd and to protect him from danger. Knipperdolling, Rottmann, the secretary Puthmann, and the chancellor Krechting followed; then the executioner and his four assistants, a train of courtiers, and servants closed the procession. The whole ceremony was as regal, as punctiliously observed, as at a royal court where the traditions date from many centuries.[205]

[205] Kerssenbroeck, p. 62; H. Montfort., p. 33; Hast, p. 363 *et seq.*; Sleidan, p. 415; "Historia von de Münsterischen Widerteuffer," f. 328 b.

When the king reached the market-place, a squire held the horse, he slowly mounted the steps of the throne, and inclining his sceptre, announced the opening of the audience.

Then the plaintiffs approached, prostrated themselves flat upon the ground twice, and spoke. The majority of the cases were matrimonial complaints, often exceedingly indecent; "the greatest abominations formulated in the most hideously cynical terms before the most cynical of judges." Capital sentences, or penalties little less severe, were pronounced against insubordinate wives.[206]

[206] Kerssenbroeck. Sleidan says, "Almost every case and complaint brought before him concerned married people and divorces. For nothing was more frequent, so that persons who had lived together for many long years now separated for the first time."—p. 415-6.

The same ceremonial was observed whenever his majesty went to hear the preaching in the market-square, with the sole exception, that on this occasion he was accompanied by the sixteen queens, magnificently dressed. Queen Divara rode a palfrey caparisoned in furs, led by a page; the court and the fifteen other queens followed on foot. On reaching the market-place, the ladies entered a house opposite the throne, and assisted at the sermon, sitting at the windows.

The pulpit and the throne were side by side; a long broad platform united them. When the sermon was concluded, the king, his queens, court, ministers, and the preacher, assembled on the platform and danced to the strains of the royal band.

It was from this platform that King John, as sovereign pontiff, blessed polygamous marriages, saying to the brides and the bridegrooms, "What God hath joined let no man put asunder; go, act according to the divine law, be fruitful and multiply, and replenish the earth." This sanction was necessary for the validity of these unions.

John, wishing to exercise all the prerogatives of royalty, struck coins of various values, bearing on one side the inscription, "Das Wort is Fleisch geworden und wohnet unter uns" (The Word was made flesh and dwelt among us); or "Wer nicht gebohren ist aus Wasser und Geist der kann nicht eingehen—" the rest on the reverse—"In das Reich Gottes. Den es ist nur ein rechter König über alle, ein Gott, ein Glaube, eine Tauffe" (who is not born of Water and the Spirit, cannot enter into the Kingdom of God. For there is only one true King over all, one God, one Faith, one Baptism). And in the middle, "Münster, 1534."

Whilst the city of Münster was thus passing from a republic to a monarchy, the siege continued; but the besiegers made no progress. Refugees informed the prince-bishop of what had taken place within the walls.

On the 25th August he assembled the captains and the princes and nobles who had come into the camp to observe the proceedings, to request them to advise him how to put an end to all these horrors and abominations. It was proposed that a deputation should be sent into the town to propose a capitulation on equitable terms; and in the event of a refusal to offer a general assault.[207]

[207] Kerssenbroeck, p. 65 *et seq.*; Montfort., pp. 27, 28.

On the 28th August an armistice of three hours' duration was concluded, and the deputation obtained a safe-conduct authorising them to enter the city. But instead of being brought before the inhabitants of the town, to whom they were commissioned to make the propositions, they were introduced to the presence of Bockelson and his court.

The envoys informed King John of the terms proposed by the bishop. They were extremely liberal. He promised a general amnesty if the place were surrendered, and arms laid down.

King John replied haughtily, that he did not need the clemency of the prince-bishop, for that he stood strengthened by the almighty and irresistible power of God. "It is your pretended bishop," said he, "who is an impious and obstinate rebel, he who makes war without previous declaration against the faithful servants of the celestial Father. Never will I lay down my arms which I have taken up for the defence of the Gospel; never in cowardly fashion will I surrender my capital: on the contrary, I know how to defend it, even to the last drop of my blood, if the honour of God requires it."[208]

[208] Kerssenbroeck, p. 21.

The bishop, when he learnt that his deputies had been refused permission to address the citizens, attached letters, sealed with his Episcopal seal, to arrows, which were shot into the town. In these letters he promised a general pardon to all those who would leave the party of the Anabaptists, and escape from the town before the following Thursday.

But Bockelson forbade, on pain of death, any one touching or opening one of these letters, and ordered the instant decapitation of man, woman, or child who testified anxiety to leave Münster.

The bishop and the princes resolved on attempting an assault without further delay. John of Leyden received information of their purpose through his spies. He at once mounted his white horse, convoked the people, and announced to them that the Father had revealed to him the day and hour of the projected attack; he appointed his post to every man, gave employment to the women and children, and displayed, at this critical moment, the zeal, energy, and readiness which would have done credit to a veteran general.[209]

[209] Kerssenbroeck, p. 68.

The assault was preluded by a bombardment of three days. The battlements yielded, breaches were effected in the walls, the roofs of the houses were shattered, the battered gates gave way, and all promised success. But the besieged neglected no precaution. During the night the walls were repaired and the gates strengthened. Women laboured under the orders of the competent directors during the hours of darkness, thus allowing their husbands to take their requisite repose. They carried stones and the munitions of war to the ramparts, and learning to handle the cross-bow, they succeeded in committing no inconsiderable amount of execution among the ranks of the Episcopal army. Other women prepared lime and boiling pitch "to cook the bishop's soup for him."[210] On the 31st August, at daybreak, the roar of the Hessian devil, as a large cannon belonging to the Landgrave Philip was called, gave the signal. Instantly the city was assaulted in six places. The ditches were filled, petards were placed under the gates, the palisades were torn down, and ladders were planted. But however vigorous might be the attack, the defence was no less vigorous. Those on the walls threw down the ladders with all upon them, and they fell bruised and mangled into the fosse, the heads of those who had reached the battlements were crushed with stones and cudgels, and their hands, clasping the parapet, were hacked off. Women hurled stones upon the besiegers, and enveloped them in boiling pitch, quicklime, and blazing sulphur.

[210] *Ibid.* p. 70.

Repulsed, they returned to the charge eight or ten times, but always in vain. The whole day was consumed in ineffectual assaults, and when the red sun went down in the west, the clarions pealed the retreat, and the army, dispirited and bearing with it a train of wounded, withdrew, leaving the ground strewn with dead.

Had the Anabaptists made a night assault, the defeat and dispersion of the Episcopal troops would have been completed. But instead, they sang a hymn and spent the night in banqueting.

The prince-bishop, despondent and at his wits' end for money, called his officers to a consultation on the 3rd September, and it was unanimously resolved to turn the investment into an effective blockade. This resolution was submitted to the electors of Cologne and Saxony, the Duke of Cleves, and the Landgrave of Hesse, and these princes approved of the design of Francis von Waldeck.

It was determined to raise seven redoubts, united by ramparts and a ditch, around the city, so as completely to close it, and prevent the exit of the besieged and the entrance of provisions. It was decided that the defence of this circle of forts should be confided to a sufficient number of tried soldiers, and that the rest of the army should be dismissed.

Accordingly, on the 7th September, all the labourers of the country round were engaged, under the direction of the engineer Wilkin von Stedingen, in raising the walls and digging the trenches. The work was carried on with vigour by relays of peasants; nevertheless, the undertaking was on so great a scale, that several months must elapse before it could be completed.[211]

[211] Kerssenbroeck, p. 75 *et seq.*; Heresbach, p. 132.

The cost of this terrible siege had already risen to 600,000 florins, the treasury was empty, and the country could bear no further taxes. Francis of Waldeck appealed to the Elector Palatine, the Electors of

Cologne, Mainz, and Trèves, to give help and subsidies; he had recourse also to the princes and nobles of the Upper and Lower Rhine; and it was decided that a diet should assemble on the 13th December, 1534, to make arrangements for the complete subjugation of the insurgent fanatics. All the princes, Catholic and Protestant, trembled for their crowns, for the Anabaptist sect ramified throughout the country, and if John of Leyden were successful in Münster, they might expect similar risings in their own principalities.[212]

[212] *Ibid.* p. 75; Bussierre, p. 372; Hast, p. 366.

Whilst the preparations for the blockade were in progress, John Bockelson, inflated with pride, placed no bounds to his prodigality, his display, and his despotism. He frequently pronounced sentences of death. Thus Elizabeth Holschers was decapitated for having refused her husband what he demanded of her; Catherine of Osnabrück underwent the same sentence for having told one of the preachers that he was building his doctrines upon the sand; Catherine Knockenbecher lost her head for having taken two husbands. Polygamy was permitted, but polyandry was regarded as an unpardonable offence.[213]

[213] Kerssenbroeck, p. 75; Bussierre, p. 372.

However, the people chafed at the tyranny they were subjected to, and murmurs, low and threatening, continued to make themselves heard; whereupon, by King John's order, Dusentscheuer announced from the pulpit, "that all those who should for the future have doubts in the verities taught them, and who should venture to blame the king whom the Father had given them, would be given over to the anointed of the Lord to be extirpated out of Israel, decapitated by the headsman, and condemned to eternal oblivion."

Amongst those who viewed with envy the rise and splendour of the tailor-king was Knipperdolling. He had opened his home to the prophet, had patronised him, introduced him to the people of Münster, and now the draper was eclipsed by the glory of the tailor. Thinking that the time was come for him to assume the pre-eminence, he made an attempt to dethrone Bockelson.

On the 12th of September he was seized with the spirit of prophecy, became as one possessed, rushed through the town howling, foaming at the mouth, making prodigious leaps and extravagant gestures, and crying in every street, "Repent! repent!" After having carried on these antics for some time, Knipperdolling dashed into the market-place, cast himself down on the ground, and fell into an ecstasy.

The people clustered around him, wondering what new revelation was about to be made, and the king, who was then holding audience, looked on uneasily at the crowd drifting from his throne towards his lieutenant-general, whose object he was unable to divine, as this performance had not been concerted between them.

He was not left long in uncertainty, for Knipperdolling, rising from the ground with livid face, scrambled up the back of a sturdy artisan standing near, and crawled on all fours "like a dog," says Sleidan, over the heads of the throng, breathing in their faces, and exclaiming, "The celestial Father has sanctified thee; receive the Holy Ghost." Then he anointed the eyes of some blind men with his spittle, saying, "Let sight be given you." Undiscomfited by the failure of this attempt to perform a miracle, he prophesied that he would die and rise again in three days; and he indicated a corner of the market-place where this was to occur. Then making his way towards the throne, he began to dance in the most grotesque and indecent manner before the king, shouting contemptuously, "Often have I danced thus before my mistresses, now the celestial Father has ordered me to perform these dances before my king."[214]

[214] Kerssenbroeck, p. 81 *et seq.*; Sleidan, p. 416.

John was highly displeased at this performance; and he ran down the steps of his throne to interrupt him. But Knipperdolling nimbly leaped upon the dais, seated himself in the place of majesty, and cried out, "The Spirit of God impels me: John Bockelson is king according to the flesh, I am king according to the Spirit; the two Testaments must be abolished and extirpated. Man must cease from obeying terrestrial laws; henceforth he shall obey only the inspirations of the Spirit and the instincts of nature."

John of Leyden sprang at him, dragged him from the throne, beat his head with his golden sceptre, and administering a kick to the rear of his lieutenant, sent him flying head over heels from the platform, and then calmly enthroning himself, he gave orders for the removal and imprisonment of the rebel.

He was obeyed.[215]

[215] Kerssenbroeck, Hast p. 366.

Knipperdolling, left to cool in the dungeon, felt that his only chance of life was to submit. He therefore sent his humble apology to the king, and assured him that he had been possessed by an evil spirit, which had driven him, against his judgment and conscience, into revolt. "And," said he, "last night the Father revealed to me that one must venerate the royal majesty, and that John is destined to reign over the whole earth."

He was at once released, for Bockelson needed him, and the failure of this attempt only secured the king's hold over him. He sent him a letter of pardon, concluding with the royal signature in this eccentric fashion:—

"In fide persiste salvus Carnis curam agit Deus. Johannes Leydanus. Potentia Dei, robur meum."[216]

[216] Persist secure in Faith. God takes care of the Flesh. John of Leyden. The Power of God is my strength.

Another event took place at Münster, which distracted the thoughts of the people from the events of the siege, and the attempt of Knipperdolling to dethrone the king.

The prophet Dusentscheuer, on the same day, the 12th September, sought the King of Zion in his palace, and said to him with an inspired air, "This is the commandment of the Lord to me: Go and say unto the chief of Israel, that he shall prepare on the Mount Zion (that is, the cathedral square) a great supper for all Christian brethren and sisters, and after supper he shall commission the teachers of my Word to go forth to the four quarters of the world, that they may teach all men the way of my righteousness, and that they may be brought into my fold."

The king accepted the message with respect, and gave orders for its immediate execution.

On the 13th September, Dusentscheuer called together the elect, traversing the streets playing upon a flute. At noon 1700 men, capable of bearing arms, 400 old men and children, and 5000 women assembled on Mount Zion.

Bockelson left his palace, habited in a scarlet tunic over which was cast a cloth of silver mantle, on his head was his crown, and his sceptre was in his right hand. Thirty-two knights, magnificently dressed, served as his bodyguard. Then came Queen Divara and the rest of the wives of the court.

When the king had taken his place, the Grand Marshal Tilbeck made the people sit down. Tables had been arranged along the sides of the great square under the trees, with an open space in the centre.

When all were seated, the king and his familiars distributed food to those invited. They were given first boiled beef and roots, then ham with other vegetables, and finally roast meat. When the plates had been removed, thin round cakes of fine wheat flour were brought in large baskets, and John, calling the faithful up before him, communicated them with the bread, saying, "Take and eat this, and show forth the Lord's death." Divara followed, holding the chalice in her jewelled hands; she made the communicants drink from it, repeating the words to each, "Drink this, and show forth the Lord's death." Then all sang the *Gloria in excelsis* in German, and this fantastic parody of the communion was over. Bockelson now ordered all his subjects to arrange themselves in a circle, and he demanded if they would faithfully obey the Word of God. All having assented, Dusentscheuer mounted the pulpit and said, "The Father has revealed to me the names of twenty-seven apostles who are to be sent into every part of the world; they will spread everywhere the pure doctrine of the celestial kingdom, and the Lord will cover them with the shadow of His wings, so that not a hair of their head shall be injured. And when they shall arrive at a place where the authorities refuse to receive the Gospel, there they shall leave a florin in gold, they shall shake off the dust of their garments, and shall go to another place." Then the prophet designated the chosen apostles—he saw himself of the number—and he added, "Go ye into all the cities and preach the Word of God." The twenty-seven stepped forward, and the king, mounting the pulpit, exhorted the people to prepare for a grand sortie.[217]

[217] Kerssenbroeck, p. 86; Montfort., p. 34; Dorpius, f. 397 b; Heresbach, p. 139, *et seq.*; Bullinger, lib. ii. c. 10; Sleidan, p. 417; this author sets the number of communicants at 5,000, the "Newe Zeitung" at 4,000, f. 329. This authority adds that the communicants distributed the sacrament they had received amongst themselves saying, "Brother and sister, take and eat thereof. As Christ gave Himself for me, so will I give myself for thee. And as the corn-wheat is baked into one, and the grape branches are pressed into one, so we being many are one." Also, "Letter of the Bishop to the Electors of Cologne," *ibid.* p. 390.

The banquet was over for the people; but John, his wives and court, and those who had been on guard upon the walls, to the number of 500, now sat down.

The second banquet was much more costly than the first. In the midst of the feast, Bockelson, rising, said that he had received an order from the Father to go round and inspect the guests. He accordingly examined those present, and recognising amongst them a soldier of the Episcopal army, who had been made prisoner, he confronted him sternly, and asked—

"Friend, what is thy faith?"

"My faith," replied the soldier, who was half drunk, "is to drink and make love."

"How didst thou dare to come in, not having on the wedding garment?" asked the king, in a voice of thunder.

"I did not come of my own accord to this debauch,"[218] answered the prisoner; "I was brought here by main force."

[218] The expression used was somewhat broad—Hurenhochzeit.

At these words, the king, transported with rage, drew his sword and smote off the head of the unfortunate reveller.

The night was spent in dancing.[219]

[219] Kerssenbroeck, p. 88 *et seq.*; Heresbach, p. 139; Dorp. f. 398.

Whilst the king was eating and drinking, the twenty-seven apostles were taking a tender farewell of their 124 legitimate wives,[220] and making their preparations to depart.

[220] Evidence of Heinrich Graess. Dorpius says that the number of apostles was twenty-eight, and gives their names and the places to which they were sent, f. 398.

When all was ready, they returned to Mount Zion; Bockelson ascended the pulpit, and gave them their mission in the following terms:—"Go, prepare the way; we will follow. Cast your florin of gold at the feet of those who despise you, that it may serve as a testimony against them, and they shall be slain, all the sort of them, or shall bow their necks to our rule."

Then the gates were thrown open, and the apostles went forth, north and south, and east and west. The blockade was not complete, and they succeeded in traversing the lines of the enemy.

However, the prince-bishop notified to the governors of the towns in his principality to watch them and arrest them, should they attempt to disseminate their peculiar doctrines.[221]

[221] Kerssenbroeck, p. 89 *et seq.*; Heresbach, pp. 89, 101, 141; Montfort., p. 35; Bullinger, lib. ii. c. 10; Sleidan, pp. 417-8; Hast, p. 368; "Historia v. d. Münst. Widerteuffer." p. 329 a.

We shall have to follow these men, and see the results of their mission, before we continue the history of the siege of Münster. In fact, on their expedition and their success, as John Bockelson probably felt, everything depended. As soon as the city was completely enclosed no food could enter: already it was becoming scarce; therefore an attack on the Episcopal army from the flank was most essential to success; the palisades and ramparts recently erected sufficiently defending the enemy against surprises and sorties from the town.

Seven of the apostles went to Osnabrück, six to Coesfeld, five to Warendorf, and eight, amongst whom was Dusentscheuer himself, betook themselves to Soest.[222]

[222] For the acts of these apostles, Kerssenbroeck, p. 92 *et seq.*; Menck. p. 1574; Montfort., p. 36 *et seq.*; Sleidan, p. 418; Bullinger, lib. ii. c. 10; Heresbach, p. 149.

On entering Soest, Dusentscheuer and his fellow-apostles opened their mission by a public frenzied appeal to repentance. Then, hearing that the senate had assembled, they entered the hall and preached to the city councillors in so noisy a fashion that the magistrates were obliged to suspend their deliberations. The burgomaster having asked them who they were, and why they entered the town-hall unsummoned and unannounced, "We are sent by the king of the New Zion, and by order of God to preach the Gospel," was the reply of Dusentscheuer; "and to execute this mission we need neither passports nor permission. The kingdom of Heaven suffereth violence, and the violent take it by storm." "Very well," said the burgomaster collectedly. "Guards, remove the preachers and throw them into prison." A few days after several of them lost their heads on the block.

John Clopris, at the head of four evangelists, entered Warendorf. They took up their abode in the house of an Anabaptist named Erpo, one of the magistrates of the town, and began to preach and prophesy in the streets. The first day they rebaptised fifty persons. Clopris preached with such fervour and persuasive eloquence, that the whole town followed him; the senate received the sign of the covenant in a body, and this was followed by a rebaptism of half the population.

Alarmed at what was taking place, and afraid of a diversion in his rear, Francis of Waldeck wrote to the magistrates ordering them to give up the apostles of error. They refused, and the prince at once invested the town and bombarded it. The magistrates sent offers of capitulation, which the prince rejected; they asked to retain their arms and their franchises. Francis of Waldeck insisted on unconditional surrender, and they were constrained to yield. Some of the senators and citizens who had repented of their craze, or who had taken no part in the movement, seized the apostles and conducted them to the town-hall. Clopris and his fellows cast down their florins of gold and declared that they shook off the dust of their feet against the traitors, and that they would carry the pure Word of God and the living Gospel elsewhere; but escape was not permitted, and they were delivered over to the prince-bishop.

Francis of Waldeck at once placed sentinels in the streets, ordered every citizen to deliver up his weapons, took the title-deeds of the city, withdrew its franchises, and executed four of the apostles and three of the ringleaders of the senators. Clopris was sent to Cologne, and was burnt there on the 1st February, 1535, by the Elector. The bishop then raised a fortress to command the town, and placed in it a garrison to keep the Warendorfians in order. Seventeen years after, the greater part of the franchises were restored, and all the rest in 1555.

The apostles of the east, under Julius Frisius, were arrested at Coesfeld, and were executed.[223]

[223] The "Newe Zeitung v. d. Widerteuffer. zu Münster," f. 329 b, 330 a, gives a summary of the confessions of these men, and their account of the condition of affairs in the city. They said that every man there had five, six, seven, or eight wives, and that every girl over the age of twelve was forced to marry; that if one wife showed resentment against another, or jealousy, or complained, she was sentenced by the king to death.

Those of the north reached Osnabrück. Denis Vinnius was at their head. They entered the house of a certain Otto Spiecher, whom they believed to be of their persuasion, and they laid at his feet their gold florins bearing the title and superscription of King John, as tokens of their mission. Spiecher picked up the gold pieces, pocketed them, and then informed his visitors that he did not belong to their sect, and that the only salvation for their necks would be reticence on the subject of their mission.

But this was advice Vinnius and his fellow-fanatics were by no means disposed to accept. They ran forth into the streets and market-place, yelling, dancing, foaming, and calling to repentance. Then Vinnius, having collected a crowd, preached to them the setting up of the Millennial kingdom at Münster. Thereupon the city-guard arrived with orders from the burgomaster, arrested the missionaries, and carried them off to the Goat-tower, where they shut them in, and barred fast the doors.[224]

[224] Kerssenbroeck, p. 100 *et seq.*

The rabble showed signs of violence, threatened, blustered, armed themselves with axes and hammers, and vowed they would batter open the prison-gates unless the true ministers of God's Word, pure from all human additions, were set at liberty. The magistrates replied with great firmness that the first man who attempted to force the doors should be shot, and no one caring to be the first man, though very urgent to his neighbours to lead the assault, the mob sang a psalm and dispersed, and the ministers were left to console themselves with the promises of Dusentscheuer that not a hair of their head should fall.

A messenger was sent by the magistrates post haste to the prince-bishop, and before morning the evangelists were in his grasp at Iburg.

As they were led past Francis of Waldeck, one of them, Heinrich Graess, exclaimed in Latin, "Has not the prince power to release the captive?" and the prince, disposed in his favour, sent for him. Graess then confessed that the whole affair was a mixture of fanaticism and imposture, the ingredients being mixed in pretty equal proportions, and promised, if his life were spared, to abandon Anabaptism, and, what was more to the point, to prove an Ahitophel to the Absalom in Zion.

Graess was pardoned, Strahl died in prison, the other four were brought to the block.

Graess was the sole surviving apostle of the seventy-seven, and the miserable failure of their mission had rudely shaken out of him all belief in its divine character, and he became as zealous in unmasking Anabaptism as he had been enthusiastic in its propagation.

There is no reason to believe that the man was an unprincipled traitor. On the contrary, he appears to have been thoroughly in earnest as long as he believed in his mission, but his confidence had been shaken before he left the city, and the signal collapse of the mission sufficed to convince him of his previous error, and make him resolute to oppose it.

Laden with chains, he was brought to the gates of Münster one dark night and there abandoned. In the morning he was recognised by the sentinels, and was brought into the city, and led in triumph before the king, by a vast concourse chanting German hymns.[225]

[225] Kerssenbroeck, p. 103 *et seq.*; Montfort., pp. 40- 1; Hast p. 368.

And thus he accounted for his presence:—"I was last night at Iburg in a dark dungeon, when suddenly a brilliant light filled my prison, and I saw before me an angel of God, who took me by the hand and led me forth, and delivered me from the death which has befallen all my companions, and which the ungodly determined to inflict on me upon the morrow. The angel transported me asleep to the gate of Münster, and that none may doubt my story, lo! the chains, wherewith I was laden by the enemies of Israel, still encumber me."

Some of the courtiers doubted the miracle, but not so the people, and the king gave implicit credence to his word, or perhaps thought the event capable of a very simple explanation, which had been magnified and rendered supernatural by the heated fancy of the mystic.

Graess became the idol of the people and the favourite of Bockelson. The king passed a ring upon his finger, and covered him with a robe of distinction, half grey, half green—the first the symbol of persistence, the other typical of gratitude to God.[226] Graess profited by his position to closely observe all that transpired of the royal schemes.

[226] Montfort., p. 40.

John Bockelson became more and more tyrannical and sanguinary. He hung a starving child, aged ten, for having stolen some turnips. A woman lost her head for having spit in the face of a preacher of the Gospel. An Episcopal soldier having been taken, the king exhorted him to embrace the pure Word of God, freed from the traditions of men. The prisoner having had the audacity to reply that the pure Gospel as practised in the city seemed to him to be adultery, fornication, and all uncleanness; the king, foaming with rage, hacked off his head with his own hand.[227]

[227] Kerssenbroeck, p. 110.

Provisions became scarce in Münster, and the inhabitants were driven to consume horse-flesh; and the powder ran short in the magazine.

The Diet of Coblenz assembled on the 13th December. The envoys of the Elector Palatine, the prince-bishops of Maintz, Cologne, and of Trier, the princes and nobles of the Upper and Lower Rhine and of Westphalia appeared. Francis of Waldeck, unable to be present in person, sent deputies to represent him.[228]

[228] *Ibid.* p. 114.

These deputies having announced that the cost of the siege had already amounted to 700,000 florins, besought the assembled princes to combine to terminate this disastrous war. A long deliberation followed, and the principle was admitted that as the establishment of an Anabaptist kingdom in Münster would be a disaster affecting the whole empire, it was just that the bishop should not be obliged to bear the whole expenses of the reduction of Münster. The Elector John Frederick of Saxony, though not belonging to the three circles convoked, through his deputies sent to the Diet, promised to take part in the extirpation of the heretics.[229] It was finally agreed that the bishop should be supplied with 300 horse soldiers, 3000 infantry, and that an experienced General, Count Ulrich von Ueberstein, should command them and take the general conduct of the war.[230]

[229] *Ibid.*; Sleidan, p. 419; Heresbach, p. 132.
[230] Sleidan, p. 419.

The monthly subsidy of 15,000 florins was also promised to be contributed till the fall of Münster. It was also agreed that the prince-bishop should be guaranteed the integrity of his domains; that each prince, Catholic or Protestant, should use his utmost endeavours to extirpate Anabaptism from his estates; that the Bishop of Münster should request Ferdinand, King of the Romans, and the seven Electors, to meet on the 4th April, at Worms, to consult with those then assembled at Worms on measures to crush the rebellion, to divide the cost of the war, and to punish the leaders of the revolt at Münster.

Lastly, the Diet addressed a letter to the guilty city, summoning it to surrender at discretion, unless it were prepared to resist the combined effort of all estates of the empire.

But if the princes were combining against the Anabaptist New Jerusalem, the sectarians were in agitation, and were arming to march to its relief from all sides, from Leyden, Freisland, Amsterdam, Deventer, from Brabant and Strassburg.

The Anabaptists of Deventer were on the point of rising and massacring the "unbelievers" in this city, and then marching on Münster, when the plot was discovered, and the four ringleaders were executed. The vigilance of the Regent of the Netherlands prevented the adherents of the mystic sect, who were then very numerous, from rolling in a wave upon Westphalia, and sweeping the undisciplined Episcopal army away and consolidating the power of their pontiff-king.

It was towards the Low Countries that John of Leyden looked with impatience. When would the expected delivery come out of the west? Why were not the thousands and tens of thousands of the sons of Israel rising from their fens, joined by trained bands from the cities, marching by the light of blazing cities, singing the songs of Zion?

Graess offered the king to hie to the Low Countries and rouse the faithful seed. "The Father," said he, "has ordered me to gather together the brethren dispersed at Wesel, at Deventer, at Amsterdam, and in Lower Germany; to form of them a mighty army that shall deliver this city and smite asunder the enemies of Israel. I will accomplish this mission with joy in the interest of the faithful. I fear no danger, since I go to fulfil the will of God, and I am sure that our brethren, when they know our extremity, and that it is the will of their king, will rise and hasten to the relief."[231]

[231] Montfort., p. 40; Kerssenbroeck, p. 104 *et seq.*; Hast, p. 368.

John Bockelson was satisfied; he furnished Graess with letters of credit, sealed with the royal signet. The letters were couched in the following terms:—"We, John, King of Righteousness in the new Temple, and servant of the Most High, do you to wit by these presents, that the bearer of these letters, Heinrich Graess, prophet illumined by the celestial Father, is sent by us to assemble, for the increase of our realm, our brethren dispersed abroad throughout the German lands. He will make them to hear the words of life, and he will execute the commandments which he has received from God and from us. We therefore order and demand of all those who belong to our kingdom to confide in him as in ourselves. Given at Münster, city of God, and sealed with our signet, in the twenty-sixth year of our age and the second of our reign, the second day of the first month, in the year 1535 after the nativity of Jesus Christ, Son of God."

Graess, furnished with this letter and with 300 florins from the treasury, left the city, and betook himself direct to Iburg, which he reached on the vigil of the Epiphany;[232] and appeared before the bishop, told him the whole project, the names of the principal members of the sect at Wesel, Amsterdam, Leyden, &c., the places where their arms were deposited, and their plan of a general rising and massacring their enemies on a preconcerted day.

[232] Montfort., p. 40.

The bishop sent dispatches at once to the Duke of Juliers and the Governors of the Low Countries to warn them to be on their guard. They replied, requesting his assistance in suppressing the insurrection;

and as the most effectual aid he could render would be to send Graess, he commissioned him to visit Wesel, and arrest the execution of the project.

Graess at once betook himself to Wesel, where he denounced the ringleaders and indicated the places where their arms and ammunition were secreted in enormous quantities. A tumult broke out; but the Duke of Juliers entered Wesel on the 5th April (1535), at the head of some squadrons of cavalry, seized the ringleaders, who were members of the principal houses in the place and of the senate, and on the 13th executed six of them. The rest were compelled to do penance in white sheets, were deprived of their arms, and put under close surveillance.

Another division of the Anabaptists attempted to gain possession of Leyden, but were discomfited, fifteen of the principal men of the party were executed, and five of the women most distinguished for their fanaticism were drowned, amongst whom was the original wife of John Bockelson.[233]

[233] Hast, p. 370; Bussierre, p. 403.

In Gröningen, the partisans of the sect were numerous; orders reached them from the king to rise and massacre the magistrates, and march to the relief of the invested city. As the Anabaptists there were not all disposed to recognise the royalty of John of Leyden, an altercation broke out between them, and the attempt failed; but rising and marching under Peter Shomacker, their prophet, they were defeated on January 24th, by the Baron of Leutenburg, and the prophet was executed.

We must now return to what took place in the town of Münster at the opening of the year 1535.

Bockelson inaugurated that year by publishing, on January 2nd, an edict in twenty-eight Articles. It was addressed "To all lovers of the Truth and the Divine Righteousness, learned in and ignorant of the mysteries of God, to let them know how those Christians ought to live or act who are fighting under the banner of Justice, as true Israelites of the new Temple predestined for long ages, announced by the mouths of all the holy prophets, founded in the power of the Holy Ghost, by Christ and his Apostles, and finally established by John, the righteous King, seated on the throne of David."

The Articles were to this effect:—

"1. In this new temple there was to be only one king to rule over the people of God.

2. This king was to be a minister of righteousness, and to bear the sword of justice.

3. None of the subjects were to desert their allotted places.

4. None were to interpret Holy Scripture wrongfully.

5. Should a prophet arise teaching anything contrary to the plain letter of Holy Scripture, he was to be avoided.

6. Drunkenness, avarice, fornication, and adultery were forbidden.

7. Rebellion to be punished with death.

8. Duels to be suppressed.

9. Calumny forbidden.

10. Egress from the camp forbidden without permission.

11. Any one absenting himself from his wife for three days, without leave from his officer, the wife to take another husband.

12. Approaching the enemy's sentinels without leave forbidden.

13. All violence forbidden among the elect.

14. Spoil taken from the enemy to go into a common fund.

15. No renegade to be re-admitted.

16. Caution to be observed in admitting a Christian into one society who leaves another.

17. Converts not to be repelled.

18. Any desiring to live at peace with the Christians, in trade, friendship, and by treaty, not to be rejected.

19. Permission given to dealers and traders to traffic with the elect.

20. No Christian to oppose and revolt against any Gentile magistrate, except the servants of the bishops and the monks.

21. A Gentile culprit not to be remitted the penalty of his crime by joining the Christian sect.

22. Directions about bonds.

23. Sentence to be pronounced against those who violate these laws and despise the Word of God, but not hastily, without the knowledge of the king.

24. No constraint to be used to force on marriages.

25. None afflicted with epilepsy, leprosy, and other diseases, to contract marriage without informing the other contracting party of their condition.

26. Nulla virginis specie, cum virgo non sit, fratrem defraudabit; alioquin serio punietur.

27. Every woman who has not a legitimate husband, to choose from among the community a man to be her guardian and protector.

"Given by God and King John the Just, minister of the Most High God, and of the new Temple, in the 26th year of his age and the first of his reign, on the second day of the first month after the nativity of Jesus Christ, Son of God, 1535."[234]

[234] Kerssenbroeck, p. 132 *et seq.*

The object Bockelson had in view in issuing this edict was to produce a diversion in his favour among the Lutherans. He already felt the danger he was in, from a coalescence of Catholics and Protestants, and he hoped by temperate proclamations and protestations of his adhesion to the Bible, and the Bible only, as his authority, to dispose them, if not to make common cause with him, at least to withdraw their assistance from the common enemy, the Catholic bishop.

For the same object he sent letters on the 13th January to the Landgrave of Hesse, and with them a book called "The Restitution" (Von der Wiederbringung), intended to place Anabaptism in a favourable light.[235]

[235] Kerssenbroeck, p. 128; Sleidan, p. 420; Hast, p. 373 *et seq.*; "Acta, Handlungen," &c., f. 365 b. The king's letter began "Leve Lips" ("Dear Phil").

The Landgrave replied at length, rebuking the fanatics for their rebellion, for their profligacy, and for their heresy in teaching that man had a free will.[236]

[236] Sleidan, p. 421.

This reply irritated the Anabaptists, and they wrote to him again, to prove that they clave to the pure Word of God, freed from all doctrines and traditions of men, and that they followed the direct inspiration of God through their prophet. They also retorted on Philip with some effect. The Landgrave, said they, had no right to censure them for attacking their bishop, for he had done precisely the same in his own dominions. He had expelled all the religious from their convents, and had appropriated their lands; he had re-established the Duke of Wurtemburg in opposition to the will of the Emperor; he had changed the religion of his subjects, and was unable to allege, as his authority for thus acting, the direct orders of Heaven, transmitted to him by the prophets of the living God. They might have retorted upon the Landgrave also, the charge of immorality, but they forbore; their object was to persuade the champion of the Protestant cause to favour them, not to exasperate him by driving the *tu quoque* too deep home.

With this letter was sent a treatise by Rottmann, entitled, "On the Secret Significance of Scripture."

Philip of Hesse wavered. He wrote once more; and after having attempted to excuse himself for those things wherewith he had been reproached, he said, "If the thing depended on me only, you would not have to plead in vain your *just* cause, and you would obtain all that you demand; but you ought ere this to have addressed the princes of the empire, instead of taking the law into your own hands; flying to arms, erecting a kingdom, electing a king, and sending prophets and apostles abroad to stir up the towns and the people. Nevertheless, it is possible that even now your demands may be favourably listened to, if you recall on equitable conditions those whom you have driven out of the town and despoiled of their goods, and restore your ancient constitutions and your former authorities."[237]

[237] Kerssenbroeck, p. 129; Sleidan, p. 421.

Luther now thundered out of Wittemberg. Sleidan epitomises this treatise. Five Hessian ministers also issued an answer to the doctrine of the Anabaptists of Münster, which was probably drawn up for them by Luther himself, or was at least submitted to him for his approval, for it is published among his German works.[238] It is full of invective and argument in about equal doses. A passage or two only can be quoted here:—

338

"Since you are led astray by the devil into such blasphemous error, drunk and utterly imprisoned you wish, as is Satan's way, to make yourselves into angels of light, and to paint in brightness and colour your devilish doings. For the devil will be no devil, but a holy angel, yea, even God himself, and his works, however bad they may be before God and all the world, he will have unrebuked, and himself be honoured and reverenced as the Most Holy. For that purpose he and you, his obedient disciples, use Holy Scripture as all heretics have ever done."[239]

[238] Luth. "Sämmtliche Werke," Wittenb. 1545-51, ii. ff. 367-375; "Von der Teuffelischen Secte d. Widerteuffer. zu Münster."
[239] *Ibid.* f. 367.

"What shall I say? You let all the world see that you understand far less about the kingdom of Christ than did the Jews, who blame you for your want of understanding, and yet none spoke or believed more ignorantly of that same kingdom than they. For the Scripture and the prophets point to Messiah, through whom all was to be fulfilled, and this the Jews also believed. But you want to make it point to your Tailor-King, to the great disgrace and mockery of Christ, our only true King, Saviour, and Redeemer."[240]

[240] *Ibid.* f. 369.

But this was the grievous rub with the Reformer—that the Anabaptist had gone a step beyond himself. "You have cast away all that Dr. Martin Luther taught you, and yet it is from him that you have received, next to God, all sound learning out of the Scripture; you have given another definition of faith, after your new fashion, with various additional articles, so that you have not only darkened, but have utterly annihilated the value of saving faith."[241]

[241] *Ibid.* f. 373.

In a treatise of Justus Menius, published with Luther's approval, and with a preface by him, "On the Spirit of the Anabaptists," it is angrily complained, that these sectaries bring against the Lutheran Church the following charges:—"First, that our churches are idol-temples, since God dwelleth not in temples made with hands. Secondly, that we do not preach the truth, and have true Divine worship therein. Thirdly, that our preachers are sinners, and are therefore unfit to teach others. Fourthly, that the common people do not mend their morals by our preaching." All which charges Justus Menius answers as well as he can, sword in one hand against the Papists, trowel in the other patching up the walls of his Jerusalem.[242]

[242] *Ibid.* ii. ff. 298-325.

Melancthon also wrote against the Anabaptist book, combating all its propositions, and to do so falling back on the maxim, *Abusus non tollit substantiam,* a maxim completely ignored by the Reformers when they attacked the Catholics.[243] Thus the new sect fought Lutheranism with precisely the same weapons wherewith the Lutherans had fought the Church; and the Lutherans, to maintain their ground, were obliged to take refuge in the authority of the Church and tradition—positions they had assailed formerly, and to use arguments they had previously rejected.

[243] *Ibid.* ii. ff. 334-363. Melancthon says that things had come to such a pass in Münster, that no child knew who was its father, brother, or sister.

In the treatise of the five Hessian divines, drawn up by Philip of Hesse's orders, the errors of the Anabaptists are epitomised and condemned; they are as follows:—
"1. They do not believe that men are justified by faith only, but by faith and works conjointly.
2. They refer the redemption of Christ alone to the fall of Adam, and to its consequences on those born of him.
3. They hold community of goods.
4. They blame Martin Luther as having taught nothing about good works.
5. They proclaim the freedom of man's will.

6. They reject infant baptism.

7. They take the Bible alone, uninterpreted by any commentary.

8. They declare for plurality of wives.

9. They do not correctly teach the Incarnation of Christ."[244]

[244] "Acta Handlung." &c. f. 366 a.

This "Kurtze: und in der eile gestelte Antwort," is signed by John Campis, John Fontius, John Kymeus, John Lessing, and Anthony Corvinus.

It was high time that the siege should come to an end, so every one said; but every one had said the same for the last twelve months, and Münster held out notwithstanding.

An ultimatum was sent into the city by the general in command, offering the inhabitants liberal terms if they would surrender, and warning them that, in case of refusal, the city would be taken by storm, and would be delivered over to plunder.[245] No answer was made to the letter; nevertheless, it produced a profound impression on the citizens, who were already suffering from want of victuals. A party was formed which resolved to seize the person of the king, and to open the gates and make terms with the bishop.[246] Bockelson, hearing of the plot, assembled the whole of the population in the cathedral square, and solemnly announced to them by revelation from the Father that at Easter the siege would be raised, and the city experience a wonderful deliverance. He also divided the town into twelve portions, and placed at the head of each a duke of his own creation, charged with the suppression of treason and the protection of the gates. Each duke was provided with twenty-four guards for the defence of his person, and the infliction of punishment on those citizens who proved restive under the rule of the King of Zion.[247] These dukes were promised the government of the empire, when the kingdoms of Germany became the kingdom of John of Leyden. Denecker, a grocer, was Duke of Saxony; Moer, the tailor, Duke of Brunswick; the Kerkerings were appointed to reign over Westphalia; Redecker, the cobbler, to bear rule in Juliers and Cleves. John Palk was created Duke of Guelders and Utrecht; Edinck was to be supreme in Brabant and Holland; Faust, a coppersmith, in Mainz and Cologne; Henry Kock was to be Duke of Trier; Ratterberg to be Duke of Bremen, Werden, and Minden; Reininck took his title from Hildesheim and Magdeburg; and Nicolas Strip from Frisia and Gröningen. As these men were for the most part butchers, blacksmiths, tailors, and shoemakers, their titles, ducal coronets and mantles, and the prospect of governing, turned their heads, and made them zealous tools in the hands of Bockelson.

[245] Kerssenbroeck, p. 130.

[246] *Ibid.* p. 140.

[247] Sleidan, p. 419; Bullinger, l. ii. c. 9; Heresbach, p. 156; Dorp. f. 498.

The king made one more attempt to rouse the country. He issued letters offering the pillage of the whole world to all those who would join the standard. But the bishop was informed of the preparation of these missives by a Danish soldier in Münster; he was much alarmed, as his *lantzknechts* were ready to sell their services to the highest bidder. He therefore pressed on the circumvallation of the city, kept a vigilant guard, and captured every emissary sent forth to distribute these tempting offers. On the 11th February, 1535, the moat, mound, and palisade around the city were complete; and it was thenceforth impossible for access to or egress from the city to be effected without the knowledge of the prince and his generals. The unfortunate people of Münster discovered attempting to escape were by the king's orders decapitated. Many men and women perished thus; amongst them was a mistress of Knipperdolling named Dreyer, who, weary of her life, fled, but was caught and delivered over to the executioner. When her turn came, the headsman hesitated. Knipperdolling, perceiving it, took from him the sword, and without changing colour smote off her head. "The Father," said he, "irresistibly inspired me to this, and I have thus become, without willing it or knowing it, an instrument of vengeance in the hands of the Lord."[248]

[248] Kerssenbroeck, p. 148.

The legitimate wife of Knipperdolling, for having disparaged polygamy, escaped death with difficulty; she was sentenced to do public penance, kneeling in the great square, in the midst of the people, with a naked sword in her hands.[249]

[249] *Ibid.* p. 149.

Easter came, the time of the promised delivery, and the armies of the faithful from Holland and Friesland and Brabant had not arrived. The position of Bockelson became embarrassing. He extricated himself from the dilemma with characteristic effrontery. During six days he remained in his own house, invisible to every one. At the expiration of the time he issued forth, assembled the people on Mount Zion, and informed them that the deliverance predicted of the Father *had* taken place, but that it was a deliverance different in kind from what they had anticipated. "The Father," said he, "has laid on my shoulders the iniquities of the Israelites. I have been bowed down under their burden, and was well-nigh crushed beneath their weight. Now, by the grace of the Lord, health has been restored to me, and you have been all released from your sins. This spiritual deliverance is the most excellent of all, and must precede that which is purely exterior and temporal. Wait, therefore, patiently, it is promised and it will arrive, if you do not fall back into your sins, but maintain your confidence in God, who never deserts His chosen people, though He may subject them to trials and tribulations, to prove their constancy."[250] One would fain believe that John Bockelson was in earnest, and the subject of religious infatuation, like his subjects, but after this it is impossible to so regard him.

[250] Kerssenbroeck, pp. 153, 154; Sleidan, p. 422; Bullinger, lib. ii. c. 2; Heresbach, pp. 159, 160.

The princes, when separating after the assembly of Coblenz, had agreed to reassemble on the 4th of April. Ferdinand, King of the Romans, convoked all the Estates of the empire to meet on that day at Worms. The deputies of several towns protested against the decisions taken at Coblenz without their participation, and the deliberations were at the outset very tumultuous. An understanding was at length arrived at, and a monthly subsidy of 20,000 florins for five months was agreed upon, to maintain the efficacy of the investment of Münster. But before separating, a final effort to obtain a pacific termination to the war was resolved upon, and the burgomasters of Frankfort and Nürnberg were sent as a deputation into the city. This attempt proved as sterile as all those previously essayed. "We have nothing in common with the Roman empire," answered the chiefs of Zion; "for that empire is the fourth beast whereof Daniel prophesied. We have set up again the kingdom of Israel, by the Father's command, and we engage you to abstain for the future from assailing this realm, as you fear the wrath of God and eternal damnation."[251]

[251] Kerssenbroeck, p. 155; Hast, 394.

The famine in Münster now became terrible. Cats, rats, dogs, and horses were eaten; the starving people attempted various expedients to satisfy their craving hunger. They ate leather, wood, even cow-dung dried in the sun, the bark of trees, and candles. Corpses lately buried were dug up during the night and secretly devoured. Mothers even ate their children. "Terrible maladies," says Kerssenbroeck, "the consequence of famine, aggravated the position of the inhabitants of the town; their flesh decomposed, they rotted living, their skin became livid, their lips retreated; their eyes, fixed and round, seemed ready to start out of their orbits; they wandered about, haggard, hideous, like mummies, and died by hundreds in the streets. The king, to prevent infection, had the bodies cast into large common ditches, whence the starving withdrew them furtively to devour them. Night and day the houses and streets re-echoed with tears, cries, and moans;—men, women, old men, and children sank into the darkest despair."[252]

[252] Kerssenbroeck, p. 157 *et seq.*; Heresbach, pp. 151, 152; Hast, p. 395; Montfort., p. 46.

In the midst of the general famine, John of Leyden lived in abundance. His storehouses, into which the victuals found in every house had been collected, supplied his own table and that of his immediate followers. His revelry and pomp were unabated, whilst his deluded subjects died of want around him.[253]

[253] *Ibid.* p. 157.

When starvation was at its worst, a letter from Heinrich Graess circulated in the town, informing the people that his miraculous escape had been a fable, and that he had rejected the follies of Anabaptism, disgusted at the extravagance to which it had led its votaries, and assuring them that their king was an impostor, exploiting to his advantage the credulity of an infatuated mob.[254]

[254] Montfort., p. 47.

This letter produced an effect which made the king tremble. He summoned his disciples before him, reproached them for putting the hand to the plough and turning back, and gave leave to all those whose faith wavered to go out from the city. "As for me," said he, "I shall remain here, even if I remain alone with the angels which the Father will not fail to send to aid me to defend this place."[255]

[255] Kerssenbroeck, p. 161.

When the king had given permission to leave the city, numbers of every age and sex poured through the gates, leaving behind only the most fanatical who were resolved to conquer or die with John of Leyden.

Outside the city walls extended a trampled and desolate tract to the fosse and earthworks of the besiegers, strewn with the ruins of houses and of farmsteads. The unfortunate creatures escaping from Zion, wasted and haggard like spectres, spread over this devastated region. The investing army drove them back towards the city, unwilling to allow the rebels to protract the siege by disembarrassing themselves of all the useless mouths in the place. They refused, however, to re-enter the walls, and remained in the Königreich, as this desert tract was called, to the number of 900, living on roots and grass, for four weeks, lying on the bare earth. Some were too feeble to walk, and crawled about on all fours; their hunger was so terrible that they filled their mouths with sand, earth, or leaves, and died choked, in terrible convulsions. Night and day their moans, howls, and cries ascended. The children presented a yet more deplorable spectacle; they implored their mothers to give them something to eat, and they, poor creatures, could only answer them with tears and sobs; often they approached the lines of the camp, and sought to excite the compassion of the soldiers.

The General in command, Graff Ueberstein, sent information, on April 22nd, to the bishop, who was ill in his castle at Wollbeck, and asked what was to be done with these unfortunates who were perishing in the Königreich. The bishop shed tears, and protested his sorrow at the sufferings of the poor wretches, but did not venture to give orders for their removal, without consulting the Duke of Cleves and the Elector of Cologne. Thus much precious time was lost, and only on the 28th May, a month after, were the starving wretches permitted to leave the Königreich, upon the following terms: 1st. That they should be transported to the neighbouring town of Diekhausen, where they should be examined, and those who were guilty among them executed; 2nd. That the rest should be pardoned and dispersed in different places, after having undertaken to renounce Anabaptism, and to abstain from negotiations, open or secret, with their comrades in the beleagured city.[256] These conditions having been made, the refugees were transported on tumbrils and in carts to Diekhausen, at a foot's pace, their excessive exhaustion rendering them incapable of bearing more rapid motion. They numbered 200; 700 had perished of famine between the lines of the investing army and the walls of the besieged town. On the 30th May, those found guilty of prominent participation in the revolt were executed.

[256] Kerssenbroeck, pp. 161-8.

The prince-bishop might have spared his tears and sent loaves. His hesitation and want of genuine sympathy with the starving unfortunates serve to mark his character as not only weak, but selfish and cowardly.

Whilst this was taking place outside the walls of Münster, John van Gheel, an emissary of Bockelson, was actively engaged in rousing the Anabaptists of Amsterdam. Having insinuated himself into the good graces of the Princess Mary, regent of the Netherlands, he persuaded her that he was desirous of restraining the sectaries waiting their call to march to the relief of Münster. She even furnished him with an authorisation to raise troops for this purpose. He profited by this order to arm his friends and lay a plot for obtaining the mastery of Amsterdam. His design was to make that city a place of rendezvous for all the Anabaptists of the Low Countries, who would flock into it as a city of refuge, when once it was in his power, and then he would be able to organise out of them an army sufficiently numerous and well appointed to raise the siege of Münster.

On the 11th May he placed himself at the head of 600 friends, seized on the town, massacred half the guards, and one of the burgomasters. Amsterdam would inevitably have been in the power of the sectaries in another hour, had not one of the guard escaped up the tower and rung the alarm-bell. As the tocsin pealed over the city, the citizens armed and rushed to the market-place, fell upon the Anabaptists and retook the town-hall, notwithstanding a desperate resistance. Crowds of fanatics from the country, who had received secret intimation to assemble before the walls of Amsterdam, and wait till the gates were opened to admit them, finding that the plan had been defeated, threw away their arms and fled with precipitation.[257]

[257] Kerssenbroeck, pp. 73, 74; Hast, p. 37; Montfort., p. 58 *et seq.*

Van Gheel had fallen in the encounter. The prisoners were executed. Amongst these was Campé whom John of Leyden had created Anabaptist bishop of Amsterdam. His execution was performed with great barbarity; first his tongue, then his hand, and finally his head was cut off.[258]

[258] Montfort., pp. 68, 69.

We must look once more into the doomed city.

In the midst of the general desolation John Bockelson and his court lived in splendour and luxury. Every one who murmured against his excesses was executed. Heads were struck off on the smallest charge, and scarcely a day passed in May and June without blood flowing on Mount Zion. One of the most remarkable of these executions was that of Elizabeth Wandtscherer, one of the queens.

This woman had had three husbands; the first was dead, the second marriage had been annulled, and Bockelson had taken her to wife because she was pretty and well made.

She was a great favourite with her royal husband, and for six months she seemed to be delighted with her position; but at length, disgusted with the unbridled licence of the royal harem, the hypocrisy and the mad revelry of the court, contrasted with the famine of the citizens, a prey to remorse, she tore off her jewels and her queenly robes, and asked John of Leyden permission to leave the city. This was on the 12th June. The king, furious at an apostacy in his own house, dragged her into the market-place, and there in the presence of his wives and the populace, smote off her head with his own hands, stamped on her body, and then chanting the "Gloria in excelsis" with his queens, danced round the corpse weltering in its blood.[259]

[259] Kerssenbroeck, pp. 176-7; Dorpius, f. 498 b; Sleidan, p. 422, says she was executed for having observed to some of her companions that it could not be the will of God that they should live in abundance whilst the subjects perished from want of necessaries. Hast, p. 395; Heresbach, p. 145.

However, the royal magazines were now nearly exhausted, and the king was informed that there remained provisions for only a few days. He resolved to carry on his joyous life of debauchery without thought of the morrow, and when all was expended, to fire the city in every quarter, and then to rush forth, arms in hand, and break through the investing girdle, or perish in the attempt.[260] This project was not executed, for the siege was abruptly ended before the moment had arrived for its accomplishment.

[260] Kerssenbroeck, p. 177.

Late in the preceding year, a soldier of the Episcopal army, John Eck, of Langenstraten, or, as he was called from his diminutive stature, Hansel Eck, having been punished as he deemed excessively or unjustly for some dereliction in his duty, deserted to the Anabaptists, and found an asylum in the city, where John Bockelson, perceiving his abilities and practical acquaintance with military operations, made him one of his captains.

But Hansel soon repented bitterly this step he had taken. Little men are proverbially peppery and ready to stand on their dignity. His desertion had been the result of an outburst of wounded self-pride, and when his wrath cooled down, and his judgment obtained the upper hand, he was angry with himself for what he had done. Feeling confident that the city must eventually fall, and knowing that small mercies would be shown to a deserter caught in arms, however insignificant he might be in stature, Hansel took counsel with eight other discontented soldiers in his company, and they resolved to escape from Münster and ask pardon of the bishop.

They effected the first part of their object on the night of the 17th June, and crossed the Königreich towards the lines of the investing force. The sentinels, observing a party of armed men advancing, with the moon flashing from their morions and breastplates, fired on them and killed seven. His diminutive stature stood Hansel in good stead, and he, with one other named Sobb, succeeded in escalading the ramparts unobserved, and in making their way to the nearest fort of Hamm, where the old officer, Meinhardt von Hamm, under whom he had formerly served, was in command. Hansel and Sobb were conducted into his presence, and offered to deliver the city into the hands of the prince-bishop if he would accord them a free pardon; but they added that no time must be lost, as it was but a question of hours rather than of days before the city was fired, and the final sortie was executed.[261]

[261] Kerssenbroeck, p. 179 *et seq.*; Sleidan, p. 427; Montfort., p. 71; Heresbach, p. 162 *et seq.*; Hast, p. 395 *et seq.*; Dorpius, f. 499.

Meinhardt listened to his plan, approved of it, and wrote to Francis of Waldeck, asking a safe-conduct for Hansel, and urging the utmost secrecy, as on the preservation of the secret depended the success of the scheme.

The safe-conduct was readily granted, and the deserter was brought to Willinghegen concealed amidst game in a cart covered with boughs of trees. Willinghegen is a small place one mile outside the circumvallation. The chiefs of the besieging army met here to consider the plan of Hansel Eck. The little man protested that with 300 men he could take the city. He knew the weak points, and he could escalade the walls where they were unguarded. Four hundred soldiers were, however, decided to be sent on the expedition, under the command of Wilkin Steding, "a terrible enemy but a devoted friend;" John of Twickel was to be standard-bearer, and Hansel was to act as guide; and the attempt was to be made on the eve of St. John the Baptist's day.[262] However, the bishop and Count Ueberstein, desirous of avoiding unnecessary effusion of blood, summoned the inhabitants to surrender, for the last time, on the 22nd June.

[262] Kerssenbroeck, p. 169; and the authors before cited.

Rottmann replied to the deputies that "the city should be surrendered only when they received the order to do so from the Father by a revelation."

Midsummer eve was a hot, sultry day. Towards evening dark heavy clouds rolled up against the wind, and a violent storm of thunder, lightning, and hail burst over the doomed city. The sentinels of Münster, exhausted by hunger, and alarmed at the rage of the elements, quitted their posts and retreated under shelter. The darkness, the growl of the wind, and the boom of the thunder concealed the approach of the Episcopal troops. The 400, under Steding, guided by the deserter, marched into the Königreich between ten and eleven o'clock, and met with no obstacles till they reached the Holy-cross Gate. Here they filled the ditch with faggots, trees, and bundles of straw; a bridge was improvised, the curtain of palisades masking the bastion was surmounted, ladders were planted, and without meeting with the least resistance, the 400 reached the summit of the walls. The sentinels, whom they found asleep, were killed, with the exception of one who purchased his life by giving up the pass-word, "Die Erde." The soldiers then advanced along the paved road which lay between the double walls, captured and killed the sentinels at every watch tower, and then, entering the streets, crossed the cemetery of Ueberwasser, the River Aa by its bridge, and debouched on the cathedral square, where the faint flashes of the retreating lightning illumined at intervals the gaunt scaffolding of the throne and gallery and pulpit of the Anabaptist king, looking now not unlike the preparations for an execution.

The cathedral had been converted into the arsenal. Hansel led the Episcopal soldiers to the western gates, gave the word "Die Erde," and the guards were killed before they could give the alarm. The artillery was now in the hands of the 400.[263]

[263] Kerssenbroeck, p. 176 *et seq.*; and the authors before cited.

The Anabaptists had slept through the rumble of the thunder, but suddenly the rattle of the drum on their hill of Zion woke them with a start. They sprang from their beds, armed in haste, and rushed to the cathedral square, where their own cannons opened on them their mouths of fire, and poured an iron shower down the main thoroughfares which led from the Minster green. But they were not discouraged. Through backways, and under the shelter of the surrounding houses, they reached the Chapel of St. Michael, which commanded the position of the Episcopal soldiers, and thence fired upon them with deadly precision.

Steding turned the guns against the chapel, but its massive walls could not be broken through, and the balls bounded from them without effecting more than a trivial damage. The Anabaptists pursued their advantage. Whilst Steding was occupied with those who held the Chapel of St. Michael, a large number assembled in the market-place and marched in close ranks upon the cathedral square.

The 400, unable to withstand the numbers opposed to them, were driven from their positions, and retreated into the narrow Margaret Street, where they were unable to use their arms with advantage. Steding burst open the door of a house, and sent 200 of his men through it; they issued through the back door, filled up a narrow lane running parallel with the street, and attacked the Anabaptists in the rear, who, thinking that the city was in the hands of the enemy, and that they were being assailed by a reinforcement, fled precipitately.

By an unpardonable oversight, Steding had forgotten to leave a guard at the postern by which he had entered the city. The Anabaptists discovered this mistake and profited by it, so that when the reinforcements sent to support Steding arrived, the gates were closed, and the walls were defended by the women, who cast stones and firebrands, and shot arrows amongst them, taunting them with the failure of the attempt to surprise the city; and they, uncertain whether to believe that the plot of Hansel Eck had failed or not, remained without till break of day, vainly attempting to escalade the walls. The Anabaptists, who had fled in the Margaret Street, soon rallied, and the 400 were again exposed to the fury of a multitude three times their number, who assailed them in front and in rear, and they were struck down by stones and furniture cast out of the windows upon them by the women in the houses.

Nevertheless they bravely defended themselves for several hours, and their assailants began to lose courage, as news of the onslaught upon the walls reached them. It was now midnight. King John proposed a temporary cessation of hostilities, which Steding gladly accepted, and the messengers of Bockelson offered the 400 their life if they would lay down their arms, kneel before him, and ask his pardon.[264]

[264] Kerssenbroeck, p. 385; Heresbach, pp. 162-6; Montfort., p. 72; Hast, p. 396 *et seq.*

The soldiers indignantly rejected this offer, but proposed to quit the town with their arms and ensigns. A long discussion ensued, which Steding protracted till break of day.

At the opening of the negotiations, Steding bade John von Twickel, the ensign, hasten to the ramparts with three men, as secretly as possible, and urge on the reinforcements. Twickel reached the bastions as day began to dawn, and he shouted to his comrades without to help Steding and his gallant band before all was lost. The Episcopalians, dreading a ruse of the besieged to draw them into an ambush, hesitated; but Twickel called the watchword, which was *Waldeck*, and announced the partial success of the 400.

Having accomplished his mission, Twickel returned to his comrades within, cheering them at the top of his voice with the cry from afar, "Courage, friends, help is at hand!"

At these words the remains of the gallant band of 400 recommenced the combat with irresistible energy. They fell on the Anabaptists with such vehemence that they drove them back on all sides; they gave no quarter, but breaking into divisions, swept the streets, meeting now with only a feeble resistance, for the soldiers without were battering at the gates. In vain did the sectarians offer to leave the town, their offer came too late, and the little band drove them from one rallying point to another.[265]

[265] Kerssenbroeck, pp. 188, 189.

Rottmann, feeling that all was lost, cast himself on their lances and fell. John of Leyden, instead of heading his party, attempted to fly, but was recognised as he was escaping through the gate of St. Giles, and was thrown into chains.

In the meantime the reinforcement had mounted the walls, beaten in the gates, and was pouring up the streets, rolling back the waves of discomfited Anabaptists on the swords and spears of the decimated 400. Two hundred of the most determined among the fanatics entrenched themselves in a round tower commanding the market-place, and continued firing on the soldiers of the prince. The generals, seeing that the town was in their power, and that it would cost an expenditure of time and life to reduce those in the tower, offered them their life, and permission to march out of Münster unmolested if they would surrender.

On these terms the Anabaptists in the bastion laid down their arms. The besiegers now spread throughout the city, hunting out and killing the rebels. Hermann Tilbeck, the former burgomaster, who had played into the hands of the Anabaptists till he declared himself, and who had been one of the twelve elders of Israel, was found concealed, half submerged, in a privy, near the gate of St. Giles, was killed, and his body left where he had hidden, "thus being buried," says Kerssenbroeck, "with worse than the burial of an ass." When the butchery was over, the bodies were brought together into the cathedral square and were examined. That of Knipperdolling was not amongst them. He was, in fact, hiding in the house of Catherine Hobbels, a zealous Anabaptist; she kept him in safety the whole of the 26th, but finding that every house was being searched, and fearing lest she should suffer for having sheltered him, she ordered him to leave and attempt an escape over the walls.[266]

[266] Kerssenbroeck, p. 195.

On the 27th all the women were collected in the market-square, and were ordered to leave the city and never to set foot in it again. But just as they were about to depart, Ueberstein announced that any one of them who could deliver up Knipperdolling should be allowed to remain and retain her possessions. The bait was tempting. Catherine Hobbels stepped forward, and offered to point out the hiding-place of the man they sought. She was given a renewed assurance that her house and goods would be respected, and she then delivered up Knipperdolling, who had not quitted his place of refuge. The promise made to her was rigorously observed; but her husband, not being included in the pardon, and being a ringleader of the fanatics, was executed.[267] The women were accompanied by the soldiers as far as the Lieb-Frau gate; they took with them their children, and were ordered to leave the diocese and principality forthwith.

[267] *Ibid.* p. 196; Heresbach, p. 166.

Divara, the head queen of John of Leyden, the wife of Knipperdolling, and three other women, were refused permission to leave. They were executed on the 7th July.

Münster was then delivered over to pillage; but all those who had left the town during the government of the Anabaptists were given their furniture and houses and such of their goods as could be identified.

All the property of the Anabaptists was confiscated and sold to pay the debts contracted by the prince for defraying the expenses of the war. The division of the booty occasioned several troubles, parties of soldiers mutinied, and attempted a second pillage, but the mutineers were put down rigorously.

Several more executions took place during the following days, and men hidden away in cellars, garrets and sewers were discovered and killed or carried off to prison. Among these were Bernard Krechting and Kerkering.[268]

[268] Kerssenbroeck, pp. 198-200. Dorpius says, "In the capture of the city, women and children were spared; and none were killed after the first fight, except the ringleaders."—f. 399.

On the 28th June, Francis of Waldeck entered the city at the head of 800 men. The sword, crown, and spurs of John of Leyden, together with the keys of the city, were presented to him.[269]

[269] Montfort., p. 73.

The prince received, as had been stipulated, half the booty, and the articles and the treasure deposited in the town-hall and in the royal palace, which amounted to 100,000 gold florins.[270]

[270] Kerssenbroeck, Heresbach, p. 168; Hast, p. 400.

Francis remained in Münster only three days. Having named the new magistrates, and organised the civil government of the city, he departed for his castle of Iburg. On the 13th July he ordered a Te Deum to be sung in the churches throughout the diocese, in thanks to God for having restored tranquillity; and the Chapter inaugurated a yearly thanksgiving procession to take place on the 25th June.[271]

[271] *Ibid.* p. 200.

On the 15th July, the Elector of Cologne, the Duke of Juliers, and Francis of Waldeck, met at Neuss to concert measures for preventing a repetition of these disorders. The leading Protestant divines wrote, urging the extermination of the heretics, and reminding the princes that the sword had been given them for this purpose.

On the same day, the diet of Worms agreed that the Anabaptists should be extirpated as a sect dangerous alike to morals and to the safety of the commonwealth, and that an assembly should be held in the month of November, to decide upon defraying the cost of the war, and on the form of government which was to be established in the city.[272]

[272] *Ibid.* p. 201

The diet met on the 1st November, and decided,—That everything should be re-established in Münster on the old footing, and that the clergy should have their property and privileges restored to them. That all who had fled the city to escape the government of the Anabaptists should be reinstated in the possession of their offices, privileges, and houses. That all the goods of the rebels should remain confiscated to defray the expense of the war. That the princes of neighbouring states should send deputies to Münster to provide that the innocent should not suffer with the guilty. That the fortifications should be in part demolished, as an example; but that Münster should not be degraded from its rank as a city. That the bishop and chapter and nobles should demolish the bastions within the town as soon as the city walls had been razed. That the bishops, the nobles, and the citizens should solemnly engage, for themselves and for their successors, never to attempt to refortify the city. Finally, that the envoys of the King of the Romans and of the princes should visit the said town on the 5th March, 1536, to see that these articles of the convention had been executed.

All these articles were not observed. The bishop did not demolish the fortifications, and the point was not insisted upon.

As for the civil constitution of Münster, its privileges and franchises, they were not entirely restored till 1553.

Francis of Waldeck now set to work repairing and purifying the churches, and restoring everything as it had been before. Catholic worship was everywhere restored without a single voice in the city rising in opposition. The people were sick of Protestantism, whether in its mitigated form as Lutheranism, or in its aggravated development as Anabaptism.

But Lutherans of other states were by no means satisfied. The reconciliation of the great city with the Catholic Church, from which half its inhabitants had previously separated, was not pleasant news to the Reformers, and they protested loudly. "On the Friday after St. John's day," wrote Dorpius "in midsummer, God came and destroyed this hell and drove the devil out, but the devil's mother came in again.... The Anabaptists were on that day rooted out, and the Papists planted in again."[273]

[273] "Hernach auff freitag S. Johanstag mitten in Sommer, kommet Gott und zerstöret die Helle, und jaget den Teuffel heraus, und komet sein Mutter wider hinein ... und sind die Widerteuffer an obgemeltem tag ausgerottet worden, die Papisten aber wider eingepflantzet."—Dorp. f. 399 (by misprint 499).

It is time to look at John of Leyden and his fellow-prisoners: they were Knipperdolling and Bernard Krechting. There could be no doubt that their fate would be terrible. It was additional cruelty to delay it. But the bishop and the Lutheran divines were curious to see and argue with the captives, and they were taken from place to place to gratify their curiosity.

When King John appeared before Francis of Waldeck, the bishop asked him angrily how he could protract the siege whilst his people were starving around him. "Francis of Waldeck," he answered, "they should all have died of hunger before I surrendered, had things gone as I desired."[274] He retained his spirits and affected to joke. At Dulmen the people crowded round him asking, "Is this the king who took to himself so many wives?" "I ask your pardon," answered Bockelson, "I took maidens and made them wives."[275]

[274] Dorp. ff. 399 a, 400 a, b.
[275] Dorp. f. 399 b.

It has been often stated that the three unfortunates were carried round the country in iron cages. This is inaccurate. They were taken in chains on horseback, with two soldiers on either side; their bodies were placed in iron cages and hung to the steeple of the church of St. Lambert, after they were dead.

At Bevergern the Lutheran divine, Anthony Corvinus, and other ministers "interviewed" the fallen king, and a long and very curious account of their discussion remains.[276]

[276] Luther's "Sämmtliche Werke." Wittenb. 1545-51. Band, ii. ff. 376-386.

"First, when the king was brought out of prison into the room, we greeted him in a friendly manner and bade him be seated before us four. Also, we asked in a friendly manner how he was getting on in the prison, and whether he was cold or sick? Answer of the king: Although he was obliged to endure the frost, and the sins weighing on his heart, yet he must, as such was God's will, bear patiently. And these and other similar conversations led us so far—for nothing can be got out of him by direct questions—that we were able right craftily to converse with him about his government."

Then followed a lengthy controversy on all the heretical doctrines of the Anabaptist sect, in which the king exhibited no little skill. The preachers having brought the charge of novelty against Anabaptism, John of Leyden very promptly showed that those living in glass houses should not throw stones, by pointing out that Lutheranism was not much older than Anabaptism, that he had proved his mission by miracles, whereas Luther had nothing to show to demonstrate his call to establish a new creed.

The discussion on Justification by Faith only was most affectionate, for both parties were quite agreed on this doctrine—surely a very satisfactory one and very full of comfort to John of Leyden. But on the doctrine of the Eucharist they could not agree, the king holding to Zwingli.[277]

[277] "Denn wiewol ichs fur dieser zeit mit dem Zwingel gehalten," &c., f. 384.

"That in this Sacrament the faithful, who are baptised, receive the Body and Blood of Christ believe I," said the king; "for though I hold for this time with Zwingli, nevertheless I find that the words of Christ (This is my Body, This is my Blood) must remain in their worth. But that unbelievers also receive the Body and Blood of Christ, that I cannot believe."

The Preachers: "How that? Shall our unbelief avail more than the word, command and ordinance of God?"

The King: "Unbelief is such a dreadful thing, that I cannot believe that the unbelievers can partake of the Body and Blood of Christ."

The Preachers: "It is a perverse thing that you should ever try to set our faith, or want of faith, above the words and ordinance of God. But it is evident that our faith can add nothing to God's ordinance, nor can my unbelief detract anything therefrom. Faith must be there, that I may benefit by such eating and drinking; but yet in this matter must we repose more on God's command and word than on our faith or unbelief."

The King: "If this your meaning hold, then all unbelievers must have partaken of the Communion of the Body and Blood of Christ. But such I cannot believe."

The Preachers: "You must understand that our unbelief cannot make the ordinance of God unavailing. Say now, for what end was the sun created?"

The King: "Scripture teaches that it was made to rule the day and to shine."

The Preachers: "Now if we or you were blind, would the sun fail to execute its office for which it was created?"

The King: "I know well that my blindness or yours would not make the sun fail to shine."

The Preachers: "So is it with all the works and ordinances of God, especially with the Sacraments. When I am baptised it is well if faith be there; but if it be not, baptism does not for all that fail to be a precious, noble, and holy Sacrament, yes, what St. Paul calls it, a regeneration and renewal of the Holy Ghost, because it is ordered by God's word and given His promise. So also with respect to the Lord's Supper; if those who partake shall have faith to grasp the promise of Christ, as it is written, *Oportet accedentem credere*, but none the less does God's word, ordinance, and command remain, even if my faith never more turned thereto. But of this we have said enough."[278]

[278] *Ibid.* f. 384 b.

The preachers next catechised John of Leyden on his heresy concerning the Incarnation. He did not deny that Jesus Christ was born of Mary, but he denied that He derived from her His flesh and blood, as he considered that Mary being sinful, out of sinful flesh sinful offspring must issue.

The catechising on the subject of marriage follows.

The Preachers: "How have you regarded marriage, and what is your belief thereupon?"

The King: "We have ever held marriage to be God's work and ordinance, and we hold this now, that no higher or better estate exists in the world than the estate of matrimony."

The Preachers: "Why have you so wildly treated this same estate, against God's word and common order, and taken one wife after another? How can you justify such a proceeding?"

The King: "What was permitted to the patriarchs in the Old Testament, why should it be denied to us? What we have held is this: he who wished to have only one wife had not other wives forced upon him; but him who wished to have more wives than one, we left free to do so, according to God's command, Be fruitful and multiply."

This the preachers combat by saying that the patriarchs were guiltless, because the law of the land (*die gemeine Policey*) did not then forbid concubinage, but that now that is forbidden by common law, it is sinful.[279] Then they asked the king what other texts he could quote to establish polygamy.

[279] Wei zweiveln nicht wenn ein bestendig Policey und Regiment gewesen were, wie itzt est, es würden sich die Vetter freilich aug der selbigen gehalten haben.

The King: "Paul says of the bishop, let him be the husband of one wife; now if a bishop is to have only one wife, surely, in the time of Paul, laymen must have been allowed two or three apiece, as pleased them. There you have your text."

The Preachers: "As we said before, marriage is an affair of common police regulation, *res Politica*. And as now the law of the land is different from what it was in the time of Paul, so that many wives are forbidden and not tolerated, you will have to answer for your innovations before God and man."

The King: "Well, I have the consolation that what was permitted to the fathers cannot damn us. I had rather be with the fathers than with you."

The Preachers: "Well, we prefer obedience to the State."[280]

[280] Predicanten: So wöllen wir in diesemfäll viel lieber der Oberkeit gehorsam sein, f. 386 b.

Here we see Corvinus, Kymens, and the other ministers placing matrimony on exactly the same low footing as did Luther.

Having "interviewed" the king, these crows settled on Knipperdolling and Krechting in Horstmar, and with these unfortunates they carried on a paper controversy.

The captivity of the king and his two accomplices lasted six months. The Lutheran preachers had swarmed about him and buzzed in his ears, and the poor wretch believed that by yielding a few points he could save his life. He offered to labour along with Melchior Hoffmann, to bring the numerous Anabaptists in Friesland, Holland, Brabant, and Flanders into submission, if he were given his liberty; but finding that the preachers had been giving him false hopes and leading him into recantations, he refused to see them again, and awaited his execution in sullen despair.

The pastors failing to convert the Anabaptists, and finding that the sectaries used against them scripture and private judgment with such efficacy that they were unable in argument to overcome them, called upon the princes to exterminate them by fire and sword.

The gentle Melancthon wrote a tract or letter to urge the princes on; it was entitled, "Das weltliche Oberkeiten den Widerteuffern mit leiblicher straffe zu wehren schüldig sey. Etlicher bedenken zu Wittemberg gestellet durch Philip Melancthon, 1536. Ob Christliche Fürsten schüldig sind der Widerteuffer unchristlicher Sect mit leiblicher straffe und mit dem schwert zu wehren." He enumerates the doctrines of the unfortunate sectarians at Münster and elsewhere, and then he says that it is the duty of all princes and nobles to root out with the sword all heresy from their dominions; but then, with this proviso, they must first be instructed out of God's Word by the pure reformed Church what doctrines are heretical, that they may only exterminate those who differ from the Lutheran communion.

He then quotes to the Protestant princes the example of the Jewish kings: "The kings in the Old Testament, not only the Jewish kings, but also the converted heathen kings, judged and killed the false prophets and unbelievers. Such examples show the office of princes. As Paul says, the law is good that blasphemers are to be punished. The government is not to rule men for their bodily welfare, so much as for God's honour, for they are God's ministers; let them remember that and value their office."

But it is argued on the other side that it is written, "Let both grow together till the harvest. Now this is not spoken to the temporal power," says Melancthon, "but to the preachers, that they should not use physical power under the excuse of their office. From all this it is plain that the worldly government is bound to drive away blasphemy, false doctrine, heresies, and to punish in their persons those who hold to these things.... Let the judge know that this sect of Anabaptists is from the devil, and as a prudent preacher instructs different stations how they are to conduct themselves, as he teaches a wife that to breed children is to please God well, so he teaches the temporal authorities how they are to serve God's honour, and openly drive away heresy."[281]

[281] "Das weltliche Oberkeit," &c., in Luth. "Sämt. Werke." 1545-51, ii. ff. 327-8.

So also did Justus Menius write to urge on an exterminatory persecution of the sectaries; he also argues that "Let both grow together till the harvest," is not to be quoted by the princes as an excuse for sparing lives and properties.[282]

[282] "Von dem Geist d. Widerteuffer." in Luth. "Samt. Werke." 1545-51, ii. f. 325 b.

On the 12th January, 1536, John of Leyden, Knipperdolling, and Krechting were brought back to Münster to undergo sentence of death.[283]

[283] Kerssenbroeck, p. 209; Kurtze Hist. f. 400.

A platform was erected in the square before the townhall on the 21st, and on this platform was planted a large stake with iron collars attached to it.

When John Bockelson was told, on the 21st, that he was to die on the morrow, he asked for the chaplain of the bishop, John von Siburg, who spent the night with him. With the fear of a terrible death before him, the confidence of the wretched man gave way, and he made his confession with every sign of true contrition.

Knipperdolling and Krechting, who were also offered the assistance of a priest, rejected the offer with contempt. They declared that the presence of God sufficed them, that they were conscious of having committed no sin, and that all their actions had been done the sole glory of to God, that moreover they were freely justified by faith in Christ.

On Monday the 22nd, at eight o'clock in the morning, the ex-king of Münster and his companions were led to execution. The gates of the city had been closed, and a large detachment of troops surrounded the scaffold. Outside this iron ring was a dense crowd of people, and the windows were filled with heads. Francis of Waldeck occupied a window immediately opposite the scaffold, and remained there throughout the hideous tragedy.[284] As an historian has well observed, "Francis of Waldeck, in default of other virtues, might at least have not forgotten what was due to his high rank and his Episcopal character; he regarded neither—but showed himself as ferocious as had been John Bockelson, by becoming a spectator of the long and horrible torture of the three criminals."[285] John and his accomplices having reached the townhall, received their sentence from Wesseling, the city judge. It was that they should be burned with red-hot pincers, and finally stabbed with daggers heated in the fire.[286]

[284] Kerssenbroeck, p. 210; Kurtze Hist. f. 400.
[285] Bussierre, p. 462.
[286] Kerssenbroeck, p. 211; Bullinger, lib. ii. c. 10; Montfort., p. 74; Heresbach, pp. 166-7; Hast, pp. 405-6; Kurtze Historia, f. 400.

The king was the first to mount the scaffold and be tortured.

"The king endured three grips with the pincers without speaking or crying, but then he burst forth into cries of, "Father, have mercy on me! God of mercy and loving kindness!" and he besought pardon of his sins and help. The bystanders were pierced to the heart by his shrieks of agony, the scent of the roast flesh filled the market-place; his body was one great wound. At length the sign was given, his tongue was torn out with the red pincers, and a dagger pierced his heart.

Knipperdolling and Krechting were put to the torture directly after the agonies of the king had begun. Knipperdolling endeavoured to beat his brains out against the stake, and when prevented, he tried to strangle himself with his own collar. To prevent him accomplishing his design, a rope was put through his mouth and attached to the stake so as totally to incapacitate him from moving. When these unfortunates were dead, their bodies were placed in three iron cages, and were hung up on the tower of the church of St. Lambert, the king in the middle.[287]

[287] Kerssenbroeck, p. 211; Kurtze Hist. f. 401.

Thus ended this hideous drama, which produced an effect throughout Germany. The excess of the scandal inspired all the Catholic governments with horror, and warned them of the immensity of the danger they ran in allowing the spread of Protestant mysticism. Cities and principalities which wavered in their allegiance to the Church took a decided position at once.

At Münster, Catholicism was re-established. As has been already mentioned, the debauched, cruel bishop was a Lutheran at heart, and his ambition was to convert Münster into an hereditary principality in his family, after the example of certain other princes.

Accordingly, in 1543, he proposed to the States of the diocese to accept the Confession of Augsburg and abandon Catholicism. The proposition of the prince was unanimously rejected. Nevertheless the prince joined the Protestant union of Smalkald the following year, but having been complained of to the Pope and the Emperor, and fearing the fate of Hermann von Wied, Archbishop of Cologne, he excused himself as best he could through his relative, Jost Hodefilter, bishop of Lübeck, and Franz von Dei, suffragan bishop of Osnabrück.

Before the Smalkald war the prince-bishop had secretly engaged the help of the Union against his old enemy, the "wild" Duke Henry of Brunswick. After the war, the Duke of Oldenburg revenged himself on the principality severely, with fire and sword, and only spared Münster itself for 100,000 guilders. The bishop died of grief. He left three natural sons by Anna Polmann. They bore as their arms a half star, a whole star being the arms of Waldeck.

AUTHORITIES

Hermann von Kerssenbroeck; Geschichte der Wiederthaüffer zu Münster in Westphalen. Münster, 1771. There is an abbreviated edition in Latin in Menckenii Scriptores Rerum Germanicaum, Leipsig, 1728-30. T. iii. pp. 1503-1618.

Wie das Evangelium zu Münster erstlich angefangen, und die Widerteuffer verstöret widerauffgehöret hat. Darnach was die teufflische Secte der Widerteuffer fur grewliche Gotteslesterung und unsagliche grawsamkeit ... in der Stad geübt und getrieben; beschrieben durch Henrichum Dorpium Monasteriensem; in Luther's Sammtliche Werke. Wittemb. 1545-51. Band ii. ff. 391-401.

Historia von den Münsterischen Widerteuffern.

Ibid. ff. 328-363.

Acta, Handlungen, Legationen und Schriften, &c., d. Munsterischen sachen geschehen. *Ibid.*, ff. 363-391.

Kurtze Historia wie endlich der König sampt zweien gerichted, &c. *Ibid.* ff. 400-9.

D. Lambertus Hortensius Monfortius, Tumultuum Anabaptistarum Liber unus. Amsterdam, 1636.

Histoire de la Réformation, ou Mémoires de Jean Sleidan. Trad. de Courrayer. La Haye, 1667. Vol. ii. lib. x. [This is the edition quoted in the article.]

Sleidanus: Commentarium rerum in Orbe gestarum, &c. Argent. 1555; ed. alt. 1559.

I. Hast, Geschichte der Wiederthaüffer von ihren Entstehen in Zwickau bis auf ihren Sturz zu Münster in Westphalen Münster. 1836.

A Book of Ghosts

I. — JEAN BOUCHON

I WAS in Orléans a good many years ago. At the time it was my purpose to write a life of Joan of Arc, and I considered it advisable to visit the scenes of her exploits, so as to be able to give to my narrative some local colour.

But I did not find Orléans answer to my expectations. It is a dull town, very modern in appearance, but with that measly and decrepit look which is so general in French towns. There was a Place Jeanne d'Arc, with an equestrian statue of her in the midst, flourishing a banner. There was the house that the Maid had occupied after the taking of the city, but, with the exception of the walls and rafters, it had undergone so much alteration and modernisation as to have lost its interest. A museum of memorials of la Pucelle had been formed, but possessed no genuine relics, only arms and tapestries of a later date.

The city walls she had besieged, the gate through which she had burst, had been levelled, and their places taken by boulevards. The very cathedral in which she had knelt to return thanks for her victory was not the same. That had been blown up by the Huguenots, and the cathedral that now stands was erected on its ruins in 1601.

There was an ormolu figure of Jeanne on the clock—never wound up—upon the mantelshelf in my room at the hotel, and there were chocolate figures of her in the confectioners' shop-windows for children to suck. When I sat down at 7 p.m. to table d'hôte, at my inn, I was out of heart. The result of my exploration of sites had been unsatisfactory; but I trusted on the morrow to be able to find material to serve my purpose in the municipal archives of the town library.

My dinner ended, I sauntered to a café.

That I selected opened on to the Place, but there was a back entrance near to my hotel, leading through a long, stone-paved passage at the back of the houses in the street, and by ascending three or four stone steps one entered the long, well-lighted café. I came into it from the back by this means, and not from the front.

I took my place and called for a café-cognac. Then I picked up a French paper and proceeded to read it—all but the feuilleton. In my experience I have never yet come across anyone who reads the feuilletons in a French paper; and my impression is that these snippets of novel are printed solely for the purpose of filling up space and disguising the lack of news at the disposal of the editors. The French papers borrow their information relative to foreign affairs largely from the English journals, so that they are a day behind ours in the foreign news that they publish.

Whilst I was engaged in reading, something caused me to look up, and I noticed standing by the white marble-topped table, on which was my coffee, a waiter, with a pale face and black whiskers, in an expectant attitude.

I was a little nettled at his precipitancy in applying for payment, but I put it down to my being a total stranger there; and without a word I set down half a franc and a ten centimes coin, the latter as his *pourboire*. Then I proceeded with my reading.

I think a quarter of an hour had elapsed, when I rose to depart, and then, to my surprise, I noticed the half-franc still on the table, but the sous piece was gone.

I beckoned to a waiter, and said: "One of you came to me a little while ago demanding payment. I think he was somewhat hasty in pressing for it; however, I set the money down, and the fellow has taken the tip, and has neglected the charge for the coffee."

"*Sapristi!*" exclaimed the *garçon*; "Jean Bouchon has been at his tricks again."

I said nothing further; asked no questions. The matter did not concern me, or indeed interest me in the smallest degree; and I left.

Next day I worked hard in the town library. I cannot say that I lighted on any unpublished documents that might serve my purpose.

I had to go through the controversial literature relative to whether Jeanne d'Arc was burnt or not, for it has been maintained that a person of the same name, and also of Arques, died a natural death some time later, and who postured as the original warrior-maid. I read a good many monographs on the Pucelle, of various values; some real contributions to history, others mere second-hand cookings-up of well-known and often-used material. The sauce in these latter was all that was new.

In the evening, after dinner, I went back to the same café and called for black coffee with a nip of brandy. I drank it leisurely, and then retreated to the desk where I could write some letters.

I had finished one, and was folding it, when I saw the same pale-visaged waiter standing by with his hand extended for payment. I put my hand into my pocket, pulled out a fifty centimes piece and a coin of two sous, and placed both beside me, near the man, and proceeded to put my letter in an envelope, which I then directed.

Next I wrote a second letter, and that concluded, I rose to go to one of the tables and to call for stamps, when I noticed that again the silver coin had been left untouched, but the copper piece had been taken away.

I tapped for a waiter.

"*Tiens*," said I, "that fellow of yours has been bungling again. He has taken the tip and has left the half-franc."

"Ah! Jean Bouchon once more!"

"But who is Jean Bouchon?"

The man shrugged his shoulders, and, instead of answering my query, said: "I should recommend monsieur to refuse to pay Jean Bouchon again—that is, supposing monsieur intends revisiting this café."

"I most assuredly will not pay such a noodle," I said; "and it passes my comprehension how you can keep such a fellow on your staff."

I revisited the library next day, and then walked by the Loire, that rolls in winter such a full and turbid stream, and in summer, with a reduced flood, exposes gravel and sand-banks. I wandered around the town, and endeavoured vainly to picture it, enclosed by walls and drums of towers, when on April 29th, 1429, Jeanne threw herself into the town and forced the English to retire, discomfited and perplexed.

In the evening I revisited the café and made my wants known as before. Then I looked at my notes, and began to arrange them.

Whilst thus engaged I observed the waiter, named Jean Bouchon, standing near the table in an expectant attitude as before. I now looked him full in the face and observed his countenance. He had puffy white cheeks, small black eyes, thick dark mutton-chop whiskers, and a broken nose. He was decidedly an ugly man, but not a man with a repulsive expression of face.

"No," said I, "I will give you nothing. I will not pay you. Send another *garçon* to me."

As I looked at him to see how he took this refusal, he seemed to fall back out of my range, or, to be more exact, the lines of his form and features became confused. It was much as though I had been gazing on a reflection in still water; that something had ruffled the surface, and all was broken up and obliterated. I could see him no more. I was puzzled and a bit startled, and I rapped my coffee-cup with the spoon to call the attention of a waiter. One sprang to me immediately.

"See!" said I, "Jean Bouchon has been here again; I told him that I would not pay him one sou, and he has vanished in a most perplexing manner. I do not see him in the room."

"No, he is not in the room."

"When he comes in again, send him to me. I want to have a word with him."

The waiter looked confused, and replied: "I do not think that Jean will return."

"How long has he been on your staff?"

"Oh! he has not been on our staff for some years."

"Then why does he come here and ask for payment for coffee and what else one may order?"

"He never takes payment for anything that has been consumed. He takes only the tips."

"But why do you permit him to do that?"

"We cannot help ourselves."

"He should not be allowed to enter the café."

"No one can keep him out."

"This is surpassing strange. He has no right to the tips. You should communicate with the police."

The waiter shook his head. "They can do nothing. Jean Bouchon died in 1869."

"Died in 1869!" I repeated.

"It is so. But he still comes here. He never pesters the old customers, the inhabitants of the town—only visitors, strangers."

"Tell me all about him."

"Monsieur must pardon me now. We have many in the place, and I have my duties."

"In that case I will drop in here to-morrow morning when you are disengaged, and I will ask you to inform me about him. What is your name?"

"At monsieur's pleasure—Alphonse."

Next morning, in place of pursuing the traces of the Maid of Orléans, I went to the café to hunt up Jean Bouchon. I found Alphonse with a duster wiping down the tables. I invited him to a table and made him sit down opposite me. I will give his story in substance, only where advisable recording his exact words.

Jean Bouchon had been a waiter at this particular café. Now in some of these establishments the attendants are wont to have a box, into which they drop all the tips that are received; and at the end of the week it is opened, and the sum found in it is divided *pro rata* among the waiters, the head waiter receiving a larger portion than the others. This is not customary in all such places of refreshment, but it is in some, and it was so in this café. The average is pretty constant, except on special occasions, as when a fête occurs; and the waiters know within a few francs what their perquisites will be.

But in the café where served Jean Bouchon the sum did not reach the weekly total that might have been anticipated; and after this deficit had been noted for a couple of months the waiters were convinced that there was something wrong, somewhere or somehow. Either the common box was tampered with, or one of them did not put in his tips received. A watch was set, and it was discovered that Jean Bouchon was the defaulter. When he had received a gratuity, he went to the box, and pretended to put in the coin, but no sound followed, as would have been the case had one been dropped in.

There ensued, of course, a great commotion among the waiters when this was discovered. Jean Bouchon endeavoured to brave it out, but the *patron* was appealed to, the case stated, and he was dismissed. As he left by the back entrance, one of the younger *garçons* put out his leg and tripped Bouchon up, so that he stumbled and fell headlong down the steps with a crash on the stone floor of the passage. He fell with such violence on his forehead that he was taken up insensible. His bones were fractured, there was concussion of the brain, and he died within a few hours without recovering consciousness.

"We were all very sorry and greatly shocked," said Alphonse; "we did not like the man, he had dealt dishonourably by us, but we wished him no ill, and our resentment was at an end when he was dead. The waiter who had tripped him up was arrested, and was sent to prison for some months, but the accident was due to *une mauvaise plaisanterie* and no malice was in it, so that the young fellow got off with a light sentence. He afterwards married a widow with a café at Vierzon, and is there, I believe, doing well.

"Jean Bouchon was buried," continued Alphonse; "and we waiters attended the funeral and held white kerchiefs to our eyes. Our head waiter even put a lemon into his, that by squeezing it he might draw tears from his eyes. We all subscribed for the interment, that it should be dignified—majestic as becomes a waiter."

"And do you mean to tell me that Jean Bouchon has haunted this café ever since?"

"Ever since 1869," replied Alphonse.

"And there is no way of getting rid of him?"

"None at all, monsieur. One of the Canons of Bourges came in here one evening. We did suppose that Jean Bouchon would not approach, molest an ecclesiastic, but he did. He took his *pourboire* and left the rest, just as he treated monsieur. Ah! monsieur! but Jean Bouchon did well in 1870 and 1871 when those pigs of Prussians were here in occupation. The officers came nightly to our café, and Jean Bouchon was greatly on the alert. He must have carried away half of the gratuities they offered. It was a sad loss to us."

"This is a very extraordinary story," said I.

"But it is true," replied Alphonse.

Next day I left Orléans. I gave up the notion of writing the life of Joan of Arc, as I found that there was absolutely no new material to be gleaned on her history—in fact, she had been thrashed out.

Years passed, and I had almost forgotten about Jean Bouchon, when, the other day, I was in Orléans once more, on my way south, and at once the whole story recurred to me.

I went that evening to the same café. It had been smartened up since I was there before. There was more plate glass, more gilding; electric light had been introduced, there were more mirrors, and there were also ornaments that had not been in the café before.

I called for café-cognac and looked at a journal, but turned my eyes on one side occasionally, on the look-out for Jean Bouchon. But he did not put in an appearance. I waited for a quarter of an hour in expectation, but saw no sign of him.

Presently I summoned a waiter, and when he came up I inquired: "But where is Jean Bouchon?"

"Monsieur asks after Jean Bouchon?" The man looked surprised.

"Yes, I have seen him here previously. Where is he at present?"

"Monsieur has seen Jean Bouchon? Monsieur perhaps knew him. He died in 1869."

"I know that he died in 1869, but I made his acquaintance in 1874. I saw him then thrice, and he accepted some small gratuities of me."

"Monsieur tipped Jean Bouchon?"

"Yes, and Jean Bouchon accepted my tips."

"*Tiens*, and Jean Bouchon died five years before."

"Yes, and what I want to know is how you have rid yourselves of Jean Bouchon, for that you have cleared the place of him is evident, or he would have been pestering me this evening." The man looked disconcerted and irresolute.

"Hold," said I; "is Alphonse here?"

"No, monsieur, Alphonse has left two or three years ago. And monsieur saw Jean Bouchon in 1874. I was not then here. I have been here only six years."

"But you can in all probability inform me of the manner of getting quit of Jean."

"Monsieur! I am very busy this evening, there are so many gentlemen come in."

"I will give you five francs if you will tell me all—all—succinctly about Jean Bouchon."

"Will monsieur be so good as to come here to-morrow during the morning? and then I place myself at the disposition of monsieur."

"I shall be here at eleven o'clock."

At the appointed time I was at the café. If there is an institution that looks ragged and dejected and dissipated, it is a café in the morning, when the chairs are turned upside-down, the waiters are in aprons and shirt-sleeves, and a smell of stale tobacco lurks about the air, mixed with various other unpleasant odours.

The waiter I had spoken to on the previous evening was looking out for me. I made him seat himself at a table with me. No one else was in the saloon except another *garçon*, who was dusting with a long feather-brush.

"Monsieur," began the waiter, "I will tell you the whole truth. The story is curious, and perhaps everyone would not believe it, but it is well *documentée*. Jean Bouchon was at one time in service here. We had a box. When I say we, I do not mean myself included, for I was not here at the time."

"I know about the common box. I know the story down to my visit to Orléans in 1874, when I saw the man."

"Monsieur has perhaps been informed that he was buried in the cemetery?"

"I do know that, at the cost of his fellow-waiters."

"Well, monsieur, he was poor, and his fellow-waiters, though well-disposed, were not rich. So he did not have a grave *en perpétuité*. Accordingly, after many years, when the term of consignment was expired, and it might well be supposed that Jean Bouchon had mouldered away, his grave was cleared out to make room for a fresh occupant. Then a very remarkable discovery was made. It was found that his corroded coffin was crammed—literally stuffed—with five and ten centimes pieces, and with them were also some German coins, no doubt received from those pigs of Prussians during the occupation of Orléans. This discovery was much talked about. Our proprietor of the café and the head waiter went to the mayor and represented to him how matters stood—that all this money had been filched during a series of years since 1869 from the waiters. And our *patron* represented to him that it should in all propriety and justice be restored to us. The mayor was a man of intelligence and heart, and he quite accepted this view of the matter, and ordered the surrender of the whole coffin-load of coins to us, the waiters of the café."

"So you divided it amongst you."

"Pardon, monsieur; we did not. It is true that the money might legitimately be regarded as belonging to us. But then those defrauded, or most of them, had left long ago, and there were among us some who had not been in service in the café more than a year or eighteen months. We could not trace the old waiters. Some were dead, some had married and left this part of the country. We were not a corporation. So we held a meeting to discuss what was to be done with the money. We feared, moreover, that unless the spirit of Jean Bouchon were satisfied, he might continue revisiting the café and go on sweeping away the tips. It was of paramount importance to please Jean Bouchon, to lay out the money in such a manner as would commend itself to his feelings. One suggested one thing, one another. One proposed that the sum should be expended on masses for the repose of Jean's soul. But the head waiter objected to that. He said that he thought he knew the mind of Jean Bouchon, and that this would not commend itself to it. He said, did our head waiter, that he knew Jean Bouchon from head to heels. And he proposed that all the coins should be melted up, and that out of them should be cast a statue of Jean Bouchon in bronze, to be set up here in the café, as there were not enough coins to make one large enough to be erected in a Place. If monsieur will step with me he will see the statue; it is a superb work of art."

He led the way, and I followed.

In the midst of the café stood a pedestal, and on this basis a bronze figure about four feet high. It represented a man reeling backward, with a banner in his left hand, and the right raised towards his brow, as though he had been struck there by a bullet. A sabre, apparently fallen from his grasp, lay at his feet. I studied the face, and it most assuredly was utterly unlike Jean Bouchon with his puffy cheeks, mutton-chop whiskers, and broken nose, as I recalled him.

"But," said I, "the features do not—pardon me—at all resemble those of Jean Bouchon. This might be the young Augustus, or Napoleon I. The profile is quite Greek."

"It may be so," replied the waiter. "But we had no photograph to go by. We had to allow the artist to exercise his genius, and, above all, we had to gratify the spirit of Jean Bouchon."

"I see. But the attitude is inexact. Jean Bouchon fell down the steps headlong, and this represents a man staggering backwards."

"It would have been inartistic to have shown him precipitated forwards; besides, the spirit of Jean might not have liked it."

"Quite so. I understand. But the flag?"

"That was an idea of the artist. Jean could not be made holding a coffee-cup. You will see the whole makes a superb subject. Art has its exigencies. Monsieur will see underneath is an inscription on the pedestal."

I stooped, and with some astonishment read—

"JEAN BOUCHON MORT SUR LE CHAMP DE GLOIRE 1870 DULCE ET DECORUM EST PRO PATRIA MORI."

"Why!" objected I, "he died from falling a cropper in the back passage, not on the field of glory."

"Monsieur! all Orléans is a field of glory. Under S. Aignan did we not repel Attila and his Huns in 451? Under Jeanne d'Arc did we not repulse the English—monsieur will excuse the allusion—in 1429. Did we not recapture Orléans from the Germans in November, 1870?"

"That is all very true," I broke in. "But Jean Bouchon neither fought against Attila nor with la Pucelle, nor against the Prussians. Then '*Dulce et decorum est pro patria mori*' is rather strong, considering the facts."

"How? Does not monsieur see that the sentiment is patriotic and magnificent?"

"I admit that, but dispute the application."

"Then why apply it? The sentiment is all right."

"But by implication it refers to Jean Bouchon, who died, not for his country, but in a sordid coffee-house brawl. Then, again, the date is wrong. Jean Bouchon died in 1869, not in 1870."

"That is only out by a year."

"Yes, but with this mistake of a year, and with the quotation from Horace, and with the attitude given to the figure, anyone would suppose that Jean Bouchon had fallen in the retaking of Orléans from the Prussians."

"Ah! monsieur, who looks on a monument and expects to find thereon the literal truth relative to the deceased?"

"This is something of a sacrifice to truth," I demurred.

"Sacrifice is superb!" said the waiter. "There is nothing more noble, more heroic than sacrifice."

"But not the sacrifice of truth."

"Sacrifice is always sacrifice."

"Well," said I, unwilling further to dispute, "this is certainly a great creation out of nothing."

"Not out of nothing; out of the coppers that Jean Bouchon had filched from us, and which choked up his coffin."

"Jean Bouchon has been seen no more?"

"No, monsieur. And yet—yes, once, when the statue was unveiled. Our *patron* did that. The café was crowded. All our *habitués* were there. The *patron* made a magnificent oration; he drew a superb picture of the moral, intellectual, social, and political merits of Jean Bouchon. There was not a dry eye among the audience, and the speaker choked with emotion. Then, as we stood in a ring, not too near, we saw—I was there and I distinctly saw, so did the others—Jean Bouchon standing with his back to us, looking intently at the statue of himself. Monsieur, as he thus stood I could discern his black mutton-chop whiskers projecting upon each side of his head. Well, sir, not one word was spoken. A dead silence fell upon all. Our *patron* ceased to speak, and wiped his eyes and blew his nose. A sort of holy awe possessed us all. Then, after the lapse of some minutes, Jean Bouchon turned himself about, and we all saw his puffy pale cheeks, his thick sensual lips, his broken nose, his little pig's eyes. He was very unlike his idealised portrait in the statue; but what matters that? It gratified the deceased, and it injured no one. Well, monsieur, Jean Bouchon stood facing us, and he turned his head from one side to another, and gave us all what I may term a greasy smile. Then he lifted up his hands as though invoking a blessing on us all, and vanished. Since then he has not been seen."

II. — POMPS AND VANITIES

COLONEL MOUNTJOY had an appointment in India that kept him there permanently. Consequently he was constrained to send his two daughters to England when they were quite children. His wife had died of cholera at Madras. The girls were Letice and Betty. There was a year's difference in their ages, but they were extraordinarily alike, so much so that they might have been supposed to be twins.

Letice was given up to the charge of Miss Mountjoy, her father's sister, and Betty to that of Lady Lacy, her maternal aunt. Their father would have preferred that his daughters should have been together, but there were difficulties in the way; neither of the ladies was inclined to be burdened with both, and if both had been placed with one the other might have regarded and resented this as a slight.

As the children grew up their likeness in feature became more close, but they diverged exceedingly in expression. A sullenness, an unhappy look, a towering fire of resentment characterised that of Letice, whereas the face of Betty was open and gay.

This difference was due to the difference in their bringing up.

Lady Lacy, who had a small house in North Devon, was a kindly, intellectual, and broad-minded old lady, of sweet disposition but a decided will. She saw a good deal of society, and did her best to train Betty to be an educated and liberal-minded woman of culture and graceful manners. She did not send her to school, but had her taught at home; and on the excuse that her eyes were weak by artificial light she made the girl read to her in the evenings, and always read books that were standard and calculated to increase her knowledge and to develop her understanding. Lady Lacy detested all shams, and under her influence Betty grew up to be thoroughly straightforward, healthy-minded, and true.

On the other hand, Miss Mountjoy was, as Letice called her, a Killjoy. She had herself been reared in the midst of the Clapham sect; had become rigid in all her ideas, narrow in all her sympathies, and a bundle of prejudices.

The present generation of young people know nothing of the system of repression that was exercised in that of their fathers and mothers. Now the tendency is wholly in the other direction, and too greatly so. It is possibly due to a revulsion of feeling against a training that is looked back upon with a shudder.

To that narrow school there existed but two categories of men and women, the Christians and the Worldlings, and those who pertained to it arrogated to themselves the former title. The Judgment had already begun with the severance of the sheep from the goats, and the saints who judged the world had their Jerusalem at Clapham.

In that school the works of the great masters of English literature, Shakespeare, Pope, Scott, Byron, were taboo; no work of imagination was tolerated save the Apocalypse, and that was degraded into a polemic by such scribblers as Elliot and Cumming.

No entertainments, not even the oratorios of Handel, were tolerated; they savoured of the world. The nearest approach to excitement was found in a missionary meeting. The Chinese contract the feet of their daughters, but those English Claphamites cramped the minds of their children. The Venetians made use of an iron prison, with gradually contracting walls, that finally crushed the life out of the captive. But these elect Christians put their sons and daughters into a school that squeezed their energies and their intelligences to death.

Dickens caricatured such people in Mrs. Jellyby and Mr. Chadband; but he sketched them only in their external aspect, and left untouched their private action in distorting young minds, maiming their wills, damping down all youthful buoyancy.

But the result did not answer the expectations of those who adopted this system with the young. Some daughters, indeed, of weaker wills were permanently stunted and shaped on the approved model, but nearly all the sons, and most of the daughters, on obtaining their freedom, broke away into utter frivolity and dissipation, or, if they retained any religious impressions, galloped through the Church of England, performing strange antics on the way, and plunged into the arms of Rome.

Such was the system to which the high-spirited, strong-willed Letice was subjected, and from which was no escape. The consequence was that Letice tossed and bit at her chains, and that there ensued frequent outbreaks of resentment against her aunt.

"Oh, Aunt Hannah! I want something to read."

After some demur, and disdainful rejection of more serious works, she was allowed Milton.

Then she said, "Oh! I do love *Comus*."

"*Comus!*" gasped Miss Mountjoy.

"And *L'Allegro* and *Il Penseroso*, they are not bad."

"My child. These were the compositions of the immortal bard before his eyes were opened."

"I thought, aunt, that he had dictated the *Paradise Lost and Regained* after he was blind."

"I refer to the eyes of his soul," said the old lady sternly.

"I want a story-book."

"There is the *Dairyman's Daughter*."

"I have read it, and hate it."

"I fear, Leticia, that you are in the gall of bitterness and the bond of iniquity."

Unhappily the sisters very rarely met one another. It was but occasionally that Lady Lacy and Betty came to town, and when they did, Miss Mountjoy put as many difficulties as she could in the way of their associating together.

On one such visit to London, Lady Lacy called and asked if she might take Letice with herself to the theatre. Miss Mountjoy shivered with horror, reared herself, and expressed her opinion of stage-plays and those who went to see them in strong and uncomplimentary terms. As she had the custody of Letice, she would by no persuasion be induced to allow her to imperil her soul by going to such a wicked place. Lady Lacy was fain to withdraw in some dismay and much regret.

Poor Letice, who had heard this offer made, had flashed into sudden brightness and a tremor of joy; when it was refused, she burst into a flood of tears and an ecstasy of rage. She ran up to her room, and took and tore to pieces a volume of *Clayton's Sermons*, scattered the leaves over the floor, and stamped upon them.

"Letice," said Miss Mountjoy, when she saw the devastation, "you are a child of wrath."

"Why mayn't I go where there is something pretty to see? Why may I not hear good music? Why must I be kept forever in the Doleful Dumps?"

"Because all these things are of the world, worldly."

"If God hates all that is fair and beautiful, why did He create the peacock, the humming-bird, and the bird of paradise, instead of filling the world with barn-door fowls?"

"You have a carnal mind. You will never go to heaven."

"Lucky I—if the saints there do nothing but hold missionary meetings to convert one another. Pray what else can they do?"

"They are engaged in the worship of God."

"I don't know what that means. All I am acquainted with is the worship of the congregation. At Salem Chapel the minister faces it, mouths at it, gesticulates to it, harangues, flatters, fawns at it, and, indeed, prays at it. If that be all, heaven must be a deadly dull hole."

Miss Mountjoy reared herself, she became livid with wrath. "You wicked girl."

"Aunt," said Letice, intent on further incensing her, "I do wish you would let me go—just for once—to a Catholic church to see what the worship of God is."

"I would rather see you dead at my feet!" exclaimed the incensed lady, and stalked, rigid as a poker, out of the room.

Thus the unhappy girl grew up to woman's estate, her heart seething with rebellion.

And then a terrible thing occurred. She caught scarlet fever, which took an unfavourable turn, and her life was despaired of. Miss Mountjoy was not one to conceal from the girl that her days were few, and her future condition hopeless.

Letice fought against the idea of dying so young.

"Oh, aunt! I won't die! I can't die! I have seen nothing of the pomps and vanities. I want to just taste them, and know what they are like. Oh! save me, make the doctor give me something to revive me. I want the pomps and vanities, oh! so much. I will not, I cannot die!" But her will, her struggle, availed nothing, and she passed away into the Great Unseen.

Miss Mountjoy wrote a formal letter to her brother, who had now become a general, to inform him of the lamented decease of his eldest daughter. It was not a comforting letter. It dwelt unnecessarily on the faults of Letice, it expressed no hopes as to her happiness in the world to which she had passed. There had been no signs of resignation at the last; no turning from the world with its pomps and vanities to better things, only a vain longing after what she could not have; a bitter resentment against Providence for having denied them to her; and a steeling of her heart against good and pious influences.

A year had passed.

Lady Lacy had come to town along with her niece. A dear friend had placed her house at her disposal. She had herself gone to Dresden with her daughters to finish them off in music and German. Lady Lacy was very glad of the occasion, for Betty was now of an age to be brought out. There was to be a great ball at the house of the Countess of Belgrove, unto whom Lady Lacy was related, and at the ball Betty was to make her début.

The girl was in a condition of boundless excitement. A beautiful ball-dress of white satin, trimmed with rich Valenciennes lace, was laid over her chair for her to wear. Neat little white satin shoes stood on the floor, quite new, for her feet. In a flower-glass stood a red camellia that was destined to adorn her hair, and on the dressing-table, in a morocco case, was a pearl necklace that had belonged to her mother.

The maid did her hair, but the camellia, which was to be the only point of colour about her, except her rosy lips and flushed cheeks—that camellia was not to be put into her hair till the last minute.

The maid offered to help her to dress.

"No, thank you, Martha; I can do that perfectly well myself. I am accustomed to use my own hands, and I can take my own time about it."

"But really, miss, I think you should allow me."

"Indeed, indeed, no. There is plenty of time, and I shall go leisurely to work. When the carriage comes just tap at the door and tell me, and I will rejoin my aunt."

When the maid was gone, Betty locked her door. She lighted the candles beside the cheval-glass, and looked at herself in the mirror and laughed. For the first time, with glad surprise and innocent pleasure, she realised how pretty she was. And pretty she was indeed, with her pleasant face, honest eyes, finely arched brows, and twinkling smile that produced dimples in her cheeks.

"There is plenty of time," she said. "I shan't take a hundred years in dressing now that my hair is done."

She yawned. A great heaviness had come over her.

"I really think I shall have a nap first. I am dead sleepy now, and forty winks will set me up for the night."

Then she laid herself upon the bed. A numbing, over-powering lethargy weighed on her, and almost at once she sank into a dreamless sleep. So unconscious was she that she did not hear Martha's tap at the door nor the roll of the carriage as it took her aunt away.

She woke with a start. It was full day.

For some moments she did not realise this fact, nor that she was still dressed in the gown in which she had lain down the previous evening.

She rose in dismay. She had slept so soundly that she had missed the ball.

She rang her bell and unlocked the door.

"What, miss, up already?" asked the maid, coming in with a tray on which were tea and bread and butter.

"Yes, Martha. Oh! what will aunt say? I have slept so long and like a log, and never went to the ball. Why did you not call me?"

"Please, miss, you have forgotten. You went to the ball last night."

"No; I did not. I overslept myself."

The maid smiled. "If I may be so bold as to say so, I think, Miss Betty, you are dreaming still."

"No; I did not go."

The maid took up the satin dress. It was crumpled, the lace was a little torn, and the train showed unmistakable signs of having been drawn over a floor.

She then held up the shoes. They had been worn, and well worn, as if danced in all night.

"Look here, miss; here is your programme! Why, deary me! you must have had a lot of dancing. It is quite full."

Betty looked at the programme with dazed eyes; then at the camellia. It had lost some of its petals, and these had not fallen on the toilet-cover. Where were they? What was the meaning of this?

"Martha, bring me my hot water, and leave me alone."

Betty was sorely perplexed. There were evidences that her dress had been worn. The pearl necklace was in the case, but not as she had left it—outside. She bathed her head in cold water. She racked her brain. She could not recall the smallest particular of the ball. She perused the programme. A light colour came into her cheek as she recognised the initials "C. F.," those of Captain Charles Fontanel, of whom of late she had seen a good deal. Other characters expressed nothing to her mind.

"How very strange!" she said; "and I was lying on the bed in the dress I had on yesterday evening. I cannot explain it."

Twenty minutes later, Betty went downstairs and entered the breakfast-room. Lady Lacy was there. She went up to her aunt and kissed her.

"I am so sorry that I overslept myself," she said. "I was like one of the Seven Sleepers."

"My dear, I should not have minded if you had not come down till midday. After a first ball you must be tired."

"I meant—last night."

"How, last night?"

"I mean when I went to dress."

"Oh, you were punctual enough. When I was ready you were already in the hall."

The bewilderment of the girl grew apace.

"I am sure," said her aunt, "you enjoyed yourself. But you gave the lion's share of the dances to Captain Fontanel. If this had been at Exeter, it would have caused talk; but here you are known only to a few; however, Lady Belgrove observed it."

"I hope you are not very tired, auntie darling," said Betty, to change slightly the theme that perplexed her.

"Nothing to speak of. I like to go to a ball; it recalls my old dancing days. But I thought you looked white and fagged all the evening. Perhaps it was excitement."

As soon as breakfast was concluded, Betty escaped to her room. A fear was oppressing her. The only explanation of the mystery was that she had been to the dance in her sleep. She was a somnambulist. What had she said and done when unconscious? What a dreadful thing it would have been had she woke up in the middle of a dance! She must have dressed herself, gone to Lady Belgrove's, danced all night, returned, taken off her dress, put on her afternoon tea-gown, lain down and concluded her sleep—all in one long tract of unconsciousness.

"By the way," said her aunt next day, "I have taken tickets for *Carmen*, at Her Majesty's. You would like to go?"

"Oh, delighted, aunt. I know some of the music—of course, the Toreador song; but I have never heard the whole opera. It will be delightful."

"And you are not too tired to go?"

"No—ten thousand times, no—I shall love to see it."

"What dress will you go in?"

"I think my black, and put a rose in my hair."

"That will do very well. The black becomes you. I think you could not do better."

Betty was highly delighted. She had been to plays, never to a real opera.

In the evening, dinner was early, unnecessarily early, and Betty knew that it would not take her long to dress, so she went into the little conservatory and seated herself there. The scent of the heliotropes was strong. Betty called them cherry-pie. She had got the libretto, and she looked it over; but as she looked, her eyes closed, and without being aware that she was going to sleep, in a moment she was completely unconscious.

She woke, feeling stiff and cold.

"Goodness!" said she, "I hope I am not late. Why—what is that light?"

The glimmer of dawn shone in at the conservatory windows.

Much astonished, she left it. The hall, the staircase were dark. She groped her way to her room, and switched on the electric light.

Before her lay her black-and-white muslin dress on the bed; on the table were her white twelve-button gloves folded about her fan. She took them up, and below them, somewhat crumpled, lay the play-bill, scented.

"How very unaccountable this is," she said; and removing the dress, seated herself on the bed and thought.

"Why did they turn out the lights?" she asked herself, then sprang to her feet, switched off the electric current, and saw that actually the morning light was entering the room. She resumed her seat; put her hands to her brow.

"It cannot—it cannot be that this dreadful thing has happened again."

Presently she heard the servants stirring. She hastily undressed and retired between the sheets, but not to sleep. Her mind worked. She was seriously alarmed.

At the usual time Martha arrived with tea.

"Awake, Miss Betty!" she said. "I hope you had a nice evening. I dare say it was beautiful."

"But," began the girl, then checked herself, and said—

"Is my aunt getting up? Is she very tired?"

"Oh, miss, my lady is a wonderful person; she never seems to tire. She is always down at the same time."

Betty dressed, but her mind was in a turmoil. On one thing she was resolved. She must see a doctor. But she would not frighten her aunt, she would keep the matter close from her.

When she came into the breakfast-room, Lady Lacy said—

"I thought Maas's voice was superb, but I did not so much care for the Carmen. What did you think, dear?"

"Aunt," said Betty, anxious to change the topic, "would you mind my seeing a doctor? I don't think I am quite well."

"Not well! Why what is the matter with you?"

"I have such dead fits of drowsiness."

"My dearest, is that to be wondered at with this racketing about; balls and theatres—very other than the quiet life at home? But I will admit that you struck me as looking very pale last night. You shall certainly see Dr. Groves."

When the medical man arrived, Betty intimated that she wished to speak with him alone, and he was shown with her into the morning-room.

"Oh, Dr. Groves," she said nervously, "it is such a strange thing I have to say. I believe I walk in my sleep."

"You have eaten something that disagreed with you."

"But it lasted so long."

"How do you mean? Have you long been subject to it?"

"Dear, no. I never had any signs of it before I came to London this season."

"And how were you roused? How did you become aware of it?"

"I was not roused at all; the fact is I went asleep to Lady Belgrove's ball, and danced there and came back, and woke up in the morning without knowing I had been."

"What!"

"And then, last night, I went in my sleep to Her Majesty's and heard *Carmen*; but I woke up in the conservatory here at early dawn, and I remember nothing about it."

"This is a very extraordinary story. Are you sure you went to the ball and to the opera?"

"Quite sure. My dress had been used on both occasions, and my shoes and fan and gloves as well."

"Did you go with Lady Lacy?"

"Oh, yes. I was with her all the time. But I remember nothing about it."

"I must speak to her ladyship."

"Please, please do not. It would frighten her; and I do not wish her to suspect anything, except that I am a little out of sorts. She gets nervous about me."

Dr. Groves mused for some while, then he said: "I cannot see that this is at all a case of somnambulism."

"What is it, then?"

"Lapse of memory. Have you ever suffered from that previously?"

"Nothing to speak of. Of course I do not always remember everything. I do not always recollect commissions given to me, unless I write them down. And I cannot say that I remember all the novels I have read, or what was the menu at dinner yesterday."

"That is quite a different matter. What I refer to is spaces of blank in your memory. How often has this occurred?"

"Twice."

"And quite recently?"

"Yes, I never knew anything of the kind before."

"I think that the sooner you return to the country the better. It is possible that the strain of coming out and the change of entering into gay life in town has been too much for you. Take care and economise your pleasures. Do not attempt too much; and if anything of the sort happens again, send for me."

"Then you won't mention this to my aunt?"

"No, not this time. I will say that you have been a little over-wrought and must be spared too much excitement."

"Thank you so much, Dr. Groves."

Now it was that a new mystery came to confound Betty. She rang her bell.

"Martha," said she, when her maid appeared, "where is that novel I had yesterday from the circulating library? I put it on the boudoir table."

"I have not noticed it, miss."

"Please look for it. I have hunted everywhere for it, and it cannot be found."

"I will look in the parlour, miss, and the schoolroom."

"I have not been into the schoolroom at all, and I know that it is not in the drawing-room."

A search was instituted, but the book could not be found. On the morrow it was in the boudoir, where Betty had placed it on her return from Mudie's.

"One of the maids took it," was her explanation. She did not much care for the book; perhaps that was due to her preoccupation, and not to any lack of stirring incident in the story. She sent it back and took out another. Next morning that also had disappeared.

It now became customary, as surely as she drew a novel from the library, that it vanished clean away. Betty was greatly amazed. She could not read a novel she had brought home till a day or two later. She took to putting the book, so soon as it was in the house, into one of her drawers, or into a cupboard. But the result was the same. Finally, when she had locked the newly acquired volume in her desk, and it had disappeared thence also, her patience gave way. There must be one of the domestics with a ravenous appetite for fiction, which drove her to carry off a book of the sort whenever it came into the house, and even to tamper with a lock to obtain it. Betty had been most reluctant to speak of the matter to her aunt, but now she made to her a formal complaint.

The servants were all questioned, and strongly protested their innocence. Not one of them had ventured to do such a thing as that with which they were charged.

However, from this time forward the annoyance ceased, and Betty and Lady Lacy naturally concluded that this was the result of the stir that had been made.

"Betty," said Lady Lacy, "what do you say to going to the new play at the Gaiety? I hear it very highly spoken of. Mrs. Fontanel has a box and has asked if we will join her."

"I should love it," replied the girl; "we have been rather quiet of late." But her heart was oppressed with fear.

She said to her maid: "Martha, will you dress me this evening—and—pray stay with me till my aunt is ready and calls for me?"

"Yes, miss, I shall be pleased to do so." But the girl looked somewhat surprised at the latter part of the request.

Betty thought well to explain: "I don't know what it is, but I feel somewhat out of spirits and nervous, and am afraid of being left alone, lest something should happen."

"Happen, miss! If you are not feeling well, would it not be as well to stay at home?"

"Oh, not for the world! I must go. I shall be all right so soon as I am in the carriage. It will pass off then."

"Shall I get you a glass of sherry, or anything?"

"No, no, it is not that. You remain with me and I shall be myself again."

That evening Betty went to the theatre. There was no recurrence of the sleeping fit with its concomitants. Captain Fontanel was in the box, and made himself vastly agreeable. He had his seat by Betty, and talked to her not only between the acts, but also a good deal whilst the actors were on the stage. With this she could have dispensed. She was not such an *habituée* of the theatre as not to be intensely interested with what was enacted before her.

Between two of the acts he said to her: "My mother is engaging Lady Lacy. She has a scheme in her head, but wants her consent to carry it out, to make it quite too charming. And I am deputed to get you to acquiesce."

"What is it?"

"We purpose having a boat and going to the Henley Regatta. Will you come?"

"I should enjoy it above everything. I have never seen a regatta—that is to say, not one so famous, and not of this kind. There were regattas at Ilfracombe, but they were different."

"Very well, then; the party shall consist only of my mother and sister and your two selves, and young Fulwell, who is dancing attendance on Jannet, and Putsey, who is a tame cat. I am sure my mother will persuade your aunt. What a lively old lady she is, and for her years how she does enjoy life!"

"It will be a most happy conclusion to our stay in town," said Betty. "We are going back to auntie's little cottage in Devon in a few days; she wants to be at home for Good Friday and Easter Day."

So it was settled. Lady Lacy had raised no objection, and now she and her niece had to consider what Betty should wear. Thin garments were out of the question; the weather was too cold, and it would be especially chilly on the river. Betty was still in slight mourning, so she chose a silver-grey cloth costume, with a black band about her waist, and a white straw hat, with a ribbon to match her gown.

On the day of the regatta Betty said to herself; "How ignorant I am! Fancy my not knowing where Henley is! That it is on the Thames or Isis I really do not know, but I fancy on the former—yes, I am almost positive it is on the Thames. I have seen pictures in the *Graphic* and *Illustrated* of the race last year, and I know the river was represented as broad, and the Isis can only be an insignificant stream. I will run into the schoolroom and find a map of the environs of London and post myself up in the geography. One hates to look like a fool."

Without a word to anyone, Betty found her way to the apartment given up to lessons when children were in the house. It lay at the back, down a passage. Since Lady Lacy had occupied the place, neither she nor Betty had been in it more than casually and rarely; and accordingly the servants had neglected to keep it clean. A good deal of dust lay about, and Betty, laughing, wrote her name in the fine powder on the school-table, then looked at her finger, found it black, and said, "Oh, bother! I forgot that the dust of London is smut."

She went to the bookcase, and groped for a map of the Metropolis and the country round, but could not find one. Nor could she lay her hand on a gazetteer.

"This must do," said she, drawing out a large, thick *Johnston's Atlas*, "if the scale be not too small to give Henley."

She put the heavy volume on the table and opened it. England, she found, was in two parts, one map of the Northern, the second of the Southern division. She spread out the latter, placed her finger on the blue line of the Thames, and began to trace it up.

Whilst her eyes were on it, searching the small print, they closed, and without being conscious that she was sleepy, her head bowed forward on the map, and she was breathing evenly, steeped in the most profound slumber.

She woke slowly. Her consciousness returned to her little by little. She saw the atlas without understanding what it meant. She looked about her, and wondered how she could be in the schoolroom, and she then observed that darkness was closing in. Only then, suddenly, did she recall what had brought her where she was.

Next, with a rush, upon her came the remembrance that she was due at the boat-race.

She must again have overslept herself, for the evening had come on, and through the window she could see the glimmer of gaslights in the street. Was this to be accompanied by her former experiences?

With throbbing heart she went into the passage. Then she noticed that the hall was lighted up, and she heard her aunt speaking, and the slam of the front door, and the maid say, "Shall I take off your wraps, my lady?"

She stepped forth upon the landing and proceeded to descend, when—with a shock that sent the blood coursing to her heart, and that paralysed her movements—she saw *herself* ascending the stair in her silver-grey costume and straw hat.

She clung to the banister, with convulsive grip, lest she should fall, and stared, without power to utter a sound, as she saw herself quietly mount, step by step, pass her, go beyond to her own room.

For fully ten minutes she remained rooted to the spot, unable to stir even a finger. Her tongue was stiff, her muscles set, her heart ceased to beat.

Then slowly her blood began again to circulate, her nerves to relax, power of movement returned. With a hoarse gasp she reeled from her place, and giddy, touching the banister every moment to prevent herself from falling, she crept downstairs. But when once in the hall, she had recovered flexibility. She ran towards the morning-room, whither Lady Lacy had gone to gather up the letters that had arrived by post during her absence.

Betty stood looking at her, speechless.

Her aunt raised her face from an envelope she was considering. "Why, Betty," said she, "how expeditiously you have changed your dress!"

The girl could not speak, but fell unconscious on the floor.

When she came to herself, she was aware of a strong smell of vinegar. She was lying on the sofa, and Martha was applying a moistened kerchief to her brow. Lady Lacy stood by, alarmed and anxious, with a bottle of smelling-salts in her hand.

"Oh, aunt, I saw——" then she ceased. It would not do to tell of the apparition. She would not be believed.

"My darling," said Lady Lacy, "you are overdone, and it was foolish of you tearing upstairs and scrambling into your morning-gown. I have sent for Groves. Are you able now to rise? Can you manage to reach your room?"

"My room!" she shuddered. "Let me lie here a little longer. I cannot walk. Let me be here till the doctor comes."

"Certainly, dearest. I thought you looked very unlike yourself all day at the regatta. If you had felt out of sorts you ought not to have gone."

"Auntie! I was quite well in the morning."

Presently the medical man arrived, and was shown in. Betty saw that Lady Lacy purposed staying through the interview. Accordingly she said nothing to Dr. Groves about what she had seen.

"She is overdone," said he. "The sooner you move her down to Devonshire the better. Someone had better be in her room to-night."

"Yes," said Lady Lacy; "I had thought of that and have given orders. Martha can make up her bed on the sofa in the adjoining dressing-room or boudoir."

This was a relief to Betty, who dreaded a return to her room—her room into which her other self had gone.

"I will call again in the morning," said the medical man; "keep her in bed to-morrow, at all events till I have seen her."

When he left, Betty found herself able to ascend the stairs. She cast a frightened glance about her room. The straw hat, the grey dress were there. No one was in it.

She was helped to bed, and although laid in it with her head among the pillows, she could not sleep. Racking thoughts tortured her. What was the signification of that encounter? What of her strange sleeps? What of those mysterious appearances of herself, where she had not been? The theory that she had walked in her sleep was untenable. How was she to solve the riddle? That she was going out of her mind was no explanation.

Only towards morning did she doze off.

When Dr. Groves came, about eleven o'clock, Betty made a point of speaking to him alone, which was what she greatly desired.

She said to him: "Oh! it has been worse this last occasion, far worse than before. I do not walk in my sleep. Whilst I am buried in slumber, someone else takes my place."

"Whom do you mean? Surely not one of the maids?"

"Oh, no. I met her on the stairs last night, that is what made me faint."

"Whom did you meet?"

"Myself—my double."

"Nonsense, Miss Mountjoy."

"But it is a fact. I saw myself as clearly as I see you now. I was going down into the hall."

"You saw yourself! You saw your own pleasant, pretty face in a looking-glass."

"There is no looking-glass on the staircase. Besides, I was in my alpaca morning-gown, and my double had on my pearl-grey cloth costume, with my straw hat. She was mounting as I was descending."

"Tell me the story."

"I went yesterday—an hour or so before I had to dress—into the schoolroom. I am awfully ignorant, and I did want to see a map and find out where was Henley, because, you know, I was going to the boat-race. And I dropped off into one of those dreadful dead sleeps, with my head on the atlas. When I awoke it was evening, and the gas-lamps were lighted. I was frightened, and ran out to the landing and I heard them arrive, just come back from Henley, and as I was going down the stairs, I saw my double coming up, and we met face to face. She passed me by, and went on to my room—to this room. So you see this is proof pos that I am not a somnambulist."

"I never said that you were. I never for a moment admitted the supposition. That, if you remember, was your own idea. What I said before is what I repeat now, that you suffer from failure of memory."

"But that cannot be so, Dr. Groves."

"Pray, why not?"

"Because I saw my double, wearing my regatta costume."

"I hold to my opinion, Miss Mountjoy. If you will listen to me I shall be able to offer a satisfactory explanation. Satisfactory, I mean, so far as to make your experiences intelligible to you. I do not at all imply that your condition is satisfactory."

"Well, tell me. I cannot make heads or tails of this matter."

"It is this, young lady. On several recent occasions you have suffered from lapses of memory. All recollection of what you did, where you went, what you said, has been clean wiped out. But on this last— it was somewhat different. The failure took place on your return, and you forgot everything that had happened since you were engaged in the schoolroom looking at the atlas."

"Yes."

"Then, on your arrival here, as Lady Lacy told me, you ran upstairs, and in a prodigious hurry changed your clothes and put on your——"

"My alpaca."

"Your alpaca, yes. Then, in descending to the hall, your memory came back, but was still entangled with flying reminiscences of what had taken place during the intervening period. Amongst other things——"

"I remember no other things."

"You recalled confusedly one thing only, that you had mounted the stairs in your—your——"

"My pearl-grey cloth, with the straw hat and satin ribbon."

"Precisely. Whilst in your morning gown, into which you had scrambled, you recalled yourself in your regatta costume going upstairs to change. This fragmentary reminiscence presented itself before you as a vision. Actually you saw nothing. The impression on your brain of a scrap recollected appeared to you as if it had been an actual object depicted on the retina of your eye. Such things happen, and happen not infrequently. In cases of D. T.——"

"But I haven't D. T. I don't drink."

"I do not say that. If you will allow me to proceed. In cases of D. T. the patient fancies he sees rats, devils, all sorts of objects. They appear to him as obvious realities, he thinks that he sees them with his eyes. But he does not. These are mere pictures formed on the brain."

"Then you hold that I really was at the boat-race?"

"I am positive that you were."

"And that I danced at Lady Belgrove's ball?"

"Most assuredly."

"And heard *Carmen* at Her Majesty's?"

"I have not the remotest doubt that you did."

Betty drew a long breath, and remained in consideration.

Then she said very gravely: "I want you to tell me, Dr. Groves, quite truthfully, quite frankly—do not think that I shall be frightened whatever you say; I shall merely prepare for what may be—do you consider that I am going out of my mind?"

"I have not the least occasion for supposing so."

"That," said Betty, "would be the most terrible thing of all. If I thought that, I would say right out to my aunt that I wished at once to be sent to an asylum."

"You may set your mind at rest on that score."

"But loss of memory is bad, but better than the other. Will these fits of failure come on again?"

"That is more than I can prognosticate; let us hope for the best. A complete change of scene, change of air, change of association——"

"Not to leave auntie!"

"No. I do not mean that, but to get away from London society. It may restore you to what you were. You never had those fits before?"

"Never, never, till I came to town."

"And when you have left town they may not recur."

"I shall take precious good care not to revisit London if it is going to play these tricks with me."

That day Captain Fontanel called, and was vastly concerned to hear that Betty was unwell. She was not looking herself, he said, at the boat-race. He feared that the cold on the river had been too much for her. But he did trust that he might be allowed to have a word with her before she returned to Devonshire.

Although he did not see Betty, he had an hour's conversation with Lady Lacy, and he departed with a smile on his face.

On the morrow he called again. Betty had so completely recovered that she was cheerful, and the pleasant colour had returned to her cheeks. She was in the drawing-room along with her aunt when he arrived.

The captain offered his condolences, and expressed his satisfaction that her indisposition had been so quickly got over.

"Oh!" said the girl, "I am as right as a trivet. It has all passed off. I need not have soaked in bed all yesterday, but that aunt would have it so. We are going down to our home to-morrow. Yesterday auntie was scared and thought she would have to postpone our return."

Lady Lacy rose, made the excuse that she had the packing to attend to, and left the young people alone together. When the door was shut behind her, Captain Fontanel drew his chair close to that of the girl and said—

"Betty, you do not know how happy I have felt since you accepted me. It was a hurried affair in the boat-house, but really, time was running short; as you were off so soon to Devonshire, I had to snatch at the occasion when there was no one by, so I seized old Time by the forelock, and you were so good as to say 'Yes.'"

"I—I——" stammered Betty.

"But as the thing was done in such haste, I came here to-day to renew my offer of myself, and to make sure of my happiness. You have had time to reflect, and I trust you do not repent."

"Oh, you are so good and kind to me!"

"Dearest Betty, what a thing to say! It is I—poor, wretched, good-for-naught—who have cause to speak such words to you. Put your hand into mine; it is a short courtship of a soldier, like that of Harry V. and the fair Maid of France. 'I love you: then if you urge me farther than to say, "Do you in faith?" I wear out my suit. Give me your answer; i' faith, do: and so clap hands and a bargain.' Am I quoting aright?"

Shyly, hesitatingly, she extended her fingers, and he clasped them. Then, shrinking back and looking down, she said: "But I ought to tell you something first, something very serious, which may make you change your mind. I do not, in conscience, feel it right that you should commit yourself till you know."

"It must be something very dreadful to make me do that."

"It is dreadful. I am apt to be terribly forgetful."

"Bless me! So am I. I have passed several of my acquaintances lately and have not recognised them, but that was because I was thinking of you. And I fear I have been very oblivious about my bills; and as to answering letters—good heavens! I am a shocking defaulter."

"I do not mean that. I have lapses of memory. Why, I do not even remember——"

He sealed her lips with a kiss. "You will not forget this, at any rate, Betty."

"Oh, Charlie, no!"

"Then consider this, Betty. Our engagement cannot be for long. I am ordered to Egypt, and I positively must take my dear little wife with me and show her the Pyramids. You would like to see them, would you not?"

"I should love to."

"And the Sphynx?"

"Indeed I should."

"And Pompey's Pillar?"

"Oh, Charlie! I shall love above everything to see you every day."

"That is prettily said. I see we understand one another. Now, hearken to me, give me your close attention, and no fits of lapse of memory over what I now say, please. We must be married very shortly. I positively will not go out without you. I would rather throw up my commission."

"But what about papa's consent?"

"I shall wire to him full particulars as to my position, income, and prospects, also how much I love you, and how I will do my level best to make you happy. That is the approved formula in addressing paterfamilias, I think. Then he will telegraph back, 'Bless you, my boy'; and all is settled. I know that Lady Lacy approves."

"But dear, dear aunt. She will be so awfully lonely without me."

"She shall not be. She has no ties to hold her to the little cottage in Devon. She shall come out to us in Cairo, and we will bury the dear old girl up to her neck in the sand of the desert, and make a second Sphynx of her, and bake the rheumatism out of her bones. It will cure her of all her aches, as sure as my name is Charlie, and yours will be Fontanel."

"Don't be too sure of that."

"But I am sure—you cannot forget."

"I will try not to do so. Oh, Charlie, don't!"

Mrs. Thomas, the dressmaker, and Miss Crock, the milliner, had their hands full. Betty's trousseau had to be got ready expeditiously. Patterns of materials specially adapted for a hot climate—light, beautiful, artistic, of silks and muslins and prints—had to be commanded from Liberty's. Then came the selection, then the ordering, then the discussions with the dressmaker, and the measurings. Next the fittings, for which repeated visits had to be made to Mrs. Thomas. Adjustments, alterations were made, easements under the arms, tightenings about the waist. There were fulnesses to be taken in and skimpiness to be redressed. The skirts had to be sufficiently short in front and sufficiently long behind.

As for the wedding-dress, Mrs. Thomas was not regarded as quite competent to execute such a masterpiece. For that an expedition had to be made to Exeter.

The wedding-cake must be ordered from Murch, in the cathedral city. Lady Lacy was particular that as much as possible of the outfit should be given to county tradesmen. A riding habit, tailor-made, was ordered, to fit like a glove, and a lady's saddle must be taken out to Egypt. Boxes, basket-trunks were to be procured, and a correspondence carried on as to the amount of personal luggage allowed.

Lady Lacy and Betty were constantly running up by express to Exeter about this, that, and everything.

Then ensued the sending out of the invitations, and the arrival of wedding presents, that entailed the writing of gushing letters of acknowledgment and thanks, by Betty herself. But these were not allowed to interfere with the scribbling of four pages every day to Captain Fontanel, intended for his eyes alone.

Interviews were sought by the editors or agents of local newspapers to ascertain whether reporters were desired to describe the wedding, and as to the length of the notices that were to be inserted, whether all the names of the donors of presents were to be included, and their gifts registered. Verily Lady Lacy and Betty were kept in a whirl of excitement, and their time occupied from morning till night, and their brains exercised from night to morning. Glass and china and plate had to be hired for the occasion, wine ordered. Fruit, cake, ices commanded. But all things come to an end, even the preparations for a wedding.

At last the eventful day arrived, bright and sunny, a true May morning.

The bridesmaids arrived, each wearing the pretty brooch presented by Captain Fontanel. Their costume was suitable to the season, of primrose-yellow, with hats turned up, white, with primroses. The pages were in green velvet, with knee-breeches and three-cornered hats, lace ruffles and lace fronts. The butler had made the claret-cup and the champagne-cup, and after a skirmish over the neighbourhood some borage had been obtained to float on the top. Lady Lacy was to hold a reception after the ceremony, and a marquee had been erected in the grounds, as the cottage could not contain all the guests invited. The dining-room was delivered over for the exposing of the presents. A carriage had been commanded to convey the happy couple to the station, horses and driver with white favours. With a sigh of relief in the morning, Lady Lacy declared that she believed that nothing had been forgotten.

The trunks stood ready packed, all but one, and labelled with the name of Mrs. Fontanel.

A flag flew on the church tower. The villagers had constructed a triumphal arch at the entrance to the grounds. The people from farms and cottages had all turned out, and were already congregating about the churchyard, with smiles and heartfelt wishes for the happiness of the bride, who was a mighty favourite with them, as indeed was also Lady Lacy.

The Sunday-school children had clubbed their pence, and had presented Betty, who had taught them, with a silver set of mustard-pot, pepper caster, and salt-cellar.

"Oh, dear!" said Betty, "what shall I do with all these sets of mustard- and pepper-pots? I have now received eight."

"A little later, dear," replied her aunt, "you can exchange those that you do not require."

"But never that set given me by my Sunday-school pets," said Betty.

Then came in flights of telegrams of congratulation.

And at the last moment arrived some more wedding presents.

"Good gracious me!" exclaimed the girl, "I really must manage to acknowledge these. There will be just time before I begin to dress."

So she tripped upstairs to her boudoir, a little room given over to herself in which to do her water-colour painting, her reading, to practise her music. A bright little room to which now, as she felt with an ache, she was to bid an eternal good-bye!

What happy hours had been spent in it! What day-dreams had been spun there!

She opened her writing-case and wrote the required letters of thanks.

"There," said she, when she had signed the fifth. "This is the last time I shall subscribe myself Elizabeth Mountjoy, except when I sign my name in the church register. Oh! how my back is hurting me.

I was not in bed till two o'clock and was up again at seven, and I have been on the tear for the whole week. There will be just time for me to rest it before the business of the dressing begins."

She threw herself on the sofa and put up her feet. Instantly she was asleep—in a sound, dreamless sleep.

When Betty opened her eyes she heard the church bells ringing a merry peal. Then she raised her lids, and turning her head on the sofa cushion saw—a bride, herself in full bridal dress, with the white veil and the orange-blossoms, seated at her side. The gloves had been removed and lay on the lap.

An indescribable terror held her fast. She could not cry out. She could not stir. She could only look.

Then the bride put back the veil, and Betty, studying the white face, saw that this actually was not herself; it was her dead sister, Letice.

Then the bride put back her veil, and Betty, studying the white face,
saw that this actually was not herself; it was her dead sister Letice.

The apparition put forth a hand and laid it on her and spoke: "Do not be frightened. I will do you no harm. I love you too dearly for that, Betty. I have been married in your name; I have exchanged vows in your name; I have received the ring for you; put it on your finger, it is not mine; it in no way belongs to me. In your name I signed the register. You are married to Charles Fontanel and not I. Listen to me. I will tell you all, and when I have told you everything you will see me no more. I will trouble you no further; I shall enter into my rest. You will see before you only the wedding garments remaining. I shall be gone. Hearken to me. When I was dying, I died in frantic despair, because I had never known what were the pleasures of life. My last cries, my last regrets, my last longings were for the pomps and vanities."

She paused, and slipped the gold hoop on to the forefinger of Betty's hand.

Then she proceeded—

"When my spirit parted from my body, it remained a while irresolute whither to go. But then, remembering that my aunt had declared that I never would go to Heaven, I resolved on forcing my way in there out of defiance; and I soared till I reached the gates of Paradise. At them stood an angel with a fiery sword drawn in his hand, and he laid it athwart the entrance. I approached, but he waved me off, and when the point of the flaming blade touched my heart, there passed a pang through it, I know not whether of joy or of sorrow. And he said: 'Letice, you have not been a good girl; you were sullen, resentful, rebellious, and therefore are unfit to enter here. Your longings through life, and to the moment of death, were for the world and its pomps and vanities. The last throb of your heart was given to repining for them. But your faults were due largely to the mistakes of your rearing. And now hear your judgment. You shall not pass within these gates till you have returned to earth and partaken of and had your fill of its pomps and vanities. As for that old cat, your aunt'—but no, Betty, he did not say quite that; I put it in, and I ought not to have done so. I bear her no resentment; I wish her no ill. She did by me what she believed to be right. She acted towards me up to her lights; alas for me that the light which was in her was darkness! The angel said: 'As for your aunt, before she can enter here, she will want illumining, enlarging, and sweetening, and will have to pass through Purgatory.' And oh, Betty, that will be gall and bitterness to her, for she did not believe in Purgatory, and she wrote a controversial pamphlet against it. Then said the angel: 'Return, return to the pomps and vanities.' I fell on my knees, and said: 'Oh, suffer me but to have one glimpse of that which is within!' 'Be it so,' he replied. 'One glimpse only whilst I cast my sword on high.' Thereat he threw up the flaming brand, and it was as though a glorious flash of lightning filled all space. At the same moment the gates swung apart, and I saw what was beyond. It was but for one brief moment, for the sword came down, and the angel caught it by the handle, and instantly the gates were shut. Then, sorrowfully, I turned myself about and went back to earth. And, Betty, it was I who took and read your novels. It was I who went to Lady Belgrove's ball in your place. It was I who sat instead of you at Her Majesty's and heard *Carmen*. It was I who took your place at Henley Regatta, and I—I, instead of you, received the protestation of Charles Fontanel's affection, and there in the boat-house I received the first and last kiss of love. And it was I, Betty, as I have told you, who took your place at the altar to-day. I had the pleasures that were designed for you—the ball-dress, the dances, the fair words, the music of the opera, the courtship, the excitement of the regatta, the reading of sensational novels. It was I who had what all girls most long for, their most supreme bliss of wearing the wedding-veil and the orange-blossoms. But I have reached my limit. I am full of the pomps and vanities, and I return on high. You will see me no more."

"Oh, Letice," said Betty, obtaining her speech, "you do not grudge me the joys of life?"

The fair white being at her side shook her head.

"And you desire no more of the pomps and vanities?"

"No, Betty. I have looked through the gates."

Then Betty put forth her hands to clasp the waist of her sister, as she said fervently—

"Tell me, Letice, what you saw beyond."

"Betty—everything the reverse of Salem Chapel."

III. — McALISTER

THE city of Bayonne, lying on the left bank of the Adour, and serving as its port, is one that ought to present much interest to the British tourist, on account of its associations. For three hundred years, along with Bordeaux, it belonged to the English crown. The cathedral, a noble structure of the fourteenth century, was reared by the English, and on the bosses of its vaulting are carved the arms of England, of the Talbots, and of other great English noble families. It was probably designed by English architects, for it possesses, in its vaulting, the long central rib so characteristic of English architecture, and wholly unlike what was the prevailing French fashion of vaulting in compartments, and always without that connecting rib, like the inverted keel of a ship, with which we are acquainted in our English minsters. Under some of the modern houses in the town are cellars of far earlier construction, also vaulted, and in them as well may be seen the arms of the English noble families which had their dwellings above.

But Bayonne has later associations with us. At the close of the Peninsular War, when Wellington had driven Marshal Soult and the French out of Spain, and had crossed the Pyrenees, his forces, under Sir John Hope, invested the citadel. In February, 1814, Sir John threw a bridge of boats across the Adour, boats being provided by the fleet of Admiral Penrose, in the teeth of a garrison of 15,000 men, and French gunboats which guarded the river and raked the English whilst conducting this hazardous and masterly achievement. This brilliant exploit was effected whilst Wellington engaged the attention of Soult about the Gaves, affluents of the Adour, near Orthez. It is further interesting, with a tragic interest, on account of an incident in that campaign which shall be referred to presently.

The cathedral of Bayonne, some years ago, possessed no towers—the English were driven out of Aquitaine before these had been completed. The west front was mean to the last degree, masked by a shabby penthouse, plastered white, or rather dirty white, on which in large characters was inscribed, "Liberté égalité et fraternité."

This has now disappeared, and a modern west front and twin towers and spires have been added, in passable architecture. When I was at Bayonne, more years ago than I care to say, I paid a visit to the little cemetery on the north bank of the river, in which were laid the English officers who fell during the investment of Bayonne.

The north bank is in the Department of the Landes, whereas that on the south is in the Department of the Basses Pyrénées.

About the time when the English were expelled from France, and lost Aquitaine, the Adour changed its course. Formerly it had turned sharply round at the city, and had flowed north and found an outlet some miles away at Cap Breton, but the entrance was choked by the moving sand-dunes, and the impatient river burst its way into the Bay of Biscay by the mouth through which it still flows. But the old course is marked by lagoons of still blue water in the midst of a vast forest of pines and cork trees. I had spent a day wandering among these tree-covered *landes*, seeking out the lonely lakes, and in the evening I returned in the direction of Bayonne, diverging somewhat from my course to visit the cemetery of the English. This was a square walled enclosure with an iron gate, rank with weeds, utterly neglected, and with the tombstones, some leaning, some prostrate, all covered with lichen and moss. I could not get within to decipher the inscriptions, for the gate was locked and I had not the key, and was quite ignorant who was the custodian of the place.

Being tired with my trudge in the sand, I sat down outside, with my back to the wall, and saw the setting sun paint with saffron the boles of the pines. I took out my Murray that I had in my knapsack, and read the following passage:—

"To the N., rises the citadel, the most formidable of the works laid out by Vauban, and greatly strengthened, especially since 1814, when it formed the key to an entrenched camp of Marshal Soult, and was invested by a detachment of the army of the Duke of Wellington, but not taken, the peace having put a stop to the siege after some bloody encounters. The last of these, a dreadful and useless expenditure of human life, took place after peace was declared, and the British forces put off their guard in consequence. They were thus entirely taken by surprise by a sally of the garrison, made early on the morning of April 14th; which, though repulsed, was attended with the loss of 830 men of the British, and by the capture of their commander, Sir John Hope, whose horse was shot under him, and himself wounded. The French attack was supported by the fire of their gunboats on the river, which opened indiscriminately on friend and foe. Nine hundred and ten of the French were killed."

When I had concluded, the sun had set, and already a grey mist began to form over the course of the Adour. I thought that now it was high time for me to return to Bayonne, and to table d'hôte, which is at 7.30 p.m., but for which I knew I should be late. However, before rising, I pulled out my flask of Scotch whisky, and drained it to the last drop.

I had scarcely finished, and was about to heave myself to my feet, when I heard a voice from behind and above me say—"It is grateful, varra grateful to a Scotchman."

I turned myself about, and drew back from the wall, for I saw a very remarkable object perched upon it. It was the upper portion of a man in military accoutrements. He was not sitting on the wall, for, if so, his legs would have been dangling over on the outside. And yet he could not have heaved himself up to the level of the parapet, with the legs depending inside, for he appeared to be on the wall itself down to the middle.

"Are you a Scotchman or an Englishman?" he inquired.

"An Englishman," I replied, hardly knowing what to make of the apparition.

"It's mabbe a bit airly in the nicht for me to be stirring," he said; "but the smell of the whisky drew me from my grave."

"From your grave!" I exclaimed.

"And pray, what is the blend?" he asked.

I answered.

"Weel," said he, "ye might do better, but it's guid enough. I am Captain Alister McAlister of Auchimachie, at your service, that is to say, his superior half. I fell in one of the attacks on the citadel. Those"—he employed a strong qualification which need not be reproduced—"those Johnny Crapauds used chain-shot; and they cut me in half at the waistbelt, and my legs are in Scotland."

Having somewhat recovered from my astonishment, I was able to take a further look at him, and could not restrain a laugh. He so much resembled Humpty Dumpty, who, as I had learned in childhood, did sit on a wall.

"Is there anything so rideeculous about me?" asked Captain McAlister in a tone of irritation. "You seem to be in a jocular mood, sir."

"I assure you," I responded, "I was only laughing from joy of heart at the happy chance of meeting you, Alister McAlister."

"Of Auchimachie, and my title is Captain," he said. "There is only half of me here—the etceteras are in the family vault in Scotland."

I expressed my genuine surprise at this announcement. "You must understand, sir," continued he, "that I am but the speeritual presentment of my buried trunk. The speeritual presentment of my nether half is not here, and I should scorn to use those of Captain O'Hooligan."

I pressed my hand to my brow. Was I in my right senses? Had the hot sun during the day affected my brain, or had the last drain of whisky upset my reason?

"You may be pleased to know," said the half-captain, "that my father, the Laird of Auchimachie, and Colonel Graham of Ours, were on terms of the greatest intimacy. Before I started for the war under Wellington—he was at the time but Sir Arthur Wellesley—my father took Colonel Graham apart and confided to him: 'If anything should happen to my son in the campaign, you'll obleege me greatly if you will forward his remains to Auchimachie. I am a staunch Presbyterian, and I shouldn't feel happy that his poor body should lie in the land of idolaters, who worship the Virgin Mary. And as to the expense, I will manage to meet that; but be careful not to do the job in an extravagant manner.'"

"And the untoward Fates cut you short?"

"Yes, the chain-shot did, but not in the Peninsula. I passed safely through that, but it was here. When we were makin' the bridge, the enemy's ships were up the river, and they fired on us with chain-shot, which ye ken are mainly used for cutting the rigging of vessels. But they employed them on us as we were engaged over the pontoons, and I was just cut in half by a pair of these shot at the junction of the tunic and the trews."

"I cannot understand how that your legs should be in Scotland and your trunk here."

"That's just what I'm aboot to tell you. There was a Captain O'Hooligan and I used to meet; we were in the same detachment. I need not inform you, if you're a man of understanding, that O'Hooligan is an Irish name, and Captain Timothy O'Hooligan was a born Irishman and an ignorant papist to boot. Now, I am by education and conveection a staunch Presbyterian. I believe in John Calvin, John Knox, and Jeannie Geddes. That's my creed; and if ye are disposed for an argument——"

"Not in the least."

"Weel, then, it was other with Captain O'Hooligan, and we often had words; but he hadn't any arguments at all, only assertions, and he lost his temper accordingly, and I was angry at the unreasonableness of the man. I had had an ancestor in Derry at the siege and at the Battle of the Boyne, and he spitted three Irish kerns on his sabre. I glory in it, and I told O'Hooligan as much, and I drank a glass of toddy to the memory of William III., and I shouted out Lillibulero! I believe in the end we would have fought a duel, after the siege was over, unless one of us had thought better of it. But it was not to be. At the same time that I was cut in half, so was he also by chain-shot."

"And is he buried here?"

"The half of him—his confounded legs, and the knees that have bowed to the image of Baal."

"Then, what became of his body?"

"If you'll pay me reasonable attention, and not interrupt, I'll tell you the whole story. But—sure enough! Here come those legs!"

Instantly the half-man rolled off the wall, on the outside, and heaving himself along on his hands, scuttled behind a tree-trunk.

Next moment I saw a pair of nimble lower limbs, in white ducks and straps under the boots, leap the wall, and run about, up and down, much like a setter after a partridge.

I did not know what to make of this.

Then the head of McAlister peered from behind the tree, and screamed "Lillibulero! God save King William!" Instantly the legs went after him, and catching him up kicked him like a football about the enclosure. I cannot recall precisely how many times the circuit was made, twice or thrice, but all the while the head of McAlister kept screaming "Lillibulero!" and "D—— the Pope!"

Recovering myself from my astonishment, and desirous of putting a term to this not very edifying scene, I picked up a leaf of shamrock, that grew at my feet, and ran between the legs and the trunk, and presented the symbol of St. Patrick to the former. The legs at once desisted from pursuit, and made a not ungraceful bow to the leaf, and as I advanced they retired, still bowing reverentially, till they reached the wall, which they stepped over with the utmost ease.

The half-Scotchman now hobbled up to me on his hands, and said: "I'm varra much obleeged to you for your intervention, sir." Then he scrambled, by means of the rails of the gate, to his former perch on the wall.

"You must understand, sir," said McAlister, settling himself comfortably, "that this produces no pheesical inconvenience to me at all. For O'Hooligan's boots are speeritual, and so is my trunk speeritual. And at best it only touches my speeritual feelings. Still, I thank you."

"You certainly administered to him some spiritual aggravation," I observed.

"Ay, ay, sir, I did. And I glory in it."

"And now, Captain McAlister, if it is not troubling you too greatly, after this interruption would you kindly explain to me how it comes about that the nobler part of you is here and the less noble in Scotland?"

"I will do so with pleasure. Captain O'Hooligan's upper story is at Auchimachie."

"How came that about?"

"If you had a particle of patience, you would not interrupt me in my narrative. I told you, did I not, that my dear father had enjoined on Colonel Graham, should anything untoward occur, that he should send my body home to be interred in the vault of my ancestors? Well, this is how it came about that the awkward mistake was made. When it was reported that I had been killed, Colonel Graham issued orders that my remains should be carefully attended to and put aside to be sent home to Scotland."

"By boat, I presume?"

"Certainly, by boat. But, unfortunately, he commissioned some Irishmen of his company to attend to it. And whether it was that they wished to do honour to their own countryman, or whether it was that, like most Irishmen, they could not fail to blunder in the discharge of their duty, I cannot say. They might have recognised me, even if they hadn't known my face, by my goold repeater watch; but some wretched camp-followers had been before them. On the watch were engraved the McAlister arms. But the watch had been stolen. So they picked up—either out of purpose, or by mistake—O'Hooligan's trunk, and my nether portion, and put them together into one case. You see, a man's legs are not so easily identified. So his body and my lower limbs were made ready together to be forwarded to Scotland."

"But how—did not Colonel Graham see personally to the matter?"

"He could not. He was so much engaged over regimental duties. Still, he might have stretched a point, I think."

"It must have been difficult to send the portions so far. Was the body embalmed?"

"Embalmed! no. There was no one in Bayonne who knew how to do it. There was a bird-stuffer in the Rue Pannceau, but he had done nothing larger than a seagull. So there could be no question of embalming. We, that is, the bit of O'Hooligan and the bit of me, were put into a cask of eau-de-vie, and so forwarded by a sailing-vessel. And either on the way to Southampton, or on another boat from that port to Edinburgh, the sailors ran a gimlet into the barrel, and inserted a straw, and drank up all the spirits. It was all gone by the time the hogshead reached Auchimachie. Whether O'Hooligan gave a smack to the liquor I cannot say, but I can answer for my legs, they would impart a grateful flavour of whisky. I was always a drinker of whisky, and when I had taken a considerable amount it always went to my legs; they swerved, and gave way under me. That is proof certain that the liquor went to my extremities and not to my head. Trust to a Scotchman's head for standing any amount of whisky. When the remains arrived at Auchimachie for interment, it was supposed that some mistake had been made. My hair is sandy, that of O'Hooligan is black, or nearly so; but there was no knowing what chemical action the alcohol might have on the hair in altering its colour. But my mother identified the legs past mistake, by a mole on the left calf and a varicose vein on the right. Anyhow, half a loaf is better than no bread, so all the mortal relics were consigned to the McAlister vault. It was aggravating to my feelings that the minister should pronounce a varra eloquent and moving discourse on the occasion over the trunk of a confounded Irishman and a papist."

"You must really excuse me," interrupted I, "but how the dickens do you know all this?"

"There is always an etherial current of communication between the parts of a man's body," replied McAlister, "and there is speeritual intercommunication between a man's head and his toes, however pairted they may be. I tell you, sir, in the speeritual world we know a thing or two."

"And now," said I, "what may be your wishes in this most unfortunate matter?"

"I am coming to that, if you'll exercise a little rational patience. This that I tell you of occurred in 1814, a considerable time ago. I shall be varra pleased if, on your return to England, you will make it your business to run up to Scotland, and interview my great-nephew. I am quite sure he will do the right thing by me, for the honour of the family, and to ease my soul. He never would have come into the estate at all if it had not been for my lamented decease. There's another little unpleasantness to which I desire you to call his attention. A tombstone has been erected over my trunk and O'Hooligan's legs, here in this cemetery, and on it is: 'Sacred to the Memory of Captain Timothy O'Hooligan, who fell on the field of Glory. R. I. P.' Now this is liable to a misunderstanding for it is me—I mean I, to be grammatical—who lies underneath. I make no account of the Irishman's nether extremities. And being a convinced and zealous Presbyterian, I altogether conscientiously object to having 'Requiescat in pace' inscribed over my

372

bodily remains. And my great-nephew, the present laird, if he be true to the principles of the Covenant, will object just as strongly as myself. I know very weel those letters are attached to the name of O'Hooligan, but they mark the place of deposition of my body rather than his. So I wish you just to put it clearly and logically to the laird, and he will take steps, at any cost, to have me transferred to Auchimachie. What he may do with the relics of that Irish rogue I don't care for, not one stick of barley sugar."

I promised solemnly to fulfil the commission entrusted to me, and then Captain McAlister wished me a good night, and retired behind the cemetery wall.

I did not quit the South of France that same year, for I spent the winter at Pau. In the following May I returned to England, and there found that a good many matters connected with my family called for my immediate attention. It was accordingly just a year and five months after my interview with Captain McAlister that I was able to discharge my promise. I had never forgotten my undertaking—I had merely postponed it. Charity begins at home, and my own concerns engrossed my time too fully to allow me the leisure for a trip to the North.

However, in the end I did go. I took the express to Edinburgh. That city, I think candidly, is the finest for situation in the world, as far as I have seen of it. I did not then visit it. I never had previously been in the Athens of the North, and I should have liked to spend a couple of days at least in it, to look over the castle and to walk through Holyrood. But duty stands before pleasure, and I went on directly to my destination, postponing acquaintance with Edinburgh till I had accomplished my undertaking.

I had written to Mr. Fergus McAlister to inform him of my desire to see him. I had not entered into the matter of my communication. I thought it best to leave this till I could tell him the whole story by word of mouth. I merely informed him by letter that I had something to speak to him about that greatly concerned his family.

On reaching the station his carriage awaited me, and I was driven to his house.

He received me with the greatest cordiality, and offered me the kindest hospitality.

The house was large and rambling, not in the best repair, and the grounds, as I was driven through them, did not appear to be trimly kept. I was introduced to his wife and to his five daughters, fair-haired, freckled girls, certainly not beautiful, but pleasing enough in manner. His eldest son was away in the army, and his second was in a lawyer's office in Edinburgh; so I saw nothing of them.

After dinner, when the ladies had retired, I told him the entire story as freely and as fully as possible, and he listened to me with courtesy, patience, and the deepest attention.

"Yes," he said, when I had concluded, "I was aware that doubts had been cast on the genuineness of the trunk. But under the circumstances it was considered advisable to allow the matter to stand as it was. There were insuperable difficulties in the way of an investigation and a certain identification. But the legs were all right. And I hope to show you to-morrow, in the kirk, a very handsome tablet against the wall, recording the name and the date of decease of my great-uncle, and some very laudatory words on his character, beside an appropriate text from the Screeptures."

"Now, however, that the facts are known, you will, of course, take steps for the translation of the half of Captain Alister to your family vault."

"I foresee considerable difficulties in the way," he replied. "The authorities at Bayonne might raise objections to the exhuming of the remains in the grave marked by the tombstone of Captain O'Hooligan. They might very reasonably say: 'What the hang has Mr. Fergus McAlister to do with the body of Captain O'Hooligan?' We must consult the family of that officer in Ireland."

"But," said I, "a representation of the case—of the mistake made—would render all clear to them. I do not see that there is any necessity for complicating the story by saying that you have only half of your relative here, and that the other half is in O'Hooligan's grave. State that orders had been given for the transmission of the body of your great-uncle to Auchimachie, and that, through error, the corpse of Captain O'Hooligan had been sent, and Captain McAlister buried by mistake as that of the Irishman. That makes a simple, intelligible, and straightforward tale. Then you could dispose of the superfluous legs when they arrived in the manner you think best."

The laird remained silent for a while, rubbing his chin, and looking at the tablecloth.

Presently he stood up, and going to the sideboard, said: "I'll just take a wash of whisky to clear my thoughts. Will you have some?"

"Thank you; I am enjoying your old and excellent port."

Mr. Fergus McAlister returned leisurely to the table after his "wash," remained silent a few minutes longer, then lifted his head and said: "I don't see that I am called upon to transport those legs."

"No," I answered; "but you had best take the remains in a lump and sort them on their arrival."

"I am afraid it will be seriously expensive. My good sir, the property is not now worth what it was in Captain Alister's time. Land has gone down in value, and rents have been seriously reduced. Besides, farmers are now more exacting than formerly; they will not put up with the byres that served their fathers. Then my son in the army is a great expense to me, and my second son is not yet earning his livelihood, and my daughters have not yet found suitors, so that I shall have to leave them something on which to live; besides"—he drew a long breath—"I want to build on to the house a billiard-room."

"I do not think," protested I, "that the cost would be very serious."

"What do you mean by serious?" he asked.

"I think that these relics of humanity might be transported to Auchimachie in a hogshead of cognac, much as the others were."

"What is the price of cognac down there?" asked he.

"Well," I replied, "that is more than I can say as to the cask. Best cognac, three stars, is five francs fifty centimes a bottle."

"That's a long price. But one star?"

"I cannot say; I never bought that. Possibly three francs and a half."

"And how many bottles to a cask?"

"I am not sure, something over two hundred litres."

"Two hundred three shillings," mused Mr. Fergus; and then looking up, "there is the duty in England, very heavy on spirits, and charges for the digging-up, and fees to the officials, and the transport by water——" He shook his head.

"You must remember," said I, "that your relative is subjected to great indignities from those legs, getting toed three or four times round the enclosure." I said three or four, but I believe it was only twice or thrice. "It hardly comports with the family honour to suffer it."

"I think," replied Mr. Fergus, "that you said it was but the speeritual presentment of a boot, and that there was no pheesical inconvenience felt, only a speeritual impression?"

"Just so."

"For my part, judging from my personal experience," said the laird, "speeritual impressions are most evanescent."

"Then," said I, "Captain Alister's trunk lies in a foreign land."

"But not," replied he, "in Roman Catholic consecrated soil. That is a great satisfaction."

"You, however, have the trunk of a Roman Catholic in your family vault."

"It is so, according to what you say. But there are a score of McAlisters there, all staunch Presbyterians, and if it came to an argument among them—I won't say he would not have a leg to stand on, as he hasn't those anyhow, but he would find himself just nowhere."

Then Mr. Fergus McAlister stood up and said: "Shall we join the ladies? As to what you have said, sir, and have recommended, I assure you that I will give it my most serious consideration."

IV. — THE LEADEN RING

"IT is not possible, Julia. I cannot conceive how the idea of attending the county ball can have entered your head after what has happened. Poor young Hattersley's dreadful death suffices to stop that."

"But, aunt, Mr. Hattersley is no relation of ours."

"No relation—but you know that the poor fellow would not have shot himself if it had not been for you."

"Oh, Aunt Elizabeth, how can you say so, when the verdict was that he committed suicide when in an unsound condition of mind? How could I help his blowing out his brains, when those brains were deranged?"

"Julia, do not talk like this. If he did go off his head, it was you who upset him by first drawing him on, leading him to believe that you liked him, and then throwing him over so soon as the Hon. James Lawlor appeared on the *tapis*. Consider: what will people say if you go to the assembly?"

"What will they say if I do not go? They will immediately set it down to my caring deeply for James Hattersley, and they will think that there was some sort of engagement."

"They are not likely to suppose that. But really, Julia, you were for a while all smiles and encouragement. Tell me, now, did Mr. Hattersley propose to you?"

"Well—yes, he did, and I refused him."

"And then he went and shot himself in despair. Julia, you cannot with any face go to the ball."

"Nobody knows that he proposed. And precisely because I do go everyone will conclude that he did not propose. I do not wish it to be supposed that he did."

"His family, of course, must have been aware. They will see your name among those present at the assembly."

"Aunt, they are in too great trouble to look at the paper to see who were at the dance."

"His terrible death lies at your door. How you can have the heart, Julia——"

"I don't see it. Of course, I feel it. I am awfully sorry, and awfully sorry for his father, the admiral. I cannot set him up again. I wish that when I rejected him he had gone and done as did Joe Pomeroy, marry one of his landlady's daughters."

"There, Julia, is another of your delinquencies. You lured on young Pomeroy till he proposed, then you refused him, and in a fit of vexation and mortified vanity he married a girl greatly beneath him in social position. If the *ménage* prove a failure you will have it on your conscience that you have wrecked his life and perhaps hers as well."

"I cannot throw myself away as a charity to save this man or that from doing a foolish thing."

"What I complain of, Julia, is that you encouraged young Mr. Pomeroy till Mr. Hattersley appeared, whom you thought more eligible, and then you tossed him aside; and you did precisely the same with James Hattersley as soon as you came to know Mr. Lawlor. After all, Julia, I am not so sure that Mr. Pomeroy has not chosen the better part. The girl, I dare say, is simple, fresh, and affectionate."

"Your implication is not complimentary, Aunt Elizabeth."

"My dear, I have no patience with the young lady of the present day, who is shallow, self-willed, and indifferent to the feelings and happiness of others, who craves for excitement and pleasure, and desires nothing that is useful and good. Where now will you see a girl like Viola's sister, who let concealment, like a worm i' the bud, feed on her damask cheek? Nowadays a girl lays herself at the feet of a man if she likes him, turns herself inside-out to let him and all the world read her heart."

"I have no relish to be like Viola's sister, and have my story—a blank. I never grovelled at the feet of Joe Pomeroy or James Hattersley."

"No, but you led each to consider himself the favoured one till he proposed, and then you refused him. It was like smiling at a man and then stabbing him to the heart."

"Well—I don't want people to think that James Hattersley cared for me—I certainly never cared for him—nor that he proposed; so I shall go to the ball."

Julia Demant was an orphan. She had been retained at school till she was eighteen, and then had been removed just at the age when a girl begins to take an interest in her studies, and not to regard them as drudgery. On her removal she had cast away all that she had acquired, and had been plunged into the whirl of Society. Then suddenly her father died—she had lost her mother some years before—and she went to live with her aunt, Miss Flemming. Julia had inherited a sum of about five hundred pounds a year, and would probably come in for a good estate and funds as well on the death of her aunt. She had been flattered as a girl at home, and at school as a beauty, and she certainly thought no small bones of herself.

Miss Flemming was an elderly lady with a sharp tongue, very outspoken, and very decided in her opinions; but her action was weak, and Julia soon discovered that she could bend the aunt to do anything she willed, though she could not modify or alter her opinions.

In the matter of Joe Pomeroy and James Hattersley, it was as Miss Flemming had said. Julia had encouraged Mr. Pomeroy, and had only cast him off because she thought better of the suit of Mr. Hattersley, son of an admiral of that name. She had seen a good deal of young Hattersley, had given him every encouragement, had so entangled him, that he was madly in love with her; and then, when she came to know the Hon. James Lawlor, and saw that he was fascinated, she rejected Hattersley with the consequences alluded to in the conversation above given.

Julia was particularly anxious to be present at the county ball, for she had been already booked by Mr. Lawlor for several dances, and she was quite resolved to make an attempt to bring him to a declaration.

On the evening of the ball Miss Flemming and Julia entered the carriage. The aunt had given way, as was her wont, but under protest.

For about ten minutes neither spoke, and then Miss Flemming said, "Well, you know my feelings about this dance. I do not approve. I distinctly disapprove. I do not consider your going to the ball in good taste, or, as you would put it, in good form. Poor young Hattersley——"

"Oh, dear aunt, do let us put young Hattersley aside. He was buried with the regular forms, I suppose?"

"Yes, Julia."

"Then the rector accepted the verdict of the jury at the inquest. Why should not we? A man who is unsound in his mind is not responsible for his actions."

"I suppose not."

"Much less, then, I who live ten miles away."

"I do not say that you are responsible for his death, but for the condition of mind that led him to do the dreadful deed. Really, Julia, you are one of those into whose head or heart only by a surgical operation could the thought be introduced that you could be in the wrong. A hypodermic syringe would be too weak an instrument to effect such a radical change in you. Everyone else may be in the wrong, you—never. As for me, I cannot get young Hattersley out of my head."

"And I," retorted Julia with asperity, for her aunt's words had stung her—"I, for my part, do not give him a thought."

She had hardly spoken the words before a chill wind began to pass round her. She drew the Barège shawl that was over her bare shoulders closer about her, and said—"Auntie! is the glass down on your side?"

"No, Julia; why do you ask?"

"There is such a draught."

"Draught!—I do not feel one; perhaps the window on your side hitches."

"Indeed, that is all right. It is blowing harder and is deadly cold. Can one of the front panes be broken?"

"No. Rogers would have told me had that been the case. Besides, I can see that they are sound."

The wind of which Julia complained swirled and whistled about her. It increased in force; it plucked at her shawl and slewed it about her throat; it tore at the lace on her dress. It snatched at her hair, it wrenched it away from the pins, the combs that held it in place; one long tress was lashed across the face of Miss Flemming. Then the hair, completely released, eddied up above the girl's head, and next moment was carried as a drift before her, blinding her. Then—a sudden explosion, as though a gun had been fired into her ear; and with a scream of terror she sank back among the cushions. Miss Flemming, in great alarm, pulled the checkstring, and the carriage stopped. The footman descended from the box and came to the side. The old lady drew down the window and said: "Oh! Phillips, bring the lamp. Something has happened to Miss Demant."

The man obeyed, and sent a flood of light into the carriage. Julia was lying back, white and senseless. Her hair was scattered over her face, neck, and shoulders; the flowers that had been stuck in it, the pins that had fastened it in place, the pads that had given shape to the convolutions lay strewn, some on her lap, some in the rug at the bottom of the carriage.

"Phillips!" ordered the old lady in great agitation, "tell Rogers to turn the horses and drive home at once; and do you run as fast as you can for Dr. Crate."

A few minutes after the carriage was again in motion, Julia revived. Her aunt was chafing her hand.

"Oh, aunt!" she said, "are all the glasses broken?"

"Broken—what glasses?"

"Those of the carriage—with the explosion."

"Explosion, my dear!"

"Yes. That gun which was discharged. It stunned me. Were you hurt?"

"I heard no gun—no explosion."

"But I did. It was as though a bullet had been discharged into my brain. I wonder that I escaped. Who can have fired at us?"

"My dear, no one fired. I heard nothing. I know what it was. I had the same experience many years ago. I slept in a damp bed, and awoke stone deaf in my right ear. I remained so for three weeks. But one night when I was at a ball and was dancing, all at once I heard a report as of a pistol in my right ear, and immediately heard quite clearly again. It was wax."

"But, Aunt Elizabeth, I have not been deaf."

"You have not noticed that you were deaf."

"Oh! but look at my hair; it was that wind that blew it about."

"You are labouring under a delusion, Julia. There was no wind."

"But look—feel how my hair is down."

"That has been done by the motion of the carriage. There are many ruts in the road."

They reached home, and Julia, feeling sick, frightened, and bewildered, retired to bed. Dr. Crate arrived, said that she was hysterical, and ordered something to soothe her nerves. Julia was not convinced. The explanation offered by Miss Flemming did not satisfy her. That she was a victim to hysteria she did not in the least believe. Neither her aunt, nor the coachman, nor Phillips had heard the discharge of a gun. As to the rushing wind, Julia was satisfied that she had experienced it. The lace was ripped, as by a hand, from her dress, and the shawl was twisted about her throat; besides, her hair had not been so slightly arranged that the jolting of the carnage would completely disarrange it. She was vastly perplexed over what she had undergone. She thought and thought, but could get no nearer to a solution of the mystery.

Next day, as she was almost herself again, she rose and went about as usual.

In the afternoon the Hon. James Lawlor called and asked after Miss Flemming. The butler replied that his mistress was out making calls, but that Miss Demant was at home, and he believed was on the terrace. Mr. Lawlor at once asked to see her.

He did not find Julia in the parlour or on the terrace, but in a lower garden to which she had descended to feed the goldfish in the pond.

"Oh! Miss Demant," said he, "I was so disappointed not to see you at the ball last night."

"I was very unwell; I had a fainting fit and could not go."

"It threw a damp on our spirits—that is to say, on mine. I had you booked for several dances."

"You were able to give them to others."

"But that was not the same to me. I did an act of charity and self-denial. I danced instead with the ugly Miss Burgons and with Miss Pounding, and that was like dragging about a sack of potatoes. I believe it would have been a jolly evening, but for that shocking affair of young Hattersley which kept some of the better sort away. I mean those who know the Hattersleys. Of course, for me that did not matter, we were not acquainted. I never even spoke with the fellow. You knew him, I believe? I heard some people say so, and that you had not come because of him. The supper, for a subscription ball, was not atrociously bad."

"What did they say of me?"

"Oh!—if you will know—that you did not attend the ball because you liked him very much, and were awfully cut up."

"I—I! What a shame that people should talk! I never cared a rush for him. He was nice enough in his way, not a bounder, but tolerable as young men go."

Mr. Lawlor laughed. "I should not relish to have such a qualified estimate made of me."

"Nor need you. You are interesting. He became so only when he had shot himself. It will be by this alone that he will be remembered."

"But there is no smoke without fire. Did he like you—much?"

"Dear Mr. Lawlor, I am not a clairvoyante, and never was able to see into the brains or hearts of people—least of all of young men. Perhaps it is fortunate for me that I cannot."

"One lady told me that he had proposed to you."

"Who was that? The potato-sack?"

"I will not give her name. Is there any truth in it? Did he?"

"No."

At the moment she spoke there sounded in her ear a whistle of wind, and she felt a current like a cord of ice creep round her throat, increasing in force and compression, her hat was blown off, and next instant a detonation rang through her head as though a gun had been fired into her ear. She uttered a cry and sank upon the ground.

Her hat was blown off, and next instant a detonation rang
through her head as though a gun had been fired into her ear.

James Lawlor was bewildered. His first impulse was to run to the house for assistance; then he considered that he could not leave her lying on the wet soil, and he stooped to raise her in his arms and to carry her within. In novels young men perform such a feat without difficulty; but in fact they are not able to do it, especially when the girl is tall and big-boned. Moreover, one in a faint is a dead weight. Lawlor staggered under his burden to the steps. It was as much as he could perform to carry her up to the terrace, and there he placed her on a seat. Panting, and with his muscles quivering after the strain, he hastened to the drawing-room, rang the bell, and when the butler appeared, he gasped: "Miss Demant has fainted; you and I and the footman must carry her within."

"She fainted last night in the carriage," said the butler.

When Julia came to her senses, she was in bed attended by the housekeeper and her maid. A few moments later Miss Flemming arrived.

"Oh, aunt! I have heard it again."

"Heard what, dear?"

"The discharge of a gun."

"It is nothing but wax," said the old lady. "I will drop a little sweet-oil into your ear, and then have it syringed with warm water."

"I want to tell you something—in private."

Miss Flemming signed to the servants to withdraw.

"Aunt," said the girl, "I must say something. This is the second time that this has happened. I am sure it is significant. James Lawlor was with me in the sunken garden, and he began to speak about James Hattersley. You know it was when we were talking about him last night that I heard that awful noise. It was precisely as if a gun had been discharged into my ear. I felt as if all the nerves and tissues of my head were being torn, and all the bones of my skull shattered—just what Mr. Hattersley must have undergone when he pulled the trigger. It was an agony for a moment perhaps, but it felt as if it lasted an hour. Mr. Lawlor had asked me point blank if James Hattersley had proposed to me, and I said, 'No.' I was perfectly justified in so answering, because he had no right to ask me such a question. It was an impertinence on his part, and I answered him shortly and sharply with a negative. But actually James Hattersley proposed twice to me. He would not accept a first refusal, but came next day bothering me again, and I was pretty curt with him. He made some remarks that were rude about how I had treated him, and which I will not repeat, and as he left, in a state of great agitation, he said, 'Julia, I vow that you shall not forget this, and you shall belong to no one but me, alive or dead.' I considered this great nonsense, and did not accord it another thought. But, really, these terrible annoyances, this wind and the bursts of noise, do seem to me to come from him. It is just as though he felt a malignant delight in distressing me, now that he is dead. I should like to defy him, and I will do it if I can, but I cannot bear more of these experiences—they will kill me."

Several days elapsed.

Mr. Lawlor called repeatedly to inquire, but a week passed before Julia was sufficiently recovered to receive him, and then the visit was one of courtesy and of sympathy, and the conversation turned upon her health, and on indifferent themes.

But some few days later it was otherwise. She was in the conservatory alone, pretty much herself again, when Mr. Lawlor was announced.

Physically she had recovered, or believed that she had, but her nerves had actually received a severe shock. She had made up her mind that the phenomena of the circling wind and the explosion were in some mysterious manner connected with Hattersley.

She bitterly resented this, but she was in mortal terror of a recurrence; and she felt no compunction for her treatment of the unfortunate young man, but rather a sense of deep resentment against him. If he were dead, why did he not lie quiet and cease from vexing her?

To be a martyr was to her no gratification, for hers was not a martyrdom that provoked sympathy, and which could make her interesting.

She had hitherto supposed that when a man died there was an end of him; his condition was determined for good or for ill. But that a disembodied spirit should hover about and make itself a nuisance to the living, had never entered into her calculations.

"Julia—if I may be allowed so to call you"—began Mr. Lawlor, "I have brought you a bouquet of flowers. Will you accept them?"

"Oh!" she said, as he handed the bunch to her, "how kind of you. At this time of the year they are so rare, and aunt's gardener is so miserly that he will spare me none for my room but some miserable bits of geranium. It is too bad of you wasting your money like this upon me."

"It is no waste, if it afford you pleasure."

"It is a pleasure. I dearly love flowers."

"To give you pleasure," said Mr. Lawlor, "is the great object of my life. If I could assure you happiness—if you would allow me to hope—to seize this opportunity, now that we are alone together——"

He drew near and caught her hand. His features were agitated, his lips trembled, there was earnestness in his eyes.

At once a cold blast touched Julia and began to circle about her and to flutter her hair. She trembled and drew back. That paralysing experience was about to be renewed. She turned deadly white, and put her hand to her right ear. "Oh, James! James!" she gasped. "Do not, pray do not speak what you want to say, or I shall faint. It is coming on. I am not yet well enough to hear it. Write to me and I will answer. For pity's sake do not speak it." Then she sank upon a seat—and at that moment her aunt entered the conservatory.

On the following day a note was put into her hand, containing a formal proposal from the Hon. James Lawlor; and by return of post Julia answered with an acceptance.

There was no reason whatever why the engagement should be long; and the only alternative mooted was whether the wedding should take place before Lent or after Easter. Finally, it was settled that it should be celebrated on Shrove Tuesday. This left a short time for the necessary preparations. Miss Flemming would have to go to town with her niece concerning a trousseau, and a trousseau is not turned out rapidly any more than an armed cruiser.

There is usually a certain period allowed to young people who have become engaged, to see much of each other, to get better acquainted with one another, to build their castles in the air, and to indulge in little passages of affection, vulgarly called "spooning." But in this case the spooning had to be curtailed and postponed.

At the outset, when alone with James, Julia was nervous. She feared a recurrence of those phenomena that so affected her. But, although every now and then the wind curled and soughed about her, it was not violent, nor was it chilling; and she came to regard it as a wail of discomfiture. Moreover, there was no recurrence of the detonation, and she fondly hoped that with her marriage the vexation would completely cease.

In her heart was deep down a sense of exultation. She was defying James Hattersley and setting his prediction at naught. She was not in love with Mr. Lawlor; she liked him, in her cold manner, and was not insensible to the social advantage that would be hers when she became the Honourable Mrs. Lawlor.

The day of the wedding arrived. Happily it was fine. "Blessed is the bride the sun shines on," said the cheery Miss Flemming; "an omen, I trust, of a bright and unruffled life in your new condition."

All the neighbourhood was present at the church. Miss Flemming had many friends. Mr. Lawlor had fewer present, as he belonged to a distant county. The church path had been laid with red cloth, the church decorated with flowers, and a choir was present to twitter "The voice that breathed o'er Eden."

The rector stood by the altar, and two cushions had been laid at the chancel step. The rector was to be assisted by an uncle of the bridegroom who was in Holy Orders; the rector, being old-fashioned, had drawn on pale grey kid gloves.

First arrived the bridegroom with his best man, and stood in a nervous condition balancing himself first on one foot, then on the other, waiting, observed by all eyes.

Next entered the procession of the bride, attended by her maids, to the "Wedding March" in *Lohengrin*, on a wheezy organ. Then Julia and her intended took their places at the chancel step for the performance of the first portion of the ceremony, and the two clergy descended to them from the altar.

"Wilt thou have this woman to thy wedded wife?"

"I will."

"Wilt thou have this man to thy wedded husband?"

"I will."

"I, James, take thee, Julia, to my wedded wife, to have and to hold——" and so on.

As the words were being spoken, a cold rush of air passed over the clasped hands, numbing them, and began to creep round the bride, and to flutter her veil. She set her lips and knitted her brows. In a few minutes she would be beyond the reach of these manifestations.

When it came to her turn to speak, she began firmly: "I, Julia, take thee, James——" but as she proceeded the wind became fierce; it raged about her, it caught her veil on one side and buffeted her cheek; it switched the veil about her throat, as though strangling her with a drift of snow contracting into ice. But she persevered to the end.

Then James Lawlor produced the ring, and was about to place it on her finger with the prescribed words: "With this ring I thee wed——" when a report rang in her ear, followed by a heaving of her skull, as though the bones were being burst asunder, and she sank unconscious on the chancel step.

In the midst of profound commotion, she was raised and conveyed to the vestry, followed by James Lawlor, trembling and pale. He had slipped the ring back into his waistcoat pocket. Dr. Crate, who was present, hastened to offer his professional assistance.

In the vestry Julia rested in a Glastonbury chair, white and still, with her hands resting in her lap. And to the amazement of those present, it was seen that on the third finger of her left hand was a leaden ring, rude and solid as though fashioned out of a bullet. Restoratives were applied, but full a quarter of an hour elapsed before Julia opened her eyes, and a little colour returned to her lips and cheek. But, as she raised her hands to her brow to wipe away the damps that had formed on it, her eye caught sight of the leaden ring, and with a cry of horror she sank again into insensibility.

The congregation slowly left the church, awestruck, whispering, asking questions, receiving no satisfactory answers, forming surmises all incorrect.

"I am very much afraid, Mr. Lawlor," said the rector, "that it will be impossible to proceed with the service to-day; it must be postponed till Miss Demant is in a condition to conclude her part, and to sign the register. I do not see how it can be gone on with to-day. She is quite unequal to the effort."

The carriage which was to have conveyed the couple to Miss Flemming's house, and then, later, to have taken them to the station for their honeymoon, the horses decorated with white rosettes, the whip adorned with a white bow, had now to convey Julia, hardly conscious, supported by her aunt, to her home.

No rice could be thrown. The bell-ringers, prepared to give a joyous peal, were constrained to depart.

The reception at Miss Flemming's was postponed. No one thought of attending. The cakes, the ices, were consumed in the kitchen.

The bridegroom, bewildered, almost frantic, ran hither and thither, not knowing what to do, what to say.

Julia lay as a stone for fully two hours; and when she came to herself could not speak. When conscious, she raised her left hand, looked on the leaden ring, and sank back again into senselessness.

Not till late in the evening was she sufficiently recovered to speak, and then she begged her aunt, who had remained by her bed without stirring, to dismiss the attendants. She desired to speak with her alone. When no one was in the room with her, save Miss Flemming, she said in a whisper: "Oh, Aunt Elizabeth! Oh, auntie! such an awful thing has happened. I can never marry Mr. Lawlor, never. I have married James Hattersley; I am a dead man's wife. At the time that James Lawlor was making the responses, I heard a piping voice in my ear, an unearthly voice, saying the same words. When I said: 'I, Julia, take you, James, to my wedded husband'—you know Mr. Hattersley is James as well as Mr. Lawlor—then the words applied to him as much or as well as to the other. And then, when it came to the giving of the ring, there was the explosion in my ear, as before—and the leaden ring was forced on to my finger, and not James Lawlor's golden ring. It is of no use my resisting any more. I am a dead man's wife, and I cannot marry James Lawlor."

Some years have elapsed since that disastrous day and that incomplete marriage.

Miss Demant is Miss Demant still, and she has never been able to remove the leaden ring from the third finger of her left hand. Whenever the attempt has been made, either to disengage it by drawing it off or by cutting through it, there has ensued that terrifying discharge as of a gun into her ear, causing insensibility. The prostration that has followed, the terror it has inspired, have so affected her nerves, that she has desisted from every attempt to rid herself of the ring.

She invariably wears a glove on her left hand, and it is bulged over the third finger, where lies that leaden ring.

She is not a happy woman, although her aunt is dead and has left her a handsome estate. She has not got many acquaintances. She has no friends; for her temper is unamiable, and her tongue is bitter. She supposes that the world, as far as she knows it, is in league against her.

Towards the memory of James Hattersley she entertains a deadly hate. If an incantation could lay his spirit, if prayer could give him repose, she would have recourse to none of these expedients, even though they might relieve her, so bitter is her resentment. And she harbours a silent wrath against Providence for allowing the dead to walk and to molest the living.

V. — THE MOTHER OF PANSIES

ANNA VOSS, of Siebenstein, was the prettiest girl in her village. Never was she absent from a fair or a dance. No one ever saw her abroad anything but merry. If she had her fits of bad temper, she kept them for her mother, in the secrecy of the house. Her voice was like that of the lark, and her smile like the May morning. She had plenty of suitors, for she was possessed of what a young peasant desires more in a wife than beauty, and that is money.

But of all the young men who hovered about her, and sought her favour, none was destined to win it save Joseph Arler, the ranger, a man in a government position, whose duty was to watch the frontier against smugglers, and to keep an eye on the game against poachers.

The eve of the marriage had come.

One thing weighed on the pleasure-loving mind of Anna. She dreaded becoming a mother of a family which would keep her at home, and occupy her from morn to eve in attendance on her children, and break the sweetness of her sleep at night.

So she visited an old hag named Schändelwein, who was a reputed witch, and to whom she confided her trouble.

The old woman said that she had looked into the mirror of destiny, before Anna arrived, and she had seen that Providence had ordained that Anna should have seven children, three girls and four boys, and that one of the latter was destined to be a priest.

But Mother Schändelwein had great powers; she could set at naught the determinations of Providence; and she gave to Anna seven pips, very much like apple-pips, which she placed in a cornet of paper; and she bade her cast these one by one into the mill-race, and as each went over the mill-wheel, it ceased to have a future, and in each pip was a child's soul.

So Anna put money into Mother Schändelwein's hand and departed, and when it was growing dusk she stole to the wooden bridge over the mill-stream, and dropped in one pip after another. As each fell into the water she heard a little sigh.

But when it came to casting in the last of the seven she felt a sudden qualm, and a battle in her soul.

However, she threw it in, and then, overcome by an impulse of remorse, threw herself into the stream to recover it, and as she did so she uttered a cry.

But the water was dark, the floating pip was small, she could not see it, and the current was rapidly carrying her to the mill-wheel, when the miller ran out and rescued her.

On the following morning she had completely recovered her spirits, and laughingly told her bridesmaids how that in the dusk, in crossing the wooden bridge, her foot had slipped, she had fallen into the stream, and had been nearly drowned. "And then," added she, "if I really had been drowned, what would Joseph have done?"

The married life of Anna was not unhappy. It could hardly be that in association with so genial, kind, and simple a man as Joseph. But it was not altogether the ideal happiness anticipated by both. Joseph had to be much away from home, sometimes for days and nights together, and Anna found it very tedious to be alone. And Joseph might have calculated on a more considerate wife. After a hard day of climbing and chasing in the mountains, he might have expected that she would have a good hot supper ready for him. But Anna set before him whatever came to hand and cost least trouble. A healthy appetite is the best of sauces, she remarked.

Moreover, the nature of his avocation, scrambling up rocks and breaking through an undergrowth of brambles and thorns, produced rents and fraying of stockings and cloth garments. Instead of cheerfully undertaking the repairs, Anna grumbled over each rent, and put out his garments to be mended by others. It was only when repair was urgent that she consented to undertake it herself, and then it was done with sulky looks, muttered reproaches, and was executed so badly that it had to be done over again, and by a hired workwoman.

But Joseph's nature was so amiable, and he was so fond of his pretty wife, that he bore with those defects, and turned off her murmurs with a joke, or sealed her pouting lips with a kiss.

There was one thing about Joseph that Anna could not relish. Whenever he came into the village, he was surrounded, besieged by the children. Hardly had he turned the corner into the square, before it was known that he was there, and the little ones burst out of their parents' houses, broke from their sister nurse's arms, to scamper up to Joseph and to jump about him. For Joseph somehow always had nuts or almonds or sweets in his pockets, and for these he made the children leap, or catch, or scramble, or sometimes beg, by putting a sweet on a boy's nose and bidding him hold it there, till he said "Catch!"

Joseph had one particular favourite among all this crew, and that was a little lame boy with a white, pinched face, who hobbled about on crutches.

Him Joseph would single out, take him on his knee, seat himself on the steps of the village cross or of the churchyard, and tell him stories of his adventures, of the habits of the beasts of the forest.

Anna, looking out of her window, could see all this; and see how before Joseph set the poor cripple down, the child would throw its arms round his neck and kiss him.

Then Joseph would come home with his swinging step and joyous face.

Anna resented that his first attention should be given to the children, regarding it as her due, and she often showed her displeasure by the chill of her reception of her husband. She did not reproach him in set words, but she did not run to meet him, jump into his arms, and respond to his warm kisses.

Once he did venture on a mild expostulation. "Annerl, why do you not knit my socks or stocking-legs? Home-made is heart-made. It is a pity to spend money on buying what is poor stuff, when those made by you would not only last on my calves and feet, but warm the cockles of my heart."

To which she replied testily: "It is you who set the example of throwing money away on sweet things for those pestilent little village brats."

One evening Anna heard an unusual hubbub in the square, shouts and laughter, not of children alone, but of women and men as well, and next moment into the house burst Joseph very red, carrying a cradle on his head.

"What is this fooling for?" asked Anna, turning crimson.

"An experiment, Annerl, dearest," answered Joseph, setting down the cradle. "I have heard it said that a wife who rocks an empty cradle soon rocks a baby into it. So I have bought this and brought it to you. Rock, rock, rock, and when I see a little rosebud in it among the snowy linen, I shall cry for joy."

Never before had Anna known how dull and dead life could be in an empty house. When she had lived with her mother, that mother had made her do much of the necessary work of the house; now there was not much to be done, and there was no one to exercise compulsion.

If Anna ran out and visited her neighbours, they proved to be disinclined for a gossip. During the day they had to scrub and bake and cook, and in the evening they had their husbands and children with them, and did not relish the intrusion of a neighbour.

The days were weary days, and Anna had not the energy or the love of work to prompt her to occupy herself more than was absolutely necessary. Consequently, the house was not kept scrupulously clean. The glass and the pewter and the saucepans did not shine. The window-panes were dull. The house linen was unhemmed.

One evening Joseph sat in a meditative mood over the fire, looking into the red embers, and what was unusual with him, he did not speak.

Anna was inclined to take umbrage at this, when all at once he looked round at her with his bright pleasant smile and said, "Annerl! I have been thinking. One thing is wanted to make us supremely happy—a baby in the house. It has not pleased God to send us one, so I propose that we both go on pilgrimage to Mariahilf to ask for one."

"Go yourself—I want no baby here," retorted Anna.

A few days after this, like a thunderbolt out of a clear sky, came the great affliction on Anna of her husband's death.

Joseph had been found shot in the mountains. He was quite dead. The bullet had pierced his heart. He was brought home borne on green fir-boughs interlaced, by four fellow-jägers, and they carried him into his house. He had, in all probability, met his death at the hand of smugglers.

With a cry of horror and grief Anna threw herself on Joseph's body and kissed his pale lips. Now only did she realise how deeply all along she had loved him—now that she had lost him.

Joseph was laid in his coffin preparatory to the interment on the morrow. A crucifix and two candles stood at his head on a little table covered with a white cloth. On a stool at his feet was a bowl containing holy water and a sprig of rue.

A neighbour had volunteered to keep company with Anna during the night, but she had impatiently, without speaking, repelled the offer. She would spend the last night that he was above ground alone with her dead—alone with her thoughts.

And what were those thoughts?

Now she remembered how indifferent she had been to his wishes, how careless of his comforts; how little she had valued his love, had appreciated his cheerfulness, his kindness, his forbearance, his equable temper.

Now she recalled studied coldness on her part, sharp words, mortifying gestures, outbursts of unreasoning and unreasonable petulance.

Now she recalled Joseph scattering nuts among the children, addressing kind words to old crones, giving wholesome advice to giddy youths.

She remembered now little endearments shown to her, the presents brought her from the fair, the efforts made to cheer her with his pleasant stories and quaint jokes. She heard again his cheerful voice as he strove to interest her in his adventures of the chase.

As she thus sat silent, numbed by her sorrow, in the faint light cast by the two candles, with the shadow of the coffin lying black on the floor at her feet, she heard a stumping without; then a hand was laid on the latch, the door was timidly opened, and in upon his crutches came the crippled boy. He looked wistfully at her, but she made no sign, and then he hobbled to the coffin and burst into tears, and stooped and kissed the brow of his dead friend.

Leaning on his crutches, he took his rosary and said the prayers for the rest of her and his Joseph's soul; then shuffled awkwardly to the foot, dipped the spray of rue, and sprinkled the dead with the blessed water.

Next moment the ungainly creature was stumping forth, but after he had passed through the door, he turned, looked once more towards the dead, put his hand to his lips, and wafted to it his final farewell.

Anna now took her beads and tried to pray, but her prayers would not leave her lips; they were choked and driven back by the thoughts which crowded up and bewildered her. The chain fell from her fingers upon her lap, lay there neglected, and then slipped to the floor. How the time passed she knew not, neither did she care. The clock ticked, and she heard it not; the hours sounded, and she regarded them not till in at her ear and through her brain came clear the call of the wooden cuckoo announcing midnight.

Her eyes had been closed. Now suddenly she was roused, and they opened and saw that all was changed.

The coffin was gone, but by her instead was the cradle that years ago Joseph had brought home, and which she had chopped up for firewood. And now in that cradle lay a babe asleep, and with her foot she rocked it, and found a strange comfort in so doing.

She was conscious of no sense of surprise, only a great welling up of joy in her heart. Presently she heard a feeble whimper and saw a stirring in the cradle; little hands were put forth gropingly. Then she stooped and lifted the child to her lap, and clasped it to her heart. Oh, how lovely was that tiny creature! Oh, how sweet in her ears its appealing cry! As she held it to her bosom the warm hands touched her throat, and the little lips were pressed to her bosom. She pressed it to her. She had entered into a new world, a world of love and light and beauty and happiness unspeakable. Oh! the babe—the babe—the babe! She laughed and cried, and cried and laughed and sobbed for very exuberance of joy. It brought warmth to her heart, it made every vein tingle, it ingrained her brain with pride. It was hers!—her own!—

her very own! She could have been content to spend an eternity thus, with that little one close, close to her heart.

Then as suddenly all faded away—the child in her arms was gone as a shadow; her tears congealed, her heart was cramped, and a voice spoke within her: "It is not, because you would not. You cast the soul away, and it went over the mill-wheel."

Wild with terror, uttering a despairing cry, she started up, straining her arms after the lost child, and grasping nothing. She looked about her. The light of the candles flickered over the face of her dead Joseph. And tick, tick, tick went the clock.

She could endure this no more. She opened the door to leave the room, and stepped into the outer chamber and cast herself into a chair. And lo! it was no more night. The sun, the red evening sun, shone in at the window, and on the sill were pots of pinks and mignonette that filled the air with fragrance.

And there at her side stood a little girl with shining fair hair, and the evening sun was on it like the glory about a saint. The child raised its large blue eyes to her, pure innocent eyes, and said: "Mother, may I say my Catechism and prayers before I go to bed?"

Then Anna answered and said: "Oh, my darling! My dearest Bärbchen! All the Catechism is comprehended in this: Love God, fear God, always do what is your duty. Do His will, and do not seek only your own pleasure and ease. And this will give you peace—peace—peace."

The little girl knelt and laid her golden head on her folded hands upon Anna's knee and began: "God bless dear father, and mother, and all my dear brothers and sisters."

Instantly a sharp pang as a knife went through the heart of Anna, and she cried: "Thou hast no father and no mother and no brothers and no sisters, for thou art not, because I would not have thee. I cast away thy soul, and it went over the mill-wheel."

The cuckoo called one. The child had vanished. But the door was thrown open, and in the doorway stood a young couple—one a youth with fair hair and the down of a moustache on his lip, and oh, in face so like to the dead Joseph. He held by the hand a girl, in black bodice and with white sleeves, looking modestly on the ground. At once Anna knew what this signified. It was her son Florian come to announce that he was engaged, and to ask his mother's sanction.

Then said the young man, as he came forward leading the girl: "Mother, sweetest mother, this is Susie, the baker's daughter, and child of your old and dear friend Vronie. We love one another; we have loved since we were little children together at school, and did our lessons out of one book, sitting on one bench. And, mother, the bakehouse is to be passed on to me and to Susie, and I shall bake for all the parish. The good Jesus fed the multitude, distributing the loaves through the hands of His apostles. And I shall be His minister feeding His people here. Mother, give us your blessing."

Then Florian and the girl knelt to Anna, and with tears of happiness in her eyes she raised her hands over them. But ere she could touch them all had vanished. The room was dark, and a voice spake within her: "There is no Florian; there would have been, but you would not. You cast his soul into the water, and it passed away for ever over the mill-wheel."

In an agony of terror Anna sprang from her seat. She could not endure the room, the air stifled her; her brain was on fire. She rushed to the back door that opened on a kitchen garden, where grew the pot-herbs and cabbages for use, tended by Joseph when he returned from his work in the mountains.

But she came forth on a strange scene. She was on a battlefield. The air was charged with smoke and the smell of gunpowder. The roar of cannon and the rattle of musketry, the cries of the wounded, and shouts of encouragement rang in her ears in a confused din.

As she stood, panting, her hands to her breast, staring with wondering eyes, before her charged past a battalion of soldiers, and she knew by their uniforms that they were Bavarians. One of them, as he passed, turned his face towards her; it was the face of an Arler, fired with enthusiasm, she knew it; it was that of her son Fritz.

Then came a withering volley, and many of the gallant fellows fell, among them he who carried the standard. Instantly, Fritz snatched it from his hand, waved it over his head, shouted, "Charge, brothers, fill up the ranks! Charge, and the day is ours!"

Then the remnant closed up and went forward with bayonets fixed, tramp, tramp. Again an explosion of firearms and a dense cloud of smoke rolled before her and she could not see the result.

She waited, quivering in every limb, holding her breath—hoping, fearing, waiting. And as the smoke cleared she saw men carrying to the rear one who had been wounded, and in his hand he grasped the flag. They laid him at Anna's feet, and she recognised that it was her Fritz. She fell on her knees, and snatching the kerchief from her throat and breast, strove to stanch the blood that welled from his heart. He looked up into her eyes, with such love in them as made her choke with emotion, and he said faintly: "Mütterchen, do not grieve for me; we have stormed the redoubt, the day is ours. Be of good cheer. They fly, they fly, those French rascals! Mother, remember me—I die for the dear Fatherland."

And a comrade standing by said: "Do not give way to your grief, Anna Arler; your son has died the death of a hero."

Then she stooped over him, and saw the glaze of death in his eyes, and his lips moved. She bent her ear to them and caught the words: "I am not, because you would not. There is no Fritz; you cast my soul into the brook and I was carried over the mill-wheel."

All passed away, the smell of the powder, the roar of the cannon, the volumes of smoke, the cry of the battle, all—to a dead hush. Anna staggered to her feet, and turned to go back to her cottage, and as she opened the door, heard the cuckoo call two.

But, as she entered, she found herself to be, not in her own room and house—she had strayed into another, and she found herself not in a lone chamber, not in her desolate home, but in the midst of a strange family scene.

A woman, a mother, was dying. Her head reposed on her husband's breast as he sat on the bed and held her in his arms.

The man had grey hair, his face was overflowed with tears, and his eyes rested with an expression of devouring love on her whom he supported, and whose brow he now and again bent over to kiss.

About the bed were gathered her children, ay, and also her grandchildren, quite young, looking on with solemn, wondering eyes on the last throes of her whom they had learned to cling to and love with all the fervour of their simple hearts. One mite held her doll, dangling by the arm, and the forefinger of her other hand was in her mouth. Her eyes were brimming, and sobs came from her infant breast. She did not understand what was being taken from her, but she wept in sympathy with the rest.

Kneeling by the bed was the eldest daughter of the expiring woman, reciting the Litany of the Dying, and the sons and another daughter and a daughter-in-law repeated the responses in voices broken with tears.

When the recitation of the prayers ceased, there ensued for a while a great stillness, and all eyes rested on the dying woman. Her lips moved, and she poured forth her last petitions, that left her as rising flakes of fire, kindled by her pure and ardent soul. "O God, comfort and bless my dear husband, and ever keep Thy watchful guard over my children and my children's children, that they may walk in the way that leads to Thee, and that in Thine own good time we may all—all be gathered in Thy Paradise together, united for evermore. Amen."

A spasm contracted Anna's heart. This woman with ecstatic, upturned gaze, this woman breathing forth her peaceful soul on her husband's breast, was her own daughter Elizabeth, and in the fine outline of her features was Joseph's profile.

All again was hushed. The father slowly rose and quitted his position on the bed, gently laid the head on the pillow, put one hand over the eyes that still looked up to heaven, and with the fingers of the other tenderly arranged the straggling hair on each side of the brow. Then standing and turning to the rest, with a subdued voice he said: "My children, it has pleased the Lord to take to Himself your dear mother and my faithful companion. The Lord's will be done."

Then ensued a great burst of weeping, and Anna's eyes brimmed till she could see no more. The church bell began to toll for a departing spirit. And following each stroke there came to her, as the after-clang of the boom: "There is not, there has not been, an Elizabeth. There would have been all this—but thou wouldest it not. For the soul of thy Elizabeth thou didst send down the mill-stream and over the wheel."

Frantic with shame, with sorrow, not knowing what she did, or whither she went, Anna made for the front door of the house, ran forth and stood in the village square.

To her unutterable amazement it was vastly changed. Moreover, the sun was shining brightly, and it gleamed over a new parish church, of cut white stone, very stately, with a gilded spire, with windows of wondrous lacework. Flags were flying, festoons of flowers hung everywhere. A triumphal arch of leaves and young birch trees was at the graveyard gate. The square was crowded with the peasants, all in their holiday attire.

Silent, Anna stood and looked around. And as she stood she heard the talk of the people about her.

One said: "It is a great thing that Johann von Arler has done for his native village. But see, he is a good man, and he is a great architect."

"But why," asked another, "do you call him Von Arler? He was the son of that Joseph the Jäger who was killed by the smugglers in the mountains."

"That is true. But do you not know that the king has ennobled him? He has done such great things in the Residenz. He built the new Town Hall, which is thought to be the finest thing in Bavaria. He added a new wing to the Palace, and he has rebuilt very many churches, and designed mansions for the rich citizens and the nobles. But although he is such a famous man his heart is in the right place. He never forgets that he was born in Siebenstein. Look what a beautiful house he has built for himself and his family on the mountain-side. He is there in summer, and it is furnished magnificently. But he will not suffer the old, humble Arler cottage here to be meddled with. They say that he values it above gold. And this is the new church he has erected in his native village—that is good."

"Oh! he is a good man is Johann; he was always a good and serious boy, and never happy without a pencil in his hand. You mark what I say. Some day hence, when he is dead, there will be a statue erected in his honour here in this market-place, to commemorate the one famous man that has been produced by Siebenstein. But see—see! Here he comes to the dedication of the new church."

Then, through the throng advanced a blonde, middle-aged man, with broad forehead, clear, bright blue eyes, and a flowing light beard. All the men present plucked off their hats to him, and made way for him as he advanced. But, full of smiles, he had a hand and a warm pressure, and a kindly word and a question as to family concerns, for each who was near.

All at once his eye encountered that of Anna. A flash of recognition and joy kindled it up, and, extending his arms, he thrust his way towards her, crying: "My mother! my own mother!"

Then—just as she was about to be folded to his heart, all faded away, and a voice said in her soul: "He is no son of thine, Anna Arler. He is not, because thou wouldest not. He might have been, God had so purposed; but thou madest His purpose of none effect. Thou didst send his soul over the mill-wheel."

And then faintly, as from a far distance, sounded in her ear the call of the cuckoo—three.

The magnificent new church had shrivelled up to the original mean little edifice Anna had known all her life. The square was deserted, the cold faint glimmer of coming dawn was visible over the eastern mountain-tops, but stars still shone in the sky.

With a cry of pain, like a wounded beast, Anna ran hither and thither seeking a refuge, and then fled to the one home and resting-place of the troubled soul—the church. She thrust open the swing-door, pushed in, sped over the uneven floor, and flung herself on her knees before the altar.

But see! before that altar stood a priest in a vestment of black-and-silver; and a serving-boy knelt on his right hand on a lower stage. The candles were lighted, for the priest was about to say Mass. There was a rustling of feet, a sound as of people entering, and many were kneeling, shortly after, on each side of Anna, and still they came on; she turned about and looked and saw a great crowd pressing in, and strange did it seem to her eyes that all—men, women, and children, young and old—seemed to bear in their faces something, a trace only in many, of the Arler or the Voss features. And the little serving-boy, as he shifted his position, showed her his profile—it was like her little brother who had died when he was sixteen.

Then the priest turned himself about, and said, "Oremus." And she knew him—he was her own son—her Joseph, named after his dear father.

The Mass began, and proceeded to the "Sursum corda"—"Lift up your hearts!"—when the celebrant stood facing the congregation with extended arms, and all responded: "We lift them up unto the Lord."

But then, instead of proceeding with the accustomed invocation, he raised his hands high above his head, with the palms towards the congregation, and in a loud, stern voice exclaimed—

"Cursed is the unfruitful field!"

"Amen."

"Cursed is the barren tree!"

"Amen."

"Cursed is the empty house!"

"Amen."

"Cursed is the fishless lake!"

"Amen."

"Forasmuch as Anna Arler, born Voss, might have been the mother of countless generations, as the sand of the seashore for number, as the stars of heaven for brightness, of generations unto the end of time, even of all of us now gathered together here, but she would not—therefore shall she be alone, with none to comfort her; sick, with none to minister to her; broken in heart, with none to bind up her wounds; feeble, and none to stay her up; dead, and none to pray for her, for she would not—she shall have an unforgotten and unforgettable past, and have no future; remorse, but no hope; she shall have tears, but no laughter—for she would not. Woe! woe! woe!"

He lowered his hands, and the tapers were extinguished, the celebrant faded as a vision of the night, the server vanished as an incense-cloud, the congregation disappeared, melting into shadows, and then from shadows to nothingness, without stirring from their places, and without a sound.

And Anna, with a scream of despair, flung herself forward with her face on the pavement, and her hands extended.

* * * * *

Two years ago, during the first week in June, an English traveller arrived at Siebenstein and put up at the "Krone," where, as he was tired and hungry, he ordered an early supper. When that was discussed, he strolled forth into the village square, and leaned against the wall of the churchyard. The sun had set in the valley, but the mountain-peaks were still in the glory of its rays, surrounding the place as a golden crown. He lighted a cigar, and, looking into the cemetery, observed there an old woman, bowed over a grave, above which stood a cross, inscribed "Joseph Arler," and she was tending the flowers on it, and laying over the arms of the cross a little wreath of heart's-ease or pansy. She had in her hand a small basket. Presently she rose and walked towards the gate, by which stood the traveller.

As she passed, he said kindly to her: "Grüss Gott, Mütterchen."

She looked steadily at him and replied: "Honoured sir! that which is past may be repented of, but can never be undone!" and went on her way.

He was struck with her face. He had never before seen one so full of boundless sorrow—almost of despair.

His eyes followed her as she walked towards the mill-stream, and there she took her place on the wooden bridge that crossed it, leaning over the handrail, and looking down into the water. An impulse of curiosity and of interest led him to follow her at a distance, and he saw her pick a flower, a pansy, out of her basket, and drop it into the current, which caught and carried it forward. Then she took a second, and allowed it to fall into the water. Then, after an interval, a third—a fourth; and he counted seven in all. After that she bowed her head on her hands; her grey hair fell over them, and she broke into a paroxysm of weeping.

The traveller, standing by the stream, saw the seven pansies swept down, and one by one pass over the revolving wheel and vanish.

He turned himself about to return to his inn, when, seeing a grave peasant near, he asked: "Who is that poor old woman who seems so broken down with sorrow?"

"That," replied the man, "is the Mother of Pansies."

"The Mother of Pansies!" he repeated.

"Well—it is the name she has acquired in the place. Actually, she is called Anna Arler, and is a widow. She was the wife of one Joseph Arler, a jäger, who was shot by smugglers. But that is many, many years ago. She is not right in her head, but she is harmless. When her husband was brought home dead, she insisted on being left alone in the night by him, before he was buried alone,—with his coffin. And what happened in that night no one knows. Some affirm that she saw ghosts. I do not know—she may have had Thoughts. The French word for these flowers is *pensées*—thoughts—and she will have none others. When they are in her garden she collects them, and does as she has done now. When she has none, she goes about to her neighbours and begs them. She comes here every evening and throws in seven—just seven, no more and no less—and then weeps as one whose heart would split. My wife on one occasion offered her forget-me-nots. 'No,' she said; 'I cannot send forget-me-nots after those who never were, I can send only Pansies.'"

VI. — THE RED-HAIRED GIRL
A WIFE'S STORY

IN 1876 we took a house in one of the best streets and parts of B——. I do not give the name of the street or the number of the house, because the circumstances that occurred in that place were such as to make people nervous, and shy—unreasonably so—of taking those lodgings, after reading our experiences therein.

We were a small family—my husband, a grown-up daughter, and myself; and we had two maids—a cook, and the other was house- and parlourmaid in one. We had not been a fortnight in the house before my daughter said to me one morning: "Mamma, I do not like Jane"—that was our house-parlourmaid.

"Why so?" I asked. "She seems respectable, and she does her work systematically. I have no fault to find with her, none whatever."

"She may do her work," said Bessie, my daughter, "but I dislike inquisitiveness."

"Inquisitiveness!" I exclaimed. "What do you mean? Has she been looking into your drawers?"

"No, mamma, but she watches me. It is hot weather now, and when I am in my room, occasionally, I leave my door open whilst writing a letter, or doing any little bit of needlework, and then I am almost certain to hear her outside. If I turn sharply round, I see her slipping out of sight. It is most annoying. I really was unaware that I was such an interesting personage as to make it worth anyone's while to spy out my proceedings."

"Nonsense, my dear. You are sure it is Jane?"

"Well—I suppose so." There was a slight hesitation in her voice. "If not Jane, who can it be?"

"Are you sure it is not cook?"

"Oh, no, it is not cook; she is busy in the kitchen. I have heard her there, when I have gone outside my room upon the landing, after having caught that girl watching me."

"If you have caught her," said I, "I suppose you spoke to her about the impropriety of her conduct."

"Well, caught is the wrong word. I have not actually *caught* her at it. Only to-day I distinctly heard her at my door, and I saw her back as she turned to run away, when I went towards her."

"But you followed her, of course?"

"Yes, but I did not find her on the landing when I got outside."

"Where was she, then?"

"I don't know."

"But did you not go and see?"

"She slipped away with astonishing celerity," said Bessie.

"I can take no steps in the matter. If she does it again, speak to her and remonstrate."

"But I never have a chance. She is gone in a moment."

"She cannot get away so quickly as all that."

"Somehow she does."

"And you are sure it is Jane?" again I asked; and again she replied: "If not Jane, who else can it be? There is no one else in the house."

So this unpleasant matter ended, for the time. The next intimation of something of the sort proceeded from another quarter—in fact, from Jane herself. She came to me some days later and said, with some embarrassment in her tone—

"If you please, ma'am, if I do not give satisfaction, I would rather leave the situation."

"Leave!" I exclaimed. "Why, I have not given you the slightest cause. I have not found fault with you for anything as yet, have I, Jane? On the contrary, I have been much pleased with the thoroughness of your work. And you are always tidy and obliging."

"It isn't that, ma'am; but I don't like being watched whatever I do."

"Watched!" I repeated. "What do you mean? You surely do not suppose that I am running after you when you are engaged on your occupations. I assure you I have other and more important things to do."

"No, ma'am, I don't suppose you do."

"Then who watches you?"

"I think it must be Miss Bessie."

"Miss Bessie!" I could say no more, I was so astounded.

"Yes, ma'am. When I am sweeping out a room, and my back is turned, I hear her at the door; and when I turn myself about, I just catch a glimpse of her running away. I see her skirts——"

"Miss Bessie is above doing anything of the sort."

"If it is not Miss Bessie, who is it, ma'am?"

There was a tone of indecision in her voice.

"My good Jane," said I, "set your mind at rest. Miss Bessie could not act as you suppose. Have you seen her on these occasions and assured yourself that it is she?"

"No, ma'am, I've not, so to speak, seen her face; but I know it ain't cook, and I'm sure it ain't you, ma'am; so who else can it be?"

I considered for some moments, and the maid stood before me in dubious mood.

"You say you saw her skirts. Did you recognise the gown? What did she wear?"

"It was a light cotton print—more like a maid's morning dress."

"Well, set your mind at ease; Miss Bessie has not got such a frock as you describe."

"I don't think she has," said Jane; "but there was someone at the door, watching me, who ran away when I turned myself about."

"Did she run upstairs or down?"

"I don't know. I did go out on the landing, but there was no one there. I'm sure it wasn't cook, for I heard her clattering the dishes down in the kitchen at the time."

"Well, Jane, there is some mystery in this. I will not accept your notice; we will let matters stand over till we can look into this complaint of yours and discover the rights of it."

"Thank you, ma'am. I'm very comfortable here, but it is unpleasant to suppose that one is not trusted, and is spied on wherever one goes and whatever one is about."

A week later, after dinner one evening, when Bessie and I had quitted the table and left my husband to his smoke, Bessie said to me, when we were in the drawing-room together: "Mamma, it is not Jane."

"What is not Jane?" I asked.

"It is not Jane who watches me."

"Who can it be, then?"

"I don't know."

"And how is it that you are confident that you are not being observed by Jane?"

"Because I have seen her—that is to say, her head."

"When? where?"

"Whilst dressing for dinner, I was before the glass doing my hair, when I saw in the mirror someone behind me. I had only the two candles lighted on the table, and the room was otherwise dark. I thought I heard someone stirring—just the sort of stealthy step I have come to recognise as having troubled me so often. I did not turn, but looked steadily before me into the glass, and I could see reflected therein someone—a woman with red hair. Then I moved from my place quickly. I heard steps of some person hurrying away, but I saw no one then."

"The door was open?"

"No, it was shut."

"But where did she go?"

"I do not know, mamma. I looked everywhere in the room and could find no one. I have been quite upset. I cannot tell what to think of this. I feel utterly unhinged."

"I noticed at table that you did not appear well, but I said nothing about it. Your father gets so alarmed, and fidgets and fusses, if he thinks that there is anything the matter with you. But this is a most extraordinary story."

"It is an extraordinary fact," said Bessie.

"You have searched your room thoroughly?"

"I have looked into every corner."

"And there is no one there?"

"No one. Would you mind, mamma, sleeping with me to-night? I am so frightened. Do you think it can be a ghost?"

"Ghost? Fiddlesticks!"

I made some excuse to my husband and spent the night in Bessie's room. There was no disturbance that night of any sort, and although my daughter was excited and unable to sleep till long after midnight, she did fall into refreshing slumber at last, and in the morning said to me: "Mamma, I think I must have fancied that I saw something in the glass. I dare say my nerves were over-wrought."

I was greatly relieved to hear this, and I arrived at much the same conclusion as did Bessie, but was again bewildered, and my mind unsettled by Jane, who came to me just before lunch, when I was alone, and said—

"Please, ma'am, it's only fair to say, but it's not Miss Bessie."

"What is not Miss Bessie? I mean, who is not Miss Bessie?"

"Her as is spying on me."

"I told you it could not be she. Who is it?"

"Please, ma'am, I don't know. It's a red-haired girl."

"But, Jane, be serious. There is no red-haired girl in the house."

"I know there ain't, ma'am. But for all that, she spies on me."

"Be reasonable, Jane," I said, disguising the shock her words produced on me. "If there be no red-haired girl in the house, how can you have one watching you?"

"I don't know; but one does."

"How do you know that she is red-haired?"

"Because I have seen her."

"When?"

"This morning."

"Indeed?"

"Yes, ma'am. I was going upstairs, when I heard steps coming softly after me—the backstairs, ma'am; they're rather dark and steep, and there's no carpet on them, as on the front stairs, and I was sure I heard someone following me; so I twisted about, thinking it might be cook, but it wasn't. I saw a young woman in a print dress, and the light as came from the window at the side fell on her head, and it was carrots—reg'lar carrots."

"Did you see her face?"

"No, ma'am; she put her arm up and turned and ran downstairs, and I went after her, but I never found her."

"You followed her—how far?"

"To the kitchen. Cook was there. And I said to cook, says I: 'Did you see a girl come this way?' And she said, short-like: 'No.'"

"And cook saw nothing at all?"

"Nothing. She didn't seem best pleased at my axing. I suppose I frightened her, as I'd been telling her about how I was followed and spied on."

I mused a moment only, and then said solemnly—

"Jane, what you want is a *pill*. You are suffering from hallucinations. I know a case very much like yours; and take my word for it that, in your condition of liver or digestion, a pill is a sovereign remedy. Set your mind at rest; this is a mere delusion, caused by pressure on the optic nerve. I will give you a pill to-night when you go to bed, another to-morrow, a third on the day after, and that will settle the red-haired girl. You will see no more of her."

"You think so, ma'am?"

"I am sure of it."

On consideration, I thought it as well to mention the matter to the cook, a strange, reserved woman, not given to talking, who did her work admirably, but whom, for some inexplicable reason, I did not like. If I had considered a little further as to how to broach the subject, I should perhaps have proved more successful; but by not doing so I rushed the question and obtained no satisfaction.

I had gone down to the kitchen to order dinner, and the difficult question had arisen how to dispose of the scraps from yesterday's joint.

"Rissoles, ma'am?"

"No," said I, "not rissoles. Your master objects to them."

"Then perhaps croquettes?"

"They are only rissoles in disguise."

"Perhaps cottage pie?"

"No; that is inorganic rissole, a sort of protoplasm out of which rissoles are developed."

"Then, ma'am, I might make a hash."

"Not an ordinary, barefaced, rudimentary hash?"

"No, ma'am, with French mushrooms, or truffles, or tomatoes."

"Well—yes—perhaps. By the way, talking of tomatoes, who is that red-haired girl who has been about the house?"

"Can't say, ma'am."

I noticed at once that the eyes of the cook contracted, her lips tightened, and her face assumed a half-defiant, half-terrified look.

"You have not many friends in this place, have you, cook?"

"No, ma'am, none."

"Then who can she be?"

"Can't say, ma'am."

"You can throw no light on the matter? It is very unsatisfactory having a person about the house—and she has been seen upstairs—of whom one knows nothing."

"No doubt, ma'am."

"And you cannot enlighten me?"

"She is no friend of mine."

"Nor is she of Jane's. Jane spoke to me about her. Has she remarked concerning this girl to you?"

"Can't say, ma'am, as I notice all Jane says. She talks a good deal."

"You see, there must be someone who is a stranger and who has access to this house. It is most awkward."

"Very so, ma'am."

I could get nothing more from the cook. I might as well have talked to a log; and, indeed, her face assumed a wooden look as I continued to speak to her on the matter. So I sighed, and said—

"Very well, hash with tomato," and went upstairs.

A few days later the house-parlourmaid said to me, "Please, ma'am, may I have another pill?"

"Pill!" I exclaimed. "Why?"

"Because I have seen her again. She was behind the curtains, and I caught her putting out her red head to look at me."

"Did you see her face?"

"No; she up with her arm over it and scuttled away."

"This is strange. I do not think I have more than two podophyllin pills left in the box, but to those you are welcome. Only I should recommend a different treatment. Instead of taking them yourself, the moment you see, or fancy that you see, the red-haired girl, go at her with the box and threaten to administer the pills to her. That will rout her, if anything will."

"But she will not stop for the pills."

"The threat of having them forced on her every time she shows herself will disconcert her. Conceive, I am supposing, that on each occasion Miss Bessie, or I, were to meet you on the stairs, in a room, on the landing, in the hall, we were to rush on you and force, let us say, castor-oil globules between your lips. You would give notice at once."

"Yes; so I should, ma'am."

"Well, try this upon the red-haired girl. It will prove infallible."

"Thank you, ma'am; what you say seems reasonable."

Whether Bessie saw more of the puzzling apparition, I cannot say. She spoke no further on the matter to me; but that may have been so as to cause me no further uneasiness. I was unable to resolve the question to my own satisfaction—whether what had been seen was a real person, who obtained access to the house in some unaccountable manner, or whether it was, what I have called it, an apparition.

As far as I could ascertain, nothing had been taken away. The movements of the red-haired girl were not those of one who sought to pilfer. They seemed to me rather those of one not in her right mind; and on this supposition I made inquiries in the neighbourhood as to the existence in our street, in any of the adjoining houses, of a person wanting in her wits, who was suffered to run about at will. But I could obtain no information that at all threw light on a point to me so perplexing.

Hitherto I had not mentioned the topic to my husband. I knew so well that I should obtain no help from him, that I made no effort to seek it. He would "Pish!" and "Pshaw!" and make some slighting reference to women's intellects, and not further trouble himself about the matter.

But one day, to my great astonishment, he referred to it himself.

"Julia," said he, "do you observe how I have cut myself in shaving?"

"Yes, dear," I replied. "You have cotton-wool sticking to your jaw, as if you were growing a white whisker on one side."

"It bled a great deal," said he.

"I am sorry to hear it."

"And I mopped up the blood with the new toilet-cover."

"Never!" I exclaimed. "You haven't been so foolish as to do that?"

"Yes. And that is just like you. You are much more concerned about your toilet-cover being stained than about my poor cheek which is gashed."

"You were very clumsy to do it," was all I could say. Married people are not always careful to preserve the amenities in private life. It is a pity, but it is so.

"It was due to no clumsiness on my part," said he; "though I do allow my nerves have been so shaken, broken, by married life, that I cannot always command my hand, as was the case when I was a bachelor. But this time it was due to that new, stupid, red-haired servant you have introduced into the house without consulting me or my pocket."

"Red-haired servant!" I echoed.

"Yes, that red-haired girl I have seen about. She thrusts herself into my study in a most offensive and objectionable way. But the climax of all was this morning, when I was shaving. I stood in my shirt before the glass, and had lathered my face, and was engaged on my right jaw, when that red-haired girl rushed between me and the mirror with both her elbows up, screening her face with her arms, and her head bowed. I started back, and in so doing cut myself."

"Where did she come from?"

"How can I tell? I did not expect to see anyone."

"Then where did she go?"

"I do not know; I was too concerned about my bleeding jaw to look about me. That girl must be dismissed."

"I wish she could be dismissed," I said.

"What do you mean?"

I did not answer my husband, for I really did not know what answer to make.

I was now the only person in the house who had not seen the red-haired girl, except possibly the cook, from whom I could gather nothing, but whom I suspected of knowing more concerning this mysterious apparition than she chose to admit. That what had been seen by Bessie and Jane was a supernatural visitant, I now felt convinced, seeing that it had appeared to that least imaginative and most commonplace of all individuals, my husband. By no mental process could he have been got to imagine anything. He certainly did see this red-haired girl, and that no living, corporeal maid had been in his dressing-room at the time I was perfectly certain.

I was soon, however, myself to be included in the number of those before whose eyes she appeared. It was in this wise.

Cook had gone out to do some marketing. I was in the breakfast-room, when, wanting a funnel to fill a little phial of brandy I always keep on the washstand in case of emergencies, I went to the head of the kitchen stairs, to descend and fetch what I required. Then I was aware of a great clattering of the fire-irons below, and a banging about of the boiler and grate. I went down the steps very hastily and entered the kitchen.

There I saw a figure of a short, set girl in a shabby cotton gown, not over clean, and slipshod, stooping before the stove, and striking the fender with the iron poker. She had fiery red hair, very untidy.

I uttered an exclamation.

Instantly she dropped the poker, and covering her face with her arms, uttering a strange, low cry, she dashed round the kitchen table, making nearly the complete circuit, and then swept past me, and I heard her clattering up the kitchen stairs.

I was too much taken aback to follow. I stood as one petrified. I felt dazed and unable to trust either my eyes or my ears.

Something like a minute must have elapsed before I had sufficiently recovered to turn and leave the kitchen. Then I ascended slowly and, I confess, nervously. I was fearful lest I should find the red-haired girl cowering against the wall, and that I should have to pass her.

But nothing was to be seen. I reached the hall, and saw that no door was open from it except that of the breakfast-room. I entered and thoroughly examined every recess, corner, and conceivable hiding-place, but could find no one there. Then I ascended the staircase, with my hand on the balustrade, and searched all the rooms on the first floor, without the least success. Above were the servants' apartments, and I now resolved on mounting to them. Here the staircase was uncarpeted. As I was ascending, I heard Jane at work in her room. I then heard her come out hastily upon the landing. At the same moment, with a rush past me, uttering the same moan, went the red-haired girl. I am sure I felt her skirts sweep my dress. I did not notice her till she was close upon me, but I did distinctly see her as she passed. I turned, and saw no more.

I at once mounted to the landing where was Jane.

"What is it?" I asked.

"Please, ma'am, I've seen the red-haired girl again, and I did as you recommended. I went at her rattling the pill-box, and she turned and ran downstairs. Did you see her, ma'am, as you came up?"

"How inexplicable!" I said. I would not admit to Jane that I had seen the apparition.

The situation remained unaltered for a week. The mystery was unsolved. No fresh light had been thrown on it. I did not again see or hear anything out of the way; nor did my husband, I presume, for he made no further remarks relative to the extra servant who had caused him so much annoyance. I presume he supposed that I had summarily dismissed her. This I conjectured from a smugness assumed by his face, such as it always acquired when he had carried a point against me—which was not often.

However, one evening, abruptly, we had a new sensation. My husband, Bessie, and I were at dinner, and we were partaking of the soup, Jane standing by, waiting to change our plates and to remove the tureen, when we dropped our spoons, alarmed by fearful screams issuing from the kitchen. By the way, characteristically, my husband finished his soup before he laid down the spoon and said—

"Good gracious! What is that?"

Bessie, Jane, and I were by this time at the door, and we rushed together to the kitchen stairs, and one after the other ran down them. I was the first to enter, and I saw cook wrapped in flames, and a paraffin lamp on the floor broken, and the blazing oil flowing over it.

I had sufficient presence of mind to catch up the cocoanut matting which was not impregnated with the oil, and to throw it round cook, wrap her tightly in it, and force her down on the floor where not overflowed by the oil. I held her thus, and Bessie succoured me. Jane was too frightened to do other than scream. The cries of the burnt woman were terrible. Presently my husband appeared.

"Dear me! Bless me! Good gracious!" he said.

"You go away and fetch a doctor," I called to him; "you can be of no possible service here—you only get in our way."

"But the dinner?"

"Bother the dinner! Run for a surgeon."

In a little while we had removed the poor woman to her room, she shrieking the whole way upstairs; and, when there, we laid her on the bed, and kept her folded in the cocoanut matting till a medical man arrived, in spite of her struggles to be free. My husband, on this occasion, acted with commendable promptness; but whether because he was impatient for the completion of his meal, or whether his sluggish nature was for once touched with human sympathy, it is not for me to say.

All I know is that, so soon as the surgeon was there, I dismissed Jane with "There, go and get your master the rest of his dinner, and leave us with cook."

The poor creature was frightfully burnt. She was attended to devotedly by Bessie and myself, till a nurse was obtained from the hospital. For hours she was as one mad with terror as much as with pain.

Next day she was quieter and sent for me. I hastened to her, and she begged the nurse to leave the room. I took a chair and seated myself by her bedside, and expressed my profound commiseration, and told her that I should like to know how the accident had taken place.

"Ma'am, it was the red-haired girl did it."

"The red-haired girl!"

"Yes, ma'am. I took a lamp to look how the fish was getting on, and all at once I saw her rush straight at me, and I—I backed, thinking she would knock me down, and the lamp fell over and smashed, and my clothes caught, and——"

"Oh, cook! you should not have taken the lamp."

"It's done. And she would never leave me alone till she had burnt or scalded me. You needn't be afraid—she don't haunt the house. It is *me* she has haunted, because of what I did to her."

"Then you know her?"

"She was in service with me, as kitchenmaid, at my last place, near Cambridge. I took a sort of hate against her, she was such a slattern and so inquisitive. She peeped into my letters, and turned out my box and drawers, she was ever prying; and when I spoke to her, she was that saucy! I reg'lar hated her. And one day she was kneeling by the stove, and I was there, too, and I suppose the devil possessed me, for I upset the boiler as was on the hot-plate right upon her, just as she looked up, and it poured over her face and bosom, and arms, and scalded her that dreadful, she died. And since then she has haunted me. But she'll do so no more. She won't trouble you further. She has done for me, as she has always minded to do, since I scalded her to death."

The unhappy woman did not recover.

"Dear me! no hope?" said my husband, when informed that the surgeon despaired of her. "And good cooks are so scarce. By the way, that red-haired girl?"

"Gone—gone for ever," I said.

VII. — A PROFESSIONAL SECRET

MR. LEVERIDGE was in a solicitor's office at Swanton. Mr. Leveridge had been brought up well by a sensible father and an excellent mother. His principles left nothing to be desired. His father was now dead, and his mother did not reside at Swanton, but near her own relations in another part of England. Joseph Leveridge was a mild, inoffensive man, with fair hair and a full head. He was so shy that he did not move in Society as he might have done had he been self-assertive. But he was fairly happy—not so happy as he might have been, for reasons to be shortly given.

Swanton was a small market-town, that woke into life every Friday, which was market-day, burst into boisterous levity at the Michaelmas fair, and then lapsed back into decorum; it was, except on Fridays, somnolent during the day and asleep at night.

Swanton was not a manufacturing town. It possessed one iron foundry and a brewery, so that it afforded little employment for the labouring classes, yet the labouring classes crowded into it, although cottage rents were high, because the farmers could not afford, owing to the hard times, to employ many hands on the land, and because their wives and daughters desired the distractions and dissipations of a town, and supposed that both were to be found in superfluity at Swanton.

There was a large town hall with a magistrates' court, where the bench sat every month once. The church, in the centre of the town, was an imposing structure of stone, very cold within. The presentation was in the hands of the Simeonite Trustees, so that the vicar was of the theological school—if that can be called a school where nothing is taught—called Evangelical. The services ever long and dismal. The Vicar slowly and impressively declaimed the prayers, preached lengthy sermons, and condemned the congregation to sing out of the Mitre hymnal.

The principal solicitor, Mr. Stork, was clerk of the petty sessions and registrar. He did a limited amount of legal work for the landed gentry round, was trustee to some widows and orphans, and was consulted by tottering yeomen as to their financial difficulties, lent them some money to relieve their immediate embarrassments, on the security of their land, which ultimately passed into his possession.

To this gentleman Mr. Leveridge had been articled. He had been induced to adopt the legal profession, not from any true vocation, but at the instigation of his mother, who had urged him to follow in the professional footsteps of his revered father. But the occupation was not one that accorded with the tastes of the young man, who, notwithstanding his apparent mildness and softness, was not deficient in brains. He was a shrewd observer, and was endowed with a redundant imagination.

From a child he had scribbled stories, and with his pencil had illustrated them; but this had brought upon him severe rebukes from his mother, who looked with disfavour on works of imagination, and his father had taken him across his knee, of course before he was adult, and had castigated him with the flat of the hairbrush for surreptitiously reading the *Arabian Nights*.

Mr. Leveridge's days passed evenly enough; there was some business coming into the office on Fridays, and none at all on Sundays, on which day he wrote a long and affectionate letter to his widowed mother.

He would have been a happy man, happy in a mild, lotus-eating way, but for three things. In the first place, he became conscious that he was not working in his proper vocation. He took no pleasure in engrossing deeds; indentures his soul abhorred. He knew himself to be capable of better things, and feared lest the higher faculties of his mind should become atrophied by lack of exercise. In the second place, he was not satisfied that his superior was a man of strict integrity. He had no reason whatever for supposing that anything dishonest went on in the office, but he had discovered that his "boss" was a daring and venturesome speculator, and he feared lest temptation should induce him to speculate with the funds of those to whom he acted as trustee. And Joseph, with his high sense of rectitude, was apprehensive lest some day something might there be done, which would cause a crash. Lastly, Joseph Leveridge had lost his heart. He was consumed by a hopeless passion for Miss Asphodel Vincent, a young lady with a small fortune of about £400 per annum, to whom Mr. Stork was guardian and trustee.

This young lady was tall, slender, willowy, had a sweet, Madonna-like face, and like Joseph himself was constitutionally shy; and she was unconscious of her personal and pecuniary attractions. She moved in the best society, she was taken up by the county people. No doubt she would be secured by the son of some squire, and settle down as Lady Bountiful in some parish; or else some wily curate with a moustache would step in and carry her off. But her bashfulness and her indifference to men's society had so far protected her. She loved her garden, cultivated herbaceous plants, and was specially addicted to a rockery in which she acclimatised flowers from the Alps.

As Mr. Stork was her guardian, she often visited the office, when Joseph flew, with heightened colour, to offer her a chair till Mr. Stork was disengaged. But conversation between them had never passed beyond generalities. Mr. Leveridge occasionally met her in his country walks, but never advanced in intimacy beyond raising his hat and remarking on the weather.

Probably it was the stimulus of this devouring and despairing passion which drove Mr. Leveridge to writing a novel, in which he could paint Asphodel, under another name, in all her perfections. She should move through his story diffusing an atmosphere of sweetness and saintliness, but he could not bring himself to provide her with a lover, and to conclude his romance with her union to a being of the male sex.

Impressed as he had been in early youth by the admonitions of his mother, and the applications of the hairbrush by his father, that the imagination was a dangerous and delusive gift, to be restrained, not indulged, he resolved that he would create no characters for his story, but make direct studies from life. Consequently, when the work was completed, it presented the most close portraits of a certain number of the residents in Swanton, and the town in which the scene was laid was very much like Swanton, though he called it Buzbury.

But to find a publisher was a more difficult work than to write the novel. Mr. Leveridge sent his MS. type-written to several firms, and it was declined by one after another. At last, however, it fell into the hands of an unusually discerning reader, who saw in it distinct tokens of ability. It was not one to appeal to the general public. It contained no blood-curdling episodes, no hair-breadth escapes, no risky situations; it was simply a transcript of life in a little English country town. Though not high-spiced to suit the vulgar taste, still the reader and the publisher considered that there was a discerning public, small and select, that relished good, honest work of the Jane Austen kind, and the latter resolved on risking the production. Accordingly he offered the author fifty pounds for the work, he buying all rights. Joseph Leveridge was overwhelmed at the munificence of the offer, and accepted it gratefully and with alacrity.

The next stage in the proceedings consisted in the revision of the proofs. And who that has not experienced it can judge of the sensation of exquisite delight afforded by this to the young author? After the correction of his romance—if romance such a prosaic tale can be called—in print, with characteristic modesty Leveridge insisted that his story should appear under an assumed name. What the name adopted was it does not concern the reader of this narrative to know. Some time now elapsed before the book appeared, at the usual publishing time, in October.

Eventually it came out, and Mr. Leveridge received his six copies, neatly and quietly bound in cloth. He cut and read one with avidity, and at once perceived that he had overlooked several typographical errors, and wrote to the publisher to beg that these might be corrected in the event of a second edition being called for.

On the morning following the publication and dissemination of the book, Joseph Leveridge lay in bed a little longer than usual, smiling in happy self-gratification at the thought that he had become an author. On the table by his bed stood his extinguished candle, his watch, and the book. He had looked at it the last thing before he closed his eyes in sleep. It was moreover the first thing that his eyes rested on when they opened. A fond mother could not have gazed on her new-born babe with greater pride and affection.

Whilst he thus lay and said to himself, "I really must—I positively must get up and dress!" he heard a stumping on the stairs, and a few moments later his door was burst open, and in came Major Dolgelly Jones, a retired officer, resident in Swanton, who had never before done him the honour of a call—and now he actually penetrated to Joseph's bedroom.

The major was hot in the face. He panted for breath, his cheeks quivered. The major was a man who, judging by what could be perceived of his intellectual gifts, could not have been a great acquisition to the Army. He was a man who never could have been trusted to act a brilliant part. He was a creature of routine, a martinet; and since his retirement to Swanton had been a passionate golf-player and nothing else.

"What do you mean, sir? What do you mean?" spluttered he, "by putting me into your book?"

"My book!" echoed Joseph, affecting surprise. "What book do you refer to?"

"Oh! it's all very well your assuming that air of injured innocence, your trying to evade my question. Your sheepish expression does not deceive me. Why—there is the book in question by your bedside."

"I have, I admit, been reading that novel, which has recently appeared."

"You wrote it. Everyone in Swanton knows it. I don't object to your writing a book; any fool can do that—especially a novel. What I do object to is your putting me into it."

"If I remember rightly," said Joseph, quaking under the bedclothes, and then wiping his upper lip on which a dew was forming, "If I remember aright, there is in it a major who plays golf, and does nothing else; but his name is Piper."

"What do I care about a name? It is I—I. You have put me in."

"Really, Major Jones, you have no justification in thus accusing me. The book does not bear my name on the back and title-page."

"Neither does the golfing retired military officer bear my name, but that does not matter. It is I myself. I am in your book. I would horsewhip you had I any energy left in me, but all is gone, gone with my personality into your book. Nothing is left of me—nothing but a body and a light tweed suit. I—I—have been taken out of myself and transferred to that——" he used a naughty word, "that book. How can I golf any more? Walk the links any more with any heart? How can I putt a ball and follow it up with any feeling of interest? I am but a carcass. My soul, my character, my individuality have been burgled. You have broken into my inside, and have despoiled me of my personality." And he began to cry.

"Possibly," suggested Mr. Leveridge, "the author might——"

"The author can do nothing. I have been robbed—my fine ethereal self has been purloined. I—Dolgelly Jones—am only an outside husk. You have despoiled me of my richest jewel—myself."

"I really can do nothing, major."

"I know you can do nothing, that is the pity of it. You have sucked all my spiritual being with its concomitants out of me, and cannot put it back again. *You have used me up.*"

Then, wringing his hands, the major left the room, stumped slowly downstairs, and quitted the house.

Joseph Leveridge rose from his bed and dressed in great perturbation of mind. Here was a condition of affairs on which he had not reckoned. He was so distracted in mind that he forgot to brush his teeth.

When he reached his little sitting-room he found that the table was laid for his breakfast, and that his landlady had just brought up the usual rashers of bacon and two boiled eggs. She was sobbing.

"What is the matter, Mrs. Baker?" asked Joseph. "Has Lasinia"—that was the name of the servant—"broken any more dishes?"

"Everything has happened," replied the woman; "you have taken away my character."

"I—I never did such a thing."

"Oh, yes, sir, you have. All the time you've been writing, I've felt it going out of me like perspiration, and now it is all in your book."

"My book!"

"Yes, sir, under the name of Mrs. Brooks. But law! sir, what is there in a name? You might have taken the name of Baker and used that as you likes. There be plenty of Bakers in England and the Colonies. But it's my character, sir, you've taken away, and shoved it into your book." Then the woman wiped her eyes with her apron.

"But really, Mrs. Baker, if there be a landlady in this novel of which you complain——"

"There is, and it is me."

"But it is a mere work of fiction."

"It is not a work of fiction, it is a work of fact, and that a cruel fact. What has a poor lorn widow like me got to boast of but her character? I'm sure I've done well by you, and never boiled your eggs hard—and to use me like this."

"Good gracious, dear Mrs. Baker!"

"Don't dear me, sir. If you had loved me, if you had been decently grateful for all I have done for you, and mended your socks too, you'd not have stolen my character from me, and put it into your book. Ah, sir! you have dealt by me what I call regular shameful, and not like a gentleman. You *have used me up.*"

Joseph was silent, cowed. He turned the rashers about on the dish with his fork in an abstracted manner. All desire to eat was gone from him.

Then the landlady went on: "And it's not me only as has to complain. There are three gentlemen outside, sitting on the doorstep, awaiting of you. And they say that there they will remain, till you go out to your office. And they intend to have it out with you."

Joseph started from the chair he had taken, and went to the window, and threw up the sash.

Leaning out, he saw three hats below. It was as Mrs. Baker had intimated. Three gentlemen were seated on the doorstep. One was the vicar, another his "boss" Mr. Stork, and the third was Mr. Wotherspoon.

There could be no mistake about the vicar; he wore a chimney-pot hat of silk, that had begun to curl at the brim, anticipatory of being adapted as that of an archdeacon. Moreover, he wore extensive, well-cultivated grey whiskers on each cheek. If we were inclined to adopt the modern careless usage, we might say that he grew whiskers on *either* cheek. But in strict accuracy that would mean that the whiskers grew indifferently, or alternatively, intermittently on one cheek or the other. This, however, was not the case, consequently we say on *each* cheek. These whiskers now waved and fluttered in the light air passing up and down the street.

The second was Mr. Stork; he wore a stiff felt hat, his fiery hair showed beneath it, behind, and in front; when he lifted his head, the end of his pointed nose showed distinctly to Joseph Leveridge who looked down from above. The third, Mr. Wotherspoon, had a crushed brown cap on; he sat with his hands between his knees, dejected, and looking on the ground.

Mr. Wotherspoon lived in Swanton with his mother and three sisters. The mother was the widow of an officer, not well off. He was an agreeable man, an excellent player at lawn-tennis, croquet, golf, rackets, billiards, and cards. His age was thirty, and he had as yet no occupation. His mother gently, his sisters sharply, urged him to do something, so as to earn his livelihood. With his mother's death her pension would cease, and he could not then depend on his sisters. He always answered that something would turn up. Occasionally he ran to town to look for employment, but invariably returned without having secured any, and with his pockets empty. He was so cheerful, so good-natured, was such good company, that everyone liked him, but also everyone was provoked at his sponging on his mother and sisters.

"Really," said Mr. Leveridge, "I cannot encounter those three. It is true that I have drawn them pretty accurately in my novel, and here they are ready to take me to account for so doing. I will leave the house by the back door."

Without his breakfast, Joseph fled; and having escaped from those who had hoped to intercept him, he made his way to the river. Here were pleasant grounds, with walks laid out, and benches provided. The place was not likely to be frequented at that time of the morning, and Mr. Leveridge had half an hour to spare before he was due at the office. There, later, he was likely to meet his "boss"; but it was better to face him alone, than him accompanied by two others who had a similar grievance against him.

He seated himself on a bench and thought. He did not smoke; he had promised his "mamma" not to do so, and he was a dutiful son, and regarded his undertaking.

What should he do? He was becoming involved in serious embarrassments. Would it be possible to induce the publisher to withdraw the book from circulation and to receive back the fifty pounds? That was hardly possible. He had signed away all his rights in the novel, and the publisher had been to a considerable expense for paper, printing, binding, and advertising.

He was roused from his troubled thoughts by seeing Miss Asphodel Vincent coming along the walk towards him. Her step had lost its wonted spring, her carriage its usual buoyancy. In a minute or two she would reach him. Would she deign to speak? He felt no compunction towards her. He had made her his heroine in the tale. By not a word had he cast a shadow over her character or her abilities. Indeed, he had pictured her as the highest ideal of an English girl. She might be flattered, she could not be offended. And yet there was no flattery in his pencil—he had sketched her in as she was.

As she approached she noticed the young author. She did not hasten her step. She displayed a strange listlessness in her movements, and lack of vivacity in her eye.

When she stood over against him, Joseph Leveridge rose and removed his hat. "An early promenade, Miss Vincent," he said.

"Oh!" she said, "I am glad to meet you here where we cannot be overheard. I have something about which I must speak to you, to complain of a great injury done to me."

"You do me a high honour," exclaimed Joseph. "If I can do anything to alleviate your distress and to redress the wrong, command me."

"You can do nothing. It is impossible to undo what has already been done. You put me into your book."

"Miss Vincent," protested Leveridge with vehemence, "if I have, what then? I have not in the least overcharged the colours, by a line caricatured you." It was in vain for him further to pretend not to be the author and to have merely read the book.

"That may be, or it may not. But you have taken strange liberties with me in transferring me to your pages."

"And you really recognised yourself?"

"It is myself, my very self, who is there."

"And yet you are here, before my humble self."

"That is only my outer shell. All my individuality, all that goes to make up the Ego—I myself—has been taken from me and put into your book."

"Surely that cannot be."

"But it is so. I feel precisely as I suppose felt my doll when I was a child, when it became unstitched and all the bran ran out; it hung limp like a rag. But it is not bran you have deprived me of, it is my personality."

"In my novel is your portraiture indeed—but you yourself are here," said Leveridge.

"It is my very self, my noblest and best part, my moral and intellectual self, which has been carried off and put into your book."

"This is quite impossible, Miss Vincent."

"A moment's thought," said she, "will convince you that it is as I say. If I pick an Alpine flower and transfer it to my blotting-book, it remains in the herbarium. It is no longer on the Alp where it bloomed."

"But——" urged Joseph.

"No," she interrupted, "you cannot undeceive me. No one can be in two places at the same time. If I am in your book, I cannot be here—except so far as goes my animal nature and frame. You have subjected me, Mr. Leveridge, to the greatest humiliation. I am by you reduced to the level of a score of girls that I know, with no pursuits, no fixed principles, no opinions of their own, no ideas. They are swayed by every fashion, they are moulded by their surroundings; they are destitute of what some would call moral fibre, and I would term character. I had all this, but you have deprived me of it, by putting it into your book. I shall henceforth be the sport of every breath, be influenced by every folly, be without self-confidence and decision, the prey to any adventurer."

"For Heaven's sake, do not say that."

"I cannot say anything other. If I had a sovereign in my purse, and a pickpocket stole it, I should no longer have the purse and sovereign, only the pocket; and I am a mere pocket now without the coin of my personality that you have filched from me. Mr. Leveridge, it was a cruel wrong you did me, *when you used me up*."

Then, sighing, Miss Asphodel went languidly on her way. Joseph was as one stunned. He buried his face in his hands. The person of all others with whom he desired to stand well, that person looked upon him as her most deadly enemy, at all events as the one who had most cruelly aggrieved her.

Presently, hearing the clock strike, he started. He was due at the office, and Joseph Leveridge had always made a point of punctuality.

He now went to the office, and learned from his fellow-clerk that Mr. Stork had not returned; he had been there, and then had gone away to seek Leveridge at his lodgings. Joseph considered it incumbent on him to resume his hat and go in quest of his "boss."

On his way it occurred to him that there was monotony in bacon and eggs for breakfast every morning, and he would like a change. Moreover, he was hungry; he had left the house of Mrs. Baker without taking a mouthful, and if he returned now for a snack the eggs and the bacon would be cold. So he stepped into the shop of Mr. Box, the grocer, for a tin of sardines in oil.

When the grocer saw him he said: "Will you favour me with a word, sir, in the back shop?"

"I am pressed for time," replied Leveridge nervously.

"But one word; I will not detain you," said Mr. Box, and led the way. Joseph walked after him.

"Sir," said the grocer, shutting the glass door, "you have done me a prodigious wrong. You have deprived me of what I would not have lost for a thousand pounds. You have put me into your book. How my business will get on without me—I mean my intellect, my powers of organisation, my trade instincts, in a word, myself—I do not know. You have taken them from me and put them into your book. I am consigned to a novel, when I want all my powers behind the counter. Possibly my affairs for a while will go on by the weight of their own momentum, but it cannot be for long without my controlling brain. Sir, you have brought me and my family to ruin—*you have used me up*."

Leveridge could bear this no more; he seized the handle of the door, rushed through the outer shop, precipitated himself into the street, carrying the sardine tin in his hand, and hurried to his lodgings.

But there new trouble awaited him. On the doorstep still sat the three gentlemen.

When they saw him they rose to their feet.

"I know, I know what you have to say," gasped Joseph. "In pity do not attack me all together. One at a time. With your leave, Mr. Vicar, will you step up first into my humble little sanctum, and I will receive the others later. I believe that the smell of bacon and eggs is gone from the room. I left the window open."

"I will most certainly follow you," said the Vicar of Swanton. "This is a most serious matter."

"Excuse me, will you take a chair?"

"No, thank you; I can speak best when on my legs. I lose impressiveness when seated. But I fear, alas! that gift has been taken from me. Sir! sir! you have put me into your book. My earthly tabernacle may be here, standing on your—or Mrs. Baker's drugget—but all my great oratorical powers have gone. I have been despoiled of what was in me my highest, noblest, most spiritual parts. What my preaching henceforth will be I fear to contemplate. I may be able to string together a number of texts, and tack on an application, but that is mere mechanical work. I used to dredge in much florid eloquence, to stick in the flowers of elocution between every joint. And now!—I am despoiled of all. I, the Vicar of Swanton, shall be as a mere stick; I shall no more be a power in the pulpit, a force on the platform. My prospects in the diocese are put an end to. Miserable, miserable young man, you might have pumped others, but why me? I know but too surely that *you have used me up*." The vicar had taken off his hat, his bald forehead was beaded, his bristling grey whiskers drooped, his unctuous expression had faded away. His eyes, usually bearing the look as though turned inward in ecstatic contemplation of his personal piety, with only a watery stare on the world without, were now dull.

He turned to the door. "I will send up Stork," he said.

"Do so by all means, sir," was all that Joseph could say.

When the solicitor entered his red hair had assumed a darker dye, through the moisture that exuded from his head.

"Mr. Leveridge," said he, "this is a scurvy trick you have played me. You have put me into your book."

"I only sketched a not over-scrupulous lawyer," protested Joseph. "Why should you put the cap on your own head?"

"Because it fits. It is myself you have put into your book, and by no legal process can I get out of it. I shall not be competent to advise the magistrates on the bench, and, good heavens! what a mess they will get into. I do not know whether your fellow-clerk can carry on the business. *I have been used up.* I'll tell you what. You go away; I want you no more at the office. Whenever you revisit Swanton you will see only the ruins of the respected firm of Stork. It cannot go on when I am not in it, but in your book."

The last to arrive was Mr. Wotherspoon. He was in a most depressed condition. "There was not much in me," said he, "not at any time. You might have spared such a trifle as me, and not put me also into your book and *used me up*. Oh, dear, dear! what will my poor mother do! And how Sarah and Jane will bully me."

* * * * *

That same day Mr. Leveridge packed up his traps and departed from Swanton for his mother's house.

That she was delighted to see him need not be said; that something was wrong, her maternal instinct told her. But it was not for some days that he confided to her so much as this: "Oh, mother, I have written a novel, and have put into it the people of Swanton—and so have had to leave."

"My dear Joe," said the old lady, "you have done wrong and made a great mistake. You never should introduce actual living personages into a work of fiction. You should pulp them first, and then run out your characters fresh from the pulp."

"I was so afraid of using my imagination," explained Joe.

Some months elapsed, and Leveridge could not resolve on an employment that would suit him and at the same time maintain him. The fifty pounds he had earned would not last long. He began to be sensible of the impulse to be again writing. He resisted it for a while, but when he got a letter from his publisher, saying that the novel had sold well, far better than had been expected, and that he would be pleased to consider another from Mr. Leveridge's pen, and could promise him for it more liberal terms, then Joseph's scruples vanished. But on one thing he was resolved. He would now create his characters. They should not be taken from observation.

Moreover, he determined to differentiate his new work from the old in other material points. His characters should be the reverse of those in the first novel. For his heroine he imagined a girl of boisterous spirits, straightforward, true, but somewhat unconventional, and given to use slang expressions. He had never met with such a girl, so that she would be a pure creation of his brain, and he made up his mind to call her Poppy. Then he would avoid drawing the portrait of an Evangelical parson, and introduce one decidedly High Church; he would have no heavy, narrow tradesman like Box, but a man full of venture and speculative push. Moreover, having used up the not over-scrupulous lawyer, he would portray one, the soul of honour, the confidant of not only the county gentry but of the county nobility. And as he had caused so much trouble by the introduction of good old Mother Baker, he would trace the line of a lively, skittish young widow, always on the hunt after admirers, and endeavouring to entangle the youths who lodged with her.

As he went on with his story, it worked out to his satisfaction, and what especially gratified him and gave repose to his mind was the consciousness that he was using no one up, with whom he was acquainted, and that all his characters were pure creations.

The work was complete, and the publisher agreed to give a hundred pounds for it. Then it passed through the press, and in due course Leveridge heard from the publisher that his six free copies had been sent off to him by train. Joseph was almost as excited over his second novel as he was over the first.

He was too impatient to wait till the parcels were sent round in the ordinary way. He hurried to the station in the evening, to meet the train from town, by which he expected his consignment; and having secured it, he hurried home, carrying the heavy parcel.

399

His mother's house was comparatively large; she occupied but a corner of it, and she had given over to her son a little cosy sitting-room, in which he might write and read. Into this room Joseph carried his parcel, full of impatience to cut the string and disclose the volumes.

But he had hardly passed through his door before he was startled to see that his room was full of people; all but one were seated about the table. That one who was not, lounged against the bookcase, standing on one foot. With a shock of surprise, Joseph recognised all those there gathered together. They were the characters in his book, his own creations. And that individual who stood, in an indifferent attitude, was his new heroine, Poppy. The first shock of surprise rapidly passed. Joseph Leveridge felt no fear, but rather a sense of pleasure. He was in the presence of his own creations, and knew them familiarly. There were seven in all. At his appearance they all saluted him respectfully as their creator—all except Poppy, who gave him a wink and a nod.

At the head of the table sat the High Church parson, shaven, with a long coat and a grave face, next to him, on the right, Lady Mabel Forraby, a tall, elderly, aristocratic-looking woman, the aunt of Poppy. One element of lightness in the book had consisted in the struggles of Lady Mabel to control her wayward niece and the revolt of the latter. Mr. Leveridge had never known a person of title in his life, so that Lady Mabel was a pure creation; so also, brought up, as he had been, by a Calvinistic mother, and afterwards thrown under the ministry of the Vicar of Swanton, he had not once come across a Ritualist. Consequently his parson, in this instance, was also a pure creation. A young gentleman, the hero of the novel, a bright intelligent fellow, full of vigour and good sense, and highly cultured, sat next to Lady Mabel. Joseph had never been thrown into association with men of quite this type. He had met nice respectable clerks and amusing and agreeable travellers for commercial houses, so that this personage also was a creation. So most certainly was the bold, pert little widow who rolled her eyes and put on winsome airs. Joseph had kept clear of all such instances, but he had heard and read of them. She could look to him as her creator.

And that naughty little Poppy! Her naughtiness was all mischief, put on to aggravate her staid old aunt, so full of daring, and yet withal so steady of heart; so full of frolic, but with principle underlying it all. Joseph had never encountered anyone like her, anyone approaching to her. The young ladies to whom his mother introduced him were all very prim and proper. At Swanton he had been little in society: the vicar's daughter was a tract distributer and a mission woman, and Mr. Stork's daughter a domestic drudge. Of all the characters in Joseph's book she was his most especial and delightful creation.

Then the white-haired family lawyer, fond of his jokes, able to tell a good story, close as a walnut relative to all matters communicated to him, strict and honourable in all his dealings, content with his small earnings, and frugally laying them by. Joseph had not met such a man, but he had idealised him as the sort of lawyer he would wish to be should he stick to his profession. He also, accordingly, was a creation. And last, but not least, was the red-faced, audacious stockbroker; a man of sharp and quick determination, who saw a chance in a moment and closed on it, who was keen of scent and smelt a risky investment the moment it came before him. Joseph knew no stockbroker—had only heard of them by rumour. He, therefore, was a creation.

"Well, my children, not of my loins, but of my brain," said the author. "What do you all want?"

"Bodies," they replied with one voice.

"Bodies!" gasped Joseph, stepping backwards. "Why, what possesses you all? You can't expect me to furnish you with them."

"But, indeed, we do, old chap," said Poppy.

"Niece!" said Lady Mabel, turning about in her chair, "address your creator with more respect."

"Stay, my lady," said the parson. "Allow me to explain matters to Mr. Leveridge. He is young and an inexperienced writer of fiction, and is therefore unaware of the exigencies of his profession. You must know, dear author of our being, that every author of a work of imagination, such as you have been, lays himself under a moral and an inexorable obligation to find bodies for all those whom he has called into existence through his fertile brain. Mr. Leveridge has not mixed in the literary world. He does not belong to the Society of Authors. He is—he will excuse the expression—raw in his profession. It is a well-known law among novelists that they must furnish bodies for such as they have called into existence out of their pure imagination. For this reason they invariably call their observation to their assistance, and they balance in their books the creations with the transcripts from life. The only exception to this rule that I am aware of," continued the parson, "is where the author is able to get his piece dramatised, in which case, of course, the difficulty ceases."

"I should love to go on the stage," threw in Poppy.

"Niece, you do not know what you say," remarked Lady Mabel, turning herself about.

"Allow me, my lady," said the parson. "What I have said is fact, is it not?"

"Most certainly," replied all. Lady Mabel said: "I suppose it is."

"Then," pursued the parson, "the situation is this: Have you secured the dramatisation of your novel?"

"I never gave it a thought," said Joseph.

"In that case, as there is no prospect of our being so accommodated, the position is this: We shall have to haunt you night and day, mainly at night, till you have accommodated us with bodies; we cannot remain as phantom creations of a highly imaginative soul such as is yours, Mr. Leveridge. If you have your rights, so have we. And we insist on ours, and will insist till we are satisfied."

At once all vanished.

Joseph Leveridge felt that he had got himself into a worse hobble than before. From his former difficulties he had escaped by flight. But there was, he feared, no flying from these seven impatient creations all clamouring for bodies, and to provide them with such was beyond his powers. All his delight in the publication of his new novel was spent. It had brought with it care and perplexity.

He went to bed.

During the night, he was troubled with his characters; they peeped in at him. Poppy got a peacock's feather and tickled his nose just as he was dropping asleep. "You bounder!" she said; "I shall give you no peace till you have settled me into a body—but oh! get me on to the stage if you can."

"Poppy, come away," called Lady Mabel. "Don't be improper. Mr. Leveridge will do his best. I want a body quite as much as do you, but I know how to ask for it properly."

"And I," said the parson, "should like to have mine before Easter, but have one I must."

Mr. Leveridge's state now was worse than the first. One or other of his creatures was ever watching him. His every movement was spied on. There was no escaping their vigilance. Sometimes they attended him in groups of two or three; sometimes they were all around him.

At meals not one was missing, and they eyed every mouthful of his food as he raised it to his lips. His mother saw nothing—the creations were invisible to all eyes save those of their creator.

If he went out for a country walk, they trotted forth with him, some before, looking round at every turn to see which way he purposed going, some following. Poppy and the skittish widow managed to attach themselves to him, one on each side. "I hate that little woman," said Poppy. "Why did you call her into being?"

*If he went out for a walk they trotted
forth with him, some before, some following.*

"I never dreamed that things would come to this pass."

"I am convinced, creator dear, that there is a vein of wickedness in your composition, or you would never have imagined such a minx, good and amiable and butter-won't-melt-in-your-mouth though you may look. And there must be a frolicsome devil in your heart, or I should never have become."

"Indeed, Poppy, I am very glad that I gave you being. But one may have too much even of a good thing, and there are moments when I could dispense with your presence."

"I know, when you want to carry on with the widow. She is always casting sheep's eyes at you."

"But, Poppy, you forget my hero, whom I created on purpose for you."

"All my attention is now engrossed in you, and will be till you provide me with a body."

When Leveridge was in his room reading, if he raised his eyes from his book they met the stare of one of his characters. If he went up to his bedroom, he was followed. If he sat with his mother, one kept guard.

This was become so intolerable, that one evening he protested to the stockbroker, who was then in attendance. "Do, I entreat you, leave me to myself. You treat me as if I were a lunatic and about to commit *felo de se*, and you were my warders."

"We watch you, sir," said the stockbroker, "in our own interest. We cannot suffer you to give us the slip. We are all expectant and impatient for the completion of what you have begun."

Then the parson undertook to administer a lecture on Duty, on responsibilities contracted to those called into partial existence by a writer of fiction. He cannot be allowed to half do his work. His creations must be realised, and can only be realised by being given a material existence.

"But what the dickens can I do? I cannot fabricate bodies for you. I never in my life even made a doll."

"Have you no thought of dramatising us?"

"I know no dramatic writers."

"Do it yourself."

"Does not this sort of work require a certain familiarity with the technique of the stage which I do not possess?"

"That might be attended to later. Pass your MS. through the hands of a dramatic expert, and pay him a percentage of your profits in recognition of his services. Only one thing I bargain for, do not present me on the stage in such a manner as to discredit my cloth."

"Have I done so in my book?"

"No, indeed, I have nothing to complain of in that. But there is no counting on what Poppy may persuade you into doing, and I fear that she is gaining influence over you. Remember, she is your creation, and you must not suffer her to mould you."

The idea took root. The suggestion was taken up, and Joseph Leveridge applied himself to his task with zest. But he had to conceal what he was about from his mother, who had no opinion of the drama, and regarded the theatre as a sink of iniquity.

But now new difficulties arose. Joseph's creations would not leave him alone for a moment. Each had a suggestion, each wanted his or her own part accentuated at the expense of the other. Each desired the heightening of the situations in which they severally appeared. The clamour, the bickering, the interference made it impossible for Joseph to collect his thoughts, keep cool, and proceed with his work.

Sunday arrived, and Joseph drew on his gloves, put on his box-hat, and offered his arm to his mother, to conduct her to chapel. All the characters were drawn up in the hall to accompany them. Joseph and his mother walking down the street to Ebenezer Chapel presented a picture of a good and dutiful son and of a pious widow not to be surpassed. Poppy and the widow entered into a struggle as to which was to walk on the unoccupied side of Joseph. If this had been introduced into the picture it would have marred it; but happily this was invisible to all eyes save those of Joseph. The rest of the imaginary party walked arm in arm behind till the chapel was reached, when the parson started back.

"I am not going in there! It is a schism-shop," he exclaimed. "Nothing in the world would induce me to cross the threshold."

"And I," said Lady Mabel, "I have no idea of attending a place of worship not of the Established Church."

"I'll go in—if only to protect Creator from the widow," said Poppy.

Joseph and his mother entered, and occupied their pew. The characters, with the exception of the parson and the old lady, grouped themselves where they were able. The stockbroker stood in the aisle with his arms on the pew door, to ensure that Joseph was kept a prisoner there. But before the service had advanced far he had gone to sleep. This was the more to be regretted, as the minister delivered a very strong appeal to the unconverted, and if ever there was an unconverted worldling, it was that stockbroker.

The skittish widow was leering at a deacon of an amorous complexion, but as he did not, and, in fact, could not see her, all her efforts were cast away. The solicitor sat with stolid face and folded hands, and allowed the discourse to flow over him like a refreshing douche. Poppy had got very tired of the show, and had slunk away to rejoin her aunt. The hero closed his eyes and seemed resigned.

After nearly an hour had elapsed, whilst a hymn was being sung, Joseph, more to himself than to his mother, said: "Can I escape?"

"Escape what? Wretch?" inquired the widowed lady.

"I think I can do it. There's a room at the side for earnest inquirers, or a vestry or something, with an outer door. I will risk it, and make a bolt for my liberty."

He very gently and cautiously unhasped the door of the pew, and as he slid it open, the sleeping stockbroker, still sleeping and unconscious, slipped back, and Joseph was out. He made his way into the room at the side, forth from the actual chapel, ran through it, and tried the door that opened into a side lane. It was locked, but happily the key was in its place. He turned it, plunged forth, and fell into the arms of his characters. They were all there. The solicitor had been observing him out of the corner of his eye, and had given the alarm. The stockbroker was aroused, and he, the solicitor, the hero, ran out, gave the alarm to the three without, and Joseph was intercepted, and his attempt at escape frustrated. He was reconducted home by them, himself dejected, they triumphant.

When his mother returned she was full of solicitude.

"What was the matter, Joe dear?" she inquired.

"I wasn't feeling very well," he explained. "But I shall be better presently."

"I hope it will not interfere with your appetite, Joe. I have cold lamb and mint-sauce for our early dinner."

"I shall peck a bit, I trust," said Mr. Leveridge.

But during dinner he was abstracted and silent. All at once he brought down his fist on the table. "I've hit it!" he exclaimed, and a flush of colour mantled his face to the temples.

"My dear," said his mother; "you have made all the plates and dishes jump, and have nearly upset the water-bottle."

"Excuse me, mother; I really must go to my room."

He rose, made a sign to his characters, and they all rose and trooped after him into his private apartment.

When they were within he said to his hero: "May I trouble you kindly to shut the door and turn the key? My mother will be anxious and come after me, and I want a word with you all. It will not take two minutes. I see my way to our mutual accommodation. Do not be uneasy and suspicious; I will make no further attempt at evasion. Meet me to-morrow morning at the 9.48 down train. I am going to take you all with me to Swanton."

A tap at the door.

"Open—it is my mother," said Joseph.

Mrs. Leveridge entered with a face of concern. "What is the matter with you, Joe?" she said. "If we were not both of us water-drinkers, I should say that you had been indulging in—spirits."

"Mother, I must positively be off to Swanton to-morrow morning. I see my way now, all will come right."

"How, my precious boy?"

"I cannot explain. I see my way to clearing up the unpleasantness caused by that unfortunate novel of mine. Pack my trunk, mother."

"Not on the Sabbath, lovie."

"No—to-morrow morning. I start by the 9.48 a.m. We all go together."

"We—am I to accompany you?"

"No, no. We—did I say? It is a habit I have got into as an author. Authors, like royal personages, speak of themselves as We."

Joseph Leveridge was occupied during the afternoon in writing to his victims at Swanton.

First, he penned a notice to Mrs. Baker that he would require his lodgings from the morrow, and that he had something to say to her that would afford her much gratification.

Then he wrote to the vicar, expressed his regret for having deprived him of his personality, and requested him, if he would do him the favour, to call in the evening at 7.30, at his lodgings in West Street. He had something of special importance to communicate to him. He apologised for not himself calling at the vicarage, but said that there were circumstances that made it more desirable that he should see his reverence privately in his own lodgings.

Next, he addressed an epistle to Mr. Stork. He assured him that he, Joseph Leveridge, had felt keenly the wrong he had done him, that he had forfeited his esteem, had ill repaid his kindness, had acted in a manner towards his employer that was dishonourable. But, he added, he had found a means of rectifying what was wrong. He placed himself unreservedly in the hands of Mr. Stork, and entreated him to meet him at his rooms in West Street on the ensuing Monday evening at 7.45, when he sincerely trusted that the past would be forgotten, and a brighter future would be assured.

This was followed by a formal letter couched to Mr. Box. He invited him to call at Mrs. Baker's lodgings on that same evening at 8 p.m., as he had business of an important and far-reaching nature to discuss with him. If Mr. Box considered that he, Joseph Leveridge, had done him an injury, he was ready to make what reparation lay in his power.

Taking a fresh sheet of notepaper, he now wrote a fifth letter, this to Mr. Wotherspoon, requesting the honour of a call at his "diggings" at 8.15 p.m., when matters of controversy between them could be amicably adjusted.

The ensuing letter demanded some deliberation. It was to Asphodel. He wrote it out twice before he was satisfied with the mode in which it was expressed. He endeavoured to disguise under words full of respect, yet not disguise too completely, the sentiments of his heart. But he was careful to let drop nothing at which she might take umbrage. He entreated her to be so gracious as to allow him an interview by the side of the river at the hour of 8.30 on the Monday evening. He apologised for venturing to make such a demand, but he intimated that the matter he had to communicate was so important and so urgent, that it could not well be postponed till Tuesday, and that it was also most necessary that the interview should be private. It was something he had to say that would materially—no, not materially, but morally—affect her, and would relieve his mind from a burden of remorse that had become to him wholly intolerable.

The final, the seventh letter, was to Major Dolgelly Jones, and was more brief. It merely intimated that he had something of the utmost importance to communicate to his private ear, and for this purpose he desired the favour of a call at Mrs. Baker's lodgings, at 8.45 on Monday evening.

These letters despatched, Mr. Leveridge felt easier in mind and lighter at heart. He slept well the ensuing night, better than he had for long. His creations did not so greatly disturb him. He was aware that he was still kept under surveillance, but the watch was not so strict, nor so galling as hitherto.

On the Monday morning he was at the station, and took his ticket for Swanton. One ticket sufficed, as his companions, who awaited him on the platform, were imaginary characters.

When he took his seat, they pressed into the carriage after him. Poppy secured the seat next him, but the widow placed herself opposite, and exerted all her blandishment with the hope of engrossing his whole attention. At a junction all got out, and Joseph provided himself with a luncheon-basket and mineral water. The characters watched him discussing the half-chicken and slabs of ham, with the liveliest interest, and were especially observant of his treatment of the thin paper napkin, wherewith he wiped his fingers and mouth.

At last he arrived at Swanton and engaged a cab, as he was encumbered with a portmanteau. Lady Mabel, Poppy, and the widow could be easily accommodated within, the two latter with their backs to the horses. Joseph would willingly have resigned his seat to either of these, but they would not hear of it. A gentle altercation ensued between the parson and the solicitor, as to which should ride on the box. The lawyer desired to yield the place to "the cloth," but the parson would not hear of this—the silver hairs of the other claimed precedence. The stockbroker mounted to the roof of the fly and the clerical gentleman hung on behind. The hero professed his readiness to walk.

Eventually the cab drew up at Mrs. Baker's door.

That stout, elderly lady received her old lodger without effusion, and with languid interest. The look of the house was not what it had been. It had deteriorated. The windows had not been cleaned nor the banisters dusted.

"My dear old landlady, I am so glad to see you again," said Joseph.

"Thank you, sir. You ordered no meal, but I have got two mutton chops in the larder, and can mash some potatoes. At what time would you like your supper, sir?" She had become a machine, a thing of routine.

"Not yet, thank you. I have business to transact first, and I shall not be disengaged before nine o'clock. But I have something to say to you, Mrs. Baker, and I will say it at once and get it over, if you will kindly step up into my parlour."

She did so, sighing at each step of the stairs as she ascended.

All the characters mounted as well, and entering the little sitting-room, ranged themselves against the wall facing the door.

Mrs. Baker was a portly woman, aged about forty-five, and plain featured. She had formerly been neat, now she was dowdy. Before she had lost her character she never appeared in that room without removing her apron, but on this occasion she wore it, and it was not clean.

"Widow!" said Joseph, addressing his character, "will you kindly step forward?"

"I would do anything for *you*," with a roll of the eyes.

"Dear Mrs. Baker," said Leveridge, "I feel that I have done you a grievous wrong."

"Well, sir, I ain't been myself since you put me into your book."

"My purpose is now to undo the past, and to provide you with a character."

Then, turning to the skittish widow of his creation, he said, "Now, then, slip into and occupy her."

"I don't like the tenement," said the widow, pouting.

"Whether you like it or not," protested Joseph, "you must have that or no other." He waved his hand. "Presto!" he exclaimed.

Instantly a wondrous change was effected in Mrs. Baker. She whipped off the apron, and crammed it under the sofa cushion. She wriggled in her movements, she eyed herself in the glass, and exclaimed: "Oh, my! what a fright I am. I'll be back again in a minute when I have changed my gown and done up my hair."

"We can dispense with your presence, Mrs. Baker," said Leveridge sternly. "I will ring for you when you are wanted."

At that moment a rap at the door was heard; and Mrs. Baker, having first dropped a coquettish curtsy to her lodger, tripped downstairs to admit the vicar, and to show him up to Mr. Leveridge's apartment.

"You may go, Mrs. Baker," said he; for she seemed inclined to linger.

When she had left the room, Joseph contemplated the reverend gentleman. He bore a crestfallen appearance. He looked as if he had been out in the rain all night without a paletot. His cheeks were flabby, his mouth drooped at the corners, his eyes were vacant, and his whiskers no longer stuck out horrescent and assertive.

"Dear vicar," said Leveridge, "I cannot forgive myself." In former times, Mr. Leveridge would not have dreamed of addressing the reverend gentleman in this familiar manner, but it was other now that the latter looked so limp and forlorn. "My dear vicar, I cannot forgive myself for the trouble I have brought upon you. It has weighed on me as a nightmare, for I know that it is not you only who have suffered, but also the whole parish of Swanton. Happily a remedy is at hand. I have here——" he waved to the parson of his creation, "I have here an individuality I can give to you, and henceforth, if you will not be precisely yourself again, you will be a personality in your parish and the diocese." He waved his hand. "Presto!"

In the twinkling of an eye all was changed in the Vicar of Swanton. He straightened himself. His expression altered to what it never had been before. The cheeks became firm, and lines formed about the mouth indicative of force of character and of self-restraint. The eye assumed an eager look as into far distances, as seeking something beyond the horizon.

The vicar walked to the mirror over the mantelshelf.

"Bless me!" he said, "I must go to the barber's and have these whiskers off." And he hurried downstairs.

After a little pause in the proceedings, Mrs. Baker, now very trim, with a blue ribbon round her neck hanging down in streamers behind, ushered up Mr. Stork. The lawyer had a faded appearance, as if he had been exposed to too strong sunlight; he walked in with an air of lack of interest, and sank into a chair.

"My dear old master," said Leveridge, "it is my purpose to restore to you all your former energy, and to supply you with what you may possibly have lacked previously."

He signed to the white-haired family solicitor he had called into fictitious being, and waved his hand.

At once Mr. Stork stood up and shook his legs, as though shaking out crumbs from his trousers. His breast swelled, he threw back his head, his eye shone clear and was steady.

"Mr. Leveridge," said he, "I have long had my eye on you, sir—had my eye on you. I have marked your character as one of uncompromising probity. I hate shiftiness, I abhor duplicity. I have been disappointed with my clerks. I could not always trust them to do the right thing. I want to strengthen and brace my firm. But I will not take into partnership with myself any but one of the strictest integrity. Sir! I have marked you—I have marked you, Mr. Leveridge. Call on me to-morrow morning, and we will consider the preliminaries for a partnership. Don't talk to me of buying a partnership."

"I have not done so, sir."

"I know you have not. I will take you in, sir, for your intrinsic value. An honest man is worth his weight in gold, and is as scarce as the precious metal."

Then, with dignity, Mr. Stork withdrew, and passed Mr. Box, the grocer, mounting the stairs.

"Well, Mr. Box," said Leveridge, "how wags the world with you?"

"Badly, sir, badly since you booked me. I mentioned to you, sir, that I trusted my little business would for a while go on by its own momentum. It has, sir, it has, but the momentum has been downhill. I can't control it. I have not the personality to do so, to serve as a drag, to urge it upwards. I am in daily expectation, sir, of a regular smash up."

"I am sorry to hear this," said Leveridge. "But I think I have found a means of putting all to rights. Presto!" He waved his hand and the imaginary character of the stockbroker had actualised himself in the body of Mr. Box.

"I see how to do it. By ginger, I do!" exclaimed the grocer, a spark coming into his eye. "I'll run my little concern on quite other lines. And look ye here, Mr. Leveridge. I bet you my bottom dollar that I'll run it to a tremendous success, become a second Lipton, and keep a yacht."

As Mr. Box bounced out of the room and proceeded to run downstairs, he ran against and nearly knocked over Mrs. Baker; the lady was whispering to and coquetting with Mr. Wotherspoon, who was on the landing. That gentleman, in his condition of lack of individuality, was like a teetotum spun in the hands of the designing Mrs. Baker, who put forth all the witchery she possessed, or supposed that she possessed, to entangle him in an amorous intrigue.

"Come in," shouted Joseph Leveridge, and Mr. Wotherspoon, looking hot and frightened and very shy, tottered in and sank into a chair. He was too much shaken and perturbed by the advances of Mrs. Baker to be able to speak.

"There," said Joseph, addressing his hero. "You cannot do better than animate that feeble creature. Go!"

Instantly Mr. Wotherspoon sprang to his feet. "By George!" said he. "I wonder that never struck me before. I'll at once volunteer to go out to South Africa, and have a shot at those canting, lying, treacherous Boers. If I come back with a score of their scalps at my waist, I shall have deserved well of my country. I will volunteer at once. But—I say, Leveridge—clear that hulking, fat old landlady out of the way. She blocks the stairs, and I can't kick down a woman."

When Mr. Wotherspoon was gone—"Well," said Poppy, "what have you got for me?"

"If you will come with me, Poppy dear, I will serve you as well as the rest."

"I hope better than you did that odious little widow. But she is well paid out."

"Follow me to the riverside," said Joseph; "at 8.33 p.m. I am due there, and so is another—a lady."

"And pray why did you not make her come here instead of lugging me all the way down there?"

"Because I could not make an appointment with a young lady in my bachelor's apartments."

"That's all very fine. But I am there."

"Yes, you—but you are only an imaginary character, and she is a substantial reality."

"I think I had better accompany you," said Lady Mabel.

"I think not. If your ladyship will kindly occupy my fauteuil till I return, that chair will ever after be sacred to me. Come along, Poppy."

"I'm game," said she.

On reaching the riverside Joseph saw that Miss Vincent was walking there in a listless manner, not straight, but swerving from side to side. She saw him, but did not quicken her pace, nor did her face light up with interest.

"Now, then," said he to Poppy, "what do you think of her?"

"She ain't bad," answered the fictitious character; "she is very pretty certainly, but inanimate."

"You will change all that."

"I'll try—you bet."

Asphodel came up. She bowed, but did not extend her hand.

"Miss Vincent," said Joseph. "How good of you to come."

"Not at all. I could not help. I have no free-will left. When you wrote Come—I came, I could do no other. I have no initiative, no power of resistance."

"I do hope, Miss Vincent, that the thing you so feared has not happened."

"What thing?"

"You have not been snapped up by a fortune-hunter?"

"No. People have not as yet found out that I have lost my individuality. I have kept very much to myself—that is to say, not to myself, as I have no proper myself left—I mean to the semblance of myself. People have thought I was anæmic."

Leveridge turned aside: "Well, Poppy!"

"Right you are."

Leveridge waved his hand. Instantly all the inertia passed away from the girl, she stood erect and firm. A merry twinkle kindled in her eye, a flush was on her cheek, and mischievous devilry played about her lips.

"I feel," said she, "as another person."

"Oh! I am so glad, Miss Vincent."

"That is a pretty speech to make to a lady! Glad I am different from what I was before."

"I did not mean that—I meant—in fact, I meant that as you were and as you are you are always charming."

"Thank you, sir!" said Asphodel, curtsying and laughing.

"Ah! Miss Vincent, at all times you have seemed to me the ideal of womanhood. I have worshipped the very ground you have trod upon."

"Fiddlesticks."

He looked at her. For the moment he was bewildered, oblivious that the old personality of Asphodel had passed into his book and that the new personality of Poppy had invaded Asphodel.

"Well," said she, "is that all you have to say to me?"

"All?—oh, no. I could say a great deal—I have ordered my supper for nine o'clock."

"Oh, how obtuse you men are! Come—is this leap year?"

"I really believe that it is."

"Then I shall take the privilege of the year, and offer you my hand and heart and fortune—there! Now it only remains with you to name the day."

"Oh! Miss Vincent, you overcome me."

"Stuff and nonsense. Call me Asphodel, do Joe."

* * * * *

Mr. Leveridge walked back to his lodgings as if he trod on air. As he passed by the churchyard, he noticed the vicar, now shaven and shorn, labouring at a laden wheelbarrow. He halted at the rails and said: "Why, vicar, what are you about?"

"The sexton has begun a grave for old Betty Goodman, and it is unfinished. He must dig another." He turned over the wheelbarrow and shot its contents into the grave.

"But what are you doing?" again asked Joseph.

"Burying the Mitre hymnals," replied the vicar.

The clock struck a quarter to nine.

"I must hurry!" exclaimed Joseph.

On reaching his lodgings he found Major Dolgelly Jones in his sitting-room, sitting on the edge of his table tossing up a tennis-ball. In the armchair, invisible to the major, reclined Lady Mabel.

"I am so sorry to be late," apologised Joseph. "How are you, sir?"

"Below par. I have been so ever since you put me into your book. I have no appetite for golf. I can do nothing to pass the weary hours but toss up and down a tennis-ball."

"I hope——" began Joseph; and then a horror seized on him. He had no personality of his creation left but that of Lady Mabel. Would it be possible to translate that into the major?

He remained silent, musing for a while, and then said hesitatingly to the lady: "Here, my lady, is the body you are to individualise."

"But it is that of a man!"

"There is no other left."

"It is hardly delicate."

"There is no help for it." Then turning to the major, he said: "I am very sorry—it really is no fault of mine, but I have only a female personality to offer to you, and that elderly."

"It is all one to me," replied the major, "catch"—he caught the ball. "Many of our generals are old women. I am agreeable. *Place aux dames.*"

"But," protested Lady Mabel, "you made me a member of a very ancient titled house that came over with the Conqueror."

"The personality I offer you," said I to the major, "though female is noble; the family is named in the roll of Battle Abbey."

"Oh!" said Dolgelly Jones, "I descend from one of the royal families of Powys, lineally from Caswallon Llanhir and Maelgwn Gwynedd, long before the Conqueror was thought of."

"Well, then," said Leveridge, and waved his hand.

In Swanton it is known that the major now never plays golf; he keeps rabbits.

* * * * *

It is with some scruple that I insert this record in the *Book of Ghosts*, for actually it is not a story of ghosts. But a greater scruple moved me as to whether I should be justified in revealing a professional secret, known only among such as belong to the Confraternity of Writers of Fiction. But I have observed so much perplexity arise, so much friction caused, by persons suddenly breaking out into a course of conduct, or into actions, so entirely inconsistent with their former conduct as to stagger their acquaintances and friends. Henceforth, to use a vulgarism, since I have let the cat out of the bag, they will know that such persons have been used up by novel writers that have known them, and who have replaced the stolen individualities with others freshly created. This is the explanation, and the explanation has up to the present remained a professional secret.

VIII. — H.P.

THE river Vézère leaps to life among the granite of the Limousin, forms a fine cascade, the Saut de la Virolle, then after a rapid descent over mica-schist, it passes into the region of red sandstone at Brive, and swelled with affluents it suddenly penetrates a chalk district, where it has scooped out for itself a valley between precipices some two to three hundred feet high.

These precipices are not perpendicular, but overhang, because the upper crust is harder than the stone it caps; and atmospheric influences, rain and frost, have gnawed into the chalk below, so that the cliffs hang forward as penthouse roofs, forming shelters beneath them. And these shelters have been utilised by man from the period when the first occupants of the district arrived at a vastly remote period, almost uninterruptedly to the present day. When peasants live beneath these roofs of nature's providing, they simply wall up the face and ends to form houses of the cheapest description of construction, with the earth as the floor, and one wall and the roof of living rock, into which they burrow to form cupboards, bedplaces, and cellars.

The refuse of all ages is superposed, like the leaves of a book, one stratum above another in orderly succession. If we shear down through these beds, we can read the history of the land, so far as its manufacture goes, beginning at the present day and going down, down to the times of primeval man. Now, after every meal, the peasant casts down the bones he has picked, he does not stoop to collect and cast forth the sherds of a broken pot, and if a sou falls and rolls away, in the dust of these gloomy habitations it gets trampled into the soil, to form another token of the period of occupation.

When the first man settled here the climatic conditions were different. The mammoth or woolly elephant, the hyæna, the cave bear, and the reindeer ranged the land. Then naked savages, using only flint tools, crouched under these rocks. They knew nothing of metals and of pottery. They hunted and ate the horse; they had no dogs, no oxen, no sheep. Glaciers covered the centre of France, and reached down the Vézère valley as far as to Brive.

These people passed away, whither we know not. The reindeer retreated to the north, the hyæna to Africa, which was then united to Europe. The mammoth became extinct altogether.

After long ages another people, in a higher condition of culture, but who also used flint tools and weapons, appeared on the scene, and took possession of the abandoned rock shelters. They fashioned their implements in a different manner by flaking the flint in place of chipping it. They understood the art of the potter. They grew flax and wove linen. They had domestic animals, and the dog had become the friend of man. And their flint weapons they succeeded in bringing to a high polish by incredible labour and perseverance.

Then came in the Age of Bronze, introduced from abroad, probably from the East, as its great depôt was in the basin of the Po. Next arrived the Gauls, armed with weapons of iron. They were subjugated by the Romans, and Roman Gaul in turn became a prey to the Goth and the Frank. History has begun and is in full swing.

The mediæval period succeeded, and finally the modern age, and man now lives on top of the accumulation of all preceding epochs of men and stages of civilisation. In no other part of France, indeed of Europe, is the story of man told so plainly, that he who runs may read; and ever since the middle of last century, when this fact was recognised, the district has been studied, and explorations have been made there, some slovenly, others scientifically.

A few years ago I was induced to visit this remarkable region and to examine it attentively. I had been furnished with letters of recommendation from the authorities of the great Museum of National Antiquities at St. Germain, to enable me to prosecute my researches unmolested by over-suspicious gendarmes and ignorant mayors.

Under one over-hanging rock was a cabaret or tavern, announcing that wine was sold there, by a withered bush above the door.

The place seemed to me to be a probable spot for my exploration. I entered into an arrangement with the proprietor to enable me to dig, he stipulating that I should not undermine and throw down his walls. I engaged six labourers, and began proceedings by driving a tunnel some little way below the tavern into the vast bed of débris.

The upper series of deposits did not concern me much. The point I desired to investigate, and if possible to determine, was the approximate length of time that had elapsed between the disappearance of the reindeer hunters and the coming on the scene of the next race, that which used polished stone implements and had domestic animals.

Although it may seem at first sight as if both races had been savage, as both lived in the Stone Age, yet an enormous stride forward had been taken when men had learned the arts of weaving, of pottery, and had tamed the dog, the horse, and the cow. These new folk had passed out of the mere wild condition of the hunter, and had become pastoral and to some extent agricultural.

Of course, the data for determining the length of a period might be few, but I could judge whether a very long or a very brief period had elapsed between the two occupations by the depth of débris—chalk fallen from the roof, brought down by frost, in which were no traces of human workmanship.

It was with this distinct object in view that I drove my adit into the slope of rubbish some way below the cabaret, and I chanced to have hit on the level of the deposits of the men of bronze. Not that we found much bronze—all we secured was a broken pin—but we came on fragments of pottery marked with the chevron and nail and twisted thong ornament peculiar to that people and age.

My men were engaged for about a week before we reached the face of the chalk cliff. We found the work not so easy as I had anticipated. Masses of rock had become detached from above and had fallen, so that we had either to quarry through them or to circumvent them. The soil was of that curious coffee colour so inseparable from the chalk formation. We found many things brought down from above, a coin commemorative of the storming of the Bastille, and some small pieces of the later Roman emperors. But all of these were, of course, not in the solid ground below, but near the surface.

When we had reached the face of the cliff, instead of sinking a shaft I determined on carrying a gallery down an incline, keeping the rock as a wall on my right, till I reached the bottom of all.

The advantage of making an incline was that there was no hauling up of the earth by a bucket let down over a pulley, and it was easier for myself to descend.

I had not made my tunnel wide enough, and it was tortuous. When I began to sink, I set two of the men to smash up the masses of fallen chalk rock, so as to widen the tunnel, so that I might use barrows. I gave strict orders that all the material brought up was to be picked over by two of the most intelligent of the men, outside in the blaze of the sun. I was not desirous of sinking too expeditiously; I wished to proceed slowly, cautiously, observing every stage as we went deeper.

We got below the layer in which were the relics of the Bronze Age and of the men of polished stone, and then we passed through many feet of earth that rendered nothing, and finally came on the traces of the reindeer period.

To understand how that there should be a considerable depth of the débris of the men of the rude stone implements, it must be explained that these men made their hearths on the bare ground, and feasted around their fires, throwing about them the bones they had picked, and the ashes, and broken and disused implements, till the ground was inconveniently encumbered. Then they swept all the refuse together over their old hearth, and established another on top. So the process went on from generation to generation.

For the scientific results of my exploration I must refer the reader to the journals and memoirs of learned societies. I will not trouble him with them here.

On the ninth day after we had come to the face of the cliff, and when we had reached a considerable depth, we uncovered some human bones. I immediately adopted special precautions, so that these should not be disturbed. With the utmost care the soil was removed from over them, and it took us half a day to completely clear a perfect skeleton. It was that of a full-grown man, lying on his back, with the skull supported against the wall of chalk rock. He did not seem to have been buried. Had he been so, he would doubtless have been laid on his side in a contracted posture, with the chin resting on the knees.

409

One of the men pointed out to me that a mass of fallen rock lay beyond his feet, and had apparently shut him in, so that he had died through suffocation, buried under the earth that the rock had brought down with it.

I at once despatched a man to my hotel to fetch my camera, that I might by flashlight take a photograph of the skeleton as it lay; and another I sent to get from the chemist and grocer as much gum arabic and isinglass as could be procured. My object was to give to the bones a bath of gum to render them less brittle when removed, restoring to them the gelatine that had been absorbed by the earth and lime in which they lay.

Thus I was left alone at the bottom of my passage, the four men above being engaged in straightening the adit and sifting the earth.

I was quite content to be alone, so that I might at my ease search for traces of personal ornament worn by the man who had thus met his death. The place was somewhat cramped, and there really was not room in it for more than one person to work freely.

Whilst I was thus engaged, I suddenly heard a shout, followed by a crash, and, to my dismay, an avalanche of rubble shot down the inclined passage of descent. I at once left the skeleton, and hastened to effect my exit, but found that this was impossible. Much of the superincumbent earth and stone had fallen, dislodged by the vibrations caused by the picks of the men smashing up the chalk blocks, and the passage was completely choked. I was sealed up in the hollow where I was, and thankful that the earth above me had not fallen as well, and buried me, a man of the present enlightened age, along with the primeval savage of eight thousand years ago.

A large amount of matter must have fallen, for I could not hear the voices of the men.

I was not seriously alarmed. The workmen would procure assistance and labour indefatigably to release me; of that I could be certain. But how much earth had fallen? How much of the passage was choked, and how long would they take before I was released? All that was uncertain. I had a candle, or, rather, a bit of one, and it was not probable that it would last till the passage was cleared. What made me most anxious was the question whether the supply of air in the hollow in which I was enclosed would suffice.

My enthusiasm for prehistoric research failed me just then. All my interests were concentrated on the present, and I gave up groping about the skeleton for relics. I seated myself on a stone, set the candle in a socket of chalk I had scooped out with my pocket-knife, and awaited events with my eyes on the skeleton.

Time passed somewhat wearily. I could hear an occasional thud, thud, when the men were using the pick; but they mostly employed the shovel, as I supposed. I set my elbows on my knees and rested my chin in my hands. The air was not cold, nor was the soil damp; it was dry as snuff. The flicker of my light played over the man of bones, and especially illumined the skull. It may have been fancy on my part, it probably was fancy, but it seemed to me as though something sparkled in the eye-sockets. Drops of water possibly lodged there, or crystals formed within the skull; but the effect was much as of eyes leering and winking at me. I lighted my pipe, and to my disgust found that my supply of matches was running short. In France the manufacture belongs to the state, and one gets but sixty *allumettes* for a penny.

I had not brought my watch with me below ground, fearing lest it might meet with an accident; consequently I was unable to reckon how time passed. I began counting and ticking off the minutes on my fingers, but soon tired of doing this.

My candle was getting short; it would not last much longer, and then I should be in the dark. I consoled myself with the thought that with the extinction of the light the consumption of the oxygen in the air would be less rapid. My eyes now rested on the flame of the candle, and I watched the gradual diminution of the composite. It was one of those abominable *bougies* with holes in them to economise the wax, and which consequently had less than the proper amount of material for feeding and maintaining a flame. At length the light went out, and I was left in total darkness. I might have used up the rest of my matches, one after another, but to what good?—they would prolong the period of illumination for but a very little while.

A sense of numbness stole over me, but I was not as yet sensible of deficiency of air to breathe. I found that the stone on which I was seated was pointed and hard, but I did not like to shift my position for fear of getting among and disturbing the bones, and I was still desirous of having them photographed *in situ* before they were moved.

I was not alarmed at my situation; I knew that I must be released eventually. But the tedium of sitting there in the dark and on a pointed stone was becoming intolerable.

Some time must have elapsed before I became, dimly at first, and then distinctly, aware of a bluish phosphorescent emanation from the skeleton. This seemed to rise above it like a faint smoke, which gradually gained consistency, took form, and became distinct; and I saw before me the misty, luminous form of a naked man, with wolfish countenance, prognathous jaws, glaring at me out of eyes deeply sunk under projecting brows. Although I thus describe what I saw, yet it gave me no idea of substance; it was vaporous, and yet it was articulate. Indeed, I cannot say at this moment whether I actually saw this apparition with my eyes, or whether it was a dream-like vision of the brain. Though luminous, it cast no light on the walls of the cave; if I raised my hand it did not obscure any portion of the form presented to me. Then I heard: "I will tear you with the nails of my fingers and toes, and rip you with my teeth."

"What have I done to injure and incense you?" I asked.

And here I must explain. No word was uttered by either of us; no word could have been uttered by this vaporous form. It had no material lungs, nor throat, nor mouth to form vocal sounds. It had but the semblance of a man. It was a spook, not a human being. But from it proceeded thought-waves, odylic force which smote on the tympanum of my mind or soul, and thereon registered the ideas formed by it. So in like manner I thought my replies, and they were communicated back in the same manner. If vocal words had passed between us neither would have been intelligible to the other. No dictionary was ever compiled, or would be compiled, of the tongue of prehistoric man; moreover, the grammar of the speech of that race would be absolutely incomprehensible to man now. But thoughts can be interchanged without words. When we think we do not think in any language. It is only when we desire to communicate our thoughts to other men that we shape them into words and express them vocally in structural, grammatical sentences. The beasts have never attained to this, yet they can communicate with one another, not by language, but by thought vibrations.

I must further remark that when I give what ensued as a conversation, I have to render the thought intercommunication that passed between the Homo Præhistoricus—the prehistoric man—and me, in English as best I can render it. I knew as we conversed that I was not speaking to him in English, nor in French, nor Latin, nor in any tongue whatever. Moreover, when I use the words "said" or "spoke," I mean no more than that the impression was formed on my brain-pan or the receptive drum of my soul, was produced by the rhythmic, orderly sequence of thought-waves. When, however, I express the words "screamed" or "shrieked," I signify that those vibrations came sharp and swift; and when I say "laughed," that they came in a choppy, irregular fashion, conveying the idea, not the sound of laughter.

"I will tear you! I will rend you to bits and throw you in pieces about this cave!" shrieked the Homo Præhistoricus, or primeval man.

Again I remonstrated, and inquired how I had incensed him. But yelling with rage, he threw himself upon me. In a moment I was enveloped in a luminous haze, strips of phosphorescent vapour laid themselves about me, but I received no injury whatever, only my spiritual nature was subjected to something like a magnetic storm. After a few moments the spook disengaged itself from me, and drew back to where it was before, screaming broken exclamations of meaningless rage, and jabbering savagely. It rapidly cooled down.

"Why do you wish me ill?" I asked again.

"I cannot hurt you. I am spirit, you are matter, and spirit cannot injure matter; my nails are psychic phenomena. Your soul you can lacerate yourself, but I can effect nothing, nothing."

"Then why have you attacked me? What is the cause of your impotent resentment?"

"Because you are a son of the twentieth century, and I lived eight thousand years ago. Why are you nursed in the lap of luxury? Why do you enjoy comforts, a civilisation that we knew nothing of? It is not just. It is cruel on us. We had nothing, nothing, literally nothing, not even lucifer matches!"

Again he fell to screaming, as might a caged monkey rendered furious by failure to obtain an apple which he could not reach.

"I am very sorry, but it is no fault of mine."

"Whether it be your fault or not does not matter to me. You have these things—we had not. Why, I saw you just now strike a light on the sole of your boot. It was done in a moment. We had only flint and iron-stone, and it took half a day with us to kindle a fire, and then it flayed our knuckles with continuous knocking. No! we had nothing, nothing—no lucifer matches, no commercial travellers, no Benedictine, no pottery, no metal, no education, no elections, no *chocolat menier*."

"How do you know about these products of the present age, here, buried under fifty feet of soil for eight thousand years?"

"It is my spirit which speaks with your spirit. My spook does not always remain with my bones. I can go up; rocks and stones and earth heaped over me do not hold me down. I am often above. I am in the tavern overhead. I have seen men drink there. I have seen a bottle of Benedictine. I have applied my psychical lips to it, but I could taste, absorb nothing. I have seen commercial travellers there, cajoling the patron into buying things he did not want. They are mysterious, marvellous beings, their powers of persuasion are little short of miraculous. What do you think of doing with me?"

"Well, I propose first of all photographing you, then soaking you in gum arabic, and finally transferring you to a museum."

He screamed as though with pain, and gasped: "Don't! don't do it. It will be torture insufferable."

"But why so? You will be under glass, in a polished oak or mahogany box."

"Don't! You cannot understand what it will be to me—a spirit more or less attached to my body, to spend ages upon ages in a museum with fibulæ, triskelli, palstaves, celts, torques, scarabs. We cannot travel very far from our bones—our range is limited. And conceive of my feelings for centuries condemned to wander among glass cases containing prehistoric antiquities, and to hear the talk of scientific men alone. Now here, it is otherwise. Here I can pass up when I like into the tavern, and can see men get drunk, and hear commercial travellers hoodwink the patron, and then when the taverner finds he has been induced to buy what he did not want, I can see him beat his wife and smack his children. There is something human, humorous, in that, but fibulæ, palstaves, torques—bah!"

"You seem to have a lively knowledge of antiquities," I observed.

"Of course I have. There come archæologists here and eat their sandwiches above me, and talk prehistoric antiquities till I am sick. Give me life! Give me something interesting!"

"But what do you mean when you say that you cannot travel far from your bones?"

"I mean that there is a sort of filmy attachment that connects our psychic nature with our mortal remains. It is like a spider and its web. Suppose the soul to be the spider and the skeleton to be the web. If you break the thread the spider will never find its way back to its home. So it is with us; there is an attachment, a faint thread of luminous spiritual matter that unites us to our earthly husk. It is liable to accidents. It sometimes gets broken, sometimes dissolved by water. If a blackbeetle crawls across it it suffers a sort of paralysis. I have never been to the other side of the river, I have feared to do so, though very anxious to look at that creature like a large black caterpillar called the Train."

"This is news to me. Do you know of any cases of rupture of connection?"

"Yes," he replied. "My old father, after he was dead some years, got his link of attachment broken, and he wandered about disconsolate. He could not find his own body, but he lighted on that of a young female of seventeen, and he got into that. It happened most singularly that her spook, being frolicsome and inconsiderate, had got its bond also broken, and she, that is her spirit, straying about in quest of her body, lighted on that of my venerable parent, and for want of a better took possession of it. It so chanced that after a while they met and became chummy. In the world of spirits there is no marriage, but there grow up spiritual attachments, and these two got rather fond of each other, but never could puzzle it out which was which and what each was; for a female soul had entered into an old male body, and a male soul had taken up its residence in a female body. Neither could riddle out of which sex each was. You see they had no education. But I know that my father's soul became quite sportive in that young woman's skeleton."

"Did they continue chummy?"

"No; they quarrelled as to which was which, and they are not now on speaking terms. I have two great-uncles. Theirs is a sad tale. Their souls were out wandering one day, and inadvertently they crossed and recrossed each other's tracks so that their spiritual threads of attachment got twisted. They found this out, and that they were getting tangled up. What one of them should have done would have been to have stood still and let the other jump over and dive under his brother's thread till he had cleared himself. But my maternal great-uncles—I think I forgot to say they were related to me through my mother—they were men of peppery tempers and they could not understand this. They had no education. So they jumped one this way and one another, each abusing the other, and made the tangle more complete. That was about six thousand years ago, and they are now so knotted up that I do not suppose they will be clear of one another till time is no more."

He paused and laughed.

Then I said: "It must have been very hard for you to be without pottery of any sort."

"It was," replied H. P. (this stands for Homo Præhistoricus, not for House-Parlourmaid or Hardy Perennial), "very hard. We had skins for water and milk——"

"Oh! you had milk. I supposed you had no cows."

"Nor had we, but the reindeer were beginning to get docile and be tamed. If we caught young deer we brought them up to be pets for our children. And so it came about that as they grew up we found out that we could milk them into skins. But that gave it a smack, and whenever we desired a fresh draught there was nothing for it but to lie flat on the ground under a doe reindeer and suck for all we were worth. It was hard. Horses were hunted. It did not occur to us that they could be tamed and saddled and mounted. Oh! it was not right. It was not fair that you should have everything and we nothing—nothing—nothing! Why should you have all and we have had naught?"

"Because I belong to the twentieth century. Thirty-three generations go to a thousand years. There are some two hundred and sixty-four or two hundred and seventy generations intervening between you and me. Each generation makes some discovery that advances civilisation a stage, the next enters on the discoveries of the preceding generations, and so culture advances stage by stage. Man is infinitely progressive, the brute beast is not."

"That is true," he replied. "I invented butter, which was unknown to my ancestors, the unbuttered man."

"Indeed!"

"It was so," he said, and I saw a flush of light ripple over the emanation. I suppose it was a glow of self-satisfaction. "It came about thus. One of my wives had nearly let the fire out. I was very angry, and catching up one of the skins of milk, I banged her about the head with it till she fell insensible to the earth. The other wives were very pleased and applauded. When I came to take a drink, for my exertions had heated me, I found that the milk was curdled into butter. At first I did not know what it was, so I made one of my other wives taste it, and as she pronounced it to be good, I ate the rest myself. That was how butter was invented. For four hundred years that was the way it was made, by banging a milk-skin about the head of a woman till she was knocked down insensible. But at last a woman found out that by churning the milk with her hand butter could be made equally well, and then the former process was discontinued except by some men who clung to ancestral customs."

"But," said I, "nowadays you would not be suffered to knock your wife about, even with a milk-skin."

"Why not?"

"Because it is barbarous. You would be sent to gaol."

"But she was my wife."

"Nevertheless it would not be tolerated. The law steps in and protects women from ill-usage."

"How shameful! Not allowed to do what you like with your own wife!"

"Most assuredly not. Then you remarked that this was how you dealt with one of your wives. How many did you possess?"

"Off and on, seventeen."

"*Now*, no man is suffered to have more than one."

"What—one at a time?"

"Yes," I replied.

"Ah, well. Then if you had an old and ugly wife, or one who was a scold, you could kill her and get another, young and pretty."

"That would not be allowed."

"Not even if she were a scold?"

"No, you would have to put up with her to the bitter end."

"Humph!" H. P. remained silent for a while wrapped in thought. Presently he said: "There is one thing I do not understand. In the wine-shop overhead the men get very quarrelsome, others drunk, but they never kill one another."

"No. If one man killed another he would have his head cut off—here in France—unless extenuating circumstances were found. With us in England he would be hanged by the neck till he was dead."

"Then—what is your sport?"

"We hunt the fox."

"The fox is bad eating. I never could stomach it. If I did kill a fox I made my wives eat it, and had some mammoth meat for myself. But hunting is business with us—or was so—not sport."

"Nevertheless with us it is our great sport."

"Business is business and sport is sport," he said. "Now, we hunted as business, and had little fights and killed one another as our sport."

"We are not suffered to kill one another."

"But take the case," said he, "that a man has a nose-ring, or a pretty wife, and you want one or the other. Surely you might kill him and possess yourself of what you so ardently covet?"

"By no means. Now, to change the topic," I went on, "you are totally destitute of clothing. You do not even wear the traditional garment of fig leaves."

"What avail fig leaves? There is no warmth in them."

"Perhaps not—but out of delicacy."

413

"What is that? I don't understand." There was clearly no corresponding sensation in the vibrating tympanum of his psychic nature.

"Did you never wear clothes?" I inquired.

"Certainly, when it was cold we wore skins, skins of the beasts we killed. But in summer what is the use of clothing? Besides, we only wore them out of doors. When we entered our homes, made of skins hitched up to the rock overhead, we threw them off. It was hot within, and we perspired freely."

"What, were naked in your homes! you and your wives?"

"Of course we were. Why not? It was very warm within with the fire always kept up."

"Why—good gracious me!" I exclaimed, "that would never be tolerated nowadays. If you attempted to go about the country unclothed, even get out of your clothes freely at home, you would be sent to a lunatic asylum and kept there."

"Humph!" He again lapsed into silence.

Presently he exclaimed: "After all, I think that we were better off as we were eight thousand years ago, even without your matches, Benedictine, education, *chocolat menier*, and commercials, for then we were able to enjoy real sport—we could kill one another, we could knock old wives on the head, we could have a dozen or more squaws according to our circumstances, young and pretty, and we could career about the country or sit and enjoy a social chat at home, stark naked. We were best off as we were. There are compensations in life at every period of man. Vive la liberté!"

At that moment I heard a shout—saw a flash of light. The workmen had pierced the barrier. A rush of fresh air entered. I staggered to my feet.

"Oh! mon Dieu! Monsieur vit encore!"

I felt dizzy. Kind hands grasped me. I was dragged forth. Brandy was poured down my throat. When I came to myself I gasped: "Fill in the hole! Fill it all up. Let H. P. lie where he is. He shall not go to the British Museum. I have had enough of prehistoric antiquities. Adieu, pour toujours la Vézère."

IX. — GLÁMR

THE following story is found in the Gretla, an Icelandic Saga, composed in the thirteenth century, or that comes to us in the form then given to it; but it is a redaction of a Saga of much earlier date. Most of it is thoroughly historical, and its statements are corroborated by other Sagas. The following incident was introduced to account for the fact that the outlaw Grettir would run any risk rather than spend the long winter nights alone in the dark.

At the beginning of the eleventh century there stood, a little way up the Valley of Shadows in the north of Iceland, a small farm, occupied by a worthy bonder, named Thorhall, and his wife. The farmer was not exactly a chieftain, but he was well enough connected to be considered respectable; to back up his gentility he possessed numerous flocks of sheep and a goodly drove of oxen. Thorhall would have been a happy man but for one circumstance—his sheepwalks were haunted.

Not a herdsman would remain with him; he bribed, he threatened, entreated, all to no purpose; one shepherd after another left his service, and things came to such a pass that he determined on asking advice at the next annual council. Thorhall saddled his horses, adjusted his packs, provided himself with hobbles, cracked his long Icelandic whip, and cantered along the road, and in due time reached Thingvellir.

Skapti Thorodd's son was lawgiver at that time, and as everyone considered him a man of the utmost prudence and able to give the best advice, our friend from the Vale of Shadows made straight for his booth.

"An awkward predicament, certainly—to have large droves of sheep and no one to look after them," said Skapti, nibbling the nail of his thumb, and shaking his wise head—a head as stuffed with law as a ptarmigan's crop is stuffed with blaeberries. "Now I'll tell you what—as you have asked my advice, I will help you to a shepherd; a character in his way, a man of dull intellect, to be sure but strong as a bull."

"I do not care about his wits so long as he can look after sheep," answered Thorhall.

"You may rely on his being able to do that," said Skapti. "He is a stout, plucky fellow; a Swede from Sylgsdale, if you know where that is."

Towards the break-up of the council—"Thing" they call it in Iceland—two greyish-white horses belonging to Thorhall slipped their hobbles and strayed; so the good man had to hunt after them himself, which shows how short of servants he was. He crossed Sletha-asi, thence he bent his way to Armann's-fell, and just by the Priest's Wood he met a strange-looking man driving before him a horse laden with faggots. The fellow was tall and stalwart; his face involuntarily attracted Thorhall's attention, for the eyes, of an ashen grey, were large and staring, the powerful jaw was furnished with very white protruding teeth, and around the low forehead hung bunches of coarse wolf-grey hair.

"Pray, what is your name, my man?" asked the farmer pulling up.

"Glámr, an please you," replied the wood-cutter.

Thorhall stared; then, with a preliminary cough, he asked how Glámr liked faggot-picking.

"Not much," was the answer; "I prefer shepherd life."

"Will you come with me?" asked Thorhall; "Skapti has handed you over to me, and I want a shepherd this winter uncommonly."

"If I serve you, it is on the understanding that I come or go as it pleases me. I tell you I am a bit truculent if things do not go just to my thinking."

"I shall not object to this," answered the bonder. "So I may count on your services?"

"Wait a moment! You have not told me whether there be any drawback."

"I must acknowledge that there is one," said Thorhall; "in fact, the sheepwalks have got a bad name for bogies."

"Pshaw! I'm not the man to be scared at shadows," laughed Glámr; "so here's my hand to it; I'll be with you at the beginning of the winter night."

Well, after this they parted, and presently the farmer found his ponies. Having thanked Skapti for his advice and assistance, he got his horses together and trotted home.

Summer, and then autumn passed, but not a word about the new shepherd reached the Valley of Shadows. The winter storms began to bluster up the glen, driving the flying snow-flakes and massing the white drifts at every winding of the vale. Ice formed in the shallows of the river; and the streams, which in summer trickled down the ribbed scarps, were now transmuted into icicles.

One gusty night a violent blow at the door startled all in the farm. In another moment Glámr, tall as a troll, stood in the hall glowering out of his wild eyes, his grey hair matted with frost, his teeth rattling and snapping with cold, his face blood-red in the glare of the fire which smouldered in the centre of the hall. Thorhall jumped up and greeted him warmly, but the housewife was too frightened to be very cordial.

Weeks passed, and the new shepherd was daily on the moors with his flock; his loud and deep-toned voice was often borne down on the blast as he shouted to the sheep driving them into fold. His presence in the house always produced gloom, and if he spoke it sent a thrill through the women, who openly proclaimed their aversion for him.

There was a church near the byre, but Glámr never crossed the threshold; he hated psalmody; apparently he was an indifferent Christian. On the vigil of the Nativity Glámr rose early and shouted for meat.

"Meat!" exclaimed the housewife; "no man calling himself a Christian touches flesh to-day. To-morrow is the holy Christmas Day, and this is a fast."

"All superstition!" roared Glámr. "As far as I can see, men are no better now than they were in the bonny heathen time. Bring me meat, and make no more ado about it."

"You may be quite certain," protested the good wife, "if Church rule be not kept, ill-luck will follow."

Glámr ground his teeth and clenched his hands. "Meat! I will have meat, or——" In fear and trembling the poor woman obeyed.

The day was raw and windy; masses of grey vapour rolled up from the Arctic Ocean, and hung in piles about the mountain-tops. Now and then a scud of frozen fog, composed of minute particles of ice, swept along the glen, covering bar and beam with feathery hoar-frost. As the day declined, snow began to fall in large flakes like the down of the eider-duck. One moment there was a lull in the wind, and then the deep-toned shout of Glámr, high up the moor slopes, was heard distinctly by the congregation assembling for the first vespers of Christmas Day. Darkness came on, deep as that in the rayless abysses of the caverns under the lava, and still the snow fell thicker. The lights from the church windows sent a yellow haze far out into the night, and every flake burned golden as it swept within the ray. The bell in the lych-gate clanged for evensong, and the wind puffed the sound far up the glen; perhaps it reached the herdsman's ear. Hark! Someone caught a distant sound or shriek, which it was he could not tell, for the wind muttered and mumbled about the church eaves, and then with a fierce whistle scudded over the graveyard fence. Glámr had not returned when the service was over. Thorhall suggested a search, but no man would accompany him; and no wonder! it was not a night for a dog to be out in; besides, the tracks were a foot deep in snow. The family sat up all night, waiting, listening, trembling; but no Glámr came home. Dawn broke at last, wan and blear in the south. The clouds hung down like great sheets, full of snow, almost to bursting.

A party was soon formed to search for the missing man. A sharp scramble brought them to high land, and the ridge between the two rivers which join in Vatnsdalr was thoroughly examined. Here and there were found the scattered sheep, shuddering under an icicled rock, or half buried in a snow-drift. No trace yet of the keeper. A dead ewe lay at the bottom of a crag; it had staggered over in the gloom, and had been dashed to pieces.

Presently the whole party were called together about a trampled spot in the heath, where evidently a death-struggle had taken place, for earth and stone were tossed about, and the snow was blotched with large splashes of blood. A gory track led up the mountain, and the farm-servants were following it, when a cry, almost of agony, from one of the lads, made them turn. In looking behind a rock, the boy had come upon the corpse of the shepherd; it was livid and swollen to the size of a bullock. It lay on its back with the arms extended. The snow had been scrabbled up by the puffed hands in the death-agony, and the staring glassy eyes gazed out of the ashen-grey, upturned face into the vaporous canopy overhead. From the purple lips lolled the tongue, which in the last throes had been bitten through by the white fangs, and a discoloured stream which had flowed from it was now an icicle.

With trouble the dead man was raised on a litter, and carried to a gill-edge, but beyond this he could not be borne; his weight waxed more and more, the bearers toiled beneath their burden, their foreheads became beaded with sweat; though strong men they were crushed to the ground. Consequently, the corpse was left at the ravine-head, and the men returned to the farm. Next day their efforts to lift Glámr's bloated carcass, and remove it to consecrated ground, were unavailing. On the third day a priest accompanied them, but the body was nowhere to be found. Another expedition without the priest was made, and on this occasion the corpse was discovered; so a cairn was raised over the spot.

Two nights after this one of the thralls who had gone after the cows burst into the hall with a face blank and scared; he staggered to a seat and fainted. On recovering his senses, in a broken voice he assured all who crowded about him that he had seen Glámr walking past him as he left the door of the stable. On the following evening a houseboy was found in a fit under the farmyard wall, and he remained an idiot to his dying day. Some of the women next saw a face which, though blown out and discoloured, they recognised as that of Glámr, looking in upon them through a window of the dairy. In the twilight, Thorhall himself met the dead man, who stood and glowered at him, but made no attempt to injure his master. The haunting did not end there. Nightly a heavy tread was heard around the house, and a hand feeling along the walls, sometimes thrust in at the windows, at others clutching the woodwork, and breaking it to splinters. However, when the spring came round the disturbances lessened, and as the sun obtained full power, ceased altogether.

That summer a vessel from Norway dropped anchor in the nearest bay. Thorhall visited it, and found on board a man named Thorgaut, who was in search of work.

"What do you say to being my shepherd?" asked the bonder.

"I should very much like the office," answered Thorgaut. "I am as strong as two ordinary men, and a handy fellow to boot."

"I will not engage you without forewarning you of the terrible things you may have to encounter during the winter night."

"Pray, what may they be?"

"Ghosts and hobgoblins," answered the farmer; "a fine dance they lead me, I can promise you."

"I fear them not," answered Thorgaut; "I shall be with you at cattle-slaughtering time."

At the appointed season the man came, and soon established himself as a favourite in the house; he romped with the children, chucked the maidens under the chin, helped his fellow-servants, gratified the housewife by admiring her curd, and was just as much liked as his predecessor had been detested. He was a devil-may-care fellow, too, and made no bones of his contempt for the ghost, expressing hopes of meeting him face to face, which made his master look grave, and his mistress shudderingly cross herself. As the winter came on, strange sights and sounds began to alarm the folk, but these never frightened Thorgaut; he slept too soundly at night to hear the tread of feet about the door, and was too short-sighted to catch glimpses of a grizzly monster striding up and down, in the twilight, before its cairn.

At last Christmas Eve came round, and Thorgaut went out as usual with his sheep.

"Have a care, man," urged the bonder; "go not near to the gill-head, where Glámr lies."

"Tut, tut! fear not for me. I shall be back by vespers."

"God grant it," sighed the housewife; "but 'tis not a day for risks, to be sure."

Twilight came on: a feeble light hung over the south, one white streak above the heath land to the south. Far off in southern lands it was still day, but here the darkness gathered in apace, and men came from Vatnsdalr for evensong, to herald in the night when Christ was born. Christmas Eve! How different in Saxon England! There the great ashen faggot is rolled along the hall with torch and taper; the mummers dance with their merry jingling bells; the boar's head, with gilded tusks, "bedecked with holly and rosemary," is brought in by the steward to a flourish of trumpets.

How different, too, where the Varanger cluster round the imperial throne in the mighty church of the Eternal Wisdom at this very hour. Outside, the air is soft from breathing over the Bosphorus, which flashes tremulously beneath the stars. The orange and laurel leaves in the palace gardens are still exhaling fragrance in the hush of the Christmas night.

But it is different here. The wind is piercing as a two-edged sword; blocks of ice crash and grind along the coast, and the lake waters are congealed to stone. Aloft, the Aurora flames crimson, flinging long streamers to the zenith, and then suddenly dissolving into a sea of pale green light. The natives are waiting round the church-door, but no Thorgaut has returned.

They find him next morning, lying across Glámr's cairn, with his spine, his leg, and arm-bones shattered. He is conveyed to the churchyard, and a cross is set up at his head. He sleeps peacefully. Not so Glámr; he becomes more furious than ever. No one will remain with Thorhall now, except an old cowherd who has always served the family, and who had long ago dandled his present master on his knee.

"All the cattle will be lost if I leave," said the carle; "it shall never be told of me that I deserted Thorhall from fear of a spectre."

Matters grew rapidly worse. Outbuildings were broken into of a night, and their woodwork was rent and shattered; the house door was violently shaken, and great pieces of it were torn away; the gables of the house were also pulled furiously to and fro.

One morning before dawn, the old man went to the stable. An hour later, his mistress arose, and taking her milking pails, followed him. As she reached the door of the stable, a terrible sound from within—the bellowing of the cattle, mingled with the deep notes of an unearthly voice—sent her back shrieking to the house. Thorhall leaped out of bed, caught up a weapon, and hastened to the cow-house. On opening the door, he found the cattle goring each other. Slung across the stone that separated the stalls was something. Thorhall stepped up to it, felt it, looked close; it was the cowherd, perfectly dead, his feet on one side of the slab, his head on the other, and his spine snapped in twain. The bonder now moved with his family to Tunga, another farm owned by him lower down the valley; it was too venturesome living during the mid-winter night at the haunted farm; and it was not till the sun had returned as a bridegroom out of his chamber, and had dispelled night with its phantoms, that he went back to the Vale of Shadows. In the meantime, his little girl's health had given way under the repeated alarms of the winter; she became paler every day; with the autumn flowers she faded, and was laid beneath the mould of the churchyard in time for the first snows to spread a virgin pall over her small grave.

At this time Grettir—a hero of great fame, and a native of the north of the island—was in Iceland, and as the hauntings of this vale were matters of gossip throughout the district, he inquired about them, and resolved on visiting the scene. So Grettir busked himself for a cold ride, mounted his horse, and in due course of time drew rein at the door of Thorhall's farm with the request that he might be accommodated there for the night.

"Ahem!" coughed the bonder; "perhaps you are not aware——"

"I am perfectly aware of all. I want to catch sight of the troll."

"But your horse is sure to be killed."

"I will risk it. Glámr I must meet, so there's an end of it."

"I am delighted to see you," spoke the bonder; "at the same time, should mischief befall you, don't lay the blame at my door."

"Never fear, man."

So they shook hands; the horse was put into the strongest stable, Thorhall made Grettir as good cheer as he was able, and then, as the visitor was sleepy, all retired to rest.

The night passed quietly, and no sounds indicated the presence of a restless spirit. The horse, moreover, was found next morning in good condition, enjoying his hay.

"This is unexpected!" exclaimed the bonder, gleefully. "Now, where's the saddle? We'll clap it on, and then good-bye, and a merry journey to you."

"Good-bye!" echoed Grettir; "I am going to stay here another night."

"You had best be advised," urged Thorhall; "if misfortune should overtake you, I know that all your kinsmen would visit it on my head."

"I have made up my mind to stay," said Grettir, and he looked so dogged that Thorhall opposed him no more.

All was quiet next night; not a sound roused Grettir from his slumber. Next morning he went with the farmer to the stable. The strong wooden door was shivered and driven in. They stepped across it; Grettir called to his horse, but there was no responsive whinny.

"I am afraid——" began Thorhall. Grettir leaped in, and found the poor brute dead, and with its neck broken.

"Now," said Thorhall quickly, "I've got a capital horse—a skewbald—down by Tunga, I shall not be many hours in fetching it; your saddle is here, I think, and then you will just have time to reach——"

"I stay here another night," interrupted Grettir.

"I implore you to depart," said Thorhall.

"My horse is slain!"

"But I will provide you with another."

"Friend," answered Grettir, turning so sharply round that the farmer jumped back, half frightened, "no man ever did me an injury without rueing it. Now, your demon herdsman has been the death of my horse. He must be taught a lesson."

"Would that he were!" groaned Thorhall; "but mortal must not face him. Go in peace and receive compensation from me for what has happened."

"I must revenge my horse."

"An obstinate man will have his own way! But if you run your head against a stone wall, don't be angry because you get a broken pate."

Night came on; Grettir ate a hearty supper and was right jovial; not so Thorhall, who had his misgivings. At bedtime the latter crept into his crib, which, in the manner of old Icelandic beds, opened out of the hall, as berths do out of a cabin. Grettir, however, determined on remaining up; so he flung himself on a bench with his feet against the posts of the high seat, and his back against Thorhall's crib; then he wrapped one lappet of his fur coat round his feet, the other about his head, keeping the neck-opening in front of his face, so that he could look through into the hall.

There was a fire burning on the hearth, a smouldering heap of red embers; every now and then a twig flared up and crackled, giving Grettir glimpses of the rafters, as he lay with his eyes wandering among the mysteries of the smoke-blackened roof. The wind whistled softly overhead. The clerestory windows, covered with the amnion of sheep, admitted now and then a sickly yellow glare from the full moon, which, however, shot a beam of pure silver through the smoke-hole in the roof. A dog without began to howl; the cat, which had long been sitting demurely watching the fire, stood up with raised back and bristling tail, then darted behind some chests in a corner. The hall door was in a sad plight. It had been so riven by the spectre that it was made firm by wattles only, and the moon glinted athwart the crevices. Soothingly the river, not yet frozen over, prattled over its shingly bed as it swept round the knoll on which stood the farm. Grettir heard the breathing of the sleeping women in the adjoining chamber, and the sigh of the housewife as she turned in her bed.

Click! click!—It is only the frozen turf on the roof cracking with the cold. The wind lulls completely. The night is very still without. Hark! a heavy tread, beneath which the snow yields. Every footfall goes straight to Grettir's heart. A crash on the turf overhead! By all the saints in paradise! The monster is treading on the roof. For one moment the chimney-gap is completely darkened: Glámr is looking down it; the flash of the red ash is reflected in the two lustreless eyes. Then the moon glances sweetly in once more, and the heavy tramp of Glámr is audibly moving towards the farther end of the hall. A thud—he has leaped down. Grettir feels the board at his back quivering, for Thorhall is awake and is trembling in his bed. The steps pass round to the back of the house, and then the snapping of the wood shows that the creature is destroying some of the outhouse doors. He tires of this apparently, for his footfall comes clear towards the main entrance to the hall. The moon is veiled behind a watery cloud, and by the uncertain glimmer Grettir fancies that he sees two dark hands thrust in above the door. His apprehensions are verified, for, with a loud snap, a long strip of panel breaks, and light is admitted. Snap—snap! another portion gives way, and the gap becomes larger. Then the wattles slip from their places, and a dark arm rips them out in bunches, and flings them away. There is a cross-beam to the door, holding a bolt which slides into a stone groove. Against the grey light, Grettir sees a huge black figure heaving itself over the bar. Crack! that has given way, and the rest of the door falls in shivers to the earth.

"Oh, heavens above!" exclaims the bonder.

Stealthily the dead man creeps on, feeling at the beams as he comes; then he stands in the hall, with the firelight on him. A fearful sight; the tall figure distended with the corruption of the grave, the nose fallen off, the wandering, vacant eyes, with the glaze of death on them, the sallow flesh patched with green masses of decay; the wolf-grey hair and beard have grown in the tomb, and hang matted about the shoulders and breast; the nails, too, they have grown. It is a sickening sight—a thing to shudder at, not to see.

Motionless, with no nerve quivering now, Thorhall and Grettir held their breath.

Glámr's lifeless glance strayed round the chamber; it rested on the shaggy bundle by the high seat. Cautiously he stepped towards it. Grettir felt him groping about the lower lappet and pulling at it. The cloak did not give way. Another jerk; Grettir kept his feet firmly pressed against the posts, so that the rug was not pulled off. The vampire seemed puzzled, he plucked at the upper flap and tugged. Grettir held to the bench and bed-board, so that he was not moved, but the cloak was rent in twain, and the corpse staggered back, holding half in its hands, and gazing wonderingly at it. Before it had done examining the shred, Grettir started to his feet, bowed his body, flung his arms about the carcass, and, driving his head into the chest, strove to bend it backward and snap the spine. A vain attempt! The cold hands came down on Grettir's arms with diabolical force, riving them from their hold. Grettir clasped them about the body again; then the arms closed round him, and began dragging him along. The brave man clung by his feet to benches and posts, but the strength of the vampire was the greater; posts gave way, benches were heaved from their places, and the wrestlers at each moment neared the door. Sharply writhing loose, Grettir flung his hands round a roof-beam. He was dragged from his feet; the numbing arms clenched him round the waist, and tore at him; every tendon in his breast was strained; the strain under his shoulders became excruciating, the muscles stood out in knots. Still he held on; his fingers were bloodless; the pulses of his temples throbbed in jerks; the breath came in a whistle through his rigid nostrils. All the while, too, the long nails of the dead man cut into his side, and Grettir could feel them piercing like knives between his ribs. Then at once his hands gave way, and the monster bore him reeling towards the porch, crashing over the broken fragments of the door. Hard as the battle had gone with him indoors, Grettir knew that it would go worse outside, so he gathered up all his remaining strength for one final desperate struggle. The door had been shut with a swivel into a groove; this groove was in a stone, which formed the jamb on one side, and there was a similar block on the other, into which the hinges had been driven. As the wrestlers neared the opening, Grettir planted both his feet against the stone posts, holding Glámr by the middle. He had the advantage now. The dead man writhed in his arms, drove his talons into Grettir's back, and tore up great ribbons of flesh, but the stone jambs held firm.

"Now," thought Grettir, "I can break his back," and thrusting his head under the chin, so that the grizzly beard covered his eyes, he forced the face from him, and the back was bent as a hazel-rod.

"If I can but hold on," thought Grettir, and he tried to shout for Thorhall, but his voice was muffled in the hair of the corpse.

Suddenly one or both of the door-posts gave way. Down crashed the gable trees, ripping beams and rafters from their beds; frozen clods of earth rattled from the roof and thumped into the snow. Glámr fell on his back, and Grettir staggered down on top of him. The moon was at her full; large white clouds chased each other across the sky, and as they swept before her disk she looked through them with a brown halo round her. The snow-cap of Jorundarfell, however, glowed like a planet, then the white mountain ridge was kindled, the light ran down the hillside, the bright disk stared out of the veil and flashed at this moment full on the vampire's face. Grettir's strength was failing him, his hands quivered in the snow, and he knew that he could not support himself from dropping flat on the dead man's face, eye to eye, lip to lip. The eyes of the corpse were fixed on him, lit with the cold glare of the moon. His head swam as his heart sent a hot stream to his brain. Then a voice from the grey lips said—

"Thou hast acted madly in seeking to match thyself with me. Now learn that henceforth ill-luck shall constantly attend thee; that thy strength shall never exceed what it now is, and that by night these eyes of mine shall stare at thee through the darkness till thy dying day, so that for very horror thou shalt not endure to be alone."

Grettir at this moment noticed that his dirk had slipped from its sheath during the fall, and that it now lay conveniently near his hand. The giddiness which had oppressed him passed away, he clutched at the sword-haft, and with a blow severed the vampire's throat. Then, kneeling on the breast, he hacked till the head came off.

Thorhall appeared now, his face blanched with terror, but when he saw how the fray had terminated he assisted Grettir gleefully to roll the corpse on the top of a pile of faggots, which had been collected for winter fuel. Fire was applied, and soon far down the valley the flames of the pyre startled people, and made them wonder what new horror was being enacted in the upper portion of the Vale of Shadows.

Next day the charred bones were conveyed to a spot remote from the habitations of men, and were there buried.

What Glámr had predicted came to pass. Never after did Grettir dare to be alone in the dark.

X. — COLONEL HALIFAX'S GHOST STORY

I HAD just come back to England, after having been some years in India, and was looking forward to meet my friends, among whom there was none I was more anxious to see than Sir Francis Lynton. We had been at Eton together, and for the short time I had been at Oxford before entering the Army we had been at the same college. Then we had been parted. He came into the title and estates of the family in Yorkshire on the death of his grandfather—his father had predeceased—and I had been over a good part of the world. One visit, indeed, I had made him in his Yorkshire home, before leaving for India, of but a few days.

It will easily be imagined how pleasant it was, two or three days after my arrival in London, to receive a letter from Lynton saying he had just seen in the papers that I had arrived, and begging me to come down at once to Byfield, his place in Yorkshire.

"You are not to tell me," he said, "that you cannot come. I allow you a week in which to order and try on your clothes, to report yourself at the War Office, to pay your respects to the Duke, and to see your sister at Hampton Court; but after that I shall expect you. In fact, you are to come on Monday. I have a couple of horses which will just suit you; the carriage shall meet you at Packham, and all you have got to do is to put yourself in the train which leaves King's Cross at twelve o'clock."

Accordingly, on the day appointed I started; in due time reached Packham, losing much time on a detestable branch line, and there found the dogcart of Sir Francis awaiting me. I drove at once to Byfield.

The house I remembered. It was a low, gabled structure of no great size, with old-fashioned lattice windows, separated from the park, where were deer, by a charming terraced garden.

No sooner did the wheels crunch the gravel by the principal entrance, than, almost before the bell was rung, the porch door opened, and there stood Lynton himself, whom I had not seen for so many years, hardly altered, and with all the joy of welcome beaming in his face. Taking me by both hands, he drew me into the house, got rid of my hat and wraps, looked me all over, and then, in a breath, began to say how glad he was to see me, what a real delight it was to have got me at last under his roof, and what a good time we would have together, like the old days over again.

He had sent my luggage up to my room, which was ready for me, and he bade me make haste and dress for dinner.

So saying, he took me through a panelled hall up an oak staircase, and showed me my room, which, hurried as I was, I observed was hung with tapestry, and had a large fourpost bed, with velvet curtains, opposite the window.

They had gone into dinner when I came down, despite all the haste I made in dressing; but a place had been kept for me next Lady Lynton.

Besides my hosts, there were their two daughters, Colonel Lynton, a brother of Sir Francis, the chaplain, and some others whom I do not remember distinctly.

After dinner there was some music in the hall, and a game of whist in the drawing-room, and after the ladies had gone upstairs, Lynton and I retired to the smoking-room, where we sat up talking the best part of the night. I think it must have been near three when I retired. Once in bed, I slept so soundly that my servant's entrance the next morning failed to arouse me, and it was past nine when I awoke.

After breakfast and the disposal of the newspapers, Lynton retired to his letters, and I asked Lady Lynton if one of her daughters might show me the house. Elizabeth, the eldest, was summoned, and seemed in no way to dislike the task.

The house was, as already intimated, by no means large; it occupied three sides of a square, the entrance and one end of the stables making the fourth side. The interior was full of interest—passages, rooms, galleries, as well as hall, were panelled in dark wood and hung with pictures. I was shown everything on the ground floor, and then on the first floor. Then my guide proposed that we should ascend a narrow twisting staircase that led to a gallery. We did as proposed, and entered a handsome long room or passage, leading to a small chamber at one end, in which my guide told me her father kept books and papers.

I asked if anyone slept in this gallery, as I noticed a bed, and fireplace, and rods, by means of which curtains might be drawn, enclosing one portion where were bed and fireplace, so as to convert it into a very cosy chamber.

She answered "No," the place was not really used except as a playroom, though sometimes, if the house happened to be very full, in her great-grandfather's time, she had heard that it had been occupied.

By the time we had been over the house, and I had also been shown the garden and the stables, and introduced to the dogs, it was nearly one o'clock. We were to have an early luncheon, and to drive afterwards to see the ruins of one of the grand old Yorkshire abbeys.

This was a pleasant expedition, and we got back just in time for tea, after which there was some reading aloud. The evening passed much in the same way as the preceding one, except that Lynton, who had some business, did not go down to the smoking-room, and I took the opportunity of retiring early in order to write a letter for the Indian mail, something having been said as to the prospect of hunting the next day.

I had finished my letter, which was a long one, together with two or three others, and had just got into bed when I heard a step overhead as of someone walking along the gallery, which I now knew ran immediately above my room. It was a slow, heavy, measured tread which I could hear getting gradually louder and nearer, and then as gradually fading away as it retreated into the distance.

I was startled for a moment, having been informed that the gallery was unused; but the next instant it occurred to me that I had been told it communicated with a chamber where Sir Francis kept books and papers. I knew he had some writing to do, and I thought no more on the matter.

I was down the next morning at breakfast in good time. "How late you were last night!" I said to Lynton, in the middle of breakfast. "I heard you overhead after one o'clock."

Lynton replied rather shortly, "Indeed you did not, for I was in bed last night before twelve."

"There was someone certainly moving overhead last night," I answered, "for I heard his steps as distinctly as I ever heard anything in my life, going down the gallery."

Upon which Colonel Lynton remarked that he had often fancied he had heard steps on his staircase, when he knew that no one was about. He was apparently disposed to say more, when his brother interrupted him somewhat curtly, as I fancied, and asked me if I should feel inclined after breakfast to have a horse and go out and look for the hounds. They met a considerable way off, but if they did not find in the coverts they should first draw, a thing not improbable, they would come our way, and we might fall in with them about one o'clock and have a run. I said there was nothing I should like better. Lynton mounted me on a very nice chestnut, and the rest of the party having gone out shooting, and the young ladies being otherwise engaged, he and I started about eleven o'clock for our ride.

The day was beautiful, soft, with a bright sun, one of those delightful days which so frequently occur in the early part of November.

On reaching the hilltop where Lynton had expected to meet the hounds no trace of them was to be discovered. They must have found at once, and run in a different direction. At three o'clock, after we had eaten our sandwiches, Lynton reluctantly abandoned all hopes of falling in with the hounds, and said we would return home by a slightly different route.

We had not descended the hill before we came on an old chalk quarry and the remains of a disused kiln.

I recollected the spot at once. I had been here with Sir Francis on my former visit, many years ago. "Why—bless me!" said I. "Do you remember, Lynton, what happened here when I was with you before? There had been men engaged removing chalk, and they came on a skeleton under some depth of rubble. We went together to see it removed, and you said you would have it preserved till it could be examined by some ethnologist or anthropologist, one or other of those dry-as-dusts, to decide whether the remains are dolichocephalous or brachycephalous, whether British, Danish, or—modern. What was the result?"

Sir Francis hesitated for a moment, and then answered: "It is true, I had the remains removed."

"Was there an inquest?"

"No. I had been opening some of the tumuli on the Wolds. I had sent a crouched skeleton and some skulls to the Scarborough Museum. This I was doubtful about, whether it was a prehistoric interment—in fact, to what date it belonged. No one thought of an inquest."

On reaching the house, one of the grooms who took the horses, in answer to a question from Lynton, said that Colonel and Mrs. Hampshire had arrived about an hour ago, and that, one of the horses being lame, the carriage in which they had driven over from Castle Frampton was to put up for the night. In the drawing-room we found Lady Lynton pouring out tea for her husband's youngest sister and her husband, who, as we came in, exclaimed: "We have come to beg a night's lodging."

It appeared that they had been on a visit in the neighbourhood, and had been obliged to leave at a moment's notice in consequence of a sudden death in the house where they were staying, and that, in the impossibility of getting a fly, their hosts had sent them over to Byfield.

"We thought," Mrs. Hampshire went on to say, "that as we were coming here the end of next week, you would not mind having us a little sooner; or that, if the house were quite full, you would be willing to put us up anywhere till Monday, and let us come back later."

Lady Lynton interposed with the remark that it was all settled; and then, turning to her husband, added: "But I want to speak to you for a moment."

They both left the room together.

Lynton came back almost immediately, and, making an excuse to show me on a map in the hall the point to which we had ridden, said as soon as we were alone, with a look of considerable annoyance: "I am afraid we must ask you to change your room. Shall you mind very much? I think we can make you quite comfortable upstairs in the gallery, which is the only room available. Lady Lynton has had a good fire lit; the place is really not cold, and it will be for only a night or two. Your servant has been told to put your things together, but Lady Lynton did not like to give orders to have them actually moved before my speaking to you."

I assured him that I did not mind in the very least, that I should be quite as comfortable upstairs, but that I did mind very much their making such a fuss about a matter of that sort with an old friend like myself.

Certainly nothing could look more comfortable than my new lodging when I went upstairs to dress. There was a bright fire in the large grate, an armchair had been drawn up beside it, and all my books and writing things had been put in, with a reading-lamp in the central position, and the heavy tapestry curtains were drawn, converting this part of the gallery into a room to itself. Indeed, I felt somewhat inclined to congratulate myself on the change. The spiral staircase had been one reason against this place having been given to the Hampshires. No lady's long dress trunk could have mounted it.

Sir Francis was necessarily a good deal occupied in the evening with his sister and her husband, whom he had not seen for some time. Colonel Hampshire had also just heard that he was likely to be ordered to Egypt, and when Lynton and he retired to the smoking-room, instead of going there I went upstairs to my own room to finish a book in which I was interested. I did not, however, sit up long, and very soon went to bed.

Before doing so, I drew back the curtains on the rod, partly because I like plenty of air where I sleep, and partly also because I thought I might like to see the play of the moonlight on the floor in the portion of the gallery beyond where I lay, and where the blinds had not been drawn.

I must have been asleep for some time, for the fire, which I had left in full blaze, was gone to a few sparks wandering among the ashes, when I suddenly awoke with the impression of having heard a latch click at the further extremity of the gallery, where was the chamber containing books and papers.

I had always been a light sleeper, but on the present occasion I woke at once to complete and acute consciousness, and with a sense of stretched attention which seemed to intensify all my faculties. The wind had risen, and was blowing in fitful gusts round the house.

A minute or two passed, and I began almost to fancy I must have been mistaken, when I distinctly heard the creak of the door, and then the click of the latch falling back into its place. Then I heard a sound on the boards as of one moving in the gallery. I sat up to listen, and as I did so I distinctly heard steps coming down the gallery. I heard them approach and pass my bed. I could see nothing, all was dark; but I heard the tread proceeding towards the further portion of the gallery where were the uncurtained and unshuttered windows, two in number; but the moon shone through only one of these, the nearer; the other was dark, shadowed by the chapel or some other building at right angles. The tread seemed to me to pause now and again, and then continue as before.

I now fixed my eyes intently on the one illumined window, and it appeared to me as if some dark body passed across it: but what? I listened intently, and heard the step proceed to the end of the gallery and then return.

I again watched the lighted window, and immediately that the sound reached that portion of the long passage it ceased momentarily, and I saw, as distinctly as I ever saw anything in my life, by moonlight, a figure of a man with marked features, in what appeared to be a fur cap drawn over the brows.

It stood in the embrasure of the window, and the outline of the face was in silhouette; then it moved on, and as it moved I again heard the tread. I was as certain as I could be that the thing, whatever it was, or the person, whoever he was, was approaching my bed.

I threw myself back in the bed, and as I did so a mass of charred wood on the hearth fell down and sent up a flash of—I fancy sparks, that gave out a glare in the darkness, and by that—red as blood—I saw a face near me.

With a cry, over which I had as little control as the scream uttered by a sleeper in the agony of a nightmare, I called: "Who are you?"

There was an instant during which my hair bristled on my head, as in the horror of the darkness I prepared to grapple with the being at my side; when a board creaked as if someone had moved, and I heard the footsteps retreat, and again the click of the latch.

The next instant there was a rush on the stairs and Lynton burst into the room, just as he had sprung out of bed, crying: "For God's sake, what is the matter? Are you ill?"

I could not answer. Lynton struck a light and leant over the bed. Then I seized him by the arm, and said without moving: "There has been something in this room—gone in thither."

The words were hardly out of my mouth when Lynton, following the direction of my eyes, had sprung to the end of the corridor and thrown open the door there.

He went into the room beyond, looked round it, returned, and said: "You must have been dreaming."

By this time I was out of bed.

"Look for yourself," said he, and he led me into the little room. It was bare, with cupboards and boxes, a sort of lumber-place. "There is nothing beyond this," said he, "no door, no staircase. It is a *cul-de-sac*." Then he added: "Now pull on your dressing-gown and come downstairs to my sanctum."

I followed him, and after he had spoken to Lady Lynton, who was standing with the door of her room ajar in a state of great agitation, he turned to me and said: "No one can have been in your room. You see my and my wife's apartments are close below, and no one could come up the spiral staircase without passing my door. You must have had a nightmare. Directly you screamed I rushed up the steps, and met no one descending; and there is no place of concealment in the lumber-room at the end of the gallery."

Then he took me into his private snuggery, blew up the fire, lighted a lamp, and said: "I shall be really grateful if you will say nothing about this. There are some in the house and neighbourhood who are silly enough as it is. You stay here, and if you do not feel inclined to go to bed, read—here are books. I must go to Lady Lynton, who is a good deal frightened, and does not like to be left alone."

He then went to his bedroom.

Sleep, as far as I was concerned, was out of the question, nor do I think that Sir Francis or his wife slept much either.

I made up the fire, and after a time took up a book, and tried to read, but it was useless.

I sat absorbed in thoughts and questionings till I heard the servants stirring in the morning. I then went to my own room, left the candle burning, and got into bed. I had just fallen asleep when my servant brought me a cup of tea at eight o'clock.

At breakfast Colonel Hampshire and his wife asked if anything had happened in the night, as they had been much disturbed by noises overhead, to which Lynton replied that I had not been very well, and had an attack of cramp, and that he had been upstairs to look after me. From his manner I could see that he wished me to be silent, and I said nothing accordingly.

In the afternoon, when everyone had gone out, Sir Francis took me into his snuggery and said: "Halifax, I am very sorry about that matter last night. It is quite true, as my brother said, that steps have been heard about this house, but I never gave heed to such things, putting all noises down to rats. But after your experiences I feel that it is due to you to tell you something, and also to make to you an explanation. There is—there was—no one in the room at the end of the corridor, except the skeleton that was discovered in the chalk-pit when you were here many years ago. I confess I had not paid much heed to it. My archæological fancies passed; I had no visits from anthropologists; the bones and skull were never shown to experts, but remained packed in a chest in that lumber-room. I confess I ought to have buried them, having no more scientific use for them, but I did not—on my word, I forgot all about them, or, at least, gave no heed to them. However, what you have gone through, and have described to me, has made me uneasy, and has also given me a suspicion that I can account for that body in a manner that had never occurred to me before."

After a pause, he added: "What I am going to tell you is known to no one else, and must not be mentioned by you—anyhow, in my lifetime, You know now that, owing to the death of my father when quite young, I and my brother and sister were brought up here with our grandfather, Sir Richard. He was an old, imperious, short-tempered man. I will tell you what I have made out of a matter that was a mystery for long, and I will tell you afterwards how I came to unravel it. My grandfather was in the habit of going out at night with a young under-keeper, of whom he was very fond, to look after the game and see if any poachers, whom he regarded as his natural enemies, were about.

"One night, as I suppose, my grandfather had been out with the young man in question, and, returning by the plantations, where the hill is steepest, and not far from that chalk-pit you remarked on yesterday, they came upon a man, who, though not actually belonging to the country, was well known in it as a sort of travelling tinker of indifferent character, and a notorious poacher. Mind this, I am not sure it was at the place I mention; I only now surmise it. On the particular night in question, my grandfather and the keeper must have caught this man setting snares; there must have been a tussle, in the course of which as subsequent circumstances have led me to imagine, the man showed fight and was knocked down by one or other of the two—my grandfather or the keeper. I believe that after having made various attempts to restore him, they found that the man was actually dead.

"They were both in great alarm and concern—my grandfather especially. He had been prominent in putting down some factory riots, and had acted as magistrate with promptitude, and had given orders to the military to fire, whereby a couple of lives had been lost. There was a vast outcry against him, and a certain political party had denounced him as an assassin. No man was more vituperated; yet, in my conscience, I believe that he acted with both discretion and pluck, and arrested a mischievous movement that might have led to much bloodshed. Be that as it may, my impression is that he lost his head over this fatal affair with the tinker, and that he and the keeper together buried the body secretly, not far from the place where he was killed. I now think it was in the chalk-pit, and that the skeleton found years after there belonged to this man."

"Good heavens!" I exclaimed, as at once my mind rushed back to the figure with the fur cap that I had seen against the window.

Sir Francis went on: "The sudden disappearance of the tramp, in view of his well-known habits and wandering mode of life, did not for some time excite surprise; but, later on, one or two circumstances having led to suspicion, an inquiry was set on foot, and among others, my grandfather's keepers were examined before the magistrates. It was remembered afterwards that the under-keeper in question was absent at the time of the inquiry, my grandfather having sent him with some dogs to a brother-in-law of his who lived upon the moors; but whether no one noticed the fact, or if they did, preferred to be silent, I know not, no observations were made. Nothing came of the investigation, and the whole subject would have dropped if it had not been that two years later, for some reasons I do not understand, but at the instigation of a magistrate recently imported into the division, whom my grandfather greatly disliked, and who was opposed to him in politics, a fresh inquiry was instituted. In the course of that inquiry it transpired that, owing to some unguarded words dropped by the under-keeper, a warrant was about to be issued for his arrest. My grandfather, who had had a fit of the gout, was away from home at the time, but on hearing the news he came home at once. The evening he returned he had a long interview with the young man, who left the house after he had supped in the servants' hall. It was observed that he looked much depressed. The warrant was issued the next day, but in the meantime the keeper had disappeared. My grandfather gave orders to all his own people to do everything in their power to assist the authorities in the search that was at once set on foot, but was unable himself to take any share in it.

"No trace of the keeper was found, although at a subsequent period rumours circulated that he had been heard of in America. But the man having been unmarried, he gradually dropped out of remembrance, and as my grandfather never allowed the subject to be mentioned in his presence, I should probably never have known anything about it but for the vague tradition which always attaches to such events, and for this fact: that after my grandfather's death a letter came addressed to him from somewhere in the United States from someone—the name different from that of the keeper—but alluding to the past, and implying the presence of a common secret, and, of course, with it came a request for money. I replied, mentioning the death of Sir Richard, and asking for an explanation. I did get an answer, and it is from that that I am able to fill in so much of the story. But I never learned *where* the man had been killed and buried, and my next letter to the fellow was returned with 'Deceased' written across it. Somehow, it never occurred to me till I heard your story that possibly the skeleton in the chalk-pit might be that of the poaching tinker. I will now most assuredly have it buried in the churchyard."

"That certainly ought to be done," said I.

"And—" said Sir Francis, after a pause, "I give you my word. After the burial of the bones, and you are gone, I will sleep for a week in the bed in the gallery, and report to you if I see or hear anything. If all be quiet, then—well, you form your own conclusions."

I left a day after. Before long I got a letter from my friend, brief but to the point: "All quiet, old boy; come again."

XI. — THE MEREWIGS

DURING the time that I lived in Essex, I had the pleasure of knowing Major Donelly, retired on half-pay, who had spent many years in India; he was a man of great powers of observation, and possessed an inexhaustible fund of information of the most valuable quality, which he was ready to communicate to his intimates, among whom was I.

Major Donelly is now no more, and the world is thereby the poorer. Major Donelly took an interest in everything—anthropology, mechanics, archæology, physical science, natural history, the stock market, politics. In fact, it was not possible in conversation to broach a subject with which he was wholly unacquainted, and concerning which he was not desirous of acquiring further information. A man of this description is not to be held by lightly. I grappled him to my heart.

One day when we were taking a constitutional walk together, I casually mentioned the "Red Hills." He had never heard of them, inquired, and I told him what little I knew on the matter. The Red Hills are mounds of burnt clay of a brick-red colour, found at intervals along the fringe of the marshes on the east coast. Of the date of their formation and the purpose they were destined to discharge, nothing has been certainly ascertained. Theories have been formed, and have been held to with tenacity, but these are unsupported by sound evidence. And yet, one would have supposed that these mysterious mounds would have been subjected to a careful scientific exploration to determine by the discovery of flint tools, potsherds, or coins to what epoch they belong, and that some clue should be discovered as to their purport. But at the time when I was in Essex, no such study had been attempted; whether any has been undertaken since I am unable to say.

I mentioned to Donelly some of the suppositions offered as to the origin of these Red Hills; that they represented salt-making works, that they were funereal erections, that they were artificial bases for the huts of fishers.

"That is it," said the major, "no doubt about it. To keep off the ague. Do you not know that burnt clay is a sure protection against ague, which was the curse of the Essex marsh land? In Central Africa, in the districts that lie low and there is morass, the natives are quite aware of the fact, and systematically form a bed of burnt clay as a platform on which to erect their hovels. Now look here, my dear friend, I'd most uncommonly like to take a boat along with you, and explore both sides of the Blackwater to begin with, and its inlets, and to tick down on the ordnance map every red hill we can find."

"I am quite ready," I replied. "There is one thing to remember. A vast number of these hills have been ploughed down, but you can certainly detect where they were by the colour of the soil."

Accordingly, on the next fine day we engaged a boat—not a rower—for we could manage it between us, and started on our expedition.

The country around the Blackwater is flat, and the land slides into the sea and river with so slight an incline, that a good extent of debatable ground exists, which may be reckoned as belonging to both. Vast marshes are found occasionally flooded, covered with the wild lavender, and in June flushed with the seathrift. They nourish a coarse grass, and a bastard samphire. These marshes are threaded, cobweb fashion, by myriads of lines of water and mud that intercommunicate. Woe to the man who either stumbles into, or in jumping falls into, one of these breaks in the surface of land. He sinks to his waist in mud. At certain times, when no high tides are expected, sheep are driven upon these marshes and thrive. They manage to leap the runnels, and the shepherd is aware when danger threatens, and they must be driven off.

Nearer the mainland are dykes thrown up, none know when, to reclaim certain tracts of soil, and on the land side are invariably stagnant ditches, where mosquitoes breed in myriads. Further up grow oak trees, and in summer to these the mosquitoes betake themselves in swarms, and may be seen in the evening swaying in such dense clouds above the trees that these latter seem to be on fire and smoking. Major Donelly and I leisurely paddled about, running into creeks, leaving our boat, identifying our position on the map, and marking in the position of such red hills or their traces as we lighted on.

Major Donelly and I pretty well explored the left bank up to a certain point, when he proposed that we should push across to the other.

"I should advise doing thoroughly the upper reach of the Blackwater," said he, "and we shall then have completed one section."

"All right," I responded, and we turned the boat's head to cross. Unhappily, we had not calculated that the estuary was full of mudbanks. Moreover, the tide was ebbing, and before very long we grounded.

"Confound it!" said the major, "we are on a mudbank. What a fix we are in."

We laboured with the oars to thrust off, but could touch no solid ground, to obtain purchase sufficient for our purpose.

Then said Donelly: "The only thing to be done is for one of us to step onto the bank and thrust the boat off. I will do that. I have on an old shabby pair of trousers that don't matter."

"No, indeed, you shall not. I will go," and at the word I sprang overboard. But the major had jumped simultaneously, and simultaneously we sank in the horrible slime. It had the consistency of spinach. I do not mean such as English cooks send us to table, half-mashed and often gritty, but the spinach as served at a French table d'hôte, that has been pulped through a fine hair sieve. And what is more, it apparently had no bottom. For aught I know it might go down a mile in depth towards the centre of the globe, and it stank abominably. We both clung to the sides of the boat to save ourselves from sinking altogether.

There we were, one on each side, clinging to the bulwarks and looking at one another. For a moment or two neither spoke. Donelly was the first to recover his presence of mind, and after wiping his mouth on the gunwale from the mud that had squirted over it, he said: "Can you get out?"

"Hardly," said I.

We tugged at the boat, it squelched about, splashing the slime over us, till it plastered our heads and faces and covered our hands.

"This will never do," said he. "We must get in together, and by instalments. Look here! when I say 'three,' throw in your left leg if you can get it out of the mud."

"I will do my best."

"And," he said further, "we must do so both at the same moment. Now, don't be a sneak and try to get in your body whilst I am putting in my leg, or you will upset the boat."

"I never was a sneak," I retorted angrily, "and I certainly will not be one in what may be the throes of death."

"All right," said the major. "One—two—three!"

Instantly both of us drew our left legs out of the mud, and projected them over the sides into the boat.

"How are you?" asked he. "Got your leg in all right?"

"All but my boot," I replied, "and that has been sucked off my foot."

"Oh, bother the boot," said the major, "so long as your leg is safe within, and has not been sucked off. That would have disturbed the equipoise. Now then—next we must have our trunks and right legs within. Take a long breath, and wait till I call 'three.'"

We paused, panting with the strain; then Donelly, in a stentorian voice, shouted: "One—two—three!"

Instantly we writhed and strained, and finally, after a convulsive effort, both were landed in the bottom of the boat. We picked ourselves up and seated ourselves, each on one bulwark, looking at one another.

We were covered with the foul slime from head to foot, our clothes were caked, so were our hands and faces. But we were secure.

"Here," said Donelly, "we shall have to remain for six hours till the tide flows, and the boat is lifted. It is of no earthly use for us to shout for help. Even if our calls were heard, no one could come out to us. Here, then, we stick and must make the best of it. Happily the sun is hot, and will cake the mud about us, and then we can pick off some of it."

The prospect was not inviting. But I saw no means of escape.

Presently Donelly said: "It is good that we brought our luncheon with us, and above all some whisky, which is the staff of life. Look here, my dear fellow. I wish it were possible to get this stinking stuff off our hands and faces; it smells like the scouring poured down the sink in Satan's own back kitchen. Is there not a bottle of claret in the basket?"

"Yes, I put one in."

"Then," said he, "the best use we can put it to is to wash our faces and hands in it. Claret is poor drink, and there is the whisky to fall back on."

"The water has all ebbed away," I remarked "We cannot clean ourselves in that."

"Then uncork the *Saint Julien*."

There was really no help for it. The smell of the mud was disgusting, and it turned one's stomach. So I pulled out the cork, and we performed our ablutions in the claret.

That done, we returned to our seats on the gunwale, one on each side, and looked sadly at one another. Six hours! That was an interminable time to spend on a mudflat in the Blackwater. Neither of us was much inclined to speak. After the lapse of a quarter of an hour, the major proposed refreshments.

Accordingly we crept together into the bottom of the boat and there discussed the contents of the hamper, and we certainly did full justice to the whisky bottle. For we were wet to the skin, and beplastered from head to foot in the ill-savoured mud.

When we had done the chicken and ham, and drained the whisky jar, we returned to our several positions *vis-à-vis*. It was essential that the balance of the boat should be maintained.

Major Donelly was now in a communicative mood.

"I will say this," observed he; "that you are the best-informed and most agreeable man I have met with in Colchester and Chelmsford."

I would not record this remark but for what it led up to.

I replied—I dare say I blushed—but the claret in my face made it red, anyhow. I replied: "You flatter me."

"Not at all. I always say what I think. You have plenty of information, and you'll grow your wings, and put on rainbow colours."

"What on earth do you mean?" I inquired.

"Do you not know," said he, "that we shall all of us, some day, develop wings? Grow into angels! What do you suppose that ethereal pinions spring out of? They do not develop out of nothing. Ex nihilo nihil fit. You cannot think that they are the ultimate produce of ham and chicken."

"Nor of whisky."

"Nor of whisky," he repeated. "You know it is so with the grub."

"Grub is ambiguous," I observed.

"I do not mean victuals, but the caterpillar. That creature spends its short life in eating, eating, eating. Look at a cabbage-leaf, it is riddled with holes; the grub has consumed all that vegetable matter, and I will inform you for what purpose. It retires into its chrysalis, and during the winter a transformation takes place, and in spring it breaks forth as a glorious butterfly. The painted wings of the insect in its second stage of existence are the sublimated cabbage it has devoured in its condition of larva."

"Quite so. What has that to do with me?"

"We are also in our larva condition. But do not for a moment suppose that the wings we shall put on with rainbow painting are the produce of what we eat here—of ham and chicken, kidneys, beef, and the like. No, sir, certainly not. They are fashioned out of the information we have absorbed, the knowledge we have acquired during the first stage of life."

"How do you know that?"

"I will tell you," he answered. "I had a remarkable experience once. It is a rather long story, but as we have some five hours and a half to sit here looking at one another till the tide rises and floats us, I may as well tell you, and it will help to the laying on of the colours on your pinions when you acquire them. You would like to hear the tale?"

"Above all things."

"There is a sort of prologue to it," he went on. "I cannot well dispense with it as it leads up to what I particularly want to say."

"By all means let me have the prologue, if it be instructive."

"It is eminently instructive," he said. "But before I begin, just pass me the bottle, if there is any whisky left."

"It is drained," I said.

"Well, well, it can't be helped. When I was in India, I moved from one place to another, and I had pitched my tent in a certain spot. I had a native servant. I forget what his real name was, and it does not matter. I always called him Alec. He was a curious fellow, and the other servants stood in awe of him. They thought that he saw ghosts and had familiar dealings with the spiritual world. He was honest as natives go. He would not allow anyone else to rob me; but, of course, he filched things of mine himself. We are accustomed to that, and think nothing of it. But it was a satisfaction that he kept the fingers of the others off my property. Well, one night, when, as I have informed you, my tent was pitched on a spot I considered eminently convenient, I slept very uncomfortably. It was as though a centipede were crawling over me. Next morning I spoke to Alec, and told him my experiences, and bade him search well my mattress and the floor of my tent. A Hindu's face is impassive, but I thought I detected in his eyes a twinkle of understanding. Nevertheless I did not give it much thought. Next night it was as bad, and in the morning I found my panjams slit from head to foot. I called Alec to me and held up the garment, and said how uncomfortable I had been. 'Ah! sahib,' said he, 'that is the doings of Abdulhamid, the blood-thirsty scoundrel!'"

"Excuse me," I interrupted. "Did he mean the present Sultan of Turkey?"

427

"No, quite another, of the same name."

"I beg your pardon," I said. "But when you mentioned him as a blood-thirsty scoundrel, I supposed it must be he."

"It was not he. It was another. Call him, if you like, the other Abdul. But to proceed with my story."

"One inquiry more," said I. "Surely Abdulhamid cannot be a Hindu name?"

"I did not say that it was," retorted the major with a touch of asperity in his tone. "He was doubtless a Mohammedan."

"But the name is rather Turkish or Arabic."

"I am not responsible for that; I was not his godfathers and godmothers at his baptism. I am merely repeating what Alec told me. If you are so captious, I shall shut up and relate no more."

"Do not take umbrage," said I. "I surely have a right to test the quality of the material I take in, out of which my wings are to be evolved. Go ahead; I will interrupt no further."

"Very well, then, let that be understood between us. Are you caking?"

"Slowly," I replied. "The sun is hot; I am drying up on one side of my body."

"I think that we had best shift sides of the boat," said the major. "It is the same with me."

Accordingly, with caution, we crossed over, and each took the seat on the gunwale lately occupied by the other.

"There," said Donelly. "How goes the enemy? My watch got smothered in the mud, and has stopped."

"Mine," I explained, "is plastered into my waistcoat pocket, and I cannot get at it without messing my fingers, and there is no more claret left for a wash; the whisky is all inside us."

"Well," said the major, "it does not matter; there is plenty of time before us for the rest of my story. Let me see—where was I? Oh! where Alec mentioned Abdulhamid, the inferior scoundrel, not the Sultan. Alec went on to say that he was himself possessed of a remarkably keen scent for blood, even though it had been shed a century before his time, and that my tent had been pitched and my bed spread over a spot marked by a most atrocious crime. That Abdul of whom he had made mention had been a man steeped in crimes of the most atrocious character. Of course, he did not come up in wickedness to his illustrious namesake, but that was because he lacked the opportunities with which the other is so favoured. On the very identical spot where I then was, this same bloodstained villain had perpetrated his worst iniquity—he had murdered his father and mother, and aunt, and his children. After that he was taken and hanged. When his soul parted from his body, in the ordinary course it would have entered into the shell of a scorpion or some other noxious creature, and so have mounted through the scale of beings, by one incarnation after another, till he attained once more to the high estate of man."

"Excuse the interruption," said I, "but I think you intimated that this Abdulhamid was a Mohammedan, and the sons of the Prophet do not believe in the transmigration of souls."

"That," said Donelly, "is precisely the objection I raised to Alec. But he told me that souls after death are not accommodated with a future according to the creeds they hold, but according to Destiny: that whatever a man might suppose during life as to the condition of his future state, there was but one truth to which they would all have their eyes opened—the truth held by the Hindus, viz. the transmigration of souls from stage to stage, ever progressing upward to man, and then to recommence the interminable circle of reincarnation. 'So,' said I, 'it was Abdul in the form of a scorpion who was tickling my ribs all night.' 'No, sahib,' replied my native servant very gravely. He was too wicked to be suffered to set his foot, so to speak, on the lowest rung of the ladder of existences. The doom went forth against him that he must haunt the scenes of his former crimes, till he found a man sleeping over one of them, and on that man must be a mole, and out of that mole must grow three hairs. These hairs he must pluck out and plant on the grave of his final victims, and water them with his tears. And the flowing of these first drops of penitence would enable him to pass at once into the first stage of the circle of incarnations.' 'Why,' said I, 'that unredeemed ruffian was mole-hunting over me the last two nights! But what do you say to these slit panjams?' 'Sahib,' replied Alec, 'he did that with his nails. I presume he turned you over, and ripped them so as to get at your back and feel for the so-much-desired mole.' 'I'll have the tent shifted,' said I. 'Nothing will induce me to sleep another night on this accursed spot.'"

Donelly paused, and proceeded to take off some flakes of mud that had formed on his sleeve. We really were beginning to get drier, but in drying we stiffened, as the mud became hard about us like pie-crust.

"So far," said I, "we have had no wings."

"I am coming to them," replied the major; "I have now concluded the prologue."

"Oh! that was the prologue, was it?"

"Yes. Have you anything against it? It was the prologue. Now I will go on with the main substance of my story. About a year after that incident I retired on half-pay, and returned to England. What became of Alec I did not know, nor care a hang. I had been in England for a little over two years, when one day I was walking along Great Russell Street, and passing the gates of the British Museum, I noticed a Hindu standing there, looking wretchedly cold and shabby. He had a tray containing bangles and necklaces and gewgaws, made in Germany, which he was selling as oriental works of art. As I passed, he saluted me, and, looking steadily at him, I recognised Alec. 'Why, what brings you here?' I inquired, vastly astonished. 'Sahib may well ask,' he replied. 'I came over because I thought I might better my condition. I had heard speak of a Psychical Research Society established in London; and with my really extraordinary gifts, I thought that I might be of value to it, and be taken in and paid an annuity if I supplied it continuously with well-authenticated, first-hand ghost stories.' 'Well,' said I, 'and have you succeeded?' 'No, sahib. I cannot find it. I have inquired after it from several of the crossing-sweepers, and they could not inform me of its whereabouts; and if I applied to the police, they bade me take myself off, there was no such a thing. I should have starved, sahib, if it had not been that I had taken to this line'; he pointed to his tray. 'Does that pay well?' I asked. He shook his head sadly. 'Very poorly. I can live—that is all. There goes in a Merewig.' 'How many of these rubbishy bangles can you dispose of in a day?' I inquired. 'That depends, sahib. It varies so greatly, and the profits are very small. So small that I can barely get along. There goes in another Merewig.' 'Where are all these things made?' I asked. 'In Germany or in Birmingham?' 'Oh, sahib, how can I tell? I get them from a Jew dealer. He supplies various street-hawkers. But I shall give it up—it does not pay—and shall set up a stall and dispose of Turkish Delight. There is always a run on that. You English have a sweet tooth. That's a Merewig,' and he pointed to a dowdy female, with a reticule on her arm, who, at that moment, went through the painted iron gates. 'What do you mean by Merewigs?' said I. 'Does not sahib know?' Alec's face expressed genuine surprise. 'If sahib will go into the great reading-room, he will see scores of them there. It is their great London haunt; they pass in all day, mainly in the morning—some are in very early, so soon as the museum is open at nine o'clock. And they usually remain there all day picking up information, acquiring knowledge.' 'You mean the students.' 'Not all the students, but a large percentage of them. I know them in a moment. Sahib is aware that I have great gifts for the discernment of spirits.'

"By the way," broke off Donelly, "do you understand Hindustani?"

"Not a word of it," I replied.

"I am sorry for that," said he, "because I could tell you what passed between us so much easier in Hindustani. I am able to speak and understand it as readily as English, and the matter I am going to relate would come off my tongue so much easier in that language."

"You might as well speak it in Chinese. I should be none the wiser. Wait a moment. I am cracking."

It was so. The heat of the sun was sensibly affecting my crust of mud. I think I must have resembled a fine old painting, the varnish of which is stained and traversed by an infinity of minute fissures, a perfect network of cracks. I stood up and stretched myself, and split in several places. Moreover, portions of my muddy envelope began to curl at the edges.

"Don't be in too great a hurry to peel," advised Donelly.

"We have abundance of time still before us, and I want to proceed with my narrative."

"Go on, then. When are we coming to the wings?"

"Directly," replied he. "Well, then—if you cannot receive what I have to say in Hindustani, I must do my best to give you the substance of Alec's communication in the vulgar tongue. I will epitomise it. The Hindu went on to explain in this fashion. He informed me that with us, Christians and white people, it is not the same as with the dusky and the yellow races. After death we do not pass into the bodies of the lower animals, which is a great privilege and ought to afford us immense satisfaction. We at once progress into a higher condition of life. We develop wings, as does the butterfly when it emerges from its condition of grub. But the matter out of which the wings are produced is nothing gross. They are formed, or form themselves, out of the information with which we have filled our brains during life. We lay up, during our mortal career here, a large amount of knowledge, of scientific, historical, philosophic, and like acquisitions, and these form the so-to-speak psychic pulp out of which, by an internal and mysterious and altogether inexplicable process, the transmutation takes place into our future wings. The more we have stored, the larger are our wings; the more varied the nature, the more radiant and coloured is their painting. When, at death, the brain is empty, there can be no wing-development. Out of nothing, nothing can arise. That is a law of nature absolutely inexorable in its application. And this is why you will never have to regret sticking in the mud to-day, my friend. I have supplied you with such an amount of fresh and valuable knowledge, that I believe you will have pinions painted hereafter with peacock's eyes."

"I am most obliged to you," said I, splitting into a thousand cakes with the emotion that agitated me.

Donelly proceeded. "I was so interested in what Alec told me, that I said to him, 'Come along with me into the Nineveh room, and we shall be able to thrash this matter out.' 'Ah, sahib,' he replied, 'they will not allow me to take in my tray.' 'Very well,' said I, 'then we will find a step before the portico, one not too much frequented by the pigeons, and will sit there.' He agreed. But the porter at the gate demurred to letting the Hindu through. He protested that no trafficking was allowed on the premises. I explained that none was purposed; that the man and I proposed a discussion on psychological topics. This seemed to content the porter, and he suffered Alec to pass through with me. We picked out as clean a portion of the steps as we could, and seated ourselves on it side by side, and then the Hindu went on with what he was saying."

Donelly and I were now drying rapidly. As we sat facing each other we must have looked very much like the chocolate men one sees in confectioners' shops—of course, I mean on a much larger scale, and not of the same warm tint, and, of course, also, we did not exhale the same aromatic odour.

"When we were seated," proceeded Donelly, "I felt the cold of the stone steps strike up into my system, and as I have had a touch or two of lumbago since I came home, I stood up again, took a copy of the *Standard* out of my pocket, folded it, and placed it between myself and the step. I did, however, pull out the inner leaf, that containing the leaders, and presented it to Alec for the same purpose. Orientals are insensible to kindness, and are deficient in the virtue of gratitude. But this delicate trait of attention did touch the benighted heathen. His lip quivered, and he became, if possible, more than ever communicative. He nudged me with his tray and said, 'There goes out a Merewig. I wonder why she leaves so soon?' I saw a middle-aged woman in a gown of grey, with greasy splotches on it, and the braid unsewn at the skirt trailing in a loop behind. 'What are the Merewigs?' I asked. I will give you what I learned in my own words. All men and women—I allude only to Europeans and Americans—in the first stage of their life are bound morally, and in their own interest, to acquire and store up in their brains as much information as these will hold, for it is out of this that their wings will be evolved in their second stage of existence. Of course, the more varied this information is, the better. Men inevitably accumulate knowledge. Even if they assimilate very little at school, yet, as young men, they necessarily take in a good deal—of course, I exempt the mashers, who never learn anything. Even in sport they obtain something; but in business, by reading, by association, by travel, they go on piling up a store. You see that in common conversation they cannot escape doing this; politics, social questions, points of natural history, scientific discoveries form the staple of their talk, so that the mind of a man is necessarily kept replenished. But with women this is not the case. Young girls read nothing whatever but novels—they might as well feed on soap-bubbles. In their conversation with one another they twaddle, they do not talk."

"But," protested I, "in our civilised society young women associate freely with men."

"That is true," replied he. "But to what is their dialogue limited?—to ragging, to frivolous jokes. Men do not talk to them on rational topics, for they know well enough that such topics do not interest girls, and that they are wholly incapable of applying their minds to them. It is wondered why so many Englishmen look out for American wives. That is because the American girl takes pains to cultivate her mind, becomes a rational and well-educated woman. She can enter into her husband's interests, she can converse with him on almost every topic. She becomes his companion. That the modern English girl cannot be. Her head is as hollow as a drum. Now, if she grows up and marries, or even remains an old maid, the case is altered; she takes to keeping poultry, she becomes passionately fond of gardening, and she acquires a fund of information on the habits and customs of the domestic servant. The consequence of this is, that the vast majority of English young women who die early, die with nothing stored up in their brains out of which the wings may be evolved. In the larva condition they have consumed nothing that can serve them to bring them into the higher state."

"So," said I, "we are all, you and I, in the larva condition as well as girls."

"Quite so, we are larvæ like them, only they are more so. To proceed. When girls die, without having acquired any profitable knowledge, as you well see, they cannot rise. They become Merewigs."

"Oh, that is Merewigs," said I, greatly astonished.

"Yes, but the Merewigs I had seen pass in and out of the British Museum, whether to study the collections or to work in the reading-room, were middle-aged for the most part."

"How do you explain that?" I asked.

"I give you only what I received from Alec. There are male Merewigs, but they are few and far between, for the reasons I have given to you. I suppose there are ninety-nine female Merewigs to one male."

"You astonish me."

"I was astonished when I learned this from Alec. Now I will tell you something further. All the souls of the girls who have died empty-headed in the preceding twenty-four hours in England assemble at four o'clock every morning, or rather a few minutes before the stroke of the clock, about the statue of Queen Anne in front of St. Paul's Cathedral, with a possible sprinkling of male masher souls among them. At the stroke of the clock, off the whole swarm rushes up Holborn Hill, along Oxford Street, whither I cannot certainly say. Alec told me that it is for all the world like the rush of an army of rats in the sewers."

"But what can that Hindu know of underground London?"

"He knows because he lodges in the house of a sewer-man, with whom he has become on friendly terms."

"Then you do not know whither this galloping legion runs?"

"Not exactly, for Alec was not sure. But he tells me they tear away to the great *garde-robe* of discarded female bodies. They must get into these, so as to make up for the past, and acquire knowledge, out of which wings may be developed. Of course there is a scramble for these bodies, for there are at least half a dozen applicants. At first only the abandoned husks of old maids were given them, but the supply having proved to be altogether inadequate, they are obliged to put up with those of married women and widows. There was some demur as to this, but beggars must not be choosers. And so they become Merewigs. There are more than a sufficiency of old bachelors' outer cases hanging up in the *garde-robe*, but the girls will not get into them at any price. Now you understand what Merewigs are, and why they swarm in the reading-room of the British Museum. They are there picking up information as hard as they can pick."

"This is extremely interesting," said I, "and novel."

"I thought you would say so. How goes on the drying?"

"I have been picking off clots of clay while you have been talking."

"I hope you are interested," said Donelly.

"Interested," I replied, "is not the word for it."

"I am glad you think so," said the major; "I was intensely interested in what Alec told me, so much so that I proposed he should come with me into the reading-room, and point out to me such as he perceived by his remarkable gift of discernment of spirits were actual Merewigs. But again the difficulty of his tray was objected, and Alec further intimated that he was missing opportunities of disposing of his trinkets by spending so much time conversing with me. 'As to that,' said I, 'I will buy half a dozen of your bangles and present them to my lady friends; as coming from me, an oriental traveller, they will believe them to be genuine——'"

"As your experiences," interpolated I.

"What do you mean by that?" he inquired sharply.

"Nothing more than this," rejoined I, "that faith is grown weak among females nowadays."

"That is certainly true. It is becoming a sadly incredulous sex. I further got over Alec's difficulty about the tray by saying that it could be left in the custody of one of the officials at the entrance. Then he consented. We passed through the swing-door and deposited the tray with the functionary who presides over umbrellas and walking-sticks. Then I went forward along with my Hindu towards the reading-room. But here another hindrance arose. Alec had no ticket, and therefore might not enter beyond the glass screen interposed between the door and the readers. Some demur was made as to his being allowed to remain there for any considerable time, but I got over that by means of a little persuasion. 'Sahib,' said Alec 'I should suggest your marking the Merewigs, so as to be able to recognise them elsewhere.' 'How can I do that?' I inquired. 'I have here with me a piece of French chalk,' he answered. 'You go within, sahib, and walk up and down by the tables, behind the chairs of the readers, or around the circular cases that contain the catalogues, and where the students are looking out for the books they desire to consult. When you pass a female, either seated or standing, glance towards the glass screen, and when you are by a Merewig I will hold up my hand above the screen, and you will know her to be one; then just scrawl a W or M, or any letter or cabalistic symbol that occurs to you, upon her back with the French chalk. Then whenever you meet her in the street, in society, at an A. B. C. place of refreshment, on a railway platform, you will recognise her infallibly.' 'Not likely,' I objected. 'Of course, so soon as she gets home, she will brush off the mark.' 'You do not know much of the Merewigs,' he said. 'When the spirits of those frivolous girls were in their first stage of existence, they were most particular about their personal appearance, about the neatness and stylishness of their dress, and the puffing and piling up of their hair. Now all that is changed. They are so disgusted at having to get into any unsouled body that they can lay hold of in the *garde-robe*, such a body being usually plain in features, middle-aged, and with no waist to speak of, or rather too ample in the waist to be elegant, that they have abandoned all concern about dress and tidiness.

Besides, they are engrossed in the acquisition of knowledge, and the burning desire that consumes them is to get out of these borrowed cases as speedily as may be. Consequently, so long as they are dressed and their hair done up anyhow, that is all they care about. As to threads, or feathers, or French chalk marks on their clothes, they would not think of looking for them.' Then Alec handed to me a little piece of French chalk, such as tailors and dressmakers employ to indicate alterations when fitting on garments. So provided, I passed wholly into the spacious reading-room, leaving the Hindu behind the screen.

"I slowly strayed down the first line of desks and chairs, which were fully engaged. There were many men there, with piles of books at their sides. There were also some women. I stepped behind one, and turned my head towards the screen, but Alec made no sign. At the second, however, up went his hand above it, and I hastily scrawled M, on her back as she stooped over her studies. I had time, moreover, to see what she was engaged upon. She was working up deep-sea soundings, beginning with that recorded by Schiller in his ballad of 'The Diver,' down to the last scientific researches in the bottom of the Atlantic and the Pacific, and the dredgings in the North Sea. She was engrossed in her work, and was picking up facts at a prodigious rate. She was a woman of, I should say, forty, with a cadaverous face, a shapeless nose, and enormous hands. Her dress was grey, badly fitted, and her boots were even worse made. Her hair was drawn back and knotted in a bunch behind, with the pins sticking out. It might have been better brushed. I passed on behind her back; the next occupants of seats were gentlemen, so I stepped to another row of desks, and looking round saw Alec's hand go up. I was behind a young lady in a felt hat, crunched in at top, and with a feather at the side; she wore a pea-jacket, with large smoked buttons, and beneath it a dull green gown, very short in the skirt, and brown boots. Her hair was cut short like that of a man. As I halted, she looked round, and I saw that she had hard, brown eyes, like pebbles, without a gleam of tenderness or sympathy in them. I cannot say whether this was due to the body she had assumed, or to the soul which had entered into the body—whether the lack was in the organ, or in the psychic force which employed the organ. I merely state the fact. I looked over her shoulder to see what she was engaged upon, and found that she was working her way diligently through Herbert Spencer. I scored a W on her back and went on. The next Merewig I had to scribble on was a wizen old lady, with little grey curls on the temples, very shabby in dress, and very antiquated in costume. Her fingers were dirty with ink, and the ink did not appear to me to be all of that day's application. Besides, I saw that she had been rubbing her nose. I presume it had been tickling, and she had done this with a finger still wet with ink, so that there was a smear on her face. She was engaged on the peerage. She had Dod, Burke, and Foster before her, and was getting up the authentic pedigrees of our noble families and their ramifications. I noticed with her as with the other Merewigs, that when they had swallowed a certain amount of information they held up their heads much like fowls after drinking.

"The next that I marked was a very thin woman of an age I was quite unable to determine. She had a pointed nose, and was dressed in red. She looked like a stick of sealing-wax. The gown had probably enough been good and showy at one time, but it was ripped behind now, and the stitches showed, besides, a little bit of what was beneath. There was a frilling, or ruche, or tucker, about the throat that I think had been sewn into it three weeks before. I drew a note of interrogation on her back with my bit of French chalk. I wanted much to find out what she was studying, but could not. She turned round and asked sharply what I was stooping over for and breathing on the back of her neck. So I was forced to go on to the next. This was a lady fairly well dressed in the dingiest of colours, wearing spectacles. I believe that she wore divided skirts, but as she did not stand up and walk, I cannot be certain. I am particular never to make a statement of which I am not absolutely certain. She was engaged upon the subject of the land laws in various countries, on common land, and property in land; and she was at that time devoting her special attention to the constitution of the Russian *mir*, and the tenure of land under it. I scrawled on her back the zodiacal sign for Venus, the Virgin, and went further. But when I had marked seventeen I gave it up. I had already gone over the desks to L, beginning backward, and that sufficed, so I returned to Alec, paid him for the bangles, and we separated. I did, however, give him a letter to the Secretary of the Psychical Research Society, and addressed it, having found what I wanted in the *London Directory*, which was in the reading-room of the British Museum. Two days later I met, by appointment, my Hindu once more, and for the last time. He had not been received as he had anticipated by the Psychical Research Society, and thought of getting back to India at the first opportunity.

"It is remarkable that, a few days later, I saw in the Underground one of those I had marked. The chalk mark was still quite distinct. She was not in my compartment, but I noticed her as she stepped out on to the platform at Baker Street. I suspect she was on her way to Madame Tussaud's waxwork exhibition, to instruct her mind there. But I was more fortunate a week later when I was at St. Albans. I had an uncle living there from whom I had expectations, and I paid him a visit. Whilst there, a lecture was to be given on the spectroscope, and as my acquaintance with that remarkable invention of modern times was limited, I resolved to go. Have you, my friend, ever taken up the subject of the photosphere of the sun?"

"Never."

"Then let me press it upon you. It will really supply a large amount of wing-pulp, if properly assimilated. It is a most astonishing thought that we are able, at the remote distance at which we are from the solar orb, to detect the various incandescent metals which go to make up the luminous envelope of the sun. Not only so, but we are able to discover, by the bars in the spectroscope, of what Jupiter, Saturn, and so on are composed. What a stride astronomy has made since the days of Newton!"

"No doubt about it. But I do not want to hear about the bars, but of the chalk marks on the Merewigs."

"Well, then, I noticed two elderly ladies sitting in the row before me, and there—as distinctly as if sketched in only yesterday—were the symbols I had scribbled on their backs. I did not have an opportunity of speaking with them then; indeed, I had no introduction to them, and could hardly take on me to address them without it. I was, however, more successful a week or two later. There was a meeting of the Hertfordshire Archæological Society organised, to last a week, with excursions to ancient Verulam and to other objects of interest in the county. Hertfordshire is not a large county. It is, in fact, one of the smallest in England, but it yields to none in the points of interest that it contains, apart from the venerable abbey church that has been so fearfully mauled and maltreated by ignorant so-called restoration. One must really hope that the next generation, which will be more enlightened than our own, will undo all the villainous work that has been perpetrated to disfigure it in our own. The local secretaries and managers had arranged for char-à-bancs and brakes to take the party about, and men—learned, or thinking themselves to be learned, on the several antiquities—were to deliver lectures on the spot explanatory of what we saw. On three days there were to be evening gatherings, at which papers would be read. You may conceive that this was a supreme opportunity for storing the mind with information, and knowing what I did, I resolved on taking advantage of it. I entered my name as a subscriber to all the excursions. On the first day we went over the remains of the old Roman city of Verulam, and were shown its plan and walls, and further, the spot where the protomartyr of Britain passed over the stream, and the hill on which he was martyred. Nothing could have been more interesting and more instructive. Among those present were three middle-aged personages of the female sex, all of whom were chalk-marked on the back. One of these marks was somewhat effaced, as though the lady whose gown was scored had made a faint effort to brush it off, but had tired of the attempt and had abandoned it. The other two scorings were quite distinct.

"On this, the first day, though I sidled up to these three Merewigs, I did not succeed in ingratiating myself into their favour sufficiently to converse with them. You may well understand, my friend, that such an opportunity of getting out of them some of their Merewigian experiences was not to be allowed to slip. On the second day I was more successful. I managed to obtain a seat in a brake between two of them. We were to drive to a distant spot where was a church of considerable architectural interest.

"Well, in these excursions a sort of freemasonry exists between the archæologists who share in them, and no ceremonious introductions are needed. For instance, you say to the lady next to you, 'Am I squeezing you?' And the ice is broken. I did not, however, attempt to draw any information from those between whom I was seated, till after luncheon, a most sumptuous repast, with champagne, liberally given to the Society by a gentleman of property, to whose house we drove up just about one o'clock. There was plenty of champagne supplied, and I did not stint myself. I felt it necessary to take in a certain amount of Dutch courage before broaching to my companions in the brake the theme that lay near my heart. When, however, we got into the conveyance, all in great spirits, after the conclusion of the lunch, I turned to my right-hand lady, and said to her: 'Well, miss, I fear it will be a long time before you become angelic.' She turned her back upon me and made no reply. Somewhat disconcerted, I now addressed myself to the chalk-marked lady on my left hand, and asked: 'Have you anything at all in your head except archæology?' Instead of answering me in the kindly mood in which I spoke, she began at once to enter into a lively discussion with her neighbour on the opposite side of the carriage, and ignored me. I was not to be done in this way. I wanted information. But, of course, I could enter into the feelings of both. Merewigs do not like to converse about themselves in their former stage of existence, of which they are ashamed, nor of the efforts they are making in this transitional stage to acquire a fund of knowledge for the purpose of ultimately discarding their acquired bodies, and developing their ethereal wings as they pass into the higher and nobler condition.

"We left the carriage to go to a spot about a mile off, through lanes, muddy and rutty, for the purpose of inspecting some remarkable stones. All the party would not walk, and the conveyances could proceed no nearer. The more enthusiastic did go on, and I was of the number. What further stimulated me to do so was the fact that the third Merewig, she who had partially cleaned my scoring off her back, plucked up her skirts, and strode ahead. I hurried after and caught her up. 'I beg your pardon,' said I. 'You must excuse the interest I take in antiquities, but I suppose it is a long time since you were a girl.' Of course, my meaning was obvious; I referred to her earlier existence, before she borrowed her present body. But she stopped abruptly, gave me a withering look, and went back to rejoin another group of pedestrians. Ha! my friend, I verily believe that the boat is being lifted. The tide is flowing in."

"The tide is flowing," I said; and then added, "really, Major Donelly, your story ought not to be confined to the narrow circle of your intimates."

"That is true," he replied. "But my desire to make it known has been damped by the way in which Alec was received, or rather rejected, by the Secretary of the Society for Psychical Research."

"But I do not mean that you should tell it to the Society for Psychical Research."

"To whom, then?"

"Tell it to the Horse Marines."

XII. — THE "BOLD VENTURE"

THE little fisher-town of Portstephen comprised two strings of houses facing each other at the bottom of a narrow valley, down which the merest trickle of a stream decanted into the harbour. The street was so narrow that it was at intervals alone that sufficient space was accorded for two wheeled vehicles to pass one another, and the road-way was for the most part so narrow that each house door was set back in the depth of the wall, to permit the foot-passenger to step into the recess to avoid being overrun by the wheels of a cart that ascended or descended the street.

The inhabitants lived upon the sea and its produce. Such as were not fishers were mariners, and but a small percentage remained that were neither—the butcher, the baker, the smith, and the doctor; and these also lived by the sea, for they lived upon the sailors and fishermen.

For the most part, the seafaring men were furnished with large families. The net in which they drew children was almost as well filled as the seine in which they trapped pilchards.

Jonas Rea, however, was an exception; he had been married for ten years, and had but one child, and that a son.

"You've a very poor haul, Jonas," said to him his neighbour, Samuel Carnsew; "I've been married so long as you and I've twelve. My wife has had twins twice."

"It's not a poor haul for me, Samuel," replied Jonas, "I may have but one child, but he's a buster."

Jonas had a mother alive, known as Old Betty Rea. When he married, he had proposed that his mother, who was a widow, should live with him. But man proposes and woman disposes. The arrangement did not commend itself to the views of Mrs. Rea, junior—that is to say, of Jane, Jonas's wife.

Betty had always been a managing woman. She had managed her house, her children, and her husband; but she speedily was made aware that her daughter-in-law refused to be managed by her.

Jane was, in her way, also a managing woman: she kept her house clean, her husband's clothes in order, her child neat, and herself the very pink of tidiness. She was a somewhat hard woman, much given to grumbling and finding fault.

Jane and her mother-in-law did not come to an open and flagrant quarrel, but the fret between them waxed intolerable; and the curtain-lectures, of which the text and topic was Old Betty, were so frequent and so protracted that Jonas convinced himself that there was smoother water in the worst sea than in his own house.

He was constrained to break to his mother the unpleasant information that she must go elsewhere; but he softened the blow by informing her that he had secured for her residence a tiny cottage up an alley, that consisted of two rooms only, one a kitchen, above that a bedchamber.

The old woman received the communication without annoyance. She rose to the offer, for she had also herself considered that the situation had become unendurable. Accordingly, with goodwill, she removed to her new quarters, and soon made the house look keen and cosy.

But, so soon as Jane gave indications of becoming a mother, it was agreed that Betty should attend on her daughter-in-law. To this Jane consented. After all, Betty could not be worse than another woman, a stranger.

And when Jane was in bed, and unable to quit it, then Betty once more reigned supreme in the house and managed everything—even her daughter-in-law.

But the time of Jane's lying upstairs was brief, and at the earliest possible moment she reappeared in the kitchen, pale indeed and weak, but resolute, and with firm hand withdrew the reins from the grasp of Betty.

In leaving her son's house, the only thing that Betty regretted was the baby. To that she had taken a mighty affection, and she did not quit till she had poured forth into the deaf ear of Jane a thousand instructions as to how the babe was to be fed, clothed, and reared.

As a devoted son, Jonas never returned from sea without visiting his mother, and when on shore saw her every day. He sat with her by the hour, told her of all that concerned him—except about his wife—and communicated to her all his hopes and wishes. The babe, whose name was Peter, was a topic on which neither weaned of talking or of listening; and often did Jonas bring the child over to be kissed and admired by his grandmother.

Jane raised objections—the weather was cold and the child would take a chill; grandmother was inconsiderate, and upset its stomach with sweetstuff; it had not a tidy dress in which to be seen: but Jonas overruled all her objections. He was a mild and yielding man, but on this one point he was inflexible—his child should grow up to know, love, and reverence his mother as sincerely as did he himself. And these were delightful hours to the old woman, when she could have the infant on her lap, croon to it, and talk to it all the delightful nonsense that flows from the lips of a woman when caressing a child.

Moreover, when the boy was not there, Betty was knitting socks or contriving pin-cases, or making little garments for him; and all the small savings she could gather from the allowance made by her son, and from the sale of some of her needlework, were devoted to the same grandchild.

As the little fellow found his feet and was allowed to toddle, he often wanted to "go to granny," not much to the approval of Mrs. Jane. And, later, when he went to school, he found his way to her cottage before he returned home so soon as his work hours in class were over. He very early developed a love for the sea and ships.

This did not accord with Mrs. Jane's ideas; she came of a family that had ever been on the land, and she disapproved of the sea. "But," remonstrated her husband, "he is my son, and I and my father and grandfather were all of us sea-dogs, so that, naturally, my part in the boy takes to the water."

And now an idea entered the head of Old Betty. She resolved on making a ship for Peter. She provided herself with a stout piece of deal of suitable size and shape, and proceeded to fashion it into the form of a cutter, and to scoop out the interior. At this Peter assisted. After school hours he was with his grandmother watching the process, giving his opinion as to shape, and how the boat was to be rigged and furnished. The aged woman had but an old knife, no proper carpentering tools, consequently the progress made was slow. Moreover, she worked at the ship only when Peter was by. The interest excited in the child by the process was an attraction to her house, and it served to keep him there. Further, when he was at home, he was being incessantly scolded by his mother, and the preference he developed for granny's cottage caused many a pang of jealousy in Jane's heart.

Peter was now nine years old, and remained the only child, when a sad thing happened. One evening, when the little ship was rigged and almost complete, after leaving his grandmother, Peter went down to the port. There happened to be no one about, and in craning over the quay to look into his father's boat, he overbalanced, fell in, and was drowned.

The grandmother supposed that the boy had returned home, the mother that he was with his grandmother, and a couple of hours passed before search for him was instituted, and the body was brought home an hour after that. Mrs. Jane's grief at losing her child was united with resentment against Old Betty for having drawn the child away from home, and against her husband for having encouraged it. She poured forth the vials of her wrath upon Jonas. He it was who had done his utmost to have the boy killed, because he had allowed him to wander at large, and had provided him with an excuse by allowing him to tarry with Old Betty after leaving school, so that no one knew where he was. Had Jonas been a reasonable man, and a docile husband, he would have insisted on Peter returning promptly home every day, in which case this disaster would not have occurred. "But," said Jane bitterly, "you never have considered my feelings, and I believe you did not love Peter, and wanted to be rid of him."

The blow to Betty was terrible; her heart-strings were wrapped about the little fellow; and his loss was to her the eclipse of all light, the death of all her happiness.

When Peter was in his coffin, then the old woman went to the house, carrying the little ship. It was now complete with sails and rigging.

"Jane," said she, "I want thickey ship to be put in with Peter. 'Twere made for he, and I can't let another have it, and I can't keep it myself."

"Nonsense," retorted Mrs. Rea, junior. "The boat can be no use to he, now."

"I wouldn't say that. There's naught revealed on them matters. But I'm cruel certain that up aloft there'll be a rumpus if Peter wakes up and don't find his ship."

"You may take it away; I'll have none of it," said Jane.

So the old woman departed, but was not disposed to accept discomfiture. She went to the undertaker.

"Mr. Matthews, I want you to put this here boat in wi' my gran'child Peter. It will go in fitty at his feet."

"Very sorry, ma'am, but not unless I break off the bowsprit. You see the coffin is too narrow."

"Then put'n in sideways and longways."

"Very sorry, ma'am, but the mast is in the way. I'd be forced to break that so as to get the lid down."

Disconcerted, the old woman retired; she would not suffer Peter's boat to be maltreated.

On the occasion of the funeral, the grandmother appeared as one of the principal mourners. For certain reasons, Mrs. Jane did not attend at the church and grave.

As the procession left the house, Old Betty took her place beside her son, and carried the boat in her hand. At the close of the service at the grave, she said to the sexton: "I'll trouble you, John Hext, to put this here little ship right o' top o' his coffin. I made'n for Peter, and Peter'll expect to have'n." This was done, and not a step from the grave would the grandmother take till the first shovelfuls had fallen on the coffin and had partially buried the white ship.

When Granny Rea returned to her cottage, the fire was out. She seated herself beside the dead hearth, with hands folded and the tears coursing down her withered cheeks. Her heart was as dead and dreary as that hearth. She had now no object in life, and she murmured a prayer that the Lord might please to take her, that she might see her Peter sailing his boat in paradise.

Her prayer was interrupted by the entry of Jonas, who shouted: "Mother, we want your help again. There's Jane took bad; wi' the worrit and the sorrow it's come on a bit earlier than she reckoned, and you're to come along as quick as you can. 'Tisn't the Lord gave and the Lord hath taken away, but topsy-turvy, the Lord hath taken away and is givin' again."

Betty rose at once, and went to the house with her son, and again—as nine years previously—for a while she assumed the management of the house; and when a baby arrived, another boy, she managed that as well.

The reign of Betty in the house of Jonas and Jane was not for long. The mother was soon downstairs, and with her reappearance came the departure of the grandmother.

And now began once more the same old life as had been initiated nine years previously. The child carried to its grandmother, who dandled it, crooned and talked to it. Then, as it grew, it was supplied with socks and garments knitted and cut out and put together by Betty; there ensued the visits of the toddling child, and the remonstrances of the mother. School time arrived, and with it a break in the journey to or from school at granny's house, to partake of bread and jam, hear stories, and, finally, to assist at the making of a new ship.

If, with increase of years, Betty's powers had begun to fail, there had been no corresponding decrease in energy of will. Her eyes were not so clear as of old, nor her hearing so acute, but her hand was not unsteady. She would this time make and rig a schooner and not a cutter.

Experience had made her more able, and she aspired to accomplish a greater task than she had previously undertaken. It was really remarkable how the old course was resumed almost in every particular. But the new grandson was called Jonas, like his father, and Old Betty loved him, if possible, with a more intense love than had been given to the first child. He closely resembled his father, and to her it was a renewal of her life long ago, when she nursed and cared for the first Jonas. And, if possible, Jane became more jealous of the aged woman, who was drawing to her so large a portion of her child's affection. The schooner was nearly complete. It was somewhat rude, having been worked with no better tool than a penknife, and its masts being made of knitting-pins.

On the day before little Jonas's ninth birthday, Betty carried the ship to the painter.

"Mr. Elway," said she, "there be one thing I do want your help in. I cannot put the name on the vessel. I can't fashion the letters, and I want you to do it for me."

"All right, ma'am. What name?"

"Well, now," said she, "my husband, the father of Jonas, and the grandfather of the little Jonas, he always sailed in a schooner, and the ship was the *Bold Venture*."

"The *Bonaventura*, I think. I remember her."

"I'm sure she was the *Bold Venture*."

"I think not, Mrs. Rea."

"It must have been the *Bold Venture* or *Bold Adventurer*. What sense is there in such a name as *Boneventure*? I never heard of no such venture, unless it were that of Jack Smithson, who jumped out of a garret window, and sure enough he broke a bone of his leg. No, Mr. Elway, I'll have her entitled the *Bold Venture*."

"I'll not gainsay you. *Bold Venture* she shall be."

Then the painter very dexterously and daintily put the name in black paint on the white strip at the stern.

"Will it be dry by to-morrow?" asked the old woman. "That's the little lad's birthday, and I promised to have his schooner ready for him to sail her then."

"I've put dryers in the paint," answered Mr. Elway, "and you may reckon it will be right for to-morrow."

That night Betty was unable to sleep, so eager was she for the day when the little boy would attain his ninth year and become the possessor of the beautiful ship she had fashioned for him with her own hands, and on which, in fact, she had been engaged for more than a twelvemonth.

Nor was she able to eat her simple breakfast and noonday meal, so thrilled was her old heart with love for the child and expectation of his delight when the *Bold Venture* was made over to him as his own.

She heard his little feet on the cobblestones of the alley: he came on, dancing, jumping, fidgeted at the lock, threw the door open and burst in with a shout—

"See! see, granny! my new ship! Mother has give it me. A real frigate—with three masts, all red and green, and cost her seven shillings at Camelot Fair yesterday." He bore aloft a very magnificent toy ship. It had pennants at the mast-top and a flag at stern. "Granny! look! look! ain't she a beauty? Now I shan't want your drashy old schooner when I have my grand new frigate."

"Won't you have your ship—the *Bold Venture*?"

"No, granny; chuck it away. It's a shabby bit o' rubbish, mother says; and see! there's a brass cannon, a real cannon that will go off with a bang, on my frigate. Ain't it a beauty?"

"Oh, Jonas! look at the *Bold Venture*!"

"No, granny, I can't stay. I want to be off and swim my beautiful seven-shilling ship."

Then he dashed away as boisterous as he had dashed in, and forgot to shut the door. It was evening when the elder Jonas returned home, and he was welcomed by his son with exclamations of delight, and was shown the new ship.

"But, daddy, her won't sail; over her will flop in the water."

"There is no lead on the keel," remarked the father. "The vessel is built for show only."

Then he walked away to his mother's cottage. He was vexed. He knew that his wife had bought the toy with the deliberate intent of disappointing and wounding her mother-in-law; and he was afraid that he would find the old lady deeply mortified and incensed. As he entered the dingy lane, he noticed that her door was partly open.

The aged woman was on the seat by the table at the window, lying forward clasping the ship, and the two masts were run through her white hair; her head rested, partly on the new ship and partly on the table.

"Mother!" said he. "Mother!"

There was no answer.

The feeble old heart had given way under the blow, and had ceased to beat.

* * * * *

I was accustomed, a few summers past, to spend a couple of months at Portstephen. Jonas Rea took me often in his boat, either mackerel fishing, or on excursions to the islets off the coast, in quest of wild birds. We became familiar, and I would now and then spend an evening with him in his cottage, and talk about the sea, and the chances of a harbour of refuge being made at Portstephen, and sometimes we spoke of our own family affairs. Thus it was that, little by little, the story of the ship *Bold Venture* was told me.

Mrs. Jane was no more in the house.

"It's a curious thing," said Jonas Rea, "but the first ship my mother made was no sooner done than my boy Peter died, and when she made another, with two masts, as soon as ever it was finished she died herself, and shortly after my wife, Jane, who took a chill at mother's funeral. It settled on her chest, and she died in a fortnight."

"Is that the boat?" I inquired, pointing to a glass case on a cupboard, in which was a rudely executed schooner.

"That's her," replied Jonas; "and I'd like you to have a look close at her."

I walked to the cupboard and looked.

"Do you see anything particular?" asked the fisherman.

"I can't say that I do."

"Look at her masthead. What is there?"

After a pause I said: "There is a grey hair, that is all, like a pennant."

"I mean that," said Jonas. "I can't say whether my old mother put a hair from her white head there for the purpose, or whether it caught and fixed itself when she fell forward clasping the boat, and the masts and spars and shrouds were all tangled in her hair. Anyhow, there it be, and that's one reason why I've had the *Bold Venture* put in a glass case—that the white hair may never by no chance get brushed away from it. Now, look again. Do you see nothing more?"

"Can't say I do."

"Look at the bows."

I did so. Presently I remarked: "I see nothing except, perhaps, some bruises, and a little bit of red paint."

"Ah! that's it, and where did the red paint come from?"

I was, of course, quite unable to suggest an explanation.

Presently, after Mr. Rea had waited—as if to draw from me the answer he expected—he said: "Well, no, I reckon you can't tell. It was thus. When mother died, I brought the *Bold Venture* here and set her where she is now, on the cupboard, and Jonas, he had set the new ship, all red and green, the *Saucy Jane* it was called, on the bureau. Will you believe me, next morning when I came downstairs the frigate was on the floor, and some of her spars broken and all the rigging in a muddle."

"There was no lead on the bottom. It fell down."

"It was not once that happened. It came to the same thing every night; and what is more, the *Bold Venture* began to show signs of having fouled her."

"How so?"

"Run against her. She had bruises, and had brought away some of the paint of the *Saucy Jane*. Every morning the frigate, if she were'nt on the floor, were rammed into a corner, and battered as if she'd been in a bad sea."

"But it is impossible."

"Of course, lots o' things is impossible, but they happen all the same."

"Well, what next?"

"Jane, she was ill, and took wus and wus, and just as she got wus so it took wus as well with the *Saucy Jane*. And on the night she died, I reckon that there was a reg'lar pitched sea-fight."

"But not at sea."

"Well, no; but the frigate seemed to have been rammed, and she was on the floor and split from stem to stern."

"And, pray, has the *Bold Venture* made no attempt since? The glass case is not broken."

"There's been no occasion. I chucked what remained of the *Saucy Jane* into the fire."

XIII. — MUSTAPHA

I

AMONG the many hangers-on at the Hôtel de l'Europe at Luxor—donkey-boys, porters, guides, antiquity dealers—was one, a young man named Mustapha, who proved a general favourite.

I spent three winters at Luxor, partly for my health, partly for pleasure, mainly to make artistic studies, as I am by profession a painter. So I came to know Mustapha fairly well in three stages, during those three winters.

When first I made his acquaintance he was in the transition condition from boyhood to manhood. He had an intelligent face, with bright eyes, a skin soft as brown silk, with a velvety hue on it. His features were regular, and if his face was a little too round to quite satisfy an English artistic eye, yet this was a peculiarity to which one soon became accustomed. He was unflaggingly good-natured and obliging. A mongrel, no doubt, he was; Arab and native Egyptian blood were mingled in his veins. But the result was happy; he combined the patience and gentleness of the child of Mizraim with the energy and pluck of the son of the desert.

Mustapha had been a donkey-boy, but had risen a stage higher, and looked, as the object of his supreme ambition, to become some day a dragoman, and blaze like one of these gilded beetles in lace and chains, rings and weapons. To become a dragoman—one of the most obsequious of men till engaged, one of the veriest tyrants when engaged—to what higher could an Egyptian boy aspire?

To become a dragoman means to go in broadcloth and with gold chains when his fellows are half naked; to lounge and twist the moustache when his kinsfolk are toiling under the water-buckets; to be able to extort backsheesh from all the tradesmen to whom he can introduce a master; to do nothing himself and make others work for him; to be able to look to purchase two, three, even four wives when his father contented himself with one; to soar out of the region of native virtues into that of foreign vices; to be superior to all instilled prejudices against spirits and wine—that is the ideal set before young Egypt through contact with the English and the American tourist.

We all liked Mustapha. No one had a bad word to say of him. Some pious individuals rejoiced to see that he had broken with the Koran, as if this were a first step towards taking up with the Bible. A free-thinking professor was glad to find that Mustapha had emancipated himself from some of those shackles which religion places on august, divine humanity, and that by getting drunk he gave pledge that he had risen into a sphere of pure emancipation, which eventuates in ideal perfection.

As I made my studies I engaged Mustapha to carry my easel and canvas, or camp-stool. I was glad to have him as a study, to make him stand by a wall or sit on a pillar that was prostrate, as artistic exigencies required. He was always ready to accompany me. There was an understanding between us that when a drove of tourists came to Luxor he might leave me for the day to pick up what he could then from the natural prey; but I found him not always keen to be off duty to me. Though he could get more from the occasional visitor than from me, he was above the ravenous appetite for backsheesh which consumed his fellows.

He who has much to do with the native Egyptian will have discovered that there are in him a fund of kindliness and a treasure of good qualities. He is delighted to be treated with humanity, pleased to be noticed, and ready to repay attention with touching gratitude. He is by no means as rapacious for backsheesh as the passing traveller supposes; he is shrewd to distinguish between man and man; likes this one, and will do anything for him unrewarded, and will do naught for another for any bribe.

The Egyptian is now in a transitional state. If it be quite true that the touch of England is restoring life to his crippled limbs, and the voice of England bidding him rise up and walk, there are occasions on which association with Englishmen is a disadvantage to him. Such an instance is that of poor, good Mustapha.

It was not my place to caution Mustapha against the pernicious influences to which he was subjected, and, to speak plainly, I did not know what line to adopt, on what ground to take my stand, if I did. He was breaking with the old life, and taking up with what was new, retaining of the old only what was bad in it, and acquiring of the new none of its good parts. Civilisation—European civilisation—is excellent, but cannot be swallowed at a gulp, nor does it wholly suit the oriental digestion.

That which impelled Mustapha still further in his course was the attitude assumed towards him by his own relatives and the natives of his own village. They were strict Moslems, and they regarded him as one on the highway to becoming a renegade. They treated him with mistrust, showed him aversion, and loaded him with reproaches. Mustapha had a high spirit, and he resented rebuke. Let his fellows grumble and objurgate, said he; they would cringe to him when he became a dragoman, with his pockets stuffed with piastres.

There was in our hotel, the second winter, a young fellow of the name of Jameson, a man with plenty of money, superficial good nature, little intellect, very conceited and egotistic, and this fellow was Mustapha's evil genius. It was Jameson's delight to encourage Mustapha in drinking and gambling. Time hung heavy on his hands. He cared nothing for hieroglyphics, scenery bored him, antiquities, art, had no charm for him. Natural history presented to him no attraction, and the only amusement level with his mental faculties was that of hoaxing natives, or breaking down their religious prejudices.

Matters were in this condition as regarded Mustapha, when an incident occurred during my second winter at Luxor that completely altered the tenor of Mustapha's life.

One night a fire broke out in the nearest village. It originated in a mud hovel belonging to a fellah; his wife had spilled some oil on the hearth, and the flames leaping up had caught the low thatch, which immediately burst into a blaze. A wind was blowing from the direction of the Arabian desert, and it carried the flames and ignited the thatch before it on other roofs; the conflagration spread, and the whole village was menaced with destruction. The greatest excitement and alarm prevailed. The inhabitants lost their heads. Men ran about rescuing from their hovels their only treasures—old sardine tins and empty marmalade pots; women wailed, children sobbed; no one made any attempt to stay the fire; and, above all, were heard the screams of the woman whose incaution had caused the mischief, and who was being beaten unmercifully by her husband.

The few English in the hotel came on the scene, and with their instinctive energy and system set to work to organise a corps and subdue the flames. The women and girls who were rescued from the menaced hovels, or plucked out of those already on fire, were in many cases unveiled, and so it came to pass that Mustapha, who, under English direction, was ablest and most vigorous in his efforts to stop the conflagration, met his fate in the shape of the daughter of Ibraim the Farrier.

By the light of the flames he saw her, and at once resolved to make that fair girl his wife.

No reasonable obstacle intervened, so thought Mustapha. He had amassed a sufficient sum to entitle him to buy a wife and set up a household of his own. A house consists of four mud walls and a low thatch, and housekeeping in an Egyptian house is as elementary and economical as the domestic architecture. The maintenance of a wife and family is not costly after the first outlay, which consists in indemnifying the father for the expense to which he has been put in rearing a daughter.

The ceremony of courting is also elementary, and the addresses of the suitor are not paid to the bride, but to her father, and not in person by the candidate, but by an intermediary.

Mustapha negotiated with a friend, a fellow hanger-on at the hotel, to open proceedings with the farrier. He was to represent to the worthy man that the suitor entertained the most ardent admiration for the virtues of Ibraim personally, that he was inspired with but one ambition, which was alliance with so distinguished a family as his. He was to assure the father of the damsel that Mustapha undertook to proclaim through Upper and Lower Egypt, in the ears of Egyptians, Arabs, and Europeans, that Ibraim was the most remarkable man that ever existed for solidity of judgment, excellence of parts, uprightness of dealing, nobility of sentiment, strictness in observance of the precepts of the Koran, and that finally Mustapha was anxious to indemnify this same paragon of genius and virtue for his condescension in having cared to breed and clothe and feed for several years a certain girl, his daughter, if Mustapha might have that daughter as his wife. Not that he cared for the daughter in herself, but as a means whereby he might have the honour of entering into alliance with one so distinguished and so esteemed of Allah as Ibraim the Farrier.

To the infinite surprise of the intermediary, and to the no less surprise and mortification of the suitor, Mustapha was refused. He was a bad Moslem. Ibraim would have no alliance with one who had turned his back on the Prophet and drunk bottled beer.

Till this moment Mustapha had not realised how great was the alienation between his fellows and himself—what a barrier he had set up between himself and the men of his own blood. The refusal of his suit struck the young man to the quick. He had known and played with the farrier's daughter in childhood, till she had come of age to veil her face; now that he had seen her in her ripe charms, his heart was deeply stirred and engaged. He entered into himself, and going to the mosque he there made a solemn vow that if he ever touched wine, ale, or spirits again he would cut his throat, and he sent word to Ibraim that he had done so, and begged that he would not dispose of his daughter and finally reject him till he had seen how that he who had turned in thought and manner of life from the Prophet would return with firm resolution to the right way.

II

FROM this time Mustapha changed his conduct. He was obliging and attentive as before, ready to exert himself to do for me what I wanted, ready also to extort money from the ordinary tourist for doing nothing, to go with me and carry my tools when I went forth painting, and to joke and laugh with Jameson; but, unless he were unavoidably detained, he said his prayers five times daily in the mosque, and no inducement whatever would make him touch anything save sherbet, milk, or water.

Mustapha had no easy time of it. The strict Mohammedans mistrusted this sudden conversion, and believed that he was playing a part. Ibraim gave him no encouragement. His relatives maintained their reserve and stiffness towards him.

His companions, moreover, who were in the transitional stage, and those who had completely shaken off all faith in Allah and trust in the Prophet and respect for the Koran, were incensed at his desertion. He was ridiculed, insulted; he was waylaid and beaten. The young fellows mimicked him, the elder scoffed at him.

Jameson took his change to heart, and laid himself out to bring him out of his pot of scruples.

"Mustapha ain't any sport at all now," said he. "I'm hanged if he has another para from me." He offered him bribes in gold, he united with the others in ridicule, he turned his back on him, and refused to employ him. Nothing availed. Mustapha was respectful, courteous, obliging as before, but he had returned, he said, to the faith and rule of life in which he had been brought up, and he would never again leave it.

"I have sworn," said he, "that if I do I will cut my throat."

I had been, perhaps, negligent in cautioning the young fellow the first winter that I knew him against the harm likely to be done him by taking up with European habits contrary to his law and the feelings and prejudices of his people. Now, however, I had no hesitation in expressing to him the satisfaction I felt at the courageous and determined manner in which he had broken with acquired habits that could do him no good. For one thing, we were now better acquaintances, and I felt that as one who had known him for more than a few months in the winter, I had a good right to speak. And, again, it is always easier or pleasanter to praise than to reprimand.

One day when sketching I cut my pencil with a pruning-knife I happened to have in my pocket; my proper knife of many blades had been left behind by misadventure.

Mustapha noticed the knife and admired it, and asked if it had cost a great sum.

"Not at all," I answered. "I did not even buy it. It was given me. I ordered some flower seeds from a seeds-man, and when he sent me the consignment he included this knife in the case as a present. It is not worth more than a shilling in England."

He turned it about, with looks of admiration.

"It is just the sort that would suit me," he said. "I know your other knife with many blades. It is very fine, but it is too small. I do not want it to cut pencils. It has other things in it, a hook for taking stones from a horse's hoof, a pair of tweezers for removing hairs. I do not want such, but a knife such as this, with such a curve, is just the thing."

"Then you shall have it," said I. "You are welcome. It was for rough work only that I brought the knife to Egypt with me."

I finished a painting that winter that gave me real satisfaction. It was of the great court of the temple of Luxor by evening light, with the last red glare of the sun over the distant desert hills, and the eastern sky above of a purple depth. What colours I used! the intensest on my palette, and yet fell short of the effect.

The picture was in the Academy, was well hung, abominably represented in one of the illustrated guides to the galleries, as a blotch, by some sort of photographic process on gelatine; my picture sold, which concerned me most of all, and not only did it sell at a respectable figure, but it also brought me two or three orders for Egyptian pictures. So many English and Americans go up the Nile, and carry away with them pleasant reminiscences of the Land of the Pharaohs, that when in England they are fain to buy pictures which shall remind them of scenes in that land.

I returned to my hotel at Luxor in November, to spend there a third winter. The fellaheen about there saluted me as a friend with an affectionate delight, which I am quite certain was not assumed, as they got nothing out of me save kindly salutations. I had the Egyptian fever on me, which, when once acquired, is not to be shaken off—an enthusiasm for everything Egyptian, the antiquities, the history of the Pharaohs, the very desert, the brown Nile, the desolate hill ranges, the ever blue sky, the marvellous colorations at rise and set of sun, and last, but not least, the prosperity of the poor peasants.

I am quite certain that the very warmest welcome accorded to me was from Mustapha, and almost the first words he said to me on my meeting him again were: "I have been very good. I say my prayers. I drink no wine, and Ibraim will give me his daughter in the second Iomada—what you call January."

"Not before, Mustapha?"

"No, sir; he says I must be tried for one whole year, and he is right."

"Then soon after Christmas you will be happy!"

"I have got a house and made it ready. Yes. After Christmas there will be one very happy man—one very, very happy man in Egypt, and that will be your humble servant, Mustapha."

III

WE were a pleasant party at Luxor, this third winter, not numerous, but for the most part of congenial tastes. For the most part we were keen on hieroglyphics, we admired Queen Hatasou and we hated Rameses II. We could distinguish the artistic work of one dynasty from that of another. We were learned on cartouches, and flourished our knowledge before the tourists dropping in.

One of those staying in the hotel was an Oxford don, very good company, interested in everything, and able to talk well on everything—I mean everything more or less remotely connected with Egypt. Another was a young fellow who had been an attaché at Berlin, but was out of health—nothing organic the matter with his lungs, but they were weak. He was keen on the political situation, and very anti-Gallican, as every man who has been in Egypt naturally is, who is not a Frenchman.

There was also staying in the hotel an American lady, fresh and delightful, whose mind and conversation twinkled like frost crystals in the sun, a woman full of good-humour, of the most generous sympathies, and so droll that she kept us ever amused.

And, alas! Jameson was back again, not entering into any of our pursuits, not understanding our little jokes, not at all content to be there. He grumbled at the food—and, indeed, that might have been better; at the monotony of the life at Luxor, at his London doctor for putting the veto on Cairo because of its drainage, or rather the absence of all drainage. I really think we did our utmost to draw Jameson into our circle, to amuse him, to interest him in something; but one by one we gave him up, and the last to do this was the little American lady.

From the outset he had attacked Mustapha, and endeavoured to persuade him to shake off his "squeamish nonsense," as Jameson called his resolve. "I'll tell you what it is, old fellow," he said, "life isn't worth living without good liquor, and as for that blessed Prophet of yours, he showed he was a fool when he put a bar on drinks."

But as Mustapha was not pliable he gave him up. "He's become just as great a bore as that old Rameses," said he. "I'm sick of the whole concern, and I don't think anything of fresh dates, that you fellows make such a fuss about. As for that stupid old Nile—there ain't a fish worth eating comes out of it. And those old Egyptians were arrant humbugs. I haven't seen a lotus since I came here, and they made such a fuss about them too."

The little American lady was not weary of asking questions relative to English home life, and especially to country-house living and amusements.

"Oh, my dear!" said she, "I would give my ears to spend a Christmas in the fine old fashion in a good ancient manor-house in the country."

"There is nothing remarkable in that," said an English lady.

"Not to you, maybe; but there would be to us. What we read of and make pictures of in our fancies, that is what you live. Your facts are our fairy tales. Look at your hunting."

"That, if you like, is fun," threw in Jameson. "But I don't myself think anything save Luxor can be a bigger bore than country-house life at Christmas time—when all the boys are back from school."

"With us," said the little American, "our sportsmen dress in pink like yours—the whole thing—and canter after a bag of anise seed that is trailed before them."

"Why do they not import foxes?"

"Because a fox would not keep to the road. Our farmers object pretty freely to trespass; so the hunting must of necessity be done on the highway, and the game is but a bag of anise seed. I would like to see an English meet and a run."

This subject was thrashed out after having been prolonged unduly for the sake of Jameson.

"Oh, dear me!" said the Yankee lady. "If but that chef could be persuaded to give us plum-puddings for Christmas, I would try to think I was in England."

"Plum-pudding is exploded," said Jameson. "Only children ask for it now. A good trifle or a tipsy-cake is much more to my taste; but this hanged cook here can give us nothing but his blooming custard pudding and burnt sugar."

"I do not think it would be wise to let him attempt a plum-pudding," said the English lady. "But if we can persuade him to permit me I will mix and make the pudding, and then he cannot go far wrong in the boiling and dishing up."

"That is the only thing wanting to make me perfectly happy," said the American. "I'll confront monsieur. I am sure I can talk him into a good humour, and we shall have our plum-pudding."

No one has yet been found, I do believe, who could resist that little woman. She carried everything before her. The cook placed himself and all his culinary apparatus at her feet. We took part in the stoning of the raisins, and the washing of the currants, even the chopping of the suet; we stirred the pudding, threw in sixpence apiece, and a ring, and then it was tied up in a cloth, and set aside to be boiled. Christmas Day came, and the English chaplain preached us a practical sermon on "Goodwill towards men." That was his text, and his sermon was but a swelling out of the words just as rice is swelled to thrice its size by boiling.

We dined. There was an attempt at roast beef—it was more like baked leather. The event of the dinner was to be the bringing in and eating of the plum-pudding.

Surely all would be perfect. We could answer for the materials and the mixing. The English lady could guarantee the boiling. She had seen the plum-pudding "on the boil," and had given strict injunctions as to the length of time during which it was to boil.

But, alas! the pudding was not right when brought on the table. It was not enveloped in lambent blue flame—it was not crackling in the burning brandy. It was sent in dry, and the brandy arrived separate in a white sauce-boat, hot indeed, and sugared, but not on fire.

There ensued outcries of disappointment. Attempts were made to redress the mistake by setting fire to the brandy in a spoon, but the spoon was cold. The flame would not catch, and finally, with a sigh, we had to take our plum-pudding as served.

"I say, chaplain!" exclaimed Jameson, "practice is better than precept, is it not?"

"To be sure it is."

"You gave us a deuced good sermon. It was short, as it ought to be; but I'll go better on it, I'll practise where you preached, and have larks, too!"

Then Jameson started from table with a plate of plum-pudding in one hand and the sauce-boat in the other. "By Jove!" he said, "I'll teach these fellows to open their eyes. I'll show them that we know how to feed. We can't turn out scarabs and cartouches in England, that are no good to anyone, but we can produce the finest roast beef in the world, and do a thing or two in puddings."

And he left the room.

We paid no heed to anything Jameson said or did. We were rather relieved that he was out of the room, and did not concern ourselves about the "larks" he promised himself, and which we were quite certain would be as insipid as were the quails of the Israelites.

In ten minutes he was back, laughing and red in the face.

"I've had splitting fun," he said. "You should have been there."

"Where, Jameson?"

"Why, outside. There were a lot of old moolahs and other hoky-pokies sitting and contemplating the setting sun and all that sort of thing, and I gave Mustapha the pudding. I told him I wished him to try our great national English dish, on which her Majesty the Queen dines daily. Well, he ate and enjoyed it, by George. Then I said, 'Old fellow, it's uncommonly dry, so you must take the sauce to it.' He asked if it was only sauce—flour and water. 'It's sauce, by Jove,' said I, 'a little sugar to it; no bar on the sugar, Musty.' So I put the boat to his lips and gave him a pull. By George, you should have seen his face! It was just thundering fun. 'I've done you at last, old Musty,' I said. 'It is best cognac.' He gave me such a look! He'd have eaten me, I believe—and he walked away. It was just splitting fun. I wish you had been there to see it."

I went out after dinner, to take my usual stroll along the river-bank, and to watch the evening lights die away on the columns and obelisk. On my return I saw at once that something had happened which had produced commotion among the servants of the hotel. I had reached the salon before I inquired what was the matter.

The boy who was taking the coffee round said: "Mustapha is dead. He cut his throat at the door of the mosque. He could not help himself. He had broken his vow."

I looked at Jameson without a word. Indeed, I could not speak; I was choking. The little American lady was trembling, the English lady crying. The gentlemen stood silent in the windows, not speaking a word.

Jameson's colour changed. He was honestly distressed, uneasy, and tried to cover his confusion with bravado and a jest.

"After all," he said, "it is only a nigger the less."

"Nigger!" said the American lady. "He was no nigger, but an Egyptian."

"Oh! I don't pretend to distinguish between your blacks and whity-browns any more than I do between your cartouches," returned Jameson.

"He was no black," said the American lady, standing up. "But I do mean to say that I consider you an utterly unredeemed black——"

"My dear, don't," said the Englishwoman, drawing the other down. "It's no good. The thing is done. He meant no harm."

IV

I COULD not sleep. My blood was in a boil. I felt that I could not speak to Jameson again. He would have to leave Luxor. That was tacitly understood among us. Coventry was the place to which he would be consigned.

I tried to finish in a little sketch I had made in my notebook when I was in my room, but my hand shook, and I was constrained to lay my pencil aside. Then I took up an Egyptian grammar, but could not fix my mind on study. The hotel was very still. Everyone had gone to bed at an early hour that night, disinclined for conversation. No one was moving. There was a lamp in the passage; it was partly turned down. Jameson's room was next to mine. I heard him stir as he undressed, and talk to himself. Then he was quiet. I wound up my watch, and emptying my pocket, put my purse under the pillow. I was not in the least heavy with sleep. If I did go to bed I should not be able to close my eyes. But then—if I sat up I could do nothing.

I was about leisurely to undress, when I heard a sharp cry, or exclamation of mingled pain and alarm, from the adjoining room. In another moment there was a rap at my door. I opened, and Jameson came in. He was in his night-shirt, and looking agitated and frightened.

"Look here, old fellow," said he in a shaking voice, "there is Musty in my room. He has been hiding there, and just as I dropped asleep he ran that knife of yours into my throat."

"My knife?"

"Yes—that pruning-knife you gave him, you know. Look here—I must have the place sewn up. Do go for a doctor, there's a good chap."

"Where is the place?"

"Here on my right gill."

Jameson turned his head to the left, and I raised the lamp. There was no wound of any sort there. I told him so.

"Oh, yes! That's fine—I tell you I felt his knife go in."

"Nonsense, you were dreaming."

"Dreaming! Not I. I saw Musty as distinctly as I now see you."

"This is a delusion, Jameson," I replied. "The poor fellow is dead."

"Oh, that's very fine," said Jameson. "It is not the first of April, and I don't believe the yarns that you've been spinning. You tried to make believe he was dead, but I know he is not. He has got into my room, and he made a dig at my throat with your pruning-knife."

"I'll go into your room with you."

"Do so. But he's gone by this time. Trust him to cut and run."

I followed Jameson, and looked about. There was no trace of anyone beside himself having been in the room. Moreover, there was no place but the nut-wood wardrobe in the bedroom in which anyone could have secreted himself. I opened this and showed that it was empty.

After a while I pacified Jameson, and induced him to go to bed again, and then I left his room. I did not now attempt to court sleep. I wrote letters with a hand not the steadiest, and did my accounts.

As the hour approached midnight I was again startled by a cry from the adjoining room, and in another moment Jameson was at my door.

"That blooming fellow Musty is in my room still," said he. "He has been at my throat again."

"Nonsense," I said. "You are labouring under hallucinations. You locked your door."

"Oh, by Jove, yes—of course I did; but, hang it, in this hole, neither doors nor windows fit, and the locks are no good, and the bolts nowhere. He got in again somehow, and if I had not started up the moment I felt the knife, he'd have done for me. He would, by George. I wish I had a revolver."

I went into Jameson's room. Again he insisted on my looking at his throat.

"It's very good of you to say there is no wound," said he. "But you won't gull me with words. I felt his knife in my windpipe, and if I had not jumped out of bed——"

"You locked your door. No one could enter. Look in the glass, there is not even a scratch. This is pure imagination."

"I'll tell you what, old fellow, I won't sleep in that room again. Change with me, there's a charitable buffer. If you don't believe in Musty, Musty won't hurt you, maybe—anyhow you can try if he's solid or a phantom. Blow me if the knife felt like a phantom."

"I do not quite see my way to changing rooms," I replied; "but this I will do for you. If you like to go to bed again in your own apartment, I will sit up with you till morning."

"All right," answered Jameson. "And if Musty comes in again, let out at him and do not spare him. Swear that."

I accompanied Jameson once more to his bedroom, Little as I liked the man, I could not deny him my presence and assistance at this time. It was obvious that his nerves were shaken by what had occurred, and he felt his relation to Mustapha much more than he cared to show. The thought that he had been the cause of the poor fellow's death preyed on his mind, never strong, and now it was upset with imaginary terrors.

I gave up letter writing, and brought my Baedeker's *Upper Egypt* into Jameson's room, one of the best of all guide-books, and one crammed with information. I seated myself near the light, and with my back to the bed, on which the young man had once more flung himself.

"I say," said Jameson, raising his head, "is it too late for a brandy-and-soda?"

"Everyone is in bed."

"What lazy dogs they are. One never can get anything one wants here."

"Well, try to go to sleep."

He tossed from side to side for some time, but after a while, either he was quiet, or I was engrossed in my Baedeker, and I heard nothing till a clock struck twelve. At the last stroke I heard a snort and then a gasp and a cry from the bed. I started up, and looked round. Jameson was slipping out with his feet onto the floor.

"Confound you!" said he angrily, "you are a fine watch, you are, to let Mustapha steal in on tiptoe whilst you are cartouching and all that sort of rubbish. He was at me again, and if I had not been sharp he'd have cut my throat. I won't go to bed any more!"

"Well, sit up. But I assure you no one has been here."

"That's fine. How can you tell? You had your back to me, and these devils of fellows steal about like cats. You can't hear them till they are at you."

It was of no use arguing with Jameson, so I let him have his way.

"I can feel all the three places in my throat where he ran the knife in," said he. "And—don't you notice?—I speak with difficulty."

So we sat up together the rest of the night. He became more reasonable as dawn came on, and inclined to admit that he had been a prey to fancies.

The day passed very much as did others—Jameson was dull and sulky. After déjeuner he sat on at table when the ladies had risen and retired, and the gentlemen had formed in knots at the window, discussing what was to be done in the afternoon.

Suddenly Jameson, whose head had begun to nod, started up with an oath and threw down his chair.

"You fellows!" he said, "you are all in league against me. You let that Mustapha come in without a word, and try to stick his knife into me."

"You let that Mustapha come in, and try and stick his knife into me."

"He has not been here."

"It's a plant. You are combined to bully me and drive me away. You don't like me. You have engaged Mustapha to murder me. This is the fourth time he has tried to cut my throat, and in the *salle à manger*, too, with you all standing round. You ought to be ashamed to call yourselves Englishmen. I'll go to Cairo. I'll complain."

It really seemed that the feeble brain of Jameson was affected. The Oxford don undertook to sit up in the room the following night.

The young man was fagged and sleep-weary, but no sooner did his eyes close, and clouds form about his head, than he was brought to wakefulness again by the same fancy or dream. The Oxford don had more trouble with him on the second night than I had on the first, for his lapses into sleep were more frequent, and each such lapse was succeeded by a start and a panic.

The next day he was worse, and we felt that he could no longer be left alone. The third night the attaché sat up to watch him.

Jameson had now sunk into a sullen mood. He would not speak, except to himself, and then only to grumble.

During the night, without being aware of it, the young attaché, who had taken a couple of magazines with him to read, fell asleep. When he went off he did not know. He woke just before dawn, and in a spasm of terror and self-reproach saw that Jameson's chair was empty.

Jameson was not on his bed. He could not be found in the hotel.

At dawn he was found—dead, at the door of the mosque, with his throat cut.

XIV. — LITTLE JOE GANDER

"THERE'S no good in him," said his stepmother, "not a mossul!" With these words she thrust little Joe forward by applying her knee to the small of his back, and thereby jerking him into the middle of the school before the master. "There's no making nothing out of him, whack him as you will."

Little Joe Lambole was a child of ten, dressed in second-hand, nay, third-hand garments that did not fit. His coat had been a soldier's scarlet uniform, that had gone when discarded to a dealer, who had dealt it to a carter, and when the carter had worn it out it was reduced and adapted to the wear of the child. The nether garments had, in like manner, served a full-grown man till worn out; then they had been cut down at the knees. Though shortened in leg, they maintained their former copiousness of seat, and served as an inexhaustible receptacle for dust. Often as little Joe was "licked" there issued from the dense mass of drapery clouds of dust. It was like beating a puff-ball.

"Only a seven-month child," said Mrs. Lambole contemptuously, "born without his nails on fingers and toes; they growed later. His wits have never come right, and a deal, a deal of larruping it will take to make 'em grow. Use the rod; we won't grumble at you for doing so."

Little Joe Lambole when he came into the world had not been expected to live. He was a poor, small, miserable baby, that could not roar, but whimpered. He had been privately baptised directly he was born, because, at the first, Mrs. Lambole said, "The child is mine, though it be such a creetur, and I wouldn't like it, according, to be buried like a dog."

He was called Joseph. The scriptural Joseph had been sold as a bondman into Egypt; this little Joseph seemed to have been brought into the world to be a slave. In all propriety he ought to have died as a baby, and that happy consummation was almost desired, but he disappointed expectations and lived. His mother died soon after, and his father married again, and his father and stepmother loved him, doubtless; but love is manifested in many ways, and the Lamboles showed theirs in a rough way, by slaps and blows and kicks. The father was ashamed of him because he was a weakling, and the stepmother because he was ugly, and was not her own child. He was a meagre little fellow, with a long neck and a white face and sunken cheeks, a pigeon breast, and a big stomach. He walked with his head forward and his great pale blue eyes staring before him into the far distance, as if he were always looking out of the world. His walk was a waddle, and he tumbled over every obstacle, because he never looked where he was going, always looked to something beyond the horizon.

Because of his walk and his long neck, and staring eyes and big stomach, the village children called him "Gander Joe" or "Joe Gander"; and his parents were not sorry, for they were ashamed that such a creature should be known as a Lambole.

The Lamboles were a sturdy, hearty people, with cheeks like quarrender apples, and bones set firm and knit with iron sinews. They were a hard-working, practical people who fattened pigs and kept poultry at home. Lambole was a roadmaker. In breaking stones one day a bit of one had struck his eye and blinded it. After that he wore a black patch upon it. He saw well enough out of the other; he never missed seeing his own interests. Lambole could have made a few pence with his son had his son been worth anything. He could have sent him to scrape the road, and bring the manure off it in a shovel to his garden. But Joe never took heartily to scraping the dung up. In a word, the boy was good for nothing.

He had hair like tow, and a little straw hat on his head with the top torn, so that the hair forced its way out, and as he walked the top bobbed about like the lid of a boiling saucepan.

When the whortleberries were ripe in June, Mrs. Lambole sent Joe out with other children to collect the berries in a tin can; she sold them for fourpence a quart, and any child could earn eightpence a day in whortleberry time; one that was active might earn a shilling.

But Joe would not remain with the other children. They teased him, imitated ganders and geese, and poked out their necks and uttered sounds in imitation of the voices of these birds. Moreover, they stole the berries he had picked, and put them into their own cans.

When Joe Gander left them and found himself alone in the woods, then he lay down among the brown heather and green fern, and looked up through the oak leaves at the sky, and listened to the singing of the birds. Oh, wondrous music of the woods! the hum of the summer air among the leaves, the drone of the bees about the flowers, the twittering and fluting and piping of the finches and blackbirds and thrushes, and the cool soft cooing of the wood pigeons, like the lowing of aerial oxen; then the tapping of the green woodpecker and a glimpse of its crimson head, like a carbuncle running up the tree trunk, and the powdering down of old husks of fir cones or of the tender rind of the topmost shoot of a Scottish pine; for aloft a red squirrel was barking a beautiful tree out of wantonness and frolic. A rabbit would come forth from the bracken and sit up in the sun, and clean its face with the fore paws and stroke its long ears; then, seeing the soiled red coat, would skip up—little Joe lying very still—and screw its nose and turn its eyes from side to side, and skip nearer again, till it was quite close to Joe Gander; and then the boy laughed, and the rabbit was gone with a flash of white tail.

Happy days! days of listening to mysterious music, of looking into mysteries of sun and foliage, of spiritual intercourse with the great mother-soul of nature.

In the evenings, when Gander Joe came without his can, or with his can empty, he would say to his stepmother: "Oh, steppy! it was so nice; everything was singing."

"I'll make you sing in the chorus too!" cried Mrs. Lambole, and laid a stick across his shoulders. Experience had taught her the futility of dusting at a lower level.

Then Gander Joe cried and writhed, and promised to be more diligent in picking whortleberries in future. But when he went again into the wood it was again the same. The spell of the wood spirits was on him; he forgot about the berries at fourpence a quart, and lay on his back and listened. And the whole wood whispered and sang to him and consoled him for his beating, and the wind played lullabies among the fir spines and whistled in the grass, and the aspen clashed its myriad tiny cymbals together, producing an orchestra of sound that filled the soul of the dreaming boy with love and delight and unutterable yearning.

It fared no better in autumn, when the blackberry season set in. Joe went with his can to an old quarry where the brambles sent their runners over the masses of rubble thrown out from the pits, and warmed and ripened their fruit on the hot stones. It was a marvel to see how the blackberries grew in this deserted quarry; how large the fruit swelled, how thick they were—like mulberries. On the road side of the quarry was a belt of pines, and the sun drew out of their bark scents of unsurpassed sweetness. About the blackberries hovered spotted white and yellow and black moths, beautiful as butterflies. Butterflies did not fail either. The red admiral was there, resting on the bark of the trees, asleep in the sun with wings expanded, or drifting about the clumps of yellow ragwort, doubtful whether to perch or not.

Here, hidden behind the trees, among the leaves of overgrown rubble, was a one-story cottage of wood and clay, covered with thatch, in which lived Roger Gale, the postman.

Roger Gale had ten miles to walk every morning, delivering letters, and the same number of miles every evening, for which twenty miles he received the liberal pay of six shillings a week. He had to be at the post office at half-past six in the morning to receive the letters, and at seven in the evening to deliver them. His work took him about six hours. The middle of the day he had to himself. Roger Gale was an old soldier, and enjoyed a pension. He occupied himself, when at home, as a shoemaker; but the walks took so much out of him, being an old man, that he had not the strength and energy to do much cobbling when at home. Therefore he idled a good deal, and he amused his idle hours with a violin. Now, when Joe Gander came to the quarry before the return of the postman from his rounds, he picked blackberries; but no sooner had Roger Gale unlocked his door, taken down his fiddle, and drawn the bow across the strings, than Joe set down the can and listened. And when old Roger began to play an air from the *Daughter of the Regiment*, then Joe crept towards his cottage in little stages of wonderment and hunger to hear more and hear better, much in the same way as now and again in the wood the inquisitive rabbits had approached his red jacket. Presently Joe was seated on the doorstep, with his ear against the wooden door, and the blackberries and the can, and stepmother's orders and father's stick, and his hard bed and his meagre meals, even the whole world had passed away as a scroll that is rolled up and laid aside, and he lived only in the world of music.

Though his great eyes were wide he saw nothing through them; though the rain began to fall, and the north-east wind to blow, he felt nothing: he had but one faculty that was awake, and that was hearing.

One day Roger came to his door and opened it suddenly, so that the child, leaning against it, fell across his threshold.

"Whom have we here? What is this? What do you want?" asked the postman.

Then Gander Joe stood up, craning his long neck and staring out of his goggle eyes, with his rough flaxen hair standing up in a ruffle above his head and his great stomach protruded, and said nothing. So Roger burst out laughing. But he did not kick him off the step; he gave him a bit of bread and a drop of cider, and presently drew from the boy the confession that he had been listening to the fiddle. This was flattering to the postman, and it was the initiation of a friendship between them.

But when Joe came home with an empty can and said: "Oh, steppy, Master Roger Gale did fiddle so beautiful!" the woman said: "Fiddle! I'll fiddle your back pretty smartly, you idle vagabond"; and she was a truthful woman who never fell short of her word.

To break him of his bad habits—that is, of his dreaminess and uselessness—Mrs. Lambole took Joe to school.

At school he had a bad time of it. He could not learn the letters. He was mentally incapable of doing a subtraction sum. He sat on a bench staring at the teacher, and was unable to answer an ordinary question what the lesson was about. The school-children tormented him, the monitor scolded, and the master beat. Then little Joe Gander took to absenting himself from school. He was sent off every morning by his stepmother, but instead of going to the school he went to the cottage in the quarry, and listened to the fiddle of Roger Gale.

Little Joe got hold of an old box, and with a knife he cut holes in it; and he fashioned a bridge, and then a handle, and he strung horsehair over the latter, and made a bow, and drew very faint sounds from this improvised violin, that made the postman laugh, but which gave great pleasure to Joe. The sound that issued from his instrument was like the humming of flies, but he got distinct notes out of his strings, though the notes were faint.

After he had played truant for some time his father heard what he had done, and he beat the boy till he was like a battered apple that had been flung from the tree by a storm upon a road.

For a while Joe did not venture to the quarry except on Saturdays and Sundays. He was forbidden by his father to go to church, because the organ and the singing there drove him half crazed. When a beautiful, touching melody was played his eyes became clouded and the tears ran down his cheeks; and when the organ played the "Hallelujah Chorus," or some grand and stirring march, his eyes flashed, and his little body quivered, and he made such faces that the congregation were disturbed and the parson remonstrated with his mother. The child was clearly imbecile, and unfit to attend divine worship.

Mr. Lambole got an idea into his head, he would bring up Joe to be a butcher, and he informed Joe that he was going to place him with a gentleman of that profession in town. Joe cried. He turned sick at the sight of blood, and the smell of raw meat was abhorrent to him. But Joe's likings were of no account with his father, and he took him to the town and placed him with a butcher there. He was invested in a blue smock, and was informed that his duties would consist in taking meat about to the customers. Joe was left. It was the first time he had been from home, and he cried himself to sleep the first night, and he cried all the next day when sent around with meat on his shoulder.

Now on his journey through the streets he had to pass the window of a toy-shop. In the window were dolls and horses and little carts. For these Joe did not care, but there were also some little violins, some high priced, and some very low, and over these Joe lingered with loving, covetous eyes. There was one little fiddle to which his heart went out, that cost only three shillings and sixpence. Each day, as he passed the shop, he was drawn to it, and stood looking in, and longed daily more ardently than on the previous day for this three-and-sixpenny violin.

One day he was so lost in admiration and on the schemes he framed as to how he might eventually become possessed of the instrument, that he was unconscious of some boys stealing the meat out of the sort of trough on his shoulder in which he carried it about.

This was the climax of his misdeeds—he had been reprimanded for his blunders, delivering the wrong meat at the customers' doors; for his dilatory ways in going on his errands. The butcher could endure him no more, and sent him home to his father, who thrashed him, as his welcome.

But he carried home with him the haunting recollections of that beautiful little red fiddle, with its fine black keys. The bow, he remembered, was strung with white horsehair. Joe had now a fixed ambition—

something to live for. He would be perfectly happy if he could have that three-shillings-and-sixpenny fiddle. But how were three shillings and sixpence to be earned?

He confided his difficulty to postman Roger Gale, and Roger Gale said he would consider the matter.

A couple of days after the postman said to Joe—

"Gander, they want a lad to sweep the leaves in the drive at the great house. The squire's coachman told me, and I mentioned you. You'll have to do it on Saturday, and be paid sixpence."

Joe's face brightened. He went home and told his stepmother.

"For once you are going to be useful," said Mrs. Lambole. "Very well, you shall sweep the drive; then fivepence will come to us, and you shall have a penny every week to spend in sweetstuff at the post office."

Joe tried to reckon how long it would be before he could purchase the fiddle, but the calculation was beyond his powers; so he asked the postman, who assured him it would take him forty weeks—that is, about ten months.

Little Joe was not cast down. What was time with such an end in view? Jacob served fourteen years for Rachel, and this was only forty weeks for a fiddle!

Joe was diligent every Saturday sweeping the drive. He was ordered whenever a carriage entered to dive behind the rhododendrons and laurels and disappear. He was of a too ragged and idiotic appearance to show in a gentleman's grounds.

Once or twice he encountered the squire and stood quaking, with his fingers spread out, his mouth and eyes open, and the broom at his feet. The squire spoke kindly to him, but Joe Gander was too frightened to reply.

"Poor fellow," said the squire to the gardener. "I suppose it is a charity to employ him, but I must say I should have preferred someone else with his wits about him. I will see to having him sent to an asylum for idiots in which I have some interest. There's no knowing," said the squire, "no knowing but that with wholesome food, cleanliness, and kindness his feeble mind may be got to understand that two and two make four, which I learn he has not yet mastered."

Every Saturday evening Joe Gander brought his sixpence home to his stepmother. The woman was not so regular in allowing him his penny out.

"Your edication costs such a lot of money," she said.

"Steppy, need I go to school any more?" He never could frame his mouth to call her mother.

"Of course you must. You haven't passed your standard."

"But I don't think that I ever shall."

"Then," said Mrs. Lambole, "what masses of good food you do eat. You're perfectly insatiable. You cost us more than it would to keep a cow."

"Oh, steppy, I won't eat so much if I may have my penny!"

"Very well. Eating such a lot does no one good. If you will be content with one slice of bread for breakfast instead of two, and the same for supper, you shall have your penny. If you are so very hungry you can always get a swede or a mangold out of Farmer Eggins's field. Swedes and mangolds are cooling to the blood and sit light on the stomick," said Mrs. Lambole.

So the compact was made; but it nearly killed Joe. His cheeks and chest fell in deeper and deeper, and his stomach protruded more than ever. His legs seemed hardly able to support him, and his great pale blue wandering eyes appeared ready to start out of his head like the horns of a snail. As for his voice, it was thin and toneless, like the notes on his improvised fiddle, on which he played incessantly.

"The child will always be a discredit to us," said Lambole. "He don't look like a human child. He don't think and feel like a Christian. The shovelfuls of dung he might have brought to cover our garden if he had only given his heart to it!"

"I've heard of changelings," said Mrs. Lambole; "and with this creetur on our hands I mainly believe the tale. They do say that the pixies steal away the babies of Christian folk, and put their own bantlings in their stead. The only way to find out is to heat a poker red-hot and ram it down the throat of the child; and when you do that the door opens, and in comes the pixy mother and runs off with her own child, and leaves your proper babe behind. That's what we ought to ha' done wi' Joe."

"I doubt, wife, the law wouldn't have upheld us," said Lambole, thrusting hot coals back on to the hearth with his foot.

"I don't suppose it would," said Mrs. Lambole. "And yet we call this a land of liberty! Law ain't made for the poor, but for the rich."

"It is wickedness," argued the father. "It is just the same with colts—all wickedness. You must drive it out with the stick."

And now a great temptation fell on little Gander Joe. The squire and his family were at home, and the daughter of the house, Miss Amory, was musical. Her mother played on the piano and the young lady on the violin. The fashion for ladies to play on this instrument had come in, and Miss Amory had taken lessons from the best masters in town. She played vastly better than poor Roger Gale, and she played to an accompaniment.

Sometimes whilst Joe was sweeping he heard the music; then he stole nearer and nearer to the house, hiding behind rhododendron bushes, and listening with eyes and mouth and nostrils and ears. The music exercised on him an irresistible attraction. He forgot his obligation to work; he forgot the strict orders he had received not to approach the garden-front of the house. The music acted on him like a spell. Occasionally he was roused from his dream by the gardener, who boxed his ears, knocked him over, and bade him get back to his sweeping. Once a servant came out from Miss Amory to tell the ragged little boy not to stand in front of the drawing-room window staring in. On another occasion he was found by Miss Amory crouched behind a rose bush outside her boudoir, listening whilst she practised.

No one supposed that the music drew him. They thought him a fool, and that he had the inquisitiveness of the half-witted to peer in at windows and see the pretty sights within.

He was reprimanded, and threatened with dismissal. The gardener complained to the lad's father and advised a good hiding, such as Joe should not forget.

"These sort of chaps," said the gardener, "have no senses like rational beings, except only the feeling, and you must teach them as you feed the Polar bears—with the end of a stick."

One day Miss Amory, seeing how thin and hollow-eyed the child was, and hearing him cough, brought him out a cup of hot coffee and some bread.

He took it without a word, only pulling off his torn straw hat and throwing it at his feet, exposing the full shock of tow-like hair; then he stared at her out of his great eyes, speechless.

"Joe," she said, "poor little man, how old are you?"

"Dun'now," he answered.

"Can you read and write?"

"No."

"Nor do sums?"

"No."

"What can you do?"

"Fiddle."

"Have you got a fiddle?"

"Yes."

"I should like to see it, and hear you play."

Next day was Sunday. Little Joe forgot about the day, and forgot that Miss Amory would probably be in church in the morning. She had asked to see his fiddle, so in the morning he took it and went down with it to the park. The church was within the grounds, and he had to pass it. As he went by he heard the roll of the organ and the strains of the choir. He stopped to hearken, then went up the steps of the churchyard, listening. A desire came on him to catch the air on his improvised violin, and he put it to his shoulder and drew his bow across the slender cords. The sound was very faint, so faint as to be drowned by the greater volume of the organ and the choir. Nevertheless he could hear the feeble tones close to his ear, and his heart danced at the pleasure of playing to an accompaniment, like Miss Amory. The choir, the congregation, were singing the Advent hymn to Luther's tune—

"Great God, what do I see and hear? The end of things created."

Little Joe, playing his inaudible instrument, came creeping up the avenue, treading on the fallen yellow lime leaves, passing between the tombstones, drawn on by the solemn, beautiful music. Presently he stood in the porch, then he went on; he was unconscious of everything but the music and the joy of playing with it; he walked on softly into the church without even removing his ragged straw cap, though the squire and the squire's wife, and the rector and the reverend the Mrs. Rector, and the parish churchwarden and the rector's churchwarden, and the overseer and the waywarden, and all the farmers and their wives were present. He had forgotten about his broken cap in the delight that made the tears fill his eyes and trickle over his pale cheeks.

Then when with a shock the parson and the churchwardens saw the ragged urchin coming up the nave fiddling, with his hat on, regardless of the sacredness of the place, and above all of the sacredness of the presence of the squire, J.P. and D.L., the rector coughed very loud and looked hard at his churchwarden, Farmer Eggins, who turned red as the sun in a November fog, and rose. At the same instant the people's churchwarden rose, and both advanced upon Joe Gander from opposite sides of the church.

At the moment that they touched him the organ and the singing ceased; and it was to Joe a sudden wakening from a golden dream to a black and raw reality. He looked up with dazed face first at one man, then at the other: both their faces blazed with equal indignation; both were equally speechless with wrath. They conducted him, each holding an arm, out of the porch and down the avenue. Joe heard indistinctly behind him the droning of the rector's voice continuing the prayers. He looked back over his shoulder and saw the faces of the school-children straining after him through the open door from their places near it. On reaching the steps—there was a flight of five leading to the road—the people's churchwarden uttered a loud and disgusted "Ugh!" then with his heavy hand slapped the head of the child towards the parson's churchwarden, who with his still heavier hand boxed it back again; then the people's churchwarden gave him a blow which sent him staggering forward, and this was supplemented by a kick from the parson's churchwarden, which sent Joe Gander spinning down the five steps at once and cast him prostrate into the road, where he fell and crushed his extemporised violin.

Then the churchwardens turned, blew their noses, and re-entered the church, where they sat out the rest of the service, grateful in their hearts that they had been enabled that day to show that their office was no sinecure.

The churchwardens were unaware that in banging and kicking the little boy out of the churchyard and into the road they had flung him so that he fell with his head upon the curbstone of the footpath, which stone was of slate, and sharp. They did not find this out through the prayers, nor through the sermon. But when the whole congregation left the church they were startled to find little Joe Gander insensible, with his head cut, and a pool of blood on the footway. The squire was shocked, as were his wife and daughter, and the churchwardens were in consternation. Fortunately the squire's stables were near the church, and there was a running fountain there, so that water was procured, and the child revived.

Mrs. Amory had in the meantime hastened home and returned with a roll of diachylon plaster and a pair of small scissors. Strips of the adhesive plaster were applied to the wound, and the boy was soon sufficiently recovered to stand on his feet, when the churchwardens very considerately undertook to march him home. On reaching his cottage the churchwardens described what had taken place, painting the insult offered to the worshippers in the most hideous colours, and representing the accident of the cut as due to the violent resistance offered by the culprit to their ejectment of him. Then each pressed a half-crown into the hand of Mr. Lambole and departed to his dinner.

"Now then, young shaver," exclaimed the father, "at your pranks again! How often have I told you not to go intruding into a place of worship? Church ain't for such as you. If you had'nt been punished a bit already, wouldn't I larrup you neither? Oh, no!"

Little Joe's head was bad for some days. His cheeks were flushed and his eyes bright, and he talked strangely—he who was usually so silent. What troubled him was the loss of his fiddle; he did not know what had become of it, whether it had been stolen or confiscated. He asked after it, and when at last it was produced, smashed to chips, with the strings torn and hanging loose about it like the cordage of a broken vessel, he cried bitterly. Miss Amory came to the cottage to see him, and finding father and stepmother out, went in and pressed five shillings into his hand. Then he laughed with delight, and clapped his hands, and hid the money away in his pocket, but he said nothing, and Miss Amory went away convinced that the child was half a fool. But little Joe had sense in his head, though his head was different from those of others; he knew that now he had the money wherewith to buy the beautiful fiddle he had seen in the shop window many months before, and to get which he had worked and denied himself food.

When Miss Amory was gone, and his stepmother had not returned, he opened the door of the cottage and stole out. He was afraid of being seen, so he crept along in the hedge, and when he thought anyone was coming he got through a gate or lay down in a ditch, till he was some way on his road to the town. Then he ran till he was tired. He had a bandage round his head, and, as his head was hot, he took the rag off, dipped it in water, and tied it round his head again. Never in his life had his mind been clearer than it was now, for now he had a distinct purpose, and an object easily attainable, before him. He held the money in his hand, and looked at it, and kissed it; then pressed it to his beating heart, then ran on. He lost breath. He could run no more. He sat down in the hedge and gasped. The perspiration was streaming off his face. Then he thought he heard steps coming fast along the road he had run, and as he feared pursuit, he got up and ran on.

He went through the village four miles from home just as the children were leaving school, and when they saw him some of the elder cried out that here was "Gander Joe! quack! quack! Joe the Gander! quack! quack! quack!" and the little ones joined in the banter. The boy ran on, though hot and exhausted, and with his head swimming, to escape their merriment.

He got some way beyond the village when he came to a turnpike. There he felt dizzy, and he timidly asked if he might have a piece of bread. He would pay for it if they would change a shilling. The woman at the 'pike pitied the pale, hollow-eyed child, and questioned him; but her questions bewildered him, and he feared she would send him home, so that he either answered nothing, or in a way which made her think him distraught. She gave him some bread and water, and watched him going on towards the town till he was out of sight. The day was already declining; it would be dark by the time he reached the town. But he did not think of that. He did not consider where he would sleep, whether he would have strength to return ten miles to his home. He thought only of the beautiful red violin with the yellow bridge hung in the shop window, and offered for three shillings and sixpence. Three-and-sixpence! Why, he had five shillings. He had money to spend on other things beside the fiddle. He had been sadly disappointed about his savings from the weekly sixpence. He had asked for them; he had earned them, not by his work only, but by his abstention from two pieces of bread per diem. When he asked for the money, his stepmother answered that she had put it away in the savings bank. If he had it he would waste it on sweetstuff; if it were hoarded up it would help him on in life when left to shift for himself; and if he died, why it would go towards his burying.

So the child had been disappointed in his calculations, and had worked and starved for nothing. Then came Miss Amory with her present, and he had run away with that, lest his mother should take it from him to put in the savings bank for setting him up in life or for his burying. What cared he for either? All his ambition was to have a fiddle, and a fiddle was to be had for three-and-sixpence.

Joe Gander was tired. He was fain to sit down at intervals on the heaps of stones by the roadside to rest. His shoes were very poor, with soles worn through, so that the stones hurt his feet. At this time of the year the highways were fresh metalled, and as he stumbled over the newly broken stones they cut his soles and his ankles turned. He was footsore and weary in body, but his heart never failed him. Before him shone the red violin with the yellow bridge, and the beautiful bow strung with shining white hair. When he had that all his weariness would pass as a dream; he would hunger no more, cry no more, feel no more sickness or faintness. He would draw the bow over the strings and play with his fingers on the catgut, and the waves of music would thrill and flow, and away on those melodious waves his soul would float far from trouble, far from want, far from tears, into a shining, sunny world of music.

So he picked himself up when he fell, and staggered to his feet from the stones on which he rested, and pressed on.

The sun was setting as he entered the town. He went straight to the shop he so well remembered, and to his inexpressible delight saw still in the window the coveted violin, price three shillings and sixpence.

Then he timidly entered the shop, and with trembling hand held out the money.

"What do you want?"

"It," said the boy. It. To him the shop held but one article. The dolls, the wooden horses, the tin steam-engines, the bats, the kites, were unconsidered. He had seen and remembered only one thing—the red violin. "It," said the boy, and pointed.

When little Joe had got the violin he pressed it to his shoulder, and his heart bounded as though it would have burst the pigeon breast. His dull eyes lightened, and into his white sunken cheeks shot a hectic flame. He went forth with his head erect and with firm foot, holding his fiddle to the shoulder and the bow in hand.

He turned his face homeward. Now he would return to father and stepmother, to his little bed at the head of the stairs, to his scanty meals, to the school, to the sweeping of the park drive, and to his stepmother's scoldings and his father's beatings. He had his fiddle, and he cared for nothing else.

He waited till he was out of the town before he tried it. Then, when he was on a lonely part of the road, he seated himself in the hedge, under a holly tree covered with scarlet berries, and tried his instrument. Alas! it had hung many years in the shop window, and the catgut was old and the glue had lost its tenacity. One string started; then when he tried to screw up a second, it sprang as well, and then the bridge collapsed and fell. Moreover, the hairs on the bow came out. They were unresined.

Then little Joe's spirits gave way. He laid the bow and the violin on his knees and began to cry.

As he cried he heard the sound of approaching wheels and the clatter of a horse's hoofs.

He heard, but he was immersed in sorrow and did not heed and raise his head to see who was coming. Had he done so he would have seen nothing, as his eyes were swimming with tears. Looking out of them he saw only as one sees who opens his eyes when diving.

"Halloa, young shaver! Dang you! What do you mean giving me such a cursed hunt after you as this—you as ain't worth the trouble, eh?"

The voice was that of his father, who drew up before him. Mr. Lambole had made inquiries when it was discovered that Joe was lost, first at the school, where it was most unlikely he would be found, then at the public-house, at the gardener's and the gamekeeper's; then he had looked down the well and then up the chimney. After that he went to the cottage in the quarry. Roger Gale knew nothing of him. Presently someone coming from the nearest village mentioned that he had been seen there; whereupon Lambole borrowed Farmer Eggins's trap and went after him, peering right and left of the road with his one eye.

Sure enough he had been through the village. He had passed the turnpike. The woman there described him accurately as "a sort of a tottle" (fool).

Mr. Lambole was not a pleasant-looking man; he was as solidly built as a navvy. The backs of his hands were hairy, and his fist was so hard, and his blows so weighty, that for sport he was wont to knock down and kill at a blow the oxen sent to Butcher Robbins for slaughter, and that he did with his fist alone, hitting the animal on the head between the horns, a little forward of the horns. That was a great feat of strength, and Lambole was proud of it. He had a long back and short legs. The back was not pliable or bending; it was hard, braced with sinews tough as hawsers, and supported a pair of shoulders that could sustain the weight of an ox.

His face was of a coppery colour, caused by exposure to the air and drinking. His hair was light: that was almost the only feature his son had derived from him. It was very light, too light for his dark red face. It grew about his neck and under his chin as a Newgate collar; there was a great deal of it, and his face, encircled by the pale hair, looked like an angry moon surrounded by a fog bow.

Mr. Lambole had a queer temper. He bottled up his anger, but when it blew the cork out it spurted over and splashed all his home; it flew in the faces and soused everyone who came near him.

Mr. Lambole took his son roughly by the arm and lifted him into the tax cart. The boy offered no resistance. His spirit was broken, his hopes extinguished. For months he had yearned for the red fiddle, price three-and-six, and now that, after great pains and privations, he had acquired it, the fiddle would not sound.

"Ain't you ashamed of yourself, giving your dear dada such trouble, eh, Viper?"

Mr. Lambole turned the horse's head homeward. He had his black patch towards the little Gander, seated in the bottom of the cart, hugging his wrecked violin. When Mr. Lambole spoke he turned his face round to bring the active eye to bear on the shrinking, crouching little figure below.

The Viper made no answer, but looked up. Mr. Lambole turned his face away, and the seeing eye watched the horse's ears, and the black patch was towards a frightened, piteous, pleading little face, looking up, with the light of the evening sky irradiating it, showing how wan it was, how hollow were the cheeks, how sunken the eyes, how sharp the little pinched nose. The boy put up his arm, that held the bow, and wiped his eyes with his sleeve. In so doing he poked his father in the ribs with the end of the bow.

"Now, then!" exclaimed Mr. Lambole with an oath, "what darn'd insolence be you up to now, Gorilla?"

If he had not held the whip in one hand and the reins in the other he would have taken the bow from the child and flung it into the road. He contented himself with rapping Joe's head with the end of the whip.

"What's that you've got there, eh?" he asked.

The child replied timidly: "Please, father, a fiddle."

"Where did you get 'un—steal it, eh?"

Joe answered, trembling: "No, dada, I bought it."

"Bought it! Where did you get the money?"

"Miss Amory gave it me."

"How much?"

The Gander answered: "Her gave me five shilling."

"Five shillings! And what did that blessed" (he did not say "blessed," but something quite the reverse) "fiddle cost you?"

"Three-and-sixpence."

"So you've only one-and-six left?"

"I've none, dada."

"Why not?"

"Because I spent one shilling on a pipe for you, and sixpence on a thimble for stepmother as a present," answered the child, with a flicker of hope in his dim eyes that this would propitiate his father.

"Dash me," roared the roadmaker, "if you ain't worse nor Mr. Chamberlain, as would rob us of the cheap loaf! What in the name of Thunder and Bones do you mean squandering the precious money over fooleries like that for? I've got my pipe, black as your back shall be before to-morrow, and mother has an old thimble as full o' holes as I'll make your skin before the night is much older. Wait till we get home, and I'll make pretty music out of that there fiddle! just you see if I don't."

Joe shivered in his seat, and his head fell.

Mr. Lambole had a playful wit. He beguiled his journey home by indulging in it, and his humour flashed above the head of the child like summer lightning. "You're hardly expecting the abundance of the supper that's awaiting you," he said, with his black patch glowering down at the irresponsive heap in the corner of the cart. "No stinting of the dressing, I can tell you. You like your meat well basted, don't you? The basting shall not incur your disapproval as insufficient. Underdone? Oh, dear, no! Nothing underdone for me. Pickles? I can promise you that there is something in pickle for you, hot—very hot and stinging. Plenty of capers—mutton and capers. Mashed potatoes? Was the request for that on the tip of your tongue? Sorry I can give you only half what you want—the mash, not the potatoes. There is nothing comparable in my mind to young pig with crackling. The hide is well striped, cut in lines from the neck to the tail. I think we'll have crackling on our pig before morning."

He now threw his seeing eye into the depths of the cart, to note the effect his fun had on the child, but he was disappointed. It had evoked no hilarity. Joe had fallen asleep, exhausted by his walk, worn out with disappointments, with his head on his fiddle, that lay on his knees. The jogging of the cart, the attitude, affected his wound; the plaster had given way, and the blood was running over the little red fiddle and dripping into its hollow body through the S-hole on each side.

It was too dark for Mr. Lambole to notice this. He set his lips. His self-esteem was hurt at the child not relishing his waggery.

Mrs. Lambole observed it when, shortly after, the cart drew up at the cottage and she lifted the sleeping child out.

"I must take the cart back to Farmer Eggins," said her husband; "duty fust, and pleasure after."

When his father was gone Mrs. Lambole said, "Now then, Joe, you've been a very wicked, bad boy, and God will never forgive you for the naughtiness you have committed and the trouble to which you have put your poor father and me." She would have spoken more sharply but that his head needed her care and the sight of the blood disarmed her. Moreover, she knew that her husband would not pass over what had occurred with a reprimand. "Get off your clothes and go to bed, Joe," she said when she had readjusted the plaster. "You may take a piece of dry bread with you, and I'll see if I can't persuade your father to put off whipping of you for a day or two."

Joe began to cry.

"There," she said, "don't cry. When wicked children do wicked things they must suffer for them. It is the law of nature. And," she went on, "you ought to be that ashamed of yourself that you'd be glad for the earth to open under you and swallow you up like Korah, Dathan, and Abiram. Running away from so good and happy a home and such tender parents! But I reckon you be lost to natural affection as you be to reason."

"May I take my fiddle with me?" asked the boy.

"Oh, take your fiddle if you like," answered his mother. "Much good may it do you. Here, it is all smeared wi' blood. Let me wipe it first, or you'll mess the bedclothes with it. There," she said as she gave him the broken instrument. "Say your prayers and go to sleep; though I reckon your prayers will never reach to heaven, coming out of such a wicked unnatural heart."

So the little Gander went to his bed. The cottage had but one bedroom and a landing above the steep and narrow flight of steps that led to it from the kitchen. On this landing was a small truckle bed, on which Joe slept. He took off his clothes and stood in his little short shirt of very coarse white linen. He knelt down and said his prayers, with both his hands spread over his fiddle. Then he got into bed, and until his stepmother fetched away the benzoline lamp he examined the instrument. He saw that the bridge might be set up again with a little glue, and that fresh catgut strings might be supplied. He would take his fiddle next day to Roger Gale and ask him to help to mend it for him. He was sure Roger would take an interest in it. Roger had been mysterious of late, hinting that the time was coming when Joey would have a first-rate instrument and learn to play like a Paganini. Yes; the case of the red fiddle was not desperate.

Just then he heard the door below open, and his father's step.

"Where is the toad?" said Mr. Lambole.

Joe held his breath, and his blood ran cold. He could hear every word, every sound in the room below.

"He's gone to bed," answered Mrs. Lambole. "Leave the poor little creetur alone to-night, Samuel; his head has been bad, and he don't look well. He's overdone."

"Susan," said the roadmaker, "I've been simmering all the way to town, and bubbling and boiling all the way back, and busting is what I be now, and bust I will."

Little Joe sat up in bed, hugging the violin, and his tow-like hair stood up on his head. His great stupid eyes stared wide with fear; in the dark the iris in each had grown big, and deep, and solemn.

"Give me my stick," said Mr. Lambole. "I've promised him a taste of it, and a taste won't suffice to-night; he must have a gorge of it."

"I've put it away," said Mrs. Lambole. "Samuel, right is right, and I'm not one to stand between the child and what he deserves, but he ain't in condition for it to-night. He wants feeding up to it."

Without wasting another word on her the roadmaker went upstairs.

The shuddering, cowering little fellow saw first the red face, surrounded by a halo of pale hair, rise above the floor, then the strong square shoulders, then the clenched hands, and then his father stood before him, revealed down to his thick boots. The child crept back in the bed against the wall, and would have disappeared through it had the wall been soft-hearted, as in fairy tales, and opened to receive him. He clasped his little violin tight to his heart, and then the blood that had fallen into it trickled out and ran down his shirt, staining it—upon the bedclothes, staining them. But the father did not see this. He was effervescing with fury. His pulses went at a gallop, and his great fists clutched spasmodically.

"You Judas Iscariot, come here!" he shouted.

But the child only pressed closer against the wall.

"What! disobedient and daring? Do you hear? Come to me!"

The trembling child pointed to a pretty little pipe on the bedclothes. He had drawn it from his pocket and taken the paper off it, and laid it there, and stuck the silver-headed thimble in the bowl for his stepmother when she came upstairs to take the lamp.

"Come here, vagabond!"

He could not; he had not the courage nor the strength.

He still pointed pleadingly to the little presents he had bought with his eighteenpence.

"You won't, you dogged, insulting being?" roared the roadmaker, and rushed at him, knocking over the pipe, which fell and broke on the floor, and trampling flat the thimble. "You won't yet? Always full of sulks and defiance! Oh, you ungrateful one, you!" Then he had him by the collar of his night-shirt and dragged him from his bed, and with his violence tore the button off, and with his other hand he wrenched the violin away and beat the child over the back with it as he dragged him from the bed.

"Oh, my mammy! my mammy!" cried Joe.

He was not crying out for his stepmother. It was the agonised cry of his frightened heart for the one only being who had ever loved him, and whom God had removed from him.

Suddenly Samuel Lambole started back.

Before him, and between him and the child, stood a pale, ghostly form, and he knew his first wife.

He stood speechless and quaking. Then, gradually recovering himself, he stumbled down the stairs, and seated himself, looking pasty and scared, by the fire below.

"What is the matter with you, Samuel?" asked his wife.

"I've seen her," he gasped. "Don't ask no more questions."

Now when he was gone, little Joe, filled with terror—not at the apparition, which he had not seen, for his eyes were too dazed to behold it, but with apprehension of the chastisement that awaited him, scrambled out of the window and dropped on the pigsty roof, and from thence jumped to the ground.

Then he ran—ran as fast as his legs could carry him, still hugging his instrument—to the churchyard; and on reaching that he threw himself on his mother's grave and sobbed: "Oh, mammy, mammy! father wants to beat me and take away my beautiful violin—but oh, mammy! my violin won't play."

And when he had spoken, from out the grave rose the form of his lost mother, and looked kindly on him.

Joe saw her, and he had no fear.

"Mammy!" said he, "mammy, my violin cost three shillings and sixpence, and I can't make it play no-ways."

"Mammy," said he, "mammy, my violin cost three shillings
and sixpence, and I can't make it play no-ways."

Then the spirit of his mother passed a hand over the the strings, and smiled. Joe looked into her eyes, and they were as stars. And he put the violin under his chin, and drew the bow across the strings—and lo! they sounded wondrously. His soul thrilled, his heart bounded, his dull eye brightened. He was as though caught up in a chariot of fire and carried to heavenly places. His bow worked rapidly, such strains poured from the little instrument as he had never heard before. It was to him as though heaven opened, and he heard the angels performing there, and he with his fiddle was taking a part in the mighty symphony. He felt not the cold, the night was not dark to him. His head no longer ached. It was as though after long seeking through life he had gained an undreamed-of prize, reached some glorious consummation.

* * * * *

There was a musical party that same evening at the Hall. Miss Amory played beautifully, with extraordinary feeling and execution, both with and without accompaniment on the piano. Several ladies and gentlemen sang and played; there were duets and trios.

During the performances the guests talked to each other in low tones about various topics.

Said one lady to Mrs. Amory: "How strange it is that among the English lower classes there is no love of music."

"There is none at all," answered Mrs. Amory; "our rector's wife has given herself great trouble to get up parochial entertainments, but we find that nothing takes with the people but comic songs, and these, instead of elevating, vulgarise them."

"They have no music in them. The only people with music in their souls are the Germans and the Italians."

"Yes," said Mrs. Amory with a sigh; "it is sad, but true: there is neither poetry, nor picturesqueness, nor music among the English peasantry."

"You have never heard of one, self-taught, with a real love of music in this country?"

"Never: such do not exist among us."

* * * * *

The parish churchwarden was walking along the road on his way to his farmhouse, and the road passed under the churchyard wall.

As he walked along the way—with a not too steady step, for he was returning from the public-house—he was surprised and frightened to hear music proceed from among the graves.

It was too dark for him to see any figure then, only the tombstones loomed on him in ghostly shapes. He began to quake, and finally turned and ran, nor did he slacken his pace till he reached the tavern, where he burst in shouting: "There's ghosts abroad. I've heard 'em in the churchyard making music."

The revellers rose from their cups.

"Shall we go and hear?" they asked.

"I'll go for one," said a man; "if others will go with me."

"Ay," said a third, "and if the ghosts be playing a jolly good tune, we'll chip in."

So the whole half-tipsy party reeled along the road, talking very loud, to encourage themselves and the others, till they approached the church, the spire of which stood up dark against the night sky.

"There's no lights in the windows," said one.

"No," observed the churchwarden, "I didn't notice any myself; it was from the graves the music came, as if all the dead was squeakin' like pigs."

"Hush!" All kept silence—not a sound could be heard.

"I'm sure I heard music afore," said the churchwarden. "I'll bet a gallon of ale I did."

"There ain't no music now, though," remarked one of the men.

"Nor more there ain't," said others.

"Well, I don't care—I say I heard it," asseverated the churchwarden. "Let's go up closer."

All of the party drew nearer to the wall of the graveyard. One man, incapable of maintaining his legs unaided, sustained himself on the arm of another.

"Well, I do believe, Churchwarden Eggins, as how you have been leading us a wild goose chase!" said a fellow.

Then the clouds broke, and a bright, dazzling pure ray shot down on a grave in the churchyard, and revealed a little figure lying on it.

"I do believe," said one man, "as how, if he ain't led us a goose chase, he's brought us after a Gander—surely that is little Joe."

Thus encouraged, and their fears dispelled, the whole half-tipsy party stumbled up the graveyard steps, staggered among the tombs, some tripping on the mounds and falling prostrate. All laughed, talked, joked with one another.

The only one silent there was little Joe Gander—and he was gone to join in the great symphony above.

XV. — A DEAD FINGER

I

WHY the National Gallery should not attract so many visitors as, say, the British Museum, I cannot explain. The latter does not contain much that, one would suppose, appeals to the interest of the ordinary sightseer. What knows such of prehistoric flints and scratched bones? Of Assyrian sculpture? Of Egyptian hieroglyphics? The Greek and Roman statuary is cold and dead. The paintings in the National Gallery glow with colour, and are instinct with life. Yet, somehow, a few listless wanderers saunter yawning through the National Gallery, whereas swarms pour through the halls of the British Museum, and talk and pass remarks about the objects there exposed, of the date and meaning of which they have not the faintest conception.

I was thinking of this problem, and endeavouring to unravel it, one morning whilst sitting in the room for English masters at the great collection in Trafalgar Square. At the same time another thought forced itself upon me. I had been through the rooms devoted to foreign schools, and had then come into that given over to Reynolds, Morland, Gainsborough, Constable, and Hogarth. The morning had been for a while propitious, but towards noon a dense umber-tinted fog had come on, making it all but impossible to see the pictures, and quite impossible to do them justice. I was tired, and so seated myself on one of the chairs, and fell into the consideration first of all of—why the National Gallery is not as popular as it should be; and secondly, how it was that the British School had no beginnings, like those of Italy and the Netherlands. We can see the art of the painter from its first initiation in the Italian peninsula, and among the Flemings. It starts on its progress like a child, and we can trace every stage of its growth. Not so with English art. It springs to life in full and splendid maturity. Who were there before Reynolds and Gainsborough and Hogarth? The great names of those portrait and subject painters who have left their canvases upon the walls of our country houses were those of foreigners—Holbein, Kneller, Van Dyck, and Lely for portraits, and Monnoyer for flower and fruit pieces. Landscapes, figure subjects were all importations, none home-grown. How came that about? Was there no limner that was native? Was it that fashion trampled on home-grown pictorial beginnings as it flouted and spurned native music?

Here was food for contemplation. Dreaming in the brown fog, looking through it without seeing its beauties, at Hogarth's painting of Lavinia Fenton as Polly Peachum, without wondering how so indifferent a beauty could have captivated the Duke of Bolton and held him for thirty years, I was recalled to myself and my surroundings by the strange conduct of a lady who had seated herself on a chair near me, also discouraged by the fog, and awaiting its dispersion.

I had not noticed her particularly. At the present moment I do not remember particularly what she was like. So far as I can recollect she was middle-aged, and was quietly yet well dressed. It was not her face nor her dress that attracted my attention and disturbed the current of my thoughts; the effect I speak of was produced by her strange movements and behaviour.

She had been sitting listless, probably thinking of nothing at all, or nothing in particular, when, in turning her eyes round, and finding that she could see nothing of the paintings, she began to study me. This did concern me greatly. A cat may look at the king; but to be contemplated by a lady is a compliment sufficient to please any gentleman. It was not gratified vanity that troubled my thoughts, but the consciousness that my appearance produced—first of all a startled surprise, then undisguised alarm, and, finally, indescribable horror.

Now a man can sit quietly leaning on the head of his umbrella, and glow internally, warmed and illumined by the consciousness that he is being surveyed with admiration by a lovely woman, even when he is middle-aged and not fashionably dressed; but no man can maintain his composure when he discovers himself to be an object of aversion and terror.

What was it? I passed my hand over my chin and upper lip, thinking it not impossible that I might have forgotten to shave that morning, and in my confusion not considering that the fog would prevent the lady from discovering neglect in this particular, had it occurred, which it had not. I am a little careless, perhaps, about shaving when in the country; but when in town, never.

The next idea that occurred to me was—a smut. Had a London black, curdled in that dense pea-soup atmosphere, descended on my nose and blackened it? I hastily drew my silk handkerchief from my pocket, moistened it, and passed it over my nose, and then each cheek. I then turned my eyes into the corners and looked at the lady, to see whether by this means I had got rid of what was objectionable in my personal appearance.

Then I saw that her eyes, dilated with horror, were riveted, not on my face, but on my leg.

My leg! What on earth could that harmless member have in it so terrifying? The morning had been dull; there had been rain in the night, and I admit that on leaving my hotel I had turned up the bottoms of my trousers. That is a proceeding not so uncommon, not so outrageous as to account for the stony stare of this woman's eyes.

If that were all I would turn my trousers down.

Then I saw her shrink from the chair on which she sat to one further removed from me, but still with her eyes fixed on my leg—about the level of my knee. She had let fall her umbrella, and was grasping the seat of her chair with both hands, as she backed from me.

I need hardly say that I was greatly disturbed in mind and feelings, and forgot all about the origin of the English schools of painters, and the question why the British Museum is more popular than the National Gallery.

Thinking that I might have been spattered by a hansom whilst crossing Oxford Street, I passed my hand down my side hastily, with a sense of annoyance, and all at once touched something cold, clammy, that sent a thrill to my heart, and made me start and take a step forward. At the same moment, the lady, with a cry of horror, sprang to her feet, and with raised hands fled from the room, leaving her umbrella where it had fallen.

There were other visitors to the Picture Gallery besides ourselves, who had been passing through the saloon, and they turned at her cry, and looked in surprise after her.

The policeman stationed in the room came to me and asked what had happened. I was in such agitation that I hardly knew what to answer. I told him that I could explain what had occurred little better than himself. I had noticed that the lady had worn an odd expression, and had behaved in most extraordinary fashion, and that he had best take charge of her umbrella, and wait for her return to claim it.

This questioning by the official was vexing, as it prevented me from at once and on the spot investigating the cause of her alarm and mine—hers at something she must have seen on my leg, and mine at something I had distinctly felt creeping up my leg.

The numbing and sickening effect on me of the touch of the object I had not seen was not to be shaken off at once. Indeed, I felt as though my hand were contaminated, and that I could have no rest till I had thoroughly washed the hand, and, if possible, washed away the feeling that had been produced.

I looked on the floor, I examined my leg, but saw nothing. As I wore my overcoat, it was probable that in rising from my seat the skirt had fallen over my trousers and hidden the thing, whatever it was. I therefore hastily removed my overcoat and shook it, then I looked at my trousers. There was nothing whatever on my leg, and nothing fell from my overcoat when shaken.

Accordingly I reinvested myself, and hastily left the Gallery; then took my way as speedily as I could, without actually running, to Charing Cross Station and down the narrow way leading to the Metropolitan, where I went into Faulkner's bath and hairdressing establishment, and asked for hot water to thoroughly wash my hand and well soap it. I bathed my hand in water as hot as I could endure it, employed carbolic soap, and then, after having a good brush down, especially on my left side where my hand had encountered the object that had so affected me, I left. I had entertained the intention of going to the Princess's Theatre that evening, and of securing a ticket in the morning; but all thought of theatre-going was gone from me. I could not free my heart from the sense of nausea and cold that had been produced by the touch. I went into Gatti's to have lunch, and ordered something, I forget what, but, when served, I found that my appetite was gone. I could eat nothing; the food inspired me with disgust. I thrust it from me untasted, and, after drinking a couple of glasses of claret, left the restaurant, and returned to my hotel.

Feeling sick and faint, I threw my overcoat over the sofa-back, and cast myself on my bed.

I do not know that there was any particular reason for my doing so, but as I lay my eyes were on my great-coat.

The density of the fog had passed away, and there was light again, not of first quality, but sufficient for a Londoner to swear by, so that I could see everything in my room, though through a veil, darkly.

I do not think my mind was occupied in any way. About the only occasions on which, to my knowledge, my mind is actually passive or inert is when crossing the Channel in *The Foam* from Dover to Calais, when I am always, in every weather, abjectly seasick—and thoughtless. But as I now lay on my bed, uncomfortable, squeamish, without knowing why—I was in the same inactive mental condition. But not for long.

I saw something that startled me.

First, it appeared to me as if the lappet of my overcoat pocket were in movement, being raised. I did not pay much attention to this, as I supposed that the garment was sliding down on to the seat of the sofa, from the back, and that this displacement of gravity caused the movement I observed. But this I soon saw was not the case. That which moved the lappet was something in the pocket that was struggling to get out. I could see now that it was working its way up the inside, and that when it reached the opening it lost balance and fell down again. I could make this out by the projections and indentations in the cloth; these moved as the creature, or whatever it was, worked its way up the lining.

"A mouse," I said, and forgot my seediness; I was interested. "The little rascal! However did he contrive to seat himself in my pocket? and I have worn that overcoat all the morning!" But no—it was not a mouse. I saw something white poke its way out from under the lappet; and in another moment an object was revealed that, though revealed, I could not understand, nor could I distinguish what it was.

Now roused by curiosity, I raised myself on my elbow. In doing this I made some noise, the bed creaked. Instantly the something dropped on the floor, lay outstretched for a moment, to recover itself, and then began, with the motions of a maggot, to run along the floor.

There is a caterpillar called "The Measurer," because, when it advances, it draws its tail up to where its head is and then throws forward its full length, and again draws up its extremity, forming at each time a loop; and with each step measuring its total length. The object I now saw on the floor was advancing precisely like the measuring caterpillar. It had the colour of a cheese-maggot, and in length was about three and a half inches. It was not, however, like a caterpillar, which is flexible throughout its entire length, but this was, as it seemed to me, jointed in two places, one joint being more conspicuous than the other. For some moments I was so completely paralysed by astonishment that I remained motionless, looking at the thing as it crawled along the carpet—a dull green carpet with darker green, almost black, flowers in it.

It had, as it seemed to me, a glossy head, distinctly marked; but, as the light was not brilliant, I could not make out very clearly, and, moreover, the rapid movements prevented close scrutiny.

Presently, with a shock still more startling than that produced by its apparition at the opening of the pocket of my great-coat, I became convinced that what I saw was a finger, a human forefinger, and that the glossy head was no other than the nail.

The finger did not seem to have been amputated. There was no sign of blood or laceration where the knuckle should be, but the extremity of the finger, or root rather, faded away to indistinctness, and I was unable to make out the root of the finger.

I could see no hand, no body behind this finger, nothing whatever except a finger that had little token of warm life in it, no coloration as though blood circulated in it; and this finger was in active motion creeping along the carpet towards a wardrobe that stood against the wall by the fireplace.

I sprang off the bed and pursued it.

Evidently the finger was alarmed, for it redoubled its pace, reached the wardrobe, and went under it. By the time I had arrived at the article of furniture it had disappeared. I lit a vesta match and held it beneath the wardrobe, that was raised above the carpet by about two inches, on turned feet, but I could see nothing more of the finger.

I got my umbrella and thrust it beneath, and raked forwards and backwards, right and left, and raked out flue, and nothing more solid.

II

I PACKED my portmanteau next day and returned to my home in the country. All desire for amusement in town was gone, and the faculty to transact business had departed as well.

A languor and qualms had come over me, and my head was in a maze. I was unable to fix my thoughts on anything. At times I was disposed to believe that my wits were deserting me, at others that I was on the verge of a severe illness. Anyhow, whether likely to go off my head or not, or take to my bed, home was the only place for me, and homeward I sped, accordingly. On reaching my country habitation, my servant, as usual, took my portmanteau to my bedroom, unstrapped it, but did not unpack it. I object to his throwing out the contents of my Gladstone bag; not that there is anything in it he may not see, but that he puts my things where I cannot find them again. My clothes—he is welcome to place them where he likes and where they belong, and this latter he knows better than I do; but, then, I carry about with me other things than a dress suit, and changes of linen and flannel. There are letters, papers, books—and the proper destinations of these are known only to myself. A servant has a singular and evil knack of putting away literary matter and odd volumes in such places that it takes the owner half a day to find them again. Although I was uncomfortable, and my head in a whirl, I opened and unpacked my own portmanteau. As I was thus engaged I saw something curled up in my collar-box, the lid of which had got broken in by a boot-heel impinging on it. I had pulled off the damaged cover to see if my collars had been spoiled, when something curled up inside suddenly rose on end and leapt, just like a cheese-jumper, out of the box, over the edge of the Gladstone bag, and scurried away across the floor in a manner already familiar to me.

I could not doubt for a moment what it was—here was the finger again. It had come with me from London to the country.

Whither it went in its run over the floor I do not know, I was too bewildered to observe.

Somewhat later, towards evening, I seated myself in my easy-chair, took up a book, and tried to read. I was tired with the journey, with the knocking about in town, and the discomfort and alarm produced by the apparition of the finger. I felt worn out. I was unable to give my attention to what I read, and before I was aware was asleep. Roused for an instant by the fall of the book from my hands, I speedily relapsed into unconsciousness. I am not sure that a doze in an armchair ever does good. It usually leaves me in a semi-stupid condition and with a headache. Five minutes in a horizontal position on my bed is worth thirty in a chair. That is my experience. In sleeping in a sedentary position the head is a difficulty; it drops forward or lolls on one side or the other, and has to be brought back into a position in which the line to the centre of gravity runs through the trunk, otherwise the head carries the body over in a sort of general capsize out of the chair on to the floor.

I slept, on the occasion of which I am speaking, pretty healthily, because deadly weary; but I was brought to waking, not by my head falling over the arm of the chair, and my trunk tumbling after it, but by a feeling of cold extending from my throat to my heart. When I awoke I was in a diagonal position, with my right ear resting on my right shoulder, and exposing the left side of my throat, and it was here—where the jugular vein throbs—that I felt the greatest intensity of cold. At once I shrugged my left shoulder, rubbing my neck with the collar of my coat in so doing. Immediately something fell off, upon the floor, and I again saw the finger.

My disgust—horror, were intensified when I perceived that it was dragging something after it, which might have been an old stocking, and which I took at first glance for something of the sort.

The evening sun shone in through my window, in a brilliant golden ray that lighted the object as it scrambled along. With this illumination I was able to distinguish what the object was. It is not easy to describe it, but I will make the attempt.

The finger I saw was solid and material; what it drew after it was neither, or was in a nebulous, protoplasmic condition. The finger was attached to a hand that was curdling into matter and in process of acquiring solidity; attached to the hand was an arm in a very filmy condition, and this arm belonged to a human body in a still more vaporous, immaterial condition. This was being dragged along the floor by the finger, just as a silkworm might pull after it the tangle of its web. I could see legs and arms, and head, and coat-tail tumbling about and interlacing and disentangling again in a promiscuous manner. There were no bone, no muscle, no substance in the figure; the members were attached to the trunk, which was spineless, but they had evidently no functions, and were wholly dependent on the finger which pulled them along in a jumble of parts as it advanced.

In such confusion did the whole vaporous matter seem, that I think—I cannot say for certain it was so, but the impression left on my mind was—that one of the eyeballs was looking out at a nostril, and the tongue lolling out of one of the ears.

It was, however, only for a moment that I saw this germ-body; I cannot call by another name that which had not more substance than smoke. I saw it only so long as it was being dragged athwart the ray of sunlight. The moment it was pulled jerkily out of the beam into the shadow beyond, I could see nothing of it, only the crawling finger.

I had not sufficient moral energy or physical force in me to rise, pursue, and stamp on the finger, and grind it with my heel into the floor. Both seemed drained out of me. What became of the finger, whither it went, how it managed to secrete itself, I do not know. I had lost the power to inquire. I sat in my chair, chilled, staring before me into space.

"Please, sir," a voice said, "there's Mr. Square below, electrical engineer."

"Eh?" I looked dreamily round.

My valet was at the door.

"Please, sir, the gentleman would be glad to be allowed to go over the house and see that all the electrical apparatus is in order."

"Oh, indeed! Yes—show him up."

III

I HAD recently placed the lighting of my house in the hands of an electrical engineer, a very intelligent man, Mr. Square, for whom I had contracted a sincere friendship.

He had built a shed with a dynamo out of sight, and had entrusted the laying of the wires to subordinates, as he had been busy with other orders and could not personally watch every detail. But he was not the man to let anything pass unobserved, and he knew that electricity was not a force to be played with. Bad or careless workmen will often insufficiently protect the wires, or neglect the insertion of the lead which serves as a safety-valve in the event of the current being too strong. Houses may be set on fire, human beings fatally shocked, by the neglect of a bad or slovenly workman.

The apparatus for my mansion was but just completed, and Mr. Square had come to inspect it and make sure that all was right.

He was an enthusiast in the matter of electricity, and saw for it a vast perspective, the limits of which could not be predicted.

"All forces," said he, "are correlated. When you have force in one form, you may just turn it into this or that, as you like. In one form it is motive power, in another it is light, in another heat. Now we have electricity for illumination. We employ it, but not as freely as in the States, for propelling vehicles. Why should we have horses drawing our buses? We should use only electric trams. Why do we burn coal to warm our shins? There is electricity, which throws out no filthy smoke as does coal. Why should we let the tides waste their energies in the Thames? in other estuaries? There we have Nature supplying us—free, gratis, and for nothing—with all the force we want for propelling, for heating, for lighting. I will tell you something more, my dear sir," said Mr. Square. "I have mentioned but three modes of force, and have instanced but a limited number of uses to which electricity may be turned. How is it with photography? Is not electric light becoming an artistic agent? I bet you," said he, "before long it will become a therapeutic agent as well."

"Oh, yes; I have heard of certain impostors with their life-belts."

Mr. Square did not relish this little dig I gave him. He winced, but returned to the charge. "We don't know how to direct it aright, that is all," said he. "I haven't taken the matter up, but others will, I bet; and we shall have electricity used as freely as now we use powders and pills. I don't believe in doctors' stuffs myself. I hold that disease lays hold of a man because he lacks physical force to resist it. Now, is it not obvious that you are beginning at the wrong end when you attack the disease? What you want is to supply force, make up for the lack of physical power, and force is force wherever you find it—here motive, there illuminating, and so on. I don't see why a physician should not utilise the tide rushing out under London Bridge for restoring the feeble vigour of all who are languid and a prey to disorder in the Metropolis. It will come to that, I bet, and that is not all. Force is force, everywhere. Political, moral force, physical force, dynamic force, heat, light, tidal waves, and so on—all are one, all is one. In time we shall know how to galvanise into aptitude and moral energy all the limp and crooked consciences and wills that need taking in hand, and such there always will be in modern civilisation. I don't know how to do it. I don't know how it will be done, but in the future the priest as well as the doctor will turn electricity on as his principal, nay, his only agent. And he can get his force anywhere, out of the running stream, out of the wind, out of the tidal wave.

"I'll give you an instance," continued Mr. Square, chuckling and rubbing his hands, "to show you the great possibilities in electricity, used in a crude fashion. In a certain great city away far west in the States, a go-ahead place, too, more so than New York, they had electric trams all up and down and along the roads to everywhere. The union men working for the company demanded that the non-unionists should be turned off. But the company didn't see it. Instead, it turned off the union men. It had up its sleeve a sufficiency of the others, and filled all places at once. Union men didn't like it, and passed word that at a given hour on a certain day every wire was to be cut. The company knew this by means of its spies, and turned on, ready for them, three times the power into all the wires. At the fixed moment, up the poles went the strikers to cut the cables, and down they came a dozen times quicker than they went up, I bet. Then there came wires to the hospitals from all quarters for stretchers to carry off the disabled men, some with broken legs, arms, ribs; two or three had their necks broken. I reckon the company was wonderfully merciful—it didn't put on sufficient force to make cinders of them then and there; possibly opinion might not have liked it. Stopped the strike, did that. Great moral effect—all done by electricity."

In this manner Mr. Square was wont to rattle on. He interested me, and I came to think that there might be something in what he said—that his suggestions were not mere nonsense. I was glad to see Mr. Square enter my room, shown in by my man. I did not rise from my chair to shake his hand, for I had not sufficient energy to do so. In a languid tone I welcomed him and signed to him to take a seat. Mr. Square looked at me with some surprise.

"Why, what's the matter?" he said. "You seem unwell. Not got the 'flue, have you?"

"I beg your pardon?"

"The influenza. Every third person is crying out that he has it, and the sale of eucalyptus is enormous, not that eucalyptus is any good. Influenza microbes indeed! What care they for eucalyptus? You've gone down some steps of the ladder of life since I saw you last, squire. How do you account for that?"

I hesitated about mentioning the extraordinary circumstances that had occurred; but Square was a man who would not allow any beating about the bush. He was downright and straight, and in ten minutes had got the entire story out of me.

"Rather boisterous for your nerves that—a crawling finger," said he. "It's a queer story taken on end."

Then he was silent, considering.

After a few minutes he rose, and said: "I'll go and look at the fittings, and then I'll turn this little matter of yours over again, and see if I can't knock the bottom out of it, I'm kinder fond of these sort of things."

Mr. Square was not a Yankee, but he had lived for some time in America, and affected to speak like an American. He used expressions, terms of speech common in the States, but had none of the Transatlantic twang. He was a man absolutely without affectation in every other particular; this was his sole weakness, and it was harmless.

The man was so thorough in all he did that I did not expect his return immediately. He was certain to examine every portion of the dynamo engine, and all the connections and burners. This would necessarily engage him for some hours. As the day was nearly done, I knew he could not accomplish what he wanted that evening, and accordingly gave orders that a room should be prepared for him. Then, as my head was full of pain, and my skin was burning, I told my servant to apologise for my absence from dinner, and tell Mr. Square that I was really forced to return to my bed by sickness, and that I believed I was about to be prostrated by an attack of influenza.

The valet—a worthy fellow, who has been with me for six years—was concerned at my appearance, and urged me to allow him to send for a doctor. I had no confidence in the local practitioner, and if I sent for another from the nearest town I should offend him, and a row would perhaps ensue, so I declined. If I were really in for an influenza attack, I knew about as much as any doctor how to deal with it. Quinine,

quinine—that was all. I bade my man light a small lamp, lower it, so as to give sufficient illumination to enable me to find some lime-juice at my bed head, and my pocket-handkerchief, and to be able to read my watch. When he had done this, I bade him leave me.

I lay in bed, burning, racked with pain in my head, and with my eyeballs on fire.

Whether I fell asleep or went off my head for a while I cannot tell. I may have fainted. I have no recollection of anything after having gone to bed and taken a sip of lime-juice that tasted to me like soap—till I was roused by a sense of pain in my ribs—a slow, gnawing, torturing pain, waxing momentarily more intense. In half-consciousness I was partly dreaming and partly aware of actual suffering. The pain was real; but in my fancy I thought that a great maggot was working its way into my side between my ribs. I seemed to see it. It twisted itself half round, then reverted to its former position, and again twisted itself, moving like a bradawl, not like a gimlet, which latter forms a complete revolution.

This, obviously, must have been a dream, hallucination only, as I was lying on my back and my eyes were directed towards the bottom of the bed, and the coverlet and blankets and sheet intervened between my eyes and my side. But in fever one sees without eyes, and in every direction, and through all obstructions.

Roused thoroughly by an excruciating twinge, I tried to cry out, and succeeded in throwing myself over on my right side, that which was in pain. At once I felt the thing withdrawn that was awling—if I may use the word—in between my ribs.

And now I saw, standing beside the bed, a figure that had its arm under the bedclothes, and was slowly removing it. The hand was leisurely drawn from under the coverings and rested on the eider-down coverlet, with the forefinger extended.

The figure was that of a man, in shabby clothes, with a sallow, mean face, a retreating forehead, with hair cut after the French fashion, and a moustache, dark. The jaws and chin were covered with a bristly growth, as if shaving had been neglected for a fortnight. The figure did not appear to be thoroughly solid, but to be of the consistency of curd, and the face was of the complexion of curd. As I looked at this object it withdrew, sliding backward in an odd sort of manner, and as though overweighted by the hand, which was the most substantial, indeed the only substantial portion of it. Though the figure retreated stooping, yet it was no longer huddled along by the finger, as if it had no material existence. If the same, it had acquired a consistency and a solidity which it did not possess before.

How it vanished I do not know, nor whither it went. The door opened, and Square came in.

"What!" he exclaimed with cheery voice; "influenza is it?"

"I don't know—I think it's that finger again."

IV

"NOW, look here," said Square, "I'm not going to have that cuss at its pranks any more. Tell me all about it."

I was now so exhausted, so feeble, that I was not able to give a connected account of what had taken place, but Square put to me just a few pointed questions and elicited the main facts. He pieced them together in his own orderly mind, so as to form a connected whole. "There is a feature in the case," said he, "that strikes me as remarkable and important. At first—a finger only, then a hand, then a nebulous figure attached to the hand, without backbone, without consistency. Lastly, a complete form, with consistency and with backbone, but the latter in a gelatinous condition, and the entire figure overweighted by the hand, just as hand and figure were previously overweighted by the finger. Simultaneously with this compacting and consolidating of the figure, came your degeneration and loss of vital force and, in a word, of health. What you lose, that object acquires, and what it acquires, it gains by contact with you. That's clear enough, is it not?"

"I dare say. I don't know. I can't think."

"I suppose not; the faculty of thought is drained out of you. Very well, I must think for you, and I will. Force is force, and see if I can't deal with your visitant in such a way as will prove just as truly a moral dissuasive as that employed on the union men on strike in—never mind where it was. That's not to the point."

"Will you kindly give me some lime-juice?" I entreated.

I sipped the acid draught, but without relief. I listened to Square, but without hope. I wanted to be left alone. I was weary of my pain, weary of everything, even of life. It was a matter of indifference to me whether I recovered or slipped out of existence.

"It will be here again shortly," said the engineer. "As the French say, *l'appetit vient en mangeant*. It has been at you thrice, it won't be content without another peck. And if it does get another, I guess it will pretty well about finish you."

Mr. Square rubbed his chin, and then put his hands into his trouser pockets. That also was a trick acquired in the States, an inelegant one. His hands, when not actively occupied, went into his pockets, inevitably they gravitated thither. Ladies did not like Square; they said he was not a gentleman. But it was not that he said or did anything "off colour," only he spoke to them, looked at them, walked with them, always with his hands in his pockets. I have seen a lady turn her back on him deliberately because of this trick.

Standing now with his hands in his pockets, he studied my bed, and said contemptuously: "Old-fashioned and bad, fourposter. Oughtn't to be allowed, I guess; unwholesome all the way round."

I was not in a condition to dispute this. I like a fourposter with curtains at head and feet; not that I ever draw them, but it gives a sense of privacy that is wanting in one of your half-tester beds.

If there is a window at one's feet, one can lie in bed without the glare in one's eyes, and yet without darkening the room by drawing the blinds. There is much to be said for a fourposter, but this is not the place in which to say it.

Mr. Square pulled his hands out of his pockets and began fiddling with the electric point near the head of my bed, attached a wire, swept it in a semicircle along the floor, and then thrust the knob at the end into my hand in the bed.

"Keep your eye open," said he, "and your hand shut and covered. If that finger comes again tickling your ribs, try it with the point. I'll manage the switch, from behind the curtain."

Then he disappeared.

I was too indifferent in my misery to turn my head and observe where he was. I remained inert, with the knob in my hand, and my eyes closed, suffering and thinking of nothing but the shooting pains through my head and the aches in my loins and back and legs.

Some time probably elapsed before I felt the finger again at work at my ribs; it groped, but no longer bored. I now felt the entire hand, not a single finger, and the hand was substantial, cold, and clammy. I was aware, how, I know not, that if the finger-point reached the region of my heart, on the left side, the hand would, so to speak, sit down on it, with the cold palm over it, and that then immediately my heart would cease to beat, and it would be, as Square might express it, "gone coon" with me.

In self-preservation I brought up the knob of the electric wire against the hand—against one of the ringers, I think—and at once was aware of a rapping, squealing noise. I turned my head languidly, and saw the form, now more substantial than before, capering in an ecstasy of pain, endeavouring fruitlessly to withdraw its arm from under the bedclothes, and the hand from the electric point.

At the same moment Square stepped from behind the curtain, with a dry laugh, and said: "I thought we should fix him. He has the coil about him, and can't escape. Now let us drop to particulars. But I shan't let you off till I know all about you."

The last sentence was addressed, not to me, but to the apparition.

Thereupon he bade me take the point away from the hand of the figure—being—whatever it was, but to be ready with it at a moment's notice. He then proceeded to catechise my visitor, who moved restlessly within the circle of wire, but could not escape from it. It replied in a thin, squealing voice that sounded as if it came from a distance, and had a querulous tone in it. I do not pretend to give all that was said. I cannot recollect everything that passed. My memory was affected by my illness, as well as my body. Yet I prefer giving the scraps that I recollect to what Square told me he had heard.

"Yes—I was unsuccessful, always was. Nothing answered with me. The world was against me. Society was. I hate Society. I don't like work neither, never did. But I like agitating against what is established. I hate the Royal Family, the landed interest, the parsons, everything that is, except the people—that is, the unemployed. I always did. I couldn't get work as suited me. When I died they buried me in a cheap coffin, dirt cheap, and gave me a nasty grave, cheap, and a service rattled away cheap, and no monument. Didn't want none. Oh! there are lots of us. All discontented. Discontent! That's a passion, it is—it gets into the veins, it fills the brain, it occupies the heart; it's a sort of divine cancer that takes possession of the entire man, and makes him dissatisfied with everything, and hate everybody. But we must have our share of happiness at some time. We all crave for it in one way or other. Some think there's a future state of blessedness and so have hope, and look to attain to it, for hope is a cable and anchor that attaches to what is real. But when you have no hope of that sort, don't believe in any future state, you must look for happiness in life here. We didn't get it when we were alive, so we seek to procure it after we are dead. We can do it, if we can get out of our cheap and nasty coffins. But not till the greater part of us is mouldered away. If a finger or two remains, that can work its way up to the surface, those cheap deal coffins go to pieces quick enough. Then the only solid part of us left can pull the rest of us that has gone to nothing after it. Then we grope about after the living. The well-to-do if we can get at them—the honest working poor if we can't—we hate them too, because they are content and happy. If we reach any of these, and can touch them, then we can draw their vital force out of them into ourselves, and recuperate at their expense. That was about what I was going to do with you. Getting on famous. Nearly solidified into a new man; and given another chance in life. But I've missed it this time. Just like my luck. Miss everything. Always have, except misery and disappointment. Get plenty of that."

"What are you all?" asked Square. "Anarchists out of employ?"

"Some of us go by that name, some by other designations, but we are all one, and own allegiance to but one monarch—Sovereign discontent. We are bred to have a distaste for manual work; and we grow up loafers, grumbling at everything and quarrelling with Society that is around us and the Providence that is above us."

"And what do you call yourselves now?"

"Call ourselves? Nothing; we are the same, in another condition, that is all. Folk called us once Anarchists, Nihilists, Socialists, Levellers, now they call us the Influenza. The learned talk of microbes, and bacilli, and bacteria. Microbes, bacilli, and bacteria be blowed! We are the Influenza; we the social failures, the generally discontented, coming up out of our cheap and nasty graves in the form of physical disease. We are the Influenza."

"There you are, I guess!" exclaimed Square triumphantly. "Did I not say that all forces were correlated? If so, then all negations, deficiencies of force are one in their several manifestations. Talk of Divine discontent as a force impelling to progress! Rubbish, it is a paralysis of energy. It turns all it absorbs to acid, to envy, spite, gall. It inspires nothing, but rots the whole moral system. Here you have it—moral, social, political discontent in another form, nay aspect—that is all. What Anarchism is in the body Politic, that Influenza is in the body Physical. Do you see that?"

"Ye-e-s-e-s," I believe I answered, and dropped away into the land of dreams.

I recovered. What Square did with the Thing I know not, but believe that he reduced it again to its former negative and self-decomposing condition.

XVI. — BLACK RAM

I DO not know when I had spent a more pleasant evening, or had enjoyed a dinner more than that at Mr. Weatherwood's hospitable house. For one thing, the hostess knew how to keep her guests interested and in good-humour. The dinner was all that could be desired, and so were the wines. But what conduced above all to my pleasure was that at table I sat by Miss Fulton, a bright, intelligent girl, well read and entertaining. My wife had a cold, and had sent her excuses by me. Miss Fulton and I talked of this, that, and every thing. Towards the end of dinner she said: "I shall be obliged to run away so soon as the ladies leave the room to you and your cigarettes and gossip. It is rather mean, but Mrs. Weatherwood has been forewarned, and understands. To-morrow is our village feast at Marksleigh, and I have a host of things on my hand. I shall have to be up at seven, and I do object to cut a slice off my night's rest at both ends."

"Rather an unusual time of the year for a village feast," said I. "These things are generally got over in the summer."

"You see, our church is dedicated to St. Mark, and to-morrow is his festival, and it has been observed in one fashion or another in our parish from time immemorial. In your parts have they any notions about St. Mark's eve?"

"What sort of notions?"

"That if you sit in the church porch from midnight till the clock strikes one, you will see the apparitions pass before you of those destined to die within the year."

"I fancy our good people see themselves, and nothing but themselves, on every day and hour throughout the twelvemonth."

"Joking apart, have you any such superstition hanging on in your neighbourhood?"

"Not that I am aware of. That sort of thing belonged to the Golden Age that has passed away. Board schools have reduced us to that of lead."

"At Marksleigh the villagers believe in it, and recently their faith has received corroboration."

"How so?" I asked.

"Last year, in a fit of bravado, a young carpenter ventured to sit in the porch at the witching hour, and saw himself enter the church. He came home, looking as blank as a sheet, moped, lost flesh, and died nine months later."

"Of course he died, if he had made up his mind to do so."

"Yes—that is explicable. But how do you account for his having seen his double?"

"He had been drinking at the public-house. A good many people see double after that."

"It was not so. He was perfectly sober at the time."

"Then I give it up."

"Would you venture on a visit to a church porch on this night—St. Mark's eve?"

"Certainly I would, if well wrapped up, and I had my pipe."

"I bar the pipe," said Miss Fulton. "No apparition can stand tobacco smoke. But there is Lady Eastleigh rising. When you come to rejoin the ladies, I shall be gone."

I did not leave the house of the Weatherwoods till late. My dogcart was driven by my groom, Richard. The night was cold, or rather chilly, but I had my fur-lined overcoat, and did not mind that. The stars shone out of a frosty sky. All went smoothly enough till the road dipped into a valley, where a dense white fog hung over the river and the water-meadows. Anyone who has had much experience in driving at night is aware that in such a case the carriage lamps are worse than useless; they bewilder the horse and the driver. I cannot blame Dick if he ran his wheel over a heap of stones that upset the trap. We were both thrown out, and I fell on my head. I sang out: "Mind the cob, Dick; I am all right."

The boy at once mastered the horse. I did not rise immediately, for I had been somewhat jarred by the fall; when I did I found Dick engaged in mending a ruptured trace. One of the shafts was broken, and a carriage lamp had been shattered.

"Dick," said I, "there are a couple of steep hills to descend, and that is risky with a single shaft. I will lighten the dogcart by walking home, and do you take care at the hills."

"I think we can manage, sir."

"I should prefer to walk the rest of the way. I am rather shaken by my fall, and a good step out in the cool night will do more to put me to rights than anything else. When you get home, send up a message to your mistress that she is not to expect me at once. I shall arrive in due time, and she is not to be alarmed."

"It's a good trudge before you, sir. And I dare say we could get the shaft tied up at Fifewell."

"What—at this time of night? No, Dick, do as I say."

Accordingly the groom drove off, and I started on my walk. I was glad to get out of the clinging fog, when I reached higher ground. I looked back, and by the starlight saw the river bottom filled with the mist, lying apparently dense as snow.

After a swinging walk of a quarter of an hour I entered the outskirts of Fifewell, a village of some importance, with shops, the seat of the petty sessions, and with a small boot and shoe factory in it.

The street was deserted. Some bedroom windows were lighted, for our people have the habit of burning their paraffin lamps all night. Every door was shut, no one was stirring.

As I passed along the churchyard wall, the story of the young carpenter, told by Miss Fulton, recurred to me.

"By Jove!" thought I, "it is now close upon midnight, a rare opportunity for me to see the wonders of St. Mark's eve. I will go into the porch and rest there for a few minutes, and then I shall be able, when I meet that girl again, to tell her that I had done what she challenged me to do, without any idea that I would take her challenge up."

I turned in at the gate, and walked up the pathway. The headstones bore a somewhat ghostly look in the starlight. A cross of white stone, recently set up, I supposed, had almost the appearance of phosphorescence. The church windows were dark.

I seated myself in the roomy porch on a stone bench against the wall, and felt for my pipe. I am not sure that I contemplated smoking it then and there, partly because Miss Fulton had forbidden it, but also because I felt that it was not quite the right thing to do on consecrated ground. But it would be a satisfaction to finger it, and I might plug it, so as to be ready to light up so soon as I left the churchyard. To my vexation I found that I had lost it. The tobacco-pouch was there, and the matches. My pipe must have fallen out of my pocket when I was pitched from the trap. That pipe was a favourite of mine.

"What a howling nuisance," said I. "If I send Dick back over the road to-morrow morning, ten chances to one if he finds it, for to-morrow is market-day, and people will be passing early."

As I said this, the clock struck twelve.

I counted each stroke. I wore my fur-lined coat, and was not cold—in fact, I had been too warm walking in it. At the last stroke of twelve I noticed lines of very brilliant light appear about the door into the church. The door must have fitted well, as the light did no more than show about it, and did not gush forth at all the crevices. But from the keyhole shot a ray of intense brilliancy.

Whether the church windows were illumined I did not see—in fact, it did not occur to me to look, either then or later—but I am pretty certain that they were not, or the light streaming from them would have brought the gravestones into prominence. When you come to think of it, it was remarkable that the light of so dazzling a nature should shine through the crannies of the door, and that none should issue, as far as I could see, from the windows. At the time I did not give this a thought; my attention was otherwise taken up. For I saw distinctly Miss Venville, a very nice girl of my acquaintance, coming up the path with that swinging walk so characteristic of an English young lady.

How often it has happened to me, when I have been sitting in a public park or in the gardens of a Cursaal abroad, and some young girls have passed by, that I have said to my wife: "I bet you a bob those are English."

"Yes, of course," she has replied; "you can see that by their dress."

"I don't know anything about dress," I have said; "I judge by the walk."

Well, there was Miss Venville coming towards the porch.

"This is a joke," said I. "She is going to sit here on the look-out for ghosts, and if I stand up or speak she will be scared out of her wits. Hang it, I wish I had my pipe now; if I gave a whiff it would reveal the presence of a mortal, without alarming her. I think I shall whistle."

I had screwed up my lips to begin "Rocked in the cradle of the deep"—that is my great song I perform whenever there is a village concert, or I am asked out to dinner, and am entreated afterwards to sing—I say I had screwed up my lips to whistle, when I saw something that scared me so that I made no attempt at the melody.

The ray of light through the keyhole was shut off, and I saw standing in the porch before me the form of Mrs. Venville, the girl's mother, who had died two years before. The ray of white light arrested by her filled her as a lamp—was diffused as a mild glow from her.

"Halloo, mother, what brings you here?" asked the girl.

"Gwendoline, I have come to warn you back. You cannot enter; you have not got the key."

"The key, mother?"

"Yes, everyone who would pass within must have his or her own key."

"Well, where am I to get one?"

"It must be forged for you, Gwen. You are wholly unfit to enter. What good have you ever done to deserve it?"

"Why, mother, everyone knows I'm an awfully good sort."

"No one in here knows it. That is no qualification."

"And I always dressed in good taste."

"Nor is that."

"And I was splendid at lawn tennis."

Her mother shook her head.

"Look here, little mummy. I won a brooch at the archery match."

"That will not do, Gwendoline. What good have you ever done to anyone else beside yourself?"

The girl considered a minute, then laughed, and said: "I put into a raffle at a bazaar—no, it was a bran-pie for an orphanage—and I drew out a pair of braces. I had rare fun over those braces, I sold them to Captain Fitzakerly for half a crown, and that I gave to the charity."

"You went for what you could get, not what you could give."

Then the mother stepped on one side, and the ray shot directly at the girl. I saw that it had something of the quality of the X-ray. It was not arrested by her garments, or her flesh or muscles. It revealed in her breast, in her brain—penetrating her whole body—a hard, dark core.

"Black Ram, I bet," said I.

Now Black Ram is the local name for a substance found in our land, especially in the low ground that ought to be the most fertile, but is not so, on account of this material found in it.

The substance lies some two or three feet below the surface, and forms a crust of the consistency of cast iron. No plough can possibly be driven through it. No water can percolate athwart it, and consequently where it is, there the superincumbent soil is resolved into a quagmire. No tree can grow in it, for the moment the taproot touches the Black Ram the tree dies.

Of what Black Ram consists is more than I can say; the popular opinion is that it is a bastard manganese. Now I happen to own several fields accursed with the presence in them of Black Ram—fields that ought to be luxuriant meadows, but which, in consequence of its presence, are worth almost nothing at all.

"No, Gwen," said her mother, looking sorrowfully at her, "there is not a chance of your admission till you have got rid of the Black Ram that is in you."

"Sure," said I, as I slapped my knee, "I thought I knew the article, and now my opinion has been confirmed."

"How can I get rid of it?" asked the girl.

"Gwendoline, you will have to pass into little Polly Finch, and work it out of your system. She is dying of scarlet fever, and you must enter into her body, and so rid yourself in time of the Black Ram."

"Mother!—the Finches are common people."

"So much the better chance for you."

"And I am eighteen, Polly is about ten."

"You will have to become a little child if you would enter her."

"I don't like it. What is the alternative?"

"To remain without in the darkness till you come to a better mind. And now, Gwen, no time is to be lost; you must pass into Polly Finch's body before it grows cold."

"Well, then—here goes!"

Gwen Venville turned, and her mother accompanied her down the path. The girl moved reluctantly, and pouted. Passing out of the churchyard, both traversed the street and disappeared within a cottage, from the upper window of which light from behind a white blind was diffused.

I did not follow, I leaned back against the wall. I felt that my head was throbbing. I was a little afraid lest my fall had done more injury than I had at first anticipated. I put my hand to my head, and held it there for a moment.

Then it was as though a book were opened before me—the book of the life of Polly Finch—or rather of Gwendoline's soul in Polly Finch's body. It was but one page that I saw, and the figures in it were moving.

The girl was struggling under the burden of a heavy baby brother. She coaxed him, she sang to him, she played with him, talked to him, broke off bits of her bread and butter, given to her for breakfast, and made him eat them; she wiped his nose and eyes with her pocket-handkerchief, she tried to dance him in her arms. He was a fractious urchin, and most exacting, but her patience, her good-nature, never failed. The drops stood on her brow, and her limbs tottered under the weight, but her heart was strong, and her eyes shone with love.

I drew my hand from my head. It was burning. I put my hand to the cold stone bench to cool it, and then applied it once more to my brow.

Instantly it was as though another page were revealed. I saw Polly in her widowed father's cottage. She was now a grown girl; she was on her knees scrubbing the floor. A bell tinkled. Then she put down the soap and brush, turned down her sleeves, rose and went into the outer shop to serve a customer with half a pound of tea. That done, she was back again, and the scrubbing was renewed. Again a tinkle, and again she stood up and went into the shop to a child who desired to buy a pennyworth of lemon drops.

On her return, in came her little brother crying—he had cut his finger. Polly at once applied cobweb, and then stitched a rag about the wounded member.

"There, there, Tommy! don't cry any more. I have kissed the bad place, and it will soon be well."

"Poll! it hurts! it hurts!" sobbed the boy.

"Come to me," said his sister. She drew a low chair to the fireside, took Tommy on her lap, and began to tell him the story of Jack the Giant-killer.

I removed my hand, and the vision was gone.

I put my other hand to my head, and at once saw a further scene in the life-story of Polly.

She was now a middle-aged woman, and had a cottage of her own. She was despatching her children to school. They had bright, rosy faces, their hair was neatly combed, their pinafores were white as snow. One after another, before leaving, put up the cherry lips to kiss mammy; and when they were gone, for a moment she stood in the door looking after them, then sharply turned, brought out a basket, and emptied its contents on the table. There were little girls' stockings with "potatoes" in them to be darned, torn jackets to be mended, a little boy's trousers to be reseated, pocket-handkerchiefs to be hemmed. She laboured on with her needle the greater part of the day, then put away the garments, some finished, others to be finished, and going to the flour-bin took forth flour and began to knead dough, and then to roll it out to make pasties for her husband and the children.

"Poll!" called a voice from without; she ran to the door.

"Back, Joe! I have your dinner hot in the oven."

"I must say, Poll, you are the best of good wives, and there isn't a mother like you in the shire. My word! that was a lucky day when I chose you, and didn't take Mary Matters, who was setting her cap at me. See what a slattern she has turned out. Why, I do believe, Poll, if I'd took her she'd have drove me long ago to the public-house."

I saw the mother of Gwendoline standing by me and looking out on this scene, and I heard her say: "The Black Ram is run out, and the key is forged."

All had vanished. I thought now I might as well rise and continue my journey. But before I had left the bench I observed the rector of Fifewell sauntering up the path, with uncertain step, as he fumbled in his coat-tail pockets, and said: "Where the deuce is the key?"

The Reverend William Hexworthy was a man of good private means, and was just the sort of man that a bishop delights to honour. He was one who would never cause him an hour's anxiety; he was not the man to indulge in ecclesiastical vagaries. He flattered himself that he was strictly a *via media* man. He kept dogs, he was a good judge of horses, was fond of sport. He did not hunt, but he shot and fished. He was a favourite in Society, was of irreproachable conduct, and was a magistrate on the bench.

As the ray from the keyhole smote on him he seemed to be wholly dark,—made up of nothing but Black Ram. He came on slowly, as though not very sure of his way.

"Bless me! where can be the key?" he asked.

Then from out of the graves, and from over the wall of the churchyard, came rushing up a crowd of his dead parishioners, and blocked his way to the porch.

"Please, your reverence!" said one, "you did not visit me when I was dying."

"I sent you a bottle of my best port," said the parson.

"Ay, sir, and thank you for it. But that went into my stomick, and what I wanted was medicine for my soul. You never said a prayer by me. You never urged me to repentance for my bad life, and you let me go out of the world with all my sins about me."

"And I, sir," said another, thrusting himself before Mr. Hexworthy—"I was a young man, sir, going wild, and you never said a word to restrain me; never sent for me and gave me a bit of warning and advice which would have checked me. You just shrugged your shoulders and laughed, and said that a young chap like me must sow his wild oats."

"And we," shouted the rest—"we were never taught by you anything at all."

"Now this is really too bad," said the rector. "I preached twice every Sunday."

"Oh, yes—right enough that. But precious little good it did when nothing came out of your heart, and all out of your pocket—and that you did give us was copied in your library. Why, sir, not one of your sermons ever did anybody a farthing of good."

"We were your sheep," protested others, "and you let us wander where we would! You didn't seem to know yourself that there was a fold into which to draw us."

"And we," said others, "went off to chapel, and all the good we ever got was from the dissenting minister—never a mite from you."

"And some of us," cried out others, "went to the bad altogether, through your neglect. What did you care about our souls so long as your terriers were washed and combed, and your horses well groomed? You were a fisherman, but all you fished for were trout—not souls. And if some of us turned out well, it was in spite of your neglect—no thanks to you."

Then some children's voices were raised: "Sir, you never taught us no Catechism, nor our duty to God and to man, and we grew up regular heathens."

"That was your fathers' and mothers' duty."

"But our fathers and mothers never taught us anything."

"Come, this is intolerable," shouted Mr. Hexworthy. "Get out of the way, all of you. I can't be bothered with you now. I want to go in there."

"You can't, parson! the door is shut, and you have not got your key."

Mr. Hexworthy stood bewildered and irresolute. He rubbed his chin.

"What the dickens am I to do?" he asked.

Then the crowd closed about him, and thrust him back towards the gate. "You must go whither we send you," they said.

I stood up to follow. It was curious to see a flock drive its shepherd, who, indeed, had never attempted to lead. I walked in the rear, and it seemed as though we were all swept forward as by a mighty wind. I did not gain my breath, or realise whither I was going, till I found myself in the slums of a large manufacturing town before a mean house such as those occupied by artisans, with the conventional one window on one side of the door and two windows above. Out of one of these latter shone a scarlet glow.

The crowd hustled Mr. Hexworthy in at the door, which was opened by a hospital nurse.

I stood hesitating what to do, and not understanding what had taken place. On the opposite side of the street was a mission church, and the windows were lighted. I entered, and saw that there were at least a score of people, shabbily dressed, and belonging to the lowest class, on their knees in prayer. There was a sort of door-opener or verger at the entrance, and I said to him: "What is the meaning of all this?"

"Oh, sir!" said he, "*he* is ill, he has been attacked by smallpox. It has been raging in the place, and he has been with all the sick, and now he has taken it himself, and we are terribly afraid that he is dying. So we are praying God to spare him to us."

Then one of those who was kneeling turned to me and said: "I was an hungred, and he gave me meat."

And another rose up and said: "I was a stranger, and he took me in."

Then a third said: "I was naked, and he clothed me."

And a fourth: "I was sick, and he visited me."

Then said a fifth, with bowed head, sobbing: "I was in prison, and he came to me."

Thereupon I went out and looked up at the red window, and I felt as if I must see the man for whom so many prayed. I tapped at the door, and a woman opened.

"I should so much like to see him, if I may," said I.

"Well, sir," spoke the woman, a plain, middle-aged, rough creature, but her eyes were full of tears: "Oh, sir, I think you may, if you will go up softly. There has come over him a great change. It is as though a new life had entered into him."

I mounted the narrow staircase of very steep steps and entered the sick-room. There was an all-pervading glow of red. The fire was low—no flame, and a screen was before it. The lamp had a scarlet shade over it. I stepped to the side of the bed, where stood a nurse. I looked on the patient. He was an awful object. His face had been smeared over with some dark solution, with the purpose of keeping all light from the skin, with the object of saving it from permanent disfigurement.

The sick priest lay with eyes raised, and I thought I saw in them those of Mr. Hexworthy, but with a new light, a new faith, a new fervour, a new love in them. The lips were moving in prayer, and the hands were folded over the breast. The nurse whispered to me: "We thought he was passing away, but the prayers of those he loved have prevailed. A great change has come over him. The last words he spoke were: 'God's will be done. If I live, I will live only—only for my dear sheep, and die among them'; and now he is in an ecstasy, and says nothing. But he is praying still—for his people."

As I stood looking I saw what might have been tears, but seemed to be molten Black Ram, roll over the painted cheeks. The spirit of Mr. Hexworthy was in this body.

Then, without a word, I turned to the door, went through, groped my way down the steps, passed out into the street, and found myself back in the porch of Fifewell Church.

"Upon my word," said I, "I have been here long enough." I wrapped my fur coat about me, and prepared to go, when I saw a well-known figure, that of Mr. Fothergill, advancing up the path.

I knew the old gentleman well. His age must have been seventy. He was a spare man, he was rather bald, and had sunken cheeks. He was a bachelor, living in a pretty little villa of his own. He had a good fortune, and was a harmless, but self-centred, old fellow. He prided himself on his cellar and his cook. He always dressed well, and was scrupulously neat. I had often played a game of chess with him.

I would have run towards him to remonstrate with him for exposing himself to the night air, but I was forestalled. Slipping past me, his old manservant, David, went to meet him. David had died three years before. Mr. Fothergill had then been dangerously ill with typhoid fever, and the man had attended to him night and day. The old gentleman, as I heard, had been most irritable and exacting in his illness. When his malady took a turn, and he was on the way to convalescence, David had succumbed in his turn, and in three days was dead.

This man now met his master, touched his cap, and said: "Beg pardon, sir, you will not be admitted."

"Not admitted? Why not, Davie?"

"I really am very sorry, sir. If my key would have availed, you would have been welcome to it; but, sir, there's such a terrible lot of Black Ram in you, sir. That must be got out first."

"I don't understand, Davie."

"I'm sorry, sir, to have to say it; but you've never done anyone any good."

470

"I paid you your wages regularly."

"Yes, sir, to be sure, sir, for my services to yourself."

"And I've always subscribed when asked for money."

"Yes, that is very true, sir, but that was because you thought it was expected of you, not because you had any sympathy with those in need, and sickness, and suffering."

"I'm sure I never did anyone any harm."

"No, sir, and never anyone any good. You'll excuse me for mentioning it."

"But, Davie, what do you mean? I can't get in?"

"No, sir, not till you have the key."

"But, bless my soul! what is to become of me? Am I to stick out here?"

"Yes, sir, unless——"

"In this damp, and cold, and darkness?"

"There is no help for it, Mr. Fothergill, unless——"

"Unless what, Davie?"

"Unless you become a mother, sir!"

"What?"

"Of twins, sir."

"Fiddlesticks!"

"Indeed, it is so, sir, and you will have to nurse them."

"I can't do it. I'm physically incapable."

"It must be done, sir. Very sorry to mention it, but there is no alternative. There's Sally Bowker is approaching her confinement, and it's going terribly hard with her. The doctor thinks she'll never pull through. But if you'd consent to pass into her and become a mother——"

"And nurse the twins? Oh, Davie, I shall need a great amount of stout."

"I grieve to say it, Mr. Fothergill, but you'll be too poor to afford it."

"Is there no alternative?"

"None in the world, sir."

"I don't know my way to the place."

"If you'd do me the honour, sir, to take my arm, I would lead you to the house."

"It's hard—cruel hard on an old bachelor. Must it be twins? It's a rather large order."

"It really must, sir."

Then I saw David lend his arm to his former master and conduct him out of the churchyard, across the street, into the house of Seth Bowker, the shoemaker.

I was so interested in the fate of my old friend, and so curious as to the result, that I followed, and went into the cobbler's house. I found myself in the little room on the ground floor. Seth Bowker was sitting over the fire with his face in his hands, swaying himself, and moaning: "Oh dear! dear life! whatever shall I do without her? and she the best woman as breathed, and knew all my little ways."

Overhead was a trampling. The doctor and the midwife were with the woman. Seth looked up, and listened. Then he flung himself on his knees at the deal table, and prayed: "Oh, good God in heaven! have pity on me, and spare me my wife. I shall be a lost man without her—and no one to sew on my shirt-buttons!"

At the moment I heard a feeble twitter aloft, then it grew in volume, and presently became cries. Seth looked up; his face was bathed in tears. Still that strange sound like the chirping of sparrows. He rose to his feet and made for the stairs, and held on to the banister.

Forth from the chamber above came the doctor, and leisurely descended the stairs.

"Well, Bowker," said he, "I congratulate you; you have two fine boys."

"And my Sally—my wife?"

"She has pulled through. But really, upon my soul, I did fear for her at one time. But she rallied marvellously."

"Can I go up to her?"

"In a minute or two, not just now, the babes are being washed."

"And my wife will get over it?"

"I trust so, Bowker; a new life came into her as she gave birth to twins."

"God be praised!" Seth's mouth quivered, all his face worked, and he clasped his hands.

Presently the door of the chamber upstairs was opened, the nurse looked down, and said: "Mr. Bowker, you may come up. Your wife wants you. Lawk! you will see the beautifullest twins that ever was."

I followed Seth upstairs, and entered the sick-room. It was humble enough, with whitewashed walls, all scrupulously clean. The happy mother lay in the bed, her pale face on the pillow, but the eyes were lighted up with ineffable love and pride.

"Kiss them, Bowker," said she, exhibiting at her side two little pink heads, with down on them. But her husband just stooped and pressed his lips to her brow, and after that kissed the tiny morsels at her side.

"Ain't they loves!" exclaimed the midwife.

But oh! what a rapture of triumph, pity, fervour, love, was in that mother's face, and—the eyes looking on those children were the eyes of Mr. Fothergill. Never had I seen such an expression in them, not even when he had exclaimed "Checkmate" over a game of chess.

Then I knew what would follow. How night and day that mother would live only for her twins, how she would cheerfully sacrifice her night's rest to them; how she would go downstairs, even before it was judicious, to see to her husband's meals. Verily, with the mother's milk that fed those babes, the Black Ram would run out of the Fothergill soul. There was no need for me to tarry. I went forth, and as I issued into the street heard the clock strike one.

"Bless me!" I exclaimed, "I have spent an hour in the porch. What will my wife say?"

I walked home as fast as I could in my fur coat. When I arrived I found Bessie up.

"Oh, Bessie!" said I, "with your cold you ought to have been in bed."

"My dear Edward," she replied, "how could I? I had lain down, but when I heard of the accident I could not rest. Have you been hurt?"

"My head is somewhat contused," I replied.

"Let me feel. Indeed, it is burning. I will put on some cold compresses."

"But, Bessie, I have a story to tell you."

"Oh! never mind the story, we'll have that another day. I'll send for some ice from the fishmonger to-morrow for your head."

* * * * *

I did eventually tell my wife the story of my experience in the porch of Fifewell on St. Mark's eve.

I have since regretted that I did so; for whenever I cross her will, or express my determination to do something of which she does not approve, she says: "Edward, Edward! I very much fear there is still in you too much Black Ram."

XVII. — A HAPPY RELEASE

MR. BENJAMIN WOOLFIELD was a widower. For twelve months he put on mourning. The mourning was external, and by no means represented the condition of his feelings; for his married life had not been happy. He and Kesiah had been unequally yoked together. The Mosaic law forbade the union of the ox and the ass to draw one plough; and two more uncongenial creatures than Benjamin and Kesiah could hardly have been coupled to draw the matrimonial furrow.

She was a Plymouth Sister, and he, as she repeatedly informed him whenever he indulged in light reading, laughed, smoked, went out shooting, or drank a glass of wine, was of the earth, earthy, and a miserable worldling.

For some years Mr. Woolfield had been made to feel as though he were a moral and religious pariah. Kesiah had invited to the house and to meals, those of her own way of thinking, and on such occasions had spared no pains to have the table well served, for the elect are particular about their feeding, if indifferent as to their drinks. On such occasions, moreover, when Benjamin had sat at the bottom of his own table, he had been made to feel that he was a worm to be trodden on. The topics of conversation were such as were far beyond his horizon, and concerned matters of which he was ignorant. He attempted at intervals to enter into the circle of talk. He knew that such themes as football matches, horse races, and cricket were taboo, but he did suppose that home or foreign politics might interest the guests of Kesiah. But he soon learned that this was not the case, unless such matters tended to the fulfilment of prophecy.

When, however, in his turn, Benjamin invited home to dinner some of his old friends, he found that all provided for them was hashed mutton, cottage pie, and tapioca pudding. But even these could have been stomached, had not Mrs. Woolfield sat stern and silent at the head of the table, not uttering a word, but giving vent to occasional, very audible sighs.

When the year of mourning was well over, Mr. Woolfield put on a light suit, and contented himself, as an indication of bereavement, with a slight black band round the left arm. He also began to look about him for someone who might make up for the years during which he had felt like a crushed strawberry.

And in casting his inquiring eye about, it lighted upon Philippa Weston, a bright, vigorous young lady, well educated and intelligent. She was aged twenty-four and he was but eighteen years older, a difference on the right side.

It took Mr. Woolfield but a short courtship to reach an understanding, and he became engaged.

On the same evening upon which he had received a satisfactory answer to the question put to her, and had pressed for an early marriage, to which also consent had been accorded, he sat by his study fire, with his hands on his knees, looking into the embers and building love-castles there. Then he smiled and patted his knees.

He was startled from his honey reveries by a sniff. He looked round. There was a familiar ring in that sniff which was unpleasant to him.

What he then saw dissipated his rosy dreams, and sent his blood to his heart.

At the table sat his Kesiah, looking at him with her beady black eyes, and with stern lines in her face. He was so startled and shocked that he could not speak.

"Benjamin," said the apparition, "I know your purpose. It shall never be carried to accomplishment. I will prevent it."

"Prevent what, my love, my treasure?" he gathered up his faculties to reply.

"It is in vain that you assume that infantile look of innocence," said his deceased wife. "You shall never—never—lead her to the hymeneal altar."

"Lead whom, my idol? You astound me."

"I know all. I can read your heart. A lost being though you be, you have still me to watch over you. When you quit this earthly tabernacle, if you have given up taking in the *Field*, and have come to realise your fallen condition, there is a chance—a distant chance—but yet one of our union becoming eternal."

"You don't mean to say so," said Mr. Woolfield, his jaw falling.

"There is—there is that to look to. That to lead you to turn over a new leaf. But it can never be if you become united to that Flibbertigibbet."

Mentally, Benjamin said: "I must hurry up with my marriage!" Vocally he said: "Dear me! Dear me!"

"My care for you is still so great," continued the apparition, "that I intend to haunt you by night and by day, till that engagement be broken off."

"I would not put you to so much trouble," said he.

"It is my duty," replied the late Mrs. Woolfield sternly.

"You are oppressively kind," sighed the widower.

At dinner that evening Mr. Woolfield had a friend to keep him company, a friend to whom he had poured out his heart. To his dismay, he saw seated opposite him the form of his deceased wife.

He tried to be lively; he cracked jokes, but the sight of the grim face and the stony eyes riveted on him damped his spirits, and all his mirth died away.

"You seem to be out of sorts to-night," said his friend.

"I am sorry that I act so bad a host," apologised Mr. Woolfield. "Two is company, three is none."

"But we are only two here to-night."

"My wife is with me in spirit."

"Which, she that was, or she that is to be?"

Mr. Woolfield looked with timid eyes towards her who sat at the end of the table. She was raising her hands in holy horror, and her face was black with frowns.

His friend said to himself when he left: "Oh, these lovers! They are never themselves so long as the fit lasts."

Mr. Woolfield retired early to bed. When a man has screwed himself up to proposing to a lady, it has taken a great deal out of him, and nature demands rest. It was so with Benjamin; he was sleepy. A nice little fire burned in his grate. He undressed and slipped between the sheets.

Before he put out the light he became aware that the late Mrs. Woolfield was standing by his bedside with a nightcap on her head.

"I am cold," said she, "bitterly cold."

"I am sorry to hear it, my dear," said Benjamin.

"The grave is cold as ice," she said. "I am going to step into bed."

"No—never!" exclaimed the widower, sitting up. "It won't do. It really won't. You will draw all the vital heat out of me, and I shall be laid up with rheumatic fever. It will be ten times worse than damp sheets."

"I am coming to bed," repeated the deceased lady, inflexible as ever in carrying out her will.

As she stepped in Mr. Woolfield crept out on the side of the fire and seated himself by the grate.

He sat there some considerable time, and then, feeling cold, he fetched his dressing-gown and enveloped himself in that.

He looked at the bed. In it lay the deceased lady with her long slit of a mouth shut like a rat-trap, and her hard eyes fixed on him.

"It is of no use your thinking of marrying, Benjamin," she said. "I shall haunt you till you give it up."

Mr. Woolfield sat by his fire all night, and only dozed off towards morning.

During the day he called at the house of Miss Weston, and was shown into the drawing-room. But there, standing behind her chair, was his deceased wife with her arms folded on the back of the seat, glowering at him.

It was impossible for the usual tender passages to ensue between the lovers with a witness present, expressing by gesture her disapproval of such matters and her inflexible determination to force on a rupture.

The dear departed did not attend Mr. Woolfield continuously during the day, but appeared at intervals. He could never say when he would be free, when she would not turn up.

In the evening he rang for the housemaid. "Jemima," he said, "put two hot bottles into my bed to-night. It is somewhat chilly."

"Yes, sir."

"And let the water be boiling—not with the chill off."

"Yes, sir."

When somewhat late Mr. Woolfield retired to his room he found, as he had feared, that his late wife was there before him. She lay in the bed with her mouth snapped, her eyes like black balls, staring at him.

"My dear," said Benjamin, "I hope you are more comfortable."

"I'm cold, deadly cold."

"But I trust you are enjoying the hot bottles."

"I lack animal heat," replied the late Mrs. Woolfield.

Benjamin fled the room and returned to his study, where he unlocked his spirit case and filled his pipe. The fire was burning. He made it up. He would sit there all night During the passing hours, however, he was not left quite alone. At intervals the door was gently opened, and the night-capped head of the late Mrs. Woolfield was thrust in.

"Don't think, Benjamin, that your engagement will lead to anything," she would say, "because it will not. I shall stop it."

So time passed. Mr. Woolfield found it impossible to escape this persecution. He lost spirits; he lost flesh.

At last, after sad thought, he saw but one way of relief, and that was to submit. And in order to break off the engagement he must have a prolonged interview with Philippa. He went to the theatre and bought two stall tickets, and sent one to her with the earnest request that she would accept it and meet him that evening at the theatre. He had something to communicate of the utmost importance.

At the theatre he knew that he would be safe; the principles of Kesiah would not suffer her to enter there.

At the proper time Mr. Woolfield drove round to Miss Weston's, picked her up, and together they went to the theatre and took their places in the stalls. Their seats were side by side.

"I am so glad you have been able to come," said Benjamin. "I have a most shocking disclosure to make to you. I am afraid that—but I hardly know how to say it—that—I really must break it off."

"Break what off?"

"Our engagement."

"Nonsense. I have been fitted for my trousseau."

"Your what?"

"My wedding-dresses."

"Oh, I beg pardon. I did not understand your French pronunciation. I thought—but it does not matter what I thought."

"Pray what is the sense of this?"

"Philippa, my affection for you is unabated. Do not suppose that I love you one whit the less. But I am oppressed by a horrible nightmare—daymare as well. I am haunted."

"Haunted, indeed!"

"Yes; by my late wife. She allows me no peace. She has made up her mind that I shall not marry you."

"Oh! Is that all? I am haunted also."

"Surely not?"

"It is a fact."

"Hush, hush!" from persons in front and at the side. Neither Ben nor Philippa had noticed that the curtain had risen and that the play had begun.

"We are disturbing the audience," whispered Mr. Woolfield. "Let us go out into the passage and promenade there, and then we can talk freely."

So both rose, left their stalls, and went into the *couloir*.

"Look here, Philippa," said he, offering the girl his arm, which she took, "the case is serious. I am badgered out of my reason, out of my health, by the late Mrs. Woolfield. She always had an iron will, and she has intimated to me that she will force me to give you up."

"Defy her."

"I cannot."

"Tut! these ghosts are exacting. Give them an inch and they take an ell. They are like old servants; if you yield to them they tyrannise over you."

"But how do you know, Philippa, dearest?"

"Because, as I said, I also am haunted."

"That only makes the matter more hopeless."

"On the contrary, it only shows how well suited we are to each other. We are in one box."

"Philippa, it is a dreadful thing. When my wife was dying she told me she was going to a better world, and that we should never meet again. *And she has not kept her word.*"

The girl laughed. "Rag her with it."

"How can I?"

"You can do it perfectly. Ask her why she is left out in the cold. Give her a piece of your mind. Make it unpleasant for her. I give Jehu no good time."

"Who is Jehu?"

"Jehu Post is the ghost who haunts me. When in the flesh he was a great admirer of mine, and in his cumbrous way tried to court me; but I never liked him, and gave him no encouragement. I snubbed him unmercifully, but he was one of those self-satisfied, self-assured creatures incapable of taking a snubbing. He was a Plymouth Brother."

"My wife was a Plymouth Sister."

"I know she was, and I always felt for you. It was so sad. Well, to go on with my story. In a frivolous mood Jehu took to a bicycle, and the very first time he scorched he was thrown, and so injured his back that he died in a week. Before he departed he entreated that I would see him; so I could not be nasty, and I went. And he told me then that he was about to be wrapped in glory. I asked him if this were so certain. 'Cocksure' was his reply; and they were his last words. And *he has not kept his word.*"

"And he haunts you now?"

"Yes. He dangles about with his great ox-eyes fixed on me. But as to his envelope of glory I have not seen a fag end of it, and I have told him so."

"Do you really mean this, Philippa?"

"I do. He wrings his hands and sighs. He gets no change out of me, I promise you."

"This is a very strange condition of affairs."

"It only shows how well matched we are. I do not suppose you will find two other people in England so situated as we are, and therefore so admirably suited to one another."

"There is much in what you say. But how are we to rid ourselves of the nuisance—for it is a nuisance being thus haunted. We cannot spend all our time in a theatre."

"We must defy them. Marry in spite of them."

"I never did defy my wife when she was alive. I do not know how to pluck up courage now that she is dead. Feel my hand, Philippa, how it trembles. She has broken my nerve. When I was young I could play spellikins—my hand was so steady. Now I am quite incapable of doing anything with the little sticks."

"Well, hearken to what I propose," said Miss Weston. "I will beard the old cat——"

"Hush, not so disrespectful; she was my wife."

"Well, then, the ghostly old lady, in her den. You think she will appear if I go to pay you a visit?"

"Sure of it. She is consumed with jealousy. She had no personal attractions herself, and you have a thousand. I never knew whether she loved me, but she was always confoundedly jealous of me."

"Very well, then. You have often spoken to me about changes in the decoration of your villa. Suppose I call on you to-morrow afternoon, and you shall show me what your schemes are."

"And your ghost, will he attend you?"

"Most probably. He also is as jealous as a ghost can well be."

"Well, so be it. I shall await your coming with impatience. Now, then, we may as well go to our respective homes."

A cab was accordingly summoned, and after Mr. Woolfield had handed Philippa in, and she had taken her seat in the back, he entered and planted himself with his back to the driver.

"Why do you not sit by me?" asked the girl.

"I can't," replied Benjamin. "Perhaps you may not see, but I do, my deceased wife is in the cab, and occupies the place on your left."

"Sit on her," urged Philippa.

"I haven't the effrontery to do it," gasped Ben.

"Will you believe me," whispered the young lady, leaning over to speak to Mr. Woolfield, "I have seen Jehu Post hovering about the theatre door, wringing his white hands and turning up his eyes. I suspect he is running after the cab."

As soon as Mr. Woolfield had deposited his bride-elect at her residence he ordered the cabman to drive him home. Then he was alone in the conveyance with the ghost. As each gaslight was passed the flash came over the cadaverous face opposite him, and sparks of fire kindled momentarily in the stony eyes.

"Benjamin!" she said, "Benjamin! Oh, Benjamin! Do not suppose that I shall permit it. You may writhe and twist, you may plot and contrive how you will, I will stand between you and her as a wall of ice."

Next day, in the afternoon, Philippa Weston arrived at the house. The late Mrs. Woolfield had, however, apparently obtained an inkling of what was intended, for she was already there, in the drawing-room, seated in an armchair with her hands raised and clasped, looking stonily before her. She had a white face, no lips that showed, and her dark hair was dressed in two black slabs, one on each side of the temples. It was done in a knot behind. She wore no ornaments of any kind.

In came Miss Weston, a pretty girl, coquettishly dressed in colours, with sparkling eyes and laughing lips. As she had predicted, she was followed by her attendant spectre, a tall, gaunt young man in a black frock-coat, with a melancholy face and large ox-eyes. He shambled in shyly, looking from side to side. He had white hands and long, lean fingers. Every now and then he put his hands behind him, up his back, under the tails of his coat, and rubbed his spine where he had received his mortal injury in cycling. Almost as soon as he entered he noticed the ghost of Mrs. Woolfield that was, and made an awkward bow. Her eyebrows rose, and a faint wintry smile of recognition lighted up her cheeks.

"I believe I have the honour of saluting Sister Kesiah," said the ghost of Jehu Post, and he assumed a posture of ecstasy.

"It is even so, Brother Jehu."

"And how do you find yourself, sister—out of the flesh?"

The late Mrs. Woolfield looked disconcerted, hesitated a moment, as if she found some difficulty in answering, and then, after a while, said: "I suppose, much as do you, brother."

"It is a melancholy duty that detains me here below," said Jehu Post's ghost.

"The same may be said of me," observed the spirit of the deceased Mrs. Woolfield. "Pray take a chair."

"I am greatly obliged, sister. My back——"

Philippa nudged Benjamin, and unobserved by the ghosts, both slipped into the adjoining room by a doorway over which hung velvet curtains.

In this room, on the table, Mr. Woolfield had collected patterns of chintzes and books of wall-papers.

There the engaged pair remained, discussing what curtains would go with the chintz coverings of the sofa and chairs, and what papers would harmonise with both.

"I see," said Philippa, "that you have plates hung on the walls. I don't like them: it is no longer in good form. If they be worth anything you must have a cabinet with glass doors for the china. How about the carpets?"

"There is the drawing-room," said Benjamin.

"No, we won't go in there and disturb the ghosts," said Philippa. "We'll take the drawing-room for granted."

"Well—come with me to the dining-room. We can reach it by another door."

In the room they now entered the carpet was in fairly good condition, except at the head and bottom of the table, where it was worn. This was especially the case at the bottom, where Mr. Woolfield had usually sat. There, when his wife had lectured, moralised, and harangued, he had rubbed his feet up and down and had fretted the nap off the Brussels carpet.

"I think," remarked Philippa, "that we can turn it about, and by taking out one width and putting that under the bookcase and inserting the strip that was there in its room, we can save the expense of a new carpet. But—the engravings—those Landseers. What do you think of them, Ben, dear?"

She pointed to the two familiar engravings of the "Deer in Winter," and "Dignity and Impudence."

"Don't you think, Ben, that one has got a little tired of those pictures?"

"My late wife did not object to them, they were so perfectly harmless."

"But your coming wife does. We will have something more up-to-date in their room. By the way, I wonder how the ghosts are getting on. They have let us alone so far. I will run back and have a peep at them through the curtains."

The lively girl left the dining apartment, and her husband-elect, studying the pictures to which Philippa had objected. Presently she returned.

"Oh, Ben! such fun!" she said, laughing. "My ghost has drawn up his chair close to that of the late Mrs. Woolfield, and is fondling her hand. But I believe that they are only talking goody-goody."

"I believe that they are talking goody-goody."

"And now about the china," said Mr. Woolfield. "It is in a closet near the pantry—that is to say, the best china. I will get a benzoline lamp, and we will examine it. We had it out only when Mrs. Woolfield had a party of her elect brothers and sisters. I fear a good deal is broken. I know that the soup tureen has lost a lid, and I believe we are short of vegetable dishes. How many plates remain I do not know. We had a parlourmaid, Dorcas, who was a sad smasher, but as she was one who had made her election sure, my late wife would not part with her."

"And how are you off for glass?"

"The wine-glasses are fairly complete. I fancy the cut-glass decanters are in a bad way. My late wife chipped them, I really believe out of spite."

It took the couple some time to go through the china and the glass.

"And the plate?" asked Philippa.

"Oh, that is right. All the real old silver is at the bank, as Kesiah preferred plated goods."

"How about the kitchen utensils?"

"Upon my word I cannot say. We had a rather nice-looking cook, and so my late wife never allowed me to step inside the kitchen."

"Is she here still?" inquired Philippa sharply.

"No; my wife, when she was dying, gave her the sack."

"Bless me, Ben!" exclaimed Philippa. "It is growing dark. I have been here an age. I really must go home. I wonder the ghosts have not worried us. I'll have another look at them."

She tripped off.

In five minutes she was back. She stood for a minute looking at Mr. Woolfield, laughing so heartily that she had to hold her sides.

"What is it, Philippa?" he inquired.

"Oh, Ben! A happy release. They will never dare to show their faces again. They have eloped together."

XVIII. — THE 9.30 UP-TRAIN

IN a well-authenticated ghost story, names and dates should be distinctly specified. In the following story I am unfortunately able to give only the year and the month, for I have forgotten the date of the day, and I do not keep a diary. With regard to names, my own figures as a guarantee as that of the principal personage to whom the following extraordinary circumstances occurred, but the minor actors are provided with fictitious names, for I am not warranted to make their real ones public. I may add that the believer in ghosts may make use of the facts which I relate to establish his theories, if he finds that they will be of service to him—when he has read through and weighed well the startling account which I am about to give from my own experiences.

On a fine evening in June, 1860, I paid a visit to Mrs. Lyons, on my way to the Hassocks Gate Station, on the London and Brighton line. This station is the first out of Brighton.

As I rose to leave, I mentioned to the lady whom I was visiting that I expected a parcel of books from town, and that I was going to the station to inquire whether it had arrived.

"Oh!" said she, readily, "I expect Dr. Lyons out from Brighton by the 9.30 train; if you like to drive the pony chaise down and meet him, you are welcome, and you can bring your parcel back with you in it."

I gladly accepted her offer, and in a few minutes I was seated in a little low basket-carriage, drawn by a pretty iron-grey Welsh pony.

The station road commands the line of the South Downs from Chantonbury Ring, with its cap of dark firs, to Mount Harry, the scene of the memorable battle of Lewes. Woolsonbury stands out like a headland above the dark Danny woods, over which the rooks were wheeling and cawing previous to settling themselves in for the night. Ditchling beacon—its steep sides gashed with chalk-pits—was faintly flushed with light. The Clayton windmills, with their sails motionless, stood out darkly against the green evening sky. Close beneath opens the tunnel in which, not so long before, had happened one of the most fearful railway accidents on record.

The evening was exquisite. The sky was kindled with light, though the sun was set. A few gilded bars of cloud lay in the west. Two or three stars looked forth—one I noticed twinkling green, crimson, and gold, like a gem. From a field of young wheat hard by I heard the harsh, grating note of the corncrake. Mist was lying on the low meadows like a mantle of snow, pure, smooth, and white; the cattle stood in it to their knees. The effect was so singular that I drew up to look at it attentively. At the same moment I heard the scream of an engine, and on looking towards the downs I noticed the up-train shooting out of the tunnel, its red signal lamps flashing brightly out of the purple gloom which bathed the roots of the hills.

Seeing that I was late, I whipped the Welsh pony on, and proceeded at a fast trot.

At about a quarter mile from the station there is a turnpike—an odd-looking building, tenanted then by a strange old man, usually dressed in a white smock, over which his long white beard flowed to his breast. This toll-collector—he is dead now—had amused himself in bygone days by carving life-size heads out of wood, and these were stuck along the eaves. One is the face of a drunkard, round and blotched, leering out of misty eyes at the passers-by; the next has the crumpled features of a miser, worn out with toil and moil; a third has the wild scowl of a maniac; and a fourth the stare of an idiot.

I drove past, flinging the toll to the door, and shouting to the old man to pick it up, for I was in a vast hurry to reach the station before Dr. Lyons left it. I whipped the little pony on, and he began to trot down a cutting in the greensand, through which leads the station road.

Suddenly, Taffy stood still, planted his feet resolutely on the ground, threw up his head, snorted, and refused to move a peg. I "gee-uped," and "tshed," all to no purpose; not a step would the little fellow advance. I saw that he was thoroughly alarmed; his flanks were quivering, and his ears were thrown back. I was on the point of leaving the chaise, when the pony made a bound on one side and ran the carriage up into the hedge, thereby upsetting me on the road. I picked myself up, and took the beast's head. I could not conceive what had frightened him; there was positively nothing to be seen, except a puff of dust running up the road, such as might be blown along by a passing current of air. There was nothing to be heard, except the rattle of a gig or tax-cart with one wheel loose: probably a vehicle of this kind was being driven down the London road, which branches off at the turnpike at right angles. The sound became fainter, and at last died away in the distance.

The pony now no longer refused to advance. It trembled violently, and was covered with sweat.

"Well, upon my word, you have been driving hard!" exclaimed Dr. Lyons, when I met him at the station.

"I have not, indeed," was my reply; "but something has frightened Taffy, but what that something was, is more than I can tell."

"Oh, ah!" said the doctor, looking round with a certain degree of interest in his face; "so you met it, did you?"

"Met what?"

"Oh, nothing;—only I have heard of horses being frightened along this road after the arrival of the 9.30 up-train. Flys never leave the moment that the train comes in, or the horses become restive—a wonderful thing for a fly-horse to become restive, isn't it?"

"But what causes this alarm? I saw nothing!"

"You ask me more than I can answer. I am as ignorant of the cause as yourself. I take things as they stand, and make no inquiries. When the flyman tells me that he can't start for a minute or two after the train has arrived, or urges on his horses to reach the station before the arrival of this train, giving as his reason that his brutes become wild if he does not do so, then I merely say, 'Do as you think best, cabby,' and bother my head no more about the matter."

"I shall search this matter out," said I resolutely. "What has taken place so strangely corroborates the superstition, that I shall not leave it uninvestigated."

"Take my advice and banish it from your thoughts. When you have come to the end, you will be sadly disappointed, and will find that all the mystery evaporates, and leaves a dull, commonplace residuum. It is best that the few mysteries which remain to us unexplained should still remain mysteries, or we shall disbelieve in supernatural agencies altogether. We have searched out the arcana of nature, and exposed all her secrets to the garish eye of day, and we find, in despair, that the poetry and romance of life are gone. Are we the happier for knowing that there are no ghosts, no fairies, no witches, no mermaids, no wood spirits? Were not our forefathers happier in thinking every lake to be the abode of a fairy, every forest to be a bower of yellow-haired sylphs, every moorland sweep to be tripped over by elf and pixie? I found my little boy one day lying on his face in a fairy-ring, crying: 'You dear, dear little fairies, I *will* believe in you, though papa says you are all nonsense.' I used, in my childish days, to think, when a silence fell upon a company, that an angel was passing through the room. Alas! I now know that it results only from the subject of weather having been talked to death, and no new subject having been started. Believe me, science has done good to mankind, but it has done mischief too. If we wish to be poetical or romantic, we must shut our eyes to facts. The head and the heart wage mutual war now. A lover preserves a lock of his mistress's hair as a holy relic, yet he must know perfectly well that for all practical purposes a bit of rhinoceros hide would do as well—the chemical constituents are identical. If I adore a fair lady, and feel a thrill through all my veins when I touch her hand, a moment's consideration tells me that phosphate of lime No. 1 is touching phosphate of lime No. 2—nothing more. If for a moment I forget myself so far as to wave my cap and cheer for king, or queen, or prince, I laugh at my folly next moment for having paid reverence to one digesting machine above another."

I cut the doctor short as he was lapsing into his favourite subject of discussion, and asked him whether he would lend me the pony-chaise on the following evening, that I might drive to the station again and try to unravel the mystery.

"I will lend you the pony," said he, "but not the chaise, as I am afraid of its being injured should Taffy take fright and run up into the hedge again. I have got a saddle."

Next evening I was on my way to the station considerably before the time at which the train was due.

I stopped at the turnpike and chatted with the old man who kept it. I asked him whether he could throw any light on the matter which I was investigating. He shrugged his shoulders, saying that he "knowed nothink about it."

"What! Nothing at all?"

"I don't trouble my head with matters of this sort," was the reply. "People *do* say that something out of the common sort passes along the road and turns down the other road leading to Clayton and Brighton; but I pays no attention to what them people says."

"Do you ever hear anything?"

"After the arrival of the 9.30 train I does at times hear the rattle as of a mail-cart and the trot of a horse along the road; and the sound is as though one of the wheels was loose. I've a been out many a time to take the toll; but, Lor' bless 'ee! them sperits—if sperits them be—don't go for to pay toll."

"Have you never inquired into the matter?"

"Why should I? Anythink as don't go for to pay toll don't concern me. Do ye think as I knows 'ow many people and dogs goes through this heer geatt in a day? Not I—them don't pay toll, so them's no odds to me."

"Look here, my man!" said I. "Do you object to my putting the bar across the road, immediately on the arrival of the train?"

"Not a bit! Please yersel'; but you han't got much time to lose, for theer comes thickey train out of Clayton tunnel."

I shut the gate, mounted Taffy, and drew up across the road a little way below the turnpike. I heard the train arrive—I saw it puff off. At the same moment I distinctly heard a trap coming up the road, one of the wheels rattling as though it were loose. I repeat deliberately that I *heard* it—I cannot account for it—but, though I heard it, yet I saw nothing whatever.

At the same time the pony became restless, it tossed its head, pricked up its ears, it started, pranced, and then made a bound to one side, entirely regardless of whip and rein. It tried to scramble up the sand-bank in its alarm, and I had to throw myself off and catch its head. I then cast a glance behind me at the turnpike. I saw the bar bent, as though someone were pressing against it; then, with a click, it flew open, and was dashed violently back against the white post to which it was usually hasped in the day-time. There it remained, quivering from the shock.

Immediately I heard the rattle—rattle—rattle—of the tax-cart. I confess that my first impulse was to laugh, the idea of a ghostly tax-cart was so essentially ludicrous; but the *reality* of the whole scene soon brought me to a graver mood, and, remounting Taffy, I rode down to the station.

The officials were taking their ease, as another train was not due for some while; so I stepped up to the station-master and entered into conversation with him. After a few desultory remarks, I mentioned the circumstances which had occurred to me on the road, and my inability to account for them.

"So that's what you're after!" said the master somewhat bluntly. "Well, I can tell you nothing about it; sperits don't come in my way, saving and excepting those which can be taken inwardly; and mighty comfortable warming things they be when so taken. If you ask me about other sorts of sperits, I tell you flat I don't believe in 'em, though I don't mind drinking the health of them what does."

"Perhaps you may have the chance, if you are a little more communicative," said I.

"Well, I'll tell you all I know, and that is precious little," answered the worthy man. "I know one thing for certain—that one compartment of a second-class carriage is always left vacant between Brighton and Hassocks Gate, by the 9.30 up-train."

"For what purpose?"

"Ah! that's more than I can fully explain. Before the orders came to this effect, people went into fits and that like, in one of the carriages."

"Any particular carriage?"

"The first compartment of the second-class carriage nearest to the engine. It is locked at Brighton, and I unlock it at this station."

"What do you mean by saying that people had fits?"

"I mean that I used to find men and women a-screeching and a-hollering like mad to be let out; they'd seen some'ut as had frightened them as they was passing through the Clayton tunnel. That was before they made the arrangement I told y' of."

"Very strange!" said I meditatively.

"Wery much so, but true for all that. *I* don't believe in nothing but sperits of a warming and cheering nature, and them sort ain't to be found in Clayton tunn'l to my thinking."

There was evidently nothing more to be got out of my friend. I hope that he drank my health that night; if he omitted to do so, it was his fault, not mine.

As I rode home revolving in my mind all that I had heard and seen, I became more and more settled in my determination to thoroughly investigate the matter. The best means that I could adopt for so doing would be to come out from Brighton by the 9.30 train in the very compartment of the second-class carriage from which the public were considerately excluded.

Somehow I felt no shrinking from the attempt; my curiosity was so intense that it overcame all apprehension as to the consequences.

My next free day was Thursday, and I hoped then to execute my plan. In this, however, I was disappointed, as I found that a battalion drill was fixed for that very evening, and I was desirous of attending it, being somewhat behindhand in the regulation number of drills. I was consequently obliged to postpone my Brighton trip.

On the Thursday evening about five o'clock I started in regimentals with my rifle over my shoulder, for the drilling ground—a piece of furzy common near the railway station.

I was speedily overtaken by Mr. Ball, a corporal in the rifle corps, a capital shot and most efficient in his drill. Mr. Ball was driving his gig. He stopped on seeing me and offered me a seat beside him. I gladly accepted, as the distance to the station is a mile and three-quarters by the road, and two miles by what is commonly supposed to be the short cut across the fields.

After some conversation on volunteering matters, about which Corporal Ball was an enthusiast, we turned out of the lanes into the station road, and I took the opportunity of adverting to the subject which was uppermost in my mind.

"Ah! I have heard a good deal about that," said the corporal. "My workmen have often told me some cock-and-bull stories of that kind, but I can't say has 'ow I believed them. What you tell me is, 'owever, very remarkable. I never 'ad it on such good authority afore. Still, I can't believe that there's hanything supernatural about it."

"I do not yet know what to believe," I replied, "for the whole matter is to me perfectly inexplicable."

"You know, of course, the story which gave rise to the superstition?"

"Not I. Pray tell it me."

"Just about seven years agone—why, you must remember the circumstances as well as I do—there was a man druv over from I can't say where, for that was never exact-ly hascertained,—but from the Henfield direction, in a light cart. He went to the Station Inn, and throwing the reins to John Thomas, the ostler, bade him take the trap and bring it round to meet the 9.30 train, by which he calculated to return from Brighton. John Thomas said as 'ow the stranger was quite unbeknown to him, and that he looked as though he 'ad some matter on his mind when he went to the train; he was a queer sort of a man, with thick grey hair and beard, and delicate white 'ands, jist like a lady's. The trap was round to the station door as hordered by the arrival of the 9.30 train. The ostler observed then that the man was ashen pale, and that his 'ands trembled as he took the reins, that the stranger stared at him in a wild habstracted way, and that he would have driven off without tendering payment had he not been respectfully reminded that the 'orse had been given a feed of hoats. John Thomas made a hobservation to the gent relative to the wheel which was loose, but that hobservation met with no corresponding hanswer. The driver whipped his 'orse and went off. He passed the turnpike, and was seen to take the Brighton road hinstead of that by which he had come. A workman hobserved the trap next on the downs above Clayton chalk-pits. He didn't pay much attention to it, but he saw that the driver was on his legs at the 'ead of the 'orse. Next, morning, when the quarrymen went to the pit, they found a shattered tax-cart at the bottom, and the 'orse and driver dead, the latter with his neck broken. What was curious, too, was that an 'andkerchief was bound round the brute's heyes, so that he must have been driven over the edge blindfold. Hodd, wasn't it? Well, folks say that the gent and his tax-cart pass along the road every hevening after the arrival of the 9.30 train; but I don't believe it; I ain't a bit superstitious—not I!"

Next week I was again disappointed in my expectation of being able to put my scheme in execution; but on the third Saturday after my conversation with Corporal Ball, I walked into Brighton in the afternoon, the distance being about nine miles. I spent an hour on the shore watching the boats, and then I sauntered round the Pavilion, ardently longing that fire might break forth and consume that architectural monstrosity. I believe that I afterwards had a cup of coffee at the refreshment-rooms of the station, and capital refreshment-rooms they are, or were—very moderate and very good. I think that I partook of a bun, but if put on my oath I could not swear to the fact; a floating reminiscence of bun lingers in the chambers of memory, but I cannot be positive, and I wish in this paper to advance nothing but reliable facts. I squandered precious time in reading the advertisements of baby-jumpers—which no mother should be without—which are indispensable in the nursery and the greatest acquisition in the parlour, the greatest discovery of modern times, etc., etc. I perused a notice of the advantage of metallic brushes, and admired the young lady with her hair white on one side and black on the other; I studied the Chinese letter commendatory of Horniman's tea and the inferior English translation, and counted up the number of agents in Great Britain and Ireland. At length the ticket-office opened, and I booked for Hassocks Gate, second class, fare one shilling.

I ran along the platform till I came to the compartment of the second-class carriage which I wanted. The door was locked, so I shouted for a guard.

"Put me in here, please."

"Can't there, s'r; next, please, nearly empty, one woman and baby."

"I particularly wish to enter *this* carriage," said I.

"Can't be, lock'd, orders, comp'ny," replied the guard, turning on his heel.

"What reason is there for the public's being excluded, may I ask?"

"Dn'ow, 'spress ord'rs—c'n't let you in; next caridge, pl'se; now then, quick, pl'se."

I knew the guard and he knew me—by sight, for I often travelled to and fro on the line, so I thought it best to be candid with him. I briefly told him my reason for making the request, and begged him to assist me in executing my plan. He then consented, though with reluctance.

"'Ave y'r own way," said he; "only if an'thing 'appens, don't blame me!"

"Never fear," laughed I, jumping into the carriage.

The guard left the carriage unlocked, and in two minutes we were off.

I did not feel in the slightest degree nervous. There was no light in the carriage, but that did not matter, as there was twilight. I sat facing the engine on the left side, and every now and then I looked out at the downs with a soft haze of light still hanging over them. We swept into a cutting, and I watched the lines of flint in the chalk, and longed to be geologising among them with my hammer, picking out "shepherds' crowns" and sharks' teeth, the delicate rhynconella and the quaint ventriculite. I remembered a not very distant occasion on which I had actually ventured there, and been chased off by the guard, after having brought down an avalanche of chalk débris in a manner dangerous to traffic whilst endeavouring to extricate a magnificent ammonite which I found, and—alas! left—protruding from the side of the cutting. I wondered whether that ammonite was still there; I looked about to identify the exact spot as we whizzed along; and at that moment we shot into the tunnel.

There are two tunnels, with a bit of chalk cutting between them. We passed through the first, which is short, and in another moment plunged into the second.

I cannot explain how it was that *now*, all of a sudden, a feeling of terror came over me; it seemed to drop over me like a wet sheet and wrap me round and round.

I felt that *someone* was seated opposite me—someone in the darkness with his eyes fixed on me.

Many persons possessed of keen nervous sensibility are well aware when they are in the presence of another, even though they can see no one, and I believe that I possess this power strongly. If I were blindfolded, I think that I should know when anyone was looking fixedly at me, and I am certain that I should instinctively know that I was not alone if I entered a dark room in which another person was seated, even though he made no noise. I remember a college friend of mine, who dabbled in anatomy, telling me that a little Italian violinist once called on him to give a lesson on his instrument. The foreigner—a singularly nervous individual—moved restlessly from the place where he had been standing, casting many a furtive glance over his shoulder at a press which was behind him. At last the little fellow tossed aside his violin, saying—

"I can note give de lesson if someone weel look at me from behind! Dare is somebodee in de cupboard, I know!"

"You are right, there is!" laughed my anatomical friend, flinging open the door of the press and discovering a skeleton.

The horror which oppressed me was numbing. For a few moments I could neither lift my hands nor stir a finger. I was tongue-tied. I seemed paralysed in every member. I fancied that I *felt* eyes staring at me through the gloom. A cold breath seemed to play over my face. I believed that fingers touched my chest and plucked at my coat. I drew back against the partition; my heart stood still, my flesh became stiff, my muscles rigid.

I do not know whether I breathed—a blue mist swam before my eyes, and my head span.

The rattle and roar of the train dashing through the tunnel drowned every other sound.

Suddenly we rushed past a light fixed against the wall in the side, and it sent a flash, instantaneous as that of lightning, through the carriage. In that moment I saw what I shall never, never forget. I saw a face opposite me, livid as that of a corpse, hideous with passion like that of a gorilla.

I cannot describe it accurately, for I saw it but for a second; yet there rises before me now, as I write, the low broad brow seamed with wrinkles, the shaggy, over-hanging grey eyebrows; the wild ashen eyes, which glared as those of a demoniac; the coarse mouth, with its fleshy lips compressed till they were white; the profusion of wolf-grey hair about the cheeks and chin; the thin, bloodless hands, raised and half-open, extended towards me as though they would clutch and tear me.

In the madness of terror, I flung myself along the seat to the further window.

Then I felt that *it* was moving slowly down, and was opposite me again. I lifted my hand to let down the window, and I touched something: I thought it was a hand—yes, yes! it *was* a hand, for it folded over mine and began to contract on it. I felt each finger separately; they were cold, dully cold. I wrenched my hand away. I slipped back to my former place in the carriage by the open window, and in frantic horror I opened the door, clinging to it with both my hands round the window-jamb, swung myself out with my feet on the floor and my head turned from the carriage. If the cold fingers had but touched my woven hands, mine would have given way; had I but turned my head and seen that hellish countenance peering out at me, I must have lost my hold.

Ah! I saw the light from the tunnel mouth; it smote on my face. The engine rushed out with a piercing whistle. The roaring echoes of the tunnel died away. The cool fresh breeze blew over my face and tossed my hair; the speed of the train was relaxed; the lights of the station became brighter. I heard the bell ringing loudly; I saw people waiting for the train; I felt the vibration as the brake was put on. We stopped; and then my fingers gave way. I dropped as a sack on the platform, and then, then—not till then—I awoke. There now! from beginning to end the whole had been a frightful dream caused by my having too many blankets over my bed. If I must append a moral—Don't sleep too hot.

XIX. — ON THE LEADS

HAVING realised a competence in Australia, and having a hankering after country life for the remainder of my days in the old home, on my return to England I went to an agent with the object of renting a house with shooting attached, over at least three thousand acres, with the option of a purchase should the place suit me. I was no more intending to buy a country seat without having tried what it was like, than is a king disposed to go to war without knowing something of the force that can be brought against him. I was rather taken with photographs of a manor called Fernwood, and I was still further engaged when I saw the place itself on a beautiful October day, when St. Luke's summer was turning the country into a world of rainbow tints under a warm sun, and a soft vaporous blue haze tinted all shadows cobalt, and gave to the hills a stateliness that made them look like mountains. Fernwood was an old house, built in the shape of the letter H, and therefore, presumably, dating from the time of the early Tudor monarchs. The porch opened into the hall which was on the left of the cross-stroke, and the drawing-room was on the right. There was one inconvenience about the house; it had a staircase at each extremity of the cross-stroke, and there was no upstair communication between the two wings of the mansion. But, as a practical man, I saw how this might be remedied. The front door faced the south, and the hall was windowless on the north. Nothing easier than to run a corridor along at the back, giving communication both upstairs and downstairs, without passing through the hall. The whole thing could be done for, at the outside, two hundred pounds, and would be no disfigurement to the place. I agreed to become tenant of Fernwood for a twelvemonth, in which time I should be able to judge whether the place would suit me, the neighbours be pleasant, and the climate agree with my wife. We went down to Fernwood at once, and settled ourselves comfortably in by the first week in November.

The house was furnished; it was the property of an elderly gentleman, a bachelor named Framett, who lived in rooms in town, and spent most of his time at the club. He was supposed to have been jilted by his intended, after which he eschewed female society, and remained unmarried.

I called on him before taking up our residence at Fernwood, and found him a somewhat blasé, languid, cold-blooded creature, not at all proud of having a noble manor-house that had belonged to his family for four centuries; very willing to sell it, so as to spite a cousin who calculated on coming in for the estate, and whom Mr. Framett, with the malignity that is sometimes found in old people, was particularly desirous of disappointing.

"The house has been let before, I suppose?" said I.

"Oh, yes," he replied indifferently, "I believe so, several times."

"For long?"

"No—o. I believe, not for long."

"Have the tenants had any particular reasons for not remaining on there—if I may be so bold as to inquire?"

"All people have reasons to offer, but what they offer you are not supposed to receive as genuine."

I could get no more from him than this. "I think, sir, if I were you I would not go down to Fernwood till after November was out."

"But," said I, "I want the shooting."

"Ah, to be sure—the shooting, ah! I should have preferred if you could have waited till December began."

"That would not suit me," I said, and so the matter ended.

When we were settled in, we occupied the right wing of the house. The left or west wing was but scantily furnished and looked cheerless, as though rarely tenanted. We were not a large family, my wife and myself alone; there was consequently ample accommodation in the east wing for us. The servants were placed above the kitchen, in a portion of the house I have not yet described. It was a half-wing, if I may so describe it, built on the north side parallel with the upper arm of the western limb of the hall and the [Symbol: H]. This block had a gable to the north like the wings, and a broad lead valley was between them, that, as I learned from the agent, had to be attended to after the fall of the leaf, and in times of snow, to clear it.

Access to this valley could be had from within by means of a little window in the roof, formed as a dormer. A short ladder allowed anyone to ascend from the passage to this window and open or shut it. The western staircase gave access to this passage, from which the servants' rooms in the new block were reached, as also the untenanted apartments in the old wing. And as there were no windows in the extremities of this passage that ran due north and south, it derived all its light from the aforementioned dormer window.

One night, after we had been in the house about a week, I was sitting up smoking, with a little whisky-and-water at my elbow, reading a review of an absurd, ignorantly written book on New South Wales, when I heard a tap at the door, and the parlourmaid came in, and said in a nervous tone of voice: "Beg your pardon, sir, but cook nor I, nor none of us dare go to bed."

"Why not?" I asked, looking up in surprise.

"Please, sir, we dursn't go into the passage to get to our rooms."

"Whatever is the matter with the passage?"

"Oh, nothing, sir, with the passage. Would you mind, sir, just coming to see? We don't know what to make of it."

I put down my review with a grunt of dissatisfaction, laid my pipe aside, and followed the maid.

She led me through the hall, and up the staircase at the western extremity.

On reaching the upper landing I saw all the maids there in a cluster, and all evidently much scared.

"Whatever is all this nonsense about?" I asked.

"Please, sir, will you look? We can't say."

The parlourmaid pointed to an oblong patch of moonlight on the wall of the passage. The night was cloudless, and the full moon shone slanting in through the dormer and painted a brilliant silver strip on the wall opposite. The window being on the side of the roof to the east, we could not see that, but did see the light thrown through it against the wall. This patch of reflected light was about seven feet above the floor.

The window itself was some ten feet up, and the passage was but four feet wide. I enter into these particulars for reasons that will presently appear.

The window was divided into three parts by wooden mullions, and was composed of four panes of glass in each compartment.

Now I could distinctly see the reflection of the moon through the window with the black bars up and down, and the division of the panes. But I saw more than that: I saw the shadow of a lean arm with a hand and thin, lengthy fingers across a portion of the window, apparently groping at where was the latch by which the casement could be opened.

My impression at the moment was that there was a burglar on the leads trying to enter the house by means of this dormer.

Without a minute's hesitation I ran into the passage and looked up at the window, but could see only a portion of it, as in shape it was low, though broad, and, as already stated, was set at a great height. But at that moment something fluttered past it, like a rush of flapping draperies obscuring the light.

I had placed the ladder, which I found hooked up to the wall, in position, and planted my foot on the lowest rung, when my wife arrived. She had been alarmed by the housemaid, and now she clung to me, and protested that I was not to ascend without my pistol.

To satisfy her I got my Colt's revolver that I always kept loaded, and then, but only hesitatingly, did she allow me to mount. I ascended to the casement, unhasped it, and looked out. I could see nothing. The ladder was over-short, and it required an effort to heave oneself from it through the casement on to the leads. I am stout, and not so nimble as I was when younger. After one or two efforts, and after presenting from below an appearance that would have provoked laughter at any other time, I succeeded in getting through and upon the leads.

I looked up and down the valley—there was absolutely nothing to be seen except an accumulation of leaves carried there from the trees that were shedding their foliage.

The situation was vastly puzzling. As far as I could judge there was no way off the roof, no other window opening into the valley; I did not go along upon the leads, as it was night, and moonlight is treacherous. Moreover, I was wholly unacquainted with the arrangement of the roof, and had no wish to risk a fall.

I descended from the window with my feet groping for the upper rung of the ladder in a manner even more grotesque than my ascent through the casement, but neither my wife—usually extremely alive to anything ridiculous in my appearance—nor the domestics were in a mood to make merry. I fastened the window after me, and had hardly reached the bottom of the ladder before again a shadow flickered across the patch of moonlight.

I was fairly perplexed, and stood musing. Then I recalled that immediately behind the house the ground rose; that, in fact, the house lay under a considerable hill. It was just possible by ascending the slope to reach the level of the gutter and rake the leads from one extremity to the other with my eye.

I mentioned this to my wife, and at once the whole set of maids trailed down the stairs after us. They were afraid to remain in the passage, and they were curious to see if there was really some person on the leads.

We went out at the back of the house, and ascended the bank till we were on a level with the broad gutter between the gables. I now saw that this gutter did not run through, but stopped against the hall roof; consequently, unless there were some opening of which I knew nothing, the person on the leads could not leave the place, save by the dormer window, when open, or by swarming down the fall pipe.

It at once occurred to me that if what I had seen were the shadow of a burglar, he might have mounted by means of the rain-water pipe. But if so—how had he vanished the moment my head was protruded through the window? and how was it that I had seen the shadow flicker past the light immediately after I had descended the ladder? It was conceivable that the man had concealed himself in the shadow of the hall roof, and had taken advantage of my withdrawal to run past the window so as to reach the fall pipe, and let himself down by that.

I could, however, see no one running away, as I must have done, going outside so soon after his supposed descent.

But the whole affair became more perplexing when, looking towards the leads, I saw in the moonlight something with fluttering garments running up and down them.

There could be no mistake—the object was a woman, and her garments were mere tatters. We could not hear a sound.

I looked round at my wife and the servants,—they saw this weird object as distinctly as myself. It was more like a gigantic bat than a human being, and yet, that it was a woman we could not doubt, for the arms were now and then thrown above the head in wild gesticulation, and at moments a profile was presented, and then we saw, or thought we saw, long flapping hair, unbound.

"I must go back to the ladder," said I; "you remain where you are, watching."

"Oh, Edward! not alone," pleaded my wife.

"My dear, who is to go with me?"

I went. I had left the back door unlocked, and I ascended the staircase and entered the passage. Again I saw the shadow flicker past the moonlit patch on the wall opposite the window.

I ascended the ladder and opened the casement.

Then I heard the clock in the hall strike one.

I heaved myself up to the sill with great labour, and I endeavoured to thrust my short body through the window, when I heard feet on the stairs, and next moment my wife's voice from below, at the foot of the ladder. "Oh, Edward, Edward! please do not go out there again. It has vanished. All at once. There is nothing there now to be seen."

I returned, touched the ladder tentatively with my feet, refastened the window, and descended— perhaps inelegantly. I then went down with my wife, and with her returned up the bank, to the spot where stood clustered our servants.

They had seen nothing further; and although I remained on the spot watching for half an hour, I also saw nothing more.

The maids were too frightened to go to bed, and so agreed to sit up in the kitchen for the rest of the night by a good fire, and I gave them a bottle of sherry to mull, and make themselves comfortable upon, and to help them to recover their courage.

Although I went to bed, I could not sleep. I was completely baffled by what I had seen. I could in no way explain what the object was and how it had left the leads.

Next day I sent for the village mason and asked him to set a long ladder against the well-head of the fall pipe, and examine the valley between the gables. At the same time I would mount to the little window and contemplate proceedings through that.

The man had to send for a ladder sufficiently long, and that occupied some time. However, at length he had it planted, and then mounted. When he approached the dormer window—

"Give me a hand," said I, "and haul me up; I would like to satisfy myself with my own eyes that there is no other means of getting upon or leaving the leads."

He took me under both shoulders and heaved me out, and I stood with him in the broad lead gutter.

"There's no other opening whatever," said he, "and, Lord love you, sir, I believe that what you saw was no more than this," and he pointed to a branch of a noble cedar that grew hard by the west side of the house.

"I warrant, sir," said he, "that what you saw was this here bough as has been carried by a storm and thrown here, and the wind last night swept it up and down the leads."

"But was there any wind?" I asked. "I do not remember that there was."

"I can't say," said he; "before twelve o'clock I was fast asleep, and it might have blown a gale and I hear nothing of it."

"I suppose there must have been some wind," said I, "and that I was too surprised and the women too frightened to observe it," I laughed. "So this marvellous spectral phenomenon receives a very prosaic and natural explanation. Mason, throw down the bough and we will burn it to-night."

The branch was cast over the edge, and fell at the back of the house. I left the leads, descended, and going out picked up the cedar branch, brought it into the hall, summoned the servants, and said derisively: "Here is an illustration of the way in which weak-minded women get scared. Now we will burn the burglar or ghost that we saw. It turns out to be nothing but this branch, blown up and down the leads by the wind."

"But, Edward," said my wife, "there was not a breath stirring."

"There must have been. Only where we were we were sheltered and did not observe it. Aloft, it blew across the roofs, and formed an eddy that caught the broken bough, lifted it, carried it first one way, then spun it round and carried it the reverse way. In fact, the wind between the two roofs assumed a spiral movement. I hope now you are all satisfied. I am."

So the bough was burned, and our fears—I mean those of the females—were allayed.

In the evening, after dinner, as I sat with my wife, she said to me: "Half a bottle would have been enough, Edward. Indeed, I think half a bottle would be too much; you should not give the girls a liking for sherry, it may lead to bad results. If it had been elderberry wine, that would have been different."

"But there is no elderberry wine in the house," I objected.

"Well, I hope no harm will come of it, but I greatly mistrust——"

"Please, sir, it is there again."

The parlourmaid, with a blanched face, was at the door.

"Nonsense," said I, "we burnt it."

"This comes of the sherry," observed my wife. "They will be seeing ghosts every night."

"But, my dear, you saw it as well as myself!"

I rose, my wife followed, and we went to the landing as before, and, sure enough, against the patch of moonlight cast through the window in the roof, was the arm again, and then a flutter of shadows, as if cast by garments.

"It was not the bough," said my wife. "If this had been seen immediately after the sherry I should not have been surprised, but—as it is now it is most extraordinary."

"I'll have this part of the house shut up," said I. Then I bade the maids once more spend the night in the kitchen, "and make yourselves lively on tea," I said—for I knew my wife would not allow another bottle of sherry to be given them. "To-morrow your beds shall be moved to the east wing."

"Beg pardon," said the cook, "I speaks in the name of all. We don't think we can remain in the house, but must leave the situation."

"That comes of the tea," said I to my wife. "Now," to the cook, "as you have had another fright, I will let you have a bottle of mulled port to-night."

"Sir," said the cook, "if you can get rid of the ghost, we don't want to leave so good a master. We withdraw the notice."

Next day I had all the servants' goods transferred to the east wing, and rooms were fitted up for them to sleep in. As their portion of the house was completely cut off from the west wing, the alarm of the domestics died away.

A heavy, stormy rain came on next week, the first token of winter misery.

I then found that, whether caused by the cedar bough, or by the nailed boots of the mason, I cannot say, but the lead of the valley between the roofs was torn, and water came in, streaming down the walls, and threatening to severely damage the ceilings. I had to send for a plumber as soon as the weather mended. At the same time I started for town to see Mr. Framett. I had made up my mind that Fernwood was not suitable, and by the terms of my agreement I might be off my bargain if I gave notice the first month, and then my tenancy would be for the six months only. I found the squire at his club.

"Ah!" said he, "I told you not to go there in November. No one likes Fernwood in November; it is all right at other times."

"What do you mean?"

"There is no bother except in November."

"Why should there be bother, as you term it, then?"

Mr. Framett shrugged his shoulders. "How the deuce can I tell you? I've never been a spirit, and all that sort of thing. Mme. Blavatsky might possibly tell you. I can't. But it is a fact."

"What is a fact?"

"Why, that there is no apparition at any other time It is only in November, when she met with a little misfortune. That is when she is seen."

"Who is seen?"

"My aunt Eliza—I mean my great-aunt."

"You speak mysteries."

"I don't know much about it, and care less," said Mr. Framett, and called for a lemon squash. "It was this: I had a great-aunt who was deranged. The family kept it quiet, and did not send her to an asylum, but fastened her in a room in the west wing. You see, that part of the house is partially separated from the rest. I believe she was rather shabbily treated, but she was difficult to manage, and tore her clothes to pieces. Somehow, she succeeded in getting out on the roof, and would race up and down there. They allowed her to do so, as by that means she obtained fresh air. But one night in November she scrambled up and, I believe, tumbled over. It was hushed up. Sorry you went there in November. I should have liked you to buy the place. I am sick of it."

I did buy Fernwood. What decided me was this: the plumbers, in mending the leads, with that ingenuity to do mischief which they sometimes display, succeeded in setting fire to the roof, and the result was that the west wing was burnt down. Happily, a wall so completely separated the wing from the rest of the house, that the fire was arrested. The wing was not rebuilt, and I, thinking that with the disappearance of the leads I should be freed from the apparition that haunted them, purchased Fernwood. I am happy to say we have been undisturbed since.

XX. — AUNT JOANNA

IN the Land's End district is the little church-town of Zennor. There is no village to speak of—a few scattered farms, and here and there a cluster of cottages. The district is bleak, the soil does not lie deep over granite that peers through the surface on exposed spots, where the furious gales from the ocean sweep the land. If trees ever existed there, they have been swept away by the blast, but the golden furze or gorse defies all winds, and clothes the moorland with a robe of splendour, and the heather flushes the slopes with crimson towards the decline of summer, and mantles them in soft, warm brown in winter, like the fur of an animal.

In Zennor is a little church, built of granite, rude and simple of construction, crouching low, to avoid the gales, but with a tower that has defied the winds and the lashing rains, because wholly devoid of sculptured detail, which would have afforded the blasts something to lay hold of and eat away. In Zennor parish is one of the finest cromlechs in Cornwall, a huge slab of unwrought stone like a table, poised on the points of standing upright blocks as rude as the mass they sustain.

Near this monument of a hoar and indeed unknown antiquity lived an old woman by herself, in a small cottage of one story in height, built of moor stones set in earth, and pointed only with lime. It was thatched with heather, and possessed but a single chimney that rose but little above the apex of the roof, and had two slates set on the top to protect the rising smoke from being blown down the chimney into the cottage when the wind was from the west or from the east. When, however, it drove from north or south, then the smoke must take care of itself. On such occasions it was wont to find its way out of the door, and little or none went up the chimney.

The only fuel burnt in this cottage was peat—not the solid black peat from deep bogs, but turf of only a spade graft, taken from the surface, and composed of undissolved roots. Such fuel gives flame, which the other does not; but, on the other hand, it does not throw out the same amount of heat, nor does it last one half the time.

The woman who lived in the cottage was called by the people of the neighbourhood Aunt Joanna. What her family name was but few remembered, nor did it concern herself much. She had no relations at all, with the exception of a grand-niece, who was married to a small tradesman, a wheelwright near the church. But Joanna and her great-niece were not on speaking terms. The girl had mortally offended the old woman by going to a dance at St. Ives, against her express orders. It was at this dance that she had met the wheelwright, and this meeting, and the treatment the girl had met with from her aunt for having gone to it, had led to the marriage. For Aunt Joanna was very strict in her Wesleyanism, and bitterly hostile to all such carnal amusements as dancing and play-acting. Of the latter there was none in that wild west Cornish district, and no temptation ever afforded by a strolling company setting up its booth within reach of Zennor. But dancing, though denounced, still drew the more independent spirits together. Rose Penaluna had been with her great-aunt after her mother's death. She was a lively girl, and when she heard of a dance at St. Ives, and had been asked to go to it, although forbidden by Aunt Joanna, she stole from the cottage at night, and found her way to St. Ives.

Her conduct was reprehensible certainly. But that of Aunt Joanna was even more so, for when she discovered that the girl had left the house she barred her door, and refused to allow Rose to re-enter it. The poor girl had been obliged to take refuge the same night at the nearest farm and sleep in an outhouse, and next morning to go into St. Ives and entreat an acquaintance to take her in till she could enter into service. Into service she did not go, for when Abraham Hext, the carpenter, heard how she had been treated, he at once proposed, and in three weeks married her. Since then no communication had taken place between the old woman and her grand-niece. As Rose knew, Joanna was implacable in her resentments, and considered that she had been acting aright in what she had done.

The nearest farm to Aunt Joanna's cottage was occupied by the Hockins. One day Elizabeth, the farmer's wife, saw the old woman outside the cottage as she was herself returning from market; and, noticing how bent and feeble Joanna was, she halted, and talked to her, and gave her good advice.

"See you now, auntie, you'm gettin' old and crimmed wi' rheumatics. How can you get about? An' there's no knowin' but you might be took bad in the night. You ought to have some little lass wi' you to mind you."

"I don't want nobody, thank the Lord."

"Not just now, auntie, but suppose any chance ill-luck were to come on you. And then, in the bad weather, you'm not fit to go abroad after the turves, and you can't get all you want—tay and sugar and milk for yourself now. It would be handy to have a little maid by you."

"Who should I have?" asked Joanna.

"Well, now, you couldn't do better than take little Mary, Rose Hext's eldest girl. She's a handy maid, and bright and pleasant to speak to."

"No," answered the old woman, "I'll have none o' they Hexts, not I. The Lord is agin Rose and all her family, I know it. I'll have none of them."

"But, auntie, you must be nigh on ninety."

"I be ower that. But what o' that? Didn't Sarah, the wife of Abraham, live to an hundred and seven and twenty years, and that in spite of him worritin' of her wi' that owdacious maid of hern, Hagar? If it hadn't been for their goings on, of Abraham and Hagar, it's my belief that she'd ha' held on to a hundred and fifty-seven. I thank the Lord I've never had no man to worrit me. So why I shouldn't equal Sarah's life I don't see."

Then she went indoors and shut the door.

After that a week elapsed without Mrs. Hockin seeing the old woman. She passed the cottage, but no Joanna was about. The door was not open, and usually it was. Elizabeth spoke about this to her husband. "Jabez," said she, "I don't like the looks o' this; I've kept my eye open, and there be no Auntie Joanna hoppin' about. Whativer can be up? It's my opinion us ought to go and see."

"Well, I've naught on my hands now," said the farmer, "so I reckon we will go."

The two walked together to the cottage. No smoke issued from the chimney, and the door was shut. Jabez knocked, but there came no answer; so he entered, followed by his wife.

There was in the cottage but the kitchen, with one bedroom at the side. The hearth was cold.

"There's some'ut up," said Mrs. Hockin.

"I reckon it's the old lady be down," replied her husband, and, throwing open the bedroom door, he said: "Sure enough, and no mistake—there her be, dead as a dried pilchard."

And in fact Auntie Joanna had died in the night, after having so confidently affirmed her conviction that she would live to the age of a hundred and twenty-seven.

"Whativer shall we do?" asked Mrs. Hockin.

"I reckon," said her husband, "us had better take an inventory of what is here, lest wicked rascals come in and steal anything and everything."

"Folks bain't so bad as that, and a corpse in the house," observed Mrs. Hockin.

"Don't be sure o' that—these be terrible wicked times," said the husband. "And I sez, sez I, no harm is done in seein' what the old creetur had got."

"Well, surely," acquiesced Elizabeth, "there is no harm in that."

In the bedroom was an old oak chest, and this the farmer and his wife opened. To their surprise they found in it a silver teapot, and half a dozen silver spoons.

"Well, now," exclaimed Elizabeth Hockin, "fancy her havin' these—and me only Britannia metal."

"I reckon she came of a good family," said Jabez. "Leastwise, I've heard as how she were once well off."

"And look here!" exclaimed Elizabeth, "there's fine and beautiful linen underneath—sheets and pillow-cases."

"But look here!" cried Jabez, "blessed if the taypot bain't chock-full o' money! Whereiver did she get it from?"

"Her's been in the way of showing folk the Zennor Quoit, visitors from St. Ives and Penzance, and she's had scores o' shillings that way."

"Lord!" exclaimed Jabez. "I wish she'd left it to me, and I could buy a cow; I want another cruel bad."

"Ay, we do, terrible," said Elizabeth. "But just look to her bed, what torn and wretched linen be on that—and here these fine bedclothes all in the chest."

"Who'll get the silver taypot and spoons, and the money?" inquired Jabez.

"Her had no kin—none but Rose Hext, and her couldn't abide her. Last words her said to me was that she'd 'have never naught to do wi' the Hexts, they and all their belongings.'"

"That was her last words?"

"The very last words her spoke to me—or to anyone."

"Then," said Jabez, "I'll tell ye what, Elizabeth, it's our moral dooty to abide by the wishes of Aunt Joanna. It never does to go agin what is right. And as her expressed herself that strong, why us, as honest folks, must carry out her wishes, and see that none of all her savings go to them darned and dratted Hexts."

"But who be they to go to, then?"

"Well—we'll see. Fust us will have her removed, and provide that her be daycent buried. Them Hexts be in a poor way, and couldn't afford the expense, and it do seem to me, Elizabeth, as it would be a liberal and a kindly act in us to take all the charges on ourselves. Us is the closest neighbours."

"Ay—and her have had milk of me these ten or twelve years, and I've never charged her a penny, thinking her couldn't afford it. But her could, her were a-hoardin' of her money—and not paying me. That were not honest, and what I say is, that I have a right to some of her savin's, to pay the milk bill—and it's butter I've let her have now and then in a liberal way."

"Very well, Elizabeth. Fust of all, we'll take the silver taypot and the spoons wi' us, to get 'em out of harm's way."

"And I'll carry the linen sheets and pillow-cases. My word!—why didn't she use 'em, instead of them rags?"

All Zennor declared that the Hockins were a most neighbourly and generous couple, when it was known that they took upon themselves to defray the funeral expenses.

Mrs. Hext came to the farm, and said that she was willing to do what she could, but Mrs. Hockin replied: "My good Rose, it's no good. I seed your aunt when her was ailin', and nigh on death, and her laid it on me solemn as could be that we was to bury her, and that she'd have nothin' to do wi' the Hexts at no price."

Rose sighed, and went away.

Rose had not expected to receive anything from her aunt. She had never been allowed to look at the treasures in the oak chest. As far as she had been aware, Aunt Joanna had been extremely poor. But she remembered that the old woman had at one time befriended her, and she was ready to forgive the harsh treatment to which she had finally been subjected. In fact, she had repeatedly made overtures to her great-aunt to be reconciled, but these overtures had been always rejected. She was, accordingly, not surprised to learn from Mrs. Hockin that the old woman's last words had been as reported.

But, although disowned and disinherited, Rose, her husband, and children dressed in black, and were chief mourners at the funeral. Now it had so happened that when it came to the laying out of Aunt Joanna, Mrs. Hockin had looked at the beautiful linen sheets she had found in the oak chest, with the object of furnishing the corpse with one as a winding-sheet. But—she said to herself—it would really be a shame to spoil a pair, and where else could she get such fine and beautiful old linen as was this? So she put the sheets away, and furnished for the purpose a clean but coarse and ragged sheet such as Aunt Joanna had in common use. That was good enough to moulder in the grave. It would be positively sinful, because wasteful, to give up to corruption and the worm such fine white linen as Aunt Joanna had hoarded. The funeral was conducted, otherwise, liberally. Aunt Joanna was given an elm, and not a mean deal board coffin, such as is provided for paupers; and a handsome escutcheon of white metal was put on the lid.

Moreover, plenty of gin was drunk, and cake and cheese eaten at the house, all at the expense of the Hockins. And the conversation among those who attended, and ate and drank, and wiped their eyes, was rather anent the generosity of the Hockins than of the virtues of the departed.

Mr. and Mrs. Hockin heard this, and their hearts swelled within them. Nothing so swells the heart as the consciousness of virtue being recognised. Jabez in an undertone informed a neighbour that he weren't goin' to stick at the funeral expenses, not he; he'd have a neat stone erected above the grave with work on it, at twopence a letter. The name and the date of departure of Aunt Joanna, and her age, and two lines of a favourite hymn of his, all about earth being no dwelling-place, heaven being properly her home.

It was not often that Elizabeth Hockin cried, but she did this day; she wept tears of sympathy with the deceased, and happiness at the ovation accorded to herself and her husband. At length, as the short winter day closed in, the last of those who had attended the funeral, and had returned to the farm to recruit and regale after it, departed, and the Hockins were left to themselves.

"It were a beautiful day," said Jabez.

"Ay," responded Elizabeth, "and what a sight o' people came here."

"This here buryin' of Aunt Joanna have set us up tremendous in the estimation of the neighbours."

"I'd like to know who else would ha' done it for a poor old creetur as is no relation; ay—and one as owed a purty long bill to me for milk and butter through ten or twelve years."

"Well," said Jabez, "I've allus heard say that a good deed brings its own reward wi' it—and it's a fine proverb. I feels it in my insides."

"P'raps it's the gin, Jabez."

"No—it's virtue. It's warmer nor gin a long sight. Gin gives a smouldering spark, but a good conscience is a blaze of furze."

The farm of the Hockins was small, and Hockin looked after his cattle himself. One maid was kept, but no man in the house. All were wont to retire early to bed; neither Hockin nor his wife had literary tastes, and were not disposed to consume much oil, so as to read at night.

During the night, at what time she did not know, Mrs. Hockin awoke with a start, and found that her husband was sitting up in bed listening. There was a moon that night, and no clouds in the sky. The room was full of silver light. Elizabeth Hockin heard a sound of feet in the kitchen, which was immediately under the bedroom of the couple.

"There's someone about," she whispered; "go down, Jabez."

"I wonder, now, who it be. P'raps its Sally."

"It can't be Sally—how can it, when she can't get out o' her room wi'out passin' through ours?"

"Run down, Elizabeth, and see."

"It's your place to go, Jabez."

"But if it was a woman—and me in my night-shirt?"

"And, Jabez, if it was a man, a robber—and me in my night-shirt? It 'ud be shameful."

"I reckon us had best go down together."

"We'll do so—but I hope it's not——"

"What?"

Mrs. Hockin did not answer. She and her husband crept from bed, and, treading on tiptoe across the room, descended the stair.

There was no door at the bottom, but the staircase was boarded up at the side; it opened into the kitchen.

They descended very softly and cautiously, holding each other, and when they reached the bottom, peered timorously into the apartment that served many purposes—kitchen, sitting-room, and dining-place. The moonlight poured in through the broad, low window.

By it they saw a figure. There could be no mistaking it—it was that of Aunt Joanna, clothed in the tattered sheet that Elizabeth Hockin had allowed for her grave-clothes. The old woman had taken one of the fine linen sheets out of the cupboard in which it had been placed, and had spread it over the long table, and was smoothing it down with her bony hands.

The Hockins trembled, not with cold, though it was mid-winter, but with terror. They dared not advance, and they felt powerless to retreat.

Then they saw Aunt Joanna go to the cupboard, open it, and return with the silver spoons; she placed all six on the sheet, and with a lean finger counted them.

She turned her face towards those who were watching her proceedings, but it was in shadow, and they could not distinguish the features nor note the expression with which she regarded them.

Presently she went back to the cupboard, and returned with the silver teapot. She stood at one end of the table, and now the reflection of the moon on the linen sheet was cast upon her face, and they saw that she was moving her lips—but no sound issued from them.

She thrust her hand into the teapot and drew forth the coins, one by one, and rolled them along the table. The Hockins saw the glint of the metal, and the shadow cast by each piece of money as it rolled. The first coin lodged at the further left-hand corner and the second rested near it; and so on, the pieces were rolled, and ranged themselves in order, ten in a row. Then the next ten were run across the white cloth in the same manner, and dropped over on their sides below the first row; thus also the third ten. And all the time the dead woman was mouthing, as though counting, but still inaudibly.

She thrust her hand into the teapot and drew forth
the coins, one by one, and rolled them along the table.

The couple stood motionless observing proceedings, till suddenly a cloud passed before the face of the moon, so dense as to eclipse the light.

Then in a paroxysm of terror both turned and fled up the stairs, bolted their bedroom door, and jumped into bed.

There was no sleep for them that night. In the gloom when the moon was concealed, in the glare when it shone forth, it was the same, they could hear the light rolling of the coins along the table, and the click as they fell over. Was the supply inexhaustible? It was not so, but apparently the dead woman did not weary of counting the coins. When all had been ranged, she could be heard moving to the further end of the table, and there recommencing the same proceeding of coin-rolling.

Not till near daybreak did this sound cease, and not till the maid, Sally, had begun to stir in the inner bedchamber did Hockin and his wife venture to rise. Neither would suffer the servant girl to descend till they had been down to see in what condition the kitchen was. They found that the table had been cleared, the coins were all back in the teapot, and that and the spoons were where they had themselves placed them. The sheet, moreover, was neatly folded, and replaced where it had been before.

The Hockins did not speak to one another of their experiences during the past night, so long as they were in the house, but when Jabez was in the field, Elizabeth went to him and said: "Husband, what about Aunt Joanna?"

"I don't know—maybe it were a dream."

"Curious us should ha' dreamed alike."

"I don't know that; 'twere the gin made us dream, and us both had gin, so us dreamed the same thing."

"'Twere more like real truth than dream," observed Elizabeth.

"We'll take it as dream," said Jabez. "Mebbe it won't happen again."

But precisely the same sounds were heard on the following night. The moon was obscured by thick clouds, and neither of the two had the courage to descend to the kitchen. But they could hear the patter of feet, and then the roll and click of the coins. Again sleep was impossible.

"Whatever shall we do?" asked Elizabeth Hockin next morning of her husband. "Us can't go on like this wi' the dead woman about our house nightly. There's no tellin' she might take it into her head to come upstairs and pull the sheets off us. As we took hers, she may think it fair to carry off ours."

"I think," said Jabez sorrowfully, "we'll have to return 'em."

"But how?"

After some consultation the couple resolved on conveying all the deceased woman's goods to the churchyard, by night, and placing them on her grave.

"I reckon," said Hockin, "we'll bide in the porch and watch what happens. If they be left there till mornin', why we may carry 'em back wi' an easy conscience. We've spent some pounds over her buryin'."

"What have it come to?"

"Three pounds five and fourpence, as I make it out."

"Well," said Elizabeth, "we must risk it."

When night had fallen murk, the farmer and his wife crept from their house, carrying the linen sheets, the teapot, and the silver spoons. They did not start till late, for fear of encountering any villagers on the way, and not till after the maid, Sally, had gone to bed.

They fastened the farm door behind them. The night was dark and stormy, with scudding clouds, so dense as to make deep night, when they did not part and allow the moon to peer forth.

They walked timorously, and side by side, looking about them as they proceeded, and on reaching the churchyard gate they halted to pluck up courage before opening and venturing within. Jabez had furnished himself with a bottle of gin, to give courage to himself and his wife.

Together they heaped the articles that had belonged to Aunt Joanna upon the fresh grave, but as they did so the wind caught the linen and unfurled and flapped it, and they were forced to place stones upon it to hold it down.

Then, quaking with fear, they retreated to the church porch, and Jabez, uncorking the bottle, first took a long pull himself, and then presented it to his wife.

And now down came a tearing rain, driven by a blast from the Atlantic, howling among the gravestones, and screaming in the battlements of the tower and its bell-chamber windows. The night was so dark, and the rain fell so heavily, that they could see nothing for full half an hour. But then the clouds were rent asunder, and the moon glared white and ghastly over the churchyard.

Elizabeth caught her husband by the arm and pointed. There was, however, no need for her to indicate that on which his eyes were fixed already.

Both saw a lean hand come up out of the grave, and lay hold of one of the fine linen sheets and drag at it. They saw it drag the sheet by one corner, and then it went down underground, and the sheet followed, as though sucked down in a vortex; fold on fold it descended, till the entire sheet had disappeared.

"Her have taken it for her windin' sheet," whispered Elizabeth. "Whativer will her do wi' the rest?"

"Have a drop o' gin; this be terrible tryin'," said Jabez in an undertone; and again the couple put their lips to the bottle, which came away considerably lighter after the draughts.

"Look!" gasped Elizabeth.

Again the lean hand with long fingers appeared above the soil, and this was seen groping about the grass till it laid hold of the teapot. Then it groped again, and gathered up the spoons, that flashed in the moonbeams. Next, up came the second hand, and a long arm that stretched along the grave till it reached the other sheets. At once, on being raised, these sheets were caught by the wind, and flapped and fluttered like half-hoisted sails. The hands retained them for a while till they bellied with the wind, and then let them go, and they were swept away by the blast across the churchyard, over the wall, and lodged in the carpenter's yard that adjoined, among his timber.

"She have sent 'em to the Hexts," whispered Elizabeth.

Next the hands began to trifle with the teapot, and to shake out some of the coins.

In a minute some silver pieces were flung with so true an aim that they fell clinking down on the floor of the porch.

How many coins, how much money was cast, the couple were in no mood to estimate.

Then they saw the hands collect the pillow-cases, and proceed to roll up the teapot and silver spoons in them, and, that done, the white bundle was cast into the air, and caught by the wind and carried over the churchyard wall into the wheelwright's yard.

At once a curtain of vapour rushed across the face of the moon, and again the graveyard was buried in darkness. Half an hour elapsed before the moon shone out again. Then the Hockins saw that nothing was stirring in the cemetery.

"I reckon us may go now," said Jabez.

"Let us gather up what she chucked to us," advised Elizabeth.

So the couple felt about the floor, and collected a number of coins. What they were they could not tell till they reached their home, and had lighted a candle.

"How much be it?" asked Elizabeth.

"Three pound five and fourpence, exact," answered Jabez.

XXI. — THE WHITE FLAG

A PERCENTAGE of the South African Boers—how large or how small that percentage is has not been determined—is possessed of a rudimentary conscience, much as the oyster has incipient eyes, and the snake initiatory articulations for feet, which in the course of long ages may, under suitable conditions, develop into an active faculty.

If Jacob Van Heeren possessed any conscience at all it was the merest protoplasm of one.

He occupied Heerendorp, a ramshackle farmhouse under a kopje, and had cattle and horses, also a wife and grown-up sons and daughters.

When the war broke out Jacob hoisted the white flag at the gable, and he and his sons indulged their sporting instincts by shooting down such officers and men of the British army as went to the farm, unsuspecting treachery.

Heerendorp by this means obtained an evil notoriety, and it was ordered to be burnt, and the women of Jacob's family to be transferred to a concentration camp where they would be mollycoddled at the expense of the English taxpayer. Thus Jacob and his sons were delivered from all anxiety as to their womankind, and were given a free field in which to exercise their mischievous ingenuity. As to their cattle and horses that had been commandeered, they held receipts which would entitle them to claim full value for the beasts at the termination of hostilities.

Jacob and his sons might have joined one of the companies under a Boer general, but they preferred independent action, and their peculiar tactics, which proved eminently successful.

That achievement in which Jacob exhibited most slimness, and of which he was pre-eminently proud, was as follows: feigning himself to be wounded, he rolled on the ground, waving a white kerchief, and crying out for water. A young English lieutenant at once filled a cup and ran to his assistance, when Jacob shot him through the heart.

When the war was over Van Heeren got his farm rebuilt and restocked at the expense of the British taxpayer, and received his wife and daughters from the concentration camp, plump as partridges.

So soon as the new Heerendorp was ready for occupation, Jacob took a large knife and cut seventeen notches in the doorpost.

"What is that for, Jacob?" asked his wife.

"They are reminders of the Britishers I have shot."

"Well," said she, "if I hadn't killed more Rooineks than that, I'd be ashamed of myself."

"Oh, I shot more in open fight. I didn't count them; I only reckon such as I've been slim enough to befool with the white flag," said the Boer.

Now the lieutenant whom Jacob Van Heeren had killed when bringing him a cup of cold water, was Aneurin Jones, and he was the only son of his mother, and she a widow in North Wales. On Aneurin her heart had been set, in him was all her pride. Beyond him she had no ambition. About him every fibre of her heart was entwined. Life had to her no charms apart from him. When the news of his death reached her, unaccompanied by particulars, she was smitten with a sorrow that almost reached despair. The joy was gone out of her life, the light from her sky. The prospect was a blank before her. She sank into profound despondency, and would have welcomed death as an end to an aimless, a hopeless life.

But when peace was concluded, and some comrades of Aneurin returned home, the story of how he had met his death was divulged to her.

Then the passionate Welsh mother's heart became as a live coal within her breast. An impotent rage against his murderer consumed her. She did not know the name of the man who had killed him, she but ill understood where her son had fallen. Had she known, had she been able, she would have gone out to South Africa, and have gloried in being able to stab to the heart the man who had so treacherously murdered her Aneurin. But how was he to be identified?

The fact that she was powerless to avenge his death was a torture to her. She could not sleep, she could not eat, she writhed, she moaned, she bit her fingers, she chafed at her incapacity to execute justice on the murderer. A feverish flame was lit in her hollow cheeks. Her lips became parched, her tongue dry, her dark eyes glittered as if sparks of unquenchable fire had been kindled in them.

She sat with clenched hands and set teeth before her dead grate, and the purple veins swelled and throbbed in her temples.

Oh! if only she knew the name of the man who had shot her Aneurin!

Oh! if only she could find out a way to recompense him for the wrong he had done!

These were her only thoughts. And the sole passage in her Bible she could read, and which she read over and over again, was the story of the Importunate Widow who cried to the judge, "Avenge me of mine adversary!" and who was heard for her persistent asking.

Thus passed a fortnight. She was visibly wasting in flesh, but the fire within her burned only the fiercer as her bodily strength failed.

Then, all at once, an idea shot like a meteor through her brain. She remembered to have heard of the Cursing Well of St. Elian, near Colwyn. She recalled the fact that the last "Priest of the Well," an old man who had lived hard by, and who had initiated postulants into the mysteries of the well, had been brought before the magistrates for obtaining money under false pretences, and had been sent to gaol at Chester; and that the parson of Llanelian had taken a crowbar and had ripped up the wall that enclosed the spring, and had done what lay in his power to destroy it and blot out the remembrance of the powers of the well, or to ruin its efficacy.

But the spring still flowed. Had it lost its virtues? Could a parson, could magistrates bring to naught what had been for centuries?

She remembered, further, that the granddaughter of the "Priest of the Well" was then an inmate of the workhouse at Denbigh. Was it not possible that she should know the ritual of St. Elian's spring?—should be able to assist her in the desire of her heart?

Mrs. Winifred Jones resolved on trying. She went to the workhouse and sought out the woman, an old and infirm creature, and had a conference with her. She found the woman, a poor, decrepit creature, very shy of speaking about the well, very unwilling to be drawn into a confession of the extent of her knowledge, very much afraid of the magistrates and the master of the workhouse punishing her if she had anything to do with the well; but the intensity of Mrs. Jones, her vehemence in prosecuting her inquiries, and, above all, the gift of half a sovereign pressed into her palm, with the promise of another if she assisted Mrs. Winifred in the prosecution of her purpose, finally overcame her scruples, and she told all that she knew.

"You must visit St. Elian's, madam," said she, "when the moon is at the wane. You must write the name of him whose death you desire on a pebble, and drop it into the water, and recite the sixty-ninth Psalm."

"But," objected the widow, "I do not know his name, and I have no means of discovering it. I want to kill the man who murdered my son."

The old woman considered, and then said: "In this case it is different. There is a way under these circumstances. Murdered, was your son?"

"Yes, he was treacherously shot."

"Then you will have to call on your son by name, as you let fall the pebble, and say: 'Let him be wiped out of the book of the living. Avenge me of mine adversary, O my God.' And you must go on dropping in pebbles, reciting the same prayer, till you see the water of the spring boil up black as ink. Then you will know that your prayer has been heard, and that the curse has wrought."

Winifred Jones departed in some elation.

She waited till the moon changed, and then she went to the spring. It was near a hedge; there were trees by it. Apparently it had been unsought for many years. But it still flowed. About it lay scattered a few stones that had once formed the bounds.

She looked about her. No one was by. The sun was declining, and would soon set. She bent over the water—it was perfectly clear. She had collected a lapful of rounded stones.

Then she cried out: "Aneurin! come to my aid against your murderer. Let him be blotted out of the book of the living. Avenge me on my adversary, O my God!" and she dropped a pebble into the water.

Then rose a bubble. That was all.

She paused but for a moment, then again she cried: "Aneurin! come to my aid against your murderer. Let him be blotted out of the book of the living. Avenge me on my adversary, O my God!"

Once more a pebble was let fall. It splashed into the spring, but there was no change save that ripples were sent against the side.

A third—then a fourth—she went on; the sun sent a shaft of yellow glory through the trees over the spring.

Then someone passed along the road hard by, and Mrs. Winifred Jones held her breath, and desisted till the footfall had died away.

But then she continued, stone after stone was dropped, and the ritual was followed, till the seventeenth had disappeared in the well, when up rose a column of black fluid boiling as it were from below, the colour of ink; and the widow pressed her hands together, and drew a sigh of relief; her prayer had been heard, and her curse had taken effect.

She cast away the rest of the pebbles, let down her skirt, and went away rejoicing.

* * * * *

It so fell out that on this very evening Jacob Van Heeren had gone to bed early, as he had risen before daybreak, and had been riding all day. His family were in the outer room, when they were startled by a hoarse cry from the bedroom. He was a short-tempered, imperious man, accustomed to yell at his wife and children when he needed them; but this cry was of an unusual character, it had in it the ring of alarm. His wife went to him to inquire what was the matter. She found the old Boer sitting up in bed with one leg extended, his face like dirty stained leather, his eyes starting out of his head, and his mouth opening and shutting, lifting and depressing his shaggy, grey beard, as though he were trying to speak, but could not utter words.

"Pete!" she called to her eldest son, "come here, and see what ails your father."

Pete and others entered, and stood about the bed, staring stupidly at the old man, unable to comprehend what had come over him.

"Fetch him some brandy, Pete," said the mother; "he looks as if he had a fit."

When some spirits had been poured down his throat the farmer was revived, and said huskily: "Take it away! Quick, take it off!"

"Take what away?"

"The white flag."

"There is none here."

"It is there—there, wrapped about my foot."

The wife looked at the outstretched leg, and saw nothing. Jacob became angry, he swore at her, and yelled: "Take it off; it is chilling me to the bone."

"There is nothing there."

"But I say it is. I saw him come in——"

"Saw whom, father?" asked one of the sons.

"I saw that Rooinek lieutenant I shot when he was bringing me drink, thinking I was wounded. He came in through the door——"

"That is not possible—he must have passed us."

"I say he did come. I saw him, and he held the white rag, and he came upon me and gave me a twist with the flag about my foot, and there it is—it numbs me. I cannot move it. Quick, quick, take it away."

"I repeat there is nothing there," said his wife.

"Pull off his stocking," said Pete Van Heeren; "he has got a chill in his foot, and fancies this nonsense. He has been dreaming."

"It was not a dream," roared Jacob; "I saw him as clearly as I see you, and he wrapped my foot up in that accursed flag."

"Accursed flag!" exclaimed Samuel, the second son. "That's a fine way to speak of it, father, when it served you so well."

"Take it off, you dogs!" yelled the old man, "and don't stand staring and barking round me."

The stocking was removed from his leg, and then it was seen that his foot—the left foot—had turned a livid white.

"Go and heat a brick," said the housewife to one of her daughters; "it is just the circulation has stopped."

But no artificial warmth served to restore the flow of blood, and the natural heat.

Jacob passed a sleepless night.

Next morning he rose, but limped; all feeling had gone out of the foot. His wife vainly urged him to keep to his bed. He was obstinate, and would get up; but he could not walk without the help of a stick. When clothed, he hobbled into the kitchen and put the numbed foot to the fire, and the stocking sole began to smoke, it was singed and went to pieces, but his foot was insensible to the heat. Then he went forth, aided by the stick, to his farmyard, hoping that movement would restore feeling and warmth; but this also was in vain. In the evening he seated himself on a bench outside the door, whilst his family ate supper. He ordered them to bring food to him. He felt easier in the open air than within doors.

Whilst his wife and children were about the table at their meal, they heard a scream without, more like that of a wounded horse than a man, and all rushed forth, to find Jacob in a paroxysm of terror only less severe than that of the preceding night.

"He came on me again," he gasped; "the same man, I do not know from whence—he seemed to spring out of the distance. I saw him first like smoke, but with a white flicker in it; and then he got nearer and became more distinct, and I knew it was he; and he had another of those white napkins in his hand. I could not call for help—I tried, I could utter no sound, till he wrapped it—that white rag—round my calf, and then, with the cold and pain, I cried out, and he vanished."

"Father," said Pete, "you fell asleep and dreamt this."

"I did not. I saw him, and I felt what he did. Give me your hand. I cannot rise. I must go within. Good Lord, when will this come to an end?"

When lifted from his seat it was seen that his left leg dragged. He had to lean heavily on his son on one side and his wife on the other, and he allowed himself, without remonstrance, to be put to bed.

It was then seen that the dead whiteness, as of a corpse, had spread from the foot up the calf.

"He is going to have a paralytic stroke, that is it," said Pete. "You, Samuel, must ride for a doctor to-morrow morning, not that he can do much good, if what I think be the case."

On the second day the old man persisted in his determination to rise. He was deaf to all remonstrance, he would get up and go about, as far as he was able. But his ability was small. In the evening, as the sun went down, he was sitting crouched over the fire. The family had finished supper, and all had left the room except his wife, who was removing the dishes, when she heard a gasping and struggling by the fire, and, turning her head, saw her husband writhing on his stool, clinging to it with his hands, with his left leg out, his mouth foaming, and he was snorting with terror or pain.

She ran to him at once.

"Jacob, what is it?"

"He is at me again! Beat him off with the broom!" he screamed. "Keep him away. He is wrapping the white flag round my knee."

Pete and the others ran in, and raised their father, who was falling out of his seat, and conveyed him to bed.

It was now seen that his knee had become hard and stiff, his calf was as if frozen; the whiteness had extended upwards to the knee.

Next day a surgeon arrived. He examined the old man, and expressed his conviction that he had a stroke. But it was a paralytic attack of an unusual character, as it had in no way affected his speech or his left arm and hand. He recommended hot fomentations.

Still the farmer would not be confined to bed; he insisted on being dressed and assisted into the kitchen.

One stick was not now sufficient for him, and Samuel contrived for him crutches. With these he could drag himself about, and on the fourth evening he laboriously worked his way to a cowstall to look at one of his beasts that was ill.

Whilst there he had a fourth attack. Pete, who was without, heard him yell and beat at the door with one of his crutches. He entered, and found his father lying on the floor, quivering with terror, and spluttering unintelligible words. He lifted him, and drew him without, then shouted to Samuel, who came up, and together they carried him to the house.

Only when there, and when he had drunk some brandy, was he able to give an account of what had taken place. He had been looking at the cow, and feeling it, when down out of the hayloft had come leaping the form of the Rooinek lieutenant, which had sprung in between him and the cow, and, stooping, had wrapped a white rag round his thigh, above the knee. And now the whole of his leg was dead and livid.

"There is nothing for it, father, but to have your leg amputated," said Pete. "The doctor told me as much. He said that mortification would set in if there was no return of circulation."

"I won't have it off! What good shall I be with only one leg?" exclaimed the old man.

"But father, it will be the sole means of saving your life."

"I won't have my leg off!" again repeated Jacob.

Pete said in a low tone to his mother: "Have you seen any dark spots on his leg? The doctor said we must look for them, and, when they come, send for him at once."

"No," she replied, "I have not noticed any, so far."

"Then we will wait till they appear."

On the fifth day the farmer was constrained to keep his bed.

He had now become a prey to abject terror. So sure as the hour of sunset came, did a new visitation occur. He listened for the clock to sound each hour of the day, and as the afternoon drew on he dreaded with unspeakable horror the advent of the moment when again the apparition would be seen, and a fresh chill be inflicted. He insisted that his wife or Pete should remain in the room with him. They took it in turns to sit by his bedside.

Through the little window the fire of the setting sun smote in and fell across the suffering man.

It was his wife's turn to be in attendance.

All at once a gurgling sound broke from his throat. His eyes started from his face, his hair bristled, and with his hands he worked himself into a sitting posture, and he heaved himself on to his pillow, and would have broken his way through the backboard of his bed, could he have done so.

"What is it, Jacob?" asked his wife, throwing down the garment which she was mending, and coming to his assistance. "Lie down again. There is nothing here."

He could not speak. His teeth were chattering, and his beard shaking, foam-bubbles formed on his lips, and great sweatdrops on his brow.

"Pete! Samuel!" she called, "come to your father."

The young men ran in, and they forcibly laid the old Boer in bed, prostrate.

And now it was found that the right foot had turned dead, like the left.

* * * * *

On the evening of the seventeenth day after the visit to the well of Llanelian, Mrs. Winifred Jones was sitting on the side of her bed in the twilight. She had lighted no candle. She was musing, always on the same engrossing topic, the wrong that had been done to her and her son, and thirsting with a feverish thirst for vengeance on the wrongdoer.

Her confidence in the expedient to which she had resorted was beginning to fail. What was this recourse to the well but a falling in with an old superstition that had died out with the advance of knowledge, and under the influence of a wholesome feeling? Was any trust to be placed in that woman at the workhouse? Was she deceiving her for the sake of the half-sovereign? And yet—she had seen a token that her prayer would prove efficacious. There had risen through the crystal water a column of black fluid.

Could it be that a widow's prayer should meet with no response? Was wrong to prevail in the world? Were the weak and oppressed to have no means of procuring the execution of justice on the evildoers? Was not God righteous in all His ways? Would it be righteous in Him to suffer the murderer of her son to thrive? If God be merciful, He is also just. If His ear is open to the prayer for help, He must as well listen to the cry for vengeance.

Since that evening at the spring she had been unable to pray as usual, to pray for herself—her only cry had been: "Avenge me on my adversary!" If she tried to frame the words of the Lord's Prayer, she could not do so. They escaped her; her thoughts travelled to the South African veldt. Her soul could not rise to God in the ecstasy of love and devotion; it was choked with hate—an overwhelming hate.

She was in her black weeds; the hands, thin and white, were on her lap, nervously clasping and unclasping the fingers. Had anyone been there, in the grey twilight of a summer night, he would have been saddened to see how hard and lined the face had become, how all softness had passed from the lips, how sunken were the eyes, in which was only a glitter of wrath.

Suddenly she saw standing before her, indistinct indeed, but unmistakable, the form of her lost son, her Aneurin, and he held a white napkin in his right hand, and this napkin emitted a phosphorescent glow.

She tried to cry out; to utter the beloved name; she tried to spring to her feet and throw herself into his arms! But she was unable to stir hand, or foot, or tongue. She was as one paralysed, but her heart bounded within her bosom.

"Mother," said the apparition, in a voice that seemed to come from a vast distance, yet was articulate and audible—"Mother, you called me back from the world of spirits, and sent me to discharge a task. I have done it. I have touched him on the foot and calf and knee and thigh, on hand and elbow and shoulder, on one side and on the other, on his head, and lastly on his heart, with the white flag—and now he is dead. I did it in all sixteen times, and with the sixteenth he died. I chilled him piecemeal with the white flag; the sixteenth was laid on his heart, and that stopped beating."

Then she lifted her hands slightly, and her stiffened tongue relaxed so far that she was able to murmur: "God be thanked!"

"Mother," continued the apparition, "there is a seventeenth remaining."

She tried to clasp her hands on her lap, but the fingers were no longer under her control; they had fallen to the side of the chair-bed, and hung there lifeless. Her eyes stared wildly at the spectre of her son, but without love in them; love had faded out of her heart, and given place to hate of his murderer.

"Mother," proceeded the vision, "you summoned me, and even in the world of spirits the soul of a child must respond to the cry of a mother, and I have been permitted to come back and to do your will. And now I am suffered to reveal something to you: to show you what my life would have been had it not been cut short by the shot of the Boer."

He stepped towards her, and put forth a vaporous hand and touched her eyes. She felt as though a feather had been passed over them. Then he raised the luminous sheet and shook it. Instantly all about her was changed.

Mrs. Winifred Jones was not in her little Welsh cottage; nor was it night. She was no longer alone. She stood in a court, in full daylight. She saw before her the judge on his seat, the barristers in wig and gown, the press reporters with their notebooks and pens, a dense crowd thronging every portion of the court. And she knew instinctively, before a word was spoken, without an intimation from the spirit of her son, that she was standing in the Divorce Court. And she saw there as co-respondent her son, older, changed in face, but more altered in expression. And she heard a tale unfolded—full of dishonour, and rousing disgust.

She was now able to raise her hands—she covered her ears; her face, crimson with shame, sank on her bosom. She could endure the sight, the words spoken, the revelations made, no longer, and she cried out: "Aneurin! Aneurin! for the Lord's sake, no more of this! Oh, the day, the day, that I have seen you standing here."

At once all passed; and she was again in her bedroom in Honeysuckle Cottage, North Wales, seated with folded hands on her lap, and looking before her wonderingly at the ghostly form of her son.

"Is that enough, mother?"

She lifted her hands deprecatingly.

Again he shook the glimmering white sheet, and it was as though drops of pearly fire fell out of it.

And again—all was changed.

She found herself at Monte Carlo; she knew it instinctively. She was in the great saloon, where were the gaming-tables. The electric lights glittered, and the decorations were superb. But all her attention was engrossed on her son, whom she saw at one of the tables, staking his last napoleon.

It was indeed her own Aneurin, but with a face on which vice and its consequent degradation were written indelibly.

He lost, and turned away, and left the hall and its lights. His mother followed him. He went forth into the gardens. The full moon was shining, and the gravel of the terraces was white as snow. The air was fragrant with the scent of oranges and myrtles. The palms cast black shadows on the soil. The sea lay still as if asleep, with a gleam over it from the moon.

Mrs. Winifred Jones tracked her son, as he stole in and out among the shrubs, amid the trees, with a sickening fear at her heart. Then she saw him pause by some oleanders, and draw a revolver from his pocket and place it at his ear. She uttered a cry of agony and horror, and tried to spring forward to dash the weapon from his hand.

Then all changed.

She was again in her little room in the dusk, and the shadowy form of Aneurin was before her.

"Mother," said the spirit, "I have been permitted to come to you and to show to you what would have been my career if I had not died whilst young, and fresh, and innocent. You have to thank Jacob Van Heeren that he saved me from such a life of infamy, and such an evil death by my own hand. You should thank, and not curse him." She was breathing heavily. Her heart beat so fast that her brain span; she fell on her knees.

"Mother," the apparition continued, "there were seventeen pebbles cast into the well."

"Yes, Aneurin," she whispered.

"And there is a seventeenth white flag. With the sixteenth Jacob Van Heeren died. The seventeenth is reserved for you."

"Aneurin! I am not fit to die."

"Mother, it must be, I must lay the white flag over your head."

"Oh! my son, my son!"

"It is so ordained," he proceeded; "but there are Love and Mercy on high, and you shall not be veiled with it till you have made your peace. You have sinned. You have thrust yourself into the council-chamber of God. You have claimed to exercise vengeance yourself, and not left it to Him to whom vengeance in right belongs."

"I know it now," breathed the widow.

"And now you must atone for the curses by prayers. You have brought Jacob Van Heeren to his death by your imprecations, and now, fold your hands and pray to God for him—for him, your son's murderer. Little have you considered that his acts were due to ignorance, resentment for what he fancied were wrongs, and to having been reared in a mutilated and debased form of Christianity. Pray for him, that God may pardon his many and great transgressions, his falsehood, his treachery, his self-righteousness. You who have been so greatly wronged are the right person to forgive and to pray for his soul. In no other way can you so fully show that your heart is turned from wrath to love. Forgive us our trespasses as we forgive them that trespass against us."

She breathed a "Yes."

Then she clasped her hands. She was already on her knees, and she prayed first the great Exemplar's prayer, and then particularly for the man who had wrecked her life, with all its hopes.

And as she prayed the lines in her face softened, and the lips lost their hardness, and the fierce light passed utterly away from her eyes, in which the lamp of Charity was once more lighted, and the tears formed and rolled down her cheeks.

And still she prayed on, bathed in the pearly light from the summer sky at night. Without, in the firmament, twinkled a star; and a night-bird began to sing.

"And now, mother, pray for yourself."

Then she crossed her hands over her bosom, and bowed her head, full of self-reproach and shame; and as she prayed, the spirit of her son raised the White Flag above her and let it sail down softly, lightly over the loved head, and as it descended there fell from it as it were a dew of pale fire, and it rested on her head, and fell about her, and she sank forward with her face upon the floor. R.I.P.

Made in the USA
Middletown, DE
31 January 2023

23553263R00278